*City*

"[Humes' talent] is as authentic a gift for fiction as has appeared in a long time. . . . One of the best accounts of the underground resistance movement and the risks and problems of working with Communist allies that I have ever read." —*The New York Times*

"An amazingly fine and thoughtful first novel . . . It is so competent that Humes may find himself hard put to better his own mark." —*Chicago Sunday Tribune*

"A work of power, maturity and distinction." —*Newsweek*

"*The Underground City,* in its complexity, its host of characters, its visions of a harassed and bloody continent . . . is unlike any other war novel." —*Wichita Falls Times*

"[A] tremendous first novel." —*Boston Sunday Herald*

"Because what these people say is of serious importance and because the author has made his characters memorable, his ambitious work is a major achievement." —*New York Herald Tribune Book Review*

"[Humes] has written one of the two or three best first novels of the season, a work of intellectual maturity, intensity and feeling, with a powerful narrative drive." —*Chicago Sunday Tribune Magazine of Books*

"If you like character developed in three dimensions, the conflict of muscles and ideas, the high drama of truth—and restraint—you'll like *The Underground City.*" —*The Houston Post*

ALSO BY H. L. HUMES

Men Die

THE
UNDERGROUND
CITY

H. L. HUMES

RANDOM HOUSE TRADE PAPERBACKS
NEW YORK

*This book is dedicated to its patron and mine,
my father, with respect and gratitude and in hope
that he will forgive its faults and the author's;
& to W.F. who taught us all—whether he likes it or not.*

—History, Stephen said, is a nightmare from which I am trying to awake.

From the playfield the boys raised a shout. A whirring whistle: goal. What if that nightmare gave you a back kick?

—The ways of the Creator are not our ways, Mr. Deasy said. All history moves towards one great goal, the manifestation of God.

Stephen jerked his thumb towards the window, saying:

—That is God.

Hooray! Ay! Whrrwhee!

—What? Mr. Deasy asked.

—A shout in the street, Stephen answered, shrugging his shoulders.

—JAMES JOYCE: *Ulysses*

INTRODUCTION

Alan Cheuse

As much as I would like to offer a thoroughly persuasive and wholly sound critical appraisal of these two novels by Harold "Doc" Humes, one of the least-known and most enigmatic members of his writing generation, I won't be able to speak about the books without first explaining how they intertwined with my own education. Or more precisely, how they became *part* of my education, in the way that some fine (or sometimes merely ordinary) books often do during that special phase in your life when raw minutes and art bind together in what, years later, you might recognize as the first blush of vocation.

I was completing my sophomore year at Rutgers and had taken over the editorship of the literary magazine, *The Anthologist,* from a fellow named James Shokoff (whose whereabouts today I sometimes wonder about) when William Sloane, who directed the Bread Loaf Writers' Conference with another teacher of mine, John Ciardi, offered me and a few others the chance to wait tables at the workshop that summer of 1958. We drove up to Vermont and carried trays for various famous writers and not-so-famous editors. One of them, a trim, dark-haired woman named Mary Heathcote, became a friend to the tall, stoop-shouldered, enthusiastic would-be bohemian that I was.

That autumn she invited me and a few other Rutgers boys to parties at her apartment in Greenwich Village. At one of these pleasant little fiestas, I met a chunk-boned, jocular man a little shorter than me, with his lovely wife and some small children in arms. He turned out to be Harold Humes, a founder of the *Paris Review,* recently returned from a long postwar sojourn in Europe. His first novel, *The Underground City,* had just been published in New York. Unlike the work of some of the other writers I had met that summer (Norman Mailer, Ralph Ellison, and Richard Yates, among others), Humes' fiction was unknown to me. Mary Heathcote sent me a copy of his massive book; I put aside my regular reading (an act *not* unknown to me in my student years) and spent some days in my dustbin of an apartment a few blocks from the Rutgers campus in dilapidated New Brunswick, New Jersey, feasting on Humes' story of politics and the disasters of war and love and peace and paternity in France circa 1944–47.

That year—in the spring of 1959—we inaugurated a regular reading series by accomplished visiting writers, something that we take for granted as part of an undergraduate literature education these days. But in the late fifties and early sixties it was a trick that we had to learn to do by trying it out. With a little financial help and a lot of encouragement from a few sympathetic instructors in the Rutgers English department, those of us on the magazine staff invited Yates (who came to read), Mailer (who did not), Ciardi (who was already in place), and a few others, including Harold Humes.

Humes showed up. In the front room of a splendid nineteenth-century townhouse appropriated by the university years before and with book in hand, he read vigorously from *The Underground City*. Head bobbing, arms waving, he looked like a middleweight boxer with his fight strategy in front of him. He then led a question-and-answer period about modern writing.

"Let me ask *you* a question," he said to the audience. "How many of you"— there were about forty of us in the crowd before him, mostly students, a few faculty members including John McCormick (critic, bullfight expert, and biographer), and Ciardi and Sloane—"have read a book called *Under the Volcano?*"

McCormick's hand shot up. Mine did, too, except that I hadn't read it, though as was often the case with my education in those days I found a copy of the novel and took care of that deficiency in my life soon after.

"Three of us!" Humes chuckled. "Three good readers. The rest of you will remain flawed until you know that novel. Not damaged. But flawed somewhat. You're missing out on a great feast, a great fiesta of human frailty and extraordinary writing."

Talk about frailty—the next season saw Humes publish his second and only other novel, *Men Die,* a book as compact in its genius as *The Underground City* was huge and overbearing. Then he seemed to disappear from the New York scene. One heard rumors that he was experimenting with a new drug called LSD—and later in the decade I read accounts in the New York press that he was seen distributing five-dollar bills to crowds at the entrance to Columbia University. A scheme of his for building houses out of paper drew a write-up in *The New York Times.* But no more fiction came from him.

I encountered him again in Bennington, Vermont, in the early seventies. I was teaching there and one of his daughters was a student. Humes seemed to have made himself over into a character from a novel in progress. He was a graying, shambling wrack of paranoia and good cheer, talking of a massage cure for heroin addicts, which he had tried to promote in Italy and the United States, and explaining that it was well understood in certain circles that the CIA could monitor the progress of radical dissidents, of whom he was one, from seemingly innocuous clouds that traveled above them on roadways across the country. He bunked in his daughter's dormitory. Students gathered around him. They had just read the *The Rime of the Ancient Mariner,* and here was the mariner in the flesh.

I never saw Humes again after his Bennington visitations, but fifteen years later his remark about Malcolm Lowry's work came to mind when, invited by David Madden to contribute to the second of his "Rediscoveries" volumes, I chose Humes' books as the fiction I thought ought to come back into print. I discovered upon rereading them that he made rare books in the best sense, great feasts and fiestas, and my reencounters with them convinced me that in the raw, instinctual days of early recognitions, my admiration for Humes' writing was not at all misplaced. I recommended them at nineteen because I found the books thrilling in ways that I could not at the time explain. In my late forties, I found them just as thrilling, and in addition I could muster a few ideas as to why.

The Underground City stands as one of those rare birds of American fiction, a true novel of ideas with credible characters and a powerful realistic plot. Humes divides the book into three large chunks, and by the way he sets his first scene, with a vast canvas of cloud and sky above Paris at the opening of a day about a year or so following the end of World War II, he seems to have nothing less in mind than the desire to create a monumental story of epic range:

> The eastern sun, full and fiery orange, just risen clear of the horizon, began slowly to sink back into the gray ocean of clouds as the plane started down; the sky altered; clouds changed aspects. To the southeast, delicate as frozen breath, an icy herd of mare's tails rode high and sparkling in the upper light of the vanishing sun; they were veiled in crystalline haze as the plane descended through stratocirrus, the sun in iridescent halo at its disappearing upper limb. And below, slowly rising closer, the soft floor of carpeting clouds gradually changed into an ugly boil of endless gray billows, ominous, huge. Against the east, rayed out in a vast standing fan: five fingers of the plummeting sun. . . .

That airplane carries the crippled and ailing American ambassador to France, the portentously named Bruce Peel Sheppard, back to Paris after a medical leave, in order to deal with an impending crisis: the war-crimes trial of a collaborator named Dujardin, whose case the French Communist Party has just taken up—on the side of the supposed war criminal—as a way of attacking the U.S. presence in postwar Europe. Caught in the middle of this rising political storm is New Jersey–born John Stone, a heroic but now burned-out alcoholic American undercover agent. Under the code-name "Dante," Stone led a group of commandos who smuggled arms to the French Resistance in advance of the Allied invasion. Stone, appropriately enough, now works in the civilian wing of the U.S. embassy under the guise of a graves registration official. As Ambassador Peel's aircraft prepares to make its descent below the clouds into what Humes, with deliberate homage to Andre Malraux (author of that great novel of ideas, *Man's Fate*) calls "the world of men," we encounter a broad cast of characters and become engaged in a masterly setup for a dramatization of the world of modern Western geopolitical affairs. Just as the trial will rip open the wounds on the French body politic still fresh from the war, the large central portion of the novel gives us the narrative of Stone's undercover work during the war—a dense, dramatic novel within the novel that may be the best story of the Resistance told by anyone in English (which stands as the testimony Stone will give at the trial of the accused and contentious Dujardin). The last third of the novel shows us the aftermath of the trial, and the unfolding fates of Ambassador Sheppard, Stone, a Resistance leader named Merseault, the Communists Picard and Carnot, and a number of other characters involved in the wartime and postwar drama.

Humes' treatment of the military and political aspects of the events alone would have been brilliant enough, but he undergirds these public matters with the burning psychology of personal motives, stories of lost sons and troubled fathers that involve both Ambassador Sheppard and Stone, as well as a mysterious member of the Resistance code-named Berger (again Humes plays tribute to Malraux by using the writer's own wartime code name). There is, too, a philosophical level to the book: the presentation of a number of warring views of history and politics, from the ill-fated notions of the ambassador on through the paranoid psycho-historical theories of the Communist manipulator Picard (which, as critic James Bloom pointed out in the original version of a brief note on Humes—perhaps the only critical notice that the book has received in the thirty years since its publication—portends the now-fashionable strategies of paranoiac fiction as exemplified by the work of Thomas Pynchon). Moreover, there is a rich mythological overlay to the story, beginning with the ambassador's descent from the heavens at the beginning of the book, on through the central return back in time to the years of the Resistance in the Stone narrative—as well as a lot of seeming counterparts to figures out of European poetry and myth among various characters, including Stone ("Dante") who makes his physical descent into the underworld of the sewers in the final section of the novel.

If *The Underground City* appears, deceptively at first, to be one of those loose and baggy monsters of which Henry James complained, the compactness of *Men Die,* published less than a year later, might give the initial impression of simplistic storytelling about a complex period: the months leading up to the United States' entry into the Pacific War. *The Underground City* seems almost wholly anomalous in its essence, a work that no other American writer tried to write before Humes (except for the neophyte attempt of Humes' *Paris Review* compatriot Peter Matthiessen, whose now deservedly forgotten early novel, *Partisans,* unlike his triumphant later work, comes nowhere near the success of Humes' book). *Men Die* has a number of echoes and companion works, beginning with James Jones' *From Here to Eternity,* Warren Eyster's (equally) ignored *Far From the Customary Skies,* William Styron's novella *The Long March,* and George Garrett's *Which Ones are the Enemy?*—these last two being, of course, books with postwar settings.

Men Die is set in a United States–occupied Caribbean island that has been carved out into a honeycomb of tunnels by a battalion of black navy laborers in anticipation of the outbreak of World War II. Lording over the operation is

Commander Bonuso Hake, a Captain Queeg–like figure who fascinates young Lieutenant Everett Sulgrave, the officer in charge of the actual tunneling and stockpiling operations. Ben Dolfuss, Hake's former first in command, is the third white man on the island. He appears to have had an affair with Vannessa Hake, the commander's sensual wife. The entire narrative explodes at the outset as the ammunition dump goes sky-high, leaving alive only Sulgrave and six black mutineers, who piece together the corpse of the commander—and the story of his life and command. Thus the novel itself is a series of highly charged narrative fragments that take us back and forth in time, from Hake's assumption of command on through the explosion, the funeral of Hake in Washington, and Sulgrave's pathetic love affair with Vannessa. Some sec+tions include overtly stream-of-consciousness vignettes from the untimely widowed Vannessa's point of view.

With all this you might think that the book itself was a disaster, as though James Jones had never recovered from a reading of *The Sound and the Fury*. But Humes' novel is tersely and convincingly composed, and while it echoes other works it never seems derivative, the result perhaps of its powerfully made scenes (such as a fire drill on the arsenal island in which a fire hose takes on a life of its own and nearly kills some men) and the essentially clear and direct nature of Humes' prose. Fathers searching for sons, sons looking for fathers, and a military structure destroying that which it is meant to defend: These are some of the motifs from Humes' first novel that we notice at work again in this second book. In the philosophical musings of the slightly demented Commander Hake we find some of the paranoid theories of *The Underground City* emerging as a prelude for war in another theater (and clearly echoing some of the chords struck by Mailer in his portrayal of the commanding general in *The Naked and the Dead*). *Men Die* is a finely executed, dramatic curtain raiser to the great story of the war, whose last year and aftermath Humes himself portrays with such breadth in his earlier novel.

It is nearly fifty years later, and now both books have come back into print. It remains unclear to me why they ever disappeared, except that perhaps when Humes himself went, in his own way, "underground," there was no one else partisan enough to lobby on behalf of further editions. Taken together they show the hand of a writer whose inventive projections and first-rate narratives deserve to see the light of day again. These books hold up the way *Under the Volcano* holds up. Until you read them, as Humes himself remarked to us all those many decades ago about the Lowry novel, "you will remain flawed. Not damaged. But flawed somewhat. You're missing out on a great feast, a great fiesta of human frailty and extraordinary writing."

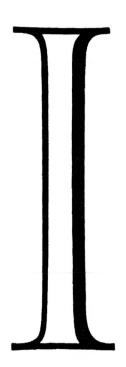

The eastern sun, full and fiery orange, just risen clear of the horizon, began slowly to sink back into the gray ocean of clouds as the plane started down; the sky altered; clouds changed aspects. To the southeast, delicate as frozen breath, an icy herd of mare's tails rode high and sparkling in the upper light of the vanishing sun; they were veiled in crystalline haze as the plane descended through stratocirrus, the sun in iridescent halo at its disappearing upper limb. And below, slowly rising closer, the soft floor of carpeting clouds gradually changed into an ugly boil of endless gray billows, ominous, huge. Against the east, rayed out in a vast standing fan: five fingers of the plummeting sun . . .

I

In the deep blue shadow of the Quai an old man stands beneath a naked winter elm making a twig broom. The false light of January dawn barely penetrates the still air, and the broad avenue along the river is still in darkness, empty. The streetsweeper wears no overcoat, only a hard black suit; a muffler is wrapped around his face covering his nose and mouth against the chill, the fringe tucked under his beret to keep it from unwinding. The broom handle lies on the ground at his feet, broomless.

Beyond him, in the cold and solitary arc of the streetlight, the paving stones near the bridge glisten feebly, still wet with vanished ice from the freezing drizzle which stopped after midnight. Working silently in the wavering darkness, he wraps the twigs in a bundle at their thick ends. Crisscrossing the bindings, he pulls each turn tight by hand; then, catching the loop of twine under the point of his peg foot and jerking up sharply, he cinches it wire-taut before tying it off. Overhead the ragged sky is almost clear and the last still stars are visible before the dark winter dawn. Hunched over his hands, his back is bent, methodical.

When the ragged fasces is wrapped and bound in three places at one end, he takes up the handle and patiently sharpens it to a new point with his knife. The broom is assembled upside down: forcing the pointed stick into the tight-bound end of the twig bundle, he taps the butt end steadily on the sidewalk, bouncing it rhythmically, without effort, driving the broom onto its handle by its own inert mass. When he is sure the stick is well jammed into the bundle of twigs, he turns it right side up and pulls on it to test the friction of the fit; he sweeps a few trial strokes. Satisfied, he gathers up the leftover willow twigs at his

3

feet and returns them to a tiny shack almost hidden under the shadow of the wall of the Ministry of Foreign Affairs. He puts them inside, closes the door, flaps shut the ill-fitted hasp and snaps the padlock. When he walks, he lurches from side to side and his left trouser flaps uselessly about the wooden peg leg. He is dressed entirely in black; the beret, the muffler, the worn ironcloth suit, the single black shoe. The one bright exception is the odd tricolor ribbon of festive silk which he wears like a mourner's arm band.

Suddenly an automobile appears; it turns the corner and coasts out of the blackness with its lights off, its muffled motor barely purring. The old man is standing in the shadow of his shack. Alerted by the wet-rubber whisper, he watches from the shadows as the car drifts to a stop at the curb a short distance from where he is standing. In the darkness under the trees the six burly figures in dark clothing are almost invisible; they get out, leaving the car doors quietly ajar. The motor of the car is still running. Now their new white tennis shoes are visible, their running footsteps grotesquely soundless on the sidewalk. They move quickly, efficiently, without words. Two of them take up stations ahead and behind the car and look up and down the street. The old man watches intently, unseen in the darkness. He stands stock-still, holding his broom. The two lookouts motion each in turn to the other four, who quickly remove several buckets from the interior of the car. Taking out several long stick-like objects, they silently cross the sidewalk, indistinct shadows, until even the quick automatic white tennis shoes are lost under the huge stone shadow of the ministry wall. The old man strains his eyes, waiting, sees nothing.

The sudden sharp crackle of new paper unrolls in the cold silence and a huge square of magic white materializes on the black stone wall. The old man is close enough to hear the soft slapping of the long-handled brushes as they smooth paste over the poster on the wall. In a few seconds the men are finished. They are picking up their paste buckets as one of the lookouts stiffens; he snaps a warning finger and points toward the old man standing off in the shadows. The second lookout peers for a moment, motions a brusque command to the other four. The brushes and buckets are thrown hastily, but without noise, into the back of the car. The leader, a squat man with heavy shoulders, waits until the other five are in the car before he moves. Then he walks slowly toward the streetsweeper. When he is close enough for the old man to reach out and touch him with his broom he stops. He looks at the old man for a long moment, as though examining him. He looks at the broom, at the door of the shack, at the broom again.

The old man says: "It is forbidden to post anything on these walls."

The other, expressionless, nerveless, continues to look at him; then, without a word, he turns on the ball of his white rubber shoe and strides soundlessly back to the car. As he walks away, the old man notices the stick in his hand, like a police baton, only shorter, and black.

Silently the car floats away from the curb, out and past the old man. At the bridge its lights flow on; the four doors slam. The yellow headlights wash across the bridge and are gone.

The old man limps out of the shadows, dragging his broom, and walks along the wall. The huge poster, wet and white in the darkness, looks like a dim window cut in the time-blackened stone. He sniffs the smell of the fresh paste, and stands before the poster gazing at it. Even in the darkness he can read the top part of the poster:

LIBEREZ DUJARDIN!

—in bold black letters. Below, there is a close-packed text, and he fumbles in his pocket for a match.

He scans pieces of the text in the flickering match light from his cupped hands. The poster glistens with wet paste: . . . *victim of warmongering imperialists. A Hero of the Resistance is being martyred by the government of France to cover up the international capitalists' blundering plot to destroy the People's Revolution . . . present French Government is the lackey of Wall Street . . . warmongering imperialists . . .* He reads slowly, with random effort, and the match burns down to his fingers. Shaking his head, he drops it, lights another: *. . . government of murderers would take the life of an innocent man, a Hero of France, rather than offend their American masters . . . bought with dollars dripping blood, the profits of capitalist war.* The old man reads silently in the light of the dying match, wagging his head slowly. Behind him he hears the fast whisper of a passing bicycle and the whirring of its light generator. He hears the bicycle turn off and cross the bridge. . . . *a plan by the American militarist leaders to bribe the world into slavery. France is being betrayed! You, the workers of France . . .* He lights another match, his last one, and skips quickly over the long, detailed text to the bottom. . . . *the true meaning of capitalist economic aid, so called to mask its true nature: "If there is war with Russia it is far better that we sacrifice our money than our blood. It is better that twelve Europeans die rather than one American"—quoted from a speech on the floor of the American Senate. France is being led into slaughter in an imperialist war against the Soviet Union. The present government stands accused! Workingmen of France, you must . . .*

The match is blown out by someone standing beside the old man. Startled, he straightens up and sees a young man standing directly beside him. Behind him are three others holding bicycles. The three lay down their bicycles and begin defacing the poster with carpenter's scrapers. The old man is gently shouldered aside. They work fast and efficiently. Very shortly most of the poster lies in long peels under their feet. The wet paste makes the task easier. Then one of them takes a handful of small stickers out of his pocket and sets them into the paste still wet on the wall. One of them, standing off watching, turns to the old man. "We save money on paste this way," he says, and laughs softly.

"It is forbidden to post anything on these walls," the old man says.

"Much is forbidden. Little is forgiven," says the one who is pressing the little squares onto the wall. They are ordinary medicine labels, marked with skull and crossbones and the word *Poison*.

Then they are gone. The old man watches them as they pedal toward the bridge. The weak yellow streaks of light from their generator headlights weave a wavering pattern. He watches until they reach the other end of the bridge and disappear. The old man shrugs, turns, rests his broom against the wall and wearily begins picking off the half-dozen stickers along with what's left of the ruined poster.

With his broom he pushes the shredded paper into a wet mound. Then he makes two trips to the edge of the sidewalk, carrying the soggy debris between his hands, and dumps it into the gutter. Satisfying himself that he hasn't missed any scraps, he recovers his broom and limps back to his shack.

At the corner, in the wavering blue light of the arc, he stoops and lifts a small iron cover set flush in the curbstone, and turns on the water with a small hand wrench. Leaning on his new broom, he watches the water flow down the edge of the street, pushing curb-side refuse before it—the shredded poster, winter leaves, the discarded twigs of his old broom. Slowly he starts to sweep, humming a cracked nasal tune through his muffler, pushing the curb water along with his broom. His breath steams white in the purple morning air as he helps the flow along, limping with each step on his wooden leg. At the next corner he stops and reaches down to turn on another valve. Then he sweeps the water around the corner of the curb, his streetlamp shadow falling long across the avenue; humming his solitary tune, he disappears behind the buildings into the side street away from the river. Overhead the flat black begins to soften before dawn, to deepen.

For a long while the stillness is unbroken except for the tremor of an underground train rumbling deep beneath the surface of the quivering earth. The only movement is the water coursing silently at the edge of the street.

Then, first faintly, there is the distant sound of heavy motors, approaching trucks. The sound slowly comes nearer; louder, closer, until finally the noise presses urgently on the silence, a sourceless drone muffled behind nearby buildings. Building to a roar, imminently present, yet not yet in sight. Suddenly sweeping around the corner: screaming yellow headlights, a mad stampede of army trucks disgorging from the side street. Motor roaring, the first driver double-clutches down into second gear, reverses his turn, and twists sharply onto the bridge, followed hardly a length behind by the second; the third lumbers into the violent turn and the noise mounts. The whine of four-wheel transmissions increases to crescendo as a bigger truck, swinging wide, treads heavily into the turn, followed by another, gears gnashing,

6

then another. On they come, each one jammed closer behind the other like berserk elephants trunk-to-tail, merged in one enormous glowing roar of yellow light.

Then, as suddenly as they came, the herd is gone. A jeep runs by like a lagging terrier.

Across the bridge, the retreating drone of motors is lost in the tangle of streets and trees and buildings; but one last truck, dropped out of the convoy, moves slowly and quietly around the corner, lights off, motor purring, makes a careful U-turn, and backs over the curb into the stealthy shadows of the trees commanding the approach to the bridge. Like the others it is a covered military van. The engine idles quietly for a moment, a cold feather of exhaust rising white and drifting, and then stops. There is no sound of voices. Only the slow irregular winking of cigarettes gives evidence of the dozen-odd men sitting in the blackness under the canvas tarpaulin, rifles between their knees, waiting.

The old man limps around the corner dragging his broom, halts, and looks around for the truck. The wooden leg taps sharply on the sidewalk. He stoops to turn off the water flowing into the side street. Then, still dragging his broom, he crosses the street on the long diagonal to where the truck is parked near the bridge.

A roll of canvas hangs halfway down the open back of the truck. He approaches it slowly, peering bird-necked over the tailgate into the back. Inside someone coughs, carefully spits past him. The old man watches.

Muffled behind a coat collar far back inside the truck: "What are you doing up?"

"He's probably been out drunk all night," says another voice. "You always sweep the streets before you go to bed, don't you, old man?"

The old man cackles. "I thought they let the new Army sleep till noon," he says. From the glow of cigarettes, he can just make out the shapes where they sit huddled in greatcoats behind upturned collars on the benches along either side.

The soldier on the right nearest the back lifts the roll of canvas and sticks his head out. He is young, with a pinched face and small black eyes set too close together. His helmet is too big for his head. "Why do you water the streets just after it's rained?" he asks.

"I'm paid to sweep the streets, not watch the rain," the old man says.

"You should join the Army again, grandpère," says the first voice. "That's all we do. Watch the rain. We do nothing. We do it slowly, but conscientiously."

Silence inside the truck for a moment.

"I wonder if I could ask a favor," says the old man. No one says anything. "I was wondering if someone could lend me a cigarette. I forgot mine this morning."

Again there is silence in the truck. The thin-faced soldier shrugs,

7

turns, and looks back inside. The old man shifts his weight from his peg leg.

"What's the matter, grandpère? Can't find any dry butts today?" Someone passes the pinch-faced soldier a crumpled pack and he hands it down to the old man. "Can you still smoke Elégantes, or have you been out of the Army too long?" he asks.

"Thank you," says the old man. He leans his broom against the truck and takes a cigarette in his numbed fingers. There are three in the pack; he hands it back with the two left. The soldier gives him a light from his.

"Let him have them," says the muffled voice from deep inside. "Tell grandpère to keep the pack. I've got more."

The thin-faced soldier looks around and receives the pack again; shrugging, he gives it back to the old man.

"Thank you. Very much," says the old man. "Thank you." He folds the pack and puts it under his beret.

"Don't smoke them all in one place, grandpère," says the first voice. "They'll last longer."

"I wouldn't smoke them at all," says a different voice. "They make them out of camel dung. They put big sacks under the camels and dry it in the sun."

"At least they kill the stink of the stuff you burn in that pipe," says the first voice. "He's a Corsican, grandpère. He doesn't appreciate camels. He'd rather smoke goat droppings."

There is a grumble of amusement among the men in the truck; a quick scuffle, someone laughs. Then the other soldier sitting by the tailgate sticks his head out under the roll of canvas at the left. He is young, fat-faced and thick-lipped, and shapeless in his outsize greatcoat. He stares blankly out at the streetsweeper for a moment, and then looks at the ribbon on his arm. The old man looks down at it also.

"Do you always wear the colors of the Republic when you sweep the streets?" he asks. He speaks in the piping voice of a schoolboy.

"I'm going to march today," says the old man.

"There won't be any parade today, my friend," says the thin-faced one, shaking his head slowly. The helmet is loose on his head. "That's what we're here for."

"Are you a Communist, grandpère?" asks the donor of the cigarettes, far back inside.

"I am a patriot," says the old man, peering vainly into the truck to see whom he is answering. "I am a veteran of Verdun," he says, knocking the broom handle on the wooden leg through the trouser cloth. The fat-faced one stares, drops the canvas, and disappears inside.

"If you try to join the demonstration you are also a fool, grandpère. Dujardin is a traitor."

"March if you want to, old man," says another voice. "But don't lose your arm band or someone like this pig might clout you on the head."

8

"Merde."

"You are a fool also, Guillaume," says the muffled voice. "You are a fool if you believe what you read in *l'Humanité.*"

"We're all fools," a new voice comments. "Or we wouldn't be in the Army."

"I believe Dujardin is a patriot," says the old man, "and I will march in his cause. It's not a question of politics."

The soldier to the right shrugs, drops the roll of canvas back in place so that only his knees show again. There is a long silence inside the truck. A spent cigarette is flipped over the tailgate and drops at the old man's feet.

"Good luck, grandpère," says the first voice, muffled deep in cloth again. "You are welcome to the cigarettes. Don't get your head broken."

"Thank you," says the streetsweeper.

He turns and limps across the street, the wooden leg skidding a little with each step on the wet film of ice over the paving stones, the broom still dragging behind him. He stoops to turn off the last of the water and drops the iron cover with a clang. After he stands the broom in the tiny wooden locker and snaps the padlock again, he turns and waves a salute toward the truck and walks away, weighting the favored leg in a broken rhythm. A short distance along the wall, he comes to a small iron door beside the gates of the Ministry. He turns a key, opens it, disappears inside, shuts it, locks it.

A single taxi rattles along the other quai across the river, headlights on, swings across the vast emptiness of the Place de la Concorde, and disappears into the chasm of the Rue St. Florentin. Far off, a dog barks; the frozen lonely sound carries on the motionless air. Then, near where the truck is hidden, one of the tall winter elms groans, and a high branch overhanging the river ruptures its sheath of melting ice and sends it cascading down in sudden splinters onto the river's edge of white ice. Then silence. Feebly the sun kindles the horizon under the clouds. Farther up, the façades of the other offices are pockmarked with sparse rectangles of yellow light that wink on and off as charwomen move from room to room, emptying ashtrays, wastebaskets, readying for the day. The Ministry itself, however, unshuttered and elegant behind the high walls, has been a splendor of light since midnight.

Inside the courtyard of the ministry building, the streetsweeper, now a gatekeeper, hurries out of hiding from inside the tiny guardbox behind the great grilled gates. There is the hollow clatter of sluggish iron as he wrestles the huge key into the ancient lock. He now wears a military greatcape, and he works with exaggerated deliberation. Somewhere behind him an automobile door opens and slams; there is the long, labored milling of the cold electric starter. Silence. Then the starter is struck again, held growling. The old man pauses to look over his shoulder. The cold engine coughs, rolls over once, and dies; the sound of the starter rises to a snarl. The old man faces the gate again.

9

Suddenly the engine, awakened, purrs easily to life. In the cold silence behind him a black Delahaye, without lights, backs out of the shadows in a hard sinuous arc, its tires crunching on wet gravel, faces the un-opened gate on an angle; a small tricolor bullseye lights up behind the windshield, shining like a cat's eye in the darkness. The old man reaches up and grips the wet iron grills with both hands, pulling his slow weight against the gates. Behind him the motor is prodded to an angry roar, drowning the chill squeal of the resisting hinges; the amber headlights stab on, lighting the spread silhouette of the gatekeeper's cape across the gate. For a brief instant, as the gates separate slowly inward, he hangs pinned against the grill by the lights, the cape spread flat like the wings of a huge black moth. Arms lifted, pulling with his back, he swings the gates slowly; slowly they open. Stepping out onto the sidewalk, he looks both ways, and waves the car forward. The limousine roars, lifts, and leaps forward through the gate, clawing gravel onto the sidewalk, and turns in a tight semicircle into the street. The gatekeeper salutes and stands looking after the car a moment longer, then turns and shuffles back inside, shaking his head. Method-ically he closes the gates; first the one on his left, then crossing to the other. The key rattles loosely into the hollow lock and grinds over once. Still wagging his head, he turns and disappears into his box.

Later, with the passing of the hour and the scattered tolling of distant bells, the sky begins to lift and lighten sharply. Then, muffled in dis-tance, an airplane's shrouded presence oppresses the silence. Invisible among the fast-clearing clouds, insistent on its tiny purpose, for a long while it throbs softly on the lonely air. Far below, its widening ribbon of sound unwinds through the thin dawn, a cold incessant drone, un-seen, remote. It unrolls over the earth's pale distance like black silk, gently settles down on the silence, smothers the stillness of the stand-ing trees.

The cold sound wavers on the diminishing air, on the river frozen in cold gloom; then it is gone, and there is nothing.

Sunrise breaks, the river is quiet.

The chill rays of the dull red January sun slant over the gray build-ings and old trees of the Quai d'Orsay and make the ice-covered branches, soft and glistening and bending under the weight, look like modelings in black wax by the river. Only the river is blacker. Under the massive shadow of the stone river walls, it moves imperceptibly between edges of white ice. The narrow vein of flawless water, like black onyx, reflects the long shadows of the black buildings that line the quai; and the yellow lights, the deep amber lights of the bridge, seem disembodied, imprisoned at the bottom of the water. Atop the cold stone balustrade on the other bank, the gas lights are suddenly turned down, and the dying gas mantles glow redly in the rich air. The sky overhead is lightening from purple to rapid grays; around the rim of the city, silhouetting the uneven roofs and smoke-tufted chimney pots, the sky steals color from the blood-red sun.

II

On a rooftop behind a crenelated stone parapet, two men, nameless, dressed in black, watching: the tall one, not clearly a man but a regal shadow in the darkness, holds a pair of huge binoculars to his eyes; the other, his attendant, holds a notebook and pencil poised. The diffused light of the darkened city reflects a faint reddish halo off the patchy black underside of the wet winter sky. Against the dim nightshine of this lifting shroud the two watchers stand in motionless silhouette, observing, waiting, intent. At their backs, away from the parapet, a cluster of chimney pipes stands stark and irreal, a twisted grove of winter cactus on a void plain; there is a table with an umbrella over it, and tied to the table, motionless, a pair of animals: dogs, sitting. Behind them stand two tripods, one mounting a telescope, its lenses capped with loose cloth covers against the weather. Nearby is the small structure like a guardbox that houses the door into the building from the roof. And past the chimneys, beyond the farther flat expanse of graveled roof, across the near distance and other buildings, the river lies buried in blue-black darkness.

After a few minutes the sound of an automobile rises coldly from the streets below. The tall man peers through the binoculars with minute concentration, absorbed. He follows the sound with his glasses as it diminishes.

"Homage to Galileo," he says under his breath, not removing the glasses from his eyes. He speaks French with a certain archaic elegance, hardly moving his lips.

"Ah, so?" his assistant replies.

"The automobile has indeed those lovely yellow license plates. Diplomatic Corps. CD8484." He paused. "That should be the last of the reception committee on their way to the airport."

The short man writes. "CD8484. Citroën 15. Black?"

"Of course black. The emblematic color. Really no color at all but rather anticolor, the death of color. Have you ever remarked the three classes of humanity who enjoy black vehicles?" He removes the glasses from his eyes, turns his head.

"I have not remarked them."

"Then observe that they are as follows: criminals, because black is the color of night; men of esteem, because black is the color of their art; and the dead, because black is the color of nothing."

"I should have observed it myself," the short one says. "And would you add the priestly class?"

"My dear fellow, observe further that they are covered in the three categories I gave you."

"Ah, yes."

"Before attempting to improve my teaching, you should reflect, and in reflection you will improve your learning."

"I humble myself for presuming on your good nature," the short one says with a slight deferential bow.

"And my nature is not good. You must strive with me to correct these unfortunate habits of speech and thought which cloud your vision."

"Again I see that I am in error."

"Precisely and forever," the tall one adds. "But you are still an apprentice in this profession. Yet you show a propensity for learning. That is why you were assigned to me." He lifts the glasses again and peers into the dark void below.

"I am greatly encouraged to be your assistant."

"I would be greatly assisted and more encouraged if you would check that number for me."

"Yes, my Prince."

The tall man drops the binoculars from his eyes and turns fully to look at his assistant for the first time. A frown of irritation flickers about his eyes. "And another thing, my dear fellow. Some men of noble origin are flattered in being addressed by their hereditary titles. I, however, am decidedly not. I appreciate that you are moved by dedication to your monarch, however naïve and out-of-date that dedication may be, but the fact that I am a prince is merely an accident of birth and death. And furthermore, be advised that I consider being born the son of a Russian landowner more a joke than an honor. I would rather not be reminded of my dispossession and disability, my father's fall from grace and favor. My exile is not a rewarding memory."

"Had I known . . ."

"You know now. Understand further that in this work anonymity is everything. It is the badge you will wear for the rest of your life. My earthly title—for understand that my title went with the land and the Czar's favor—is not evidence of any signal deed or accomplishment. Rather it reminds me only that my fathers toadied to a weakling for the right to oppress a hundred serfs. I am in the profession for no cause but my own. I am useful to whoever purchases my skills and services. But I am useful. That is why men respect me and court my favor."

"I will check this number right away," the short man says, chagrined.

The tall man turns again to the stone parapet and gazes down as though lost in his thoughts. His assistant goes across the roof to the table with the umbrella over it and sits down with the pad of paper at his elbow. The dogs follow him with their eyes, not moving.

The table is arranged like a small command headquarters, with three dun-colored field telephones on it. The telephones have been deftly spliced into the city system by means of a long lead wire brought up through a chimney from a room below. Also on the table are another pair of binoculars, two cameras, and a device for attaching the Leica to the eyepiece of the large telescope standing covered on its tripod. Next to the table, on the other tripod, is a listening device with a parabolic dish that can be focused down on the street to pick up conversations on the steps of the building opposite. A large suitcase beside it contains the recording apparatus. Next to that is a large stuffed chair, obviously abandoned, damp from the previous rain; and a low charcoal brazier on three legs, with a casserole full of dull red coals.

The telephone communication takes only a few minutes. The assistant brings the jotted information back to the parapet and stands waiting for recognition before speaking.

The tall man breaks his gaze from the ghostly black panorama of streets and buildings. He says: "Am I correct?"

"Yes. The number is assigned to the Americans. It belongs to the Embassy transportation pool."

"And did they trace the taxi that arrived at the apartment in the Rue Babylon?"

"Yes. You were right. It was the same one that passed here thirty minutes ago. The police followed it from the Ministry of Justice."

"Hmm. My powers of clairvoyance are improving. Who went in the Delahaye?"

"They don't know yet."

"It doesn't matter. Everything is proceeding as planned. Doesn't that please you?"

"I am pleased if you are pleased. As for the plan, I don't know what the plan is." The short man laughs, a high-pitched self-conscious giggle. "As you say, I don't even know whom I am working for."

"Are you satisfied with your work?"

"Oh, yes. Very satisfied."

"You have no wish to abrogate the terms of your contract?"

"Oh, no. I didn't mean . . . Besides, that's not possible, is it?"

The tall man muses a moment. "It's been done a few times."

"I can't possibly imagine what anyone could gain by doing such a thing."

"I will teach you imagination when you're ready for it," the tall man snaps.

"I didn't mean to say . . ."

The tall man softens. "You will make a capable agent," he says. "All it takes is time."

"I am encouraged."

"Don't be. It takes a lifetime and longer to become a good agent. Have you any idea of how long I have been in this profession?"

"No."

"It is just as well. You wouldn't believe it. By the way, let me compliment you on your choice of this location. I can see everything from here."

"When I worked for the telephone company before the war I installed the trunk lines here. That's how I knew where the main junction box was."

"We need more men of your talents in the service."

"Perhaps I might be able to help recruit some of my former colleagues . . ."

"You leave the recruiting to us, my dear fellow. You are not ready for anything so delicate as recruitment."

"Someday I should like to know . . . I mean . . . why I was chosen."

"We watched you for a long time. You were chosen because you were ambitious and uneducated."

"I see."

"No, you don't. But perhaps someday you will. Don't be too anxious."

"I'm sorry if my curiosity . . ."

"Perhaps the time has come to satisfy some of your curiosity. Curiosity and ambition are two serpents whose fangs must be periodically drawn."

"These are my private sins, you are right."

"Now tell me, are you certain that you have no residual moral compunctions left over from your former life among the hypocrites?"

"Quite certain. I see the world more clearly since I've been in training with you."

"Would you say that you have become enlightened?"

"I would hesitate to use such a word in your presence, but otherwise . . ."

"Excellent. You are learning."

"I try to see the world as it is, as you have taught me."

"Excellent. Then tell me, how is the world?"

The assistant stammers slightly. "Ah—I, ah—I'm not sure I understand how you want me to answer."

"Come now, my dear fellow, I am about to satisfy some of your curiosity. Just answer my questions candidly. You are curious to know what we have been working on these past days, are you not?"

"Why, yes. But . . ."

"Then we must start at the beginning. Tell me now, how *is* the world?"

"Do you want a short answer or a long one?"

"Give me a studied answer."

The assistant lowers his head and thinks a moment. In the sudden distance across the rooftops a single lighted window silently appears in a tall apartment building. The tall man idly raises his glasses to peer at it. After a few seconds the assistant raises his head to answer.

"I would say the world presents a picture of confused conflicts."

Without lowering his glasses, the tall man asks: "Are these conflicts real?"

"I don't quite . . ."

"Are these conflicts material?"

"To the world? No."

"Then why do they continue?"

"I don't know why. I have often wondered why. Except that I suppose it is human nature to fabricate conflicts."

"You give human nature too much credit. And what of superhuman nature?"

"Again, I must confess my lack of . . ."

"All right, perhaps we should begin at the beginning again. You and I, would you say we were human?" He continues to peer through the glasses at the window.

"Obviously you are driving at a point I'm missing. That is, I . . ."

"I am watching a woman sitting on a bed with a baby. The baby has awakened her and is crying. She is trying to put it back to sleep by rocking it in her arms. Would you say she is human?"

"I would say so, yes."

"Do you think she knows I am watching her? Do you think she even suspects that there is another being in whose mind she actively exists?"

"No, not unless she is praying."

"She is not praying," the tall one says sharply. "She has two existences, one in her own mind, and one in mine. If her existence is human and can yet in itself exist in my mind without her knowledge or permission, then what is my existence? At this time and in this place is my existence not precisely superhuman?"

"You mean because you are standing on top of a building? You mean superhuman in the sense of being above humans, is that it?"

The tall man sighs. "Yes, I suppose there's a literal interpretation for everything, even metaphysics. Perhaps you had better simply do your work and not ponder these simpler matters."

"But it is because I have not had proper instruction . . ."

"True, true," the tall man says gently. He pauses, watching through the glasses. "She is putting the baby back into bed. And now she is standing in front of a mirror looking at herself."

"I do want to understand, but you yourself said it takes time . . ."

"Well, then. We'll leave generalities and pursue specifics. You want to know something about your work, is that right?"

"Yes."

"Particularly you are curious about the present project."

"I would never ask questions, of course."

"Yes. Well, of all the confusion and conflict, what do you make of it? No, never mind, that's too general again. For the moment you are a French citizen. Now, as a French citizen, what conflict is uppermost in your mind? Come now, what do you suspect we're working on? You must have guessed it at one time and another."

"The Dujardin thing?"

"Why, of course. Now, have I told you anything you didn't know already?"

"I suppose not."

"Do you wish now to ask questions?"

"You said I was a French citizen for the moment. Am I to be transferred?"

The tall man laughs. "You fail entirely to appreciate the greatness of the profession. You are a French citizen for the purpose of your daily survival and for the immediate purpose of my leading question. But tell me, when you walk among them, do you feel yourself to be one of them?"

"Well, no . . ."

"Of course not. And furthermore, you don't know whether you are a traitor or a savior, and that further isolates you from them."

"But I feel that they are all like me and I am like them."

"Nonsense. What ordinary human has eyes that stretch across cities, eyes that pierce the night and uncover their nakedness? What ordinary mortal has ears that listen in a hundred places at once, ears that hear through walls? And what human being has a memory for the casual conversation, for the face in a crowd, a memory that defies time and distance. With your cameras, listening devices . . ."

"But I'm only a technician."

"You've only begun your apprenticeship. I commenced as a dilettante. We all have to start from somewhere." The tall man shrugs. "You have difficulty grasping abstract ideas," he says, a trace of irritation in his voice.

"There *is* one question I would like to ask," the assistant says.

"I have given you leave. Ask it."

"I don't understand the Dujardin case. Who is guilty?"

The tall man laughs. "Guilty. Who is not guilty? They are all guilty, the whole world. If they weren't you and I would have to seek other employment."

"I mean practically speaking. In the trial, who was guilty?"

"The same as always. The jury."

"I think you are mocking me for my ignorance," the short man says, hurt.

"Why, quite the contrary, my dear fellow. Perhaps I should explain to you what a trial is among men on this earth. Are you prepared to follow me?"

"I am prepared."

"A trial is a ritual whereby miserable men are relieved of their share of the common guilt by compassionate men, who then take this extra burden of guilt on their own shoulders. The condemned man is thenceforth blameless forevermore. His guilt is portioned out among his judges. Thus there is on earth no guiltier man than an aged judge, for an aged judge is among the most generous of men."

"But which side are we working for?"

16

"She is rocking the baby again."

"She? Oh. You mean the woman in the window. I didn't understand."

"Why should we favor one side over the other? Is it not true that we hear only what is spoken, and see only what is there to be seen?"

"You mean we are useful to both sides?"

The tall man doesn't answer, but continues to study the dark distance through the glasses, his lips a tight thin line as though sealed.

The assistant says: "It seems useless, all this conflict. Like a game with no prize."

The tall man wheels about with sudden passion. "You are wrong!" he hisses. "There *is* a prize. Would you like to see it?"

The surprised assistant nods dumbly. The tall man grasps his arm in iron-hard fingers and propels him across the roof to the other side. There, before the stone parapet, he hands the wide-eyed assistant the binoculars and says, "Look, look at the prize. Look at the Place de la Concorde. What do you see?"

The assistant silently looks through the glasses. Then he says, "It's dark, but I can see them."

"Look under the streetlights. They gather around light like moths, like planets around a hundred suns. What are they?"

"People. At least they look like . . ."

"Correct. People. The people are a great beast, so we are told, and yet the prize is their allegiance. The struggle is for their mindless hearts."

"I spoke hastily."

"And what are they doing?"

"I can't tell. They are all huddled up together. It looks like they are sleeping."

"Idiot! They are *waiting*. They are waiting for the demonstration. They may have come from anywhere and nowhere, but they came. Because they believe."

"Yes, they are waiting."

"Who is taking care of them? Is it cold?"

"Why, I don't see anyone taking care of . . ."

"Who fathered them? Hath the rain a father?"

The assistant drops the glasses and stares at the tall man.

"Don't look at me as if I were mad," the tall man says sharply.

"I—I'm sorry. I didn't mean . . ."

"I'll tell you the answer: They are fatherless. They are poor and fatherless. Bastards!" The tall man's anger mounts momentarily to a rage. "They are bastards! Do you understand me?"

"Yes, I . . ."

"Then stop looking at them in their shame and misery!" He snatches the glasses away from the assistant. The assistant stares at his empty hands in confusion.

Suddenly the other's wrath vanishes. He hands the glasses back to the assistant as though returning a plaything to an injured child. "Come," he says gently, "carry the binoculars back to the table. You must be very cold."

The other nods in dumb assent and smiles tentatively. They walk together to the table. The tall man says, "You must understand that I demand more from you than I do from others. I am not hard on you for my pleasure, but rather for your survival. In this profession there is no room for mistaken thinking. Mistaken thought is the mother of blundering enterprise. Therefore in all things you must see and think clearly."

"I understand," the assistant says.

The tall man picks up his notepad from the table and with it begins to fan the coals in the brazier to life. Sparks fly from the glowing charcoal with each rapid pass of the fan, and presently tiny blue-orange flames snap among the traceries of black and red. The idle assistant stands over his superior's bent back looking awkward and embarrassed. Then to make up for having let his superior remake the fire, he is suddenly inspired to make a comfortable place for him to enjoy its warmth. He recovers the newspaper lying dry on the roof gravel under the table, and sets about spreading it carefully over the dampness of the ruptured chair's upholstery. When the coals are glowing well and throwing good heat, the tall man straightens and looks around. He takes the prepared seat without a word of acknowledgment. The assistant makes haste to drag the brazier in front of the chair, where his superior can get the full effect of its warmth.

The tall man says, "No, I built it for you. You must be cold. I never feel the cold. Here, you sit here." He starts to get up from the chair.

The assistant refuses, with gestures of such vehemence that the tall man half risen from the chair looks at him doubtfully a moment, and then falls back. The pale glow from the brazier reflects a warm red off his thin, handsome features.

The assistant smiles his satisfaction. He says, "I have some cheese left from earlier."

"I'm not hungry." The tall man stares into the heap of coals, which glow and wane in the cold motionless air like a thing alive and breathing. He seems to relax into a reverie. The assistant rummages in his pocket for the cheese and bread, unwraps it, and falls to finishing it. Then his superior says: "They move me to a great pity. In this work one comes to see the irony of existence, but it only deepens one's capacity for pity. And that's the final irony. That woman, for example . . ."

"The woman in the window?"

"Do you think she was thinking of herself as 'the woman in the window'?"

"No."

"And yet to us she is the woman in the window. Strange. She was tired, and not beautiful."

"It is difficult to be a mother these days."

"And she was young. Too young yet to know that her baby is going to die."

"Her baby? Die? How can you know that?"

The tall man gazes into the fire as though not hearing. Then abruptly he comes back from his thoughts and looks up at his assistant, into his face, as though searching for a clue. Then he says: "Is her child not mortal like the rest?"

"Now I understand you."

The tall man smiles and leans forward. "Do you?" he asks intently. "Then please explain *me*. What am I doing here? Who am I?"

"I—I'm sorry," the assistant says in confusion, backing away slightly.

The older man leans back wearily in his chair again. The firelight plays on the drawn lines in his face. "So am I," he says. "Profoundly sorry."

He falls silent and looks up at the predawn sky. As he watches, the sky overhead deepens to a regal purple; in the east the first light of dawn appears beneath the lifting shroud of winter clouds; in the distance, the sound of an airplane. The two dogs raise their heads, listening.

III

John Stone looked at the clock—the shining pendulum blinked like a steady eye behind its peephole—silently reminded himself again that this was the last night. After tonight no more questions. He let his eyes go out of focus—it was the next best thing to closing them—and tried to think about the document on the desk.

For the third night in a row, Stone was closeted with an official at the Ministry of Justice. The main job was done; all that remained was to double-check details. The air in the room was close, smelled of steam heat and paint from the newly painted radiators. Bare-walled, official, the second-floor office in the Ministry seemed isolated from the rest of the darkened building merely by the fact that it was lighted and occupied. The door to the corridor was open, but the corridor was only a black maw of shadows. The cleaning women had turned off the corridor lights when they'd left the floor for the night. Now there were only Stone, the advocate whose name Stone couldn't recall, and the young man, the stenographer. And they were alone, three men capsuled in a lighted room in an abandoned building.

On the wall the clock ticked, mechanical, tired—the flat brass pendulum passing back and forth behind the tiny oval window was no longer a distraction, but a relief. Stone watched it as though hypnotized. The stenographer, a thin young man with an acne-scarred face, sat near the window looking out into the glazed blackness; he yawned incessantly in restrained furtive silence, hardly opening his mouth. The advocate sat immobile, his chin in both hands, grimly concentrating on the slow pages of the thick document on the desk before him. Every few minutes there was a thin rattle of onionskin as he leafed over another page. From a green glass ashtray at his elbow, a cigarette unreeled a ribbon of delicate blue smoke, slowly turned to perfect fragile ash.

Every now and then the lawyer looked up to ask a question, hear Stone's answer, make a note. Once he broke the point of his pencil; the monotony was broken as he stopped to sharpen it with a tiny gold penknife he carried on his watch chain. Even the scraping blade sounded loud in the room. The fatigue was hypnotic. Stone watched, thinking without will, gazed at the document: his history, his life.

A hundred closely typewritten pages—and what was it? He had answered each of their questions as honestly as he could—and how honest was that? Could any man be honest about the past? A week ago he could have been certain he knew the past. But intense questioning had an effect. Had things really happened the way he remembered them, or was memory fatigued by present events, present desires, regrets too deep to be remembered at all? He knew he was now too tired to think. When so tired, it was dangerous to think; it was like struggling in a bag.

Stone thought: They want to understand the present, not the past. They saw the present as a logical extension of the past, and if the present was to be logical they first had to impose a logic on the past. That sums it up, Stone thought; they are not interested in what happened then, but in what they want to happen now.

The document on the desk, then, was futile—he turned it over in his mind—a hundred pages of irrelevant questions, accommodating answers. Several times he *had* tried to explain, but explanations only seemed to frustrate their effort of comprehension. They listened, tolerant, polite, even at times suspicious, confused. But always after such an attempt to explain the complexities of the past, Stone would notice that the stenographer had stopped recording, was waiting patiently for an end to the digression, the irrelevancy. Perhaps the truth wasn't subject to being recorded.

Stone felt the warning twinges of a headache. His mind was full of things that still needed saying, that still required the utmost care and explanation. But over the past week he'd had a growing sense of discouragement, of frustration, of bitterness. Flattered at first by their attention, he'd learned finally that they weren't interested in him, nor in what had really happened to him. And now the document, their collection of details, was finished. When he answered their prepared questions they had listened to him with absorbed interest, but when he tried to explain, to transmit his feelings, they listened as though to a friendly madman. Lack of sleep hadn't helped matters, he knew. He had a tendency to be voluble and subjective when tired. He was still tired tonight, only now he was also numb. He felt trapped and helpless as he stared at the useless dialogue on the desk. It was too late to tear it up and start over again. A curious chill went through him—it was as though they were accusing him—and he felt sick again with suppressed irritation. The feeling passed. He knew he was overtired, felt drenched in failure like cold sick sweat. Time passed slowly and the smoke-laden air in the room was oppressive. I am a friendly witness, he thought cynically. He looked at the man behind the desk. And you, he thought, are the friendly inquisitor.

The interrogator looked up from the document, almost as though he'd heard Stone's silent mind. "This first conversation with the prison doctor . . ." he began, gazing myopically at Stone over his bifocal spectacles. Although a younger man than Stone—Stone put his age at about thirty-five—the glasses gave him the lawyerly manner of an old man.

"Yes?"

"This conversation took place in his office at the prison, is that correct?"

"It was a room upstairs from my cell. There was a first-aid kit on the wall . . ."

"And that's where he passed you the drug that you were to take to make you appear to be ill?"

"Yes," Stone said.

"He gave you no warning?"

"Warning?"

The interrogator paused, ripped open a fresh pack of cigarettes and dumped them out into his desk. Idly he stacked them into a pile like a tiny cord of wood. "That there was an informer among your group," he said, clipping his words.

Stone paused, collecting his words carefully. "I'm afraid I've given you the wrong impression. It is only my guess that there might have been an informer. I never knew for certain . . ." Stone let the sentence trail off, conscious of the interrogator's steady gaze. Besides, it was all written down now. Explanations only confirmed the deeper confusion. It was like trying to recast the die.

"Of course," he said. He looked at Stone a moment longer and went back to his task, making a small cryptic mark in the margin, neat, precise, a mark that meant something only to him.

Stone felt an odd moment of pity for the man across the desk. It came like an illumination that the man didn't dare try to understand what lay beneath the surface of the expressed facts. Deeper explanations were too intimate, too sweaty and personal, and he was afraid of embarrassment. He took refuge in dry official logic. It was only human.

The stenographer meanwhile yawned, nodded slightly, looked furtively at Stone to see if the yawn had been noticed. Stone looked up at the clock again to avoid contact with the young man's sad pale eyes.

For Stone it was the end of a strange week. A week of no sleep, of restlessness, a week dedicated to the remembrance of a dead past. Under the press of urgent circumstances he'd been forced to dredge up the details of lost events, order them in his mind, recount them, edit them, justify them. It had been like a week of forced retreat and meditation, a pilgrimage back, to places and events that had formed him, had determined his life. He remembered more than he told them, went further back than he'd been asked to. When he thought about it objectively it all seemed sane and logical, but privately it was becoming an eerie experience—memory, once provoked, went further: recalling early manhood led back to childhood. Never before had he attempted to explain himself to another human being. Never before had he been compelled to. Nor was he compelled now—for he was still a "voluntary witness"—but once started he had sensed that there could be no turning back. For oddly enough he knew that he had never explained himself to himself. And now he wondered if indeed he ever could. Still smarting from the polite rebuffs he'd suffered in attempting to communicate the bruised truth of his experience, he'd finally resolved to abandon all efforts at communication in favor of the longer task of simple understanding. He had finally seen that it was *he*, not they, who didn't understand. Communication had had to fail. Thereafter he gave them simply what they asked for: facts. Places. Names. Dates. Actions. He'd told no lies. But had he told the truth? And yet it hadn't all been in vain. They had taught him a hard lesson: true facts often tell no truth. To tell the truth, the facts must be invented. It was a startling failure. Order they wanted, not truth.

And what of that *other* investigation: the brief sharp nightmare of the Army's security investigation into his past life? Before that clumsy investigation had been abruptly and mysteriously called off—had higher brass intervened?—he had passed morning and afternoon with the two young civilian security specialists who had come from Washington to interview him. At first they had asked him no questions at all. Rather they gave him to understand that they were not at liberty to discuss any "derogatory information" that might be in his file. Therefore, for the first morning and afternoon, they merely sat and waited for Stone to "talk openly," as they put it. Like two ravens on the doorstep, they sat in Stone's office talking studiously about nothing significant, ominously pleasant, friendly, generous with cigarettes. But the three-way conversation had a system to it: Stone was told that they weren't interested in his wartime work since that was classified still as secret. But in Stone's own mind the Resistance loomed large. He was still under oath not to discuss his job as an agent, and yet one secret word hovered in his conscience like a circling albatross: the word *Communists*.

One agency of the government was begging him to confess; the other was forbidding him to talk. And yet what was there to confess? The war was over, and won. And the two security men kept emphasizing that they weren't interested in his wartime work, that they had been warned not to tempt him to a violation of a service oath. What then had been the threat?

It was pleasant enough on the surface, their curious aimless approach; but underneath was where Stone had sensed danger. They were too young and too humorless. As requested, he recounted the details of his adult life, accounting carefully for his time on earth. It made him feel uncomfortable and silly, even defensive, feminine—like a housewife proving to deliberate children that the inheritance was really spent, not lost, not squandered.

Stone's thoughts were abruptly interrupted.

The interrogator had asked a question from his desk without looking up: "I take it you weren't in Marseilles again after your first mission?"

Stone said, "No." He waited for another question, but there was nothing more.

He resumed his thoughts.

What had he finally told them? He smiled inwardly, sadly. He'd told them facts. He'd told them nothing. In his mind's eye he saw the "fact sheet" they had shrewdly asked him to check over for accuracy: *John Stone: Born, January 1, 1906, Trenton, New Jersey. Name at birth: Giovanni Sasso. Father: Michael Angelo America Sasso; occupation monument-maker. Mother: Edna Sasso (maiden name Baumgarten); occupation teacher (music).* Stone remembered the little three-page document clearly: they'd surprised him with it. But what did it really tell about John Stone? They would have to have lived on Mulberry Street themselves to know anything about who he was and why he was born. Noted correctly in the fact sheet, for example, was the fact that the Sasso family moved to another neighborhood in 1914, that the family name was changed from Sasso to Stone in that same year, and that in 1922 they built a house in Lawrence Township, just outside of Trenton. But standing by itself the fact said nothing. What was important was that the family had moved the first time and changed their name as a result of their boy's having been nicknamed "Sassy Sasso" by some of his third-grade schoolmates. His father had been proud of his Italian name—another important thing that didn't appear on the fact sheet—and never parted with it entirely. He changed the name of his business to "Sasso & Stone, Monuments and Tombstones," referring afterward to Sasso as "the man who started the business before Stone took it over."

Before this dreamlike week of questions and more questions, he never would have thought to remember this. But to Stone, caught between the painful memory of the past and the anxious uncertainty of the present, these things had suddenly become important again. Despite the bitterness and numb anger and fear and uncertainty that ran trapped around the cage of his heart, dogs snapping in a slow sullen whirl, there was still a dim sense of discovery, rejoicing vaguely realized. The odd circumstance of these two separate and mutually exclusive secret investigations had forcibly projected him into the past, into two pasts eternally separate: a secret wartime past, and a prior life of peace. Like night and day. Separated by an oath. In peace he'd taught schoolchildren, had taught them music and French. Once, as an adolescent, he had even dreamed of being a cellist. But that was the somber day of peace; during the long bright night of war he dreamed of nothing, not even victory. He had expected to die.

He had even then disciplined himself to think of death as his proper object. It was the only practical way of conquering fear, the only sensible contract to make with himself. An agent on suicidal missions into enemy territory, he had had to learn to make the bargain. But after the war, when the war was incredibly and strangely and melodramatically over and life continued, he felt his own life become pale, vague, unreal. And only recently, during the last week, a week which was not an orbit of time but only a confused and sleepless question, had he learned why —an illumination, it was clear: In disciplining himself to death he had, in part, achieved it.

That wasn't on the fact sheet either.

The things that were important in his peacetime life were not the things he had told them either, nor were they included there in the massive document on the desk. What *was* important was the whole disconnected mass of sudden memory—that his father had lost two fingers in the old country when a block of marble slipped out of its sling and crushed his hand; that his father couldn't therefore serve his adopted country in the First World War; that he made monuments and honor rolls for its dead: these things were important. His father could recite long passages of Dante by heart, but was uneducated, lost two fingers, was an apprentice at seventeen—if this wasn't important, why should his mind repeat it, suddenly dwell on it so? He knew it was significant, but not why—the secret was still locked in the powerful remembered image, mysterious to the child, of his father's hand: a three-fingered hand, white, covered with limestone dust. As a child it had awed him. And now it suddenly awed him again. Until this week it seemed he'd never known what memory really was.

There were other things he hadn't told them. Details left out. He'd told them he'd been to Paris as a child—and later as a tourist schoolteacher—but he hadn't told them why. Or how. He hadn't even thought about it until they asked him if he'd ever been out of the United States at any time before the war. He had to count back twice on ten fingers to figure out what year it was. The first trip involved his mother, and music, and that dim gay tragic time before Depression:

Up to the time he entered high school, in 1919, his mother gave him music lessons, piano and violin. Even after that, Miss Ogilvy, the spinster music teacher in the elementary school, still gave him private lessons whenever she could. He joined the high school orchestra, but, the school being short of instruments, the only chair open the year he entered was for a cello. He was a phenomenal success on the cello; being awkward in sports and studies, he threw all his energies into music, in which he excelled. He also developed a facility for languages, concealing the fact that he knew Italian from birth and had learned some French from his mother. He even knew a few words of Yiddish and German from her friends. In Latin and French he was often first in his class.

About the time of his second year in high school, on the recommendation of his music teacher and with his mother's strong concurrence, his father agreed to let him go into New York each Saturday to study with a celebrated cellist, Alphone Paz, who held first chair in the New York Philharmonic. The father bought his son a fine cello for his fifteenth birthday. But even then he still clung to the hope that John would grow up to be a lawyer, "maybe someday a big judge."

In a national competition his last year in high school, he won a prize for music that offered him two years of study at any conservatory of his choosing. His teacher in New York was enthusiastic in his insistence that the boy be sent to study under Poggi at the Paris Conservatoire de Musique. The boy's father, with some misgivings that this might be "carrying a hobby too far," finally gave in under the combined forces of his wife and his son's two music teachers. At eighteen the boy went to Paris with six other young American music students on arrangements made under the auspices of the committee awarding the prize. What finally won his father's permission was the fact that Poggi was an Italian. His father wrote a letter to the celebrated man asking him to look after his son and not to encourage him beyond his talents since, as he explained, the only cellist who could make a living in America was a first-rate cellist and even then there was some question. That was 1924. John stayed on in Paris through 1925, living with a French family, working very hard, and leading a very circumscribed life. The family was named Sessions. Madame Sessions had four young American students living in their huge apartment in the sixteenth *arrondissement*. Monsieur Sessions was an exporter of musical instruments, mostly specializing in brass and woodwinds, with oboes his special specialty. A musician himself, his hobby was playing antique music on the original antique instruments—his apartment was a magnificent showcase for his collection; they were kept in glass cases and taken out only on Thursday evenings, when a group of musicians would gather *chez Sessions* to play old scores they copied out of odd archives during their travels all over Europe.

Madame Sessions. She was more a fact than a memory; she was still alive.

Stone watched the advocate leaf over another page, and thought about old Madame Sessions. It was one more thing he could never explain to them. Madame Sessions had a double aspect: she was flesh and blood, also a memory. Twenty years ago she was a handsome woman—but it was more than twenty years ago, Stone thought—1925. It was hard to connect the beautiful active woman of the past with the frail and withered old lady who was Madame Sessions now. She still had the gracious manner, and when she wasn't "resting" she still poured afternoon tea with style. But her eyesight was failing fast. Her face, now powdered and chalkwhite, was smaller and more fragile. She had changed with the room. The priceless collection of ancient instruments was gone; the glass cases lined with bottle-green velvet still stood around the walls of the unused music room, but they were empty. The piano was locked. Stone assumed she had been forced to sell the collection one by one, but he couldn't bring himself to ask. When he had come to visit her after the war they were already gone, every one of them.

Abruptly the interrogator looked up at Stone. He said, "This is taking me longer than I thought. I'm almost through."

Stone said, "I understand."

The stenographer yawned again, no longer making any effort to hide it.

The advocate said, "One of us had to make a final check. We drew lots, you know. I lost. I'm almost to the end."

"Yes."

"So far we're doing very well. No inconsistencies."

Stone said, "That's good." The stenographer glanced at Stone, looked away as Stone turned his head toward him.

"You've been patient," the advocate said, automatically returning his eyes to the manuscript.

Stone nodded. The advocate lowered his chin onto his hands again, resumed reading, sighed inadvertently. The stenographer began to fidget again, uncomfortable in his enforced idleness. He'd been able to be of service only once during the entire evening; otherwise his talents had gone to waste this night.

Suddenly in the silence the clock stopped ticking—it simply stopped, run down. Stone looked to see if the other two had noticed. Neither gave any sign. But just as Stone was about to comment, the advocate, without looking up, said, "Félix, would you mind winding it up for me? Usually the cleaning women take care of it."

The stenographer rose without a word.

The advocate said, "The key is inside. You'll have to stand on a chair." Then he looked at Stone and shrugged. "This office hasn't been cleaned for three nights now," he said, as though complaining of a wrong. He shrugged again and went back to reading, shaking his head to himself.

Stone watched him read, watched his eyes. His eyes moved behind the spectacles, magnified like doll's eyes as they mechanically scanned the close text. Stone let the face drift out of focus; Madame Sessions was still in his mind.

Something had become clear. He hadn't thought of it before; at least he hadn't seen its significance. Now it was abruptly clear why he'd gone to stay at Madame Sessions' apartment a week ago. True, he needed temporary refuge from clamoring newspaper reporters; but it was also true that there were perhaps a dozen other places he might have escaped to. It was clear: during recent weeks the past had become important, and Madame Sessions was a living link with the past.

He had a fleeting sense of piercing the design. There *was* a design, a pattern, a rewarding logic. It was no accident, he saw now, that it had suddenly occurred to him to accept her conversational invitation, an invitation he hadn't even remembered until that moment ten days ago. (It had been right after Paris was liberated, when he came to visit her, still in uniform: she had recognized him instantly, even after twenty-odd years and a war which had changed them both more than age. All he could remember now of the strained nostalgic conversation was her saying, "Your old room is still here for you, when you decide to come back.") He knew she needed the money; instead he'd arranged to get food from the PX and bring packages to her regularly. Now, of course, she steadfastly refused to accept payment from him for the room he was occupying, his old room; he had had to insist.

That was it: his old room. Not only was he dredging into the memory of the past, but suddenly he realized that in a small way he was living in the past. And *that* was what had made the experience of the past week so eerie. That *was* it. Again he felt possessed of an insight, a sense of logic beyond explanation.

He gazed at the thick document the advocate was preparing for the printer, and thought of the empty glass cases with their beautiful linings of old green velvet. He'd spent many satisfying evenings in that room, listening to ancient chamber music with the other young music students who then boarded with the Sessions. He'd even been privileged to play some of the priceless old instruments of Monsieur Sessions' collection—but that was in another decade, and besides, their owner was dead.

1925. That was a year that changed everything.

He remembered that the telegram came in the late afternoon, while they were all gathered in the music room for tea. A late winter afternoon. The telegram was from his father: his mother was sick. Madame Sessions took care of everything.

He left school in midterm and followed his trunk aboard the train at St. Lazare and amid anxious cries of farewell departed for Le Havre for America. The last thing he saw through the steamy glass was Madame Sessions, handsome in a fur muff and Cossack-style fur hat, searching anxiously for him among the faces behind the moving train windows. He didn't let her see him, because he was crying. Outside of Paris the train moved through the flat winter twilight and a light snow began to fall, bleak and gray.

The passenger steamer on which he made the empty winter crossing was deserted. The first night out was rough, Christmas Eve, and the band played Christmas carols and gay music to an immense and empty ballroom. There was a girl his age who danced atilt with her father, as the polished floor rose and dropped.

The next day he saw the girl again. It upset him. He practiced his cello four dutiful hours, even though he was sick from the rough winter seas. And tried not to think of anything. But there was the girl, a pretty girl he remembered, with her carefree family; and a longing and sudden loneliness that was new to him. In the afternoon he watched her playing shuffleboard with her father. Her bright laughter awakened something like guilty fear in him, and thoughts of his mother sick.

On the third day the girl spoke to him; she had heard him practicing on his cello in the deserted lounge, and complimented him. She took him by surprise; and he insulted her with his incurable shyness. He wasn't able to answer a word. She turned away embarrassed, and left him standing, his heart wrung with anger, vaguely realized desire. If only she hadn't mentioned the cello.

That night in the shivering sensual roll of the sea he was unable to sleep, thinking about her, feverish and full of bewildering lust. Unworthy, unclean, therefore unable to pray, on that night he knew for certain that his mother would die. It was a terrible night, a night he would never forget. He cried for the nearly last time; and the embers of childhood, at nineteen, died and went cold. Near dawn, finally exhausted in the rhythmic heaving of the winter sea, he gave up his tormented vigil; swallowed in the vast intimate confusion of lost love, he fell asleep.

He was twenty years old on the day of his arrival in New York, January 1, 1926. No one met him in spite of the cablegram Madame Sessions had sent, and he made his way alone to Trenton, leaving his baggage for later. He carried only his cello with him. When he arrived home he knew the moment he saw the house, its shades drawn, that his mother was already dead.

There was no one in the house. He sat down in the living room alone. In the gathering winter dusk, he opened his cello case and played a few bars of a nursery song she'd taught him. He tried to cry but couldn't. At dusk his father returned with his grandmother Sasso. They were returning from the funeral. His father greeted him; the boy was shocked. His father had aged as much in a year as another man might in ten.

His father never recovered from the impact of his wife's death. He began turning all his assets into real estate, buying properties without even looking at them, as though the transaction held no meaning or even interest for him. He left the management of his business more and more in the hands of his yard foreman, Williams, making him boss and partner in 1928. He grew increasingly irritable, being especially resentful of his mother, old Mama Sasso, then seventy-four and full of the querulous ill nature of uprooted old age. She had never learned English and the only language spoken at home now was Italian. In the spring of 1929 he hired a housekeeper, an Italian woman, to look after the old woman's needs. He hardly ever left his bedroom any more; he would get up at seven and dress and sit at a desk writing "letters." One Sunday morning he left the house to go to Mass, an unusual thing for him. He walked out of the house and was never seen again.

No one ever knew where he went. The "letters" he had been writing as he muttered to himself in his locked bedroom over the months past were detailed admonitions and instructions to his son as to what to do in case of his death. No one knew when or how or if he died. His father left no power of attorney among his papers, and the fact that he was not known to be dead made legal obstacles. But the question of the estate was settled by the stock-market crash that fall, which so devalued the few securities that his father had left in a safe-deposit box of the Trenton Trust Company that the problem of ownership became largely academic. The decade ended in chaos; and John, in January of 1930, sold the house for what he owed, and set about following his father's injunction that he get a college education. He was twenty-four, a late starter.

Stone's clocklike reverie was interrupted by a decorous fit of coughing from the stenographer. The young man coughed behind the back of his thin left hand, glancing anxiously at the advocate—the advocate ignored him. It was almost as though the coughing was intended merely to break the ticking monotony of the silence. Suddenly he stopped coughing, looked out the window again.

The silence broken, the advocate took the advantage, looked up and asked Stone quickly, "Do you mind if I ask a personal question? You don't have to answer it."

Stone said, "Not at all."

"Have you ever had—and I mean this question in a general way— have you ever had any private, ah, shall we say, *connections* with the Party in your own country?"

"In America? No."

"Of course I wouldn't presume to ask you about your private sympathies . . ." the advocate said, tactfully leaving it to Stone whether to answer or not.

"I have never had private sympathies in the matter. My work in France was simply a matter of carrying out my mission. I was under orders to use my judgment."

"I see."

"Ah, this man who was with you . . ." The advocate let his eyes drop to the document for an instant. ". . . this man you call Orchard —he was a Communist?"

Stone demurred. "Orchard was killed. So was my radio operator. I had to make my decisions alone."

"Yes, of course. I was merely curious in a general way . . ." The advocate went back to reading.

Stone thought: He'll bring it up again before the night's out.

The two special investigators from Washington had brought it up several times before they got discouraged—they were especially interested in his political life during the Depression. Stone smiled to himself: he had no political life, not in the thirties, not now. He remembered the look of sharp suspicion that had crossed the faces of both the civilian investigators when he blandly informed them that he hadn't voted in the 1932 election because at the time he didn't feel he understood the issues clearly enough. They asked him if he didn't think it was every American's duty to vote, and he had answered, "Not if he knows he's ignorant." He wanted to ask the two investigators if they voted in the 1932 election, but he thought better of it; neither one of them could have been old enough to shave in 1932. In fact the younger one, a fresh young college graduate who masked his uncertainty with a studied air of seriousness, was probably still playing marbles in that sad year of trial and disappointed hope. But the attitude sharply reminded Stone of his own uncertain—although different—youth, and he said nothing.

There had been incidents in those days of Depression that he could have related, but it would have only embarrassed the clean-cut structure of fact they were seeking. He could have told them what life had been like, what it meant to survive without a family. He could have told them a lot. He could have even told them about the sharp-faced woman with the red hair . . .

From 1930 to 1933 he lived in a rooming house in Trenton and worked at odd jobs to support himself through New Jersey State Teachers College. He had never made any conscious decision to abandon music, but after his mother's death, amid all the postponements and indecisions that followed, months of silence had lengthened into years. He knew his fingers had gone stiff without practice. For two months after his mother's death, partly to atone for missing her funeral, but mainly to take his mind off the aimless confusion that attended waiting on his father's decision as to what he should do next, he had worked in the stoneyard of Stone & Sasso, Architectural Stonework. It was hard satisfying work, moving blocks of marble and limestone about, quartering and polishing them, but it didn't help preserve the sensitivity of his string fingers. In 1931 he went back to the old house and repossessed his cello from the downstairs closet where he had locked it over four years ago. He had left it there by agreement with the new owner, a former friend of his father's.

He took it back with him to his rented room and spent an hour replacing the dead strings and tuning it. He played that evening for two hours before he had to go to work—he had a job stringing telephone cables through sewer conduits, working from eight in the evening to four in the morning. During the day he went to classes and slept; he was studying to be a French teacher. His French was nearly perfect but he needed the diploma to get a job.

The day after his two hours with the cello he took it into New York and sold it to a dealer for nearly what his father had paid for it, and put the money in a bank.

The following year, in addition to his job with the telephone company, which paid him fifteen dollars a week, he took a weekend job as a chauffeur for an undertaker, or mortician, as that gentleman preferred to entitle his calling—a curious euphemistic reversal that impressed Stone as humorously macabre. The job added five dollars to his weekly income and he moved to better quarters.

In 1932 his grandmother died, and after her death Mr. Williams made an informal cash settlement with Stone for his father's share of the partnership. Considering the year, it was a fair settlement. Mr. Williams had no way of knowing whether the elder Stone was deceased or still alive to return someday and reclaim his share of the business. Stone was delighted, especially since it came at a time when the telephone company was laying off men. He added the money to what he already had in the bank from the sale of his instrument. He was saving then to get married. A girl, a fellow student named Faith Masters, equally harried herself by a night job as a waitress in a White Tower hamburger shop, had more or less surrendered to his sleepless off-hours courtship.

But three weeks after the bank failure of 1932 she broke the engagement, what there was of it to break, and John Stone, at twenty-six, decided he'd missed his chance for marriage.

His savings wiped out, Stone was graduated in 1933 in a borrowed double-breasted blue suit, the one lent him by the mortician for chauffeuring the hearse on weekends. By going to school summers, and even sometimes nights, he'd made it in three years. He was in arrears to the college and got his teaching certificate only on promise to pay. But the time he had spent in getting it had dissipated the opportunity of getting the job it qualified him for. For in 1933, even Ph.D.s were unemployed and looking for work.

After applying for jobs at nearly a score of high schools Stone gave up in disgust and joined the Civilian Conservation Corps. He did this the day after he had spent six hours waiting in an employment office for a job as a day laborer. He hadn't got the job, and on emerging into the street at six o'clock, hungry and full of dull rage, he was handed a leaflet by a meanly anonymous woman with mousy red hair. He remembered her that way: the woman with the red hair. The leaflet said, "Had enough? Join the Communist Party of America and take ACTION!" The leaflet gave the address of an office in a local bank building. It was the same bank where he'd lost his savings. Standing in the failing winter light of 1933, staring at the brassy invitation he held in his hand, he experienced a sinking sensation, of wrathful panic, a feeling oddly like being cornered in a trap. The mousy woman, watching him as he read the leaflet, made the error of smirking a jaded last-laugh smirk. He looked at her a moment and suddenly all the fury he had pent up over

31

the months burst out. He cursed the startled woman off the sidewalk into the street, to the grim amusement of several onlookers, and capped his spated anathema by tearing the leaflet into a hundred bits and snowing it into the air over his head. Then he laughed and clapped the woman amiably on the back and went home.

The next day he made the decision, and spent the year in the C.C.C. building a picnic park near the Delaware Water Gap.

In 1935, as the rusty wheels of industry moved off dead center again and the Ph.D.s started drifting back into cobwebbed laboratories, he got a job as a substitute teacher in the Trenton school system. His duties consisted of filling in for regular teachers out with colds, and from one day to the next he never knew what subject he would be teaching, or indeed if he'd be teaching at all. Mainly he developed a certain astuteness in ferreting out cooperative students who would inform on their classmates and tell him what the previous day's homework assignment had been. Then he would confine himself to examining the victims as to the state of their unpreparedness, which was, in 1935 in that city, usually gross if unblamable; many of the students, like their teachers, were holding down after-school jobs. Stone worked at odd jobs on the side, played the Sunday organ at a corrective school for girls.

The following year, at the late age of thirty, John Stone became a regular teacher. The year in the C.C.C. had turned him into a fairly muscular example of a man. He was strong enough to engage in most sports on a more than equal footing, having become in the rough-and-tumble of Corps life particularly adept at the manly pastimes of boxing and wrestling, making up in science what he lacked in brute experience. When, therefore, an opening became available at the high school in the neighboring community of Princeton for someone who could teach French and help coach athletics, he borrowed a fellow pedagogue's asthmatic automobile and whipped the reluctant machine thirteen miles through the driving rain; he was still dripping as he stood on the principal's carpet inquiring about the job. The principal stated in a businesslike way the salary, duties, et al., and then dropped the chilling remark that there had been five other applicants that morning. Stone played his trump over his own ace and offered in addition to take on some of the duties of a music coach. The principal's eyebrows went up a fraction of an inch. He politely inquired after Stone's credentials, obviously expecting to find them thin if not desperate. But as Stone ran down the dusty list of bright names, the men and places, Alphone Paz, Poggi, Paris, the Conservatoire, the prizes and medals, he saw the principal's face change. Stone knew he had the job, but he hadn't driven from Trenton to wait in uncertainty. Instead of bargaining on hours and salary, he asked to know immediately if he could have the job, lying that he had another offer to reply to that afternoon. The principal's eyes narrowed in thought and he surveyed Stone as though deciding whether to risk buying the horse without looking at its teeth. Finally he asked Stone to wait outside while he conferred with the superintendent of schools by telephone.

Stone left Princeton as a new citizen of the town and went back to Trenton only to return the car and collect his monies owed and his belongings. The new salary was astronomical: $150 per month; it had been upped voluntarily by the superintendent in consideration of his added duties as, of all things, bandmaster. Stone sang most of the first act of *Rigoletto* on the way back in the rain. As bandmaster he knew he had a plum: outside income as a music tutor. As he drove singing in the blinding cold spring rain he flexed his fingers to limber them and wondered if he could still do a sixty-fourth-note trill as cleanly as he could for Poggi. He picked up a rain-sodden hitchhiker on the other side of Lawrenceville and sang to him until they reached Trenton. The man smiled embarrassedly all the way. Stone asked him if he had eaten. The man said no. Stone gave him a half-dollar and dropped him off in front of a beanery on Brunswick Avenue. It was one of the first times in nearly a decade that Stone had felt utterly good, or had thrown away a dollar.

He plunged into his work; he recruited the band, organized a chamber-music group, planned a concert. The students, lifted out of themselves by his enthusiasm—incredible even to them, for they were not deaf to their own distempered harmonies—played doggedly on; soon to everyone's amazement their flair developed to the point where the ambiguities they manufactured passed unnoticed in the youthful outpouring of confidence and musical sounds. Deaf to cacophonies he plowed ahead. He began to organize the chamber group into a nucleus for an orchestra. One summer he went to Europe on a budget tour.

Finally he organized a French Club that met each Thursday during the morning study period. Students flocked to it to avoid the silent tedium of study under watchful eyes. In no time at all, the orchestra was playing spring concerts outdoors, the band was traveling with the football team each fall. And in no time at all it was 1939. The French Club made trips to New York to speak French and get lost and eat things at the World's Fair. And Hitler invaded Poland.

Stone rose out of his vat of activity to find that the world had moved on as he had unwittingly grown older and, in an active bachelor's small measure, happier. The world had turned the elusive corner to prosperity and found war. He thought more and more of the apartment house in the sixteenth *arrondissement,* of Monsieur and Madame Sessions, of the priceless antique instruments in their velvet-lined glass cases. He had tried to look up the Sessions on his brief schoolteachers' tour of France, but the apartment was closed; they were away for their *vacances.* He thought later of writing them but dismissed the idea, uncertain if they would remember him. Nearly fourteen years had passed. He could hardly believe it. Fourteen years.

The day France fell and the swastika flew from buildings in the

Rue de Rivoli—the "phony war," the lull after Poland, was no longer phony—he went home to the room where he lived comfortably in the bosom of a ministerial family. It was a large old rambling house and his was the upstairs apartment, rear—he had his board in exchange for piano lessons for the three children. He sat in his room until dinnertime thinking: of China, of Spain, of his father's Italy now under a pompous stage-actor who, in newsreel after newsreel, played Juliet to the nation's Romeo. And of his mother, who had been French, and a Jew. There was a pattern here, he thought, but it evaded him. Finally he thought of Finland and Ethiopia. It seemed that they'd all been practicing; and that was the pattern. He'd been watching the rehearsals for a drama that was just beginning, not ending.

That evening at dinner, as though an answer had merely emerged from the gnashing mill of his unconscious mind, he announced almost without thinking that he was going to join the Army. He surprised himself more than he did the Reverend Meagher, his wife, three children, and the other boarder, Mr. Curtain, the Y.M.C.A. secretary. The latter put down his spoon and said merely, "What in Heaven's name for?"

Stone, unseeing, watched the blue ribbon of smoke rising from the advocate's endless cigarette. A fleeting image of the Reverend Meagher's wife, a bosomy woman prone to easy sentimental tears—he remembered how she would sniffle over newspaper accounts of weddings and funerals of people she only vaguely knew—a fleeting image of her great meaty face floated across his reminiscent vision. He remembered with extraordinary lucidity the cookbook she kept on the window ledge in the kitchen. In his mind's eye he could see it: a thick page-loose book with a broken spine and grease-stained pages, bulged to the point of bursting with newspaper clippings, recipes from magazines, and a lifetime's collection of leather souvenir-bookmarks—idiotic souvenirs from places she had never been. But she had been kind to him. He wondered what made him remember, of all the oddly assorted things she collected, a cookbook. He wondered if she were still alive.

Suddenly the advocate thumped the heavy manuscript with the flat of his hand and stood up. His chair scraped loudly on the wooden floor. The stenographer jumped, guiltily at attention.

"Finished!" the advocate said, twisting his back from side to side to stretch the cramped muscles—if it weren't for the smile on his face he might have been writhing in pain. He took off his bifocal spectacles and kneaded the bridge of his nose. His face looked naked without the glasses, his eyes wide and childlike, innocent. He put the spectacles back on again, became an agency of law once more. He said again, "Finished!" and sighed with heavy delight.

Stone looked at him, unaccountably found himself laughing. Instantly the smile faded from the advocate's face. Stone stood up, serious, apologetic.

The rest was confusion. A spate of busy instructions to the stenographer—he was responsible for taking the manuscript to the printer. Stone grasped that the printer was waiting for it. Coats. Hats. Gloves. A tangle of scarves was sorted out from the pile on the extra chair. Handshakes. The inevitable confusion of official good-bys.

In the hallway, the lights suddenly went on as though by magic. And then they met a tiny phalanx of freshly slept lawyers coming up the stairway to relieve Stone's companion of his lone vigil. Stone said good-by and went on alone, hearing the echoing empty talk long after he was out of the light. He groped his way out through the dark lower corridor and found himself standing in the dark courtyard. It was cold; he could see his breath. Outside in the street he found a taxi; he had to wake the driver.

IV

Standing in the darkness of the Rue Babylon, John Stone paid off the taxi driver through the window of the cab. The old man had kept up a steady stream of garlic-accented French all the way from the Ministry of Justice to the Rue Babylon, discoursing on politics with all the flair of a professional entertainer; he had worked hard for his tip and he accepted it with an accomplished doffing of his chauffeur's cap. He examined the money quickly in the feeble light, then looked narrowly at Stone, as though taking his measure, his eyes glinting conspiratorially in the tiny yellow light of the taxicab meter. Finally he leaned across the front seat and motioned to Stone to come closer. Stone put his head inside the window. Even in the predawn chill he could smell the faintly pleasant odor of garlic on the old man's visible breath.

"Because you are a good type," the old man began, by way of explanation. "Don't turn your head to look, but a car has been following us."

Stone laughed softly. "Thank you," he said. "I am aware of it. They're just as unhappy about it as I am."

"Ah, good," the old man said. "Ordinarily I wouldn't say anything, since they came out of the Ministry. But—" he shrugged "—you seemed all right to me."

"You're all right yourself," Stone said, lifted momentarily from fatigue.

"Sometimes the police are sneaky," the old man said with an apologetic shrug. "Citizens have to stick together, not so?" He blew his nose and briskly put the cab in gear. Stone saluted him. The old man said, *"Bonne chance,"* and drove off, around the corner.

Stone watched the taxi disappear; then turned and walked slowly back to where the car was parked in the darkness, its lights turned off. The two men in it were smoking; the glowing points of their cigarettes were visible through the windshield. They ignored Stone as he approached; he had to tap on the window. The nearest one shrugged, looked uncertainly at his companion, and rolled it down.

"Would you like to come inside for a cup of coffee?" Stone asked.

The near one turned to the one sitting behind the wheel.

"Orders are to stay outside," the driver said shortly. He was looking straight ahead.

"Where are my other two friends?" Stone asked, looking around.

"Night off."

A voice snapped something distorted and incomprehensible on the police radio, then the radio was silent again. The two inside ignored it.

"If you get cold, come on up," Stone said.

Neither of them answered. The nearest one nodded and shrugged, and Stone turned to walk away.

"Are you going out again this morning?" the driver called, as though against his better judgment. He was clearly being practical in spite of his irritation.

Stone paused. "Not until eight-thirty or so. I'll make sure to wake you," he said. "You can trust me."

The driver grunted and jerked his head at the open window to indicate that the other should roll it up.

Stone walked back toward the apartment. A gauntly husky man— young-looking in his forties—he walked with his shoulders hunched up. He wore no hat. His unruly straight black hair seemed to bother him. He combed his fingers through it twice as he stood waiting for the concierge to wake up and answer the bell. Against the penetrating January cold he wore a well-used light raincoat and a wool scarf stretched long through hard wear. The scarf was wrapped carelessly twice about his neck and hung down outside the raincoat, one end in front, the other in back.

The only light in the dark street was from the streetlamp directly in front of the apartment door. The pavement glistened black with the melting film of ice from the night's drizzle. When the concierge buzzed the electric lock-release from inside, Stone pushed the door open, waved tiredly back in the direction of the invisible parked car, and stepped inside. The massive door swung to behind him with a hollow heavy boom that reverberated in the silent street. Then it was quiet. The only sound was from over the wall, the soft waspish noise of the isolated streetlamp.

Stone crossed the cobbled courtyard inside, groped about for the button of the *minuterie,* and slowly mounted the stairs to Madame Sessions' apartment on the *premier étage.* In his mind he counted carefully to thirty, when he knew the light would go out. It was a game he had played ever since he came to stay in Madame Sessions' apartment.

He took out his key and unlocked the door, waiting to finish his count. The light went out on twenty-four; his timing was badly off tonight.

In the apartment he found the light in the foyer on for him. Silently, so as not to wake Madame Sessions, whose bedroom was off the corridor, nearest the front door, he took off his coat, turned out the light on the table in the foyer, and tiptoed to the end of the long hall toward the sitting room at the farther end. It was too late to go to bed; he would have to get up again in a couple of hours.

From the bookcase in the pitch-dark hall he extracted a book; it was too dark to look at the title. It didn't matter what he read. With the book and his coat under his arm, the scarf dangling loosely around his neck, he went into the darkened sitting room—the music room it had been called in earlier days—and turned on the lamp over the big chair. . . .

For one shocked moment he stood transfixed, staring down at the figure of a woman curled like a cat in the chair asleep; then he recognized Solange Récamier. It was cold in the room, and she had drawn a foot blanket around her for warmth. In her sleep, disturbed by the light, she groped for the blanket and pulled it closer.

"Solange," he said softly. The figure stirred again. She opened her eyes wide. He asked in English, "What are you doing here?"

Even on awaking from uncomfortable sleep Solange Récamier was handsome, Stone thought. He knew her as a close friend of old Madame Sessions, had met her for the first time at dinner a few nights before. She was related in some distant way to the Sessions family and had lost her husband during the war. Stone suddenly recalled that he was to have had dinner with her and Madame last night.

Solange lifted her head and looked around in sleep-heavy bewilderment. She was about thirty, but seen suddenly in this momentary unpoised posture, she looked younger, almost a young girl.

"What *time* is it?" she asked groggily in French.

"It's nearly dawn. I'm sorry about last night. I've been at the Ministry since yesterday afternoon." He answered her automatically in French.

"Doing what?"

"Answering questions for them, what else?"

She sat up and drew her knees under her. She was graceful, easily waking from sleep. She was not small, but was compactly built. She pushed her fingers through the hair at her temples, rubbing the skin, and shook her head violently from side to side.

"Who covered me up?" she asked, touching the blanket.

"Madame Sessions must have."

"She must have turned out the light too," Solange said. Her voice was low, warm with sleep, even huskier than usual.

"Why didn't you go home?" Stone asked.

"I didn't think you'd be so late. I thought I'd wait and let you take me. I don't like to go walking for a cab after midnight."

"You were waiting for me?"

"Of course," she said, stretching candidly. She controlled her movement unconsciously, like a cat. "You must be dead."

"I should be, but I'm not."

"I brought the cello," she said, pointing to the dark corner of the room.

"You did *what?*"

"I said I would."

"I thought you were joking." Stone was astounded.

"It hasn't been played since my father died. All the horsehairs in the bow are dried out, but you can fix that. It's a good one."

"But I haven't touched the cello for years," he said, laughing incredulously. "I'd be afraid to pick it up."

"You gave lessons before the war, you said."

"To high-school students, yes. But to play—" He paused and brushed his hair back off his forehead. He held out his hands and looked at them. "Do these look like a cellist's hands?"

"They're beautiful hands," she said. "It's the only thing I really like about you," she added, smiling. She stretched again, luxuriously, with tense grace, and yawned. "Are you shocked to find a strange girl waiting for you?"

He shook his head slowly, turning his hands over, examining them. For a long time he said nothing. Then he looked at Solange and said, very deliberately, "I think you and Madame Sessions are in league." He didn't smile, glanced uneasily toward the instrument in the corner.

"Of course we are," she admitted. "Why do you think she invited me to dinner? She's very worried about you. After all, you were one of Poggi's favorites. And her husband was very fond of you. She says you were like a son to them. I suppose because they never had children."

"You hardly know me," he said. "Are you worried about me too?"

"Shouldn't I be?" she asked seriously. "You're worried about yourself."

"I behaved rather like a fool after dinner the other night. I was upset."

"You drink too much."

"I'll be all right once this damned inquest is over," he said defensively.

"I'm not sure," she said.

"Why do you say that?"

"You're by yourself too much. You don't seem to have any friends. You'd still be living in that box you call an apartment if you hadn't had to come here to escape the reporters."

"I'm a lone sheep in wolf's clothing," he said glumly. "I don't mind my solitude."

"Am I intruding on your solitude?" she asked with light irony.

He looked at her in surprise. "No—no. I'm—I'm glad to see you. Really glad. Only I didn't expect to find . . ."

"My father was indebted to the Sessions. I'm very fond of Madame myself. She is fond of you. She said you needed someone to get you out of yourself. Is that so terribly complicated? Or can't you comprehend friendship?"

"Friendship? I understand friendship," he said. "I think."

"You worked for the same thing my husband died for. Is it really so difficult to understand? Don't let the fact that I'm a woman confuse you. A woman can offer friendship where it is needed. I don't love you except as I love my friends."

"Curious," he mused. "I must be tired. Everything seems a little unreal."

"What's curious?"

"You're very direct. I think something must be missing in me. I can't be as direct as you are. When you pumped me about myself the other night, I wondered about your motives. I'm sorry."

"You don't trust people very much, do you?" she said.

"And now you show up here with that cello—" He shook his head. "I want you to know how much—"

"You do better not to thank me. What I do I do because it is necessary. And I make decisions easily."

"I wish I could explain to you. It's like coming into a different world. I've just come from an all-night session at the Ministry of Justice. Outside, there's a police car with two armed individuals in it who are pledged to see that I'm not killed by some lunatic. I can't even go to my own bed to sleep, or I'll find the international press corps standing over me when I wake up. I can't explain it. But a *cello!* Lovely and touching. Don't you see? It doesn't fit."

"Music refreshes the soul," she said with a small unconcerned shrug.

"That's not it. In another way it's like dredging up mud from the bottom of the river. Can you imagine what memories a cello conjures up in my mind? My family. Music. All of it. All the buried life. It's like resurrecting a corpse."

"Your dead self," Solange said, staring at the cello case in the shadows.

"Things hit you harder when you're tired, I suppose. Yes, my dead self."

"Why didn't you go back after the war?"

"I don't know. Why do people stay anywhere?"

"Don't you have any roots in America?"

"My family is gone. All of them." He paused. "I've wondered why I didn't go back. I know partly why."

"Why?"

Stone was silent for a long moment. He held his hands out in front of him and turned them over again, slowly looking at them.

"I've ruined more than my hands. I don't want to be melodramatic, but it's true. I was in and out of this country a dozen times before the invasion. I fought here. I fought for this damn country, and when you fight for a country it makes you part of it. Your roots are in the dirt you fight for." Stone paused and lowered his hands. He turned his head and stared into the shadows where the cello case leaned against the wall. "But a cello— That's part of something else. It makes me feel like two people. It seems as though I had ten years lifted out of my life—like something removed by surgery. A whole decade. I went into the Army when I had everything ahead of me. Everything worth doing in life you start between the ages of thirty and forty. But I'm past forty—for me that whole decade is gone. It never existed. I have no family to go back to, nothing to pull me back home. I'm tired. I feel used up. I don't know what that means." Suddenly he looked up and smiled. "And I can't even play the cello any more. As a kid, that's the only thing I ever knew how to do well."

"Madame Sessions says you were a brilliant musician."

"I might be of some use if there was another war, I suppose," he said, not listening. "But my heart wouldn't be in it. A man is good for only one war."

"You depress me," Solange said, getting up abruptly. She lurched sideways, and fell back into the chair again.

"What's the matter?"

"My foot's asleep."

"Rub it between your hands."

"Get me my handbag off the hall table," she commanded irritably. "I feel as if I need some color on my face."

He brought the leather bag back into the room, after having groped about for it on the table in the dark hall. He handed it to her.

"What's going to happen today?" she asked matter-of-factly, staring critically into a tiny mirror as she examined her face. Stone walked to the window and gazed out into the dark street. "Are they going to execute Dujardin or not?"

"The stage is set," he said. "We'll know from the debate this afternoon. It seems someone is going to pull a rabbit out of a hat—another eyewitness of the massacre who will impugn my testimony." Stone sounded tired.

"Will they?" she asked, drawing her lips taut as she applied lipstick. "I thought there were no survivors. Except you, I mean."

"I don't know. It could be a hoax. But there *was* one body unaccounted for. He could have escaped."

"What will happen if it's not a hoax?"

"The government will have to stay his execution pending investigation. They have no choice. Dujardin is a queened pawn. Otherwise they might have to risk a vote of confidence." Stone added, "The Ambassador is arriving today."

Solange dropped her hands apart into her lap, the mirror in one, the lipstick in the other. She looked at Stone's back. "You mean *your* ambassador? I thought he was in a hospital in America."

"He was. But he's arriving here this morning. At least that's the rumor."

"Whom did you hear it from?"

"I'm to be at the Embassy at nine this morning, to meet an unspecified very important person. I've suddenly become a major embarrassment to the government of the United States, it appears. They want to make sure I'm telling the truth before they back me up through the Embassy."

"Well, you're not the first," she said, resuming her examination of her face in the mirror. She drew her silk-stockinged feet up under her again and fluffed her brown hair in short, delicate, darting motions of her fingers, scrutinizing the results in the mirror. The first pale imitation of light empurpled the windows.

"Do you mind if I ask you something?" she asked, looking at Stone's back as he stared out the window. "I know you must have been answering questions all night."

"One more question tonight won't kill me," he said. "If it's friendly."

"Is it true that the Army wants you to quit your job?"

"You know better than to ask that," he said, turning around halfway to look at her.

"You mean you'd rather not discuss it," she said ironically.

Stone didn't answer. He turned his back to the room.

"I'm sorry," she said.

Stone was still silent. Finally he said, "I can't blame the Army. I'm only another civilian employee now. How can they be certain I'm right? They can't risk offending French public opinion."

"You don't have to discuss it if you don't want to," she said.

"I trust you," Stone said. He compressed his lips, combed his hair back with his fingers, a quick, harassed gesture; continued to stare out the window.

There was a moment of strained silence.

"There are already people in the Place de la Concorde," he said abstractedly. "The taxi driver said some of them have been there since midnight."

"Did the Assembly stay in session?"

"Until three hours ago. There was another fist fight on the floor, not serious."

Solange made a wry face. "Was your name mentioned?"

"Not exactly," Stone answered glumly. "They're saving that for today."

"And the strike?"

"There won't be any chance of settling that until this Dujardin affair is settled. I'll never know how they managed to tie the two together, but they have. The Party won't relax their pressure now." Stone yawned openly. "They're going on with the demonstration."

"How can they get in without public transportation?"

"They're going to bring them in trucks. Any way they can—on ass-

41

back, muleback, camel back, maybe—but they'll come and camp in the streets."

Solange mused, "It's strange—the face of a crowd. Their presence is power."

Stone said nothing, made a distracted gesture as he gazed into the street.

Solange gazed at the back of his head.

Stone muttered as though thinking to himself, "They are always there."

"Did you ever notice how faces . . . ?" Solange left the question hanging.

"The worst part is that this will all be forgotten," Stone said abruptly. "They'll forget that Dujardin existed."

"People forget," Solange said simply, and shrugged.

"Oh, hell," he said, irritated.

"At least keep your dignity," she said severely. "Before strangers and women," she added.

"Do you want a drink?" he asked morosely, turning away from the window.

"No. And neither do you." She snapped her handbag shut and dropped it into her lap. She looked calm, almost serene, patient.

"I know what I want."

"Have you always made a habit of drinking alone in your room?" There was a moment of silence.

"I can't believe Madame would be snooping around my room."

"She's not," Solange said. "But the maid goes in to make the bed."

Stone sank into an armchair, dropping his raincoat in a heap on the carpet. "I'm tired," he said, sighing. "I'm worn out from thinking."

Solange said nothing.

"I'm damned if I even know what I am," he said. "Mainly I'm tired. And naïve. I'm naïve and tired." He laughed without humor. "Everyone tells me that."

"Can you close your mind to it?" she asked.

"I'm sick with waiting." Stone covered his eyes with his hands, rubbing his forehead. Then, removing his hands, he held them arrested in midair. "Do *you* know what I want?" he asked, half sarcastically.

"I think so," she said, staring at the figure in the carpet.

"Perhaps someday you'll lead me into the light."

"Perhaps," she said. "One can't be sure."

"There's something missing in me," he said, half aloud. "I should be angry with somebody, but I'm not."

"There's something lacking in all of us," she said. "There's an absence . . ." She fell silent, thinking to herself; suddenly looked up as though about to say something; said nothing.

It was quiet in the room. From the muted depths of the building, in another apartment somewhere below them, an alarm clock went off. Outside the windows the sky was changing. The muffled ringing went on for a long moment, then stopped. From somewhere came the sound of a wakened child crying.

"Solange," Stone said. "It was very kind of you to wait here for me."

Solange rose from her chair and padded in her stocking feet across the carpet to the window. Stone followed her with his eyes. She drew the patterned lace curtain aside and looked up at the sky. The winter dawn was fading from deep dark blue to the blue-gray of January.

"I like this time of day," she said quietly. "Everything is beginning again."

Stone laughed. "If you have the temerity to face it," he said.

She said softly: "I remember a time when I hated the light of a new day. That's why I love it now."

"I envy you," Stone said, smiling at her, brushing his hair back. Solange dropped the curtain and returned to her chair.

At that moment the telephone rang, and Stone jumped. He stared at Solange an instant. "Are you expecting a call?" he asked her.

"Certainly not at this hour," she said.

"Would you please answer it? If it's the newspapers . . ."

Solange put her finger to her lips, reached for the telephone.

"Hello."

There was a pause.

"Who?"

Another pause.

"I'm sorry, we must have a bad connection. I can't hear you. Would you repeat that?"

Hurriedly Solange clapped her hand over the mouthpiece and whispered to Stone, "It's someone from the Ministry of Justice for you."

Stone nodded, relieved.

"Yes, he's here," Solange said. "Just a moment, please."

She gave the instrument to Stone and sat back in her chair. Stone took the receiver and stood beside the chair. "This is Stone," he said.

There was a long pause. Then he said, "Let me get a pencil."

Solange opened her bag and rooted in it. She found an eyebrow pencil and handed it to Stone with an old envelope.

"Dr. Georges—what is the last name?" he asked, writing with difficulty. The soft point of the eyebrow pencil kept crumbling. "Would you spell it? M-E-R-S-E-A-U-L-T. Merseault. I have it, Dr. Georges Merseault. Yes, I've got the number. I'll call him right away. Is he expecting my call?"

There was another long pause. "I understand. I appreciate your consideration. I'll try to help him if I can. You don't know what it's about? . . . All right. I'll call him right now," Stone said. "Good night."

He hung up the receiver and raised his eyebrows at Solange.

"Something cooks," he said. "I asked the Ministry not to give out this number to anyone. So they called me and asked me to call him. I hope it didn't wake Madame."

"Shall I leave you in private?" Solange asked, making a move to get up.

"No. Stay here. If I can't trust you I can't trust anyone."

Stone picked up the telephone again and dialed the number, this time turning his back to the chair and looking out the windows. "It's getting light fast," he said, waiting for the number to answer. He heard a click in the earpiece and was surprised to hear a man's voice answer with the words, "Ministry of Foreign Affairs."

"Dr. Georges Merseault. Please," Stone said.

"One moment, please." There was a dead pause, then the voice came back: "Who is calling, please?"

"Monsieur Stone."

"One moment, please."

Stone heard several clicks and then: "Mr. Stone, I'm sorry to bother you, but I'm very pressed for time." Merseault spoke rapid English.

"The Justice Ministry just called me," Stone said. "They didn't explain anything."

The voice answered: "I'm not at liberty to go into details just now, but I wonder if you would be so kind as to give me some information. I have to meet your Ambassador in a few minutes at Orly—the car's waiting for me. I understand you're to see him this morning."

"I have an appointment at the Embassy, that's correct—although I haven't been told officially that I was to meet the Ambassador."

"Fine. We'll leave it unofficial, then."

"Can you give me some idea what sort of information . . . ?" Stone began. He was trying to compose a mental picture of Merseault from the voice in the earpiece.

". . . I have just received an interesting communication that needs verifying. You may be able to help me."

"I'll try," Stone said.

"A matter of detail concerning the Montpelle incident: Do you recall whether any one of the prisoners had a right arm missing from the shoulder?"

"No, there was no one with a missing arm."

"Can you be absolutely certain of that?"

"Positive. I would have noticed someone like that. They had us cutting down trees for several hours. I wouldn't forget a one-armed man if there'd been one there."

"Did any of the prisoners have beards during the time you knew them?"

"No. In the prison they were afraid of typhus—they made us shave every week on account of lice."

"Do you think you could positively identify a photograph?"

"I think so. I'd know Berger, for sure. Carnot, yes. Lautrec, yes. The doctor, probably. The others I can't say definitely. Until I see it, of course."

"Even if he had a beard?"

"It depends on the picture, but I think so. Do you mind if I ask why?"

"You'll be at the Embassy at nine, do I have that correct? I can't say more now. I'm sure you understand."

"Nine. Yes."

"Good. In the meantime, I have to ask you to discuss this with absolutely no one. I'm sorry I'm pressed. You understand, of course."

"I understand. If I can be of any further help . . ."

". . . I'll be in touch with you. I'm looking forward to meeting you again. I'm sorry to have to rush like this, but they have a car waiting for me outside. I'll have to say good-by. Thank you for the help."

"I'm afraid I haven't been . . ." The receiver went dead in his ear; Merseault had hung up. Stone looked balefully at the telephone in his hand, shrugged, and put it back on its cradle. "Thank *you*," he said to the mute instrument. He brushed his hair back and handed Solange her blunted pencil. "He said he was looking forward to meeting me *again*. I don't think I've ever met a Georges Merseault. I don't even know who he is."

"He had something to do with reorganizing our intelligence services after the war," Solange said. "I remember reading about him. Legion of Honor."

"But have I met him?"

Solange shrugged. "Perhaps during the war," she said. "He was in the same dirty business you were."

"The Ministry said his interest would be unofficial. Isn't he with the government any more?"

"I think he's retired. Before the war I think he was a professor of history and political science at the Sorbonne. Then he did something very important with the Resistance. I don't believe he teaches any more. I haven't heard anything about him in the last two years."

"I'd tell you what he said, but he asked me to be discreet. I hope you don't mind."

"I don't mind," Solange said. "I figured most of it out anyway, from your end of the conversation. They've found the missing corpse, am I right?"

"I don't know. He wouldn't say much on the telephone. But I horribly suspect you're on the right track. I only hope the corpse is *really* a corpse—I don't mean that—I only hope to God this doesn't open up the whole case again."

Stone was preoccupied, lost in his own thoughts. "I just can't believe anyone else could have gotten out alive," he said, smacking his fist abruptly into the palm of his hand. "I can't believe it. I *saw* . . ." He checked himself, relaxed. "I just can't believe it. He would have come forward by now if he were alive." Stone noticed that Solange in her turn seemed not to be listening.

"*He?*" Solange said distantly. She turned her head and looked queerly at Stone, interrupted in her own thoughts.

"*He* . . . that is, whoever might have escaped besides me," Stone replied, confused. He sat down on the piano bench.

"You think you know who it is, don't you," Solange stated flatly, her voice strained with an odd accusing tone.

"At this point I don't know what to think. I admit it," Stone said. "For one of us, me, to be still alive is incredible enough. By rights, I shouldn't be here. I should be dead. But two? That would take a miracle. I don't think I'd believe it if he walked into this room in the flesh."

"Doubting Thomas," Solange said. Again she appeared to lose herself in reflection.

"I know. It's just that in my mind I can still see the whole thing. I can close my eyes and see them lying on the ground. In my *mind* they are dead, every last one of them. *I've* killed them off. For a while I hoped that one got out, just one, just one besides me, so I wouldn't be alone, so I wouldn't be the *only* one. Then I knew I had to stop hoping or go insane. In my mind they are dead. I can't change that." Stone looked at Solange. "How can I change that?"

Solange gazed at him speculatively. Then she said, "The dead die in the flesh and are resurrected in the mind. You would have it the other way around. Why should you be alone if you're alive? Let the dead return to haunt the dead. I once hoped, and had to stop hoping. When I first heard he was dead I felt like laughing because I couldn't believe it. But then I found that to stop hoping I had to stop loving too. It was enough that I had his child in me. Then I lost the child. I can't feel pity for you any more than I can for myself. We've all lost pieces of ourselves . . ." Her face suddenly became flushed and angry. "I can't help being alive and alone any more than you can. Perhaps I can't sympathize with you, because I'm a woman. Let the dead return? I have no pity for them because I have none for myself. We've mourned them, haven't we? Why must we be damned with them?"

She stopped and stared straight ahead. Stone looked at her and saw her. He saw her face, her eyes. He saw that her eyes had an odd, glazed look, blank, as though hardened to the remembrances of suffering; her face was open and smoothed of all outward pain, drawn, empty, numb. He saw her then as a woman, a woman who had endured, who had loved and hoped and, surrendering totally to life, had sought to live again. And he knew that this was his vision of her, private, secret unto himself, as no man living had ever seen her, and in that instant the question hung like a black and silver banner across the entrance of his mind, cold, clear, rational: *What is love?* And he heard it too, loud, sourceless, black; as black as the whisper in a dream.

Yet detachment overruled him; sick with fatigue, disfigured by fear and speechless longing, he could not surrender to the moment. Benumbed, a man too tired to sleep, a man drained of volition, he could only watch her through the dim distance of his mind; touch her, no.

V

Small, bald, condemned to die, he passed his days as usual, taking his meals, returning his tray, walking twice a day with his guards, knitting, crocheting, saying his prayers. His jailers weren't sure that he even knew; after his conviction and incarceration something had seemed to happen to his mind. The light was never off in his cell. He lived in his niche under the ever-burning light like an ikon, for he couldn't sleep in the dark.

For the public, the flesh didn't exist. Only the name existed. And the name split the country. Families were sullenly divided over it; fathers forbade sons to mention it at table. Fist fights broke out in cafés over it. In the south a Saturday soccer match was turned into a riot when a banner bearing it was raised in the stands. Thirty-nine were killed when a section of grandstand collapsed under the weight of people who swarmed up as the fight started. A demented woman who had recently escaped from a lunatic asylum was found one morning squatting on the steps of Notre Dame bellowing obscenities at two young priests, holding them at bay with an ice pick as she tried to make a votive bonfire of her hair. She had the name incised backward on her forehead, a bridal hand mirror by her side. Later she laid claim to receiving the stigmata from God, who had saved her from the embrace of the Devil just as the Devil was about to take her for his bride. She was treated for multiple lacerations of the scalp and minor burns of the hands, and sent back to the asylum. But the newspapers made much of the bizarre ceremonial, to the amusement and disgust of their respective readers. Photographers reached the scene before the police.

The fatal name was everywhere, known all over France. In two weeks it had been printed millions of times in hundreds of newspapers, on posters, in government reports; scrawled crudely on walls in chalk, red paint; lettered on black-bordered street banners. The government found itself struggling to control the vacillating elements of its shaky coalition to face a vote of confidence that could, and very likely would, topple it. For the country was wasting in the second week of a paralyzing general strike—a strike that had almost been avoided until the name, wrathfully shouted on the floor of the National Assembly, broke the grim calm that surrounded the delicately balanced wage negotiations.

The name no longer symbolized a man; it symbolized a cause. And the man was all but lost in the crash of events. He sat in prison, mindless, cut off from the world outside. The pebble in the avalanche, he seemed unaware, innocent of the calamities his name had caused. Nor did he seem to have any clear idea who his new lawyers were or why they were there. The only question he ever asked—he asked it only once—was who was paying for their services. (It was a question other people asked, not at first, but later. Later, they would get their clear answer.) His eyesight was failing, and in the beginning the lawyers read to him in the hope of impressing him with what was happening, of eliciting some response, some enthusiasm. But he only smiled and nodded, apologized for taking up their time; and after a while the lawyers simply left the newspapers. He thanked them each time, and used the newspapers to wrap his knitted squares in neat bundles. He completed several squares a day. Each time he finished a square he scratched a mark on the wall. There were over a thousand of these tiny scratches: one of the lawyers had counted them. The detail was duly reported in the press.

That the name no longer symbolized the man was evidenced by the fact that, although he was the center of the storm, journalists no longer tried to see him. Every newspaper in France combed through its back issues for stories about his trial, year-old leftovers that could be warmed up and served again. But not one newspaper, not a single one, printed his picture. To half the press he wasn't noble enough of countenance to make a good martyr's portrait; to the other half, he didn't look evil enough to be the murderous traitor they pictured in their printed columns. There were no papers in between. Expressions of moderate opinion were shouted down by both sides, reviled by both sides, crushed and damned by both sides. If a politician had a moderate opinion, he had no opinion; he kept it to himself. Not even the Church, the traditional last refuge, was safe from division. Squabbling erupted from pulpits. Unity was restored only when the priests were finally silenced by mandate from the stony upper reaches of hieratic power.

As the government wrestled frantically to maintain its slippery hold on sweating politicians, the one thing that prevented their wholesale bolt was their agonized uncertainty as to which side of the argument was the frying pan, which the fire. There was widespread talk that the government had a trump up its sleeve in certain "mysterious documents" that would settle the question of murderer-versus-martyr with devastating finality. The government, perhaps realizing that it was wise to understate a bluff, hastened to deny the rumors with suspicious alacrity. One of the spokesmen smiled broadly as he handed out the mimeographed statement of denial to the assembled press; even his smile made news. There had indeed been some question at the time of the trial about certain missing "personal files" which the defendant's original lawyers claimed had been stolen, but which the prosecution claimed he had destroyed. The government's denial skirted specific mention of these files, but the newspapers printed stories studded with enigmatic references to them, with quotations from unnamed sources close to the government. If the tactic worried the partisans of martyrdom, their worry didn't show through the ridicule they heaped on the idea of "mysterious documents." They challenged the government to produce them. Indeed, if the government was in possession of "certain documents"—a contingency it had already studiously denied—it seemed content to bide its time for a more propitious moment. The government's larger tactic was to keep its strategy melodramatically secret—so secret, in fact, that several members of the Cabinet doubted the existence of any strategy at all. But so far they had kept their misgivings to themselves. It wasn't necessary to abandon the present hapless ship of state until it was clear that it was actually sinking. There was time enough for that before the final vote of confidence. And with time there was room to maneuver—to break the strike, delay the vote. Anything was possible with time. But the problem remained unchanged: Would the name die with the man, or would it issue up from its futile grave, and, like King Hamlet's ghost, drift among the battlements and council halls demanding its proper vengeance?

For in two weeks, the Dujardin affair had been driven into the national psyche like the honed point of a wedge finding the long straight grain in oak. A nation's conscience, which an army of conquerors in four years hadn't been able to hack through crosswise, had been split cleanly down the middle by one of their own, a small man in his fifties who knitted away the days to his death and knew the world as a small barred patch of gray sky.

Even now, hearing the story for the second time, it was hard for citizens to grasp the sequence of events. The trial a year ago of Théophile Dujardin, former police official in the Department of the Var, had been a simple affair. His defense had been unspectacular, a tawdry parade of the usual character witnesses, a great deal of pointless reading of dusty official records by an unenthusiastic defense lawyer. Indeed, such trials had long since lost the public's interest; they were part of the dreary business of slow justice, a nagging reminder of the nuisance of war. The press, by that time, had sensed the public apathy and reported only the beginnings and the outcomes. The heads that rolled right after the war were the prominent ones; the rest, the collaborators, the petty spies, the black-marketeers, came to anticlimactic justice. It was, as one judge put it, a dirty job that had to be done; these criminals were "merely a part of the rubble and dirt of war" that had to be swept away before reconstruction could begin. Justice was rendered fairly, therefore slowly, and the newspapers became preoccupied with other things. The Dujardin case might have escaped public notice entirely except for Dujardin's alleged involvement in the Montpelle massacre, an incident that could still elicit a thrill of horror in the public soul. Though Dujardin's responsibility for the massacre was not established beyond all doubt, the surprise eyewitness testimony of an American agent named Stone was sufficient to catapult the trial onto the front pages for a few days. After that, it lapsed back into long dry sessions of analysis of old records, and people forgot about it until they read that Théophile Dujardin had been convicted of treason. Then the sentence passed quietly into history for a time.

Hunted down by the English, captured by the Americans, tried by the French, Théophile Dujardin, condemned, had seemed well content to die. In fact, as far as the public was concerned, he might already have been dead.

So when a year later his name struck bold black headlines across the nation's newspapers, it was as though he were a man disinterred from the grave. And where before there had been only the apathy of a people bored by war and its grievances, now, as the painful memory of war's ignominies became bleached and faded with time, there was interest. And as the larger issues were spelled out, the name Dujardin came to symbolize something that heretofore had existed in the public mind as only a vague feeling, a feeling unarticulated and disturbing. It gave shape and eerie substance to an idea that people had been aching to pin down, a ghost they had been trying to lay by divination of its living name. In the end, as the Dujardin affair became a cause, even the morbid apathy of a war-weary people gave way to public passion.

The name became a cause only when a deputy named Picard, formerly a lawyer in the Department of the Var, read on the floor of the Assembly an affidavit signed by Dujardin. The affidavit charged that the Americans had beaten a false confession out of him; since this written confession had been the cornerstone of the case implicating him in the Montpelle massacre, the validity of the whole trial and its outcome was thrown into doubt. The Provost Marshal General of the American Army vigorously denied the charge contained in Dujardin's sworn statement, but the denial did nothing to dissipate the charge.

When Deputy Picard was shouted down before he came to the end of the document, what had begun as the final heated debate on economic policy ended in a fist fight on the floor of the Assembly. The fist fight made news, and thus so did the thing that caused it. The affidavit's content was not news—it had been briefly reported in the press the previous day—but once read in the Assembly, it rolled onto the public stage like a time bomb from the wings, and tempers flared in the open. The workers had been restive, but for a while it had appeared that they would accept, however sullenly, the government's emergency wage measures. But as physical violence exploded in the

Cabinet and the Assembly, the general strike, so long threatened and so nearly averted, now broke out almost spontaneously. The city of Paris, long the smoldering volcano of undirected passions, erupted in violence the first day of the strike.

It took the newspapers two days to catch up with these events, since most of the printers struck too. By the time the papers were circulating again, the public was desperately confused by the sudden intrusion of the Dujardin case into the issues of the strike. The Party press was now grinding out vehement articles about "the martyr Dujardin," but no one, the striking workers included, seemed to have an accurate idea of what Dujardin had to do with raising wages or reducing the price of bread. However, demonstrations were dutifully carried out, posters were printed, and Dujardin's name was carried about the streets on placards by striking workers who had little else to do. They obeyed orders. By the time the progovernment presses overcame the opposition's head start, it was becoming gradually clear that a carefully wrought strategy was in operation. Whether by luck or by sheer insight into the public mind, the Party was obviously using the Dujardin case as a wedge to split apart the government coalition, divide the nation, topple the Cabinet on a vote of confidence. It was obvious that the Party was hoping to pick up the pieces and put them together in a fashion more accommodating to its long-term aims; that reducing the price of bread was one of these aims was hammered home daily to the readers of the Party press. And the Party press, like the Party itself, was the largest in France, a fact which did not escape the acute attention of politicians who felt uncomfortable or insecure in the Premier's coalition. Already one cabinet minister had deserted the government, resigning because of his "health"; privately he gave reporters to understand that he did not wish to be "embarrassed" by the Premier's attempt to defend the government's handling of *l'affaire Dujardin*.

Indeed, if the allegations put forth in the Dujardin statement could be made to stick, the government would be hard put to answer. And on the heels of the first affidavit came new charges in the opposition press: charges of brutality, of withheld evidence, of deliberate perjuring of evidence, of intimidating witnesses—all these electrified the nation not so much because of their nature—such charges had been made before and investigated and forgotten—but because of the boldness and absolute confidence with which they were made. The fact of the Party's springing to the immediate defense of an accused collaborator, in the minds of many, noncommunist as well as Communist, tended automatically to exonerate him. The Party would not risk the reputation it had earned in the heroic days of the Resistance to defend an obscure fascist traitor unless he were falsely convicted—so went the reasoning. Even in the moderate press there was severe criticism—criticism which grew harsher with each passing day of the government's delay in answering the additional charges. One ordinarily progovernment paper, in an acid editorial, remarked that the scandal of the trial was nothing compared to the scandal of allowing the Communist Party the honor of uncovering it. "Every time we allow an honest cause," said the editorial, "to fall into the hands of the Communist Party, we have armed them with a weapon against which there is no defense—truth."

The effectiveness of the Party's continuing attack was adequately evidenced by the stalemate that resulted. After the first flurry of government denial, there was nearly a week of official silence while the records of the trial were dug out of dusty archives and reviewed and the government assembled its detailed rebuttals.

Both sides took advantage of the temporary lull to repair their shattered ranks, cement and justify new alliances, adjust themselves to strange, often embarrassing, bedfellows. The first full excitement of the general strike wore off; wage earners began to feel the honest pinch of revolution. But even as the populace steeled itself for what might be a long slow grind of attrition, the prevailing mood of the nation, especially among the workers, was still one of mild surprise. So much had happened so quickly; a nation had been brought to utter standstill by the very people who composed it. They were surprised, even a little apprehensive, at the power they suddenly found residing in their hands. But most startling of all was still the issue which had touched the spark, which had catalyzed the strike and opened up the old wounds of war, bitter scars supposedly healed.

The newspapers also settled down to take stock of the wreckage, count the casualties, augur the future; to fill in their readers with what they could dig out of their own back issues. And since the only thing about the trial itself that had excited the press's interest was the intrusion of the Montpelle massacre, most of the background stories again exploited the details of that atrocity.

The massacre at Montpelle had been one of the many events that intensified and saddened the end of the war. It occurred in the last days of the fighting, and even to a nation hardened to four years of brutality during the occupation, it seemed an act of wanton, insensible destruction. The discovery of the ruins of the village, and the funeral pyre on the mountaintop nearby, shocked the world. But Montpelle was shocking only because it was the first to be found. It was soon forgotten in the smoking horror of even greater enormities that came to light immediately afterward in the wake of the general German retreat. All that remained to remind men of what had happened to the village of Montpelle was a plain granite marker where the village had stood. Now, once again, photographers were sent back to the site, and pictures of the monument appeared in the newspapers, together with the local stonecutter's explanation of why there was no inscription on the stark gray obelisk: "Such grief is without words," he said. A few of the people who had survived, by being out of the village on the day of the massacre, were tracked down and interviewed for the third time by reporters; but their accounts seemed sparse and vague, as though they too had submerged the painful memory of that day.

From a legal point of view the American agent Stone hadn't been a key figure in the Dujardin trial. His testimony reduced to the fact that he had merely heard Dujardin's voice near the scene of the massacre before the murders took place. The prosecution could not finally prove Stone's contention that Dujardin had deliberately conspired to hand over his prisoners to the SS battalion, the same battalion that also burned the village, since Dujardin had a witness to testify that he had been in St. Maxime on the day of the massacre. Though Stone's testimony was of doubtful value to the prosecution, it was of sensational interest to the public, since it was the only eyewitness report of a survivor of the actual massacre.

As a former secret wartime agent in France, Stone first had to be released from his official vow of silence before he could testify publicly. Through delicate overtures of the French Government, the release was granted on the condition that Stone would testify only on matters relating directly to the Montpelle incident. It was established in the course of the questioning, however, that the government had known the details of the massacre for some time, having been provided with a copy of the secret stenographic record of the British War Crimes Field Commission of Inquiry which first investigated the Montpelle massacre and linked Dujardin's name to it. Stone stated at the trial that he had testified at the Inquiry before the case was turned over to the then newly constituted French Government.

During questioning by Dujardin's defense counsel Stone pointed out that there was at least one other possible survivor of the "sunset executions," as the murder of the ten prisoners was called to distinguish it from the mass murder of the villagers which took place earlier in the day. The fact that there were originally twelve prisoners was clearly established by Stone, and so was the fact that the remains of only ten corpses were found in the funeral pyre. Stone, escaped, made eleven. Who was the twelfth? There were no unidentified corpses found among the dead villagers. More puzzling than the question of who was the twelfth was the question of what happened to him. If he had been killed, where was his body? If he was alive, why had he not come forward? Stone provided the court with a list of names, as he had known them, of the eleven other prisoners besides himself. However, for the other American agent who by that time was known to have been among the twelve at the massacre, Stone knew only the wartime code name Antoine Berger.

Now, in the heat of revived interest in the trial, Dujardin's lawyers stressed the fact that this agent's true name had been omitted, although at the time of the trial it had been clearly established that the American security services were under no obligation to reveal the true names of agents they had in France during the German occupation. Routine security was the reason given at the time, and at the time it was accepted by everyone. It was believed that among the twelve prisoners, according to Stone's own testimony and the mute testimony of the circumstances of their sudden arrest, there had been an informer. Stone had refused to speculate on his identity; Stone had also been unable to give information on the other American agent; at least one other person had escaped and might possibly be still alive. Was this the other American? If so, what was Stone's motive in remaining silent? Finally, who was the informer? Was his escape planned by the Germans as his reward? That would explain the missing corpse.

Every newspaper in France now reviewed these questions while French government specialists prepared their answer and weighed the decision as to how far they should go in defending their handling of the Dujardin case. Every newspaperman in France searched in vain for a clue to the American Stone's whereabouts. How would he answer these same questions today?

Stone, it was believed, had returned to America shortly after the trial. In fact, he had never left France.

In its second week the general strike widened, as expected, to most of metropolitan France. While the government stood still, workers went about the sullen empty streets collecting contributions from each other, for a fund to liberate a man whom a few weeks ago they would have reviled: Dujardin. The strike had an ingenious, bizarre quality, even to veteran observers of France's tangled politics. It seemed on one hand that the strike proceeded only from the most monstrous non sequitur, and yet on the other hand it had every chance of success in bringing down the government. Troops were held in readiness outside the city to reinforce police if it became necessary; yet this was precisely the sort of dilemma the government had sought to avoid.

When the government finally answered the latest charges, it quietly branded them as false, and made clear that it would defend its handling of the case. The opposition was not very skillful at concealing its elation over the government's decision. After the Premier released his statement to the press, it began to dawn on the government advisers that they might be stumbling into a trap. For it was reliably forecast that the defense lawyers were about to strike back with documents which they would state were exact copies from captured German war archives. The documents would prove beyond a shadow of a doubt that the Germans had, at several points during the progress of the war, received evidence that Dujardin was secretly cooperating with the Resistance forces in his area. One photocopied document was reputed to be a German intelligence memo which suggested that Dujardin be left in his police post so that he might lead the Gestapo on to bigger game, but that he should be watched with the utmost care, and arrested if he betrayed the slightest suspicion that he was suspect. How the Dujardin lawyers had found these documents in the staggering mountain of largely unsorted captured papers was a mystery, but among the experts there was no doubt that if they existed they would be genuine and would accurately reflect the German intelligence service's appraisal of Dujardin. It suddenly appeared that the government had put its neck in the noose, and the noose was about to be pulled tight.

The day following the rumor of the German documents there was rioting near Pantin, and a troup of police were forced to fire into a crowd to save themselves from being torn to pieces. Regrettably, a fifty-year-old woman demonstrator, mother of three children, was struck in the hip by a police bullet and died of shock after being trampled by the retreating crowd. One of the encircled policemen died a few days later of stab wounds in the groin and lower abdomen. His death was not reported on the front pages; his death made no widow, orphaned no children; the public had no sympathy to waste. Both were equally dead.

Now the streets were strangely empty and silent. No buses ran, the subways had stopped, taxis were a rarity. Paris looked like a city of the dead. The winter skies remained dull and sullen, as though reflecting the temper of the city. Food was in critically short supply because farmers, during the first few days of the strike, had been reluctant to risk having stones thrown at their trucks as they entered the city. Fuel was scarcer than ever. In many sections shops were closed and shuttered tight. Behind the façade of ominous quiet the political maneuvering became more furious as the government marshaled its forces for an open battle for its life. The politicians were resigned to it. There would have to be a vote of confidence in the Assembly; but by the time the vote came the real struggle would be already over. The struggle was being decided beforehand in internecine party meetings where heads were traded for allegiances. Reputations would be broken, some careers would be abruptly ended, and if the government coalition survived, many of the men who helped forge it would not. Meanwhile nothing moved in the winter streets, as though a plague had hit. Even the undertakers had struck, and for days there was no one to bury the dead.

Ambassadors alerted their governments, called absent personnel back from winter vacations, and kept a judicious silence. The British Ambassador quietly canceled all his public engagements and kept a doubled staff of couriers standing by on twenty-four-hour call. The Swiss Ambassador developed a diplomatic illness to keep his time free of importunate visitors. But the American Embassy, the target of the crisis, was caught without instructions. In the absence of the Ambassador the Embassy staff maintained a stony silence before ferreting newsmen who pressed for information on the American agent who had figured in the trial a year before. The only information the Embassy press officer, stalling for time while awaiting the Ambassador's return, had given out, was the noncommittal fact of Stone's honorable discharge from the armed services shortly after the trial. Stone had been attached to the Graves Registration Command in Paris during the final days of the war, and had been discharged a civilian about a year ago.

The Embassy would provide no further information as to his whereabouts. Still the reporters pressed the information officer, and snuffled around the office of the military attaché, who sent out word with his empty coffee cups that he regretted he had no time to see the press but he had nothing to give them anyway. It was becoming obvious that the Dujardin affair was, among other things, being subtly turned into a propaganda foray on the American Government by the powerful, efficient press of the far left. Stone, a relatively minor figure in the original trial, was being artificially catapulted into the key position. His very absence made him an ideal target. Innuendoes were not leveled at any of the other prosecution witnesses, were saved for the American alone. The picture presented in the opposition press ignored the other witnesses entirely and concentrated the attack on Stone, whose one distinguishing feature was that he was the only foreign witness at the trial. The Embassy was being careful. The public impression, however, was unfortunate. What appeared an official desire of the Americans to remain aloof from the furor only had the effect of further isolating the French Government in its embarrassment.

Nor could anybody be sure afterward who the reporter was who found Stone, although several people mentioned a man named Mac-Naughton, a Paris correspondent for a half-dozen Scottish newspapers. In the uproar that followed, his name was overlooked, and he didn't step forward to claim the public honor. It was known only that this man, who at the time didn't identify himself as a reporter, had gone to the place of Stone's last command, the Army Graves Registration Command for the European Theater; he had walked into the old Hotel Astoria Building and asked for Major John Stone. He had probably expected nothing more than a lead—if that. But the guard merely scribbled a room number on a slip of paper and told him they were waiting for him upstairs. The astounded reporter took the paper and nodded. "Only he don't like to be called Major any more," the guard had remarked. "He's a civilian now."

What happened then depended on which version one heard or read. The reporter, in any event, knocked on Stone's door and was told to come in. It was clear that the assembled colonels in the smoke-filled room were expecting someone else. The lone civilian sitting among them, gaunt and tired, was certainly Stone. The group of officers stared at the intruder; he quickly excused himself and backed out of the room, but was apprehended as he left the building. When it was learned that he was a reporter instead of the civilian security officer who had been expected, the colonels succeeded in detaining him long enough to call the Embassy and patch together a hurried statement for Stone to give to the press by telephone, thus beating the hapless reporter to the punch.

For no one had suspected that Major Stone had taken his discharge only to return to his old job, as a civilian employee. As it turned out he had even kept the same office, the same desk, and had merely had the military title before his name scraped off the opaque glass panel on the door. He hadn't left France once, not even when he took his separation leave before returning to his old job in his new status.

In the headlines of the sensational press, the plot thickened rapidly. Stone, long since dubbed "the American intelligence agent," was now wildly reported as being "still at large in France." The question of the identity and whereabouts of the "other American agent" was bandied about by these papers with the same horrified relish they lavished on Stone himself.

In the midst of the sensation, the day following Stone's clumsily staged statement to the press, the American Ambassador's plane left Washington unannounced on its return flight to Paris. Despite precautions, word leaked back to Paris from London, and reporters swarmed like flies to Orly airport to harass his return. In the end everyone at the airport settled down for an around-the-clock vigil—everyone who had a valid press pass. A middle-aged woman reporter from a Stockholm paper came equipped with a sleeping bag, a Primus stove, a coffee maker.

VI

The farmcart loomed up abruptly. The battered truck bouncing over the uneven paving stones, its single yellow headlight jumping and dancing like a wild eye loose and rolling in its socket, was almost upon the cart before it swerved out to pass. The truck's brief light washed shakily over the cart and illuminated a peasant family—sack-like shapes huddled together on its flat-bedded back. The farmcart moved in darkness, and after the truck had rattled away into the distance, it still came slowly on, its boards popping in the cold, its iron-banded wheels squealing and grinding over the cracked uneven pavement. The wagon lurched slowly from side to side over the frost heaves and sagging potholes, a dirty ruby lantern swinging from the rear axle.

The lantern flickered in a smoky red arc between the rear wheels.

The reins were snapped and the crack of harness leather sounded sharply on the cold air. As the cart came out from the tunnel of shadow beside the airport buildings it was suddenly etched again in a flash of light by the brilliant sweep of the revolving beacon. The faces on the back showed white for an instant, then vanished. Then the cart again labored in darkness until the next flash came around.

It moved down the slow road toward the city, a series of flashing apparitions, until it was very small in the distance. Finally, after a long time, it was gone. The road past the airport was silent again; the first light before dawn had just begun to fog the eastern sky.

Only a few other occasional vehicles passed during the hour before dawn: a military van, a few produce trucks, an isolated automobile that sped past, leaving a long trail of cold sound in the silence.

The road stretched along the edge of the airfield, a long straight ribbon of dirty paving stones, mottled black from large and small bomb patches hastily laid down in the final days of the war, not intended to survive the frost of two winters. The old highway was separated from the newly paved airfield by a heavy wire fence topped with mousy barbed wire on wooden supports. In several places the fence was buckled from bomb blasts and the barbed wire trailed in limp strands along the ground. The midsection of the fence, the section containing the watchman's cubicle and the main gates to the airport buildings, was new, rebuilt after the war. Unlike the buildings, which were also rebuilt but largely in temporary-army-barracks style, the fence gates really looked new and permanent.

A parking area bridged the narrow gap between the fence and the steps of the administration building. Inside were the waiting lounge and reception center, offices of the various international airlines, customs inspection counters, a bar, a restaurant. In the restaurant several dozen people—reporters and Embassy people—dozed fitfully on hard chairs.

Outside, the roof of the low two-story building had been made into an observation deck. Out of the center jutted the glassed-in control tower with its revolving two-faced beacon that flashed red and blinding white into the far corners of the darkness.

Straight up, the sky was still black, but toward the east the first filmy skyshine of winter dawn traced out an indistinct horizon. The high overcast was breaking up, and overhead the winter stars turned on and off as clouds, otherwise invisible against the blacker limits of empty space, scudded past beneath them like silent floes of black ice. The wet runways stretched out into the darkness, flanked by long rows of blinking marker lights. Red, green, here and there amber, blue, they blinked in unmatched cadences. Under the lee of the buildings they studded the ground like vigilant jewels, eyelike, winking; as they stretched away into the night's distance they became bleared, indistinct, long streaks of color smeared across the waterslick. Except for these, and the stabbing beam of the beacon, the landscape was motionless and black. The fields and distant farms lay frozen and useless under the black winter dawn. The beacon swung its blade of light over the wasted land, reaping the last of its eerie harvest of darkness; the nearer houses, shuttered tight and cowering in the dark, leaped to light and collapsed with each pass of the shuddering flash.

The restaurant was a large barnlike room with a concrete floor, and a glass wall that looked out on the paved staging area toward the runways. The room was cold and dark; at the farther end two huge polished coffee machines loomed behind the upended bar stools piled along the deserted length of the long counter. The huge urns glinted silver each time the revolving beacon passed over the wetly shining pavement outside, glossy black beyond the cold glass wall. Most of the tables in the room were piled high with chairs, and their shadows made spider-legged patterns that crawled across the farther wall and flitted into darkness with each ghosting pass of the light.

Those reporters who hadn't been lucky enough to lay claim to a comfortable chair in the lounge slept in the restaurant. A few of them had improvised beds by pushing two tables together and stretching themselves out across their length. They lay on their backs, wrapped in greatcoats like hatted mummies; one of them snored wetly. Others in the room slept fitfully, sitting slumped over tables as though in grief, heads buried in their arms. The woman from Stockholm had un-stacked a few stools and set up her sleeping bag on the bar, safe from scavenging mice that scurried across the floor and rustled among the refuse behind the counter. But not everyone was asleep. The plate-glass wall had two glass doors, one at either end; midway between them a small group of reporters conversed in low tones around a chess game that was being played in the intermittent light of the beacon.

One of the players, the Englishman named MacNaughton, sat back-ward on his chair smoking a large pipe; the other, a stringer for a news weekly in Prague, rocked meditatively back and forth studying the board, kneading his chin with one hand and hugging himself with the other. Around them stood a handful of kibitzers, whispering among themselves. The silent tableau was framed against the black glass with each revolution of the beacon. Abruptly the Czech reached forward and with a single sweeping movement of his bishop deftly struck a black knight off the board and removed it in his fingers. There was a mumble of disapproval from the spectators. MacNaughton reached forward and pushed an idle pawn with the bit of his pipe.

"Check," he said. "Discovered."

His opponent had started to move his king when one of the spec-tators, a bald man with glasses, stepped forward saying, *"Nyet, nyet,"* and moved a defensive knight into the breach instead. Than he stepped back. The Czech looked at the Englishman across the board, shrugged eloquently, and removed his hand from the king.

"Ivan there seems to take our game more seriously than we do," MacNaughton said musingly.

"He is my professor," said the Czech in English.

"You may as well humor him."

"Yes. He's Russian."

The Englishman gave a short silent laugh and pushed the pawn again. "However, I think his move *is* better," he said. "Not much. But some."

"I can't stop that pawn. I resign—with your permission." The Czech leaned back and stretched out his arms. Then he reached forward and symbolically turned his own king onto its side.

There was an angry rattle of Russian from the bespectacled on-looker.

"What is our Ivan saying?" the Englishman asked after a moment.

"He is telling me where I made my fatal error."

The Russian continued his staccato commentary and, leaning over the board, began backing up the pieces to an earlier position. The other spectators drifted away. The Czech nodded wearily at each pause in the unsolicited analysis and shrugged again at the Englishman. The Russian triumphantly played out both sides and demonstrated what appeared to be the winning position for white. MacNaughton leaned forward, frankly interested. He studied the board for a long time as the Russian watched confidently. At last MacNaughton looked up and announced his contention that in this position the game was probably a draw. The Russian pumped the Czech for a translation. The Czech told him, and the Russian made a guttural noise of contempt and pulled a chair up to the table.

"Ivan wants to play me?" the Englishman asked with mild surprise.

The Russian caught the meaning and nodded vigorously at the board. The Czech moved his chair aside. As the pieces stood on the board it was black's move. Without hesitation the Englishman, for his first move, made what appeared to be a questionable rook sacrifice. The other onlookers came back to the table.

The Russian clearly hadn't weighed all the ramifications of the sacrifice move. He studied the board for a long time. No one made a sound. Across the room someone groaned in uncomfortable sleep and coughed. After a while the snorer, who had been silent for a while, began to gargle in his sleep again. Finally the Russian made a move.

"Ivan has blown the game," MacNaughton announced, grinning. "It *was* a draw." He picked up his king's rook and pretended to spit on the bottom of it; then he screwed it into the board at the foot of the vacant queen's file as though gluing it into place. The Russian frowned at the board and said nothing. The Czech smiled. It was obvious that black would control the file on the next move. White's queen would be pinned and useless unless a king's protecting pawn was given up.

"Stalingrad," the Czech said. The Russian looked at him and smiled for the first time. He looked a trifle sheepish, took his predicament good-naturedly.

"Da," he said. Then he frowned at the board again. The English-

man refilled his pipe from his pouch that lay on the table, tamping it absently with his thumb as he gazed at the board.

"He has no way out," he said. Abruptly he stood up and stretched. "Let me know if he moves. I want to stretch my legs." The Czech nodded.

Suddenly the room was flooded with harsh white light from a single large bulb high in the center of the ceiling. Everybody blinked. An old man stood by the door, his hand on the switch, looking in surprise at the bodies draped around the room. He carried a bucket and a mop.

"Here comes Aurora of the rosy finger," said the Englishman.

Around the room, one by one, the stiffened sleepers sat up, scowling with sleep, rubbing their eyes, their faces puffy and bloodless. The old man made an apologetic gesture and began clattering about the room with his bucket and mop. He left the door open, and from the dim, echoing corridor came the faint crackle of the radio upstairs in the tower. A young reporter who had been watching MacNaughton's chess game cocked his head in the direction of the sound and spoke to the Englishman. His voice stamped him as American.

"Do you think he'll come in here or at Le Bourget?" he asked.

MacNaughton shrugged.

"I gave the radio operator a little something to keep us informed."

MacNaughton looked surprised. "Such enterprise," he said. "I don't think he'll go to Bourget. Those runways aren't so accommodating for these big cross-water planes. But we can take my car if we have to."

"Do you think he'll try to duck through?"

"Well, the old lion might be able to shake off one or two of these jackals, but he can't ignore the whole bloody pack. At the least he'll throw us a few scraps to fight over, and leave a press attaché to cover his retreat. I've never seen him duck the press yet."

"He's been sick, though," said the American reporter.

"Do you know the straight story on what's wrong with him?" MacNaughton asked. "All this veiled medical mumbo-jumbo your Embassy has been putting out sounds very suspicious."

"I think it's just his legs. I know he has trouble bending his knees."

"He's always had trouble with that, the proud old bastard. Probably spent too much time in church as a child. No, I mean—are you sure this isn't just a cover-up for an old warrior about to drop dead?"

"He's not a soldier any more."

"Blessed be the peacemakers," said MacNaughton. "You haven't answered my question. Why did he offer his resignation last week?"

"I don't know," said the American. "But knowing him I wouldn't imagine it would have anything to do with being in the hospital. He's been in too many of them during his life for anything like that to shake him up."

"Well, why then?"

61

"I don't know. There are a few congressmen after his scalp, I suppose. What surprises me is not that he offered his resignation, but that the President didn't accept it. It would get him off the hook in Congress."

"That's another thing. Why do your legislative people honor him with their august disapproval? He seems to be the first sensible chap you've had in France since Ben Franklin opened your ruddy Embassy."

"I'd have to give you the whole history of the United States to answer that. It's just that he takes the idea of the brotherhood of man a bit too literally for good Texas Christians."

"What, pray, is a Texas Christian?"

"For a Texas Christian the brotherhood of man ends with tideland oil rights. Or at the federal three-mile limit."

"You mean Sheppard's an internationalist."

"Not only that. He's a do-gooder, wants to give money away to foreigners instead of to deserving Texans."

"Tell me about Texans. I'm curious about them. You don't like them, I take it?"

"Not at all. Everybody picks on Texas and Brooklyn. I love Texans —in Texas. Outside of Texas they develop a fearful inferiority complex and damn everything they don't understand."

"Like Sheppard."

"Like Sheppard, or what they think a man like Sheppard stands for."

"They sound like wonderful people. Full of beans and vitality."

"They are really, you know. When they take their silly ten-gallon hats off and stop jangling their spurs at the dinner table. They have a great intellectual future ahead of them when they discover how bright they are."

"Are they really bright?" MacNaughton asked.

"And they have money too. But they waste their time playing at being shrewd instead of being profound. It will come. It will come. With money they can travel, and that's what will save them from extinction."

"It's true, you know," MacNaughton said. "I've seen them checking into the George V with their Cadillacs and truckloads of luggage. Heroic confusion. I ate dinner next to one of them one night at the Escargot. The first and only oil well I ever met. He came in with his wife, white Stetson and all, and they got the table next to mine. Well, they both ordered steak—they asked for a T-bone and threw the headwaiter into a sweat. There is no such cut in France."

"I know. They split it up and make Chateaubriands or something out of it."

"I'm not sure what in hell they do with it. Maybe French cows just don't have any bloody T-bone, for all I know. Anyway, there was a long discussion, during which the head chef came out. Your compatriot drew a picture of what he wanted on the tablecloth. He used a ball-point pen, and I saw the headwaiter suffering quietly. Finally the chef nodded and went back to the kitchen. I must say he was very patient. Well, the steaks came. Two beautiful *filets,* as big as my clasped hands. I've never seen such steaks. The master chef himself brought them out and stood by to see the first reaction. Our friend was very polite, very friendly. They chewed into the steaks and nodded wildly to the chef. Our friend rubbed his paunch and pantomimed his highest approval. This was all silent, in sign language, you see. I was having trouble to keep from laughing. That chap should have been a clown."

"Was the chef happy?"

"They made him the happiest man in the world. But I'll never forget what happened next."

"What happened next?"

"Well, the chef went back to the kitchen, and for a while they didn't say anything. Then the man turned to his wife, holding this beautiful steak on the end of his fork like it was a dead rat. He looked at it sadly and shook his head. 'Blanche, isn't that a shame,' he said. 'When will these Frenchies learn how to cut up a cow?' Well, I almost choked on that. I was afraid I had offended the poor chap, for he saw me. But no. He just pointed the steak at me and said, 'It's a sin to waste the Lord's divine fire on a piece of gristle like this.' "

"In the Escargot?" asked the American, laughing.

"Those were two of the most lovely pieces of meat I have ever seen in my entire life," the Englishman said, shaking his head in slow amazement over the recollection.

"Did you talk to them?"

"Oh Lord yes. We closed the place. I was so full of brandy I couldn't walk. I've never seen money thrown around the way he did it. He didn't do it offensively at all. He was completely innocent and naïvely trusting. He delivered a thousand-franc tip in person to the head chef. He just got up—everyone else had left long before—and walked out into the kitchen. I've never seen anything like it. I think even the headwaiter wound up liking him. He drank with us and even refused to accept a tip for himself—which is not normal behavior for him. The chef told me a long time afterward that Monsieur le Texas had eaten there several times after that, and when they returned to the States, he shipped him an entire steer packed in ice. It was butchered Texas style."

"My God."

"What time have you got?" asked MacNaughton.

The American shook his watch and listened to it. "It's stopped, but it must be nearly seven o'clock."

"I'm going to see if I can get anything out of the dispatcher upstairs. You want to come along?"

"What about your chess game?"

MacNaughton looked blank for an instant and then turned around and looked at the table, where the Russian correspondent was still bent over the board, frowning in profound concentration. One by one, the kibitzers had drifted away.

"Ivan doesn't lose easily, does he?" MacNaughton asked.

"The honor of his country rests on his shoulders," said the American. "And it's a big country." The Czech was asleep in his chair beside the Russian.

"Were you watching our game?"

"I saw the last of it."

"That Czech chap plays a jolly sharp game. I've played him before."

"He's not much of a match for you, it seems."

"Well, I played as a semiprofessional for nearly four years, in my youth," MacNaughton said. "Don't tell Ivan, though. I've been trying to suck him into a game for the last two years."

"Is he good?"

"Damn good, but not much of a sporting type. Plays for blood."

"Why do you want to play him?"

"Don't you know who he is?" asked the Englishman.

"I'm new to this beat."

"He's head man from Tass. Lovely contact if I could ever cultivate the sour little bastard. Look, I'm sorry, I don't know your name. I've talked to you a dozen times around town but we were never introduced."

"Striker. Willie Striker," the American said, extending his hand.

"MacNaughton," said the other as they shook hands. "What paper are you with?"

"None. Associated Wire Service. Night desk."

"You must know old Sharktooth," said MacNaughton. "He'd be your boss?"

"He's only around days. We're on the same coffee pot."

"Evil."

"He knows what's happening," said Striker.

"I'll say he does. He's a necromancer. I've never seen him use anything but a telephone, but he's always on it. I think he's talking with Lucifer. Used to work with him for Reuters. Messy bastard. Does he still leave coffee cups all over the premises with cigar stubs floating in them?"

"He still smokes cigars."

MacNaughton said, "Give him my love when you see him. What do you think is keeping that damn plane? I wasn't able to get even a rough E.T.A. Do you think it fell in the pond?"

"My mercenary friend upstairs says that they fueled in Iceland before midnight."

"Iceland? What in hell are they doing 'way up there? They must be dropping someone in London. Did you check on Shannon?"

"Closed in by fog."

"Well, even allowing for stopovers . . ." MacNaughton said.

"Maybe we can get something upstairs."

"I'd like to get out of here anyway," said MacNaughton. "The place smells like a gymnasium. That disinfectant our aged friend is slopping all over the floor doesn't help things either. My God, look at that." MacNaughton stopped short and pointed across the room.

The Swedish woman had rolled up her sleeping bag and was now squatting on the floor cooking something in a collapsible pan over her camp stove. The coffee pot steamed on the floor beside her. At the moment she was ferreting in a small rucksack with one hand while holding the sizzling pan with the other. She came up with a half-loaf of bread.

"Half a loaf is better than none," MacNaughton commented, watching her. "Why doesn't she use a table?"

"Probably likes to rough it," said Striker.

"I don't know what I'm doing here. I must be out of my mind. This kind of thing is for young bucks like you, and Swedes. I haven't had a drink all night, not one bloody dram. I'm ruining my health. I wish Hercules would finish with his Augean stable so we could turn that bloody light out and I wouldn't have to look at that goddamned healthy Swedish hausfrau."

"The radioman has a bottle of cognac upstairs."

"Good news, how do you know?"

"Because I gave it to him."

MacNaughton looked disappointed. "Hell, he won't open it. He'll take it home and save it for Christmas, or give it to his mistress."

"I took care of that. I opened it before I gave it to him."

"Ah. Brilliant move. For a neophyte in the artful science of separating people from their private knowledge, you show rare promise. I must take you to lunch on a Glasgow editor or two."

"It wasn't exactly my idea . . . I—"

"Sharktooth. I should have recognized the signature. I must be getting foggy from that bloody witch's brew that old chap is dissolving the floor with. Let's get out of here and rescue the fair princess from the tower. We'll leave Ivan to turn into a pillar of salt. He's forgotten that he's even got an opponent. In fact, that's the whole trouble with his game. He forgets that there are two players. I must tell him that when I learn to speak Russian."

They crossed the floor together. The old man stood before the doorway tangled in his mop and bucket. MacNaughton stopped and watched the old man wring dirty yellow fluid out of the thick acid-eaten mop. "Here we have a boy," MacNaughton said in flawless French to the old man, "a mere boy, and he's already schooled in the blacker arts. A good tutor can make all the difference, isn't that true? All the difference in the world." The old man turned around to see if MacNaughton could be talking to someone behind him, but there was no one in the corridor. MacNaughton brushed on past him, Striker following automatically. The old man stared after the two of them in confusion. "All the difference in the world," MacNaughton repeated as he disappeared into the deeper gloom of the corridor.

The old man shook his head and went back to wringing his mop. The tower radio, remote, unseen, snapped out a few dimly intelligible words and went silent again. Then the old man gathered his mop, his bucket, turned off the light, went out. He closed the door softly behind him. Outside, beyond the vast expanse of the room's transparent wall, the sky was deepening in ragged running patches to an ink-like purple.

VII

As they came over the western coast of France the navigator called out the new compass heading to the pilot, and the giant plane began its slow turn onto the final leg of its course. The radio operator sat behind his panel, his head sandwiched between huge black rubber-cushioned earphones, scribbling what he heard on a yellow pad of paper clamped in a clipboard. He took off the earphones and ripped the message off the pad and took it to the pilot, who scanned it quickly and passed it to the navigator, jerking his thumb toward the passenger compartment. The navigator, a young Air Force lieutenant, folded the message and took his uniform jacket down from a hook and put it on. He buttoned the collar of his shirt and slipped his tie into place. Straightening the peak of his cap, he opened the door leading aft and closed it behind him.

The Ambassador hadn't slept all night. The navigator, being the member of the crew with the most time on his hands, had ministered to his needs. Twice he had made coffee for himself and the crew, and had taken a cup back to the Ambassador. The Ambassador had thanked him civilly each time, but the coffee remained untouched at his elbow. He worked in his shirtsleeves with an old-fashioned green eyeshade over his nose. Once during the night he had asked for a blanket to put across his knees as he worked, and for more heat in the cabin. The polished top of the mahogany desk was stacked with thick documents bound at the edge with red ribbon. The Ambassador went through them page by page like a proofreader, stopping every now and then to pencil a note in the margin. He read over the stingy print with a large rectangular magnifying glass. He had sent his secretary to bed hours ago; her covered typewriter sat neat and severe in the center of her cleared desk. The cabin was furnished with simple but efficient luxury, green leather armchairs, a thick pile carpet on the floor, hunting lithographs secured in frames on the bulkheads fore and aft. Aft were the sleeping quarters.

As the plane leaned into its gently banked turn, the Ambassador looked up and saw the navigator coming through the brightly lighted doorway with a message in his hand. He put down his pencil and removed the eyeshade and peered out the window into the blackness.

"Crossing the beach already, Lieutenant?" asked Sheppard.

"It's under us right now, sir."

"The Ark comes again to Ararat. Send out the raven. Hold the dove until you see the rainbow."

"Sir?"

"Have you got something for me there?" asked the Ambassador, pointing.

The lieutenant looked down at the paper in his hand. "This just came in, sir." He gave it to the Ambassador and stepped back smartly. Sheppard unfolded the paper and gazed sternly at it. His hands were gnarled and looked much older than his face. He sat stiffly erect, his face half in darkness where the bright light from the desk lamp cut across it, his white hair gray in the shadow. He compressed his lips into a thin line of exasperation as he read the message.

"I don't understand what they want. So there are reporters. What did they expect there'd be? Lieutenant, can you offer me the reason why every press officer I've ever had, in the Army and out, seems to be frightened out of his meager wits at the mere appearance of reporters?"

"I don't know, sir," said the lieutenant. "Battle fatigue maybe."

"Yes," said the Ambassador. "Although I think it's more a case of Greek meeting Greek." The Ambassador scribbled rapidly on the back of the message, talking as he wrote. "What do you think of a press officer who keeps the working members of the press up all night waiting in a drafty air terminal while he's probably home in bed?"

"It doesn't sound like a very good way to butter them up, sir, I'd say."

"And you'd say rightly, Lieutenant. If I ever fire you as a navigator I'll make you my press officer. How's that?"

"I'd rather take a beating, sir, than try to handle reporters."

"That's exactly what you would take as a press officer, Lieutenant," said the Ambassador. "Nobody loves a press officer."

Sheppard finished writing his message with a flourish and folded the paper with a sharp crease. "That should fix Cadwalader. It will scare him out of the last few wits he has left. The radio operator can edit it if it isn't clear enough. The main point to get across to them is to see that those wolves are watered and fed before I get there. At the Embassy's expense. A hungry reporter is a dangerous animal, Lieutenant. Even more dangerous than a sober one. You'd better learn that before you reach staff rank."

"Yes, sir."

"Get that sent immediately. Then go aft and wake Mr. Sweet. He wants to be up in plenty of time before we land. Let the steward sleep as late as possible, but get him up in time to serve breakfast. Don't wake my secretary at all. If she sleeps through the landing just let her sleep. You can tell her I won't want her at the office before noon. That little girl worked like a Trojan last night."

"I'll tell her, sir."

"Then you might make some more coffee if you have a mind to," said Sheppard. "And I'll drink it this time. I can't do any more on this now. My eyes feel like they're wrapped in cobwebs."

"Would you like a doughnut with your coffee, sir?"

"Give me a doughnut and bring one for yourself. You may as well keep me company and help relax my mind a bit."

The plane came out of its long slow turn and righted itself. The round-bottomed smoking stands, weighted to the floor beside each of the armchairs, responded in unison to upright positions again, in dumb affinity for the invisible forces of the earth far below. The steady churning of the engines filled the cabin with their dull concussive roar and the plane, still high above the weather strata, flew on toward the eastern dawn which spread its clear light over an endless cloud blanket of gray wool covering the world of men far below.

The smell of fresh coffee filled the pressurized cabin, and the lieutenant came back carrying two steaming mugs with spoons jutting from them. He also brought the doughnuts. As he was setting them out on the desk the radioman slid the door open forward and waved another yellow message sheet. The lieutenant took it and brought it to Sheppard.

"Sit down, Lieutenant, while I look at this."

"Sugar, sir?"

"No, thank you. I like it black as sin and strong as the Lord's right arm."

The younger man laughed stiffly and spooned sugar into his own cup as Sheppard read. "Well, now, Lieutenant, what do you think of this?"

"What's that, sir?"

"Mr. Cadwalader wants me to compromise—just a short statement to the press at the airport and a formal press conference later in the day. Do you think we should let him have his way?"

"Well, sir, I know how to find my way across the Atlantic, but—"

"I think we should take the offensive on the enemy's territory rather than indulge in chicken-hearted delaying actions. What's your opinion?"

"I'm not sure my opinion would—"

"Relax, Lieutenant. I'm not a general officer any more. I didn't invite you to have coffee with me to hear that you have no opinions."

"Well, sir, you do win more games in your own ballpark, I suppose."

"You mean you favor holding the press conference at the Embassy. Perhaps you're right, Lieutenant. We'll let Cadwalader earn his salary." He wrote a single word on the back of the message: *AGREED*.

"Send that," he said, handing the paper unfolded to the navigator. "And ask them to send me my revised schedule of appointments for the day."

The lieutenant was back in a minute. He took his seat again, still sitting stiffly, not knowing quite what to do with his hands.

"Is Mr. Sweet awake?" asked the Ambassador.

"He was reading in bed when I went in, sir. He said he was about to dress. He asked me to tell you he would like to talk to you before we land."

"Anything else, Lieutenant?"

"Well, sir, he asked me if you had been to bed."

"Mr. Sweet worries me, Lieutenant. He worries too much. Well, it can't be helped, I suppose."

"Sir, what is the proper way to address him? I mean do you ever use a title—Mr. Secretary, or something?"

"It is quite proper to address him as Mister. Only the Secretary or Undersecretary would require anything more. Mr. Sweet is not properly an Assistant Secretary of State, although you probably have him listed that way on your passenger manifest, since as Chief of Security he has the equivalent rank. It's only to help protocol officers decide where to put him at the dinner table."

"One of these days I'm going to get a book and get these things all straight," said the lieutenant.

"Save your strength. Protocol is one of the more abstruse disciplines of metaphysics. Not only must you decide how many angels can sit on the head of the pin, but in what order."

"It sounds like a terrible waste of energy."

"It can be, Lieutenant. But sometimes a good protocol man can tell you more about the latest shifts in a government's pecking order than your best intelligence officers. All he does is watch how they line up for chow or for funerals. Some of them are nearly uncanny, Lieutenant. As I say, it's an abstruse science."

"I see."

"Tell me, Lieutenant, where are you from?"

"From Boston, sir."

"Did you go to school there?"

"Yes, sir. I studied airframe design for two years at Wentworth Institute. But I just didn't have the head for it."

"Mathematics too tough for you?" asked the Ambassador.

"No, sir. I got through that part of it all right. But I guess I just don't have the imagination to be a good designer. I went in the Air Corps and they made me a navigator."

"How do you like being a navigator, Lieutenant?"

"I like it better than anything I've ever done. I get a real emotional kick out of looking at my watch and saying to myself, 'In six minutes and ten seconds you should see the Eiffel Tower,' or something like that. And then, if you haven't made any goofups, there it is. Each time it happens it's just like the first time. I always think I'll get over it, but each time I feel just like a kid on his birthday. You know. It's just as though someone said, 'Shut your eyes, I have a present for you'—all along you know what it is because you've been pestering your folks for weeks for a bicycle or something like that. Then you open your eyes, and there it is. It never seems real at first."

"Whom do you pester for the Eiffel Tower?" asked Sheppard.

The young man looked uncomfortable. "I guess I've prayed a couple of times. Anybody gets scared enough'll pray."

"It's nothing to be afraid to admit, Lieutenant."

"Well, I'm not very religious. I guess that's the reason."

"How do you know?" asked Sheppard. He blew on his coffee.

"That I'm not religious? I hate to admit it, sir, but I haven't been in a church since I was a kid."

"Well, cheer up, Lieutenant. Perhaps the church has wings. Keep in mind, they build cathedrals with spires in order to get closer to heaven."

"Well, I know one thing. The higher up you go, the humbler you get."

"I don't know about that. Lucifer started his fall from a long way up."

"That's just what I mean, don't you see?" said the lieutenant. He was beginning to relax, although he was still sitting well forward in the leather armchair. "When you're flying, for example, you have to keep on the lookout for all sorts of things. Have you ever flown through a cold-front storm, sir?"

"I don't think so, Lieutenant. That's the sort of thing I fire pilots and navigators for," said Sheppard, smiling slightly as he sipped his coffee.

"Well, when I was in training, I got caught in one once. It was my own fault, you see. I laid the course without getting a last-minute weather report on a stationary front we were going to fly over around Topeka. It was just after I was beginning to feel invincible. I didn't have my beginner's fear to keep me in line any more, you see. Well, we hit this mess in the distance and didn't want to use up gas trying to go over it—it didn't look that bad from a hundred miles away, you see. Well, we tried to sneak through a pair of thunderheads—we were all pretty green by then. Anyway, we went in at six thousand feet—this was twenty tons of airplane, don't forget—two engines—we went in and then all hell broke loose. I've never seen anything like it. Lightning all over the plane like it was on fire—hailstones that made dents the size of fists all over the *underside* of the plane. The pilot holds that plane in a full dive at full throttle. I think he's gone crazy. We're spinning around like a leaf in a propblast. Then I see the altimeter needle spinning around like it was a wind-up top. We're going *up!* In a full dive with both engines over the red line, we're going *up*. Then I figure the altimeter is busted. I can see the pilot watching it. He's wondering the same thing. Six thousand feet is not a long way from the ground. I remember thinking then I wasn't scared any longer. I was wondering whether I would have time to know we'd hit the ground or whether I just wouldn't ever know. It was black as night outside even though I knew it was only five o'clock in the afternoon. We couldn't see a thing except rain and lightning."

"I take it you survived," said Sheppard.

"Yeah, the thing spit us out at eighteen thousand feet. We'd gone up more than two miles against a full dive. I still get the willies just thinking about it."

"That sounds like quite an experience," said Sheppard.

"I forget why I was telling you this—oh, yes—you see I got over-confident. I forgot what can happen to you when you begin thinking you're bigger than you really are Anyway, we were a lot more humble at eighteen thousand feet than we were at six, I can tell you that."

Sheppard laughed. "I think it's a rather special case, but I see your point." He put down his cup. "By the way, Lieutenant, my compliments on your coffee. It's strong enough for a fly to walk across."

"My grandmother used to say that the way to make good coffee was to put some in it," said the navigator. "She called that her secret recipe."

"Your grandmother was a smart woman. Do you have any brothers or sisters?"

"I have two brothers, both older, and a younger sister. She's getting married next week. My mother's all upset, thinks she's too young and all that. You know how mothers can get over a wedding."

"Four children. Your parents have reason to be proud of themselves."

"Have you got any children, sir?"

"My son was lost during the war, Lieutenant," Sheppard said.

"I'm sorry, sir. Was he your only child?"

"He was our first and only. My wife died when he was born."

The younger man flushed slightly. "I—I didn't mean to . . ."

"Stir up unhappy memories? Don't worry, Lieutenant, you learn to take things like that philosophically as you get older. I never knew my son very well. The Army is a hard mistress, I'm afraid. His mother's family really brought him up, and I could only manage to see him during summers or over his vacations at Christmas and Easter. Of course, I visited him and had him with me whenever I could, but it's not the same thing as having a family, is it? If you're going to make a career of the Army, Lieutenant, marry young, have your children early, and retire before you're too old to understand them. That's good advice, young man, in case you're looking for it."

"Yes, sir."

"Were you in the war, Lieutenant?"

"Yes, sir. I was in North Africa when you were there with President Roosevelt. We flew in a couple of tons of your file cabinets for the conference at Casablanca."

"You've been flying the Atlantic a long time, then. How many trips have you made?"

"I don't keep track any more," said the lieutenant. "Over a hundred."

"Have you ever been down?"

"You mean in the drink? Not yet, sir." The lieutenant leaned over and knocked on the polished mahogany desk top. "I've been in practice ditchings, but never the real thing. That's one thing I'm a bug on. I check the survival gear myself before and after every flight. Even if it's already been checked out. I don't take anybody's word for it. The boys think I'm a pessimist, but I've heard of more cases of rafts that wouldn't inflate right because someone had loaded cargo on top of them and broken the valve or something. Or rubber so old that it cracks when it fills up. These four-engined birds sink too fast to start putting tire patches on a leaky raft when water is boiling in around your knees."

"I think you're very wise. I'd be inclined to check the gear myself if I were in your position."

"You are in my position," the lieutenant said.

"That's a thought." Sheppard smiled.

"You know that door aft, the one next to your—your washroom? The one with the red release bar across it? It's a flyaway door. Well, when they converted this plane into a flying apartment house they had to relocate the door release in order to get the plumbing in for the sink and the shower. There's just a few inches' clearance there. Well, it worked fine on the ground. But there's a little valve on the cold-water supply that's used to drain the line when the plane is out of use, so the water won't freeze and bust the pipes. I was checking that door one day and I found it wouldn't release. The whole door's supposed to drop off when you hit that red bar down hard. What it was, was that valve—when it's screwed all the way in it's fine, but when it's open it sticks out just far enough to jam the release latch. On the ground it was easy to see what was happening—but what if we came down in the drink at night and that valve was under two feet of salt water? Anyway, I sawed the damn thing off. If they want to drain the pipes they can turn it with a pair of pliers."

"Well, Lieutenant, I hope you never have to use that door."

"Oh, we use it all the time to bring cargo aboard. Your desk came in that way."

The sky outside was growing lighter. Far to the south a tall cloud was cut in half by the sharp line between shadow and light from the rising sun. Sheppard looked at it. The sun, barely risen, appeared to hover on the horizon as the plane began a gradual descent to lower altitude.

"That's quite a sight, Lieutenant. We must be starting down."

"When you're up here you can really *see* a sunrise. Sometimes you even get the feeling you can actually see the earth turning. It's hard to realize that it's night down there. It'll still be pretty dark when we land. Unless that soup breaks up some."

"Lieutenant, I hope I'm not keeping you from your duties."

"No, sir. I'm free as a bird until we start in on our approach. You'll feel it in your ears."

"Good. I'm enjoying talking with you. It helps me unwind my mind after all this foolishness." Sheppard waved his hand over the thick pile of documents stacked before him on his desk. "This is what you'll be doing if you stay in the Army too long, Lieutenant. Let me warn you."

"Generals don't just ride horseback any more, do they?"

"Lieutenant, the Army was child's play compared to this. Fighting a war is far less complicated than avoiding one. If I hadn't already fought two in my time I don't think I'd have the courage to avoid another one. It's a lot of work, and there's no such thing as clear-cut success or failure. In war, you either win it, draw it, or lose it. In any event, *something* tangible happens, and success, a victory, is usually obvious. The object of diplomacy, however, is to see that nothing happens. Your ambassador has his victory only when he can tell the people that nothing is still happening, and that nothing will continue to happen. It's rather negative, don't you think, Lieutenant? It's why generals are always fated to be known as either bumblers or heroes, while diplomats will never be anything but tiresome scalawags with a passion for making things complicated. Unfortunately, Lieutenant, things *are* complicated. What you see here on my desk is merely a *digest* of documents that grew out of a single economic conference on the future of those people who are sound asleep in their beds down there."

"It must give you a funny feeling sometimes."

"I imagine you've had the same feeling, Lieutenant. Have you ever been lost with a planeload of passengers at your back?"

The navigator laughed. "A navigator never gets lost, sir. When a navigator doesn't know where he is he calls it a 'rough estimate of position.' Say like 'east of the Rockies.' There was a story I remember from training school about a navigator who got lost and ran the plane into a mountain. The pilot manages to pancake the plane, and as they're all climbing out of the wreckage the pilot is mad as hell and starts chewing out the navigator. The navigator takes it for a while, then he gets very insulted and says to the pilot, 'Wadda ya mean *lost?* Don't you think I know the name of this mountain?'"

The Ambassador leaned back in his upholstered swivel chair and laughed. "Ha, that's an excellent story. I'll keep it in mind. The unfunny thing is that I've known that story to be too true."

"But I know the feeling you mean, sir. I've had it. It's as though you have people's lives in your hands, and I guess you really do. Only they don't know it."

"Ah. That's the point. They don't know you're lost. *You* know it but they don't. You have knowledge of the uncertainty of their destinies,

73

due to your own uncertainty. And that, Lieutenant, is precisely the knowledge that irrevocably separates you from them. You see them in a new perspective. They go on eating their dinners, drinking their cocktails, laughing, enjoying the mild pleasures of the storm, trying not to show their nervousness. Because they trust in your infallibility."

"I've often wondered what would happen if I ever told them, in a case like that, that I wasn't so damned infallible, and that in fact I didn't have the foggiest idea of where we were."

"It's cruel to disabuse people of their trust, Lieutenant, although every once in a while I suppose it might help put the fear of God into them."

"Sometimes they make you feel like a little tin god the way they assume—I don't know how to put it. They assume that nothing can go wrong. But if there's a little rough weather, it's the pilot's fault, since he's responsible for everything having to do with their personal comfort. They never see the guy sweating it out up front. They just hear a voice over the loudspeaker that's full of confidence and authority. I flew commercially for a while, but I got sick of it and joined up in the Air Force again. This is my second hitch."

Sheppard looked at the navigator. He was sitting forward in the armchair, his back straight as a ramrod, his hands on his knees. The light from the desk caught his hands, but his face was in shadow.

"How old are you, Lieutenant?"

"Twenty-seven, sir."

"My son would be just about your age now. The worst part of serving the public, Lieutenant, is that the public rarely appreciates you for it. That is, they insist on flattering you for the wrong reasons—which can be worse than no flattery at all."

"How do *you* feel, sir? I mean, you stay up all night reading about what's going to happen down there. And there's this strike all over France. And now riots. I've been reading about it in the papers, about the demonstrations in front of the Embassy and all . . ."

"What do you think about that, Lieutenant?"

"It looks like they're having open season on Americans to me, sir. I don't think I'd like to have your job. I mean, all those people down there—well, they—"

"Hate me?"

"I didn't mean that, sir."

"Unrequited love is a terrible thing," said Sheppard, smiling. "To tell you the truth, I don't mind the personal attacks so much. That's part of politics. You get used to it in public life. But it hurts to see so many honest people being misled. As a matter of fact, earlier this morning I was trying to sort out my feelings on the subject. That's why I asked you about yours."

"But I don't feel the responsibility that you—"

"Exactly," said Sheppard. "Which perhaps gives you the clearer

74

perspective. From what you've told me, you've spent the better part of your adult life—you're twenty-seven, you say—"

"Yes, sir."

"—flying over the destinies of men, and that should qualify you as some sort of expert in the overall viewpoint. As for me, all I feel is the pressure—the pressure of what you call responsibility—the pressure of events that are beyond my control. Still, I feel responsibility for them. Like this strike. I'm like anybody else, afraid of mistakes. I worry about past errors. We all make errors, Lieutenant, only when you get to be a public man my age they call them blunders. I feel much as I imagine you must have felt in a storm when you were low on gas and didn't know where you were. This strike is a terrible thing. I don't even know if quicker economic aid from the United States could have helped France prevent it. It's left over from the war, Lieutenant. It's part of the legacy of war. It's been black weather in France since the war. We've had to improvise as we went along, to fly by the seat of our pants, so to speak."

"Well, sir, at least now you know the name of the mountain."

Sheppard looked blank for a moment and then laughed. "There you're absolutely right. At least it's not worse than a strike. It could have been a civil war, I suppose."

"We're starting down through the weather, sir," said the lieutenant. The plane yawed slightly. He looked at his watch. "There's some chewing gum in that little cubbyhole there if you want it—it will help equalize the pressure. Gum is the Air Force substitute for pressurizing."

"Young man, you forget I started life as an artilleryman. I know how to clear my ears," said Sheppard, smiling. He looked out the window, and down. "I don't think you'll see your Eiffel Tower this trip, Lieutenant."

"Well, it won't stop me from looking for it. We'll be in in about thirty minutes, sir. Do you want me to tell Mr. Sweet? I hear the steward knocking around in the galley."

"Tell Mr. Sweet, Lieutenant. And thank you for your company. This is always the longest part of the flight for me, too tired to work, too late to sleep."

"Don't thank *me*, sir. Usually I have to talk to myself on these flights."

"Go back there and show that steward how to make coffee, Lieutenant. I won't drink another cup of that bath water he put out last night."

"Yes, sir. Right away. I'll tell the pilot to roost her easy so your secretary can sleep. He'll have to give his permission, though. If it looks too sloppy when we get down there, he'll want her in a seat belt, I'm afraid."

"By all means, Lieutenant," said Sheppard. "He's responsible for his command."

The plane turned in a wide bank toward the northeast, lost altitude

75

in the clear air, and the light began slowly to change. As the plane descended, the sun which had only a moment earlier risen suddenly appeared to reverse itself; the downward movement of the aircraft halted the rising of the sun, then made it set.

They continued down. The air grew bumpier. The plane began to pitch with a more unbridled yawing motion as it floated into the careening twilight. Finally the aircraft passed from sunlight into the earth's shadow; the sun set below the thickening bandage of clouds and was lost at the distant blood-red edge of the world.

Lower, the plane shredded the looming tops off the standing clouds; tatters of thick gray scud fled past the windows. Suddenly, almost without warning, the aircraft lurched deep into the heavy earthbound shroud of clouds and the light failed completely. The plane plunged through turbulent darkness. Instantly rain slithered in ropes across the black glass and froze in delicate veins, like tendrils of a vine. A black gust of water slapped the metal hull like an open hand; sleet, like a wall of gravel, staggered the huge aircraft as it dropped and recovered in a shuddering downdraft. Just as suddenly, the rain stopped; they were under it, in clear air again, and the flight leveled out. Close below were the lights of a sleeping town; ahead, the skyshine of the city.

As the plane approached Paris, the overcast cleared slightly; it was lifting. The aircraft wheeled in a slow bank over the slag-gray rooftops and dark canyons of the city and turned eastward. Directly below, the dim phosphors of yellow headlights wormed through the dark maze of streets. The *boulevard extérieur,* banding the city along the ancient site of vanished walls, was etched in a bluish glow of streetlights. And beyond the boulevard, crouching outside the city's final gates, the two airports lay like somnolent watchdogs, their great saucer-eyed beacons swinging ceaselessly over the dark, opposite land. Dawn began again.

VIII

The police arrived in plenty of time to check papers. A whole platoon entered the building a few minutes after the old man had finished mopping the restaurant and had moved on to the men's room. The old man had turned out the light; the police turned it on again. This time everybody in the room had to get up. The police asked for *cartes d'identité* as well as *cartes de presse.* Everyone's papers seemed to be in order; out in the corridor, however, there was a commotion, a babble of argument; other police were seen politely hustling two unidentified persons in black overcoats past the door out to a waiting car. Everyone in the room heard the car drive off outside. In the room even the police were curious. But to the reporters' annoyance no one would discuss the matter.

Just then the American Embassy press officer arrived, a man named Wardell Cadwalader, otherwise known simply as "the Cad" or, elaborately, as "Cadwaddillac." The latter name was invented in the dimmer reaches of the Embassy file rooms and transmitted to the outside by a garrulous young lady who was later dismissed for emotional instability, a convivial security risk. The more ponderous name incorporated a simultaneous reference to Cadwalader's taste in automobiles and his rather unfortunate fat man's gait; the shorter name embraced certain shrewder aspects of his personality. At first he had been called "the Caddy" for the way he followed the Ambassador's staff around, carrying the clubs, so to speak; however, the reporters soon learned the hard way that he knew more about the game than some of the duffers he was hired to serve. Thus he earned a grudging promotion in the estimate of the press; the name was shortened to "the Cad." A former city editor on a tough Boston daily, he knew the arcane mysteries of journalism better than many of the reporters who depended on his favor. Worse, he had more than once demonstrated that he knew how to rap knuckles: a delayed invitation to an important press conference (for which he apologized profusely afterward); a tip gratuitously withheld; a misapprehension allowed to pass uncorrected—these were but a few of the weapons he had and, on occasion, wielded. In general it was admitted, though, that he was fair; some even held in more generous moments that he was the best press officer in Paris. But unfortunately, from the reporters' point of view, like Rommel the Fox he was on the other side.

Cadwalader entered the room, stout and solemn in a black chesterfield and homburg. A huge wet cigar, an incurable leftover from his days on the city desk, made an odd contrast with his diplomatic regalia; the cigar jutted from his broad flat face like the bung in a beer barrel.

MacNaughton stared at him. "Daniel enters the lions' den," he said, "like a gangster at a funeral. We ought to tear him limb from limb for making us freeze in this barn all night."

Striker said nothing. Cadwalader walked over to the captain of police and shook hands with him. The captain smiled broadly; they were plainly business friends.

"You'd think he was running for office," said MacNaughton. "I think he knows every *flic* in town by his first name."

"That comes from working a desk in Boston," said Striker, amused. "They say the mayor once tried to get him arrested on some sort of trumped-up charge to get him off his back, but the cops tipped him off and he spilled the whole thing across page one."

"I think he likes playing diplomat."

"He must. He could make three times the salary in the States."

"Is he really that good, your chap?" asked MacNaughton seriously.

"I only know what I hear the Old China Hands say when they get drunk."

"How'd he come to Sheppard?"

"The story goes that Sheppard went to him. Asked him personally to take the job. Made a special trip to talk him into it. The Cad worked for Sheppard during the war."

"Sheppard seems to have a lot of his wartime buddies still with him, doesn't he?" said MacNaughton. "Cutler was a colonel under him when I was working the Sicily Landings. Stark's another. Burns. That chap who doesn't like me—what's his name?—Lasher. And his air attaché—I can never remember his name."

"A lot of people have moved up with Sheppard. He's a stickler on loyalty. He gets good men to stay with him that way. He has a talent for surrounding himself with good men."

"When he moves, they move with him, is that it?"

"That's why he can get a character like the Cad for a third of what he's worth," said Striker.

"How does a young rabbit like you know so much about the ins and outs of Mount Olympus?" asked MacNaughton.

"I worked for the Embassy for a while, cranking a mimeograph. It was the only job I could get and I wanted to stay in Paris. The only other job was guard at the Talleyrand."

"Sounds a lot easier than being a printer's devil," said MacNaughton.

"You can learn a lot running a mimeograph if you read everything that comes out of the machine."

"Apparently," said MacNaughton, absently filling his pipe again as he gazed across the room at Cadwalader and the captain of police, who were talking and laughing with their heads together. "Where did the Cad learn his French?"

"God knows," said Striker. "I've never heard anything like it. It is absolutely perfect grammatically, but the accent . . . God."

"Amazing chaps, Americans," said MacNaughton. "He probably learned it in a book on the way over. Hello, what's this?"

Two white-coated attendants wheeled in a huge stainless-steel cart on rubber tires. Behind it came another cart bearing trays, napkins, silverware.

"Why, bless his little pig eyes," said MacNaughton. "He's going to feed us! Cadwalader, I love you, you shrewd old rhinoceros. Come on, Willie boy. Before the others get over the shock we can eat it all if we work fast."

The reporters stood around looking at the food carts in surprise and disbelief. The two attendants, without a word, placed three tables in a line and spread a sparkling white tablecloth over them. The starched linen opened with an expensive snap. Trays were stacked at one end, silverware at the other. The steaming carts were placed behind. Cadwalader walked among the reporters beaming like a host at a surprise party—which indeed it was. He addressed each journalist by name as he saw him, smiling hugely and waving an expansive hand toward the food. His face was as red as a slab of roast beef; in the middle was the plug of cigar held clenched in his teeth. He never found it necessary to remove it.

In the round wells of the portable steam table were scrambled eggs, two kinds of hot cereal, hot milk; in the flat trays were uncovered rows of fresh bacon done to perfection—crisp and hot—country sausages, and slabs of grilled ham. On the other cart, packed in ice, were fruit juices of several kinds, applesauce, cold milk, chilled pats of butter. There was a complete assortment of small individual boxes of corn flakes, puffed rice and other cold cereals. This was the American-style breakfast; there was also a complete European selection. Warm rolls, perfectly formed *croissants, brioches, tartines au beurre*. Finally, two portable urns were rolled in. One contained American coffee, the other French. There was also a small pitcher of hot chocolate, which the Swedish woman had entirely to herself. And there were napkins, white linen napkins that also unfolded with a starched snap.

The reporters jostled each other into line. As they passed before the table and held their trays and made their choices there was a great deal of pleased chatter. But as they went their separate ways with their trays and sat down at tables—Cadwalader had been going around unstacking chairs, sweating in his heavy double-breasted overcoat—the voices were stilled. The reporters got down to the serious business of eating. After a while the only sound in the room was of spoons and forks tinkling against the metal trays. The correspondent from Tass even left his single-handed chess game for the time it took to fill his tray. He was the only one to thank Cadwalader formally for his government's thoughtfulness. He did it with a stiff little bow and returned to his chessboard; Cadwalader was caught slightly off balance and his voice rose to an awkward boom in the empty echoing room as he called after the Russian, in his execrable French, that he was welcome. After the Russian's example, everyone else thanked him too, when they finished eating. It made a somewhat comic picture, Cadwalader with his huge soggy cigar, his black homburg still on, standing at the steam table as they brought back the wreckage of trays and cutlery, receiving handshakes of thanks like a Chicago matron seeing her guests off. The party was over, but nobody went home. As though to keep things from flagging, Cadwalader rounded up the police and also herded them toward the tables. He sent the captain out to get the others who were checking papers in the lounge, and the captain came back with several more hungry reporters and astounded police. They fell on the table like wolves. Everybody ate well. There was plenty of food. The coffee was strong and hot. A few of the airport personnel came down from their tower to join the unlooked-for banqueting. A half-empty bottle of cognac was generously passed around to slug the coffee and put an edge on it. The last one to pass before the desecrated table was the old man, who bashfully abandoned his mop at the door and, still protesting weakly, allowed himself to be steered over by Cadwalader. The old man was still eating when the first sound of the plane descended on the gray morning air and trembled the wall of glass.

It was just light when they heard the plane—the official Embassy crowd had arrived quietly and was already waiting outside. The distant pulse of its engines was faint but unmistakable. Reporters set their cups down, picked up their hats and started toward the door. Outside, the sky was still a dark dawn, but toward the east the horizon was well defined and lightening rapidly under the ragged clouds. The line beteen earth and sky was distinct; a light winter mist was collecting in mysterious pools over the distant meadows, blurring the farthest approach lights. The plane was still a good distance away: the throb of engines fixed the direction it was coming from. They watched the sky to the northwest.

They looked out over the vast black reach of tarred runway, still wet from the night's rain, that stretched away toward nothing. The long lines of ground lights converged in the distance; and the white light from the beacon over their heads flashed monotonously over the field, each flash like light from a silent explosion. Striker found himself standing next to MacNaughton again. Striker said, "I wonder how those guys up in the tower can stand that damned light night after night."

MacNaughton turned and looked at him. His face was a shadow, sleepless and cheese-white. "You get used to it," he said. "After a while you don't notice it. It's like the ticking of a clock. You don't hear it." The light slashed across his face. His head was turned slightly sideways; his drawn face looked oddly sad.

They saw the plane the instant the twin-beamed landing lights stabbed down out of the far-off murk. It came across the field banking in a ponderous slow circle; made a high trial run and went out again for the final approach, losing altitude. As it passed over their heads it made the glass behind them rattle. Then it went off again into the morning gloom. Everyone was outside now. Reporters stood stamping their feet and talking; a photographer accidentally discharged a flashbulb as he was straightening his tie in the wet reflecting glass. He muttered and threw the spent bulb on the ground: it broke with a muffled pop.

Briefly the reporters watched Cadwalader as he came out through the glass doors. He called the Ambassador's chauffeur over when he saw him. Those standing nearest could overhear him telling the driver to bring the car in close to the foot of the passenger stairs when the plane landed. A uniformed policeman passed, followed by two others. One of them turned at the sound of Cadwalader's voice and saluted politely in the semidarkness. He nodded; the other two turned and saluted also. The three went off talking in low tones, the question "Who was that?" whispered, the other two answering out of earshot. One of them paused to look back for an instant. The sound of the motors swelled again.

Everyone looked toward the north runway, where the plane would appear, and waited. The runway lights lay winking in rhythmic opposition. As they watched, the greens lagged behind the reds; slowly they fell into perfect unison for a time. Then, little by little, they slipped out of phase into opposition again. The cycle was repeated several times before the plane, tiny in the distance, suddenly appeared far beyond the end of the runway. It floated in low over the darkened houses ringing the distance, nearly invisible against the gray sky except for its lights. It looked like a huge flying insect, lights eyelike, piercing, the thin, brilliant beams shivering like sensitive feelers. The noise of engines increased as the shadow loomed closer; seen head on, it seemed hardly to be moving but simply hanging, suspended, floating, incredibly growing in size. As it approached it increased until its hugeness made it seem that it would surely fall. The winglights swept over the blown winter grass and came rippling toward the paved runway, as the machine felt its way down, the beams sweeping onto the wet pavement as the plane roared closer, flaps down, braking hard against the sluggish air; as it came toward the administration building its silver size and speed suddenly became real. Eating up the distance in seconds, it roared down the fleeting length of airstrip and swept immensely past the tiny group of men, one huge wheel glancing the earth a smoking kiss. The wings lurched slightly and lifted with the bounce; then there was a final yelp of rubber, and the big plane was down. Overhead, the passenger floodlights went on, bleaching the staging area in brilliant white light.

They watched and listened as the plane spent its speed to the far end of the runway. Finally it turned back, running awkwardly, crippled on the ground. It lumbered hugely out of the ambient darkness and slowed to a halt directly in front of where the reporters were standing. It stood a moment, engines idling with the detonating sputter of ten thousand horsepower. The starboard brakes set, it started to turn. The whole length of the plane vibrated as the pilot revved up the outboard port engine. The thin silver skin of the wingpanels reflected a pattern of shivering light. Slowly it turned, wingtips heaving with the weight of the straining engines, the blast of air from the propellers drying the pavement behind in a wide arc. The plane pivoted slowly, majestically, the deadly transparency of propellers changing to nervous glitter with the angle of light. Suddenly, appearing from nowhere, attendants rushed out onto the field: mechanics, cargo handlers, rolling a stairway, pushing carts. They were followed by a small tractor.

Striker became aware that someone was talking to him over the racketing of the engines' idling. He turned his head. It was MacNaughton.

"What?" shouted Striker.

"I said, the stable hands of Pegasus!" said MacNaughton, shouting over the din. "The stable hands of Pegasus come to life! Never mind."

Striker nodded and smiled. The police were forming a formal cordon

81

to keep the reporters back. A gendarme nodded and saluted at the Embassy group as they passed through, and cautioned one of them about a cigarette he was carrying in his left hand. The man stopped and stared at the cigarette a moment. It was unlighted. He'd been carrying it unconsciously. He grinned and gave it to the policeman, who took it and smiled and saluted again as he stepped back to let him pass. They walked in a solemn black file toward the plane as the reporters watched. "Gangster's funeral," MacNaughton shouted over the noise; he was enjoying himself. Then, one by one, the poppeting engines choked to a stop and the four spinning discs of light were transformed to triple blades frozen motionless in the astounding silence.

The passenger stairway was rolled into place and secured. The light from the floods seemed feeble over the short distance, and the airport attendants cast long jerky shadows as they hurried about their tasks, chocking wheels, placing ladders. A fuel truck moved into place under one wing, and even before the passenger door was open the tiny shapes of men swarmed over the plane, dragging hoses to fuel it, currying it, grooming it again for flight.

The police allowed the reporters to move out onto the field behind the official reception committee. They formed a cordon again just under the wingtip. One of the police gaped up at the huge engine over his head. A thin-blown lather of hot oil streaked the bright metal skin of each nacelle, and in the dark light of sunrise the half-hidden manifold rings still glowed a faint cherry-red. Down the dark length of runway the colored lights were mirrored off the plane's glistening metal; and flashing silently off its silver flanks, the beacon swept past again.

IX

The plane door opened. For a long moment no one appeared from inside. Then an Air Force officer looked out; light glinted off the gold oak leaves on his shoulder. The major looked briefly over the heads of the small Embassy group at the ring of reporters standing behind the police, as though he was counting them. He beckoned to Cadwalader and ducked back out of sight. Cadwalader threw away a fresh cigar and came forward, taking a pair of gray gloves from his pocket as he mounted the stairway into the plane.

The Ambassador's black limousine slowly nosed its way forward. The reporters stepped apart to let it through. The car, dwarfed in the mammoth shadow of the aircraft, turned slowly toward the rear of the plane behind the reception committee and stopped, angled on a line between wingtip and tail. The white breath of its exhaust rose silently in the chill half-light. The chauffeur got out and stood stiffly by the door as the other official cars moved slowly onto the field and parked in a line outside the ring of reporters. Near the main gate a double file of motorcycle police leaned against their black machines.

"Where did *they* come from?" asked MacNaughton, pointing. Striker turned around and looked at the motorcycle escort.

"I didn't see them come, did you?"

"We would have heard them," said MacNaughton. "They must have arrived when the plane did."

It was cold standing on the wet tarmac. Several minutes passed. Cadwalader hadn't reappeared from inside the plane. Then some hand luggage was slid out onto the upper stair platform. The Ambassador's chauffeur recognized the bags and hurried up the stairs and gathered them up. He stopped to peer into the dark interior of the plane an instant, and waved. He came back down the stairs with the small bags. Cadwalader appeared again while the chauffeur was putting the bags in the car's luggage trunk. He came down the stairs and walked along under the trailing edge of the wing out to where the reporters were standing.

"The Ambassador is very tired," he said without prelude. "I don't want you gentlemen to keep him longer than necessary. He will give you a statement and answer a few questions. A *few* questions. I suggest you get together among yourselves on the questions so everyone won't be shouting at once. There will be a formal press conference later today. You'll all be notified. So for now, keep the questions simple and *few*. I'll be glad to try and fill you in on anything that's not clear afterward. I'll stay here as long as you want me to. I'm not tired."

"What did I tell you?" whispered MacNaughton to Striker. Striker nodded without looking away from Cadwalader.

Cadwalader turned to the captain of police, who was standing nearby, and said loudly enough for everyone else to hear: "When I give you the signal, Captain, you can let the photographers through. The *photographers*." The captain smiled and saluted, nodding emphatically. Cadwalader said, "All right?" Without waiting for complaints he turned on his heel and rejoined the Embassy group. He stood at the rear, his hands in gray gloves clasped behind his back.

"He's like an old mother hen," said MacNaughton. "He actually flutters at a time like this."

"Are you going to try a question?"

"No. I just listen at times like this. You?"

Striker shrugged noncommittally.

The reporters pressed forward, crowding the police. It was like a crafty game between old opponents; the police were giving ground from a carefully advanced position while the reporters in the front rank advanced innocently on motive power surreptitiously supplied from the rear. In this fashion, the phalanx moved forward behind massed shields of murmured apologies. The police pursued their retreat with grudging good grace, until finally they reached the line both sides had known in advance they would settle for—a line just behind the circle of officials. There they stopped. The reporters stopped pressing.

A tall man, not the Ambassador, stepped out of the plane and came down the stairs carrying an attaché case. He was met at the bottom with deferential handshakes and soft conversation.

MacNaughton turned to Striker and whispered, "Who's His Nibs?"

Striker leaned over and whispered back, "That's Sweet."

"Byron Sweet? The Grand Inquisitor himself? What's he doing here?"

Striker shrugged. "God knows what he's doing anywhere."

From behind, another reporter leaned over Striker's shoulder. "Who'd you say he was?"

"He doesn't know," said MacNaughton. The reporter shot Mac-Naughton a dirty look.

MacNaughton said, "He told me, but he just forgot again." The reporter stepped back, scowling.

MacNaughton leaned over and whispered to Striker, "That chap is one of my unpleasant memories of Hong Kong. He gave me a rather bad time. I wouldn't give him a drink of water."

Striker shrugged.

In the cold gray light the reporters watched the plane and waited. The door stood open in dark expectancy for the Ambassador to make his appearance. Cadwalader, like a nervous stage manager, stepped through the group of officials and shook hands with Sweet without taking his eyes off the empty doorway. Abruptly he turned and nodded quickly to the captain of police, but a dozen photographers were already scurrying forward out of hiding. They'd been crouching unnoticed in enfilading positions. Jockeying Cadwalader out of their way, they swarmed around the foot of the stairway, standing, some kneeling, most bent over cameras in a half-crouch, focusing, elbowing, muttering curses as they got out of each other's way, adjusting flashguns.

There was a short pause, then a snicker of triggered shutters and a blazing eruption of white light; the tall figure bending through the doorway was frozen in motion, a captured image burned on the retina. In that blinding instant everyone saw the photograph as it would appear before the world, stern image, an imposing picture: the Ambassador holding a black cane and steadying himself with one hand on the door in the act of stepping over the doorsill. A black military cape hung straight from his bent shoulders and broke in folds over his forearms. He wore no hat and his hair was very white against the dark interior of the plane. His face was fixed in a tight-lipped smile, the firm, severe smile so characteristic it had almost become his trademark.

After the first flash blinded everyone, there was a moment of darkness. *Hold it, Mr. Ambassador!* But the photographers worked fast;

there was a feverish click-clacking of film holders, a clatter of spent flashbulbs dropped on the soft tarmac. The Ambassador stepped clear of the plane door into another blinding tattoo of popping flashguns. *Let's have a wave, Mr. Ambassador.* Moving like a jerky image on motion-picture film, he raised his flashing arm and waved casually for the photographers; now they were chattering at him in a half-dozen different languages: *Wave again, Señor Ambassador; Herr Ambassador; Mister; Monsieur. One more; jetz ein andern; encore une.* Patiently the Ambassador smiled and repeated the gesture several times.

Finally Cadwalader passed among the photographers and tapped them one by one on the shoulder. "If you haven't got it by now you'll never get it." He repeated this pet phrase over and over in English and in Cadwalader French. Reluctantly the photographers began slowly to back off, several of them still blazing away as they went. A few squatting diehards broadened their photographic collections with a point-blank shot of Cadwalader's huge double-breasted paunch bearing down on them. Between Cadwalader and the police the photographers were finally squeezed back out of flashgun range. "You'll get another crack at him later," Cadwalader told them.

A young Air Force officer emerged from the plane's doorway and offered the Ambassador his arm. Beside the officer the Ambassador's height became real; he hadn't seemed so tall standing alone at the top of the stairs, even though they'd seen he'd had to stoop through the door. Slowly they came down the stairs together. The Ambassador didn't lean on the younger man for support, although he started to negotiate the stairs awkwardly, stiff-leggedly.

The escorting officer successfully made it appear that he was merely standing by out of respect due a ranking elder. But the man Byron Sweet, seeing the Ambassador start down the stairs, broke away from a conversation and mounted the bottom steps extending an anxious hand upward, as though out of solicitude for an invalid. An alert photographer stepped around the end of the police line and raised his camera; just as quickly Cadwalader turned and walked across his field of view. The camera flashed and Cadwalader jumped in surprise; another closeup of Cadwalader's overcoat was added to the files of international journalism. Cadwalader apologized and innocently bent down to pick up the nearly whole cigar he'd thrown away a short while earlier. The reporter's anger faded in confusion as Cadwalader dusted the cigar on his sleeve and jammed it back in his teeth, reaching into his pocket and offering the man one like it. The bewildered cameraman accepted the cigar. Cadwalader walked away.

"Did you see that?" MacNaughton asked Striker in a whisper. Striker nodded. "The old beer keg has a lot of brass, I'll say that for him."

The reporters were beginning to press from the rear again. The police stood with their hands behind them, watching Cadwalader, who was talking to the Ambassador. They kept their feet planted firmly and didn't budge, and this time the front rank of reporters was caught in the squeeze. The Ambassador was standing on the lowest step of the stairs. He looked out over the heads of the small crowd before him, and leaned over to ask Cadwalader an inaudible question. Cadwalader shook his head. A vexed frown crossed the Ambassador's face; again he looked around as though looking for someone. Cadwalader said a few words to him. The Ambassador nodded slowly, asked another question; Cadwalader nodded, then shrugged. The Ambassador laughed and clapped him on the shoulder.

One by one the half-dozen officials stepped up and shook hands with the Ambassador while Cadwalader eyed the press corps warily. The chill gray of morning light made Cadwalader's normally beefy face look pale and bloodless. The officials filed off to one side. Cadwalader nodded to the police captain. The police moved forward in a ring around the foot of the stairs and let the reporters close in behind them. The Ambassador remained standing on the lower step, one hand holding the cane by the middle, the other braced on the handrail. He stood straight, his bearing informal but still military. He was smiling. The reporters waited; only a few held notebooks.

"I understand you gentlemen have been waiting," said the Ambassador. He spoke slow, flawless French. "I apologize for that."

The reporters waited.

"It is a real pleasure to step onto French soil again—" The Ambassador stopped abruptly, looked down at his feet, and laughed. "Although I see I haven't done it yet." He stepped off the step onto the ground. "The act is done. I'm glad to be back." There was a polite scatter of gloved applause from the reporters, semiserious.

"Knowing how fond you all are of prepared statements . . ." the Ambassador began. He paused. The reporters grimaced on cue. ". . . I have taken the liberty of not preparing one." Cadwalader frowned and studied the ground at his feet, absorbed; then he put his hands behind his back and gazed up into the morning sky.

"Therefore, one question at a time, gentlemen," said the Ambassador. The signal touched off a babble of voices. The Ambassador held up both hands defensively and shook his head from side to side, smiling weakly. Finally he got silence again.

"You are a multitude," he said. "I doubt if my small loaf will feed all these hungry ears. We'll let the lady go first." He nodded at the Swedish newspaperwoman standing directly in front of Cadwalader. She flashed a mouthful of white teeth, smiling her thanks. She held up a small notebook and, by the superfluous light of a tiny pencil flashlight, began to read her question, speaking French as an Englishman might. It was a long, difficult question involving commitment of counterpart funds for refunding of national debts versus expansion of export production facilities. The question displayed considerable knowledge of the European Recovery Program. The other reporters sagged; there were a few subversive groans. The Ambassador stroked his chin with his hand, giving careful thought before answering.

"The administration of counterpart funds," he said finally, "must be left on a fairly flexible basis, in my opinion. How they are used in a given country should depend on the specific problems facing that country. In instances where the debt position is severe, debt retirement should of course receive high priority. But in all cases counterpart funds will be administered on the basis of common agreement between the signatories of the bilateral agreements. Does that answer your question? I'm not the expert on these matters. Mr. Bruce, or Mr. Harriman at the Talleyrand, can give you more authoritative information."

One of the reporters asked, puzzled, "Mr. Bruce? Who . . ."

The Ambassador corrected himself. "I'm sorry. I meant Barry Bingham."

"Thank you, sir," said the Swedish woman. "What effect will the speech of Senator Taft have on United States tariff policy, can you say?" This time there were loud sighs of exasperation from the other reporters, a few rude snorts.

"None, immediately. Mr. Harriman at the—"

"Thank you, sir." She scribbled furiously.

The Ambassador pointed his cane at a reporter standing directly in front of him. It was MacNaughton.

"I didn't really have a question, Mr. Ambassador, but since you've done me the honor I may as well end the suspense. What are you going to do about the Dujardin mess?" MacNaughton asked the question in English, casually, almost offhandedly. But at the mention of the name Dujardin the reporters came to life again and picked up their ears.

The Ambassador laughed easily. "Mess is right," he said, also in English. Then he switched back to French. "The Dujardin affair. What is there to do? It is a domestic problem of France. The United States has no right to pass judgment on the internal affairs of a friendly nation. Personally, however, I deeply regret the bitterness it seems to have caused here. Anything which divides a nation in a time of crisis is cause for grief. But this is a family affair of the French nation. I can only hope that justice will be done. Toward that end the United States will do anything it can to help, nothing to interfere."

"What about Major Stone?" asked a reporter for a rightist daily.

The Ambassador reacted sharply to the question: "*Mister* Stone is a private citizen who left private life only to serve his country in time of war. He has since returned to private life. His employment as a specialist by the United States Army Graves Registration here in Paris doesn't distinguish him in any way from the millions of other private citizens in the employ of the United States Government. I see no reason for referring to him by his temporary wartime rank. He is not a professional army officer retired."

"They won't let us in to see him, Mr. Ambassador," said another.

"Let me point out," said the Ambassador, smiling again, "that not everyone in this world is as happy to see your smiling faces as I am. Mr. Stone is a private citizen, and as such has every right to avoid you like the plague if he so wishes. However, Mr. Stone wishes to cooperate in every way possible with the French authorities; he has given his assurance that he is at their disposal. In addition, I have made arrangements for Mr. Stone to appear at a press conference with me this afternoon at the Embassy to answer your questions. I will also have a statement for you afterward. I have spoken with the Minister of Justice. But let me say one thing—and, of course, you may quote me if you like. I would like to say here that it is my firm belief that the Dujardin case is being deliberately exploited for partisan political advantage, and not in the interests of securing justice. The manner in which the documents from German intelligence archives are being introduced to the public is hardly calculated to preserve the atmosphere of judicial calm necessary to obtaining justice for a man whose life hangs in the balance. Rather, it appears that his life is of no consequence. If that were not so, why are the documents still being withheld?"

"How do we know they didn't just obtain them, sir?" asked a young Swiss reporter. "And how do we know such documents even exist?"

The Ambassador turned casually toward the young man standing under the shadow of the stairs. "How do we know? Well, now, we wouldn't know, would we? That is, we wouldn't unless the custodian of the Army's Historical Section in Berlin had done a little checking for me."

The reporters looked up as one man. There was a long moment of absolute silence as the Ambassador held them with his eye. He in turn scanned the circle of faces.

"Those documents were obtained several months ago," he said finally. He said it with a sort of offhand dismissal, as though the subject were already ancient history.

"Sir, does the French Government know this?"

"They have been advised, yes," said the Ambassador casually.

"Will it be possible to prove this?"

"I'm not in the habit of making unfounded statements."

Cadwalader stepped forward in front of the Ambassador. "You've got it all now. Now let's go to press." He looked at his watch. "You may be able to make the late morning editions, *if you hurry.*"

"Mr. Ambassador—"

"Sir, just one more question—"

Cadwalader again: "School's out. No more questions now. The Ambassador's had a long trip. The Ambassador is tired. The Ambassador didn't get a good night's rest on a restaurant table like you all did. Party's over."

"Sir, do you think—"

"No more thinking," said Cadwalader. "Go home." The police widened their circle. The Ambassador stood alone in the center smiling apologetically and shrugging with mock helplessness as Cadwalader took matters completely out of his hands. A few reporters started running for the telephones, then a few more; then a general foot race was

88

on across the staging area. Striker, MacNaughton, and the Russian from Tass found themselves walking alone almost together. Behind them came the officials walking toward their cars. The Ambassador and Byron Sweet were standing with Cadwalader at the Ambassador's car. The chauffeur held the door open, waiting patiently while the three men hung back, still talking.

Suddenly another limousine came around the building from the front parking lot on the other side. MacNaughton put his hand on Striker's forearm and halted in his tracks.

"French," he said. "Let's see if we can see who it is."

"It's been there all the time?" asked Striker.

"Must have been."

The car moved slowly between the alleyway of motorcycle police, circled around the string of official Embassy Citroëns and came to a halt. The Ambassador saw it and waved. A man inside waved back. The Ambassador said a few more hurried words to Sweet and Cadwalader. Cadwalader ran after the departing group of lesser officials and called, "Colonel Lasher. Colonel Lasher." A small man in civilian clothes turned around. "The Ambassador would like you to ride back in his car with Mr. Sweet." The man fairly bolted forward. "Glad to. Glad to."

He walked back with Cadwalader. A few police stood about the Ambassador's car idly looking at the newly arrived limousine, admiring it. Mounted behind the glass of the windshield, a small round bullseye bore the illuminated colors of the Republic.

The motorcycles exploded in unison and rolled slowly forward through the open double gates. The gatekeeper stepped well back to let them pass. They turned slowly onto the highway, waiting for the rest of the motorcade to catch up to them. Two Citroëns followed directly after them, then Lasher and Sweet in the Ambassador's car, then the black Delahaye, sleek and low, then three more Citroëns. One Citroën remained behind, Cadwalader's. MacNaughton walked over to it. Cadwalader was standing beside it shucking his gray gloves, an actor getting out of costume, a freshly lit cigar in his mouth.

"Handled like a master, Ward, old man," said MacNaughton.

"The Ambassador is riding with an old personal friend, if that's what you want to know," Cadwalader said without looking up, his mouth thin, determined.

"In an official car?"

"It's borrowed for the occasion." Cadwalader looked at him. "That's the straight truth, MacNaughton. It's on loan from one of the ministries."

"I believe you, Ward," said MacNaughton. "Personal friends are out of your line, I suppose."

"Official business I got in carload lots. Whatever you want. But the Ambassador's personal business is his personal business. I'm not paid to edit a society column. The man he's with is not an active official of government, so for me he doesn't exist."

"I appreciate your position, Ward," said MacNaughton. "You don't mind if we snoop around on our own, Willie and I?"

"Your personal business is your personal business," said Cadwalader, shrugging. "Striker, you've fallen in with bad company, I see."

"It takes a thief to tell a thief," said MacNaughton, grinning.

"I never been caught stealing in my life. You're not a thief until they catch you."

"Cadwalader, after what you did to that photographer out there you should be ashamed to talk to me, a member of the honest working press," said MacNaughton. "Talk about your bad company."

Cadwalader grinned modestly. "You saw that little bit, did you? I'm glad someone appreciates me at times. You have to admit you couldn't have done better, MacNaughton."

"How's his health?"

"You want a straight answer just for your own information or a crooked answer to print?"

"I'll keep this to myself. The good burghers of Glasgow won't miss it."

"We don't know. We won't know until he goes in for a checkup again. But his knees give him trouble. He's got to stay off his feet as much as possible. If he hadn't off-loaded the doctor in Boston last night he never would have gotten away with standing around to answer a lot of fool questions."

"Just the knees?"

"Lord, isn't that enough?"

"Thanks for the fill-in, Ward, old man," said MacNaughton. "Appreciate it."

"Give my best red garters to Sharktooth, Willie," said Cadwalader.

"I will," said Striker.

Cadwalader got into his car. They watched him drive off.

Inside the restaurant the bar was opening for the day. MacNaughton bought the captain of police several *fins*—he was off duty. The Englishman had a few himself and Striker joined them. After a while the conversation came around to the beautiful black Delahaye. Then, casually, to the man in it. The captain responded.

"That was Colonel Owl," said the captain expansively. "You've heard of him, no doubt, my friend?"

MacNaughton pursed his lips and nodded gravely. "So," he said. Striker looked blank. "Who's Colonel Owl?" he asked.

MacNaughton turned slowly and looked at him. He rolled the small glass of amber brandy between his palms carefully. "A legend," he said. "A myth. He doesn't exist."

The captain threw his head back and roared with laughter. *"C'est exact,"* he said, laughing still. It seemed a private joke. *"Un mythe. Il n'existait pas."*

MacNaughton's smile was distant, nostalgic. "The Owl was a figment of the imagination, Willie, who haunted people during the war.

People who didn't belong here. The man who dreamed up the nightmare was named Professor Georges Merseault. That was him in the car."

"Merseault?" asked Striker. "Have I heard of him?"

"I doubt it," said MacNaughton. "Not many people have. He taught history."

"One more drink for the Owl," said the captain. He was getting quite happy, a little flushed, but happy nonetheless. "I'm off duty."

"No," said MacNaughton, frowning. "The Owl hoots thrice, remember?"

The captain roared with laughter.

They had some more drinks.

Finally Striker had to beg off to call his office. MacNaughton, who was getting slightly drunk, insisted on coming along and saying hello to the man on the daytime desk—old Sharktooth. They avoided the public phones where a few reporters were still trying to put calls through, and slipped upstairs unnoticed.

The radioman was also well along; he was also off duty now and the bottle was nearly gone. They had left the captain of police at the bar, saturated with nostalgia over the discussion of Colonel Owl, under whom he thought he had once served—no one could ever be sure, he said.

Willie Striker called in a recital of what had happened, what was said, everything. He had barely finished when MacNaughton impatiently snatched the instrument out of his hand and bellowed into it: "This is Captain Littletoe of his Majesty's Foot."

There was a long silence. MacNaughton held the receiver out so Striker could hear: "For Christ's sake," the metallic voice rapped in the earpiece, "I told Willie to give that bottle to— Wadda you doing to my night shift?"

"I'm buying his liquor for him, you old reptile."

"You take him on one of your daytime bats and I'll eat out your eyeballs. Lemme talk to Willie, Mac."

"He can hear you," said MacNaughton. "He's only on the other side of the room."

"Willie, you get the hell on home and get some sleep. Tell MacNaughton to go to hell. You hear me?"

Willie nodded.

"He hears you," said MacNaughton. "You hear him, Willie?"

"I hear him," said Willie.

"He even says he hears you," said MacNaughton into the phone. "You want to hear him say he hears you?"

"Go to hell, both of you. Get him in here on time, that's all, Mac." The voice in the telephone went dead. There was a click.

"Rang off," said MacNaughton. " 'Hung up,' to you, that is."

There were more drinks at the bar, during which MacNaughton and the police captain talked about the last days of the war in France. The captain dismissed Dujardin with a wave of the hand when MacNaughton mentioned his name, but the name seemed to throw a pall over the conversation. The captain became quieter, finished his glass, ordered another, stood staring down into his drink. He kept waving his hand from time to time as though arguing with himself. MacNaughton was quite excited now and talking brilliantly, as he admitted. Striker was feeling more tired than intoxicated. But he listened. The police captain was completely absorbed in his own dark thoughts as he scowled at one glass after another.

MacNaughton was talking loudly, slipping from French into English and back again, pounding the bar to emphasize his points. He had the curious habit of pounding *before* he made his points rather than at the same time or after. Bang! "Do you want to know why Sharktooth is a good reporter? Well"—bang!—"I'll tell you . . ."

His speech kept shifting through a dozen accents and idioms. He talked like a suitcase with hotel labels from every part of the British Isles plastered all over it. He did the same thing in French. If he was talking about the south, he would unconsciously fall into the accent of the Midi. He was a man who seemed to have never had a home, or whose home was wherever he went, wherever he chose it to be. When he talked about Sharktooth, he unconsciously salted his speech with Americanisms and hard cadences. But he talked with extreme clarity; it was his eyes, not his tongue, that betrayed the liquor in him.

". . . a good reporter knows good from evil. Accepts both as necessary. Halves of total human experience. But he *knows* one from the other. He doesn't prefer one over the other. He observes. He reports. He makes no prophecies. He's sentimental, but cold as ice. He isn't moralistic. He doesn't preach. He's merely right. He has no nerves at all, only feelings. Cosmic feelings. He feels sorry for people, pities them. But he has a sense of fate, a sense of dramatic irony. He knows he can't tamper with their destiny since he's a part of it. Who, where, what, when, how. Five questions. Five acts of tragedy?"

MacNaughton fumbled in his pocket and took out his wallet. "I carry this clipping around to illustrate my point. This isn't the first time I've given this lecture." He gave the clipping to Striker. Striker unfolded it carefully. It was worn, and about to come apart at the creases.

TRAIN KILLS HOMELESS CHILD UNDER BRIDGE

Charlotte, N.C. Oct. 14 (AP)—A frail 10-year-old girl was crushed to death by a locomotive as she huddled with her brother and sister in a Southern railroad underpass.

They were keeping out of the rain while their destitute father, Henry N. Duncan, 54, sought coffee for his shivering family which had spent the night in some woods.

Mamie Lilian apparently didn't hear the approaching switch engine.

"I grabbed for her, but I didn't get her," related Hazel,

17, who jumped with her brother, Alvin, 11, just in time. "We weren't asleep then. We were just sitting there on the track out of the rain. We were spelling words. I was trying to learn my little sister how to spell."

Striker fingered the clipping, reading it again before handing it back.

"Up to the last line, that clipping is merely an accident report," MacNaughton said. "Last line raises it to the level of tragedy. It's the difference between Sophocles and Thucydides. That's why there are no good Marxist reporters. Their point of view is historical rather than tragic."

"You think a reporter is a tragedian?"

"That puzzled me for a long time." An airline hostess went past the window carrying a small dog with a yellow shipping tag hanging from its collar. "He's not really a tragedian because he's in the tragedy himself. It's a paradox. The tragedians themselves felt it, so they invented the chorus. In *this* bloody tragedy the working press is the chorus." He slapped the solid wood of the bar with his open palm.

They stood at the bar until noon. The captain of police insisted on paying for his share of the drinks, but MacNaughton threatened to throw himself under the wheels of a car if the barman accepted the money. MacNaughton finally paid. There was great affection all around.

Willie Striker was tired—he'd been awake all night watching Mac-Naughton play chess with the Prague stringer. When he finally said good-by, he walked outside and passed the glass wall. He saw Mac-Naughton sitting inside talking, this time to the lone barman, pounding on the bar and nodding his head. The barman leaned on the counter, listening with what looked like interest.

X

The limousine crept slowly along the runway toward the gates, waiting to follow the motorcycle escort.

"How do you feel?" Merseault asked in English.

"Tired, Georges," Sheppard said, sighing heavily. "I'm tired to the marrow of my bones. It's good to see you."

"You don't look cheerful, Bruce," Merseault said. "What's wrong?"

"Tired. Tired tired tired." Sheppard leaned his head back and closed his eyes. "Thank God you were here. It's a relief—to be able . . ."

". . . to drop the mask?"

Sheppard nodded, eyes closed, and smiled faintly. "To drop the mask. Precisely."

"I thought you were bringing the doctor with you," Merseault said.

"Tricked you."

"I was told he was in your party when you left Washington."

"We jettisoned him in Boston. Off-loaded, I believe, is the technical phrase."

Merseault looked at Sheppard, studying his stern profile. The lines around his closed eyes were heavy with fatigue. A blue vein pulsed at the temple under the parchment-white skin, just below the gray-white line of hair. Without the steel light of the eyes the face lost its illumination; it was lined and revealed the secret of age with awful clarity.

"I can still hear the roar of the engines," Sheppard said. "It's like a dull ache somewhere in the back of my head."

"No sleep, as usual, I suppose," Merseault said.

Sheppard didn't answer.

The limousine halted, waiting; the chauffeur got out and stood beside the car. Ahead the police were assembling their escort.

"You're killing yourself," Merseault said.

They sat in silence, the idling motor muffled in the deep upholstery, the automobile shivering slightly with the vibration.

"Was the resignation just for effect?" Merseault asked finally.

"A maneuver," Sheppard said, opening his eyes. "But I'm finished, Georges. It's a job for a younger man. I'm going to have to step down as gracefully as I can."

"How does the President feel?"

"He wants to avoid having it appear that he's knuckling under."

"Your esteemed Congressman Kreuger?" Merseault asked.

"He's merely a nuisance. The Senate is something else again. All Kreuger and his clan can do is tamper with appropriations. He can't actually block legislation. I've outlived my usefulness to the administration, Georges."

"When is this polite little knife fight going to come out in the open?"

"Never, if I can help it," Sheppard said. "Why should I let the President damage his position? There's no point to it. Some of his appointments are already being held up in committee. Dr. Jessup, for example, is more important to the future security of the United States than I am."

"I don't see how anything can be gained by capitulating. Battles aren't won by retreating."

"Wars are," Sheppard said. He sighed, and fingered the upholstery beside him.

"That's an odd reflection for a victorious general."

Sheppard smiled. "A commander who knows how to attack can win battles. But give me a general who knows how to manage a skillfully timed retreat, and I'll give you a man who can win wars."

"You must have Russian blood," Merseault said, smiling. "It certainly doesn't sound like the English puritan in you talking. Or the student of Clausewitz."

"Clausewitz reflects the military situation of a nation that has no place to retreat to. Germany is a landlocked island. That's why he stressed the fight, the battle in attack, so strongly. But in politics the terrain is limitless, and you can retreat indefinitely into silence. The adversary is most tactically vulnerable when he's strategically overextended."

"Interesting theory," Merseault said. "But it overlooks the talkative nature of man. Also, silence can be liquidated. It's the logical extension."

"It might come to that," Sheppard said. "Why are we talking about this?"

"Did the President seem in good health?"

"He looked very well. But every time I see him he looks older. I imagine I strike him the same way. It makes me realize how fast my time is running out."

"Did he send you back because of . . ." Merseault paused. "I'm being tactless."

". . . because of my personal stake in the matter?"

"Is that the reason?" Merseault asked. "It's perhaps not my affair."

"We didn't discuss it in those terms," Sheppard said. "But, yes. That's one reason. There are other reasons, of course."

"Of course."

The two limousines idled at the edge of the runway while the police assembled the other cars among the escort vehicles beyond the gate. A rear guard of six motorcycles and one carload of plainclothes police circled around behind the second limousine, the Delahaye, and now also came to a halt, waiting.

Merseault's chauffeur considerately produced two lap robes and was in the process of spreading them across his passengers' knees when the squad guide's shrilling whistle pierced the racketing motorcycles' din. Motorcycles ahead and behind fell instantly into strict three-filed ranks and halted, alert for the second signal that would start the procession on its way. Merseault's chauffeur carefully finished tucking the blanket around the Ambassador's knees, saluted, and backed out of the door. He rolled up the windows and tested the handles of both rear doors to make sure that they were properly locked from inside before closing them. Then he walked around the long black vehicle one last time and gave each of the four tires a proving kick, removing as he did so the black leather cover from the official seal of state that emblazoned the front of the car. Satisfied that all was in order, he opened his own door and stood for a moment, conscious that all eyes were on him. All chauffeurs of lesser responsibility were in their vehicles already.

Finally he nodded with grave dignity to the squad guide, who was watching him from the head of the procession outside the chain-wire fence. Instantly there was a piercing whistle blast and an explosion of motorcycles as the advance escort moved smartly off in closely dressed formation. The chauffeur swung into his driver's seat.

"Félix is a very conscientious chauffeur," Merseault said, smiling. "He has driven for three presidents and a dozen premiers. He has demoted himself to cabinet rank now, to Minister of Foreign Affairs." Sitting stiff and straight behind his glass partition, Félix put the car smoothly in gear, and the heavy black limousine moved precisely off with the rest of the procession.

The Ambassador smiled absently. His face was drawn and tired.

Merseault continued, "He feels that driving presidents is a job for a younger man. Also, he feels that the key to France's destiny now lies in its foreign policy. Remarkable chap. Remarkable."

The Ambassador shifted his position abruptly to face Merseault. The intense preoccupation that showed in his face dissolved as he looked at Merseault as though the time had come to open a direct attack on the question occupying his mind. The car glided smoothly through the gates—Merseault returned the old watchman's informal salute—and turned right onto the highway behind the Ambassador's own Cadillac limousine. The space between vehicles lengthened as they picked up speed. The tires made a soft drubbing sound on the cobbled paving stones, momentarily stifling the closed interior of the Delahaye with brain-dulling sound; as the speed increased the oppressive vibration diminished and ceased.

"What is happening, Georges?" Sheppard asked.

Merseault shrugged. "Where do you want me to start?" he asked.

"I had a special briefing before I left the hospital—Washington, that is. It was totally inadequate. Even your French Ambassador seemed a little bewildered. He was obviously waiting for clarification himself. This strike . . ." Sheppard shook his head. "The only really solid advice I got was from Jeff Caffery—he was in town for a few days."

Merseault smiled. "This is an affair of passion, not logic."

"Start by explaining to me how the Dujardin case got tied into the strike in the first place. I fail utterly to see any connection."

"There is no real connection," Merseault said. "The connection has been manufactured."

"And what is Stone's part in all this?"

Merseault shrugged again. "Simple. Here we have a drama. He is an American. He was in the Army and still works for the Army as a civilian. Also, he was an 'agent' during the war. Thus he is perfectly qualified for the role of villain in the dialectical folklore. The Party has a great flair for reducing political drama to its simplest terms."

"But why . . . ?" asked Sheppard.

"True, the finished drama may have nothing to do with reality, but on the other hand don't underestimate the power of a work of fiction. Facts have nothing to do with this production, which is what makes it hard to refute. Dujardin—the Dujardin being presented here —never existed. Neither does Stone. They are both pure inventions. They are creatures of the printed page, of the press. Dujardin is no more a martyr than you are."

"But surely there can be no doubt in the public mind that he collaborated with the Germans."

"Bruce, my good literal-minded friend, I'm trying to tell you that this whole business has nothing to do with facts. Do you realize that you are now almost universally referred to in the press not as 'Ambassador Sheppard' but as 'General Sheppard'? Even the *Paris Tribune* has fallen into the trap once or twice, but *l'Humanité* started it all. The rest have merely slipped into it out of misplaced respect, I imagine."

"Have you pointed this out to Cadwalader?" Sheppard asked.

"It only dawned on me last night while I was going over some press summaries. It was a subtle change. Stone is being referred to in the Party press as working for the 'American Occupation Army in France.' "

"But that's too stupid."

"Is it? Do you know what subconscious associations the word 'occupation' carries in France? *Le Zone d'Occupation?*"

Sheppard nodded slowly, frowning.

Merseault continued, "Words are symbols, Bruce. Agent. It is true that Stone was an agent in France. General. Ever since the Dreyfus case the word 'general'—"

Sheppard interrupted. "Yes, yes," he said, irritated.

There was silence for a moment as the car sped past a knot of black-shawled women gaping at the edge of the road.

Merseault asked, "What are you going to do with Stone?"

Sheppard sighed and let his head fall back on the cushion. He spoke with his eyes closed. "The Army is panicky about all the public attention they've been getting. Stone has refused to take a leave of absence until the Dujardin thing is settled." He opened his eyes again.

"I can't say that I would do any differently in his place."

"Some fool captain in Washington—a public relations officer—came up with the bright idea of getting rid of Stone, as a security risk. They had actually got to the point of an investigation when my old classmate Colonel Thaw heard about it and gave the captain a billet in the Philippines."

"I heard about the investigation. We had a request from one of your security people . . ."

"You have a file on Stone?" Sheppard asked, not surprised.

Merseault smiled. "Just a history. Anyone who worked in France during the war . . ."

"Yes, of course."

There was another brief silence.

Merseault asked, "What's going to happen to him?"

Sheppard said, "I agreed to take Colonel Thaw off the hook. I'm asking to have Stone transferred as of today to the Embassy payroll, to the office of the military attaché. He's been working in Liaison with them anyway. It doesn't matter which end he's paid from."

"Do you think you'll be criticized?"

"Georges, who knows any more? I've been criticized all my life and I've survived it."

Sheppard smiled and turned away to look out the window at the dismal winter countryside flashing past. They were passing through the farthest outskirts of the still-distant city, a no man's land of city-style houses and small farm buildings wall-painted with faded prewar advertisements for liqueurs, magazines long defunct, and automobile tires. He said, "It would be happier if I understood what it meant."

Merseault glanced at the Ambassador's averted profile, but said nothing.

Then Sheppard said, "Georges, tell me what is going to happen."

Merseault shrugged. "I don't know."

"What's your guess?"

"My guess?" Merseault pondered, absently turning his walking stick between his hands. "My guess is that there is going to be a more concerted effort to discredit American policy. First they will try to discredit its representatives, that is, you. The only real threat to the Party's long-range power ambitions in France is American economic aid. The Party seems to be working on the theory that a little calculated ingratitude will curdle the milk of American generosity."

"Go on."

"The danger of course is that American policy will trip over its own mixed motives. The strategy will be to anger you to the point where you abandon generosity, and discredit yourself."

"Of course, our generosity, as you call it, is not quite so noble as you make it sound. We have an obvious self-interest in European stability."

"You Americans don't recognize nobility when you see it. Within the range of human frailty these policies are noble enough—I can't vouch for what you might do in the future, however."

"Unfortunately, neither can I," Sheppard said glumly.

"First, every effort will be bent to establishing in the popular mind the idea that the American Ambassador is really a military chief of staff in disguise, that the American Army is dabbling in French domestic politics. This might explain the curious attempt to impeach Stone's old testimony before the Allied Court of Inquiry. Unhappily, this requires that the Party undertake to whiten Dujardin a little."

"But, good Lord, Georges, the man is guilty. Your own trial records clearly show that—"

Merseault sighed heavily, interrupting. "Not everyone reads trial records. You must understand that no decent Frenchman wants to believe that one of his own countrymen was a worse animal than any German SS officer. They will search for any explanation which saves them the indignity and pain of accepting the ugly fact at face value. Moreover, Dujardin was tried as a pro-Nazi, but now the Communist Party has taken up his cause and is defending him in their press, in posters, even to providing legal aid and money. Now, to many average Frenchmen, right or wrong, the Communists still wear the collective mantle of *Héros de la Résistance* and they can't swallow the contradiction of the Party's defending an ex-Nazi. Therefore—the reasoning goes—Dujardin was not really pro-Nazi—especially when all this follows on that affidavit about being tortured and forced to sign a confession dictated by the American C.I.D. Dujardin is not clever enough to have carried it off alone. He was put up to it. Precisely by whom and for what purpose I don't know, but I hope to find out. I told you at the time that I thought Stone was making a mistake when he offered testimony at Dujardin's trial. It should have been exclusively a French affair. I am sure he made a mistake. I know how you feel. You and others felt bound by conscience to allow him to tell what he knew and to see a criminal get a just punishment. But from a legal point of view, his testimony turned out to be unnecessary. And you may have succeeded in making Dujardin a nice fat Party martyr, if not a national hero."

"Georges, I don't have to remind you that Stone was given leave to testify only at the invitation of the French Government and with the approval of the Ministry of Justice. After all, it looked as though Dujardin was going to get off scot-free simply because he had successfully murdered everyone who might have witnessed against him. Even his chambermaid was afraid to testify against him for fear of being implicated."

"Morally you did the sober thing. Politically you made a mistake," said Merseault. "You could have refused to clear Stone's appearance at the trial on grounds of military security."

"I have never been completely convinced of the wisdom of separating moral from political judgments, Georges."

Merseault was silent for a moment, turning the cane slowly on the point of his toe. He shifted his weight as though preparing an attack from a new position. Then he turned his black homburg upside down on his knees and pulled the sweatband inside out and stared into it as if it were a crystal ball.

"Bruce, my excellent friend, I am only the best political brain in all of France, if not Europe, and it is true that I don't know much, but I do know when we are embarked on a large subject. In French politics, at least, wisdom consists in reconciling moral and political judgments. Otherwise nothing is done. But it is too large a subject. One could write a book about it. I prefer to confine the conversation to more modest pastures, where the cow is not so easily lost. I am a practical man. That is why I am a student of history. If I were less practical I would be President of France and die younger. But fortunately, I am a late riser and have been spared the burden of a political career."

"You are being modest, Georges," said Sheppard, smiling at his fingernails.

"Not modest, just amusing. I am trying to cheer you up, Bruce. You are upset about the dirty business afoot. Am I right?"

"I am sick of it, Georges," Sheppard said, "because it might succeed."

"I am sick too, but my illness is of the spleen," said Merseault. "If the stakes were not so high I would not be angry, for it is a childish trick they have done. But I know France. Two things I must tell you, more than two, perhaps, and I want you to listen. First, remember that in spite of the fact that I lived in the United States for several years, at bottom I am still French. I have the gift of being able to speak the heart and mind of my country perhaps because I lived away from her for so long before the war. Second, I believe your cause coincides with my cause. I am a skeptical man, but I believe your own interest in my country is something personal, something better than common politics. And I will do everything I can to help you, not only as a political analyst on your private ambassadorial payroll, but as a friend. The situation you are faced with is dangerous. It is dangerous because it is at one time sinister and imaginative. It is based on a profoundly accurate knowledge of human beings, in particular those human beings who call themselves Europeans. Take the business of your being labeled a general. We French have a profound distrust of political generals. That's why we call them marshals. We also distrust politicians. You are no doubt familiar with the old French cynicism, 'Elect the stupidest.' Nine-tenths of the Party's success in France is based on the fact that on the surface they don't look like politicians. Their deputies attend the Assembly in their shirtsleeves and indulge themselves in fist fights on the floor. Underneath, they are superb politicians—more interested in power than in decorum. In this Dujardin case, for example, they are playing on the wounded national pride of every man and woman in France. Let me be blunt. My country has a national inferiority complex. We didn't win our own war. France was liberated from the outside. That is a fact to make an honest Frenchman squirm. After all, even I wept when France fell. The fact that many Frenchmen collaborated with the enemy is a deep-rooted source of guilt. Every Frenchman who did not actively risk his life resisting the Germans feels in his heart that he was a passive collaborator. The French bitterly resent the fact that they had to be liberated, and every time a collaborator comes up for trial every man in France remembers the dozen eggs he sold to a German soldier or the beer he served them in his café. We were all collaborators, Bruce, because we are all human. In one small way or another, we are all guilty. It is only a question of degree. But in a man's soul guilt knows no degrees. It is only a question of guilty or not guilty. In the soul there is no leniency. So when one man, any man, even a piece of scum like Dujardin, says, 'I am not guilty. I was beaten into submission,' he is speaking an unarticulated protest that lies deep in the most secret recess of my country's heart. For even those of us who were in the Resistance by night were forced to wear another countenance by day. We trafficked with the Germans in order to survive, to live, to get permits, ration cards, to save ourselves and our children from starvation. But there is perhaps a more profound guilt. For we talked to them because they were lonely. Many of them were sorrier souls than we were. They were the spawn of a sick nation. And toward the end some of them came dimly to understand the horror of their own creation. Starvation is bad, but human bewilderment can be worse. I would far rather starve as a Frenchman than live in plenty and suffer the hatred of the nation of Frenchmen. For the French hate as they love—with passion and finesse. But few of us really starved. If we had, the burden of guilt wouldn't be so great. If all of us could have suffered in the camps, if we could all have tasted the torture, the degradation, the abysmal misery, then we would have atoned for our guilt. It was bad, yes. We were hungry, sick, depressed, yes. But we survived, and we are a nation shackled in guilt and shame by nothing so much as that simple fact. That we survived."

There was a long moment of silence.

"Aren't you going rather far, Georges, too far, perhaps?" asked Sheppard quietly. "After all, such generalizations . . ."

"Yes, I am going too far," said Merseault in clipped tones. "It is always necessary to go too far in order to make one's point. The first rule of rhetoric."

"Then if I take what you're saying correctly, the Party seeks to peddle the Dujardin affair as balm for the wounded dignity of France."

"Dignity in the largest sense. Precisely," said Merseault. "The only thing that stands in their way is one piece of irrefutable testimony condemning him, of which testimony Stone was the author. It may have little legal weight, but it has immense moral weight. Let me warn you: They are counting on you to behave as an honorable man. So beware of acting as an honorable man. At least don't make the obvious moves. I got a hint last night of what's in store."

Sheppard said, "In store?"

"The first Party speech attacking you on the floor. Up to now they have attacked you only in their press. But last night, in the very first speech, you were inaccurately referred to as an 'OSS general' . . . and the O was slurred over so that it sounded like 'SS general.' I must say that was a swinish bit. One of the other deputies interrupted to demand an apology for the affront to the Assembly. He pointed out that your proper title was either His Excellency or Ambassador. The lout who made the attack very politely apologized for what he said was poor enunciation caused by bad teeth. He played to the gallery for a laugh. Then he dragged out the old canard about an ambassador being an honest man sent to lie abroad for his country. Several times he made reference to the fact that you had publicly approved of Stone's giving testimony. Then one of the Socialist deputies shouted out and called the speaker a coward, and there was almost a riot."

"Did Picard say anything?"

"Curious thing. Picard left shortly before the attack on you was made. I think he anticipated trouble. He came back for the vote, though."

"Did any of the other deputies leave?"

"No. He was the only one."

"At least he had the decency to leave," said Sheppard.

"I don't think it was decency that motivated him." Merseault said. "I saw him get a signal from someone in the back. I'm pretty sure they didn't want to risk his having to answer anything on the floor. They're saving him for the big show today."

"Then you definitely think he's thrown in his lot once and for all with the Party?"

"I don't think he's sitting on the fence any more. The independence is merely a pose."

"A useful pose."

Sheppard turned again to look out the window. The cars ahead had gathered speed again after slowing down for a section of road under repair. Merseault was watching Byron Sweet and the civilian colonel, Lasher, in the Ambassador's Cadillac directly ahead. Lasher was talking animatedly; Sweet kept nodding his head at polite intervals. The Ambassador noticed Merseault watching them.

"Lasher will talk his arm off," Sheppard said.

"What's your chief security officer doing here?" Merseault asked.

"Nothing, yet," Sheppard said.

Merseault didn't press the subject. There was another silence.

"I suppose you're wondering what my cablegram was all about?" asked Merseault. He passed his hand lightly over his smooth, wiglike hair and hung the homburg on the black walking stick held upright between his knees and relaxed. Sheppard looked at him before answering. Merseault was a small man, heavy but animated; his round face gave an impression of joviality that was contradicted by his quick black eyes. The black hair grew long and was plastered severely in place over the bald spots. On the right side it looked as though it had been cut on a straight-edge; it was like a square black cap. He could have been a prosperous wineshop proprietor from the provinces, except for the homburg.

"I've never known you to use the word 'urgent' in a telegram before," said the Ambassador. "I'm curious, yes."

"At the time I heard you were coming back, it *was* urgent. Things have slowed down a bit since. This is a little off the beaten track; it's an asylum problem. Political, not mental, that is. I don't want to go into details just now. I'll merely cover the main points. If you're free later today I can tell you the rest."

"I've kept a large hole free around ten. If I'd got your message sooner I could have done better."

"That sounds fine. You can be thinking up questions you'd like to have answered. Now I'll just give you the story in broad outline. But before I get into that there's a totally unrelated matter that's come up in the meantime," said Merseault. "It's a little off the subject."

"Of course," said Sheppard. "What is it?"

"I've been rather interested about this person Carnot—the one they're going to spring as the other eyewitness."

"Then it's true? Carnot is really alive?"

Merseault nodded. "There's no doubt of it any more."

"Then that rules out any other possibility . . . of the boy's being alive."

"I'm afraid we both knew that a long time ago."

"Yes," Sheppard said. He sighed tiredly. "At least it removes a final uncertainty. There was always that last slim chance—you must understand."

Merseault nodded.

"I must really be getting old, Georges. The hope of old age is desperation. I *feel* old. I feel the weight of my mortality, I suppose. I keep thinking of that line from Yeats '. . . sick with desire and fastened to a dying animal.' The heart of the father always seeks to live again in the heart of the son, I imagine."

There was a long pause. Sheppard turned and looked out the window at the passing houses. "At least the doubt is laid once and for all. Have they located this Carnot individual?"

Merseault nodded. "Located but not contacted. The Party has him here in Paris somewhere."

"He's genuine?"

"Half genuine. He has no criminal record or anything we could confound them with."

"Is there anything I can do for you?"

"I'd like you to have your intelligence people check their files for anything they may have. There must be something. Stone must have mentioned Carnot in his reports."

"I'm sure I can do that for you. Is this delicate?"

"No. Not really. I can arrange for your people to see what we have on him, if they'd like. Not much they'd be interested in, I'm afraid."

"Is there anything else?"

"Yes. This *is* delicate. My suspicion is that they will not spring Carnot in person, but will read a statement or something like that—sometime today during the debate in the Assembly. After they introduce the German records. They could call a press conference, I suppose, but my guess is that they'll make a statement on the floor of the Assembly."

"The government knows, of course."

"They've known for days. But no one can get to Carnot. But the government is prepared to let them spring their little surprise. They have one to spring in return."

"What's delicate about this?"

"Stone knew Carnot. Stone should be advised of what's coming, so he'll be prepared for it. Otherwise he might be caught badly off guard. But that's a detail we can take care of this morning. I'd like to talk with Stone: that's what's delicate. In person. I spoke to him on the telephone this morning."

"You're not obliged to ask my permission, Georges."

"Will you prepare a statement to release to the press on—" Merseault caught himself, looked at the chauffeur; there was a soundless glass partition between them—"I'm sure he can't hear me, but . . . will you make a statement about your son?"

"Yes. Washington has agreed with me that it will be better to release it myself than have it discovered accidentally. It was difficult for them."

"And for you."

There was a pause.

"Did you discuss this with Stone at all?" Sheppard asked.

"No. I have no official reason to. He spent the night at the Ministry of Justice going over his old testimony line by line."

"Would you like to see him at my office this morning? He's coming to see Cadwalader and Lasher to arrange his statement for the press conference this afternoon."

"Yes."

"That's what you wanted?"

"Yes. I'd like to see his reaction in person."

"About Carnot?"

"Yes."

"Stone hasn't acted like a man who has anything to hide," Sheppard said.

"I realize what a tremendous personal stake you have in all this, Bruce. Whether I need your permission to talk to him or not is entirely beside the point. I *prefer* to have your permission. I feel that I need it. It is absolutely essential that he tell me everything he remembers about Carnot. About his relationship with him. There must be some detail . . ."

"Do you think Stone lied?"

"At the trial? No, I certainly don't."

"Neither do I."

The conversation lapsed. The car sped along. The houses were closer together as they neared the metropolis. Far in front, the motorcycle police were using their whistles to warn traffic ahead. Lasher was still talking to Sweet in the Cadillac. Sweet still nodded from time to time.

"Getting back to the asylum matter I cabled you about—if it weren't somewhat urgent it would be routine," said Merseault. "Asylum cases are not usually difficult. The Canadians might help, of course. You see, as it stands—"

"Before you start on that, Georges, let me ask you—what is going to become of this Dujardin business? As far as the vote of confidence goes, that is. Is the government going to fall on it?"

"On the Dujardin thing? I don't think so. If the government falls it will be on economic policy. Dujardin is insignificant, really. The whole affair is being used as a smokescreen to cover up the real issue: higher wages versus stabilization of the franc. You'll see after the smoke clears it will be the same old battle again."

"I don't know if that's reassuring or not."

"Neither does the government. Nor I either, for that matter."

"The Party seems to be concentrating its fire pretty heavily on the Recovery Program."

"As I say, I believe the whole Dujardin thing is just a small part of the pattern."

"How do you see the schedule of events?"

"I think you can expect something rather serious in the way of a propaganda campaign—against you in particular and your compatriots in general. The specific object, of course, would be to break the back of the aid programs. The Party has found that the surplus-dumping argument doesn't carry much weight in France. We French are very practical. If the United States is dumping surpluses we'd rather you dumped them here than elsewhere. Spiritually, France is still very much a country of farmers, and among farmers surpluses are acts of God, like droughts and famines. Therefore the United States can't be made out a villain merely because it has surpluses to dump. I think the next line of attack will be more to the point—to brand you as militarists. Prussianism."

"That seems to be in the wind, is that it?"

"I've noticed a few signs. Since I left active government service I don't keep up with things as I used to, but it has all the earmarks of a long-range program."

"I see."

"I have a few people working on it for me privately. I'll let you know if I turn anything up, of course. But time is against them. If the aid program is even slightly successful it could stabilize the center this year. The Party fears a strong center much more than it does a strong right. Aristotle said something about the inertia of a large middle class being essential to the stability of a state. The Party has read Aristotle as well as Lenin."

Sheppard smiled.

"Also, the Party still numbers among its ranks a number of people who have never known material poverty. Under the Germans the whole country was reduced to poverty, spiritual poverty—just as compelling a motive for revolution as material poverty. Europe is full of young militant baronesses who call themselves Communists. Very brave. Very guilty. It doesn't matter to the Party. Especially in France. Even ninnies vote in a republic. Especially ninnies."

"The old vested interest in poverty," said Sheppard.

"The Party provides the illusions that make poverty bearable. After all, Bruce, illusions are easier to find than remedies. The perfect proletarian state is functionally not much different from the City of God—it holds the same promise of blissful release from the black toils of this earth. Take China. Yes. You've chosen to maintain the wrong illusion. You talk freedom and liberty to a Chinese peasant who was born in war, grew up in war, has never known anything but war, and all you do is puzzle him with concepts he has no vocabulary for. You should have started merely with a loaf of bread. Gigantic posters all over China with nothing on them but a picture of a bowl of rice, saying, *This is what we will give you.* The Russians understand China better because they haven't been spoiled by high standards of living. We face the same problem in Indochina. The Russians are closer to the soil and hence to poverty. The Chinese want change. They don't care if the Devil himself brings it."

Sheppard smiled politely. "What was it you wanted to ask me?"

"Oh, yes. The other thing. As I said, it's slightly off the whole subject—but could you arrange asylum in the States for a hot Party member? I think he might be in a position to provide a few pieces of extremely useful information. If he'll go, that is."

"How high up is he?"

"He's in a pivotal position at the present moment. Otherwise he's not important."

"I won't press you."

"This thing may take money," said Merseault. "Anonymous money."

"I have unvouchered, unearmarked funds at my disposal for such things."

"I know," said Merseault. "I don't know how much yet, but it might be a lot."

"This is a detail," said Sheppard. "I could have our people take over all payments directly if you think it necessary."

"That is just what I'm trying to prevent. The point is—*I* will need the money and *I* will have to make the payments personally. And I won't be able to give you an accounting. There are several people involved in this who must be protected, including the victim himself."

"I see."

"Besides, I think I can save you money in the long run. The regular intelligence brokers have been bidding the price of information up, I'm afraid. Americans are notorious over-tippers. My modest operations have always been the pastime of a gentleman-scholar. But since most of my sources are neither gentlemen nor scholars, they are beginning to cost money. They haven't the same objectivity in these matters that I have, and unfortunately my friendship with you is fairly well known. A man is known by the conspiracy he keeps. And charged accordingly."

Sheppard laughed. "How is your book coming along?"

"I don't know. By the time they've gone through it and taken out all the state secrets there won't be anything left of it. I can't boast of my proudest achievements."

"I thought it was going to be sort of a textbook."

"Every writer likes to boast a little while he has the chance," said Merseault. "I may never have it again."

There was a short silence. The car sped along over the paving stones, floating softly over the pits in the road. Morning traffic was becoming less sparse.

"I won't be able to tell you very much today," said Merseault. "In fact, I'll be frank with you—I'm absolutely paralyzed at the thought of an American agent stumbling on this. He'd scare the life out of my quarry. I'm just egotistical enough to think that I'm the only person in the world right now who can manage this. The individual whose soul I'm wrestling for has got himself into a rather dangerous situation and he doesn't know what to do. He is an extremely frightened man. Furthermore, he has reason to be. More reason than he knows, I've found out. I don't know that he will accept my solution to his difficulties, but as far as I can see it's the only way he can save his skin."

"You can't tell me the nature of his difficulties?"

"Let's say for now that he's put the Party's future in jeopardy by playing a little game with Party properties. Sooner or later it is going to be found out. I'm not saying this is the case now, but it will be before I'm through. I've even thought of trying to blackmail him for his own good. He's been on the verge of trying to get out of the country already, but he'd never make it alone, and he knows it. And that's the only thing that's kept him from making an irrevocable break. He can't help clinging to the hope that somehow everything will turn out all right. It won't. They are on to him already, I think. Only he doesn't know it yet."

"I'll do all I can. I don't think asylum will be hard to arrange if the case warrants it."

"Bruce, the reason I'm not telling you any more than I have to is also to protect you. I know you take your official responsibilities seriously, and I imagine that you put them ahead of any purely personal friendship—which is as it should be. I don't have a complete picture of this situation yet, but I have some terribly dark suspicions as to what the completed picture is going to look like. If I told you even what I think I think, you'd probably consider yourself derelict in your duties if you didn't call in your top intelligence man and repeat to him what I told you I thought I thought."

"Why don't you go to the top and take out an official hunting license? You could get one."

"Too much chance of a leak," said Merseault. "I've been gathering information through some pretty low channels. Sewers, you might even say. Until I'm quit of these associates I think I had better rely on simple anonymity."

"What do these low persons think your motive is?"

"Money," said Merseault. "Criminal blackmail. I may even have to go through with it if they get suspicious."

"Good Lord, Georges," said Sheppard, shaking his head slowly. "You're playing with rather sticky cards, aren't you?"

"I only hope the deck isn't marked."

"The stakes *are* rather high," said Sheppard.

"And the players are all armed. I'm holding four aces. Everyone is very nervous."

"Including you."

"Especially me." Merseault smiled grimly. "Poker is not my game. I prefer chess."

"This sounds more like Russian roulette," said Sheppard.

"I hope I know what I'm doing," Merseault said with a comic grimace.

Sheppard laughed.

Ahead the motorcycle police were slowing. Still farther ahead, a crowd of people, small in the distance, was gathered at one side of the road around what appeared to be an accident. Merseault pointed silently. Sheppard followed his gaze and saw the crowd. Foot police were trying to clear the street, waving with their white batons for the traffic to continue past. A few cars and trucks slowed down out of curiosity and caused the motorcade to telescope slowly on its own length as the first cars were forced to relinquish speed.

Two parked ambulances were angled out into the road, causing a constriction around which traffic had to pass. The motorcycles filtered through easily in single file. The first two Citroëns slowly skirted the crowd and passed on. As the Delahaye came closer they saw that a large military truck had collided with the rear of another vehicle, a horse-drawn farmcart. Two soldiers helped a third into one of the ambulances and closed the rear doors. Immediately, the ambulance pulled out into the road ahead of the Ambassador's car, sounding its mournful signal. It cut the motorcade in half.

Merseault turned to Sheppard. "Do we need the escort?" he asked. Sheppard shook his head. Merseault leaned forward and rapped on the glass partition, and, gesturing in a wide circle, signaled the chauffeur to pull around past the scene of the accident and stop. As the limousine crept past, two forms on stretchers were slid into the back of the other ambulance. The motorcycle escort was in total disorder: half had gone on slowly with the two Citroëns, finally halting far ahead; the other half had turned back to wait for the cars cut off behind the ambulance.

A police officer appeared immediately at the rear window of the

Delahaye as it stopped. Merseault reached across Sheppard's knees and rolled down the glass.

"Call one of the escort," said Merseault. The harried gendarme fumbled for his whistle and blew a short blast, not loud but very piercing, and beckoned with his whole arm. It made his cape fly up over his shoulder, where it stayed. A motorcyclist spurred his machine and turned in a tight circle and stopped beside the opposite door. Merseault pointed mutely through the closed glass at the ambulance working its way forward around traffic ahead. The policeman astride his sputtering black machine understood. He nodded. Merseault held up three fingers. The motorcyclist nodded again and saluted and broke away in a blast of noise, swerving gracefully away and lifting his left foot as he went.

The motorcycle veered around the ambulance; the rider waved his arm, signaling the driver; motorcycle and ambulance passed the two halted Citroëns, waving them farther off the road to wait for the other cars. Two other motorcycles bolted forward, following the first; the ambulance disappeared in the distance behind the three black motorcycles. The rest of the escort turned back in wide circles to mend the division in the procession.

"What about the other ambulance?" Merseault asked the gendarme. "Is it ready to leave?"

The police officer standing beside the door shook his head slowly. His face was drawn and white; he looked really sick. "Those ones there have forever to get where they are going," he said.

"How many?" asked Merseault, his voice flat and colorless.

"Two men. One boy. The child died instantly. The other two—the doctor did what he could." The policeman's bloodshot eyes were wide and his voice was unsteady. "I heard the—" He stopped. He kept glancing away. He seemed to be unconsciously watching something from the corner of his eye. Merseault and Sheppard turned at the same time to look.

A woman squatted impassively at the side of the road behind them. She was watching nothing; her face was blank. Around her stood a circle of younger women, one half-kneeling with an arm awkwardly around her shoulder. In front of the woman, at her feet, was what at first appeared to be a pile of clothing. It was the body of the child, covered with coats.

"She's been sitting there like that since it happened," said the gendarme.

"You got the boy out?" asked Merseault.

The policeman nodded mutely at a smear of blood on his cape. He seemed to be in a state of physical fatigue. "She hasn't said a word. I can't even get her to tell me her name. She hasn't cried." The policeman shuddered slightly and took a deep breath. "If you don't want anything further . . ."

"Of course," said Merseault. "And the driver of the truck?"

The policeman pointed. Across the street on the stone steps of a house, a young soldier sat with his head buried in his arms. Beside him stood two uncomfortable gendarmes, not looking at him or each other, and an Army officer. A jeep was parked at the curb, its lights still on, a huge buggy-whip antenna shivering with the vibration of its idling motor. There was no one in the jeep.

"Is that the ranking officer present?" asked Merseault.

"I think so," said the gendarme.

"Would you ask him to step over here a moment?"

The officer was young, not more than twenty-three. He looked frightened and nervous as he approached the car. He saluted smartly, glancing at the official insignia on the windshield. He looked at the other official cars parked ahead.

"Lieutenant," said Merseault, "I'd like you to see that these people are treated at Army expense. They should get the best of care, the same as your own men who were hurt."

"My driver couldn't have seen them, sir. It was dark. It was not his fault—I—"

"It is not a question of whose fault it was, Lieutenant," said Merseault gently. "Whose fault is it that in this century people have to drive horse carts on roads designed for high-speed automobiles?" Merseault reached into his breast pocket and extracted a card case. He handed the lieutenant his personal card and said, "You may have to take shortcuts on your own authority to get things done quickly. If you get into trouble, telephone me. I'm sure it can be straightened out."

The lieutenant stared openly at the name on the card for a long instant. Then he saluted with extra snap. "Yes, sir," he said. "I think I can arrange it by radio. May I use your name—discreetly of course, sir. But it might—"

"Discreetly. Of course, Lieutenant. But naturally *you* will be taking the responsibility. I have no official authority any more, you realize."

"Yes, sir. I understand perfectly, sir." The lieutenant started to turn around; then he added, "Thank you, sir. I feel less helpless if I can do something."

Merseault was looking back at the wreckage of the wagon through the rear window of the car. "Lieutenant," he said abruptly, "what happened to the horse?"

The lieutenant raised his arm and pointed straight ahead. Some very small children were squatting beside the road looking down into a small ditch at the right-hand side; a part of the horse's flank was just visible in the declivity. "He had to be shot," said the lieutenant.

One of the children, a tiny girl about four years old, was kneeling, poking the lifeless horse with a stick. She held her head tilted all the way over to one side as though to see the horse's face right side up. She seemed absorbed in the puzzle of a horse lying on its side. Suddenly a thin, hatchet-faced woman, obviously the child's mother, broke away from a black cluster of older women standing in a doorway and flew down on the child like an angry hen. She yanked the stick away from her and slapped her hand, wrenched her upright by the arm, and set the surprised child on her feet. Then she knelt and waggled an angry finger in her face. The little girl began crying. The distraught mother stood up, turned, and went back to the other women. The child stood looking at the horse a long moment, wide-eyed, sobbing slightly; slowly she backed off to a safe distance, still watching the other children playing around the dead horse. She stood with her thumb in her mouth, sobbing, and didn't move.

"We can do nothing more here but add to the confusion," said Merseault.

Sheppard nodded. He had been silent since they had first come on the accident. Around the two limousines, a group of curious, sullen watchers was slowly gathering: children, adults, old women.

Suddenly there was a piercing shriek from behind them. Everyone turned and looked.

The mother of the dead boy was leaning forward on her knees, holding onto the legs of one of the two ambulance attendants. The child's body lay covered on the stretcher they supported between them. The gendarme who had spoken to Merseault bent down and gently pulled her fingers away one by one until she let go her hold and sagged back on her heels. She made no sound after that eerie shout of anguish. Her eyes were dry, gazing straight ahead. Her face showed no emotion, seemed unmoved, almost peaceful.

She sat on her heels in the dust for a long time, staring at the dark splotch where the child's body had lain. Then as they watched, the tears came and she leaned forward, her shoulders sloped with grief and weariness and slow days of labor. Tenderly she began to gather the wet, blood-stained dust into her apron.

The police officer jerked his eyes away and turned his back and walked slowly away from the farmcart, his arm involuntarily across his forehead. No one tried to stop the woman. There was a moment of utter silence that shriveled in sudden piping laughter—the children daring each other to touch the dead horse. The woman paused and raised her head, listening, her face twisted, blind with tears.

There was a slight delay in starting; the cars behind were held up, waiting for an old man to finish sweeping a refuse of broken red glass out of the road. A mangled lantern, thrown loose from the cart, trailed a red spray of splintered glass across the paving stones; the rearward cars followed the old man at a snail's pace as he swept it up, conscientious and unperturbed. Only when the last shard was swept away did he step aside himself. He doffed his cap and motioned for the cars to proceed, leaning on his broom and nodding gravely as they passed. The Delahaye turned into line behind the Ambassador's car. The cortege moved more slowly than before.

Sheppard and Merseault didn't speak until they were into the city.

111

"We didn't even see the child," said Merseault.

"Did you see what she was doing?"

Merseault nodded slowly. "If you read it in a newspaper it wouldn't touch you."

Sheppard mused, "It's odd to think that if we had taken one turn instead of another, that wouldn't exist for us. If we'd taken another route, another turn . . ."

Merseault reflected quietly for a moment. "Life is not a fiction in which you can divine the intention and refuse to turn the page. People try, I suppose, but they only isolate themselves from humanity—from the dirt, the filth, the suffering, death. Did you see the strength in that woman?"

"But *is* that humanity, Georges?"

"Is what?"

"The dirt, the suffering," said Sheppard. "I suppose it is."

"It's what's at the root of everything. It's the bedrock. Everything else is mere civilization, a construction. The bedrock trembles. An earthquake. Civilization has nothing more in common with humanity than a house does with its foundation; it merely rests on it. Humanity has never needed gentle manners to survive. You know, they may wipe out this civilization. They'll never wipe out humanity. Man is an idiot, but he will survive. Because he is an idiot."

"Why do you say man is an idiot?" asked Sheppard.

"Because he hasn't the sense to shoot himself in the head," Merseault said. He looked at Sheppard's face and relented. "I'm joking," he said.

XI

The offices of Associated Wire Service, Limited, the European subsidiary of the parent American concern, were in the building opposite the *Continental Daily Mail,* a sandlot edition of the *London Daily Mail* used for training editors. Like the *Paris Herald Tribune,* the *Daily Mail* was a stepping stone into the big leagues, and though both of these English-language dailies often operated at a loss, they justified their existence as journalistic finishing schools by virtue of their long lists of valuable and distinguished alumni. As such, despite a painfully low salary scale, these two papers attracted some of the finest newspaper talent of two continents and they could afford to be selective about whom they employed. It was occasionally said by old hands that a night wire clerk on the *Paris Tribune* was worth three staffers in New York. In New York they ate too well and went soft, but in Paris they were kept lean and hungry and developed the competitive instincts of alley cats. Otherwise they made a tight and friendly fraternity, kept loyal by mild hunger and the exigencies of survival. Some of them found they liked the life and stayed on year after year; others did their stint and moved on to bigger things. Thus they were divided into two distinct groups, one much older and wiser and permanently adjusted to the ways of exile; the other young, bright, inexperienced, and ambitious to be finished with apprenticeship and transient existence. And since neither group was overcovetous of the other's aims in life, they worked together in excellent harmony. The old hands taught; the journeymen listened and, in general, learned.

If Sharktooth was one of the old school, Will Striker was certainly one of the new. A graduate of Bucknell who came to France for the summer, he'd ferreted out the job under Sharktooth before anyone else in town knew it was open. Sharktooth had deliberately kept it secret to avoid having an avalanche of summer-brown Smith girls wreck the office in their rush for the job. He was waiting for the hungrier ones who would recklessly cash in their return passages and start looking around for ways to keep the Atlantic Ocean between them and their parents. He had a girl in mind, and when Striker came in and said he wanted the job he turned him down. But Striker was more desperate than Sharktooth had bargained for. He'd been working for the Embassy and had quit "to do something foolish like write a novel." He was getting the art knocked out of him trying to make ends meet on a small G.I. disability check. He wouldn't shake. He kept coming around. Finally he brought in a story he'd dug up somewhere out of the bowels of the Embassy about old man Sheppard being in Walter Reed Hospital with bad knee joints or something. When the story checked out, Sharktooth decided to take him on. He was green, very green, but on the other hand he wasn't stupid. And he looked good and hungry. Besides abandoning the novel forever, in four months he'd learned a lot. . . .

When Willie telephoned from the airport, Sharktooth was just coming in for the day. He took down the story with his hat still on; then he scanned the night wire and leisurely began setting up shop. He was in early.

It was going to be a bad day; he could feel it. He made an estimate of what would happen today, and a rough guess of how much wordage would cover it. There were several stories cooking, which meant that he could send developments as they came along. No heavy background work, no research; coverage would be the headache for today. The Dujardin thing. The general strike. *Sheppard's Arrival Hailed.* These items passed in review in his mind. They were relatively fixed points of departure, solid islands in the day's shifting sea of unmade news. There was the attack on Sheppard in the Senate. He frowned. That was less certain. The papers hadn't played it up in the States yet, but anything could happen. And Representative Krueger was just stupid enough to be unpredictable too; he had a sense for the uglier passions of a news-hungry nation. Sharktooth wondered if the story had been picked up in Europe. Later, he would look at the clips. He felt uneasy about that story. That one wasn't fixed. It could bring a reaction. Not yet, not today, but later. Look for it in about a week or so.

And then there was that poor goat Stone. He would try to see him in person. Late afternoon.

The government would parry the move in the Assembly by granting a stay of execution. That would end the morning session. A slow investigation would postpone the whole business until spring. In the spring there would be bigger fish to fry. *Foreign Ministers Conference Planned for Paris in the Spring.* He often thought in headlines and wrote the news backward—from the headline he wanted to produce to the peg that he would hang it on. Paris in the spring. Trite. *Peace Conference Plotted for Paris Springtime.* That one was going to require background. He'd put Striker on it next week. It needed a slow but steady advance buildup; they'd have to start early. There were some contacts in the Quai d'Orsay it wouldn't hurt to polish up a little. Couldn't wait much longer or it would be too obvious what he was after. He ripped off a sheet of his calendar and scribbled, "Drinks with R at Q. d'O. sometime this week."

He'd go to the Assembly himself for the morning session. It looked like the tip about the mystery witness business might be based on something. If the Party had something besides the German documents up their sleeve this was the day to pull it out. The question was: Where would this leave Stone? He glanced over the papers on his littered desk. Down the hall he heard the night man come back from coffee and go into the machine room. He looked at a query from New York: "Does your estimate of vote results still stand?" He frowned in annoyance and penciled a reply on the same sheet—"See no reason change estimate. Best guess coalition will offer compromise get off hook." He marked it "routine" and threw it in the out basket.

Sharktooth was an old hand, a digression from common history. He had shipped on a bumboat out of San Francisco as a captain's hand when he was fourteen years old. He knew the Orient by the time he was seventeen, shipping aboard a beatup freighter. The captain was usually drunk in port and assigned him the touchy duty of clearing the manifests with the various quarantine and customs authorities. On him, at the age of sixteen, rested the responsibility of more than one ship's sailing. He learned to type on Chinese typewriters; learned to haggle with Malayan bribe brokers; learned to understand a half-dozen Eastern dialects; learned to look stupid and pretend to understand nothing. He had seen wars, negotiated truces with Singapore dock workers, and had once saved his ship from being looted and possibly burned. At the age of twenty, Sharktooth could swing through the dense jungle of oriental graft like a monkey on an errand of love. Born of a pair of renegade Americans in a Mexican slum in Los Angeles, left to shift for himself at the age of eight when his father was killed in an argument over a poolroom debt and his mother died avenging him (successfully, it should be noted)—by the time he was ten he was wiser in the devious ways of existence than a Boston banker on his deathbed. Poverty didn't revolt him, because he understood it, and in the Orient this knowledge stood him in good stead. People trusted him because he made no effort to be trustworthy. He rarely felt pity for the downtrodden; even more rarely did he feel antipathy for the rich and powerful. He accepted everything on its own terms, and pretended to nothing. He had made a fortune of his own by the time he was twenty-five, and he understood something of the emptiness of that victory. He made his fortune selling guns that didn't fit their ammunition. Afterward he claimed he'd done a service to mankind: the war didn't come off, the guns rusted, and eventually the two bandits made a treaty that brought peace to the region. He had sold the ammunition too. Sharktooth liked to recall the story when he was in a mellow mood, and underline the lesson in it. He'd taught both sides, he claimed, the costliness of war without their having the agony of waging one. He'd drained the coffers of the bandit lords by charging them twice what the weapons were worth; their treasuries empty, they had no choice but to make peace. To be fair, he had sold the spurious munitions to both sides.

At twenty-five, the possessor of a cheerful fortune, he started an English-language newspaper in Calcutta. A year later, after a social contretemps with the British resident governor, he found his funds impounded pending an investigation of his dealings in the gold market. But he forced the government's hand by selling his assets and donating the entire amount to a struggling Indian hospital for the blind—on the one condition that the governor release the funds. He announced the gift on the front page of the last edition he ever published, making the governor out a wicked ogre who was standing in the way of health, eyesight and progress. Caught between two stools, the governor gave way; Sharktooth left India uninvestigated, unreconstructed, penniless, and content with life. The statement he made as he landed in London was classic. He was remembered for it. "One gets tired of money," he said.

With war in the Orient, real war this time, Sharktooth came into his own. He reported for a dozen papers during the first few months of the confusing Japanese *démarche* into China; the phrase "China Incident" was first used in one of his dispatches, a scathing cynicism that passed the Tokyo censors and was tragically lost on those who seized on the phrase to avoid the embarrassing bad-for-business word "war." From that time on, whenever war broke out, whenever anything outlandish happened, Sharktooth was there ahead of time. It got so that he couldn't go to Ethiopia for a vacation without a tiny phalanx of fellow journalists booking passage on the same ship—just in case. He left a bullring in Seville to file the first detailed report of the civil war in Spain. Whether by luck or by prescience, he always seemed to be there.

In those days he had a photographer he worked with, a man known variously as "Little Sharktooth," the "Prophet's Disciple," or "Wiseapple" (from his name, Weissapfel). Together they would descend from the cool upper reaches of some semitropical hotel, and stroll out into a quiet noontime street where a few minutes later fighting would uncannily erupt: a pocket revolution would be under way. By four o'clock the dispatch would be in Reuters' London office, often interrupting debate over recent outlandish items on his expense account—or as he often called it, his "persuasion account"—bribery being a word that ruffled his superiors' calm and ordered view of human affairs. His dispatches usually ended with the two words: Photos follow. This phrase too came to be one of Max Weissapfel's nicknames. Weissapfel's many names, together with those of Sharktooth's reminiscences that were printable, made up the bulk of "Wiseapple's Testament," the obituary Sharktooth wrote of him when he was killed in an anti-Jewish riot in Bremerhaven on a day when the world wasn't looking. The rest of the obituary was a warning, a warning that the world ignored.

Sharktooth covered the Munich Pact without a photographer. He got to the conference late, in time only for the signing ceremony. But when war finally came, he was there before anyone else. His rasping eyewitness broadcast from Radio Warsaw came to the stunned English-speaking world like a message from the grave. He reminded them tactlessly of Munich. The broadcast earned him a price which he wore on his head like a halo throughout the war. He escaped from Poland and the amiable collision of German and Russian forces by buying a boat and leaving from the north, slipping out of grasp like a bar of wet soap, to the furious annoyance of Dr. Goebbels, whom he'd spat on over the microphone—literally, audibly, spat on. Later Sharktooth dubbed it "the goober that was heard around the world."

Sharktooth's real name was Caesar Douglas Lutelacker. It was a name known only to the archives of the city of Los Angeles, the juvenile court records of the city of San Francisco, and Sharktooth himself. On his passport, by dint of proper manipulation of legal affidavits, the name appeared as Douglas Lutelacker. He strongly disliked his first name, which had been given him by his diffident elders to honor a certain Caesaro Marcasiano, an open-handed ward politician who, having no children of his own, made a generous policy of giving five dollars to the parents of any neighborhood children named after him. Sharktooth had reason to be grateful, however, since once he'd gone to old Mister Marcasiano as his namesake and had successfully fended off an attempt to put him in a school for wayward children. As political training, the incident was not lost on the eleven-year-old Caesar. However, fond as he was of his political godfather, the name didn't harmonize with Lutelacker. When Marcasiano was done in by some friends in a squabble over liquor franchises, Sharktooth, then fourteen, joined the hundreds of other Caesars at his funeral, and quietly interred the name with its erstwhile owner. It was the only time in his life that Sharktooth could ever remember crying. Even the food was good. It was some funeral.

The name Sharktooth had two origins. There was some question as to which took priority. It was true that Sharktooth did indeed wear an enormous shark's tooth on his watch chain. He called it his Phi Beta Kappa key. It was also true that he told an excellent story of besting the former owner of the tooth—the shark, that is—in mortal combat somewhere in the waters of the Philippine Sea. But whether the story was actually true in every detail was more than most careful men would gamble on while sober. It was far likelier that Sharktooth had done a little editing of Jack London and invented the story to cover the real reason for the name. The fact was that Sharktooth did indeed have very pointed teeth, although no one but a dentist could have known that. For Sharktooth held his mouth in an unchanging inscrutable line, his lips drawn tightly down; he looked at you, but he never smiled. He liked jokes but he never laughed. He grunted. It might have been that when he was younger he smiled often, perhaps showing his teeth, and that gained him the name. Although he hardly opened his mouth even to talk, there was good reason to believe that this was the real origin of his name. The best evidence was the extraordinary punctures that defaced the lip ends of the endless rubble of cigar stubs he left around the office.

But whatever the origins, the name was Sharktooth, and however sharp his teeth, his mind and tongue were that much sharper. Although he never raised his voice above a menacing whisper when you faced him in person, on the telephone he changed completely. He could roar and rant with the best of them. But it was the curious tight-lipped constriction of his words, even when shouting, that made him a terror to those under him. He never really lost his temper except in a false histrionic way, as though he'd taught himself to pretend he'd lost his temper because people expected it of him. His lean parchment-skin face, his blue sunken eyes, his egg-bald head, all combined to suggest that his character was tailored to his name. And as if to emphasize that fact, whenever his patience was tried he fingered the enormous shark ivory hanging from his stained vest, a trick that could disconcert even the most phlegmatic of underlings. But for some curious reason no one actively disliked him. The young men who worked for him remembered him years later with a perverse affection, made mellower no doubt by time and distance, but nevertheless real. He made them work, but he taught them the secret stingy tricks of the craft with a generosity possible only to a man who feels himself totally beyond the challenge of competition, an old hand, a master. He had ten cardinal rules for his staff. They were posted on the wall over his desk. Dimmed by time and cigar smoke, they read:

HOUSE RULES

1. Opinions change. Therefore, entertain none of your own.
2. Belief is for the idle rich. When I ask, you *know*.

3. Never violate a confidence except for money.
4. Act happy. The world will learn to love you someday.
5. Feel sorry. The world loves the wrong man.
6. Keep in mind, when writing, you're closer to your death when you finish.
7. Suicide is prohibited on an empty stomach and these premises.
8. Report what you know. Fiction pays less than crime.
9. To err is human, to forgive divine. Don't count on it.
10. I rarely do favors. When I fire you, thank me.

The rules were not made up all at once; each rule was added as the result of an incident, the suicide included. They stopped at ten because it was a round number.

Sharktooth lit a cigar, the first cigar of the day, and sat back to think.

The Ambassador would hold a press conference, probably in the afternoon. Stone would be on public display, captive. He'd send Lacy—Lacy always came to work in a clean shirt, even though he owned only three. Sharktooth looked at a memo hung on a spindle marked "current and choice." It was off the Tass wire. He merely glanced at it, but it was enough to make him decide he'd need an extra photographer for the day. He ran down his list of free-lancers. Picking up the telephone, he dialed a number, waited.

"Sorry to wake you, friend, but I wanted to get you before anyone else did. . . . This afternoon, but I'll put you down for the whole day. Demonstration. Tass is sending out a lot of muscle talk. . . . Yeah, it will come off, all right. They'll make it come off. . . . No. Don't worry. Usual terms, plus insurance for your black box if you haven't got it covered. . . . O.K. Firm? . . . All right, work out from the Crillon Bar. I'll leave word there if I need you. . . . I don't care. You watch the crowd and use your judgment. Call in."

The rest was just being ready. It was bound to be a bad day, unpredictable, with news breaking too late for the New York editions. He had to be careful not to spread them out too thin and leave no one in the office—that would be the moment they'd pick to shoot the President of France. He sat down to editing the stuff Striker had telephoned in. It could go out on the early wire—the earlier the better. Get the dogwork done and off as soon as it came in. The rush would come this afternoon. The only chance of seeing Stone would be after finishing up. Quiet day tomorrow, maybe. They'll all be busy reading about what happened today.

It was cold in the office. He plugged in the electric heater and the lights dimmed. He always kept the lights on in his office; there were no windows. He didn't like windows because they reminded him of what time it was. His was a room without windows, without clocks. He'd found that he worked faster when he wasn't sure he was on time. If it got unbearable there was a clock in the hall.

Striker came in. Sharktooth looked up at him in surprise.

"Why aren't you getting some sleep?" he asked.

"I'm just stopping by to pick up some cash," Willie replied.

"You have enough."

"It's just to pay the taxi. I'm a little low."

"Well, sign a voucher when you take it out," Sharktooth said.

"Well, yes."

"How did he look?"

"Who?"

"His Nibs, who else?"

"He had a cane. They kept it out of the photographs. He had some trouble getting down the stairs from the plane. But he looked fine otherwise."

"Kept it out of the picture, eh? A cane. Now a cane can be very distinguished. Why would they want to keep a cane out of the picture?"

"You're asking me?"

"No, Willie. I'm just thinking. Wondering if they have any guilty secrets. Was Caddy there?"

"Yes."

"He look nervous? Laugh a lot, shake hands, and all that?"

"Yes, a little," Willie said.

Sharktooth swiveled around in his chair twice, thinking. "How old is he now—over sixty, isn't he?"

"Around there," Willie said.

"Been to the hospital on the QT." Sharktooth stood up. "Willie, I want you to look in our live obit file and see if we have one made up on one Bruce Peel Sheppard. I think there's one left over from the war, but he got through the war alive, so it's very much out of date. I want you to rewrite it and file it again. Take the military flavor out of it, bring it up to date. You might make a general check and see if we're missing any other prominent obituaries. That whole file should be brought up to date. Maybe I'll give that to you as a project if you don't keep me happy."

"Right now, just Sheppard's file is all you want?"

"Yes. Now for the love of God don't leave any first drafts lying around here without marking them 'live obit.' Some fool is liable to decide that the Ambassador has passed out of the present tense and send his obit out on the wire. Don't consign him to oblivion before he's ready to cooperate. Or else you'll have to shoot him yourself."

"I'll be careful."

"Use the past tense and your imagination. The less we have to re-write the faster we can get it off."

"You think he's that sick?" asked Willie.

"The way to make a man live forever is to have his obit on file. The

119

ones who go are always the ones we haven't got a file on, and they never give you time to scrounge for background. Stick around here long enough and I'll learn you the ropes, Willie my lad." Sharktooth took a cigar out of his drawer. "Now get back here by five."

"When do you want that—file on the Ambassador?" asked Willie.

"No rush, Willie," Sharktooth said airily, relaxing in his chair. He exhaled a slow cloud of heavy smoke that enveloped his head like a ball of dirty cotton. "Any time before he dies, that's all. You decide. Don't forget, back here by five. It's going to be a bad day."

"Anything else?" Willie asked. "Are you going to see Stone this afternoon?"

"Close the door. You're letting all the smoke out."

Willie closed the door on the room without windows, without clocks. He figured to get at least six hours' sleep, if he hurried.

XII

File Copy (uncut)
LIVE OBIT
AMBASSADOR BRUCE PEEL SHEPPARD

Paris, France (DATE) (LEAD OFF WITH NAME, TIME, PLACE & CAUSE OF DEATH IF IMMEDIATELY KNOWN. ONE PARAGRAPH. OTHER DETAILS SAVE FOR NEWS STORY TO FOLLOW. LEAD IN TO NEXT PARAGRAPH.)

The Ambassador's passing has been widely noted in official circles as a great loss for the American government and its foreign service. Throughout Paris flags are being flown at half-mast from all government buildings, as well as from several private and commercial buildings along the wide avenues of this capital city. The President of France and several cabinet ministers have publicly expressed sorrow over the passing of "a great American and friend of France."

In accordance with tradition, all American government offices including the Embassy and consulates will remain closed tomorrow (OR MONDAY IF HE GOES ON A WEEKEND) throughout France, except for emergency business.

The President's appointment of General Sheppard to the post of Ambassador to France climaxed a long and distinguished career in his country's service. Born in 1885, the son of a former

Surgeon General of the United States Army, Bruce Peel Sheppard was educated at Groton before entering the United States Military Academy as a plebe in 1904. Commissioned a second lieutenant with his class in 1908, he then went on to the Artillery School, where he made his mark as an honor student. He graduated from the Army Staff College in 1912 and was one of six selected to do advanced study at the Ecole Militaire in this city, where he again distinguished himself with a paper on advanced tactics, a paper which he wrote entirely in the French language and which was widely published in military journals in France and abroad. Many French Army officers remember him with affection from those days.

As a first lieutenant, Sheppard was one of the first to stress the need for greater flexibility in the use of automatic weapons. With the outbreak of hostilities in 1914, Sheppard was promoted to captain and assigned to an observation team attached to Marshal Pétain's command headquarters during the Verdun stand.

It was as a captain that he was first propelled into the national eye, when he was called to Washington to defend a report he had written recommending the abandonment of the machine-gun company. Sheppard's view was in favor of incorporating the machine gun directly into the infantry company as a special automatic weapons squad. Newspaper stories of the period testify to the heat generated at the hearing. The young captain, defending his argument before the congressional committee, challenged his fellow artillerymen's concept of a machine-gun company and earned the ire of his more tradition-minded superiors. He was vindicated, however, in 1917, two years later, when the American Expeditionary Forces in France adopted his recommended practice. After serving as an instructor at the Army Staff College for a year, he returned to France in 1917 and there took part in the Aisne-Marne battle, and the St. Mihiel and Meuse-Argonne offensives.

In France his abilities were recognized by another rising young officer later also to become famous: George Catlett Marshall. It was Marshall who in 1919, as aide-de-camp to General John J. Pershing, first brought Sheppard off the battlefield into the limelight of public affairs and the diplomatic arena. Sheppard, then a major, accompanied the American Peace Delegation to Paris, where he attended the Ecole de Science Politique while serving as President Wilson's personal translator and technical interpreter on military matters. In later years, when asked about his service to the former President, Sheppard once recalled that the President's mastery of French was so complete that "all I did was listen."

During the peace conference, Major Sheppard married Lucille d'Avilliers (great-great-granddaughter of the Duc d'Avilliers), whom he had met while a student at the Ecole Militaire. The following year, while her husband was on urgent assignment in Panama, Lucille Sheppard died in childbirth in Paris. Their only son, Anthony Peel Sheppard, grew up in France and the United States and served both countries during the Second World War. The Ambassador's son was listed as lost while serving with a special mission of the Office of Strategic Services in France. Ambassador Sheppard leaves no survivors or immediate family.

Among military honors accorded the late Ambassador during a lifetime of public service around the world are to be listed the Distinguished Service Medal with Oak Leaf Cluster; the Silver Star; Victory Medal with three bars; Croix de Guerre with Palm; Grand Croix of the Legion of Honor; Knight Grand Cross, Order of Bath; the Order of Suvarov, first degree; and others too numerous to list. He received accolades from civilian groups all over the world for his postwar contributions to peace, and came to be generally regarded as a statesman of the highest ability. Generals Eisenhower and Marshall, both of whom worked closely with him during the recent war, have publicly testified to his ability as a general officer. Winston Churchill affectionately referred to him as Lord Excalibur, a name bestowed in respect for his talent at cutting through red tape. In the dark days of the Battle of Britain he served as special adviser to the Harriman Mission in London, and earned the Prime Minister's friendship. Sir Winston has spoken feelingly of his contribution to the Allied victory.

Between the First and Second World Wars he served variously in Panama, the Philippines, and as military attaché at the Berlin Embassy, alternating administrative posts with active commands. During the war he served actively in the North African campaign and the European Theater and finally as chairman of the President's Special Commission on Postwar Planning. He was cited by President Roosevelt at the Casablanca Conference for his work in laying the foundation for the system of American Military Government which later was employed successfully in Germany, Austria and elsewhere.

Among the several honorary degrees held by the late Ambassador were: Doctor of Military Science, Norwich University, 1937; LL.D., Boston University, 1939, Yale, 1940, Williams College, 1940, Columbia University, 1945, Kings College (Canada), 1945; Doctor of Political Science, University of Berlin, 1946; Doctor of Civil Law, Oxford University, 1946.

Funeral services will be held at (INSERT TIME AND PLACE, IF KNOWN. CHECK WITH EMBASSY PROTOCOL BEFORE PUTTING ON THE WIRE.)

PS.—AND BE SURE HE'S DEAD.

XIII

A black prewar Citroën came across the Place des Pyramides and turned slowly into the Rue de Rivoli, cruised a short way along the curb and then stopped. Two men got out; the one in the gray overcoat was Deputy Maurice Picard. The other man wore a jacket but no overcoat; the right sleeve of the jacket dangled empty and was pinned inside the pocket: Alexi Carnot looked pale, slightly ill. They came across the street and turned into the Tuileries, walking along just inside the fence in the direction of Concorde.

For a while the two simply walked slowly without talking. Behind them, the automobile with two other men in it kept up, creeping at a snail's pace. It would stop from time to time, letting the two walkers get a little ahead; then it would move abreast again, stop, wait. The park was deserted, the street almost empty of traffic. Picard stopped, and placed his hand on Carnot's left shoulder.

"Are you all right now?" Picard asked.

Carnot nodded without looking at him.

"That car stinks permanently of Boris' cigars," Picard said. Then he continued gently, "You've got stage fright. It's possible you won't have to answer questions today. Just relax. Perhaps we can even avoid the press."

"Then why do I have to be there?" Carnot asked, staring into the distance.

"You have to be available. In case we're challenged."

"You said you didn't think you'd be challenged."

Picard sighed. "I want you sitting in the gallery. I can't afford to take chances at this point. You'll have Boris and Jean to keep you company."

"Just in case I get cold feet at the last minute?"

Picard paused. He looked sharply at Carnot. "You won't get cold feet."

"I really don't feel well," Carnot said. "My head aches." But he smiled.

"You're nervous. But don't irritate me. Did you take that pill I gave you?"

Carnot nodded.

Picard said, "You'll feel more relaxed in a few minutes."

They walked in silence for a few paces. Then Picard said, "Keep in mind that I'm risking a great deal on you. The Party is risking even more."

"Stone saw him."

"Don't say anything more than what you know first-hand. No more. You don't have to embellish; you don't have to lie. You have no reason to believe that Dujardin *was* standing outside that truck. *You* didn't see him."

"You don't have to go over it," Carnot said tiredly. "Boris made it clear."

"Stone only *thinks* he heard him outside the truck. You yourself admitted to me you heard nothing. Don't forget that. You have no reason to think he was there. The point is not to disprove Stone's testimony. It will be enough to cast it in doubt."

"What's going to happen with Dujardin if he's let out of his cage?"

"Why should you care, Alexi? He's unimportant. The thing that's important is that the American is lying. You are our only means of impugning his testimony." Picard waited for Carnot to take in his meaning. "This is no time to start worrying over settled points. Dujardin is a swine, and I'll hate to see him freed. But he's the only instrument given us. We must make do. Remember that. If you fail us, Alexi, Dujardin will be just one more criminal executed on the block of petit-bourgeois justice. If you do your share, however, we can use him to advance the people's interests. Have you forgotten what you lost your right arm fighting for?"

Carnot glared at Picard. "I haven't forgotten. But the Party has made mistakes."

"True. But this is not a mistake. If it misfires it could be unpleasant, but the Party's reputation will not suffer."

Carnot walked along in silence, not answering.

"We've planned tactics for that eventuality," Picard continued. "If it misfires, we still have the means—to turn it to our advantage. The Party never commits its destiny to a single person or a single outcome."

"You'd repudiate me," Carnot said. "Is that it?"

"If we had to." Picard laughed good-naturedly. "But you're too serious, Alexi. What's at stake in this maneuver? There's much more to consider than your personal feelings, or mine."

"I'm an instrument, too," Carnot said. "You think of me as—"

"You're an instrument, that's correct," Picard said reasonably. "We are all instruments of revolution. Keep that in mind when you're sitting in the gallery at the Assembly this morning. I'll have it in mind while I'm speaking on the floor. It's never out of my mind."

Carnot said nothing. The expression on his face was contemptuous.

"Look, Alexi, we're not fools here in Paris. But we have to consider the larger picture. This is no longer a provincial or even a national issue. It is international. You think I am cynical, but I understand sentiment even if I don't make a show of it. I feel too." Carnot glanced sideways at Picard. "That shouldn't surprise you. I haven't come to where I am in politics by being a fool. Only a fool feels no sentiment —a fool or a madman. It wasn't just because you were nervous that I suggested we walk to the Assembly. I say one thing to you when Boris is around—here I am talking to you as an intelligent human being. Without slogans, without the clichés, the formulas. Those are for people who can't think, Alexi. For Boris, for Jean. The Party depends for its strength on people who can't think, who have worked too hard too long to be able to think. We make slogans for them. We make causes for them. We think for them. But we give them solidarity and hope. Is that so foolish? We give them identity by taking identity from them. The Party *is* great. As workers for the Party they partake of that greatness. They're all gathering up ahead already, in the Place de la Concorde. It's their day of sacrament. But you and I are in a different world, Alexi. We *know*." Picard paused, shrugged. Carnot was silent.

Picard continued, "We are *behind* the puppet stage. We create the great dream they believe in. I make the causes and you keep those causes alive. They sleep nights because I don't. I know how you feel about Dujardin. He should be fed to the ants. But until the revolution comes we have to make use of any weapon they put into our hands. And Dujardin is a weapon. This rotten society created him and gave him to us. We're making him our cause—for the ones who can't think. We're giving them hope. We're also strangling our enemies with a rope of their own making. Dujardin is *theirs*. We're gorging them on their own excrement."

"I'd like to kill him first," Carnot said, his face blank.

Picard looked at Carnot narrowly. Then he said slowly, "You'll have to free him first. A man can't die twice."

"I've executed men," Carnot said abstractedly. "Other men."

"You've killed one too many, perhaps," Picard said. "It's not good to like killing too much." He stopped walking. "You lost more than your arm in the war."

Carnot stopped and looked at him.

"You've lost touch with humanity, Alexi," Picard said.

Carnot stared at Picard a moment, then turned away and spat deliberately on the ground. "For humanity," he said quietly, looking sidewise at Picard with a smile of hard insolence fixed on his face. "You never killed a man with your bare hands."

"That's enough," Picard said coldly.

Carnot fell silent. He walked slowly, looking sullenly at the ground before him. Picard walked beside, looking hard at him, his face cold and inexpressive.

"I keep forgetting that people like you exist," Picard said, looking stonily at Carnot, who avoided his eyes.

For a moment they walked in silence again.

Then Picard said, "Apologize to me."

"I apologize," Carnot said, not looking up. He smiled to himself.

"Is that why you took a job in a slaughterhouse, because you like to bloody your hands?"

"They had a job for a one-armed man," Carnot said sullenly. "You eat what I slaughter."

"If you'd spoken up sooner the Party could have got you something."
Carnot grunted.

"You'll have to change if you're going to work in the Party again," Picard continued. "We've outgrown the need for butchers. This is France, not Russia, my friend."

"I'm not—" Carnot stopped. His face twisted with irritation.

Picard watched him carefully. Then he said, "You've got to guard your thoughts more carefully. I warn you now, I don't ever want to hear—"

"I'm sorry," Carnot snapped.

Picard stopped walking and put his hand on Carnot's arm. Carnot stopped and looked at him. Picard's manner seemed to soften.

"Alexi, I know you're upset. If you don't want to go to the Assembly you don't have to. I can manage without you there. I'll have Boris take you back right now if you want to go."

"You think that offering me a chance to back out will make me go?"

"That's quite correct. Sound psychology is so transparent, Alexi."

"You know I have to go."

"Yes."

"I can't do anything else," Carnot said. He smiled unexpectedly again.

"No."

"All you want me to do is sit there?"

"And if I point to you from the floor, stand up. That's all. But I don't think you'll have to stand up. I'd rather wait. I'll identify you only if there's no alternative. You have my promise on that. Have you ever been to the Assembly before?"

"No."

"Then imagine you're a tourist. You'll enjoy it more," Picard said. "Don't worry about anything. You'll be among friends in the gallery. I've seen to that. If you do have to stand up you'll be cheered as a hero." Picard made an ironic grimace. "That should please you."

Carnot said, "I'll be all right." He gestured vaguely, absently.

"I'm happy to hear it. Now, do you want to walk or go back to the car?"

"I'd rather walk," Carnot said.

"All right. You walk then," Picard said, looking at his watch. "I'm going back to the car. I have to go over Jean's instructions with him. We'll pick you up at the bridge. You have a half-hour. Take a walk and enjoy yourself and don't think about anything at all. Just enjoy yourself and relax. You'll feel better." Carnot looked sharply at Picard. Picard continued softly, "I'm not afraid you'll run out on me. Boris won't follow you. I'm going to stop off for cigarettes. Do you want Boris to get you a pack of Gitanes?"

Carnot said nothing. He looked at the ground and shook his head.

"Alexi, you don't understand," Picard said gently. "I have no wish to force you to do anything against your will. This is *your* decision. *You* will have to make it. I'll not make it for you. I gave you money yesterday." Picard laughed pleasantly. "It's enough to leave town on if you want to. I won't stop you. I'll be criticized, but if I have to force you I'd rather not have you with me. It would be too much of a risk. I'm not a fool. There's an old saying in law that an unwilling witness is a dangerous witness."

Carnot looked up. "Do you still think I'm not telling you the truth about the files?" He smiled, as though unconsciously.

"Files, files? What files?" Picard asked, shrugging. "Alexi, if you say they're not in your possession, I take your word for it. First, I don't even know that they exist. It might easily be a ruse thought up to make me lose sleep. As I told you, I did receive information that you or somebody had certain files. However, as I also told you—I've been frank with you—I wasn't able to confirm the source of that information. Therefore I suspect that it was planted. But that's beside the point. The point is that you say you have no knowledge of any such files. I believe you. I have no choice."

"You didn't believe me."

"I pressed you because I thought you might be afraid to give them to me for fear— But they're not that important to Dujardin's defense." Picard threw up his hands. "I pressed you no harder than any lawyer would press an ordinary client. All right, Alexi, tell me: Do you possess or have knowledge of any papers, documents, or other evidence concerning Théophile Dujardin, his heirs or assigns, said papers, documents, or other evidence not being presently in my hands?" Picard was smiling.

"No," Carnot said. "I don't."

"Good. I believe you," Picard said. "Now all we have to do is hope that no one else has them either."

"What would happen if—"

"If such documents should turn up? You let me worry about that. It would be an embarrassment for you, but we're prepared for it if it happens," Picard replied. He peeled back his glove from his wrist. "Check your watch against mine. I have nine o'clock exactly. We'll meet you in exactly one half-hour at the other end of the bridge—unless you decide not to cross it—in front of the Assembly."

"I'll be there," Carnot said. "And I *would* like cigarettes."

"Keep an eye out for the car. You still look like a stranger to me since you've shaved. I'm not sure I'll recognize you in that crowd without your beard."

"You'll recognize me without this," Carnot said, raising the shoulder-stub of his right arm. The sleeve slipped out of the jacket pocket and the straight pin fell out onto the ground. Picard bent and picked it up. Awkwardly he helped Carnot pin the empty cuff back in its place. Then he straightened up and shook Carnot's left hand with his.

"In a half-hour we'll begin making history," he said. "Comrade," he added, with a wry smile.

Carnot held out his left wrist. "Wind my watch for me," he said.

Picard stared at him a moment and then came close to wind the watch. Carnot, his black eyes bright, watched Picard fumble with the stem of the timepiece, dominating him. Finally, in the awkward intimacy of a moment's disadvantage, Picard used both hands.

XIV

By ten o'clock the gray haze over the city had burned off and a cold gusty wind had arisen to sway the trees and shake the last of the ice from the branches. The streets were dry and the tag-end of storm weather from the night before had blown inland. The sky was a pale brittle blue, and in spite of the wind the temperature had risen slightly since the early morning. The Ambassador was alone in his office when Georges Merseault opened the tall, narrow gilded doors and poked his head in. He saw Bruce Sheppard bent over at the far end of the room, poking the fire that had been laid earlier that morning in the huge marble and bronze Empire fireplace.

"Am I early?" asked Merseault.

Sheppard turned around, the poker still in his hand, and waved it awkwardly toward a chair. "Hello, Georges. Sit down. I want to fix this fire. As long as we must have a fire we may as well have it properly, don't you agree?"

Merseault carried his black homburg on the point of his cane. He seemed to cross the room on the balls of his feet, in spite of the slight ungainliness of his limp. He took off his coat and gloves swiftly and threw them over the red satin chaise longue that graced the corner of the room. He sat down on a straight-backed gilt chair at the farther end of the room from Sheppard, still holding between his knees the cane with the hat on it.

"Did you get any rest after I left you?" asked Merseault.

Sheppard turned the logs with effort and straightened up, rubbing the small of his back. "I caught forty winks," he said. "Have you just come from the Assembly?" He walked the length of the long room toward Merseault, one hand on the small of his back, the other outstretched to greet him. Merseault rose; they shook hands.

"Yes. Nothing much happening. That can wait for later. Stone isn't here yet?"

"He's with Cadwalader and Lasher in Lasher's office. They're putting together a statement for this afternoon."

"Have you seen him before this, Bruce?"

"I haven't seen him since that day with you after the war," said Sheppard. "I've kept an eye on his progress every now and then, though."

"Why did he stay here in Paris after his discharge?"

Sheppard shrugged. "He evidently has no family left. Like me. Likes it in France. I guess he feels at home here. A bachelor could do worse, I suppose."

"I'm rather anxious to see him again. I doubt if he'll remember having met us that day."

Sheppard winced. "As I remember, we were both traveling rather incognito." Then his face became serious. "And he was quite distraught. That day was an ordeal for all of us. But especially for him."

Merseault nodded soberly. "Lasher is going to be here this morning?"

"He's bringing Stone here in five minutes. But Lasher doesn't have to stay."

Merseault nodded.

When Lasher came in with Stone, the Ambassador rose in greeting, shook hands, and inquired how the statement was coming. Lasher replied that a copy of it was being typed for his approval. The Ambassador then asked Lasher to bring it with him when he came back at eleven with Mr. Sweet. Lasher looked mildly surprised and opened his mouth to say something; it was clear from his manner that he had been about to sit down. He left the room with a furtive glance at Merseault, undoubtedly wondering what, precisely, he was doing there. Stone, gaunt, his black hair rumpled, stood looking after him, his thin-stretched woolen scarf still around his neck and the old raincoat over his arm. For a fleeting instant he watched the door close softly, an apprehensive frown on his face. Then he turned around, tense, uncertain. There was an awkward moment of silence. The Ambassador smiled.

"Colonel Lasher has one chronic weakness," said Sheppard, obviously to put Stone at ease. "He's afraid of missing something."

Stone responded with a grateful, harried smile and looked around for a place to put his raincoat.

"Add it to the pile," said Sheppard, waving toward the chaise longue. "Let's regroup at the other end of the room. We may as well get some use out of that fire before it goes out for good. Mr. Stone, this is Dr. Georges Merseault. You spoke together on the telephone this morning."

"Yes," Stone said. He shook hands awkwardly with Merseault.

Stone sat uneasily on one of the straight-backed chairs upholstered in red silk, both feet flat on the floor in front of him, his hands restlessly idle on his knees.

"Have you eaten?" asked Sheppard. "I understand they've been keeping you busy. You understand the circumstances of your transfer to the Embassy?"

Stone smiled a quick deprecating smile. "Mr. Cadwalader bought me breakfast. He came to pick me up this morning. Mr. Lasher explained the details of my new job just now, while I was with him in his office."

"You don't sound very encouraged."

"Well, sir," Stone said, "he also gave me a few other details—for one thing he told me that I'd have to be cleared through security here."

"That's the procedure, Mr. Stone. Each agency of the government must do its own security clearances."

"But I was just cleared again by the Army—for the second or third time. In fact—"

"It's not in my hands, Mr. Stone. That's the way the law reads."

"I had hoped that sort of thing was all over—with this transfer, that is." Stone sighed. "I guess I'm being naïve."

There was a moment when no one said anything. Stone shrugged resignedly. The Ambassador laughed. "Don't let it worry you. I've been under pressure to resign all my life, but you learn to live with harassment after a while. But a lot of people *would* be happier if I gave in and resigned."

"I don't plan to resign."

"You're not really being asked to. I don't plan to resign either. At least not for a while yet."

"I wish I could be as calm as you, sir."

The Ambassador waved off the subject. There was a pause.

"You've changed since we last met," said the Ambassador. He watched Stone's utter lack of reaction and smiled, and looked at Merseault.

"You've met us both," said Merseault, "although I don't blame you for not realizing it. Not with that crowd of people. At Montpelle. We were with Colonel Jay."

The slow light of recollection flickered in Stone's pale eyes.

"That was a grim time for all of us," said Sheppard softly. "I think I felt something of what you felt, watching you re-enact that—that unhappy day."

Stone was too surprised to say anything. He looked first at Merseault and then at the Ambassador. Finally he said, "I didn't know . . . I—"

Sheppard, smiling, raised his hand and cut him off. "There are a lot of things you *still* don't know," he said. "There are a lot of things *we* still don't know. That's the chief reason I've asked you to be here this morning." His face grew serious.

Stone nodded. He looked grave, unsure, terribly tense, but he seemed to be in full possession of himself.

Sheppard continued, "Before we start, however, I'd like you to know that I have faith in your integrity, Mr. Stone. A man who went through what you survived deserves gentler treatment than I'm afraid you've received. But you mustn't blame the Army too much. There's a great deal at stake in this Dujardin business—for you personally, for me personally, but also for your country. Perhaps it *would* have been better for you to take a leave of absence, but that decision rested entirely with you. No one should ever have tried to force you to make that decision, no matter how wrongheaded they may have thought you were being. I can only point out that we are living in a frightening time, and in such times fear often supersedes common sense and common decency. I hope you'll find it in your heart not to bear the bitterness you have the right to."

Stone stared at him. "Then you *do* know about my trouble with Army security? I didn't think the word had time to get around."

"It was a mistake of judgment," said Sheppard. "It was preposterous on the face of it. Let me say this: After the service you've rendered your country, Mr. Stone, no one could doubt your loyalty. But fear is a form of madness. I only hope you're strong enough to take whatever comes."

Stone relaxed slightly.

"There is one thing I would like to ask you, however," said Sheppard. "And this is completely off the record, Mr. Stone: What in the world have you done to earn the ill will of Congressman Kreuger?" Sheppard smiled.

"I knew his finger would be in this pie somewhere," said Stone. He sighed. "Mr. Kreuger wanted to sponser a bill to dig up all military graves in Europe and transfer them back to the States. He came over here on a fact-finding mission, as he called it. He's very much a politician, very patriotic, Fourth-of-July, and all. Well, he came into my office and laid his whole draft bill in my lap and asked me to tell him how much it would cost. The war was hardly over. A lot of casket manufacturers were behind him, I think. Some sort of bill was eventually passed, and they used steel caskets that cost the taxpayers over a thousand dollars each."

"But what did you do to—"

"In the course of describing his bill to me he called it 'an act of Congress to separate the mud from the boys.' I simply quoted him to the press, that's all."

"That's *all*," said Sheppard. "It's a wonder he's still in Congress. He denied it, of course."

Stone nodded. "Threatened to sue me, even, for libel or something. I suspected I hadn't heard the last of that."

"Well, maybe you have and maybe you haven't. He bears a grudge, but there's always the question of his re-election . . ." Sheppard smiled.

Stone shrugged.

The Ambassador gazed at Stone, studying him: The man looked

younger than he actually was. He even looked somehow as though he felt younger to himself, perhaps unwittingly refusing to believe that a half-decade of war had counted as part of aging. He looked a badly used thirty-five, but Sheppard knew he was over forty. He had a nervous habit of passing his fingers like a comb through the hair behind his ear, his hand rigid, clawlike. When he talked he gestured, his hands cutting the air like blades, chopping out the rhythm of his thoughts as though hewing words out of thin air. His eyes, Sheppard noticed, were shockingly blue and pale, as if lighted from behind, and more luminous for being deep-socketed. Although he couldn't have had much sleep the night before, that alone wouldn't account for the shadows lining his eye sockets; they seemed more permanent. His face was gaunt and bony, hawkish, tough. Even with his dark complexion, the large bones of his face made the hollows under his cheekbones plainly visible. He had a brooding air about him, an intenseness, Sheppard reflected, that could make a person uncomfortable in his presence. His constrained posture communicated a restlessness, vague and terrible, and his fingers were yellow from smoking. His clothes, once tasteful and conservative and of obvious good quality, were old and unpressed.

"I know you're tired," Sheppard said, "so we probably ought to get down to business. Dr. Merseault told you he was going to be here and you're probably wondering why. Georges, I think we may as well start with the main point."

"Sometime today a statement will be released by the other person who escaped the Montpelle massacre," said Merseault without preamble.

"You mean they've found him? Who was it?"

"Alexi Carnot."

"Carnot! *He* got out? Why hasn't he come forward before this?"

"I don't know. We're trying to find out, of course. But we are sure that Maurice Picard has found Carnot and that he is alive. He was caught again after the massacre, and came back from a concentration camp after the war."

"My God. Carnot," said Stone, shaking his head. "Carnot."

"Mr. Stone," said Merseault, "there is something I'd like to ask you. It may be of a personal nature. Please don't become angry and don't ask me how I know about this."

A tiny flicker of surprised interest passed across Sheppard's face for the barest instant. Stone sat rigid, waiting. He didn't move.

"You made a trip to Germany . . ." Merseault paused.

"Two years ago," said Stone. "Yes?"

"There you saw . . ."

"I saw a woman who knew Carnot. Yes. I made that trip."

There was a sharp embarrassed silence in the room. The fire snapped.

"Do you understand why I have to ask?" Merseault asked gently. "By the way, the Ambassador didn't know I was going to ask you this."

"You want to know if I knew Carnot was alive? Is that what you're getting at?"

"Yes."

"She told me he was. I didn't believe her. Everyone from the past was alive in her mind, even the dead. She was dying. She had drugs."

"You don't have to go into it further if you don't want to," said Sheppard abruptly. "Georges has his answer, Mr. Stone."

"I don't mind discussing it," said Stone evenly.

There was another pause. Merseault said nothing, clearly waiting.

Stone went on. "Yes, she knew Carnot. . . . I didn't know what had happened to her. After the war I learned that she'd been caught shortly after we were. It took me over a year to trace her through four camps. When I found her she was dying. She was crippled, one foot gone. They couldn't straighten her spine. As near as I could piece the story together, she and several other women prisoners had been left in a camp, locked in the buildings. The Allies were coming. The German guards set the place on fire and left them. She and eleven others got out only because that one building collapsed on them before they burned to death. An old German found her alive. Her face was badly scarred. In the hospital they gave her morphine. Then the old German—he was a farmer, a hermit—took her home and took care of her. He was at least seventy years old. He's dead now too. He married her. Once, when she was lucid, she told me that he was atoning for Germany's sins. He was completely crazy, but harmless, kind to her. I sent him money until he died. I also arranged to get her morphine legally. She lived in constant pain. I wondered when someone would ask me about her."

"You don't have to explain," said Merseault. "It was only a question of Carnot—whether he was in touch with her after the massacre."

"She kept talking about a child . . ." Stone began again: "Sometimes she didn't even know who I was. Other times she confused me with other people: Berger, the other American, Carnot. But the doctor thought that she had had a child. In fact, he was sure. I'm still trying to find out if that child was born alive. I can't find anything . . ."

"She was . . . involved with Carnot?"

"She had been. Yes."

"Perhaps I can help you," said Merseault. "If you can give me all the information you have to go on . . . I don't know. I can't promise anything—but there have been similar cases. You would like to know if her child . . ."

"When I talked to her, the old German would sit in one corner of the room watching me with her. He was very suspicious and he muttered to himself all the time. He was senile, a crazy miser hermit, but he took care of her. I spoke French when I asked her questions. I lied to the old man about not being able to speak German. I just didn't want him listening. He kept falling asleep in the corner and waking up and demanding a translation from her of what I was saying. This is when she had drugs and could talk. There was a young British Army medical orderly from the hospital who'd been risking his neck getting morphine for her. I met him only once."

"There's a collection of camp birth records in Berlin . . ." said Merseault.

"I've had them searched twice," Stone said. "She would never translate my questions correctly. To the old man, I mean. She had some sort of fantasy in her mind that she told him—that I was trying to find my family, who'd been in the camps with her. It was full of details that existed only in her mind. I wondered if she even understood what *I* was saying to her sometimes. The morphine made her—made her— I've searched the records in Berlin, but they're not complete. There are other records scattered around Germany—midwives' records, foster homes. I don't know if the child was born alive. She never saw it, I'm sure. She . . ."

Stone put his hand to his forehead. "I have a headache. I wonder—" He stopped.

"Georges, there's something in that sideboard I keep for visitors. Would you like a bit of cognac, Mr. Stone? It's quite good, really."

Stone smiled slightly. "It's a shame to waste it," he said apologetically.

Merseault poured three brandies. They drank in silence.

The logs in the grate were green, unseasoned, and the fire burned with a low steady hissing, snapping and throwing sparks against the bronze screen from time to time.

Finally Stone spoke, almost as though to himself. "Carnot," he said, shaking his head in amazement. "I don't know how he did it. I saw him go down. It was nearly dark, but I saw him fall. I'm sure of it."

"It's a miracle anyone got out," said Sheppard. "There was practically no cover on top of that hill."

"Berger drew most of the fire," said Stone. "If it hadn't been for him . . . He should have been decorated—even posthumously. Will they release his identity now that they're certain he didn't get out?"

Merseault glanced at Sheppard, who was sitting impassive, watching Stone.

"Why are you curious about his identity, Mr. Stone?" asked Merseault. "Not that your curiosity is unnatural, you understand."

"I've always wondered about him. He was a strange kid. I owe my life to him, I suppose. Well . . . I don't know . . . I'm curious, I guess. The Army has made sort of a cloak-and-dagger thing out of it. I've always wondered if he wasn't the one who got out. I didn't see him fall—I was sure they must have got him, but I didn't turn around to look. I just ran. Carnot was running in the same direction I was. I eliminated him as the possibility. I *saw* them both go down. But I always thought Berger might have made it—that he might be wandering around—lost his memory or something like that. He was already in pretty bad shape before he . . . It was just a fantasy I used to keep myself awake nights thinking about."

"A release has been obtained from the Army," said Sheppard. "A statement is being prepared for release in a few days. It should have been done long ago."

"I can understand the Army's reluctance to name agents. It seems to make more enemies than friends. I wish I were still anonymous. Sometime I'll show you my collection of threatening letters. Since this thing started a year ago I've received nearly a hundred."

"Don't you turn them over to the Sûreté?" asked Merseault.

"I photostat them at the office," said Stone. "For some perverse reason I like to keep copies of them. It's a macabre thing to collect, I suppose."

"Anyone who has ever had his name in the paper gets those things," said Merseault. "Some people pass away their old age writing poison-pen letters—I've had some experience in my time with them. One letter threatening the life of the President of France sounded as though it could be the real thing. It was very professional, but we traced it to an old lady in Pantin who liked gangster movies. She was very proud of the results she got—asked if our men were armed."

"Were they?" asked Sheppard. He was still watching Stone's profile.

"They certainly were," said Merseault. "She called it her 'literary vice.' She must have been nearly eighty—a sweet little old thing." Merseault wagged his head. He was obviously diverting the conversation deliberately.

Stone and Sheppard both laughed. "I wonder if I have one from her," said Stone.

"Your collection will never be complete without it," said Sheppard.

"Carnot," Stone said again, shaking his head. "I just can't believe it."

"Do *you* have any idea of why he didn't come forward during the trial?" asked Merseault.

"No," said Stone. "But I do have an idea how the documents from the German war archives were turned up."

Merseault looked up sharply. "Oh?" he said.

"I've had some experience trying to trace things through captured files," said Stone. "Missing prisoners of war, among other things. I know that even a German can't find anything in those files unless you can tell him exactly what sort of document you're looking for. Especially the approximate date of transmission and the probable recipients or senders. Otherwise it's like sifting a mountain for a grain of sand. They must have known just where to look."

"How would Carnot—"

"Carnot took particular pleasure in having the Germans eliminate their own best friends. He told me one story—it's hazy now, but I remember it was about a painstaking frame-up of an official, in the postal service, I think."

"You mean Carnot might have planted evidence with the Germans to the effect that Dujardin was cooperating with the *Maquis?*" Merseault asked.

"Dujardin couldn't have known of the existence of adverse German intelligence reports on him. If he had, he would have brought them out at his trial in his own defense. I'm sure he will be more surprised than anybody to find the Germans didn't count him among the elect."

"But how——" Sheppard began.

"Whoever planted those documents would know precisely where and —more important for locating them—*when* they were planted," said Stone.

"If they were really planted," Sheppard added. "It seems incredible."

Merseault pursed his lips. "Hmm. Was Carnot intelligent, in your estimation?" Aside to Sheppard, he said, "It's very possible, Bruce."

"Yes," Stone answered.

Merseault gazed at his brandy glass, reflecting. "Interesting," he mused. "There's an old saying—the gravedigger knows best where his children lie buried."

There was another long pause in the conversation.

Finally Merseault, glancing at Sheppard briefly, spoke to Stone. "Mr. Stone, let me put a flat question to you: Would you have any objection to sitting down with me, say over dinner at my house—you'll dine well, at least—and telling me as much as you can remember about Carnot? His personal traits, his psychological makeup, his strong points, his weaknesses—that sort of thing? I'd like to have you spend an evening reminiscing—not what he did but what he thought and felt. I don't know how closely you were able to know him . . ."

"I would need to have some sleep," said Stone.

"Certainly. Not today, but as soon as you . . ."

"Tomorrow? In the evening?" asked Stone.

Merseault took out a card. "My secretary—I have a young law student who guards my privacy—he may tell you I'm not home if I forget to tell him—I'm becoming very absent-minded with my mellowing years. Give him this card." Merseault uncorked a fountain pen and scrawled *Laissez passer* on the back and signed it boldly with black initials, *G. M.* "One thing though, I have a rather embarrassing request to make."

"Go right ahead, sir," said Stone, sipping his brandy. He looked as if he would like to gulp it down all at once.

"I imagine you're aware that you have an extra shadow behind you from time to time."

Stone laughed. "I've had more than one. Sometimes they almost trip over one another. Colonel Lasher was distressed that I refused a bodyguard—I suspect that he's given me one anyway."

"You have a French angel watching over you as well," said Merseault, smiling. "It would be very embarrassing to us if you met with any inhospitable circumstances due to an excess of fanatic zeal on the part of one of our own countrymen. You've become something of a celebrity, you know."

"You don't think my French angel might also be interested in where I go and whom I talk to?" Stone asked, looking up, a trace of a sardonic smile flickering across his face. He was sitting forward with his elbows resting heavily on his spread knees, as though afraid to lean back for fear of breaking the delicate antique chair. He held his brandy glass between both hands.

"That is not impossible," said Merseault, his expression not changing.

Sheppard silently watched the two men in profile, smiling slightly.

"A man who has had practice evading the *Sicherheitsdienst* shouldn't have too much difficulty," said Merseault.

"Shaking them off?" asked Stone.

Merseault nodded. "I have to protect my amateur standing," he said.

Stone laughed loudly. "Would you mind if I asked you what you do, Doctor?"

"The 'Doctor' is an academic title that I take refuge in. Basically I'm a historian, Mr. Stone. That is, I hope to be remembered as one if history does as well by me as I should like to do by her. Unfortunately, there's no guarantee of reciprocity."

"Georges is working on his magnum opus, Mr. Stone," Sheppard said. "He is retired from the French intelligence service."

Stone said, "What I mean is: What is your interest in—well, Carnot, for example?"

"I still do occasional consultation work, you might say," Merseault said. "Unofficially, of course. I've put my cloak and dagger in mothballs, but every now and then I take them out just to look at them. Vanity, I suppose."

"Georges is like an old fire horse when he hears the fire bell ring," Sheppard said. "He has a taste for skulduggery."

"What is your book about? Or don't you like to discuss it?" asked Stone.

"I don't mind at all," Merseault said. "In fact, I'm always flattered if anyone shows enough interest to ask. After all, it's not a novel. It's a history of sorts, a compendium, a textbook. I've taken a field that seems to have been overlooked by historians. It is a history of political conspiracy."

"Georges likes to stay close to his material," Sheppard said, reaching out to refill their two glasses. He poured with a steady hand.

"Conspiracy is the obverse side of diplomacy," said Merseault, warming to his subject. "More history has been made in cellars than in chancelleries. Unfortunately, conspirators don't take minutes at their meetings, nor, as a rule, do they keep files. Yet the fate of nations has been altered by cellar diplomats. I have to rely on rather unscholarly sources for my material."

"I see," Stone said.

"I understand you used to teach before the war, Mr. Stone."

Stone looked at Merseault with mild interest. "Teaching music and French in a high school hardly qualifies me as a scholar," said Stone. "You seem to be familiar with my—my dossier, I would imagine you'd call it."

Merseault nodded, smiling. "You have a very flattering dossier, Mr. Stone. Your French dossier, that is."

"I'm honored that the French Government takes the interest," said Stone, grinning broadly. "I wonder if the American version is as complimentary."

"In France," said Merseault, "the writing of dossiers has become a fine art, a branch of serious literature. The dossier is a literary form, witty, penetrating, sometimes hopelessly imaginative. It takes years to develop an art form to such a level. Flaubert is our forefather, our mentor. You should read the dossier of a *crime passionnel* someday. Or a pathologist's report. France loves to write French. It will be years before the Americans will be able to write a classic dossier."

"You have the Frenchman's classic condescension, Georges," said Sheppard, smiling. "I imagine we have just as many unsung police officers writing fiction as you do."

"Ah, yes. But *good* fiction—that's another thing, you see."

"You can't beat him," Sheppard said to Stone.

"Then I can expect you to take dinner with me tomorrow evening, Mr. Stone?" asked Merseault. "If you take the Metro to Passy around six o'clock you should be able to relieve your escort from duty at the Etoile. It'll be crowded when you change trains. I used to use the Etoile myself during the war. Nothing fancy—just go in one side of the train and out the other as the door closes. That leaves them either in the train or on the other side of the track. You have a clear view from the stairs. In either case you have plenty of time to get outside and pick up a cab. If you can't free yourself, telephone me. My numbers are all on the card. The lower one rings in my study."

Sheppard laughed. "Georges, you're a menace to society."

"No more than society is to itself," said Merseault. "And to poor Georges also, for that matter. It comes out even."

Sheppard and Stone both laughed. Merseault sat poker-faced. He shrugged.

"I'm looking forward to having dinner with you," said Stone. "It'll be the first pleasant thing I've had to look forward to in two weeks."

"We will have the *spécialité de la maison, bécasse Marianne.* My cook is a genius. I haven't let her know it yet. I shout at her every now and then."

"What have you planned with Mr. Cadwalader for this afternoon?" Sheppard asked abruptly. "Are you satisfied with the draft of your statement?"

"I'd like to make it a little stronger," Stone said. "Mr. Lasher seems to want to tone it down. I think we should call a spade a spade, **Mr.** **Ambassador.**"

"For heaven's sake don't call me Mr. Ambassador, Mr. Stone. I hear that all week. It gets to be depersonalizing. I much prefer to be Mr. Sheppard, so that I know when people are addressing me. I like to think of myself as a person, not an administrative abstraction. What do you mean, 'tone it down'?"

"I think some of the innuendoes that have appeared in the press are despicable. I think Dujardin is as guilty as sin. I think his lawyers **are** *liars,* and I'd like to say so out loud. Liars."

"I see," said Sheppard. "Let me ask you a question. In your mind, are you absolutely certain that Dujardin is not, say, half-innocent?"

"Certain."

"I see. Do you think this man Carnot knows this—or rather, do you think he believes in Dujardin's innocence?"

"It was Carnot who first gave me the concrete facts of his guilt."

"So?" said Merseault, interested. "Could he have been lying to you?"

"He could have. But if Dujardin was playing a double game he abandoned it when he turned the twelve of us over to that SS battalion. That was murder."

"But he didn't personally commit it," Sheppard said. "Understand me, Mr. Stone. I'm merely playing the devil's advocate for a moment. You say Dujardin himself was at the scene of the massacre?"

"I heard him talking to the battalion commander outside the truck," said Stone. "I heard the German call him 'Herr Dujardin.' There's no doubt about it. Dujardin was bent on eliminating twelve people who could bear witness against him. And he couldn't risk bloodying his own hands, not with the Allies already on the beach. So he gave us to the SS."

"Did Carnot hear this?" asked Merseault.

"I'm certain he did. I didn't have a chance to talk to him. We were in separate trucks then. But they were right together."

"No one saw Dujardin?"

"I'm sure I saw him, but he was too far away to recognize by his features. And it was quite dark. I'd seen him before, once when they caught Carnot while he was waiting to rendezvous with me, and once during the last interrogation."

"In other words, it *is* just possible that Carnot neither saw nor heard him *at the scene of the crime.* He might be able to say—"

"He could say anything," said Stone. "But I *know* he must have heard him."

"What were they talking about?" asked Merseault.

"This was all in my testimony at the trial."

"Yes," said Merseault, "but you were vague on—"

"Of course I was vague," said Stone sharply. "As I said, I only caught a word here and there. As near as I could gather, the German wanted to give Dujardin a receipt for us—the prisoners, that is. I got that from the fact that the German didn't know the French word for 'receipt' and kept repeating the German for it. I speak both languages and I could hear them fumbling to understand each other. Dujardin said a receipt wouldn't be necessary. I don't know what happened—whether he got one anyway or not. The German was very insistent."

"I wonder if there would be a duplicate kept of such a document," Merseault said. "I doubt it. But the Germans might be just that thorough. . . ."

Stone turned and faced Sheppard. "Do you believe me?"

Sheppard nodded very slowly and very gravely. He said nothing.

"Lasher doesn't seem to have the same confidence in my integrity," Stone said bitterly. "He acts as if he were charged with whitening a black sheep."

Sheppard chuckled. "You're undoubtedly Mr. Lasher's *bête noire,* Mr. Stone. But don't think too badly of him. He has his blind spots, but he is a very capable staff officer. He's a little uncomfortable in civilian clothes."

"I'm always suspicious of military men who feel the need of a military title in civilian life," Stone said.

Sheppard threw back his head and laughed. "I'm glad I was saved from the ranks of the damned, Mr. Stone. If I weren't an ambassador people might still be calling me 'General.' "

"Some people still are," Merseault commented dryly. "Certain segments of the local press, that is."

"A general is a different matter," said Stone awkwardly. "A general becomes a public institution after he's gotten his third or fourth star."

"Like marriage and museums," offered Merseault. "Ambassadors never amount to much."

"I didn't mean that," said Stone. "Although it's possibly true, I suppose."

"Blessed be the peacemakers." Sheppard smiled.

"R.I.P." said Merseault.

Sheppard put down his brandy glass. It was hardly touched. "Well, what's left on the agenda?" he asked affably. "Are you prepared for your little meeting with Mr. Sweet, Mr. Stone? I hope you don't let anything said there get under your skin."

"I don't quite understand why this requires a *meeting,*" said Stone. "Mr. Sweet is from Washington, isn't he? Isn't he Chief of Security there?"

"Answer his questions as best you can. Mr. Lasher will be there. Between you and me, I've also asked the general counsel to be there to see that it doesn't turn into a private hearing. Then there will be a stenographer—you will be provided with an unedited stenographic record of everything that's said."

"I don't feel easy about this, I'll tell you. If I could get out of it without being ungraceful I would jump at the chance."

"It's entirely voluntary. You can refuse to appear, if you so wish," said Sheppard. "I realize it's a little intimidating to sit down to a table and have to answer all sorts of idiotic questions about yourself. But it's merely routine. The alleged object of *our* investigation is mainly to protect you. If there are any chinks in your armor, the Embassy would like to know beforehand rather than be embarrassed by surprise. After all, there's a lot more at stake in this affair than just your personal reputation or my personal reputation. It's somewhat a question of your country's reputation."

Stone smiled. "They want to make sure the sheep is really white, is that it?"

"All sheep are white when they're shorn," said Merseault. He shrugged and smiled.

"Pink," corrected Sheppard.

Stone laughed. He was beginning to feel the brandy. His face was flushed. "What color is a lamb after being led to slaughter?"

Merseault looked at Stone, his smile fading. "Red," he said.

"You're being morbid again, Georges," said Sheppard. "Georges has a warped Gallic sense of humor, Mr. Stone."

Merseault gazed at Stone. "I was speaking politically, not morbidly," he said. He frowned petulantly. "No one laughs at morbid jokes any more."

"I laugh," said Stone, trying to sound at ease.

Sheppard laughed. "I'm sure you can take care of yourself, Mr. Stone. Just don't lose your dignity or your sense of the ridiculous. One's your shield, the other your sword. If you keep those two things intact you can survive any human situation. One draws strength from the other. But if you lose one, you soon lose the other. Keep that in mind."

"Do you know what sort of things I'm going to be asked?" asked Stone.

"I never read a security file unless I'm required to." The Ambassador seemed suddenly agitated; his voice and manner took on an edge of irritated impatience. "Sorting other people's private unwashed linen is the most certain means of demoralization I know of. It leads to the chambermaid mentality. People whose main concern is other people's soiled linen—washerwomen, chambermaids and the like—always seem to turn into community gossips and common scolds. The whole object of privacy is not to protect the individual from embarrassment so much as to protect the community from demoralization. I am sorry if I seem to lecture, but this is a sore spot with me. There are no morals without privacy. To sin is man's eternal lot, and the only public defense against immorality is to maintain the privacy of sin. To force a public servant to rub his nose in dirt is the one sure way to unfit him for public service. That's one reason I try to avoid these hearings. Sin cannot be legislated out of existence. If the clergy hasn't been able to do it in two thousand years of trying, I doubt if an Act of Congress will have better success."

"It's reassuring to know that someone's on Mr. Stone's side," Merseault said, quietly ironic.

Stone began, "I realize, sir, that you can't be concerned—"

The Ambassador cut him off with a wave of the hand. "Government employees will become more cynical and hypocritical, harder to catch *in flagrante delicto*. They will learn to cover their lapses. And people who have no compassionate conception of private evil inevitably have very little understanding of the public good—like the well-meaning people who plunged the United States into the bloody whiskey bath of Prohibition. Organized virtue engenders organized vice as surely as Abel found a brother to slay him. I don't think the new security law will survive another session of Congress. If it does, if it becomes an institution, a vested interest, then as sure as milk goes sour in summer, the United States has entered her childless years. Personally, I think it's merely a temporary debility. But if the practice of polluting the consciences of government officials with these cheap collections of legal pornography continues much longer, then I fear for government, gentlemen. And I am concerned."

He paused, deep annoyance showing in his face. "No, Mr. Stone, I don't know anything of the blacker aspects of your history. I haven't the least idea what you should expect. Perhaps, in the privacy of your mind, you may be able to weigh the secrets that might have been dredged up against you. Don't be surprised at anything. But remember, this is not a confessional booth. Unhappily, there is no absolution to match the penance. You'll have to excuse me. I believe in honor as much as I do in security. I was raised in the old conservative school of individualism and privacy, and I'm a bit rabid on the subject—in private, that is. In public, I do my level best to administer a bad, unworkable inanity of a law. And I might remind you that Mr. Sweet is doing the same thing. It's not a rewarding job he's got. It's a labor of Sisyphus. Mr. Sweet's political career—which was very promising, let me assure you—has been ended. He knows this now, but it's too late for him to do anything about it. He is doing a job he didn't ask for, as best he can. He's not happy to know that he has become a political pariah. No one loves a hatchet man. So keep in mind when you get angry with Sweet that if *he* didn't have this job, someone else would. There are lots of people with keyhole mentalities who would love to have a chance to even up the score between them and the rest of this sinful world."

There was absolute silence as the Ambassador finished speaking. Stone nodded. Merseault studied his glass. There was something about the Ambassador's sudden intensity that cast a shadow of embarrassment over the room, but only for a second.

Merseault looked up at Stone and raised his glass and smiled. "Good luck, black sheep."

XV

Colonel Lasher gave a first-draft copy of the afternoon press statement to the Ambassador's secretary and waited for Stone in the outer office. The secretary disappeared through the tall gilded doors, the thin sheets of onionskin fluttering under her arm. In a moment she was back. She told Colonel Lasher that Mr. Stone would be out directly and went back to her desk, where she untangled a delicate bridle of earphones attached to a dictating machine and sat down at her typewriter. Two other typists bent to their labors without looking right or left, and the colonel sat trying to collect his wits amid the rattle of three clattering typewriters.

He looked again at the paper in his hand, gazing at it, shaking his head slowly from side to side and frowning. Ten minutes ago the report had come from the Assembly. As expected, a document purporting to be a statement from one Alexi Carnot had been read on the floor. But not as expected, the statement had come from the far right side of the house instead of from the left. Even as he read over the communication in his hand, Lasher knew the statement he and Cadwalader had just drafted for the press would have to be rewritten. Unconsciously he glared at the nearest typist, and sighed. The deputy who had read the statement was a former colonel in the French Army, a man Lasher had met once at a reception for General De Gaulle, then newly and triumphantly returned from four years of active exile in London. He had liked the French colonel, had found him friendly toward the Americans, even admiring—but now this . . . Lasher had insisted during the drafting of the statement that Cadwalader stress the fact that the Communists were alone in their insistence on Dujardin's innocence, that the whole Dujardin affair was a plot to discredit the United States, of which plot the Communist Party was the sole author. Somehow it had seemed to Lasher that the best way to refute the Dujardin charges was to point out the disreputable character of their authors. It was his deep-felt conviction that no respectable person— that is to say, nobody worth considering—would give credence to charges made by Communists. Charges authored by such persons would be discredited automatically once the authorship became publicly known. To Colonel Lasher this was only common sense. He wished he could go on the radio himself for just five minutes and explain everything to the French populace and clear up the matter once and for all. Unfortunately, he couldn't speak French, a fact which annoyed him occasionally. But not often.

What annoyed him more was that no one took his views seriously.

No one would make the effort to see the simple clarity of his argument. Even Cadwalader, who when he first came on the job had shown rare clear-headedness, was getting foggy. Working around diplomats could do that to anyone, Lasher reflected, but somehow he hadn't expected Cadwalader, hitherto a rock of strength, a tower of common sense, to succumb quite so easily to the general malaise. With the Communist Party holding a third of all the votes in France, it was clear as crystal that they had to be neutralized. The colonel was impatient.

The main thing was to convince the people of France that the Communist Party was evil. Lasher had observed that people who didn't hold firmly to the fact that communism was evil sooner or later fell into sympathy with Communist causes if not Communist methods. They fell into the error of adopting Communist ideas for their own. As a result, socialism was spreading like a disease and sapping the strength and initiative of countries that were formerly healthy. The problem, as he had told Cadwalader and that odd-ball Stone, was to strike at the source of the contagion. The Communist Party shouldn't be allowed to carry on its subversive activities under protection of the law. It should, in Lasher's forthright opinion, have been eliminated long ago. The only sensible way to weed a garden was to pull the weeds up by the roots.

Colonel Lasher was a tolerant man. But tolerance had its limits. Before evil there could be no tolerance. The fact that the Communists had already successfully connived to control a third of the votes of France made the problem doubly urgent. A third was enough to block any effective action against them, but on the other hand, he reasoned, the Almighty didn't wait to vote Lucifer out of heaven. He threw him out.

But the most benumbing evidence of how far the poison had spread was, in Colonel Lasher's eyes, the fact that a professional army man had been duped into playing the Communist's game for them—one of De Gaulle's own deputies, a man who had risked his career to follow De Gaulle to London against Pétain's explicit orders. The colonel reflected bitterly that if the United States hadn't won the war, the author of the speech he held in his hand would have been hanged as a mutineer. Colonel Lasher was vexed by ingratitude.

There had been a time when he ignored politics. For a conscientious career officer, it was the wisest course to follow. Colonel Lasher had always counted himself conscientious. He had served without complaint under six different Presidents and their administrations before he ever believed Bolshevism and other anarchist movements to be anything more than a passing threat from the lunatic fringe. He now readily admitted his political innocence of those days, telling anyone who would listen that he had once considered communism harmless. He insisted that he had formerly held no other real opinion on it. Live and let live—that had been his attitude. He had, he insisted. approached communism with an open mind. When Roosevelt came in, he served as faithfully as he had under Hoover; whatever doubts he had he took pride in keeping to himself.

However, during the war he sat on a court-martial board hearing the case of a young lieutenant charged with giving intelligence information to the Russians. Before the trial opened, Lasher listened to an intelligence officer's briefing in amazement and alarm—but the Russians were allies! The case couldn't be proved; the lieutenant got off; but the colonel received a rude baptism. Soviet espionage was not a myth; communism was not a joke. He began to read, to acquaint himself with the realities of international espionage. Inevitably it started him thinking. Lasher was certain that the young lieutenant—he hadn't been a regular, fortunately—had been involved in *something* shady or he wouldn't have been up for court-martial. It was a regrettable incident, but it was the kind of thing that was bound to happen with an army of civilians assembled under the hasty pressures of wartime. The lieutenant was lucky. The president of the court-martial was also a reserve officer, a former lawyer in civilian life with what Lasher felt were mild liberal leanings.

Then, to his heart-sick disgust, he saw with his own eyes the order General Eisenhower gave withdrawing American troops from before the gates of Prague. His wife, whom he'd met after the war, came from an old Polish family that lost everything to the Russians. His eyes were opened to the Soviet menace.

Colonel Lasher stared morosely at the secretary's crossed ankles bent at a grotesque angle under her chair, and reflected idly, not for the first time, that she would be quite an attractive girl if she would improve her posture. She was also too thin, however. Someone should make her eat more. The girl looked up unexpectedly and smiled at him. He nodded for no reason and began rereading the French officer's truculent statement he held in his hand. He was still thinking how he might tell the girl tactfully about her posture, and his eyes ran over the thick-set oratorical sentences without taking in their meaning. Then suddenly, unbidden, a phrase standing alone in the forest of confusion split away from its context and crashed across the silent stream of his thoughts like a felled tree: ". . . *was not, I repeat was not, working with the Free French forces in the area."*

He retraced his way back to the beginning of the paragraph and picked his way through the dense verbiage, reading carefully this time. It was slightly puzzling. If Stone wasn't working with the Free French, what was he doing? Who *was* he working with? Was he working on his own? Lasher had made it a point throughout his military career never to probe around areas of military intelligence that weren't his immediate operational concern. This morning, meeting Stone for the first time, he'd been tempted to ask him something about his work during the war, but knowing that the lid was still on some of the undercover work, he had refrained from seeming too inquisitive. He understood perfectly that, while the British could now allow their agents to write adventure memoirs, the American position was more delicate. The United States had recognized Vichy as a neutral and had kept up formal diplomatic relations to the point of sending an ambassador. An ambassador was not supposed to countenance sabotage. But now Stone's background had become Colonel Lasher's immediate operational concern. Byron Sweet might be open to suggestions, he reflected.

The immediate problem, however, was to rewrite the press release. Lasher was reluctant to face Cadwalader again and ask him to revise the statement, but it would have to be toned down a good deal more—there was no sense in offending a Gaullist deputy by implying that he was in league with the Communists. They would have to change it without Stone or it would never get done. It was an achievement to have got even the first draft to please him and still have it retain some dignity.

If Colonel Lasher could have had his way he would have preferred not to grace the Dujardin charges with the dignity of a reply. The least he could do was to see that Stone didn't descend to the level of calling the lawyers liars, as he had wanted to. Lawyers were, in the colonel's opinion, professional men who were carrying out their duties, doing merely what they were paid to do. There was no sense in antagonizing the legal profession by intemperate name-calling. The issue was unfortunately a controversial one, unlike anything he had ever been forced to deal with in the Army; in the Army there simply were no controversial issues unless someone blundered. But Colonel Lasher was sure that the less controversy the Embassy indulged in, the better it would be for all concerned. Also, he wasn't entirely sure about Stone. He looked like a troublemaker; he would have to be handled carefully. But the colonel saw no reason why Stone should be allowed to use the Embassy as a soapbox for an airing of his personal grievances. Colonel Lasher didn't understand why the Ambassador didn't leave Stone to fight his own battle. In fact, he saw no reason why the United States Embassy didn't simply ignore the whole business. If Karl Marx had been properly ignored in the first place, there would be no such thing as communism. But Colonel Lasher knew there was no profit in hindsight: crying over spilt milk was a waste of time. He was a practical man, realistic, and he took pride in being realistic. In fact, just that morning he had explained to Stone and Cadwalader that he was, as he called it, a practical realist. It sounded good.

He gazed across the room. A file cabinet was standing with a drawer out, its open padlock lying on top. In any other office he would have got up and closed it and locked it without saying a word—as a silent object lesson in security. Whenever anywhere in the building he found a lock lying loose with its key in it, he would simply lock the file and pocket the key, leaving a note on the padlock saying "Please see me," and signed with the abbreviated signature he habitually used instead of initials: Lash. He knew that among the office help this practice had earned him several behind-back nicknames: "Colonel Dreadful," "Old Keysnatcher," "Abominable Clarence," perhaps others. He was rather proud of them in a perverse way. And when the culprit did come for the key, he always had his revenge: he made a careful point of keeping the person waiting on pins and needles for a good half-hour. Sometimes he would then call him in and lecture him on the meaning of security. But usually he merely finally sent the key out with a secretary. He never tired of pointing out to his own staff that laziness was the greatest enemy of security.

But it wasn't prudent to antagonize anyone, even a typist, in the Ambassador's office. There were too many petty ways they could take advantage of their strategic position to hector him, and he was certain they would if given the excuse. If the thin girl looked up again, he would merely look pointedly at the file cabinet and let it go at that. She didn't look up. He glowered at the open file. His mind wandered.

"The aforementioned agent, Stone, had no direct contact with De Gaulle. . . ." the words from the speech of the Gaullist deputy kept running through his mind. Colonel Lasher wondered. Something nagged him. Why had the deputy stressed . . .

Suddenly it came to him. He snapped his fingers and sat bolt upright on his chair. The report slid off his lap and fluttered to the carpet. The girl stopped typing and looked up.

"Did you just remember something, Colonel Lasher?" she asked, smiling at him.

He reddened and bent forward to pick up the report that lay at his feet. He forgot to look at the file cabinet. "I just thought of something," he said, almost muttering.

The secretary smiled again and returned to her typing. Colonel Lasher was studying the report in earnest again. As he read, absorbed, the corners of his mouth turned slowly down and a frown of suspicion settled on his face.

XVI

The crowd came no farther than the corner of the Rue St. Florentin. There they halted before the police around the Talleyrand. There was no traffic in the streets. Taxi drivers had stayed home, not so much out of sympathy with the striking bus and subway workers as from fear that their ancient machines might suffer damage if there was trouble. And there was almost sure to be trouble before the day was out.

By eleven o'clock the bright sunshine had taken the chill off the streets and the sidewalks were almost dry, but the wind was still blowing and the people stamped up and down and flailed themselves with their arms to keep warm. Most of them wore no topcoats, only cheap dark suits, sometimes a muffler and a beret. Nearly all the men in the crowd wore bicycle clips, the badge of the French workingman. Some of them wheeled their bicycles with them. Here and there through the crowd darted trained agitators, exhorting, shouting slogans. Each agitator worked his own particular section of the crowd, constantly consulting with the others and exchanging bundles of leaflets.

Outside the main crowd of workers, who were now no longer chanting, but only singing and shouting in sporadic groups or taunting the imperturbable police, another crowd was gathering, and behind the parked police vans spectators had assembled: office workers, shopkeepers, tourists, even young seamstresses from the dress shops in their light blue work smocks. One enterprising hot-chestnut vendor, a grizzled old man with an enormous cigarette-yellowed mustache, scuttled his smoking cart back and forth in front of them, shouting in a gravel voice that could be heard across the square, *"Chaud, Chaud, Chaud! Pour chauffer le foie et l'âme. Chaud, Chaud!"* Two young priests holding bicycles stopped him. The old man handed them a newspaper rolled in a cone, full of chestnuts, and moved on, still chanting about warming the liver and the soul.

At quarter after eleven much of the crowd in the square was sitting down, on curbs, in doorways, swarming all over the two empty fountains in the center of the Place de la Concorde, and around the base of the obelisk. Bottles of label-less red wine made their appearance here and there and were passed around. But the crowd was quieter now, and the police merely went through the motions of keeping people moving. They were waiting for the announcement of the vote in the Assembly. Directly across the river in front of the Palais Bourbon, where the vote was in progress, a similar crowd was being briskly cleared away by a mounted unit of the *garde républicaine.* Their bright red uniforms and polished helmets shone in the cold sun as they waltzed their horses flank to flank backward into the crowd, gradually forcing them up onto the sidewalks of the bridge. A cordon of special police were taking up their stations locked arm in arm along the curb with their backs to the press of the crowd.

Each group of people on this side seemed to have its assigned place, for no one in the Place made any attempt to cross the bridge to where the excitement was. They only watched and talked among themselves as the police on the opposite bank finally cleared a wide path across the bridge to the foot of the Champs Elysées, where a moment later the car of the President of France would pass, followed by the Premier, or ex-Premier, and his cabinet and then, finally, the deputies. In front of the Assembly two dozen police of the motorcycle escort in their sinister black leather uniforms leaned on their machines smoking and talking. Suddenly, at a signal from someone on top of the steps, they swung onto their motorcycles and almost as one man came down hard on their kick-starters. There was a deafening roar of noise and the machines came to life and out of nowhere the black Delahaye limousine of the President appeared in position at the bottom of the steps. The crowd stepped farther back from the street as four gray Citroëns, each containing four husky men in black coats, spun recklessly around the corner of the building out of the side street where they had been waiting. Before anyone had time to notice, the President was down the stairs and in his car. Two of the men in black coats jumped out of the first Citroën and onto the running board of the President's car. The motorcycle police pulled their black leather helmets on and fixed their enormous black goggles over their eyes; the pack leaped forward, motors roaring, onto the bridge. Following at breakneck speed came the plainclothes security police, then the President's car, the red, white, and blue bullseye of the Republic of France flashing on and off at the front of the car.

Alexi Carnot looked at his watch and crossed the street toward the Place de la Concorde. He walked with his shoulders hunched slightly, his empty right sleeve tucked into the pocket of the old British Navy duffel coat. Midway across the bridge he put up the hood of his coat to avoid the slim chance of someone in the crowd recognizing him.

Although he knew no one could possibly know his face now, he could still feel the residue of the fear that had gripped him when he heard his own name spoken aloud on the floor of the Assembly. He had looked furtively around at the people sitting near him in the crowded gallery. But no one looked at him. No one turned to accuse him. It was like being present as a ghost at your own funeral. No one knew him to look at, and yet there was the strange feeling that he was no longer anonymous, as though indeed his name were written on his forehead. He had dreaded the moment when Picard would turn dramatically and point up into the gallery at him from the floor and all the hundreds of faces would turn to stare at him. He would have had to stand up; Boris and Jean would have seen to that, sitting as they were on either side of him. But the moment never came. Picard had made hardly any speech at all. He had shrewdly let the Gaullist deputy carry the whole attack. The doddering old fool really thought Dujardin was innocent— Carnot stopped thinking about it. He shook his head and put the sickening memory of his stage fright out of his mind. It was over for now. He looked around at the people coming across the bridge, searching their faces for some sign. But nothing showed in their faces, no flicker of recognition. You all know me, he told them silently in his mind. But you don't recognize me. I am Alexi Carnot. His own name sounded loud in his thoughts. *Alexi Carnot.* But the faces continued to flow past him unheeding. The crowd would all know his name by the time the afternoon newspapers came out.

But there would be no photograph. He would still be secure in his secret knowledge of his own true identity. It gave him power over them all.

He would not think about Dujardin's reprieve. The idea filled him with sick hatred, for Dujardin, for Picard, for himself. A special commission to investigate—what a comedy, he thought contemptuously. Picard had been so angry that his face was white when he left the floor. By granting the special stay of execution, the government had assured itself of winning the vote of confidence. The vote would come this afternoon, but now it was merely a formality. Carnot knew instinctively from the white anger in Picard's face that the government would win it. And Picard's frustration had given him a vicious secret satisfaction.

As he reached the end of the bridge he turned right to avoid the thickest part of the crowd. The square was quiet; an informal truce now prevailed while everyone took time out for lunch. Everyone seemed to have a lunch pail and a bottle of *pinard*. As Carnot walked the short length along the river toward the Tuileries, he passed a group of troops playing *belote* on the extended tailgate of one of the trucks. The cards were so battered that he could hardly read them as he paused to watch the play. Some were dog-eared, some torn, all mottled with wine spots. He watched the play with dull interest until the hands were thrown in. The soldier who won the hand looked up at Carnot and grinned, showing a mouthful of rotten teeth. He gathered the cards for another deal.

"I try to tell them this game is not for idiots," said the soldier. "They refuse to understand."

"You could use some new cards," Carnot observed.

"New cards? Don't be ridiculous," answered another soldier. "We couldn't tell one from another with clean cards."

"Just so. Just so," said the first soldier, dealing.

Carnot crossed the street. He mounted the few steps into the Jardin des Tuileries and walked along the wall toward the Rue de Rivoli. When he reached the far corner of the park, he stood with his back to the Jeu de Paume for a moment and leaned on the wall, looking at the crowd on the level of the square a little below him.

At the edge of the sidewalk just below, people were making a circle around a laughing red-faced man who stood with a towel tucked under his chin bellowing like a circus barker. Suspended from a cord around his neck he carried a sign: *Le Père Grenouille;* painted on it was a man with a frog's head. The man was haranguing the crowd thickening around him. He called for a little money as evidence of good faith before he performed his remarkable feat. At his feet were two large jars of water each holding several litres. In one swam three small frogs. A few coins clinked on the pavement and rolled in falling circles around his feet. He scorned even to stoop and pick them up; instead he shuffled them toward the center with the point of his toe. He laughed hugely and called the crowd misers and threatened not to swallow any frogs unless the pittance was increased; a few more coins fell. He continued his loud scolding, dancing around in a queer little dance and laughing. When the crowd finally grew large enough to make it seem worth his while, he produced a large metal funnel and stuck it in his mouth. Then he picked up the first jar and wrestled it up onto a level with the funnel he held between his lips. The jar was about the size of a mop bucket and full to the brim with water. He held it there for a moment, about to drink, then reconsidered, let the funnel fall from his mouth, shouted, "Misers!" at the crowd, laughed, and started to lower the jar. Coins turned in sunlight at his feet; he threw back his head and laughed. Still holding his head back, he lifted the huge jar again and began pouring water into himself, the funnel still rolling in a circle at his feet. He didn't seem to be swallowing the water, but simply pouring it in; it made a curious gluck-glucking sound. The crowd watched spellbound. Water dribbled from the corners of his mouth as he emptied half the water from the jar into himself, like a barrel being filled. He stopped and looked around at the crowd, slapping his foot impatiently on the pavement. More coins. When, incredibly, the jar was three-quarters empty, he stopped again; coins spun faster around his feet. Then he finished it, his stomach protruding grotesquely, and held up the empty jar. The crowd laughed and clapped. His voice was strained and rasping as he laughed and cradled his distended paunch in his hands. He reached down and dipped his hand into the other jar. A girl gave a little scream and turned her back as he caught the first wriggling frog and lifted the hapless creature by its hind legs. He swallowed it head first. Then the second frog followed after its unhappy brother. There was an apprehensive moment when the third frog nearly escaped from his grasp; an instant's juggling, the frog was retrieved, and it too disappeared down the gullet of Père Grenouille. He opened his mouth wide to show that the frogs were gone. A girl egged on by three boys looked carefully, unbelievingly, then covered her face and shrieked with laughter as she stepped back into the crowd. The red-faced Père Grenouille stood in the middle of the cleared circle in an attitude of sad-clown mourning for the three departed frogs. Then he bent on one knee and pretended to pray. The crowd howled with laughter. When the head of the first frog peeped out from between his lips several girls shrieked at once and turned away; the men laughed and teased at their discomfiture, urging them to turn around and watch. The first frog was barely dropped back into the jar when the second appeared. The third took longer to find his way back into the light.

When the three resurrected frogs were once again swimming around in their jar, Père Grenouille prepared to empty their temporary residence. Looking like a human fire hydrant, he stood with his hands on his hips, his face purple, and ejected a horizontal jet of water as round as his wrist. People in the crowd jumped back out of the way laughing and shrieking; several of them were splashed. There were a few more coins thrown; Le Père Grenouille had been wise to get his payment in advance. He shouted that he was available for celebrations and fetes, wedding parties and other events; a message left with the ticket taker at Métro Gaieté would reach him. He held his hand to his side, breathing hard, as he stooped to pick up the wet coins at his feet; alertly, discreetly, the crowd dispersed to avoid a last challenge to their generosity. "Misers!" Père Grenouille shot after them. He wasn't laughing. He wasn't dancing any more.

Carnot turned away. Before him the expanse of pavement ended in the abrupt façade of stately matched buildings that stretched in a line across the square to the barren winter trees of the Avenue Gabriel. Across the Rue de Rivoli just to his right he looked at the Talleyrand. During the war it was the German Ministry of Marine, he thought. Now Americans.

He looked again at the crowd in the square and thought of something he had once heard, that a strike is a workingman's outing—thought of the bitter cynicism in the double meaning. And yet they *were* like children on a picnic. He watched a group of two young girls and a boy. They were talking, and every once in a while one of the girls would throw back her head and laugh gaily. The boy was wearing a jacket that was too small for him and his knobby arms stuck too far out of the sleeves, which were patched in leather at the elbows. He seemed to be the object of the girl's good-natured teasing; she kept gesturing toward the other girl. Carnot immediately recognized something of himself in the shyness and awkwardness of the boy, and a sense of tenderness went through him for the girl, who was obviously gay and happy and teasing only because she was with him. She was a very plain girl but the cold had made her cheeks red and when she laughed she was beautiful to see. Carnot felt a sudden pang of unreasoning irritation and turned away from the parapet.

Before he realized what he was doing Carnot had turned around and was walking the other way. He moved slowly over the frozen grass, was still annoyed with himself. The stub of his amputated arm began to throb dully. It occurred to him that he could stop at the sculptures along the way instead of looking in shop windows full of high-priced tinsel for tourists, which nevertheless always fascinated him.

There was one group of sculpture in particular that he liked—a rhinoceros killing an enormous tiger. The rhinoceros had one massive foot planted on the huge cat's belly and you could fairly feel the tiger squirm. He tried to remember the name of the sculptor, but to his annoyance it eluded him and he decided to allow himself to look at the name only one more time. It wasn't important. But he shouldn't have forgotten it. If he didn't remember it this time, he thought, he wouldn't allow his curiosity the easy satisfaction of looking again. It's your last chance, he instructed himself.

He walked quickly, with purpose in his stride, and approached the great bronze animals, the one immobile, terrifying in victory, the other forever in the act of death; he went around the back to search for the signature on the pedestal.

XVII

The hearing room was long and narrow, and the mahogany table was shaped to fit the room. On the side opposite the long row of floor-length windows was an ornate fireplace flanked by two tall sentry-like door-handled mirrors. Stone surveyed the walls in silence. The rest of the room was without doors and unrelieved in its bareness except for the wine-red carpet and drapes. The huge table top was one solid piece of mahogany, warm and lustrous with age. It glowed red where slotted patches of late morning sunlight lay heavily across its width of ancient wood; pouring through seven brilliant gashes in the closed crimson drapes, the sun spilled its cold liquor across the wine-dark varnish and made the heavy crystal ashtrays blaze.

No one spoke. Colonel Lasher stared at the papers on the table in front of him and at the three newly sharpened pencils neatly squared and centered on the virgin pad of white paper that lay between his small idle hands. With his left hand he fingered an unlighted cigarette. Mr. Sellers, the general counsel, continued to read silently to himself with unhurried deliberation, glancing up from time to time as if to count noses. Once or twice he glanced at the thin-chained gold watch he had placed on the table before seating himself. It was a ritual.

The mirrored door to the left of the fireplace opened and a white-jacketed steward brought in three shining vacuum bottles on a tray and placed them around the table with the usual cellophane-wrapped glasses. He left without rippling the hush, pulling the tall mirror carefully shut behind him. The only sound was the ticking of Sellers' watch and the slow rustle of turned pages as he continued to study the brief in front of him. It was three minutes to eleven when Byron Sweet came in through the other door and sat down in the chair to the left of that at the head of the table without looking at anyone; the security chief opened his briefcase with a sharp snap and carefully ranged his papers in front of him. Then he sat back and lighted a cigarette. He glanced at Clarence Lasher opposite and nodded. The set expression on Lasher's face didn't change. He snapped a lighter and lighted the cigarette he'd been holding when Sweet came in. He stared at the ceiling and smoked. At his end of the long table were only Sweet and himself. The chair at the very head, where the Ambassador usually sat, was empty.

Stone reached for the shining decanter of ice water. His mouth felt dry. He moved his hands with deliberate, abrupt purpose to cover the uncertainty he felt. What *were* they going to face him with? Thoughts of the past flitted through his mind like moths from a closet. He unwrapped the loud cellophane and filled the glass. He took a sip of water and stilled his mind by staring fixedly at Sellers' watch, concentrating on it, memorizing every detail of it. It was an old trick.

These men have no power over me, thought Stone. They can't touch me if I don't let them. He tried to recall the words of Erasmus. No man is hurt except by himself—something close to that. It must be nearly time. This can't last long.

The general counsel picked up the watch from the table, winding the thin gold chain in the thick tangle of his fingers; he sat for a moment as though weighing the watch in his right hand, and then let it dangle and untwirl itself. He would hold the watch in his hand—Stone predicted silently—running the chain through his deliberate fingers, all through the meeting. At the end of the conference he would slip the watch unobtrusively into his waistcoat pocket. Now he put the watch down; Stone smiled inwardly when a moment later he saw the general counsel's right hand move toward the watch, again groping for it, finding it. He was still reading quietly as he picked it up—an almost unconscious gesture.

Sweet looked judicial. He was silent for a long moment now as he glanced around at the small group, at Sellers obliviously weighing the watch. Sellers looked like a youngish patriarch about to bend his head for grace, for blessing on the bread.

"This is repugnant business, Mr. Stone," he said at last. "For everyone here, I'm sure. Mr. Sellers and Colonel Lasher and the Ambassador have privately expressed to me their misgivings about it. I hope that you will find it in your heart to bear them no ill will, whatever the outcome of this hearing may be."

Stone nodded. "Is this a hearing?"

"More precisely, it's a review," said Lasher.

Sweet nodded. "You have certain rights under the law, Mr. Stone. And I stress the voluntary nature of your appearance. You have, as I have told you, the right to have counsel of your own choosing present at this—and any other—hearing, but I assume that a man of your experience is perfectly capable of interpreting the Act of Congress under which your record is being reviewed." Byron Sweet smiled.

"A sea lawyer likes to lose his own cases," said Stone with studied affability.

Grunts of polite laughter around the table.

"At least you save the fee," said Sweet.

The laughter was more relaxed. Stone alerted himself to the fact that Sweet was deliberately trying to allay the tension around the table.

"You will notice that the stenographer is not present yet," continued Sweet. "I have asked him to wait outside because there are a few things I want to say to clear the air before we begin. When I have had my say, there may be something that Mr. Sellers may want to add, and I think we can all speak a bit more freely without the calculated presence of an eavesdropper."

Mr. Sellers waved off his option to speak. A small dark thickset man with pale, unbelieving eyes behind watery lenses, he glanced up with quickened interest and blinked like an owl coming into the light. Stone liked him but was glad he didn't know the man. It made their present relationship easier. Stone sensed that Sellers didn't relish the proceeding.

"First, some Fourth of July oratory," said Sweet. "I never mind discussing fundamental things in fundamental situations. I'm going to allow myself the expansive luxury of moralizing a wee bit. . . .

"This type of hearing has always caused me a good deal of worry. Abe," he said, addressing Sellers, "I suppose as a lawyer you have found some way of coping with this feeling, but I must admit I haven't yet, even though it's part of my job. There are certain aspects of this type of proceeding that I simply find repugnant, largely because of its quasi-legal nature, I suppose. First, the burden of proof is on Mr. Stone. You must prove, Mr. Stone, that you are not tainted. Second, you cannot under the law demand a confrontation with your accusers —informants, agents, call them what we will. Third, you cannot cross-examine testimony because that testimony has been given in secret. Fourth, you have no guarantee that you will not be placed in double, or triple, or quadruple jeopardy. There is never any formal termination of this sort of trial. You can be called to account over and over again."

Lasher nodded again and again as Sweet struck off the points of objection. Stone felt a wary exultation. It was the first solid indication of Sweet's feelings that he had had.

"Finally, I, as mock judge of a mock trial, feel intensely the burden of that mockery. I have convened this hearing because I am requested to do so under the law, Mr. Stone, having most properly been requested to do so. I find myself in the ungraceful attitude of presuming to sit in judgment on a man over whom I have no judgment. You have a record as an efficient and faithful employee of the government. You have worked hard and well. You have discharged every task put you with vigor and forthrightness. If it were mine to judge, I would judge you well. But the fact is that I can only recommend further action. I am only another employee. My highest recommendation would still be nothing but a mock judgment, subject to the vagaries of bureaucracy. Do you understand, in a word, what I am here to do?"

Stone heard applause, an astounding flat patter of hands. He looked up and saw the owlish, unsmiling face of the general counsel. "Good speech," said Sellers. He was clapping slowly and deliberately, as though he were alone in a box at the opera, except that he hadn't bothered to remove his elbows from the table and his expression hadn't changed. There was laughter, good-natured laughter, and Stone felt like reaching across the table and shaking Sellers' pudgy right hand.

"Mr. Stone, we are not ranged against you here," said Sweet. "But it is true that I am determined not to jeopardize the foreign service at a time when our country needs it most. There are no 'charges' against you. Only certain information. Nothing unusual. It was felt in Washington that I should be here out of courtesy to you and the Ambassador, if nothing else. But on the more practical side, there are certain matters of policy which attach to this investigation—matters which Colonel Lasher quite properly felt he was not qualified to handle. Also, it is a little awkward for his chief. So they sent me to save Clarence the embarrassment."

Lasher knitted his brows and scribbled intently on his pad. He was drawing circles.

"All this the Ambassador knows, I think," Sweet went on. "I welcome the opportunity to clear myself of any charges of malice before we begin. This is indeed a repugnant business. If Clarence and I weren't here to do it, somebody else would. I am forced to perform my duties in the precise manner the law stipulates. I am answerable not only to the Secretary and the President, but to the Congress of the United States as well. You read the papers as well as I do. Now, it is true that ours is a government of laws, not of men. But just as there are imperfect men, so there are imperfect laws. This new law—the law which created my job—may be a very imperfect law. I cannot improve or discard the law. Congress must do that. I can never know whether I am performing the Lord's work or the Devil's. I only know that I am performing the will of the American people as expressed through their elected representatives."

Stone was beginning to feel uneasy at the long apology-in-advance.

"I must admit—and this is strictly off the record—that I never envisaged this kind of situation, when the law was first passed. I earnestly hope that I can, with good conscience, find some way of resolving everything in your favor, Mr. Stone. But I will be candid with you. The case against you could be serious. Unless it is mistaken. It depends on you."

Sweet pressed a button on the table. Instantly the mirrored door opened and the conference reporter, a thin birdlike man with steel spectacles, came into the room. He carried a folding chair and the stand for his stenotype machine. He unfolded the stand with professional aplomb, like a violinist setting up a music rack, and secured his instrument onto it. He sat down with professional unobtrusiveness and posed over his keys.

Sweet picked up the brief in front of him.

"The charges," he said with mock-melodramatic irony. The recorder's fingers moved dreamily over his instrument, the tape moved and stopped. He waited. "Strike that," said Sweet. The stenographer ripped it off and crumpled it.

"You've read the copy I sent you, Mr. Stone, haven't you?"

"No," said Stone, surprised. "I've received no copy of anything."

The negative answer had a curious effect. Lasher and Sellers looked up from their copies of the brief and stared. Everyone in the room, including the recorder, was looking at Stone. They knew, he could tell, that he was telling the truth. It could only be the truth. The general counsel stared at him with his pale wet lenses and suddenly laughed.

When it appeared that Stone hadn't received his copy of the brief, Sweet barred discussion of it. Nor would he allow it to be read, sprung on Stone by surprise. Lasher seemed annoyed.

For a time, totally ignored as the conversation revolved around a question of procedure, Stone occupied himself by folding a slip of paper into the shape of an airplane. Then he crumpled it and twisted it into the shape of a mouse, complete with whiskers and tail.

There were a few routine questions from Sweet about Stone's French associations. The meeting bogged for a time with Stone politely trying to pin Sweet and Lasher down as to the broad nature of the brief. Futile. There were no formal charges, Sweet insisted, emphasizing his dislike of the word "charges." This was simply a preliminary hearing. The derogatory information in Stone's file was "unevaluated." "Raw data," as Lasher called it. There was no way of telling where it came from, Sweet said. The "raw data" was gathered by the Federal Bureau of Investigation and other agencies and transmitted to the State Department unevaluated. It was impossible to know its source, since these agencies never divulged informants. Sweet pointed out rather pedantically the "utter necessity of protecting sources of information." They could be simply cranks, he said. Stone was annoyed, suddenly afraid again. The discussion around the table became acid only once, when Stone was nudged by circumstances into a vexatious exchange with Lasher, who had suddenly become voluble—as though he'd been chafing on a leash.

"Colonel Lasher," Stone asked finally, after Lasher insisted for the tenth fatuous time that Stone wasn't "on trial"—"Colonel Lasher, do you conceive of your job as being nonpolitical?"

Absently, Stone dropped the paper mouse into the mouth of the water decanter, mildly surprised that it fell in.

"Nonpolitical?" Lasher asked warily. "How do you mean?"

"Are you, in a word, above politics?" At this point Stone saw the general counsel look up. His eyes narrowed slightly as he watched Stone, interested.

"Why, of course I'm above politics. This is a completely nonpartisan . . . ."

"I don't believe you," said Stone. There was silence.

"I can't blame you for being upset," said Sweet finally. "But, Mr. Stone, there's a rather nasty implication in what you just—"

"Of course there is," said Stone.

"Well, now," said Lasher, recovered, smiling broadly. "Why don't you believe me, Mr. Stone?"

"I have known government people for several years," Stone said. "Only a politician would say he is above politics."

"Tact is sometimes a necessary form of dishonesty, Mr. Stone," said Sweet. He wasn't smiling any longer.

"You're being tactful?"

"I'm being tactful, Mr. Stone," said Sweet. "But I'm afraid you're not."

At that point Sellers stepped into the conversation and sharply changed the subject.

"It seems that you wrote a booklet, Mr. Stone," said Sellers. "It was some time ago."

"I never wrote any booklet," said Stone quickly, pouncing on the error. "I *thought* there might be something like this." His manner was a little too unrestrained in triumph.

"Evidently your booklet has been cited by a House subcommittee . . ." said Sweet, forgetting his ruling about the unread brief.

"The subcommittee," said the general counsel unexpectedly, "is a committee of sub-morons, of course. Sub-sub-subcommittee."

Sweet ignored the interruption. ". . . as being counter to the interests of the United States."

Stone said, "I never *wrote* a booklet, even several years ago. What is this booklet and whose interests does it supposedly counter to?"

"Whose United States?" asked the general counsel of no one, smiling wistfully.

"It is my understanding," said Sweet, confused, "that this booklet of yours was prepared for briefing consular personnel throughout the Far East."

"What? Me?" asked Stone, with astonished laughter.

"It was not written to be a best seller, that's true. I believe it carried a classification of 'secret.' "

"Classic texts are never best sellers," said the general counsel. "At first."

"You've read the pamphlet, Mr. Sellers?" asked Sweet, mildly surprised.

"Abe Sellers reads everything," said Lasher.

"Yes," said Sellers, nodding aimlessly.

"But I didn't write it," said Stone, completely lost.

" 'Yes,' you've read it; or 'yes,' you read everything?" Sweet asked the general counsel, with heavy humor.

Sellers looked at Lasher as if he were some rare specimen of caterpillar. Then he looked away with his watery blue owl eyes and shrugged.

There was a long silence while everyone leafed through papers or stared studiously at the ceiling. Stone sat stunned, suddenly looked around the table. They were going on as though he wasn't there. Reality slipped away like passing time.

"Both," said the general counsel finally. "But who cares?"

Stone attempted a good-natured laugh, but it escaped like a bubble of air under water, an inaudible belch.

There was more circular discussion about Stone's past work in government service. Mostly it revolved around the mysterious booklet. It was aimless, desultory.

Time dragged on, liquid and unreal; it was almost twelve. Stone was finding it impossible to concentrate at all now.

Finally he gave up trying to find out what they wanted of him, and just let himself drift, etherized with the talk. All purpose escaped him, like gas from a slow-leaking balloon. Once or twice he answered questions addressed to him, but he had stopped thinking. He was getting irritable, and getting hungry.

Finally the general counsel quietly put his watch back in his waistcoat pocket. Five minutes later the preliminary hearing was abruptly over.

As they all left the room Sellers said to Stone: "You're none the wiser." He and Stone were the last to go out. Smoke hung blue and thin in the air of the abandoned conference room; one ashtray had spilled over with debris.

"I'm wiser," said Stone. "Or I'm mad. One or the other."

"Cheer up," said Sellers. "All you can lose is your head."

"Of course."

"Crime doesn't pay," said Sellers conspiratorially. Stone liked him.

"Whose crime?" asked Stone, amused though still a little bewildered and angry.

"Our crime. Whose else? Sweet is only the Mad Hatter. You're the dormouse."

"I suppose they think I'm guilty as sin, for God's sake," said Stone, suddenly annoyed.

"Of course," said Sellers, staring with his blue owl eyes. "We're all guilty for God's sake. That's a joke. A theological joke."

"I'm going to prove that they're crazy if it's the last thing I do."

"You might. They may be. But so what?"

"We must talk about it someday."

"Let's go eat in luxury. I'd like to know you better before you go to pieces."

XVIII

The restaurant was small and unremarkable. The menu was limited and Stone ordered what Sellers recommended, *paupiette de veau*. Wine and bread were laid on the worn marble table top—there was no table-cloth—and two *couverts* were clattered into place by a bored waiter, who then vanished into the kitchen.

"You are a dead duck," Sellers said, moodily dismembering a small piece of bread. "I suppose you know that."

"No," Stone said.

"A security inquiry is like a taint of the plague. Sooner or later you'll have to resign. Even if you are cleared, the taint remains. No one will risk having you in their office for fear of the contagion. You're a leper; that is, a suspected leper. I don't know which is worse."

"You're rather pessimistic."

"I'm merely accurate," Sellers said.

"But my job isn't sensitive. I haven't seen a secret document since—I don't know when. I'm merely a graveyard worker, a caretaker of the gallant dead."

"You could sabotage the tombstones by mixing up names or something."

"I hope you're not serious."

"I hope so too," Sellers said. "You've got the wrong idea. Security has nothing to do with common sense. If it did, there wouldn't be any such thing as loyalty oaths and such idiotic nonsense—as though a dedicated spy would hesitate to take a loyalty oath—stupid nonsense. This whole business is irrational. It borders on national insanity."

"I think you're exaggerating."

"You'll see," Sellers said.

"Do you know anything I don't know?" Stone asked.

"Not really. I know that you've made a rather unfortunate enemy out of one of our Congressional sub-morons."

"Kreuger?"

"Do you need confirmation?"

"No," Stone said.

"Kreuger is a fool, but a vindictive fool. He believes that he grows in power in proportion to the number of notches he has on the handle of his meat ax. Did you know that ever since he entered politics he has kept a blacklist?"

"No."

"Well, it's true. And you, my friend, are on it. He once succeeded in getting a taxi driver's license revoked—the driver refused to take him to Philadelphia at four o'clock in the morning. Kreuger likes to tell that story to impress people with his bulldoggedness, as he calls it. Basically he's merely stupid. He knows this, I think, and tries to compensate for a fundamental lack of intelligence by seeking an excess of power."

"I'm on his list," Stone said. "You're probably right."

"I heard about the mud-from-the-boys exploit. You hit him right where he's most sensitive, right in the middle of his constituency. The Kreuger opposition back home made great political capital out of that blunder of his. He had his heart set on having his name attached to that crazy bill, you realize. Do you remember the speech he made in the House, the 'bring our boys back home, bring *all* our boys back home' speech? I'm sure he holds you partly responsible for having deprived him of his chance for immortality. He'll never get a bill named after him now. He's too well known as an idiot. He didn't even invent that remark about the mud and the boys—I heard it in the First World War."

"What has he got to do with my security status?"

"Nothing. Except that he's expressed interest in your 'case.' That means—look at it this way—if anyone hires you that person is running counter to Mr. Kreuger's expressed will. Therefore that person joins you on Mr. Kreuger's blacklist. Which is by no means fatal, but it can be a damn nuisance when you're trying to get an appropriation out of committee. He has all sorts of foolish little ways to hold you up. If ever anyone tells you the American legislature doesn't truly represent the people, you can point to Kreuger. *Someone* has to represent the illiterates. Kreuger's a natural."

"Are you saying that Kreuger is taking a personal hand in this?"

"No. He has merely let it be known several times that he considers you dangerous and un-American—whatever that means. He won't meddle directly, unless—" Sellers paused in mid-sentence.

"Unless what?"

"There's talk of a special investigating committee to look into Dujardin's charges, specifically the charge that he was beaten by American military personnel and forced to sign a phony confession."

"Kreuger's idea?"

"Not entirely. Kreuger could only be the tool. You see, he's firmly convinced that the war against Germany was a mistake. There are a lot of people who believe that Germany and Russia should have been allowed to 'destroy each other.' How that was going to come about they don't bother their little pointed heads about. Kreuger still talks of the United States' entry into the war in Europe as 'meddling in a European quarrel.' He believes that; only he's learned the hard way that it's a very unpopular thesis to expound in public, so he keeps quiet about it. But he hasn't changed his mind. There are a lot of people like him in the States. They're mostly stupid, but they have sense enough to keep their political noses clean. But any indirect way of exposing Roosevelt's folly in fighting England's battle has a natural appeal for them. It's going to come out that you worked with Communist organizations in France during the German occupation."

"I imagined that would be an issue."

"I've made it my business to look into that a little. I think you're clean. But it won't do you any good to point out that the Communist underground was fighting Germans for us here, any more than it's worth pointing out that Russia was an ally. It's all very discouraging. You're a victim of history, Stone. Caught in the middle."

"I won't resign."

"I was afraid of that."

"Look, I'm over forty. I have no particular occupational skills. I once knew how to play a fairly decent cello sonata, but I've even forgotten that. I could go back to teaching French, I suppose. But I'm happy here. I've found a job that will keep me in Paris—I studied music here as a youngster and a lot of my happiest memories are buried here in this city. I left France and went home to become a young concert artist once, so I thought. In the thirties I taught pimply adolescents how to use their fingers for something more elegant than picking their noses. For what? For nothing, really. I never thought I was an artist. In those days an artist was just another slacker out of a job, which is what an artist always is in America, perhaps. Anyway, my fingers forgot what teachers in Trenton, New York and Paris had drilled into them. In college I'd had a job working for the telephone company stringing cable underground through sewers. I did that at night and taught one little girl how not to play Schubert by day. The only really satisfying job I ever had was playing the organ at the Bordentown State School for Wayward Girls. I made four dollars every Sunday, and they had a good organ, believe it or not. Some old lady left it to them in her will. I would have done it for nothing. But there weren't enough wayward girls, so they closed the place. I taught French and music in a New Jersey high school at eighteen hundred dollars a year. I also coached the band. And that, Mr. Sellers, is the story of my life.

"In other words, Mr. Sellers, until the war came along I never knew I was a failure—I haven't even found redemption in marriage. I didn't ask for the job I've got now. I got into Graves Registration through a chance assignment—a colonel who didn't even like me. But I found that I liked the job. There's something tragic and ennobling, perhaps, about burying the dead. Anyway, I make nearly nine thousand a year as an administrative expert. And I'm in Paris."

"Scene of your boyhood triumph," Sellers said. He was nervously tearing off pieces of bread and chewing them as Stone talked.

"*Dreams* of triumph," Stone said.

"Yes."

"I won't resign. How could I resign? I'm good at what I'm doing. They call me an expert, even. I take it seriously, you see. I *like* what I'm doing."

"I feel very sorry for you, Stone."

"Are you being sarcastic?"

"No. I'm not being sarcastic," Sellers said. "You see, I don't like what I'm doing. Shaw said something about the tragedy of our age being the devotion of a man to a cause he knows in his heart to be base."

"You think it's base to work for the government?"

"No. I think it's base to work against it."

"I don't follow your—"

"I'm not working in the interest of the government by hectoring you, for example."

"Then I'm going to be axed anyway, is that right?"

"Have you read the Internal Security Act?"

"No."

"I didn't think you had. Have you read the executive orders that have grown out of it?"

"No."

"I think you should engage counsel, Mr. Stone. You're an innocent in these matters, I see."

"What will you have to do with it?"

"I am a lawyer, Mr. Stone. I am hired by the government to render opinions pertaining to matters of law. If my opinion doesn't agree with that of the persons who solicit it—"

"—they'll hire another lawyer, is that it?"

"Unfortunately, Mr. Stone, the government's conscience is the lawyer for the government's will. The government's will is very clearly expressed in the law under which you are being, shall we say, arraigned. I don't know what to say to you . . ."

"Perhaps you've said enough already."

"Yes, perhaps I have," Sellers said. He looked depressed. "Let me ask you something. Who do you think is to blame for this situation?"

"I don't know."

"*No one* is to blame, Mr. Stone. That's what makes it terrifying."

"Perhaps Karl Marx," Stone said, smiling grimly. "Or Charles Darwin."

"Marx said something about—" Sellers paused.

"About what?"

"About certain governments containing the seed of their own destruction. Would you have thought that it might come in the form of an Act of Congress?"

"Aren't you being a little dramatic?"

"What's dramatic about history?" Sellers asked mildly, pausing. "Everything about history is dramatic, Mr. Stone."

The waiter brought the food and placed it carelessly on the table. Sellers tore off the last piece of bread. He looked up at the waiter and asked, "Have you any more bread?"

The waiter shrugged, the bored expression on his face remaining unchanged. "No more bread," he said. He gestured vaguely toward the street outside. "The strike," he said, as though referring to a natural cataclysm in some distant land. He turned his back and walked toward the kitchen.

Two more customers came in off the street and looked around at the deserted restaurant. They took a table near the door.

Stone pushed his portion of bread across the table to Sellers. "I don't want mine," he said. "I wouldn't eat it anyway."

"Thanks," Sellers said. "Shall we drop the subject?"

"What subject?"

"You and Karl Marx and Darwin and the other prime movers of history."

"You're forgetting—"

"And Kreuger, too."

Stone laughed. "Perhaps we can just enjoy the meal."

"For what it's worth," Sellers said. "I feel like I'm sharing the last meal of the condemned."

"Cheer up," Stone said. "The worm will turn."

"Yes," said Sellers, brightening mawkishly, "the worst is yet to come. Are you ready for the press conference this afternoon?"

Stone looked at Sellers, shrugged helplessly, and said nothing. They ate in silence.

XIX

After lunch Stone left Sellers on the corner of the Rue St. Florentin, and returned to the Embassy alone. He was just about to enter the elevator in the front lobby when he heard his name being called. He turned around and saw the secretary from the military attaché's office. She was holding an envelope in her hand.

"I'm so glad I caught you," she said. She was a nervous woman who had a perpetually worried look on her face. "I didn't know where in the world to find you."

Stone smiled and nodded politely.

She waved the envelope in her hand. "This just came for you. It's a pneumatic, or whatever they call them." She handed Stone the message.

"*Pneumatique.*" Stone corrected her. Automatically his fingers slid under the flap.

"Why in the world do they call them that?" the secretary asked. "I've been here for six months and I still don't know what they are, except that people are always getting them."

"They call it that because it's sent through pneumatic tubes. Department stores back home used to have them." He unfolded the message, looking at it first for a signature. There was none. "Only in Paris the tubes go all over the city."

"Now isn't that clever," she said. "Who would have thought it? You mean those tubes that make a sucking sound when the clerk opens them?"

Stone looked up. "I'm sorry," he said. "I was reading what it says. Clerk?"

"In the department stores. They used to keep me waiting for hours with those things, waiting for my change."

"Oh, yes. That's right." Stone's mind was on the message.

"Bad news?" she asked with bland solicitude.

Stone looked at her. "Er—what? Bad news? Oh, no." Then he said, "It's just that my cat is sick."

The woman stood for a moment looking at him. "Your *cat?*"

"Oh, don't worry. He's always sick. He's a chronic hypochondriac."

The secretary looked uncertain. Stone kept a dead-serious expression on his face. Finally she said, "Well, I'm glad I caught you. I didn't know where in the world to find you." She turned to go, then added, "I hope he is better."

"Who?" Stone asked, taking malign pleasure in the woman's humorless gullibility.

"Your cat."

"Oh, yes. I'll tell him," he said, waving the message.

"Well, I'm glad I found you, Mr. Stone."

And she was off across the lobby. Stone watched her go, wondering if she wore a girdle or if it was just her natural walk.

The message was unsigned and he assumed without a second thought that it was from Solange. She had said she would telephone him for lunch, but she hadn't. Still, it was odd that she'd send a *pneu,* except that Parisians were addicted to them. There was no one else he could think of who would send an unsigned message.

He looked at the message again, puzzling. It read: "Meet me alone at two o'clock on the bench near the water fountain. Urgent."

The question was what bench, what water fountain. Obviously they must be in the little park between the Champs Elysées and the Avenue Gabriel, since that was the only place near the Embassy that had benches. He thought, All I have to do is find the water fountain. It must be right there.

He stuffed the message in his pocket and started toward the elevator. Just then he glanced at the clock over the reception desk. It was two o'clock exactly. He checked it against his wristwatch, which confirmed it. Automatically he buttoned his coat again.

He walked out of the Embassy wondering: What could be so urgent?

There was one bench that was closer to a water fountain than all the others. Solange wasn't there yet, and he thought: It couldn't be too urgent. Sitting on the bench beside the dry fountain was a man reading a newspaper. He had it creased lengthwise and held it in one hand, like a man reading on a bus. Stone took a seat at the other end of the bench.

There were a few nurses and governesses around on the other benches, their white uniforms peeping out at the hems of their dark winter coats. A group of red-cheeked children were disputing over who should stand near the fountain. Stone watched them, enjoying their shrill, excited babble, and tried to make out from the snatches of piping dispute what the object of the game was. Finally he figured out that the aim was to touch the fountain without being tagged by the defender of the fountain.

Just as the play was beginning, Stone became conscious that the man on the other end of the bench had moved closer, still reading the paper.

Suddenly the man said, in French, "You were three minutes late."

Stone wasn't certain he was being addressed because the man never took his eyes off the newspaper, so for the moment he said nothing.

Then the man said, "You never used to be late. Don't recognize me. We might be watched."

It was Carnot. It was actually Carnot.

For a moment Stone was too surprised to say anything. Then he asked, "Why all the cloak and dagger, Alexi? The war's over."

"The war is never over, my friend Dante."

It was the first time anyone had called him by his code name since the war. Stone was caught in confusion. "What's all this, anyway?" he asked.

"Did anyone follow you here?"

Stone said nothing.

"I have to be careful. I can't take risks. But this is a risk."

Instinctively, Stone glanced around casually. There was no one except the nurses. "What do you want to see me for?" Stone asked sharply.

"You're not pleased to see me, are you?" Carnot asked.

"From what I hear I haven't got much reason to be pleased, would you say?"

"Ah, you mean Dujardin. My deposition."

"Your perjury."

"First let me ask you. Do you think I am satisfied with what I have been forced to do? That is why I arranged to meet you. There are a few things I have to explain to you."

"No one can force you to lie," Stone said. "Or have you lost your stomach for the truth?"

"Sometimes you have to lie to make history true."

Stone shook his head slowly. "My God," he said, "I never thought you'd finally go under. What's happened, Alexi?"

For the first time, Carnot turned and looked at Stone. . . .

It was a shock, not sharp, but a slow realization that something had changed the man beyond caring. It was even hard to connect the face with the strong young face of the man Stone had known during the war. Then Stone remembered what Merseault had said on the telephone that morning, and realized that the reason Carnot was holding the paper in one hand was that he had only one. The sleeve of the other arm was empty.

Carnot said sadly, "They say I'm crazy. I know there is something wrong, but I'm not crazy. I only act crazy to get them to do what I want them to do. I only act crazy. You must remember that. But I don't have to tell you. You knew me *then*." He stressed the word then, giving it a surreptitious twist. He even looked around him when he said it, as though he was looking for eavesdroppers. He looked at the children for a long time, and then said, "They are even clever enough to make a child do their work. You must not underestimate them. They are everywhere."

"Who?"

"All of them. They are everywhere. Watching. Listening. Intercepting messages."

Carnot turned and looked full at Stone. His eyes, Stone thought, his eyes. He looks absolutely happy.

And suddenly he realized that Carnot had truly gone mad. Stone thought: His mind is gone. The poor bastard.

"You must be careful," Carnot said. Stone said nothing.

The children playing around the fountain darted in and out. Some were caught; some touched the fountain and clung to it. Three of them made a chain of hands and tried to extend the fountain's haven by conduction, but this tactic, which made defense nearly impossible, aroused strong protests from the lone defender. The game was temporarily stopped while the rules were argued. One little girl, who seemed too young to quite follow the necessities of the game, nevertheless enjoyed the argument and jumped up and down clapping her hands. When the game started again she was the first one caught.

"What is that game they're playing?" Stone asked.

"Game?" Carnot turned his head and looked at the children. "I don't know. It's a children's game. Why are you interested in the game they are playing?"

"Because I don't quite understand it, I suppose."

Carnot said nothing, but looked briefly at Stone and then looked away. His newspaper was still held open in his hand.

There was a long silence, while Stone waited for Carnot to speak again. He was wondering how Carnot had known enough to send the message to the Embassy instead of the Graves Registration Command. He decided to wait and ask him later. Finally Carnot said, as though he had read Stone's thoughts, "I knew you'd be at the Embassy because you are having a press conference there this afternoon. Isn't that true?"

"Yes, that's true."

167

"You will make a statement?"

"I don't think I am in a position to discuss the matter with anyone outside the Embassy. Are you worried, Alexi?"

"Why should I worry? They can't touch me. I have something that will take care of them." Carnot nodded to himself and muttered something Stone couldn't hear. Then he said, "They think they will drop me. But they can't drop me. When the newspapers come out this afternoon, I will be famous. Then I will have enough power to make them do what I want. You will see, my friend Dante. You think I am a fool. You think I am crazy, but you will see." Carnot laughed a forced laugh, almost like a stage laugh, full of empty menace. Then abruptly he stiffened and fell to studying his paper again. Under his breath he said, "You see that nurse over there? The one with the package on her lap?"

Stone looked. He saw a middle-aged woman sitting placidly, talking to a child who sat on the bench beside her. In her lap was a brown paper package.

"What about her?" Stone asked.

"Why isn't that child playing with the rest?" Carnot asked.

"For God's sake, Alexi. Who cares? She might be Mata Hari, but so what?"

"She has a camera in her lap, in that package. The child isn't playing because he doesn't know the other children."

Stone looked and said nothing. Carnot might be crazy, but then Stone knew nothing of what sort of game he was playing.

"It's a good thing I noticed her. She just came. I have to leave." Carnot held the paper just high enough to cover the lower half of his face. "I have stayed here too long as it is."

Carnot was up on his feet with his back to the nurse. Hurriedly he folded his newspaper. Then he said, "You must understand that I am not doing what I am doing because I like to. But it is necessary. They are right about that. But they want to take all the credit. I am sorry for you, but you will understand. But you can help me. After I leave, look beside you on the bench. There is something there I want you to keep. Don't lose it, because it is my life if you lose it. Don't look down now."

"I'm not sure I want to get mixed up in your little plot, Alexi," Stone said.

"You have no choice," Carnot said. "You will thank me someday. Say nothing of this meeting or you might cost me my . . . I've taken a great chance to see you and explain everything to you."

Carnot turned without another word and walked away. Stone watched him go. The nurse didn't turn her head or touch the package, and Stone smiled to himself. He thought, If I listened to him long enough I'd go crazy myself. Gradually he relaxed and began turning the disjointed conversation over in his mind. He looked beside him on the bench and found a key, nothing more. He covered it with his palm, and as he got up he dropped it into his pocket. He stood for a while watching the children play, wondering whether to report his meeting with Carnot to Lasher. He knew that he ought to tell someone if only to cover himself, but for the moment he had a strong disinclination to discuss it with Lasher. Then he thought of Merseault. Merseault had asked him this morning about Carnot, and Merseault seemed to be a reasonably discreet man. If it was true that Carnot was taking a real risk, then Merseault would be worth talking to. Stone decided to telephone him right away, before talking to Lasher or anyone else.

Absently, he followed the pattern of movement about the fountain.

Watching the children, thinking about Carnot, he suddenly understood their game. The fountain was both a haven and a prison. If the defender tagged a child trying to touch the fountain before he reached it, then that child became a prisoner and had to remain at the fountain until another child tagged and freed him without being caught. On the other hand, if a child could reach the fountain without being tagged he could rest there and remain invulnerable until he decided to slip away again when the defender was busy elsewhere. There seemed to be no decisive end to the game, but the children played it enthusiastically without worrying about a final object. To Stone it looked like a good game, now that he understood it. He wondered if they had just made it up or if it had a name.

The nurse who had worried Carnot with her package had unwrapped it and was giving the small boy sitting beside her something which he immediately ate. It looked like a small sandwich. Stone laughed to himself and crossed the gravel path and walked back toward the Embassy.

He placed the call to Merseault from the public booth downstairs. Someone answered and said that Merseault was busy on another telephone. He said he would call back and left his name before hanging up. Then to kill time he walked out into the courtyard again, ignoring the impulse to catch a quick drink in the Crillon Bar. Just as he stepped out the door he saw the nurse from the park. The small boy was nowhere in sight and she was hurrying along the sidewalk. Stone watched her, curious. Suddenly, as she reached the corner, a large black car with two men in the front and one in the back stopped at the curb and picked her up. She got in the car quickly, obviously not surprised to see it. Stone said aloud, "That was clumsy of them." He wondered who they were and what they were after. Anyway, Stone thought, old Carnot isn't completely crazy. He wondered who the boy was and where she had borrowed him and where she had deposited him. She didn't waste any time, Stone thought. And that was her error.

Frowning, he turned and went back up the steps of the building. The porter at the door opened it for him. He went directly to the telephone, and called Merseault.

Merseault answered the telephone himself this time. Stone explained briefly about the message and then gave an account of his unexpected meeting with Carnot. Merseault, on the other end of the connection, listened without interrupting, except to grunt affirmatively at various points. Finally Stone paused and waited for Merseault's reaction.

Merseault said nothing for a moment, then: "I'm not surprised. He's not entirely sane any more, despite what he says."

Stone said, "He asked me to say nothing to anyone. He implied that he was in some sort of danger . . ."

"Oh, I suppose he might be. I tell you, why don't we go into it when you come to dinner? In the meantime, I don't know what to advise you. I would rather you kept this to yourself for a day or two, until I can find out who . . ." Merseault paused. Then he said, "We'll discuss it at dinner. Why don't you write it all down in the form of a report—just to cover yourself against any future questions from, well, from your people at the Embassy. Or, if you wish, give them a full account. I can't advise you. However, the fewer people who know about a thing, the better it keeps."

"I saw the woman afterward. She wasn't a nurse. She got into a car with three men about fifteen minutes later."

"Oh?"

"You have any idea who—"

Merseault interrupted affably, "That's one of the things I wanted to check into. But you'll have to give me a little time. Why don't we save the details for our dinner? I have someone coming to see me right now, and I'm afraid I'm rather busy. But tomorrow we'll have time enough."

Stone stared into the mouthpiece of the telephone, thinking, I wonder if he thinks I'm crazy. Then he said, "Fine."

Merseault jumped ungracefully at the opening for ending the conversation. "Good-by, then. I'll see you tomorrow."

And Merseault had hung up. Stone stared into the dead telephone, and slowly put the receiver back on its hook.

XX

Shortly before the afternoon press conference Merseault arrived at the Ambassador's office with a complete transcript of the Carnot deposition—quoted in excerpt in the Assembly that morning—which Dujardin's lawyers had just given to the Ministry of Justice. Without a word Merseault laid the thick document on Sheppard's desk and turned to several sentences he had underlined. They constituted one of the details of Carnot's own eyewitness account of the Montpelle massacre—a detail that hadn't been quoted in the first brief news stories:

> *. . . One of the ten corpses in the pyre was the body of the Wehrmacht sergeant they had impressed into service. He was shot by the SS captain for letting one of the prisoners—it was Berger—catch him by surprise. They threw his corpse onto the pyre with the rest of the prisoners. I was watching from where I was lying. I couldn't tell who the others were. It was dark. That means only nine of the ten corpses were prisoners. Three must have escaped. Not two. . . .*

Sheppard read the words twice in silence, with Merseault watching his face closely. He looked up at Merseault. His face was drawn and tired, pale. "By that reckoning . . ." Tight-lipped, he left the sentence unfinished. "Stone is one. Carnot is two. And a third . . ."

Merseault nodded slowly. "One of the prisoners is still miss— no, unaccounted for," he said. "I'm sorry for this, but I can't see why he would lie about something like that."

"If only the dead could be buried . . ." said Sheppard, shaking his head angrily. "This is still my curse."

"Bruce, don't pursue it any further," said Merseault. "It's becoming an obsession. Let it rest."

"I can talk to Stone," said Sheppard with calm assurance. "And . . ." He gestured vaguely. ". . . others."

"He knows nothing more."

"And Carnot?"

"You are pursuing a ghost, Bruce," said Merseault. "I'm sorry to talk like that. But for nearly three years I have tried to learn for you what happened to . . . I can understand. I've never lost a son, but I lost my brother in the First War."

"Stop, Georges," said Sheppard, his voice patient, tired, resigned. "Please stop. Perhaps I am obsessed, but if I am, please keep it a secret."

"From whom?"

"From myself."

Outside there was the sound of the afternoon crowd milling idly about the square. The Ambassador looked at his watch. The press appointment was to start in twelve minutes.

The press conference was set for three-thirty but was delayed by a brief incident which arrested the attention of several reporters as they entered. They stopped and watched from the steps, idly interested.

In front of the Embassy two embarrassed gendarmes were remonstrating gently with a young Negro dressed in a white toga and a turban who paced back and forth along the narrow strip of sidewalk in front of the high iron pickets of the Embassy fence. He had been there for some time, at first standing quietly, ignored by the police. He was bare-foot despite the cold and he muttered unintelligibly to himself as he walked; the gendarmes talked quietly and earnestly as they kept pace with him. He seemed to be pacing in an effort to shake them off. But just as everyone was about to go back inside the Embassy he suddenly stopped in front of the huge open gates and whirled around. He held his fingers outstretched toward the sky and threw back his head. He gave a shout—"Ho!"—that made the two police jump.

"Ho! And the *voice* of the Lord *came* unto me and said, *'Jeremiah, what seest thou?'* " His voice pounced on words, a clear, vibrant baritone, enormous, stentorian. The two police instinctively stepped back another pace, astounded at its volume and intensity. "And I told the Lord, I *answered*. I told *Him* of the *great black army* hiding in the *night* of the dark trees."

He looked around, his eyes flashing white and rolling wildly. His booming voice and striking appearance arrested the moment completely as he stood with his arms still outstretched. He suddenly seemed tall, and huge.

"Go and *warn* my people, saith the *Lord* unto *me*. And the Lord mixed mud with *silver* spittle and bade me *speak* His prophecies with my *tongue*. Even though *no* man listens. *Even* though my tongue be *cut*. For the wicked *will* prosper and die in the *fire,* and those whose love *is* for the Lord will go *hungry* and live in caves and places dark and *underneath* the earth. So *saith* the Lord God!"

Several more people came out of the Embassy talking and laughing and stopped short at the sight of the tall figure standing, arms upraised, blocking the gate with his back to them.

"For I *will* descend and SMITE the WICKED!" he shouted. "Know that I am God! This I will visit *on* them. I shall breathe my breath, which is as the breath of the fiery sun, on their cities of corruption and they shall vanish forever. I *shall* visit. I will burn out the *eyes* of the wicked with a vision of the *light*. They shall *see* God and be blinded! Then shall I SMITE them! Men die! *Men die!* MEN DIE!"

The man made a strangling guttural cry, anguished, piercing. People watched from a block away.

"WEEP for my people. WEEP for the wicked. WEEP for them. They will *cry out* in pain and suffering and I will grant them *no* ease. *Saith* the Lord God! I shall breathe on their cities that they have builded *up* out of ashes with their *hands*. I shall *destroy* them. I shall destroy *them* and their riches shall come to nothing. I *will* set the wicked against the wicked and the houses of nations shall fall, shall *vanish* into the light and eternal darkness. The *black*birds will *fall* from the dead sky like *rain*. And there shall be *nothing*. SAITH THE LORD GOD!"

He collapsed in a white heap, his eyes rolling back in his head, his whole body shaking. His turban became unwound, ridiculous. The two policemen, flustered, embarrassed, stepped forward and picked him up gently, and laid him awkwardly against the gatepost. But his body was still shaking violently and he appeared to have lost consciousness. Someone came out of the Embassy with a white-coated doctor running behind. The doctor leaned over the young Negro and forced several tongue sticks between his teeth. Working with rapid efficiency, he opened a small bag, extracted a hypodermic and administered an injection while the two police, looking worried and uncertain, held the epileptic prophet. He was rigid from head to toe and shaking violently. His eyes had disappeared under the upper lids and only the whites showed.

Suddenly it stopped. The rigidity went out of him and the young man collapsed. The doctor questioned the two gendarmes briefly and asked the Negro several times if he was American. Finally he heard, nodded weakly. He was pouring sweat. He looked sick, terrified. The doctor signaled to two Marine guards. The white-robed figure was carried into the building on a stretcher, his teeth chattering violently. The doctor walked alongside, gently tucking a blanket around him. The small crowd pressed forward around the gendarmes, asking questions. The two shaken policemen answered questions, shrugged, answered questions, shrugged. One of them explained that they had seen him before. But never in a white robe.

The press conference was divided into two sittings: the general press gathered in the crowded conference room where Stone was to read his statement; afterward there was to be a discreet personal briefing for a few top-ranking correspondents of the friendly press in the Ambassador's private office. Standard procedure.

The conference room seemed smaller than it had that morning. A blue layer of cigarette haze hung like a canopy over the room, undulating gently with the ebb and flow of low movement and conversation. Cadwalader, Lasher, and Stone stood among a group of officials at one end of the room; the reporters, many with their coats and hats over their arms, were admitted at the farther door and pressed against the walls in a U around the opposite end of the long mahogany table. In between was a sort of no man's land with couriers shuttling back and forth passing out mimeographed bilingual copies of "background material" which the reporters accepted, scanned politely, and slid into their pockets, waiting. The conference itself would be held in English. They watched Cadwalader for the signs. Every now and then Cadwalader glanced across the room, then at his watch, sizing up the crowd like an auctioneer. Then the show started.

Stone read in a monotone the statement that Lasher had rewritten. The reporters' restiveness was a measure of their disappointment. The statement reiterated what Stone had said at the old trial, added a few cautious remarks about justice prevailing, something about Franco-American friendship, the wartime alliance. And that was all. Stone stopped reading and looked up at the reporters, shrugged apologetically.

"That's it," he said.

"Mr. Stone," a reporter called out instantly, "one of Dujardin's lawyers has implied that either you or the other American was the informer instead of his client. Would you reply to that?"

There was a hush over the room. Stone opened his mouth to answer but Cadwalader stepped forward. "Whose question?" he asked. The reporter answered with the name of his paper, a left-of-center provincial daily. Cadwalader stepped back.

"I haven't heard anyone say . . ." Stone began. He stopped. "The lawyer is a liar," he said. Behind him Lasher winced perceptibly. "But I don't hold it against him. He's trying to save a man's life." Lasher relaxed.

Several reporters shouted questions. Cadwalader stepped forward and pointed at one of them. The reporter stated his paper's name and asked his question. "Mr. Stone, what did you mean in your statement when you said you were speaking as a private citizen? Does that imply that the Embassy doesn't agree with your position?"

Stone looked blank and instinctively turned around to Lasher, but the colonel was making himself small at the back of the cluster of officials. "I don't know what it means," said Stone frankly. "I seem to be more of a public citizen than—" He was drowned out by laughter from the reporters. Cadwalader laughed with them and stepped forward to rescue Stone.

When the room was silent again Cadwalader spoke. "If everyone wrote his own press releases it would put press officers among the ranks of the unemployed," he said good-naturedly. The reporters laughed again, politely. "The Embassy's position will be made clear in a release which will be given out the day after tomorrow. But in general the Embassy stands behind Mr. Stone. Mr. Stone is an American citizen and this is, after all, *his* Embassy, gentlemen."

Cynical laughter. And more questions. Cadwalader stood in the front line of the attack, a kind of interlocutor or interpreter. He would receive the question, skillfully draw its teeth by restating it—ostensibly to make it clearer—and then he would toss it, harmless, to Stone, who in the meantime had had time to think out an answer. This continued for some time, until a few reporters began to duck around the front of the crowd and slide out the narrow doors. Cadwalader called the conference to an end and thanked the journalists for being there. Stone disappeared into the wings, leaving by the near door with Lasher and several other silent Embassy people. Cadwalader stayed behind, answering a few last questions to cover their retreat.

The closed session in the Ambassador's private office would begin after the building was cleared of the main body of reporters. A small group of well-dressed men loitered inconspicuously behind in the lower lobby, waiting to be called back for the later session. After about a half-hour had passed, Cadwalader descended in the elevator and nodded to the men. They put out their cigarettes and began to drift upstairs, talking together quietly, walking in groups of two or three up the one flight. Only a few took the elevator.

Canapés were served in the Ambassador's outer office, which the secretarial staff had evacuated for the occasion. Their covered typewriters stood mute and black, became repositories for paper plates with half-eaten sandwiches on them and for crumpled paper napkins. Drinks were passed by a white-jacketed steward carrying a tray. The deans of the Paris press corps were all there, mostly bureau chiefs, chief correspondents, wire-service managers. They dressed well and conservatively and drank sparingly. The group looked almost scholarly. Several of them smoked pipes; it could have been a gathering of middle-aged college professors. Cadwalader passed among them, talking to them familiarly and pleasantly. Then the Ambassador came out, greeted them individually, and invited them into his office.

"Bring your provisions with you," he said pleasantly. "Mr. Cadwalader, can you arrange for a general refill of glasses later on?"

Cadwalader nodded, indicating by his expression that it had already been taken care of.

Chairs were brought in from the outer office to make up the complement, and when everyone was settled, the tall doors were shut. Stone was already present with Mr. Sweet and Colonel Lasher. They sat on a couch along one wall.

The last man to enter the room was Douglas Lutelacker, just that moment arrived—dressed carefully in single-breasted gray worsted of expensive English cut, he presented a totally different appearance from his role as Sharktooth, the legendary nemesis of his young employees. It was impossible to discern any trace of the rough manner he affected among his staff. He entered the room with casual familiarity, looked about as though gauging the importance of the gathering; then went directly toward the Ambassador, who was talking, his back turned, in a group with Cadwalader. Cadwalader saw him coming, interrupted the Ambassador as though to signal him, said, "Hello, Doug."

The Ambassador turned around, smiled warmly, and stepped out to shake hands. "Douglas, I thought you weren't coming," he said. "How are you?"

Lutelacker smiled, urbanely at ease; the handshake was warm and sincere. "Am I glad to see *you* back," he said. "Since you've been gone, this place has been in chaos. Did you tell the Secretary happy birthday for me? How was the States?"

"I did that. You have his fond regards. Washington was hectic, as usual."

"I don't know why you even bother to go there any more, Bruce. No one knows anything in Washington except the President, and he's busy."

The Ambassador laughed. "Well, Douglas, some of us have to lie at home for our country."

Lutelacker said, "How did it go down at Walter Reed?"

The Ambassador smiled. "Too early to tell much. My legs are a bit stiff, but I'm still upright. I have to take exercises."

"Too upright, I'd say. Smart generals sit down. When are you going to take a decent vacation for yourself, Bruce?"

"When you quit the newspaper business," Sheppard retorted, smiling.

Cadwalader said, "I hope you'll both be very happy together." He turned to the Ambassador. "In the meantime, sir, I'd like to get this show on the road before we run out of victuals."

The Ambassador patted Lutelacker on the shoulder and said, "All right, you young hobo, sit down."

Cadwalader loudly cleared his throat in the room.

The Ambassador took a seat beside his desk, not behind it, and leaned back casually. His audience was spaced informally around the room.

The Ambassador began a careful recapitulation of the economic factors behind the current strike. He spoke slowly, making his points with quiet emphasis, explaining, unraveling, commenting. He was careful to separate his opinions from observed fact. The talk was illuminating. The Ambassador gave several new insights into the behind-scenes developments preceding the strike, including a brief summary of discussions held in Washington with the French Ambassador. A great deal of hitherto unrevealed information was put before the assembled journalists. No one took notes, in deference to the fact that this was a more or less off-the-record briefing for what Cadwalader usually referred to as "the most-favored press." The most-favored press listened, nodding occasionally with quiet interest. The only sound in the room was the occasional scratch of a match under the Ambassador's quiet voice. The Ambassador ended with an extremely frank appraisal of the United States' position vis-à-vis the touchy situation of the French Government. Then he asked for questions. For a moment there was silence. Then one of the men turned to see if anyone behind him had a question. Someone was about to raise a hand, but he deferred to the other with a polite nod. The man turned around and cleared his throat.

"About your resignation, Mr. Ambassador . . ." he said.

The Ambassador smiled broadly. "Yes, my resignation," he said. "I make a point of resigning every now and then just to prove to myself I still have the courage to do it. There's always the risk that it might be accepted." His face became more serious.

"Did you confer with the President beforehand, sir?"

"It didn't come as a surprise to him, if that's what you mean."

"Did the President want an opportunity to demonstrate publicly that he was backing you?"

"I was flattered by his statement of confidence, of course. But I'm afraid the President keeps his own counsel in these matters."

"Thank you very much, sir. You've answered my question."

"Who's next?" asked the Ambassador. He leaned forward in his chair, appearing to enjoy answering questions. "I must say it's been a long time since we've got together. It's a pleasure to be on the griddle again."

"Mr. Ambassador."

"Yes, Mr. Stephanos."

"Seriously, what is going to happen now that Dujardin has been reprieved?"

"I wish I knew, sir," said the Ambassador, laughing.

"Will the United States take any further official cognizance of . . . well, of the anti-American turn the whole thing has taken?"

The Ambassador smiled again. "Well, sir, we can hardly bury our head in the sand, can we? When someone is throwing mud all over you it doesn't do much good to duck."

Polite laughter. The Ambassador continued.

"Yes. We will take cognizance of all attacks as they occur. We will have a complete statement for you the day after tomorrow. Perhaps I can get you advance copies a little earlier, since you gentlemen have been so patient so long. It was regrettable that I was away from the Embassy when this whole thing broke."

"Will you release the data on . . ." The man turned and nodded apologetically toward Stone sitting on the couch. ". . . Mr. Stone's mission during the war? And the other agent—Berger?"

"Yes. All that will be made available. It has finally been declassified. The United States maintained an embassy in Vichy, which makes this sort of thing rather delicate, you realize. Even though the war is over. A government is naturally reluctant . . ."

The Ambassador stopped, leaving the sentence unfinished. In the rear of the small group two men were engaging in an agitated whispered conversation. One was gesticulating with the point of his pipe to the other, who was listening and nodding soberly. As the Ambassador stopped speaking, the whispering was suddenly loud in the silence. It stopped. The man seemed terribly flustered. The Ambassador smiled gently.

"Do you have a question for me, Mr. White?" asked the Ambassador.

Mr. White twisted the bit of his pipe in his hands and looked at his companion, who nodded a slow serious encouragement. "I'm not sure, sir. That is—it might be fantastic. I don't want to make an impertinent fool of myself."

The Ambassador's face became expressionless. He glanced at Sweet. Sweet raised his eyebrows a fraction and glanced warily at the questioner.

"I mean I don't quite know how to phrase this . . ." continued Mr. White. "I'm sure . . ."

"Ask your question, Mr. White," said the Ambassador, his voice colorless and level.

"Sir, this agent Berger . . . I mean, I know you had missing in the war . . ." The journalist was painfully embarrassed. "You visited the scene of . . ."

There was utter silence.

". . . *Berger* is the French word for shepherd . . . *Antoine,* Anthony . . ."

The words seemed to hang suspended in the room. No one moved. Colonel Lasher, his jaw actually gone slack, stared at the Ambassador. Stone stared at White, then slowly turned his head and looked at the Ambassador. Sweet didn't move a muscle. Seconds dragged by before the Ambassador turned his slow gaze toward the windows.

"You will have the release shortly, I suppose," said the Ambassador. "Byron?"

Everyone in the room turned and looked at Sweet. Sweet nodded slowly.

The Ambassador rose from his chair and walked around behind his desk. He picked up a round paperweight and held it in his hand as though weighing it. He put it down, centering it carefully on a blank square of paper. Then he looked up abruptly.

"My son," he said, explaining with a gesture of one empty hand.

There was a long, uncomfortable silence, an uneasy shifting of positions. Someone in the room cleared his throat. The room was hushed.

Cadwalader stepped forward quietly. "If there are no more questions," he said, "perhaps we should call it a day, gentlemen. I will be at your disposal."

"Thank you for being here, gentlemen," said the Ambassador. He smiled briefly, thinly, automatically.

The members of the press filed out. Douglas Lutelacker paused to communicate a brief glance, a query; reassured by the Ambassador's firm nod, he went out after the others, shaking his head soberly. White remained behind with Sweet, Stone, and Lasher. Cadwalader glanced dubiously at the Ambassador and followed the others out, leaving the doors ajar.

"I'm profoundly sorry, sir," White said.

Sheppard shook hands and placed a hand on his shoulder. "You're a newspaperman, Mr. White."

"But I didn't realize . . ."

"Nonsense. You've merely helped me expedite matters," said Sheppard. "I wish you had guessed it long ago. It's been difficult."

White left looking beaten. Lasher still looked stunned. Sweet stood up abruptly. "Perhaps that's the best way, Bruce," he said.

"Yes," said Sheppard, looking down at the paperweight. He breathed a long sigh of relief and looked up. "I've always found it easier to plunge when the water's cold. It's over before you know it."

The Ambassador took out his watch and looked at it. "If Mr. Merseault is outside ask him to come in, will you?" Sheppard glanced at

Stone, who was still sitting on the couch, looking at him. "We'll want to have a long talk, Mr. Stone. Later. Not now."

Stone nodded and got up. From the outside office the words of Cadwalader drifted over the monotone hum of low voices: ". . . tomorrow, tomorrow. Yes, of course, all day. Tomorrow, gentlemen. Tomorrow . . ."

XXI

Outside in the corridor Stone found Colonel Lasher waiting for him. The cadre of journalists drifted away toward the elevator, Cadwalader in their midst still answering questions, nodding, gesturing with his huge red hands, smiling as best he could in his anxious sweat to get away from them.

Wardell Cadwalader was probably already phrasing out in his mind the cable that he would have to get on the wires notifying Washington of the unexpected turn of events, so that the Department wouldn't be caught flatfooted by the flood of inquiries Cadwalader knew would pour in from Stateside editors and bureau chiefs as soon as the news reached them from Paris. He knew he could get a priority cable to Washington ahead of everybody, clearing the wires if necessary. But the knowledge didn't seem to comfort him; he stood like a nervous footman handing the last three newsmen into the elevators like royalty into a carriage, his head still nodding as though on a hinge in answer to the last inaudible sally of questions as the door closed. He stood a moment before the blank doors after they slid shut, and expelled a huge sigh. The smile vanished from his face instantly, and he turned and hurried back, his face worried, angry, his eyes on the floor, not watching where he was going. If Colonel Lasher hadn't stepped aside, Cadwalader would have run him down. He stopped and looked up, startled, first at Lasher, then at Stone.

"Stone, you still here?" he asked. He sounded harried, perhaps even slightly annoyed.

"I asked Mr. Stone to wait," Lasher said almost apologetically. "I wanted to talk with him before he leaves."

"Oh, fine, Clarence. Fine," Cadwalader said, unconsciously forcing the professional smile onto his face again. "I just wanted to make sure he got transportation. I've reserved a car for you, Mr. Stone. I'll have my girl call down and have him wait. You can't go out the front way with that mob out there. We'll smuggle you out the back way, through the truck entrance."

Stone gave him a silent nod of appreciation. Cadwalader stared at Lasher. "Looks like it hit you as hard as it hit me, Clarence."

Lasher seemed to fumble for words. "I didn't know."

"No one knew except Sweet. He told me this morning because I had to start work on the release. Best-kept secret of the whole bloody war."

Lasher looked embarrassed for some reason, as though intimidated by the mere bulk of Cadwalader. He nodded. Cadwalader took out a cigar and bit off the end of it. His face seemed to relax somewhat. He turned abruptly to Stone and looked at his face, a kind of enigmatic scrutiny in his eyes, the cigar hand arrested in midair.

After an instant he said, "You all right, Stone?"

"Yes," Stone said, his tone a guarded question, as though to inquire of Cadwalader the reason for asking.

"You don't need anything?"

"No," Stone said, this time in a tone of open puzzlement.

"Well, fine, Mr. Stone. Your car will be downstairs. Just sign the chauffeur's trip pass with the time you're through with him. If you need anything feel free to call me. Clarence, I'll see you before you go?" He jammed the cigar into his teeth and fumbled in his side pocket for matches.

"Why, yes, Ward. If you want . . . I'll stop by your office before I leave. I imagine you'll be working late tonight."

Cadwalader merely snorted at Lasher's understatement and threw a salute over his shoulder as he turned to walk off. His big back, hunched over with the pressure of time, made a curious, almost pathetic contrast with the artificial self-assurance of his public smile. Halfway down the hall he stopped to light his cigar. Then, breaking into a huge shambling trot, he disappeared around the corner at the end of the corridor.

Stone waited for Lasher to say something. Lasher cleared his throat.

"I only want to talk to you a minute, Mr. Stone. Why don't we slip into the conference room? It'll be empty. There'll be people waiting to see me back at my office. Save me having to put them off."

Lasher's manner struck Stone as different from what he'd displayed that morning at the hearing. He seemed friendly, perhaps even apologetic. Stone was tired.

They went into the deserted conference room, gloomy and stale in the failing light of gray winter and late afternoon. The room with its enormous table was still upset into two groupings of chairs from the press conference; the empty expanse of polished mahogany was littered with discarded papers at either end. Despite the faint dead reek of cigarettes the room still preserved some of the atmosphere of a field of contest, like a littered tennis court after a public match. Lasher sat with one ham on the edge of the long table, his short leg swinging in a nervous, constrained circle. He clasped his hands in front of him as though about to ask a benediction and looked at the floor, frowning in concentration. Stone remained standing, his back to the door, his worn raincoat still draped over his arm as he had been carrying it all day long. The scarf he had left in one of the half-dozen offices he'd been shuttled among during the morning and afternoon. Lasher remained silent for a long minute, obviously trying to formulate a preamble for this impromptu conversation. He looked up at Stone and leaned back.

"I imagine you are still annoyed about what happened this morning," he said. He spoke softly, without a trace of rancor or hostility.

"How would you feel if you were in my place?" Stone asked mildly.

"Yes. Yes, of course. That is why I wanted to have a talk with you. Abe Sellers tells me he took you to lunch."

Stone nodded. There was a short pause.

"I've found out why you didn't receive your copy of the specifications. My girl was to have it sent to you by hand messenger. Instead she sent it by mail. It should be back on your desk when you get there, although there's no telling about the mails with this damned strike going on. If it is not there, I've arranged for my file copy to be made available to you. You'll have to sign a receipt for it, since it is classified and the copies are numbered. You can call my secretary—she'll be here until eight o'clock tonight—and she'll bring it to you herself when she takes a car to go home. I wouldn't advise you to take it out of your office, however."

"What if I should like to show it to counsel?" Stone asked.

"There's plenty of time for that. You can show him *your* copy. Your copy carries no classification. But mine does. You are free to do with yours as you like."

"Aren't they identical?"

"Oh, yes. They're exactly the same."

"But why . . . ?"

"We couldn't send a secret document outside the office. Therefore your copy had to be declassified before we could send it to you. It is classified only for your protection, actually."

"I see."

"You will have your own declassified copy as soon as it gets to you. You can surely wait that long to show it to your lawyer."

"I haven't got a lawyer yet."

"Of course."

There was an awkward silence. Outside, the gathering crowd lifted its voice. Distantly the sound penetrated the heavy curtains and drifted into the closed room.

"Mr. Stone, I want to apologize in advance for any unpleasantness that may arise between us in the course of my doing my duty. You know what my position is here."

"You are the Embassy security officer."

"Yes. It is not a very pleasant job."

"So I've been informed several times today."

"Really?" Lasher seemed almost to brighten. "By whom?"

"Well, by the Ambassador, for one."

"It's a relief to me to know that at least some people know I don't relish interfering with people's lives. It's an unpleasant job but of course it has to be done. The security of the country must come before consideration of the individual. I don't like this job, but what I like or dislike as an individual doesn't enter into it. The job has to be done and I do it. I want you to understand that I have nothing against you personally."

"Are you also going to tell me I'm going to be fired?"

Lasher smiled. "Abe likes to exaggerate. It's a common trait among people of Jewish extraction, you know. Like explaining things with their hands."

Stone gazed at Lasher in silence. Lasher was watching for some reaction.

"Understand me, Mr. Stone. I'm not against Abe Sellers because he's a Jewish person. I know a lot of people who are prejudiced, but that is one thing I'm definitely not. I don't believe in it. Some of my best officers in the last war were Jewish boys—not all staff officers either, like some people say. Combat men."

"Yes," said Stone. He wondered what sort of trap Lasher was trying to draw him into.

"I wouldn't be surprised if you were Jewish, Mr. Stone."

"I wouldn't be surprised if we all were," Stone said quickly.

"Beg pardon?"

"Genealogies go back a long way, Colonel Lasher. To Adam, they say."

Lasher laughed, slightly relieved. "Yes, of course. I see exactly what you mean. So you see, I have nothing against Abe Sellers."

"I understand, sir," Stone said coldly.

"There's no reason to call me 'sir' in here, Mr. Stone. I asked you in here to talk man to man, I guess you'd say. But to get to the point. Mr. Sellers is on the board that is examining your security status. Now I don't think you have done anything wrong in accepting a luncheon invitation . . ."

"You mean I shouldn't have gone to lunch with him?"

"No. That's not what I mean at all, really. However, you can see that it doesn't look quite right for you to be seen leaving the Embassy with one of the men who is responsible for evaluating your case. People will always put the wrong interpretation on things if you give them half a chance. It might be thought that you were trying to influence the board—well, of course you see what I'm driving at. How could people know that he asked *you* to lunch instead of the other way around?"

"What people?"

"People, Mr. Stone. I'm sure you understand what I mean."

182

"The Ambassador?"

"Well, yes. Him too," Lasher said—reluctantly, Stone thought. "I'm only trying to help you keep from making the wrong impression, Mr. Stone. It's in your interest. You must admit that your attitude before the committee this morning was a little, well . . ."

"Truculent?"

"That sounds like what I mean," Lasher said.

"Look, Lasher, we're grown men, both of us." Stone spoke with a tone of squaring off. "Let's look at the facts and stop beating around a nonexistent bush. I wish I had a gold piece for every time I've been told today that I mustn't blame you or Mr. Sweet for any dire misfortunes that may befall me. The general feeling seems to be that this hurts you more than it does me. That's pure rot. You aren't going to suffer over the outcome of this business. I am. Even if I'm cleared it won't be without suffering, not to mention what it will cost me financially if I'm forced to retain counsel or make an appeal or fly to Washington. I'm innocent, but not that innocent. I've heard how these affairs can get involved and wreck a person's life. I make no bones about the fact that I think these security hearings are stupid and unnecessary, and I don't think you should try to make any bones about the fact that the dice are loaded against me."

"I think you're being a little emotional, Mr. Stone."

"Emotional! Wouldn't you be emotional? For three nights running I've been trying to help the French Ministry of Justice dredge through this Dujardin mess. I've been working like a dog all day sorting out dead men on paper, and sweating my brains out at night to reconstruct conversations that took place years ago. How do you think I feel? Instead of feeling that I have my Embassy behind me backing me up, I have the feeling that I'm a pariah, a leper, a security risk. You think I'm some sort of left-wing menace. The French think I'm a tool of Wall Street imperialists. If it weren't so damn tragic it would be hilarious. I'm just a political orphan with some sort of social disease. I don't mean tragic for myself. I mean tragic for everyone. The United States. You, Lasher. Those people standing out there on the pavement in the cold like cattle. I haven't had a good night's sleep since I don't know when. Or eaten a decent meal. I don't dare go out to restaurants. I've had to give up my apartment to get away from the newspaper photographers."

"Where do you stay?"

"You know perfectly well where I stay. If your office doesn't know where I stay, then you'd better start firing some of your personnel. Look, Lasher, I'm very upset about this whole thing. I don't imagine I'm the first person you've seen in these circumstances. I don't want to insult you, but on the other hand you can't ask me to pretend you're a friend bent on doing me a good turn. You're out to wreck my life. That's what you're doing. I won't resign. I won't take a leave of absence. I have a clear conscience and I mean to have a clear name."

"Of course, Mr. Stone," Lasher said, rebuffed.

"Do you know that I was asked to surrender my passport this afternoon? Did you know that, Lasher?"

"It's merely routine, Mr. Stone," Lasher murmured, apparently surprised, his eyes avoiding Stone's. "It shouldn't have been done in your case, however."

"How do you think that makes a man feel? To know that his own country doesn't have enough faith in him to— Why don't you go a little further and ask me to post bond? Why not make it properly insulting?"

"The action is not exceptional, Mr. Stone. I assure you it is a purely routine—however, I will see that it is returned to you."

"All the worse if it's routine," Stone said.

"Mr. Stone, you must realize that—"

"You are depriving me of my liberty of movement without due process of law, for one thing. Why don't you simply fire me outright or charge me with high treason and arrest me? Why this sneaky—"

"Mr. Stone. You're letting yourself get carried away. I don't see how you've been compromised in the least. Everything pertaining to your case has been carried out with complete discretion. If you should decide to resign, your resignation would receive no publicity. We could arrange to have you leave for budgetary reasons. It's quite proper . . ."

"Fine. Except you're overlooking one small thing. I'd never be able to work for the government again."

"Mr. Stone, to work for the government is not a right but a privilege. You must understand that."

"I don't understand that. I've heard that cliché before, and up to recently I never had reason to question it. It *sounds* so true, it *sounds* like perfect common sense. But it's not. It is the most insidious slogan in the history of American politics. If a qualified citizen hasn't the right to dedicate himself in his country's service, then what rights has he left?"

"Surely you see that the privilege of—"

"If it's not a right to work for the government but merely a privilege, then we now have government by a privileged class. Is that your conception of the American democracy, Lasher?"

"I think you're twisting words, Mr. Stone."

"I'm twisting them back to what they actually mean, if you like. I'm straightening out a piece of twisted logic. Rights not specifically reserved for Congress revert to the states or the *people*. Our Constitution says that, Lasher. The Tenth Amendment. The Bill of *Rights*. *Rights*, not privileges, you understand."

"But the government has a duty—"

"The citizen has a duty, Lasher. His first duty is loyalty to his country, not to his country's security officer." Stone paused. "I'm sorry I said that. I know you're not to blame. No one had to tell me."

"It's all right," Lasher said. "I know you're upset."

"Rights are engendered by duties, Lasher. And vice versa. They are opposite sides of a contract. You tell me that I have no right to serve my country and I'll tell you I have no duty to serve my country. You'd make loyalty not my duty but my option, my whim. The government has no right to demand my loyalty but is merely privileged to enjoy it when I grant it—is that what you want? Carry your logic far enough and the *only* loyalty a government will have will be that of its privileged employees, and even they won't be too unswerving if they live in the shadow of being drummed out as poor risks. Your ideas attack the very fabric of government. If you want citizens to be loyal to their government, the government must first be loyal to its citizens."

"I think you misunderstand, Mr. Stone. You're not being questioned about your loyalty. It's a matter merely of security. We're not talking about loyalty."

"I'm talking about loyalty, Lasher. Do you think my government is being loyal to me? I went to war without being asked. I volunteered, rather than be drafted. I didn't *want* to go to war. No questions. I merely went. I had my rights as a citizen; therefore I had my duty. And I did it. As it turned out I risked my life, I almost lost it. So what? Maybe I didn't do my job as well as someone else could have. But I followed orders, and did as I was told, and somehow, thank God, we survived the war. But the next time we go to war, if I'm a security risk, you can damn well draft me. Or jail me. I know when I'm not wanted."

"You ought to be more careful with what you say, Mr. Stone. A remark like that could easily be misunderstood."

"I don't see how anyone could misunderstand it."

"I understand," Lasher said.

"As you can see, Lasher, I've done a lot of thinking about this whole business. It never occurred to me to think about it before. I never thought it could happen to me, even though I read about it happening to a lot of other people. I was all in favor of cleaning the reds out of the State Department, as the saying goes. But I didn't know I was among them. I didn't know you were manufacturing reds with a paint brush."

"I see you don't take the Communist menace very seriously, Mr. Stone."

"I take it seriously enough not to lose my head over it."

"Let me tell you something that happened right here in this Embassy. This only happened a few weeks ago, and I'm going out on a limb in telling you about it because naturally all these matters are classified. But perhaps it might impress you with the seriousness of what we're up against."

Stone nodded politely, shifted his raincoat to his other arm and sat down straddling a chair, facing Lasher.

"This is only an example. It is not primarily a security matter except that it involves misappropriation of classified material. By that I mean that it was not political. We had an employee in the Food and

Agriculture Division across the way. It seems that he was a sexual deviate."

"What's that?"

"Effeminate. You know the type. Now I know you don't think much of the security program—security program I'm talking about now, not loyalty. Your loyalty has never been questioned, Mr. Stone. Your security status is what we are trying to determine. Anyway, this employee seemed to be a good worker, came to the office on time, was never absent, had a good efficiency rating and all that. In the course of his work he had to deal with French wheat allocations. I won't go into detail except to say that he knew ahead of time when large movements of wheat would be released into the French market from storage. Now you can realize that accurate information of this kind would be of interest to anyone speculating in wheat futures."

Stone nodded.

"Well, it seems they got this young man into a compromising situation while he was intoxicated and had this held over his head."

"Photographs?"

"We never learned. They only hinted at the whole thing to him. He wasn't able to tell us exactly what it was. Claims he was too drunk to recall. The point is that they began soliciting information on shipments of various commodities. They blackmailed him. When we finally found out about it and faced him with it he insisted that what he gave them was information that they could have got from reading the papers. But we have no way of knowing. The point is that he admitted giving them information."

"Classified?"

"Everything of that nature is classified. Now, this is a classic case of a security breach. The danger is always blackmail. The only thing we can do is to make a rigid scrutiny of every employee's background and associates and try to see that the bad apples are weeded out before they have a chance to be blackmailed. Our only defense is constant vigilance. I see these things every day but I can't talk about them. I know how you feel about the security program, Mr. Stone, but try to realize that no one likes it. I've been investigated. We've all been investigated. You just have to get used to the fact that we're faced with an enemy that will stop at nothing."

"Such as cribbing wheat futures," Stone said.

"That was only an example, Mr. Stone. I chose it because it is not in an area we would call 'sensitive.' But I think it illustrates my point."

"How did you finally find out about this employee?"

"One day he went to his superior and confided in him and asked him what to do. His superior had been friendly toward this boy and I think that's why he told him. Anyway, his superior advised him to make a clean breast of it."

"How were they going to blackmail him?"

"Well, they knew he'd lose his job if we ever got ahold of the photographs or whatever they were. They threatened him with the loss of his job. He said they threatened to send the photographs to the FBI."

"But you say he didn't know if photographs existed."

"No. Obviously they weren't going to release their trump card into his hands."

"But they would have shown him prints."

"We thought of that. Obviously they were cleverer than to show their hand and make themselves liable for criminal prosecution."

"What if they had nothing on him?"

"Why would he have come to us?"

"Then I take it he took his superior's advice?" Stone asked.

"Yes."

"And you fired him."

"We had no choice. The law—"

"Did he admit that he was a sexual deviate, as you put it?"

"Of course not," Lasher said. "He knew that would be automatic cause for dismissal. The law states that—"

"Then how do you know he was a—"

"After you've been in this kind of a job as long as I have you learn to spot that kind. Besides, what else could they have on him that would make him think they could blackmail him? It's a case of two and two making four, I should say. Of course, we let him resign quietly. It's not our aim to persecute people, but merely to get them out of the government. We don't care who hires them afterward."

"Did you have a psychiatrist talk to the boy?"

"We tried that system for a while. Didn't work."

"Why not?" Stone asked.

"Too inconclusive. You can't get a cut-and-dried answer from those people. They see too many sides to the question. They always hedge the main point. We want to know whether he is or he isn't."

Stone lapsed into silence. Outside, the noise of the crowd grew in volume. People were singing and shouting. Inside the room it was getting definitely darker as the city fell into the slow twilight-less gloom between late afternoon and not-yet early evening. It was the hour when crowds usually filled the streets on the way home from work, and the buses and underground trains were jammed to the doors. Tonight there would be few people going home from work because nearly all work in the city had stopped. The subways hadn't run all day. Buses had vanished off the streets.

"Things look different from my side of the desk, don't they, Mr. Stone? It's no bed of roses being responsible for the security of an organization, I can tell you. Have I been able to give you a little more insight into the complexities of the problem of security?"

Stone was silent for a long while before answering. In the gray light of the room he sat staring at the wine-red carpet. Lasher stopped swinging his foot and lit a cigarette for himself, then offered one to Stone. Stone took it and accepted a light. He blew out a long thin puff of smoke like a sigh and got up from his chair. He crossed the noiseless carpet to the windows and drew the drapes aside and stared out. When he began to speak, he spoke softly, without turning around.

"Lasher, you and I are the victims of a monstrous practical joke played on us by—by God, the Devil, Fate—I don't know who. I would like to judge you more kindly than I do. But I can't. I think you are a menace to my country—*my* country, *my* United States of America. Your United States and my United States are different countries, and you're going to nail me to the wall like a captured flag. I didn't realize until now that I haven't got a chance of surviving this hearing. Do you know why? Because I *am* subversive—I believe that people like me should own part of our own government; the government is of me, not the other way around. I never realized it until this minute, but I finally know why I won't compromise with you, the committee, or anyone else for that matter. Not with the Ambassador himself—and God knows I respect him almost more than any living man. I won't compromise with you because I'm a simple-minded puritan and I believe you are a puppet of the Devil. It's not your fault."

"Now hold on, Stone—"

"What do you mean by security? When someone says security to me, I think of the security of the *individual*—a job, a future, or at least the illusion of a future. Perhaps a family, for some people. But you tell me that my individual security must be ignored in the face of the pressing demands of national security. I can't see how you can distinguish them. I see an organization as a collection of individuals. If the individuals in an organization aren't secure, how can the organization be secure?" Stone kept his back to Lasher, still looked out the window.

Lasher's voice behind Stone was soft. "There are different kinds of security, Mr. Stone."

"Nonsense. There is only one kind of security and that's being free from unreasonable fear. If individuals in an organization feel secure in their jobs, if they can have pride in belonging, then you've got what is called *esprit de corps*. The organization is secure. But what have *you* done, Lasher, to make people secure in their jobs? If anything, you've made them completely insecure. There probably isn't a human being in this place who hasn't got some dark, innocent secret he's afraid of. Any day you may ferret that secret out—or even something which is not a secret, but merely suspicious. Out he goes. All you need, according to your new law, is grounds for reasonable doubt—I think that's what it says, isn't it? In *my* United States guilt must be proved *beyond* reasonable doubt, because all men are unreasonable when it comes to judgment of what they fear, of what they think is evil.

"Lasher, you think you're reasonable—you told me that little story about the boy being blackmailed. The security law, you say, is designed to prevent blackmail. But hasn't it occurred to you that you've set up the ideal conditions for blackmail? All I have to do to blackmail someone is to threaten to reveal their sins to *you,* the security officer.

And you say you're responsible for the security of this organization. I think, after the story you just told me, that you are responsible for *destroying* the security of this organization. Do you think they could have successfully blackmailed that boy if he knew he could come to you and confide in you, and enlist your help in restoring his own personal security? He was loyal, in his own confused way. He came to *you* finally and told *you*, "Father, I have sinned." And what did you do? You fired him for having finally *proved* his loyalty. He trusted you and you fired him. Have you ever wondered how many other people you are blackmailing? *You* are the instrument of blackmail, not the photographs—which probably never even existed anyhow, except in the frightened imagination of a stupid young man who knew about wheat shipments, to his eternal regret. Without you there could be no blackmail. Even assuming such photographs existed, how could they use them except to send them to you? Do you think the boy's parents would behave the way you did? Throw him out?"

"What else would you have us do?"

"I don't know what I would have you do. I only know that the Constitution is a lot wiser than you, in guaranteeing against the invasion of privacy. Let me ask you, do you think the next time someone finds himself being blackmailed that he'll come to you and alert you? Like hell he will. That's how secure you're making this organization. You're an *insecurity* officer."

"You sound like you want me to open a confessional booth or something. The law states—"

"You'd do a lot more for security with a confessional booth and some smart police work than you would with your star-chamber tactics, Lasher. Did you *catch* the blackmailers?" The derision in Stone's voice was unconcealed.

"I don't see what that's got to do with it, Stone. We can't interfere in French police affairs. Of course we reported it. That's all we can do."

"What happened to him?"

"The Food and Agriculture case? I don't know."

"I'd watch him if I were you, Lasher. I wouldn't blame him one bit if he went straight over to the Russian Embassy and offered his services gratis. Just to even up the score."

"You wouldn't?" Lasher's voice sounded queerly strained in the darkening empty room. Stone was about to turn around when the door at the opposite end of the long room was opened. A cleaning woman with a mop and a broom and a rag tied around her head stood in the fall of yellow light from the hallway and peered in the direction of the voices. Then, just as suddenly as she had entered, she went out again. The door closed quietly behind her, shutting out the light.

"They must want to clean up," Lasher said.

"It's late," Stone said.

"I'm sorry you feel the way you do, Stone," Lasher said. "I see your point very clearly. I see it all the time, every day, in fact. Perhaps now you see why I don't like my job." Lasher's voice was strangely gentle, apologetic again. He sounded tired. Like an old man, Stone thought.

Stone turned from the window and looked at him. The drape fell back in place and the room was nearly dark. It was hard to make out Lasher's expression. He was kneading the bridge of his nose with his hand, as though his eyes were tired. He continued speaking without looking up. "I'm not a fool, Stone. Quite a number of people think I am, including you, I suspect. I'm quite aware that to many people I look foolish. Even stupid. It's an unfair advantage I take of them. Because while a man is busy taking me for a fool I'm busy finding out what kind of a person he is. What his soul looks like, you might say. The reason I'm telling you I'm not a fool is because I think you're honest. Therefore be forewarned, Stone. The old snake is wide awake."

Stone listened, rather surprised. Lasher went on.

"I've learned more about what manner of man you are, Stone, in the last half-hour than I could possibly learn in a month of hearings. You're young for forty-odd years, very young. I'm old for fifty-odd years. All my life I've trained myself to take orders, Stone, and to carry them out. I haven't had time to read much. What I've learned I've learned by provoking young rabbits like you into telling what they know. I've provoked a lot of knowledge out of a lot of people, including you here this afternoon. I come from a different school than you, Stone. I find that the world has moved right along while I was in the Army and it's not at all like it was when I was a youngster. I have my prejudices, but I've learned to live with them in the space of three decades. I don't move against the stream, but with it. That's what I was trained for. That's what I am. The world needs people like me, Stone, to make a balance with people like you. It's people like you that pass laws, that change things from what they were. It's people like me who administer those laws. Your kind start wars, Stone, and my kind wrap them up. You see, Stone, I'm competent. When someone wants to start something they'll go to someone like you. But when they want to finish something you started, they'll come to me. I won't change this law. You'll have to do that. I'll do whatever I can to get you through this hearing in one piece. If it gets impossible, I'm going to advise you to resign. For your own salvation, not mine. I'll let you know when it looks hopeless, if it goes that far. Think twice before you write me off as a fool. I've had my talk with you, Stone. You've told me what I want to know. I'm going to have to rely heavily on the testimony of your own word. I'm not inclined to think you'll lie to me. I'm going up to my office now. There's a car for you at the truck entrance. If you want that copy, call my girl before eight."

Stone stood silently as Lasher approached him. As Lasher came closer to the windows Stone was surprised to see a slight puckish smile on his face. Lasher extended his hand; Stone shook it almost by reflex.

"Good night, Stone," Lasher said. He turned and walked toward the door. On opening it, he paused; framed in the rectangle of yellow light, he turned slowly around. "One more thing, Stone. I hope I judge you more gently than you've judged me."

He went out. The door closed.

Stone turned, frowning, and gazed out the window, lost in thought. The sky was still light enough outside, even though it was almost completely dark in the conference room. Stone, thinking about Lasher, gazed unseeing at the milling crowd. He bit at the nail of his right thumb, thinking. Had he judged Lasher? Soon the streetlights would go on outside. The crowd was restive and noisy. Below him in the square he noticed a policeman gesturing wildly before a small knot of demonstrators. He put his forehead against the cold glass and watched. The wind was rising and whipping the gendarme's cape around him. The people circling him merely stared dully at him, moving only slightly under the prod of his white stick. Suddenly, as Stone watched, a young man in a tight black suit with no overcoat stepped up behind him and flicked the policeman's cap off. The gendarme turned out to be bald. The policeman snatched up the cap from where it fell at his feet and spun around, taking a short vicious grip on his stick. But the boy had melted back into the crowd. Stone watched the policeman collar another youth by mistake, but the boy wrenched free and squirmed through the legs of the protecting crowd. The policeman blew his whistle. The crowd flowed quickly away from the policeman and left him standing alone, a furious picture of ridicule, deserted in his moment of wrath.

A new crowd, different, a merely curious crowd, replaced the former faces. They stared at the frustrated gendarme as though he were an animal in a cage at the zoo. The policeman cursed them and shook his stick at them. They merely stared at him with dumb interest and kept out of range of his stick. Stone felt an odd sense of detachment from the scene—almost peaceful, satisfying. But he smiled slightly when he realized that the boy who had knocked off the hat was now standing directly in front of the policeman, acting like a simple-minded bumpkin innocently come to view the attraction, whatever it was. Stone could see the policeman's mouth working its futile anger on the crowd. But the only sound through the cold glass was the pervading murmur, wordless, senseless, like torpid bees stirring in a winter hive.

The crowd in the Place de la Concorde had thinned out and for a short while seemed to be dissipating entirely. But with the failing light of late afternoon the tide of human beings ceased ebbing and mysteriously began to flow back into the square, as though they had merely been home for teatime. The crowd of gaping spectators exceeded the numbers of the demonstrators, who, having now a gallery to play to, became bolder and more refractory in their taunting of the police. As the afternoon grew colder and grayer and the wind began to rise, the temper of the police grew shorter and the mood of the sea of people more truculent, more ugly. It was as if both sides, having passed the day in active inactivity, were determined not to have stood about in the cold all day for nothing. A vague excitement flickered back and forth through the crowd like cold electricity every time its periphery was prodded. The mood was brittle with the promise of violence before nightfall; it hung in the dimming air like the subtle smell of nitrate.

As the afternoon grew to a close, to counter the frightening growth of the crowd the police made the first move. Without warning, a file of running police wearing black steel riot helmets moved decisively from the concealment of the Rue Boissy d'Anglais, and amputated the appendage of the crowd projecting exploringly into the Avenue Gabriel. The crowd reacted by melting back and pressing into the blending background of spectators, using them as deliberate shields between themselves and the pursuing police. The sharp division between spectators and demonstrators vanished—to the sorrow of several spectators, who became surrogates for the slippery fugitives and were hustled unceremoniously into the black riot wagons which spun into position seemingly out of nowhere; the wagons gobbled the innocent as efficiently as the guilty.

It was over almost before anyone knew what had happened, and after the first retreat the crowd repossessed the square again, this time bringing the buffeted spectators with them to swell their numbers. For nearly an hour things remained static, with the police refraining from further concerted movement, hoping that cold and fatigue and boredom and descending dusk would accomplish their work for them. Indeed, more than a few demonstrators did leave the square after the first police foray, but the hardier ones remained and merely closed their weeded ranks; the police then confined themselves to playing tag with individuals who tempted fate by dartling out and back in a sort of adult version of the children's game of prisoners' base. It seemed to be enough to divert the crowd from more advanced designs.

This was the situation as it stood when the late-afternoon special edition of the Party newspapers hit the demonstrators with the electric news that the missing Berger was the American Ambassador's son. In an inflammatory editorial, the crowd was given its orders: a demonstration march up the Champs Elysées to the Arc de Triomphe at six o'clock. The papers were passed in bundles from the back of a truck out over the heads of the crowd, floating like diminishing cakes of ice on a sea of hands, until the bundles, peeled apart and distributed, simply melted into nothing and vanished as the crowd consumed them. It was five-thirty when the last gratis newspaper carried its dangerous message from the back of the truck out to the crowd.

The crowd read their orders in sobered silence, and waited for six o'clock to come. The police brought troops into their remoter redeployment, eight truckloads, and ordered the trucks to take up stations at the far end of the Champs Elysées. The trucks stood around the edge of the great stone star, like chess pieces, waiting.

XXII

At Graves Registration Headquarters at the head of the Champs Elysées, Stone worked listlessly at cleaning out his old desk. Most of the personnel had left at five, and he had the feeling of being alone in the building. Slowly he worked through the contents of the desk drawers, emptying them into separate piles on the bare wooden floor. He worked on the floor in a squatting position. Most of the papers he crammed into the already overflowing wastebasket; the rest he placed in disorderly piles on top of the file cabinet. The file cabinet was the only thing going with him to the Embassy. Everything else stayed. One file cabinet had already been sent over during his absence that day; a clean rectangle on the floor near the wall showed where it had been. Files of the dead. The missing were still here.

The light in the room was bad; the large bulb in the ancient ornate ceiling had burned out and he'd neglected to put in a requisition to building maintenance for replacement. There was only the gooseneck desk lamp, which spread its stingy light around the room at waist level, leaving the corners and the rest of the room in gloom. The shade was of glass, a nearly opaque green. The lamp was one thing Stone was glad to be leaving behind. It had been the glaring bane of his existence; it reminded him of an old man wearing a green eyeshade. It gave the room all the bare-boarded impersonality of a ticket office in a railway station. Yet he liked the room, liked the austere bareness of it, and had done his best to keep it that way. The lamp was fine during the daytime; it was only on the rare occasion at night when he had to use it that it irritated him, for its glare never failed to give him a headache. Somehow he never got around to changing it.

Stone felt depressed, full of resentment. He was tired to the bone. The move to the Embassy ordinarily would be a step up in the world, but in this case he was moving because his presense here was embarrassing to his old colleagues—no, he thought, it was not *they* who made him feel like a pariah, the pressure came from people in Washington. In Paris it was out of their hands. They had no choice. His connection with the Army, however tenuous that connection was, had to be severed. He shrugged as he straightened up from the piles of papers on the floor. It was enough for tonight; the rest could wait for tomorrow.

From the bottom drawer of the empty desk he lifted out a half-empty bottle of vodka and gazed at it a moment. He had gone the entire day without a single drink. No, he thought, there was the cognac in the Ambassador's office. Two cognacs. But that was social. In the office he rarely drank, but a drink helped when he was tired, was a mild cure for depression. One of the other officers—even after a year as a civilian he still thought of himself on the job as an officer—had recommended the vodka. It left no smell on the breath, he said, made a good office bottle.

He washed a glass out in the bathroom, bending over the old bathtub to run the water. The sink was covered with a board and piled high with mimeographed documents. That was one advantage to having an office in a former hotel; there would be no bathtub in the office of the military attaché at the Embassy. But on the other hand, Stone thought, the floors wouldn't creak and the elevators would work. He shook the glass dry and went back to his desk. He poured a careful two fingers of the water-clear liquor, and sat down behind the naked glass-topped desk. Idly he traced a circle in the dust with his thumbnail, thinking.

The feeling of letdown, of depression, continued to dog him. He needed sleep. The events of the day turned in a circle about the center of his thoughts; their meaning was too much to attempt in his present state of fatigue. But the meaning was there, and it made him uneasy. He closed his eyes against the glare. It was a task even to collect his thoughts; they wheeled about like shadows on a wall, of moths about a central candle. Beyond the events, beyond the meaning which lay in the future, there was uncertainty. Eyes shut, the empty glass warming in his hand, he calmly asked himself: What am I afraid of? The sober answer came: I don't know—I am afraid of what I don't know.

But the uncertainty was there, beyond sense, beyond meaning. It flickered around the rim of his mind like dry summer lightning, a certain anxiety, restlessness foretelling of a storm. In his mind he sought shelter; inadvertently he looked down at the newspaper on his desk and recognized the name under the photo. A sudden wave, a sharp shock, made him shudder, it was so abrupt, so unexpected. He jumped violently to his feet. He said aloud, "No. . . ."

He squeezed the empty glass angrily in his hand, and stared around the empty room, as though waiting for the shadows to dispute him. He'd only glanced at the paper when he bought it; hadn't recognized the bearded face; it was an old picture of Carnot, the emaciated victim of a concentration camp. In the dead silence he heard a snatch of shouting from the approaching crowd beyond the window at his back. Another part of his mind reflected coolly on his action: Carnot? This face? Carnot? Yes, this was the face that had produced the face he had seen this afternoon.

He sat down, frowning. Carefully, precisely, he poured another measure of liquor from the bottle. He put the bottle down, corked it, and sat without touching the drink, lost in thought. He studied the picture.

But why? Why? Carnot had hated Dujardin, hated the *man,* not merely his works.

He thought for a long time, coming back time and again to the same puzzle: What *was* Carnot's motive? It was impossible to reconcile any logical motive with what he knew of the man he knew as Carnot. Was Carnot's statement really his? And why had Carnot arranged that strange meeting today?

Stone's thoughts were shattered by a sharp shout from the crowd. At first he doubted his hearing, then the shout came again. Quietly he put the bottle back in the drawer and closed it; the bottle rolled and boomed in the empty desk.

He rose and went to the window. Outside, the noisy shouts of the demonstrators gradually increased as they worked slowly closer to the Etoile. The police were waiting them out, blocking only the side streets and the head of the wide avenue. This was the hard core of the day's vast crowds, a stubborn few hundred who, risking arrest, refused to go home for dinner. From the window they seemed a small disorganized battalion, all but lost in the vast open space of the empty Champs Elysées. The police gave them no opposition except their constant presence, waiting. The crowd advanced along both sidewalks, spilling onto the street, sparsely separated in the middle. It was feeling its way into a cul-de-sac. Illuminated in the cold light of the winter streetlights, the whole scene had a bizarre static quality. The marchers were hardly a block away from the window where Stone watched. A few of them had flashlights that winked on and off in the center of the crowd, and, although it was too dark to read them, a few still carried signs. They kept up a steady chanting, hoarsely indistinct across the short distance.

Stone stood at the window, watching. Again he felt calm, clear-headed; the sense of depression had left him.

Thinking still about Carnot, he admitted now that Carnot had betrayed himself as a human being. He hadn't been ready to acknowledge it earlier—was that why he'd put the whole question out of his mind? What *had* happened to Carnot? Stone turned and gazed at the unreal photograph on the first page of *France-Soir:* so that's what they did to Carnot. Then he thought: He might as well have been dead.

Suddenly there was a commotion in the street, a shouting, almost accusatory in its tone. He turned back to the window. The crowd was gathering toward the building, looking up, pointing at something out of his vision. It was almost as though they were pointing at him. Then he guessed that the American flag had not been taken in at sunset; it would still be hanging from the angled flagstaff that jutted from the second floor of the building. He wondered whether the guards had left it flying on their own initiative or on orders. He shrugged; it seemed an inept gesture to alter the routine—it only made the police's job harder.

He closed the inside shutters and turned away from the window, stumbling over the full wastebasket. He caught himself and stood perfectly rigid for a moment. Had the liquor caught up with him? He sat down and opened the drawer again, knowing with perfect clarity that it was a mistake. But he also knew that one more mistake made no difference. Downstairs the door would be locked; the guards would have their orders to let no one in or out until the disturbance outside was over and danger of "incidents" past. He had time to kill, he was a prisoner of events.

He relaxed, sat at his desk slouched and silent, his legs stretched out under it, crossed at the ankles. He stared at his shoes under the desk. He could hear the ticking of his wristwatch. And although the shutters were closed, he could hear the muffled voice of the sullen crowd outside the window. The syllables were indistinct, vague, faraway, but the rhythm, the full pause between syllables, was the same. It was unmistakable. Slow, slower even than a heartbeat, in his mind's eye, he could still see the crowd stamping their feet and swaying from side to side with the chanting: One—two; one—two—three. One—two; one—two—three. Over and over again: *Shep—pard; as—sas—sin.*

The stamping, monotone beat made the name sound like two separate words, and when he first heard it he recognized only the word *assassin*—because the crowd tended to join the syllables by hissing the s's. Otherwise there was no inflection. Each syllable was given the same heavy accent and the cadence had the ugly, monotonous quality of a hammer.

Stone tried to keep himself from listening. But there was something familiar in the rhythm, in the muffled beat. For a fleeting instant he had the sensation that what he was experiencing had all happened somewhere before. And then, quite suddenly out of the depths of memory, he had a vision of the old horse straining up the hill toward the Chapelle de Ste. Anne. The hearse. The drummers. Particularly he remembered the flies, iridescent green flies, flies in whole patches all over the animal, around its eyes, nostrils, in the sores.

As long as he lived he knew he would never forget the sound as the horse's knees struck the cobblestones; nor the shame later when, after the graves had been covered, he helped butcher the animal on the spot. Nine men braked the ancient hearse down the hill and hauled it back to town. He remembered the hearse clearly. It was black, all black, even to the shaft and crosstree, with four enormous black plumes, matted and ratty from rain and time, sticking up at the corners.

He and Carnot had joined the cortege at great risk, but by that time such risks had become routine. It was a questionable thing to do, but fortunately the local German authorities had correctly gauged the ugly temper of the town and had left the procession to pass unmolested. They all felt bad about the horse, though. Everyone tried to conceal his feelings, but all felt the same; that somehow they had degraded both themselves and their dead by butchering the poor beast in the very shadow of the chapel where their friends lay buried, the dirt hardly settled in their graves.

No one had actually suggested cutting up the carcass. It was done more or less by mutual consent. In the hot sun, without proper tools, it was slow work, and after a while no one said a word but only worked. Those who were doing the cutting were drenched in sweat. They worked only in their underpants to avoid getting blood on the suits they wore to Mass. The others stood by and watched and helped carry the heavy sides of meat to the hearse, where they covered them with straw to keep the ever present flies off. It was Madame LaChaise's horse, an old horse, and the last horse in St. Tropez.

All the way down the hill no one said anything. The only sound was the scuffling of feet in the choking dust and the grunting of the men and the creaking of the wheels and springs as they worked their way down the steep hill, struggling to hold back the heavy black hearse which, a hundred years ago, had been designed to be drawn by four horses. Nearing the bottom they relaxed a moment too soon and the hearse began to move, slowly gathering speed as the men tried vainly to snatch a new foothold in the loose dust. Finally there was nothing to do but run with it and try to steer it to keep it from running off the road. Bucking and swaying, the hearse lurched down the hill with nine pairs of pinwheeling legs kicking up a column of dust behind it. The rest of the cortege, the old men and the black-shawled women, were left gaping from the ditch as the hearse with its load of meat cleaved a path down the hill. The mourning population of the town had started back as the butchering was being finished. Walking in small groups of two or three, they were all overtaken. Mothers almost yanked the arms off children as the shouting, cursing men bore down and sent them scuttling to the sides of the road. A hundred yards from the bottom of the hill the men managed to halt the hearse and dropped on the grass, exhausted. They were not young men, only younger than the others in the village—but older than those they'd just buried. One of them got up in a moment and started wearily back up the hill to find the battered old top hat he had lost coming down. At the foot of the hill he was greeted by a gabble of women who surrounded him with their questions. One of them gave him back his hat, which was none the worse for the adventure, and he put it back on his head.

"It was the meat," he said, gesturing helplessly. "Not only do we have to pull the wagon, but the horse as well. *Çà alors.*" He made a gesture with his hand as though shaking water off it, and went back to the hearse. Stone remembered that it was then, as they started off the second time, that someone had said what they had all been thinking earlier about the horse, the horse that had drawn the dead to their burial, the horse that had waited to the top of the hill before falling dead. It was the man in the top hat who said it: "At least the poor beast might have chosen to die at the foot of the hill and save himself the work. We are justly punished for our dishonor. We should have buried him."

But it was Carnot who gave them back their self-respect. Two women were arguing that it was ungallant of the horse to die at all, especially since he was the last horse in St. Tropez. Carnot got up off the grass and walked over to the hearse and climbed up onto the seat. He stilled the babble of voices with one word.

"Monsieur!" he said, looking down at the man in the top hat just below him. Everyone stopped talking and looked up. "I agree with you that he was a good horse, an honest horse. But we bury men, not horses. Horses are to eat. An honest horse serves the people in life and it is honorable and fitting that he be allowed to serve the people in death. That is the only noble end for an honest horse."

Someone in the crowd said, "Bravo."

"Look at us," he went on. "Some among us are almost starving and you talk of burying a horse! Let us bury our men, let us bury *them.* But let us remember there is still work to do, still the enemy to fight, not one but two. First we must conquer hunger or we will never live to conquer the other enemy. This horse died in a noble cause, and, dead, he can continue to serve that cause. But that does not mean he must die unhonored!" Carnot was shouting now. He stood up in the driver's place and pounded his fist on the top of the hearse. It made a noise like a huge drum. "This heroic beast is no less a victim of the Germans than were the men he dragged up the hill to their graves. And by all the ancient martyrs of France, he should be justly honored! Where are the drummers?"

A murmur went through the crowd and three old *bravadiers,* in faded red, white, and blue costumes that hadn't changed since the Revolution, stepped forward carrying their drums, which were muffled with felt. One of them was so old he could hardly walk. They took up their positions in front of the hearse and a new cortege was formed for the horse. The nine men lifted the shaft and crosstree. Carnot jumped down into the dust and walked around to form the head of the procession behind the hearse. Automatically the men began falling in behind him. Last came the women, holding their black shawls tightly about their heads. When everything was ready there was a long, unsteady drum roll and the cortege started back to town, walking the slow, measured cadence of the muted drums. The hearse tilted forward down the hill, sagging slightly to the right. It limped along the dry, dusty road with its right front spring squashed flat. During the downhill run the load of meat had shifted.

Stone knew what it was now, what it was that had brought the whole scene to the surface of his mind. He sat listening to the steady chant of the crowd outside, remembering the sound of the muffled drums, hearing them in his head. Tum—tum; tum—tum—tum. Four miles they had walked, in the sun, and never once had the beat changed. When they reached the town, people gaped from the windows and children ran wide-eyed alongside the procession asking, where was the horse, what had happened to the horse? But no one answered them. Not one of the black-clad figures in the procession answered a word, but only stared stonily ahead, marching step on step to the slow beat of the unrelenting drums. The procession wound through all the streets in town, and Stone remembered the very real fear he had felt when the cortege passed for the second time under the window of the German provost's office. The first time nothing happened. The second time two helmeted sentries with fixed bayonets stepped into the street and barked out an order to halt. One of them, in bad French, demanded to know what was the meaning of the parade, as he called it. No one said a word. The silence was fearful. Finally the man in the top hat left his place and stepped forward. No one breathed. If they should lose the meat . . . The spokesman in the top hat cleared his throat. Everyone could hear every word he said.

"Pardon, Monsieur, but . . ." He paused. ". . . the last horse . . . in St. Tropez . . ." He took off his hat. ". . . *is dead.*" He bowed his head and turned slowly and shuffled back to his place, crossing himself. The drums rolled again and the hearse lumbered past the two baffled Germans, on down the narrow cobblestone street toward the butcher's. There were a few angry smiles among the marchers in the rear, and the air was heavy with vengeance. The drums, drumming, drummed on.

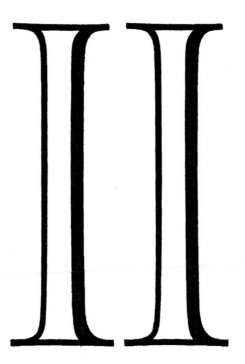

I

The storm had blown for three days and three nights without end. The white sand beach, once inviolate to all but the worn sea's aimless debris of drifting wood and cuttlebones, shells and seaweed, once barren and lovely, was ragged with the melancholy garbage of war. The wreckage lay at the lip of the tide driven high onto the sand by the same savage wind that collected the lost dead, the floating aimless life-jacketed dead, and buried them in tender froth at the lapped edge where their primeval life began. Their last agony, the fuel oil that filled their lungs, burned their faces off, drowned them, the wind skimmed off the vast embattled water like viscid black cream. Oil. Black, black oil. It lay under the howling wind, washed mirror-black by the splintering rain. Immobile, in pools, in clots, as sludge, claiming everything. Life jackets. Oars. Broken rafts, broken boats. Broken men. Everything broken, everything black and useless. And everywhere the oil asserted its domain, the edge of the sea, the final edge of the land. Tomorrow men would search these signs for knowledge, for names, of ships, of men, of countries. Clues to how the battle was going. For the sea lugged these signs from Africa, from the gates of the Atlantic, from all the beleaguered sea lanes where men struggled and hoped and despaired and died. In the shape of a charcoaled life raft or life jacket, men would read the fate of nations, an oracle of their own living destinies. The dead of all the nations were assembled there, rolling gently in the fury of the wind, waiting to be counted. The sea was an impartial recorder, and after three days and three nights the record was almost complete, and the sea was washed clean of its misery.

That was a bad year, a year when few men had time to weep before drowning. A blinding flash in the still darkness, lovely perhaps for an instant, and then the galvanizing roar, and the night erupted in terror. The ship groaning, the hiss of her steam like a knife edge slicing time and silence, as the tiny shouts of running men dot the silence of the impassive sea. A feather of smoke, fire. From the ruptured iron in her bowels the ship bleeds her oil, the black flammable blood that will be her final legacy to the living world. A fresh sinking.

At the end of the third night of the storm, three living men landed silently on that violent coastal sand. Driven in on the wind, they landed in rubber rafts painted black. The first one came in over the edge of overturning water caught in the lip of a surly wave. The tiny craft was lifted high and spun around on its axis and hung there for a moment as the wave surged under it. The man in it thrashed the back of the wave with his paddle as the next breaker towered behind him. There was a crash of white water and the raft disappeared for an instant. Then it tumbled up out of the breaker, empty, and slithered up along the tongue of long water and came to rest high on the beach. The water raced backward and tugged the man back into the sea. He fell onto his hands and knees and clawed his way forward against the sliding sand. Another wave crumpled over him and bowled him onto the beach. He crawled out of the sea's reach toward the raft. The wind lifted the raft and blew it end over end into the darkness of the night-like dawn. He crawled after it.

The second raft came farther down the beach. It came in on the curl of a roller, its occupant clawing the water with his paddle to stay with it. The tiny raft was suddenly lifted and shot forward. The man stopped paddling only when he struck sand. The raft slid up onto the beach. He stood up, reached down for a large suitcase, and got out.

While he was dragging the raft up onto the dunes, the third raft came in. It came in slowly, on a series of waves, and this third man didn't use his paddle at all but sat backward, dragging something through the water behind him on the end of a line. He took his time, playing the line as though there were a fish on it. When he landed he sat in the raft and reeled in a cone-shaped piece of white canvas, a sea anchor. He landed midway between the other two, and gathered the drogue into the raft. When he got up out of the raft he hoisted himself with the aid of the paddle, and using the paddle as a crutch, he limped up the beach dragging the raft, lifting it every few steps to let the wind help him.

Except for the steady crash of the waves and the hiss of sliding water, there was only the black lonely howling of the wind. The driving rain and the black sky cheated the feeble winter dawn of nearly all its light. In the darkness, each of the three men worked alone, first securing his raft to the paddle driven into the sand, then deflating it. The rolls of storm sand driven in on the waves isolated the three from one another. They worked with feverish but methodical haste. When the rafts were folded up and buried and covered over, only then did they begin to look for one another. The last man in remained where he was, between the other two, when he was finished, while the others worked their way along the beach toward him. They walked along the edge of the surf. Behind them the sea erased their footprints.

The meeting was wordless. The three crouched in a circle on the blackened sand for only a moment as the second man examined on his hands and knees the contents of the suitcase. When he was ready, they stood up. They were all dressed in black. There was a single handshake all around. They held their wrists together, checking the three watches against one another. Ten minutes had elapsed since the first man crawled out of the surf.

One by one, they walked away from the beach toward the woods. When the first man was out of sight, the second one followed him. The third, supporting himself on his makeshift crutch, walked backward and kicked sand over the footprints. By the time the soggy light of dawn long delayed had etched out the edge of the rain-driven sea, they had vanished as though they had never been. All that was left for the melancholy wind to mourn was the lonely wreckage of lost battles, lost ships, men dead at sea, driven home to a land that was never theirs. . . .

The rain let up before dawn and turned to a light drizzle. It was necessary to find shelter and concealment before it began to get light. Skirting the sleeping village of Croix Valmar, the three men left the main road where it branched into the *route nationale,* and followed what appeared to be an unused section of the old dirt road that the highway had replaced. It was in the woods to the left of this that they found the abandoned roadmender's shack. The roof was half gone and the fine misty rain blew in, but it was well off the road in the partial concealment of trees and scrub. They reconnoitered the surrounding area for a half-hour for signs of daytime activity, but there was nothing, no farms, no houses. It was as good as they were likely to find. It was better than sleeping in the woods.

Captain Stone's mission had not begun auspiciously. They had waited as long as they could before electing to make the landing in spite of the storm, which had already delayed them for three days. For three days they had lain on the bottom off the southern French coast rolling gently in the storm swell until they could delay no longer. They had to either risk a landing through the mountainous surf or return to Malta with the submarine, whose captain had already overstayed his orders by twenty-four hours. Just as it was beginning to seem hopeless, the furious wind relented enough to make a landing dangerous but not impossible. During the launching of the black rubber boats, the mission's leader was almost lost over the side. An enormous swell had thrown Stone against the coaming of the conning tower and wrenched his left knee so badly that now he was hardly able to walk.

After waiting near the inland spot where they were supposed to be met by agents of the men they were to contact in France, the three men gave up and proceeded on their own, keeping as far from the main road as possible. But it was slow going, and it would be another night before they would be in the village of Cogolin.

The code name for the mission was "Butter-and-Eggs," and for two of the men it was their first mission in the south. None of them had worked together before. The group chief was Captain Stone; according to the carefully manufactured papers he carried with him for this mission, he was Raymond Morel. But his code name among the Resistance along the southern coast was Dante; it was a name he had chosen himself and abandoned formally after his first successful mission in France. But it had adhered to him, so finally he had kept it and used it. He was fond of it; it had earned a reputation. It had become his nickname, and he used it to sign his radio messages to Algiers. And he had again become Dante the moment he entered France. From here on his real name had to be forgotten, even when talking to himself.

The other two men were Mike Fontana, a radio operator, and Horace Orchard, a "regional specialist."

After the soaking sea and driving rain, the roadmender's hut was comparatively dry. All three men were wet to the skin—expecting to be met, they hadn't brought raincoats. There was room for two men to stretch out on the bare earth floor and still have what was left of the roof thatching protect them from drizzle, except when it blew in strong gusts. The inside of the hut smelled of rotting straw from the thatching. Mike stowed the suitcase transmitter in the driest corner. It was necessary to decide the question of who would take the first watch.

"I can't sleep anyway with this knee," Dante said.

"Fine," the radio operator said. "I'm dead. Wake me when you get tired and I'll take the second watch."

"Did we leave any tracks coming in from the road?" Orchard asked.

"No, I looked," Dante said.

It was the first time Orchard had been on a mission, although he knew the country from before the war. Dante asked him how he liked being back in France. Orchard just shrugged.

"The hotels were better before the war," Mike said. He was sitting on the ground trying to light a wet cigarette.

"You better get rid of that American lighter," Dante said.

Mike held up the lighter. "It's not American. It's German. I got it on my last trip to Paris—off my old landlady in the Rue Garancière. She got it from her son, who lifted it off a German. They sent it to her with his personal effects. She wanted me to have it."

Mike gave up trying to light the cigarette and lay back on the ground, his head propped against the suitcase. "Orchard," he said, "you get the outside berth. I have to be near my accordion or I can't sleep."

Orchard grunted and spread his wet jacket over himself. Mike laced his fingers behind his head.

"Do you think they gave us up for lost?" Mike asked, musing.

"They might have," Dante said. "But they should have known the storm would delay us."

"Perhaps your friends didn't think we'd try to land until it was over," Orchard said.

"Perhaps," Dante said.

"You think something went wrong at their end?" Mike asked matter-of-factly.

"We'll know when we get to Madame LaChaise's," Dante said.

"What if your 'safehouse' isn't safe any more?" Orchard asked.

"Then we'll be working blind. There's no use crossing that bridge until we come to it. Lautrec gave me his word he wouldn't let anyone else use the house, so it should be all right. And I don't think Madame would compromise herself against Lautrec's orders."

"Did this bird Berger know about it?" Mike asked.

"Lautrec uses different houses for different agents. Berger wouldn't know about it—unless something has happened."

"What are we going to do if we can't find him?" Mike asked.

"Who, Lautrec or Berger?"

"Berger."

"What makes you think we won't find him?" Orchard asked, turning to look at Mike suspiciously.

Mike didn't answer. Dante said, "I guess it's time to give you a little more background. I didn't tell you everything in Algiers because both of you were better off not knowing more than you had to. But we haven't heard a word from Berger since the end of December. That's nearly four weeks. That's why we're here. Something's happened."

"I can always go to Nice," Orchard said.

"I wouldn't be too eager if I were you," Mike muttered.

"We'll save that for a last resort," Dante said to Orchard. "The less French you have to speak the better. Your accent's dangerous."

"It's none of my business, but I'm against it," Mike said.

"There's no sense talking about it now," Dante said curtly. "And from now on no more English. From here on in we talk French and nothing else until we leave this country, or until the Allies land on top of us."

Mike rolled over and faced the wall, grunting as he tried to make himself comfortable. Finally he found a position he could tolerate and lay still, his head on the suitcase as if it were a pillow. *"Bon jour,"* he said. *"Dors bien."* His teeth chattered.

No one answered him. Dante cleared a space by turning up clean sand and sat down on the wet ground to wait for daybreak and the end of the rain. After a while the sky began to lighten. Orchard turned once or twice. Mike began to snore, a loose phlegmy rattle not much louder than the wind yawning in the wet trees around them.

Dante sat in the gray light of dawn absently massaging his knee from time to time, thinking. They had cleared the first hurdle, the landing, and it was the most difficult landing he had ever made. For the other two it had been their first trip by submarine. Mike had always flown in and on two occasions jumped. Dante began taking stock: Orchard was in good physical condition, although not being an OSS regular, he lacked the extensive training Mike had. Dante could see that sleeping on the open ground in wet clothes was harder on Orchard than on Mike, who had undoubtedly been forced to do it many times before. From the relaxed way Mike snored he might have been sleeping on a feather bed. Dante was relieved that neither of them had showed any tendency to complain during the strain of waiting in the cramped and motionless submarine, an experience calculated to try any man's temper. He'd noticed one thing, however, that might cause friction, and that was Mike's needling of Orchard about his Marxism. Dante had watched them carefully and had sensed that Orchard was sensitive on the point and was beginning to resent Mike's constant ironic references to communism. Dante made a note in his mind to call Mike off before Orchard's meager sense of humor failed him and he began nursing a grudge. If it came to the point where they had to use Orchard's contacts, in the event that everything else failed, there was no sense in riling him unnecessarily now. Mike would have to humor him a little more generously, Dante decided.

That raised in his mind the unsettled question of second in command. Dante had deliberately left the matter vague in the hope that Mike, who would normally take over from Dante, would naturally assert the qualities Dante wanted to find in him. Orchard seemed the more reflective of the two, the more cautious, certainly the more aware of the political subtleties involved in the mission. Mike, on the other hand, tended to oversimplify problems and to move too quickly. Orchard had his inexperience and his commitment to Marxism against him, both of which tended to make him dogmatic, unimaginative, inflexible. Mike's inflexibility was of another sort; Mike was used to working in Paris, where the Resistance was relatively well integrated with Allied policy. In the south, where the common enemy wasn't so tangibly in evidence, the various Resistance groups constantly tended to become involved in internecine squabbles, both personal and political—a situation which could easily spell the doom of an agent who was politically tone deaf, as unfortunately Mike seemed to be.

Dante sighed to himself and tried to push the matter temporarily from his mind. But it was not a question to be left unsettled, especially under the circumstances of the vastly differing personalities of the two men. Sooner or later he would have to decide.

Dante wished he'd had time to get to know each of them individually in Algiers, but the mission had been organized in such haste that there was no opportunity. All three had shared the same cramped quarters and there had been almost no chance to be with one of them without the other's being present. There was a real question, as Colonel Jay had carefully cautioned him, of Orchard's political reliability. He had worked in Spain with the minority Communist forces, which was undoubtedly where he got his shrewd education in partisan politics.

The situation they faced in the south now, Dante reflected, was not unlike that among the Loyalists in Spain, with the groups bitterly divided, fighting among themselves, unable to agree on a common strategy against the common enemy—an enemy who in the meantime cold-bloodedly exploited the divisions and played upon disunity to suppress, to conquer. Orchard had grasped the point immediately; even Jay had been impressed with his shrewd insights and inferences. The question that remained was where his final loyalties lay, with the Allies or with the old compelling dream of proletarian revolution. Until that question was resolved, Dante knew he would have to be extremely cautious in making use of him. If the mission came to depend on Orchard's contacts—if indeed those contacts still existed after six years—Orchard would gain a subtle de facto power to neutralize Dante's de jure command. Dante tried again to stop worrying the question; it seemed that for the moment, at least, the right decision was no decision.

The rain decreased to mist, invisibly fine, and the leaden sky lightened overhead. Dante looked up, listening to a dog bark in the aimless distance. They had skirted the village mainly to avoid waking dogs, and Dante was glad now they had. He listened to the other dogs taking up the dawn chorus. He looked at his watch: it might be the patrol going through the village; it was just after the hour. He knew from previous missions that the patrols in the area were regular and kept rigidly to their timetable. But it could also be fishermen coming home or farmers getting up.

He felt automatically under his shirt for the forty-five wrapped in its plastic bag. Now that they'd gotten past the landing without incident they would have to think about getting rid of their weapons. When the transmitter was safely installed he would collect them and bury them behind the house, where they could be found again if need be. Once the transmitter was out of their immediate possession they were better off without weapons—in case they were caught in a road block or a search. The penalty for being caught with a transmitter or a weapon was immediate and final: death.

Dante listened to the barking dogs, thinking of the patrol, regretting that they had had to leave half their equipment on the submarine because of the heavy breaking seas. Even the extra submachine gun was a luxury they hadn't been able to afford, as were spare clothes, food, and raincoats. The other automatic weapon Mike had managed somehow to take apart and fit into the suitcase with his transmitter. Dante hoped fervently to himself that the "safehouse" in Cogolin was still good. Otherwise they would have to hide the transmitter and risk a hotel. Thinking of a hotel made Dante think of money: he unbuttoned his shirt and passed his hand inside to check the money belt. It was still dry and secure; the beeswax he'd dipped it in to waterproof it seemed perfectly intact. Then he picked up the canteen beside him and shook it; there was just a sound of sloshing liquid. Not even the other two knew what was in the canteen. That was a trick Dante had picked up from an old smuggler in Algiers, lining the inside of the canteen with gold coins embedded in beeswax: when the melted wax hardened you filled the canteen with cheap red wine, so raw that no one in his right mind would drink it even if offered. If he had to jettison the paper francs down a public toilet during a raid he would still have the canteen. Besides the louis d'or pieces, he was carrying the paper equivalent—at prices current in the Marseilles black market—of eight hundred and fifty troy ounces of fine gold. Most of it had originally been earmarked for Lautrec's organization. It was one more thing he would like to get off his person. Getting rid of the bulky package would be a weight psychologically and physically off his chest.

In the far distance he heard a vehicle pass on the road they'd left earlier. The sound of the unmuffled engine approached and slowly died away. He looked at his watch and made a quick calculation in his head: it had been the early patrol all right, right on time. No matter how often he heard or saw the enemy, when he was on a mission, he would never get used to the tiny knot of fear that always formed in the pit of his stomach. It was an animal reaction, a survival reflex, and after the threat passed he never failed to experience the shaky weakness caused by the adrenalin that had poured into his bloodstream in preparation for exertion and struggle that hadn't materialized. In fact he waited for the relieved weakness that followed, marveling each time at this evidence of his body's automatic readiness to adjust for survival. And each time it gave him a curious sense of being alive, a sense that heightened reality for a moment and made him feel animal-like and invulnerable. He noticed with surprise that his knee had stopped hurting.

He felt clear-headed and optimistic again. They had survived the landing; the transmitter hadn't been damaged; and now his knee was obviously not seriously damaged either.

It was getting light. They would sleep for another dozen hours and then start again, would be in Cogolin before morning. There Dante knew he would find answers to the questions and uncertainties that had plagued him since long before he left Algiers. Why hadn't Berger answered the last interrogatory? Had he been caught? What was Berger like? Who *was* Berger? He felt a sudden longing to see Lautrec's calm face again, watch him rub his pipe on his nose—making the bowl gleam with the natural skin oil—listen to his slow, assured assessment of the situation. Lautrec was a man to trust. But Berger was an unknown quantity. What were the details of the dispute between him and Lautrec? That one phrase, ". . . L. not cooperating . . . ," had worried Dante more than any other single thing. If Lautrec was not cooperating with his American liaison, then there must be something wrong with Berger, not Lautrec. Dante had given up trying to keep an open mind; already he was prejudiced against Berger, and he knew it. The only thing to do was try to hear both sides —if there were still two sides to hear. Dante brooded on the meaning of Tournant's failure to keep men on the rendezvous spot, at least until the week was out. It was not like a good operator—as Tournant reputedly was—to let his men give up so easily. Had something happened to him in his attempt to trace Lautrec's group? Something had definitely gone wrong; the best he could hope for was that it was a misunderstanding and not a catastrophe that had prevented Tournant's men from being on the beach.

Still, it was better to keep his apprehensions to himself for the moment. He was too familiar with the gnawing feeling of fear that could develop in men cut off from all sense of contact in unfamiliar territory. For him the area along the coast wasn't so unfamiliar, but he had only to recall his feelings on his first mission to know what the other two were going through. The only sense of safety they had was in trusting him, trusting that Dante knew what he was doing. It was unnecessary to add to their burden of uncertainty and nervousness: fear of that sort could unhinge a mission, cause bickering, recriminations, even deep distrust. There would be time enough for fear and disagreement later. For the present Dante decided to keep his forebodings to himself. That, at least, was a clear decision.

Dante ran down the check list of events in the offing. They would have to enter Cogolin from the back road if they weren't to run the ever present hazard of waking the dogs. Food wouldn't become a problem for at least another day; after that it wouldn't be too much of a risk to buy it. Dante realized grimly that already he was planning for the eventuality that the house in Cogolin might be unavailable. Even finding that out would take careful reconnaissance. Lautrec had talked Madame LaChaise into getting rid of her two dogs, so her house could be approached fairly easily. But it would be hard in the dark to see the windows and read the signs. The first signal that the house was safe would be the green window shade in the attic bedroom completely drawn. From the ground it would be hard to distinguish a dark green window shade at night. Then there was the second signal: the shawl on the hook in the kitchen.

Dante could see it in his mind: two shawls on two hooks that could be seen from outside the rear kitchen window. The white one—perhaps it would show up even in the dark—was never to be removed as long as the house was safe; it served a double purpose, for if Madame were to be seen wearing the white shawl in public, it would be an obvious signal that it was no longer hanging on the hook in her kitchen. Dante thought about the two shawls and dreaded the vision of a single black shawl hanging from its hook in the kitchen; if both of them were gone it would mean that Madame herself had been arrested. The idea of the shawls had been hers when Lautrec pointed out that in a lightning arrest she wouldn't have time to raise the shade in the upstairs window. Madame had said that a German wouldn't deny an old lady her shawls against the chill of prison, for all Germans fancied themselves *galants* when arresting old women.

Next there was the question of the permanent transmitting antenna Lautrec had promised to conceal in the attic. An efficient permanent antenna would cut down the need for repetition and confirmation and thus lessen the chances of the transmitter's being pinpointed by German locator posts.

Clothes would be a problem. They had plenty of ration tickets with them, carefully forged like the rest of their papers. They would need to learn the new train schedules that had gone into effect the first of the year. As a measure of military security timetables were no longer printed in France, but Lautrec would know the schedules. He reminded himself that he would have to teach Orchard how to use his ration tickets. He'd meant to do it on the trip across, and scored himself mentally for forgetting that essential detail. If there was anything that would betray a stranger, it would be fumbling with his ration tickets in a public place.

Orchard's French bothered Dante too. He spoke it with a curious mixture of Spanish and American accents. His papers had the birthplace made out accordingly, a small town near the Spanish border that Orchard himself knew and had suggested, but it wasn't an impenetrable cover. Especially if a Frenchman instead of a German listened to him carefully.

It was like making a list of assets and liabilities in his mind: Dante was mentally trying to assess their current position. Behind them lay the beach with the greatest chance for incriminating discovery; that much was past. Ahead lay the uncertainties, the unforeseen crises. Mike muttered in his sleep and rolled his head to one side. Dante smiled wryly to himself. He felt like paterfamilias worrying late over the family accounts, while the trusting household sleeps its untroubled sleep.

Orchard was lying on his back, as straight as a piece of cordwood, his hands crossed on his chest like a corpse. Dante looked at his watch; in two hours he would wake Orchard for the mid-watch. If he woke Mike, Mike would only wake Orchard climbing over him to get out.

Outside the fine mist had almost stopped, but low gray clouds pressed thick and heavy near the earth. It was going to be a dreary day, and Dante looked on it with grim satisfaction. It wasn't the kind of day to inspire a patrol to wander off the main road into the wet and dripping scrub. Sodden ground was uncomfortable to sleep on, but more than usually safe. There was also less likelihood of children and dogs nosing around. The wet ground killed scents and discouraged play.

The worst enemy likely to be encountered during the day was boredom; it was hard to resist the temptation to go out and reconnoiter the ground and see what sort of situation the night had landed them in. The spot seemed deserted enough, but Dante decided he should give formal orders to Orchard and Mike that they were not to set foot outside. Natural functions could wait for darkness.

Traveling in the inverted world of fugitives, of the underground, never failed to give Dante a curious feeling, a sense of being an animal who slept by day and hunted by night—except that they were the hunted. Even the German patrol vehicles when he'd seen them, their blue slits of blackout headlights shining like half-shut eyes in the darkness, had the catlike quality of nocturnal hunters. They generally traveled slowly, sniffing at the dark sides of the road for prey. To Dante's mind there was no more chilling sight than to see one of those squat, deadly vehicles stop, back up, and shine its Cyclops eye of a searchlight into the protecting bushes where you were hiding. He remembered once lying flat on the ground, the silent light probing all around him, expecting any second to be impaled on that stabbing blade of discovery and death. It was hard to believe afterward that the thing had been directed by human hands; it had seemed like some slow prehistoric monster, dull-witted but deadly. So deeply was the scene burned into Dante's memory that it flashed across his mind every time he thought he heard a patrol vehicle.

But there was no sound outside now, not even of dogs barking. A faraway rooster, spirits dampened by the day he was greeting, crowed a few times half-heartedly and stopped. The only sound at all was the steady dripping of the trees, the sluggish soughing of the sodden wind.

II

The villa that served as Colonel Jay's intelligence headquarters in North Africa had formerly been the summer residence of a French spice importer from Marseilles. It had been commandeered in secret, selected largely because it was well outside the city of Algiers on a little-used road. There were four main buildings, whitewashed and sparkling clean, around a rectangular court, and several guest cottages scattered about the grounds within the outer walls. There was even a tennis court made of concrete, although it had been canopied and converted into a work pit for the mechanics from the group's private motor pool. The intelligence group had its own communications, its own transport, its own kitchen, and was in all respects independent from other Allied installations in North Africa. The only men outside the group who knew of it, except for certain higher officers of the North African Command, knew of it as a convalescent rest home for psychiatric cases. Otherwise, Jay's group didn't exist.

With the coming of winter had come the first unsettling reports to the villa headquarters from the agent who had been sent down from Paris to maintain contact with the Lautrec organization. His cover name was Antoine Berger. It was apparent then that the new agent had failed to understand his function. His job had been simply to maintain the status quo and keep contact. He had been given a Canadian radio operator from Marseilles whose own mission had been called off just after he was landed.

Berger's reports were infrequent and dangerously long. Through the month of November it became increasingly obvious that Berger had his own ideas on the southern organization. He outlined a plan for welding several diverse groups into one large one with central direction, insisting that the gain would be worth the extra risk. Colonel Jay drafted an instant reply advising extreme caution and specifically ordering Berger to make no move. Stone was worried over Berger's complaining references to alleged mismanagement by Lautrec.

After the third long message Berger was ordered to cut down the length of his transmissions, and they heard nothing for nearly two weeks. Then came Berger's alarming proposal to effect an open meeting between the leaders of several unnamed organizations—all of which Berger particularly emphasized were anticommunist. The only leader named in the message was a man called Dujardin. To Stone it appeared that Berger was being dangerously unrealistic in putting political considerations ahead of military security, and he questioned Berger's motives to Colonel Jay.

It was then that Jay informed Stone for the first time that although Berger had been recommended for good work in Paris, he was a barnstormer, an agent without formal training. He had been in Paris when war was declared and had remained behind when the Germans overran France. The following day Jay sent off a strongly worded communication that unequivocally ordered Berger to drop all contacts with all groups but Lautrec's. That was in December. Stone and Jay interrupted their Christmas dinner to work for three hours in the dry North African heat to pore over the whole Lautrec file and draft the final message. No reply ever came from Berger, not even confirmation of receipt.

The days that followed were tense. Then the British passed along a chilling report from Nice of a series of night arrests all along the Côte d'Or that had commenced on New Year's Day and continued through the following week. Berger's Canadian had been lost in the carnage. Stone feared the worst. From Algiers they tried frantically to check on the authenticity of the British report, but in the wake of the arrests it was impossible to learn who had been caught and who had merely disappeared into hiding. The ominous silence gradually convinced Stone against his will that the southern resistance organization that had been so carefully built up to soften the initial savagery of the landing had been severely damaged, if not totally destroyed. Stone knew that there were undoubtedly more ways than one to win the war, but the logic of an initial southern front seemed to him utterly compelling, to the extent that he finally considered no other. His commitment to the idea of a southern landing made his failure—for he thought of the maiming of Lautrec's group as *his* failure whether it was or not— seem all the more tragic. The agent called Berger seemed unimportant in his mind. Berger was only one of the myriad vicissitudes that a well-built organization should be capable of surviving.

As the talk of invasion increased and speculation about the date multiplied, Stone grew more restless with self-recrimination. The thought of a hundred thousand probable casualties from an unsupported landing plagued him night and day. In his mind's eye he saw the fortified sweep of southern beaches with their network of inland roads. The Germans would be able to move men and matériel about with impunity, throwing divisions in wherever they were needed, while the Allied forces remained pinned immobile on their beachheads. With Allied mobility it would be an even fight. Or if the Germans were deprived of *their* mobility it would also tend to even the battle up. And that was what Lautrec had been supposed to do. Set up road blocks. Destroy bridges. Tear up railway tracks. Cave in tunnels with explosives. Rip down telephone lines. Merely picking off small reconnaissance patrols would deprive the enemy of eyes and ears at a time when he most depended on them. Lautrec had spent over a year building up a silent force of trained men to do these specialized tasks. All they had needed was more weapons. To enjoy maximum security, this special group of Lautrec's had even curtailed their normal paramilitary operations, passing up choice opportunities to inflict daily tactical damage on the enemy in the hope of crippling him when the ultimate contest came. They had trained themselves, using only a handful of weapons, until they had become experts in the arts of destruction.

The first full-scale weapons drop was to have taken place in the first moon period in January. Colonel Jay had managed to scrape up the weapons, but now there was no one to give them to. They lay useless in their parachute packing crates in a depot near the Algiers airstrip. The moon period came and went, with still no word. And the weapons still lay in their shed outside Algiers, unconsigned, useless.

There was other matériel in Gibraltar that the British had agreed to fly in. Still other weapons were scattered around remote country airfields in Britain. All of them carried the large yellow consignment tag of Jay's special operations group stapled to their warehouse lading slips. An ordnance inspector had once dubbed the farflung cache "Jay's Arsenal," and the name stuck. It was indeed a strange collection, including everything from limpet mines, magnetic time bombs that a swimmer could attach to the hull of a docked ship, to folding two-man saws that could be used to fell trees for road blocks. There were printing presses that could be fitted into a suitcase, incendiary fountain pens, capsules filled with emery dust, poison kits, a special device for forging signatures—engines designed to perpetrate every crime known to man, from counterfeiting to arson. If an agent needed a device that didn't exist there were specialists who could make it. Jay's was by no means the only arsenal of its kind among the many Allied groups competing in skulduggery, but it was one of the most complete.

It was the thought of these weapons lying idle that persuaded Stone to ask for one last mission into France. If Lautrec's group was beyond salvaging there was always the hope of building another, or if there wasn't time for that, of coming to agreement with the Communists. The Communists in the south had so far resisted efforts to be firmly integrated into the Allied effort, even though the USSR was engaged in that effort. They preferred direct and continuing action to long unspectacular training in preparation for the day of invasion. Arming them more fully would be risky, since they were liable to tip their restless hand too soon and bring down the wrath of full-scale military repression on innocent civilian populations: for every known Communist at large in France there were a dozen bewildered hostages. Stone had decided to put the idea to Colonel Jay.

Jay listened to Captain Stone's proposal without comment, and when Stone was through went to the window and stood looking out with his back to the room. Then he said, "There are political risks in arming French Communists."

"De Gaulle has formally accepted their support, however. That's a point to consider," Stone said. "We could time the drops so that they wouldn't be fully armed until just before the first beachhead is established."

Jay grunted. "You're assuming the landings will come in the south."

"Yes. Aren't you? Have you heard anything to the contrary?"

Jay shrugged. "The buildup seems to be coming in England."

"That would be logical. They'll have to invade the north corner sooner or later, but I'd think it would be later. A southern landing would end the Italian campaign, or at least take some of the pressure off Clark."

"Well, whatever the decision will be we won't be able to wait before dropping arms in. It's getting harder to get aircraft, and it will continue to get harder as the invasion date approaches. The difficulty of working at high level is that when the top brass are busy they won't give you the time of day. Yet we can't very well work any other way."

"How much time do you think we have?"

"Before we try a big landing? I don't know. I'll certainly be told before most of the others, but we haven't been clued yet."

"Do you think they're afraid of a Communist coup?"

Jay snorted. "How are a handful of revolutionists with hand grenades going to bring off a coup with the entire Allied expeditionary forces sitting on top of them? No one in his right mind is worried about the Communists pulling off a coup with the few weapons we could give them."

"But they might be able to exert local influence—municipal elections and such."

"There won't be any municipal elections for some time in France. De Gaulle will have to force his way firmly into the driver's seat before he'll hold any elections. Legally, De Gaulle is still a deserter from the French Army. Pétain was legally appointed by a constituent assembly. De Gaulle will have to convict a few people of treason before the legal basis for his government will be secure. He will have no choice. He's not fool enough to risk immediate elections. I could be wrong, I suppose."

"Then you don't see any political risk?"

"What can they do? We give them weapons now. After we get into France we take them away from them. Where's the difficulty? That's not the problem. The real problem is, first, whether they will take orders from us about the use of weapons we provide them, and second, whether they maintain enough discipline to restrain premature action on the part of individual partisans."

"You're thinking about civilian reprisals?"

"Of course I'm afraid of civilian reprisals. The Germans would be merciless. For one thing we might easily be blamed for such an occurrence by noncommunist French. I think your first idea is better."

"You mean to start over from scratch."

"There *must* be survivors from Lautrec's group. They know the ropes and could train others faster than they trained themselves. They have the benefit of their own mistakes."

"*If* there are survivors."

"Well, if there aren't, I'd say then you'd be right to investigate the local revolutionaries. It would be worth a talk in any case. But that would be strictly a last resort."

"Am I to obtain prior clearance before making a decision?"

Jay came back to his desk and sat down. He looked at Stone carefully and said, "No." He waited. Stone said nothing. Then he added, "Do you want me to tell you why?"

"Only if you want to," Stone said.

Jay leaned back in his chair and looked Stone in the eye. Then he said, "You're not in the Regular Army, Stone. I am. The Army is my profession. It is *not* yours. It may come as a surprise to you that I have been thinking the same thing you have about this mess we have on the southern coast. I understand how you feel about it. It's been your baby. But I have to consider other areas as well as yours. The spy business in Italy makes your Riviera seem like the vacation spot it should be. Sicily is still thick as lice with German agents reporting on our troop and convoy movements. In other words I have my hands full. We don't have an unlimited quantity of weapons to throw away. I've had to beg, borrow and steal everything we've got, because every plane we tie up means one less for a bombing mission, every carbine we drop into France means one less for the main show. Supplies are really tight, Stone, tighter than almost anyone knows. We've lost enough equipment in Sicily and Italy to outfit the Golden Horde. The weapons will have to go where they will do most good."

"One *maquisard* with a bazooka . . ."

"I know that and you know that. But not everyone else does, especially the division commander who has to give his men carbines instead of semiautomatics. There have been a few cases where divisions have lost or used up matériel faster than we can replace it. Every available popgun is being held back for the main show."

"I realize that."

"Now if we give a rifle to a Frenchman he can save perhaps twenty American and British and Canadian lives with it. *If he uses it at the right time in the right place.* He can keep twenty Germans busy just trying to run him down. But this doesn't mean much to the American field commander who has to postpone an action because he can't replace equipment. Nor does it mean much to the infantryman who has to use a barrel that's so worn he can't place a decent group with it. Now, why am I leaving the field decision up to you?"

Stone remained silent as Jay let the question sink in. Then Jay continued, "I've not only been thinking about your idea before you came to me, but I've done two things about it. We're in business to win a war and save casualties, not to please the D.A.R. First, I've managed to scrape up a new recruit who ought to know something about working with French Communists. Second, I've been to the top to find out how far you can go."

"What did they say?"

"You can imagine what they said. They were very cordial, but they said I would have to make the decision *according to the military necessities involved.* Do you know how you translate that phrase in the Army?"

"I'm not sure."

"It means that the decision rests squarely on my neck. And if the decision turns out to be wrong, they never heard of me."

"You mean they wouldn't approve or disapprove," Stone said.

"The higher you go in rank, Stone, the more important political considerations become. You can't blame them for not wanting to juggle a hot potato. From a military point of view there's no question in my mind that it makes sense to arm any Frenchman who can hold a steady gun. But if they specifically approve the arming of Communists, that is, give their formal considered approval, then they will be held responsible if something backfires. This way, if something goes wrong they will merely call me on the carpet and blandly demand to know why I didn't obtain prior authorization."

"I see. The old buck-passing routine," Stone said.

"No, Captain, there's a difference. When you've been in the Army as long as I have you learn that buck-passing is one of the devices that makes an efficient army possible. Notice that they haven't specifically said no. If a man believes in his action, he should be willing to take responsibility for it without buttressing his belief with official sanction. Any fool can act on official sanction. It takes courage and brains to use your judgment. There are times when official sanction must be withheld. A good general officer doesn't risk his neck unless the reason is absolutely and finally compelling. That's why the Army secretly frowns on 'front-line generals.' Spurring the troops on from a white horse is very colorful, but what happens to the plan of battle when the old man gets shot in the head?"

Stone said nothing.

"Part of the selective process that weeds out unfit professional officers is the necessity of learning how to keep from compromising oneself. A good staff general must demonstrate a good political ear for music or he's worthless in a top position, because the ones who are at the top have to deal with congressmen as well as troops. A general will never be trusted in such a position if he has demonstrated political ineptness. It's easy to forget, now that Russia is our ally, that previously the USSR was dedicated to the destruction of industrial capitalism. But I haven't forgotten. Nor have the officers I have to answer to."

"You think there will be trouble with Russia after the war?"

"Personally I doubt it. After all, she'll owe us the debt of her survival. When the chips were down we came to her aid. There'll be a lot of diplomatic jockeying, but the men that fought the war in the field will remember that they didn't build those jeeps in Russia."

"So you are going to pass the buck to me, is that it?" Stone asked, smiling.

"I'm depending on you not to make any mistakes. I said before that if a man believes in his considered action he ought to be willing to risk his future on it *if that action is absolutely necessary.*"

"Evidently this Berger agrees with you," Stone said.

"Don't get flippant with me, Captain. I'm talking to you, a mature, well-trained soldier, not to a young wastrel with a Messiah complex."

Stone looked up in surprise. "You know something about Berger?"

"We'll talk about Berger later. For the moment understand that he appears to have disobeyed an unequivocal order. I don't expect the same from you. I know your work and I doubt that I'd ever have to send you an order worded the way I worded Berger's."

"I didn't mean to . . ."

"I understand, Captain. I merely want to make certain you understand."

"Yes, sir."

"I don't know the field. You do. I rely on your judgment in any case before I make decisions. You are perfectly aware that you can thus control my decisions by the information you send me."

219

"I wouldn't distort a report just to get—"

"We all distort, Captain. According to what we know, what we hope, what we believe. We see facts the way our minds and hearts want us to see them. More than one battle commander has been deprived of victory simply because he couldn't believe victory was his."

"Yes, sir."

"I'll be perfectly honest with you. I don't believe in your scheme as strongly as you do. I don't think it can do any harm to try it as a last resort, but I don't believe we'll get any effective support from a group that has steadily refused to adjust their aims to ours. They are more interested in revolution than in war. However, the final decision will depend on the kind of men they are. If you think they are disciplined enough to be entrusted with more efficient weapons, then you'll make your decision. I can't help you with it. If it backfires, I won't call you on the carpet for it. In fact I'll defend you, because your general orders read broadly enough for you to make such a decision without prior approval. But you'll have to advise me as soon as you've made it, if and when you do."

"My general orders?"

"Didn't you mention last week that you'd like to take one more try?"

"Yes, but I didn't think you were taking me seriously. That is, I was only making a casual . . ."

". . . a casual remark to see how I'd react. A trial balloon, is that it?"

Stone smiled. "I am a little tired being a meantime instructor."

Jay reached into his desk and took out a file folder. He laid it on his desk and opened it. Then he looked at Stone and said, "This is not a final draft, but it will give you an idea of what we could do for you." Jay put on a pair of steel-rimmed spectacles and scanned the open file folder. "You would go in this time by submarine. Fly from here to Malta and be picked up there. I've got you a radio operator from Italy but he also speaks French—with a Marseilles accent, I'm told. His name is Fontana. I've also found you a man named Orchard who is or was a Communist—at least he worked with them a few years ago during the Spanish Civil War. Evidently his job was to smuggle contraband French arms from Nice and Marseilles across the Pyrenees. He seems to have had extensive contacts in the French Communist labor unions, especially among railroad workers in Nice. He's due to arrive here in a few days. They found him on a merchantman on the Atlantic run—as a storekeeper. He has two drawbacks besides his politics. His French is good but he evidently has a decided American accent. Also, he was rejected by the Army because of a splinter of Spanish shrapnel which is lodged in the bone of his heel—it might give him trouble if you have to do much walking—and he has two toes missing from the same foot."

"Has he had any training?"

"They've given him a hurry-up run-through in the States, but you can hardly call it training. However, his work in Spain and France should have made him a little more battlewise than ordinary. He's the best they could find for me."

"Who is they?"

"The Federal Bureau of Investigation," Jay said casually. Then he smiled. "They've helped us before. You remember that safecracker, the one Al Scarlatti took with him into Naples?"

"The little one with the gray skin?"

"He did a perfect job. Perfect. I put him in for a decoration."

"Maybe you'll make him into a respectable citizen," Stone said.

"Not any more," Jay said. "He's dead."

Stone nodded and said nothing. Jay looked back to the file.

"Arrangements will be made through Tournant in Marseilles to meet you on the beach with transport and dry clothes if you need them. You'll go in at a point just south of St. Tropez at a place called Cap Myrt. There's a German coastal gun near there and the beach is patrolled, but you shouldn't have any trouble if your timing is right. I'm trying to get this year's timetable for the trains around there, but at present I don't have it. We know the train schedules were changed at New Year's. Tournant will try to arrange a safehouse for you in Croix Valmar, until you can get up to Cogolin. From there on you'll be on your own. Tournant will not go with you any farther than Croix Valmar. You'll have plenty of money, two men, and a transmitter. The rest is up to you. Tournant is in your area now, trying to find out if there is anyone left of Lautrec's group that you can contact with certainty. You'll want to work as quietly as you can. If you can get a group together, you'll have to pick out a few drop areas in the immediate neighborhood. The British will use their own fields farther north if they do the dropping. You'll have to arrange transport for your own group. How does it sound so far?"

"Terrible."

"It's not much, is it?" Jay said ruefully. "Do you still think you want to do it?"

Stone simply shrugged. "I asked for it."

"Well, if you want to back out you can on this one."

"I won't back out."

"In Marseilles there are two advanced weapons instructors attached to Tournant's group. He also has a road block and demolition man. All of them are good. One of them is on loan from the British. We're keeping him busy for them until they can get him out. You'll make arrangements with Tournant for their services, *but only when that becomes necessary.* Tournant will also set up a spare maildrop for you."

"Everything depends on Tournant showing up. Have I met this Tournant?"

"No, I don't think so," Jay said, studying the file. He didn't elaborate. "I suppose you'll sign yourself Dante again. I guess that's all right, but don't overdo it."

"The name has a reputation," Stone said.

"I think you're keeping it as a talisman. It's probably got a reputation with the SD too."

Stone shrugged.

"You'll get the same name and cover story as last time. Identity cards, ration tickets, textile and tobacco cards—all of the finest London manufacture. I'll give you this whole file to go over later on." Then Jay put his finger on a typewritten paragraph. "Oh, yes," he said, "this is a little detail you will have to square with your conscience before you leave."

"What detail is that?"

"I told you that I arranged for these orders to read as broadly as possible."

"Yes," Stone said.

"I had to give a little quid pro quo for the latitude you'll enjoy. If you do contact elements of the Communist resistance, you'll have to do what you can to spy out their paramilitary organization."

"I'd do that in the normal course of inspecting their facilities."

"Not quite. These are to be detailed accounts of how they are armed and who the top men are. Also, G-2 would like to know where they hide their weapons when they're not using them."

Stone looked at Jay. Then he said, "Why did you call it spying?"

"Ordinarily you'd merely be inspecting, as you say. But I see no sense is not equipping you with the facts. You know, of course, why they want this information."

"To disarm them after the landings?"

"I don't think I have to comment further," Jay said.

"I see," Stone said.

"You're still convinced you can do something?" Jay asked.

"I'd feel bad if I didn't try."

Jay shook his head dubiously. "We'll do all we can for you here. But this will be harder than it was before. You'll get closer attention from the authorities this time."

"Yes," Stone said.

"I'll see that you are shown photographs of Tournant. You'll have a little homework to memorize again. Your operator should be here in a few days, and so will Orchard. If you're fully decided about this trip, then I see no reason for wasting any more time than necessary."

"What arrangements should I make for pickup?"

Jay looked up and closed the file. "This time I think we'll bring the Army to you. Your best bet is just to lie low and wait for us."

Stone smiled back at Colonel Jay. "You're pretty certain that the invasion will come this spring, aren't you?"

"Aren't you?" Jay asked, still smiling.

"Yes. It has to come."

Jay got up and came around his desk. He went to the door and opened it for Stone. "We'll talk more about it later. I'll arrange to have you read the file tonight. Tomorrow evening I'd like you to stop in at my quarters after mess. I'll have to talk to you again after you've done your homework, and I'd feel more comfortable there."

"Yes, sir."

"It won't take long," the Colonel said. "Now, about this lad Antoine Berger—if he's still alive, I want him back here. You may have trouble."

"You know him then," Stone said.

"Not precisely," the Colonel said. "I want him brought out of France, Captain. I don't want him held hostage."

"Brought out? I thought you said we should wait . . ."

"If he won't come on his own, you'll have to try to bring him—but not at the risk of your mission. Am I being clear?"

"You want him arrested?"

"Captain," the Colonel said, "how you do it is your problem."

"Is he important?"

Colonel Jay took a fresh cigar from the humidor on his desk and turned toward Stone. "Important enough, Captain," he said. He smiled and bit off the end of the cigar, spat it carefully into the wastebasket.

III

Before the war the village of Cogolin was quietly dedicated to the manufacture of hand-loomed carpets and brierroot pipes. In both these enterprises the local craftsmen excelled, but their output was so small that only a connoisseur of rugs or pipes would know of Cogolin. This tiny village was within walking distance of the sea and St. Tropez. It was also famous locally for a nougat-like confection that its women were fond of touting as the best in the whole of France.

The full impact of the war was not felt in Cogolin until the Germans finally occupied "unoccupied France" to protect their Mediterranean interests. As one of the old pipemakers put it, it was not Cogolin that went to war, it was the war that went to Cogolin.

However it was, when the war finally did come the Italians came with it, later the Germans. When the Allies invaded Sicily the Italians began to be reinforced by the Germans, who, it was said, didn't trust the Italians enough to leave them in control of such a strategic sector. The Italians sang a great deal and drank a great deal of wine.

The Germans were first sent merely to tighten discipline among the Italians; in the end they replaced them. The Italians were sent home. Things changed. Where the Italians had merely drunk wine, the Germans collected it and sent it home; the Germans seemed to sing only while they were marching.

Madame LaChaise's husband had been killed at Verdun. He had been a pipemaker, a middle-aged, generous man with a passion for insurance—a novelty in those days. When he was killed she was still a girl in her twenties. She insisted on managing his funeral herself. And when the body arrived, she buried him with such pomp and dignity that when other bereaved families found themselves faced with the same sad chore she was usually consulted. She told everyone she was glad to do it, that it gave her something to do to take her mind off her own loss. But the young, energetic widow had found her calling. And the village of Cogolin, which heretofore had merely thrown dirt on its blessed dead, at last came into its own with a professional undertaker who knew what it was to be correct.

The commerce in cadavers was brisk, and the business thrived. Madame LaChaise exercised her option to buy out her two male partners, a new sign that had *POMPES FUNEBRES* in great black letters replaced the small plaque beside the door, and although a few neighbors complained at first, things went well. Madame LaChaise got most of the farmers' trade. Hers was the only funeral parlor in that section of the Var that could provide silver-tasseled door hangings for the home of the deceased. Not to mention a black hearse drawn by four black horses (now only one remained, an ancient nag which she kept in St. Tropez to rent now and then to fishermen).

Monsieur LaChaise, as Madame was fond, even proud, of pointing out on every occasion, had saved her from a life of vice by plucking her out of a squad of *filles de joie* who regularly worked the late-Edwardian winter trade in the Riviera resorts. He had offered marriage the first night, and she, being at the time in a moment of broken vanity from an unhappy love affair with a young English bounder, accepted. She loved to buttress her respectability of more recent years with stories out of her squalid youth, as she called it. It was as though measuring her rise from such a low beginning made her ascendancy and final triumph that much greater than those of other women who had risen to their present positions from merely respectable beginnings. But if she had lost her heart for such youthful adventures, she kept her head for business. Many of the men in town still courted her advice, which she gave as generously as she had once given her affections, with the result that Madame LaChaise was reputed to own a piece of every man in town. Her position as long-term creditor placed her in a position of some power in the village as well as in the surrounding farms and communities. It was said that Madame LaChaise ran the town. Madame LaChaise said this was nonsense. No one else said it was nonsense.

When the war came, burials declined in their level of splendor as money became scarcer. But Madame LaChaise kept the good will of her past and future clients by burying a great many of their kin on credit, secured of course with one form of chattel or another, but on credit. When the first rumblings of the underground Resistance movement were heard in the village of Cogolin, Madame LaChaise had the prudence to realize that talk was dangerous. So she didn't discuss it. She didn't make her views known even to her closest acquaintances. It wasn't long before she knew that she had sensed the essence of the problem. Because now money was needed, and those in a position to give it who had spoken out loudly in favor of the Resistance were hard put to find ways of disguising their donations. Through channels, Madame LaChaise found out how much was needed, where, and by whom. She also found out who the active men were. Waiting until the time was ripe, she searched out one man whose discretion she trusted absolutely and made contact with him secretly. In one feverish week she raked together a million francs. She gave the man she had chosen for her single contact—a man named Lautrec—all the money he asked for with a half million to spare. Then she went underground. By agreement with Lautrec, she became discreetly but convincingly pro-Vichy. She lost most of her friends. People began burying their own dead.

Lautrec had been a good man. Madame LaChaise's judgment was more than vindicated by the scope and effectiveness of the organization he built in the course of the next few months. His disappearance was a terrible blow. For one thing, Lautrec was the only person in the world, besides the American agent he had brought to her house with her permission, who could vouch for her real political behavior. It was getting late in the war, and contempt hung in the air when she walked in the streets; Madame was no longer respectable—for more than one reason: The last real money available had, on Lautrec's suggestion, gone to buy a languishing bordello in St. Tropez, which now furnished a steady flow of information on German activities in the area.

She couldn't learn what had happened to Lautrec. One day, after Dante—the name used by the American—had left and the new agent had arrived, Lautrec had confided to her that he was worried. The new agent—a man known as Berger—wasn't working out. He took risks, he ignored security precautions. That afternoon he had greeted Lautrec in public, and it was this more than anything else that seemed to worry him. He also mentioned a split in the local department leadership and talked vaguely of stepping down. It was the first inkling Madame LaChaise had that Lautrec had risen to be head of the departmental Resistance command. But it was the agent Berger who seemed to occupy Lautrec's mind most. Madame of course had never met him.

The other agent, Dante, had requested that no one else ever be allowed to use the house, unless it was absolutely necessary.

Lautrec's last words to her re-echoed the imperative necessity of keeping her relationship to the Resistance secret, "in case we ever need the house." And he talked as though he thought he would need it. She asked him why the new liaison agent didn't use the house. Lautrec answered that it was better to have it for a safehouse "only in an emergency." She remembered these words particularly and pondered their meaning many times, and waited with the uneasy feeling that Lautrec's disappearance was a prelude to disaster. The two shawls remained on their hooks.

The real disaster came in the New Year's Day raid that wiped out the organization Lautrec and the American had built. Arrests went on all day and into the night. Over two hundred men vanished without a ripple. Madame LaChaise made discreet inquiries, only to find she had overplayed her role as a Vichyite. She met with a stone wall of silence. She decided to continue waiting.

The widow LaChaise waited. She lived indoors and survived on potatoes that were stored in the cellar. Two of her windows were smashed by rocks one night. She patched them with newspaper by the light of a candle and went back to bed.

During the days, she watched the street from behind the black-and-silver curtains in the large front room, which still smelled vaguely of the dead. Behind the house, in what had once been a proper stable, the black-painted hearse weathered in the rain that drove in under the rotting eaves. She kept the house locked.

The morning she heard the knocking on the kitchen window, she knew immediately who it was. It was the same knock. V for victory. She rose up from the cot in the small room downstairs, where she had taken to sleeping with all her clothes on, and walked through the back rooms to the kitchen. She lifted the shade and looked out the window. Then she went to the door and broke open the bolt. The last person to use the door had been Lautrec. Now it was hard to open.

"Push," she said through the door.

The door opened and Dante came in out of the rain. He turned and motioned toward the stable. In the gray morning light two more men crossed the space where once the rose garden had been. When they were all inside she shoved the door closed again.

"I wondered if you would come," she said.

"Is the house safe?"

"Not even the dead come here any more," she said. "They take their business elsewhere."

"So much the better for the dead."

"So much the better for the living," she said. "What's left of them."

"You haven't changed, Madame."

"You're wrong," she said. "Who are these two?"

"Friends."

She grunted. "One can never have too many friends," she said. "Come upstairs and get dry. I've saved your clothes."

In twenty-four hours from the time of their landing, the three men had come thirty-five kilometers without incident, until finally they were standing in the widow LaChaise's kitchen. Every step had been torture for Dante and his leg was blue and swollen, but even so it seemed too easy.

"What's wrong with your leg?" Madame LaChaise asked.

"I wrenched it getting into the raft."

There was little time for conversation the first day. Dante gave Madame LaChaise some money and she went out for the first time in several weeks to make arrangements for the food they would need. Orchard helped Mike set up the transmitter in the attic. The antenna Lautrec had promised to install was there, but it was agreed after discussion among the three of them to limit the evening transmission to three bursts of fifteen seconds' duration. Stone was skeptical as to whether it was enough.

"It's enough," said Mike. "This is a new-style piano. It squirts enough wattage to melt their earphones."

"What's our schedule?" Dante asked.

"I set it up for squirt transmission on the hour, any time from midnight on," said Mike, picking up his earphones. "For steady sending, I've a clear five minutes at six minutes past the half hour, any hour of the day or night."

"Can you receive on that thing?" asked Orchard. Mike nodded, listening in one earphone.

"They must have an aircraft jammer near here," he said.

"Isn't it asking for it, to work on the hour?" Dante asked.

Mike put down the phones and turned off the receiver. "It depends on how you look at it," he said. "It's true that the Krauts are probably glued to their sets every hour on the hour, since that's a nice logical time to schedule transmissions. But direction finders have their limitations. It's hard as hell to get a coordinate fix in fifteen seconds. By the time they get their loop tuned to my frequency, I'm all through. Then they hold their breath waiting for me to peep again. But I don't peep. In the meantime everyone else from here to Marseilles can get off their two cents' worth while the Krauts are tied up monitoring the hole I left in the band. Sometimes, when I'm feeling mean, I blast off five seconds of gibberish just to louse them up. There's another reason, too. There may be as many as four or five guys working squirt on different frequencies all at the same time. I'd hate to be a Kraut sometimes." Mike poked into his set with a long thin screwdriver, and laughed.

"Isn't there any way to make it impossible for them to locate you?" asked Orchard. "Switch frequencies around, or something?"

"That makes it just as hard on you as on them. It's not always easy to tune these things up after they're set," said Mike. "There was one time in Paris, though. The Krauts are pretty good in Paris. They've got at least a dozen bug-wagons there, and I've had them swarming around me like flies in a garbage can."

"You could see them?"

"See them? Hell, I could have smelled their bad breath, if I'd waited around. But one time we really drove them nuts."

"I think you enjoy this business," said Dante, smiling.

Mike looked at him in surprise. "Yeah, I guess I do," he said. "It's better than cops and robbers."

"You're still a kid at heart, is that it?"

"How'd you drive them nuts?" asked Orchard impatiently.

Mike sat on the edge of the table beside the transmitter and leaned back to tell the story. "Well, there was a British character we were in touch with. He'd done some sending for my boss man once, when I'd fried our set for us. It took me a few days to rustle up parts, and there was something very hot going on, so this Limey boy volunteered—it was strictly a favor for the Yanks. His Number One said it was his neck if he wanted to risk it. Anyway, we owed him a favor.

"About a month after that, they got into some kind of a jam. There was some sort of real snafu that had to be straightened out with London. High policy, or some sort of jazz like that. Anyway, it was going to take a long transmission to straighten it out. Even boiled down, it was going to take at least twenty minutes, and it was urgent as hell so they couldn't break it up over a few days. Anyway, the Limey piano player got an idea. He knew from listening that there was at least one other American sending out of Paris besides me. I didn't know who he was—he was new in town—but I had an idea my boss might be able to turn him up if he had to. I didn't think the Limey's idea would work, because his set had a tendency to drift all over the band. But we finally got the third guy and decided to give it a try. There was a lot of beating and whistling, but it worked."

"What worked?" asked Orchard.

Mike looked at him blankly. "The transmission worked," he said. "All three of us got on the same frequency and the other Yank and I kept our plates loaded with just enough power to blanket the area without reaching London. The Limey went full blast, sending like a maniac. I never heard anyone send that fast before. We were all sweating blood."

"Didn't you interfere with each other?" Dante asked.

"Oh, we just put out a carrier with nothing on it while the Limey transmitted. We just kept quiet."

"I still don't see why they couldn't—" Orchard began.

"Look," said Mike. "There are three of us. Each of us is in a different part of the city, in a big triangle."

"Oh, you weren't together," said Orchard.

"Hell, no. By us being in three different places, the Kraut bug-wagons were screwed. All they got was a signal that came from everywhere at once. There was no way they could get a fix. There was no null point. I heard afterward that there were bug-wagons going crazy all over town. I had a guy in the street keeping an eye out, and he told us how this one bug-wagon came tearing up the street and went past out of sight. A minute later it came tearing back and passed another bug-wagon doing the same thing. They both slammed on the brakes and backed up to each other. My boy was sitting on a bench reading a newspaper laughing his ass off, while the Krauts were getting ready to blow their brains out. We stayed on for a total of thirty-three minutes. I'll bet they heard that Limey in Berlin."

"Why don't you do that all the time?" asked Orchard.

Mike shrugged. "Too many people get to know each other," he said.

"What did they think in London?" Dante asked.

Mike looked at him. "I never asked. It doesn't pay to be too curious."

"I don't know about the rest of you, but I could use some sleep," Orchard said abruptly.

"Yes," Dante said. "Mike, I've asked Madame to wake you this evening in case I sleep through dinner. I'm going to wait up for her."

"She didn't seem to have much to say this morning," said Orchard.

"That's why I want to talk to her alone," said Stone. "She's bound to be a little overcautious after what's happened here."

"She doesn't trust us, is that it?" asked Orchard.

"Do you trust her?" asked Mike.

Orchard turned slowly and looked at him. "I've been in this sort of racket too long."

"Not in this war you haven't," said Mike.

"As far as I'm concerned, it's still the same war. I don't even trust you," said Orchard. "Nothing personal, of course."

"Still the old war-of-the-classes jazz, is that it?" asked Mike.

Orchard reddened slightly, and was about to open his mouth to answer when Dante cut him off. "That's enough, Mike," he said.

"What have *I* done?" asked Mike. "I only asked . . ."

"We all know where we stand," said Dante. "I think we'd better leave it that way."

"But I only asked him—"

"Well, I'm asking you to stop asking him," said Dante shortly. "This is the kind of thing that can lead to needling. In Algiers it was a joke. Here it's not quite so funny."

"I'm sorry," said Mike. "You two take me too seriously."

"If you'd been in Spain, you'd take it seriously too," said Orchard.

"Would you do me a favor, if I do you one?" asked Mike of Orchard.

"Favor?"

"Yes. Would you stop talking about how it was in Spain?" asked Mike. "I don't want to hurt your feelings, but we've had it tough enough in this damned war without hearing how you got shot at."

"Maybe you've got a guilty conscience," said Orchard. "If you and a lot of others had been in Spain, you might not be here now."

"Yeah," said Mike. "I might be dead."

"You both may be dead yet anyway," Dante said. "Don't rush things. For the time being, I think it might not be a bad idea if both of you got some sleep."

Mike was the first one to leave the room. He turned around at the door and addressed Orchard.

"Look, I'm sorry if I've really been getting under your skin," he said.

Orchard shrugged.

"Maybe the whole world's got a guilty conscience," said Mike. He stood in the doorway a moment looking at the two of them. Then he turned his back and went out. Orchard started to follow him, but Dante put a hand on his arm.

"We may be holed up here a long time before we get a break," he said. "It's a little early in the game to tense up."

Orchard looked at him for a moment, reflecting. He nodded soberly, and Dante took his hand off his arm. Orchard left the room without a word. Dante listened to his footsteps going down the stairs and along the second-floor hallway. He heard a door close, and after a long while he heard shoes drop on the wooden floor. In the silence, he sat down near the front dormer window to watch for Madame LaChaise to appear in the street below. For the first time he became aware of how cold it was in the room. The fire Madame LaChaise had set in the tiny stove near the bare chimney was undoubtedly out by now. The wood was soft and damp, the remains of an unfinished pine coffin salvaged from the old earthen cellar. He looked at the stove, and reflected. Even if the fire was out, in the mere presence of the stove there was still the illusion of heat. He amused himself and passed the time by trying to conjure up a vision of a roaring fire inside the stove. He laughed at himself and that, finally, made the room seem warmer.

Dante was surprised to learn from Madame LaChaise later that afternoon that Lautrec had actually disappeared before the New Year's Day raid. This was a fact of some significance that had not reached Algiers. It was impossible that Berger wouldn't have known it, and yet there had been no mention of it in his last report. If Berger had known of Lautrec's disappearance, why hadn't he reported it? If he didn't know of it— But that was impossible. He must have been in daily touch with Lautrec. The final report from Berger had spoken only of the merger to be effected between Lautrec's group and the other smaller groups headed by the man named Dujardin—Dante wasn't sure whether this was a cover name or not. From what could be deduced from Berger's report, Dujardin was to head the combined group with Lautrec as his operations officer. Lautrec's disappearance was bad enough in itself, but this reorganization, and Madame La-Chaise's revelation that Lautrec was worried over "a split in the leadership," was profoundly disturbing. Dante kept his anxiety to himself, however. He would not discuss this with the others until he could take more time with Madame LaChaise and pick her brain for significant details that she might have overlooked as unimportant but which might provide clues. There was nothing else to go on. That night the "safe arrival" code phrase was transmitted without difficulty. Mike even picked up an acknowledgment from Algiers.

The next morning, after debating the risks, Dante finally decided to hazard asking Madame LaChaise if the name Dujardin meant anything to her. He waited until he had her alone in the kitchen. Orchard was reading upstairs, and Mike was tinkering with the receiver.

It turned out that she knew several Dujardins, and he made her describe each one of them. When she mentioned one who was a police official, Dante remembered Berger's first report on the subject. He was sounding out, went the report, a man who had built up a small independent organization, with the idea of inducing him to join Lautrec. The man was "well-placed strategically but reluctant to consolidate." While Dante was recalling this, Madame LaChaise had continued talking. He let her run through several more Dujardins before he asked her if any of these men had been taken in the New Year's Day raid. When she said no, he let the subject drop. Several times that day he asked her to go over her conversations with Lautrec again. Patiently she repeated everything, and together they puzzled over her recollections searching out possible clues. But there was nothing new. She had told him everything the first time.

The question of Antoine Berger was a different problem. Making inquiries after a "blown" agent—an agent who'd been exposed—was risky enough, but attempting to trace a missing agent was close to folly. He decided to take the others in on the decision, since it involved their safety as well as his. He gathered them in the front room and put the question to them after filling them in on what he had gleaned from his conversations with Madame LaChaise. He told them then that Algiers had worded their orders in such a way that they were to "seek information on the agent known as Antoine Berger only insofar as consistent with the safety of the mission." Mike said he would abide by whatever decision Dante made. Orchard pointed out that if Berger hadn't been taken he was probably in hiding, and if he was in hiding, it might well place him in jeopardy to look for him. Orchard was against doing anything beyond placing the standard notice in the personal columns of the Nice paper. In the end Dante decided to place the notice immediately. If nothing came of that, he would decide then what to do next. The conference ended there, and nothing more was said about Berger.

Dante had learned to "do nothing" with as much caution as he used in active operation. He had learned that these "blind" missions were the most treacherous of all; the lack of well-established contacts made things go so slowly that even the best agent was at times sorely tempted to "feel around" for people to work with. This meant exposure to the risk of making contact with "decoys," with disastrous results. He was sure of Madame LaChaise, because he was sure of Lautrec, but even this contact was risky. They needed the house, however, so it was a risk they had to take. They might have chanced another contact through her, but Madame LaChaise was a blind wall. She was as cut off as they were, and Dante knew in his bones that in the end, unless something broke, they would have to resort to blind-man's buff if they were to break the stalemate.

Orchard brought it into the open. He spoke again of the people he had known in Nice before the war. "Some of our people," he said. He was sure they were still there. But he would have to go alone. He refused to discuss it in detail. Dante said to wait a few more days.

Madame LaChaise took a regular part in these strategy councils now. She went out each morning to buy food for all of them, and she was able to manage easily since most of the black-market operators were pro-Vichy and had no compunctions about selling to her. The meat was delivered at night. With Madame LaChaise, Mike made one trip into St. Tropez during the day and shopped the brothel while she went over the books. Lautrec had kept it a secret even from her which girls were passing on information, and Mike could make no contact. The place was crawling with Germans from a nearby coast artillery installation. There were also a couple of plainclothes German types lounging around the main room. Dante trusted Mike's estimate that the place was "hot." Mike had to show his papers once. They were perfect, he said. He also mentioned a bicycle he had seen parked in front of a shop. From Madame LaChaise he learned that the owner was a notorious collaborator. That night he went alone into St. Tropez and remained the night. In the morning he came back on schedule, riding the bicycle.

A week later Dante gave Orchard permission to try his contacts in Nice. The bicycle was disguised with some black paint that had once been used for touching up the hearse, and Orchard mounted it at dawn and went his own dark mission to Nice. A daily "normal" code was arranged for insertion in the Nice paper. If it failed to appear Stone and Mike were to leave the house. Madame LaChaise understood. Mike was quiet about Orchard's trip; Dante knew he didn't like the whole idea, but he didn't say anything. They were to expect Orchard back in three days to a week. The newspaper would warn them of his arrival. They waited.

Three days after Orchard's departure, Madame LaChaise struck paydirt. She found a Resistance contact in the brothel. It was the manageress herself. She had left a small black notebook in the cash drawer, and when Madame LaChaise opened it she had enough of a glance at its contents to realize that it was a list of German military personnel with their names and ranks. She handed it to the woman closed. The woman blanched, according to Madame LaChaise, and volunteered that it was a list of customers whose standing with the house entitled them to an occasional drink on the cuff. Madame La-Chaise told Dante that she hadn't given the woman any cause to believe that she found anything unusual about the notebook. Indeed, said Madame LaChaise, the woman was very adroit. "It is a clever woman who employs the truth to tell a lie," she said. They discussed ways this opening could be exploited, and finally Madame LaChaise suggested that she take quarters in her own "hotel" in order to supervise its management. "After all," she said, "it *is* legally a hotel. There is a sign out front to prove it." They would wait for Orchard to return before she made the move. They discussed details far into the night. When he went to bed Dante fell asleep without thinking; for the first time since they had been in the house he slept soundly. He didn't even hear Mike snoring. That was the first time, too.

In the following days they discussed the possibilities of developing the opening Madame LaChaise had found. The problem boiled down to following the trail of the money from the brothel that, on Lautrec's instructions (through Madame LaChaise), was deposited by mail each week in a bank in Lyon. The account was a blind one, a non-existent corporation purporting to be a farmers' cooperative. Although Madame LaChaise was certain that someone well placed in the bank was a Resistance member, she had steadily resisted the temptation to make inquiries for fear of exposing the enterprise as a Resistance front. She knew that her "hotel" was not the only depositor to the account, although she had no idea who the others were; the only safety lay in discretion.

Dante agreed with her that it would be dangerous to tamper with the delicate arrangement Lautrec had taken such care to set up, but he felt that if the manageress was indeed Lautrec's contact, she had to know at least one other person. If Madame failed to find this contact, he planned to go to Lyon, and from trustworthy contacts available there, to attempt the difficult task of working backward. The problem was time. Time was short. Although he had been impressed with the nearness of the invasion date, he had no way of knowing exactly when it was, or where it would come. The only thing to do, he decided, was to assume each day that it would come tomorrow, and that it would come first in the south. With time, anything could be solved, any task could be accomplished. But he had already spent weeks doing nothing, and although he was used to this as the inevitable beginning of a blind mission, in this case it was particularly frustrating. On past missions, there had never been any thought of the "end" of the war, or, indeed, that the war could ever have any end. It was only the struggle that counted, and the struggle was only in the present, with no past, no future. But now things were changed. Orchard had put it in terms that startled Dante. If Berger was in hiding, he had said, it would be best to leave him alone—"Perhaps he can hold out until the landings," he said. . . .

Orchard returned without warning. He hadn't bothered to place the notice of pending arrival since he would arrive ahead of it. He left the very day he found out. He abandoned the bicycle and took the train to make time.

He didn't come straight to the house but waited until Madame La-Chaise left late in the morning. He spoke to her from behind a thick hedge and told her to keep walking and listen. It was to her he gave the news to pass on to Dante. He also gave her a time and a place for Dante to rendezvous. He sounded nervous, Madame LaChaise said later. He had had some trouble on the train, he said, and he had something he had to do. He would wait until dark before coming back to the house. Madame LaChaise walked slowly along the tall hedge and looked straight ahead, listening carefully to him as he walked along the other side. There were people passing every now and then. She warned him under her breath when to keep silent; he would wait for the person to pass, and then continue. At the end of the hedge he repeated that he would come to the house that night. Madame LaChaise kept walking for a while and then turned and went back the way she had come.

When Dante heard the news, the first thing he did was to wake Mike. They decided it could wait until nightfall for transmission to Algiers. By then they could get more details from Orchard. But there were to be no more details. Night came and went, and Orchard didn't turn up. He didn't come that night, or the next night. No one ever saw Orchard alive again. The police found a body behind the hedge with a bullet wound in the stomach. In their opinion, Madame LaChaise reported, the man had bled a slow death.

Dante questioned Madame LaChaise over and over about the message from Orchard, with Mike listening silently. A rendezvous was set for Sunday in St. Tropez. It was to take place sometime during the noon Mass. Dante was to go alone. There were no other details. But the danger of a trap was too real to be ignored. Had Orchard meant that Dante was to rendezvous with him? But that was impossible if he was carrying the bullet inside him at the very time he was talking to Madame LaChaise. He had "had some trouble on the train" and he had "something to do." Had he fainted shortly after and fallen there behind the hedge, there to die, there to be discovered a day later by a farmer's dog? There were only the two points in Orchard's message: that the agent Berger was alive, and that someone expected to meet Dante in the church of St. Tropez on Sunday. Dante decided to keep the rendezvous, and to follow instructions and keep it alone.

The rest of that week passed slowly. In the wake of the rains that had raged since they landed, now came the first warm air moving in over the land from the south. The countryside began to look more like the prewar winter travel posters. Madame LaChaise called this the "false spring" that came every year, but to Dante it felt more like summer. The wind from the south blew steadily, and each day it seemed hotter and drier. The sun still crossed the sky low in the south and the days were short, but the palm trees were noticeably greener, and cleaner from the long rain of the short Mediterranean winter. Twice during that week Dante awoke during the night to the sound of distant explosions. The Allies were bombing German harbor batteries again. Dull tremors would thud sporadically through the foundations of the house, and Dante would lie awake and count the seconds before the explosion crumpled and died in the black silence of the moonless night. He wondered when the night would come that they would be awakened by the sound of shouting in the streets. The invasion could come any day or night. It would come without warning. And it could mean the end of his mission, it could mean failure by default.

Dante wondered how many other fugitives from time were lying awake listening to their history being hammered out in the terrible fitful silence of the night. He wondered how many of the small personal wars that were being fought in secret and in silence would be overrun and forgotten, swallowed up in the larger holocaust that would sweep in from the sea and lay waste the sad land. He wondered again if he would be alive to see the end of the war. But the question was still unreal; it was as useful to wonder if one would be alive when he passed through the gates of Heaven or the gates of Hell. Time was no longer a friend; it was an enemy. And like death, he knew it could defeat him. Each night, as he listened to the pounding in the harbor, he would think these thoughts and fall into light, uneasy sleep. Dawn would come, the bombing would stop; he would awake tired. Once he awoke from a dream; in the fleeting second between sleeping and waking he saw a vision of Orchard lying dead behind the hedge. The corpse was lying open-eyed with its finger to its lips, motionless and white, frozen in a gesture of silence.

IV

Dante stood just inside the old Cathedral of St. Tropez, unable to see for a moment. Outside, the bright sun reflected white from the powdery dust like white flour that covered the cobbled streets. It was bomb dust; it was everywhere. He stood in a tiny side door. In front of him was a blackface effigy of the patron saint of St. Tropez. Dimly he made out a red glow in the nave where the Mass was being celebrated. Then he heard the tinkle of a tiny bell and realized that the silvery-white object standing cross-like in front of the altar was the priest, his back turned and his hands upstretched. The church seemed empty and at first he thought he was almost alone in the gloom, but suddenly the crowd rose from their knees amid a rustle of cloth and he realized that he had been looking at a field of black-clad backs bent forward in prayer. He saw that the church was nearly full. For a split instant he felt panic; making contact in such a crowd would be difficult, if not impossible. Especially with the meeting blind. He went down along the side aisle and to his relief found a bench that was almost unoccupied; he was already seated before his eyes became adjusted to the gloom and he perceived the reason: at the other end of the bench sat three men in the uniform of the Wehrmacht. They were looking at him. Staring, even. From a short distance, with their caps off and in their dark uniforms, they looked like everyone else. He quelled an urge to get up and move elsewhere, deciding it would only compound the mistake. His mind raced: Why were they looking so hard at him. What was wrong? Suddenly he felt a hand on his shoulder and turned around to find a young, unsmiling priest pointing sternly to a sign over Dante's head which said: *Reservé pour les forces militaires.* That was it. The priest beckoned to Dante to follow him and pointed to an unoccupied forward seat deep in the middle of a full row. Dante moved along the row of people, stepping over feet, mumbling apologies. He could feel the blood pounding in his ears and knew the eyes of everyone behind him were watching him. In front a few people turned around and looked. There was a lull in the droning of the priest at the altar, and for one panic-stricken instant, as he was painfully shuffling his slow way past the seated people, he had the impression that the priest had stopped and was waiting for him to reach his seat. But the bell rang again and the intoning recommenced as the priest swung the censer from side to side. He reached the seat and sat down. From one of the windows in the high Romanesque clerestory a shaft of sun revealed the floating presence of blast dust in a dazzling column of silver light. It reminded him of the cheap religious chromos that adorned the walls of provincial hotel rooms before the war. He told himself that he must be on the alert since they would probably have to kneel again. In the back of his trained mind he made an automatic note to brush up on Catholic ritual in case he ever had to do this again. He was surprised that he'd overlooked the detail.

He kept his head bowed and watched the feet of the woman next to him for warning of the next genuflection. Her shoes seemed to be in better condition than those he had seen on people walking the road into town. The others were mostly farmers, fishermen perhaps. This woman must live in the town. Her shoes were brown, flat, with a fringed tongue, like the shoes Miss Ogilvy used to wear when she took her pupils walking after lessons. He could still remember how the tongues would flap up and down when she walked. He pictured in his mind his first music teacher's leggy, determined stride and recalled the maxim she would repeat when anyone complained of being tired, "If you don't learn how to walk *properly* before you're ten, you'll be in a wheelchair by the time you're fifty. You will never amount to anything unless you keep fit." Miss Ogilvy was sixty then, so his mother had said. The last he had heard of her she was still alive—and walking —at eighty. She must surely be dead by now, he reflected. She had taught him to identify different kinds of birds, and she had once taken him to New York with three other pupils to hear the big Brahms quartet in Carnegie Hall. How old would she have to be now? She was sixty-two when I was eight. I'm thirty-eight now, difference of thirty. Thirty plus sixty-two? She would have to be ninety-two. It's possible, he thought, not likely.

To calm his pulse, which was still racing from the brush with the enemy, he forced himself to recollect more about her—the way she talked, dressed—in a conscious effort to divert his mind from the panic of a moment earlier. It was an old trick. Suddenly he saw the shoes next to him disappear. He slid forward onto his knees in unison with the rest of the row, mumbling the responses as best he could. With his head bowed he could see the outline of the woman's knee and thigh stretched against the worn black-striped serge of her skirt. The brown shoes seemed out of harmony with the black cotton stockings she was wearing. Later, he told himself, he would look at her face. She must be a young woman. They knelt a long time. He tried to conjure up a vision of what she would look like, to keep his mind off his tiring knees.

Finally he was able to think only of his aching knees digging into the hardwood, and of his left foot, which was slowly going to sleep. As far as he could see without raising or turning his head, everyone else in the row had a small cushion or a roll of cloth to rest his knees on. The girl next to him knelt on what seemed to be a shawl folded into a pad.

During the final prayer, which the congregation recited mechanically, he slowly became aware that the girl next to him was not following the same words as everyone else. The singsong cadence and the monotone inflection were the same but she was repeating two phrases over and over: "Say nothing. Follow me. Say nothing. Follow me." His heart jumped. He had made contact; the young priest . . . Finally he leaned far forward, his forehead almost touching the back of the pew in front of him, and as the Amen was pronounced he nodded his head twice in what might have been a gesture of religious fervor. Beside him he heard another whispered "Amen" and felt her net gloves as she pressed his wrist with strong fingers. He thought of the Wehrmacht behind him; he didn't turn to see her face.

The congregation was standing before he could get off his knees. His left foot was completely asleep; it felt like a thousand needles when he tried to stand. With her back to him, she seemed tall. She unfurled the shawl and threw it over the tiny black veil she wore. Limping slightly, he followed her through the press of black figures toward the door, where she stopped at the font, dipped her fingers, and crossed herself. Feeling not at all awkward, he imitated her action precisely and followed her toward the door. When he had come in earlier at the side entrance the church was almost dark. But now, with the huge front doors swung wide, the bright sunlight streamed in and illuminated the motes of dust that swirled in clouds from the floor as hundreds of pairs of feet shuffled out. It was the same pulverized plaster dust that covered the streets outside, that was in his ears and hair, that he could feel thick in his nostrils and gritty between his teeth. The bombings, he thought. So fine that it rose in billows at the slightest touch, like pumice after an eruption, the dust was everywhere. It covered the town.

As it was turning out he was glad the first contact had been arranged for Sunday Mass, since the farmers from the surrounding country came into town then and the presence of a stranger would be less likely to arouse curiosity. Nobody appeared to take any notice of him as he walked along the street, keeping the girl well in sight. He had on one of the late Monsieur LaChaise's black suits. The clothes, he thought, the clothes are perfect. From the neat, worn vest to the black shoes that laced up over his ankles, the long-outdated clothes made a perfect portrait of a formerly well-off provincial entrepreneur, a pipemaker, in fact. Still, when he thought of the church and the three German soldiers, he felt a momentary emptiness in his chest. It doesn't take much, he thought; one more slip like that could finish me before I start. It occurred to him that the young priest must have been in on it. The seat had been saved for him, obviously. He wondered how many people already knew. And how much did they know? Whom was he meeting? In any event, he thought, I'll soon find out.

When she walked she held herself erect, and Dante could see now that she was not a tall girl, but very young. He lost sight of her for an instant as she passed a bend in the narrow cobblestoned street, and he crossed to the other side so he could still see her. Once she turned part way around to see if he was behind her. He saw nothing of her face because of the veil. Most of the women in the streets wore veils; St. Tropez looked like a village of mourners.

In spite of the bright sun the early spring air was cool. The sky was a crisp blue where it showed like a wide ribbon between the thick earthenware buildings that stood on either side and enclosed the street in shadow. There were no sidewalks and the street was barely wide enough for a cart. In front of each doorway was a single stone step onto the street. A few thin children sat on the steps, not talking, just watching the people coming back from Mass. Dante was close behind her when she turned out of the street into the Place de la Mairie. He felt the sun warm on his back as he followed her across the square, past the steps of the town hall, to a tiny stone archway at the opposite corner that gave into an even narrower street where there was almost no sun at all. Although the cobblestones were swept clean, faintly he could smell the dank odor of animal urine. Somewhere behind the walls he heard a man's and a woman's voices raised in argument, and farther on a racking, dry-throated sound which only after he'd passed did he recognize as a baby's crying. A group of three people walked silently past. Except for the soft echo of footsteps between the old walls, the street was quiet.

The Place des Pêcheurs was all sunshine again. The tiny café that faced the bay looked closed, but then he saw the girl open a side door and slip inside, looking back over her shoulder to make sure he was following. She left the door open. Dante crossed the square to the café and pushed aside the hanging strings of fly chain and stepped inside. For a moment he could see almost nothing. The shutters were closed and the gloom was thick like the smell of stale wine and he knew with certainty that the room before him was empty.

V

The Café des Pêcheurs had closed three months after the capitulation, and had remained closed ever since. The proprietor, Auguste Beauregard, even in those hectic days, rarely read a paper; he served the Germans and waited to see what sort of a peace France had won. And he saw. The death of his wife in her thirty-fifth year gave him the discreet reason he needed for stacking the chairs and locking the large front door for the last time. A few of his friends among the fishermen visited him in his sorrow, which was inarticulate and genuine, and it was known that on rare occasions for a short time thereafter he still served a select few from his place behind the zinc counter. But the front door remained locked. When his friends came, they entered by the side door. Then they stopped coming.

He rarely appeared outside and kept aloof from the town, where his status was still undecided. During the first months of the occupation he had been severely criticized for being cordial to the Germans and serving them in his café, but Auguste *père* had served under Pétain and Auguste *fils* had been brought up to revere the Hero of Verdun as a savior of France. The old man was long dead but his son remembered, and kept faith. He kept faith for six weeks and lost it. In six more weeks he had lost his wife. He took care not to offend the new authorities and apologized to his military customers when he closed the café. He did nothing to correct the town's impression of him, and even cultivated the stain on his honor by refusing to discuss politics with the few friends who still tried to convert him. But in his heart a black resolve for vengeance was taking shape. One man, a young man new in the village, called Carnot, saw through Auguste Beauregard's protective coloration, waited, and when the time came, made him an offer.

At first only a trickle came in, but the proprietor of the Café des Pêcheurs knew every fisherman from Cannes to Toulon, and gradually the shipments were increased. Little by little, methods were refined, operations expanded, until finally the fishermen's café looking out over the tranquil bay of St. Tropez, windows shuttered, its blue-painted letters almost illegible, grew to be a major clearing house for strategic contraband. At first it was common smuggling, olive oil, drugs, gold, Swiss francs, concealed in fish, wine bottles, gasoline cans; anything that would help finance the growing organization that was quietly spreading long roots deep into the soil all over France. Later, when the men were proven, rudimentary contact was established with Malta and Gibraltar; weapons began coming in, transmitters, short-wave receivers, two printing presses. Even by that time it was big business. But Auguste kept his part in it secret. The café was never used for storing goods; its essential function was coordination. And that function was secret. Only a handful of the men who risked their lives bringing in the stream of goods would have hesitated to add a few words of calumny to the already soiled reputation of Auguste Beauregard, the recluse café owner who had once served Germans. Only a handful knew who directed their operations; the rest had no idea whom they were working for.

Alexi Carnot had wanted Auguste for the job from the very moment the idea was first conceived. Before Auguste ruined his back he had been a fisherman—like his father before him—and his knowledge of the coast was nearly infallible. It was as though he had decided that since he couldn't fish, he would commit the coast to memory and fish it in his mind as he tended bar. During the years after he started the café, a large part of his time was taken up giving advice when it was asked, and it was asked often. His one particular pleasure was settling arguments, for he also enjoyed the authority of a referee. Friends in happier years had won many drinks from Auguste at *vingt-et-un,* for *le bonhomme Beauregard* made it firm policy never to refuse to roll the dice, double or nothing, with anyone who had a glass at the zinc.

Carnot had listened carefully when one day, before Madame Beauregard died, Auguste on that rare occasion attempted to explain his hope for Pétain's government; Carnot decided then that Beauregard's loyalties were more with his patriot father than with his father's patriot. But he only listened, and said nothing. Perhaps Carnot's own bitterness made him more acute to the subtle change that was then taking place in Auguste and culminated only with his wife's death, but he recognized that Auguste was not a man of fickle loyalties. When the disillusionment came Carnot knew it. He probed behind Auguste's silence, sounding him out. He sat night after night at the bar, rolling the three dice out of the leather cup, and watched Auguste's false smile when Germans came in to be served and saw the secret hate and rage in his eyes. It was during this time that Carnot, with careful impertinence, began addressing Auguste in the royal third person, as Auguste the Honest. A month later, when Carnot finally obtained formal permission from Nice to approach Beauregard, he asked him simply if he wanted to work for France. Auguste looked him straight in the eye. "My wife is lost," he said, shrugging his shoulders. "I have nothing more to lose. I have no choice. I have nothing."

Carnot poured a glass of cheap wine and drank a toast. "To Auguste the Honest," he said.

Auguste refilled the glass. "To no choice," he said. A dribble of wine ran down his chin and he wiped it with his sleeve.

Nothing more was said. Light from the candle butt danced among the twisted shadows of the stacked chairs, and the only sound was the rolling of the dice in the leather cup and the clicking on the metal bar as they spilled down its length. A few days later the Café des Pêcheurs quietly went out of business and its owner became the village hermit. Everyone said he was mourning his wife—which he was—and waiting for the Germans to win their war—which he was not.

"Mass should be over by now," Auguste said nervously. He sat holding the battered old alarm clock in both his ham-like hands, and stared balefully at the face. "Maybe she missed him."

"Maybe," said Carnot. He didn't seem to be listening, but concentrated on a Luger he was assembling on his side of the round table. In the center was an empty wine bottle.

"How are you so sure he'll come, Alexi? You forget what happened to the other one."

Carnot found the part he was looking for and started it in its hole. He forced it into place with the point of a bullet. "I'm sure, Auguste," he said, looking up.

"What will you do with Henri?" Auguste asked.

"Henri drinks too much."

"I think he drinks because he is afraid."

"He drinks too much," said Carnot. "When he can't have his way, he drinks."

There was a rush of water through the pipes in the wall, and from upstairs came the sound of a door opening.

"He had a job to do this morning. He didn't do it," said Auguste. "This makes the third time. I think you're taking a chance trying to use him. He tries to find courage in a bottle."

"It's not such a bad place to look," said Carnot. "He looks a little too hard."

"But why did you send him?"

Carnot looked steadily at Auguste. "Because I'd rather risk him than Adriane."

Auguste lifted a finger to his lips.

Henri came heavily down the stairs. He was obviously still drunk and his black hair was soaking wet. Leaning on the wall to steady himself, he stood at the bottom of the stairs with his cap in his hand, blinking to focus his eyes. The other two men watched him and said nothing. Henri was thin and short, and his face was infected with adolescent pimples which were worse for being picked at. He was trying hard to look sober, but even though color was slowly returning to his face, the nausea had left him shaky. He walked deliberately across the room and sat down on the cot next to the wall.

"You've almost got it together, Alexi," Henri said, trying to focus on the pistol and enunciating with drunken precision. "How long would it take me to learn how to take one like that apart and put it back together again?"

"Why don't you stay upstairs and lie down, Henri?" Auguste asked gently. "We have company coming this morning. Have you forgotten?"

"I feel fine now," said Henri, fixing a smile on his face. "You always feel better when you get rid of it." He bounced a little on the edge of the cot. Contrasted with his waxen face, the effect of his attempt at gaiety was harrowing.

"Maybe this time will cure you," said Carnot. "But you still don't look like you're alive. Your sister will think we've been beating you. Why don't you lie down on the cot for a while, until she gets back?"

"Thanks," said the boy. "I'm still a little weak, I guess."

"If you get dizzy," said Carnot, "put one foot on the floor."

"This way I'll be here if you need me to do anything." Henri lay back on the cot. "I want to earn my keep."

Carnot bent over the pistol. Auguste watched him intently. He was still holding the clock, and for a long time the only sound in the room was its clatter and the scraping of the miniature file Carnot was using. He would file a few strokes and then try the piece in the gun, then take it out and file it some more. Auguste watched as he did this several times.

"What do you do that for?" he asked finally.

"It has a heavy trigger," said Carnot. "It's an antique. Must be one of the first ones they ever made. I reblued it yesterday."

Henri was lying on the couch with his cap over his eyes. His regular breathing sounded as though he might be asleep. But he wasn't.

"Alexi?" Henri's voice was stronger. He sounded almost sober.

"Yes, Henri?"

"Alexi, I'm sorry about this morning. But I didn't know it was so important. You should have told me it was important."

"Everything is important."

"Yes, but sometimes I feel that all I ever do is run errands and bring eggs in from the farm," said Henri. He was speaking through his cap and the words had no timbre. A few times he stumbled over his pronunciation, betraying the fact that he still wasn't completely sober.

"Armies move on their bellies, my cabbage."

"What I mean is, you never tell me what anything is about. All you said was that I was supposed to bring someone back from church. You didn't tell me it was so important. I never know what anything is about. That's what I mean. I always feel like you don't trust me, or you wouldn't always leave me in the dark. I don't like being left in the dark."

"Children never do." Carnot put the pistol down and sighed a tired sigh. "I'm sorry, Henri, but you've tried my patience badly this morning. I don't imagine you remember, but we've been all through this before. Why keep nagging yourself with endless questions? The less you know, the better it will go for you when you are caught. But you don't have to act like a fourteen-year-old. Your sister didn't ask questions. She just went."

"I'm not a child, Alexi," said Henri. "They'll never learn anything from me, even if we are caught."

"Precisely, my cabbage. Because you don't know anything."

"I'm old enough to take responsibility," said Henri. "You're not that much older than I am."

"First you should learn to mimic a clam," said Carnot.

There was a long silence, then Henri sat up unsteadily. "But you let Adriane . . ." he started again.

Auguste interrupted. "Are we back to that again? I must agree with Alexi, Henri. This is getting very tiresome. I know you were drunk, but I wish you'd stop chewing on the same cud. If we didn't trust you, I personally would have chopped you up for fish bait long ago. As for your sister, she was the next logical one to go. It means we'll get a cold dinner, that's all."

Carnot signaled with his hands to let it drop, but Auguste ignored him and went on.

"Alexi couldn't go. It's too risky. You couldn't go because you were sick. If I showed up for Mass it would be a public event, it would cause talk. Someone would surely ask questions, and I'd have to stop and answer and explain how I'd had a visitation from the Virgin or something, while our customer stood in the street chewing his hat. At least Adriane knows which way to cross herself."

Carnot wanted to end the conversation. "Look, Henri, you have no reason to worry about Adriane. She knows when to keep her mouth shut and she is very reliable. Why don't you take a nap?"

"She is reliable. She is your mistress," said Henri, his thick tongue blurring the words, "and I am your mascot."

"Nom de Dieu!" Carnot picked up the pistol and slid it back onto the table with a clatter. "This has been going on for three weeks. If you can't find anything better to do than complain and get drunk, Henri, then you'd better get out. You know what your job is. To sit still and keep quiet. You talk about trusting you. Do you think your performance this morning was calculated to inspire trust? I have been very patient because you have been useful. I'd hate to lose your services. But either you stick to your job and take orders, or quit now. This is the time to decide. Which will it be?"

Henri sat looking at his hands. "I'm sorry," he said. "You know I don't want to quit." He began picking a pimple on his chin. He seemed on the verge of tears. Carnot could see that his hands were still shaking. Henri looked so beaten that Carnot's anger was frustrated.

"As for you, Auguste," he said, turning around, "you should know better."

"What have *I* done?" asked the proprietor, bewildered.

"You're older than Henri, but all morning long you've been worming at me. 'When will he come?' 'Are you sure he's coming?' Let me tell you both the facts of life again. Very few men in this world can be convincing while they pretend ignorance when in pain. In the end they convict themselves by trying to trade what they know for relief, which they get only in front of a firing squad. Only the ignorant survive. In this business, knowledge is automatic guilt. So be ignorant. I don't want to hear another word out of either of you. Henri, lie down and go to sleep."

The room was quiet for a long time. Carnot finished assembling the Luger while Auguste caught a sluggish out-of-season fly in the empty wine bottle. He made the fly move around inside by shaking the bottle, and succeeded in wetting him with a drop of wine. The fly cleaned himself and then began to buzz crazily around inside the bottle. Auguste removed the cork to see if he would fly out. Carnot heard the furious buzzing and looked up.

"The little bastard is blind drunk," said Auguste.

The fly hit the side of the glass and fell into the dregs at the bottom. He started walking up the sides, but each time he got to the place where the neck curved in he fell down to the bottom again. Auguste turned the bottle upside down and the fly slid out and fell on the table, where he floated in a dribble of wine. Auguste gave the fly a push but he didn't move.

"Dead drunk," he said. "Dead. That's better than swatting him."

"You think maybe it's more fun for the flies?" Alexi said. "You're just as dead one way as another."

Auguste sighed and righted the bottle. He picked up the clock in both hands again; the glass was missing from the clock's face and the metal base was gone. "Mass should be over by now," he said.

Carnot, tight-lipped, laughed. He wiped the pistol with the oily rag and cocked and released it several times to test the tension in the spring. Then he held it up to the light and squinted intently down the barrel. "Auguste, why don't you put that clock down?" he asked, sighting through the barrel. "Squeezing it won't make it go faster."

Auguste laid the clock face up on the table. Suddenly Henri got up from the cot and started toward the door leading to the small court around which the house was built.

"Not out there, my little cabbage," said Carnot.

"I don't feel well."

"Condolences," said Carnot. "But not out there again."

"But where?" He darted his eyes about the room like a dog trapped in a fire. His face was pale, almost gray, and sweating.

"The neighbors will hear and think Auguste is kicking off," said Carnot. "Some of them might come nosing around hoping to make sure." He carefully wrapped the pistol in the rag. "If you can't make it upstairs, put it in your beret."

Henri looked at the shaving sink on the opposite wall. "No!" shouted Auguste, trying to get out of his chair. "If you . . . No!" Skirting Auguste's outstretched arms, Henri loped around the table and across the room.

"I'm going to be . . . going to be . . . sick . . . a-gain!"

Auguste saw Henri blurt the last words into the sink, and fell back in his chair, his face buried in his hands.

"I told him to stay upstairs!" He groaned and looked up. "Pig!" he shouted. "Bail it out before it clogs!"

Carnot couldn't help laughing at Auguste. He was purple, and was making unconscious motions with his hands, as though tearing invisible hair from his bald head.

"If the neighbors catch a whiff of that, Auguste," said Carnot, still laughing, "they'll think you've been dead for a week."

Carnot turned around to Henri, who had collapsed to his knees before the basin, exhausted, his head bent forward on his chest. "I'm sorry, Alexi," he whispered. "I'm sick. You've got to get me something . . . I need it, Alexi."

"You're full of poison," said Carnot. "What were you drinking this morning?" Carnot could see Henri's hands shaking. Only then did he realize he was hiding a rosary in his hand. Henri didn't answer.

"I only gave him two *pastises* so his hands would stop shaking," Auguste said defensively. "But he went out before breakfast."

"Where did you get it, Henri?"

Henri still made no answer. Carnot got up and covered the sink with a newspaper. He gently pulled back Henri's head by the wet hair, until Henri opened his eyes and looked at him. Carnot was shocked at the color of his face. He had once seen a drowned man washed up on the beach who was that color.

"Who gave it to you, Henri?"

"No one gave it to me. I'm sorry. I took it out of Max's compass. His extra one."

"You what?" Carnot stared at him.

"The alcohol out of Max's compass."

Carnot looked at Auguste.

Auguste shrugged. "If you open a compass, it's all but ruined," he said. Carnot helped Henri to his feet.

"Go upstairs and lie down. Don't worry about this mess. Adriane will take care of it."

Carnot watched his back as he slowly went upstairs.

"He is a fool," said Auguste.

"He is a sick fool," said Carnot moodily. "It's a good thing he got rid of it. I'm not going to let him have anything."

"He'll never break the habit," said Auguste.

"He'll have to. If he doesn't, we'll have to shoot him," said Carnot. "Like a horse."

Suddenly Auguste held up his hand and turned his head to listen. He got to his feet just as they heard the side door open. The blackout curtains partitioning the room they were in from the front of the café suddenly parted and the girl stepped into the room looking flushed and frightened. She dropped her veil and shawl on the table and motioned wordlessly toward the front room.

"Is anything wrong?" Carnot asked in a whisper.

The girl shook her head and looked back at the curtains.

"Good. Go upstairs and take care of your brother. He's sick. Auguste, you stay here for a while."

They heard the whisper of the fly chains as someone entered the front room.

Unbuttoning his shirt, Carnot put the pistol wrapped in the rag into its holster. He buttoned the shirt and went to the curtains and stood listening for a moment. No sound came from the other room. He opened the curtains and saw the silhouette of a man standing inside the doorway. In the middle of the room a table stacked high with chairs stood in the line of vision and Carnot watched the man through the rungs of a chair as he moved warily away from the door into the room. He was looking around the room and hadn't yet seen Carnot, since the back room was almost as dark as the deserted café.

"Close the door and bolt it. We're in here."

The man turned and closed the door without a word. Carnot dropped the curtain back in place and took up a position behind the table beside Auguste, who had risen also and was nervously pulling at his mustache. The curtains parted and Dante stepped into the room. For a moment no one said anything. Each of the three men in the room felt the uncertainty.

Carnot's handshake was direct and firm and his hand was hard. He spoke with the accent of the Midi, rolling his r's and voicing mute e's. "We are very glad to have you with us," he said.

Dante returned the handshake and looked straight at Carnot, whose eyes did not waver. He watched Dante steadily. Even as he introduced Dante to Auguste, Carnot's eyes never left Dante's face for a second.

Dante shook hands with the café owner. "We are happy to see you," said Auguste.

Dante turned again to Carnot.

"You couldn't be any happier to see me than I am to see you," Dante said, grinning broadly.

"Unfortunately we have no fatted calf to slaughter," Carnot said, relaxing into a chair. There was an atmosphere of relief in the room—suppressed and tense, but it was there. "However, Auguste has a rabbit which he can't save much longer, can you, Auguste?"

Auguste smiled a wry smile and sat down.

"Would you keep an eye on the door outside, Auguste?" said Carnot. He watched Auguste leave the room. "I expected a younger man," he said. "Why did they pick someone as old as you?"

Dante was surprised at the blunt candor of the question. He took the chair Auguste vacated at the table and sat down. "I must admit I hadn't expected you to be quite so young. Do I look like an old man?"

"You look young enough to jump on cue. That's all that counts. We are still in the position where when they shoot we dance. We have no choice. We need weapons. Guns. Grenades. And bigger. Especially bigger. Automatic weapons are what we need worst."

"I think I can get them for you. That's why I'm here."

"When?" asked Carnot. "Assume we have the organization you're looking for."

"As soon as we can arrange pickup points and a distribution scheme. They'll do you no good in their crates."

"Yes. The big problem. We've set up a system of caches but it's obsolete. Things are moving too fast, and there is always the risk of discovery. We've lost too much already."

"One of the things I must make clear—as long as we're getting down to business so quickly," said Dante. "The quantity and type of arms you'll get will depend on the facilities you have for handling them. The decision as to amount and variety of weapons into this part of France will rest on how effectively you can use them. How many men you have. What training facilities you've got. Et cetera. We will have to divert them from elsewhere. You'll have to convince London and Algiers that it will pay off strategically, since as long as the Germans are in firm control, the only justification for diverting shipments from Italy into France will be the size of the nuisance you can create with them."

"During the landings?"

"During the landings."

"Perhaps you don't feel that the war is still going on in France, is that it?" asked Carnot, bitterness in the question.

"What should I call you?"

"Alexi."

"You use your real name?" asked Dante. "Or a cover name?"

"I managed a death certificate a long time ago. Even to his old friends, Alexi Carnot is a dead man. Carnot is the name I was born with."

"Your family is in France, also?"

"I have no father. My mother never knew his name. I was raised by Jesuits. My mother was a paid whore," he said calmly. "She paid the priests for my board, and I worked on a farm. She used to come and visit me every other Sunday. I went in to the city one Saturday and found her and I knew. But I was old enough to suspect it before."

Dante listened in silence, concealing his surprise at the gratuitous bald revelation. Carnot must have told the story many times before—it seemed glib and artificial—and he was evidently determined to tell it again. He recited it mechanically, like a penance.

"I beat her, you see. I beat her until she told me. I forced her to tell me. I made her confess that all the stories she had told me about my father were a lie. I was sorry I had to find out, because I think she loved me. I was sorry for beating her. She said she would never forgive me. I left the farm that night and never went back. Once I wrote to my half-sister. She told me my mother married a violin teacher from Strasbourg. When you deal with me, never forget you're dealing with a bastard."

Dante asked the question quietly, his mind recoiling from the brutal, unsolicited intimacy of Carnot's speech. "You've never seen her since?"

"My sister probably told her I'm dead," he said matter-of-factly. "But I like the name Alexi Carnot. It is the one link I allow myself with the world." Carnot laughed. "Don't look so serious. There are certain advantages to being officially dead. One has no social obligations, no friends to cheat you . . ."

"Well," said Dante, leaning back in his chair, "at least it has this advantage. Once dead, it will be awkward to kill you again."

"Who knows?" said Carnot. "Perhaps when this war is over and the pigs driven out of our garden, who knows? Perhaps I'll resurrect myself." Carnot stretched in his chair.

"Why did you want a death certificate?" Dante watched Carnot's face, wondering how young he was.

"I was known as a Party member," he said simply. "They had no photographs or fingerprints, though. We arranged for them to supply us with a corpse and the corpse and I went underground together. It would be impossible now. They keep a stricter accounting of corpses. But right after Dunkirk it was still possible."

"How old were you?"

"I died in the prime of life," Carnot said with a self-satisfied smile. "Three days after my nineteenth birthday."

"So now you are, what, twenty-two, -three?"

"The dead age slowly," said Carnot. "I am a child of eternity."

"I see." Dante smiled. "War is Hell. The general Sherman was right."

"The general was right," said Carnot. "War *is* Hell. And we are the damned. I feel most alive at funerals. I love funerals."

"I must say, you don't talk like a young man," Dante lied.

"Perhaps I talk like a Jesuit," said Carnot, leaning forward. "My point is that a dead man can't afford to be young. Not if he wants to stay alive. A young man is young because he makes mistakes. Mistakes are luxuries we are forced to do without. Upstairs there is a young man who still makes mistakes. He makes mistakes because he thinks he is still alive. He is not protected by the armor of death, by the knowledge that he also is dead. He still *feels* his fear, has ambition. Probably he still masturbates when he is alone in his room. He is young. He makes mistakes, as the saying goes, because he is human. I am *in*human. I have trained myself in my role of dead man, so that I no longer feel fear. I have no ambitions and no ideals. I only have my job, and I only do that so that someday I may be able to live again. But I don't think about that. For we are a nation of dead men. As you say, we live in Hell."

"What about Orchard?" Dante asked abruptly. "What happened to him?"

"What do you mean what happened? They shot him. What else do you think happened to him?"

"Is there nothing else you can tell me?" But he already knew there wasn't.

"There's nothing else to tell," said Carnot. He shrugged. "They shot him. He's dead. There's nothing else."

Neither Carnot nor Dante heard Auguste come through the curtains. His rope-soled shoes made no sound on the stone floor.

"*Le frère* wants to see you, Alexi. He won't say about what."

"Stay by the door, Auguste. Send him in here."

Dante immediately recognized the young priest, who gave no sign of recognizing him.

"What is it, Charles?"

Before answering, the priest looked at Dante.

"It's all right to talk in front of him," Carnot said.

"One of them didn't come back this morning," said the priest. "I've just been to his room. He hasn't slept in his bed."

"You shouldn't have gone there. Did anyone see you?"

"No," the priest said hesitantly, looking at Dante again. "It's Max. And he knows about this place."

"Have you told anyone else? The others must know something if you asked them about him."

"No one knows he's missing. Everyone checked in except him."

"Does Max know about the farm?"

"No one knows about the farm, except Auguste and the girl and her brother." Charles still seemed to find it painful to talk in front of the stranger in the room. He kept shifting his weight from one foot to the other and glancing awkwardly at Dante as he talked. He looked uncomfortable and was obviously anxious to say as little as possible. It dawned on Dante that the priest must not know the reason for his presence in St. Tropez. He wondered where the man Max had been that he didn't come back from. He saw that Carnot was worried.

"Why did it have to be Max?" Carnot said, half to himself. He sat motionless, thinking. He sighed heavily and stood up. "We'll have to clear out of here until we find out what happened to him."

Carnot went into the other room and Dante could hear him talking to Auguste in low tones·behind the curtain. Dante caught the priest's eye and said, "Thank you for this morning."

"It was nothing," said the priest. He seemed to disapprove of further conversation and Dante left it at that. Carnot came back into the room.

"Auguste and the others will join us this evening," he said. "You'll go with the Lord's apostle here," he said to Dante. "I hope you don't find him too talkative. I'll follow you in sight." Then to the priest: "We'll use the farm."

"How far is this farm?" asked Dante. He got up from the chair and picked up his hat. Then he recognized the piece of dark cloth on the table; it was *her* shawl. It brought back instantaneously the scene in the church—sitting beside her, alone, going through the mumbling motions of prayer and watching the movement of her shoes. Suddenly the full impact of his utter dependence on these people struck him. A girl whose face he hadn't seen; a man almost young enough to be his pupil, who he suspected was utterly ruthless nevertheless; and now this sallow-cheeked young priest who used his frock for a soldier's disguise. Out of the tail of his eye he watched the priest's bent back disappear between the curtains and a feeling of helplessness came over him— passive, even oddly satisfying, like a yawn. There were too many questions to ask even to try to begin. His only choice was complete trust. He knew now, finally, that there was no turning back. He felt indeed like an old man and knew he was tired.

Carnot was saying something. Even as Dante turned his head, his gaze hung onto the shawl, as though his eyes, independent of will, had found a lazy interest of their own. "I'm sorry. What did you say?" he asked mechanically.

"I said, it's a long walk and I hope those fancy shoes are comfortable," said Carnot. Dante shook a fleeting picture of Miss Ogilvy out of his mind. What's the matter with me? he thought.

"Shoes?" Dante said. "Oh, *these* shoes." He lifted his trouser cuff. "I'm afraid they're not a very good fit. I have blisters already. Funny, they also belong to a dead man. I have them on loan."

"Well, dust is easier on the feet than leather," said Carnot as he followed him out of the room. "If they give you too much trouble you can take them off and go barefoot. Like a true pilgrim. You won't be the only farmer carrying his shoes back from Mass. Saves leather. It's an economical penance—a cheap way to atone for your sins."

The farm was four kilometers out of town, on a slight rise of distant land that gave it a view of the village. The narrow back road toward Ramatuelle was utterly deserted, and as they walked the only sound was the starting of birds from the brush and the occasional rustle of an animal in the leaves. Once, just before they passed the last houses at the edge of town, the priest spoke.

"If you hear a motorcycle, you will leave the road. Go into the brush and lie down," he said. "We will not stay together. You go left. I'll go right. Wait until you see me come out. If anything happens, use your judgment."

"Is this road patrolled?" Dante asked.

"Yes," said the priest. "It is near the sea."

"And the farm?"

"The farm is safe. We supply two coast guns with fresh milk and eggs every day."

Dante looked at him, searching his face. "No butter?"

He seemed surprised. "Butter? Yes, sometimes butter, too."

Dante said nothing more but concentrated on matching the hard pace the priest set.

Once or twice, on stretches where the road ran straight, he looked back and saw the figure of Carnot in the distance. As they passed a fork where a narrower road joined, little more than a path, Dante saw the sharp print of tire treads in the dust. At first he thought they were automobile tracks but then he realized that he was looking at the imprint of a motorcycle with a sidecar. He noticed that the tracks seemed to weave from one side of the dust strip to the other. That patrol must have been going very slowly, he thought.

Later, the priest waited for him while he stopped to take off his shoes. The cool dust felt good between his toes. It made him think of Carnot and he involuntarily looked back again to see if Carnot had seen him stop. There was a bend in the road and he was nowhere in sight. Charles seemed determined to walk slightly ahead now and Dante watched the large ebony cross as it swung from his hip with his stride. They stopped only once more, when the priest went to the side of the road to urinate. Dante was struck by the whiteness of his legs.

As they neared the farm there was a long stretch of umbrella pines, their grotesque and twisted branches driven seaward, as though tormented by an invisible wind. They seemed to cling to the sand and the red rocks only by the tips of their roots, which strained toward the land in a shapeless tangle. The March air was cool and still, except when once or twice a gust of wind blew from nowhere, gnashing the desiccated blades of wintered palms, then died again into the stillness.

The farm was set a good distance back from the road and was nearly hidden behind a tangle of undergrowth and scrub sand pine that bordered the narrow track that led to it. Dante continued to follow his guide at several paces. The priest walked very slowly now. Three times he stopped, waited, as though halted by an unheard challenge from the brush. In each case he turned his head in the direction of the unseen sentry, nodded slowly, and waited for permission to pass. Dante avoided looking to either side but felt the invisible eyes as he passed the places where the priest had stopped.

The farm buildings were in an obvious state of disrepair and disuse. The main house was shuttered and gave the appearance of being abandoned. It was a long, low building with thick earthen walls and a sloped roof. The ancient clay tiles of the roof were broken and patched in places, and clumps of dry grass made curious toadstool-like shapes in the otherwise bare reddish sand around the base of the building.

Inside the house, the priest led him to a small room in the rear. Dante had to duck his head under the low beams that supported the ceiling in the narrow dark corridor. He was still half blinded from the bright sun outside. The priest opened the door and nodded for Dante to enter.

"This will be your room," the priest said, not looking at him. "You will wait here until I come back for you."

Dante went in and the door closed behind him. Light entered the small room from narrow slits between the sun-shrunken boards of the shutters. It cast a barred pattern on the bare brick floor. Against the wall at the left was a cot with a bare mattress on it. There was nothing else in the room except a white chamber pot in the corner opposite the foot of the cot and a small wooden plaque on the earthen wall. The plaque looked as if it might have once had a crucifix attached to it. He sat down on the cot and waited, cooling his tired feet on the cool brick floor. In another part of the building he heard a thump, like a door thudding shut.

For a long time he heard no other sound. He refused to wonder what would happen next. Finally he stretched out on the cot, his fingers laced behind his head, and stared at the ceiling, waiting, not thinking, but resting his mind, waiting.

It was about an hour later that he heard voices outside his room. He sat up just as the priest opened the door.

"Come with me," he said, standing in the doorway.

Dante reached down to put on his shoes, but the priest made an impatient gesture. "Carry them with you," he said.

The priest led him to another part of the house. Dante entered a long low room which he took to be the main room. Several men were seated on benches along both sides of a trestle-footed board table. Three of them had weapons slung on their backs. Dante assumed that these were the three sentries who'd been on duty outside the house. As Dante entered the low-voiced conversation stopped. None of the men looked up at him. He felt foolish standing holding his shoes. and turned around to find the priest, but he was gone.

252

The man at the head of the table lifted his head from a newspaper and nodded to the others. They got up, lifting their legs over the benches, and left the room, filing past without looking at him. Dante was left alone in the room with the man at the head of the table. He was a small thin man with steel spectacles. He looked up at Dante and motioned him to sit down. Dante came forward and sat down on the bench. The stone floor under his bare feet was gritty. He dropped his shoes before him and forced his feet into them one by one. The bespectacled man was reading his newspaper again, ignoring Dante's presence. Suddenly he folded the paper without looking up and said, in perfect English: "So you are the famous Dante."

Dante remained silent.

"Would you like to know what happened to Lautrec?" the man asked.

"Perhaps you should tell me who you are," Dante said.

"That isn't necessary. You'll not be seeing me again so there's no need to know my name. It is purely by chance that I'm in this region, which is perhaps fortunate for you. My colleagues aren't too well disposed toward you."

"What about Lautrec?"

"I'm down here for much the same reason I imagine you are. The New Year's Day raid was disturbing news in Paris. Even if they didn't touch our organization, you see, such an occurrence is cause for general concern."

Dante nodded. The man still didn't look at Dante as he spoke, but looked at his hands, which he kept folded before him on the table. His British-sounding English was bookish and precise, with hardly a trace of accent. He had the manner and speech of an educated man.

"You are acquainted with a person called Antoine?" the man asked.

"I've never met anyone called that," Dante said, hedging. It was true; he had never met Berger.

"Precisely. But perhaps you'd like to."

Dante said nothing.

"Lautrec's organization, as you have probably found out by now, has been completely destroyed. We are not sure who was responsible, but it might interest you to know that Lautrec is still alive. He's under guard in a villa outside St. Raphaël."

"Under whose guard?"

"Your agent Antoine came here from Paris with an introduction to a person named Dujardin. Have you heard of him?"

Dante hesitated. "Yes, I've heard of him."

"Precisely. And you are under orders to contact him."

Dante let the mistaken assumption pass uncorrected.

"Antoine apparently fears Frenchmen more than he does Germans. He was very anxious to unite Lautrec's group with others in order to compete with us."

"Where is . . ."

"Your agent?" the man finished for him. "He is alive. We saved his life, but he doesn't seem very grateful. We are holding him."

Dante remained silent.

"We have had people in Lautrec's group from the beginning. It has been necessary from time to time to know what our friends were up to. I would give you some good advice." This time the man looked at Dante. "Don't go near Dujardin."

Dante nodded noncommittally.

The man looked at his hands again. "I came here mainly to interrogate your friend Antoine. Perhaps I should tell you a little about him."

"Are you sure I'll be interested?" Dante asked.

The other ignored the remark. He made a spire of his hands and tilted his head back to gaze at the ceiling. "We first became aware of his activities in Paris. He is not a very cautious young man. I was assigned to cultivate an acquaintance with him and keep track of his movements. We did not know at the time that he was an American agent. We were under the mistaken assumption that he was a French citizen. Do you know what group he was working with in Paris?" The man turned and gazed at Stone. Stone didn't let his expression change.

The man looked at the ceiling again. Then he said, "He calls himself a *Monarchiste*. It would be an excellent cover for an American agent, except that this one is serious. That makes him very dangerous."

Dante made a gambit. He said, "Why should this interest me?"

The small man turned and looked at him. His eyes were open wide in feigned surprise. He said, "Why, my dear sir, your life may depend on it. Perhaps you might be more interested in the fact that six months ago he lost nearly twelve thousand francs at chemin de fer. He seems to have a pathological need to gamble. Suicidal types often do. And there is some evidence that he is a user of narcotics. Narcotics are still fashionable in certain of the more effete circles of European society. Your agent seems to have become attracted to the followers of splendid decadence. He displays a fondness for faded baronesses. I have information that he hopes to become a papal count after the war. For a young man in his twenties, it seems a strange ambition, don't you agree?"

Dante decided to commit himself. "How did you get to know him?" he asked.

"Why, my dear sir, I am of an excellent family," he said. There was a faint, mocking smile on his face.

"What is this monarchist group you mentioned?"

"There are several, of course. All bickering among themselves. This particular group, however, believes in direct action—counterrevolutionaries of the purest kind. They are counter to the French Revolution above all others. Their hope is to take advantage of the present conflict to restore the Count of Paris to the throne. It's nothing new in

France, of course. Unfortunately, their methods are rather reminiscent of the Medici family. Machiavellian in the extreme. I rather doubt that your superiors know the full extent of their agent's involvement in these activities, since undoubtedly he would take great care to conceal his allegiance to a cause that conflicts so violently with the American form of bourgeois republicanism."

"Do you know him intimately?" Dante asked.

"I have been careful not to—as you can well understand," the man said. "But of course now that he knows of my connection with the National Front, he will have to be taken out of France. But that's a matter I leave for you to negotiate with the local committee."

"Then he is a hostage, is that right?"

"You might put it that way. However, the only ransom we want is his removal. If it weren't for the fact that he is an American agent, he would have been tried and executed, I'm afraid."

"What do you want from me?"

"Perhaps you should put that question the other way around. What do you want from us? And what are you prepared to give in return?"

Dante said nothing.

The man continued, "Your troops are in Italy. The main landings will no doubt come here in the south. Casualties will be high. Our objectives are not different. We have an enemy in common. Do you want our help? If not, you'll get it anyway, since we will continue to kill that common enemy with whatever weapons we can lay our hands on. If you want more from us than that, you will have to provide us with the means to do it. Do I make my meaning clear?"

"And your political objectives?" Dante asked.

"Military objectives come first."

"And after the war?"

The man shrugged. "That will be up to you. Your government will enter this country as a conqueror, a friendly conqueror, but a conqueror nevertheless. You will dictate the future government of this country. You are fools if you try to install De Gaulle in power. But we are counting on you to do it. De Gaulle will make a *salade* of things, but his blunders will strengthen us in the long run. Our political objectives are simple: we will wait."

"Who has the power to speak here?"

"You'll discuss that with the committee. You have met Carnot."

"He's in charge?"

"He will tell you what you need to know. He is young but he is intelligent. If I were you I wouldn't conceal any of my motives from him."

"Where is Antoine Berger?"

"You will have a chance to talk with him. We have informed him of your arrival. The news seemed to distress him. I would advise you to be very careful in talking to him. He is a very impulsive young man, not what I'd call a good agent. He's much too conspicuous."

"Why was he distressed?"

The man looked at Dante, absently picking up the newspaper. "He is a young man who is very disturbed in his mind. He is not anxious to leave France."

"How did he escape the New Year's raid?"

"We had a young woman working as a servant in the house where he was staying. Théophile Dujardin's house. Your agent Antoine learned that her younger brother had been caught with a case of black-market cigarettes in his possession. He very foolishly arranged for her brother's release without consulting his host. He is dangerously fond of making gallant gestures. As it was, his bribe was successful. But the boy would have been safer in jail. She learned that Berger was an American agent. Can you imagine, the fool told her for no other reason than to display his bravado. When Carnot got warning of the raid we had time to snatch Berger out of Dujardin's house along with the girl."

"Dujardin, I understand, is well placed in the district police."

"Stay away from him. He's playing a double game."

"Are you certain of that?"

"Frankly? No. Why should I lie to you?"

"Why did you save Antoine and not Lautrec?"

The other turned his palms upward, as though to show them empty. "There was no time. Lautrec was picked up earlier. Besides, an American agent is more useful alive than dead."

"You were here during the raid?" Dante asked. "Or in Paris?"

"You have no need to know," the other said shortly. He rose from the table and nodded toward the doorway. A man with a rifle on his back stepped out of the shadow of the doorway into the room.

"We have finished our little talk," the man said to Dante. He turned to the guard. "See that he has whatever he needs," he instructed. His voice turned hard and was utterly different from the mild-mannered tone of his conversation with Dante. A slender man with a scholarly look, he turned to Dante and smiled slightly, as though the real secret of his nature was out between them. He extended his hand and Dante shook it automatically. "Are you hungry?" he asked gently.

Dante looked at him. "I haven't eaten much today," he said.

The little man turned stiffly to the guard. The command flickered out like an adder's tongue. "Feed him," he said. As he turned back to Dante his manner softened again. It was like seeing a knife exposed for a second and then sheathed again in its scabbard. "I regret that I haven't time to talk longer," he said politely. "After the war, perhaps."

Dante nodded. The other smiled a brittle smile and then sat down and opened the paper again. Dante turned and followed the guard out of the room. His shoes were still untied. They felt loose on his feet.

VI

The meeting was brief. Carnot remained with Dante and Berger and the door was left open. Carnot listened, but didn't interrupt.

Berger's room was smaller than Dante's. Berger sat on the cot. He was a slender blond man, almost boyish, in his early twenties. He sat with his legs crossed, his long thin hands gripping the edge of the cot. Dante noticed immediately that he was wearing expensive clothes and shoes, although the silk shirt, open at the neck, was soiled and slightly torn at the shoulder. There was a brownish spot of dried blood near the tear. His blond hair was long and carefully combed in place; his skin was pale to the point of pallor. He sat poised and distant as Dante entered the room and stood before him. There was a moment of strained silence.

"How are they treating you?" Dante asked in French.

The young man looked up at him with cool contempt. "You will find out, I imagine," Berger said. His French was clipped and correct, but strongly affected the upper-class accent of Paris.

"I'll come to the point. What is *your* opinion of this Dujardin? Evidently he's not universally trusted here."

"He's vulgar but politically clean. He won't work with these Marxist scum." He shot a glance at Carnot, who ignored him.

"They seem to think he might have tipped off . . ."

"That's ridiculous. He took Lautrec into custody for his own protection, to hide him during the raid."

Dante was startled. "He took . . ." But he thought better of showing his surprise. "Why didn't he warn the rest?"

"He knew no one else. There was no other way."

"You knew of the raid before it happened?" Dante asked.

"Of course not. But obviously he had no time to do anything else."

"I see." Stone wondered whether Berger knew anything besides what he'd been told. He decided to wait and ask later.

"Are you working with this rabble?" Berger asked, nodding at Carnot behind Dante. Dante heard Carnot laugh softly, a quiet, mirthless laugh.

"I don't know what you mean by working with them."

"You'll only help them to destroy this country," Berger said.

Dante avoided the subject. "Do you have any ideas about who could have informed on the Lautrec group?" he asked.

"Look around you," he said. "They'll admit to you they had planted spies in his organization. How do you think they managed to kidnap me?"

"How did you come to contact Dujardin?"

"That is not your affair," Berger said. "He was recommended to me by a person of the utmost reliability. A person of rank."

"Rank?"

"Yes. Rank. Or is nobility something beyond your experience?"

"I take it there is nothing else you have to tell me then," Dante said.

"Yes, one thing. You were a fool to leave Lautrec in charge. He's politically naïve."

"You were instructed to make military arrangements, not political ones," Dante said, letting his annoyance show. "Or so I thought."

Berger stared coldly at him. "I'm not aware that there's a difference."

"Have you given any information . . . ?"

Carnot stepped from behind and cut Dante short. "He has no information to give us or anyone else. I think you've talked enough for now. I'll let you see him again. Come."

Berger curled his lip in a sneering stage-laugh. The effect was ridiculous. Dante hesitated. He felt Carnot's arm on his shoulder. He looked at Berger. "Is there anything else you want to tell me now?" he suggested.

Berger reclined languidly on the cot. In a calculatedly bored tone he said, "I'd like some fresh linen. They wouldn't let me bring any clothes with me."

"Perhaps you'd like a body servant," Carnot said.

Berger answered with a cold sigh and lay back on the cot, his eyes shut. Dante noticed that his shoes were finely made; they were black morocco with thin soles, like dancing pumps. But the laces were missing.

They turned and went out of the room in silence. The door was not locked, but in the corridor outside Dante noticed a guard who hadn't been there before.

That evening Carnot inexplicably let Dante talk to Berger again, this time alone. Berger was nervously excited, flushed, with none of the affected calm he'd assumed earlier. Dante noticed the change immediately. From the first, Berger rambled on in a volatile monologue.

". . . A romantic is a puritan in the last stages of decomposition. The child raised on puritanism in adolescence comes into collision with certain biological realities of life. His puritan values fail him. He feels betrayed. The hand-me-down virtues, these precious moral heirlooms, collapse in splinters like so many antique chairs the first time he tests them for support. He is angry, hurt, guilty, bewildered. But mainly guilty—for breaking Mother's delicate furniture which she evidently prized too highly. He runs away from home in fear and sorrow and becomes an intellectual vagabond. That is what happened to me,

I suppose." Berger paused, interrupting his explanation of his background, in order to break a cigarette in two.

Berger had obviously been prepared to see him; he sat on the edge of the narrow iron bedstead, his long slender legs crossed, his thin hands folded in his lap, waiting. At first he had addressed Dante in French, but as he talked he slipped from French into English. He paused and lit the half-cut cigarette, and blew a narrow stream of smoke from between his thin lips.

"They still let me have cigarettes," he said, turning the ragged butt in his fingers, examining it with distaste. "Occasionally, that is."

Dante shifted his weight uncomfortably in the straight-backed chair, which was the only piece of furniture besides the iron cot in the cell-like room. On the wall was a crucifix.

"I'm sorry to have to receive you in such sorry circumstances," said Berger. "They won't even find me a writing table." He shrugged.

"What happened then?" asked Dante, waving aside Berger's apology for his deficient hospitality. "I mean after you came to France."

"Came *back* to France," Berger corrected. "I had spent my childhood here. I went to the University in Zurich for a year. An utter bore and waste of time, I'm afraid. I spent every weekend in Paris."

"Why did you go to Zurich if you didn't like it?" Dante asked.

"Masochism, I suppose," Berger said. "It was the death strength of the puritan in me. I was also interested in Germanic studies, hoped to do a book on Wagnerian myths. . . . You see, I was already nibbling at the large side of Alice's mushroom. I was always attracted to the romantics."

"Hitler seems to have found some official pleasure in them too," Dante said with undisguised irony.

"Hitler is merely vulgar," Berger said.

Berger spoke English with the accent of an expensive education in eastern American schools, and his manner of speaking French seemed to Dante even more affectedly upper class than it had been earlier. It had the monied inflections of a haughty child of one of the "old families." Dante, curious, asked him about his family. Berger replied, with an airy wave of the hand, *"Mon cher,* I have no family. I buried my family with my past when I left America."

Then he continued, "My dear Dante, I am merely—that is I *was,* I hope I've expunged the odium—I was the product of a number of equally vain schools, all of which attempt to justify their existence by catering to the pathetic social aspirations of the American railroad-car aristocracy. Fortunately I am of slightly better stock."

Dante quietly set about deflating the young agent. "I take it you were highborn?"

Berger blinked. "No one in America is highborn," he said. "However, I was born in Europe. As my mother was. She was highborn, as you put it. But she died when I was lowborn." His voice had a nasty edge to it, as though to warn Dante off the subject. "I assume my father holds me responsible."

"I thought you said you had no family," Dante said, regretting it.

"A father is not a family. I hate my father. He reciprocates my devotion."

It was left at that.

An hour later the conversation, while not intimate, had slowly but irreversibly laid bare the differences between the two men, and the attempt at polite formality was gradually abandoned. Dante was making no effort to conceal his impatience and annoyance with Berger, whose manner of speaking bordered on impudence. If Berger realized that his fate rested largely on Dante's being able to get him out of the country safely, he made no show of it. Dante found the younger agent's manner repulsive. There was something cruel and yet perhaps effeminate about him which disturbed Dante profoundly. Berger spoke at length in glowing terms about the return of the King to the throne of France.

Dante might have thought he had gone mad, except that he'd heard French monarchists outline their vision before. He knew some to be dedicated, if impractical, fanatics who might have been dangerous except that a devotion to the rigid tenets of good breeding predisposed them to a distaste for common intrigue and violence. He had met them when he was a student in Paris, had known several of them well, had even on one occasion allowed himself to be inveigled into attending one of their meetings. But the phenomenon of an American taking up the passion for dead queens and dead kings and backing an exiled pretender was something utterly new to him.

Dante decided that young Berger must have been a frivolous political innocent, whose head had been turned by the lazy well-bred opulence of the Faubourg St. Germain. It was evident that he utterly lacked a political or historical sense of things, of the events in which he had been participating up to the time of his "rescue" (as the man in the steel spectacles had called it), his "capture" (as Berger himself called it). Dante hesitated to bring up the subjects that clamored most loudly in his mind for answers: the history of the Lautrec debacle, the shaded personage Dujardin, who seemed to hang in the background of everything, the exact circumstances of Berger's "rescue," the role of the girl. . . .

Dante searched his mind for the precise words to describe Berger. He was monstrous, and *charming*. He seemed utterly assured that the war would end with God in His Heaven, the King on the throne, and all right with the world. He had some of the fervor of a sincere religionary when he spoke of this; the mask of bored cynicism dropped completely, his voice took on a tone of sincere and reverent awe. Dante watched him and listened, fascinated against his will. In the light of the fast-diminishing candle that was dripping wax over the iron bedstead where it was fastened in its own meltings, Berger's narrow ascetic face seemed to shine with mystic revelation. His dark eyes glistened in the light and he spoke, softly, in a steady roll of long balanced sentences, of the group he had started with in Paris. He said he was working to restore peace and order in France through the re-establishment of the monarchy; he was attached firmly to the idea that all France's misfortune since the Revolution was a curse on the nation for the regicide that ended the dynasty of the Bourbons. He saw the war as the final act of the long divine retribution.

Dante searched his mind for an understanding of how Berger could ever have been charged with the task of liaison with Lautrec's group. The blunder was incredible, could have happened only in wartime, but Berger had somehow been able to get himself officially connected with the American armed services through the helpful good offices of a military attaché at the Paris Embassy before it removed to Vichy. Dante made no comment; he let Berger talk without interruption. And gradually the essential pattern became clear. With the announcement of the French formal surrender, Berger became a Catholic. His monarchism and Catholicism crystallized: he became fanatic.

"I really am risking nothing here, since my life is totally useless otherwise," Berger was saying. "Some of us are destined to find the path of righteousness amid chaos, amid chaos only, amid war."

Dante interrupted: "What was the nature of your work in Paris?"

"I buried myself like a flea in the fur of the beast. I set up the Lisbon maildrop that everybody is using now. Monseigneur was very helpful. The Church knows no frontiers, you know. Of course, the Monseigneur had to be extremely careful not to involve the Vatican in any scandal—that silly concordat, you know—a nuisance but tactically useful, I suppose. I had one of the best organizations in the entire world entirely at my aid and disposal. Ah, but the Church is the Sublime Power."

"What did you do then?"

"Do? I did nothing except attend parties, frequent the finest restaurants, go to Mass every day and Nice every winter, gamble at the casinos. A flea in the fur of the beast. I'm to be made a papal count, you know—when I get my French citizenship after the war. Monseigneur has arranged it all. I shall probably also get some recognition from our ally, I imagine."

"Ally?"

"The United States."

"I see."

On the subject of drugs, which Dante brought up without any warning overtures, Berger was less voluble. He seemed to have expected the question and was prepared for it.

"Drugs? What are drugs? Merely doorways to perfect understanding. Coleridge took drugs. De Quincey, innumerable people. You'd never suspect how many public figures indulge their penchant for bliss in secret. Really, it's quite fashionable, you know. Although in a vulgar society where the middle class insists on imposing their silly conception of moral order on everyone of superior birth and vision, one must exercise discretion."

"Is that why you are in such a good mood now?" Dante asked.

"Good mood?" Berger's face actually twitched once. He flushed.

"Drugs?" Dante persisted.

"I'm never in any different mood. I have no moods."

"Carnot gave you—"

"Carnot is a stupid pig," Berger said heatedly. "He's worse than the middle class. He's a barbarian. He will tear down everything noble, everything worth giving your life for . . . He's a Communist, you know. Did he tell you that?"

Dante nodded.

"He deliberately tried to betray Dujardin's organization. He hates anyone who competes successfully with the Communists, you know. He's a madman."

"But he gives you drugs." Dante's face remained fixed at the mention of Dujardin's name.

"My personal affairs are not your concern, Monsieur . . . Monsieur Dante. Why did you choose such a poetic code name?" Berger asked sarcastically.

"Dante came back alive," Dante said quietly. "It's a talisman. I take it you're dependent on Carnot for your drugs. On Dujardin too?"

Berger remained coldly silent.

"You don't wish to discuss it, I take it, Antoine?" Dante was aware of having the upper hand momentarily, as though he were a headmaster reprimanding a young boy sullen with shame. Berger remained silent.

"Then we won't discuss it further," Dante said affably. Berger glanced at him and dropped his eyes again. "What happened to Lautrec?"

"He's in custody."

Dante kept a carefully controlled countenance. "I know that," he said. "But there seems to be some ambiguity concerning the circumstances of his arrest."

"Lautrec was supposed to keep a rendezvous on Christmas Day. Dujardin heard that the SD knew of the rendezvous although they didn't know the identities of the two men involved. There was no way to get a message to Lautrec to get out of the restaurant since they were watching it from the outside. So they arrested him."

"What for? Who arrested him?"

"Dujardin arrested him. For black-marketeering. He got Lautrec out under the noses of the plainclothesmen."

"Who was the other party to the rendezvous?"

Berger looked at Dante. "I was."

"You were!" Dante's surprise betrayed him. "How is it they didn't get you?"

"I came up just as the *saladier* pulled up outside. It was a perfect way of warning me off. You don't go into a restaurant to keep a rendezvous when you see a police van parked outside."

"Dujardin arrested him?" Dante's eyes narrowed slightly.

"He explained to me later. Naturally it was inconvenient, since it meant carrying out the act. But Lautrec is safe in prison. Prison is a very safe place sometimes."

"And the raid?"

Berger shrugged.

"How did you know Dujardin?"

"Through Paris. I told you. I was sent last year to contact him here on another matter. I made contact through a croupier at the casino in Monaco."

"And him? What's become of the croupier?"

"They got him several months ago. I don't dare go near the place now."

"Who got him?"

"He was kidnaped. Disappeared." Berger shrugged again.

"Dujardin, what are his politics?"

"He's very sound, you needn't worry about that. Monseigneur personally . . ."

"Who is this Monseigneur?"

"Le Pale is not his real name, of course. I can't tell you his real name."

"You don't know it?"

Berger remained purposefully silent.

"Very well," said Dante, "so Lautrec's in prison. Do you know where?"

Berger shook his head.

"Dujardin didn't tell you?"

"Dujardin survived the raid because he is the only one who knows how to keep his mouth shut. He is a professional, you see. The others were amateurs."

"And the meeting you wanted to call to merge the two groups?"

"Meeting?"

"I read your communications with Algiers. Did you call that meeting?"

Berger hesitated before answering. "Lautrec called it."

"You mean it was held in spite of Algiers' reply?" Dante asked incredulously.

"It came too late," Berger said. "Lautrec was impatient. I suggested he wait. It was not my fault."

Dante accepted the statement with an outward show of credence and went on.

"And the girl? Adriane? I understand she had something to do with your escaping the raid."

"Adriane was planted in Lautrec's organization by the Communists. She must have known the raid was coming because she got me down here on some wild pretext the day before. They knew, you see. I was valuable to them."

"Valuable?"

"As a hostage. They want weapons. They want to take control of France after the war. They're nothing but filthy revolutionists. They don't care about winning the war unless they are in control after it. Have you forgotten that they wouldn't fight until Hitler attacked the Soviet Union? Hitler was their ally. Have you forgotten the Nazi-Soviet pact? Infamous. Filthy rabble. Barbarians."

"You seem to be rather ill disposed toward your hosts."

"They welcomed the Germans into Paris. I will never forgive them for that. They actually welcomed them. Hitler gave them half of Poland for a birthday present. Dogs sniff out dogs."

"Was Lautrec in agreement with you on bringing Dujardin into the organization?"

"He had no choice. Dujardin was in a position to hold their allegiance and Lautrec was not. Lautrec allowed himself to be frightened into doing nothing. The men wanted action."

"It seems they got it on New Year's Day, doesn't it?"

"They were fools. Someone must have blundered. If Dujardin had only come in earlier . . . He's a man used to exercising authority."

"But now we have no organization here."

"See Dujardin. He needs money. With money he can get men. Without it he can do nothing."

"How much have you told Carnot?" Dante asked coldly. "For drugs?"

"Don't be a fool," Berger said. "Don't feel that you're free to insult me simply because . . ."

"You'll have to leave France. I have orders to get you out."

"I'll never leave France. This is my homeland."

"I don't think you have much choice. Not if you want to stay alive."

"Are you threatening me?"

"I'm simply telling you the facts. I'm a guest here myself, you see."

"I don't care what these swine do. I stay. I have given my word not to try to escape, and I keep my word even when I give it to swine."

"The girl saved your life, I think."

"And I should bow down and kiss the feet of the Devil? What matter if I lose my life? There are some things more sacred than life."

"I see. You have no intention of escaping from here?"

"Why should I? I have to hide anyway for a time. They have my description. That ass Carnot, the swaggering little fool . . . when I'm ready to escape I will retract my word of honor first. My word means more to me than my life, Monsieur Dante."

"I think you're half mad, Berger."

"Are you any saner?" Berger asked. "Answer me that."

"What does it matter?"

"Precisely," Berger said. They stared at each other with open hostility for several seconds.

"You haven't told me much," Dante said. "I suppose it would be useless to ask you for a formal report on what happened in Cogolin."

"I'm not working for you," Berger said.

"Who are you working for?"

"For God," said Berger airily, "and the King."

The conversation circled around aimlessly in a bog of distrust and hostility for another half-hour. Berger answered questions shortly and with a minimum of information. It was clear that he had had his mind made up from the beginning not to extend himself any further than necessary. But now he made no effort to conceal his intention not to cooperate. Several times he accused Dante of being jealous of his, Berger's, work in the French underground, and it was all Dante could do to keep his patience. There was no doubt in his mind now that Berger was mad.

As Berger let the veil of cordial decorum fall completely, he began to hiss his words and he seemed to hunch over and draw himself inward. His mind, totally exposed for the first time, was a witch's kettle of snakes and toads; jealousy, abject fear, resentment, megalomania, hatred, persecution—all suddenly spilled over like a noxious brew that befouled the close air of the tiny cell.

Dante watched the transformation taking place before his eyes. He watched with sick pity and an uncomfortable disgust—even hate—for what he was seeing. Berger talked faster and began to perspire. Dante sat passive, his face immobile, not betraying what he was feeling, and watched. Berger didn't once allow their eyes to meet. He looked like a man tormented out of his senses; the sudden change from his former debonair attitude was shocking to witness. Pacing back and forth in the room, he talked in disconnected sentences, spitting out words in thick clots of hatred, of fear. As he paced back and forth in front of Dante, who sat tensed but immobile on the hard chair, it was gradually as though Dante weren't in the room at all. Berger was speaking not to him now, but to the walls, to the huge black shadow he cast there before the candle, to imaginary enemies, to fearful memories that loomed in his mind like ghosts.

He would stop in the center of the small room and stare into mid-air and talk as though addressing someone he saw there. Twice his tirade of repressed horrors was interrupted by a peculiar feminine shriek that he made. As Dante watched him pass back and forth in his noiseless elegant shoes, the light in the room began to waver. Dante caught a glimpse of the disembodied candlewick as it slid burning down the iron bedpost in a slither of melted wax. Then the candle was no more; the room plummeted in darkness.

Outside the windowless room a night bird laughed in the distant silence; the room was now utterly black. Dante heard a rustle of movement and instinctively raised his hands to protect himself from invisible attack. He slid noiselessly sideways out of the chair toward the door. From the near darkness came a low sobbing sound; it was mingled with snatches of slobbered prayer. He reached into his pocket and carefully took out matches, and struck one. The match rasped loudly in the close darkness. In the flare of the match he saw Berger on his knees before the crucifix with his back to him. He was on all fours. He was on his hands and knees with his head drooping, so that it looked for a terrifying instant as though he'd been decapitated. His narrow shoulders shook with weeping. Dante dropped the match onto the stone floor, where it lay glowing red for a moment, then vanished. He opened the door softly behind him. As he left the room he closed the door again, but not before hearing Berger repeat several times, "I'm *not* afraid. God, God, help me. I *can't* be afraid."

The next morning at breakfast, Berger wasn't there. Dante said nothing, waiting for Carnot to volunteer an explanation. When no explanation was forthcoming, he finally asked flatly if Berger had been removed from the farmhouse. For a moment Carnot said nothing, then he smiled, broke a piece of bread in half and resumed chewing. "I never keep two birds in the same cage," he said. He said it affably enough. "In any case, you can move into his room if you wish. The bed is probably more comfortable."

VII

The days continued to be unseasonably warm, although the nights were still wintry. By the end of the week a few flies had even begun to appear, and milk curdled noticeably faster. Dante learned that the farm had been willed by the former owner, who had died childless, to the Church. Before the war it was usually rented, but now it was operated by the priests. The only one who lived permanently in the crumbling house was Charles, the young priest whom Dante had met already. He was a sort of manager. The other priests came to work in the morning and left at night. Dante noticed that none of them ever came near the main house, not even to eat. They ate where they worked, in the fields. Carnot gave strict orders that no one in the farmhouse should show himself at the windows or go outside during the day. Since the farm was allowed electricity for the hen coops, and the basement was wired, everyone was content to pass most of the day in the cellar vaults. In times past they had been used for aging wine, but now they comprised a small arsenal and smelled mostly of packing grease. In what had once been the blending room there were a few chairs in addition to the ancient stone tasting table.

On Saturday they learned that Max, the man whose failure to appear Sunday morning had been cause for the sudden removal from the café, had had his boat shot out from under him. The boy with him was killed instantly; Max escaped by forcing a length of gasoline hose through the hole in a cork net float and sliding over the side just before the searchlight from the patrol boat picked up the wreckage.

Max was brought back at midnight by the young priest Charles. He had hurt his arm and Carnot ordered him to go to bed. Dante caught only a glimpse of him as he came in. Carnot announced that there would be a meeting the next morning. The priest went out again into the night.

It was around six the next morning when Charles returned to the farm with a man Dante hadn't seen before. A stranger. At breakfast a second man, also a stranger, who must have arrived while they were all still asleep, joined the rest of them at the long table in the kitchen. There were no introductions. Conversation was saved for the meeting which followed breakfast.

After breakfast Carnot and the two strangers remained upstairs while everyone else went down into the vault. They waited in silence for the meeting to start. Dante watched Henri and Max pass the time playing cards on the massive stone tasting table. Dante himself alternated between pretending to study the maps Carnot had given him the night before and perusing a worn copy of *Lives of the Saints* which the priest had loaned him. It seemed to be the only book in the house. Carnot and the two strangers were upstairs a long time. The meeting began when they came down.

Carnot and the two men brought chairs with them and placed them at the table. One of the men was completely bald. The other was dark-skinned and taciturn, and so thin that Dante wondered if he had been in prison. He looked like a victim of starvation. The index finger on his right hand was missing. They sat down. Max looked up at Carnot and gathered up the cards. Henri continued looking at his hand. "Henri, watch the door," said Carnot. "Adriane, you go up with your brother." The girl followed Henri up the stairs; Henri was still frowning at the fan of cards he held in his hand.

When the trap door shut at the head of the stairs Carnot turned to Max. "Anton and Agathe haven't heard your story. For that matter, neither have I. Suppose you go over it for us from the beginning."

Max sat with one arm, the injured one, resting on the table, and slapped his shoe with the short length of hose that had saved his life. Speaking softly, he began his story again, this time recounting in detail his movements of the last three days. He watched his feet, crossing his legs first one way, then the other, as he talked. Carnot, Auguste, the two silent men, the priest, and Dante sat listening. Dante sat quietly. Carnot frowned from time to time as he listened to Max's story.

Max was a huge man. He looked like a blacksmith. He had white hair and was far the oldest member of the group. Dante estimated him to be much older than himself—fifty-five, maybe sixty. Dante couldn't help being struck by the singular incongruity of Max, the older man, answering to Carnot, the younger. Carnot was more than thirty years his junior, and yet it was obvious that Max's respect for him was not forced, but was genuine, even profound. Max catalogued the events of his return to the town: swimming ashore, hiding, finding a doctor, finding the priest. He didn't remember exactly when he had fractured his wrist, he said. It might have happened during the blast. Carnot nodded once or twice as he listened. He seemed preoccupied. Finally, Max came to the end of his recital and shrugged his shoulders. "And here I am," he said. There was a long silence. Then Carnot turned to Dante.

"Tell me," he said, "how can they make a direct hit when there is no moon?"

"They must be using radar."

"The only thing I saw was the sky," said Max, shrugging. He winced slightly at the pain the movement caused in his wrist. "I was at the tiller, and then I was on my back in the bilge. I may have been out for a moment. I don't know. The boy wasn't in the boat. I could feel the water coming in fast and I heard the patrol boat and saw their light. I had thought out the hose and float business one night when I had nothing else to do, and while I was rummaging under the forepeak for the hose, I kept hollering for the kid. I was still a little out of my head, I think. Then I found his arm. The water was up to my chest before I got out."

Carnot wasn't listening, but was still looking at Dante as though waiting for an answer to his question.

"I don't know for sure," said Dante. "The Germans probably have a radar-directed AA gun that can be depressed horizontally for tanks. They could use it as a harbor gun. This point is at the entrance to the bay, you say?"

"Yes," said Carnot. "So this radar is not just a myth."

"I'm afraid not. Up to recently, it's been a secret, but everyone's been using it," said Dante.

"You will have to explain it to me sometime," said Carnot. "When I first heard of it, I didn't believe it. How sure are you they are using it here?"

"There might be other possibilities." Dante shrugged. "It is the only possible way they could have scored a direct hit in pitch blackness. Unless he hit a mine. But he wouldn't be here. Besides, he saw the muzzle flash."

"Do you think," Carnot asked Max, "that they know for certain what we were bringing in?"

"Well, after I was in the water, I got the starboard air tank open and hung onto the gunwale until she filled and turned over. She didn't go down right away but she spilled it all out. We didn't lash anything down on account of the easy weather."

"Were you coming in on the motor?" asked Carnot.

"Naturally," said Max.

"How do you muffle the noise?" asked Dante.

"They line the engine housing with cork bark," said Carnot. "They cut an old inner tube and lash it onto the exhaust manifold like a hose. Weight the end and let it drag it in the water. They move like cats."

"Quieter than cats," said Max.

Carnot turned to Auguste, who had been sitting the whole time with the back of his chair against the wall, his chin on his chest and his hands in his pockets, looking glum. "What do you think, happy one?" Carnot asked. "Does it sound as though we'd better dissolve the merchant marine for a time?"

"We can still use the estate. It would be risky, though."

"I thought of that," said Carnot. "It's too close to here. They know we must warehouse the stuff somewhere. It's never occurred to them to look in their own back yard. But if they caught stuff being landed on the estate, they'd turn this whole area upside down like bears after a honey pot. No, Auguste, without an entrance from the open sea I'm afraid we've lost the bay. Now that they've actually got a boat, they are sure. Up to now, they've only suspected. The pressure is on now. They've kept quiet figuring they might get another one, and they might have, if Max hadn't dropped in to pay his respects. I think we better pull in our horns. Max, the boat has been missed. If the kid was too bad, maybe they'll assume it was you. We'll have to get you out of the province. We'll get you new papers. Where was the kid from?"

"Marseilles," said Max. "I don't think they'll connect him with this, unless they can identify him."

"Which from what you told me is doubtful," said Carnot.

"He was a good kid. Good sailor," said Max.

"Welcome to the circle of the dead," said Carnot grimly.

"I hope he didn't have any mortal sins on his soul," said Max.

"I hope for your sake, Max, that he had a soul."

Dante watched the priest, who sat on a crate beside the two close-mouthed men, looking as dour as ever. Dante couldn't help feeling that he disapproved of Carnot's remark. Carnot must have sensed it too, because he suddenly turned and addressed him.

"What do you think, Charles? Can we offer any proof to Max?"

"Max is a good Catholic." The priest answered slowly, without looking up. "He doesn't need proof."

"Well, then, tell me, if Max were to trade identities with him, would Max still have his own soul or is that part of his identity?"

"Can they trade fingerprints?" The priest looked as though he were going to say more, but remained silent.

"So one question only begets another, is that it?" asked Carnot. "There are no final answers?"

Auguste seemed uncomfortable. "Drop it, Alexi," he said. "Max's soul is his own problem. Leave Charles alone."

"Merde," said Max, disgusted.

"But it is my problem, too, Auguste," said Carnot with exaggerated seriousness. "I would like to know if I still have my own soul, or whether I lost it when I exchanged places with the corpse lying under my tombstone. It is a question of some importance."

Auguste seemed to fall so easily into the role of mediator that Dante guessed this wasn't the first time Carnot had baited the young priest. "Ignore him, Charles," said Auguste. "Alexi's spent too much time with the Jesuits."

Dante was surprised to see the priest look up and smile a constricted sad smile. It was the first time he had ever seen him smile. Carnot seemed annoyed by Auguste's remark.

"The Jesuits have nothing to do with it," said Carnot. "I merely thought the Church might have a position on the question."

One of the strangers, the thin dark one, leaned forward and struck the stone table with the flat of his hand. He fixed Carnot with a stare. "Is this what you brought us here for, to listen to this *merde?"* His voice was strained and guttural, an almost inaudible wheeze.

Carnot looked at him blankly. *"Alors, mon pot, tu es pressé?"*

"Let's get on with what we came for," said the bald man. "We haven't got all week."

"No, but you've got all day," said Carnot calmly. "You're stuck here until it gets dark. But you're right. We may as well get down to business. *Au boulot."*

Carnot pulled his chair up closer to the table and unrolled a large marine chart of the neighboring coast. Dante noticed the date on it. It was fifteen years old. Auguste went into the nearest vault and brought out four freshly unpacked grenades which he placed at the four corners to keep the chart from snapping back into the roll. Max got up and threw a large piece of driftwood into the iron stove. The smell of garlic was heavy in the small room.

The man with the missing finger watched him. "You keep that burning all the time?" he asked Max, pointing at the stove.

"Yes," Carnot answered for him. "We have to keep it dry down here or everything will rust."

"What do you do with the smoke?" he asked. He jerked his thumb toward the priest. "I thought you said he was the only one who was supposed to live here."

"The chimney comes up through the manure pile," said Carnot.

270

The man seemed satisfied and sat back in his chair. The other one lit a cigarette and shared it with his companion. He offered it to no one else.

"Monsieur Dante," said Carnot stiffly, "this is the *chef d'opérations* from Nice." The one with the missing finger nodded. "You will know him as Anton."

"*Enchanté,*" said Anton. Dante was undecided whether the man was unfriendly or whether the sarcastic note in his voice was inadvertent, caused by whatever was wrong with his throat. When the bald one was introduced he only nodded. His security name was feminine, Agathe, and it made an odd contrast with his hard weathered face and bony hands. Both men wore the clothes of Sunday peasants. Dante gathered that Sunday Mass was universally used as a cover for important movements.

"Agathe does the same job in Cannes," said Carnot. "I have told them what you told me last week about distribution and we are here to discuss arrangements. I am afraid Anton is somewhat skeptical about the whole thing."

"How much will we get, and when?" asked Anton.

"Before we start," asked Dante, "would it be a violation of security to ask which one of you is in authority? Specifically, is one of you in a position to make final agreements, or will they have to be ratified by your superiors?"

There was a long silence. Anton gave Carnot a disgusted look, as though Dante, by speaking, had finally justified his skepticism. The priest looked at the table, and Auguste rolled one of the grenades from side to side nervously. Finally Carnot spoke.

"We have no superiors," said Carnot. "Obviously you are not too familiar with the National Front."

"Who makes your decisions?" asked Dante. "Do you work independently?"

"Men have been shot for working independently," answered Anton. "The National Front works together."

"Perhaps we should start at the beginning." Dante was annoyed that the conversation had started on a negative note. "Correct me if I am wrong. The National Front is the paramilitary organization of the Communist Party, right? Now someone must have final . . ."

Carnot interrupted. "Already you are wrong. Does Charles look like a Communist?"

The priest looked down and said nothing.

"All right," said Dante. He was obviously on shifty ground; the only way was to beg off and mollify them. "Naturally, our intelligence is often misinformed, especially on complex matters such as this. Perhaps *you* should explain your organization to *me*. I have dealt only with the other groups. The National Front always seemed to prefer to work more or less separately."

"We are organized entirely horizontally," said Carnot. He spoke as though instructing a backward pupil. Dante wondered how he was going to satisfy both the priest and the militant Anton. "While it is true that the Communist Party organized the National Front, it was only because the Party was already experienced in the technical aspects of clandestine work and was best suited for the job. Many of our people had worked in Germany, under the very noses of the Nazis. But the Central Committee in Paris is made up of representative members from every profession, who have equal voices in its affairs. Labor unions, scientists, everyone is represented. The Church has two men of the cloth serving."

"What about the other groups, *Ceux de la Résistance, De la Libération,* and the others?" Dante wanted to see how close Carnot's answer was to the truth.

"They are very few. They are mostly political groups who cause the Germans very little actual discomfort. Some of them have been very brave but they are too small. They are wiped out every other week. They would be far wiser to join with us, but they would rather continue their petty political quarrels, the same quarrels which caused the 1939 disaster in the first place. In some places they are strong; here *we* are in control. If you want to kill Germans here, you must deal with us. There is no one else."

"I am aware of that," said Dante.

"But your government regrets it, is that it? They would rather make deals with De Gaulle. Here De Gaulle has no influence. He is known for a coward who sits in London and shouts bad names at the Germans, while we fight and die so he can come back a hero. A good general is not afraid to be seen by his troops." He stopped, waiting for Dante to contradict him. Dante decided not to agree or disagree and remained silent, waiting for Carnot to go on.

"De Gaulle promised arms. Look, he has said the British would send arms. I used to work near Lyon. There I worked with one of the other groups. Night after night, we'd risk our lives going out after curfew during the moon period. We'd wait and wait for planes that never came. Twice we got a drop. The first time we got a wireless that was completely smashed because it wasn't packed right. The second time we got machine guns with not enough ammunition to blow our own brains out. That is why I joined the National Front. Do you know how *we* get equipment? From the Germans, that's how. We blow up their trains and help ourselves. Lately we've been getting a trickle from felucca operations, but how much do you think we can sneak in on fishing boats?"

Auguste spoke up. "The National Front is strong because De Gaulle is weak. That's always the way it is."

"You still haven't answered my question," said Dante.

"What was your question?" asked Carnot, the oratorical fire gone out of him.

"Do you have the authority to ratify final agreements?"

"Of course," said Carnot. "However, we will have to coordinate with Paris. We will advise them of whatever actions we decide to take. Naturally we will wait for their reply."

"In other words, even though there is no chain of command, Paris has the final say."

"There is no final say," said Carnot, annoyed with Dante's obtuseness. "We don't take orders. We coordinate our decisions. There is always unanimous agreement. We work *together*. Everyone has equal voice and equal responsibilities."

"Then you, as *chef d'opérations* here, are not actually a local commander, but rather a coordinator, is that right?"

"Now you are beginning to understand."

"Do you consult with the men working with you on the decisions you make?"

"Precisely. In things that concern them, yes."

"For example, like a raid, or something like that," said Dante.

"Like a raid, precisely. We plan it together."

"Well, what happens if someone still disagrees after you've reached a coordinated decision?" Dante was just beginning to be intrigued, wondering how far he dared push Carnot's hermetic logic, when the door at the top of the stairs opened. The girl Adriane came halfway down the stairs.

"No one ever disagrees. Only a traitor or a coward would disagree. Your question isn't realistic." Carnot dismissed the subject. "What is it?" he asked the girl.

"There is smoke from the back chimney at the hotel."

The silence was tense. Dante wondered what had happened, and whether the hotel they were talking about could be Madame LaChaise's.

Carnot drummed his fingers slowly on the chart and pursed his lips. He turned to Auguste.

"What do you think, Auguste?" he asked. "Do you have any idea?"

"There are no boats out. Nothing's coming in until Thursday. I can't think what it might be. Marie is not an alarmist."

"True," said Carnot. "I can't send Henri. He'd probably get drunk and forget to come back. Max can't go."

"Charles could go," said Auguste.

"No. We need him here to front for us. This might mean visitors."

"Are you sure about the smoke?" asked Auguste.

"Henri checked it with the binoculars," said the girl.

Adriane came down to the foot of the stairs. "I could take Henri's bicycle," she said, "and be back in forty-five minutes." Obviously Carnot had already decided she was the one to go.

"Be careful approaching the house. If there is bedding hanging from any of the windows, don't go near it or come back. Go to the church and ask for a special confession and say that the hotel has been blown. Auguste, is there anything in the café?"

"No. It's clean."

"Make sure the old lady isn't around the place before you talk to Madame Marie. Check the café. Don't go near it, but see if you can see anyone standing around outside. Be careful. Take a basket of eggs with you. It's better to be a black-marketeer if you're caught than an *agent de liaison.* On the other hand, if you talk to Marie, come back here right away, if you think it's safe. Otherwise go to church, and let one of them come out. *Entendu?*"

Dante wondered if the "old lady" might be Madame LaChaise. If so, her pro-Vichy role must be still intact.

"I understand." She turned to go up the stairs.

"Send Henri down here."

Adriane went upstairs.

"Max," said Carnot, as Henri came down the stairs. "Go upstairs with Charles and help him put the stone in place. Fill the cracks with dust. There's dust in the can under the sink. Charles knows where it is. Henri will stay down here. You can come back through the tunnel. Charles will show you where it is and Henri will open it and wait for you. I'll open the drain."

Max and the priest went upstairs and Carnot went over to the wall and picked up a large rusty wrench. Dante could hear the large stone being dragged over the stair opening. Standing on a crate, Carnot unscrewed one of the pipes, which Dante estimated to be the drain from the kitchen sink. Then he put his mouth to the pipe and spoke into it.

"*Ça va?*" he said.

The voice of the priest answering through the pipe had a strange hollow sound, like a voice from the tomb. "*Ça va,*" he said. Carnot got down off the crate and sat. Throughout, the two men called Anton and Agathe sat silent and unmoving, as though what was going on around them was none of their problem. Dante realized that he must have presented much the same appearance. But far from feeling indifferent, he was worried. Not so much by the knowledge of possible danger, but by the same feeling of helplessness he had experienced in the café. He felt entirely at the mercy of causes over which he had no control, which, in fact, he hardly understood. He was completely unable to make any estimate of the situation, in the face of which he felt wholly ignorant. He only knew that *his* safety depended on their safety; his life on their lives. If the precautions they were taking were inadequate, there was nothing he would ever be able to do, nothing he might have contributed, and, in his ignorance, there was nothing to do but put his full trust in them. He was completely dependent on them, and the feeling of helplessness exasperated him.

"Is there something I can do?" he asked.

"All you have to do is stay alive," said Carnot. "Otherwise you're no good to us."

"How long do we have to stay cooped up in this mausoleum?" asked the one called Agathe. "I feel like I've been buried alive."

"It's a lot pleasanter than being buried dead," said Carnot shortly. Anton grunted at the remark. "Henri, go open the tunnel for Max."

Max and Henri came back through the vaults, covered with dirt. "I hope we never have to go through that hole in a rush," said Max, brushing himself off. "This was the only clean suit I ever owned."

"Henri," said Carnot. "You'll have to get lost. We want to talk."

Henri looked around the room. "But where?"

"Go in the back vault and play with a bomb," said Carnot. "You can't stay here. And close the door behind you."

"Alexi, there's no light in there."

"What's the matter, little one, afraid of the dark? Take a candle. Not that one. The one with the chimney," said Carnot. "And make sure you keep it away from the sawdust in those crates or they won't have to bury us twice. Take a chair and something to read. Here, what's this?" Carnot picked up the volume the priest had lent Dante. He squinted at the illegible gold-leaf title on the spine and then opened to the title page. "Ah, excellent! A collection of short stories! Henri, you are in luck. Here." He threw the book and Henri nearly dropped it.

Henri lit a twist of newspaper in the stove, lit his candle and left the room dragging a chair, the book under his arm. Carnot waited until he heard the thud of the heavy oak door before he spoke again.

"Anton feels that you should leave the distribution end of things to us, and just deliver the goods."

"If we get anything, we'll find a way to distribute it," said Anton. "Don't worry."

"That's not the point," said Dante. "I have been asked to report on several things before any decision is made to increase shipments. Two of those things are of first importance. One is what facilities you have for storing and distributing equipment. The other is the facilities you can set up for training men in the use of new weapons."

"Every man in France knows how to use a rifle," said Agathe.

"I'm not talking about rifles," said Dante.

"What is it?" asked Anton.

"It is an antitank rocket that can be fired by one man. It is capable of knocking out any tank now known to be in use. It fires an armor-piercing rocket and is extremely accurate even at a good range."

Anton was visibly impressed. Agathe nodded.

"One man can fire this?" asked Carnot.

"Yes. But it requires a team of at least two or three to be effective. Furthermore, while it is not a complicated weapon, it is not simple either. Men must be trained. In the hands of untrained personnel such a weapon is worse than useless."

"Is it portable?" asked Max.

"Completely. It can even be fired from a standing position. But for any extended use it requires a third man to carry ammunition."

"Mon Dieu," said Carnot, "what we couldn't do with that. We could wreck every train in France in a week."

Dante could tell that the attitude of the skeptic was changing. Anton appeared to be making a calculation in his head. Dante pressed his advantage.

"How many men could you arm?" Dante asked.

Carnot hesitated, looked first at Anton, then at Agathe. Neither man's expression changed. Then Carnot looked at Dante, as though debating with himself. "Do you have to know?"

Dante shrugged. "I have to know sooner or later."

"I can arm seventy-five in my area. Anton?"

"Two hundred."

Dante raised his eyebrows. Anton noticed.

"Two hundred, Monsieur," Anton repeated.

"Agathe?"

"Fifty."

Carnot said, "Three hundred and twenty-five total. And if we can arm them, we can recruit more."

Dante whistled softly. He was truly impressed. Even if they were exaggerating by doubles, it was still more than he'd anticipated. "I want to make it clear that we are most anxious to see to it that you are provided with everything you need. In spite of whatever experiences you may have had in the past, let me assure you that if you can give me convincing evidence that you can handle whatever amount you think you need, you'll get it. But keep in mind that these arms will necessarily be diverted from elsewhere. Unfortunately, that is how wars are fought. From a strategic point of view, your needs must coincide with ours; or, if you want to look at it another way, our needs must justify with yours, since the liberation of France is our common goal. If you haven't been getting enough weapons, it may have been due to ordinary stupidity on our part, but it was more likely due to the fact that nothing could be spared from the African campaign. I know of one spot where a tank crew surrendered to one of ours because they were out of ammunition. What they didn't know was that ours had only one round left. But one round was enough. That is the way this war is being fought."

Anton had finished thinking. "Can you send men in to show us how to use these things?" It was clear he was becoming more interested.

"It could be arranged."

"Alexi. I think we should show him the training camps," said Anton.

"I was thinking the same thing," said Carnot. "Perhaps it might give you a better idea."

"It's risky," said Agathe. "What about Paris? Shouldn't we ask them?"

"It would take weeks," said Anton. "And they would say no."

"He's right," said Carnot. "We can't afford to waste any time. Every

276

extra day the comrade has to stay here makes it that much more likely he'll be caught."

Dante was surprised to hear himself called "the comrade."

"There's not that much of a hurry," he said.

Carnot looked at him as though weighing his words. He looked around at the others. They nodded. "You may as well know."

"Know what?" asked Dante.

"They know you are here," said Carnot, looking at him steadily. "They are looking for you."

Dante had expected to hear this sooner or later and had prepared himself for it. Nevertheless, it came as a profound shock, considering how limited his activities had been. He counted up in his mind the number of people who knew of his presence. Madame LaChaise's was the weak spot, he thought, and he remembered how uneasy he had felt there after Orchard was killed. He wondered if Mike was all right. He decided to say nothing. He hoped Orchard had not told them where he was staying, or that there was another man still there.

"Do you know where the leak is?" asked Dante.

Carnot's answer was blunt. *"We* have no leaks," he said. "Your people have slipped up."

Carnot stood up and began pacing the room. Dante was too surprised to argue. There had been a slow insistence in Carnot's voice that to Dante indicated a refusal to discuss the matter further. Dante decided to wait until he could talk to him alone.

Within half an hour they had almost completed discussing the operational details of various types of clandestine action within the three districts—raids, sabotage, smuggling, and the printing of an illegal newspaper. It all seemed informal and unreal. Dante gathered that Anton had the largest area as well as the greatest number of men under him. Agathe seemed to be the operational planner. But Carnot was obviously the organizational expert and his opinions carried special weight. Auguste and Max sat silent on a wall bench behind Dante's back. Dante was secretly astonished at the size of some of the undertakings which were described to him—they were fully military, well planned and executed—but he gave no outward sign and asked few questions. It seemed the less he said the more information they volunteered, almost as though it were a contest to see which of the three could impress him most. Agathe seemed the most conservative of the three. He scorned Anton's suggestion that they be given large-bore weapons.

"If one man can't run with it, we don't want it," said Agathe.

"But we *could* use some heavy machine guns," said Carnot. "I'm not thinking about raids, Agathe. I'm thinking about the big day. A few well-placed road blocks could be very effective, even if we do have to abandon them. We can force them to waste time. These rocket things will be fine but we will have to protect our positions."

Agathe was skeptical, but Anton agreed. Dante then proceeded to sum up and outline a vast program for landing matériel by parachute. He detailed the tentative schedule for drops that he had worked out with Colonel Jay for just such a contingency as this, and outlined a proposal agreeing on the amount and variety of equipment to be included. When he finished, he asked for their impressions. He was anxious to reduce the discussion to absolute factors, numbers, dates, quantities, mainly to impress on them that this was no vague scheme but a concrete offer of help. He waited for their reaction. For a moment no one said anything. Then Max spoke up. He had been so quiet that Dante had almost forgotten he was sitting behind him.

"Are you a capitalist?" he asked. Dante wondered if he had heard him right. The question seemed odd coming from Max; Dante recalled the priest's words that Max was a good Catholic. He wasn't sure how to answer.

"Am I a *what?*" he asked, turning half around to see if Max was smiling. He wasn't smiling. "What has *that* got to do with it?"

"Nothing," said Max. "I was just curious. You talk like you used to run a factory."

Dante was impatient but he laughed. He knew he had to be careful. "I'm not a capitalist. I've made my living working in a sewer fixing telephone lines. Giving music lessons. Teaching French. In a bank, counting other people's money." The last was a lie, a fragment from his cover story.

"Why'd you leave the bank job?" asked Auguste.

"I was fired for making mistakes," he said. "After all, it wasn't my money."

"I hope the mistakes were in your favor." Carnot was amused. "What did you do after that?"

"Just before the war I taught French and music in public school. Before that I was a minor functionary in the government," he said, thinking with amusement of the C.C.C. camp. Dante was satisfied when he could avoid lying merely by distorting actual facts. It annoyed him to be forced to lie outright.

"What do you think of Russia?" Agathe asked abruptly.

Dante was beginning to feel awkward, like a rich man playing host at a thieves' banquet.

"Monsieur, if I told you what I thought of Russia I would have to go back and begin with the first invasion of the Tartars. And I would probably do our gallant ally an injustice. For me Russia is a great riddle."

"At least you are an honest man," said Carnot.

Just then Henri opened the door to his private crypt and asked how much longer he was going to have to stay in there.

"Not much longer, my cabbage," answered Carnot. "We regret the inconvenience."

A moment before, Dante had wanted to get the conversation back onto the subject of munitions, but now curiosity piqued him and he

278

was beginning to divine that in Max's mind his question wasn't simply an idle non sequitur. He decided to explore, deliberately addressing his question to Carnot.

"Why did you ask if I am a capitalist?"

No one said anything. Carnot seemed to be scrutinizing the chart in front of him. Finally he looked up and spoke.

"Many men have been killed, not all of them by Germans," he said. "Many Frenchmen are content with the Germans. Germans are exterminating Jews and Communists, therefore they are the saviors of the world. This is a capitalist war. The English are fighting Germany because they are economic competitors. If Russia is not beaten after the war, they will join together against Russia. The Nazis will be forgiven. In the meantime they will not launch an attack on the Continent unless Russia either is beaten or begins to win decisively. If Russia begins to roll back the Germans, the Allies will attack on the Continent in order to prevent her from reaching Atlantic ports. We have long ago seen that this is an economic war."

"And the United States?" asked Dante.

"The United States holds the balance," said Carnot. "I don't understand Roosevelt."

"Would it do any good to tell you that the attack on the mainland has been planned for over two years?"

"Why did you attack Africa first?" asked Anton.

"If the Germans had succeeded in ringing the Mediterranean through Greece and Egypt we could never have dislodged them," said Dante.

"You were protecting British Crown possessions," said Carnot flatly.

"That is purely a by-product, growing out of the fact that England holds the Suez and Gibraltar. Without those the rest is lost."

"If you had attacked the mainland, you could have cut off their sources of supply," said Agathe.

Dante was beginning to realize that the discussion was not spontaneous, that these arguments had all been gone over again and again until they were recited like a catechism. The worst of it, Dante knew, was that based as they were on the Marxian premise that all motivations of man are economic, they were unshakable in their logic. Max's question was premeditated. They were testing him. Dante hadn't coped with the rigorous frustrations of Marxian dialectic since school, when he had argued late into the night with ardent radicals, many of whom now sat on conservative school boards. Dante began to recall, in a fleeting instant, the well-worn route the argument used to take, and the old words flowed into his mind like sap.

"Alexi," he began. As far as he could remember, it was the first time that afternoon he had addressed Carnot by his first name. "I know that as a Marxist you accept unequivocally the first premise that man is an economic being. If you accept that as the keystone, then your dialectic is sound." The old dusty vocabulary was coming back to him. "If your premise goes unchallenged then your deductions are unshakable."

Anton sighed loudly and slumped back in his chair. Dante heard Max drag his chair closer, and now he could see him out of the tail of his eye. He had the hopeless sincerity of a gentle brute, interested, trying hard to flex his brain. Agathe listened politely with a slightly bored frown. Carnot's face was a mask but he watched Dante closely. Dante knew he was being tried by a biased jury, but his aim was not to convert them, only to convince them of his fundamental good will. Yet to do this he knew he had to argue honestly. In the back of his mind he sensed that his own safety was somehow at stake, as well as the success or failure of his mission; that these men were perfectly capable of a flat refusal to cooperate for reasons which had nothing to do with facts but rather with what they *thought* were facts.

"First let me tell you," Dante continued, "that from where we sit, the war doesn't appear at all as you describe it. You must have some inkling of what a heartbreaking job it is trying to build up the forces necessary for a large-scale invasion. It must be done in the face of constant bombardment and it must be done in several places at once. Second, there is the war in the Pacific, which will probably turn out to be the bloodiest in the history of the world. Perhaps the attack *might* have come sooner. I confess I don't know. But one thing overrides all other considerations: when the attack does come, *it must not fail*. Where we might attack with a division, we'll use ten divisions. Where we might use a hundred tanks, we'll use a thousand. When the landings come, *no force on earth will stop it*."

Dante hoped desperately that he was right; he was managing to convert hope into words that carried conviction. Even Anton was paying attention, against his will. Carnot remained silent.

"I tell you there are other things motivating this war besides economic determinism. For one thing, there is a madman."

Carnot looked up. "There is always a madman. But it is the forces of economics that project madmen into power and perpetuate their madness. It is a fact you cannot escape. Germany was the birthplace of Protestantism. Only the good Protestants had nothing to protest. They were fat. They were content."

"Don't you believe that ordinary people can rise up in pure indignation to fight back? Don't you believe that the wholesale slaughter of the Jews in Germany can sicken men and make them want to strike down and crush the tormentor underfoot?"

"It has been going on for many years," said Carnot, "and the world chose to ignore it. Ordinary people tried to rise up in Spain and fight back. You, the United States, refused to help them. You refused. Some of your own countrymen were slaughtered trying to help ordinary people defend a few rights they had won. Are these countrymen of yours heroes? Do you honor their memory? They were simply reds, idiots, dupes, fools, traitors. And yet I am told that nearly every man, woman and child in America was on the side of the Loyalists while the war was going on."

Dante remained silent. Carnot went on, certain he had the best of the argument for the moment.

"If the Spanish Republic was truly a Communist state, I could understand; for I understand your American fear and hatred of Communists. But they were not. They were a republic, a republic achieved by peaceful means through the peaceful consent of a monarch, who could no longer blind himself to the fact that his country was dying of rot. It was a government of college professors, foolish liberals with high ideals and principles not so very far removed from what you naïvely believe to be your own. Yet you let them be murdered; the Communists put you to shame by helping them. Now you say they deserved to be murdered. So. You talk to me of ordinary people rising in indignation. They were ordinary people. We here are ordinary people, Auguste, myself, Anton, Max, Agathe. But we've given up rising in indignation to be murdered. One learns to play dead. We've gone underground, like dead men, and we grow our mushrooms in the dark."

"The Spanish war was a sickening tragedy," said Dante.

"But it was the work of the gods, and not economics, is that what you're going to tell me?" Carnot asked sarcastically. "It is the only other logical answer."

"People didn't understand what was happening," said Dante. He knew in his heart it wasn't true; he remembered the newsreels of the bombing of Barcelona, because he had forgotten deliberately.

"Because they *didn't want* to understand," said Carnot. "They were secure in their jobs. It was none of their business. I was a child then but I read newspapers. I saw how it was. It was the same in France as everywhere else."

"Then you don't believe we have any noble motives, do you?" asked Dante.

"Nobility went out with jousting and chain mail. It is hard to talk of noble motives when you've seen women sell their daughters for a kilo of rotten potatoes."

"What about those men who went and fought in Spain of their own free will?"

"No one fights of his own free will. Men fight for survival," said Carnot. "Some men have longer vision than others. They perceived the threat sooner than the rest of you."

Auguste spoke up from behind Dante. "Do you think you'd be sitting in this tomb now if you had stopped them in Spain? Frankly, what do you think?" He asked the question respectfully.

"I don't know. Probably not. But I don't think we could have avoided war with Germany if we had," Dante answered without turning around. "And we weren't ready for it, then."

"No country is ever ready for war until it's over," said Carnot. "For us this is not a war. It is another battle."

Dante leaned back in his chair and looked at each of the three men in front of him. Each of them looked back. "Why have you brought this up now?" he asked.

It was Anton who answered him finally, speaking in his asthmatic voice.

"Did you think we would trust you?" he said.

Dante realized that he had known all along what he had refused to allow himself to consider. It was an ugly dangerous thought centered somewhere in the base of the skull. *They know you are here,* Carnot had said. It was a shrouded threat.

"You think I am here to betray you?" Dante said, his emotions rising. He felt slowly strong in the role of accuser. "An *agent provocateur?* You think I have placed my life in your hands, not to help you, but to break the back of your organization?"

"We have been betrayed before," said Anton, unmoved. Carnot kept his head down and examined one of the grenades. "Not always by friends of the Germans either, but by enemies who fight on their side."

Dante saw it clearly now. Their enthusiasm was an act to suck him in. They had even held out the bait of letting him see one of the camps. He remembered Carnot's words, all the significant ones he had forced himself to ignore, "Here *we* are in control. If you want to kill Germans here, you must deal with us. There is no one else!" Dante wondered what lay behind the words, "in control," how many had died, been betrayed, turned informer, so that Carnot could say, "Here we are in control. There is no one else." He had noticed that Anton had relapsed into his original sullen state. But there had been a point where they were with him. What had he said to lose them? He tried to think back.

"What did you find wrong with the tentative plan I outlined?" he asked. No one answered. Dante felt a panic of certainty as though he were on trial for his life: They had all discussed it previously among themselves. What they would give, what they would take, what questions they would ask. Max's question was out of character. It was merely assigned to him. They were all thinking the same thoughts. A huge thought crowded forward in his own mind; guiltily he recalled Item Six of his Special Orders, which he had been required to learn verbatim: "The assigned will endeavor, while executing arrangements for the implementation of Operation Butter-and-Eggs, to discover all possible operational details of the Communist organization in the coastal regions and elsewhere, particularly to assay their strength and political influence, and to determine, if at all possible, all factors bearing on postwar political aims, specifically whether the Communist Party will elect to join a coalition government or will attempt, by force or action of military arms, to establish government unilaterally. The assigned will give particular attention to determining the strength of their representation in key activities; in particular, police organizations, postal and telegraphic centers, railways, public and quasi-public utilities, and key factories." The last sentence of Item Six was in italics: *"The assigned will make every effort to discover the extent and organization of the paramilitary arm of the Communist Party, particularly the location, strength, degree of training, and discipline of existing operational units."* For the first time Dante thought of himself as a spy rather than an organizer. For the first time he felt their distrust justified. He felt sick, but that was the way it was. It couldn't be erased from memory.

"That's the point," said Carnot. "I found nothing wrong with it."

"It's tempting bait," said Anton.

"Bait!" Dante stood up. He felt there was no use trying to control his anger. But mainly he jumped at the opportunity to conceal the mixture of guilt and dread. "Bait!" he repeated. "Either I am too naïve or too honorable to understand you. Can't any one of you here bring yourself to believe that a man, or a nation, can disagree with your philosophy of mere survival and still offer you help, out of common cause? Perhaps someday you'll use the weapons we give you against us. But we have no choice. We must rely on you or risk losing perhaps a hundred thousand extra men. As you said, here we must deal with you. Is that logic grim enough for you? We're trading our lives for yours."

"How do we know we'll get the arms?" asked Anton. "How do we know that the schedule for the drops won't find its way into the hands of the Germans?"

Dante was stunned.

"Sit down, Dante," said Carnot. "What Anton says is true. It's happened. More than one reception party has walked into a trap and been wiped out. Schedules made in advance are always dangerous."

Dante remained standing. "But can't you see we are fighting this war together?"

"For us it is a battle," Carnot repeated.

"Whatever you say about economics may be true," said Dante, gaining better control over himself, "but the vast majority of men who are fighting this war are fighting so they can live with their consciences again; they are fighting to restore ordinary human decency in a sick world. Perhaps it is as you say. Orchard said the same thing before he was killed. They are fighting because they are guilty and ashamed, ashamed that they didn't fight sooner. In Spain, Ethiopia, Manchuria. Perhaps they are fighting to redeem themselves."

"Men fight for survival," said Carnot. "Nothing more."

"What good is survival? What good does it do a man to merely exist if he feels in his soul he is dead?"

"You used two words I don't understand," said Carnot calmly, after a long pause. "Good, and soul. Death, survival—those words I have a clear knowledge of. The others are premised on ideas which you've merely assumed."

"This isn't getting us anywhere. I'm not here to argue philosophy," said Dante.

"It's exactly what you're here for," said Carnot curtly. "Today, anyway. Tomorrow, we'll see."

"Well, I haven't got the heart for it," said Dante. "Personally, I am fighting the war so I can get home and forget it. I don't want anything out of it except my separation pay. I don't know anything about the machinations of my government. You may accept me as a pawn in the international conspiracy, or anything you please. Do you want your butter and eggs or not? If so, how much and when? I'll be damned if I risked my neck sneaking into this country to wrangle over politics in somebody's cellar. I could do that at home."

"You have been very patient," said Carnot.

"I'm not being patient," snapped Dante. "I simply have a job to do, that's all. The sooner I get it done, the sooner I'll get home and the happier I'll be."

"We will accept your offer on one condition," said Carnot.

Dante was too tired to care that the positions had reversed, that he was now the one who was doing the asking, how much, when. Poor bargaining, he thought vaguely. What did it matter?

"What's the condition?" asked Dante, resigned.

"That you arrange to stay here until the first shipments arrive. As you know, we have communication facilities which are at your disposal since you don't have any."

Dante realized that Orchard had told them nothing about Mike.

"Am I your guest or your hostage?" asked Dante politely. "Actually it makes little difference, since without your help I can't leave."

"As you say," said Carnot, "it makes little difference. Actually it is merely a routine security precaution. Perhaps you were planning to stay anyway?"

"Perhaps I was," said Dante. "I didn't come here to do a halfway job. Or lead you into any fantastic trap either. I must admit I hadn't expected to be treated like a Judas sheep. That was the one thing I was *not* prepared for. I didn't know what low store you set by human decency." Dante felt bitter, and calculated that it wouldn't hurt to let it show.

"It's hard to talk of human decency once you've been betrayed by your countrymen," Carnot said quietly. "But it is doubly hard to talk of human decency when you've been worked over and tortured by a countryman. I've known too many *collabos.*"

Out the tail of his eye, Dante saw Anton curl his fingers under his palms and cover the stump of the missing index with his thumb. Slowly the hands were drawn off the table and laid in his lap.

"Max," said Carnot, "go let Henri out of his crib."

Max got up and went to the door of the back vault. There was a murmured exchange and presently Henri followed him back into the room, dragging his chair. Dante watched him look around the room from face to face. No one acknowledged his presence, but he remained standing there as though waiting for someone to make an announcement. Each of the others seemed to have withdrawn into himself and sat moodily looking at nothing. There was no communication. It seemed a communion of private hostility.

Then Dante remembered. He glanced covertly at his watch and saw Carnot lift an eyebrow. After a long minute, Henri sat down. All the time they were talking, Dante thought, they must have been counting the time. In his own mind he saw what they had been seeing. They must have been following her mentally, counting the minutes, thinking: Now she will be on the main road, by now in town, then to the hotel, allowing time for conversation, then back on the bicycle, back on the road, then past the fork. But there must have been a moment for each of them when she should have been back, and wasn't, when the imagined sequence of her movements collapsed into a welter of unimaginable certainties at her nonappearance. Something had happened, but what? Or had they simply not noticed the passing of time, as Dante himself hadn't? Or forgotten? Henri too, sitting alone in his vault, must have followed the road, must have rehearsed the turns and visualized the slow panorama which now raced through Dante's mind like the tag end of a film strip leaving nothing but a blank. She must have gotten to town, but no, perhaps a patrol . . . Then she must have gotten to the road . . . After that it was blank. Of course, Dante thought, the church. That was it. Unless she was caught. He suddenly felt a kind of rapport again. They were waiting for the messenger, one of the priests. Dante began constructing a new picture, of the priest leaving town, the road. Would he take a bicycle? He would be here. No—Dante now saw him walking, his cross swinging—perhaps another half-hour. Then he thought of him being caught by a patrol and being led back to town. Impossible. He would evade the patrol. The priest was back on the road again. At least now, like a straggler running up from the rear, Dante felt he had caught up with the thoughts of the men around him, who still sat silent and unsmiling and alone and perhaps in fear, carefully not looking at anything. The stove iron snapped as it cooled, untended. Carnot looked lost in a daydream. In his mind Dante set the priest back on the road, and imagined him walking fast, perhaps even running. But then, perversely, he stopped and went into the bushes. All Dante could think of was the legs, the obscene spindly legs, which were fish-belly white and ridiculous.

"Something has gone wrong," Carnot said at last. He got up from his chair and started to pace again. "It is over two hours. That's too long."

"I told you you should have sent me," said Henri.

"Oh, shut up," snapped Carnot. Henri sat down abruptly.

"I have only one sister," said Henri. "You can always get another mistress."

Carnot spun around on his heel. Dante stared at Henri. The fool, he thought. Carnot walked slowly over to Henri's chair and stood rubbing his open palms on his trousers. Out of the corner of his eye Dante saw Max lean forward in his chair, ready to jump up and separate them. Carnot's eyes were half shut, his face relaxed into a mask. No one moved. Carnot walked slowly around behind the chair, as though inspecting Henri. Henri tried to follow him with his eyes without turning around, trying hard not to look frightened. Then, standing behind him, Carnot stopped. He put his hands together and cracked his knuckles. In the stone vault the sound was like a pistol shot. Henri spun to his feet. Carnot simply stood grinning at him, a curious lopsided grin without a trace of amusement in it. Dante felt an infinitesimal shudder in his stomach as he watched Carnot standing there, depersonalized, the grin frozen on his face. It wasn't fear Dante felt, but the shock of instant recognition. The corners of Carnot's mouth were drawn all the way back, baring his teeth, with the jaws clamped tight together. He looked like a man in pain, a woman in agony; or a child about to brush his teeth, Dante didn't know which or what it was. Perhaps it was not knowing, but Carnot's half-closed eyes gave him an air of dreamy malevolence, remote, detached, impersonal; and for some reason, perhaps the angle of light, he had never looked so young. Like a boy, Dante thought.

It was all over in an instant. The grin faded and Carnot shook his head slowly as if in pity, and left Henri standing beside the chair looking ashamed and frightened. Carnot took his seat at the table.

Auguste broke the silence. He spoke to Henri.

"That was a *sale* remark, Henri. I think we will hear an apology."

"If he's got the guts," said Max, disgusted.

Carnot interrupted with a wave of his hand. "Don't, Auguste. It's better if we don't make an issue of it," he said. He spoke softly, seemingly without anger. "Forget it. Everyone has the right to be reckless like that *once* in his life. I did send her."

"She volunteered to go," said Auguste.

"Because she knew I was going to send her." Carnot rolled a grenade from side to side and kept his eyes on the table. For a moment no one said anything.

"I'm sorry," said Henri. His voice was unsteady, almost as though he were going to cry. "I'm really sorry, Alexi."

Anton watched Carnot out of the corner of his eye as though trying to take his measure. Agathe sat back in silence. They seemed a bit intimidated by Carnot. Carnot at this moment seemed unpredictable, dangerous. He rolled the grenade. Back and forth. Back and forth. Dante looked at Carnot's bowed head and tried to guess what he was thinking. Carnot's black hair was scraggly and growing long, so that it fringed over his ears and the nape of his neck. Dante still couldn't get over how young he was, and was still slightly awed by the completely unalloyed respect shown him by the older men. Dante realized that he himself was coming to respect him. Or perhaps it was fear. He wondered, and thought to himself that there is no respect without fear, and tried to imagine what this young man had done that he should be thus feared.

Carnot got up abruptly. "I'm going," he said.

"Are you out of your head?" asked Auguste. He was really alarmed. "They have your description." He looked shaken.

"Alexi," said Max, pleading. "If they get you, we're through. You'd be breaking your own rules."

"Look, Alexi," said Auguste, trying to calm him. "They've been having suitcase checks for the last three weeks. She was stopped and asked about the eggs. They'll keep her for a while and she'll have to answer questions. They might even come and ask Charles, to see if she is telling the truth. But she knows her story by heart. They won't bother her if Charles vouches for her. Charles will make them a gift of the eggs and that'll be the end of it. It won't hurt to wait for another half-hour."

Before Carnot could answer, a pebble rattled down the drain overhead and shot out the curved end of the pipe and struck Dante lightly on the arm before it fell to the floor. Everyone turned and looked up at the open end of the pipe. No one said anything. Carnot leaned his chair to one side and picked up the pebble. They sat frozen, listening a moment longer. No more pebbles came.

"Only one," said Auguste, whispering. "At least it's not Germans."

Carnot motioned impatiently for silence. He climbed up onto the crate and put his ear to the pipe. His face was absolutely without expression as he listened. Nobody moved and minutes dragged by. Finally Max pointed to the stairs, a questioning look on his face; Carnot nodded. When Max came back out of the vault, he was carrying two Sten guns and a handful of magazines which he laid gingerly on the table. Dante's heart dropped a beat when he saw Carnot lift his arm and point directly at him. Max simply tiptoed around the table and handed Dante one of the Stens and nodded toward a spot beside the stairs. Max went around to the foot of the stairs, where he had full command of the descent.

From where Dante stood he had a full view of the large wooden trap door, covered above by the square of stone. Even without crouching, the stairs themselves afforded partial cover. Carnot pointed to the light, which hung by a single cord over the table. Henri jumped onto a chair and reached over the table and unscrewed the bulb a turn. Dante felt his heart pounding. The vault went pitch black. Then he heard Carnot's angry whisper.

"Turn it on, idiot! Wait until I tell you."

The light went on. Henri stood sucking his burned fingers.

"Is she with them?" whispered Auguste.

Carnot shook his head almost imperceptibly, removed his covering hand from the drain end.

Dante ran his hand along the cold steel barrel of the weapon. The contours felt totally strange to his hand even though he knew the Sten by heart. The whole scene had a nightmarish unreality, with Henri still standing on the chair and everyone standing or sitting in strained attitudes, casting contorted shadows around the vault as the light moved like a swinging censer. Carnot stood on the crate with one ear to the pipe, absently unwrapping the rag from around the Luger. He gripped the pistol under his armpit, barrel first, and meticulously refolded the oily cloth into a small triangle, almost as if he were folding a diaper, Dante thought, patting it flat and put it back in his shirt. Dante took it as a sign. After that they only waited; Dante wondered why Carnot had chosen him for the other Sten. Anton sat cleaning his fingernails with the point of what seemed to be a knitting needle. Agathe, his bald head shining in the light, sat quietly with his hands in his lap. Carnot listened at the pipe, immobile. Then Dante saw that the knitting needle was a long, delicate knife with a twine-wrapped haft, like an ice pick. Anton looked up unexpectedly and caught Dante staring at the stiletto.

"Pretty?" whispered Anton. He held the knife up in the light and dangled it by a lanyard from his wrist. "No noise. No smoke. They never even bleed. *Spécialité de la maison.*"

"Anton used to be a pig farmer," said Max's soft voice. Dante turned and could hardly see where Max was standing, but he heard him laugh softly, as if to himself. He was standing in Henri's enormous shadow, which moved gently back and forth with the pendulum of light.

Time passed slowly, but it couldn't have been fifteen minutes before the police finally left. Carnot got down off the crate and Dante heard the sound of the priest's voice hollow down the pipe.

"Ils sont partis."

They waited another half-hour before Charles called down that she was back. Max went out through the tunnel. Carnot put the Sten guns back in the vault, and presently Dante heard the stone being dragged away above the trap.

The priest, looking grim, accompanied Max and Adriane halfway down the stairs and then went back up. She leaned on Max; Auguste gave her a chair. The girl was badly shaken and obviously was undergoing a reaction of delayed fright. Dante noticed that his own knees were beginning to shake, in spite of the fact that previously he had felt clear-headed and unafraid. The priest came back down the stairs with a clear bottle and a tumbler. While he poured out two fingers of the liquid into the glass, Dante recognized the unmistakable pungent smell of licorice. The liquid was clear in the bottle but turned milky white with the water in the glass. In the bottle there was a handful of twigs. At first the girl shook her head but the priest pressed the glass on her and she took a swallow, handing it to Max, who stood beside her chair. No one had spoken. Adriane sat pale and still trembling, and Dante looked at her face, examining it closely for the first time.

When he had first seen Adriane's face, Dante had thought it ordinary, the common unexpressive Mediterranean face, with black hair wrapped tightly about the head and gathered in a tight bun at the back. Before, she had fitted perfectly her part of cook and housecleaner. She was young, perhaps nineteen, but her face had the self-contained, hard-bitten cast of fishermen's women. To Dante such faces betokened the unyielding penury, born of drawn-out petty suffering, which was the caste mark of those who, while poor, never starved. He had seen the same face thousands of times before, on peasants, farmers; on Auvergnian café owners in Paris, who dispensed alcohol at the front of their tiny bistros and coal and cordwood in the rear, on concierges, even under the trite make-up of whores all over France. But now she looked different. The fear she was trying so hard to control transfigured her; Dante tried to think whether her face was common or beautiful. But she wasn't beautiful. Her hair had worked loose as she massaged her forehead with her fingers. Once or twice she lifted her head back, her chest lifting as she gulped air, and Dante saw that her eyes were no longer dull but expressive, like the eyes of a frightened animal. She was very thin, and the bones in her face showed where the delicate hollows of cheeks and eyes were accentuated by the single yellow light above her head. Her hands looked strong and her body was young and well formed. Dante realized now that she was taller than Carnot.

"*Alors, ma vierge,*" said Carnot, smiling, "you are superb. Someday you'll be a great actress."

She smiled weakly at the compliment and reached for the tumbler in Max's hand. This time she finished it.

"It was Charles," she said. The priest only frowned.

"Well, what went wrong?" asked Auguste.

"They found out Max stayed at the hotel. They've identified the boat. They know he is alive."

"Does Marie know *how* they know?" asked Max.

"One of the girls, I think."

"I think I know which one," said Max. "One with a long scar on her belly. She was watching me, like she was trying to memorize my description."

"Did you sleep with her?" asked Carnot.

"I stayed away from her. I didn't sleep with any of them."

"That's enough to make anyone suspicious," said Carnot.

"I'm an old man," said Max. "I had other things to think about."

"What's an old man doing in a whorehouse?" asked Carnot.

"Whorehouses are always full of old men and Germans," said Auguste.

"That's the trouble. Max doesn't look that old," said Carnot. "Some one of them was bound to get wise. Do they suspect Marie?"

"I don't think so," said Adriane. "She admitted right away that Max was there."

"That was smart," said Carnot. "After all, she had no way of knowing he was wanted."

"How did you get stopped?" asked Max. "Were the police there before . . ."

"They came after I got there," she said. "They saw me go in."

"Who came?" asked Carnot.

"Dujardin himself, and two others who aren't from around here. At least I've never seen them before."

"That scum," said Max.

"She was very good," said Adriane. "Madame Marie is the actress."

"Was the old one there?"

"LaChaise? No."

Dante felt a thrill of recognition go through him at the name. As he had suspected, they were talking about Madame LaChaise's "hotel."

"Marie waited until they were almost in the room before she tried to hide the eggs. They caught her, and she lied to them until they said they had seen me come in with the basket. They made me stay there while they questioned her about Max. They showed her his picture. She was very indignant after a while and asked them how she could be expected to help them if they didn't keep her up to date on things. She was very good. When they couldn't get anything about Max, Dujardin started in about the eggs. It was the other two who did all the talking about Max. I finally had to tell them I was working here."

"Did he come out here himself?" asked Auguste.

"No," said the priest.

"They made me wait at the *gendarmerie* until they came back," said Adriane. "I went back to the hotel for the bicycle, but it was gone. I didn't go in. Maybe she took it inside."

"You lost my bicycle?" asked Henri. He was ignored.

"Before they came, she told me what it was," said Adriane.

"You mean it wasn't Max?" asked Carnot.

"She didn't know about Max until they came," said Adriane. "What she wanted to tell us was that they've taken twelve more. It isn't official yet."

"Arrested them?"

"They claim an officer was shot Saturday night. Madame Marie thinks it's a lie. She says—"

"She's right," interrupted Carnot. "He wasn't shot around here."

"They're hoping someone will crack," said Max. "Sooner or later someone will. Too many people in town know too much."

"Did she know who they've taken?" asked Carnot.

"She says she's sure there were none of ours," said Adriane.

"Then they can't know much," said Auguste.

Anton spoke up in his broken voice. "That means we can't stay at her place tonight. We'll have to go on to St. Maxime."

Carnot looked at his watch. "If you want to beat curfew you'd better get started now."

The two men got up.

"We'll get you a complete list of what we need by the middle of the week," said Agathe, looking at Dante, but speaking to Carnot. "First we'll have to talk to the others, and get their agreement."

Dante wondered uneasily how many "others" there were.

"Henri," said Carnot, "go out and check the road. You'll stay a hundred meters ahead of them. When you get to town, go to the café and stay there. Auguste will be back later. Don't go out and don't drink. Auguste, is everything locked up?"

Auguste held up a large key in the light.

"Good. Here, Henri. This will be enough to keep you warm." Carnot poured out some *pastis* and handed the tumbler to Henri. There was no water and Henri downed it straight. He put on his beret and started up the stairs alone. Each of the other two men helped themselves to the *pastis* and then followed him.

"Good luck," said Auguste, as they reached the top of the stairs.

"Merde," said Anton, saluting.

Carnot left with Auguste not long after Anton and Agathe and Henri. Max and the priest stayed, and the girl. Dante sat alone in the great kitchen, which was the communal room on the main floor, reading in the poor light about Saint Sebastian. Max, exhausted, was asleep in another part of the house. Charles was in his tiny room, which Carnot referred to as his "cell." Adriane was somewhere outside, and Dante heard the occasional squawk of a hen being relieved of her egg. Blankets covered the windows and a fire burned low in the fireplace, which was large enough for a man to stand in; it was made of cobblestones, black with smoke and time. In the center of the room there was a long heavy table with two benches. The wood was smooth and gray from a century of washings; even the scars from knives and the cleaver were worn down. The ceiling was low and two large hand-hewn beams ran the length of the room; from one, near the fireplace, an assortment of copper pots hung. It was the only room in the house besides the vault downstairs that was lit by electricity. At each end of the room a single bulb hung on its cord but only one was lit. The naked carbon filament glowed redly inside the nippled bulb that dangled over Dante's head.

Dante tried to read but his eyes still smarted from the smoke that had filled the room when he had tried to build up the fire without opening the damper completely. Adriane had taken the poker out of his hand without a word and fixed the fire while he stood by and watched uselessly. He had tried to smile at her but she hadn't looked at him again as she knelt, poking up the embers. When the fire caught she

291

had taken down a basket and gone out, throwing a shawl about her shoulders.

Dante watched her as she came back inside and bustled about the fireplace, putting water on to heat, greasing one of the large skillets. She worked with her back to him, breaking eggs into a bowl and beating them with a fork. Dante got up and silently went over to the stack of clean dishes beside the sink opposite and began setting the table. He set three places, laying out the dishes and the knives and forks, silently, and glasses for wine or milk or water. Then he sat down and pretended to read. The omelette hissed into the skillet as she rocked it gently over the fire. She placed it in its wire cradle to tend itself and straightened up. Still not looking at Dante, ignoring him almost, she went straight to the sink and got three clean plates and brought them back to the table. Dante didn't look up from his book but he could see her stop short as she saw the places already set. She was still wearing the same brown shoes with the fringed tongues.

"*Merci,*" she said. Dante looked up. She was holding the three extra plates against her breast and three stacked glasses in the crook of her arm. Her hands were full of tableware.

"It's the least I can do," Dante said.

"Even so . . ." She carried the plates back to the stack on the drainboard.

She left the kitchen and Dante heard her footsteps in the hall and her knock on the door of Charles's room. Charles followed her into the kitchen rubbing his gaunt face with the heels of his palms. He had been asleep. He went to the sink to wash his hands. He turned off the water.

"Did Alexi put the drain back?" he asked, still rubbing his eyes.

"I don't think he remembered," said Adriane.

"He never remembers," said the priest. "And we waste wood trying to keep it dry down there. I'll be right back."

The priest picked up a pail and a mop from the corner and went down the steps to the vault. Dante heard him tightening the section of drain with the wrench, and then he heard the clank of the wrench on the stone floor. The priest came up and emptied a half pailful of filthy water into the sink.

"I'm getting tired of pouring water through the same hole twice," he said. Adriane said nothing. She carried the large skillet from the fire to the table and divided the omelette in three equal parts and served it onto the plates.

"The eggs were small," she said. "Almost pullets. . . . Milk?" she asked.

"Wine," said Charles irritably. "It's time we were weaned."

"There's not much left," said Adriane.

"Is it the last bottle in France, then? Or can we drink it?"

"It might be the last for all I know. Stop blaming me because the drain wasn't put back. You should have asked before you used the water."

"I'm getting tired of pouring the same water through the same . . ."

"Then shut up," snapped Adriane. "You've already said that."

". . . hole twice," he finished.

The priest crossed himself and began to eat. They ate in silence and there was no sound except the clucking of the hens outside as the wind rose and the fire hissing in the grate and the desultory tinking of forks against the earthenware plates. It was Charles who broke the silence.

"Is there no bread?"

"When would I have got any?" asked Adriane, her anger fortified by the long silence. "This is Sunday again. The bread was finished by the middle of the week. How far do you think I can make three loaves go with this crowd?"

"You have plenty of ration cards," said Charles.

"Half of them are counterfeit. We can't use them, remember?"

Charles was silent. Dante felt uncomfortable in the continuing realization that he was not a welcome guest. Small considerations come first, he thought, and it's merely another mouth to feed, another bread eater with false papers. The priest offered him more wine. Dante smiled and placed his hand over his glass and shook his head. And yet, he thought, it's hard not to sympathize with them. They've been in this so long they can no longer see the forest for the trees. In two weeks they'll have the other things they need. I suppose we could drop in combat rations, he thought to himself. He looked at Adriane bent over her plate, not speaking. That, my dear, he said to himself, will be my bread-and-butter gift for the hostess. Then he thought, Bread always decides battles sooner than arms. He bent over his food and let his thoughts run. He had first come into wartime France feeling like Santa Claus to an orphanage, a bringer of good tidings, of gifts; he offered them the arms to free themselves. But where he had expected to find a monolithic unity, a people united under a common oppressor, he had found instead schisms, petty jealousies, internecine quarrels. Yet even with their bickering among themselves Dante had to sympathize for the hardships they endured, for the risks they accepted without question as part of their existence.

He had learned to recognize a certain ugly danger in their disagreements, though, and he could never hear them arguing without feeling a sense of foreboding, of impending disaster, of doom. He knew now for example—rather, disciplined observation told him—that the balance of cooperation between Carnot and the priest was precarious. From what he could surmise, Carnot *was* the underground. He had the brains, the courage, and the men; but the priest had above-ground organization, the physical plant, the farmhouse, freedom of movement. Dante couldn't help feeling that Carnot had played rather recklessly with the priest's feelings, that the priest was a man of unsophisticated faith uncertain of the state of his soul and not altogether impervious to Carnot's academic nagging. But it was Carnot's mordant bitterness, which seemed to Dante more like concealed disappointment, that gave his harmless witticisms a disguised quality of soul-searching questions, like barbs dipped in poison. Dante was now sure that Carnot made a chronic habit of jabbing these thorns into Charles, and it worried him. An open split would mean the damnation of the entire enterprise. Alone they both were confounded, powerless; together they might accomplish the miracle of helping to free themselves and the world. Dante watched the priest's lowered head. He was fair-haired even though his face was permanently bronzed from the sun. During the day, as they worked in the potato field, Dante had seen the priests throw back their cowls. Then Dante remembered Charles's legs, which were pale, the color of vine roots snaked up out of the earth by the plow.

They finished dinner and each one carried his plate to the sink. The priest went back to his room, and Adriane stood silently in the center of the kitchen holding the three empty wineglasses, waiting until she heard his door close. Then she turned to Dante.

"How can you stand being cooped up here?" Instead of saying, "with him," she tilted her head toward the priest's room.

"I read," said Dante, smiling—indulgently, he thought.

"Qu'est-ce que c'est?" She picked up the book and looked at it. "The Bible?"

"It's an old edition of *Lives of the Saints,*" Dante said. "It's a pleasant way to pass the time."

She squinnied at the first page of the book.

"How can you read such fine print?" she asked. "Are you a lawyer?"

"My father once wanted me to be a judge. So he said. I spent my time trying to learn music. I never went to law school."

"Was the music any good?" she asked.

"No." Dante laughed. "Unfortunately, I wouldn't have done any better in the law. I would have liked reading all the cases. But I would have failed on examinations. I always preferred the dramatic ending to the legal one. It always struck me as truer."

"Justice is not dramatic," she said.

"To be good, justice must be just dramatic enough," he said. "But it was never dramatic enough. That's why I didn't go into law."

"Your father must have been unhappy. Was he a bourgeois?"

"He was just a father, like any other father. He worked hard and worried about his son. He wanted me to have the things he had denied himself, wanted me to do all the things he had to leave undone during his time on earth. Are fathers ever any different?"

"It sounds like he was a bourgeois."

"I suppose he was," said Dante.

"And you?" she asked. She was sitting on the edge of the table with her back to the firelight. Her worn serge skirt was stretched taut and Dante could see the long muscles in her legs move under the shiny fabric as she swung her foot gently back and forth.

"I don't merit any classification," said Dante. "I am simply one of the men who make up one more generation."

"All Americans are bourgeois. You are bourgeois," she said, as though dismissing him from audience. She swung her leg off the table and turned her back and began wiping the table with a cloth. Dante, amused, watched her—this young woman who worked hard, who risked her life feeding and caring for her children of darkness, who rarely complained without justice; he watched her in front of the dying fire as she swept the table with positive, clockwise motions of the cloth, wondering then whether what he felt was truly amusement with her simplicity, or perverse admiration for her steadfast and bitter dedication. He noticed she did everything with her left hand.

Dante read till late that evening. The wind outside was dry and rising. He had gone once to his bedroom after dinner and found that one of the shutters had come unlatched in the wind and was swinging back and forth. He secured it with twine and went outside to empty the *pot de chambre*. The wind was stronger than he thought and he grabbed vainly at the cloth covering of the chamber pot, only to see it whirl up and into the darkness and away, flapping like some great nocturnal bird. Bits of sand stung his face and overhead the twisted sea pines soughed in swells with the rising and falling of the wind. Toward the road, invisible in the moonless blackness, he heard the presence of the slashing palms as they sawed unseen in the dry rush of heavy air. As he stood over the dark pit emptying out the evidence of his mortality, he tried to remember the names of the Mediterranean winds. He could recall only three, the Levant, the Mistral, the Sirocco. All the others escaped his memory and he wasn't entirely sure where the three he could remember came from precisely. He seemed to recall vaguely that there was a wind name for nearly every point of the compass. But this was the Mistral, he was sure of that. He had felt it before in Provence, before the war, and he remembered it. It was part of the fishermen's lore that the Mistral would blow for three, six, or nine days, and he remembered once in Toulon, during one nine-day blow, when an old crippled sailor had called it the breath of God.

Adriane saw him put down the book and looked up. She was sitting at the diagonally opposite end of the table under the other light, mending some heavy woolen socks. Dante rubbed his eyes with his knuckles.

"So," she said. "The saints have finally made you blind. This light was not meant for close reading."

"It takes more than light for close reading," Dante said. "It takes a nimble wit, and I'm afraid I haven't got it. I'm tired."

"I know," she said, holding up the sock she was darning. "I work more by feel than anything else. Otherwise I'd go blind."

"This is worse than any legal document," said Dante, placing a clue of raveled thread in the book to mark his place.

"My father used to have a saying," she said, working without looking at her hands. "He lost most of his land in a lawsuit. He used to say that the Devil writes in fine print. He hated lawyers."

"Was he a bourgeois?"

"He was a drunkard." She looked down at her work.

There was no more conversation and Dante sat with both elbows on the table, staring into the embers on the hearth. Outside, the wind still rose and every now and then the house shuddered in a gust.

VIII

When Carnot came into Dante's room the next morning, Dante was already awake, fully dressed, lying on his cot smoking a cigarette, his head propped up against the whitewashed stone wall. When he saw Carnot he swung his feet off the cot and sat up to greet him. Carnot's face was troubled.

"What's wrong?" asked Dante.

"They are looking for you," Carnot said. "They've got your radio operator."

Dante said nothing.

"You should have told me you weren't alone," Carnot said after a moment.

"I couldn't take that chance," Dante said.

Carnot looked at him. "You're right, of course. You had no way of knowing exactly who we were. You did what I would have done."

"How did they find out?" asked Dante.

"It worries me," Carnot said. "I don't know. They took Marie and the old lady—as well as your assistant. They came back last night."

"Marie at the hotel?"

"Yes."

"You knew Madame LaChaise was . . ."

". . . giving money to Lautrec? We knew. She was all right."

"What about my operator?" asked Dante. "Do you know where they've got him?"

"He's to be transferred to Nice by train tonight," Carnot said. "They'll probably release the women eventually."

Dante looked at him a long time. "Can you get him out?"

"I don't know."

"Will you try?"

"I don't know."

"How many men would it take?"

"We have no one who speaks German," Carnot said.

"I speak German."

"I know."

"But you don't want to risk it, is that it?" Dante asked.

"I don't want to risk you. Without you we can never get weapons. We've got to get you to a safer place, rather than let you take any chances."

"I need Mike."

"Is that his name? Mike?"

"One of them."

"I don't know," Carnot said. "It is extremely risky. We have a man in the prefecture who is keeping us informed. Your Mike is to be questioned again tonight. They don't know who they've got. We took the transmitter out of the house in Cogolin before they got there. They don't know who he is. But they know his papers are false. They got all three of them at the hotel."

"You've got the transmitter?" Dante asked incredulously.

"Marie got word out from the hotel before they were taken away. Here." Carnot handed Dante a tiny sheet of crumpled toilet paper. It read: *Transmitter in attic Cogolin. Be careful. M.* "We took six men. We got it."

"Did you tear out the antenna?"

Carnot nodded slowly.

"Good," Dante said. Carnot smiled slightly.

That afternoon Carnot argued for two hours with Charles. Dante watched and remained silent. Carnot insisted that the job couldn't be left to anyone else. Dante was the only one who spoke decent German; he, Carnot, was the only one who knew perfectly the interior layout of the prison. There was no time to bring others into it; they would have to get him out tonight or not at all. In the end Charles sullenly capitulated, and left the farmhouse to get the uniforms from the village.

The plan was simple but dangerous. They had three hours to go before Mike was to be questioned by the *Milice* again. The informant inside the prefecture said that Mike was still able to walk although badly beaten. While questioning him that morning they'd broken his nose, perhaps a rib. Carnot explained that since he was so far a routine prisoner he would be handled in a routine fashion. The French *Milice* would give him up that evening to the German SD, who would take him to the train. The SD would come from St. Raphaël by car, around midnight, and park outside, leaving the car unguarded at the gates while they attended to the formalities of transfer inside. Then they would come out—there would be two of them, perhaps three if it was a slow night in St. Raphaël—get in the car, the gates would be opened, and the car would be driven into the prison courtyard. The car would be unattended for at least five minutes, more if the Germans could be persuaded to have a cognac while inside. The port was blacked out completely because of the recent shellings and there would be only the French sentry on duty outside. He would be called to the telephone by the man Carnot's organization had inside; this man would replace the sentry while he went inside to pass a few minutes on the telephone with a local prostitute whose favors he was known to enjoy. She was ignorant of the purpose of her call to the policeman (whom Carnot said she detested) but was not ignorant of the value of a good French franc. When the two Germans emerged from the building and turned the vehicle into the courtyard through the huge gates, which would be immediately closed behind them, the car would be carrying four passengers; two in it, two more under it. It was understood that if a chauffeur was left in the car while the other two were inside—as would be the case if there were three of them instead of two—the temporary sentry would engage him in conversation and offer him a nip from a bottle he would have under his cloak for that purpose.

From there the plan had three alternatives. One was to leave the two Germans inside and simply drive out with Mike. This was the reason for the German uniforms Charles had been sent to get out of mothballs. To some extent this was the best scheme if it could be worked quietly. Whether or not it would be possible depended entirely on what opportunities might present themselves once they were inside. It would have to be a snap decision. If this course looked impossible, they would be forced to hang on under the car, resting on the ground perhaps, until Mike was in it and then leave with it. How far they would travel in this manner depended on several things: the clearance under the car, the speed of travel, the state of the roads. If they could make it to the outskirts of St. Maxime, there would be a railroad crossing with the gate in the down position. And there would be people on hand to take care of the sentry if one should appear after the shooting started. When the car stopped, the rest would be relatively simple. If, however, they couldn't make it to the railroad junction, Carnot was carrying a small, easily managed Spanish pistol which he would use to blow out a rear tire. But with this scheme they would have no assistants lurking in the shadows beside the road, as they would at the crossing. Both these plans were to be avoided if possible, since there was some question whether they would be able to hang on under the car long enough to get outside of town, even using leg straps and hooks as they planned to. The best way would be to quietly effect the "transfer" inside the prison. If it was possible.

They would take Mike to a doctor—"the clinic," Carnot said guardedly. He would need treatment in any case, and tonight's questioning might be worse.

Charles came back wearing the two uniforms under his frock. He took them off in the kitchen and laid them on the table. They'd been neatly pressed recently, and in one a small hole in the breast of the tunic had been repaired so that it was nearly invisible. It was the first time Dante had ever seen a churchman in his underwear. They would both wear coats over the uniforms into the village. There was no other practical way since Carnot ruled out risking the café by changing there. Dante suspected that he didn't want Auguste to know of the enterprise until it was all over. Carnot took Charles aside out of earshot and gave him long detailed instructions while Dante was getting into his uniform. The weapons were laid out newly cleaned and oiled on the table. There were two Lugers, two leather blackjacks with wrist thongs loaded with lead shot, two sheath knives, the small Spanish handbag pistol (Carnot had loaded it with steel-nosed bullets which he'd sharpened to needle points to make sure they would not bounce or glance off the tough rubber of the tire), a German machine pistol with a folding stock, four grenades (one a smoke grenade), several loaded clips, and two homemade silencers for the Lugers. The lethal collection was laid out in two neat, orderly rows for easy counting. It glittered under the single weak kitchen bulb like surgeons' instruments.

"What will we do with the car?" asked Dante.

"Perhaps we can wreck a train with it," Carnot said. "No sense wasting it." He grinned.

Charles walked ahead of them. It was fortunately a totally moonless night, black as tar. Charles carried a hooded flashlight to signal with in an emergency. They walked in silence, Carnot on one side of the road, Dante on the other. In the village they had to be careful. A woman in the village was dying, which gave the priest a legitimate excuse for being out after curfew, but Carnot and Dante could not risk a check of papers.

Charles proceeded well ahead of them, using the flashlight sparingly at the corners to indicate all-clear, and they reached their destination without incident. They came to the square before the prison and found Charles waiting for them. He was standing in the darkness pointing mutely. Across the square, in front of the blacked-out building, they saw the squat shadowy outlines of a car. They could hear its engine idling.

"*Mon Dieu,*" breathed Carnot, "they're here already. I don't like this."

"Wait," said the priest. He walked noiselessly across the dark cobblestones. A form stepped out of the shadows and met him. They stood together for only a second; Charles loped back toward them.

"Something's going on inside," he whispered. "You have to hurry."

"How many?"

"Two. But Roger says they've telephoned Nice, for some reason. They're still questioning him. You must hurry. The other one may come back any minute."

There was a brief firm handshake. Carnot stripped off his coat.

Dante followed his example, piling the two coats onto Charles, who stood like a harried butler in the darkness. They wore no hats, intending if necessary to remove them from their adversaries. Charles did an odd thing. In the darkness he made the sign of the cross toward each of them, and then, incongruously, blew them a burlesqued kiss. Then he turned on his heel and disappeared into the side street off the square.

It happened so quickly that neither of them had time to think. The straps were left lying where the car had been since they didn't even have time to harness themselves into them. Carnot hissed a silent curse as he rolled under the car, burning his cheek on the hot muffler. The two Germans came out of the door and fairly ran to the car, jumped in, threw the car in gear. Dante was nearly shaken loose as it went through the gates, half dragging the two men clinging frantically to the axle frame underneath. The car lurched to a halt and the motor was shut off. The two Germans, both with flashlights, jumped out, leaving the car doors winged open, and ran across the courtyard toward the cell blocks inside, followed by the man who had opened the gate. They disappeared through a lighted doorway at the end of the corridor. The door was shut behind them from the inside. Carnot peered out from under the car, scanning the deserted courtyard for life. There were two other vehicles parked for the night in the silent courtyard, a riot wagon and a Citroën.

"We're in luck," he whispered. "We have to make it here or not at all. You agree?"

"We have no choice. We have only one strap between us."

"All right. Look there. Do you see that door where they went in?"

Dante nodded in the darkness. A single cowled light went on in the courtyard under the stone archway leading to the door the two Germans had taken. The courtyard, as Carnot had explained earlier, was open to the sky, although it was so dark it was hard to believe. They rolled silently out from under the car on the side away from the archway. The archway opened into a large arched corridor with stalls on either side. Carnot had said it was once the stable for the constabulary. Now it was where the prisoners were walked on rainy days. In the center of the corridor was a large crude table which the guards had installed to play cards on. The light hung down on a long cord just above the table. The courtyard was deathly still. A slight odor of stale urine hung over the place.

"This is better than I ever dreamed," whispered Carnot. "We'll have to take the one with the keys with us."

"Why don't we just take the keys from him?"

"Did you hear that key ring he was carrying? It would take us all night to find the right keys. There are two separate keys, I know. So don't kill him."

"How do you think they'll come down?"

"They'll come back the same way. There's only one other entrance into the court and that's sealed off. There'll be anywhere from three to five of them. But probably four. One guard, French. I don't know how he'll be armed. We'll have to see. The two we came in with. The concierge. The concierge may not be armed, but don't count on it. If your friend Mike isn't too active, he may be only handcuffed. However, if the guard is armed, he'll be carrying his weapon at the ready. That's a rule in here. I'll take care of him. That light is new since the war. There's a blackout switch just inside the first stall as they come down the stairs. The door at the bottom of the stairs is locked before and after they come through."

"Who locks it?"

"The hall guard inside. He may hear us if we aren't careful. This light also turns out from upstairs. I'll wait until they are all through the door and I hear it locked behind them. As they start out I'll turn out the light. It's a lever-box switch and it won't make any noise. They'll probably think it was turned out from upstairs. Keep your eyes closed while we wait for them to come out, so your eyes will be better used to the darkness. Don't forget they're coming out of the light. The two Germans will use their flashlights, but I may be able to get the guard first. He will be the last to come out, probably. You will get whichever German is nearest you when the light goes out. I will concentrate first on the guard. Be careful you don't knife *me* by accident. It'll be pitch dark. I'll try to get the other one. If anyone comes out from inside, we'll have to play it by ear. Do you mind the cold?"

"No, why?"

"We might be wise to work in our stocking feet. Try not to leave any weapons behind. Get theirs if we have a chance. There's no sense letting them go to waste."

"How long do you think they'll be?"

"We'll have plenty of warning. It takes a few seconds to unlock that door. It's an old lock with a double-action bolt. You'll hear them. You take the farthest stall on the other side. I'll be in the first one as they come out. Can you drive one of those things?" Carnot pointed back at the German staff car standing in the courtyard, its hot engine snapping and pinging as it cooled in the cold silent darkness. There were no sounds from inside the building. The prison was as cold and dark and deathly still as a graveyard. It was hard to believe there was life inside. No light filtered from behind the heavy blackout curtains inside.

They waited. Dante stood just inside the end stall with his eyes closed. He could feel his heart pounding in his throat, and he had a curious hollow feeling like sharp hunger in the pit of his stomach. He counted backward from one hundred by twos to take his mind off waiting. He was beginning to feel the dangerous sensation of being walled in, imprisoned. Suddenly he thought of the locked gates. He opened his eyes. Carnot's head was just visible across the top of the horse stall at the opposite corner. His face was serious, his eyes shut. He could have been praying.

"You'll take the gatekeeper?" Dante whispered. Carnot nodded and kept his eyes closed.

Time pressed down on the silence. The minutes dragged past like hours. Dante strained his ears for some hint of sound from behind the huge mute door. When at last he heard steps he opened his eyes. A flash of unexpected panic went through him like an electric charge. He felt suddenly unprepared. Time fled past now, the key ground in the lock, and there they were.

Fear vanished at the sight of Mike. He was hardly recognizable. His face was puffed-out and bloody and his eyes were nearly shut. His lips and cheeks were one swollen blue bruise. His hair had been shaved off to the scalp. His hands were raised grotesquely behind his head and Dante saw that he was handcuffed at the elbows. One wrist was enormously swollen and his white shirt was black with blood and dirt and ripped in shreds. He was barefoot.

The door closed. Carnot had guessed right. Four. The concierge scuttled past Dante rattling his huge ring of keys. He looked sick. Dante was surprised that he was such an old man. His eyes were on the ground ahead of him. Dante could have reached out and touched him. In a glance, Dante saw that the guard carried a Sten. That they hadn't counted on.

Darkness.

Silence.

A voice. French. *"Merde,* the idiots have turned off the light upstairs. Wait here while I . . ." A tiny thud in the darkness. It could have been someone stubbing his toe. Dante moved like an automaton toward where the nearest German had been standing. In his mind's eye he still saw the figure standing transfixed. He shot the small heavy leather sack of lead out of his sleeve. It dangled from his wrist by the thong.

"Was ist das?" The voice was directly in front of Dante. The German had his back to him. You'll find out what's the matter, he thought. He reached out gently and found the shoulder. "Heinrich?" said the voice, soft with anxiety, the head turning.

Dante fondled the German's shoulder for a moment. *"Ja,"* he said. "Heinrich?"

Dante held onto the cloth of the uniform and let the body down gently onto the cold stone. He stepped over the inert form, his heart pounding. The blow was louder in his mind than it had really been. He stumbled into the table. Stepping back, he bumped into someone else and turned around. "Heinrich?" he said. Immediately he regretted it. If it was Carnot, Carnot would do exactly as he had just done to the other German. He stepped nimbly aside, in case. But after a short silence, a voice answered, *"Ja?"* It was unmistakably Bavarian. With immense relief he reached out and found the figure standing in the perplexed darkness and raised the blackjack as high over his head as he could reach. But before he brought it down, the body he was touching was jerked away from him. He heard it hit the floor softly. "Alexi?" he said in a bare whisper. He felt someone standing to the left of him. "I didn't get the guard," Carnot whispered. "I missed him. Get down." Dante squatted. Carnot found his ear in the blackness and put his lips to it. "I rolled Mike under the table. The guard has a Sten." Dante could feel Carnot's hand gripping his arm like a claw. The whispered words sounded huge in the dark. Dante could feel his lips moving against his ear.

They were silent for what seemed like an eternity, both thinking the same thought. Somewhere between them and the door was a man with a submachine gun, waiting for them to move. Behind them in the entrance to the arch they heard the thin inquiry of the puzzled gatekeeper.

"*Messieurs?*"

Silence.

"*Messieurs?*"

Nothing.

Suddenly Dante felt Carnot tug at his arm. "I hear him." Dante could hear nothing. "He's going crawling for the light switch." Carnot was gone, crawling noiselessly. Dante reached out quickly and just touched his heel as he jerked it away toward the door. There was silence. Dante heard a soft movement of cloth. Then nothing. A Sten gun, the noise will wake up the dead, he thought. He doesn't dare fire in the dark to get help. He'd give his position away. But with the light . . . a Sten. Dante began to stock the machine pistol, pulling it out from under his tunic and working feverishly and silently in the darkness. Twice he heard movement, or thought he did. It was from the direction of the stall with the switch in it. Whoever got control of the light would control the moment, the decision . . . a split-second advantage would make the difference. The thought came like a slow dream:

The light!

Dante laid the machine pistol on the stone floor and moved like a snake toward the table. The light. It all depended on who had the decision. The light itself. He climbed soundlessly onto the table, forcing himself to hurry. Any moment the room could burst into light and a hail of bullets. He stood up on the table in the dark, painfully conscious of the target he would make, almost feeling the bullets cut through him. He gritted his teeth and shut his eyes against the shock, groping blindly over his head for the light bulb. He couldn't find it. Seconds passed. Still the expected blast didn't come. He started over again, systematically plowing the empty air, back and forth, back and forth. Suddenly his hand grazed it. He found it, found the bulb. It wouldn't unscrew. He twisted it frantically. It wouldn't come loose.

He gave it one final twist. It made a slight noise, but it turned in his hand. His heart thumped in his chest. One hand firmly around the light bulb, he stood full-length on the table in the darkness and carefully drew the Luger. He wondered where Carnot was. The crude silencer attached to the barrel made it awkward, and the gun didn't balance in his hand. He stood stock-still, aiming in the direction of the switch, and tried unconsciously to still his galloping blood. He was afraid he wouldn't hear anything over the pounding in his ears.

Silence again. Absolute silence. The voice of the concierge brought him back to a sense of time again. Probably only a few seconds had passed.

"Vous êtes là, messieurs?" His voice sounded small and plaintive in the silence. Undoubtedly he was wondering how they could have gone back inside so quickly.

There was a thump. Loud. The handle on the hollow switch box had been thrown with all the force a man's arm could muster. But the light didn't go on. Dante started to count ten and hoped it wasn't Carnot who'd thrown the switch. Six. If only Carnot knew he was at the light bulb. Seven. Eight. There was no other choice. Nine. Ready, ready? God make him ready. Ten. He screwed in the bulb. Light.

Carnot shot the guard from over the wall of the next stall. Carnot was leaning over almost on top of him. The guard instinctively looked toward the light and dropped on all fours. He was dead before his hands touched the stone floor, a bullet in his ear point-blank. It sounded like a small cork being popped from a wine bottle. Carnot pointed mutely to the concierge, who was standing looking down at the two fallen Germans with a puzzled look on his face. Dante jumped off the table and pointed his Luger with its huge ugly snout of a silencer in the old man's face. The old man didn't raise his hands, but merely shrugged and showed his both hands empty.

"Is the gate open?"

"Not yet," said the old man. "It doesn't open by itself. Who are you?"

"We're your new employers, papa," said Carnot. Carnot worked rapidly, dragging first the guard then the two Germans into the stalls out of sight.

Suddenly Mike groaned and rolled out from under the table, his hands still locked up behind his head. Carnot prodded the gate-keeper.

"You have the keys to the handcuffs, papa?"

"I lock only doors and gates. He has them." He pointed into the stall at one of the Germans, the one at the end of the track of blood. Still carrying the knife in his other hand, unconscious of it, Carnot went to get the keys.

Carnot lifted the hats and weapons off the two Germans while Dante helped Mike to the car, his hands still up behind his head. Carnot came with the keys. Then he went and slashed the tires of the other two vehicles standing in the back of the courtyard.

Dante was trying to fit the key into the handcuff when suddenly Mike lurched away from him and crossed behind the car in a dreamlike rotation, like a dancer with his hands in the air. He collapsed before the old gatekeeper could break his fall. Dante leaned over him and got the handcuffs, more like leg irons, off his swollen arms. Carnot stood over them, watching. He still held the knife.

"He's bleeding from the mouth," Carnot said, reaching down to turn his head. "He's hurt inside."

They got the unconscious body of Mike into the rear seat of the car. Carnot stood at the door pondering. "Wait here. Watch papa. There's something I have to do." He started back toward the stalls.

When Carnot came back his face looked grim and tense. The knife wasn't in his hand. Dante looked at him. "I forgot to clean my knife," Carnot said. "All right, papa, open the gate. You're coming with us."

"If I don't wish to?" asked the old man with shaken dignity.

"Then you'll stay here," Carnot said. "I'll have to clean my knife again."

The old man opened the gate and got into the front seat. Carnot got in after him. They drove outside. Carnot got out and pulled the gates shut.

"That was risky," Dante said when Carnot got back into the car.

"Everything is risky. But it may give us a little more time," Carnot said. "Drive slowly until we get out of town. Follow my directions. You look like a real Nazi."

"Clothes make the man," Dante said grimly.

"Did that sentry look too curious when I got out?"

"I couldn't see him."

"Perhaps he's still talking to his friend."

They drove out of town in silence. Carnot pointed out the turns in the road before Dante could see them by the dim blackout headlights. The clinic was a carefully kept secret; Dante wondered what they would do with the old man.

"My name is Flageolet," the old man said suddenly.

"*Enchanté*," Carnot said. "Have you any family, Monsieur Flageolet?"

"No."

"Your family is fortunate."

"Are you going to kill me?" asked the old man with composure.

"No," Carnot said. "You'll be dead soon enough without help from us, papa. We are going to leave you with friends."

The old man was left at a farm. Dante had no clear idea where they were by then. He knew they were somewhere on the other side of Cogolin, but beyond that there had been too many turns onto narrower and narrower roads. They retraced their route after dropping the old man. Finally they turned into the clinic. It was a real clinic just outside of St. Maxime.

"But the car . . ."

"They treat everyone here," Carnot said. "We can't waste time, though. We'll have to get rid of it."

Carnot went inside and returned with two men who removed Mike onto a stretcher and took him back inside without a word.

"Let's get out of here. I can feel this car getting hot," Carnot said, taking the wheel.

He drove the car into a hollow haystack off one of the back roads. It was a perfectly camouflaged garage.

"We spend the night up there," Carnot said after they had replaced the hay door. He pointed to a large dark farmhouse on the brow of a small hill. When they got to the farm, the door was open, there were beds made on the floor of the front room and a candle burning. But no one greeted them. They saw no one. "In the morning we'll figure out how to get you to the rest camp. But first we'll go back to the clinic."

"Is it safe?"

"Safe as a nursery. It's run by a German. There's no need to ask questions."

Dante was astounded to find his own clothes lying on the pallet that had been prepared for them, but he said nothing. They dressed in their own clothes again, and Carnot wrapped the uniforms in newspaper and stuffed them into the chimney behind the fireplace. Dante fell asleep as soon as he lay down.

In the morning they awoke to food and coffee that had been left on a tray on the floor beside them.

Seven days later, after Dante and Carnot made seven fruitless trips down to the clinic, the radio operator, Mike, died. He never once regained consciousness. Not in seven days. Not in seven nights.

The German staff car was used, Carnot said, to derail a freight outside of Toulon. How they got it there Dante didn't know, and he was too depressed to ask. It was a waste, Carnot said, but it was useless for anything else. They needed the garage for other things.

IX

Mike died at dawn, a week after his futile rescue. Charles received the news in mid-morning from a messenger come to confession; the priest left the church immediately and carried the news to the farmhouse. It was noon before Carnot knocked on Dante's door and told him. He said simply: "He's dead." And turned and left, closing the door softly behind him. The simplicity of his message couldn't mask the bitterness and anger in his voice; they had been cheated of their small victory. No more words were necessary for the sharing of defeat.

Dante had expected Mike to die, had prepared himself for the happening; the irrevocable event left him unaccountably moved. And in the back of his mind he realized that he had been hoping against hope that Mike, so vital, so tough, would survive. Dante had never felt more alone, more grieved—a grief of loneliness brought home.

With his radio operator gone, Dante was in fact more alone than he wanted to admit; his only independent contact with the outside world was destroyed. He was more blind than ever.

He knew that Carnot would want to get him out of the region as quickly as possible, and the thought of an unknown journey to an unknown place filled him with sick uneasiness. There was nothing to do but trust. And try to settle a few things before he left.

But nothing was settled that day. The afternoon was spent in a heartless session of inconclusive talk. Carnot had heard nothing definite from his confreres, nor could Dante get him to give an opinion on how the matter of weapons would be decided. More disturbing was Carnot's wary refusal to discuss the whereabouts of Berger, or, what interested Dante more, what they planned finally to do with him. In the end, tiring of the nerve-racking poker game, Dante gave up further conversation and went to his room. He lay down for a nap and fell into a fitful sleep.

When he awoke it was dark, and outside the wind had risen. Instantly on waking Dante had a feeling that the rhythm of the old farmhouse had been interrupted. For one thing, it was long past suppertime and no one had awakened him. The house *felt* empty. He remembered that Carnot had seemed nervous—why hadn't he noticed it more clearly?—and had twice looked at his watch. Was there something scheduled for tonight? He put on his shoes and listened for the sounds of human movement. There was nothing, only the wind.

Dante's feet were cold on the stone floor and a draft filtered under the kitchen door. It was late; Carnot still hadn't returned. Suddenly there were three knocks on the door, a pause, and three more knocks, and then three more. Dante stood up, preparing to disappear, but Adriane motioned him to stay where he was. She went to the door.

"*Qui est?*"

The muffled reply was barely audible through the thick oak door. With relief Dante recognized Carnot's voice: "*C'est moi. Ton plus grand amour.*"

"You are alone?"

"*Tout seul.*"

Adriane lifted the heavy wooden bar from across the door and shot the bolt. The door blew open, banging the stanchion, and Carnot's black beret sailed across the threshold into the room. Carnot came in after it, seemingly propelled on the wind. Adriane threw all her weight against the door and slammed it closed against the lintel, clipping off the roaring voice of the wind that moaned against the walls outside. He was carrying three cylindrical packages rolled in newspaper. Three bottles. Dante saw that the cork was out of one of them; Carnot was carrying the cork in his teeth. He grinned crookedly and set the three bottles carefully on the table. Dante could see that he was already drunk. Adriane asked him where the others were. Carnot waved off her question, dismissing it with an offhand gesture.

"Tonight we celebrate," he said, still grinning, the cork between his teeth. "Tonight we mourn."

Adriane looked at Dante for only an instant, a question in her eyes. Carnot stood at the head of the table. He leaned down unsteadily and retrieved his beret, weaving slightly as he carefully put it back on his head.

"You are *chez toi* now," said Adriane. "Take off your hat."

Carnot turned around and looked glassily at her.

"Chez nous!" he said.

"Chéri," she began, remonstrating gently. "At least . . ."

"You have made one mistake," said Carnot. "For that, the hat stays."

Dante stood at the other end of the table watching Carnot. Adriane looked as though she were about to say something else, but shrugged and turned away. Dante was surprised to see Carnot drunk. He had evolved in his mind a picture of Carnot as a person of inflexible self-control, a person incapable of self-abandonment, of even becoming drunk. And yet he was drunk, not so drunk as to forget himself, but drunk just the same. His eyes were puffed up almost as though he'd been crying. Of the one bottle that had been opened, only the neck stuck out of the paper, and Dante wondered how much of it was gone. He could smell the licorice at the other end of the room. It was more of Auguste's homemade *pastis,* which Dante had estimated might prove out at three-quarters pure ethyl alcohol. Auguste had remarked that his *pastis* was good for bleeding gums.

Carnot sat down on the bench and slowly unwrapped the three bottles. The last was a third empty and Dante wondered if he had shared it with anyone. Suddenly Carnot leaned back on the bench and, imitating the motion of pulling the pin from a grenade, yanked the cork out of the side of his mouth; he stood up, and lobbed it across the kitchen.

"Poof!" he said. "Poof, poof, poof, poof poof." He sat down abruptly on his hands; rocking from side to side on his palm-down hands he made an odd strangling noise in his throat that faded into a hopeless-sounding moan. In the chimney the wind answered. Carnot turned around on the bench and stared into the fireplace, still sitting on his hands. Adriane glanced at Dante again, this time with a look of positive alarm. A gust shook the door frame and sucked sparks up the chimney from the blackened hearth.

"What's happened, Alexi?" she said.

Dante too felt a sense of foreboding, from something in Carnot's manner. Carnot didn't turn his head, but simply began again to rock on his hands, staring into the fireplace where a few blood-red coals lay bedded in the ashes. Adriane stared at Dante again. There was fear in her eyes. Dante wanted to do something. He started to come around the table but she grabbed his arm and stopped him. He felt her fingers amazingly strong.

"Be careful." She formed the words distinctly, silently, with her lips.

Adriane left him standing and went to Carnot. She sat down on the bench beside him. Dante could see that in her lap she held one of the woolen socks. Both her fists were clenched tight. Carnot didn't move.

"Where's Max?" she asked. "Did you get him to the boat?"

He nodded.

"The others?" she asked again.

"They're all right," Carnot said. "Henri got his bicycle back."

"What? How?"

"It was inside the hotel," said Carnot. When he talked he didn't seem drunk—it was only when he stood up or when Dante looked at his eyes. "It's been there all along."

"You let him go there?" Adriane asked, surprised. "After what happened?"

"Nobody let him. He went. He disobeyed orders. Your brother is a fool."

"Didn't he go to the café?"

"After he got his bicycle, yes. He says he made sure no one was following," said Carnot derisively. "He says . . . *merde* . . ."

Adriane was silent for a moment.

"That's not why you've been drinking," she said.

Carnot didn't answer her. He sat perfectly still, his head cocked to one side, as though listening to the wind that wailed in gusts in the trees outside and made the dying embers fade and glow and fade in the draft from under the door.

"A man drinks to celebrate," he said. An ember snapped apart and threw sparks at his feet. Deliberately, one by one, he stepped on them. "A man drinks to mourn. All else is a waste of liquor."

He turned around to Dante and smiled the same twisted grin. "We are short of liquor," he said. "But when the butcher breaks his stone he sharpens one blade against the other. So we will mourn as we celebrate."

Adriane pleaded with Dante with her eyes. "Alexi," she said. "You've had enough for tonight."

Carnot turned around and glared at her. "I'll tell you when I've had enough," he said. Then his face relaxed and he laughed. "When I've had enough I won't be able to tell you. You, my love, won't need to know. Go to bed."

She looked at Dante again. Carnot saw it.

"My friend Dante, my good friend Dante, we are going to drink together." He turned around. "Aren't we, my good friend Dante?"

Dante looked at Carnot. He no longer seemed drunk at all, and his eyes were cold and hard and steady. He was waiting for an answer to his question. The way he said it, half threatening, half begging, made Dante feel definitely uneasy. Inadvertently, he glanced at Adriane.

"She is going to bed," said Carnot without taking his eyes off Dante. Adriane's face was completely without expression and the luster was gone from her eyes. To his surprise, Dante saw her nod almost imperceptibly.

"I always drink with my friends," Dante said—he was surprised at the sound of his own voice. It was as steady and hard and inflectionless as Carnot's eyes.

"Then I must tell you what we are celebrating," said Carnot. "We are celebrating the successful completion of our negotiations. We are celebrating you, my good friend Dante."

Dante was surprised to see Carnot smile, this time candidly, even warmly. Instantly he was on his guard. He wondered if he dared trust this young man whose mercurial face could change from one second to the next, belying the shape of his thoughts. Then it occurred to him that Carnot must be seeing him in nearly the same light. Even this afternoon, despite what he had been thinking, he had played most of the game with a straight poker face, even at times to his own surprise. He smiled. Carnot's smile vanished.

"But I must also tell you what we are mourning."

Dante refused the opportunity Carnot was giving him to repeat the implied question. Instead he watched Carnot's face and waited.

"Perhaps you'd rather not know?" asked Carnot.

Dante kept silent and deliberately, very slowly, raised his eyebrows. Carnot watched him, a trace of an insolent smile about his lips.

"For we are also mourning you," said Carnot. Dante felt his stomach contract but he allowed nothing to show in his face.

"Am I worth mourning?" said Dante.

Carnot turned abruptly to Adriane. "You need sleep," he said to her.

Adriane got up and stood in front of Carnot with her back to the fireplace. She gazed at him for a long moment as though she weren't seeing him. There was something in her distant eyes of love, or contempt, or pity. Or perhaps she feels nothing, Dante thought. She abruptly gathered her shawl tighter about her shoulders and left the room without a word. Dante heard her door close in the hall off the kitchen.

Carnot looked at Dante a long time. He was sitting on his hip, his feet toward the fire with his body twisted around and his arms resting heavily on the table. He was lying half on the table. He looked uncomfortable. Dante sat directly across from him on the other bench.

Between them stood the three clear glass bottles, each with a handful of twigs in it.

Carnot's eyes closed for an instant and his head bobbed then came bolt upright. He sat up, blinking, and swung his legs over the bench to face Dante. Dante had almost forgotten how drunk he was, he had seemed in such possession of himself a moment earlier.

"Hurry," he said. "We must celebrate before I am unconscious."

"What did you mean when you said you were mourning me?" Dante asked.

"You are a brave man," said Carnot, reaching for the opened bottle. "I always mourn brave men. And you are much older than I."

"I am not dead yet," said Dante.

"Once you have joined us you are as good as dead," said Carnot. "We are a nation of the dead. Get two glasses and some water. It's only a matter of time before they get you. We are all dead. We must hurry."

Dante pushed the bench back and got to his feet. He half filled with water the wine bottle they'd emptied at dinner and brought two glasses back to the table. Carnot held the bottle and Dante could see that he was determined to do the pouring.

"Tomorrow we are taking you out of this area," said Carnot. "They have your description. Only they think you're British."

"When will I have a chance to communicate with the outside?" asked Dante. "I'd like to try to get some drops started before this moon period is over."

"We will have to know your codes," Carnot said. Dante again had the sensation that Carnot's drunkenness was feigned. His eyes were bright again.

"I think you know what I will have to say to that."

"Yes. But I was supposed to try anyway," said Carnot, smiling. He shrugged.

"There's no harm in trying. Actually, the codes I used are all phrase codes. They are never used twice. But I am not at liberty to reveal them to anyone. I will, however, be more than anxious to give you the substance of all messages I send through your facilities."

"I have been told that you can also send wireless messages through one of your own agents in Marseilles."

Dante was surprised. Did this mean Tournant's group was still in business, or was Carnot bluffing? He decided it would be wisest not to contest the accuracy of it.

"I suspect you of making an educated guess," said Dante. "But in any case . . ."

"I was guessing," said Carnot. "It is well known that the British have a very efficient transmitter in Marseilles."

"Then you have also heard of the one the Americans have in Cannes," said Dante.

"Yes, we know of that too," said Carnot. Dante suspected he was bluffing again; there had been no agent working a transmitter out of Cannes when he left Algiers.

"You don't trust me, do you?" Carnot said suddenly.

"Security is hardly a question of trust," said Dante.

Carnot leaned over the table, his eyes narrowing. "Let me tell you something. Let me tell you the most important thing I have learned in all the time I have worked with the underground."

He paused to pour water into the two tumblers. As the water mixed with the clear liquor it instantly turned milk-white. Carnot pushed one of the glasses toward Dante.

"There is no such thing as security. There is *only* trust. That is the greatest thing I have ever learned. Mistrust is the first step to self-betrayal."

"Do you still think I would betray you?"

"If you mistrusted me enough," said Carnot. "Or no. No. That's not it. If you thought *I* mistrusted you enough. One can betray a man by simply letting him down, refusing to take risks for him."

"You mean refusing to stick your neck out," said Dante.

"Precisely," said Carnot, nodding his head vehemently. "The greatest weapon of sabotage we have in France is mistrust. We have destroyed some of the worst collaborators in the Vichy government by simply causing them to be mistrusted. Because of us the Germans have sent some of their best friends to concentration camps."

"And how do you go about 'causing them to be mistrusted,' as you put it?"

"It's so simple it's amusing. For no one trusts anyone else. It's the greatest thing an organization like ours has to fear." Carnot took a long swallow of his drink. "It's simple. We use forged documents, false tips, traps, planted literature, anything. All we have to do is start it. The Gestapo does the rest."

"You mean you actually get rid of people by falsely implicating them?"

"Why should we waste bullets when we can get the Germans to execute them for nothing?" asked Carnot with a shrug. "You say that security is not a matter of trust. I say it is. It is a matter of trust and intelligence, both kinds of intelligence."

Dante remained silent. He wanted to hear more about this but knew that he must be careful not to appear to be pressing for details. He decided to remain unconvinced and give Carnot a chance to make his point more abundantly. In the back of his mind he wondered exactly what was Carnot's purpose in steering the conversation onto the subject of trust. He felt sure it had something to do with the discussion that afternoon; exactly what, he wasn't sure.

"But the Germans are usually very thorough," Dante said. "I don't see how they'd not be sure from checking a man's record . . ."

"That's exactly it. They are thorough. They also think they are more intelligent than anyone else. They can't seem to believe that we are clever enough to outwit them. It's never occurred to them that we might be brilliant enough to use their own apparatus to destroy them. But necessity is still the mother of invention. At first, when we had no weapons, we had to find other ways to attack them. In many ways the collaborators are the most dangerous. They speak the language, know the country. Without them the Germans would be powerless. Let me give you an example. We have one right here in our own back yard, this man named Dujardin. He used to be a fish cutter until he got in trouble with the police before the war. Now he has a fine house and is the regional prefect for the Vichy police. He still thinks Auguste is a friend of Pétain. Sometimes he sends him food. But he is the most dangerous man between here and Nice. He knows the coast as well as Auguste does. He knows the political opinions of every man in town. He knows who lives here and who are strangers. He knows who has left town. He even knows, pretty accurately, who works with us above ground. But he is a good Catholic and so far I don't think he suspects that half of us are priests during the weekend. Even so, Charles is the only one of them who knows that we are using this place as an arms depot. He discovered the cellar vaults by accident. They have been bricked up for a hundred years at least. You haven't touched your drink, my friend."

Dante looked down at his own drink. Carnot watched him, took a huge swallow and wiped his mouth on his sleeve. Carnot waited until Dante drank also before he went on.

"Dujardin is a far worse threat to us than any German alive. He is one of us. But we'll get him. And he will die on the guillotine of his own invention. And any successor will think twice before he serves so ably so ungrateful a master. But we will have no worry. Inevitably they replace a clever man with an unimaginative dolt. The Germans always put their final trust in stupidity. Anyone who is simple enough for them to understand completely, they trust. But all over France the same thing is happening. Sooner or later things will simply grind to a halt."

"How will you effect his removal?"

Carnot looked at Dante narrowly. "It is not my responsibility. Such things are handled by specialists who have been trained for the job."

Dante nodded and took another conspicuous swallow of his drink.

Carnot brightened. "But let me tell you a story. This one I know something about. In Nice there was a man in charge of the post office. It was a crucial position, particularly since he was very conscientious about cooperating with the Germans. We have worked hard to gain control of the postal services and this man was approached. He listened to our proposal and seemed to be interested. He finally tried to lead our agent into a trap by making a rendezvous in a café and tipping off the *Feld-gendarmerie*. His secretary had never worked for us but she went to some people she thought might know how to get in touch with us. I was warned twenty minutes before I . . ."

"Then you were the agent?"

Carnot smiled. "I hadn't meant to include that."

Dante looked toward the door leading to the other part of the house and raised his eyebrows in a question.

"Yes," said Carnot. "That is how I met her."

Dante tried hard to visualize Adriane working in an office, sitting at a typewriter, answering a telephone, but he could not reconcile the picture with her current role of peasant housekeeper. Carnot was still smiling.

"She doesn't look like a first-rate stenographer," said Carnot, guessing what was in Dante's mind. Dante smiled.

"What happened to him?" asked Dante.

"We capitalized on his failure to produce anything at the rendezvous. We began sending clandestine literature to his home address and tipped off the police. They began watching his mail. The postmaster's own mail being opened!" Carnot laughed as he thought of it again. "We gave him a code name in a gibberish letter sent to his house. Then we made up a list of false financial contributors, all code names for nonexistent people. His was high on the list. We set up an apartment to look like a neighborhood headquarters, complete with clandestine literature, gibberish codes and lists. I remember one touch I added myself. I had a long itemized list of the contents of a German warehouse I'd got the week before, complete with photographs and detailed instructions for sabotaging it. In the instructions we listed his house as a 'safehouse.' He used to carry an immense briefcase to and from the office. He did it to create the impression that he was working overtime at home. He never opened it. Adriane planted a carbon copy of the list, which by itself looked harmless enough, among a batch of papers for him to sign. It was on his office stationery. He was always in a rush to get home at night and never read anything. She used to leave all his papers on his desk, staggered so that he could run down the whole bunch and sign them. She stamped the list 'Approved as Ordered' and had him sign it. Adriane began coming in late every morning until finally there was an enormous scene in front of the whole staff and she was fired. The morning after the warehouse burned down almost a month later the police got an anonymous tip from a woman who claimed she had seen a lot of suspicious traffic in and out of the apartment after curfew. The Germans did the rest. All we ever heard was that 'incriminating papers were found on his person.' The briefcase."

"All that just for one man?" asked Dante.

"His assistant was one of us. He should have got his job. He was very secure, loudly pro-German. I don't know how many others they got in the same raid. As I say, the postmaster was the only one I knew about. We had to do the warehouse anyway. His assistant didn't get the job, but he might as well have with the idiot they put in."

"Didn't they suspect her?"

"She was questioned about him, but they knew about the business when he fired her. All they wanted to know was the names of all the people who came to visit him at his office. She obliged them and even gave them the old cover name I was using when I had first met him, which they knew but he didn't, plus a wrong description of me."

"How long did this all take?"

"Almost a year. We were busy with other things."

Dante reached for the bottle and poured himself another drink. Carnot added the water. He poured one for himself.

"Why are you telling me all this?" asked Dante.

Carnot stared into his glass for a moment. He looked up. "For two reasons, my friend Dante, my good friend Dante, for two reasons. First because you don't trust me and that is bad for security. Second, because I want you to understand that we are not idiots. We *think*. We make do with what we have. If we have nothing, we make do with that."

"Are you trying to say that if we don't help you, you can get along without our help?"

"Perhaps that is part of what I'm saying," said Carnot.

"And if we do help you, we are to expect no gratitude, is that right?"

"Your helping us is not a gratuitous act."

"We are acting out of common cause. We are acting out of enlightened self-interest, if you wish."

"I want you to trust me," said Carnot. "Therefore let me tell you something. Our causes have nothing in common. And self-interest is never enlightened. It is only either successful or stupid. You Americans have been fooling yourselves for years with your enlightened self-interest. You preach it like some new-found gospel. All it proves is that up to now your self-interest has been short-sighted and stupid. When a man has done things wrong all his life he blames the gods. But when he finally does something right, he thanks God privately and takes all the credit himself."

Dante said nothing.

"But you don't trust me, do you?" said Carnot.

"Do you recall the conversation at that first meeting?" asked Dante.

"I may be a little too drunk to recall it word for word . . ."

"Do you think I should trust you after you practically accused me of being an *agent provocateur.*"

"It wasn't I who accused you," said Carnot quietly. "Anton is almost too jumpy to be in this business."

"Jumpy?" said Dante. "He seemed rather a cool character to me."

"*Sang froid,*" said Carnot. "All dead men have cold blood. It's an occupational disease of the dead. Anton is getting careless, but even the dead are vulnerable. When I said 'jumpy,' I meant about trusting people. In this business, when you get like Anton you're ready for retirement."

"What do you mean, 'like Anton'?"

"You saw him," said Carnot. "He's been getting that way with everybody. You're no exception. Did you notice his voice?"

"How could I help it."

"Do you know who did that to him?" asked Carnot.

"The Gestapo?"

"Our ex-fish cutter. Our Prefect of Police."

"Dujardin?"

"He broke his larynx," said Carnot matter-of-factly. "And the finger."

"I saw that too."

"That was taken down on a grindstone," said Carnot. "When we finally got him out, we had to amputate the rest. We did it right here, on this table." He pounded the table with his open palm. "Right here."

"You rescued him?" asked Dante.

"We ambushed the truck taking him to the Nice Gestapo," said Carnot. He sipped thoughtfully at his glass. His eyes seemed to have a film on them. Dante was beginning to feel the effects of the *pastis,* and hoped he could at least outlast Carnot. Considering the amount Carnot had already consumed, it shouldn't be difficult. Then he remembered Adriane's silent warning to be careful and wondered what she had meant. Except for his appearance Carnot was conducting himself soberly now. His speech was clear and he didn't seem to be thinking at all like a man who was drunk. Dante wondered again if he had been acting.

"You see," said Carnot, "Anton knows too much. We had to get him back. We sent him north to where our . . . to our 'rest camp' near Nice. Dujardin had to save his own skin by insisting he was dead. He doesn't know we know that. Two months later we let word filter out that we had buried him with honors."

"I take it he was almost right," said Dante.

"It was a reasonable gamble that he wouldn't live another twenty-four hours after we got him back. He was in bad condition."

"I would think he would be recognized."

"Never in a thousand years. His own mother wouldn't recognize him. Before they got him he weighed over a hundred kilos. Now I doubt if he weighs fifty. But he is still strong as piano wire. I have seen him . . . break . . ." His voice trailed off and he stared at his glass, which was already empty.

Every time Dante talked Carnot took the opportunity to take another swallow. At first Dante had meant to try and fake it, but now he was matching Carnot drink for drink. He was counting on the hard facts of blood chemistry to leave him the survivor. He tried to estimate Carnot's intake per hour of alcohol, figuring the diluted product at thirty per cent alcohol, and calculated that unless he slowed down he would be unconscious within the hour. He was putting it in at a much faster rate than blood could oxidize it or kidneys remove it. But Dante had to be able to stay awake himself, and he decided that Carnot wouldn't notice if he relaxed his own rate of intake a little. He poured himself another drink, this time putting the water in first to cover up. A thimbleful of *pastis* was enough to turn it milky-white. He pushed the bottle across to Carnot, who just stared at it.

"I have seen him break . . ." His voice trailed off again as if he had forgotten what he was talking about. Slowly, unsteadily he refilled his glass and added water. He looked up at Dante, his eyes bleared. All at once he seemed dead drunk again. "We need more water," he said. He waved the bottle, which was still more than half full, and Dante, taking the easiest course, got up to refill it. He returned to the table with the bottle full to the top with water. Carnot waved his hand impatiently.

"I don't want to talk about Anton," he said. His speech was just beginning to thicken a little. "I don't want you to trust Anton. I want you to trust *me*. I don't care about Anton. I want you to trust *me*."

"I'll trust you if you trust me," said Dante, a little too slovenly he thought. If he did any acting it would have to be subtler than that.

"Look," said Carnot, "if I tell you something I'm not supposed to tell you, will you trust me?"

Dante looked at him. "Perhaps I already trust you," he said.

"I told you we were celebrating, didn't I?" asked Carnot. "Did I tell you that?"

"Yes."

"Yes. I told you that," said Carnot half to himself. "But I didn't tell you we were mourning, too, did I?"

"Yes. You said we were mourning me."

"Then maybe I've already told you what I'm not supposed to tell you," said Carnot. "Have I told you that?"

Dante couldn't help smiling. He was sure Carnot was not acting now.

"I don't think so," said Dante. He was beginning to relax. He picked up his glass. A large swallow almost brought tears to his eyes and he froze in the instant realization that Carnot had switched drinks while he was at the sink.

Carnot didn't blink an eye, but lifted his glass with him. "I propose a toast to mutual trust," he said.

Dante watched him drain the glass of licorice-flavored water, and forced himself to do likewise with his own glass of what must have been almost pure liquor. There was no hint in Carnot's filmy eyes of anything amiss. In fact, Dante remembered now that the two glasses had both been near the middle of the narrow table and it was perfectly possible that they had been exchanged by accident. It was also possible that Carnot's palate was too numbed to notice the difference. But the irony of the toast was too thick to be a coincidence, Dante thought.

Carnot went on as if nothing had happened, and Dante kept a perfectly straight face, in spite of the fact that for a moment he couldn't have talked if he wanted to. He could still feel the liquor searing his entrails. Finally he felt he should say something, if only to show that the object lesson wasn't lost on him, and that he bore no resentment. He had deceived and had been deceived in turn, whether by Carnot or the Furies he didn't know, and he knew he would never find out.

"This is raw stuff," he said.

Carnot's answer came immediately. "You should put more water in it," he said. "Especially if you're not accustomed to it."

Dante poured himself a moderate drink, and one for Carnot which he openly made much stronger. Carnot watched him and made no protest.

"I return your toast," said Dante, raising his glass. "To mutual trust." Carnot smiled and nodded with drunken grace and drained his glass with Dante. Dante could feel the liquor warming in his blood and he knew that it was only a matter of time before he began to feel the full effects.

"I was lying before to Adriane," said Carnot abruptly. He set his glass down quietly. "Max is gone."

There was something in the way he said it, an emptiness in his words, combined with the gesture he made, a slow, empty upturning of hands, that allowed Dante to suddenly see behind the mask, see him for the first time as human. For a brief instant Carnot had dropped all pretense and Dante saw through to the very bottom of the grief he refused to allow himself to show—because it was inexpressible. Though Dante hadn't come to know Max well, during the days they had spent in the farmhouse together, he had talked with him enough to sense his deep strength and simple honesty and loyalty. And suddenly he was perceiving for the first time what a man like Max could mean to a fatherless, remorseless child like Alexi. For in this instant Carnot was no longer the steel-bright leader of men twice his age. He was a child, and he was lost. Dante saw in his face what he should have known all along; it was implicit in the remorseless logic of suffering. He saw loneliness. It was the key to the puzzle. He saw loneliness and a child's fear of being alone.

"When?"

"An hour after we left here. Henri was supposed to come to the café after he gassed the boat. Max and I got to the café and Henri wasn't there. Naturally we couldn't take the risk of staying there, not if Henri had been caught carrying fifty litres of gasoline. He was supposed to be there. We split up, but our timing was ruined. We had timed it to miss all three patrols. I went back to head off Auguste and send him back here. Since Henri knew about the vaults, we had to start getting the stuff out. The rule is forty-eight hours, but I couldn't be sure Henri would hold out that long." Carnot looked completely beaten.

"Look, you can't let yourself go to pieces now," Dante said.

"I should have let Anton . . ."

"This is no time . . ."

"I don't know why I've let that sniveling little coward live. I don't know why. If she hadn't . . ." Carnot bit his lip and slapped his palms together.

Dante felt a sick sinking in his stomach. Then he asked, "Where did Max go?"

"He went to arrange for the hearse." Carnot paused wearily to explain aside to Dante. "That's how we transport our stuff. We hold a funeral. Max and I were to rendezvous at the side entrance of the church in thirty minutes. But I had to skirt a long way around to avoid the patrol and I missed heading off Auguste. I knew Auguste would go straight to church for a special confession when he found no one at the café. That's the standing arrangement if a contact fails to show up, even for Auguste. It's against all rules to wait if a contact isn't on time. I'd wasted twenty minutes already running around back alleys and ducking in and out of doorways, so I started back to the church. I took my time so I wouldn't be early. It was getting dark and there were a lot of people going to vespers so I stayed in the street. I arrived in the Place de la Mairie with one minute to go when Henri came through the square on his bicycle and broke another rule by waving at me. I was so angry that I walked too fast. I could see the side door and Max standing beside it. I should have known then that something was wrong, because he wasn't holding a newspaper and he wasn't making any effort to hide his face. God knows what he was thinking. He saw me just as I was about to cross the street. He turned around and started running in the opposite direction, shouting at someone. He didn't get twenty paces. There were three of them. The one in the doorway had a Sten gun, another one stood in the wineshop opposite. The third one almost knocked me down coming out of an alley behind me. Max must have had twenty bullets in him. He was crawling on his hands and knees. They all ran in the same direction Max had started in. The one near me stopped to put a bullet through the back of his head. I couldn't even run. I couldn't do anything. I . . . He trusted me. He always told me what to do. I couldn't help . . ."

Carnot sounded like a man pleading, and then Dante saw that his eyes were not bleared from drunkenness. He was crying.

"I . . . couldn't even go near him. I just had to stand there and watch him get . . . get . . . I felt like a coward."

Dante saw the whole scene in his mind; the old cathedral, the great door, the same door through which he had entered their lives, were vivid before his eyes. He remembered also the somnolent wineshop, he remembered the smell of it, and the street full of people, a street of mourners. He could imagine every detail, the cobblestones, the dust, everywhere the dust . . . and Max; Max who had asked him if he owned a factory, Max on his hands and knees. The last thing he felt then was the dust, the dust . . . He remembered Max sitting in the vault patiently beating Henri game after game, and Henri scowling at his cards. A few hours ago he had talked to Max . . . talked to him

. . . Death is always like this, he thought, always unbelief, uncomprehension.

Carnot was still talking to himself. "Why did he have to run? He wasn't armed. Why did he have to warn . . . to save . . ."

He was crying openly now. He sat with his hands clenched tight together, resting on the table, the knuckles white. His lips kept forming words and the tears were running down both cheeks, but all he could get out was soundless choking. He sat for a long time silent and absolutely rigid, his whole body racked with strangling sobs. Dante could feel the heavy oak table shaking under the pressure of Carnot's hands. Not for an instant did he turn away from Dante's eyes. Not once did he move. He only sat and cried soundlessly, pressing his knuckles into the wood. Then suddenly he looked as if he were about to burst open from inside and his lips drew back, all the way back, and for one terrible moment Dante saw him grinning, his eyes crossing slowly. Then he pitched forward and his face struck the dead oak with a sound like a butcher's mallet. And he didn't move.

Then Adriane was picking him up and laying him gently on the bench. She was crying and Dante realized immediately that she must have been listening. She could do nothing more, and helplessly she got down on her knees on the stone floor and buried her face in his chest. Blindly she worked her twisting fingers up into his hair. Alexi's beret slipped off the bench onto the floor. Dante stood transfixed, watching her. The loose black hair which fell over her back and arms had the sheen of gunmetal. Her shoulders shook long and silently, and then a harsh racking gasp muffled under her hair. Dante saw that except for an ugly muslin shift and one slipper she was naked. His legs were unsteady under him and he felt sick to his stomach. I was a fool to even try to drink, he thought. But he couldn't shake the fog out of his head. He was startled by a quiet voice beside him and turned to see Charles standing next to him, fully dressed. His eyes were soft brown in the light and his face was expressionless.

"Get some water," he said.

Dante handed the wine bottle full of water to the priest, who went around the table and pulled gently at Adriane's shoulder. She didn't respond at first and he put the bottle down on the stone hearth and tried to lift her with both hands. She shook free and sat back on her heels with her head still bent toward her knees, her white fingers gripping the long muscles of her thighs. Dante could see she was digging her nails into the flesh just below where the rough texture of the cloth ended, sobbing quietly to herself. She lifted her face, which was puffed and unlovely and streaked with jagged tears, and saw Charles standing over her looking down at her, his face immobile and hard with compassion, with pity. Dante saw his hand move in the deep folds of his robe and realized that he was rubbing the invisible cross with his thumb.

Adriane's mouth twisted and they both saw the tiny mark of blood where she was biting her lower lip between her teeth. The priest took her face in both his large peasant's hands and gently pressed the heels of his palms into her jaws until she was forced to open her teeth, the way a farmer might open the jaws of an animal. His face remained a sculpted mask of stone, but his eyes flickered for a split second at Dante. Dante came around behind her and put his hands under her arms. Her flesh was cold and hard and he could feel her ribs. When he tried to lift her she was limp, like a corpse, and she was all dead weight. Together they lifted her to her feet and Dante held her while Charles awkwardly dragged the other bench around the end of the table. Her hair was pressed against Dante's cheek and he could smell her female odor of soap and sweat and woman.

Outside the hard wind was still blowing, but steadier, so that the deep moaning in the chimney was a constant sound that Dante hardly heard any more. Charles took her hands and Dante felt life come back to her body. She walked of her own accord to the bench, walked slowly, like a sleepwalker, with her arms outstretched in Charles's hands, and for a grotesque instant Dante saw her as a ragtaggle Lady Macbeth. She sat down. Still shaken by enormous shudders, she had nonetheless stopped crying. Dante felt sudden relief, tremor of nausea, realized his knees were shaking. He went to the sink and splashed his face with water, and stood for a long moment leaning over until the nausea passed. The water cleared his head a little, as did the abrupt fear of becoming sick, but in the back of his throat he could still taste licorice.

Adriane was silent. She sat on the bench with her back to the room, facing the door. She sat straight-backed and rigid, with her head up, her black hair hanging clear of her shoulders to the small of her back. Her hands were folded and hung limp in the coarse cloth that bagged between her bare knees. She stared at the door which pushed against the bar with every pressure of the wind, her eyes dry and wide open, unblinking. As Dante watched her from profile, she shuddered once and opened her mouth in a sharp intake of breath. When she closed her mouth he heard her teeth click and chatter for a second. Charles was bending over Alexi, gently slapping his cheeks. Dante took off his shabby jacket and went to her and put it around her bare shoulders. She didn't move or look up. When he felt her skin it was cold and taut with gooseflesh. While he turned the collar up around her neck and buttoned the top button she continued to stare at the door as if he weren't there. He saw the priest reach down for the wine bottle and pour a little water on his hands and lay them on Alexi's cheeks and forehead, slapping gently. There was no response.

Dante watched Alexi's face over the priest's shoulder: though the whole side of the face was bruised, it was relaxed and peaceful and there seemed to be the trace of a smile on his lips. Suddenly he started to snore. The priest straightened up and looked down at him, shaking his head slowly. The bruises on his cheekbone and forehead were rapidly turning blue. The priest handed Dante the bottle and went to the sink to dry his hands. Dante put his thumb over the mouth of the bottle and sprinkled water on Alexi's head. The priest came back and stood beside Dante, rubbing his hands in a towel, watching. Carnot's hand slipped off his chest and hung limp on the floor.

"He was supposed to go with me this morning," said the priest.

"At this hour?" asked Dante. "What time is it?"

"It's three. It takes an hour to get to town," said Charles. "We have to go through the woods after curfew."

"What will you do there this late?"

"The fishing boats leave at four. We have business." The priest leaned down and placed his arm under Alexi's shoulders. "You'll have to help me."

They lifted Carnot up and sat him on the bench, propping his back against the table. He snored louder and his head lolled forward on his chest. Charles began slapping his cheeks, harder this time. Carnot groaned and one hand came up in a feeble gesture of defense.

"Give me the water," said Charles. Dante handed him the bottle and the priest upturned it over Alexi's head. The water came gluck-glucking out of the narrow-necked wine bottle and spilled over Carnot's head and shoulders, running in rivulets off his hair onto the table and bench and floor. Charles began to twist his ears, the way a farmer does to get a mule on its feet, and Carnot opened his mouth to mumble an incoherent protest. His eyes were closed. When he tried to cover his ears with his hands, Charles began tweaking his nose, holding his head up by the hair. Suddenly Alexi bellowed a drunken roar and thrashed out with both hands. Involuntarily the priest stepped back, and Carnot's face relaxed, his eyes still shut, and he started slipping sideways onto the bench. Dante reached out and held him until Charles could get his hands under his armpits and prop him upright again. Carnot groaned again. But he wouldn't open his eyes.

The priest stood for a moment feeling the cloth under Alexi's left armpit. Then he unbuttoned his blouse and slipped his hand inside to take the gun out of the holster. He started to withdraw the weapon and Dante was astonished to see Carnot's hand flash up and grasp the priest's wrist, bending it backward. The surprise on Charles's face changed to a wince of pain and he released his grip as Carnot snatched the Luger by the barrel with his other hand. His lips twisted in a shadow of a smile. He didn't open his eyes.

"Cochon!" said the priest, rubbing his wrist. "Are you coming with me or not?"

Alexi didn't say anything. His face relaxed and as for an answer he snored again, still clutching the blue pistol in both hands.

"Oh, leave him alone!" screamed Adriane, whirling around. "Can't you see he can't go anywhere like that?"

Dante and Charles both turned and looked at her for a long time.

She was standing up and Dante's jacket hung ridiculously from her narrow shoulders.

"Then I will have to go alone," said Charles.

"I know why you're going," she shouted. "Poor fool. You think Max is sleeping in the life preserver locker on Armand's boat. Max is dead, fool! He's dead. We traded him for a bicycle!"

Charles didn't move. She beat her fists on empty air, and she was crying again. He looked at her and didn't move. As Dante watched Adriane he understood finally. It was Henri. Henri was the one responsible. She *had* listened, standing in the dark hall with one foot bare on the cold stone floor; she had listened and heard her brother condemned in the death of Max, heard him blamed for the near-death of Alexi. At first he had been puzzled at her behavior, but now he began to imagine what she must be feeling, what she was going through as she listened in the hall. Why had he overlooked that part, the essential detail of the story? She had brought Henri into the group. If Henri hadn't gone to get the bicycle . . . if he had been where he was supposed to be . . . Then it occurred to him that it was Adriane herself who had left the bicycle in the first place. She covered her face with her hands and sat down slowly on the bench again.

Charles turned to Dante.

"Do you know about this?" he asked.

"He told me Max was shot tonight, last night that is, at the church."

"At the church!" Charles's eyes opened wide. "And nobody bothered to tell me? How many more may be dead by now!"

"He was drunk. He didn't tell anyone."

The priest's eyes blazed. He went to the door and lifted the bar. He looked back.

"How much did they find out? Was anyone else there?"

"He was killed alone," said Carnot out of the depths of his stupor. "No one else. Auguste back at café. Henri. Armand will know by now what . . ." His voice trailed off as though he were going to sleep. But suddenly he lurched to his feet. "But you're right. Have to go tell . . . Go with you." He staggered toward the door and fell sideways. Dante caught him as he was about to fall into the fireplace.

"Sit down," Dante said. To his surprise, Carnot sat down without a word.

"No good," said Carnot. "Too drunk. Can't walk quiet. I'm sorry, Charles, I'm sorry . . . have . . . go alone."

"Get him to bed," said the priest. "I'll be back at eight. Keep out of sight. They won't come for eggs until ten."

"I'd . . . just get us . . . both . . . caught." Carnot's stomach kept interrupting his speech. Dante thought he was going to vomit. "I'm sorry . . ."

Automatically, Adriane got up and dropped the bar back after the priest went out.

323

Then, without warning, eyes closed, Alexi laid back his head, and bellowed a horrendous roar, like a madman. He did it again, and then again, waving the Luger by the barrel in the air. Adriane was galvanized into action: she sprang onto him and slapped him hard, once, twice, a third time, with all the force in her arm. Each time she hit him his jaw jerked sideways over his shoulder and came back. Still he roared like a maniac and stamped his feet in a paroxysm of drunken rage. His mouth was open wide and it sounded as if he was trying deliberately to split his larynx. She hit him once again, this time with her closed fist, on the side of the head. He stopped and opened his eyes in surprise. For a second he looked as if he didn't know where he was, and he stared around the room, bewildered. He looked stupidly at the pistol in his hand and gropingly put it back in the holster. Then he saw Dante.

"Dante! My good friend Dante!" he shouted drunkenly. He got up and reeled over to where Dante was standing and grasped him by both arms, looking straight into his face. His knees kept buckling under him but he held himself up by steadying himself against Dante. "Do you trust me? I want to know do you trust me?" Dante saw tears in his eyes again. "Tell me!"

"I trust you, Alexi."

Dante felt his fingers digging into his arms.

"After all, though, do you *really* trust me? Are you fool enough?" His voice broke and tears slid down his cheeks. Dante could smell the reek of *pastis* on Carnot's breath in spite of the fact that he too had been drinking it. Alexi was losing all self-possession. Before, even though drunk, he had had enough presence of mind to switch the glasses. Now he was completely out of control and crying drunk.

"I trust you, Alexi."

"That makes me feel good," he shouted at the ceiling. "Good. So good. I'm glad you trust me, because I trust you. Don't ever forget that you promised you trusted me. You won't forget you trust me, will you? Or I'll cut your throat!" Carnot's eyes narrowed with drunken suspicion. Dante was beginning to feel pain in his arm from the pressure of his fingers.

"I don't forget who I trust," he said.

Carnot laughed. "My friend. My new friend Dante," he said. This time there was no mockery in his voice. "From now on when we drink together, we drink *together*, all right?"

Dante couldn't help smiling. There were still tears in Carnot's eyes.

"I won't drink against you," said Dante. "From now on we drink together."

"I know I'm younger than you," said Carnot, his words rushing on faster than Dante could follow the tortured sequence of his thoughts. "But it won't make any difference if you trust me, will it?"

"Why should it make any difference?"

"Will you help me?" asked Carnot.

"Help you how?"

"I don't know. Help me. I'll help you. We can work together?"

"Of course," said Dante. "Naturally."

"*Not* naturally!" said Carnot, stamping his foot like a small boy and digging his fingers harder into Dante's arms. "*Un*naturally! I want you to help me because you trust me. You'll never change your mind?"

"No."

Carnot's face broke into a great smile and he relaxed his grip. "My friend. My new friend Dante! I won't ever forget." Alexi's eyes were still watering and for a moment he simply stood looking at Dante, smiling. "It's too bad Max . . ." He left the sentence unfinished and his face went blank, his eyes relaxing into a vague gaze. He came back to himself and looked at Dante again. For a long moment he didn't say anything. Then he embraced Dante in a stiff, formal, French military embrace, first on one side and then on the other. Then he stepped back a pace, lurching a little, and saluted him. Dante was surprised to find himself returning the salute automatically. They shook hands. Carnot sat down on the bench and picked up the two empty *pastis* bottles and looked at them with drunken satisfaction. He reached into his back pocket and took out a knife; before Dante could grasp what he was doing Carnot was savagely turning the corkscrew into the cork of the last bottle.

"From now on we will drink together," said Carnot, "like friends. Whatever I have I will give you half."

"Alexi," said Dante, laughing, "if I have another drop of that embalming fluid of Auguste's, I'll be too well preserved to walk. I'm an old man, compared to you. And tired. I can't keep up your pace."

Carnot looked disappointed but sympathetic. "I'm sorry, Dante. If you are not used to this it can be very bad for you. Perhaps I've been giving you too much if you are not used to it." He smiled mischievously.

"I'm just right, now," said Dante, still amused at Carnot's stamina. "But I'm tired also."

"How can I give you anything if you won't take it?" asked Carnot. "How can we drink together if you go to bed?"

"I would gladly kill that bottle with you after I've gotten over my state of shock from the two we just finished."

"Then we'll save it," said Carnot, pulling the cork with a pop. "I'll have one in advance and we'll save it."

"Do you mind if I break down and go to bed?"

"You are tired. You are, my friend," said Carnot, trying to pour himself a drink. "You must go to bed. Take Adriane with you."

Dante wondered if he had heard correctly. He heard the words but misunderstood, perhaps. He gave no sign and continued without a pause, turning to Adriane who was sitting quietly on the other bench, still wearing his jacket. Her face was composed but she looked tired.

"Yes, Adriane," he said. "You must be tired too."

"She is never too tired to make love, this one. Even with a grandfather," said Carnot, smiling good-naturedly. Adriane, if she heard, didn't show it. Dante couldn't make his mind believe that it was registering. He was sure he had misunderstood. Something completely unreal was happening. Carnot wasn't leering; he was smiling naturally, even though he was drunk. And even though he was drunk he seemed to know what he was saying. Yet the reaction from Adriane was missing. He was trying to think of a tactful way of clearing his misunderstanding without blundering on insult, when Alexi removed the last refuge of doubt.

"She doesn't want to sleep with me. I'm too drunk," he said. "You are my friend. You are my good friend Dante. So sleep with her."

Dante sensed that anything he said could be dangerous. He tried to let nothing show on his face, but in his mind he was utterly staggered. It was as though Carnot, in the grip of grief and rage and lost love, had become a child of petulant malice, dangerous, drunk, demanding. Yet out of the distorted logic of drunken friendship, here also was a man— half brother, half son—offering him his wife to use. Wife, mistress, canon law, common law, thought Dante: it came to the same thing. What struck him hardest was the girl herself, for she didn't move or make any protest; yet Dante thought he could see hurt and fear and pain and fury in her dulled eyes as she sat watching Carnot. Then she looked up at him, her face sad but expressionless, and he was overwhelmed by an inexpressible pity for her. Carnot was drinking the *pastis* straight, without water. He put the glass down and looked at Dante. Dante, still stunned, was trying to think of something that would strike the right medium in a ragged situation of extremes. He was conscious that Carnot was watching him and he couldn't make his mind work.

"You have refused to drink with me," said Carnot. "And I understand. You are tired. She is the only other thing I have." Carnot reached into his shirt and took out the Luger and laid it on the table.

"Besides this. This I can share with no one."

"I am much too old to amuse her," Dante said, laughing lamely. He tried desperately to convey to her with his eyes that the remark was only a gambit to spare her worse indignity.

"You are not supposed to amuse her. She will amuse you."

Dante, still shocked, could not fathom Carnot's feelings. He was deadly serious, but he didn't seem to be acting merely out of drunken malice. Nor did he give the impression that he had no respect for the girl. Rather, something in his tone conveyed the feeling that he thought of her simply as a woman, that perhaps he was even doing her a favor that might earn her gratitude. Dante looked into her eyes and was no longer sure what it was he saw there. Resignation? Acceptance? Perhaps she truly didn't care. Suddenly a thought slithered below the surface of his mind uncontrolled. Had he ever before looked at her *as* a woman? Did he want it to happen? Was he going to acquiesce simply because it might be dangerous otherwise, or was it because . . . After all, there *was* Carnot, drunk. There *was* that Luger on the table. And he remembered the instant when Carnot had started shouting, berserk. Beyond that, he could always sleep on the floor . . . But perhaps, he thought, this is all a deception. There's still the chance . . . Am I hoping she will settle the decision herself? Can't I admit I want to stay with her? Why can't I admit that? She would be safe. Again he felt an immense pity for her. He stared at the bruise on her cut lip which had dried in a brown smear.

Dante turned around all the way and faced Carnot, his back to Adriane. He knew she was watching him, though.

"Perhaps she prefers to sleep alone," he said unemotionally. "This has been a bad night."

Carnot was silent. For a long moment. He seemed to be considering what Dante had said. Then he looked up past Dante toward Adriane.

"It has been a bad night," he said. "For all of us. But a bad night is not a night to be alone." He paused. Dante watched his eyes. Alexi was exhausted too. He seemed to be forcing himself to drink. His eyes looked as if they would close any moment of their own weight. Dante wondered: What would Carnot, were he sober, think of this that he was doing? Could he manage Carnot tomorrow morning? "Some things I don't understand," Carnot continued thickly, still looking past Dante at Adriane. "I am going to stay here and think about them. Do you want to sleep alone?"

Dante couldn't make himself turn around. Instead, he kept his back to her and watched Carnot, waiting for her to speak. But she didn't speak. Finally Carnot looked up at Dante. Dante was sure she had made some gesture. She had shaken her head, perhaps shrugged her shoulders. Dante watched Carnot looking at him, then watched him turn back to his drink, tilting it forward and staring into it, holding it with both hands.

"My friend. My new friend Dante," he said half to himself, rolling the glass between his palms. He seemed relaxed and content. "Go to bed. Take her with you."

Dante was about to open his mouth to speak when to his immense relief she brushed quickly and silently past him and disappeared through the curtains. That settles the matter, he thought. Thank God. If Alexi saw her go he gave no sign. Dante waited and then said good night.

As he looked back he saw Carnot still sitting as he had left him, his head bowed, staring into the empty tumbler under the cone of sick yellow light, laughing to himself. He seemed far away in his thoughts and Dante saw a grim triumph in the drunken smile on his face. He left the kitchen.

Feeling reprieved, he groped his way and opened the door to his room; he heard the wind once again. The outside shutter he had bound with twine had worked loose and was swinging gently in the diminished wind. He decided: it was a pleasant sound and he would leave it. He stepped into the blackness and closed the door softly behind him, feeling in his pocket for the candle he had left in the kitchen. As he stood with his hand on the door handle, letting his eyes adjust to the darkness, wondering whether it was worth going back after the candle, he heard the frightened shriek of a ground bird, attacked in the nest by a nocturnal prowler just outside his window. There was a furious flutter of wings and then silence. He wondered if the bird were flown or dead. He crossed the tiny room to open the window. As he did so he stepped on a slipper; stopped dead; eyes adjusting to the darkness. Finally, knowing, he turned and looked toward the bed, smelling the odor of lye soap; she was sitting on the foot of the bed with her knees drawn up under her chin, watching in the passive dark.

They slept at dawn. The first time Dante awoke, it was full light; Adriane was gone. No one came out of their rooms, even to eat, till five o'clock, and each time Dante awoke during the day he could hear the priest pacing his room and the low murmur of his voice through the wall as he prayed. The day outside was gray, even though the wind continued to blow.

At five o'clock Carnot gathered them in the kitchen to reschedule Dante's departure. The priest had foreseen that Dante wouldn't leave that morning and had communicated with the contact in Nice, postponing the meeting by one day. As Carnot explained how, in view of the increased need for security, they would proceed with an alternative plan to the one originally scheduled, he kept his hand to his forehead as he talked, his eyes averted, as though he had a severe headache. Dante watched Adriane out of the corner of his eye as she moved about the kitchen preparing food. The fire had gone out downstairs in the vault as well as in the kitchen, and Charles had had to reset them both. Only once, as the girl stood behind Alexi beating eggs and meal in the bowl under her arm, did she look at Dante. There was no expression in her eyes and her face was blank.

Charles explained the plan in detail: he would take him to the clinic as soon as they had supper, and Dante would leave for Nice the next morning, with a nun to accompany him. It was obviously something that had all been worked out ahead of time and Charles reeled off the time schedule mechanically. As Charles finished, Carnot said he wasn't hungry, and went to his room.

Charles said he was sorry for Alexi, that Max was the nearest thing he had to a Father Confessor. Dante said nothing and Charles went on, saying that since Alexi was raised a Catholic he would never be able to go very long without finding himself a confessor. Dante remembered the wry mischief of Alexi's toast to mutual trust the night before, and wondered if it was a confessor he wanted so much as a reliable drinking partner for occasional commiseration. Nothing more was said. Adriane didn't sit at the table but ate on an old milking stool by the fireplace with her plate in her lap. Charles dawdled over his omelette; for the first time since he had met him Dante had the feeling that the taciturn priest wanted to talk. Dante didn't oblige him and kept his eyes on his plate. Secretly he cursed the priest and wished he would finish and leave.

He wanted badly to talk to Adriane alone. What did he want to tell her? He tried to formulate something to say. And why was it so important? He was leaving tonight. But he didn't want her to despise him. Despise him for what? Satisfying her? No. Using her? Perhaps that was it. He felt pity for her, that was true. But he couldn't tell her he pitied her. In the back of his mind he knew all along what he *wanted* to tell this loveless, passionate child. While he was thinking about pity, in another part of his mind he was toying with an exciting idea, an immense idea. He knew he wanted to tell her he loved her. Yet he knew without ever putting the thought in words that it was impossible, ridiculous. It wasn't true. Besides, she was less than half his age; she could easily laugh in his face.

In the end he resigned himself to talking to the priest. They talked about redemption, and later, whether it was a sin in the eyes of God to kill a man in self-defense without intending to. The priest maintained that taking life under any circumstances was a sin. Dante had never seen him so talkative. Adriane was washing the dishes and her continued presence in the room obtruded on Dante's thoughts to the point where twice he lost the thread of his own argument and had to start over.

Abruptly, the priest rose and announced that it was getting late. He left the kitchen and went to his room to get his things before they left the house. Adriane put down the dish she was washing and stood with her back to him, her hands idle. Charles would be back in a minute. Dante knew what he was demanding of himself, if he had the courage. His heart jumped in his throat as he reached out and found himself touching her again. He grasped her gently by the shoulders and turned her around. She looked at him dully for a moment and made no movement to resist. He looked in her eyes, trying to see what she was feeling, but he saw nothing. Then, awkwardly, he drew himself to her and put his arms around her trying to place her head on his shoulder. But she remained stiff and straight and he found himself leaning on her to keep his balance. He tightened his arms and pulled her to him and he felt her body relax and come alive. Then she drew back and looked at him intently with something like sullen pity in her eyes. He was shocked to see her face tighten and her eyes fill with tears. She dug her fingers into his arms and shook herself free and ran out of the room. The curtains were still moving where she had passed, when they parted again: Charles entered carrying a suitcase and the clothes Dante was to wear on the train to Nice in the morning.

X

Dante thought about Adriane several times while on the train. He thought about her and put it out of his mind because he wanted to stay completely alert to the situation around him. Charles had instructed him to travel first-class, since usually the only people who had the money to travel first-class were those who had influence with the Germans or collaborated. That way he would be less likely to be bothered by questions. The nun fussed around him, arranging a pillow. Once a man entered to take a seat in their compartment, and while Dante feigned sleep with the coded newspaper over his eyes, she shrewdly managed to convey that her companion was tubercular. Then she put the new occupant at his joyless ease by adding that the disease was not always contagious and she was glad to have his company. After a decent interval the gentleman excused himself to get a drink of water. He never came back.

On the train, even while pretending to be asleep, Dante forced himself to remain on the alert and to watch the corridor through the glass with half-open eyes. Thus both times the German train police opened the door they found a man in the midst of a racking fit of coughing. One of them even put his gloves on before taking the identity papers the nun held out to him.

The picture of Adriane kept reappearing in Dante's mind, yet he put off thinking about the undigested events of the past days. He also refused to think about the experiences of the previous weeks: of Max's death, of Orchard's, of Mike's rescue and his death.

The trip was uneventful. He was accompanied all the way by the nurse-sister from the hospital. The nun sat between him and the door to the compartment. Four times they had to show their papers, twice to German railway police, twice to French police when they changed trains. When the police saw the medical certificate they read only as far as the word "tuberculosis"; only the Germans even bothered to look at the *laissez-passer*. None of them examined the *carte d'identité* very closely, or even asked to see Dante's *fiche de démobilisation*. Dante's confidence in his manufactured papers was greatly strengthened, and when they left the railroad station at Nice he was feeling very optimistic for a man attested to be dying of diseased lungs.

They were met in Nice and escorted to the bus stop by a middle-aged priest who identified himself in exactly the manner Carnot said he would—by asking if it had rained down the coast that morning. Dante replied, as prescribed, that rain would be welcome since the vines needed water. Then Dante gave the priest a newspaper in which a

330

number of words were marked with tiny numbers indicating the order in which they were to be sent. Even on close examination the numbers would hardly be noticed unless one knew they were there and was looking for them. The completed message was a series of nonsense phrases.

Dante leaned heavily on the nun as they crossed the street to a bench on the square to wait for the bus. The priest wished him well and promised that the message would go out before sundown and would be sent simultaneously from two different points. That way, Dante figured he would get a confirmation through the French Service of the BBC within a day, and an answer within a week. Carnot had assured him that the receiver at the retreat where he was going was excellent and that at night, due to the moderate elevation, the BBC came through with exceptional clarity. He was looking forward to his stay at Asprémont. From what Carnot had told him, the tiny olive-growing village sounded peaceful and lost from the world.

Although Asprémont was less than fifty kilometers inland from Nice, it was an uphill climb all the way. The bus, actually a converted delivery truck, burned producer gas from a wood-fired generator on the back, which left a trail of sparks and smoke as the ancient springless machine snorted over the crests in the road, then roared down the other side at bone-jarring speed to gain enough momentum to hurtle it rockily up the next hill.

The rest of the passengers were all peasants, except one enormous woman with a gaudy shawl and a ridiculous fringed parasol. Dante passed the first part of the journey speculating on what she was and where she was going. Twice the passengers had to get out and help push the vehicle over the crest of a hill. Dante, because of his "condition," was exempted by the driver from these exertions, but the nun pushed with the rest. Only once did they have to show papers at a German patrol point. After an old woman had been sick in the front of the bus, the other sentries only stuck their heads in and surveyed the buffeted collection of miserable beings like so many badly tied bundles on the floor, and waved them on. The stench was too much for them; the passengers had long since ceased to notice it.

A system of rotation was worked out after a while so that everyone had his turn on the two hard wooden benches along the sides of the lightless interior. Dante insisted on taking his turn on the floor with the others, which earned him the respect of the other passengers but left him with both buttocks bruised and sore. The woman with the parasol finally refused to leave her place on the bench when her time was up. Dante was surprised that no one else was resentful or even seemed to care. She sat on the bench and was ignored while the others continued to rotate in turn. But later when the old woman got sick she was careful not to miss the one with the parasol, who sputtered and fumed as she tried to wipe off her shoes with a cheap lace handkerchief. The driver stopped long enough to clean out the inside of the bus with some leaves and cover the place on the floor with dust from the road. He was wooden-faced and seemed completely unperturbed.

They stopped once or twice in small villages, where the driver got out and put more logs in the firebox and the passengers relieved themselves at the side of the road. One damp old farmer who must have had kidney trouble couldn't wait, however; he too went to the front of the bus and sat where the woman with the parasol, who was still muttering something about filthy peasants, might adequately consider the evidence of his misery.

As the bus labored up the last series of steep grades before Asprémont, Dante allowed himself to relax a little and think about Adriane. Sitting in the kitchen watching her and listening to Alexi had been like a dream. How could she even be there after the night before? How could she not show anything in her face, he wondered. Her utterly impassive look contrasted so violently with the clawing sexual hunger he had met in the dark silence of his tiny cubicle; it made his flesh crawl to think of it. He had given up trying to quiet her. He remembered her crying, panting, and the smell of her flesh, invisible—and still crying—all this though they had barely spoken a word to each other since the night she was mending while he read.

The next night, as he followed her out of the tail of his eye about the kitchen he could hardly make himself believe it had happened. But it had happened. He hadn't dreamed it. But knowing it wasn't a dream only made the present scene in the kitchen that much more dreamlike. No one alluded to anything even remotely touching on the previous night. It was as if by common consent the day had disappeared from the calendar. The only clue that it hadn't was Carnot's pretending to shade his eyes with his hand and holding his aching temples. He looked sick, and under the light his skin was waxen yellow.

Dante looked at the nun sitting placidly on the bench above him. He wondered if that body, now forever hidden from light, had ever known the ague of passion. He had never looked at Adriane as a woman until Alexi had rubbed his nose in the fact by offering her to him to use. And suddenly, out of a welter of conflicting emotions, emerged the guilty fact that he still wanted her. Before he had seen her simply as a badly dressed, self-effacing servant and housekeeper, never as a woman. He looked at the nun and wondered if, in general, he had ever really looked at women *as* women rather than simply as wives, mothers, nurses, servants, nuns, whores. He wasn't satisfied with the thought, "women as women." What did it mean? It was a tautology. It meant nothing. Yet the phrase kept circling in his mind as he went over the details of the dreamlike scene in the kitchen. Womanhood, he thought, is that what whores and nuns hide from themselves?

The bus lurched heavily around a descending curve. The passengers swayed. Dante stood up in the aisle to stretch his cramped legs. He was in the rear, next to the nun, who was still sitting on the bench. The bus was laboring over the crest of the last hill before the final climb to the top of the tiny peak and the village of Asprémont. He had to steady his footing as the floor tilted forward under him, and the chuffing vehicle began loping down the pitted incline, gathering speed. A few minutes earlier, through the tiny windows in the rear doors Dante had watched the setting sun rise again in the west as they climbed up the hill. Now it was setting again with astonishing rapidity as the bus lurched and skidded down the other side.

The passengers groaned in concert as they were thrown against each other and the walls of the bus. The old woman who had been sick was now chattering to herself and doing something busy with her hands. At first Dante thought she was knitting or sewing, then he saw the cross on the rosary as it snaked through her fingers, and he felt sorry for her. She was sick with fear.

At the bottom of the drop it was almost dusk and Dante wondered how the driver could see without lights. He decided the best thing was to try not to look. The racketing of the limber old machine, rattling and squeaking and clanking, and the moaning of the terrified occupants were punctuated by the teeth-grinding whine of changing gears and the irregular thud of the wheels caroming into potholes in the road. Dante turned his back on the scene ahead and, bracing himself, looked out the back of the truck. He watched the river of dust behind them unwind to a narrow ribbon under a pall of black smoke; a streamer of orange sparks spewed out of the tank apparatus that hung like a red-hot bustle on the rear. When they reached the top of the final hill, the driver reared back on the brake lever with both hands, completely ignoring the steering wheel. The truck squealed and grated past one, two, three, four houses and stopped in the center of the village in front of a café. The café had a sun-bleached sign, a painted red bullseye on the front: *Relai des Routiers. Bonne Table. Telephone 5*. Dante and the nun were the last out of the bus. In front of him he heard the driver apologizing to the old lady who had been sick. Her fingers were still mechanically working the rosary as the driver helped her down. The driver was still wooden-faced and apparently untired. "I'm sorry we had to go so quickly coming down," he explained gently to the old woman, "but we have to save fuel. Also, the brakes are worn out."

Dante noticed that his watch had stopped at quarter to four.

The village of Asprémont covered the summit of the peak, which was too large to be called a hill and too small to be called a mountain. From what Dante could determine the community subsisted entirely on the olive groves that covered the southern side of the hill down to the edge of the river Loup, which glistened like a silver tape in the sun at the bottom of the valley far below.

By the third day it was evident to Dante that he wasn't the only one in the hotel who had business with the underground. The day before, he had seen the messenger talking quietly to the manager of the hotel in the lobby after he'd left Dante's room. The messenger gave Dante no sign of recognition, and the manager only nodded as he walked past the desk and went to have a vermouth outside. He had been told by the manager the first night that he had free run of the town but not to miss any meals under any circumstances, since mealtimes served as a formal muster. He was also shown a special table at which he was never to sit except in the unanticipated circumstances of his having been followed to the hotel by someone he didn't recognize. If he ever saw anyone sitting at his table, he was to remain where he was until he received instructions from his waiter. A radio appeared in his room.

Dante got the impression that not just the "rest camp" but the whole village was an armed stronghold. He reasoned that the Resistance must control the police as well as everything else, and he remembered how the bus driver had winked when telling him he didn't have to help push because of his sickness. It had not occurred to him at the time that the driver was a *maquisard*. He'd thought the fellow was looking for a tip, which fortunately he hadn't attempted to give him.

The voice of the BBC had come through clear and steady; three successive times the same code phrase was reiterated: *Si les vignes ont besoin de l'eau, il faut prier pour la pluie.* Over and over the phrase repeated itself in Dante's mind. If the vines need water, pray for rain. It meant that his request for matériel was in the process of being cleared through the Allied High Command in London. He knew that Carnot must be hearing the same phrase—probably on Mike's wireless, which he knew had been set up somewhere near St. Tropez—and experiencing the same feeling of satisfaction. He had hardly expected the wheels of decision to grind so fast. If things kept up at this rate the first drop might be expected to take place within the month.

Since his arrival at the hotel-sanitarium he had decided that he would insist on being present with the reception committee when the first load of equipment was parachuted. He had arranged air drops but had never seen one; it would be satisfying to see some of the results of his efforts. Besides, in this case the personal risk would be more than offset by the increased confidence his presence might possibly inspire in the men who would be risking their lives retrieving and caching the contraband weapons. He had sent his request—to be included on the committee—to Carnot by messenger the day before.

On the morning of the fourth day Dante was awakened by a knock on his door, and the *femme de chambre* informed him that he had a visitor. He assumed it was the messenger from Carnot with a reply to his request of two days ago, and told the girl to send him to his room in five minutes, after he'd dressed. The girl said that the visitor was a woman. Dante said that it made no difference, she was to come in five minutes. He dressed immediately, wondering what Carnot would have to say to his request. While he was starting to tie his tie there was a knock on the door and he went to open it.

Adriane entered the room without a word of greeting and Dante was too surprised to say anything. She turned in the center of the room and faced him.

"Well," she said, "close the door."

He closed the door.

"What are *you* doing here?" he asked. She looked entirely different from when he had last seen her. She was still dressed simply but she had make-up on. And her hair was cut short.

"Madame LaChaise was arrested again," she said. "The day after you left I was called in for questioning."

"So they sent you here?"

"I know too much," she said simply.

"But when did you arrive?" asked Dante. "I haven't seen you in the dining room."

"I eat in my room. I came yesterday."

She seemed a different person. She no longer behaved like a servant. She seemed self-assured, even confident.

"Won't they miss you?"

"Yes," she said. "Everything has been taken out of the farm, temporarily. At Max's funeral. It was a risk. But Charles will manage them. As far as he is concerned I was a charity case sent by the Church. They don't know where I came from or where I went or what I was doing in St. Tropez. He will manage."

"And Alexi?"

"He went away with Henri. They will come back when things quiet down. Auguste is staying in the café. They are still looking for you, too."

"How do you know?"

"I could tell by the questions," she said. "But they have a very bad description of you."

"Why did they let you go?"

"They followed me. They wanted me to lead them to someone else."

"Where did you go?"

"To church."

"And you lost them?"

"It is not difficult to lose someone if you know the houses."

Dante seated her in the only chair in the room and sat down on the bed.

"I wish I had something to offer you to drink," he said.

"Why?"

"Perhaps we could go downstairs," he said.

"I'm not allowed out of my room. I had to get permission before I could see you."

"Why did you want to see me?"

"Is it unnatural I should come to see you?" she asked.

Dante could say nothing for a moment.

She said, "Had you forgotten?"

"No. It's just that I never expected . . ."

"You never expected to see me again, is that it?"

"I guess not," he said. It was true, he realized.

"Is that why you didn't want to sleep with me?"

"Do we have to attack this subject before I've had breakfast?" asked Dante. "I'm not even sure you're the same person yet. I can't believe you're here. I just woke up."

"Everyone comes here sooner or later," she said.

"I'm glad you're here."

"Why?"

"Of course I am," he said, too emphatically, he thought.

"You're embarrassed," she said. "You're wondering what I want from you."

There was a pause.

"What *do* you want?" he asked finally.

"Can we have breakfast?" she asked. "I have some sausage in my room. Auguste gave it to me."

"I have to go to the dining room," he said. "It seems to be a rule."

"I know about that. You can go down and tell René you are eating in my room."

"Who's René?" he asked. "I don't know a thing about this place. All they've told me is to appear for meals and behave like a sick man in public."

"René is the small one. The headwaiter."

"You've been here before?"

"Once."

"After the business in Nice?" he asked, without thinking.

"What business?" she asked, alerted.

"Alexi mentioned that you were once employed by a man who was arrested," said Dante, surprised at the facility with which he backtracked from his indiscretion. He watched her for a reaction. She looked at him narrowly.

"Perhaps," she said. "I've worked for a lot of people."

"I can't get over how you've changed," Dante said extraneously, to change the subject.

"How do you know I've changed?" she asked. "You never knew me."

"I . . . I mean, you weren't the same at the farm."

"You thought I was a simple child."

"No. No. Why are you taxing my wits when I'm only half awake?"

"Of course I wasn't the same," she said.

"Why did you leave the kitchen when I wanted to talk to you?" he asked.

"Why did you want to talk to me?" She asked the question with emphasis, as though it answered his own. She looked at him steadily until involuntarily he dropped his eyes. "Did you want to ease your conscience?" she asked.

Dante felt simultaneously elated and disgusted with himself. Already the anticipation of knowing her again was crowding the unarticulated regions of his mind. She was unbelievably young. But as yet desire had no solid shape in his thoughts and all he felt was an unaccountable relief, elation, at seeing her again. She was good. It was good to see her again. It was good to look at her. He remembered that he had felt like an adolescent when he tried to put his arms around her in the kitchen, and had cursed himself afterward for his awkwardness. Now he felt he had been granted a reprieve, a second chance. But his relief was confounded by the unsettling feeling that this was no longer the same woman. Somehow things were now more complex, less clearly defined. All he could remember was that he hadn't wanted her to despise him. And he was sure she did; yet here she was, sitting on the edge of a chair in his room, apparently relaxed, and yet he sensed she was not at ease. He felt with certainty that the failure was somehow his.

He thought how much she resembled Carnot in her manner, the way she kept herself in rigid control, almost playing a role. But *she* had come to see *him*. Then he remembered Carnot, and wondered what her real purpose was. He couldn't deny the warm pleasure that suffused his mind and body at seeing her again. She was so young. So young, he thought. It was the hair. Her hair was no longer tied in a bun but was cut short and loose. It seemed to go with her new character.

"I don't exactly know why," he said.

"What were you going to say?" she asked. "You were going to say something. You had your mouth open."

Dante looked at her. She still had on the same serge skirt, and the fringed shoes. But she also had on what looked like a man's shirt, except that it fit, and it was severely tucked in at her waist and showed the solid lines of her body. The collar was turned up behind her neck, which made her look taller and more slender. And she was wearing a bracelet. At the farm she had always worn only two or three rough woolen sweaters and an old leather hunter's jacket, never any makeup. He thought about her standing behind Alexi, dull-eyed and silent, whipping batter in the bowl under her arm, looking at him only once. And Alexi looking sick and pale. Again he wondered how much Alexi remembered of the night before. It was possible he remembered nothing.

"I think I wanted to tell you I loved you," he said, "because you were young." The words were out of his mouth before he could think; he was still remembering Alexi drinking in the kitchen. Then he added: "War makes old men."

"That would have been a cheap salve for your conscience," she said. "That's what *lycée* students would like to say to their first whore. But they've at least got some grounds for their declaration."

Dante said nothing. The remark was brutal, partly because it was true. Suddenly he wanted nothing to do with her. He wanted to protest, but he decided anything he might say would sound false. Most of the things he could think of offhand to say *were* false—or cynical. He said nothing.

"I don't believe you were going to say that," she said.

"I honestly don't know what I was going to say," said Dante, strongly annoyed.

"Don't I please you? Aren't you challenging me to spend the night with you again?"

Dante felt his pulse slacken. It was true, perhaps. "Please. I'm not even awake. I haven't had breakfast," he said. "I am an ordinary middle-sized human being. I need something in my stomach before I can analyze my devious motives. I'm glad to see you again."

"Come to my room," she said. "We'll have breakfast and then you'll have all morning to analyze your motives." She didn't smile.

Dante resented the quickened edge of anticipation he felt in his blood as he went downstairs to announce his absence from his table. On the stairs he had to press against the wall as a waiter passed him with a large tray with two breakfasts on it, and suddenly he was sure no one even expected him in the dining room. But he went anyway, unable to do otherwise, and carried out the motions of explaining and excusing himself from the meal. The headwaiter was very understanding and said his breakfast would be sent up to his friend's room. Dante didn't like the casual way he said friend. Before going upstairs he dawdled at the desk and read an occupation statute relating to closing hours, which, according to law, was posted on the wall. When he finished he started slowly up the stairs to her room, refusing to let himself wonder about the purpose behind this clumsily prearranged assignation. Obviously, she had been "assigned" to him. The idea filled him with sick anger. He went upstairs.

The sun spread evenly over the southern side of the slope down to the river that stretched toward the sea far below. The air was clear and the sky cloudless for the first time in over a week. It was the first day that didn't conceal the stubborn threat of tardy winter rain. The sky was blue and clear as quartz crystal, from the snow-covered peaks of the little Alps at the far distant north to the unreal Mediterranean blue of the sea only thirty kilometers to the south. As the sun climbed higher in the south, its cold white brilliance paled in the luminous blue sky.

"Spring always comes quickly in the Midi," said Adriane. She was wearing a twine-knit sweater she had finished the previous day. She rubbed her arms against the chill.

Dante offered her his leather windbreaker but she refused it. "I like it when it's like this," she said. "If I get really cold I'll go back and get a jacket."

Dante had never even suspected the existence of the tiny terrace behind the Asprémont café until she suggested they go there for breakfast. Since word had arrived from St. Tropez that her disappearance had not caused any untoward upheaval, she had been given the same freedom to move about the village as Dante and most of the other "patients." The man in room eight was now the only one who was never seen in the dining room. From the maid he had learned that the unknown occupant in number eight was male. Beyond that he knew nothing except that the man's arrival had stirred interest. He suspected that Adriane knew who he was, but he had learned that direct questions about anything were treated as a breach of manners in the hotel and had decided not to place Adriane in an uncomfortable position by asking about the new arrival. He had been here a little over a week, arriving six days after Dante.

By observing the keyboard closely every day, Dante had figured out that there were only two rooms unoccupied out of the eighteen. He had also learned, the hard way, that one didn't attempt to make conversation in the dining room, or anywhere else, for that matter. His only two efforts in this direction were greeted with a blank stare and a conversation-stopping answer, in the first case "yes," in the second a firm "no." There seemed to be no rule, however, against conversing with the waiters, as long as one confined the discussion to relatively innocuous matters, such as the points of interest worth seeing in the region, the poor quality of the wine, or even the progress of the war, as long as one was discreet. Once he had referred to the BBC, however, and the waiter had leaned down to tell him to be careful. His waiter was called André, and Dante gathered that he too was only on temporary sojourn at the hotel when he mentioned inadvertently that he had been working in Paris a few months before. Life in the hotel was strange. The idea of a hotel being converted into a sanitarium was odd in itself, but the pretense was kept up. Wheelchairs were kept in the front hall. A doctor was in residence and made strict rounds, and after the third day Dante no longer received visits from *agents de liaison,* although every now and then he still recognized one of them in the dining room, but instead the doctor was his contact with the outside. He had noticed, however, that the doctor was a frequent visitor to room eight, which was on the same floor as his own. And once he definitely smelled the vague reek of iodoform in the corridor. It was the first time it occurred to him that the man in room eight might be wounded.

Adriane dipped the corner of her *croissant* in her second cup of chicory and held it out to Dante. He took a small bite.

"The sun is deceptive up here," she said. "It always looks warm outside from the hotel."

"We're pretty high up," Dante said. "This must be a foothill of the Alps. How far away are those mountains up there? This is the first day it's been clear enough to see them."

"I'm not sure," she said, looking over her shoulder at the distant peaks up the valley to the left. "The river must come from there. I know they're a lot farther away than they look. But before the war I remember you could leave on the train from Nice in the morning and be skiing before the sun was at noon. As a little girl, I can remember how strange it was to see whole busloads of people getting off the bus in the square with their skis over their shoulders and boots on, coming back from a weekend in the snow. The sun was always shining and it was always hot and they looked so strange with their snow suits and their boots. My family used to go to Majorca, rather my mother's family, and I never even saw snow until I was twelve years old."

"What was your family like?" asked Dante. "Are they still alive?"

"My mother died when she gave birth to my younger brother."

"And your father?"

"We were raised by my maternal grandmother. She took us away when I was thirteen, just before the war. He was a drunkard."

"Your grandmother lived with you?"

"She was nearly blind but she still had some money. She hated my father and he hated her. She wouldn't give him money to drink. She came from a good family in Nice. Her father was a wine merchant. But my father was just a farmer who didn't even have the sense to stay out of law courts. He lost most of the land his father left him the year after the old man died. He refused to hire a lawyer and he refused to settle out of court. He sold the rest of the land and came to Nice to work, rolling barrels for my grandfather."

"Why did your grandmother hate him?"

"After she took us away from him . . . There was a terrible fight one night and she left the house. She was almost blind but she left the house. She was sixty-seven years old. She came back one night when he was out drunk somewhere as usual and she had two men with her. One of them used to work for my grandfather also. Grandpère left him a half interest in the business. My brother was still only a boy and I remembered he cried because he was frightened being wakened up in the middle of the night. Father always used to wake us up when he was drunk and we would have to sit and listen to him while he rambled on about nothing. If we fell asleep he would rap us on the knuckles with an ebony letter opener he used to keep. Anyway, my grandmother came and we were on the boat to Majorca almost before we could wake up. We didn't even get dressed."

Dante watched her. The sun on the terrace was taking the chill out of the stone under his feet. They sat at the only table which was upright on the terrace. The others were stacked next to the wall at one end. The table was rusty and there were cobwebs between the iron legs under it and in the umbrella hole in the center. Long ago it had been painted green.

Her cheeks were red from the brisk high air and Dante thought she looked very lovely. He still couldn't think of her as the girl at the farm. Perhaps because he had first learned what she felt like in the sightless

340

dark, how hard and strong she was—perhaps that was the reason he still couldn't get rid of the picture in his mind of her standing at the sink with the old leather jacket over the three sweaters, drab, gray, her hair tied in a bun. She had been squat-looking; it was as if she were deliberately trying to make herself look as ugly as possible. But now she looked young and alive, and there was not the same hardness in her face. He decided that she was definitely not beautiful. But she was strong. She was young. He still couldn't adjust to his guilty good fortune.

For several days he had tried to understand his own feelings toward her. First he had felt guilty, even mistrustful of her. Then as he saw how naturally she accepted their relationship, he began to feel easier. But the thought that he was nearly forty kept obtruding into his thoughts, and for the first time he forced himself to admit the meagerness of his own experience. He had always considered himself a bachelor by virtue of his own choice, but in analyzing the unease and uncertainty he felt in her presence he had come to face himself openly, perhaps for the first time in his life, with the fact that he was afraid of women, of her. That wasn't it exactly; rather it was that he had always known that no woman would ever be afraid of *him,* and somehow this was tied up with his idea of masculinity. If things hadn't happened at the farm in the incredible way they had happened, he knew—or he couldn't help feeling—that she would have found him out long ago. He told himself that he had never known how to approach a woman properly, that the iron lessons of a puzzling adolescence had settled too deep ever to be extirpated completely. He was only just beginning to understand how grimly he had battled against something he couldn't name.

He had always been the reliable bachelor who had firmly made himself unattainable, had deliberately banked his own fires. The years had fled by, and now suddenly through her he was finding out how old he really was. And how young.

But somehow time seemed to be going in reverse. The fact that she was so physically young made him feel old spiritually, but he was conscious that he was hard and that his body was well shaped by the grueling training he had been put through. And he was doing something real. He was thirty-eight. And so? For the first time in a long while he felt as if he was taking whatever life had to offer him as fast as it was offered, without picking and choosing. In the dreary landscape of existence, he had suddenly found a shortcut. He had long ago accepted fully the idea that he might never get out of France alive. And now each day was a day of grace.

It still seemed unreal. Suddenly there *she* was. She was no more his than any other man's, perhaps, but somehow he couldn't even remember thinking of any other woman as "his." It had never crossed his mind. He was enjoying a little of the experience of a child thrown into the water suddenly discovering he can swim. But this was tempered by the sobering thought that it meant he had been able to swim all along; he was beginning to see the significance of himself and the years. Many of the old defenses, like the old glibness about the shy advantages of bachelorhood, the careless charm, looked tawdry from the other side of the wall. With her he knew he was learning something about himself that he had missed as a younger man. It was as if all his life he had been struggling to atone for some unspeakable sin, only to learn that the sin was constant and ever renewing, to suspect now that the sin was perhaps the struggle of life itself. Perhaps in a different way it was the same thing that Carnot would never find out either. In any event he felt that his time was running quickly, and somehow he must find out the secret about himself that this young girl could tell him, before time and events and war swept her away from him. Or he'd never learn.

"Did you ever see your father again?" he asked.

"Once in a nightclub. He was with his mistress and some German officers. He didn't see me."

"He is a collaborator?"

"He has found his niche," she said with a shrug. "He thinks my grandmother took us to North Africa when the war started. I know he knows she's dead because he tried to get some of her money."

"Why didn't your grandmother take you away earlier?"

"She was blind. She liked to punish herself by living in the same house with him. I think he drank because of her. She used to tell him when he shouted at her that he killed his wife. That shut him up."

"Was she against the marriage?"

"She told me afterward what happened. My father was working in my grandfather's warehouse when one day he came to the house to lay some new wines in my grandfather's private cellar. He met my mother. Grandmother says he deliberately got her with child so he could marry into the family. But my grandfather liked him because he knew wines better than anyone else in the warehouse, and they were married. Three days after the wedding, my mother had a miscarriage."

"Do you hate your father?"

"Why should I hate him? He's not evil. He's weak. He collaborates with the Germans because he has no self-respect left. They accept him. They like Frenchmen who don't hate them. He sells them wine. Why should I hate him?"

Dante was silent. She went on.

"He loved my mother, I think. Whenever he got drunk he would cry and then he would scream at Henri because he said *he* had killed her. He was very drunk. Then my grandmother would come out of her room and scream at him and tell him that he couldn't blame the child. But why should I hate him? We all killed her."

"What made your grandmother finally decide to take you away after all those years?"

Adriane looked at him, her head cocked to one side.

"Why are you interested in all this?" she asked.

"You don't have to tell me anything if you don't want to," said Dante. "I simply want to know you better."

"You don't like sleeping with a stranger, is that it?" she asked, smiling.

"Please, let's not start needling me again," he said. "I don't know why you find it so amusing to look for distorted motives."

"Perhaps it's because you have never told me what your true motives are," she said. "Anyway, I'll tell you."

"How can you tell me what my motives are when I'm not even sure myself?" he asked.

"I don't mean that. I mean, I'll tell you why my grandmother finally decided to leave. Isn't that what you asked?"

Dante sighed.

"My father had been getting much worse. He was drinking so much that he couldn't shave himself any more and he always went around with a week's growth of beard. He drank over a litre of *marc* a day. He was always drunk. He had lost his last job and he couldn't get another one. He would steal money from my grandmother's purse, or else he would get it some place. We never knew where. But every now and then he would show up after a weekend with a lot of money. He cried all the time when he was home. Am I boring you?"

"No. I was just looking at the sun on the river."

"One night he came home worse than we had ever seen him. He had had a fight. My brother was still a small boy. He still slept in the crib because we couldn't afford a new bed. He was much too big for it. Anyway, on this night he had had a fight, and from the way he looked had been beaten. He wouldn't let anyone come near him to clean the blood off him, but he stayed quiet and Henri didn't wake up. When I went to bed he was sitting alone in the kitchen crying again. He had a bottle of *marc* and I couldn't get it away from him. I didn't think anything until I woke up and heard my little brother screaming. I ran into his room and there was my father standing over the crib with the bottle in his hand. He was relieving himself through the bars of the crib. His own son. My grandmother came in, and that was the last fight they ever had." She shrugged. "He was drunk, of course. He didn't know . . ."

"And after that you don't hate him?"

"My brother hates him. But that's because he is still afraid of him. In his mind, I mean. I used to be afraid of him. I'm not any more. He hates himself enough."

"Do you know where Carnot went with Henri?"

"No."

Far down on the slope, workers were cleaning the ground around the base of the olive trees, and repairing places where the terraced steps had crumbled from the rain. From where Dante sat they looked hardly human, more like ants or mason wasps as they worked over the earth.

Somehow he could no longer respond to what she was saying; it was suddenly as if she was far away, speaking to him across a chasm in another language. He felt he should make some effort, but the task seemed too enormous. He felt lost in lethargy. He knew she was watching him, perhaps even waiting for him to say something, but he couldn't unfix his eyes from the glint of the white sun on the river far below in the valley. A thought, clear, ridiculous, and simple crossed his mind; part of a quotation he had read somewhere: *drowning in the river, that glorious sun of mine, our glorious sun.*

XI

On Saturday when he awoke the first thing he was aware of was that she was missing. Without opening his eyes he had reached across the bed and found her place empty. The covers were thrown back and there was a depression in the pillow where her head had been. She was not behind the screen at the sink. She was not in the room.

At first he thought she might have gone down the hall to the w.c., but her thin robe was over the back of the chair. He saw that most of her clothes were still there, but her shoes and trenchcoat were gone. Hurriedly he slipped into a shirt and a pair of trousers and dashed water in his face.

There was no answer when he knocked on the door of her own room. He hadn't really expected any. Down the stairs, at the desk, the old watchman was still on duty; it was still dark in the hall because he hadn't yet opened the shutters for the day. The watchman dozed in a chair under an old travel poster advertising the beauties of *Les Alpes Maritimes,* which hung on the wall behind the desk next to the keyboard. On the poster were pinned yellowing notices of bus schedules and timetables for trains and buses which no longer ran.

Dante noticed that it wasn't quite seven o'clock. He wound his wristwatch; the old man's head nodded and recovered as he dozed in the old wicker chair. Dante knocked three times on the counter. The old man opened his eyes.

"Have you seen Mademoiselle go out this morning?"

The old man jumped to his feet, almost tipping over the wicker chair.

"Excuse me," said the old man. "I didn't see you standing there. I was thinking about something else."

"Have you seen Mademoiselle?"

"I opened the door for her about an hour ago. She said she was going to walk down to the river before breakfast."

"Will you do me a favor?" asked Dante.

"Mais, bien sûr," said the old man, blinking his eyes.

"If we are not back in time for breakfast, will you tell René where we have gone? I'm going out to try to find her."

"I will tell him as soon as he comes down," said the old man. "He should be here any minute. He comes down about this time."

Outside the sun was bright and he could see his breath in the clean mountain air. As he walked through the square he saw two old women taking their bundles of laundry to the ancient stone washing place in the square near the church. They stopped to talk to another woman who was taking down the shutters in front of a *laiterie*. Dante passed them on the other side of the street and he sensed the three women watching him. He continued walking until he reached the minuscule plateau at the edge of the village. From the edge of the road he could see the river through the twisted olive trees and smell the strong evidence of goats. Ten paces from the road a pile of goat dung still steamed in the morning chill. Far down the slope he could hear the bells around their necks as they picked their way down toward the river, and the distant yapping of the goatherd's dog.

He remembered her telling him on the terrace that there was a way to get down to the river through the olive groves, and that halfway down was the ruin of a stone olive press which was centuries older than the village and was said to date from the time of the Romans. He started down the steep slope looking for the path, which he soon found. The goats had left it well marked. He had gone only a short distance when the path divided in two; he took the one to the left, following the sound of the bells. He was beginning to feel hungry.

The path seemed to zigzag back and forth down the side of the slope, and once when he was walking away from the sound of the goat bells, he passed a large circular stone wall which looked as if it might have been the foundation of a windmill. The path turned sharply again and doubled back along the hillside. He found he was breathing heavily and walking downhill almost at a trot. The grade was just steep enough to make it awkward to walk slowly. After fifteen minutes he came to a level place and sat down to rest. Water had collected on the path where it hadn't drained off and the ground was soft. He was catching his breath when he noticed a footprint in the soft earth. Although it was indistinct he was sure it was her shoe. Peasants' shoes didn't have heels on them and would be larger. He was not far from the sound of the goats now. After less than a minute he got up and continued down the hill, taking a shortcut straight down through the olive trees to the path below instead of following it around.

When he turned the path again he saw the goats. Two boys were prodding them with long switches while the dog scampered at their heels barking. The dog stopped and turned as Dante approached. The animal bared its teeth and growled and the older boy spoke sharply to the dog. He was perhaps twelve or thirteen, and the younger one wasn't more than nine or ten. Dante waved at them. As soon as they turned around, the goats took advantage of the moment to scatter, munching the grass at the sides of the path. The dog ran around them in circles.

"Bonjour," said Dante. The two boys said nothing but only stared silently. The dog growled quietly once again.

"Have you seen a lady pass by here this morning?" he asked. Still there was no answer. Dante wondered if perhaps they spoke only Provençal. Suddenly the little one lifted his arm, without taking his eyes off Dante for a second, and pointed down the path in the general direction of the river. Dante thanked them and stepped past them. The dog growled and the little one hit it with his switch. Dante could smell each of them as he went by. They both smelled like goats. He turned around once and they were both still staring after him. He waved, but they didn't wave back. When he was out of sight around the path he heard them shouting at the goats in their high piping voices, and the dog barking as they rounded up the scattered animals. There must have been at least six, Dante thought.

The ground was leveling out. He had noticed from above on the terrace that there was a wide flat strip about halfway down the side of the hill, where the olive trees gave way to terraced vineyards. He could see the red earth through the trees. As he came out of the olive grove, the path ran lengthwise for some distance along the back edge of a vineyard. He stumbled over great clods of earth at the edge of the furrowed ground. The vines were just beginning to show the first yellow-green trace of new leaves.

At the corner of the plot the path turned and widened to a narrow dirt road which ran between two separate vineyards. The river was no longer visible because of the rise of the land. Down the road to the left there was a group of buildings which he assumed to be the farmhouse of the larger vineyard. Halfway between him and the farmhouse, two people were bending over a vine trellis. Dante had often watched skillful fingers tie up the young vines in the spring, and he could tell from the angle of the man's back that it was what he was doing. Suddenly the woman beside him stood up, and he recognized her. It was Adriane. She waved both arms wildly and started coming toward him.

He waved back and walked faster. When he was close enough she called to him, "Come around by the road. You can't get through here."

He went back to the road and walked until he reached the end of the row she was standing in. The vinekeeper was in the next row. It was difficult walking over the uneven earth.

"How did you ever find your way down here?" she asked, delighted. "I thought you'd still be asleep when I got back."

"I left a message for René in case we miss breakfast," he said. "Why did you run out and leave me?"

"I was only going to go for a short walk and then come back," she said. "I felt like going by myself. But I'm glad you're here. It's such a beautiful day. I didn't expect it to be such a lovely day." She had both hands in the pockets of the trenchcoat, which was buttoned all the way up to her chin.

"Well, thanks to me, you don't have to go back for breakfast," he said.

"You're a darling." She came to him and kissed him lightly on the cheek. He couldn't remember ever having seen her looking so happy. She turned around to the old man, who was standing with his hat deferentially in his hand, and introduced Dante as her husband. The old vinekeeper smiled and nodded. Adriane introduced him as Monsieur Legay. She said he was an old friend.

"I am getting lessons in tending a vineyard," she said. "Monsieur has been showing me how the vines are trained."

"Would you mind if I watch?" Dante asked the old man.

"Not at all," he said. "But it's not very difficult. All it takes is patience and gentle fingers."

The old man went back to tying up the new tendrils, working rapidly and with great skill. He finished off each bind with a curious knot that he tied so quickly Dante couldn't see how it was done. He finished the vine he was working on and moved on to the next one. Dante put his arm around Adriane's waist and together they stood watching the old man plait the string and the green shoots in his swift fingers.

"Are all vines tied up this same way?" asked Dante.

"Not all. This way is best for this place," said the old man. "Not everyone even around here does it this way. Some of them are too lazy. My wine is always the best."

"If you tie the vines differently, does it change the wine?" asked Dante.

"Everything changes the wine," said Monsieur Legay. "That's why no two years are alike."

"Will this be a red or a white wine?"

"Neither, darling," said Adriane. "All around here they produce *rosé*."

"There is some red, but it is very poor," said the old man. "Around here, that is. Farther down it is different. The soil is different near the river. And they get less sun."

"What else do you have to do to the vines before you finally harvest the grapes?" asked Adriane.

"Oh, many things," said the old man. "You have to trim and prune so the grapes won't be scrawny. You have to turn the earth. Many things. But mostly you just have to watch them grow, and figure the right time for the cutting."

"Where is the wine press?" asked Dante.

"Over there," said Adriane, pointing to the group of farm buildings. "Two years ago I watched them press the grapes, didn't I?"

"It doesn't seem like two years ago," said the old man. "Has the war been going on so long?"

"Longer," Adriane said quietly.

"It's hard taking care of all this alone." Monsieur Legay waved his hand over the vineyard. "But they had to go. They had no choice. They're both good sons."

The air was warmed as the sun rose higher across the southern sky, and Dante noticed that he was perspiring from the walk down the side of the valley. He mopped his brow with a handkerchief and put it back in his pocket.

"You must have been running down the hill," said Adriane. "Were you afraid I'd get away?"

Dante squeezed her hand and said nothing. Monsieur Legay was tying up the last vine in the row. He was talking again. He was an old man, but his face and hands were hard and brown from years of southern sun. When he spoke, his voice was old and gentle and his words full of the slow inflections of the Mediterranean. He explained that the vineyard was his life, that ever since he was old enough to remember he had helped with the harvest; and before him his father's life, and his father's father's.

"It will be my son's, my oldest son's, after me. Perhaps even my son's son," said the old man. "But I am worried for him. It is hard for a son to tend his father's vines when he has learned killing. He has killed Germans. He told me."

"No one likes to kill," said Adriane. "Even to kill Germans. He is helping to free France, like the rest of us. We only do what we must."

The old man's fingers worked dexterously, wrapping the string and knotting it. He shook his head slowly and didn't answer immediately.

"I don't know," he said. "I saw it in *dix-neuf*. When they came back, they knew things no man should ever know. A hunter must love the thing he kills or he won't be a good hunter. My son is a good son. But he has killed. He is proud. But he hasn't killed out of love. He kills in hate. I don't know." He shook his head and finished the vine and straightened up. "I don't think I'll ever understand. I'm a farmer."

"You don't think your son will want to come back after the war?" asked Dante.

"Everything is uprooted," said the old man. "My sons have both been torn away from the soil. Men die in war. But many more die after. Because their roots have been cut."

The three stood in a group around the end of the row, Dante with his arm lightly around Adriane's waist, the old man holding his box full of twine and tools. The old man seemed lost in a reflection. Then he looked up with a flickering look of bewilderment on his face.

"I don't know," he said. "In the Bible . . ." He paused, trying to think out what he was going to say. "In the Bible," he said, "I never understood until my grandfather explained it to me—the two brothers. The one who said, 'Am I my brother's keeper?,' he was a hunter of

the field. The other one, the one he killed, was a tiller of the ground."
He looked from Adriane to Dante. "It has something to do with that.
One brother lived by destroying life, while the other lived by growing
life. My grandfather explained it much better than I can. He said the
two brothers stand for all mankind."

They stood for a moment longer. Dante saw no reason to correct
Monsieur Legay's improved version of Genesis.

"I am worried for my sons," said the old man.

Overhead a flight of swallows bobbed and chirped in what seemed a
vast game of tag. The old man watched them for a moment longer,
then turned his back and started toward the farmhouse.

"It is time to have something to eat," he said over his shoulder.
"You are both my guests."

Dante looked at Adriane questioningly, and she nodded. He followed her, walking single file along the top of the ridge of red dirt
that edged the drainage furrow bounding the vineyard.

Monsieur Legay fed them and gave them some cheese and bread
and wine to take along, insisting that he would be insulted if they didn't
accept his gift. Dante felt guilty about taking it, but Adriane said they
had to accept.

Together they walked through the vineyard to the high ground at
the far end. At the bottom of the path, where Dante had come down,
they said good-by and Monsieur Legay left them. A short way up the
path Adriane turned and watched the vinekeeper walking back toward
the house. Once he turned around and they could see that he was
looking for them and they waved, but he didn't see them. There were
too many trees. Dante could still hear the old man's winey laughter in
his ears.

The tortuous path up the hill seemed much narrower and steeper
than it had coming down. It seemed a different route entirely. There
were many places where they had to walk single file, Adriane going
first, and after a while they took to resting a moment after every third
turn. Dante began counting steps to himself, and estimated that each
terrace was roughly a hundred paces wide. However, on the widely
zigzagging path they were forced to walk four or five times that distance. The olive trees on either side, although spaced apart from
one another, were all on different levels of the uneven ground and their
twisted branches totally obscured any view of the river. Once Adriane
stopped and pointed out the tiny roof of red terra cotta that was Monsieur Legay's farm. It could just be seen over the tops of the trees by
climbing up to the top of a huge rock outcropping, around which the
path made one of its hairpin turns. From up here the Mediterranean
was also visible, blue and unreal in the distance.

They sat down on top of the rock to rest. Dante put the wine in the
shade of his body. Adriane sat hugging her knees, her chin resting on
them, and looked out toward the sea. For a long time nothing had been

said and both she and Dante, still breathing hard from the climb, were satisfied simply to remain silent. Dante was surprised to see how far they had climbed. Monsieur Legay's farm was so far below that he couldn't distinguish the separate tiles in the roof. The vineyard itself was completely hidden by the trees, and the tiny patch of roof looked like a bright taggle of orange bunting caught in the twisted branches of the trees.

"When I was little I used to sit up here. You could see the whole farm then," said Adriane. "Even olive trees grow when they're not pruned."

Dante looked at her for a moment. She stared out over the land and the sea, and her eyes were remote, far away. She seemed almost to be talking to herself, as if he weren't there. He stretched back on the rock and lay down, his hands behind his head. The rock was warm from the sun, almost hot, and the muscles in his legs and back hurt pleasantly as he stretched out on the hard rock. He felt them slowly distend and finally they relaxed completely. Overhead the sky was blue-white, and vast. It was empty except for one delicate ridge of cloud, extremely permanent and high, like a wisp of combed flax, or the stroke of a dry brush. The sun was almost lost against the brilliance of the sky, and the light dazzled his eyes, making his eyelids feel drawn and heavy. His eyes closed and he watched the membranous orange dance of flashing pinpoints on his retina, whirling like corpuscles of blood. He felt her body move ever so slightly and knew she had turned her head and was looking down at him. He kept his eyes closed. Against the blind orange light he felt her shadow between him and the sun, and heard the bare whisper of the heavy fabric of her trenchcoat. Her lips barely touched his, dry and hard and austere, as she bent down to kiss him. The shadow disappeared and the light of the sun fell again on his shut lids. He smiled and kissed the warm air in return. Then he felt her hard slender hand on his forehead. It was as cold as ice.

"In my country there is an old saying," he murmured. " 'Cold hands; warm heart.' You stir an old man's blood."

"You must think I'm a child. You're not an old man. Thirty-eight is not old," she said. Then she asked, "Are my hands that cold?"

"What do you think?" he said.

She laughed, a little sadly he thought. He wondered what she was thinking about. She said nothing for a long while.

"It's hard to think that you are an American," she said suddenly. "And a spy."

The word shocked him a little. It was hard indeed to think of himself as a "spy." Unnecessarily hard, he thought.

"I can't think of myself as a spy," he said. "For one thing I'm not a professional. I'm only an amateur." He laughed at the thought.

"You are more of an amateur than you think if you don't know that you're a spy. That's what you'll be shot as. A dead amateur is as dead as a dead professional."

"If I'm caught," he said.

She said slowly, deliberately, "You have almost been caught twice."

He opened his eyes and looked at her. She was looking down at him without smiling, with something like pity in her face. The instant she saw him open his eyes her expression changed, hardened.

"When?" he said.

"The men who questioned me at Madame LaChaise's . . . and the three men who killed Max . . . and the two at the brothel that Sunday—they were all strangers," she said. "From the pattern of their questions it seems that a special detachment of *Sicherheitsdienst* men have been sent from Paris. Their orders are to find you. Alive."

Dante looked at her. "That's better than dead."

"Is it?" she said.

He said nothing.

"They are turning the whole place upside down," she said. "The SD are very thorough. They also have a special detail of *Milice*. It is very unpleasant."

"Do they know *why* I'm here?"

"Alexi is sure that they do. Dujardin tipped his hand when he was interrogating me the last time. He asked me if the words 'butter and eggs' meant anything to me. They didn't. But I told Alexi about it and he said that 'butter and eggs' meant you. The next day we dismantled the whole apparatus in the village—until things get clearer."

The mention of Dujardin's name didn't surprise him.

"In Toulon and Nice they have made over a hundred arrests in the last week," Dante said. "René told me last night at dinner. Does that have anything to do with us?" He said "us" unconsciously. "Me, that is?"

"The Germans are trying to break the southern underground. They are terrified of a landing here. You are not the only one who is here to arrange for arms. I guess you know."

"I only know that there are other agents in the field," said Dante truthfully. "I have been deliberately kept ignorant of their missions."

"The Americans work very differently from the British," she said.

"I don't know," he said. "For all I know you could be an American agent, and I probably still wouldn't know. We never let our right hand know what our left hand is doing."

"The British are much more blasé. They are very good and very brave," she said. "I know two of them who used to meet socially every afternoon in Nice for tea in a shop run by a collaborator. It was a terrible risk. One of them told me it was the only place in Nice where you could get a decent cup of tea."

Dante laughed.

"I remember my grandmother always saying that tea drinking was a dangerous vice. She was an Anglophobe," he said.

"You may be caught," she said. "They have caught others."

"Did they catch the Britishers?"

"Would you call cyanide pills an escape?"

Dante didn't answer.

"Even if you aren't caught . . ." She left the sentence unfinished and stared out over the tops of the trees toward the sea, which was almost royal blue under the sun climbing toward its zenith in the southern sky. He waited for her to finish. Then she turned and looked at him.

"You think I'm too young, don't you?" she said abruptly.

"No," he said quietly. "I don't think you're too young. Too young for what?"

"There's nothing for us, is there?" she said. Her voice was low and she stared at the rock where she had scraped a circle with her fingernail. Her face seemed harder than he ever remembered it, her voice more intimate. "Nothing touches you, does it?"

"What do you mean?" he said. " 'Nothing' is a large word."

"It's like everything. I was thinking this morning when I woke up. The coffee is ersatz. Even the bread has sawdust in it. Do you remember the first night you came to the farm? The rabbit? Well, Auguste caught it in the alley behind the café and killed it with his bare hands."

"The rabbit?" Dante tried to think back.

"It was a cat," she said. "It was a feast—and you don't remember it?"

Dante didn't say anything. She laughed unpleasantly.

"Everything goes under a false name," she said. "Even you. In this war, even love is ersatz." She clenched her fists and looked away from him. "I want to love, but I can't. I need to love someone, but I can't. Even when we make love . . . it . . . it comes to nothing. Nothing is real. When I make love it's as though my soul has left my body. My mind is in the corner of the room watching my . . . a corpse that moves. I can't feel anything . . . any more. Nothing is real."

At first Dante thought she might cry—he was sure she would if he touched her—but she only shook her head slowly from side to side and rubbed her fingernail in the same circle on the rock. The man's trenchcoat made her look small and pathetic. She rested her chin on her knees again and looked toward the sea. There was real sadness in her eyes.

"Monsieur Legay is real. This . . ." Dante said, sitting up and reaching for the wine. "This is real. Even if the bread does have sawdust in it . . . The cheese is real."

She looked at him with sudden anger in her eyes.

He stopped talking immediately, and waited for her to speak.

"Do you have any idea why I came down here this morning?" she asked. "Do you have *any* idea?"

He shook his head.

"For two weeks I have been trying to make myself come down here. This morning I dreamed that the old man was dead. I woke up and grabbed my coat and *ran* all the way down here. For two weeks I have been putting it off."

"Putting what off?"

"I am supposed to tell him that both his sons are dead," she said. "They've been dead for months. I'm supposed to *tell* him. Me. *Tell* him."

Dante remembered the picture of her laughing with the old man; for just an instant he was stunned by what she was saying, but he recovered quickly.

"How did it happen?" He tried to sound matter-of-fact, unemotional.

"Emile . . . he's the younger one. He was the first boy I ever made love with. We used to sit right here on this rock. I didn't love him." He found her candor brutal. "Emile was caught with a hotel key in his pocket. It had a number on it. He also had a receipt for a week's rent with the name of the *pension* on it. The SD put two and two together and caught Jean in the room—before he knew they had Emile. There were firearms in the room, and other things, explosives. I don't know. Jean jumped out the window. They tortured Emile until he died. I don't know if he broke or not. Anton said he did. Alexi says he didn't. Alexi hates Anton, you know."

"Will you still tell the old man?"

"No," she said slowly. She hesitated. "I told him they both sent their love."

"Oh, good Lord," said Dante.

"I didn't mean to say it," she said. "I just said it. He wanted to hear it." There were tears in her eyes now. She sounded as though she was pleading. "I didn't mean to. But he asked me how they were." She paused, looking into his eyes. "Oh, God! What if he finds out?" She said it with a kind of shock, as though thinking of it for the first time.

He put his arms around her and patted her back slowly, gently. Suddenly she pulled away from him.

"Don't do that to me!" she shouted. Tears rolled down her cheeks. But she wasn't sobbing.

"Do what?" asked Dante, completely taken aback.

"Pat me like that!" she cried. "I'm not your dog!"

He had done it without thinking, instinctively, and he was completely at a loss to understand why she reacted so violently. It was an ordinary human gesture. He reached for her again.

"Don't touch me," she said. "Leave me alone. You always pat me. I can't stand it!" She turned around and faced away from him.

He felt acutely uneasy. He was watching her back, wondering how to approach her, when suddenly he felt more sharply than he had ever felt before the conflict of his ambivalent feelings toward her. He was deeply moved by the suffering she was going through over Monsieur Legay's sons. It was too real, too embarrassing. He felt sorry for her and wanted somehow to try to help her, and to say something that would salve the wound still raw from the experience. Yet in his body, he felt rather than knew that another thought dogged his mind like a shadow. There was something heartbreaking in the too familiar slope of her strong small shoulders under the stiff fabric of the trenchcoat.

From the angle of her body, the way she was sitting, he could imagine every delicate curve and bone in the contour of her shoulders. All morning long he had tried to overlook that intimate knowledge, but now he was simply too aware of it: that underneath the trenchcoat she was naked.

This was not the first time she had refused to let him touch her. As he sat there watching her back, he thought of the first night they had spent together at the hotel. He had turned on the light over the bed without warning her and had been shocked to find her sitting up in bed staring wide-eyed at nothing. She was shaking like an animal convulsed. Her face was white and drawn and when he tried to take her in his arms her limbs were rigid. She stared past him, refusing to speak. The shaking got worse, until finally he forced her to lie down. It took all his strength. He put out the light and held her in his arms for a long while, caressing her back, covertly managing to count her pulse by the artery in her neck. It was high; he could even feel her heart hammering against his chest. Slowly she began to relax. Once she tried to say something but her teeth chattered and she remained silent. He stroked her body gently, trying hard to communicate more than carnal love with his hands, until finally he felt her muscles go limp and her breathing become deep and regular, and then she was asleep in his arms. He held her like that for a long time, listening to her regular breathing, and then he put her head on her own pillow. He had lain awake a long time that night, wondering.

He remembered now that never after making love would she let him turn on the light, or touch her. Invariably she said she wanted to sleep, but he knew that she didn't sleep. He could tell that she was lying awake in the darkness and he was sure that she always had her eyes open. He would listen to her breathing until he fell asleep. Another night he hadn't known he was asleep until he awakened with a vague feeling of danger, left over from the dream which had awakened him. He opened his eyes and saw her naked body in the darkness starkly silhouetted against the window. He could tell she was watching him, and he wondered how long. He reached out for her, groping for her hand. "Don't touch me," she had said. She whispered the words but they were startlingly loud and full of venom, as though she had been waiting all night to say them. She was crying, he knew by the choked sound of her voice. He sat up and put his arms around her forcefully, and she dug her nails painfully into his back deeper and deeper, until he could feel she was drawing blood. Then in senseless anger he freed one arm and drew back and slapped her full across the face. The slap was shockingly loud in the utter silence that followed. He couldn't see her face, but he could feel his hand tingling where he had hit her. Then suddenly she was all over him, kissing him, biting his ears and neck in a terrifying frenzy of passion, crying, begging his forgiveness. He grasped her head between his open hands in the darkness, and held her stock-still until he felt her gradually relax and her breathing return to normal. Then he kissed her gently and put his arms around her and forced her to lie down. She relaxed completely in his arms and for a long time the only sound close to his ear was the minuscule sound of her tears dropping on the rough muslin of the hard headroll. By turning his head infinitesimally toward her, he could feel the spot, damp and cool against his cheek—the memory smote him like an ax in the chest.

When sunlight streaming through the window woke him that next morning, she was still asleep in his arms. They hadn't moved at all. Her face was relaxed and she slept like a child. He watched her, thinking, wondering about her, for almost a half-hour, until without warning her eyes opened wide and soft and still, like a child's. That morning he had begun to wonder if he wasn't really falling in love with her, or whether what he felt was the pity of a father for a sick child. Somehow, at moments like this when he saw clearly how young she was, especially when at the moment separating consciousness from sleep he saw truly what a child she was, he felt overwhelmed at sleeping with her. He felt ashamed of his age, or, more exactly, he felt ashamed of himself, knew he was vulnerable. But when he wasn't thinking of his age he was happy. For somehow he felt she had *proved* to him that it didn't matter, even if too often he did feel more like a father to her than a lover—he tried to ignore that. She was so young. He took her proof at face value.

Now, under the sun, on the warm rock, the blood pulsed strongly in his veins while he tried desperately to think how to help her; rejected by his mind, that other thought and that other knowledge suffused and took root in his body instead. And although he was sure that he wasn't at fault for her present unhappiness, somehow he felt responsible, even guilty. It was an extremely uncomfortable feeling, one that he couldn't remember ever experiencing before, and it brought him up short. His chest felt sickeningly hollow and he felt his heart suddenly beating as though it had worked loose from its own cavity. He sat still and tried to analyze the feeling. What have I done, he thought. God knows I have tried. I have tried.

For a long time he sat unmoving, trying to allay the feeling by fixing it with a name. He felt helpless before her, and he admitted to himself for the first time that sometimes her behavior actually frightened him. Yet that wasn't it now. It wasn't fear. Or helplessness, exactly.

While he was thinking he had been holding the bottle of wine in his hands, staring blankly at the illegible label, too preoccupied to notice that she had turned around and was looking at him. He didn't look up until she touched his arm.

"I'm sorry," she said. "Except try to be patient. It's just something I can't stand. You do it all the time."

He looked at her blankly for a moment.

"Do what?" he asked.

"It makes me feel like you think I'm just a child. I'm not a child. Please tell me you don't think I'm too young. I know I'm young. But

I'll try to be a woman. I'll really try. I *can* make you happy. I *can*."

He looked at her in amazement. Somehow he had never even suspected another side to her usual self-sufficiency. Certainly not that it was a cover for uncertainty or anxiety. Perhaps insecurity. But it all made sense. He had been so preoccupied with uncertainties and inadequacies of his own that he had been blind to what it seemed she had been trying to communicate all along. She needed love worse than he did. In dropping her guard completely she was taking the risk of letting him know how desperate that need was. He knew he had to be careful now because she was without defense, and he knew he could hurt her if even one slight word miscarried. His heart jumped at the realization that she trusted him so completely.

He watched her, alert for the smallest movement, as though she were a bird that might start at the slightest false move. Slowly he reached out and pulled her to him, and was gratified that she yielded without the slightest resistance. She had her hands in the pocket of her coat and she made no move to take them out. He kissed her hair. In English he said, "If you knew how I love you . . ." It was barely a whisper. In his mind he was weighing the risks. There was no question of the danger. There was always danger. Spy, he thought, she said it. Where's my judgment?

"Speak French," she said.

"I want so much to tell you I love you," he said, his lips just touching her ear, which was cold. "I don't know if I dare. I want desperately to be honest with you."

He was surprised to hear her laugh. The tears were still wet on her cheeks.

"There," she said. "You're doing it again."

He drew back and looked at her.

"What am I doing?"

"You were patting me," she said. But she was smiling, wiping her eyes.

"Good God!" he said. "If I have to think about not patting you when I'm trying to tell you I love you . . . Look, please let me pat you. Perhaps I do it to reassure myself."

"Don't think I'm a child," she said, warning him.

He laughed with nervous relief. "Haven't I told you that you make me feel like an old man? I don't mean physically old. Mentally."

"And that is foolish," she said simply. There was no mistaking her sincerity.

"Well, it's true," he said. This is unwise, he thought, ridiculous. Am I doing this just because I want her?

There was an awkward silence, and he was thinking of trying to reinforce his statement, but decided that overinsistence would only increase her doubts. He let the silence run its course.

"You believe you'll live out the war, don't you?" she said.

He wished he could see her face, but he had taken her in his arms again. Through dark wisps of her hair he watched a pair of gulls sail high toward the sea. They looked a little out of place.

"I wouldn't be talking to you like this if . . . I do. Then on the other hand, perhaps I don't," he said. "I don't know. Why, don't you?"

"I used to," she said. "You haven't lived with it. You haven't seen them disappear—two hundred overnight, without a trace. No one knows until it happens."

She pulled back from him, and looked into his eyes.

"Do you know how many Gestapo agents they have in Paris alone?" she asked.

"I'm not sure."

"We are," she said. She looked at him. "There are over forty thousand."

While he was surprised at the figure, he didn't question it.

"Let's not talk about it," he said.

Suddenly she got to her feet. She looked agitated.

"Let's get off this rock," she said. "I'm tired of sitting."

He climbed down first and helped her down. He kissed her, but she only looked at him blankly, as though she was trying to see what was behind his eyes. She had changed again. He felt the mood of a few moments ago slipping away, and he turned around the rock and started up the path walking ahead of her. "My love-rock," she said—with derision, he thought.

They had gone only a little way up the path when he felt her pull on his sleeve. He stopped and turned around.

"You're walking too fast," she said. She looked at him and her eyes softened. "Don't be angry." Then she brushed past him; she walked ahead of him the rest of the way.

They climbed five terraces before she stopped, and they rested. Not a word was spoken. He sat down in the low crotch of a very old olive tree. She sat on the grass at the side of the path. He watched her idly collecting pebbles into a small circle; then he heard the faint sound of goat bells in the distance and the barking of the goatherd's dog. He listened. The wine bottle felt warm against his bare forearm, and his hands were sweaty.

They rested for a long time. He watched her profile, studied it. She seemed to relax.

"Come," she said, jumping up suddenly. "I'll show you the olive press. You remember? The one I told you about?"

"The one that's supposed to have been here before Adam and Eve?" he asked.

"It's really old," she said. "Don't make fun of our ruins."

"Was that it I passed on the way down?" he asked. "That round thing at the end of the terrace just off the path?"

"That's not the best one," she said. "There are two. I'll show you the other one."

They started up the path again. The muscles in the backs of his legs were beginning to ache, and he walked with his back bent forward to balance his weight. They passed the spot where he had met the two boys with the goats and he stepped around a pile of dung in the middle of the path. At the next bend of the path, instead of turning with it, Adriane led the way off the path into a grove of trees which looked hardly cultivated at all. The ground was terribly uneven and got worse. After a short while great boulders and brown underbrush in eroded gullies made walking difficult. Finally they came out onto a sort of tiny plateau. Adriane stopped and pointed up the hill.

"See that ridge up there?" she asked. "You saw one of the old presses up there. The path runs along the ridge."

"Where's the other one?" he asked.

"Straight ahead. First we have to find the stream."

Dante was wondering about the time. He looked at his watch. The morning was almost gone.

"Do you think we'll have time to see it and still get back in time for lunch?" he asked.

"I've decided I'm not going to lunch," she said casually. "You can go back if you want to. But René will figure out where you are."

Dante immediately doubted the wisdom of the procedure. But he knew he couldn't go back without her. In truth he didn't care about going back either, but somehow he felt obliged, as a "guest," to do as he had been told. Yet he didn't protest when she said she wasn't going back. He only hoped the message he had left with the old concierge had reached René, otherwise there might be trouble. Actually, he was surprised that he didn't care whether there was trouble or not. It was simply too beautiful a day. And it probably wouldn't happen again. He followed her. Finally they found the stream. It was a tiny, fast-flowing mountain freshet, which they both easily jumped across.

"We can have a picnic," she said. "We have cheese and bread enough for two."

"How will we open the wine?"

"You can hammer the cork in with a stick and a rock," she said. "It won't hurt the taste."

The tiny stream plunged suddenly downward at a steep angle and scattered itself over a facing of bedrock that leveled out again like a giant stairstep cut in the mountain. On the apron of the step was a clutter of huge boulders of varying sizes, each perfectly round and smooth, that looked like a monstrous handful of pebbles. Dante was puzzled, and at first he thought they had been put there for some purpose, but then it dawned on him that the stream had washed the silt from under them and lowered them onto the bedrock. He was fascinated by their almost perfect roundness and deduced that they must have been deposited by a glacier.

From the top of the rock face the view was clear and the valley was a kingdom of silence. He had a vision of a gigantic ramrod of slow ice carving out the mountain eons ago, driving these spheres of rock before it, and the horrendous grinding of that cataclysmic ball mill making sand, roaring unheard in a frigid waste. He listened, holding his breath for the sound of the goat bells. But there was nothing, only the water splashing at his feet. The scene captured his imagination completely, and he was so surprised when Adriane suddenly appeared below, like the victim into the arena or an actor come onstage, that he applauded her feat.

"Bravo!" he said, looking vainly around for the means of descent. "The goddess appears by machinery! Now, how about telling an ordinary mortal how you did it?"

"Fly!" she said. "Sprout wings!"

He was sure he would find a path, but he looked all along the upper lip of the rock without seeing any possible way down. She watched him, pleased with herself and laughing.

"You look like a little puppy on a chair who's afraid to jump off," she said. "Except you are still trying to keep your dignity."

"Do you want me to kill myself?" he asked, laughing. He refused to show that his failure to find a way down irritated him slightly. "I know *you* didn't jump. And I don't *think* you flew."

It was becoming a game and a puzzle. She had gotten down in perhaps half a minute, while he had been standing looking at the surprise panorama of sudden valley and endless sea. She had been behind him, therefore . . . He turned around and walked back so that he could no longer see her over the edge. He reasoned that there must be a path around the abrupt drop of rock, and began searching the scrubby bushes back along both sides of the stream. He went back about twenty paces and found nothing. He heard her laugh and turned around. She was standing silently an arm's reach away from him, shaking with laughter.

"How in the name of God . . . ?" he said. She threw her head back and laughed the same child's laugh he had seen that morning for the first time. He realized that they were embarked on another ritual of pleasure from the past. It made him feel instantly good.

"Shall I show you?" she asked, abruptly serious.

"If you show me, I'll never speak to you again," he said. "I want to find it myself."

"Oh, let me show you," she said. When she changed character like this he couldn't quite be sure whether she was mimicking the behavior of a child or whether her gestures and intonations were mostly unconscious. He set his mouth and frowned with exaggerated determination, unthinkingly aping a child himself, and stalked back to begin his search over again.

"You're getting warm," she said.

"How warm?"

"Just warm." She giggled.

He looked around carefully and finally distinguished the only irregularity in the surroundings that could possibly hide a solution to the problem. To the left, slightly back from the edge, was an outcropping of rock which seemed simply to jut out of the flat ground around it. He sized it up out of the corner of his eye. She was watching him.

"Close your eyes and count fifty," he said.

She put her hands over her eyes and began to count.

"One . . . two . . . three . . ."

Behind the small pinnacle of rock he was surprised to find that the ground unexpectedly fell away in a narrow fissure, which beyond was almost concealed by the heavy growth of wild blueberry bushes. Short logs split in halves had been placed with their flat sides up to form a crude stairway where long ago the soil, undermined by water, had spilled down the side of the mountain with the overflow of spring rains. The rock face on which he had stood only a moment ago turned out to be deeply undercut so that what appeared from above to be the edge of a solid cliff face was actually a huge overhang.

Below, he came out from under the table of dripping rock and looked up to see Adriane standing with her hands still over her eyes, counting.

". . . twenty-six . . . twenty-seven . . ."

"Twenty-eight," he said. She opened her eyes and looked down.

"Did you jump or fly?" she asked.

"I went underground," he said. "As we say in the trade."

She disappeared and a moment later came out from under the raining rock, shaking drops off her hair. The rock underfoot was wet, but the main flow of the stream flattened out among the boulders toward the other end of the ledge.

"Soon I won't have any secrets left," she said.

"You'll always have yourself," he said.

"You think I'm a secret?" she asked. "That's flattering—I think."

"It's not flattering. It's true. All women are secrets, at least they are to me, and, I imagine, most males."

She seemed to be thinking. The voices reflected off the rocky face and seemed to enclose them. It was like talking in an empty echoing room. Dante picked up a round stone the size of his fist and tossed it toward the boulders where the water streamed thin and flat across the table rock. The shallow splash was a socking sound of rock on rock; the water-clatter reverberated sharply in the cool shadow of the overhang. The sound was loud and clean in the struck silence.

"I have decided that's flattering," said Adriane finally.

"Do you like to be flattered?"

"If it's true," she said, after a pause. "I don't like liars."

The word instantly struck him, like a warning. But he also felt a certain challenge that might be dangerous to let pass unanswered. He felt a tiny wearied annoyance with being brought up short by untempered changes in the mood of her language, and had to force himself to pause and weigh his response before he committed it to words.

"Someone once said all lovers are liars," he said.

She looked at him quizzically and raised her eyebrows in an ambiguous gesture. It could have been coquetry or contempt.

"Whoever said that," she said, joking, "was probably an old man like you who was a better liar than he was a lover."

He couldn't help smiling. "We all make mistakes," he said. "Especially we older people."

She looked at him steadily as though trying to stare him down. "You said that to hurt me," she said. "I hate it when people do that to me."

He laughed gently. "No. You're being unreasonable. I didn't say that to hurt you. At least not deliberately. The only person I ever deliberately try to hurt is myself, and I usually deserve it." He reached out and took her by the shoulders. There was still the accusation in her eyes. "Believe me, if I hurt you I deserve worse than that. You've been hurt enough."

She looked at him hard for a long time. She had her hands in the pockets of her coat. Almost imperceptibly her expression changed. She seemed to be searching his face. She said something voicelessly; he only saw her lips move.

"What?" He bent closer to her in an unconscious gesture.

"I need your help," he heard her say, firmly this time. "You've got to help me to love someone. I do so want to love. I need to love someone, anyone. You're the only person who can help me. I know it. I know it." The words came out in a string, as though she were reciting a litany learned by heart as a child before she was old enough to understand the meaning of the words. "It's not my fault if I can't say I love you. I want it to be true and I know it's not because I can't love anyone. Please, please understand that it's not my fault and help me." She curled her lower lip under her teeth, biting it hard. He recognized the movement from the night with Carnot at the farm. That night, she had made it bleed. She turned her face away from him, her hands still in her pockets. He still held her gently by the shoulders. They felt thin. "Oh, God. Oh, God," she whispered. "Oh, God, God."

She was shaking, trembling; she wasn't crying. Dante felt the same remote helplessness he had felt before. It crept through him like the warm luxury of half-sleep, a cataleptic detachment that made it impossible to concentrate his thoughts. But it was only for a moment, and he shook it off. Then he realized she was laughing, not strained, but just laughing, and she looked up.

"I'm such a fool," she said. "Sometimes I just talk and talk. And whenever I do I talk like a complete fool. I'm not really, you know. But you think so, don't you?"

"No."

"You don't think I'm a fool, a real foolish fool?" she asked.

"No."

"Then you're the fool," she said. "Because I'm hungry."

She twisted free, still without taking her hands out of her pockets, and ran from under the shadow of the overhang to where the stream gathered again and flowed into a natural sluice at the bottom of the small ravine. She jumped nimbly from rock to rock, never taking her hands out of her pockets, and he followed her. The ravine was very short. At the far end the stream poured like a spigot into a level bed, where it slowed its headlong rush and backed up in a deep pool formed by a depression in the rock and a natural dam of stones and branches. In the very center of a flat green clearing to the left was another circular ruin like the one Dante had seen near the path. Only this one had walls that came up to his chin, at least. At one point there was a break in the wall where the stones had been toppled to make an entry into a circle. Except for a tiny path leading out, the clearing was surrounded by thick, woody bushes and stunted trees. Dante carried the bottle of wine inside his shirt. He had slipped twice coming down the ravine and his left shoe was full of water. He had needed both hands to balance, while she had never once removed her hands from her pockets and both shoes were dry. She stood waiting for him while he negotiated the last of the rocks. When she did take her hands out of her pockets, she had the bread in one and the ashen block of cheese in the other.

He put the wine in the water at the edge of the pool. She was struggling to take off one shoe with the other, without bothering to bend down and untie the laces. He watched her, amused, as she kept slipping off balance trying unsuccessfully to get the shoes off. Finally she gave up.

"What are you laughing at, idiot?" she said. She held out the bread and the cheese. "Either hold these for me or get down and untie my shoes."

"Why are you in such a rush to get your shoes off?" He leaned down and untied first one, then the other.

"Because I don't like to swim with them on" she said. "Here, take our provisions and put them over there on the wall." She gave him the food.

Just as he placed the cheese and bread on the wall, he heard a splash behind him. When he came back the trenchcoat lay in a heap half inside out on the ground beside her shoes. She was nowhere to be seen.

Then he saw her. She was still underwater, sliding along the bottom on the momentum from her dive, her arms and hands trailing close beside her. Through the distorted refractions of the disturbed water, she looked like a shimmering white fish. Her hair was the same dark color as the rock and all he could distinguish was her body; the water was much deeper than he had realized. Then he saw her rise up slowly until she broke through the surface with an explosion of air.

"Oh!" she shouted to the sky. "Is it *cold!*"

She blew water out of her mouth and flung her hair around her head with a practiced swimmer's toss. The drops of water fell in a perfect circle around her like a string of pearls breaking. "It's wonderful!" she cried across the water. She had come up almost at the other side of the pool. Dante could see her arms and legs waving gently to and fro under the glint of the sun on the water. Underwater her arms moved with the soft rhythm of a fish standing still against a current. He watched the surface of ever spreading rings of concentric ripples that radiated on the water around her head and neck. She seemed to be a natural swimmer, so effortless was the way she kept herself afloat. Her wet hair, like burnished blue-metal, clung to her head and shone like a helmet.

"Aren't you coming in?" she asked. "It's warm! Really!"

He laughed across the water at her. "It's warmer here," he said.

She gulped air and put her face in the water and swam back toward the high flat rock on the bank where he stood. She swam the entire way with slow strong overhand strokes, turning her head to breathe only once. Her feet seemed barely to move under a dollop of smooth froth and she sliced through the water with amazing speed. He felt a physical pleasure watching the slender grace of her body and the precise rhythmic beauty of her movement. Her fingers touched the rock wall just under his feet and she bobbed up.

"Why?" she asked, flinging her wet hair back in a wild arc.

"Why what?"

"It's really wonderful," she said.

"I don't feel like swimming," he said. "Besides, a man of my dignity must consider his modesty."

"Bah!" she said. "Modesty nothing. You're afraid because it's too cold."

"Perhaps," he said. "I felt it when my shoe went in." He stepped on and off the wet shoe to demonstrate, and it made a squelching sound full of water.

She laughed. "It's not exactly warm," she admitted. "Turn your back. I'm coming out."

"Why the sudden prudishness?" he asked, smiling. "I may be modest but I'm not that easily offended."

"An eye for an eye," she said. "I can't look at you; you can't look at me. I don't like being naked when somebody else has clothes on. It makes me feel naked."

He turned around with his back toward her and stepped off the rock onto the grass. He heard her heave herself up out of the water and the slap of wet flesh on the flat rock. Then he heard her bare feet just behind him. She was jumping up and down to get warm.

"Give me my coat," she said. "Don't turn around, either."

He picked up the coat from in front of him and turned the sleeves right side out. Then he held it out behind him.

"Bring it up here," she said. "I don't want to get my feet dirty."

He backed up a few steps until he felt the rock under his feet.

"Here," he said, handing the coat to her. "I suppose you want your shoes delivered to you too."

"If you please."

He went and got her shoes, and backed up to the rock again; he felt ridiculous, but he held the shoes out to her backward.

"Thanks," she said, and he felt her take the shoes. Then, suddenly he was off balance and falling backward. He felt his leather belt cutting into his midriff and her fingers at his back pulling hard. He shouted once and heard her laugh before the shockingly icy water closed over his fully clothed body and drowned his last vision of her teetering naked as a nymph on the edge of the rock, her arms windmilling backward as she tried to regain her balance. He knew she was falling too. He was on his back still going down when she fell right into his open arms, the water between them taking up the shock. He closed his arms around her in a bear hug and opened his eyes under water. Laughter twisted and distorted her face through the water and her mouth was open wide and vomiting huge quicksilver bubbles of air. He gave her a cruel squeeze and forced the last giddy spasm of air out of her lungs. Her face was still grotesquely split with laughter, but he saw her eyes open in involuntary panic and felt her struggling to free herself. He pushed her hard toward the bottom and stroked for the surface. She came up a moment later under the shadow of the rock, gasping for air and coughing water. He pulled off one shoe and tossed it up onto the grass.

"You almost drowned me," she said, coughing. She was angry.

"An eye for an eye," he said, throwing the other shoe after the first. He was himself still secretly annoyed, but he laughed. "It will take all afternoon to dry my clothes."

"That's no reason to drown me," she said, hurt. "You're not going to a reception in them."

"You took advantage of my good nature," he said. "You were planning it. You asked me to turn my back so you could get me unawares. What if my watch wasn't waterproof?"

"But you're stronger than I am," she said, coughing again.

"You should keep that in mind," he said, laughing.

He peeled off the shirt, which clung to him like new skin, and threw it flapping in a wet ball onto the rock.

"You had no intention of putting on your coat," he said.

She held herself up by one hand on the rock and didn't answer.

He took a deep breath and went under, struggling with his belt and trousers. Finally, with his feet nearly touching bottom, he got them off and surfaced again. The wool was heavy with water. When he threw them toward the rock they fell short and splashed into the water beside Adriane. Without a word she gathered them to her and rolled them carefully into a ball; instead of putting them on the rock, she threw them with all her might out into the deepest part of the pool, where they sank instantly.

He swam to the spot and dove three times without coming up with the trousers. At last he caught them and fought his way to the surface, his ears and lungs bursting; she was sitting up on the rock hugging her knees and laughing. In one hand she had one of his shoes. When she saw him she cocked her arm as though to throw it.

"Truce?" she asked.

"Truce!" he shouted. "For God's sake don't!"

"Promise?" she asked, laughing. "No revenge?"

"Yes, yes!" He swam toward the rock, pushing the waterlogged pants before him on the surface of the water. At the bank he threw them onto the grass, well out of her reach.

"Are you sorry?" she asked.

"Sorry?" He was still trying to get his breath. "Me, sorry . . . ?"

She cocked the shoe farther back.

"Yes!" he shouted. "I'm sorry!"

She put the shoe down in front of her on the rock. He clambered out onto the grassy bank a few paces away and sat down to rest. His chest was heaving from exertion. She watched him. He felt unnaturally naked outdoors.

"I think we are even," she said.

He nodded to save breath. Then he got to his feet. Cautiously she picked up the shoe again.

"You have my honor," he said.

"Bah," she said. "I have your *shoe,* which is much better."

"Than my honor?"

"I'm a materialist," she said, laughing.

"You have my honor as a gentleman," he said. "Now please give the gentleman back his shoe."

She threw him his shoe and he barely caught it. "We'll see once and for all if you are a gentleman."

"And the other one."

She picked up the three shoes around her, hers and his, and stood up and pelted him with them. He caught his own and ducked. One of hers glanced off his shoulder and the other one missed him. She jumped off the rock and bounded past him to retrieve them before he did, but he reached out his arm and caught her around the middle and swept her giggling off her feet. Her skin was wet and cold against his chest and she kicked and twisted as he picked her up off the ground in his arms. He felt his bare heels sink deep in damp turf as he carried her across the grass and through the opening in the circle of stones. He dropped to one knee and laid her struggling down on the grass.

"I told you I was stronger than you," he said, breathing hard. He held her down by both shoulders and kissed her before she had time to turn her head. She pushed against him violently, but he held her immobile, pinned to earth. Then she stopped struggling and he felt her teeth against his lips. But suddenly she was biting him beyond the point of passion, beyond the astonished point of pain; desire vanished; bewildered hurt changed to outrage, fury. Like a blood-blind animal, he struck her.

He stared at her: *"Are you crazy?"*

365

She tried to get up but he pressed her shoulder blades hard into the soft moist earth with all his weight. Finally she relaxed and lay still, looking up at him with large dull eyes. He could feel her pulse throbbing in the cold silk under her arms, and the rhythmic rise and collapse of her ribs with angry breathing. He saw her eyes, cold, blue and unblinking, fill with tears.

"I hate you," she said quietly.

She closed her fingers slowly into his wrists and he could feel her nails. He pressed his thumbs into her flesh and held her shoulders pinned fast against the warm earth. "It's hard to know what you want," he said.

"Oh, God," she whispered. "God." She turned her face away from him, then rolled her head from side to side. Her wet hair was tangled and full of grass and bits of leaves, and her white skin was cold and taut with gooseflesh and covered with droplets that glinted silver in the white sun. She stopped moving and closed her eyes. Bits of grass clung to her cheeks where the tears had smeared. She lifted her chin toward him, her eyes knit tight.

"Then kiss me," she said in an angry whisper. "Kiss me, old man."

He only kissed her lightly, and she opened her eyes.

"Take your watch off," she whispered harshly.

"Why?" he asked. "Are you commanding me?"

"You always take your watch off," she said in a small voice. "I don't want to hear it ticking."

He lifted his arm and she slipped the watch off his wrist with both hands and laid it in the grass beside her head. Inside the ringed wall of ancient moss-covered stones it was like a room, remote, hollow, and private, with a bed of soft grass that grew not in soil but had its roots in centuries of dead and withered grass before it, and would, come the end of summer, throw down its seed and wither too, lost to the sun, that new grass could grow in it. It was like a room cut off from the world with a bed of growing grass for a floor and overhead the ceiling of the white sky around an eye of sun. Outside the walls the only sound was the gurgle and chuckle of water spigoting into the pool from upstream. They made love and fell asleep to that sound.

He had fallen asleep, the sun warm on his back, with the watch ticking in the grass beside his ear, a damp tickle of hair soft against his cheek. The last thing he'd thought of was how, without a word, she had fallen asleep—really like a child, he'd thought. The moist earth felt soft and cool and yielding under his weight, and he had relaxed, feeling tired muscles pressing out his own body's mold into the drowsy, grassy sod.

He didn't know how long they'd slept but he could tell without opening his eyes that the sun hadn't moved very far from where it had been. He lay in a half-doze, then turned to Adriane and held her to him. She murmured and lay still in his arms again and he kissed her gently, half asleep. For a long time they lay still, their arms wrapped around each other. He was lying on his side with his eyes still shut against the bright sun, when he heard a small scuffing noise, and opened his eyes. Over her shoulder, directly in his line of vision, sitting silently on top of the wall swinging his black-stockinged legs gravely: *a small boy.* It was the younger one of the two boys he had met that morning with their goats. The boy regarded him blankly and made no move to go away. He merely sat there, swinging his feet, gnome-like and secret and silent, watching.

Involuntarily his fingers tightened, and Adriane, thus aroused from sleep, lay back and stretched like a cat, groaning a little in the voluptuous pleasure of the warm sun. She opened her eyes: snapped her mouth shut on a yawn halfway, and stared behind him. He turned his head around and saw the other boy sitting on the wall behind him in the identical attitude. He noticed that the bread and cheese were still on the wall untouched, where he had put them.

Adriane turned on her stomach and laid her head down on her crossed arms, kicking her calves in the air. She looked at Dante sidewise without raising her head, saw his face, and burst out laughing.

"Perhaps they'll go away," she said.

Dante lay prone beside her, his chin cupped in his palms.

"They don't seem to be making any efforts in that direction," he said glumly.

"Do you have an extra fig leaf?"

"In my pocket."

"Maybe we could dig a hole," she said.

"I'll have to get the clothes," he said.

"I don't see that it makes much difference now," she said.

"How long do you suppose they've been there?" he whispered.

"They probably live here," she said.

"I wonder what they did with the goats," he said.

She smiled slightly and patted his arm.

"Let's make a dash for the pool," she said.

"I'm game if you are."

"On three," she said, pulling her knees up into a crouch. "One. Two. Three!"

He ran after her through the opening in the wall, seeing the small boy's head turn slowly as he gazed after them. There was no change in the interested expression on his face.

Suddenly the dog was barking and running along beside him trying to nip his heels, and he had to dance and sidestep to avoid stepping on the animal. Once he almost tripped over it, and heard wild piping laughter behind him. Adriane, unencumbered by the dog, reached the rock and dove in. The dog was barking furiously and circling around Dante, enjoying the game hugely. Finally Dante got his back to the water and ran awkwardly backward to the rock, holding the dog more or less at bay. He dove sidewise into the pool. When he came up he saw the dog dragging his shirt away, prancing and tossing its head and shaking the shirt in its teeth.

Suddenly he felt her hands on his shoulders from behind and felt himself being pushed under. He came up expecting to see her laughing, but instead he was surprised to see that she looked angry.

"You looked like such a fool," she said. "Why didn't you take a rock and kill him?"

As he got out of the pool onto the grass he took a handful of small pebbles off the bottom. The dog saw him and dropped the shirt and ran toward him. He pelted him with a few pebbles and the dog retreated to a safe distance. The boys picked up stones and threw back. Doing his best to dodge the stones, he got into his damp trousers. Then he ran at the two boys, scooping up his shirt as he went. The boys ran off into the bushes. The oldest one stopped at the head of the path and yelled taunts at Dante. He was pointing at Adriane and yelling something over and over in a patois that Dante couldn't understand. Dante took a few more steps, dropping the shirt and making a menacing gesture with his fist. The boy turned and fled after his brother and finally disappeared.

Still there was no sign of the goats.

When Dante was sure that they weren't coming back he went back to the pool and sat down on the rock. Adriane was swimming on the other side, ignoring him. After a while he gathered up the shoes in the grass and got dressed, and sat down to wait for her. His clothes were still heavy with water and his shirt clung to him and he shivered. Then he thought of the wine cooling in the water and remembered that he was terribly hungry.

They ate in silence, sitting on the wall. Adriane refused to put on the coat until she was dry and sat naked except for her shoes, which she put on to keep grass off her feet. He hammered the cork into the bottle with a stick and a rock. The bottle sat on the wall between them.

"You look grotesque," he said finally. "At least tie your shoes or take them off."

"I feel grotesque," she said, her mouth full of bread and cheese.

"Look, do we have to let that spoil it?"

"They didn't spoil it."

"What do you mean?" he asked.

"Idiot," she said, chewing.

"God's chosen," he said. "You mean they didn't bother you?"

"Oh, they bothered me, I suppose," she said. "But I felt all right once I was in the water."

"What were they shouting?" he asked.

"He said that I was your she-goat."

"Was that all?"

"He said I was better than a she-goat," she said. "And I suppose I am," she added, shrugging.

"They're animals," he said.

"Does that make us more innocent?" she asked.

"Look, I'm sorry," he said. "You're right. There is more evil in my mind than in theirs, I suppose. But please don't expect me to be completely rational about it right away. I must admit that the whole thing upset me."

She didn't say anything. In the sun her body was white and her skin seemed almost translucent. She appeared completely unconscious of her nakedness. She kicked off her shoes and they fell on the grass.

"I suppose I felt guilty for exposing you to such an experience," he said. "It *was* my fault."

She arched her eyebrows and looked at him. "Your fault?" she said. "Why do you think I brought you down here in the first place?"

He looked at the ground and swung his heels against the stone wall, uncertain what to say.

"What is it that makes me sit around now with nothing on?" she asked. "Do you think I'm that innocent?"

"I don't know," he said. "Are you that innocent?"

"I really don't know either," she said. "That's the worst part."

"There's nothing wrong with being naked," he said. "There's the sun. And there's the freedom of it."

"Give me my coat," she said.

He picked up the coat beside him and handed it to her. She hesitated, then dropped it on the grass.

"I dropped it," she said, laughing. "I don't think I'm innocent."

He jumped off the wall and picked up the coat and handed it to her. With the coat in one hand, she put her arms around his neck and he lifted her down off the wall. She kissed him.

He held her for a moment, laughing.

She wriggled her foot into one shoe, and dropped the coat again, on purpose.

"Pick it up," she said.

He stooped and picked it up, and she tried to shove him off balance with her foot. He was too quick for her.

"Here, you idiot," he said, throwing the coat over her head, laughing. "It's getting late. Cover your nakedness before thy God and let's get out of here."

The bottle of wine was still cold from the stream and only half empty. He searched around for something to plug it with as a temporary cork. After trying two or three sticks he found one that fitted fairly well and jammed it in and broke it off, leaving just enough to pull it out by hand. They started across toward the path the two boys had taken. They hadn't gone far when Adriane had to stop and kneel down to retie her shoe. In the shadow of the close, uncultivated trees, Dante waited for her. Without the sun his damp clothes felt even colder and he was anxious to keep walking.

Dante didn't recognize any features of the landscape. He realized that they were much farther from the village than he had thought. In following the stream down its course they had evidently come diagonally away from the path he had taken that morning. There was no sign yet of the olive groves he had come through. In the distance he heard the faint familiar sound of goat bells, but he couldn't determine precisely the direction they came from. The land around was rugged and forbidding-looking, full of rock outcroppings and stunted trees. Every so often they passed a pile of fresh goat dung on the path, and once when they came to the top of the rise they looked down on a small sunken plateau and surprised several large black birds picking the rotting carcass of a dead goat. The animal had been dead for weeks and there was nothing left of it but the skeleton with clots of goat hair clinging to it. The head looked almost intact except where the eyes were gone from the sockets. The birds lumbered into the air and disappeared. The smell of the dead goat hung like a blanket over the ground. Farther on was a dirty spring with a sign painted on the rock. It was a crude death's head painted in weathered white paint with the words *Eau Non Potable* under it. Somebody had made several handprints in white paint beside it.

The path suddenly became steep and they walked bent over, resting every fifty or sixty paces. At the top, Dante saw where he was. Before him the olive groves stretched as far as the eye could see. He even had a clear view of Monsieur Legay's farm far below.

XII

The drop was scheduled for two hours after midnight. Dante, weary to the bone from long hours on trains and buses, sat quietly in the empty dining room of the dingy Hôtel de la Gare, waiting, per instructions. His guide and traveling companion had left him at the previous station. The laconic young girl had simply pulled her valise down from the rack and told him he was on his own; he was to get off at the next stop. She didn't even say good-by or wish him luck. He had watched her from the window of his darkened compartment as she crossed the deserted platform carrying her valise. He saw her turn in her ticket stub and show her papers at the gate to a sleepy *feldgendarme* who hardly looked at them. Then she had disappeared from view, obscured by a huge feather of cold white steam that hissed from somewhere under the car and swirled up on the wind, casting a frigid yellow halo around the single electric bulb that swung on a wire over the station platform.

The tiny, desolate towns had all looked the same. They were strung out along the decrepit railroad, unrelieved by any passing scenery, like accidental knots in a frayed string. The bleak, wind-swept plateau of south central France, seen from the dirty windows of the ancient un-heated train, seemed almost uninhabited. Twice the train had stalled, once for over an hour. In the dark Dante had noticed a woman passenger relieving herself outside beside the roadbed. For some reason all the w.c.'s in the train were locked. He decided he could wait.

The Hôtel de la Gare was a mustard-colored building attached to the station itself. It looked as if it had been hand-plastered with stucco-textured mud. He had had to ring three times before a head poked out of a pair of board shutters upstairs and grumbled something about the late hour. He waited, not knowing whether he was going to be let in or not, worrying about a possible slip-up in the arrangements. But the food had undoubtedly been saved for him in advance, and although it was stone-cold he found it as appetizing as it was reassuring. When he finished eating, there was nothing to do but wait. The proprietor seemed to have gone back to bed. He looked at his watch; it was just after midnight.

Only two hours to go.

For a moment he felt a vague sense of panic. What if the delayed train had caused them to abandon him? It was true that he wasn't essential to the operation. He wished he knew whether Carnot were here or not. It would be some assurance if there was someone he knew. He was painfully aware that his safety depended on the fragile thread of word-of-mouth communication, since nothing could be put in writing. He could have sent a coded postcard to Carnot's maildrop, but that was risky business since arrests on the southern coast had been mounting appallingly in the last weeks and maildrops were always the most vulnerable; he might be sending a postcard revealing his where-abouts straight to the *Sicherheitsdienst*. He decided there was no use worrying about it now. He would cross that bridge when he came to it. In the meantime there was nothing sensible to do but wait, and try to stay relaxed.

To pass the time he carried his candle around the tiny dining room. In a corner he found a stack of old menus and a wine card dated 1939. He sat down and decided to read them. He figured that the candle was good for an hour. He began with the wine card, wondering idly whether the building had electricity. There had been no lights at the station, although he remembered there were blackout curtains.

A half-hour must have passed and he was starting on the wine card for the second time when he heard the hollow echo of a key rasping in the enormous lock of the street door. On automatic reflex he blew out the candle an instant before he saw a flashlight beam playing on the wall of the entryway.

The flashlight came straight through the narrow portals of the dining room and danced around the room until it was shining straight in his eyes, blinding him. He hadn't heard any footsteps. Whoever was holding the flashlight looked him over for a long time; nothing was said. The snuffed candle on the table in front of him seemed to be hanging by its dead wick from a thin blue string of smoke. Deliberately, looking straight into the blinding beam, Dante moistened his thumb and forefinger and pinched off the smoking wick. Slowly he got to his feet.

"*Bon soir,*" he said, still blinded.

For a moment there was silence and then the beam snapped off. Dante could still see it as a bright red spot burned onto his retina.

"*Alors, vous êtes la grosse huile,*" declared the voice behind the red spot. And then, "Can you mount a bicycle?"

Dante said he could manage a bicycle. The man grunted.

They left by a back door. Two bicycles were waiting in the alley with a third man, who then disappeared immediately. The other man leaned down and snapped bicycle clips around his trousers. Dante tucked his trouser cuffs into his socks.

"Follow me at twenty meters," said the man. "What did you do with your baggage?"

"It's in the dining room."

"That's as good a place as any," he said, mounting his bicycle. "Are you armed?"

"No."

"Good," said the man. "We have to be careful. It's after curfew."

The road out of town was rough and the frozen ground was rutted with cart tracks, but there was just enough light from the full moon to see the ruts in time to keep the wheels out of them. Once they were stopped by an armed *maquisard*. There was a low exchange of words and the man stepped back off the road to let them pass. Dante noticed that the submachine gun the sentry was carrying was British and a recent model. He hoped the Americans would do as well tonight. In a way, it would be a test of his own word. He had perhaps oversold his case. The Americans were still relatively new at this sort of thing. The British were old hands, expert through hard and sometimes tragic experience.

Dante swerved just in time to avoid a pothole, almost losing his balance. He had to pedal hard to keep up with the other bicycle. Somehow it seemed characteristic of the whole crazy war. He smiled to himself, and addressed his thoughts to those aircraft crewmen somewhere off in the darkness. "I hope you flyboys know your business," he said under his breath. He noticed he was falling behind again and pedaled harder. His legs were getting tired.

Finally the man ahead stopped and got off his bicycle.

Dante came up to a stop beside him. "We'll walk the rest of the way," said the man. "We have some young ones with us and they might be a little trigger-nervous. It's their first time out under the stars."

They were challenged four times. The last sentry, Dante noticed, was just a boy. He couldn't have been more than fifteen. Dante could tell by his too-husky voice and manner that he was trying to hide the fact that he was frightened.

They reached the edge of a field and hid the bicycles in the bushes and crossed the field on foot. Dante almost tripped over one of the stakes that had been driven into the ground to fix the torches to. At the far side of the field, concealed from the road by a meager stand of scrubby trees, was a farmhouse. The wind was dry and rising steadily and Dante noticed that it seemed to be veering around to the west.

The farmhouse looked completely dark, but Dante noticed a delicate wisp of smoke coming out of the chimney between gusts of wind. There were a few scattered clouds in the sky, but otherwise it was a perfect night for a drop.

They knocked on the great wooden gate to the courtyard around which the farmhouse was built. A small door in the enormous gate was opened; Dante had to bend down to get through. Inside, a man with a submachine gun led them to the house and knocked three times.

Dante stepped into a long, low-ceilinged room, well lighted by smoking lamps hung from the great beams in the ceiling. He had to duck his head to avoid hitting the beams. About two dozen heavily armed peasants looked up when he came in; they were sitting along both sides of a long table that ran the length of the room, hunched over steaming bowls of soup. They were bundled up; only one of them had taken his hat off to eat. Most of them had carbines or rifles slung on their backs. They examined Dante without showing any interest and went back to spooning their soup. A fat, red-cheeked woman with a glum face ladled out a bowl of soup and set a place at the table. She came over to Dante, who turned around to look for his guide only to find that he hadn't come in with him. He felt a momentary confusion. The woman grasped his sleeve and hustled him toward the place at the table.

"You must eat quickly," she said. "There are still others outside who have not eaten."

She seated him at the table between two fierce-looking old peasants, one of whom had a brand-new Sten gun on his back; Dante could smell the packing grease. The smell almost seemed to come from the soup, which was piping hot and tasty but had a thick layer of animal fat floating on top of it.

Dante was sopping up the last of the soup with a chunk of dark bread when he felt a hand on his shoulder. He turned around to find Carnot grinning down at him. His right arm was in a black sling. Carnot put his fingers to his lips and winked before Dante had a chance to say anything. Dante got up from the table and Carnot made a motion for him to follow him. Carnot led him into a back room, closed the door, and turned around. Dante was conscious of the fact that he himself was grinning like a schoolboy. But then so was Carnot.

"I didn't want you to say my name in there," he said. "I'm glad to see you."

"I can't tell you how glad I am to see you," said Dante, holding out his hand. "I was beginning to feel like an orphan."

"This is going to be a big affair tonight," said Carnot. "There must be fifty people here. A lot has happened since we left Asprémont."

"We?" said Dante automatically.

Carnot grinned wider. "I was there almost as long as you were," he said. "I was the *blessé* in room eight."

"You?" asked Dante. "For God's sake what happened? Why didn't you let me know you were there?"

"It was a delicate question of security," said Carnot, grinning again. "You see, I was supposed to be somewhere else. I have two graves now."

"Is that how you got that?" asked Dante, nodding at Carnot's slung arm.

Carnot lifted up his arm like a broken wing. "I got it in a *bagarre* with a German officer." He offered no further explanation.

"You must have been drunk," said Dante, shaking his head.

"You make jokes," said Alexi. "But you know, I was. I was so drunk that I didn't even feel my arm. I wish Max could have been there."

"How did you get to Asprémont?"

"I walked," said Alexi. "At night. I couldn't go back to St. Tropez with that hole in my arm."

Dante was silent. He was wondering if Adriane had known Alexi was the man in room eight. He felt sure that she had. He wanted to ask Alexi but something prevented him. He thought of Adriane in the trenchcoat.

"You know," said Alexi, reflectively, "I've been trying to think. Did you ever see a turtle with its head cut off?"

"I can't say that I have," said Dante.

"When I was a boy," he said, "at the farm, a turtle was killing ducks on one of the ponds. One of the brothers—he wasn't a Jesuit—found it and cut off its head with an ax. The turtle just kept walking away until it hit a wall. It just kept walking and walking into the wall. Even without its head. We watched it for a long time."

"What made you think of that?" Dante asked.

"I don't know," Carnot said. He shrugged.

Alexi fell silent. He seemed absorbed in thought. Dante watched him, unable to get the thought of Adriane out of his mind. It annoyed him. He wondered how much Alexi knew. He thought: You gave her to me. He watched Alexi's face. He had lost a great deal of weight and his black hair had been cut. But he looked the same, maybe older. Alexi looked up and saw Dante studying him.

Dante smiled. "It's good to see you," he said. He said it off the top of his mind to cover his thoughts. But he knew that he meant it. Then he asked, "What did you finally do with Berger?"

Carnot frowned. "He is under guard in Nice. In a hotel-pension.

He'll be all right. Adriane will be keeping an eye on him. If all goes well tonight he'll be yours. It'll be up to you to find a way to get him out of the country."

Dante nodded, said nothing.

The frown vanished from Alexi's face. "Do you know that they have changed the program tonight? They aren't going to drop. They're going to land. We got the word this evening."

"Do you remember the message?" asked Dante.

"Yes. 'The hen brings the duck in her bucket.' "

"Do you know who 'the duck' is?" asked Dante.

"I'd gamble that he's your replacement?"

"I take it there was more to the message, then?" Dante asked cautiously. He knew he was not getting any replacement, but he didn't bother to correct Carnot's assumption. The message was not for him; it meant nothing to him. Carnot was merely fishing for information.

"There was," said Carnot. "Good news for you, I think. 'When the eggs are hatched, the hen will leave the coop.' "

Dante smiled. "I hope we'll get them laid before they're hatched."

"You see," Alexi said cheerfully, "you come in like a fish and go out like a fowl."

"And yet I am neither," Dante said. "Was there anything else from BBC?"

"The usual. There was only one other thing that might be for you. It's been on for the last three nights. Does 'The rooster crows at midnight' mean anything to you?"

"That's the routine confirmation of the flight time. That means they should arrive around two o'clock."

"Let's go outside," said Alexi. Dante could tell he was repressing his excitement. "The men should be on the field by now. We had to pull up the stakes and reset them when the wind changed?"

"What's the recognition signal?"

"You'll see," said Carnot. "Come on."

"Aren't you carrying arms?"

"I can't do much with this," said Carnot, lifting his arm. "I have a pistol and two grenades. And you?"

"No."

"I can give you this if you want it," said Carnot, taking out the Luger wrapped in its rag. "I can't use it too well with my left hand, anyway."

"Thanks," said Dante. "You keep it."

Carnot stuffed the heavy pistol into his shirt, barrel up. He shrugged.

"By the way," said Dante, as they were leaving the room, "are there any responses I have to know?"

"If you get separated from me and anyone challenges you, tell them to go to hell. It's the safest answer. There are about three different outfits working in this circus and nobody knows anyone else. But be careful. There are a lot of jumpy kids around. Make plenty of noise when you walk and you'll be all right. Some of the freaks from the sideshow are a little drunk."

"From the *what?*"

"From the sideshow. This is a traveling carnival. That's how we'll cart the stuff out of here. The freaks are real. They're old hands at it, but half of them are never sober. It's nerve-racking business for them. They're more afraid of the explosives than they are of the Germans. Nobody can convince them that the stuff is safe as long as the fuses aren't armed. They're all sure that they are going to be blown to hell by a bump in the road."

Dante laughed. "My God," he said.

"The freaks and the animals are genuine. So are the wagons. The rest of it is phony. The rest are our people."

The armed guard opened the tiny door in the great wooden gate and let them out. There were dark shapes of men hurrying around the field hammering down the last of the stakes that formed an arrow with the direction of the wind. Another crew was carrying freshly made torches out onto the field. Dante could smell the odor of fresh kerosene on the wind. Still a third group of silent figures were lashing the unlighted torches to the stakes. Dante felt Carnot press something into his hand. It was a flashlight.

"You take this. Don't waste the batteries. They are impossible to get."

"What will I need it for?"

"You will have to keep an eye on the unloading. You will need it to read the crates. They are sometimes written in English. Your people should think to put everything in French."

"I'll tell them."

"And don't abbreviate words. Even if we have someone who can read English, it is useless to try to read that salad they stencil on the crates. We have to unpack them to find out what we have. And the right things are never together. We find the guns and then spend all night trying to sort out ammunition to fit them."

"I can see that it is a serious problem," said Dante.

"This is nothing, tonight. When they land the plane it's easy. You should see it after a drop. Sometimes they scatter everything over ten square kilometers. And we have to find it in the dark. And don't forget, if we miss something, sooner or later some idiot always finds it and turns it in to the police and then we can never use that spot for a drop again."

They walked toward the center of the field, where a man was wrapping rags around an enormous torch. A tiny figure brushed past Dante carrying a can of kerosene. He gave the kerosene to the man making the torch and scurried off across the moonlit field.

"My God," said Dante. "What's a child doing out here?"

Alexi laughed. "That's Loki. He's the midget. The other one, the

376

big one, that's Prometheus. He's the fire-eater. All the freaks use Greek names. The show is called the *Cirque Parnasse*."

"Loki isn't Greek," said Dante, laughing.

"Who cares. They think it is," said Carnot. "They used to have a fat lady named Cleopatra. But when rationing came she got thin."

"What did she do when she got thin?"

"What did she do? She died."

Dante said he thought the death of the fat lady was tragic. Alexi said it *was* too bad because now the group was without a fat lady.

They stood a little way off from the fire-eater and watched him silently. Prometheus knew they were watching him and seemed to take special pains with the flare he was making. He obviously knew his business. After he had wrapped the long stick with rags, he bound it tightly with wire, crisscrossing it back and forth around the cloth head. It looked as if he were making a scarecrow to put up in the middle of the field. In the moonlight it could have been a scarecrow, except that it needed a coat, and some straw to make the arms stick out. But the head was the right size. When the rags were securely bound, he fastened the end of a length of rope to the butt end of the handle. Then, taking a firm stance, he tried a few practice turns with the contrivance. He swung it around his head like a hammer-thrower, letting out more and more rope until Dante and Carnot had to step back to avoid being knocked flat as the thing whooshed past like a great gray owl. It was too dark to see the rope, and the bundled stick looked like some sort of bird flying in a great lumbering circle about the fire-eater's head.

Satisfied with his creation, Prometheus reeled it in on its tether. He laid it on the ground at his feet and poured kerosene over it, leaning down to work the fuel into the spongy scarecrow-like head. Dante could smell the acrid odor. When the rags were saturated, the fire-eater expertly coiled the tether rope and sat down on the cold ground, looking up at the sky. Not once had he acknowledged their presence.

"He's waiting for his cue," said Carnot. "He has the best act in the whole show."

"It looks as if it ought to be spectacular," said Dante.

"When he gets that thing going around his head you'll think it's a pinwheel. The British told him it's the best recognition signal in France. It's gone to his head a little. He makes Loki wait on him."

"I saw that," said Dante. "The Sorcerer's Apprentice."

"The pilots even have a nickname for him. They call him Fireball. They use this method all over this part of France now. It's more distinct from the air than a bonfire. But the pilots say they can always tell when it's the Fireball at work because he makes it look like a perfect unbroken circle, a solid ring."

Dante cupped his watch under the flashlight.

"Overdue?" asked Alexi.

"By quite a bit," said Dante. "They may have detoured the flak."

"They never come straight here anyhow. At least the British don't."

"They will probably have a British navigator flying with them for this first trip," said Dante. "That was discussed, anyhow."

All around the field activity had ceased. Now there was only waiting. Suddenly there was the distant sound of a motor. Carnot grabbed Dante's arm. "Come on!" he said, running off the field. The fire-eater flopped on his face and lay still.

Dante had thought at first that the sound was a plane; then from the shadow of the scrub trees at the edge of the field, he saw the turtle-backed weapons-carriers. They were clearly visible in the moonlight. They roared slowly and ponderously along the road, their shielded blue headlights probing the rutted ground like the antennae of great blind beetles. Dante felt Carnot's fingers tighten on his arm. For an instant he felt the cold slow paralysis of fear. The trucks slowed.

"Those aren't circus wagons," Dante said.

"It's not a regular patrol," Carnot answered.

"No, they're looking for something. Probably us."

The stakes marking off a runway were plainly visible to Dante. It's because you know what they are, he told himself. They can't see them from the road.

"If only none of those idiot children take a shot at them . . ." whispered Carnot. "One of them will have to be a hero."

Dante waited to hear a shot or the stutter of a Sten gun rip the air. But there was silence. The vehicles were stopped on the road, their motors idling. Then Dante was chilled to hear an order, barked out in brittle German, drift faintly across the field. This is the enemy, he thought, troops trained to kill. These were not administrative soldiers, not service troops, not military police. These were combat troops. There was great activity around the trucks. The Germans seemed to be having a conference. Then they all went back to their vehicles.

"If they come onto the field, we're cooked," said Carnot.

There was another faraway spate of the jagged, alien language. Commands were shouted. The words sounded furious and small in the moonlit silence, but they struck sparks of terror in the stillness, like flint on steel. Then for a suspended moment there was nothing. The motors roared. The lead car, lurching mightily under the weight of its armor, moved slowly on down the road, its blind blue lights poking inquiringly into the ruts and potholes, a cockroach in search of garbage.

"Will they leave one behind?" asked Dante.

"They travel in packs," said Carnot.

Carnot was right. The other three moved off in their turn and disappeared down the road.

"And nobody fired a shot," said Dante." Thank God."

"They're probably too scared to even aim straight," said Carnot. "Come on. We've got to plug the breach."

They hurried across the field to the farm.

"What do you mean?" asked Dante.

"I'm not in command here," said Carnot. "The local commander has the guts of a chicken. He'll try to call it off if he can."

"Won't they hear the plane?" asked Dante.

"*They* won't," said Carnot, jerking his head after the Germans. "Not as long as they have their motors running. I don't think they're looking for anything in particular. They're just checking usable fields. I'm glad they got here before and not after."

"But they must suspect something. You said they're not a regular patrol."

"They probably think they're on a wild-goose chase thought up by some stupid captain to rob them of their sleep."

"Still," said Dante, "I think it's risky."

"Of course it's risky," said Carnot, sharply. "It's risky being alive. We'd all be safer dead."

Carnot's guess was right. The commander was actually in the process of giving orders to the section leaders to call it off when Carnot strode up to the group by the farmhouse wall.

"If you leave," he announced, "I'll do it myself."

He countermanded the commander's orders on the spot, and a violent argument began between Carnot and the stocky peasant. The section leaders stood around in a circle waiting, almost politely, for the issue to be decided one way or another.

They were so engrossed in the dangerously heated quarrel that none of them, not even Dante, heard the faint hum of the plane's motors. It wasn't until one of the section leaders tapped the commander on the shoulder that he turned around and saw the fire-eater preparing to light the torch. A match flared and went out. The torch caught. The commander was purple with rage. Carnot laughed. Dante realized that from where Carnot was standing he had known exactly what was going on and was simply stalling for time.

The commander broke away from the group and ran toward the center of the field, where Loki was holding the burning firebrand as the fire-eater backed off to give himself some scope. The commander was shouting in a ridiculous stage whisper that could be heard all over the field. Loki launched the torch. It faltered for a moment and then Prometheus snapped up the slack in the tether and the ball of fire began to travel its first ponderous circle. Carnot ran out on the field behind the commander. The commander reached the center of the field and stood transfixed for a moment just inside the terrible circumference of flame, watching the roaring ball of flame come straight at him. Alexi was shouting encouragement to the fire-eater and clapping his hands like a small boy. The commander dropped to his knees and crawled out of range.

Dante was astounded at the rushing roar of the enormous whirling streak. It looked like a comet and seemed to be at least an arm's-breadth in diameter at the head. It left a standing tail of fire and dripped large blobs of fire on the grass from the excess burning kerosene. The fire-eater put both hands on the rope and got it going faster and faster. It lit up the whole field, and men standing saw their sweeping shadows flicker crazily across the whole field and fall among the trees. Prometheus swung the fireball faster and faster, until finally he let out all the rope and the fiery hammer was lost in a vast, wheeling blur, a solid circle of fire.

The commander was still shouting curses at the fire-eater, but Prometheus was too completely lost in his art to acknowledge him. He was absolutely alone and secure in his ring of yellow flame. He turned like a satanic dervish in a trance. A choking billow of black smoke rose in a ring around him and the light shone on his glistening skull and face. As Dante came closer, he could see that the fire-eater was in fact completely bald.

"I told you it was worth seeing," Carnot shouted.

"I'm surprised he didn't listen to the commander," said Dante.

Carnot looked surprised. "How could he? He's a deaf mute. I thought I told you that. Loki is his ears and tongue."

The roar of the plane overhead drowned all conversation. Prometheus was still spinning like a top. The plane blinked the recognition signal, and Dante saw the midget, Loki, dodge inside the periphery of flame. Keeping his head down so he wouldn't be decapitated by the hissing cord, he reached the fire-eater and slapped him on the leg once. Prometheus took one more series of turns, building impossible speed, and then with one gigantic heave, he released the fireball hammer and it sailed up into the wind in a long, sweeping arc, leaving a trail of delicate sparks that seemed to hang for an instant like a rainbow of witch's fire. The hammer splashed fire as it struck the earth and cartwheeled end over end until its energy was spent and the fire went out. The fire-eater collapsed on the ground, his chest heaving like the bellows of a forge. Loki knelt down to him and made a pillow for his head on his knees. Far across the field lay the smoking ash of the spent firebrand, a great cotton ember, red and black, crawling with patches of feeding sparks like colonies of bright maggots in the oxidizing wind. The blackened rope trailed in the blown weeds like a dead snake. Two curious men, hardly more than boys, stood over the head examining it. As if to make sure the life was out of it, one of them turned it over with the toe of his boot, and an angry swarm of sparks flew.

The torches lashed to the stakes were lit by two men carrying brands who raced down the length of the field; they dipped fire onto each stake as though ladling it out with a spoon. Instantly the field was ablaze with a fiery arrow whipped by the wind it accused; Dante noticed that the direction was nearly accurate. Close enough for a landing, anyway.

The commander had by now accepted the situation, if only to rescue the initiative of his command. He was giving orders that guards should be deployed in double strength on all approaches. In the event of Germans appearing again, they were to be fired upon only in the extreme emergency of the plane's not yet being airborne. It would take at least fifteen minutes to unload the plane.

"My God," said Dante. "You'd think it would wake up the German High Command, all that noise."

"It is funny that such a noisy operation should be such a secret," said Carnot. He had to shout to make himself heard as the plane changed the pitch of its propellers and banked off to make the approach again.

Everyone was jumpy. This time the plane suddenly appeared over the scrub of trees, low, as though out of nowhere. Its engines were throttled back and it came in on a low glide. Dante could see the moonlight glinting off the lowered flaps. It seemed to hover like a giant moth, slowly, almost too slowly, Dante thought. The pilot was obviously afraid of overshooting. The plane began to come down fast. The engines roared once only and then it was on the ground lightly as vision. It seemed unreal and almost too huge to believe, but there it was. A moth couldn't have touched down more gracefully, more delicately.

But once on the earth the plane lost its grace. It was not made for crawling over the face of the earth, and it looked as awkward as a moth with a broken wing. Tons of metal lurched over the ground, turned slowly, taxied back to the downwind end of the field and turned once more into the wind, prepared to take off. Several of the slender stakes had been knocked over and the torches lay burning in the weeds, starting small fires. Several men ran around stamping them out. In a moment the arrow of fire was gone.

The belly of the twin-engined Dakota opened and crates started to be thrown out. Dante and Carnot were the first at the plane. Next was the fire-eater, completely recovered from his exertions. Loki wasn't far behind.

A flyer dropped out of the plane. He was in British uniform. He reached up and helped down a civilian. "The duck," said Carnot to Dante under his breath. Then the flyer turned around.

"Where's the big wheel of fire? I say, Fireball!" he said when he picked out the beaming fire-eater from the crowd of faces. He shook Fireball's hand. *"Formidable!"* he said. He turned to Loki. "Tell him I love him more than my wife." Loki conveyed the sentiment silently on his fingers to Prometheus. The fire-eater grinned and made quick fingertalk back. Loki laughed. He had a high, squeaky laugh. He turned to the flyer.

"He says thank you, but he would prefer your wife, and to learn how to fly."

The flyer roared with laughter. "The chap's got taste," he said. "I'll teach him to fly after the war."

Crates were being heaved out of the plane and carted off in a quiet frenzy of activity. Carnot advised the navigator to stay inside the plane, explaining that they'd had unwelcome visitors earlier. Dante helped as best he could to get the crates sorted out so that they were stacked in some sort of logical order. There was a tremendous load of equipment. Out of the corner of his eye Dante watched Carnot surveying the mounting pile of boxes. He looked satisfied, even impressed. Someone spoke to Dante.

"Hello." The voice was English. "I'm MacNaughton."

Dante turned around to see a tall man standing beside him. It was the civilian off the plane.

"Are you the duck?" asked Dante.

"Quack, quack," said MacNaughton, without smiling. In fact he looked rather sour.

"How do you do," said Dante, a little stupidly he thought.

"Quack, quack," MacNaughton said. "Where does one go through customs?"

The circus wagons were hidden in the trees off the road. Most of the weapons in their flat cases were packed into the animal wagons which had specially built false bottoms. In one of the loaded wagons Dante watched a mangy catlike animal with a doglike face stride back and forth over the straw-covered boards. The animal was still ruffled from having her sleep disturbed and being chained in one corner of the cage while strange men invaded her domain and uprooted the floor. Now she glared through the wooden slats, stopping in her circuit of the cage to hiss at the unfamiliar faces outside her cage. Under her softly padding feet were six cases of automatic weapons and nearly a hundred thousand rounds of special tracer ammunition. The half-starved hissing animal was an ugly deterrent to anyone who would like to search the cage.

Dante marveled at the efficiency of the method of transporting the weapons. A circus naturally had freedom of movement, and no German was likely to discover accidentally the double nature of its cargo. Dante learned that the animals would have died of starvation long ago had not the underground discovered their usefulness and provided money to feed them. But there was another surprise besides the circus.

Parked off the road on the other side were three ancient motor hearses, empty. Carnot explained with ghoulish pleasure that the hearses followed the circus by different routes, to rendezvous in previously appointed places. They were used to make local deliveries.

It was a shrewd arrangement. In small towns the local *maquis* would let it be known in advance by word of mouth that an old long-departed resident was being brought home to be buried. Hence no one in the village would be overcurious when a strange hearse arrived in the village. The grave would be dug in advance. The hearse would arrive, reeking through the streets with a load of weapons and rotten pig entrails packed together in a coffin. The coffin would be given a discreetly rapid burial with prayers by the unwitting local curé, perhaps even a few mourners. Then the hearse would leave immediately; the circus would follow the next day. The authorities were always anxious to get the malodorous "corpse" into the ground and there was never any delay over permits. No one would dream of opening the casket. In this manner, village after village would be visited simultaneously with the tawdry gaiety of a traveling circus and the macabre fulfillment of a forgotten citizen's dying wish—to be buried in the village of X, or Y, or Z. Naturally, the weapons could be dug up at any time. And the beauty of the arrangement, of course, was that everything up to and including the burial of the weapons was consummated in broad legal daylight, thus eliminating the risk of clandestine after-curfew movements. It was perfect.

After the departure of the plane, with gifts of perfume and champagne to take back to England, the plowing of the field began. It was a remarkable operation, done in silence and in the dark. A dozen plows staggered in tandem ranged across the long narrow field, the horses muzzled, their bridles oiled to make them silent. In less than an hour the telltale tracks of fifty men and an airplane were obliterated completely. The circus teams were used to help, and since the plowing wasn't deep they did almost as well as the farm animals. The horses moved like ghosts across the field, leaving a black wake in the silver sea of moonlight. Dante watched the plowing for a while. Then he went in to join the others in the farmhouse.

Inside the quiet, darkened farmhouse—which looked so shuttered and asleep from the outside—everything was light and joy. A few circus people and the peasants with rifles on their backs were crowded into the low-beamed dining room. The newly arrived British agent MacNaughton was regaling his listeners with a hair-raising tale of the flight through the flak on the French side of the Channel. Dante noticed that his French was perfect—in fact, he spoke with the accent of the region. He stood with his back to the fireplace, facing his audience, a huge glass of hot wine in his hand. He was a tall man with an easy-going style, who instantly made a friend of every man in the room. Dante had no idea what his mission was, except that MacNaughton had told him he was going directly on to Paris. He had his own arrangements, apparently.

Dante looked around for Carnot, but he didn't seem to be in the room. Most of the circus people were still outside putting the finishing touches on the stowage of the weapons. Another group outside was taking care of the burial of the bulkier equipment that couldn't be transported by the caravan—Dante had gathered from Carnot that most of the clothing, radios, transmitters and photographic equipment would be kept at the farm for later distribution. Carnot and the local commander were probably overseeing this final job.

When the plowing was finished, the rest of the men came in from outside. Carnot came in with a group of men carrying shovels who looked as grim as gravediggers. Carnot's arm sling was covered with mud. He saw Dante instantly and came up and slapped him lustily on the arm. He reached into his shirt.

"Here is a present for you," he said. He drew out a banana. "I haven't seen one of these for four years." He looked at the banana and shook his head.

Dante took the banana. "Where did you get it?" he asked.

"That pilot threw it to me just before he closed the door," Carnot said. "I give it to you in recognition of your services to France." Carnot was smiling happily. "We did it, didn't we?"

"It was perfectly timed," Dante said. "I'm glad it's over, though."

Carnot's laughing mood suddenly vanished. His face grew sober. "It's not over yet," he said.

Dante looked at Carnot.

"That patrol," Carnot said, jerking his head to one side. "If they heard that plane, the roads will be blocked and they'll be checking everything closer than usual." Carnot looked around the room. "All these men have to get home before dawn," he said. "The circus will stay in the village tonight."

Dante looked around the crowded room. The faces of the men were relaxed and happy. Everyone was drinking wine and there was a steady drone of conversation. There was an atmosphere of quiet congratulation and celebration in the room.

"What are they waiting around for?" Dante asked.

"We are waiting for word about the roads." He looked at his watch. "In twenty minutes we should know if any special precautions are being taken."

"Roadblocks?"

"Roadblocks and possible house searches. They know that if an operation is in progress, a lot of husbands won't be in their beds tonight."

Dante listened to Carnot's statement, sobered by it, and turned to look at the men in the room again. The circus people were shaking hands and filing out into the courtyard. MacNaughton was still at his place by the fireplace. He was answering questions about the progress of the war, nodding slowly to make his points. His audience, hungry for news from the outside, stood in a semicircle around him listening soberly, reflectively. A few men sat at the table, helping themselves to bread and soup. The soup steamed in a huge pot over a charcoal brazier in the center of the table. It was there for anyone who wanted it. Dante turned back to Carnot, who was staring at his feet, frowning in thought.

"Do you want some soup?" Dante asked.

Carnot looked up. He was about to answer when there was a commotion in the other room and a man burst into the room. He said nothing, but his face carried news enough. He gestured, grim-faced, toward the door behind him. Every man in the room put down his glass, his spoon, whatever he was holding. There was no need for conversation. Carnot was galvanized into action. He strode across the room to the messenger standing in the doorway. Dante was directly behind him.

"What," Carnot said. One word only, spoken like a statement rather than a question.

The man gestured again toward the outside, tossing his head to one side with a gesture of contempt. "The car," he said. He carried his weapon in the crook of his arm.

"How many?" Carnot asked.

"One. The others aren't with it."

"Is it part of the same patrol as before?"

The man shrugged. "They've stopped. One of them is looking at the field."

Carnot turned and shot a significant look at Dante. "They might have noticed that it wasn't plowed before."

A farmer behind Dante said, "I doubt it."

Carnot looked at him. "It's more obvious at night than by day," he said. "Before, it looked white. Now it looks black. Why else would they be looking at it?" Behind them someone was blowing out the oil lamps. Only one remained lit.

Carnot turned and followed the man who'd brought the message through the doorway. The rest of the men were formed up by their squad leaders and followed quietly behind.

Outside the farmhouse door they ran into the local commander. He was out of breath with running. "I told them to hold their fire," he said. He no longer seemed to dispute Carnot's authority.

They passed through the stand of trees. A cloud was over the moon. Suddenly the field came into unobstructed view. Standing on the road across the field was one of the same German patrol vehicles, its motor throbbing softly in the darkness, its blue slit-lights hardly visible through the haze over the newly plowed field. To the left, back among the trees, Dante noticed several of the circus people standing like ghostly spectators. The armed men deployed to the right and left, silently encircling the field toward the road. The weapons carrier was stopped midway between the extreme ends of the field, well out in the open. It was headed in the opposite direction from before.

"Is it the same one?" Dante asked Carnot.

Carnot stood looking calmly across the field. "It must be one of the same ones," he said.

"Why did they split up?"

"To cover more ground," Carnot said. "They must know something is up."

"Do they have two-way radios in those things?" Dante asked.

"Some do. Some don't. It will have an antenna if it does. One of them always does. Come on."

Carnot started out directly across the open field, half-running in a low crouch. Dante followed him. He noticed that Carnot was glancing over his shoulder at the cloud which was moving rapidly across the face of the moon. Just as the moon was about to come out again, Carnot fell into a shallow furrow, and Dante dropped beside him.

"There he is," Carnot whispered, looking toward the road. Dante saw the clear outline of a figure standing alone between them and the stopped vehicle. The German was standing with his hands on his hips, looking around at the field. He stood for some time, turning his head from side to side as though listening. Twice he walked to the left, stooping to pick up a handful of dirt, examining it, throwing it away. They were just close enough to hear the clod of earth fall.

Carnot grasped a handful of dirt and did likewise. "Do you think he can tell this has just been plowed?" he whispered.

"If he's a farmer he certainly can," Dante whispered.

"They must suspect something," Carnot said. "Otherwise they'd be looking for tire tracks. That's probably what they came here for."

"How many other fields in this area could land a plane?" Dante asked.

"About six."

"What will you do?" Dante asked.

"We have a method. Quiet. Listen."

Another German appeared at the top of the vehicle. His head and shoulders were silhouetted beside the up-jutting machine gun mounted ahead of the turret. He spoke softly across the short distance between him and the one standing in the field. The German words were indistinct.

"Can you hear what they're saying?"

Dante shook his head in the semidark. They lay still, listening. The Germans didn't sound alarmed, for although the words were indistinguishable, the tone was easy, conversational. Suddenly the moon drifted behind a cloud again. Carnot was up instantly and crawling toward the road. He had taken his arm out of the sling, which now hung uselessly around his neck. Dante suddenly saw that he had something huge in his teeth—he knew it was the Luger wrapped in its oily rag.

The cloud was a large one, and dense. They worked slowly forward. The shallow furrows afforded partial cover, and now they snaked over them one by one on their stomachs.

Finally they could distinguish words of the conversation. The nearer German was only a vague shadow, but the vehicle was still clear against the distant sky. They lay immobile, hardly breathing, listening. The conversation was near and clear. Dante squirmed closer to Carnot's ear and whispered, "He's not sure. The one in the truck is for going back and reporting. This one here is for looking around first."

The conversation continued. Dante listened. Then he whispered, "He says he's sure this field wasn't plowed. The other one says that if a landing *was* made here they'll all be home in bed by now anyway." Dante felt Carnot's ear move under his lips as his face constricted in a smile.

Carnot whispered, "They're in for a surprise."

"Are you going to stop them?"

Dante felt Carnot's slow deliberate nod. In the pit of his stomach Dante felt the familiar cold constriction of fear, of anticipation, excited foreboding. His heart felt loose in his chest, thumping hollowly. He turned carefully on his side and studied the cloud moving past the moon. It was nearly halfway past. There was no other cloud following it. Suddenly the two Germans came to a conclusion.

"They're going back," Dante whispered. The nearer German walked to the vehicle. Dante felt Carnot tense. He was unwrapping the Luger. The rag fell to the ground. From the pocket of his jacket Carnot took out one of his two grenades and put it into Dante's hands.

"If I miss," he said, "you won't. You can't. Get it inside."

"It will wake up the dead," Dante said, feeling the deadly cold weight in his hand.

Carnot turned his head toward him in the darkness. "Not if you get it inside," he said slowly. "Watch what I do. You won't get a second chance if you miss. Come on. They'll go north."

Carnot started off diagonally across the field toward the road to head off the weapons carrier. The German was mounting into the vehicle, and the driver was revving the engine. It hadn't started to move yet. Dante shot a quick glance backward at the moon and started after Carnot. Everything depended on the moon.

They were nearly to the corner of the field when behind them they heard the vehicle's gears mesh and it started into motion. They were just at the spot where the field ended and the trees began when Carnot flopped face down into the narrow ditch that bordered the edge of the road. Dante fell almost on top of him just as the vehicle swept lumbering past, gathering speed.

The rest happened so fast that Dante hardly had time to take it all in before it was over. He felt Carnot get up and start after the vehicle. Moonlight suddenly flooded the scene again, and just as Dante got up he saw a huge tree sway slightly over the road. It seemed to hang suspended for a second, and then float slowly down. For one mesmerized instant it seemed merely to be floating, lovely and silver in the air of the moon. He saw one of the Germans stand up in the open turret. Everything seemed suspended, immobilized. Then came the crash as the tree slammed down onto the road in a cloud of leaves and dust. It bounced all along its ponderous length just as the vehicle hit it. Dante found himself running toward the crash. He saw the hard iron outlines of the square vehicle, and then he was touching the cold bare metal. He didn't even hear the shot, but only saw the German in the turret slump and disappear, and Carnot bound in a single leap onto the rear deck, agile as a bird, his sling flapping about his neck like a rakish scarf; then he soared off backward, silhouetted against the blinding flash. Dante opened his eyes instantly and saw the moon floating in the incredible silence of the faded black sky. Pieces of falling metal were raining through the leaves around him. He was still tensed for the blast when he realized he'd heard it—it had been nothing more than the huge whoomph that billowed skyward on a geyser of flame. Then someone was pulling him to his feet, hands under his armpits. Men were swarming out of the woods with pails and mops. For a moment Dante thought he was having a hallucination. The men attacked the smoking vehicle with the wet mops, slapping at the tiny tongues of flame that licked about a wet stain of gasoline on the ground. Twenty flailing men were stomping and slapping in a wild antic dance, flame flickering about their feet as raw gasoline soaked into the dirt and spread. Dante instinctively stepped back. He stumbled over Carnot, who was sitting in the road feeling himself. He looked up at Dante and frowned critically. Then he smiled.

"How was my form?" he asked.

"Very good."

"My timing was off."

Dante stared at him, slow realization dawning on him. "You pulled the pin before . . ."

"That's the trick," Carnot said. "If you drop it in too soon, they'll just throw it out. And you can't stand around up there counting five."

Dante said nothing. He could feel the tension in his body relaxing and the familiar weakness flowing like warm fluid into his knees. He sat down on the road and simply watched.

The fire was out before it could really take hold. The hulking form still smoked in the moonlight. Suddenly the tree began to slide off into the woods, seemingly of its own power. Then Dante saw the long line of men hauling on the rope. It disappeared slowly from sight, swallowed by the dark woods. He heard it being dragged deep into the standing trees.

The local commander was supervising the attaching of more ropes to the wreck. Two paired teams were added to the man ropes, and almost before the dust of the explosion had settled, the wreck was moving away. It went off down the road still smoking. The smell of raw gasoline was still in the air. On top of the vehicle men were working like ferrets, salvaging the machine gun, which had been blown half off along with its flimsy mount. The whole area was a strange silent turmoil of activity. Carnot sighed wearily and got carefully to his feet. Dante stood up again.

"Where are they taking it?" Dante asked.

Carnot smiled. "Come on. You'll see," he said. They started together up the road after the tank, stepping carefully around the mops and buckets that were strewn across the road. Everyone seemed occupied with his own task. One man was picking up twigs and branches from the fallen tree. Others stood by with brooms. No one paid any attention to Carnot or Dante. Dante passed close to the local commander, who was leaning over doing something to his boot.

"Have the shovel crew started?" Carnot asked.

The commander looked up. Recognizing Carnot, he straightened, almost snapping to attention. "I sent them ahead so they could get started," he said.

Carnot walked on, Dante walking beside him. They walked in silence. Behind them several men were already at work with twig brooms erasing the tracks of the vehicle. One crew followed Dante and Carnot. The other started in the other direction, the direction the vehicle had come from.

They had walked for several hundred meters when Carnot suddenly turned aside. He was following the scuff marks, which were clearly visible in the moonlight. The tracks turned aside and seemed to end at the edge of the ditch, which was narrow but deep at this point. The vehicle was nowhere to be seen. Carnot jumped down into the ditch and climbed up the other side. Dante followed him.

"How did they get it across?" Dante asked.

"Boards," Carnot said. "Laid across the ditch."

They walked deeper into the woods, following what seemed to be an unused cow track. Suddenly through the trees Dante saw a light, then several. They came into a small clearing. The weapons carrier stood in front of them. The light of several lanterns lit the sweating faces and glistening torsos of the dozen men who stood waist-high in a huge pit in the center of the clearing. Several armed men stood around the pit, silently watching. The double brace of horses were out of harness, nibbling grass in the four corners of the clearing. Carnot walked up to the nearest man.

"Get back out along the road. We walked in here like Hansel and Gretel," he said sharply.

The man looked at him and saluted awkwardly. He went around the pit rounding up the other men. They filed silently past Carnot out of the circle of light toward the road. The men who were crowded into the pit worked without talking, the chink and sucking of their shovels the only sound. Dirt rose in a careful pile around three sides of the pit. The fourth was left open for the wreck. The men who had hauled the hulk to where it stood, squatted on the ground around it, resting. Two men were busy with a jack and tire tools stripping the ruptured chassis of everything that could still be removed. The salvaged machine gun lay in the grass beside them, glistening in the feeble light of the five lanterns. The shovels worked in a steady unvarying rhythm, counterpointed by the regular fall of dirt around the rim of the pit. The neat ridge of earth grew larger. The men were literally digging the ground out from under each other's feet. In the short time Dante had been watching they were already up to their middle ribs as the floor of the deepening pit sank under them.

For a long time Dante sat on the sparse grass in the chill gloom of the surrounding trees and watched. The dirt was flying up out of the pit now; the diggers were hidden from him behind the rising mount of earth. Only the glinting arcs of the spade tips were visible. The men with the horses were preparing for another haul. The horses were assembled on the far side of the pit. They stood patiently while the long cable was attached to their draw bar. One of them stood on three legs.

It was some time later that the pit was finally judged deep enough. The sweating men were helped up out of it. They put on their shirts and jackets and rested on the ground. None of them spoke.

Boards were laid across the pit, covering it. The cable attached to the wreck was laid across the middle and the horses took up the slack. The men got up wearily from the ground and prepared to push from behind. At a signal, the cable snapped taut and sawed down into the ridge of loose earth on the far side of the pit, burying itself. The machine slowly began to move forward onto the boards. A halt was called when the vehicle was poised centered over the pit, its forward half sagging slightly. The cable was removed, and one by one all the boards were removed except the two on which the naked rims rested. Then with the aid of a man rope it was inched forward. Suddenly the wheels slipped off the boards and the full weight of the hulk fell on them. There was a sharp cracking of wood and the whole thing fell neatly into the hole with a crash.

Carnot turned around to Dante. "The rest is not very interesting," he said.

"What will they do with the leftover dirt?"

"Carry it into the woods and scatter it around. They'll put leaves over it. You won't see a thing when they're through."

"I didn't think it would work."

"It's better than leaving it around. It will give them something to think about."

They walked toward the road. Overhead, through the trees the sky seemed to be deepening.

"It will be dawn soon," Dante said.

"Well, let it come. Everything is buried. We gave them a large grave, at least."

It was with a slight shock that Dante suddenly realized that the dead Germans were still inside their vehicle. He turned and looked back. All he could see was the glimmer of light through the trees; all he could hear was the slicing of the many shovels and the splash of earth and stones on the hollow armor plate.

On the road, they passed four old men making slow backward progress with their brooms. None of the old men looked up as Dante and Carnot passed at the side of the road. When they passed the place where the tree had been felled, there wasn't a trace of anything. The crowd of men had disappeared as though vanished into thin air. They turned off the road before they reached the field and went through the woods toward the farm. The circus wagons were gone.

"How is it we didn't see their tracks on the road back there?" Dante asked.

"They went across the back field to the other road. They'll be nearly to the village by now."

They walked on in silence. Twice Dante noticed armed sentries standing in the shadows near the edge of the field. They passed behind them. Carnot called out softly who they were but didn't pause. Dante noticed that he'd put his arm back in its sling and was cradling it with his other arm. The bandage on his hand was saturated with fresh blood.

"That was very good," Carnot said as they came in sight of the farmhouse through the trees.

"This is a very efficient group."

"It's three groups. Yes, they are good," Carnot said.

"How did they manage to drop that tree like that?"

"It was already cut, with a rope holding it. There was one at the other end of the field too. All they had to do was hit the rope with an ax."

"Does your arm hurt?" Dante asked.

"Yes."

"Badly?"

"It hurts too much to tell," Carnot said. "It'll be all right."

They turned off the path to the farmhouse and started toward a low barn beyond, which Dante took to be a stable. The barn looked abandoned.

"Is this where we'll stay tonight?" Dante asked.

"You mean *today*. No. This is all over. No one stays in this area. Everyone has forgotten they were ever here."

"Where will we sleep?"

"We won't. We have a long walk ahead of us."

"Where to?" Dante asked.

Carnot gestured vaguely with his good arm. "Nowhere," he said. "Just south. Our business is finished here."

XIII

The first necessity was getting settled in the quarters Carnot had arranged. Nice was not unfamiliar ground, but Dante knew he would have to be careful. Times might have changed since he'd last worked in Nice for any length of time—although with the expectation of an Allied landing in everyone's mind, things might be easier. He had agreed, after Carnot's detailed description, that the Hôtel de Home would be satisfactory; Carnot had used it once himself on a previous occasion. He had sketched for Dante its interior layout and ground plan. All outside rooms were served by balconies from which it would be a simple matter, in emergency, to climb to the ground. The building had only four stories, and the outside walls were covered with Victorian latticework that was nothing more than an elaborate fire escape, for only sparse vines grew on it. The grounds were covered with a tangle of neglected palm gardens and a thick wall which could easily be vaulted. The hotel was private, comfortable, and still enjoyed an air of run-down respectability.

It had once been a favorite resort of middle-class British spinsters, who before the war took refuge there from the bone-aching island winters of the North Atlantic and passed their afternoons and even mornings in the Casino diligently recording each spin of the wheel. *Systemières* they were called by the bored croupiers who manned the low-stakes, daytime tables. But the system players were gone with the system; the wheels no longer turned for them. The last bewildered tenants of the Hôtel de Home had been shepherded out of their lodgings by a harried young man from the British consulate in the final days before Dunkirk. Now it was more or less a convalescent home for old men whose families could somehow or other find the money to pigeonhole them in style. But essentially it was still a hotel. There were even rooms for transients, although the permanent weathered sign outside on the door still read *Complet,* a relic from more prosperous days.

What the Hôtel de Home lacked in luxury was more than made up for in musty cleanliness. The rugs were threadbare and the curtains in the rooms were laundered thin, but there was no dust anywhere. It looked as though it was still swept and scrubbed every week; the unblemished gilt on the cage-elevator that didn't work made it look as if it ought to—it seemed only temporarily out of order, the door always open invitingly, the faded red velvet cushions on the seat inside plumped and brushed until the nap stood up. On the wall beside the elevator was a sign, in English, that read, *Please not more than three persons in the lift!* Dante was struck by the place. In contrast to so many hotels he had seen in France during the war, the Hôtel de Home seemed unchanged, even cheerful in its threadbare way, as though everything was being held in readiness for the day when the old residents would return. Nothing was missing—nothing, that is, except the comma in the sign by the elevator. But undoubtedly that had always been missing.

Dante was shocked when he realized that the kindly-looking middle-aged woman, who looked rather like a British spinster herself in her worn tweeds, blithely assumed an evil purpose behind their engaging the rooms—she actually winked at him. "It is very quiet here. Your friends have the connecting rooms," she said. "She will be able to rest afterward. You shouldn't let her get up too soon, but she will have good rest here, and it is *very* private."

However, the evil presumption was reassuring—it gave the undertaking more, and thus less, of a sub rosa aspect. The place was apparently less savory than it looked—he wondered with amusement what flight of fancy had moved Carnot to invent such a cover story. At least there'd be no trouble with Madame talking.

The woman led him up one flight of stairs and showed him the room. It was actually the center room of a suite of three. The connecting doors were closed. Heavily furnished with somber brown nondescript furniture, the room was only vaguely late Victorian. It looked like a French bourgeois conception of how to make an Anglican lady feel at home. The proprietress was dressed more or less in the same spirit.

"Your friends must be napping," she said, nodding at the closed connecting doors. Then Dante got a real shock. "Do you by chance speak English?" she asked suddenly, as he walked around inspecting the room. Dante smiled, felt a chill sense of danger, and shook his head no.

"I have never been out of France in my life," he said.

"Pity," said the woman. "I'm afraid I'm forgetting it. One must practice a language to keep it up. I ask every one of my guests if they speak English. There's an old veteran upstairs who speaks a little, but not enough. Pity."

"The room is very satisfactory," said Dante, to change the subject.

"Monsieur is very fortunate," said the proprietress. "When Madame first called about a week ago I was afraid I would have nothing for some time. But then suddenly—poof!—I had this. Have you arranged for her doctor?"

Dante felt a tinge of uncertainty. "When was it Madame first came to see you?" he asked casually, mentally puzzling over Carnot's omitting to communicate the cover story he'd used.

"Oh, it was over a week ago," said the woman. "Of course I told her I had nothing and then . . ."

"Yes," said Dante, cutting her off.

"Here is your key," said the woman. Dante felt her sweaty palm on his as she pressed the wooden ball with the key attached into his hand. "There is another key, but Mademoiselle took it when she went out a while ago." For an instant he found himself staring into her watery blue eyes and was astounded at the insolent invitation he saw there. It jarred him out of himself. She held her hand on his for an instant too long; then she smiled a grotesque crockery smile and turned and went through the door, passing close to him, brushing him. He smelled her. "If you'll come downstairs I'll show you where you'll hang it," she said.

Dante almost failed to notice that the woman had forgotten herself, had referred to Adriane as "Mademoiselle," instead of the more tactful "Madame."

He followed her down the stairs, watching her hams under the tweed skirt as she labored from side to side, her legs working up and down alternately like pistons. What kind of a place is this? he wondered. He had been too dumfounded by her brassy attempt at coquetry to even answer her. On first impression she had looked like somebody's grandmother, and then, suddenly, there she was leering at him like an old and practiced jade. In the lower hall she showed him where he could hang his key, and where the button for the night bell was; and the light switch, which she said was timed to go out after four minutes.

"If you ever come in late, don't be afraid to ring the bell," she said archly. "I sleep right here on the ground floor. I only lock the front door at ten."

Dante mumbled his thanks. She flashed the chinaware smile again, and this time he saw the gold in her teeth. He was anxious to return upstairs.

When Dante went back to his room alone he found that, as Carnot had promised, Antoine Berger had been delivered intact; Carnot had given up his hostage. The only reservation Carnot had made was the armed guard who was installed as Berger's unhappy roommate.

Berger's room communicated with Dante's through a huge Edwardian bathroom which had formerly been closed off and locked on Dante's side. Together with Adriane's room on the other side of Dante's, the rooms made an interconnecting suite served by a common balcony. Dante's first reaction to Berger's presence was satisfaction. In his own curious way Carnot had proved his good faith. But on the other hand Berger was an added responsibility, a new fact to cope with. He could be trouble. And trouble at this late date could be catastrophic. For there was nothing to do now but wait for instructions to come by radio from Algiers—he had no idea how to get Berger out. But whatever happened Dante himself fully expected to sit tight and wait for the Allies.

He still hoped, against growing anxiety, for a southern landing. For otherwise the mission he'd just accomplished had been accomplished largely in vain. He thought of the two men he'd lost—Mike, his radio operator, and Orchard with his sullen vision of Utopia. If the southern landing didn't come the Germans would pull out and leave the country to anarchy, fomenting anarchy, abetting it, in a last gesture of contempt and vengeance. This anxiety overshadowed the problems of the moment—Berger and all the rest. Worse than anarchy was the very real possibility of a premature uprising which would be crushed without quarter or mercy. With weapons he was helping to procure for them, a few drunken revolutionaries could drench the countryside in blood. Innocents would be drawn to their death in a whirlpool of violence.

As the expectation of invasion increased, Dante could see a new attitude among the people, a dangerous attitude. Waiters, long sullen and silent, now showed open contempt for the Germans they served. An atmosphere as explosive as gasoline vapor pervaded the coastal towns. The first spark of armed uprising could touch off insanity and disaster. Dante felt a sharp sense of danger. His own responsibility made the realization of danger even sharper, for he knew with certain knowledge what the German authorities did not. That some men had arms—and ammunition. For he had given them to them. But he also knew that they didn't have them in sufficient quantities to sustain both an initial uprising and an effective defense against the massive reprisals which would surely follow. And the weapons were all new, of the latest American design. One man could by recklessness expose the fact that new weapons were coming in. And the hammer would fall without mercy.

Berger was the least of the problems facing him. Carnot had even offered to return Mike's transmitter to him, but he decided against having it in the hotel. Algiers had helped set up the schedule of drops and would be in a better position to assess the situation than he was. They would decide when or whether to discontinue them. At the moment he had nothing of real urgency to transmit, and although he could transmit in a pinch, his sending was slow and therefore liable to discovery. In the end he asked Carnot to keep the transmitter until such time as he might need it, and Carnot agreed.

Berger's guard was a large, uncommunicative man about forty, stout and slightly balding. He had bland gray eyes and the lined face of a man who had spent his life outdoors squinting into the sun. He had been either a fisherman or a farmer, Dante concluded. When Dante arrived and entered Berger's room the guard merely looked up from his newspaper appraisingly and nodded as Dante introduced himself. Berger sat on the bed looking pale and delicate, as if he had just recovered from a long illness. He wasn't looking at Dante when he came in, but gazing out the window down the long avenue toward the sea. When Dante spoke his name he started and got to his feet. Apparently he was glad to see him. They didn't talk, because the guard remained in the room and Dante was reluctant to ask him to leave. After a brief greeting Dante went back through the bathroom to his own room.

He knocked on Adriane's door in the hope that she might have returned, and when he got no answer he pushed the door open. Stretched out asleep on her bed was Henri.

Dante frowned and closed the door softly. Mentally he cursed Carnot for introducing Henri into their midst. It was as though Carnot had cleaned house and gotten rid of both Berger and Henri, the two weakest links in his security chain, by pushing them onto him. An adolescent drunkard in one room, Dante reflected, and an alleged narcotics addict in the other. They even looked somewhat alike; Berger's features were slightly more refined, but were similar to Henri's.

"Damn her," he said aloud to himself. Then he stopped pacing.

He kicked off his shoes, still hot from the sun-baked streets, and padded about his room in a circle. He was hot and tired, and not a breath of air stirred the heavy string-lace curtains, each insipidly embroidered with two cherubs rampant. The strain of the past few weeks suddenly broke on him in a fit of senseless irritation.

Even now he knew in the back of his mind that he was holding Adriane, not Carnot, responsible for Henri's presence. He was powerless to prevent his irritation from deflecting from Carnot onto her. After all, Henri was *her* brother. And it was she who had saved Berger's skin when she should have gone to warn Lautrec. He remembered Lautrec's betrayal with bitterness. Although he knew he had no unequivocally solid reason for believing that Berger's irresponsibility had directly caused Lautrec's capture, he was certain that Berger's method of operation constituted contributory negligence.

Suddenly he realized that his thinking had taken an ugly turn. In the dim regions of his mind he was thinking that if Berger was killed through his own foolishness it would be a vengeance for Lautrec's capture and a problem off his hands. For a brief instant he was shocked by the unbidden turn of his mind, fascinated, then revolted. In another part of his consciousness a moral alarm sounded with urgent warning. He cleared his mind completely, feeling disgusted with himself, and sat down by the window. Aside from the moral question, this was the sort of thing, he knew, that could destroy a whole mission. Although the thought had only fleetingly crossed his mind, like a fragment of a forgotten melody, he knew now that it too had been there all the time, dormant, unrealized. And that worried him more than anything else. A mere suggestion of evil, the idea of Berger's convenient death, was like the deadly tip of an iceberg dimly glimpsed through a fleeting hole in the fog. The thought of what lay below the surface worried him more now that the vision had receded, now that the fog of rational conscience had closed over the premonition of hidden danger. And like a man engulfed in fog, he stopped, listening to his own heartbeat, peering into that uniform whiteness for another sign, but seeing nothing. His irritation and fatigue were suddenly chastened, forgotten, as he gazed out over the wall toward the hazeless summer sea of turquoise, listening to the silence of the sultry afternoon, alerted to evil, to himself. There were no clouds in the sky. The air was hot and thick and still. Too still. Toward nightfall, with the first stirring of sea wind over the cooling earth, he knew with certainty that it would rain. And he knew his irritation for what it was. It was for her. Because she wasn't there.

An hour later the sun was beginning to wane and Adriane was still not back. He heard Henri get up from the bed in the next room and heard him moving aimlessly about. Partly to avoid talking to Henri, partly to find out where Adriane had gone, he got up from his seat by the window and went into Berger's room again. This time, apparently for no other reason than that he was tired of sitting in the same room, the guard got up without a word and went into Dante's room and closed the door behind him. Berger looked after him in surprise.

"That's the first time he's been out of my sight in forty-eight hours," Berger said with an exaggerated sigh of relief.

"Do you happen to know where Adriane went?" Dante asked.

"She went to the doctor."

"Is she sick?"

"No," Berger said, sighing again. "She thinks she's pregnant."

Dante held his expression rigidly immobile, but slowly experienced an astounding physical sensation throughout every muscle fiber in his body. It was like a sustained series of small electric shocks, or rather the paralyzing grip such shocks produce. It was a new and utterly unfamiliar physical reaction, and a part of his mind involuntarily marveled at the extraordinary sensation. So it wasn't merely a cover story. And yet Berger's words had hardly seemed to carry any meaning at all to him, certainly no conscious impact. It had always been a possibility. He had never consciously avoided the fact that it might happen. He heard himself saying calmly, "How do you know she thinks so? Did she tell you?"

Berger said, "No. The doctor told me. He came to look at my chest. I think I have tuberculosis, you know." Berger seemed to grasp at the idea of his problematical disease. "My mother probably had it. My grandmother told me that it was why she died when she had me. We are all weak . . ." he placed a pale starfish hand on his chest, unconsciously imitating a woman's gesture, ". . . here," he said. "On my mother's side, her family, that is. Good blood is usually thin blood, I'm afraid. Don't you think I look rather pale?" He jumped nervously off the bed and went to the mirror. "Look, my skin is getting perfectly translucent."

"Did the doctor tell her in front of you?" Dante asked, his voice edged with slight annoyance.

Berger turned around and gazed at Dante, lost for a moment. "About my skin? Oh, you mean about her being pregnant—horrible word, pregnant—I wish I could avoid it without being arch—I try not to use it any more than I have to. Don't you agree it's an ugly-sounding word?"

"Did the doctor tell . . ."

"Oh, yes. Matter of fact, he chivvied her about it a little. She was furious with him. I admit it came as a surprise to me, although I had never ruled it out as a possibility, of course. Nature exacts her payment for our smallest pleasures."

Dante stared openly at Berger, almost afraid to press him for his meaning. But Berger must have noticed his expression.

"Oh, I'll give the child a legitimate birthright. You needn't worry about that. I'm somewhat of a puritan, but I have a strong sense of family. I never thought I would marry, though, although now with this disease killing me off I must confess that I'm rather glad to leave an heir behind—any heir at all. My grandmother would never approve of her but who cares. *Noblesse oblige.*"

"What did you . . ."

"She was a servant working in Dujardin's house when I came here. I had no idea, of course, that she was planted there by that small ape Carnot. She worked her seduction for an ulterior purpose, I know that now. But I think the poor misguided girl fell in love with me. Or perhaps I'm just vain enough to have it that way. I got rather emotional after it happened the first time. I made her swear to me . . . but that doesn't matter. I was upset at first. I had always prided myself that I had never known a woman. I still insist that a woman is only a necessary instrument of procreation, essential to the preservation of the unbroken line of the family. So, naturally, I was upset at first. She got me drunk one night and . . ."

"I'd rather not listen to your fall from grace," Dante said caustically. He suppressed an astounded urge to strike Berger across the face with his open hand.

"Well, of course one can be a puritan without being stuffy . . ." Berger said, taken aback.

"Where did you get your ideas? Were you brought up on this sort of sickness?"

Berger stared at Dante coldly.

"My ideas are my own. If you call this world healthy then my ideas are sick. But then you are no doctor to judge sickness. You believe all that nonsense of the so-called rational Enlightenment. You believe in the Reformation and the sanctity of the merchant class. You believe in Rousseau and the general will and liberalism. You are against authority and the True Church. You are . . ."

"Who is the doctor?"

"What?"

"I said, who is the doctor?"

"I don't know. But I certainly know that you are not, and neither was Rousseau. He was a barbarian, a vulgar quack."

"I mean the doctor who came here, you damned fool," Dante said.

"Oh. I don't know his name. Someone Carnot got for me. A Communist, as you might guess."

"Where did she go today?"

"He couldn't examine her here. He made an appointment for her to come to his office. He's a little sort of bald man with dirty fingernails and bad breath. He probably makes his living doing abortions for the local comrades."

"Look, Berger . . ."

"How should I know what she's going for? She has no fear of eternal damnation. What's to stop her? I've *said* I'd marry her. My conscience is clear. Charles heard my confession."

"Charles?"

"The priest at the farm. He's still a Catholic, you know, in spite of the fact that he is forced to work with Carnot."

"How do you explain his working with Carnot?"

"The Church must have its reasons. I think I've almost reconverted her brother. I'm working on this oaf of a guard now. He handcuffs me to him when he goes to sleep."

"You sleep in the same bed?"

"I have to. I can't bear it but what can I do about it? I can't sleep because I can't stand anyone touching me. I have a horror of people touching me. Sometimes at night, he tries to hug me in his sleep. It turns my stomach. I think he thinks I'm some whore in his dreams."

"You lead a very hard life, Antoine," Dante said. "Is your real name Antoine Berger or is it a cover?"

"I have better reasons than you for using a false name."

"Your mother was French?"

"My lineage is none of your affair. If my mother was French, it would be none of your concern."

"And your father is American, is that it?"

"I don't recognize my father except as the Fourth Commandment requires me to. I honor him in my mother's memory. Beyond that I have nothing to do with him. I honor his memory as best I can. As I would if he were dead. But as I say, none of this concerns you."

"Are you sure you don't mean the Fifth Commandment?"

"Obviously, you favor the Protestant version in everything—in theology as well as in history."

At that moment the door from the bathroom opened and the guard came back into the room. He glanced at Dante and sat down heavily. He lit a cigarette and examined the tip of it for a long moment. Then he swung his chair around to face the window and looked out at the long splash of color that gilded the western sky of the dying sun. Cigarette smoke curled in wreaths about his head.

Dante turned to go. Berger stopped him. "Perhaps I was indiscreet to tell you what I told you. Perhaps you'd better not mention it to her. I don't want to embarrass her. It's only right that I should know, but for others . . ."

Dante was struggling to keep his gorge from rising in his throat. He listened to Berger's incredibly assured tone of intimacy, and was suddenly seized with a brutal desire to puncture Berger's blind egotism and to destroy his assurance. Dante knew that Berger had hurt him irrationally, perhaps witlessly, and yet it seemed as though Berger was deliberately baiting him. He struck at Berger by striking at her. Ignoring the presence of the guard, Dante looked calmly at Berger, who still stood with his hand on his arm. Then he said, "As one gentleman to another, I assume you know that she's Carnot's mistress."

There was a short silence. Berger fidgeted nervously. Then he smiled and said, "No, you're wrong. I made her swear to me . . ."

"How much of a fool are you really?" Dante demanded, his voice rising in unreasoning irritation at Berger's stainless armor of blind conceit.

"You don't understand. She told me that Carnot—had an accident once. He . . . he's emasculated. I asked Charles too. He confirmed it."

The speechless interval was suddenly interrupted by an explosion of laughter from the guard. He didn't turn around or move from his position of having his back to them. He could have been laughing at something he'd just remembered. Only it wasn't that way.

Berger spun toward the guard. "Do you think a priest would lie?" he demanded shrilly. The guard didn't answer him, only laughed again.

Berger appealed to Dante. "Do you think a priest would lie to me about something like that. Do you?"

Dante smiled, feeling bitter satisfaction. He turned toward the door. He opened it slowly, then paused, as though studying the grain of the wood. "Perhaps Charles has a taste for jokes," he said. Behind him he heard another grunt of amusement from the guard. Berger said nothing.

Dante stepped through the door and closed it behind him without looking around. Then through the thick door he heard a gruff shout from the guard, the scraping of a chair, a scuffling, and then a tremendous crash of bedsprings. He could picture in his mind Berger furiously attacking the guard from behind, perhaps beating with his frail fists on the balding head, the guard's surprised attempt to rise. In the end it sounded as though he had lifted Berger over his head and thrown him down onto the bed. Whatever happened, it was now all over. From the room behind him Dante heard only silence.

He was surprised to find himself shaking from the suppressed emotion and anger he had experienced in the conversation with Berger. He felt disgusted with himself, degraded, for allowing himself the petty vengeance of his final remark to Berger. One thing was certain, he would have to avoid any further conversation with Berger if he was to avoid strangling him with his bare hands. The man's weakness revolted him to the point where he simply wanted to extinguish it.

He stood in the bathroom, unwilling to open the door into his own room. He had no desire to face Adriane's brother in the wake of his encounter with Antoine Berger—who might have been Henri's brother for all the similarities between them. He leaned against the sink for a moment, conscious only of being wrenched by rage and frustration. Adriane was uppermost in his mind. She was the source of the conflict and confusion he felt within himself. He stood with his eyes closed for a long minute, trying to sort out some kind of order from the sudden chaos his mind and heart had been plunged into.

He gradually found one clear fact which was solid and sure: he was tired, badly tired. It explained a large part of his inability to cope with his feelings. A bathroom was no place to stand and think. A phrase from some forgotten book or classroom drifted across his consciousness: *To understand the universe one must begin with the simplest purpose.* A bathroom was no place to be standing, driven into limbo by his own misunderstanding of its purpose. A bathroom was to bathe in. He opened his eyes and took a deep breath. Without thinking he reached over the sink and turned on the water. But when he finished, he could find no towel to dry his hands.

Adriane made it clear that she had no time to answer questions; she sent Dante into his own room to set the places on the heavy oak trestle table. Of the three rooms, his was the only one with a table big enough for six. He dragged the long narrow table from its place by the window into the center of the room. The few pieces of silverware rattled loosely in the drawer. The table, the cutlery, the bedsheet tablecloth—everything was makeshift. But under the circumstances it was a brave effort; the prospect of a dinner made him feel less depressed.

Adriane had come back carrying the black-market groceries she'd procured. She greeted Dante as though she'd seen him yesterday. She seemed in good spirits and in a hurry to prepare the food. She didn't even take off her hat. Dante stood in the doorway between the rooms and watched as 'she prepared to start her work. She'd improvised a tiny kitchen with a gas ring in the bathroom off her own room. The blackout curtains were drawn and the room was close and stuffy. Henri sat in the corner by the bed, reading, saying nothing after Dante greeted him. Dante gathered from Adriane that the evening meal was to be a small celebration of the successful airdrop. Carnot was coming, and bringing wine. Berger was to be allowed out of his room for the occasion.

In a way, he was glad there hadn't been time to talk with her. It would be far better to wait until later, after they had eaten. He was beginning to feel hungry, and knew from experience that his upset mood would be less urgent after he'd eaten something, perhaps drunk a little wine. For the present he simply felt drained, tired.

Seeing her had given him a momentary uplift, but there was a certain distance in her manner. And when she had no time for him the cloud seemed to settle again. But he tried to keep his mood to himself. He decided he needed rest. After setting the meager silverware out on the table, he took a nap.

He hadn't really intended to sleep when he lay down on the couch. But when he awoke, he awoke to the sound of Carnot's voice hale and cheerful in the next room. The light in the room had changed; it was nearly dark. The smell of the wine sauce for the rabbit filled the room with a heavy good odor that sharpened his hunger immediately.

Feeling rested, he got up and went to the connecting bathroom. But as he opened the door, Berger and his guard came out. The guard sniffed the steamy air with approval. Berger didn't look at Dante, but avoided his eyes. He had a blue mark under his left cheekbone.

Dante went into the bathroom and closed the door after him. He took his time washing.

When he came out of the bathroom, Carnot had drawn the blackout curtains and turned the lights on and was drawing chairs to the table. The rest were standing, waiting to sit down. Adriane still had her apron on; she was picking at a knot to take it off.

Carnot saw Dante and raised the bottle of wine in his hand and waggled it back and forth like a hand bell. He was no longer wearing a sling. "He has arisen," he said to the others. Dante sensed that Carnot had already had some alcohol. Adriane smiled slightly. Carnot turned back to Dante. "You were dead to the world when I came in," he said.

"I was tired. I didn't think I'd sleep so long."

"You slept for over an hour," Adriane said. "You look better."

They sat down to the table, Adriane at the end nearest her make-shift kitchen, Carnot at the other. The other four were widely spaced along both sides of the peculiarly shaped table. It was so narrow that opposite plates would almost have touched if Dante hadn't staggered them a little to make more room. Dante found himself at Adriane's right, with Berger directly opposite. Next to Dante sat Henri, on Carnot's left. Opposite Henri was Berger's guard.

"There's only one knife," Adriane said, "so you'll have to share it."

"We won't need a knife for *your* rabbit, *ma chérie,*" Carnot said.

Carnot was in a gallant good mood; he looked better than Dante had ever seen him. He turned the corkscrew into the cork and looked at Dante, smiling. "She's a very good cook for a woman," he said. "Someone should marry her."

Berger quickly dropped his eyes to his empty plate, his pale face reddening with guilt or anger—Dante couldn't have said which. But Dante saw that both Carnot and Adriane had noticed Berger's reaction to Carnot's remark. A frown crossed Carnot's face for only an instant, then vanished. Dante avoided Carnot's eyes. The cork popped out of the bottle Carnot was wrestling with.

"First, a celebration toast," Carnot said. "A good old petit-bour-geois toast." He filled the assorted tumblers and handleless cups on the table before him and passed them down one at a time. Dante got a cup with a handle, the only one.

Carnot stood up. "A toast to our continued successes," he said, looking at Dante. Everyone rose except Berger, who sat determinedly not touching his glass. Carnot looked at him, decided to ignore him. He shrugged off Berger, and smiled again as he lifted his glass, the only proper wineglass at the table. He'd taken it for himself to dress up the toast.

The toast was drunk and everyone sat down. Berger still stared at his plate, his hands in his lap.

Adriane uncovered the tureen. A cloud of savory steam escaped, and drops of moisture dripped off the underside of the ill-fitting cover. Everyone leaned forward to look inside. Joints of rabbit floated in a heavy reddish-brown sauce. Adriane served Berger first, then Dante.

Then the bowl was slid down the center of the narrow table to Henri and the guard. There were only five plates; Carnot had to eat out of the bowl.

Bread was passed around, and everyone except Berger broke off a large piece. The wine was passed again and another bottle opened, and for a while everyone ate in silence.

Berger picked at his food, and pushed it away half finished. Carnot looked up, first at Berger, then questioningly at Dante. Dante said nothing and continued eating. Berger's guard spooned into Berger's abandoned plate without even breaking the rhythm of his moving hand. He continued to take alternately, first from his, then from Berger's plate, until finally matters resolved to mopping up sauce with a chunk of bread. This, too, he did alternately. Berger sat ignoring him.

Carnot was eating again, now mopping up the last of the sauce in the tureen with gusto, stopping now and then to wash down the bread with wine. The second bottle was passed again; the guard finished it off. Carnot reached under the table for the third bottle and gave it to the guard, who had now finished both plates.

The guard held the bottle in one huge hand, as though about to strangle it, and opened it with a single twist of the corkscrew.

The cork made a sound like a loud kiss.

Carnot looked up from his enterprise inside the tureen and glanced down the table at Adriane, who was eating slowly, her eyes on her plate. Pointing with his piece of bread at her, he said again to Dante, "She'd make some man a good *bonne à tout faire*. This sauce is good, even if you did make it in a bathroom, *ma chérie*."

There was a moment of silence. Berger self-consciously dropped his hands off the table. Dante knew that Carnot was now watching Berger carefully, despite the offhand manner. He was probing. Dante wished he had picked another time.

"I mean it," Carnot said, addressing no one but watching Berger out of the corner of his eye. "Someone should take this one back to America. She is an excellent cook. I heard before the war that American women are bad cooks. As long as you have to marry a woman, you may as well marry one who can cook."

There was another silence. Dante knew it was futile to step in. Carnot had seen Berger's reaction and was bent on exploring it fully; nothing would stop him until he had got to the bottom of the puzzle. Adriane seemed to be ignoring the turn the one-sided conversation had taken.

"She knows how to keep a man happy," Carnot continued, his voice even gayer. He was talking to the guard now, but still watching Berger out of the corner of his eye. "Even a young man," he said. The guard smirked and grunted, nudged Berger.

Berger couldn't take any more. His knuckles were white on the edge of the table, as white as the cloth. He made an agitated movement and started to get up. The guard reached behind him and pulled him down before he was even out of his chair. Berger's hand slashed the air with a furious gesture; and his untouched wine tumbler was knocked over onto the white bedsheet.

The brief violence of the spilled wine stunned the ensuing silence. Adriane's fork balanced suspended before her open mouth. The guard frowned but didn't move. Carnot feigned complete surprise at Berger's sudden outburst. Dante felt angry at Carnot's dogged courting of unpleasantness. But it had happened now. There was nothing to do about it. Henri kept his eyes on his own wine cup. Down the narrow length of the table and down the hanging side of the bedsheet, a large, slowly spreading crimson stain grew in size as it spread and was absorbed in the cloth. Everyone watched but did nothing to stop it. It continued to edge outward from the fallen glass, which had broken in two precise halves where it was knocked over. Berger sat, his face suffused with confusion and anger, looking at the broken glass. No one said anything for nearly a minute.

Finally Carnot, looking around the table, said, "What disease does he have today?" He didn't look at Berger at all.

The guard snorted. "He's crazy," he said. They were the first words Dante had heard him speak since he'd been in the hotel. His voice was raspy, as though rusty from disuse.

"I don't have to take this," Berger said, his choked voice lurching with lamed fury. His voice was almost a squeak.

"What's the matter, *petit?*" Carnot asked with false solicitude. "All I said was that our mistress was an excellent cook."

"You've been baiting me ever since . . ."

"Go on," Carnot said suddenly, dropping all pretense of gentleness. "Since when?"

"I refuse to talk to scum like you," Berger said.

"Then keep quiet and let the scum eat in peace," Carnot said sullenly.

Dante noticed that Henri was concentrating very hard on his plate. There were tiny beads of sweat on his temples. Adriane sat looking into her folded hands, nothing showing in her face. Her food was unfinished. Dante felt his anger mounting, but decided to say nothing. He hoped that Carnot, having satisfied himself, would change the subject. But Carnot wasn't ready to change it yet. After a moment of silence he turned to the guard, holding his wineglass for a refill.

"What's his trouble?" Carnot asked the guard, jerking his head toward the white-faced Berger.

The guard shrugged and poured wine into Carnot's glass.

Carnot repeated, "What's his trouble? I want to know. I came here to celebrate, but now I want to know."

The guard didn't look at Adriane. He only said, "Her." Adriane didn't move or look up. Her face was composed, as though she was listening to her own thoughts.

Carnot looked at her, his face exaggeratedly dawning comprehension. "Oh, so that's the way it is." Then he turned to Berger and asked, "What's the matter, *petit,* isn't she taking care of you like she used to?"

Berger turned and hissed, "She's your mistress, isn't she?"

For a moment Carnot looked taken aback, genuinely puzzled. "Yes," he said, "naturally she's my mistress. She's not my mother, nor my wife, nor my sister. If a woman isn't one of those things, she's your mistress. So what?"

"I won't talk with scum," Berger said. Carnot merely sighed and shook his head.

"Poor Antoine," Carnot said. "Yesterday tuberculosis. Today madness. What surprise will you have for us tomorrow, *petit?"*

Berger didn't answer. Carnot turned to the guard.

The guard took a swallow of wine. Without looking at Carnot he said, "He thought he was the only one."

Carnot looked at the guard closely, then at Berger. Berger was watching his every move. Then Carnot gave a roar of laughter, throwing his head back and laughing for several seconds while everyone watched him. It was false laughter. Then he stopped. Silence.

Carnot spoke softly, with menace in his voice. "You like to own things, don't you, *petit? My* house. *My* dog. *My* cow. *My* factory. *My* woman. If you don't own it, it's no good. All right, let me tell you a few things. You'll never be man enough to own your own woman."

Berger pursed his lips and made a funny face, as though trying to gather enough saliva between his dry cheeks to be able to spit. Carnot watched him, his eyes cold, impassive, deadly. Finally the twitching of Berger's face stopped.

"You'll never own a woman unless someone gives her to you. I gave this one to you, you little fool. I needed access to your room at Dujardin's. You always kept the door locked, do you remember?"

Berger stared at him.

"You kept it locked, and people don't lock doors unless they have something they don't want other people to have. Locks were invented by people who own things. You even locked the door at night when she was in your room."

"You pig," Berger said, turning to Adriane. She turned her head slowly and gazed at him abstractedly, her eyes not seeming to see him. Dante felt overcome by a great urge to jump up and shake her back to reality—or to strike Berger—or both. But somehow any gesture seemed useless. Forces were at work that put action beyond his reach. The time for action had swept past him, and now he felt that something like this was predestined to happen. The best thing was to let it happen. He felt suddenly very tired. An inexplicable lassitude separated him from the event. He looked at her, and understood finally: she felt the same.

"I didn't know what you had in your room, *petit,* but I found out. I found out and I have it."

Berger's eyes narrowed, like a cornered animal's.

Carnot assumed a conversational tone. "You kept a diary, a very literary sort of . . ."

Berger half rose in his chair, his body tensed, his hands pressing down on the table. The guard held him down by his belt with one hand.

"You stole my journal!" he said. He looked first at Carnot, then at Adriane, then back at Carnot. Dante watched him in disbelief.

"Your what?" Dante blurted, his voice cracking. He was shaken out of his daze. The mention of Berger's journal touched him like an electric shock. "You kept a diary? Are you completely insane?" Dante was on his feet himself now, glaring open-mouthed at Berger.

"Yes," Carnot said mildly, "and very complete too. It even had a title page: *The Journal of an Unsung Hero.* He was going to publish it after the war. It says so on page one."

Dante simply stared at Berger, unable to say anything.

"I didn't use any names in it," Berger said defensively.

Dante said, "My God." Then he dropped back onto his chair.

"Of course you used no names," said Carnot. "But how long do you think it took us to figure out who your X's and Y's and Z's were? How long? I'll tell you, *petit.* As fast as Charles could translate it, that's how long."

Dante looked up, choked again on his own words. "You wrote it in *English?*" he said. "Here, in occupied France, an agent keeps a diary in *English?*" Dante whirled around to Carnot. "You have this thing in your possession?"

"Not exactly on my person," Carnot said, smiling unpleasantly.

Dante knew better than to ask Carnot for it then and there. Carnot waited for him to ask, but Dante said nothing.

Carnot turned again to Berger. "So now, my little cabbage, you know why I gave you a woman to play with. Frankly I didn't think it would work with you. But she's a better woman than I gave her credit for. She almost made a man out of you."

This time Berger did spit, not at Carnot, but on the table in front of him. Carnot looked down at it. He said, "What do you expect that to do, *petit,* burn a hole in the cloth?"

Berger stood furiously, his face working, the guard holding onto his belt with both hands now, pulling him back down. Berger's legs collapsed and he fell like a sack of kindling wood onto his chair again. The guard's face wasn't angry, simply bored.

"What makes you think Dujardin didn't examine your diary too?" Carnot asked. "Have you thought of that, *petit?*" Berger didn't answer him.

Dante looked at Berger. The first shock had worn off. His mind raced ahead. The damage was done, he thought, but still the problem remained of getting Berger out of France—he would have to be handled carefully. He started to reason with Berger. "But didn't you realize that you were violating the most fundamental . . ."

Berger broke in. "They're scum. Can't you see that? Scum. She was coming to me at night from . . . from *him*."

"And from others," Carnot said mildly. "You may as well understand, *petit*. This group supplies itself. She is here to take care of the needs of the group. She cooks, she sews, she cleans up, she . . ."

"That's enough," Dante said angrily. Adriane hadn't changed her expression. It was as though she were in another room. Dante felt the emptiness in her eyes, and it filled him with pain and anger, and shame.

Carnot looked at Dante in surprise. "What, you too? You've been part of the group. She's taken care of you, hasn't she? Fed you, made your bed . . ."

Berger was livid. "You?" he said, leaning across toward Dante. Then he laughed a quick spasmodic laugh. "How classic," he said. "How utterly classic."

"Quiet, *petit*. If you're a good boy, perhaps I'll let you enjoy her again before you leave."

"That's enough," Dante said, rising from his chair.

"She's pregnant!" Berger said, his voice rising almost to a scream.

Carnot stopped short. He looked at Adriane. "Ah, so?" he said. "Then, my congratulations. To all of us." She didn't raise her eyes.

"She can't know whose it is," Berger said, with an ugly attempt at a sneer. Dante could have wrung his neck. Adriane's face showed nothing.

Carnot looked again at Berger. Then he said slowly, "It's no one's. No one owns a child. You like to own things, *petit*. It doesn't matter which tooth of the saw hits you."

There was silence. Adriane got up slowly and walked to her room, leaving her food unfinished. The door stayed open behind her. Henri left the table and followed her, uncertain whether Carnot would let him go. But Carnot said nothing. He watched for a moment, then filled the glasses, one for Berger included. Berger started to push the glass away. Carnot leaped up and reached across the table, grabbing Berger's wrist.

"If you don't drink this toast," he said softly, crooning his words, "I'll kill you right here. Right here." He pounded the table gently with his other fist. Berger went even paler than he was. Carnot took the Luger out of his shirt and laid it gently on the table wrapped in its oily rag. "Every drop of it, *petit*," he said softly. "Every drop of it. So don't shake too much or you'll spill it."

In utter silence they watched Carnot fill Berger's glass to the absolute brim. He filled the others only half full.

"A toast," he said. "To Adriane, and to the child. It's not *whose* it is, *petit*, but *what* it is. Do you understand? Now drink."

Dante forgot to drink watching Berger lift the glass. His hand shook. But he didn't spill a drop. When Berger put his empty glass down Dante turned to Carnot.

"To Adriane," he said. And drank.

After Berger retired with his guard to his own room, Carnot got up from the table and softly closed the other door. Then he sat down again. Dante and Carnot were alone in the room. The last bottle of wine stood half finished amid the refuse of the calamitous dinner. The wine stain had dried to a large purple splotch, the broken glass lay where Berger had knocked it over; an unfinished joint of rabbit lay congealed in the cold sauce where Adriane had left it. The bedsheet tablecloth was pulled askew where Berger had been struggling with the guard. Carnot looked around at the wreckage and shrugged. He pulled out a pack of English cigarettes and offered Dante one. Dante shook his head without looking up.

"What's the matter?" Carnot asked.

Dante eyed the pack of cigarettes moodily. "Where'd you get those?" he asked sullenly. "Have you gone crazy too?"

"I saved them. That pilot gave them to me. I was saving them for tonight."

"You made a fine celebration," Dante said sarcastically.

"It wasn't my fault," Carnot said. He sounded chagrined.

Dante looked at him. "Why say that? I watched you. You knew you were putting the needle in him."

Carnot shrugged. He said nothing, lit a cigarette.

"What's the matter with you?" Dante said, letting his irritation out. "Do you think it will be easier to get him out of the country after telling him you have his diary? I gave you credit for more sense."

"I'm sorry," Carnot said. "He gets under my skin."

Dante sighed. "I know," he said. "He got under mine this afternoon. I can't blame you without blaming myself."

Carnot said nothing.

"What are you going to do with the diary?" Dante asked.

"Whatever you say."

"I'd like to have it. I may need it."

"Need it?"

"I'll have to justify my action. You understand I'll have to place Berger under formal arrest."

"Why?"

"He's made it clear that he won't leave the country except under arrest. He's making me stick my neck out as far as he can."

"Aren't you supposed to take him back?" Carnot asked.

"Or send him. But not at gunpoint, which is what I'll be doing."

"What do you know about him?" Carnot asked, leaning back in his chair.

"If I knew anything about him, I wouldn't tell you. But the truth is I know less about him than you do. You've at least read his diary."

"Didn't they tell you anything?"

"I think his mother was French and his father American."

"His father is alive," Carnot said. "His mother is dead."

"How do you know?"

Carnot smiled. "I've read his diary."

Dante nodded. "Did Dujardin read it too?"

"I don't know. I don't think so," Carnot said. He looked at the closed door to Adriane's room. "She said he kept it well hidden. It took her three hours to find it. It was in the lining of his suitcase."

"How did she know he had it?" Dante asked.

"Every morning when she cleaned his room, there were new pencil shavings in his wastebasket. He sharpened his pencil with a pocket knife. There was always a pencil on his desk but never any paper. After she left him at night the light would stay on for an hour or so. I told her to look in his baggage. At that time we weren't sure who he was, or even if he was an agent. But he was staying in Dujardin's house. That was enough to make me curious. Finally she found it."

"I see. Who knows about it besides you?"

"Charles translated it for me. I didn't tell him what it was or where I got it. Charles doesn't ask questions. Besides her and Charles, no one knows about it except me."

"You didn't show it to your inspector general friend from Paris?" Dante asked. "The gentleman I met the first day at the farm?"

Carnot snorted. "Why should I explain where I get my information? Let them go on thinking I'm a wizard. If I told Picard how I learned Berger was an American he wouldn't be so impressed."

"If you told . . . who?"

"The name doesn't matter. Anybody," Carnot said. "If you tell all you know, everyone gets as smart as you. Then they don't need *you* any more."

"I see. Then when can you give it to me?"

"I'll put it in your hand when your feet leave the ground," Carnot said. "Or when the Americans land. Not before. But I'll let you read it, if you wish."

"That's fair enough," Dante said. "I'll have one of your Gold Flakes on that."

Carnot tossed Dante the package of cigarettes. Dante took one and leaned back in his chair to light it.

Suddenly Carnot said, "You'll have to watch him yourself tomorrow. I can't spare a single man from this operation."

"What operation?"

"The circus arrives tomorrow afternoon. After that we have a few funerals to attend. Would you like to join us?"

Dante frowned. "He needs a guard."

"Don't worry. If you come, I'll leave the guard—I'd rather have you. We'll be back the next day," Carnot said.

"Are you staying here tonight?" Dante asked. "You can have the couch."

Carnot looked at his watch. "No. I'm just killing time. I have a little spade work to do before the sun comes up. We could finish this wine, I suppose." Carnot slopped wine into two glasses and slid one across the rumpled wine stain to Dante.

"Then we're not going to the camp tomorrow. I'd still like to see your training facilities as soon as possible."

"Next week," Carnot said. "The circus comes first. When we're finished here you'll take the train by yourself to St. Raphaël. There's a bus at ten that goes to Toulon. You'll get off at La Four and walk into St. Tropez. You'll arrive ahead of the circus." Carnot looked grim. "That funeral will be a real one—we lost some hostages there last night."

"Will they release the bodies?"

"Tomorrow probably. We'll hold the funeral when we can."

"You still want to meet in the fish market at St. Tropez?"

Carnot nodded. "At twelve noon sharp every day—until further notice. I won't wait, and neither will you. If you ever miss me go to the church and find Charles. He'll have information on any change of plans."

"Cross-signs?"

"A newspaper. If it's in my left hand, don't come near me; in my right, it's clear. The same for you. I don't think you'll have to worry. Watch your step getting on the bus, though. And they'll check your papers in St. Maxime."

"Did you have any trouble coming up?"

"I came a different way," Carnot said. "I had some errands to run in Grasse."

Dante nodded. Carnot carefully broke off the glowing tip of his cigarette and slipped the unsmoked half back into the package. He sat silent for a long moment, looking at the design on the package. Then he sniffed it. Then he looked at it again.

"They actually smell English," Carnot said. Then he was silent again. Dante watched him. Suddenly Carnot put down the package and straightened up in his chair. He looked at Dante. Then he said, "Is she really pregnant?"

Dante said, "I don't know. I haven't had a chance to talk to her."

Carnot shook his head. "This is a hard year for having babies," he said.

The subject recalled the dinner to Dante's mind, and his irritation. "Every year's a hard year for having babies," he said meaninglessly. He rose. "Do you mind if I go to bed? I'm dead."

Carnot looked up at him. "I've got to go anyhow," he said. "I'll leave you the wine. I have to get started before curfew." He got up.

"I'm sorry about Berger. I feel like apologizing for him," Dante said.

"It was my fault," Carnot said. "I shouldn't even drink wine when he's around. I can't stand cowards who are ashamed of being cowards."

Dante looked at Carnot in surprise.

"I'm a coward," Carnot said. "Everyone is. But I'm not sorry about it."

Carnot walked quickly to the door, opened it quietly, and looked out into the corridor. Then he turned back to Dante. "Good night," he said.

"And take my advice," Carnot said, "don't be sorry about Berger. Just be careful." Then he was gone.

After Carnot had left, Dante turned out the light and drew open the blackout curtain on the half-open window. He stood for a long time looking out at the night. Then he went to Adriane's door and knocked softly. There was no answer. He knocked again and waited. No sound came from within. Finally he tried the knob—it turned, but the door didn't open. The door was locked from the other side. He went back to the window.

He looked out at the warm silent night for nearly an hour. Then he turned away from the window and softly tried the door again. And it was locked. Finally, without taking off his clothes, he went to the other side of the room and lay down in darkness on the unmade bed. It was a long while before he could fall asleep. The darkness was stale and heavy with the smell of wine.

Hours later he awoke to thunder, a flash of lightning that whitened the walls. He awoke startled, his mouth dry, his tongue thick and moistureless, instantly conscious of overpowering thirst. His tongue felt glued.

He got up, fumbled toward the window—the trestle table had been roughly shoved back in place, and he remembered that there was a little wine left in one of the bottles. In another flash of lightning he found it; he sat down before the partly open window and carefully poured some into a glass. It was enough to wet his tongue, and he was grateful.

Outside, the rain suddenly broke. It came on gusts of rapid lightning that blanched the landscape, occasional thunder. Sitting at the table he watched it come, stared out over the ironwork balcony that rounded the window, out into the flickering black. The dreary sheets of rain bellied out and passed in review on the procession of illumined gusts; he watched them pass and vanish, rank on rank, blown spirits of the aimless driven dead, into farther darkness. The thunderstorm was from the east.

How long he sat watching before he fell asleep at the table he didn't know. But when he awoke, he awoke from a dream; he found himself fallen in a heap on the floor, clutching the rungs of the chair that had toppled with him. Outside, it was already first light. The wind was freshening, the rain clearing. Had he fallen asleep at the table before he dreamed? Or was falling asleep at the table *part* of the dream? Or had he really been lying across the bed and dreaming that he'd fallen asleep at the table? In the monstrous confusion of the dream, this question would have to be solved first. Everything hinged on it. Everything.

This was a dream he couldn't remember having before, yet it was familiar, and as usual it was paralyzing. He knew it immediately, recognized it, and struggled only half-heartedly to break out of the strangling grip. The dream couldn't have lasted more than a few seconds—he had entered the room using a key someone had given him. He entered and saw a figure hunched over a table, the head asleep on its arms. So far everything was right, just as he'd left it. The figure slumped over the table was his own, that much was logical enough. But the room was enormous, hollow, and the floors and walls were stone. Someone was beating an irregular drum, offstage. Yet there was a certain luxury here, a monumental dignity, an agitated rustling of black judicial taffeta. Raising his head from the table he sank to his knees before the long judicial bench. Justice would be done, and because this was a dream the situation was more dangerous—he had to stay alert, find the right words, make the right arguments, the proper deferences.

Behind the long raised counter sat his judges, silhouetted dimly against uncertain light; he stood up to face them. Yet each time he faced them he found himself being tried in a different place on new, more ingenious grounds than the time before. He stared at his feet marshaling his tactics, keying himself to an alert pitch of mind. Suddenly he discerned under the dust at his feet the vague outlines of an ancient mosaic—the legend was printed in an endless unpunctuated circle:

The value of knowledge in advance was priceless, yet he could tell from the impatient rustle of garments that his judges were waiting. In a moment he would have to look up again.

But in that instant he heard a long howl of glee from one of the judges sitting up on the bench. Ah, ha! Then the trial wasn't a dream. He looked up boldly at the semicircle of curtains which were drawn up now out of the way, and saw the pointed silhouette of a howling dog on top of the judiciary. Then he saw that the others were dogs too—all dressed in careful robes of judicial black. Some were lying down with their heads between their forepaws watching him. Others were sleeping. And at the left end of the long carved-oak counter, in full view, two middle-aged dogs were obscenely coupled in the frenzied *allegro con brio*—nor were they disencumbered of their judicial trappings while in the process. Suddenly the central dog again pointed his snout into the air and bayed a long and morose note that belled and echoed in the stone-walled room long after the black-robed animal lowered his head. The accused covered his face with his hands, and heard the dog howl for the third time since he'd come to trial. Then he stumbled backward, tripped, and fell entangled in a huge wooden cross he hadn't seen behind him. Stunned, he rested a moment. Under his hands he felt for the stone floor, found only familiar wooden boards. The embracing cross was a cane-seated chair. He awakened from the dream wondering where and precisely how he'd fallen—had he fallen asleep at the table?

Repossessing himself, he got to his feet and righted the chair—the muscles in his back were stiff and knotted. He was cold. Outside the first light was beginning to break. The last of the storm was blowing out.

He sat down again, now fully awake, and bit by bit reconstructed what he could of the dream; his conscious purpose was to put it out of his mind. As the wind freshened the gusts came at less frequent intervals, carried less violent rain. Water had blown in from the half-open window and wet the table. I must try to see her, he thought, even if she refuses. I still want to see her.

The wind had shifted to the southeast, blew salt spray mixed with rain, a flying mist like spindrift. He saw a gust moving across the gray landscape; a hard sheet of finespun drizzle veiled the moving wall of wind. It soared through the disembodied palms like a dragging curtain of wet gauze ripped at the earthward hem. It rose over the whispering flails of the drowned palms and sucked past the open window, fetching the glass a sharp wet slap as it passed. He shut his mind to the dream, shook it off.

XIV

The rain had stopped completely when Dante awoke again. It was fully light. He rose and went to the bathroom and washed his face. In the next room he could hear Berger's guard snoring.

When he came out he went to Adriane's door and turned the knob, but the door was still locked. He was standing wondering if he could speak to her through the door, when the door suddenly opened. She was fully dressed. Behind her, Henri was asleep on a mattress on the floor. Dante looked at her blankly for an instant.

"Are you coming in?" she asked quietly.

"No . . . that is, I thought you might like to go out," he said. "The rain has stopped for a while. We could get some coffee."

She stood looking at him for a moment without saying anything. Then she turned and crossed the room to the armoire and took out her trenchcoat. He didn't enter the room but waited for her outside.

When she came out, pulling the door closed behind her, she didn't look at him.

He followed her out and down the stairs. Downstairs, out of the corner of his eye he saw one of the drapes covering the entrance to the proprietress' quarters move almost imperceptibly. Without turning his head he said, *"Bonjour, Madame."* There was no answer and the drape fell back into place.

When they got outside Adriane turned around and faced him.

"Why did you do that?" she asked.

"Do what?"

"It doesn't matter," she said. She turned and walked ahead of him slightly, just enough so he couldn't see her face. They walked in silence. The streets were still wet from the night's rain. Then he took her arm. She made no move to resist.

They walked for a long time, not saying anything, crossing behind the old part of town until they reached the outskirts. Then they turned around as if by common consent and started back the way they'd come. They passed an old man dragging an enormous overstuffed chair down the middle of the street. The chair was rain-soaked and ruptured in several places and left a clotted trail of cotton stuffing on the pavement. After they'd passed, Adriane turned once to look back.

"He used to know me," she said.

Dante said nothing.

"He used to have a *confiserie*," she went on. "He used to give candy to my brother and me when we were children."

"What happened to his business?" asked Dante.

Adriane looked at him narrowly, as though taking his measure.

"He's a Jew," she said. "That's what happened."

"I see," said Dante.

"Like me," she said.

Dante felt the bitterness in her words. He wanted to tell her it was beside the point, but he checked himself in time. He knew it wasn't. In fact it explained a lot. He remembered the time he had tried to take her in his arms in the kitchen at the farm. He thought: She isn't going to give me any quarter. She wants to make sure I know what she's suffered. He thought of telling her that his mother had been a Jew, but his mother hadn't suffered the same way.

"Does that surprise you?" she asked, deadly casual.

"What difference does it make?" he asked sharply. He stopped walking and faced her. He wasn't going to be able to take being badgered. She knew he couldn't stand any more after last night, he thought.

"Perhaps you can tell me," she said.

"Oh, for Christ's sake . . ." he started, and stopped, caught.

"Yes," she said softly. "That's one difference."

She stood looking at him with a hard little smile on her face that could have been either contempt or pity, or both.

"Oh, God," he said, putting both palms on his temples, "what are you trying to do to yourself? What do you want from me? I'm sorry if I've loved you. I . . ."

"You don't any more?"

"Oh, please please don't come at me again like that. I can't take any more. I don't know what love is. I thought I did. I thought I knew until a bitter lovely child . . . taught me . . ."

"You still think I'm a child, is that it?"

He didn't answer, but took a deep breath and began walking slowly. She took his arm again and walked along beside him looking up at him. He avoided looking directly at her.

"I could almost be your daughter, is that it? That excuses everything?"

"What do you want me to do?" he asked quietly, looking at the wet ground under his feet. "I don't know what I am any more. You've made me out a monster. And I'm not sure you're not right."

They walked together in silence for a while and then crossed the street. The sun was trying to come out, but the scudding gray clouds were still low in the sky. Suddenly they turned a corner and came face to face with a group of military police who had the street blocked off. Dante felt her fingers tighten on his arm.

"I left my papers in the room," she said in a hoarse whisper.

It was too late to turn around. One of the police was already watching them, he saw.

"Come on," he said. "I'll try to get you through on mine."

It was a risk. He would have to rely on the influence of his after-curfew pass, and it was known by the authorities that a number of these special passes bearing the prefect's signature were forgeries. It was not unusual practice to detain the bearer until the validity of his papers could be verified by telephone. Such a proceeding was always handled with deference, though, since such a pass, if genuine, was automatic evidence that the bearer was a man of some importance. But since curfew was over, there was a chance that they wouldn't check. When they arrived at the barrier Dante went directly to the ranking officer who was overseeing the operation. The officer saluted him politely.

"Good morning," said Dante. "I wonder if you could give me some assistance."

"*Mais assurément, cher Monsieur,*" the officer said with a slight bow. He had small suspicious eyes that belied his *politesse.*

"Mademoiselle is a . . . friend," he said, pausing just long enough on the word "friend" to give it a delicately ulterior meaning. The officer nodded understandingly.

"She has left her papers in my . . . ah . . . my study. I find myself in an *embarras* of the first order. You see, my wife . . . She could wait here, of course, while I go fetch them—her papers—for her. You see . . ."

"May I see your papers?" asked the officer, coldly polite.

Dante was worried. This one was plainly conscientious. He didn't know if he dared try money. It might arouse suspicions to be too generous. He took out his wallet and extracted his *carte d'identité*, carefully exposing the corner of the prefect's personal signature on the curfew pass. He couldn't be sure that the officer noticed it. But he couldn't risk being too obvious. The officer scrutinized the card Dante gave him, then handed it back.

"Have you other pieces of identity?"

"Only this," said Dante, unfolding his *fiche de demobilisation.* This time he let the curfew card fall on the ground. The officer bent agilely and picked it up for him, looking at it with interest. "And of course that," said Dante casually. "But I'm afraid that's not much good at this time of day, is it?"

The officer glanced at the card for only an instant before handing it back. His manner changed completely and Dante knew he was in the clear, at least for the time being. He gave the officer the *fiche de demobilisation.* He was glad he was dealing with a Frenchman instead of a German.

"I'm sorry to put you to so much trouble," Dante said. He watched the officer's face as he scanned the document in his hand. Out of the corner of his eye he saw Adriane looking in a shop window, apparently unconcerned. He decided to take the plunge. "I was going to buy Mademoiselle a little gift," he said. "But perhaps she should pay for her carelessness. Perhaps you would be so kind as to offer your men a drink in my behalf—after all, it is trouble for them."

The officer began folding up the paper and shrugged. He didn't smile. "It is cold weather," said the officer. "They wouldn't refuse it."

As he put the wallet back in his pocket Dante extracted a bill and pressed it into the officer's gloved palm as they shook hands. Adriane was suddenly at his side. She smiled broadly at the officer, who pulled back one of the wooden barriers to let them pass. The officer hadn't returned Adriane's smile, and Dante was a little surprised to see him give an unsmiling wink as he followed her through the opening. Dante realized that he was being unbending for the benefit of his men, who were all watching them at that point. He thanked the officer and took

Adriane's arm again. They walked slowly, making a point of browsing the meager windows of the shops that lined the streets.

After they were out of sight of the checkpoint, Dante felt his heart begin to pound. He steered Adriane across two streets and into the first café that was open. They sat down at a table in the empty gloom of the back room. In the center of the room was a billiard table with a great rip in its surface of green cloth. The only other person was the old man mopping the floor near the entrance. Adriane looked around. If the incident of the papers check had upset her she didn't show it. When they were seated, the old man put down his mop and dried his hands on his gray apron, which he then took off and changed for a white one. He was still tying it on when he approached the table to take their order. Dante ordered coffee and a *tartine*. Adriane ordered a cognac with her coffee. The old man shuffled away. She unbuttoned her coat and made herself comfortable. She gestured at the walls of the room, then at the billiard table.

"My grandfather used to hold the mortgage on this place," she said. "It's a good thing he didn't own it."

"Why's that?" asked Dante.

She dropped her hand and turned and looked straight at him. "Why?" she said. Her eyes had an almost dreamy look, of reminiscence, nostalgia. "Why? My grandfather was a Jew."

After two cups of the harsh acorn coffee, Dante felt better. Adriane decided she didn't want the cognac so Dante finished it in his second cup of coffee. The two tastes tended to cancel each other and the liquid was almost palatable. They sat in silence. He watched her as she drew designs on the worn marble table with the tip of her spoon, dipping it from time to time in the dregs of her coffee. The old man had changed back to his gray apron and had resumed his role of janitor and floor-washer. The only sound in the place was the soft sloshing of his mop as he worked his way back toward them from the entrance.

"Why did you lock the door?" Dante asked suddenly.

The spoon stopped moving but she didn't look up. "Why do you ask?"

"Curiosity, I suppose," he said honestly.

"I don't know why," she said. "I didn't want to be taken by surprise, I'm not sure. I just felt better with the door locked, that's all."

"It wasn't to keep me out?"

She looked up at him.

"Why should I want to keep you out?" she asked. "You pay for the room. Or your government does."

"I can't apologize for last night," he said, surprised that he'd said it.

"At least you're honest about that anyway," she said. She began drawing again. Her thoughts seemed to be concentrated on the tip of the spoon.

"That's not the way I meant it," he said. "I mean nothing I could say could make it . . . make it . . ."

"Make it hurt any less? No, I suppose there isn't anything you could say. It didn't hurt me. I hurt myself."

"You said you were going to have revenge," he said. "Do you remember that? You said it a long time ago. As a joke."

"Did I really say that?" she asked, bemused. "I suppose it's true, but I don't remember saying it."

"Do you want the child?" Dante asked. "Look at me. Do you?"

She smeared the design she was making and dropped the spoon in her cup with a clatter.

"Why do you ask the question that way?" she asked. "Do you want to know if it is yours? Why try to make me think you're stupid."

Dante winced. "Please don't fight me any more," he said. "I'm too tired. Can't we try not to hurt each other any more than we have already?"

"Weren't you trying to hurt me when you asked that?"

"Look," he said, trying to sound dispassionate. "Is the fact that I want to know if it is my child—does that mean I'm trying to hurt you? Doesn't that hold any meaning for you?"

"No."

"You don't want the child?" he asked.

"That's not the point," she said. "Do *you* want it?"

"I never asked you to marry me, simply because with the war it seemed impossible."

"Yes," she said.

"But now I ask you to marry me," he said. "War or no war."

"Is marriage the only way you know of salvaging your honor?" she asked. "I'm not interested in your honor."

"You don't *want* the child, do you," he said. "Tell me the truth."

"It's not my child to want," she said. "The child doesn't want me. You don't want either me or the child."

"That's not true," he said.

"You wish it weren't true, you mean."

She fell silent. He watched her, studying her face. He thought: She doesn't want the child. Why? Is she right? Yet what is so ignoble about honor that it shouldn't be salvaged? He came to the conclusion that she had made up her mind before he spoke. She had never meant to have the child. But she didn't want the responsibility of the decision. He was being cheated of something that was his. And yet, was it? He had asked her to marry him, even though marriage could only remain an unreal dream. That clearly wasn't what she wanted. What was it, then? Did she want him to take the responsibility for the decision, to act for her? To absolve her?

He looked at his hands on the table in front of him. The wrinkles were deep across his palms. After all, what else has she got to lose? he thought. I will never have a child. She will have as many as she wants. She's a child herself, and she's afraid.

"What are you looking at your hands for?" she asked.

"What are you afraid of?" he asked.

She seemed to think a moment before answering. "There's only one thing I'm really afraid of," she said finally. "When I was a child I was afraid of being left alone in the dark. I always had a light in my room."

"You're still afraid of the dark," he said.

"I never really was afraid of the dark. It was being left alone I was afraid of," she said. "I'm still afraid of that. I don't like sleeping by myself."

Dante hadn't expected as candid an answer. But there it was, the answer to everything. Could it really be so brutally simple? She was looking at him oddly, with her head cocked slightly to one side. He could tell from her face she was tired. He wondered if she'd slept.

"You didn't answer my question," she said. "Do you want the child?"

"That was my question to you, I think," said Dante.

"Of course I want it," she said quickly. "That's not the point either. At least I'm certain that it's mine. The question is do *you* want it."

He felt certain she was lying. There was something flippant, perhaps challenging, in her tone. He suddenly felt very tired and depressed.

"Perhaps we should discuss it later when we've both had a better sleep," he said. "I haven't the heart to fight with you."

"No," she said. "I want you to answer me now."

To be absolved, he thought wearily. He knew that she wouldn't relax her pressure until she had from him what she wanted to hear. If only I could be sure, he thought. Yet he knew in his heart that he was sure. But what was the use? He was sure now that she had lied to him simply to make it less obvious. He tried to think of some way of putting it off. Perhaps he could make her change her mind later. He longed to lie down somewhere and sleep. She was young. She had life to burn. She could keep it up indefinitely. He turned and looked at her for a long while. She refused to lower her eyes. She knows I know she's lying, he thought. Her eyes were bright and unblinking as he looked at her. She was in the advantage. So young, he thought, to be absolved . . .

"Answer me," she said. "Please answer me. I must know."

"I only want this child if you want it," he said. "Not otherwise."

"I knew you didn't want it," she said. She sounded almost triumphant.

"You have your absolution," he mumbled, looking at his hands again.

"What did you say?" she asked sharply. Her face was flushed and excited.

"Nothing," he said, listening to the soft sloshing of the old man's mop. He was too tired to argue any more. He felt sick from lack of sleep, and the bad coffee was beginning to roil in his knotted stomach. He felt a cramp in his intestines—he knew he would have to go to the toilet immediately—it always happened when he didn't get enough sleep. He felt that he wanted simply to lie down on the dusty green expanse of the unused billiard table and sleep. He felt cheated and angry, an immense fatigue. The war would drag on. The war was endless. The only dream was survival.

Berger's guard waked Dante the next day, and he got up after another sleepless night to take the train down the coast to meet Carnot. The circus had left for St. Maxime the night before, and the funeral had been rescheduled.

Dante put his things together in a paper sack and, fully dressed, knocked on Adriane's door to say good-by. But the door was locked and there was no answer. He went to say good-by to the guard instead. The guard was in the bathroom. Berger was still sleeping.

"When will you be back?" the guard rasped. He was sitting on the toilet.

"Perhaps a week."

The guard grunted. Then he said casually, "Your friends have landed."

Dante didn't understand. "My friends?"

"The Americans."

Dante dropped the paper sack and stepped into the bathroom. "What!" he exclaimed. "When? Where?"

"All last night. In Normandy," the guard said. He might have been announcing a change in the weather for all the excitement he showed.

"Is it a large invasion or just a raid?" Dante asked, stunned.

"Several divisions. No one knows for sure."

"What's the date today?"

"June sixth, maybe the seventh, I don't know," the guard said.

"My God," Dante said. "So they came in the north after all."

"You're going to miss your train," the guard said.

Dante looked at his watch. "I guess I'd better start," he said. "I can't believe it."

"You'll hear about it when you get outside," the guard said. "The BBC has been talking about it. They bombed down the coast last night."

"Thanks," Dante said.

"Don't mention it," the guard answered. He leaned back and inspected one of his feet. "The war will be over soon."

Dante went back to Adriane's door and pounded on it. She called out sleepily to ask him what he wanted.

"The invasion has started up north," he shouted.

"That's good," she said. "But I want to sleep."

"Don't do anything until I get back," he said. She didn't answer.

X V

It was a Friday when they caught Carnot. As usual, Dante was supposed to rendezvous with him at precisely noon at the fish market. The tiny square in St. Tropez was crowded with jabbering fishwives washing down the cobblestones, sweeping the last bright entrails off the ancient stone cutting tables. Carnot came through the opposite arch at twelve o'clock to the second.

They appeared from nowhere, four of them. Just as Dante was approaching him, Carnot casually shifted the newspaper from his right hand to his left. Dante halted in his tracks, inspecting a small squid on one of the tables. Out of the corner of his eye he saw Carnot throw the newspaper at the head of the nearest one. Then there was shouting and running. Dante saw Carnot knocked to the ground. It was one minute after twelve. But it hardly seemed as though more than ten seconds had passed.

Carnot lay on the ground, face down on the small hard round wet cobbles discolored black from centuries of fish gore and polished smooth as jasper. He made no effort to get up, but after a moment rolled slowly over and stared at the sky. They stood in a ring around him, weapons drawn. Carnot laced his fingers behind his head and stared beyond them, ignoring them. Dante stood frozen, watching, too stunned to move. Suddenly one of them thought to handcuff Carnot. Carnot passively offered his hands to the man as he bent over him. The man was laughing at Carnot, when suddenly his laugh turned to a scream of pain: Carnot had hooked his toe behind the man's foot and then kicked him hard just under the kneecap, bending the leg the wrong way. The man dropped his weapon and fell like a log; he was rolling on his back clutching his knee as the others closed in. Carnot was kicked and mauled and dragged to his feet. He bent double to cover his groin, and might have succeeded in getting himself shot on the spot had it not been for the intervention of a short, rotund man. He entered through the arch and barked a command; his men backed away. The injured man rose limping to his feet, the small round leader laughed heartily at his misfortune. It was the first time in his life that Dante saw Monsieur le Préfet, Théophile Dujardin, and then only for an instant. For the rest of his life he would remember him primarily as a small, rotund, jovial-looking man with a drawn revolver, holding his sides and shaking with good-natured laughter.

Dante was afraid to move, afraid of drawing attention—although he was dressed like a fisherman and looked like anyone else in the tiny enclosed square. Finally, he started to edge toward the archway where he had entered. The other archway was blocked by the disguised police. Suddenly he felt a broom being pressed into his hands and smelled the strong fish-oil smell of the shapeless old creature who passed it to him behind her back. The woman nudged another woman and together they closed in in front of him, partially hiding him. He watched one of the police search the faces of the silent black-shawled women and old men standing behind their stands with their backs to the wall. He waited for the shout, "There's the other one!" and longed for a weapon. But no shout came. Tensed like a spring to bolt out through the archway, he felt the eyes pass over him. In his mind, he was sorting a hundred possible escape routes, discarding, weighing; the streets of the town passed through his mind like riffled photographs. In a split second he made a thousand perfect decisions, which way, where to walk, where to run, where to duck (at the corners), avoid which streets —it all led to the cathedral. He knew this was dangerous, but there was no other place. By now they would know, he was certain, of Carnot's capture—someone would be hurrying through the streets at this very moment carrying the news. He wouldn't be able to hide, but he must get a weapon, a weapon. Not for them. Like a lightning calculator—fear was meaningless—his mind without conscious direction programmed his own destruction. He was counting the number of leaps to reach the arch, then how much time to the first corner . . . then how far . . .

Suddenly a huge red-faced woman with enormous hands and wild gray hair stepped forward and shook her broom at the tableau of police standing around Carnot.

"You've finished your game," she said sharply, in an astounding cracked voice that oscillated between a man's basso and a piping excited treble. "Now get out so honest people can wash out the stink before the sun sets it in the stones."

One of the police, a thin yellow-faced boy, made a surly gesture toward her with his pistol. The beefy woman sneered at him, and gestured toward the pistol.

"Save that to make your whore happy," she said, grabbing her crotch fore and aft and hiking as though to lift herself off the ground. When her skirts lifted, the flesh of her huge white legs showed. Dujardin turned and walked out, still laughing.

Then they were gone, unbelievably gone, gone. They disappeared dragging Carnot through the archway. The big fishwife waved good-by to the murderous-faced boy by holding up her huge hamlike hand and wiggling the tip of her little finger. The boy had to be restrained from coming back at her. Pausing to cough up a generous rattle of phlegm, she stood with her hands on her hips and laughed at him. Then she spat on the ground at his feet.

"De la merde," she said. She was no longer laughing. And then they were gone, the last of them. Dante heard a voice raised in anger beyond the arch, and once again Dujardin's indulgent laughter.

Then hands were at his back, women pushing him toward the opposite exit like mother hens herding a strayed chick. There were no words, only the urgent, eloquent pressure of the hands. Through the dank eternal shadow of the earthen arch, up a step, another, through a doorway, into a room, into another room, down stone stairs into a cave, dark, cold and musty with dampness. It was the big woman from the square, behind him; he knew without turning around because she wheezed in the same cracked way that she shouted. He could hear water dripping.

"Stay here," she said. He felt a Luger being pressed into his hand. "The magazine is full. Be sure to save one. It is his pistol, Alexi's."

"Who are you?"

For a second he thought she wasn't going to reply. Then she spoke, and her voice was turgid with rage, he thought.

"You knew Max?"

"Yes."

"I used to be called Max's whore."

He felt awkward in the darkness, blind in the face of the huge fearless woman's passion. The suppressed force of her clenched words made her anger a terrible thing; he was glad he couldn't see her face—rather, that she couldn't see his.

"Now they call *me* Max," she said. "Max."

"I see," he said, immediately knowing his own remark was nakedly gratuitous. She let it stand for what it was.

After a pause she said, "You think so."

Then she was gone up the stairs, and the wooden trap slammed shut.

Dante knew he was standing on hard bare dirt, maybe clay or wet sand, he thought. It was black, black, sightless and black. The pistol was warm as flesh in his hand and sickeningly heavy. Before his mind he saw the whole scene in the fish market unroll again, as though it had been permanently burned onto his retina by the brilliant white sun. He tried to close it out so he could think of something else, but it was no use. The still-life of Carnot on the ground seemed projected inside his forehead just above eye level, floating upward, ever upward. When he looked up it floated out of eye reach; when he looked straight ahead it hovered down again.

There seemed no room in his mind for directed thought; it was as though his brain and body, in a moment of fear, had commandeered all available channels of his brain and had mobilized them to the single end of escape. Every fiber of his brain was jammed with that few seconds' worth of recorded detail and emergency calculation; the conscious intellect, too slow, clumsy, too wasteful, had been temporarily swept out of command, had abdicated to its secret master. Even fear had been crowded out; he knew he was perfectly prepared to kill, to be killed, to run, to fight, or, finally, to destroy himself.

He still felt a terrifying exhilaration; he gulped air for a few seconds more, waiting for the reaction. And finally his knees began to shake uncontrollably, and he was cold. Then, at last, he was afraid. He sat down on the cold wet earth, hugging his knees, completely blind with eyes open, and rested his head on his knees. In some part of his mind he remembered to be careful not to get dirt in the barrel of the pistol. He rested the heavy loaded weapon across his shoes. A shudder went through him and he rubbed his arms. He knew he was sweating, but wasn't sure whether the wetness on his cheeks was sweat or tears. He didn't lift his hand to find out, but he kept his eyes strained wide open, staring into nothing, into the blackness. After a time the blackness seemed to be behind his eyes, not in front of them, as if he were staring into the warm dark round of his own skull.

He tried to stop the shivering by rubbing himself with his free hand. His whole body was tense with the cold of the cellar. He didn't realize how tightly he was gripping the Luger until it went off.

The flash blinded him. The pistol exploded with a paralyzing roar directly in front of his face. He felt a sharp pain in his shin and pinpricks on his face, stinging in his eyes—powder grains, he thought instantly, or sand kicked up by the blast. The pain in his ear doubled him forward. The flash and the blast seemed to last for minutes—time stopped; there seemed only the unending duration of pain. The other monstrous sound, like the drunken humming of a great hilarious bee, was the bullet ricocheting off the stone walls, slam slam slam, with a high-velocity fluttering whine as it tumbled lopsidedly through the deadly air. A fraction of a second, the wink of an eye, and it was over; Dante had seen the room in the split second of the flash. He had charted the short instant of the bullet's flight and heard it hit each time—he knew it was impossible—as it spent itself methodically, step by step, with agonizing slowness against the walls of the vault. It was spent in the instant before the flash subsided. The pain in his ear was agonizing. The only thing in his mind besides pain was a singsong piece of Army training-poster doggerel jammed inanely in his brain:

Jones left the safety off a loaded gun;
Jones blew his foot off, all in fun.

He felt his shin carefully, steeling himself to find jagged shards of bone, but he felt nothing. He pulled up his pant leg and searched again—still nothing. Then he realized that the recoil must have kicked the heavy weapon against his shin. His right ear still hurt; his head was ringing so badly that he hardly realized what it was, it was so intense and high-pitched.

He got shakily to his feet to be ready when, as his imagination saw it, the police would throw open the trap door. He didn't feel anything any more except a vast, weary resignation. He felt disgusted. A cosmic disgust. Somehow, it seemed right that he should pay for such a stupid blunder—with his life if necessary. He tried to shake the ringing out of his head. Then a feeble shaft of light fell from where the trap was. He was shocked and sickened to realize that he had got turned around in the darkness and was facing in the wrong direction. His *back* was to the trap. The resignation only deepened, and he turned around slowly, deliberately making himself an easy target. Nothing happened. He waited. *Someone* had opened the trap. He could see an outline, above.

"Mama says to ask you if you killed yourself." He made out the outlines of the small girl's upside-down face peering down from one corner of the trap. A terrible urge to laugh came over him. The little girl's tone was serious, matter of fact, funny and horrible at the same time. She couldn't have been more than ten years old from the sound of the voice. Suppressing the urge to laugh as a relief, he couldn't find words for a moment. The little girl withdrew her head and spoke to someone in the room above.

"He must be dead," she said. "But he's still standing up."

The upside-down head reappeared; this time he could see pigtails hanging down.

"Why are you standing up if you killed yourself?" she asked.

"I'm not dead," he said simply. He felt very foolish trying not to laugh. But he felt that if he once laughed, he wouldn't be able to stop.

"Mama can't talk to you," she said.

"Why?" he asked. "Why can't she?" He snickered uncontrollably.

"She has to watch at the window for the men that are coming to kill you. She says it's a big raid all over town."

He heard sharp indistinguishable words from behind the child. The child withdrew her head again. There were more words, instructions.

"Mama wants to know what you are shooting at and to stop it," said the girl with grave authority. "You'll wake up the dead, she says."

Dante got serious. "Tell her I shot a demon," he said, feeling unaccountably light-hearted. "It was self-defense."

More instructions from across the room upstairs. The child listened and then relayed them down to Dante.

"Mother says to watch out for Max's Luger," she said knowledgeably. "It has a hairy trigger."

Dante felt himself almost break down and cry. He wanted to laugh but couldn't. Laughter sat heavy in his belly like a stone.

"Mama says not to kill yourself just yet," relayed the child. She looked down at Dante wide-eyed and serious and upside-down as though she were inspecting him. He might have been a bear in a pit at the zoo.

Dante heard the woman order the child to close the trap. Instead the child asked him what his name was.

"My name?" he repeated. The child inspired an upsetting mixture of emotions in him. She had a serious, unchildlike face, and dark unsmiling eyes. She was funny, as children are in their innocence; and yet, he thought, tragic in her innocence. The thought came to him clearly.

He heard the mother's command again, louder this time, to shut the trap. The child dallied, propping the trap open with her head, holding it from closing all the way.

"I'm the demon-shooter," he said.

"I'm going to a masquerade ball when I grow up," she said.

"What's *your* name?" Dante asked impulsively.

Once again the command to close the trap, this time angry. Then over his head he heard angry footsteps coming across the floor toward the child.

"My name is Max," she said. "That's short for . . ."

Bang! The trap dropped shut cutting off the word "Maxine" as her mother yanked her away. He heard the rug being slipped into place over the trap, and the child crying. Dante pictured her holding her seat where her mother had impressed the lesson in obedience. He felt completely collected as he stood in the dark watching the square of light of the trap's image fade from the eye's memory, and mused to himself on the whereabouts of the spent bullet he had fired. He doubted now that the shot had been heard outside the house. He hadn't been able to hear what the woman was saying to her daughter, even when the trap was open.

The little girl delighted but also troubled him. It was wrong that she was endangered because . . . he left the thought hanging in his mind.

"Max," he breathed aloud, "thy name is legion."

Then he got down on his hands and knees to search for the bullet.

XVI

He couldn't tell how long it had been, except for the heat. It was summer heat, heat that penetrated even the stone damp of the lightless cell. It had been still spring when he was captured. When his head was clear enough to think he reckoned the days and nights by the coming and going of the prison orderly who came to empty the bucket. There were days when there was no food. There was no regularity about food. But they never failed to come and empty the bucket. They were afraid of typhus, even among the prisoners. Disease made no distinctions.

Ordinarily he would have opened up after forty-eight hours; that was all the silence rule required. At first it seemed that they knew everything. But they tipped their hand. "Who is Dante?" The question still plagued him in dreams, even now, long after they had ceased to ask it. The only defense was total silence. They had shown him photographs of his dead radio operator, and asked him over and over again, "Where is Dante?" After the required forty-eight hours were up, he might have spoken if it hadn't been for the slips they made: "We know Dante came here to contact you," the fat one said. It was all he had to say. For one reason or another they had decided their prisoner was French, that the American was still at large. And the prisoner's stubborn silence confirmed them in their error.

Dante sat in his cell self-condemned to silence, kept alive by the fear that one slip, one English word twisted from him in sleep would spell his doom. He forced himself to think in French, to dream in French, to forget English. He had reached the point, living in the saturated knowledge of death, where an English phrase rising from the mists of a dream was enough to awaken him in clammy terror.

He was certain that neither Carnot, nor whoever else had been taken at the same time, knew for sure that he had been captured the day after they were, because there had been no confrontations. He puzzled over the fact that he had always been questioned alone. Either they were inept or the others were already dead. They *were* inept, he thought, all except the fat one. The fat one: Dujardin. But the fat one seemed to have lost interest. After the first excitement died down, he hadn't attended any more interrogations. Dante worried more about him than any of the others. The fat Dujardin was shrewd. He was dangerous. It was only his pompous anxiety to display his omniscience that had caused him to make the slip that silenced Dante permanently. Now they called their prisoner the "quiet one," the "crazy one," for each day he continued to greet them with cataleptic silence, opening his mouth only to scream and gargle in pain when there was no other choice. He behaved like an animal, and this had come to have its advantages. For they treated him like one. They fed him like an animal, but they also questioned him like an animal. That is to say, they'd given up questioning him as though he were human. A few kicks, a punch or two, a great deal of cursing, and then back to the kennel with him. They only went through the motions now. They had their orders, but they refused to make fools of themselves by expecting speech from an animal. Dante was thankful.

The day before he had taken a foolish risk. He had confounded them. Signaling for a pad of paper and a pencil, he took it and in the deliberate scrawl of a six-year-old wrote the single word, "cigarette." As if he were a deaf mute, they discussed the development among themselves in his presence. One of them gave him a cigarette and told the guard to take him out. Today the doctor had come to his cell.

"Open your mouth," the doctor said.

Dante opened his mouth.

"You're not deaf then," the doctor concluded calmly. He peered down Dante's throat with a tiny flashlight. The guards remained outside the cell door, out of hearing. One of them kept poking his head in nervously, as though concerned for the doctor's safety.

The doctor looked cryptically at Dante over the beam of the flashlight. "I think I'd better have you up to the infirmary."

The doctor turned around. "Guard. Take this man up to the infirmary. I want to examine him further."

"We have no orders . . ." The first guard looked dubiously at the second, who merely shrugged and shook his head, refusing any responsibility for decision.

"I just gave them to you," the doctor said sharply. He walked out, not waiting for a contradiction. The first guard shrugged this time and came into the cell.

The handcuffs were tighter than usual and the leg irons made the stairs difficult to negotiate. It was the first time Dante had been anywhere except to the small interrogation cubicle at the end of the cell block. The "infirmary" was a small office with double-barred doors, a converted single cell on the second floor. An old barber chair was bolted to the floor in the center of the dusty room and a tray of dentist's forceps, also covered with dust, lay on the floor beside it. The only other medical emblem in the room was a white cabinet with a red cross on it that hung on one wall; it had a cracked mirror. A desk and two chairs completed the furnishings.

"Stand outside the door. Come in when I call you," the doctor said.

Dante was surprised when the guards did as they were told. The doctor closed the outside door, went through after Dante, then closed the inner door. The inner door had a paper window shade hanging from a wooden roller that was wired onto the bars. It gave the room a semblance of privacy.

The doctor silently motioned Dante to a chair. He took the other.

"Do they know who you are?" the doctor asked softly, glancing at the door. Dante's heart jumped. He remained silent, unmoving. His mind raced through the doctor's words and their implications, weighing the gamble of answering.

The doctor, reading his thoughts, said, "It's a chance you have to take. I could be trying to trap you."

"They don't know," Dante said, his heart pounding out of control.

The doctor sucked through his teeth softly, shaking his head slowly. "How long have you been here?"

"I was caught the next day. There were no witnesses."

"We haven't much time," the doctor said. "I will try to get word to the others. An escape is being planned."

"They are alive?"

"Some of them. They have communication among them. I come here only on Wednesdays. I will give you pills to make you feverish. You will also vomit, be very sick. You will complain of cramps. Seven days from now."

"I understand."

"I will try to get word to the others before. You will be able to walk.

428

After you vomit you will feel better but don't let it show. You will be part of an epidemic. Three guards will be sick also. With luck you'll be removed under guard to the clinic. Do you understand?"

"Yes."

The doctor opened the top drawer of his desk and took out a small bottle. He shook four pills into his palm. "Take them after food so you will have something to stink up the cell with. Put them into the cuff of your trouser." The doctor glanced warily at the door. "I've been setting the stage this week in the village. I'll diagnose you as typhus. An 'epidemic' is just getting started. I have to be very careful. Sooner or later there will be an investigation. German doctors do not fool easily."

"What will you do?"

The doctor shrugged. "I will be puzzled, like them. It will be a strange malady."

"Why the escape?"

"Because it is known that the Allies will be here soon."

"Soon?" Dante asked. So the war had gone on without him.

"You don't know? They are in Paris."

Dante could only stare.

"Or near it," the doctor amended. "The news is very confused."

"But if . . ."

"I know. Why don't we simply wait for them to come? Is that what you're wondering?"

Dante nodded, dumb.

"Because your host is getting panicky. The Allies have announced their intention to try all war criminals. Dujardin has blood on his hands. His only hope is to get rid of the evidence. You are the last surviving prisoners who could testify against him."

"But people must know . . ."

"Dujardin has never dirtied his hands with killing. He has always let the *Boche* do that for him. Otherwise there would be too many witnesses. He is a sadist. He tortures them, but he lets the SD finish the job. He's shrewd. But this time . . ."

"This time?"

"This time, even the Germans don't want his prisoners. They are pulling out. Two divisions are already gone. Even the Gestapo won't take Dujardin's latest batch off his hands. He's worried. They're all worried. Judgment Day is coming. They are all trying to wash their hands."

"But . . ."

"We haven't time to go into it. Only this. The minute the Allies land here, you're doomed unless we can get you out. Dujardin is making a last attempt to get you all to Germany, off his hands, that is. The alternative is being caught red-handed."

"I see."

"If anyone comes to you with a message, it will be a guard with a long face and no hair. He's the only one you can trust completely, do you understand? Even he doesn't know who you are. You won't tell him."

Dante nodded.

"I will report that you seem to be suffering aphasia induced by shock. That will do for now. It means you've lost the ability to speak. We will have to end your 'examination' now. Those two outside might get the idea that I'm becoming too humanitarian if I keep you any longer. Did you know they used to be prisoners here themselves?"

"Those two?"

"All of them. These two were in for murder. Specially picked for the job. Fortunately a few others—thieves mostly—are still loyal to the country that jailed them."

The doctor stood up. "Guards!" he roared. "Come and get this imbecile."

Back in his cell Dante sat in a state of elated shock for a long time. The invasion had come off! In the nearly total darkness he sat on the mattressless iron bed and fingered freedom in the shape of four pellets hidden in the cuff of his trouser. They seemed the only testimony of reality. If it weren't for the solid evidence of the four pills, he might have thought in the giddiness of isolation and hunger that he had only dreamed again. But the pills were there. He felt them, counted them, touched one to the tip of his tongue. It was bitter. But real. He fell asleep with the bitter secret still in his mouth, a taste of freedom.

That night—night or day he never knew, but called the time when he slept night—that night he awakened to the crash of an explosion. He felt it through the stone. It must have been close for the sound to penetrate the walls. The one was followed by another. At first he thought of bombing. But then from the regularity of the silent intervals he concluded that it must be a naval bombardment. This was no sporadic affair, he realized. After lying in darkness listening he knew that they were pounding the coast for an invasion.

The next night the bombers came. One explosion was so loud that it shook dust from the crevices of the stone over his head, and for a while he felt the terror of possibly being buried alive. No one came, despite the fact that in the dim upper reaches of the prison he could hear an air-raid gong sounding, muffled, distant. Somewhere in the building someone was pounding on a pipe. Beyond that he could hear nothing. He spent the night listening in fear and elation.

No one came to empty the bucket the next day. He began to wonder if he would starve to death, forgotten in the bowels of the earth. He began to think of himself as a corpse already buried, a corpse sealed off from the light and the remoter furies of men. Nightly he listened to the bombardment that shook the earth and stone under the iron legs of his bed. The room stank. He slept all the time now, too weak from hunger and immobility to do anything else.

He had no idea how many days had passed when he heard them

come to take him out. He didn't open his eyes even when he felt someone shaking him. Then he heard several voices, felt the stab of a flashlight on his eyes. Someone said, "He's alive. Get him out of here." It was the fat one's voice. "Search his clothes." He felt fingers rummaging in his trouser cuff. They took the pills. He didn't care particularly. He opened his eyes only for an instant.

Outside the cell, light slammed onto his closed eyes like the flat of an ax. Supported between two guards he felt himself dragged up a flight of stairs. A door opened and the light struck his brain. It was agony. How many days had it been? How many? Had he let a week slip by uncounted? He couldn't think, and besides, he was surprised that he didn't care. But they made him eat. Soup. Nothing would come clearly into focus. Was this rescue? But then what was Dujardin doing here? Had he been there? He sucked the soup with his eyes closed against the excruciating pain of the light. He heard someone say, "His eyes are inflamed." He didn't care. He felt detached from his rotting body, from his suppurating eyes. It was the doctor's voice. Was he a prisoner too?

Later, after the forced-feeding, they questioned them in rounds. When they weren't questioning them they forced more food into them. But there was no sleep. They forced them to stay awake. The fat one did the questioning. Daylight came and went. They gave them injections of glucose to bring back energy. The facts began to order themselves. The room took on shape. The people in it became real. A huge room. At one end they questioned. At the other end they fed them, cleaned them, injected them with sugar so that they would be able to answer the questions.

The fat one did the questions. He stalked back and forth behind the small table, sweating under the glaring light. He stopped only to go away and sleep, turning the questioning over to an officer of the SD. It became obvious that he was trying to accomplish something with this questioning. Two other SD officers drifted in and out of the marathon proceedings. Finally, after over forty-eight hours of questioning, they resorted to amphetamine. The drug bolted them upright, and it also cleared their minds.

Dante had seen Carnot when they first dragged him into the light. But there were others. There was the doctor. Charles the priest was there. Auguste. Adriane and Henri were missing.

There must have been nearly twenty-four of them. They came in one by one. Dante didn't know them all. Most surprising was Lautrec. He was alive but he came in badly beaten, freshly beaten. He didn't look starved. He looked healthy except for the swollen flesh and the cuts. Later they brought in Berger and Anton. Berger looked like a corpse. Then came the man Dante knew as Agathe. They sat on the floor along one wall, moving up as they went to the table for questioning. Over and over, the same questions, the same senseless round.

Only the last time it was different. When Dante was jerked to his feet, he approached the table between the two guards. Berger was already there. He was sitting opposite the chair where Dante was seated. Beside him were two of the SD officers. In front of him, back and forth, paced Dujardin. Dujardin was more obviously angry and frustrated than Dante had seen him before. He stopped pacing, hands behind his back, and stared at Dante. His fat face was puffy from lack of sleep, and his left eye twitched.

"We come to you again," he said contemptuously.

Dante noticed that Berger avoided his eye. He was worried. It was essential to communicate to Berger the fact that his identity was still unknown. He would have to speak. While he was thinking how to break his long silence, one of the Germans gave him the opening he was looking for.

"This one has only wasted our time," he said. The Germans were different. They were obviously at ease, rested, even bored. Dujardin seemed to be trying to prove that he had an important prisoner in Berger.

"Do you know this man?" Dujardin asked Berger.

"He knows me," Dante said before Berger could answer.

"So! You finally condescend to speak!" Dujardin dropped Berger and whirled around to face Dante. "How does he know you?"

"I'm not the only Frenchman he knows." It was enough. He saw Berger catch it. It was enough.

Dujardin saw nothing. He turned to Berger. "Where did you know this man?"

"At the farm."

"What name did you know him under?"

"I knew him as Antoine. I remember because it was the same first name as mine."

Dante was startled at Berger's nerve but he didn't let it show. Dujardin fumed.

"You are a liar. Your name is not Antoine."

"Yes it is," said Berger.

"I know what your name is. Don't think I'm a fool."

Berger smiled idiotically. One of the Germans tapped a pencil impatiently.

"What did he do at the farm?"

"I don't know. I only saw him once. I never talked to him."

Dante felt that Berger was doing fairly well.

"Do you admit you were at the farm?"

"What farm?" Dante asked. "There are lots of farms."

"You know what farm."

"I don't remember."

"You are a Communist," Dujardin said.

"I don't remember," Dante said.

"You are trying my patience."

"I didn't know you had any," one of the Germans said. The other two laughed. "Monsieur Dujardin, this is getting us nowhere. You led us to believe that you had important prisoners. We didn't come all the way from Nice to . . ."

"No, wait, I can show that one of these . . ." Dujardin was not even trying to conceal his anxiety any more. It bordered on panic. He turned to Dante. Dramatically he pointed a finger at Dante. "I know who you are. I've eliminated all the others." He turned back to the Germans. *"This* man is Alexi Carnot," he pronounced.

There was silence. One of the Germans turned to his two colleagues with a smug smile, as though to say, "I told you so." Then he turned to Dujardin. "We are wasting our time here. *Carnot is dead.* You have brought us down here on a stupid duck hunt." He waved his arm around the room. The other prisoners, crouching out of earshot against the wall, looked up at the group of men around the table as the German raised his voice. "These are nothing but garbage. You are wasting our time, Monsieur." He pushed his chair and licked his thin lips in a malicious smile. "I'm afraid we can't help you. So far you've merely wasted our time. We have to be back before nightfall and we have a long way to go. The roads are damaged. Are you ready, gentlemen?" The other two Germans got up.

"No, wait! You are making a mistake." Dujardin actually wrung his hands.

"So far you have proved that they sold eggs on the black market. You said you found arms. Three pistols."

"But that in itself . . ."

"Monsieur, I cannot be blunter. We came here because you went over our heads and we were *ordered* to come here. Now I tell you: *We don't want your prisoners.* Even if you have Mr. Roosevelt's son among this rabble, we haven't time to listen to you trying to find him. What's more, *we don't want him.* Is that clear?"

"I'll have to report what you've told me," Dujardin said. "You're making interrogation impossible, you realize."

The German smiled. "And who will you report it to, Monsieur?" He laughed bitterly. "The Allied High Command?"

"If you will only have the patience to . . ."

One of the other two Germans made a wry face and turned to leave the room. Over his shoulder he said, "Sweep up your own dirt. We have enough of our own."

"Guards!" Dujardin shouted. "Take them back to their cells."

Dujardin followed the three Germans out, sputtering angrily at them. The prisoners were taken back to their cells. Dante, still nervous from the effects of the drug, lay awake on a bare-springed cot and listened in the darkness for the sound of the bombardment to begin. It came soft and distant, like distant summer thunder, and he fell asleep.

That night the east wing of the prison was demolished by a direct hit. Dante heard it only dully, an effigy of sound paraded through the alleys of a dream.

The bombardment clamored day and night now. The invasion was imminent. Even the prison orderly who resumed emptying the bucket talked of it. The guards didn't shut him up. He brought gossip, rumors. Dante learned that the orderly was a prisoner himself. Not political, he said. "I am only a thief," he said, shrugging. "The war is not my doing."

The orderly told of reports of troops, of parachutes spotted. But *hélas,* nothing confirmed, he said, nothing sure. One of the guards sighed malevolently. The orderly picked up the bucket and withdrew. "I won't be seeing you tomorrow," he said. The door thudded. Dante heard them walking away.

He fell asleep again, slipped back into the semiconscious confusion of a dream that settled over his mind like mist, a dream that flickered like a candle in the wind with each rumble of the distant earth. In half-sleep he heard the crash of shells and knew without volition that they were smashing the harbor half a kilometer away. Crump. Pale images of sound, like delicate paper lanterns, hung for a moment in the caverns of his mind, receded to pinpoints, and vanished to oblivion. Crump. Crump. Then three close together: Crumpcrumpcrump. Silence. He slept soundly.

They were given a meal before they were herded into the trucks. It happened so suddenly that Dante stepped from the fringes of the dream into the glare of reality without marking the exact moment of awakening. He had learned to survive in a habit-state of dream, and at first he was dreaming he was being dragged upstairs, then he *was* being dragged upstairs. The meal was another forced-feeding. The guards allowed no talking. Dante found himself sitting next to the doctor.

Slowly the fact took shape in his mind that the escape plan had been betrayed. He knew already that the doctor was a prisoner; he was at the interrogation. But he hadn't connected it. It was the first hint that his mind had been giving way. He wondered at what point he had stopped thinking, had stopped rationalizing the irrational world of his cell. For the first time in weeks he wondered what was going to happen next.

He reflected that the food had rescued him from oblivion. He was once again a thinking suffering being, no longer accepting things as an animal accepts them, without thought. A guard was standing over them. When he turned his back, Dante spoke to the doctor without moving his lips.

"Why are they feeding us?"

The doctor answered boldly in a normal tone: "It is either a routine or an oversight." The guard turned sharply around. "Eat. You'll need it," said the doctor.

"No talking," said the guard.

An explosion close by shook the enamelware bowls on the table. Everyone stopped sucking soup and looked up, waiting. Dust settled from the roof rafters.

"I'll talk if I please, garbage," the doctor said. He had difficulty articulating because his lips were swollen and cut. One eye was completely closed. Dante braced himself for the expected fall of the truncheon. But the guard merely muttered something unintelligible and turned his back again.

"The fortunes of battle are turning," the doctor observed, and went back to his soup. The others were eating again.

"What is happening?" Dante asked.

"We are going to Germany, my friend. To be exterminated offstage."

A panic of despair sliced mind and body apart as Dante heard the words. His mind raced around a single thought: escape. His body relaxed out of control into a deep apathy of no-movement. He laid down his bowl and stared into it. The doctor's voice roused him moments later.

"What are you looking at?"

Dante shrugged. "My bowl." He felt unable to lift his head or turn his eyes.

" '. . . To see the world in a jade cup,' " the doctor mused.

"What?"

"It's from a Chinese poem."

Dante looked up.

"Can we escape?" he asked.

"We have to be careful," the doctor said. "There is an informer among us. That is, if he wasn't killed the other night."

Dante realized for the first time that half the prisoners who had been at the interrogation were gone.

"Where are the . . . the others?"

"The east wing collapsed. A direct hit. Some of them may be still alive, but I doubt it."

"No one tried to . . ." Dante looked around. Carnot and Berger were at another table.

"To get them out? It would be inefficient," the doctor said. "They would only have to be buried twice."

Dante was silent. He tried to spread his hands but the manacles snapped taut.

"Stay close to me," the doctor said. "Carnot will join us if he can lag behind. There are two trucks. We will try to get into the second truck."

"It's insane. Why don't they simply . . . get it over with?"

"Protocol must be observed."

Outside, the shelling increased in intensity.

"Oh, my God," Dante moaned. "Listen to them."

"Finish your soup. Don't drink it too fast or you might vomit. You must hold onto your soup. Don't talk. Eat. Conserve your strength."

As they left for the courtyard, where the trucks were waiting in the dark, Carnot was caught lagging behind. He was jerked around and pushed into the first truck. Dante had a chance to count them. Twelve, including himself. Auguste was gone. So were Anton and Agathe. Charles, the priest, was gone. Lautrec was in the first truck. So was Carnot. Of the prisoners in the second truck, the doctor was the only one Dante knew. Then suddenly he recognized Berger. Antoine Berger had been beaten almost beyond recognition, but he was still walking. A pang of horror went through Dante when he saw his face. He knew Berger had seen him. Two men he knew in the first truck. Berger and the doctor he knew in the second. Of the other seven prisoners, only a few looked familiar.

The trucks left the courtyard and started, not along the coast road but inland, to avoid the harbor and the shelling, which now had grown deafening to ears used to nothing but silence. It was some time before conversation could be attempted. Two guards rode postilion on the rear platform outside the wire mesh. The night was pitch black.

Dante edged closer toward the doctor until he was sure that he could talk without being heard by any of the prisoners he didn't know.

"What happened to the escape?"

"Someone talked," the doctor said. In his mind's eye Dante could imagine the resigned shrug that went with the words. It was totally dark. The truck drove slowly, blacked out. The roads were pitted, and the prisoners shot painfully to and fro as the springless vehicle lurched over the potholes or veered to avoid bomb damage.

"What happened to Berger?" Dante asked in a whisper. "He looks bad."

"The same thing that happens to everyone else. You looked that way when I first saw you. I should have let you look in the mirror."

"Do I look better?"

"You're healing," the doctor said. "But you've lost weight."

"I don't understand this."

"Don't try. Dujardin has lost his mind with fear. He is going to try to take us to Germany himself."

"What! Is he with us?"

"Look through the grill. Behind us. See those blue lights? He's managed to get a car that runs."

In the darkness Dante strained his eyes to see. Slowly he made out the ghosting blue blackout headlights far behind them. They disappeared again as the truck rounded a curve in the road. Then they came back.

"He's a madman. The war is over," Dante said.

"Not for us. Not for him. Yes, he's a madman," the doctor said softly, almost sadly, with a sigh of fatigue that sounded like regret.

"We must talk to Berger."

"Leave him alone. He's been gone over for the last forty-eight hours without sleep. They think he's you now. He will have to sleep. We have plenty of time for talk. Germany is a long way off. You must sleep also. There is a strong Resistance in Grenoble. I think they've been alerted to look for us. I don't know if the word got through. Hope."

"Yes."

"But for now, sleep. We will hold council when the guards get tired of standing on the back and looking in. Sooner or later they will sit down and look at where we've been. Then we can change our places around. Berger is close enough."

"When will we reach Grenoble?"

"Don't be a fool with questions," the doctor said sharply. "Sleep."

"No talking in there," barked the guard.

"Merde," someone said. There was silence. Only the motor throbbing. And they slept.

XVII

Invasive war, Leviathan, came now from the south. In shifting fortunes of terror and hope and confusion, decisions were made and revised and remade and unmade; plans triumphed, plans failed, and men were at the mercy of chance, excited by fear, humbled by immensity, tormented by conscience. Swept on the roaring river of war and events, submerged in headlong defeat, in pellmell thanksgiving and victory, in blood and the smell of death, the strategies and mere designs of men were hourly reforged to fit the fluid moment, to cleave to the flying design. Having untrammeled the blood-crazy stallions, men were no longer masters, but slaves to hope and catastrophe; unhorsed, they plunged across the burning eye of Hell in pursuit, carrying empty bridles. The invasions came. The war moved; and men, where they could, moved with it. Boiling up out of the churning sea, the war moved across the beaches and followed the rivers: first the Seine, the Loire. Now, later, the Rhone.

Foot soldiers and chiefs of state, men would remember these days of blast and decision. Some would remember these days only vaguely, a slow delirium of mud and confusion memorized by touch and taste and smell. Others would recall only the battle orders, the placement of platoons and rubber-tired guns, the relentless heartache of dog-tired decision. Each man would suffer out his part, would remember it the way he felt and saw it, would try, in the unshattered years left him, to fit that remem-

bered part into the whole. Very few would remember the whole, the maddening whole as it was then, the whole of the agony and failure and imperfection of men. But a certain few men, having borne the full weight, would remember it uniquely, would in the intervening years piece together the architectonic moments of destiny, lay bare the matrices of decision. And one man, a leader in particular, looking backward from the peace yet to come, would remember it all and record it, would tell the cataclysmic tale. He would, in his own measured time, order this event and give it meaning, palpable and whole again, would tell it in his own words, his own way:

* * * * *

. . . I visited Eisenhower at his headquarters near Portsmouth and unfolded to him my last hope of stopping the "Dragoon" operation. After an agreeable luncheon we had a long and serious conversation. Eisenhower had with him Bedell Smith and Admiral Ramsay. I had brought the First Sea Lord, as the movement of shipping was the key. Briefly, what I proposed was to continue loading the "Dragoon" expedition, but when the troops were in the ships to send them through the Straits of Gibraltar and enter France at Bordeaux. The matter had been long considered by the British Chiefs of Staff, and the operation was considered feasible. I showed Eisenhower the telegram I had sent to the President, whose reply I had not yet received, and did my best to convince him. The First Sea Lord strongly supported me. Admiral Ramsay argued against any change of plan. Bedell Smith, on the contrary, declared himself strongly in favour of this sudden deflection of the attack, which would have all the surprise that sea-power can bestow. Eisenhower in no way resented the views of his Chief of Staff. He always encouraged free expression of opinion in council at the summit, though of course whatever was settled would receive every loyalty in execution.

However, I was quite unable to move him, and next day I received the President's reply.

President Roosevelt to Prime Minister   8 Aug. 44

I have consulted by telegraph with my Chiefs of Staff, and am unable to agree that the resources allocated to "Dragoon" should be considered available for a move into France via ports on the coast of Brittany.

On the contrary, it is my considered opinion that "Dragoon" should be launched as planned at the earliest practicable date, and I have full confidence that it will be successful and of great assistance to Eisenhower in driving the Huns from France.

There was no more to be done about it. It is worth noting that we had now passed the day in July when for the first time in the war the movement of the great American armies into Europe and their growth in the Far East made their numbers in action for the first time greater than our own. Influence on Allied operations is usually increased by large reinforcements. It must also be remembered that had the British views on this strategic issue been accepted, the tactical preparations might well have caused some delay, which again would have reacted on the general argument.

> *Prime Minister to President Roosevelt* 8 Aug. 44
> I pray God that you may be right. We shall of course do everything in our power to help you achieve success.

* * * * *

The days were so crowded with Cabinet business that my dates receded. On August 9 I telegraphed to Mr. Duff Cooper that I hoped to arrive at the Maison Blanche airfield, outside Algiers, about 6:30 A.M. on Friday, August 11, and would stay there for about three hours on my way to Naples. I added, "You may tell de Gaulle in case he wishes to see me at your house or the Admiral's villa. The visit is quite informal."

We arrived punctually. Duff Cooper met me, and took me to his house, which his wife had made most comfortable. He told me he had conveyed my invitation or suggestion to de Gaulle, and that the General had refused. He did not wish to intrude upon the repose I should need at this brief halt on my journey. I thought this needlessly haughty, considering all the business we had in hand and what I could have told him. He was however still offended by what had happened at "Overlord," and thought this was a good chance of marking his displeasure. I did not in fact see him again for several months.

I reached Naples that afternoon, and was installed in the palatial though somewhat dilapidated Villa Rivalta, with a glorious view of Vesuvius and the bay. Here General Wilson explained to me that all arrangements had been made for a conference next morning with Tito and Subašić, the new Yugoslav Prime Minister of King Peter's Government in London. They had already arrived in Naples, and would dine with us the next night.

* * * * *

On all these three days at Naples I mingled pleasure with toil. Admiral Morse, who commanded the naval forces, took me each day in his barge on an expedition, of which the prime feature was a bathe. On the first we went to the island of Ischia, with its hot springs, and on the return we ran through an immense United States troop convoy sailing for the landing on the Riviera. All the ships were crowded with men, and as we passed along their lines they cheered enthusiastically. They did not know that if I had had my way they would be sailing in a different direction. However, I was proud to wave to these gallant soldiers. We also visited Capri. I had never seen the Blue Grotto before. It is indeed a miracle of transparent, sparkling water of a most intense, vivid blue. We bathed in a small, warm bay, and repaired to luncheon at a comfortable inn. I summoned up in my mind all I could remember about the Emperor Tiberius. Certainly in Capri he had chosen an agreeable headquarters from which to rule the world.

These days, apart from business, were a sunshine holiday.

* * * * *

On the afternoon of August 14 I flew in General Wilson's Dakota to Corsica in order to see the landing of "Anvil" which I had tried so hard to stop, but to which I wished all success. We had a pleasant flight to Ajaccio, in the harbour of which General Wilson and Admiral John Cunningham had posted themselves on board a British headquarters ship. The airfield was very small and not easily approached. The pilot was excellent. He had to come in between two bluffs, and his port wing was scarcely fifteen feet from one of them. The General and the Admiral brought me aboard, and we spent a long evening on our affairs. I was to start at daylight in the British destroyer *Kimberley.* I took with me two members of the American Administration, General Somervell and Mr. Patterson, the Assistant Secretary of War, who were on the spot to see their venture. Captain Allen, whose help in these volumes I have acknowledged, was sent by the Admiral to see that we did not get into trouble. We were five hours sailing before we reached the line of battle-ships bombarding at about fifteen thousand yards. I now learned from Captain Allen that we were not supposed to go beyond the ten-thousand-yard limit for fear of mines. If I had known this when we passed the *Ramillies,* which was firing at intervals, I could have asked for a picket-boat and gone ashore. As it was we did not go nearer than about seven thousand yards. Here we saw the long rows of boats filled with American storm troops steaming in continuously to the Bay of St. Tropez. As far as I could see or hear not a shot was fired either at the approaching flotillas or on the beaches. The battleships had now stopped firing, as there seemed to be nobody there. We then returned to Ajaccio. I had at least done the civil to "Anvil," and indeed I thought it was a good thing I was near the scene to show the interest I took in it. On the way back I found a lively novel, *Grand Hotel,* in the captain's cabin, and this kept me in good temper till I got back to the Supreme Commander and the Naval Commander-in-Chief, who had passed an equally dull day sitting in the stern cabin.

On August 16 I got back to Naples, and rested there for the night before going up to meet Alexander at the front. I telegraphed to the King, from whom I had received a very kind telegram.

Prime Minister to the King   17 Aug. 44
    With humble duty.
    From my distant view of the "Dragoon" operation, the landing seemed to be effected with the utmost smoothness. How much time will be taken in the advance first to Marseilles and then up the Rhone valley, and how these operations will relate themselves

to the far greater and possibly decisive operations in the north [Normandy], are the questions that now arise.

2. I am proceeding today to General Alexander's headquarters. It is very important that we ensure that Alexander's army is not so mauled and milked that it cannot have a theme or plan of campaign. This will certainly require a conference on something like the "Quadrant" scale, and at the same place [Quebec].

3. My vigour has been greatly restored by the change and movement and the warm weather. I hope to see various people, including Mr. Papandreou, in Rome, where I expect to be on the 21st. May I express to Your Majesty the pleasure and encouragement which Your Majesty's gracious message gave me.

And to General Eisenhower:

Prime Minister to General Eisenhower (France)   18 Aug. 44

I am following with thrilled attention the magnificent developments of operations in Normandy and Anjou. I offer you again my sincere congratulations on the truly marvellous results achieved, and hope for surpassing victory. You have certainly among other things effected a very important diversion from our attack at "Dragoon." I watched this landing yesterday from afar. All I have learnt here makes me admire the perfect precision with which the landing was arranged and the intimate collaboration of British-American forces and organisations. I shall hope to come and see you and Montgomery before the end of the month. Much will have happened by them. It seems to me that the results might well eclipse all the Russian victories up to the present. All good wishes to you and Bedell.

*   *   *   *   *

This chapter may close with an outline of the "Anvil-Dragoon" operations themselves.

The Seventh Army, under General Patch, had been formed to carry out the attack. It consisted of seven French and three U.S. divisions, together with a mixed American and British airborne division. The three American divisions comprised General Truscott's VIth Corps, which had formed an important part of General Clark's Fifth Army in Italy. In addition, up to four French divisions and a considerable part of the Allied air forces were withdrawn from Alexander's command.

The new expedition was mounted from both Italy and North Africa, Naples, Taranto, Brindisi, and Oran being used as the chief loading-ports. Great preparations had been made throughout the year to convert Corsica into an advanced air base and to use Ajaccio as a staging-port for landing-craft proceeding to the assault from Italy. All these arrangements now bore fruit. Under the Commander-in-Chief, Admiral Sir John Cunningham, the naval attack was entrusted to Vice-Admiral

Hewitt, U.S.N., who had had much experience in similar operations in the Mediterranean. Lieutenant-General Eaker, U.S.A.A.F., commanded the air forces, with Air Marshal Slessor as his deputy.

Landing-craft restricted the first seaborne landing to three divisions, and the more experienced Americans led the van. Shore defences all along the coast were strong, but the enemy were weak in numbers and some were of poor quality. In June there had been fourteen German divisions in Southern France, but four of these were drawn away to the fighting in Normandy, and no more than ten remained to guard the 200 miles of coastline. Only three of these lay near the beaches on which we landed. The enemy were also short of aircraft. Against our total of 5000 in the Mediterranean, of which 2000 were based in Corsica and Sardinia, they could muster a bare two hundred, and these were mauled in the days before the invasion. In the midst of the Germans in Southern France over 25,000 armed men of the Resistance were ready to revolt. We had sent them their weapons, and, as in so many other parts of France, they had been organised by some of that devoted band of men and women trained in Britain for the purpose during the past three years.

The strength of the enemy's defences demanded a heavy preliminary bombardment, which was provided from the air for the previous fortnight all along the coast, and, jointly with the Allied Navies, on the landing beaches immediately before our descent. No fewer than six battleships, twenty-one cruisers, and a hundred destroyers took part. The three U.S. divisions, with American and French Commandos on their left, landed early on August 15 between Cannes and Hyères. Thanks to the bombardment, successful deception plans, continuous fighter cover, and good staff work, our casualties were relatively few. During the previous night the airborne division had dropped around Le Muy, and soon joined hands with the seaborne attack.

By noon on the 16th the three American divisions were ashore. One of them moved northward to Sisteron, and the other two struck north-west towards Avignon. The IInd French Corps landed immediately behind them and made for Toulon and Marseilles. Both places were strongly defended, and although the French were built up to a force of five divisions the ports were not fully occupied till the end of the month. The installations were severely damaged, but Port de Bouc had been captured intact with the aid of the Resistance, and supplies soon began to flow. This was a valuable contribution by the French forces under General de Lattre de Tassigny. In the meantime the Americans had been moving fast, and on August 28 were beyond Grenoble and Valence. The enemy made no serious attempt to stop the advance, except for a stiff fight at Montélimar by a Panzer division. The Allied Tactical Air Force was treating them roughly and destroying their transport. Eisenhower's pursuit from Normandy was cutting in behind them, having reached the Seine at Fontainebleau on August 20, and five days later it was well past Troyes. No wonder the surviving elements of the German Nineteenth

Army, amounting to a nominal five divisions, were in full retreat, leaving 50,000 prisoners in our hands. Lyons was taken on September 3, Besançon on the 8th, and Dijon was liberated by the Resistance Movement on the 11th. On that day "Dragoon" and "Overlord" joined hands at Sombernon. In the triangle of Southwest France, trapped by these concentric thrusts, were the isolated remnants of the German First Army, over 20,000 strong, who freely gave themselves up.

* * * * *

To sum up the "Anvil-Dragoon" story, the original proposal at Teheran in November 1943, was for a descent on the south of France to help take the weight off "Overlord" [the landing in Normandy]. The timing was to be either in the week before or the week after D-Day. All this was changed by what happened in the interval. The latent threat from the Mediterranean sufficed in itself to keep ten German divisions on the Riviera. Anzio alone had meant that the equivalent of four enemy divisions was lost to other fronts. When, with the help of Anzio, our whole battle line advanced, captured Rome and threatened the Gothic Line, the Germans hurried a further eight divisions to Italy. Delay in the capture of Rome and the despatch of landing-craft from the Mediterranean to help "Overlord" caused the postponement of "Anvil-Dragoon" till mid-August or two months later than had been proposed. It therefore did not in any way affect "Overlord." When it was belatedly launched, it drew no enemy down from the Normandy battle theatre. Therefore none of the reasons present in our minds at Teheran had any relation to what was done and "Dragoon" caused no diversion from the forces opposing General Eisenhower. In fact instead of helping him, he helped it by threatening the rear of the Germans retiring up the Rhone valley. This is not to deny that the operation as carried out eventually brought important assistance to General Eisenhower by the arrival of another army on his right flank, and the opening of another line of communications thither. For this a heavy price was paid. The army of Italy was deprived of its opportunity to strike a most formidable blow at the Germans, and very possibly to reach Vienna before the Russians, with all that might have followed therefrom. But once the final decision was reached I of course gave "Dragoon" my full support, though I had done my best to constrain or deflect it.

* * * * *

At this time I received some pregnant messages from Smuts, now back at the Cape. He had always agreed wholeheartedly with my views on "Dragoon," "but," he now wrote (August 30), "please do not let strategy absorb all your attention to the damage of the greater issue now looming up.

"From now on it would be wise to keep a very close eye on all matters bearing on the future settlement of Europe. This is the crucial issue on which the future of the world for generations will depend. In its solution

your vision, experience, and great influence may prove a main factor." *

I have been taxed in the years since the war with pressing after Teheran, and particularly during these weeks under review, for a large-scale Allied invasion of the Balkans in defiance of American thinking on the grand strategy of the war.

The essence of my oft-repeated view is contained in the following reply to these messages from Smuts:

> *Prime Minister to Field-Marshal Smuts*   31 Aug. 44
> Local success of "Dragoon" has quite delighted Americans, who intend to use this route to thrust in every reinforcement. Of course 45,000 prisoners have been taken, and there will be many more. Their idea now, from which nothing will turn them, is to work in a whole Army Group through the captured ports instead of using the much easier ports on the Atlantic.

"My object now," I said, "is to keep what we have got in Italy, which should be sufficient since the enemy has withdrawn four of his best divisions. With this I hope to turn and break the Gothic Line, break into the Po valley, and ultimately advance by Trieste and the Ljubljana Gap to Vienna. Even if the war came to an end at an early date I have told Alexander to be ready for a dash with armoured cars."

* My italics.—W.S.C.

XVIII

Toward midnight the moon came out. The men in the truck were jolted awake as the truck stopped suddenly. There was silence for a moment when the motor was cut. Outside there was nothing but night. It was cooler.

Outside there was the sound of voices shouting far up the road ahead, thin, cold, detached. A question. And answer. Both unintelligible, strange and small in the black emptiness of the night.

"Where are we?" asked a voice thick with sleep and pain.

"Look at the map," came the sarcastic answer.

"No talking," said the guard.

"Merde."

"No talking."

"Merde."

"Merde encore."

"Quiet," the doctor hissed, straining to make out what the dim voices were saying. Everyone listened.

"German," the doctor said. "We must have run into a convoy."

Someone was approaching. The conversation was getting nearer.

"They're stopping us," the doctor said. "Do you understand German?"

"They're asking for papers," Dante said. There was a long silence. Dante could visualize the German scanning the papers by flashlight, then shining his light into the cab. Further up the road, where the first truck had been stopped, Dante concluded, he heard more shouted orders. The words were sharp and deadly, terrifying even in their smallness under the vast black sky and passive moon. Like animals barking, for remote unknown reasons, in the vast unintelligible silence of the night. Then the near German shouted up the road to his companions. Beside the road the crickets dinned the silence.

"He's calling for an officer," Dante said.

Suddenly the blade of a flashlight stabbed into the feral darkness of the truck. One at a time the faces of the men, white with sleep and fear, were impaled on the beam. They looked like animals caught in the light. Their eyes shone wide, trapped, transfixed. Suddenly Dante was blinded in his turn. The light snapped off. They listened to the receding bootsteps.

"Where are we?" a voice asked.

"For Christ's sake, shut up," someone pleaded.

Someone groaned. Dante knew it was Berger. In the brief flash of light he had seen him lying prone athwart the truck bed up forward. He was probably still unconscious in sleep.

For a long time there was silence.

"Where is Dujardin?" Dante asked the doctor.

"They passed us a while back. He must have expected something like this."

"Were you awake?"

"Occasionally," the doctor said.

Outside there was no wind, no sound: only the chinking of the overheated engine as it cooled and contracted in the night air.

"We've been going up," the doctor said. "We're probably entering the lower Alps."

"Yes," Dante said. "It's cooler. You can feel it."

Both guards had left their posts. They were standing in the road behind. The ruby point of a cigarette glowed in alternation as they passed it back and forth between them.

Time dragged. Outside there was still no sign of movement, no sound.

"What do you suppose they're up to?" asked Dante.

"Dujardin is probably trying to peddle us off. Selling his sheep to the caravan."

After a short while they heard the two drivers leave the cab. Both doors slammed, one after the other. The drivers went up ahead.

"Two drivers," the doctor counted. "Two guards. With Dujardin

445

and his bodyguard and the other truck, that makes ten. We outnumber them by two at least." He grunted. "Ha," he said, disgusted.

Finally they heard the drivers coming back. Someone was explaining something in German-tortured French. Then the German gave up and reverted to his own language.

"We can't go past," Dante said. "They are clearing the road up ahead. There's a whole convoy stalled. Wait." Dante listened. "Wreckage. Sabotage. I can't catch it all."

There was one more spate of brittle words. Then they heard the German walking back up the road again, and the two drivers cursing quietly between themselves. The doors of the cab opened. They felt the truck respond to the weight of the drivers as they came aboard again. The doors slammed together. Nothing happened. Silence.

"He said we could wait until morning or turn back," Dante translated.

"He sounded drunk," the doctor said.

"Yes."

They heard the drivers shifting around to make themselves comfortable in the cab. Then there was silence again. Slowly, the nightsound of insects whirring in the grass beside the road penetrated the empty stillness again.

"Go to sleep," the doctor said.

After a time, in a half-doze, Dante heard a scuffling sound overhead. One of the guards had climbed up onto the top of the truck and stretched out. Dante opened his eyes. The other one lay stretched out on the platform behind. His weapon leaned against it, the barrel jutting upright and glinting in the glimmer of the dying moon. He guarded it in the crook of his arm. The spaces in the heavy wire grillwork were too small to get a hand through. After that Dante remembered nothing. Once as in a dream, he thought he heard drunken singing up ahead.

When he awoke again it was still dark. He lay awake listening absently to the chattering sound that woke him: dim snappings in the distance. Then he sat upright, bolted awake, and turned to shake the doctor. What had awakened him he suddenly recognized as the rattle of gunfire. The doctor was already awake, tense and silent in the darkness, listening.

For nearly an hour they sat in darkness, listening. After the first furious spate of gunfire, there was only sporadic shooting.

"What do you think?" Dante asked the doctor.

"It could be an ambush. Try to wake up Berger."

"It will be dawn soon."

"Yes," said the doctor. "We have to be ready."

Berger was sleeping so deeply that Dante thought he was dead. He felt his pulse. The beat was slow but strong. He shook him without results. Finally he slapped him awake. Berger rolled over. "No," he said.

"Wake up," Dante hissed in his ear.

"I won't tell you anything more," Berger said brokenly, in English. It startled Dante. Two of the prisoners Dante didn't know whispered to each other. Dante put his hand over Berger's mouth in the darkness. Berger struggled, still drugged with sleep. Dante whispered in his ear to calm him. "It's me, Dante," he whispered. *"Don't speak English."* Gradually he felt Berger relax. He removed his hand carefully, ready to clap it back again at the first syllable of English.

"I'm sorry," Berger whispered in French. "What's happened? Where is this?"

"We're in a truck. They're taking us to Germany."

Berger gave a low moan, like a man in grief. "I'm sorry," he said.

Dante felt a chill go through him. He was torn between contempt and pity for the inert form lying in the darkness. Berger made a sound like sobbing. Dante fought down a temptation to question him then and there.

"There's nothing to be sorry for," Dante said. "We're all in this together. You'll have to wake up. We have to be ready in case of attack. It might be our chance."

Berger sat up slowly. Dante felt the doctor at his elbow.

"How is he?" the doctor whispered.

"I'm all right," Berger said.

"What happened?" Dante asked Berger urgently.

"Happened?"

"Adriane. Where is she?"

"I don't know. She was out when they came."

"What about Henri?"

"Henri?"

"Her brother." Dante shook Berger's shoulder.

"He was shot. In front of the hotel. He ran."

"Ran?" He shook Berger again. "Damn you, wake up."

"She was out getting food."

"Do you think she came back?"

"I don't know. Maybe she saw the cars. I don't know."

"How many men came?"

"I don't know. Maybe she stayed away. Why are you . . ."

"All right." He released his grip on Berger's arm.

Berger mumbled, "I don't know. Leave me alone."

The doctor turned to the other three prisoners, who were all awake now.

"Who is for escaping?" he asked in a low voice. No one answered.

"You don't think we'll get out of this alive, do you?" the doctor asked, addressing all of them.

"The war will be over in a few days," one of the prisoners said.

"We'd be shot down before we got out of the truck," another one said. The three other prisoners sat apart from Dante, Berger and the doctor. They'd been whispering among themselves and had evidently come to some sort of decision.

447

The doctor said, "You won't join us?"

"You're not going anywhere," the first prisoner said. He was evidently the spokesman for the three. His tone was clearly menacing. "If you tried, they'd shoot us too."

There was sullen silence in the truck.

"You are fools," the doctor said. "We're on our way to be executed."

"We don't think so," said the spokesman. Dante tried to see his face but it was too dark. "If they were going to kill us they would have already done it."

"If there is to be an attack, it will come at dawn," the doctor said.

"Let it come."

"Will you interfere if we try?" Dante asked.

"You won't try," the prisoner said. "We would pay for your success."

"The war is almost over," another prisoner whined softly. "Why make trouble?"

"You'll be shot, war or no war," the doctor said.

"We've made the decision," the spokesman said. "There'll be no escape."

Berger suddenly laughed a high-pitched choked laugh. It made Dante shudder. He wondered if Berger's mind was cracking.

"For your own safety," the doctor said softly, "you three had better keep out of my reach."

"There's no point fighting among ourselves," the spokesman said. "You'll thank me when the war is over. I'll buy you a glass of wine, Doctor."

"I don't drink with cowards," the doctor said. "Even in hell."

"Perhaps someday you'll apologize for that remark, Doctor," the prisoner said. "After we've saved you from killing yourself and your good friends."

"If I am wrong, I'll apologize," the doctor said.

"You'll be in a happier mood," the prisoner said. "In happier times."

The doctor turned around and spoke in a whisper to Dante and Berger. "We'll have to be careful. Perhaps they'll change their minds, but we'll have to work on them gradually. They're afraid."

"But how *could* we escape?" Dante asked in a whisper. "Even if they agreed not to stop us."

"With this."

Dante felt the doctor press an open wire into his hand.

"The lock is already open. I opened it while you were all asleep."

"But the guards?" Dante asked incredulously.

"One was on the roof sleeping. The other is bought. That's why I wanted Carnot in this truck. But the one guard has to be careful of his friend."

"But how . . ."

"I've worked in the prison for a long time. One learns to prepare for the day when one is caught. I arranged this a long time ago. It was luck that he was assigned to go along on this journey. I couldn't believe it when I saw him."

"But the lock . . ."

"I used to practice. One learns to look ahead."

"Do you think if we told the others . . ."

"Right now it's too risky. They're not properly disposed to the idea."

"But if we trusted them enough to tell them that . . ."

"Trust is a spiritual thing. They blame us for their misfortune."

"What do you mean?" Berger asked in a hoarse whisper.

"They're innocent. They've never had anything to do with the underground. They just happened to be in a certain café at the wrong time, but now they know too much and Dujardin can't let them go. I understand how they feel. We have to be very careful with them. I think I can bring them around before we get to Grenoble."

"But what if there's an attack this morning?"

"I don't know," said the doctor. "It worries me. I wish I knew what was going on outside. I'd like to know what the shooting was about."

"What if they find the lock open?"

"They'll close it, I suppose," the doctor said.

"I don't like this," Dante said. He turned and looked toward the back of the truck. A strange light flickered on the faces of the guards standing off to the side of the road. They were watching something up ahead. "Look," Dante said. "Something's burning up ahead. You can see the light reflected."

The doctor looked. The reflected firelight showed vague shadows in the road. The two guards looked nervous. They fingered their weapons and glanced from time to time at the side of the road. The other three prisoners had noticed it too.

No one said anything.

They watched the strange light for a long time, wondering what it was that was burning. The firing up ahead had stopped completely now. Slowly the light waned, and silence was once more intensified by darkness. But the sky was beginning to show the first gray streaks of dawn. Two of the other prisoners went back to sleep while the third remained awake, sitting up watching the doctor, Dante and Berger. Finally Berger lay down and dozed off again. The doctor didn't stop him.

"If there were going to be an attack they would have started it by now," the doctor said to Dante.

"Perhaps that *was* the attack, and it failed."

"I doubt if that was the main attack. It's more likely that they've just blocked the road to stop the trucks, so that we'll be vulnerable from the air. We may get strafed if they don't get the road cleared by daylight."

"You don't think this is a large group?"

"No. We are not strong in this area. They probably just mined the road. If they leave us here to be strafed we can get out. Our three innocents will probably come with us," the doctor said. "Pray for rain."

As it got lighter outside, the two guards came back to the truck and sat down on the back platform. They didn't talk. One of the other prisoners woke up and asked the guards where they were. Neither of them answered. After that there was complete silence. The predawn sky turned gray and purple and the first dark streaks of red appeared at the far horizon. The outline of the road became visible, stretching off behind them. What little of the landscape they could see from the back of the truck was hilly, almost mountainous.

Just before dawn there were voices outside the truck. Dante was half dozing in a sitting position when the doctor jabbed him with an elbow.

"What's he saying?" the doctor demanded urgently. It was a German insisting about something. Dante listened.

"Something about a receipt. I don't quite understand."

Then came a flurry of French. The speakers sounded as if they were standing some distance from the truck, because it was nearly impossible to make out what they were saying.

"Do you recognize your friend?" the doctor asked mildly.

"My friend?"

"That's Dujardin. I'd recognize that squeak anywhere," the doctor said.

Dante listened.

"There seems to be some sort of disagreement," he said.

"I gathered that. Can you make out what it's about?"

"They're too far away."

"What sort of receipt?" the doctor asked.

"I don't know."

The voices continued for some time and then went away. There was silence again. Suddenly there was the sound of marching feet. A squad of Germans appeared around the end of the truck and halted in full view.

"SS," the doctor whispered.

For a long time nothing happened. Dante woke Berger by pinching him surreptitiously. The other three prisoners were all awake.

Up ahead there was the sound of engines starting, one after the other, and of vehicles backing and filling. There were a great many vehicles from the sound of it.

"They're getting them off the road," Dante said. The doctor nodded, not taking his eyes off the squad of men standing at the back of the truck. The Germans didn't talk among themselves, but simply stood at ease, waiting. They didn't look at the prisoners.

"Something's going to happen," the doctor said.

Suddenly the old Citroën that Dujardin had come in passed around the truck and halted some distance down the road. It was headed back toward the coast. Three Germans ran down the road after it and got in. The doors slammed and the car ground into gear.

Dante looked at the doctor as the car disappeared around a far bend in the road. "What do you think?" he asked.

"I think we've been sold to a new owner," the doctor said somberly. "That's what the receipt was for."

At that moment the squad of men snapped to attention and a large unkempt man in the uniform of an SS colonel appeared at the back of the truck and stared in at the six prisoners. He looked as though he'd just been roused from sleeping in his clothes. His eyes were red and irritated and his face was flushed with sullen ugly anger. He looked drunk and had difficulty focusing his eyes. There was something animal-like about him, a cruelty that molded his features in a permanent mask. The black uniform with the death's head insignia made a chilling harmony with the face of the man who wore it. Dante couldn't take his eyes off him. The SS colonel stared for a long moment, his eyes rheumy with dead malevolence, and then he turned away and gave an order to the men. He signaled to the two prison guards to open the back of the truck. One of them sprang forward and fumbled his key in the open lock, and opened the grill. No one seemed to notice that the lock had been open. The guard was white with fear; Dante realized that he had known.

Dante and the other prisoners were herded out of the truck and gathered in a group with the six from the other truck. They stood at the side of the road under guard and watched the two trucks back up and turn around. When the trucks were completely turned around they stopped and the four guards got into the back of the second truck. The two trucks started down the road. The prisoners watched them go. The open grilled doors flapped to and fro as the empty trucks made good their flight.

A lieutenant came from the head of the convoy to take over the prisoners. He was a thin man, old for a lieutenant, with a lean haggard face. Dante linked the face with the voice he had heard earlier outside the truck. He seemed ill at ease before the detail of men standing guard on the prisoners. For one thing, Dante noted, the sergeant treated him with a deference that bordered on mockery. The lieutenant gave orders to the sergeant to put the prisoners to work clearing two wrecks off the road ahead. He spoke in a curious voice, soft almost to the point of being feminine. The sergeant amused his men by mimicking him. The lieutenant didn't seem to notice it.

In the east the sky was lightening to gray.

What happened in that hour before dawn would never be completely known even by those few who survived it. What happened during the rest of the day crippled the imagination. It was as though the very demons of Hell had been spewed up out of the fissured earth with orders to destroy. In the cold darkness of that lonely mountain road only a handful met death. But before the day was over, in a fury of insane drunken vengeance a whole village perished, the population put to death, the buildings burned; what wouldn't burn was pulverized. In an orgy of destruction the village of Montpelle was swept off its mountainside into oblivion. The populace was locked inside the church; the church burned.

When the destroyers left at nightfall they left behind them, as a final signature to their achievement, a flaming monument of flesh and gasoline, a human torch that flared in the desolate wind atop the mountain. It burned into the night and excited wonder in the distant inhabitants of the surrounding region. In the morning the peasants came, cautiously, for they had heard the explosions the day before.

They came, and at first they didn't believe. They sifted the village through puzzled fingers and let the dust and ashes fall at their feet. Had the people been taken hostage? Even when they found the first few charred bodies they were unable to believe they were all dead. For mostly they were peasants, unnoticed by the war. But the grim word spread, and they came like pilgrims to a shrine of death. The mysteries of the shrine were beyond the profanity of mere belief. Among those who came first there was only dumbstruck awe, wonder impossibly beyond belief, even beyond horror.

The destroyers had come by night, vanished by night. The peasants had heard their distant engines roaring and clanking along the roads during the week's stealthy retreat; from their beds, in shuttered secret fear they listened to the conqueror leaving the land under cover of night, and husbands whispered to wives. It was too soon yet to breathe relief. They wondered who was chasing this phantom. Amid rumors of invasion, of wild battles, of liberation, of the war's end, they listened alertly, their eyes open in darkness, waiting. Then one night the nightlong rumbling convoys were gone; there was only the occasional passing of trucks, in groups, at irregular intervals through the night. Most of the armored divisions were gone, withdrawn.

But the scorpion carries death in his tail; the SS unit that destroyed the village of Montpelle prided themselves on their name: the Scorpion Battalion. If there could be any answer to why the village was massacred, if there could be any rational knowledge of that insanity, that answer and that knowledge died with the madness. For the Scorpion Battalion later dragged its bloody trail across the Rhine and was followed, cut off, and surrounded. And finally, in one of the cruelest engagements that has ever been fought on the face of the earth, in the very last week of the war, the destroyers themselves were destroyed.

In a single circuit of the sun, a town and its population were destroyed and no one would later be available or alive to be blamed, except an insignificant official, an accessory before the fact, who supplied the twelve prisoners whose final light illuminated the night and beckoned the first pilgrims to the devil's altar where these victims were sacrificed. Théophile Dujardin. There was no one else to share the guilt. The others were dead or disappeared, in any case destroyed. The reasoned attempt to reconstruct what happened during that day would later occupy seven volumes, including: the First Report of the Field Investigation Team, the Preliminary Sessional Documents of the War Crimes Court of Inquiry, the Record of the Extraordinary Tribunal of Paris, and finally, the pertinent sections of the Nuremberg War Crimes Proceedings. Aside from the eventual conviction of Théophile Dujardin as accessory to the massacre, the two years of juridical inquiry would find only that, insofar as could be determined, the principals, the criminals, were dead. And if any were then alive they were vanished.

From captured enemy archives, it would be learned that the SS Scorpion Battalion had originally been assigned to stay behind with the few German divisions that were to try to blunt the southern invasion. But when it became obvious even to Hitler that he couldn't hope to stem the southern advance up the Rhone Valley, the battalion's orders were changed. From the south came the Allied Seventh Army, from the east the Third Army; like a huge pair of jaws they threatened to close on the German Nineteenth Army. Hitler was determined to prevent this encirclement at all costs. The only escape route was the pass between the Vosges and the Jura mountain ranges, the Belfort Gap. Some of Hitler's most vicious troops were rushed in to hold the jaws open. And at the last minute, the Scorpion Battalion was among them.

And where the village of Montpelle stood, all that remains is a plain stone marker standing mute and inscriptionless, an angular abstract sphinx riddling the world with its query.

XIX

Lieutenant Schneider had passed most of the war in Germany as an administrative officer in the SS. His specialty was finance, and finance was a specialty of the SS. The SS was financed like a corporation, a gigantic holding company that owned large pieces of German industries, and was thus beyond the reach of any group that might attempt to curb it through control of its funds. As the Führer's personal army and bodyguard it was even beyond the reach of the Wehrmacht and of the General Staff. For Hitler never fully trusted his regular generals; although they originally promoted him to power, he could never be sure that power was truly his until he deprived them of power to rescind the gift they'd bestowed. In creating the SS, Hitler tied their hands. For the SS answered to no one except its creator.

It was to insure this that Emil Schneider, forty-two, former professor of economics, was impressed into the Death's Head Elite. And up to the last days of the war, Lieutenant Schneider, married, childless, passed the war engaged in the quiet management of the huge complex investment trust that was the backbone and blood of the SS. Though he'd taken the oath and bore the tattoo, he looked on the war with mild detachment. The job was absorbing, unique in its challenges, and full of interesting problems. He did what was required of him, asked no questions. In essence, his job would have been the same had he been managing the securities of a life insurance company, a subject he'd written his doctoral dissertation on years before. Except that he went to work in uniform.

It was a strange job, full of irony, but until the closing days of the war the irony was lost on Lieutenant Schneider, who spent his evenings making notes for the book he would publish after the war. For he had several heavy books to his credit already. He liked writing; it made up for childlessness. War was thus something he simply accepted; it never occurred to him to wonder who would win it. The worst that could happen would be a repetition of 1918. Germany would negotiate for an adjusted peace, perhaps give up some of her hard-won territory on the Continent in return for her old colonies back. Then there would be the problems of adjustment to peacetime economy, of controlling inflation—serious problems, but not insoluble, and at any rate interesting. Especially so to a professional economist. Professor Schneider planned his postwar book around the problem of inflation and credit management. There would be need for his ideas in the postwar period. It would generate a timely interest. Emil Schneider liked to think in the future. It gave perspective and balance to the present, and made the months pass in easy routine. With his wife he discussed his book; never the war.

But suddenly everything changed. The air raids could no longer be ignored. Even so, it was not the air raids that jarred him so much as the secret knowledge of their results. It came to him first in the reports that crossed his desk, long lists of production figures that weren't in agreement with published statements appearing in the carefully briefed press. It made him uneasy. Then suddenly he was shifted to another job, production and supply distribution. It brought him closer to the war; the ciphers he worked with were no longer financial but logistical. Then came the terrible months when each morning he awoke to reports of another German city shattered. It all happened too fast to comprehend.

And finally, the morning came when he bicycled through the smoky haze of the night's bombing—they came night and day now—and his eyes were opened to what was happening. All at once, as he pedaled his bicycle down the plaster-strewn streets, he knew with clear certainty that Germany was doomed. The conviction came unbidden; once it entered into his mind, it was an unshakable, terrible knowledge. And when he got to the building where he worked, it was gone.

Gone too were the notes for his book, which he'd left in the middle left-hand drawer of his desk. For Emil Schneider, the rest of the war was a dream. He sent his wife to her parents, in the country.

On orders that issued down from central command, a vague disembodied authority unlocatable even in his own mind, he drifted closer and closer to the war, to combat, to the death he somehow knew to be certain. He never tried to explain it, except that he identified himself with the cities, places of his youth, places that no longer really existed except as disfigurements of the land. Germany was dying; he was Germany. There was no logic in questioning the destiny he could read in the ruins around him. He had been able to imagine defeat, never destruction. He did whatever was required of him, asked no questions. It was long past a time for questions, and in his mind there were none. There was only the deep acceptance of what he saw around him: total defeat.

He came to a final understanding of the ridiculous oath he had taken, for in defeat lay a sadness deeper than death. The only absolution for defeat *was* death. The only thing that troubled him now was thoughts of his wife, who was barren. Hers was a defeat he could hardly understand. Hers was a fate that baffled him.

He was shifted from post to post, doing jobs he was never trained for, giving orders he hardly understood. He was always replacing some officer who had gone eastward to replace another officer, who perhaps had gone eastward to replace still another. He was a transportation officer, a supply officer, an intelligence officer; he was impressed into service on a military court, moving on before a verdict was reached. He arrived at the German border in time to deliver a lecture on first aid to a group of old men who'd been scraped up from the bottom of the barrel. He directed a movement of obsolete tanks across a bridge into France. For three weeks he was a demolition officer, charged with laying explosives on bridge abutments along the east bank of the Rhine.

He was a company commander, a general inspector; he was a whole army rolled into one man. He stayed in one place only until *his* replacement arrived. He seemed to be marked as a fill-in; wherever a vacancy appeared Lieutenant Schneider was sent to fill it. In this bewildering series of commands, Lieutenant Schneider developed a technique. It became almost a reflex with him. He would ask the senior noncommissioned officer what needed to be done, listen carefully to what the man said, and then order that thing to be done. Rarely would he be around long enough to see the order carried out. Someone would arrive, present him with a paper, salute gravely, and take over. Usually he brought with him the orders for Lieutenant Schneider's next assignment. The Americans were in France, but that didn't seem strange. They had been there before, one war ago. He moved from one decapitated unit to another, doing what he could to keep order, to mend discipline. Twice he received commendations from unknown superiors, once for obtaining gasoline for a stalled convoy, once for putting out a fire in a field ambulance. He got very little sleep, ate carelessly, and often went two days without shaving.

Each time new orders came, he was moved closer to the war. He didn't think about it any more. He was an unflagging replacement. He moved into France toward that last-act curtain of steel that would sweep across the tragic stage of Germany and end life. Everything was confusion, constant bombardment, harassment from the sky. Convoys passed each other on the road going in opposite directions. Trains were derailed, sabotaged, blasted into junk iron from the sky, died in an expiring hiss of live steam. He descended into the maelstrom, filling vacancies, signing orders others wrote, drawn by the vacuum of war, of death.

Suddenly he was shifted to the south. It was like passing through the calm eye of the storm. In a staff car with three others on separate business, he made the trip in a single night. He slept to avoid talking.

The Scorpion Battalion had to be brought north immediately to consolidate the stand-or-die defense of the Belfort Gap. The Allied southern landings of the previous days made speed essential. Communications from the south were confused, and Lieutenant Schneider was given broad orders to commandeer whatever matériel might be needed in order to get the battalion out intact, ahead of the pursuing Allied divisions. He felt it would be his last assignment of the war.

Lieutenant Schneider never reached the coast, for the Scorpion Battalion had already managed to get what they needed. They stripped a Wehrmacht group of its vehicles and gasoline and commandeered the field kitchen, together with the cooks that went with it. The three cooks were hardly more than boys; the oldest, a corporal, was seventeen and new to the war. The battalion had started north immediately on receiving their orders, without waiting even for a confirmation of their reply. They left at nightfall, and their colonel allowed his men to celebrate their retreat to battle by looting a wineshop. Lieutenant Schneider didn't even have to look for them; he found them stalled on the road. Only at the time, each thought the other was the enemy. If the lieutenant's staff car hadn't been traveling with lights, a risk taken to make time, it would have collided with the half-track that lay wrecked on its side blocking the culvert bridge.

The fact that no one in the staff car was hit by the fusillade of bullets that thunked into the vehicle was pure accident. Both headlights were shot out instantly, and the driver threw the car into reverse and backed out of effective range. But the staff car was finished. The engine stopped and the smell of raw gasoline filled the air as the men jumped out.

A tracer bullet from a submachine gun ignited the gasoline pouring from the ruptured gas line of the staff car. Its former occupants lay scattered far away in the bushes helplessly watching it burn. They heard shouting in German but elected to wait until the sky lightened before attempting to walk back up the road. It was an inauspicious beginning for a replacement officer, but in the confusion of that drunken hour no one knew precisely who was firing on whom.

It was only with the coming of dawn and light that the sporadic firing stopped. The whole story would never be clear; even when, an hour later, contact was established and the identities of the benighted antagonists became clear, the situation was only confused further by the curious fact that the battalion commander had slept through the entire incident. Lieutenant Schneider presented his orders to him as formally as possible under the circumstances, but from the moment he saw him Lieutenant Schneider recognized that the colonel and half his battalion were completely drunk. There was nothing to do but keep quiet. The colonel peered through the orders searching for the signature of the general who'd signed them, muttering about sabotage and Frenchmen. He was convinced that the half-track was wrecked by saboteurs in order to stall the convoy and expose it to a strafing attack. Once one of Lieutenant Schneider's traveling companions, an old man in the uniform of a Wehrmacht captain, attempted to suggest that perhaps the driver had struck the abutment of the bridge—it was obvious from his wild story of seeing three men in pitch blackness that he'd invented the story of sabotage, of being fired upon, to cover the fact that he was blind drunk and had missed the narrow turn leading onto the bridge, which would have been easy to do even in daylight and sober, since the turn was sharp and not marked, the road narrow onto the bridge and banked the wrong way—but the half-track was riddled with bullet holes, evidence which the colonel accepted as absolute proof of the attack. The fact that in the first frantic moment of panic as they ran from the staff car, the sergeant-chauffeur had emptied a clip from a machine pistol in the general direction of the bridge wouldn't sway the colonel from his conviction. It was impossible, he said, to hit anything in the dark at that range. He was very drunk, and building indignation into a slow rage. He tried to ignore the fact that he had slept through the whole thing, and believed that three of his men had been wounded after the staff car was burned. He pointed at the burned car as further proof. He was in a very ugly mood and made it absolutely clear that he would be challenged no further on his statement of fact: the convoy had been attacked. He asked for further comment, and no one made any.

For, in fact, there was actually not much evidence to dispute him. It was not untypical of the type of tactic employed by *Maquis* groups to harass troop movements—and there was a possibility that such an attack had indeed been made. The shaken driver of the wrecked half-track could have fired on the staff car for the obvious reason that it was irregular to have a car bear down on you with its lights full on—it was rare even to meet a car on this road at night. That, plus the panic that must have ensued after having the half-track turn over, could easily account for the fusillade of mistaken bullets. No one had been able to rouse the colonel at the moment when crucial leadership was most urgently needed, and the fact that the staff car roared around the corner just shortly after the wreck occurred, when the men were leaderless and sensible of their vulnerability in the darkness, must have added to the panic and confusion. The three wounded men were a puzzle, unless, as someone suggested, they might have been firing at each other —it was established that two groups did move forward independently on opposite sides of the road in an attempt to flank the staff car—before it caught fire.

"There was no cause for it," the colonel said drunkenly. "Does anyone here disagree with me? Such acts should not be allowed to go unpunished."

No one answered.

"Get the road clear. Take the rest of the vehicles and spread them around off to the sides of the road."

Lieutenant Schneider looked around at the drunken battalion. It annoyed him. The colonel annoyed him. Everything annoyed him. He felt as though he'd come on a useless errand. "Since your orders state that you're to report to me, you'll report to me, Lieutenant," the colonel said, in an ugly tone of drunken truculence. He didn't like being caught, so to speak, in a state of undress by an outsider. "You'll follow me around until we get this mess cleared off the road."

The colonel looked at the two wrecked vehicles up the road, the one lying grotesquely on its side, the other charred black and still smoking where it had been abandoned.

The two Wehrmacht officers and the sergeant-chauffeur drifted off toward the rear of the convoy. No one wondered where they went, whether they set out for Nice on foot or what, but Lieutenant Schneider never saw them again. He assumed that they negotiated a ride back with the Frenchman, the crazy little fat man with the twelve prisoners. The Frenchman had evidently been waiting a long time to see the colonel; he was red-eyed and extremely nervous. His eyes were so red that they looked puffed up, as though he'd been crying. The colonel at first argued with him in German, which the Frenchman didn't speak. Finally the colonel turned away in disgust, ordering Lieutenant Schneider to find out what he wanted and to accommodate him and get rid of him. After everything was made clear, the colonel knitted his brows in sullen drunken reflection.

"Give him a receipt for them. Keep a copy," the colonel finally said.

Then the colonel turned to the Frenchman. "You are positive these are criminals. They have killed Germans?"

The Frenchman nodded vehemently, relieved, it seemed, that his main point had finally penetrated the fogged brain of the colonel. He even understood it in German.

Lieutenant Schneider had to argue with the Frenchman a long time before he would accept the receipt for the twelve prisoners. It seemed strange, since the colonel's instruction that he give a receipt struck him as merely a stupid effort to appear official and correct. All the Frenchman had to do was to tear it up. Lieutenant Schneider had his orders, foolish as they were, and he took a perverse satisfaction in carrying them out to the letter. He made the little fat Frenchman take the receipt. He seemed a little crazy, but his papers were in order. Some sort of police official. Lieutenant Schneider hadn't quite understood why the prisoners were being delivered to the battalion and it was too much trouble to try and decipher it all again; he did as he was told. The colonel looked a little crazy too. It made no logic to do otherwise, because, crazy or not, he was a colonel and he was in charge.

The sun was nearly up before the road was cleared. Two men were left behind to repair the righted half-track and catch up with the battalion in the village just ahead. The colonel asked Lieutenant Schneider what the name of the next town was. Lieutenant Schneider didn't know. No one knew. The colonel got out the map from the weapons carrier. He put his finger on the road, traced it to the bridge at the tiny stream, and traced it north around the back side of the mountain until he reached a tiny red dot marking a village. He ground the blunt point of his finger into the paper and poked a hole through it where the village was. He didn't attempt to read its name. The colonel put his finger on the point of highest elevation, a point overlooking the village and some distance away from it. He looked up the slope far ahead. There was a stand of green, pine trees of some sort, that capped the nearly bald hill. The village was around the other side and not all visible, although not far ahead on the road.

"Up there," the colonel said, pointing, "I want a pen built, Lieutenant. I'll give you exact directions as to how I want it built. It will take you all day to do it right, and it will be hard work. But you're not afraid of hard work, are you, Lieutenant?"

There was something mocking, almost malevolent, in the colonel's smile. Lieutenant Schneider thought: Hard work—polite phrase for torture.

"Anyway, you'll spend the day up there building your log house. And I want a good house. You will use the twelve French to help you. I'll give you one of my best sergeants to supervise the guard. He knows what to do. I'll be busy down on the slope. The battalion is very badly in need of target drill."

The colonel spread out the map. "You'll take three trucks and use this road here." He traced out a thin tiny thread of a red line indicating the mountain road. "Here's your sergeant, Lieutenant. He's built houses before. It was his trade before the war. Keep in mind that he

459

turned down a field commission in North Africa. I offered him a captaincy, Lieutenant. Make sure you keep him busy, Lieutenant. Get those French murderers to clean up their own vomit. Have them clear the road before you go. I'll teach them to commit sabotage. I'll kill them a hundred to one."

Lieutenant Schneider felt only tired annoyance at the colonel's gratuitous animosity. The sergeant was obviously a brute type. He looked illiterate. He looked like a crude version of the colonel. Lieutenant Schneider thought of protesting, but at least he wouldn't have to watch the battalion run the village out of their homes and destroy them. It didn't occur to him that it was a holy day and nearly every living being would be at early Mass.

After they got their instructions, and after the seventeen-year-old Wehrmacht cook had been impressed into duty as a guard, they went to get the prisoners. They were to leave ahead of the battalion, as soon as the road was cleared. The idea of senselessly brutalizing prisoners made the lieutenant sick with disgust. Even if they were criminals. It was the colonel who disgusted him most. The battalion commander seemed to relish the idea. The lieutenant knew what had to be done—still, it was hard to obey such a man.

Lieutenant Schneider got into a staff car. Ahead he watched the three trucks lurch into motion, one after the other like prodded elephants, and bounce off down the narrow, rutted road toward the bridge where the wreck had just been cleared; they left behind them, rising unbroken on the immobile air, three identical columns of exhaust vapor where they had stood, their engines idling fast, while the prisoners were loaded into them. The sergeant, standing with one foot on the running board, cocked his arm to throw away his cigarette. He hesitated, measuring with his eye the short stub in his oversized black leather motorcycle glove, and calculated it good for one last puff. He drew quick and deeply and the glowing end burned back into the leather thumb of the glove and filled the staff car with an acrid stench like burning hair. He threw the butt away and coughed retchingly, water springing to his eyes, and cursed. Still coughing, he climbed into the bucket seat behind the driver and slammed the door as the driver put the car in gear. The lieutenant sat in front and they jounced over the chilled mud in silence, except for a couple of times when he coughed. Beside the sergeant sat the young Wehrmacht corporal, the cook whom the sergeant had bullied into service to fill out his complement of guards.

They waited at the bridge while some men kicked the last shards of glass out of the road. The car stopped, almost touching the tailboard of the truck ahead, and Lieutenant Schneider found himself searching the expressionless faces of the four silent men who stared back at him from the crisscrossed shadow of the heavy wire grillwork. He thought they looked completely uninterested in what was happening to them.

He had seen that look before on many faces. It was the look of prisoners, resigned prisoners, and he knew that when they had that look there would be no trouble.

The lieutenant sighed and turned his head to look out of the window, his chin cupped in his palm. The sun, rising cold and orange at the end of the valley, was bleared behind the gutted outline of an old ruin just off the side of the road close by. After looking for a moment at the peaceful aspect of the chill morning, he began to feel partly relieved of his impatience.

"When the sun's like that," said the corporal unexpectedly, "it looks like that old place is on fire, don't it?"

No one answered him. He was obviously making nervous conversation.

"It looks like it was a church or something."

"Hospice," said the lieutenant automatically.

"Hospice?"

"An inn for travelers."

"An inn?" said the corporal. "It's got a steeple. If you look close you can even see the cross hanging cockeyed from the part on top that's almost caved in."

"The steeple was for bells," said the lieutenant. "During snowstorms they were rung continuously so that people could find their way down through the pass." This has got to stop, he thought, and paused. He felt sorry for the boy but the totally irrelevant conversation irritated him beyond reason. He felt it imperative that he shut him up and re-establish privacy and silence. Pitching his voice to a tone of finality intended to convey the authority of rank, he looked stonily out of the window and added, "It was established and maintained by the monks of the Cistercian order." The plausibility of the last invention instantaneously pleased him and he smiled. He let his eye wander back along the crooked shadow of the buckled spire where it tapered obliquely across the intervening ground and fell tangled among the great wheels of the truck ahead. I should have dreamed him up the date of founding too, he thought to himself. The sergeant only grunted.

Once across the bridge, the four vehicles started the long climb up the road which wound like a ribbon-worm up to the summit of the ridge, dipping and rising with the contour of the mountain. About two kilometers farther they crossed over the high point on the road and emerged from the cold shadow of the western slope into the dazzling morning sunshine. The lieutenant shielded his eyes and looked toward the north, where for a brief instant he caught a glimpse of their destination. They started down the incline, picking up speed, and the barred shadows of tall pines rose on either side of the road and closed in his vision. A steamy morning mist rolled down off the forest floor and curled catlike into the warm sun on the road. The rhythmic flicker of the sun through the passing pines had a hypnotic effect on him. He put his hand over his eyes, but he still felt the steady drubbing in his brain.

Very irritating, he thought, feeling drowsy again, *light flashing about five cycles per second. Almost maddening.* A short while later, lulled by the steady hissing of the gasoline heater under the dashboard, he felt himself slipping into sleep, and was half conscious of grinding up a long climb in low gear and the high whine of the engine and the oppressive heat in the cab.

He woke up when they turned off the paved road, wondering vaguely how long he had slept. Five minutes? Ten? He knew the two enlisted men would make no attempt at conversation so long as he kept his eyes closed. For all his contempt, the sergeant still respected rank. A sudden wave of disgust went through him. The stupid asses, he thought, the carefully indoctrinated, stupid asses. For an instant he saw his relation with the service in a sharply defined light. The sergeant has earned his right to joke with me by having refused a field commission in North Africa, but he will never earn the right to wake me up without authorization. It's crystal clear. The army consists of two kinds of dullards who are profoundly afraid of each other. A flatulent expedagogue like myself and two specimens like these: there we've got an army, he thought. He opened one eye and looked past the driver's hawk-like profile to the passing scenery and was surprised to see that there were very few trees now. They were up among wind-swept rock and scrub pine. The heat in the cab was terrific. He sat up. Behind him the sergeant stirred.

"Can we turn off this damned heat for a while?" he said. "If the lieutenant has no objections?"

"You awake, sir?" the driver asked the lieutenant.

"I'm awake. It is getting hot in here."

"Yes, sir. If you'll just turn that little handle to the left . . . no . . . the red one. That's it. No, you're making it hotter. Turn it to the left, the other way. That's got it."

The hissing stopped, making words hang abnormally loud in the silence, even over the roar of the motor. The road became steadily worse and the trucks ahead lurched after each other, rolling from side to side like three fat old women. As they got up higher the wind increased and outside the stony ground was swept almost bare. Ahead there was dense pine on both sides of the road.

As they approached the summit, the lead driver signaled and turned his truck off the road, heaving and pitching over the uneven ground, into a large flat clearing. The others followed in their turn and formed a half-circle around the clearing. The driver of the staff car looked dubiously at the terrain and decided against trying to take the lighter vehicle into the clearing, preferring instead to park it at the edge of the road.

The lieutenant waited in the car and watched while the sergeant, with the other guards and the drivers standing in a circle around him, gave them their instructions. They stood at the edge of the clearing. The sergeant finished and nodded at the lieutenant. As he got out of the car the dry cold cut through him like a blade. It was hardly summer up here. He realized he must have perspired profusely while he was sleeping. The sergeant saluted in a perfunctory manner as the lieutenant approached the group.

"I have given them the briefing the colonel gave me," he said. "Is there anything else the lieutenant wishes?"

"You may as well give them their rations before they start work. They are probably hungry."

"Yes, sir," said the sergeant. He smiled a twisted contemptuous smile.

"Have you had any police experience?" the lieutenant asked the young Wehrmacht corporal. The corporal looked out of place among the circle of black uniforms.

"I'm just on temporary assignment, sir. I'm only a cook."

"Sergeant, see that you instruct this man before you give him a weapon."

"Yes, sir," the sergeant said. He turned to the corporal. "There is a machine pistol in the seat holster of the staff car. It hasn't been fired since it was made, I think. Secure the stock in place. I'll show you how to fire it. You will work the rest of the day with me. Is that all clear?"

"Yes, sir," said the corporal, stepping smartly back into the group.

"I'll take over, Sergeant," the lieutenant said. He turned to the group. "Now. I want to go over quickly what the colonel told you. There are twelve prisoners. There are four guards. I want one guard to two prisoners. That means no more than eight out of the trucks at one time. You'll work them in shifts." Lieutenant Schneider looked around for questions. There were none so he continued. Out of the tail of his eye he saw the sergeant smirking. "There are two saws. Thus four of the prisoners will be down on the slope with the saws. The other four will drag the trees up here. There are two hatchets for trimming the branches. With the hatchets in use, I want the rest of the prisoners back in the trucks. You'll trim the trees and cut them to length up here. Make sure you pick trees no bigger around than the calf of a man's leg, and straight ones. Under no circumstances are you to allow them to work close to each other when they have tools. Is that clear?" They nodded as one man. "I'm making the drivers responsible for keeping constant surveillance over the prisoners remaining in the truck."

He dismissed the drivers and they went back to the warmth of their cabs. He addressed the guards in a subdued tone. "I want the rest of you to be particularly careful. Don't let the scenic beauties of the Alps distract you. I don't want any escapes, but if it should become necessary, shoot for the hips and legs. They've been warned that if they try to escape we will *not* shoot to kill, that, on the contrary, they will be allowed to go through it alive." He paused and looked at them for a moment. "So you see, I don't think any of them will try it."

"Might be a new experience," the sergeant said, and laughed.

The lieutenant ignored him. "We'll break off for lunch later, but give them a ration before they start."

Lieutenant Schneider turned the detail over to the sergeant and watched with satisfaction as he went about briskly parceling out the work. He stood watching for a minute as the tools were laid out on the ground and then walked to the far edge of the clearing and lit a cigarette. The wind was beginning to abate as the sun climbed higher into the crystalline sky. He watched the tip of the cigarette glow a fierce red in the fanning wind and turned the details of the morning's rapid events over in his mind. The whole thing was disgusting.

He decided that there was nothing the sergeant wasn't brutally competent to handle. He wanted no part of it. He would use the time to write a long letter to his wife, to keep from going mad. The wind momentarily dropped completely and he was watching the turbulent ribbon of smoke from his cigarette rise in the suddenly stilled air when the cold silence was pierced with the stitching of the machine pistol. He dropped his cigarette. He forced himself to bend down casually and pick up the cigarette without turning around. He felt the sergeant's eyes on his back, but he didn't turn around, even when he heard the echo.

He finished the cigarette and went back to the staff car. The heater was still hot enough to start without priming. He took out his letter paper and began the letter to his wife. I owe her a long letter, he thought, and, like a long-distance runner, he set a slow, loping pace in the very first paragraph, unwinding his reminiscence of her last letter in long sentences broken up into easy-breathing phrases and clauses. The knowledge of his wife's habit of saving his letters and rereading them years afterward had a curious effect on his prose style; he wrote as he might to the editors of a magazine, concealing behind casual formality a half-disdainful hope of being published. From the slope below the clearing he could hear, through the window he had left slightly open for ventilation, the sound of sawing. When he had filled two pages covering his routine activities of the previous two weeks, he paused and fell to gazing out over the vast panorama of forest and mountain and tried to capture in words, for his wife, the peculiar feeling of isolated grandeur which settled in him. It has been a long time, he thought, since I have written her a poem. He felt a wave of nostalgia and cast his thoughts back to the early days of their correspondence, before their marriage, when it was his habit to compose a few lines every week and send them to her. We are both getting old, he thought. He felt his stomach growl and wondered if he was hungry. I will write her a poem after lunch when I feel more like it.

He wrote another page about imaginary plans to go skiing at Garmisch at Christmas, when he would have leave; and then dozed a little until noontime. Below, he could hear the artillery pounding the village.

The sun was at its zenith in the southern sky when he became aware that the sound of the sawing had stopped. He opened his eyes as the first pair of prisoners with their guard came up over the edge of the clearing. He stretched and got out of the staff car and was surprised to find that it was agreeably warmer outside. In the distance he could hear the explosions as they destroyed the village. There was no wind at all now. He saw the sergeant come into the clearing, squinting up at the sun as he pulled off his work gloves.

"Sergeant," he called, "put them all back in the trucks and give them their rations there. Let them have seconds if they want it. This is heavy work."

"How long do we give them?"

"How much more do you have down on the slopes?" asked the lieutenant.

"Another three hours maybe."

"Then take your time. Give them an hour." The lieutenant stepped close to the sergeant. "Are they behaving?" he asked quietly.

"Like saints," the sergeant said. "Don't you worry, Lieutenant."

Lieutenant Schneider felt he ought to be hungry but wasn't. He walked down the slope toward the stand of pines with a purposeful air, to give the deliberate impression that he was going down to inspect the progress of the work. A little walk will give me my appetite back, he thought.

There was still snow on the ground in the cool gloom of the pines, where neither sun nor wind had been able to penetrate in full force. The hewn trees hung at violent angles, their branches caught in the bigger trees standing untouched. Here and there a tree lay completely fallen. The only movement was the silent vapor from his own breathing, and occasionally a distant rumble of an explosion.

He stood for a long time in the cold stillness looking at the carnage, hearing the pulsing of his own blood in his ears, smelling the clean, cold fragrance of the pines in his nostrils. He leaned down and touched the raw end of one of the up-jutting stumps and looked at the two-man saw, with its precise line of steel teeth, which lay arched over the fallen tree.

In his mind he found himself carried back to a childhood scene at his great-aunt's house where his family had visited each summer. He had had a nightmare. He dreamed that he was in his aunt's garden where the gardener was cutting clusters of rambler roses and the roses were screaming with pain, but the gardener paid no attention and went right on cutting. He was crying, begging his aunt to make the gardener stop cutting the roses, and then he was wide awake and still crying with his great-aunt holding him close to her and he could smell the rose water and glycerine that she put on herself at night. He had never seen her in her nightgown before, with her hair down, and the scene remained vividly printed on his memory. He could still remember the insistent, tender inflection of her voice as she tried to calm him.

"But the roses are not like people, my little Frederick, roses have no feeling when they are cut. They are not like you and me. God made you with a soul. Roses have no souls, my little Frederick." He could still recall how, when he had stopped crying, she had read to him from the Bible, reading in her low sonorous voice the stories he knew and liked, looking very strange and terrible in her white nightgown with her hair down, not at all like his great-aunt, until finally he closed his eyes and only listened to her voice.

"It is too bad," he said aloud, shaking his head from side to side, as though addressing the company of trees. "This is a very untidy way to do things."

Back up in the clearing Lieutenant Schneider made a brisk show of personally supervising the resumption of work and then took his own rations back to the staff car, where he ate, less from hunger than routine, by himself. He knew that the men, encouraged by their sergeant, laughed at him. He wanted no part of them. When he finished eating, he took a clean sheet of paper out of the glove compartment and placed it on the clipboard, covering the unfinished letter, and began setting down words and phrases about the desecrated trees, trying to rework them into images of isolation. He thought of likening a half-fallen tree to a dying soldier upheld by his comrades in arms, but after the first flush of the inspiration had passed, he dismissed the metaphor as maudlin, if not actually bad. Then he wrote, set apart from the other words on the page: "Roses have no souls," and underlined it. Then his mind wandered and he drew a box around it, then a box around the box. Finally, he crosshatched the space between the inner and the outer boxes. The heat was increasing in the cab. He reached for the red knob and tried to adjust the heater for less heat but it went out with a barely audible pop. An all-or-nothing device, he thought, either we roast or we freeze. Everything connected with the war, he thought, it's the same. No happy medium. He reached under the dash to re-light the heater and burned his thumb on the hot gasoline burner and cursed. Roast or freeze or burn-your-thumb, but no in-between. He went back to the poem but found himself unable to concentrate. He was more conscious than ever of the heat in the cab.

By late afternoon the logs were being trimmed and cut into approximate five-meter lengths and neatly stacked. The branches which had been trimmed off the trunks of the trees already made an enormous pile near the center of the clearing. All but the few prisoners trimming branches had been locked back in the trucks. The sergeant left the corporal with the machine pistol in charge of the detail and came over to the staff car. The lieutenant stopped writing and rolled down the window.

"We're almost ready to begin, Lieutenant," said the sergeant.

"Your men have complete instructions?"

"As complete as the colonel gave me, sir."

"Then you can begin. Lay the logs in a square as he told you and

466

notch the ends where they overlap. I don't want any of them to roll out when the walls get high," said the lieutenant. "Make sure each layer is properly bedded down with branches before you add the next one."

"They've already been notched," said the sergeant. He shifted his weight impatiently from one foot to the other. "Like he told me, remember?"

"Yes. Very good."

"When they're all tucked in," said the sergeant, suppressing a trace of sarcasm in his smile, "you can come and kiss them good night, sir."

"It shouldn't be necessary," the lieutenant said flatly, and rolled up the window.

When the last two prisoners had finished stacking the logs and were put back in their truck, Lieutenant Schneider got out of the staff car and looked at his watch. He turned and looked behind him and noted that the sun was already in the tops of the trees. He walked over to the clearing and watched as the first four prisoners were led out. From inside the first truck came a mournful noise like singing, but a wind was springing up now and the words were carried away.

The four prisoners were all as thin as the rest. Their heads were shaved and they had the same abject uninterested look on their faces. There was one guard for each prisoner. They carried two logs from the stack and placed them on the ground in the center of the clearing, parallel to each other about a log's length apart, and then they placed two more across the ends, forming a square. He watched them fit the ends carefully into their notches so they wouldn't roll. They added more logs on top of the bottom ones until the structure was three tiers high and then they filled it up with large armfuls of branches. When it was quite full one of the guards gave a quiet order. There was a hesitation and then each of the four prisoners climbed onto the bed of pine branches and knelt down. The guards took up their stations at each corner of the square. Lieutenant Schneider walked over to the sergeant, who had been supervising two of the other enlisted men as they unlashed a large steel drum from the running board of the last truck. One of them was the young Wehrmacht corporal. His face was white.

"I want no part in this, Sergeant," the lieutenant said finally.

"I'll call you if anything comes up, sir," the sergeant said contemptuously.

"I'll be in the car. I have my report to finish," said the lieutenant. He knew the sergeant didn't believe he was writing a report, but it hardly mattered now. It would be good to get out of the chill. The wind was still rising and getting colder and he was beginning to shiver standing around doing nothing. He couldn't understand its being so cold.

He turned his back on the sergeant and walked to the staff car. The slow, deliberate chanting was being taken up by the other two trucks. As he opened the door he heard the brief, metallic ripping noise behind him and he stood motionless for a moment waiting for the echo. He got in the car and looked back toward the clearing. Four more prisoners were being let out of the second truck and the guards were throwing pine branches over the other four. He watched them add three more tiers of logs, jogging them into their notches, and fill up the inside with evergreen brush. The sun had fallen behind the slope. It was getting dark rapidly. It almost seemed as though it wasn't summer at all, but winter. The sky was clouding up in the west.

Lieutenant Schneider watched against his will.

The third group—the last group of four—was taken out of the third truck. They started toward the pile of logs, the guards beside them.

Suddenly there was gunfire and everything was confusion. Men were running, falling, getting up again. More gunfire. One of the prisoners had rushed the young Wehrmacht corporal and knocked him down. The other three ran in different directions. The lieutenant jumped out of the car. Before he could open his mouth to shout he saw the sergeant step up behind the corporal, who was on his hands and knees on the ground. The sergeant leaned down and put a pistol at the back of the corporal's head and pulled the trigger. The corporal's body was slammed face down to earth by the impact of the bullet. The guards plunged off in pursuit. Then it was silent.

There was nothing to do. He wanted no part of it. He got back in the car and watched them pick up the bodies. He was shaking, sick with rage. He had just seen the sergeant commit murder. At the proper time he would get him court-martialed for it. Instinctively he knew that it would do no good to report it to the battalion commander. He felt his mind starting to give way at the insanity of it all. To keep from thinking he plunged back into writing the letter. The main thing was to keep from thinking.

By final twilight Lieutenant Schneider hadn't finished what he was writing, when he stopped and gathered up the crumpled pages at his feet and smoothed them out again on his knee. He'd been writing in near-darkness and couldn't read what he'd written. He looked at the pages, feeling dissatisfied, and folded them up with the page he had been writing on and put them in the left breast pocket of his tunic. Then he put a hasty blind-written ending on his wife's letter and looked out the window. It was getting too dark even to write blind. He noticed that the dark shadows from the tall trees on the slope behind him had crept up toward the clearing. But where they fell into the clearing they were obliterated by the light from the pine-log house, five meters square, eighteen logs high, that blazed wildly in the gathering breeze.

By nightfall the sky had cleared again. The destruction of the village was finished, and the entire battalion was drunk again and on the move. Lieutenant Schneider privately determined that he would seek a court-martial of both the sergeant, for murdering a German soldier, and the colonel, for disobeying orders. The colonel had lost nearly a full day by stopping on the march, in willful disregard of the urgent terms of his orders. The shabby disorder of the continually drunk battalion depressed Lieutenant Schneider, but he kept his own counsel. He planned to write a detailed report when they reached their destination.

The report was never written. The Scorpion Battalion reached its destination, but Lieutenant Emil Schneider wasn't with it. Three days after joining the battalion, Lieutenant Schneider took his own life. It happened outside a small town near Grenoble. In a fit of depression, he added a final postscript to his journal to his wife, walked to the side of the road, and put a bullet through his heart. He was tired of war.

X X

"What's your name?" the tall soldier asked for the second time.

"Are we behind American lines?" Dante asked. He was too tired to try to explain everything. "Look, why don't you take me to your commanding officer?"

"Don't get anxious. You'll get there sooner or later."

"I need a little medical attention."

"So I notice. What's your name?"

"Are we behind . . ."

"Who knows. This is a crazy war."

"What's your unit?"

"I'll ask the questions. What's your name?"

"Dante. Look, I have to get in touch with Colonel Jay. Can you pass that on to your captain?"

"Don't know where the captain is, Dante old buddy. He'll catch up with us sooner or later. Then you can talk to him yourself."

"Look, you don't have to keep a gun on me. I'm an American, I tell you."

"Why did you answer us in Kraut?"

"Because you called out in German, that's why."

"We thought you were a Kraut," the short one said.

"Shut up, Schoolboy. He may still be a Kraut for all you know. You speak Kraut pretty good, Dante old buddy. For an American, that is. Better'n Schoolboy."

"I've been working as an agent here. I'm an American agent sent into France . . . Look, I don't even know if I should be telling you why I'm here. I've got to get in touch with Colonel Jay."

"Leave him alone, Maxie. He's right. If he's what he says he is, he can't say nothing about it."

469

"You speak pretty good Kraut, Dante old buddy. What were you going to do with that Kraut grenade?"

"What do you think I was going to do?"

"You play rough, Dante old buddy. Like a Kraut. Where'd you get it?"

The tall soldier turned the German-made grenade over in his hand, tossing it up and down slowly, like a small ten pin.

"It was thrown at me. Only they forgot to pull the pin."

"Pretty wild story, Dante old buddy," the tall one said. "Pretty wild."

"Look, would I have given you the damned thing if I hadn't recognized you as Americans? I thought at first you were Germans—part of the same patrol."

"How'd you get that nick in your arm?" the short one asked.

"I don't know."

"What do you mean you don't know?" the tall one asked.

"Look, I've been dodging patrols for three days. I don't know when I got it or how. I've been shot at four separate times, not counting the escape. This place has been lousy with Germans, jumpy Germans. Every time one of them would shoot at a bush, I'd be in it."

"That escape sounds a little wild too, Dante old buddy."

"Leave him alone, Maxie. The guy's had a rough time," Schoolboy said.

"He damn near gave us a rougher one," Maxie said. "How come you didn't spot Schoolboy's lousy German, Dante old buddy?"

"I speak good German," Schoolboy said. "Milwaukee German is good German."

"His German is very good," Dante said wearily.

"That arm hurt you much?" the tall one said.

"No. I'm only afraid of it getting infected."

"Schoolboy'll clean you up. Clean him up, Schoolboy. Then we'll start back. I've had enough goddamn war for today. They ought to have that road block out of the way. Schoolboy, how far back did you leave the jeep?"

"I figure we've come about a thousand yards."

"O.K. Let's clean him up and get back before somebody steals it. Did you take the rotor out of the distributor?"

"You think I'm crazy? I want that damn thing to start if I'm being chased by something. I didn't know what you guys had found up here."

"O.K. Get everybody on their feet. We're starting back. They've had a nice goof in the sun." The tall one turned to the rest of the small patrol squad who were sprawled on both sides of the road. "O.K., deadheads, rustle your butts! We're going back," he shouted. He turned back to Schoolboy. "Shake 'em up. I want to get out of here before anything else pops out of the bushes."

Schoolboy roused the squad, and started a quick bandage around the flesh wound on Dante's upper arm.

"Boy do you stink," Schoolboy said. "That's some haircut they gave you."

"I've been in prison for a few months waiting for you."

"Did they really wreck that town like you said—for nothing? How'd they do it?"

"Tanks. They used it for target practice. We heard them pounding it all day. When the tanks were through they finished it off with a demolition crew, I think. I doubt if there's much left."

Schoolboy shook his head and finished taking turns around Dante's arm with the sterile gauze.

"These Germans have gone loony. What happened to the people?"

"I don't know. I didn't see it and I didn't stay around."

"Where were you all this time?"

"It was night by the time I got down off the mountain. For a while they had a big search party in the woods, but they were too drunk to find their way around. They almost stepped on me once."

"You the only one that got out?"

"I don't know. There were three others when we made the break."

"There. That isn't much of a bandage, but I doused it up with sulfa. Too tight?"

"I can't feel anything at all in that arm."

"I think you may have a piece of iron in you. Any of them grenades go off?"

"Two."

"You may have caught some of it. It's a funny-shaped hole, and there's only one." He smiled. "Something went in that didn't come out."

"I appreciate your fixing it up for me. It worries me that I don't feel anything there."

"You'll have a medic looking at it inside of half an hour. Look, don't mind Maxie too much. He's a little bitter about being here. They flew him here from the Pacific. So far he hasn't seen one damned German he can shoot at."

"They don't seem to be staying around, do they? I've been watching them come through here like a flood. I don't see how you can keep up with them."

"Maxie's getting a little anxious. He thinks they've sent him on a wild-goose chase. You don't know how close you came to getting perforated. He was all set to go to work on you with that Singer Sewing Machine. Maxie loves the sound of a B.A.R. Especially when he's making it."

"I guess I've got you to thank . . ."

"You were just lucky, friend. This morning I flipped Maxie for who gets first shot at the first superman we see."

"You won the toss?"

471

"I won."

"I see."

"I guess you do. Can you walk O.K.? You look pretty beat."

"If it's in the right direction, I can walk."

"Don't worry about Maxie. He's a damn fine guy. Don't squawk about him walking behind you with his sewing machine. He learned the hard way once. He don't trust the King of England. You get that way out in the islands. He almost got his when a dead Jap turned out to be not so dead as he thought."

"I'll keep my mouth shut."

"You don't *look* much like an American, you know."

"I guess I don't look much like anything. I must be down to ninety pounds."

"You seen yourself in a mirror lately?"

"No."

"It's going to be a shock, friend."

On the way back in the jeep—the rest of the patrol followed on foot—the soldier named Maxie sat in back with his weapon across his knees while Schoolboy drove. Maxie suddenly seemed to be in a better mood. He even seemed mildly solicitous of Dante's condition.

"We're going to have to fatten you up some before we shoot you," he said jovially. "You're too skinny a target even for a firing squad."

"Lay off, Maxie," Schoolboy said over his shoulder. "The guy's had a hard time, even if he is a spy."

Dante laughed in spite of himself. Schoolboy and Maxie were a wild pair, but he felt enormously at home in this jeep. It was something solid, something real and familiar, something from Detroit.

"At least you got a better sense of humor than Schoolboy here, Dante old buddy. What's Dante? Your first or last name?"

"It's my code name, Maxie," Dante said, feeling relaxed and safe for the first time in months.

"You see, Schoolboy, I told you this guy was a spy."

"An agent," Dante corrected good-naturedly.

"Fancy talk," Maxie said. "I hope you're on the right side, Dante old buddy."

"I hope so too, Maxie," Dante said.

"Don't mind Maxie. He's a joker," Schoolboy said, frowning slightly.

"I love you both like brothers," Dante said, throwing his head back. "Where do you come from, Maxie?"

"Detroit."

"I'll vote for you if you ever run for office," Dante said.

"The only thing Maxie'll ever run for will be the nearest exit," Schoolboy said.

"You're goddamned lucky today, Dante old buddy," Maxie said. "Schoolboy here had you for his pigeon. If you'd a been mine, we'd be crating you up for shipment right now."

"My luck had to change sometime," Dante said.

472

"Schoolboy here still hollers 'halt' before he lets go. That'll get him killed one of these days. In the islands you never hollered halt until the corpse stopped kicking."

"This is a different kind of war here, Maxie," Schoolboy said.

"Like hell. You'll find out when them Krauts stop running and turn around. War ain't no different here than anywhere else."

"Yeah, but you guys get pretty loose out on the islands."

"You're goddamned right. That's why I'm still alive, Schoolboy. Some of these Stateside bums don't understand that. They'd come out there to Guadalcanal with the Geneva Convention rolled up in their pockets, and then raise hell with everybody because . . ."

Maxie stopped and was silent a moment, and then laughed reminiscently. "Hell, the stories I could tell you . . ." he said.

"Go on, Maxie. Tell us how it was out in the islands," Schoolboy said, laughing. He turned to Dante. "Maxie got kicked outa the Eighth Marines, so he joined the Army."

"Don't get so goddamned wise or I won't tell you nothing, Schoolboy. Then what will you do for bedtime stories? You better treat your Uncle Maxie right, boy."

"Maxie can really tell some good stories," Schoolboy said to Dante. "Go on, Maxie. We got about twenty minutes before we get back."

The jeep struck a pothole in the road and bucked sharply, jarring its passengers.

"Well, slow down, Schoolboy. I don't want to bite my tongue off."

Schoolboy slowed down. It was warm down in the valley, and the noontime sun was bright overhead in a clear blue-white sky. The road was dusty, and the jeep left a long plume of dust along the road behind them.

"You think I'm trigger-happy. Hell, you shoulda seen some of the guys I came back with. They couldn't even hold a piece without they fired it."

Maxie shifted his position forward to get closer to his audience. His B.A.R. made it awkward and he had to shout over the engine. "There was this guy with me out there. They sent us back to the States together. He was up for discharge because he had a hole in his head or something. Anyway, they gave us this temporary guard duty at this relocation center down in Maryland some place. Never did know where the damn place was. Flew us in. Flew us out.

"Anyway, one night—it was just getting dark, you know, like it does down there in summer—one night old Strange has got the duty on the main gate. It was a Sunday evening. There wasn't a goddamned soul on the base except us—everyone who wasn't waiting on orders was off on weekend pass. Well, this guy Strange—you gotta know something about him first. He comes from Kentucky. He was born with a squirrel gun in his hand. All his life he's hunted and fished and that sort of stuff. You know, a real Daniel Boone character only a little crazy. Anyway, I was down to keep him company this evening, and I was sitting in the guard shack reading a comic book. He was outside—

he was never comfortable inside four walls, always liked to watch the sun go down and all that. Anyway, I'm sitting there reading. Everything is quiet. The crickets are starting to chirp. When all of a sudden I hear a sound like a cannon going off. My nerves were all shot then, and I must have jumped three feet out of that damned swivel chair. In comes old Strange with a goddamned ring-necked pheasant. The damn thing was dead but still flapping. You see, we had forty-fives when we were on gate duty. You ever heard one of those damn things go off when you ain't ready for it? You, Schoolboy?"

"Yeah, Maxie. They make a lot of racket."

"You?" Maxie asked Dante.

"Unhappily I have," Dante answered.

"Well, then I don't have to tell you. Anyway, Strange drags in this bloody chicken, grinning like a fool, and stuffs it in the bottom drawer of the file cabinet. Well, it wasn't two minutes before the officer of the guard is down there in his goddamned jeep wanting to know who fired the shot. He must have heard it all the way up to the administration building. Strange says he was cleaning his gun and all that jazz, and for a while it looks like he's going to get away with it. Then this four-eyed shavetail sees the blood on the ground outside and follows it into the shack straight over to the file cabinet."

Maxie paused to see if his audience was with him.

"What happened, Maxie?" Schoolboy asked.

"So anyway, the night before the court-martial we all go down to the jug where old Strange is cooling his heels, and have ourselves a roast-pheasant dinner. We gave him his through the goddamned bars. The next day they have the court-martial, and I have to be there because I'm a witness, see? Well, it starts in the morning, and there's a tough-looking old buzzard of a colonel running the show. And it's obvious he takes a dim view of our boy Strange."

The jeep swerved around a washout at the edge of the road.

"For Christ's sake, Schoolboy! Keep this lousy iron on the goddamned tar, will you? How do you expect me to tell a story with you trying to make lumber out of all the goddamned trees all around?"

"I'm sorry, Maxie. There was a hole there."

"Now where was I? You made me forget where I was."

"The colonel was taking a dim view," Dante said.

"Yeah. This old buzzard makes it clear at the start that he's going to roast my boy for dinner. He asks for presentation of the evidence, or some crap like that. Everybody looks blank. The pheasant, he wants to know. Where's the Exhibit A? Well, this shavetail gets very red and sputters around and stands on his head and finally says plain that he don't know. Then everybody starts asking everybody what happened to the evidence. When the colonel finds out that I cooked the goddamned evidence and took it down to the stockade, he's fit to blow his cork. First he chews out the shavetail. Then, one by one, he chews out everyone else in the room. Finally he comes to me, and says that he's got a good mind to court-martial me and maybe he will. It's funny now, but it's not so funny when you're sitting and looking down the wrong end of the cannon. You know how they start one of them courts? You, Schoolboy?"

"No."

"Well, they start out by this guy stands up and says, 'The United States of America against Andrew Jackson Strange.' It ain't so goddamned funny when you look at it that way. Old Strange just shrugged his shoulders and sat down looking tired. So anyway, right off things look bad. He has a young punk captain who's scared silly of the colonel—they gave him a lawyer at least. The guy had been to law school. So after they find out we ate the evidence, they take a break for lunch. Strange goes to his sitting room, and comes back after lunch looking like he's already quit hoping for anything better than ten years in Leavenworth. All that afternoon they just spend fixing up the noose so that it looks pretty around his neck. Finally they're all ready to wind it up, and the colonel asks Strange if the prisoner has anything to say in his own behalf—'The prisoner will stand,' they say. For a while Strange just stands there mumbling. You could hear the flies buzzing around the fan he's talking so quiet. The colonel tells him to speak up."

Maxie paused, laughed privately, waiting to let the picture sink in.

"Damn if that wasn't something," he said as though to himself.

"Well, what did he say, Maxie?" Schoolboy asked, in a tired routine way.

"What'd he say?"

"Yeah, what did he say?"

"Well, he stands there, and looks the colonel right in the eye, and raises his voice so everyone can hear. He really spoke up like the old buzzard said to. He said, 'Well, sir. It was getting pretty dark about that time and I seen this thing move and I heard a rustling, so I said halt. I said halt again. I said halt three times. When it didn't halt the third time—I *shot* the sonovabitch.' Well, that broke it up for fair. The old colonel was trying to get order, pounding with his goddamned mallet, but he can't keep a straight face himself. Finally he starts to laugh himself, and that's all."

"What happened to your friend?" Dante asked, laughing also—it was still a good story, and Maxie's version was better than others he'd heard.

Schoolboy was doubled over the wheel, shaking all over. The swerving jeep nearly went off the road.

"God *damn*, Schoolboy!" Maxie shouted, truly alarmed, as the jeep veered wildly back onto the road. Maxie was on his feet ready to jump. Slowly he sat down. "You trying to kill us?" he demanded, outraged.

"I'm sorry, Maxie," Schoolboy said, trying to sound serious. "There was a hole back . . ."

"The only hole you got to worry about, Schoolboy, is in your goddamned head."

"Maxie tells a good story," Schoolboy said to Dante apologetically. "I told you he could tell a good story." He was still laughing, but he looked a little sheepish. Dante turned around to look at Maxie. Maxie was staring at the side of the road and the long drop they had almost taken down to the riverbank.

"I'm glad I got my goddamned G.I. insurance," Maxie said morosely.

"A lot of good it would do you," Schoolboy said.

"You better hang onto your Uncle Maxie, Schoolboy, or some German will blow your goddamned head off while you're trying to scratch it," Maxie said.

"I'm sorry, Maxie," Schoolboy said again. And this time, in a more sobered state, he meant it. It had been a close shave.

"What finally happened to your friend?" Dante asked Maxie.

"My friend?"

"The one who shot the pheasant."

"Oh, him. Hell, what do you think happened to him. They gave him ninety days in the slam. What did you think?"

The jeep reached the command outpost in time to miss noontime chow, but Schoolboy rustled up some stew from the field kitchen. It was the first Dante had eaten in three days, and he couldn't keep it down. The captain was off at some other headquarters. A young serious-faced lieutenant listened to Dante's story, taking notes, and then assigned him a bunk in a field ambulance.

He slept away the whole afternoon. That night they moved him into a large house. Dante found himself bunking down in the lower hall with his two acquaintances, Schoolboy and Maxie. Dante had become, unknown to him, something of a celebrity around the place; the story of the destroyed village had been confirmed by air reconnaissance that afternoon while he slept. He had slept in the heat of the ambulance with the rear doors open, while curious G.I.s passed by to look in on him, almost as though at a body lying in state. The lieutenant had passed Dante's story on to the captain, and the captain had ordered him to be given space in the house and had assigned Maxie and Schoolboy to look after his needs. The house was a larger sort of command headquarters and it had electric lights. Dante was only half awake as Schoolboy helped him out of his filthy clothes and into bed. He heard Maxie and Schoolboy getting into the cots that flanked his. Maxie was having trouble working the switch to turn the light off. It was a rococo table lamp that had come out of one of the rooms upstairs.

"The hell with it," Maxie said. "I'll leave the damn thing on."

There was silence for a long moment. Then Schoolboy raised his head.

"For Christ's sake, Maxie, can't you turn it off? I can't sleep with a light on."

There was another long silence. Dante opened his eyes and turned to look at Maxie, who was lying face down like a dead man on the cot next to him. He was fully dressed. If he intended to do anything more about the light, it wasn't obvious from his heavy relaxed breathing. After a short while Schoolboy spoke up again.

"Come on, Maxie, don't make me get up. Snap off the light."

No response.

"Come on goddamn it, don't play dead on me. Snap off the god-damned light."

Then, next to him, Dante saw Maxie's arm go up under the silk tasseled shade—he was still face down on the cot. His hand groped around under the shade for a moment, then there was a sharp snap, a blue flash, and a tinkle of broken glass. The room was in utter darkness. From the next cot came a low grunt of laughter, muffled by the pillow around Maxie's face. He dropped the broken bulb on the floor.

Dante heard Schoolboy come bolt upright in bed: "Jee-*sus*, Maxie, I didn't mean for you to go to all *that* trouble . . ." the words choked to a giggle.

Maxie grunted, "Anything else you want snapped off, Schoolboy?" He sounded hugely self-satisfied.

Dante fell asleep laughing silently to himself.

XXI

The war moved north and with it the armies, pursued and pursuing. In their wake came the service troops, and the Riviera became known, inaccurately perhaps, as the "champagne front."

The unexpectedly rapid withdrawal of the German armies left a vacuum of civil disorder. Arms distributed clandestinely to underground groups fell into vengeful hands; with no enemy left to fight, these weapons were put to the unreasoning service of civil warfare. Hundreds and thousands of civilians, some guilty, some innocent, were put to death in those unlucky days of shame and revenge. It was impossible to distinguish real *Résistants* from those who had only recently discerned the true path of righteousness. And the latecomers were the more vicious for being late. They expunged their private guilt in a bath of public blood; collaborators, real and imaginary, were summarily put to death. Women had their heads shaved and were run naked through the streets to be stoned and scorned by jeering mobs. It was a time of fear and terror and secret guilt. Anyone who dared speak up for moderation was automatically suspect. For most, it was an attempt at vengeance; but for others, riding the bloody tiger of revenge, it was an attempt at power. For them the war was only beginning. They used the public madness to cloak private ambitions, and it was not always by accident that the innocent were denounced with the guilty, condemned with the guilty, shot with the guilty. For every innocent who died by accident, another died by design. As the public insanity was manipulated, secret grudges were satisfied, old scores were settled, political foes were eliminated. The invading armies landed to find a war they hadn't looked for, a civil war. It was short, but it was real. And it was bloody.

Dante reported finally to a Colonel Wolfe in Nice. He waited in the lobby of the commandeered hotel while harried officers came and went from their audiences with their commander. Finally, after an hour's wait, an aide ushered him into the colonel's office. A short man in the uniform of a French officer was just leaving. Over the door, Dante noticed a sign in French and English, a relic of less hectic days. It read: *Hotel Manager*.

"Who are you?" the colonel asked abruptly as Dante entered the room.

The aide, a captain, interposed. "This is Major Stone, Colonel. Colonel Jay sent you a communication about . . ."

"Why the hell aren't you in uniform, Major?" the Colonel demanded.

"I haven't been able to lay my hands on one yet, sir. I didn't even know I was a major until just this minute."

"Don't you keep up with . . ."

Again the captain interceded. "Major Stone is the one who has been working as an agent here in France, Colonel. If you want me to get Colonel Jay's memorandum for you I'm sure you'll recall the details . . ."

"No. No. I remember it now," the colonel said.

"Yes, sir," the aide said.

"Go out and get a uniform for this man, Captain. I don't care if it's a private's, but bring it back here before he leaves."

"Yes, sir."

The captain left, closing the door softly behind him.

"You're one of the ones responsible for giving these madmen weapons to shoot each other up with, from what I gather," the colonel said.

"Sir?"

"I have nothing against you personally, Major," the colonel said irritably. "But this is the goddamnedest mess I've ever got into. I know you're probably a hero and been through hell and all that. But I've had a bad morning here. A bad bad morning. Here, have a cigarette. Did you know that officer who was in here before you were?"

"No, sir. I didn't notice him particularly."

"We can't do anything about this mess. We've had to call the French in on it. That man you just saw leaving is going to handle it. I don't know where to start. I can't even understand who in hell is fighting whom. Do you know? I thought this country was fighting Germans, not Frenchmen."

"The Germans promoted divide-and-conquer politics in France."

"I'll say they have. Here, look at this."

The colonel picked up a sheet of paper from his desk and passed it to Stone.

"I got that this morning. If I didn't know my intelligence officer I'd think he was crazy. What you've got in your hands is an inventory of arms delivered by *Germans, the Germans,* mind you, to the local Communist Party. Can you figure *that* out? I can't. We know positively from intercepted messages that the Germans deliberately tipped off the local Communists as to where these weapons were—in an unguarded warehouse. They think they captured them, but we know the Germans *let* them have them. What in hell kind of war are we fighting here anyhow?"

"The Germans are doing everything they can to intensify . . ."

"You're damn right they are. I haven't had a moment's peace since I moved into this damned town. Every time I try to appoint a mayor, somebody takes a shot at the poor sonovabitch. I've had to get the French in on it. It took damn near a whole division to restore order here. They've gone crazy."

"I . . ."

"I don't know who in Washington was responsible for giving popguns to these characters, but whoever it was should have his head examined."

"There was no way of knowing that the Germans would pull out without putting up a fight."

"What's that got to do with it?"

"The landing came too late. But it would have saved a lot of lives if . . ."

"Hindsight."

"Yes, sir. I suppose it is. A few months ago it was foresight. I don't know when the landings were originally scheduled, but I got the idea that they were to come a lot sooner than they did."

"Everybody thought we'd have Italy sewed up a lot sooner, too. We couldn't divert anything until Italy folded. Well, as I say, Stone, I have nothing against you personally, but you've certainly given me a lovely headache here. You're not the only one who's been shipping bean-blowers in. The British have been doing just fine. I hope to God that Frenchman they sent me knows what he's doing. I don't even know who the hell to arrest. As far as I'm concerned one Frenchman is just like any other Frenchman. It wasn't like this in 1918, I can tell you that."

"Who did they assign, or shouldn't I ask?"

"Hell, you can ask. If Jay trusts you, you must know how to keep your mouth shut. His name is Merseault. That was him you just saw leaving. He's just been commissioned as a colonel by De Gaulle. He popped up out of the woodwork with a small army under his command. God knows where he got it, but at least he seems to know what's going on here. *He* didn't have a uniform either. *Nobody* has a uniform. I don't know what kind of a war I'm supposed to be running here. The military is quiet and peaceful, while all the goddamned civilians are running around in armies shooting up the countryside. Did you ever hear of him?"

"Who?"

"This Merseault character. He's evidently got to be a big pain in the neck to the Germans with his little band of merry men."

"Merseault? No, I don't think I have."

"He used a different name. They called him Colonel Owl. But he says there are a dozen Colonel Owls around France. I don't know. You tell me."

"Yes, I have heard of the Owl."

"From what he told me, he did all right up around the Swiss border. He's evidently a specialist in making hamburger out of choo-choo trains. De Gaulle sent along a half-dozen citations when he sent his commission. I just commissioned him in De Gaulle's name. Just a few minutes ago. I hope to God he can unsnarl this mess."

"I hope so too, sir."

"Don't be upset if I stay mad at you, Major. I've been in the Army over thirty years and I've never seen anything like this. Someone shot at my chauffeur last night. Now why in hell does anyone want to shoot my chauffeur?"

"What do you plan to do?"

"Find out who's got the damned guns and take them away from them, I guess. Can you think of another way? By the way, did you give a list of . . ."

"I gave it to the captain before I came in, sir. Most of my contacts are dead, I'm afraid. I mentioned a couple of places where weapons might be cached."

"That's fine. Now what about yourself? Do you want to sit on your tail for a while, or do you want an assignment? Jay has given you into my charge until he gets here. You look like you might take some time off in a hospital."

"Well, sir, if you don't mind, the doctors said . . ."

"I've got your medical report right here, Major. I know what the doctors said. I want to know what *you* say. You've been okayed for light duty. But you're entitled to a rest if you want it."

"I'd rather have some sort of assignment if you don't mind, sir. I've been sitting in prison for a long time. A hospital wouldn't be much of a rest for me mentally, I'm afraid."

"Hm."

The colonel scanned a sheet of paper on his desk in front of him. "Do you have any preference? What did you do in civilian life?"

"I was a teacher, but I'd rather not do that for the time being, if you don't mind."

"Well, I could use you to teach French to some of the deadheads I have on my staff, but . . ."

"I'd really rather wait for a while before . . ."

"How about Graves Registration? Major Greeves is laid up with an infection in his foot. Stepped on a nail."

"Well, I worked my way through New Jersey State Teachers by driving a hearse on weekends, if that's any qualification."

The colonel laughed for the first time since Stone had come in.

"That's more qualification than Greeves had. He used to be a wholesale liquor salesman. You want the job? It's not a happy berth, but fortunately we've had very low death casualties this trip in. It's mostly detective work from now on. There's still a number of 'missing' we have to classify. They're either captured, dead, or deserted. You want it?"

"I'll take it, sir."

"If I had my way I'd send you home to the States. But as long as you have to stick around I think you're doing the smart thing. I want you to take care of yourself. I don't want you to wind up a customer in your own emporium, Stone."

"I'll be seeing the doctor daily for the next couple of weeks."

"But I *can't* send you home. Have you seen this?"

The colonel handed Stone another paper. Stone scanned it quickly. "No, sir. This is news to me. Although I sort of half expected something like this."

"You're ordered to stick around for the investigation. There'll be a field commission arriving here in about three days. War Crimes Court of Inquiry, or some such. You may have to go up there with them if the doctor says it's all right. They really did that town in. I saw some photographs yesterday."

"I was sure there wouldn't be much left of it."

"So far, you're the only survivor. Your testimony will be very important."

"I'm . . . the . . . *only* survivor? But the people in the village . . ."

"You didn't know? They burned the church down with the whole town in it."

"Oh, dear God, not *all* of them."

"Men, women . . ."

"And children?"

The colonel nodded slowly, watching Stone closely. There was a long silence.

"Are you all right?" the colonel asked quietly after a moment.

"I'm all right."

"You look a little . . ."

"I'm all right. It's just that I never dreamed . . ."

"I didn't know you hadn't been informed, Major," the colonel said. "I would have broken it more gently."

"How many?"

"It's not certain yet. They're still trying to . . . Hell, this is no time to talk about this. You look really gray. I'm sorry . . . This has been a bad day for me. I haven't been able to keep my wits about me."

"I'm all right. How many?"

"About two hundred or so," the colonel said, surreptitiously covering up a stack of photographs with a piece of paper on his desk. "Look, I don't want you to start your job until next Monday at least. Come in and see me in a couple of days. I'm going to give you quarters upstairs. This hotel is fairly comfortable, better than where you are."

Stone nodded absently.

The colonel got up and went to the door and opened it. "Captain," he called.

A sergeant came up. "He's gone out to get a uniform, sir."

"Sergeant, this is Major Stone. I want you to give him quarters upstairs. Pick a comfortable room with a decent bed. Have the captain send the uniform up there when he gets back."

"But we're billeted full, sir."

"So you throw out whoever's got the lowest priority. Draw up an eviction notice and I'll sign the damned thing."

The colonel closed the door.

"Really, I . . ." Stone began.

"I give the orders around here, Major," the colonel said. And then in a gentler tone, "The Commission of Inquiry will have to be put up here. You may as well be right here with them. It's a mixed commission, I understand, American and British. The French will have someone on it too. You better get some rest."

"Thank you very much, Colonel," Stone said, shrugging.

"Hell, don't thank me. Thank the manager, whoever that might be. Maybe after the war, you'll get your chance."

"I'll wait outside for the captain."

"You sure you're all right now?"

"I'm fine."

"You've got a little color back at least. All right, Major, I'll see you in a couple of days. If you need anything, I want you to come straight to me, you understand?" The colonel opened the door for Major Stone. "Tell the next one on that bench out there to come in, will you?"

The next man on the long wooden bench outside was the former police official, Théophile Dujardin.

Stone stood rooted to the spot. Dujardin didn't look up.

"Colonel, close the door," Stone whispered.

The colonel stared at Stone in perplexity. He closed the door.

"I don't know what you can do," Stone began, confused.

"What's the matter?" asked the colonel.

482

"That man out there on the bench. His name I'm sure is Dujardin. He's a police official, a collaborator."

"You mean the short fat one? He's been around here looking for a job. He's got the backing of some sort of group, veterans or something. Are you sure?"

"If his name is Dujardin I'm sure. He's the one that—my God, am I going crazy, or is that really him? I feel like . . ."

"Yes?"

"I don't know what I feel like. I'd like to murder him with my own hands. I can't believe it's him. Open the door just a crack. I want to have another look."

"You don't need another look. His name is Dujardin all right. What's he done?"

"He's the one who turned us over to the SS, for one thing."

"Are you able to prove that? I'll have him arrested immediately if you can."

"No, wait. Let me think. I don't know if I can prove it. If I'm the only survivor . . ."

"I can make sure that he doesn't go anywhere. But are you positive?"

"I'll never forget him as long as I live. I'm positive."

"I'll have him detained. I can keep him for questioning."

"But he'll know what's up when he sees me come out that door."

"Then go out *this* door," the colonel said. "This one leads out into the ballroom. You can walk around behind him and up the stairs."

Stone went out the other door just as the colonel went out to greet his caller. But when Stone came through the ballroom arch he met the colonel face to face.

"He flew the coop," the colonel said. "He must have seen you."

"I didn't notice him looking at me."

The colonel bawled, *"SERGEANT!"* The sergeant sprang out of nowhere. "There was a short fat man in a black suit, well dressed, sort of bald . . ."

"Yes, sir," the sergeant said. "He just left."

"I want that man found and held for questioning. Get going. He knows you're looking for him."

The sergeant went off on the double, shouting to two M.P.s who were standing guard at the door of the hotel lobby.

"You go upstairs, Stone, before you collapse. You look like you've seen a ghost."

"I feel more like I've seen the devil himself."

"I'll call you when they bring him in."

But it was a long time before Théophile Dujardin was brought in. Almost a year. And by that time the war was over.

XXII

The thin-faced young man at the speaker's table interrupted his political harangue and peered over the heads of the men toward the shadows at the rear of the schoolhouse. There was a commotion in the rear
of the room. The door opened and a young guard backed into the
room, his Sten gun at the ready. The two dozen men sitting before the
speaker turned their heads to see a small round man in a semimilitary
uniform being held at bay by the guard.

A huge old peasant with a rifle on his back stepped into the aisle.
"What is it, *petit?*" he asked gruffly.

The young guard with the Sten backed up warily and turned halfway around, still keeping an eye on the intruder. "He says he has a
message," he said.

Ignoring the guard, the intruder came forward, casually brushed
the guard's weapon aside and stepped past him. The confused guard
looked around for orders, but the short man entered the room with
such an air of assured authority that no one rose to intercept him. The
big peasant made no move to stop him, but stepped aside, watching him
narrowly as he passed. The newcomer's mud-caked boots sounded hollowly on the board floor as he walked down the aisle to the speaker's
table. He looked neither to the right nor to the left. The speaker
stared at him open-mouthed, and was about to challenge him when
the man saluted, a weary but eloquent salute. Then he turned around
and repeated the gesture at the men assembled in the room.

"What do you want here?" the thin-faced young man asked in a
tone of suppressed outrage. The man turned slowly around.

"Are you in command here?" he asked politely.

"You can state your business to me," the young man said. He
seemed flushed and excitable, much younger than the other men in
the room, certainly too young to be in command.

"I have a message for you," the man said. "I have a message for all
of you." This time he turned around and faced the audience.

The old rifle-backed peasant was still standing in the aisle between
the school desks. "If you have a message let us hear it," he said. A
few men grumbled agreement.

"It may take a little time to deliver it."

"We have a lot of that," the peasant said. He moved back to his
place and sat down, looking impassive and critical.

The short man reached into his tunic and took out a paper and
started around the end of the table. Automatically the speaker

moved aside, yielding his place behind the table; then, realizing what he had done, he grew flustered.

"Who are you, and by whose authority are you here?" the young man asked, too obviously trying to reassert his abdicated authority.

The newcomer looked calmly at him, his face blank. Slowly he withdrew a revolver from his holster and placed it gently on the table. "I am here by the same authority as you," he said, smiling slightly. "Only I have additional credentials."

From the rear of the room the young guard with the Sten stepped quickly forward, his weapon raised to the ready. There was a second of tension in the room. Then the short man behind the table smiled and waved his hand casually.

"That won't be necessary," he said to the guard in the rear.

The tension relaxed. The guard looked around for moral support, but no one was paying any attention to him. He lowered the barrel of his weapon and retired sullenly to the rear again. He remained standing in an attitude of exaggerated vigilance, looking very young and self-conscious and vaguely ridiculous. He held the weapon awkwardly, with two hands, as perhaps he'd seen gangsters do in motion pictures.

The newcomer unfolded the sheet of paper and placed it on the table beside the revolver. Then he took out his pocket watch, winding it briefly, and placed it on top of the paper. Lastly, he unfolded a pair of horn-rimmed spectacles and held them in his left hand without putting them on. The men in the room were shifting impatiently in their seats. The man standing at the table looked up at them a moment, and then began to count noses, counting with his forefinger as though he were poking holes in the tobacco smoke that hung in the room. The displaced young speaker compromised between taking a seat in the audience and standing uselessly beside the table: he perched himself on a high stool before a standing blackboard and lit a cigarette. But his effort to be casual was spoiled; his hand shook slightly as he lit the match. He looked up to see if anyone was watching him.

When the counting was finished, the man at the table looked down at his watch. He stood that way for several seconds, as though waiting. A few men stirred restlessly in their seats. One man coughed. There was an impatient shuffling of feet and creaking of chairs on the bare wooden floor. Suddenly he looked up from the timepiece and spoke.

"I regret the delay," he said, "but unfortunately it was necessary. I bring you greetings from the new government in Paris and congratulations from Colonel Owl. In the name of the Republic of France, you are being asked to surrender all arms and ammunition currently in your possession."

There was a stunned moment of silence and disbelief. Then uproar. The men half rose from their seats. Suddenly the young speaker was standing on the rungs of his stool shouting over the angry babble of voices.

"De Gaulle is a fascist," he shouted. "We take our orders from the

Central Committee. Not from London. Not from Colonel Owl, either."

"Why doesn't Colonel Owl come and take them from us himself?" came a taunting voice from the rear of the room. There was immediate laughter, raucous and not laughter at all, but derision, contempt. The man at the head of the table raised his hand for silence. After a moment he got it.

"Colonel Owl sends you his *personal* greetings and congratulations. I am Colonel Owl."

This time the young speaker was the one to raise his hand for silence. When the last murmur had died out, he lowered his head, as though deep in thought or about to intone a prayer. His face was white and drawn with anger. He seemed to address his question to a spot just in front of his feet. He spoke slowly, weighing his words. But his voice quivered.

"What makes you think these men will give up the weapons they have risked their lives to get? For us, the war is not over until the last traitor, the last fascist exploiter, is out of France, and the state is returned to the working people who rightfully own it." Then he turned and looked up at the men, mostly standing now, and cried out, "Are we going to stop now?"

There were a few angry shouts of "No!" But most of the older men simply remained impassive. The speaker stilled the few with a single disciplining wave of his hand. He turned to Colonel Owl, who stood with a troubled expression on his face.

"You are outvoted, Monsieur," said the speaker excitedly. "Now I suggest that you leave while you can."

Colonel Owl shrugged resignedly and absently fished a handkerchief out of his pocket and wiped his spectacles. The room was silent. In the back, a man's raspy breathing could be heard. It was the only sound in the room. Still rubbing the spectacles, he began to speak, softly and slowly at first, without looking up. In the back, men strained to hear what he was saying. As he spoke, every now and then he would pause and hold the lenses up to the light, inspect them, and then go on talking, polishing, polishing.

"Some of you men," he was saying, "have fought bravely and well in the face of every extremity. Hunger. Hopelessness. Fear. Torture. You have never slackened even though for many long, black months you hadn't even the assurance of eventual victory. For many of you it was better to die in what seemed certain defeat than to live in the spiritual misery of a land of petty tyrants. And I admire you. And France admires you. In generations to come French children will learn what you have done. And all the sons of France will admire you. For you have helped break the back of the blackest tyranny in our history. Some of you have been fighting for years. Others among you have only recently taken up arms. But now you would embark on an adventure. The tyrant is withdrawing in the north. He is retreating in Italy. He is being driven back in Russia. There are rumors even that he is already dead. But as he withdraws he leaves the spirit of his tyranny behind him. The land is infected with the spirit of tyranny. You would eliminate tyranny by gathering tyranny unto yourselves. But we are done with the tyrant, and now we must be done with his methods. We must be done with the cruelties and inhumanities that he has taught us, or we shall be cruel and inhumane ourselves. Now you want revolution. In principle I am not against revolution. You have the right to make revolutions as you wish. But the government has the duty to attempt to put them down. The right is yours. The duty is the government's. But the government is restricted to the legal use of force. You are not. And that is as it should be to make the balance of numbers even. But a schoolhouse is not an appropriate place to plot a revolution. This paper you see here on the desk before me is an authorization from Paris empowering me to employ legal force in halting your revolution. This I propose to do. And why should I have thrown my lot in with the government and not with you? It is not because I am opposed to revolution, however misguided, however bloody. It is because this would *not* be revolution; it would be—and is—civil war. You are not trying to destroy a government. You are trying to destroy a class. But you are inclined to overlook the fact that a class is people. And to destroy a class you must destroy people. And where is the end to this destruction?" He paused and looked around.

"In coming here, I come as a Frenchman to Frenchmen. I have come here at the risk of my life. First, I risked my life in carrying this document here on my person through German lines. Second, I have risked my life coming in here myself to demand that you surrender your weapons —not just those you have on you right now, but also those you have buried anywhere and everywhere under the soil of France. It would have been easier and perhaps safer to have merely surrounded this meeting and demanded that you come out with your hands in the air. But I am familiar with the record of some of the older men among you, and I doubt if such an appeal would have found much sympathy with you. Many of you who are listening to me at this moment, sitting here alive and angry and thinking, would be lying in your own blood by now."

Colonel Owl paused as the huge old rifle-backed peasant from the back of the room shouldered his way through the standing men. He came forward to the table and stood directly in front of Colonel Owl, his huge farmer's hands hanging awkwardly at his sides. His face was a mask of stone. Every eye in the room was on him as he addressed the Owl in a low rumbling voice full of the phlegm of hard old age.

"You have men around this place outside, is that it?"

"Yes."

"How many?"

"Twenty."

"You don't lie," the old man said. His eyes were clear blue and never blinked once as he talked.

"I don't lie."

"How are they armed?"

"Six submachine guns. Two light machine guns, mounted. Twelve carbines. One light mortar with ten rounds. Two dozen grenades. Each man carries a Mauser besides his other weapons."

"And you?"

"Just this," the colonel said, nodding at the revolver on the table in front of him.

The thin-faced young man who had been speaking at the table when the Owl came in stepped forward agitatedly. The old man glared at him to keep silent. "This is a military affair, not a political one," the old man said to the other. "If you want to be useful count the ammunition and keep quiet."

The old man turned back to the Owl. "He's been to school, that one, but he hasn't learned yet when to keep quiet," he said. "Have these men of yours fought Germans?" he asked.

"Professionally," said Colonel Owl. The men were crowding forward to hear better. "Are you in charge here?" Owl asked the old man.

"It doesn't matter who's in charge."

"Who's the one who was speaking when I came in?" Owl asked.

"He's political."

"I see. He's very young to be a commissar."

"Why didn't you bring more than twenty? We outnumber you by four men."

"I lost four. We came north behind German lines."

"How did you lose them?"

"One dead. Two wounded. One captured."

"What were you doing?"

"Derailing. Attacking convoys. The same as you."

"What have you planned if we refuse your demands?"

"General attack, commencing with slow fire at 0400, followed by advance under cover of light machine fire at 0415. At 0430 you will be offered a chance to abandon further resistance in return for a guarantee of safe exit."

"Provided we give up our weapons."

"On that condition, yes."

"And if we refuse?"

"Advance will continue. Submachine guns at the east and west windows. Grenades at north and south. Carbines will continue to cover the doors and maintain steady random fire through the wooden parts of the walls. The mortar will be used only as a last resort if approach with grenades is impossible."

"Ammunition?"

"Ample for the operation."

The other chief, the young political one, was working his way through the back fringes of the group. Questions and answers flowed between him and the men in low anxious tones as the men checked their ammunition. Finally he finished and totted up the results on a scrap of paper and pushed to the fore, holding the paper so that no one could read it as he passed. The old man took the paper and studied it. He frowned slightly and made a calculation in his head and then passed the paper to the man on his left, who read it and passed it on. One by one they all read it. The old man was silent, thinking. Everyone watched him, waiting for him to speak. But the Owl spoke first.

"Tomorrow, with or without me, my group goes back to the north. We have food and supplies there in excellent quantity. Anyone who wishes to join them is invited to do so."

"Without our weapons?" someone asked sarcastically.

"You will be issued new weapons and clothing, as well as extra ration cards," said the Owl.

"He's trying to trap you," said the political leader from the side of the room. He was staring out the window into the black night. "You'll all be jailed."

"And you?" said the old man. "You'll be dead, *petit.*"

"Maybe."

There was a long silence in the room. The old man reached out for Colonel Owl's watch, scowled at it, and put it back. He didn't touch the revolver. There was another silence. Someone passed the slip of paper back up to the front of the group. It ended in the old man's hand.

"I don't see anyone out there," said the political one from the window. The old man turned and looked toward him. Across the bare room at the window the other's back was bent before the black glass. The old man shook his head.

"How long could you hold out?" Colonel Owl asked the old peasant quietly. The old man stood before him like a grizzled warrior out of the past, and stared into the air over the Owl's head. Then he looked down at the paper in his hand and dropped it on the table in front of the Owl. Colonel Owl looked at the old man for a moment, and then glanced down at the paper. He studied it carefully, then picked it up and gave it back to the old man. "In the daytime," said Colonel Owl, "you might manage with that."

"0400 is not daytime in this part of the world," said the old man.

"I am sorry, really," said Colonel Owl. "This must be embarrassing for you."

"It was a mistake to meet here," said the old man. "We've got careless since the Germans left."

"Why kill your own countrymen in the south when you can fight the invader in the north?" asked Colonel Owl.

The man at the window whirled around. "Fascist!" he hissed. He was shaking with anger. "You're all fools and peasants forever if you listen to him," he said to the group. "We have more than just ammunition. We have the great Colonel Owl for a hostage. Do you think his own men will fire on us as long as he is here?"

All heads turned in unison back to the colonel to hear what he would say. Colonel Owl rubbed his nose out of shape as he stood thinking before he answered. When finally he spoke, he spoke as though speaking to himself. No one made a sound.

"My men opposed my coming in here for precisely the reason that I would be automatically your hostage if you so chose. But they have their orders, and they will carry them out. We will be attacked by a force of twenty heavily armed experienced men at precisely 0400, if that is what you choose. But the choice is yours, not mine. I made my choice when I walked in that door."

"You might have been killed on the spot," said the old man. "The boy had orders to challenge."

"He didn't have time," said the Owl.

"You could have made your demand from outside," said the old man. "As it is, if we fight, we have no choice but to hold you, you understand."

"It would be poor tactics to add to your enemy's number, I agree."

"Are you so tired of war that you take such risks?" asked the old man.

Colonel Owl looked at the old man and broke into a smile. "Perhaps you have shrewder insight than I," he said. "My reasoning is hard to explain."

"Why didn't you stay outside?" asked the old man.

The Owl looked at him. "I took a calculated risk. I could not believe that you would fight if you knew in advance you were committing your men to suicide."

"Sometimes men don't count the cost."

"There is another reason. More personal," said Colonel Owl. "You were right. I am tired of war. But I am more tired of seeing Frenchmen killing their brothers. If civil war is the reward we have fought for—this spectacle of blood—if there is to be more of Frenchmen killing Frenchmen, then I would rather be counted on the side of the dead against the living."

"Fine words," sneered the political one from his place by the window.

The old man ignored him and went back to questioning the Owl. "What are our chances if we make a break for it out of both doors?"

"I don't know."

"What would you say?"

"I don't know. It is dark, but the doors are covered by the Stens. Risky. One or two might make it. Maybe more."

"How are your men deployed?"

"I don't know. I didn't want to carry that knowledge in here, so I left it up to my second. My opening of the door was the signal for him to commence deployment. That was why I delayed starting."

"I say kill him right now," said the political youth.

"We could be back in action in forty-eight hours if we got started tonight," said the Owl quietly to the old man, who appeared to be weighing the question.

"He's trying to trap you," said the younger man. He was still standing on the other side of the room by the window.

"What's the matter, Armand? Is killing Germans too dangerous for you?" asked the old man. "How many have you killed already?"

"Are you saying I'm a coward?" shouted Armand. "I'll show you who the cowards are." He turned and addressed the group of men. "All the cowards stay over there. All those who want to fight, come over here with your weapons."

"Are you tired of handing out literature for us to read, *petit?*" the old man said, goading Armand.

There was a moment of tense silence. Then the young guard with the Sten moved across the room to join the other leader. Two more looked at each other, and then moved hesitantly, making sure of each other's intent, and finally strode across the room. Their heavy tread on the old wood boards echoed emptily in the bare schoolroom. One more left the group. Then another. Then three broke away simultaneously and walked across the invisible line between the two groups. That made nine including the one named Armand.

"Take your time," Armand said caustically. "You're not a coward if you're slow. Only if you stay."

One more hefted his weapon off the floor, shrugged, and crossed the floor. That made ten, just less than half the men in the room.

There was a long wait, but no more came. Finally the old man spoke.

"Now we are rid of the fools and the children," he said, and turned back to Colonel Owl.

It was true. The remark was startling for its accuracy. They were all young who had crossed over. The ten of them stood isolated from the older men, and their isolation made them look even younger. Scattered among the men, they had looked like men; gathered in one group, they looked like boys. Actually they were boys, including their leader, the sharp-faced one called Armand. He looked a thin twenty, perhaps less. It was hard to tell. But there were ten years between the oldest one of his group and the youngest one of the old rifle-backed peasant's group. The young ones tried to hide their fear, but their faces were white, and the Owl could guess by looking at them that the blood was pounding in their stomach pits. Armand stood seized with a cataleptic fury and glared across the room in silence.

"However, I have not decided what I am going to do," the old man continued. "But I will not be pushed into madness by an angry child."

"He is lying to you," Armand shouted to the men across from him. They regarded him passively, nothing showing on their faces.

The old man turned slowly to face Armand. "The point is not whether he is lying to us, *petit,* but whether we have any choice other than believing him. But I, for one, don't believe he is lying. He is a brave man. He has no need to lie."

"Brave man. Brave man," taunted Armand, almost hysterical with fury. "With a pistol in front of him, he is a brave man."

"You have a pistol, Armand," said the old man reasonably. "Shoot him."

"Why does he need a pistol, if he is so brave? Why?" Armand continued shouting, unheeding.

"You don't understand a brave man, Armand," the old man said. "You only understand brave talk." He calmly reached forward and lifted the revolver off the table from in front of the Owl. Before the Owl realized his intent he had tossed the pistol underhand across the room to Armand, who caught it hard. For a split second Armand stared at the pistol in his hand. But the old man had misjudged him: instantly he raised the revolver at arm's length, aimed straight at Owl. The blast rocked the room and hung ringing in the startled air for a long second. Everyone stared transfixed at Colonel Owl. His face was dirtied by the blast from across the room, but he didn't fall. He didn't move. The old man cursed and leaped across the room toward Armand, but before he could reach him the room was rent with the sound of splitting wood and the whine of bullets thunking into the timbers high overhead. Everyone hit the floor between the chairs. The old man hit Armand in passing, a tremendous blow which bounced him off the wall. The pistol slithered and clattered across the boards and lay there. Everyone was flat on the floor and there was utter silence in the room. Colonel Owl was the only one still standing, fully erect, his face smudged with gun soot. He was wiping his face with his handkerchief. After the single high volley from outside there was complete ear-splitting silence. They didn't fire again. Several of the older men were on their feet immediately, holding the nine defectors at gunpoint. One of them grabbed the Sten.

"*Merde,*" grunted the old man as he got warily to his feet. As he did so he fetched Armand a terrible kick that made him bounce. He turned to Colonel Owl. "Your friends outside are early. I'm sorry. I thought the little fool had more sense. Did he hit you?"

Colonel Owl wiped the gray smudge off his face as best he could and stuffed the handkerchief back into his pocket. "Who is actually in command here?" he asked one of the men who'd dropped to the floor directly in front of him. The man cocked his head toward the old farmer, who stood now looking awkward and embarrassed.

"Do the rest of you men on this side of the room recognize him as your commander?"

There were no dissents. Owl turned formally toward the farmer.

"In the name of the Republic of France I offer you a field commission with the rank of captain in the Army of that Republic. Reply whether you receive that commission and whether you accept the responsibilities of both subordination and command attaching to your acceptance."

"What?" asked the old man. Some of the others were at last getting slowly and cautiously to their feet.

"Will you accept a commission as a captain of the Army, and will you take and give orders as prescribed?"

The huge peasant looked blankly at the men in front of him. One of them nodded. Then, one by one, each man made his own small sign. Finally the old man turned back to Colonel Owl. "My name is Marius, and I accept your commission."

"We'll take care of the oath later. In the meantime, I order you to arrest that idiot there, put a guard over the others until I decide what to do with them, and have the rest of your men—those not on guard duty—fall out outside on parade. Have them leave their weapons in here until such time as we can reissue them to you. If you go out with your hands up no one will take a shot at you. But walk slowly just to be on the safe side. Ask my second to come in here a moment and to bring four men to replace your guards. If any of these young hotheads refuse to give up their arms, or otherwise offer resistance, shoot them out of hand." The nine defectors made no move to resist giving up their arms.

"I don't see how he missed you," said Marius, shaking his huge head of hair, which was rumpled from his dive onto the floor and Armand. Marius gave Owl back his revolver. Armand was just getting his wind back and was sitting up on the floor. The fight was out of him.

"He didn't miss me. I got the paper wad right in the chest. That was a blank round in there. It was to signal my second for a high volley, in case you wanted proof that I wasn't bluffing. There's your high volley," Owl said, pointing up to the rafters. "I didn't have time to stop you before you threw him my pistol."

The wooden wall along the level of the eaves was ripped open in a dozen different places. Wood splinters the size of spikes projected from the wall where the bullets had entered. There was also a neat round hole in the top of the blackboard.

Marius gave orders self-consciously, stiffly, but he gave them. Outside, the men were searched by Owl's second and led back one by one into the schoolroom. Their weapons were all mounted and stacked in one of the corners.

Owl's second had the new recruits lined up at attention awaiting their induction, when Owl called him over and a whispered conference was held with a number of Owl's men. Captain Marius was not included. There was much discussion in agitated whispers. The nine young prisoners seemed to realize that their fate was being discussed.

Finally the second went over to the wall and methodically began loading rifles. The arrested Armand stood in the corner trying to look dangerous and surly to hide his youth and fear. Two of Owl's men watched him. The rest of Marius' men stood at attention in two ranks.

The trial was formal but over quickly. Armand was found guilty by the three-man court-martial of attempted murder with a firearm. Nine loaded rifles were brought out into the center of the room and stacked in threes.

"Prepare to carry out the court's sentence," Colonel Owl intoned from behind the table. The nine young *bravards* who had recently given their allegiance to the prisoner were led out from their corner single file. Owl's second personally passed them each a rifle. They lined up facing the condemned man, who was being held against the wall by two tough-looking *maquisards*. Behind each man of the impromptu firing squad was one of Owl's men with his own weapon. The crowd of men watching at attention were beginning to stir uneasily. It was clear that they didn't like what they saw shaping up before their eyes. A few of them were shaking their heads, though they remained standing stiffly.

"If any man fails to carry out the order of this court by not aiming and shooting straight, he will be shot out of hand."

The air was thick with the smell of sweat, of fear. Everyone shared the prisoner's terror. The young men of the firing squad stood white-faced, benumbed with fear. It was happening too fast to absorb. The men standing in ranks stared in disbelief at what was unrolling before their eyes. Everyone was waiting for someone else to protest at the severity of what they were witnessing. But there was fear, and no one spoke.

With brutal dispatch the firing squad, made up of the prisoner's former loyal followers, was accurately positioned at parade-rest. Then the Owl asked the prisoner if he had anything to say. The prisoner's face was ashen. He opened his mouth, unbelieving, tried to speak, but no words came out. Then he simply shook his head no, biting his lip. The two guards positioned him roughly against the wall and withdrew out of range, one to either side. The prisoner's knees were visibly buckling under him, but he remained tight-lipped and refused a blindfold. His youthful attempt at final sullen bravery collapsed only when he shut his eyes; visible tears rolled down his thin cheeks.

The Owl's second barked out the command, "At the ready!"

"Take your aim!" The line of barrels wove and shook pitiably as the fear and horror of what was happening pressed down on them with the slow passing seconds. In the silence of that instant, not a man breathed.

"Fire!"

Pain stabbed out in all directions from the confined roar of nine rifles. The prisoner's knees bent slightly and he staggered forward into the flash, falling on one knee. He remained there in that kneeling position and a look of rapt astonishment crossed his face as he looked up at the nine frightened young men ringed before him. Slowly, very slowly, he got up, feeling himself without looking. Then he went over to a chair and sat down on it and broke into great racking sobs that sounded like gusts of inane laughter. The nine stood dumb, staring at him. Slowly, one by one, everyone turned to look at the Owl, who sat impassive at his table.

"If any man here thinks I did that for a joke, let him think again."

Brusquely, the second collected the rifles from the nine, who still stood in a state of stunned comprehension.

The men stood shaken and staring at the sobbing victim of the mock execution. Suddenly the old peasant, Marius, broke away from the group and strode forward. He stood in front of Colonel Owl, glaring at him, breathing in hard anger. When he spoke, his voice quavered and his words were choked with anger.

"That was a swinish trick," he said. His hands shook with emotion.

Colonel Owl looked at him, his eyes cold and remote. For a moment he said nothing. Then he said, "Would you rather have seen him killed?"

The farmer snorted in contempt. "He would have killed you," he said.

"True," the Owl said reflectively. "I have you to thank that he didn't. The next bullet might have had enough weight to carry your argument. Only the first round was blank." The Owl picked up the pistol from the table and broke it open, spilling the empty shell with the other unfired rounds into his hand. He carefully picked out one unfired bullet and held it up. "This is the one that might have killed me—or you," he added. He tossed it to the old peasant, who caught it automatically in his hand without looking down. "If it were a medal I'd give it to you with a kiss on both cheeks—for gallantry. As it is it's only a bullet."

The old man didn't move a muscle.

Colonel Owl sighed. He shrugged. "When I came in here I came alone," he said. "I told you that if there was to be any more killing of Frenchmen by Frenchmen it would not be I who would give the command. True, I have the legal power to execute criminals and traitors. But this man here is neither a criminal nor a traitor. He is merely young, unwise, and weak. As it is, his punishment fit his crime."

"You would have done better to . . ."

Colonel Owl looked up sharply. "Are you so certain? I'm not. Perhaps we should ask the victim." Owl turned sharply to his second. "Bring that boy here," he ordered.

They had to help him to his feet. Everyone stood tense and silent. The only sound was the stifled breathing sobs which still shook the boy's body even as he stood up and faced the table. Colonel Owl didn't look up at him until the prisoner had himself under control. The boy made no more attempt at bravado. The old peasant stood to one side.

Finally Colonel Owl said, "You tried to kill an officer of the French Army." He spoke so softly that it was almost as though he were addressing someone in private conversation. No one breathed; they heard every word. "Did you realize the significance of your act at the time you performed it?"

The boy shook his head, looking at the floor. His back was to the men in the room.

"Have you ever been in combat?" Colonel Owl asked, looking at the boy.

The boy shook his head again. He stood between his two guards, looking very thin and beaten.

"When did you join the active Resistance? Don't lie to me."

The boy mumbled something indistinct at the floor. There was a long silence.

"That's not a very long time," Colonel Owl said finally. His manner was deliberate, even gentle in an unbending way.

"How old are you?"

"Seventeen," the boy answered, looking up this time.

"You look very old for seventeen. Have you ever killed a man?"

The boy shook his head no and looked at his feet again.

"At seventeen that's not necessarily something to be ashamed of," Colonel Owl said. "Even in war."

The boy said nothing.

"You realize I'll have to hold you in custody, don't you?"

The boy looked up quickly, but said nothing. The reference to future time seemed to bring him to life.

"Would you have preferred a real execution to the one you had?"

The boy mumbled something at the floor. He was beginning to reassert his sullenness.

"Stand at attention," Colonel Owl snapped. "Speak up when you answer me."

"No," the boy answered again. He straightened up.

"No, *sir.*"

"No, sir."

"You realize I can still press a charge of attempted murder against you, don't you?"

"Yes, sir."

"Are you glad you're alive?" Colonel Owl asked coldly.

"Yes, sir," the boy said, involuntarily dropping his eyes again.

"So am I," Colonel Owl said grimly. "Perhaps you'll value life more highly in the future. At least you'll think twice before attempting to destroy it."

"Yes, sir."

"You have grown up in war. War teaches contempt for human life. Do you feel that your punishment has been unfair so far? Or cruel?"

"No, sir." The tone of voice was stronger, grudging but no longer sullen.

"Do you understand it?"

"Yes, sir."

Colonel Owl turned to his second. "This man will go back to Nice tonight with André's group. Make arrangements for him to be given into Captain Fanon's custody. I'll decide what charges to prefer later." He turned back to the young man. "Dismissed," he said.

The two guards turned the prisoner around.

"Wait," Colonel Owl said. They turned him back.

"Perhaps the prisoner would like the opportunity to apologize," the Owl said gently. "Not to me, but to these citizens who would have been the ultimate victims of his lawlessness." He looked the prisoner straight in the eye. "Some of them might be dead on your account, you realize," he said. He looked away from the prisoner now, at old Marius, who was standing off in the shadows.

"I apologize," the prisoner said, turning toward the men but looking at the floor.

The two guards steered the prisoner toward the door. The men stepped aside to make a path for them. The room watched in silence as the two guards led him outside. The door closed behind them.

Captain Owl looked around the room at the silent watching faces, then at old Marius. "I apologize too," he said, sighing heavily.

It took just six days, two hundred arrests, forty-nine trials, seventeen imprisonments, to locate the six largest arms caches in the coastal area. The rest were left to rust, which in time they did. On the twelfth day Colonel Owl sent north a quiet army of twenty-three hundred carefully picked men, traveling separately in small groups. Most of them returned home later. But that was a year later, and the war was over.

XXIII

It took the inspection team the better part of two days to retrace the last hours of Major Stone's captivity. The War Crimes Commission of Inquiry had already gone through what was left of the prison—it had been badly bombed. They now proceeded north along the route taken by the Scorpion Battalion and the small unlucky convoy of prisoners.

Of the twelve prisoners being herded to extinction that fearful night, Stone was the only one known to have escaped his planned fate. Atop the summit of the Montpelle ridge overlooking the vanished village, the remains of only ten corpses were recovered from the rain-sodden mound of ashes. Stone would have made the eleventh. The twelfth body was missing, unaccounted for; thus one other prisoner could conceivably have escaped alive. The possibility that the unaccounted one had been wounded and was still in hiding was not ruled out, although a thorough search of the surrounding countryside had failed to turn up anyone who'd sheltered a wounded man. But neither had the searchers discovered a corpse or anyone who'd found and buried one. The question of the missing prisoner remained for the time unresolved. Also, there was the mystery of the belt buckle and metal buttons that were sifted from the ashes and positively identified as being from the uniform of a Wehrmacht common soldier. Then, for lack of a better explanation, it was assumed that one of the prisoners was wearing a stolen jacket.

The last phase of the investigation required a visit to the site itself for the grim reconstruction of the events leading up to the crime. It was a wet and weary day. It began to rain at dawn and continued throughout the rest of the day. The sky was a wet gray blanket of clouds that pressed close to the earth. Rain fell steadily in strings, straight down; there was no wind to deflect it in its fall. The procession of nine dun-colored vehicles proceeded slowly and carefully northward, threading their way across the map, up along the battle-pocked road into the lower Alps. Major Stone was in the third car with Colonel Wolfe from Nice; the colonel had elected on his own to come on the grim pilgrimage. In the lead were two Military Police jeeps. The vehicles all traveled with their lights on, the customary signal of being in convoy.

At noon the caravan stopped, by prearrangement, for lunch. A bleak rain-washed command headquarters had been set up temporarily in a former roadside inn. Lunch was eaten in silence, and in a half-hour the group was ready to start on their way again. They came out from lunch, stepping over puddles toward the automobiles, and Colonel Wolfe noticed that a tenth car had joined the procession. It was a limousine staff car. He pointed it out to Stone.

"I wonder who that is? The rank plates are covered." The newly arrived vehicle was a type issued only to high-ranking officers, usually generals; as Stone knew, the rank plaque was usually covered with its black leather sheath only when the officer it was assigned to wasn't in it.

All the cars of the procession turned their headlights on again; on this day it was almost dark enough to need them anyway. The new arrival had turned on its lights just as Major Stone and Colonel Wolfe were coming out of the inn. Above the steady drubbing of rain the only other sound was the purr of engines and the unceasing whisper of a score of windshield wipers. Stone and the colonel sloshed across the open ground to the colonel's car. The captain, the colonel's aide, ran ahead to hold the door open. Once the colonel was inside, the captain closed the door and went around and got in the front beside the driver.

There was a strong smell of wet wool in the car. The colonel looked back uneasily at the newly arrived limousine.

"Hold it a minute," he said suddenly. "I want to find out who that is back there."

The colonel opened the door decisively and stepped out into the rain again, slamming the door. The driver squinted into the rear-view mirror.

"There's rank in that wagon, Captain," he said, without looking away from the mirror. "One, two, three of them. Plus a driver."

Next to him the captain nodded moodily and stared through the cold glass at the rain-splashed ground beside the car. The rain was slowly turning the ground to a sea of mud. "This is a hell of a day for an outing," he said.

The colonel came back to the car and got in again. He was frowning. For a while he didn't say anything. As the two jeeps ahead started up, the driver straightened his cap to a snappy angle and slid on a pair of leather gloves. He put the car in gear and pulled expertly onto the road behind the slow-rolling jeeps. The car swayed softly sideways as the rear wheels slipped and spun in the mud before they gripped the solid pavement. The driver drove slowly in low gear, bumper to bumper with the second jeep, watching in the rear-view mirror for the others to catch up. At a signal from the lead jeep he stepped into high gear and the cortege was on its way again.

Finally the colonel said, "That's your friend Colonel Jay back there, Major."

Stone was surprised and pleased, but he simply nodded. He knew that Jay had arrived the day before and had half expected him to show up.

"Who's that with him?" the captain finally asked, with a too-studied casualness.

The colonel didn't answer right away. Finally he said, "That Frenchman, Merseault. And a visitor down from Paris. Here unofficially."

"Traveling incognito?" the captain asked.

"I'm in no mood for wit," the colonel rebuked him. "How far are we from this place?" he asked the driver.

"Half-hour. Maybe an hour," the driver said, not taking his eyes off the road. "Depends on how bad the road's shot up, Colonel."

They drove in silence after that; the only sound above the engine was the splash of water as they plowed through pools in the road, and the steady whish-slap, whish-slap, of the windshield wiper. The captain sat looking straight and sullenly ahead.

It was midafternoon before they reached the bombed and broken culvert bridge and the line of cars made their first stop. Stone got out with the others. He was surprised to find that he had a distorted memory of the surrounding countryside. Although the bridge was familiar, the landscape was totally different from what he remembered. It was as though he were seeing it for the first time. True, it had been fairly dark just before that fatal dawn, but nevertheless his lapse of recall surprised him. The sharp mental picture he had built up of this place where the bridge was resembled nothing of the reality. The bridge, repaired temporarily since its bombing, was actually at a low point in the entrance to the valley; he had pictured it as much higher up. Also, his memory of distances was completely distorted. The valley of memory was longer, the mountain higher; actually it wasn't a full-grown mountain, but rather a large foothill. Everything seemed to have shrunk. Distances that in remembrance seemed interminable turned out in reality to have been a stone's throw. It gave Stone a sharp sense of unreality. It was somehow hard to believe that this innocent rain-soaked countryside was truly the sinister locale he remembered. The site of those tragic events had, on that terrible day, seemed grander, more portentous.

When everyone had stretched their legs, the reconstruction of events began. Stone stood in the circle of rain-soaked officers, American, British, and French, explaining first the placement of the German convoy, then about the two wrecks near the bridge, and then, little by little, all the rest. Somehow, to him, it sounded unreal in his mouth, untrue, as though it had never happened, but was merely a fantastic nightmare, a lie. It made him uncomfortable. It took twenty minutes from start to finish. Then came questions, precise questions, questions with steel edges to them; it only made him doubly uncomfortable. A sergeant of the Engineers Corps directed the laying of a steel tape to the earth; he called off the measured distances to a companion; their colloquy made the background against which Stone spoke. It added to the unreality. As though anything that happened here could be measured, even with a steel surveyor's tape.

The rain plopped ceaselessly on the soft mud around them. Major Stone would say what he could, recall what he could remember, answer the questions he could answer. But it seemed, to Major Stone, inadequate. The events he was talking about might have happened, he felt, on another planet. But he answered questions until the members of the Commission were satisfied they had grasped the situation. The legal men took notes as best they could in the straight and windless rain. The recorders recorded; the surveyors surveyed. Finally they all went back and joined those who'd remained in the cars, those officials who were not directly concerned with this particular part of the inquiry.

The convoy started again. In no time at all they were at the summit of the ridge. Stone remembered the journey as a long one, and yet they seemed to be there now in fifteen or twenty minutes. The road up to the summit branched off the main road before it reached the village. The village they would see last; they would approach other things in the order Stone approached them. They would see more, because they weren't confined in trucks; they would see less, because they wouldn't see through confined eyes. At the summit, to his immense secret relief, Stone recognized the clearing the instant it came into view. As they drove up the long muddy road, the landscape had become more and more unfamiliar, until in a moment of unreasoning panic Stone wondered if he would be able to identify at all the spot where he had so narrowly escaped with his life only a few weeks ago. But the upper ground seemed suddenly more familiar; some of it he had crawled over on his hands and knees in the dark; this ground he knew by touch, from memory according to the fact. Here, even several of the drivers got out and stood in the rain to follow the major through the reconstruction of his spectacular escape. Just as the group was assembling, Stone suddenly recognized Colonel Jay standing off to one side. He was with two other men. One was a French officer, a short round man with an unsoldierly bearing, the other an older American officer, a tall man whose insignia of rank was covered up by his raincoat. Stone found the American officer's face vaguely familiar, a public face, like a face seen once in a newsreel. The man turned away when Stone glanced at him; he was being as unobtrusive as possible. Stone concluded that he had a reason to remain aloof; later he would ask Jay privately who he was. Jay nodded at him gravely; Stone nodded back. It was the first time they'd seen each other since Stone left Algiers. It seemed like several years ago.

The members of the Inquiry Group asked careful questions. Twice over, Stone explained the disposition of the trucks, of the German staff car. Rain continued hanging in flat gray strings, plashing gently on the sodden earth. Again in the background the two engineers called out cryptic measurements to each other, one of them writing them down in a small notebook he shielded from the rain under his raincoat. The milling of the two dozen people had already begun to churn the ground into mud. A few umbrellas had been put up; most of the group simply stood, hands in pockets, collars turned up against the draining skies.

Major Stone explained precisely how the tools had been laid out on the ground; how none of the prisoners guessed the precise purpose of what they were building until the Germans broke out the gasoline drum; and how by that time they were back in the trucks waiting for their final exit into the pyre. The recorders jotted as best they could in the rain. Then Stone took them all down onto the slopes; here there was real evidence. It had a sobering effect on the group. It brought them closer to the reality. The mute stumps of the freshly vanished trees impressed everyone in the group more than anything so far. A few of them reached down and fingered the stumps in something like rapt disbelief. Stone pointed out exactly which ones he himself had helped cut down. They stared at him, as though he were impossibly alive, a ghost returned. That was a detail he hadn't forgotten: each tree, and in what order. That he would never be able to forget.

"You have said, Major Stone," the senior British legal officer asked, "that none of the twelve prisoners was aware of the purpose of this construction?"

"That is correct, sir. Not until the very end. It dawned on the doctor and me about the same time."

"Did you discuss it among yourselves? I mean those of you who realized what was going to happen."

"No. Not exactly. That is, it's difficult to explain. I saw by the doctor's face—his expression changed at just about the same instant I put it together for myself. You see, they'd brought a drum of gasoline along. Originally we thought we were in for a long trip, and logically that explained the gasoline. It was strapped onto the running board of the first truck."

"I see. Then it was the gasoline drum that . . ."

"I don't know. Yes. All of us assumed somehow that they were going to lock us up in this thing—it looked like it was going to be a pen, a sort of stockade, you know. And that explained it. When I first saw the thing as a pyre, I was afraid almost to think of it. It was only after the other two groups had been shot that I think we all tacitly agreed that we would have to try to break. It was all done with the eyes. It's hard to explain. We hadn't been able to make any plans out loud because they would allow no talking. The guards were standing right over us."

"I see. Then when they locked you all back up in the trucks, you did finally agree—tacitly, as you say—on some sort of group action, action that culminated in the break?"

"I don't know if the others thought about it in that way. As I remember, during the morning the doctor said, 'If anyone sees an out, take it,' and Carnot said, 'No two in the same direction.' When they took us out they took us out one at a time—in single file. I said, 'Whoever goes in the lead will start it.' That's all I got out, because the guard hit me in the ribs for talking."

"And Antoine Berger was first?"

"Yes."

"He rushed the guard?"

"Yes. I saw that one of them was off guard, and I reached out to nudge Berger—to alert him. He saw him at the same time and rushed him. I didn't turn around to see how the others broke, but I heard them run. Then there was too much shouting to hear anything."

"You say Berger rushed his guard. That was the Wehrmacht soldier you alluded to in your statement?"

"Yes, sir."

Another British officer spoke up. "Major, you say that he was 'off guard.' Can you explain that more precisely?" He spoke without lifting his eyes from the notebook in his hand, but continued writing.

Stone hesitated. He looked at the officer.

"He was crying," he said. "I knew he couldn't see . . ."

502

The officer stiffened, the pencil halted. He straightened up and looked away. "And that's why you rushed him, of course." He added gently, "You had to."

There was an awkward silence. Finally the legal officer asked, "He was knocked to the ground?" He spoke very quietly.

"Who?" Stone asked. "The soldier?"

"Yes, Major. The one you said was, ah, said was crying."

"Of course he was knocked to the ground," Stone felt unaccountably irritated. "I had to jump over him."

"I see," the officer said. "Did you see him get up?"

"I didn't look around," Stone said.

Someone breathed, "Good God." Then silence.

One of the drivers had unobtrusively retrieved a flattened bullet out of a dead tree trunk with a penknife. He showed it to one of the legal officers; the officer decided that the bullet was too deformed by heat of impact to be of any practical use. There were several bullets still imbedded in trees, although most of them had been removed on orders of the legal staff in an effort to learn exactly what types of weapons were used and, if possible, someday to help identify their users. No evidence, not even the most fanciful, was being overlooked. The soldier pocketed his bullet for a souvenir.

Back up in the clearing, Stone stood where the pyre had been. He said nothing; there was no need for words. Where the pyre was there was now nothing. The ground had been brushed and swept until it was bare of ashes. Every scrap of the pyre's remains had been removed to be sifted and resifted for additional evidence. All that remained was a bare patch of grayish rain-soaked mud. The last of the funeral mound was gone.

After the ground was covered in the main tour, the inspection party split into two groups. Most of the American military personnel went with the recorders and surveyors in the larger group to visit the site of the village. Arrangements were made to rendezvous on the main road —everyone checked his watch—and the party left for the village. Stone was glad of a chance to avoid seeing the village at close range.

Stone remained behind with the legal officers, both British, and a recorder. The car that brought Colonel Jay and the other two officers didn't leave with the others but remained also. It was parked a short distance away from the center of the clearing; Stone noted that it was parked in the same spot the staff car of the German SS lieutenant had once parked in. The colonel had left his staff car and chauffeur behind for Stone and the two legal officers, and had gone down into the village in the lead jeep.

"That was decent of the colonel," the captain said. He looked very serious, the more so for his young face. He couldn't have been more than twenty-eight, young for a legal officer. They stood in the rain.

The other British officer was a gentle old major. He had the manners of a King's Solicitor, and had been a barrister in civilian life. Colonel

Wolfe had briefed Stone on everyone's history before leaving Nice. This man's name was Ponsonby. The captain seemed to be a sort of junior law partner to Major Ponsonby. The major was old enough to have been his father, and the captain deferred to him with genuine respect.

Colonel Jay and his two companions had gone to their car and were sitting out of the rain. The rear door was open. Out of the tail of his eye Stone could see Jay conversing with the unidentified American officer and the French colonel. He felt terribly anxious to see Jay, but wished he could have talked to him first in different circumstances. The rain was depressing. Stone felt wet around his trouser cuffs and ankles, and water seeped down the upturned collar of his service raincoat.

"These are two different cases, Major Stone," Major Ponsonby was saying.

Stone realized he was being addressed. "I'm sorry, Major," he said. "My mind was wandering. What was that?"

"I say these are two different cases. Procedurally, of course. The destruction of the village involved no Allied military personnel. We still haven't entirely settled the problem of jurisdiction in this matter of war crimes. For one thing there isn't much in the way of precedent to go by. This may turn out to be a French show before we're through, but we want to get on with it while the trail is still warm."

"Yes," Stone said. He felt uncomfortably detached from this scene. It bothered him, and he had a hard time keeping his mind on it. He was thinking about Colonel Jay. Somehow he felt that he had failed before the inspectors. He hadn't been able to communicate the reality, the terror, of what had happened here. He had a hard time, he realized, convincing himself. It all seemed so remote and impossible now. The mind, even his own mind, recoiled from the nightmare. The routine seemed to stultify the reality.

"I'm sorry to have to insist on details," Ponsonby said, "but we have to build a careful case. If the Allies do incorporate a tribunal, we'll have to have airtight evidence. Otherwise it could backfire, and that would be a terrible tragedy."

"I understand."

"I know this must be very painful for you, Major," the captain offered with genuine solicitude. "But you'll be glad to know we've already identified the SS unit."

"Yes, Captain," Stone said. "It's like trying to remember a nightmare you've already forgotten."

There was a short silence. The recorder, an American corporal, stood a short distance off, holding a pad and pencil under his raincoat, waiting to be called upon to take down conversation. The rain fell slowly and steadily, and underfoot the ground was reduced to a churn of gray mud. A light breeze had risen and the curtain of gray rain undulated steadily back and forth with a steady unceasing whisper.

"Particularly we will need witnesses, Major," Ponsonby said. He

504

looked at the ground and kicked a clod of mud off the toe of his boot. "Witnesses," he repeated wearily. Stone looked at him sharply. Did Ponsonby feel something of the enormous impossibility of trying to embrace the unimaginable? Stone felt a sharp pang—he searched his mind for the exact word. What was it? Sympathy? It was more like love, he knew. Ponsonby's poised mask had dropped for an instant and revealed a confused human being under the careful attitude of official objectivity.

Stone realized for the first time that he was tired to the point of nervous exhaustion. He found release in a deep sigh. Ponsonby looked up quickly, and for one short instant they stared at each other in absolute recognition of the agony that they shared. Ponsonby nodded slowly, wordlessly.

Stone looked away. He felt his emotions taking complete control of him. He was too tired to try and check them. "I—hadn't realized how this thing has hit me," he said. He felt suddenly the full unexpected flood of grief and confusion. "I must be overtired." There was a knot of rage, an impotent desire for vengeance that weighed like lead inside him. Unconsciously he clenched his fists. He realized that there were tears forming in his eyes. He made no effort to hide them. Ponsonby and the young captain averted their eyes out of consideration.

"I've managed to keep from thinking about it too long," Stone said, embarrassed. "Why? Why? Why did they have to do this?"

"In all my years in the law . . ." Ponsonby began, and then broke off, leaving his unsatisfactory thought unfinished. He shook his head. "Major Stone," he said angrily, "this is only a small part. I haven't seen the other places. This is my first inspection tour. But I've read reports. They've already found worse. Worse. And we're not even across the Rhine yet. I fear sometimes that God has abandoned us."

"Worse?" Stone asked dully.

"This incident is only part of a huge pattern. This—this massacre was not an accident. This is part of a policy, a carefully considered, coldly calculated policy."

Stone looked from the major to the captain. He realized but couldn't feel the meaning of the major's words. He said nothing.

"I'm afraid of what we'll find in Germany. In the camps," Ponsonby said. "I—I try to keep my sanity. But I'm afraid of what we'll find."

"Sanity?"

"Sanity," Ponsonby said. "This is insanity. It's not merely evil. It's a black disease, a plague of the mind and soul. I'm not sure that it might not be best to hide these things from the world. I fear for the effect it will have on the world's sanity. Man exposed as totally bestial—I don't know. It could mean the collapse of order, of moral law. If the world believes it, that is."

"You don't think people will believe *this* happened?"

"I don't know, Major. In the law you gain an odd insight into humanity's capacity for disbelief. When faced with a fact that threatens their sanity, they simply reject it. Nothing can make them believe it. If they believed it they'd go mad."

No one said anything. The young captain fidgeted nervously with a button that was hanging by only a single thread on his drenched raincoat. Suddenly he yanked it off and slipped it into his pocket.

"I sometimes wonder if I'll ever be able to believe in the validity of the law again," Ponsonby said. "This is hard for an old Victorian like me. There are some illusions that are necessary for life. Hamlet has no place in the law—or politics either, for that matter. This could incapacitate a man in my career. After the war I had always planned—"

Ponsonby looked up from his reflection. "Enough of that," he said, interrupting himself. "War will incapacitate a lot of us. Let's get on with it, what do you say, Major. There'll be time enough for mourning mankind after this is all over, what?"

"I'll try to help you," Stone said abstractedly. "I don't know what I can tell you besides what I've already told you."

"Stone." It was Colonel Jay.

Stone turned around. Jay stood there behind him. Stone wondered how long he'd been standing there. The rain had masked his approaching footsteps. His thin hawklike face was serious and worried. Stone was shocked at how much Jay had aged since he'd last seen him in Algiers. Then Stone realized that Jay must have been thinking the same thing about him; his face couldn't hide the shock. Stone knew that he must still present a harrowing appearance, in spite of his days of rest in Nice. He'd lost nearly fifty pounds since Jay had last seen him.

"I didn't want to interrupt you gentlemen," Jay said apologetically to Ponsonby. He seemed embarrassed before Stone. He turned and stared openly into Stone's face. "You've been through it, John. Lord, am I glad to see you again."

"It's good to see you, sir," Stone said, smiling. It *was* good to see Jay.

"Could you spare the major for a moment?" Jay asked Ponsonby. "Of course, Colonel."

"The gentlemen with me have to start back to Nice," he explained. "I want them to meet the major." He turned back to Stone. "Would you come over to the car with me, John?"

At the car Stone had to bend down to see the two men in the rear of the limousine. The driver sat straight as a ramrod, looking ahead. The motor was purring quietly, and a trail of white exhaust mingled with the falling rain.

"This is Major Stone, sir," Jay said into the open rear door. He appeared to be addressing the American officer, who was sitting on the far side.

Stone bent further and saluted into the murky interior. The two officers saluted informally in return.

"This is Colonel Merseault," Jay said to Stone. "Your list of arms caches has been of great help to him."

"You have done this country a service, Major," Merseault said in English. "I salute you for it." Merseault saluted again, this time formally. Stone murmured his thanks. He didn't look directly at the French colonel's face. He felt vaguely embarrassed.

"I'm sorry I have to go back so quickly, John," Jay said. "But I'll be in Nice for the rest of the week. What have they got you doing there?"

"Graves Registration," Stone said.

Jay bent and glanced ambiguously into the car, a question on his face. He must have received a signal from the other American officer inside, for he straightened up and looked at Stone and asked, "Is there anything else you'd rather have?"

"I don't mind Graves Registration," Stone said. "I've only been at it for a few days, but I think I'm going to get along."

"Would you like a spot in Military Government, John? With your experience . . ." Jay left the suggestion unfinished. There was a pause.

Stone realized that the offer must have emanated from the ranking person inside the staff car. He was careful to phrase his refusal to indicate his appreciation of the proffered favor. "I'd like to give this other thing a try first, if you don't mind. It's removed from—from . . ."

"From the war?" Jay offered. He spoke gently, with understanding. "You must be pretty battle weary by now, John."

"It's not quite that," Stone said. "It's removed from politics. I've gotten a little disillusioned with the affairs of the living, I'm afraid. It appears I made a botch of—"

"Nonsense. I won't hear that kind of talk from you. You've done a fine job here. It's not your fault we were slowed down in Italy. It's ours, perhaps, but certainly not yours. You did exactly what I would have done under the circumstances."

Stone grinned. "You've talked to the colonel?"

"I've not only talked to him, John. I've straightened him out on a few things." Jay turned into the car. "Haven't we, Georges?" The French officer nodded. Stone could see only his chin as it went up and down; the roof of the car cut off the rest of his view. He could also see the long gnarled hands of the American officer resting on the dun-colored blanket across his knees. They looked like hands made old by arthritis, Stone thought, or hard labor.

"Well, the offer is open any time you want to take it, John," Colonel Jay said. "How about a change of post?"

"From Nice you mean?"

"We need Graves Registration people in Paris, John. We need them badly, I'm unhappy to say. The going up north has been rougher than the broadcast figures indicate."

"Casualties?"

"Very heavy, John. Especially the last two weeks. Keep that under your hat. We're having a little morale problem among troops coming in green for replacements. Things will be all right." He looked troubled.

"I'd like to go to Paris. I'll know my trade better in a few weeks here, though."

"I'll get in touch with you, John," Jay said, extending his hand.

"Are you in my plush hotel?" Stone asked.

"No, we have a villa, as usual. Somewhere in France," Jay said, smiling.

"Still at it?"

"Lord, yes. The Germans left us a pretty mess to untangle. No one knows friend from foe in this damned war."

Jay got into the car beside the French colonel. He held the door open a moment longer, bending toward Stone with his arm outstretched on the door handle.

"Do you need anything?" he asked privately.

"No."

"You know why I didn't ask to have you back, I imagine."

"I'm stale," Stone said, smiling.

"I thought you'd know. You've signed enough orders for me to know my mind. I think you're wise to keep active. How's your state of mind?"

Stone smiled. "It's very peaceful working among the dead."

"No politics, at least," Jay said grimly.

"Somehow it makes me feel constructive. Did you see the cemetery our friends the engineers built in their spare time? They did a good job."

"I'll drive out and take a look at it," Jay said.

From inside the car, the other American officer spoke. His voice surprised Stone with a quality of clear kindness and sure authority. It was a handsome voice. He addressed himself to Jay. "If the major would like to have leave with his family, I'm sure you could arrange it, Colonel," he said.

Jay looked at Stone; he seemed flustered. Stone answered the question implied in his look. Jay knew that Major Stone had no family.

"My family is gone, sir," Stone said, bending down and peering into the car. He saw the older officer's face in profile against the wet glass of the opposite window. The officer said nothing, but simply nodded his apprehension of Stone's statement. Stone straightened up and accepted Colonel Jay's handshake. It was a warm hard handshake, full of feeling. Jay held it for a long time, looking straight into Stone's face. Then he said, "We'd given you up, you know."

"I almost gave myself up," Stone said.

"Welcome back to the world of the living, John. Take decent care of yourself. I'll be in touch with you."

The car door clicked shut with a heavy expensive click. He watched the car turn around. Not every officer had a limousine for his staff car, Stone reflected—must be a general. Old training had long ago taught him not to be curious about Jay's affairs. He automatically closed his mind to speculation; he had no desire to know anything he didn't need to know. As the car started down the hill he held his hand to wave a salute, but no one inside turned his head. The three men looked straight ahead. The car swept past him through the rain. As it started down the hill the lights went on. Stone stood in the rain and watched the diminishing ruby gleam of the twin taillights; they winked in bright unison as the driver braked the car around the first steep bend. And then the car was out of sight. He turned and walked back.

Colonel Ponsonby and the captain were sitting out of the rain in the colonel's loaned car, and the rear door left ajar. Ponsonby was taking advantage of the interlude to dictate a few final notes to the recorder, who sat awkwardly facing around on the front seat beside Colonel Wolfe's bored driver. Ponsonby finished his terse clipped sentence and pushed the door wider for Stone, who stood waiting beside the car, his hands in the pockets of his raincoat.

"Get in, Major," Ponsonby said. "It's getting too dark to do much else here today. In fact I'm not sure there's much else we can do, as you say."

"You're going back?" Stone asked. In his mind he was still preoccupied with Jay. He'd always thought of Jay as a contemporary in spite of rank difference. But Jay had changed. He was no longer a vigorous young colonel.

Stone shook the rain off his new officer's cap and got into the car. The back seat was barely wide enough for three.

"May as well," Ponsonby said. "It'll be totally dark before long. I'd like to get down off this infernal mountain before then. We have to rendezvous with the others at the broken bridge."

"The aerial photographs will be ready tomorrow, sir," the captain said. "We might be able to work from them, if we have to do any more on the physical layout."

The driver, unbidden, suddenly started the car.

"Who *was* that?" Ponsonby asked casually, cocking his head in the direction of the departed limousine. "Looked like visiting royalty."

"Colonel Jay—Nice Intelligence."

"Oh, I've met Jay. I meant the other two. One was French, wasn't he?"

Stone was amused at the way Ponsonby and the others had all smelled out rank in the strange staff car. The driver swore under his breath as he wrestled the car out of the mud and turned around onto the road.

"A colonel, yes," Stone said. He tried not to remember the French officer's name. "The name slipped by me," he said. He sighed. "I must be tired; I can't seem to keep anything in my head for more than two minutes."

The car slithered into the mud ruts left by the other vehicles, and started downhill.

"I must say," Colonel Ponsonby said, surveying the interior of the car—it was a Buick and it still smelled new in spite of the odor of wet wool. "I must say, you chaps know how to provide the finer things in war. It's too bad it has to be painted the color of mud, this lovely vehicle."

"Mud is the color of my true love's hair," the chauffeur said unexpectedly. It was definitely said in a disrespectfully flippant tone. Ponsonby opened his mouth with a tiny recoil of well-bred surprise; but being a guest in the American colonel's car he was at a disadvantage. He couldn't bring himself to correct his host's servant. Stone avoided Ponsonby's eyes and looked out the window. Outside the dismal rain-sodden landscape stretched away into the late afternoon. Stone felt depressed, wet, tired. He realized with depressing clarity how far he had to go before he would get his former strength back. Without thinking, he said, "Mud is the color of war."

They rode the rest of the way down to the bridge in silence, lulled by the soft hypnotic heartbeat of the windshield wipers. Every so often the driver would whistle under his breath, a tuneless toothy sissing that mildly irritated Stone. Next to him Ponsonby was lost in the unexplored wilderness of the law as he leafed through the notes he'd gathered earlier into his morocco-bound zippered ring-binder briefcase. The young captain turned over in his fingers the button he'd wrenched off his trenchcoat, staring solemnly at it as though trying to memorize it. The recorder up front beside the driver amused himself by alternately breathing fog on his window and then erasing it furtively with his sleeve. It seemed to take longer coming down the mountain than it had going up. It was darkening quickly as they descended into the valley. As they reached level ground on the way to the broken bridge, Colonel Ponsonby slapped his briefcase shut and zipped it up sharply and sat staring straight ahead. He sighed a heavy sigh of fatigue.

"Tired, Colonel?" Stone asked, to break the silence.

"Dead," the colonel answered. "Absolutely, utterly dead."

Spring arrived too late to be spring; the last wet winter skies lifted only as the April sap shot up; the trees exploded into leafy bursts of clear green. The long gray days of winter had dragged their leaden misery out too long; too long had people gone about the wet streets of spring dressed in wool-smelling black, their collars up, like mourners. The sudden sun's spectacular return, dazzling the sky and the eye, struck the city like a blow; the city started awake. Then, as though caressed, it sank back, thankfully stunned into happy paralysis, warmed witless. The sun, the soporific sun, smoothed its forgiving warmth over the tight fatigue of winter and beguiled the urban soul; and that is how winter vanished. Like that, it was over; winter was gone, suffering was gone, whatever was overriding and grim was for that first welcome week forgotten, lost in the sun's oblivion. Summer was come in April; and spring was hardly missed.

I

John Stone stepped through the tall doors and felt the carpet thicken under his feet. The carpet absorbed all sound in the room, even the click of the door as the secretary closed it behind him. Stone waited respectfully. The Ambassador, absorbed, didn't look up. He penciled a note in the margin of a pink information copy of a cablegram—Stone recognized the familiar format—and slid it aside. Stone had never seen him before with the tiny steel-rimmed half-spectacles. It gave him a stern academic air, reinforced by the hushed austerity of the large room. Stone was sure that the Ambassador knew he was standing there. He waited calmly to be recognized, conscious of feeling uncomfortably like a wayward student awaiting the headmaster's pleasure.

It was the room that did it. The tapestried walls reflected no sound, nor did the thick carpet. The room possessed a respectful decorum, a calculated dignity that intimidated the beholder and gave strong advantage to the man who occupied it. It was truly the Ambassador's quarters. It was here that decisions were taken, crises met; it was here that certain final questions were asked and answered; it was here that the destinies of a certain portion of the world's people were conjured with, threatened, defended. The room was at once austere and grand. Its furnishings couldn't be called expensive, for they had never seen a market place; they were merely without price, quiet, superb, unique. If a chair in this room had value it was derived not from its age or its honest craftsmanship, but rather from the men who had sat in it. Invisible history gilded these articles, hung from the walls like invisible moss, rich, luxurious, as though all the words spoken in this room over the decades and centuries had permeated the walls and remained there. The room had a patina of solemn mystery about it, and although Stone had been in this room twice before in his life, he realized that he was really sensing this for the first time. On the last occasion it was arranged for the press conference and had a public air, like a small theater. Before that Merseault had been here with him. But now, on his own request, he was here alone, a petitioner before the king's chamberlain so to speak, and the room suddenly reasserted its intimate personal quality—a privy chamber, an inner sanctum sanctorum. It was a little like finding oneself in a royal bedchamber, a room heavy with long privacy and untendered secrets.

"Sit down, Mr. Stone. Let me clear up these few things. Then we can talk without interruption. I'd like to get these out in the early pouch." The Ambassador gestured with his pen, an old-fashioned gold fountain pen with a huge flexible nib that flowed ink into the brusque signature. He turned the paper over and blotted it carefully. Without looking up he pointed toward a chair.

Stone cleared his throat politely and sat down. The Ambassador continued to read, scanning each document; occasionally scribbling a comment in the margin of a document, he affixed his initial at the lower right-hand corner as he put each aside. He finished the crop of cables and turned to the letters. Stone had the feeling that the man was completely submerged in the problems before him, oblivious to everything else in the room, including his visitor. Stone felt invisible, a ghostly intruder on the privacy of a public man. He watched the Ambassador as he read, the stern face reflecting unabashedly his reactions to whatever it was that was impinging on his consciousness at the moment. At one point, when he was halfway down the neatly staggered pile of letters, he extracted one and frowned at it in vexation, reaching by reflex for the intercom button.

"Yes, sir?" came the voice from the box, feminine, metallic, efficient.

"Get me Dr. Edwards on the telephone, please, Mrs. Steele." There was a trace of irritation in his manner.

"Yes, sir."

The Ambassador signed two more letters before the telephone buzzed softly. He reached for it, not taking his eyes off the letter he was reading.

"How'd you sleep last night, Arthur?" the Ambassador asked, smiling into space. A pause. The Ambassador laughed. "Arthur, you know my bark is worse than my bite. I'm sorry if I was a bit critical of your shop, but we're under pressure for a reply. We've got to get it off to Washington in time for the President's budget session." A pause, longer this time. The Ambassador listened, a slight frown appearing across his forehead. He took off his spectacles and rubbed the bridge of his nose. "I've got it here in my hand. I've been reading it." He picked up the letter. The heavy parchment bond snapped stiffly as he shook off the envelope and tissue copies that were neatly paper-clipped to it at the top. "I was wondering, Arthur, if you might not be wise to cover yourself a little better. I don't want to put my signature to anything that's going to rise up and haunt you." Stone could hear the thin vibrations of the reply in the earpiece. "Precisely," said the Ambassador. Another long pause. "Well, Arthur, it's my fault. I should have warned you about that. It's not the director you have to worry about. Everyone in Budget understands our problem. They're an administrative agency themselves. No, I think Webb will be sympathetic enough—I can assure you personally—I talked with him at some length when I was in Washington last winter. He's not insensible to your dilemma." A pause. The Ambassador idly picked up his pen and signed another letter, the letter in front of him. "All right, Arthur, I'll sign this, then, and send it out by pouch today. I'll send it direct, but I'm going to make it personal. Is that all right with the three consultants? I'll make a note on it that this is not a firm policy recommendation, but merely to provide background to help the President come to a decision. Now does that square with your thinking?"

Stone suddenly realized what it was that made him feel so intrusive in the present situation. The Ambassador was in his shirtsleeves. But that wasn't it alone. It was the elastic bands he wore, like an old-fashioned telegraph operator, to keep the cuffs back. It was the revealed intimate secret that made the mind run on to other details. Did the Ambassador wear garters? Stone reflected that public figures always seemed whole and inviolate; to wonder whether Caesar wore underwear beneath his toga when he bled in the Senate was to compromise the legend. The Ambassador's spectacles, which he never wore in public, the elastic sleeve garters—these things betokened a human being, a personal living individual whose humanity was suddenly brought into sharp focus. Stone lost track of the Ambassador's end of the conversation. He thought about the story he'd heard during the war sometime of Winston Churchill's cavorting about his White House bedroom in his birthday suit deep in earnest conversation with the President of the United States; how Churchill had suddenly, impressively, become more real. People wanted pomp and decorum in their public men. Why? Was it because they distrusted the frailties of the human man? Or was it an attempt to elevate their servants above mortality? And yet the frailties and weakness of humanity defined humanity. Stone felt that he had seen something clearly for the first time. The attempt to rise above one's own humanity was to deny that humanity. And then for no reason he thought of Calvin, who in striving after righteousness finally lived to burn a man at the stake. Suddenly it all seemed so clear, so ironic. So just.

Stone came back to the Ambassador. He was listening quietly, and had been for several minutes, to the tiny voice like a claw in the earpiece, scratching in the silence. Every now and then he nodded soberly and stared at the point of his fountain pen, which he turned in his fingers. Stone shifted unconsciously and the Ambassador's gaze flickered in his direction. It was as though he'd just remembered Stone was there. He sat suddenly upright in his chair. "Fine, Arthur," he said, speaking in a tone that conveyed an end to the conversation. "Now let's make sure we have our strategy clear between us. You want me to send this along now, with my little comment post scriptum. We'll then follow it up with our final suggestions, a copy of which will go, over my signature, to the chairman of the Appropriations Committee for his guidance and information. But you're agreed that we can't send this to them, right? They'd eat you alive. Just be careful that you don't say anything that would embarrass them before their constituents. It is my experience, Arthur, that a member of Congress will show you just the understanding and sympathy for your problems that you show for his. It's not easy to represent the people." The Ambassador nodded, listening to the reply. "Well, don't let it upset you, Arthur. After all, you're new to government. This is a far cry from the cloisters of the law faculty." The Ambassador listened and laughed. "You're learning, Dr. Edwards. I agree completely. Now, can you let me have a draft—just a first draft, nothing fancy—say, by ten tomorrow morning? Bring it with you and we'll go over it. Fine. Fine. It's on my calendar then." The Ambassador hung up.

"I'm sorry, Mr. Stone. Just one more minute." The Ambassador pushed the intercom button. The same secretarial voice answered.

"Did you get my signal?" the Ambassador asked.

"Yes, sir."

"Good. Will you type up a copy of that for my personal file, please? Not the whole thing—just the long part in the middle. By the way, some of those figures come from the President's Interim Report—I think you'd better up the classification of the entire file. What's it carry now?"

"Confidential, sir."

"Yes. Go through and up that to 'secret' for the time being. There are six copies of that file out among the division chiefs, take care of them too while you're at it, Mrs. Steele. Will you do that for me?"

"Yes, sir. The mission chiefs have had a summary sent them. It went out as a circular airgram this morning. Shall I . . . ?"

"No. There's nothing specific there. I just don't want a repetition of what happened last week. We were lucky that the press didn't catch the discrepancy, but Washington did. You saw that little billet-doux?"

"Yes, sir."

"See that the press section has their nose rubbed in it. Gently of course, Mrs. Steele. I know your sharp tongue." The Ambassador smiled and looked at Stone.

"I'll tell Mr. Washburn, sir."

"I want you to muzzle Mr. Washburn, Mrs. Steele. I know he's bursting to tell the world of his accomplishment, but this is one story that must be broken by Washington. As much as it pains him. You can come in now and clear my desk, if you will."

Stone wondered who Mr. Washburn was.

The Ambassador glanced over the last few letters, each of which was no longer than a few lines each, and scrawled his careful signature on each in succession. Mrs. Steele entered noiselessly and waited for him to finish. She didn't even glance at Stone. When the Ambassador had signed the last letter she handed him a slip of paper and gathered up the papers. The Ambassador read the slip she gave him, and frowned.

"Ask him to wait, please. Apologize for me."

"Yes, sir."

"No, wait. Would you ask Mr. Lasher to see him first? Ask him if he would mind doing that for me? If he prefers not to see Lasher, take him into Mr. Chalmers' office—he's in London today, isn't he?—and make him comfortable until I can see him."

"Yes, sir."

Mrs. Steele glided out with a rustle of papers in both hands and closed the tall doors. Stone watched the brass handle turn carefully, silently, as she closed the doors from the outside without a sound. The Ambassador reached once more for the intercom.

"And, Mrs. Steele, please screen all my calls. We'd like to be undisturbed if possible."

"Shall I cancel the Frankfurt call, sir?"

"No, I'll take that. Also, if Chalmers calls, I want to talk to him." The Ambassador glanced at his watch. "It's getting late. The Geneva cable can wait until morning. Have Dr. Edwards draft a reply and bring it with him tomorrow."

"You asked me to remind you to get your hair cut, today."

"Yes, and you forgot."

"You didn't have time today. I'll remind you tomorrow before you go to the reception."

"Reception?"

"The Quai d'Orsay. You accepted."

"Is that thing tomorrow? Have Cicero draft some appropriate remarks for me. No rhetoric. Straightforward."

"He's already started on the speech, sir. I told him to make it no more than five or ten minutes long and to avoid the sterling question."

"Fine. Have him call me between six and seven tomorrow morning and read me what he's got over the telephone. That way he won't have to get out of bed. You call him and wake him before you call me."

"Yes, sir."

The Ambassador snapped the switch and leaned back in his chair, his fingers laced behind his head.

"Well, Mr. Stone, you've been very kind to let me get my afternoon cleaned up while I've kept you waiting."

"Not at all, sir. I'm sorry to intrude on your time like this."

"By interesting coincidence, there's a friend of ours waiting to see me outside," the Ambassador said. Stone looked blank. The Ambassador reached forward and took the slip of paper his secretary had given him and passed it across the enormous writing table. The green leather inlay was worn smooth with polished use and time, and the paper slid off the desk and fluttered to the carpet at Stone's feet. "Oh, excuse me," the Ambassador said.

Stone had already retrieved the elusive scrap and held it before him. In a carefully legible feminine script it read: *Dr. Merseault to see you. Says important, that you know what about.*

"I haven't seen him since I last talked with you here in this office. Don't you think that's a fateful circumstance?" the Ambassador said. "It all seems like ancient history. Spring is here and everyone forgets—except Georges Merseault. What do you think of that, Mr. Stone?"

"For myself I'm glad. I don't have to go around ducking photographers any more." Stone paused. "What's happening to that business, anyway?"

"I imagine Merseault is keeping track of it. Picard's been unusually quiet. As to Dujardin himself, who knows what they'll finally do?"

"I've heard rumors that he is to be let out—on some sort of parole. Does that mean . . . ?"

"It's hard to say what anything means. One thing is certain, however. The Party's interest has long since evaporated. As soon as the winter strikes were over they dropped the whole affair like the rind of a juiced lemon. Did you notice that coincidence?"

Stone frowned, hesitating. Then he said, "Well, frankly, I'm fed up with it. It upsets me to think about it. Besides, I'm taking up your time—I'd rather use the time you've given me to better advantage."

"Well, then, Mr. Stone, do I know why you're here?"

"I think so, sir."

"Well, we're both grown men," the Ambassador said soberly. "There's not much point in waltzing about the bush. Let's get at it. Is that all right with you?"

"Yes, sir."

"I think that for the time being you'd better stop calling me 'sir.' It sometimes seems to get in the way of discussion, where people's emotions are involved. And I understand your emotions are involved in this."

"Yes, sir." Stone smiled uneasily. "That is, yes, my emotions are involved."

"Well, so are mine—if that's any consolation to you. I've worked in the service of my country for more years than I care to count, but I've never yet been able to reconcile every public act with all my private feelings. You realize, of course, that in asking to see me personally you're slightly out of line. Jumping the chain of command, as we'd say in the service."

"I realize that it might seem that way. However, I didn't want to see you for myself alone. That is, this thing has long ago ceased to be a purely personal matter for me. In a way, I suppose I'm taking it all very ungracefully, but I've come to see that there's more at stake than just my future as an individual. I'm not the only one. There are others."

"Precisely. And none of them will speak up because they're ashamed or afraid of the stigma that attaches to being singled out for investigation. No, it's not precisely that. It's more that secretly every human soul harbors doubts as to his worthiness. Very few of us have led simon-pure lives, I suppose. I suppose every one of us feels guilty for some of our secret thoughts, if not for our secret actions—persecution is one of the most successful means of intimidation, usually because its victims secretly feel that it's justified, if not absolutely just. Neither then are we absolutely guiltless. This kind of thing operates in the gray regions of the soul. I assume, however, that you didn't come here to have me lecture you on metaphysics. Why have you come here? I'll tell you. You have come here because you think that somehow I have it in my power to rectify the situation. Is that right?"

"Yes. I wouldn't have put it that way, but I suppose it's a fair way to look at it."

"Well, Mr. Stone—I'm going to call you John if you don't mind. It's hard to admit failure to someone you call 'mister.' Because that is exactly what I am going to do. I have failed to justify your faith in me. I have no remedy. I don't know where to tell you to go to find one."

"I didn't mean . . ."

"And furthermore, I am a cog in the very rack you're being drawn on. And I'm powerless to help you."

"But I don't . . ."

"Please pardon me for saying this. It sounds unnecessarily cruel but it isn't intended as a criticism of you. But unfortunately, a person's sense of injustice is rarely excited in the cause of others until an injustice is visited on him personally. Every citizen in our land knows that unjust acts are being committed in the name of the nation's honor, and yet they have remained blind to them. Now I tell you that this situation will be put to rights only when enough people get a personal taste of what it means to suffer under it. If that seems cruel and unreasonable, I'm sorry. But penance comes before absolution, I'm afraid. Before our country can rededicate itself in the cause of simple justice, apparently they will have to have a strong dose of simple *injustice*. Not complicated injustice, but simple injustice. All I can do in my position of public trust is to carry out the law as it is read to me and to keep these injustices simple. In your case I would say that we've succeeded admirably, wouldn't you say?"

Stone had to smile. "This is all very disarming, but the fact remains that I'm not being allowed to earn my keep here."

"Yes. Lasher forwarded your, ah, bill of particulars, shall we say. An impressive document."

"I merely listed the specific incidents. It's impossible to convey the atmosphere down there. I come to work every morning. Sit at my desk until noon. Go out to lunch. Come back. Sit at my desk until it's time to go home, and then I go home. No one talks to me unless he has to—understand me, there's no malice on their part. But I've become a leper. People are afraid to be seen talking with me. Oh, there are a few who couldn't care less who they talk to, but they're in the minority. No one gives me any work to do. The files are never left unlocked. I have no access to documents. Even documents I wrote. If they're classified, I can't see them. I've given up embarrassing people by asking for them. I keep the overtime records. It's the least I can do."

"It was unfortunate your job was classified as sensitive."

"Ever since I was denied access to classified material—in fact, ever since this whole investigation started—I've been just putting in time. I don't dare stay home, because I'm sure personnel would take any graceful way out to get me off the payroll. But I can't quit now. You see that, don't you? And I can't accept a less sensitive job, either. If I give an inch, it's an admission of guilt. I've heard it myself: 'So-and-so was transferred to the cultural attaché's office, and you know what *that* means.' It's incredible. I was hoping you could help me get my old job back at Graves Registration."

The Ambassador looked at Stone for a long minute. "John, I've got some unpleasant news for you. Do you think it was an accident that you were transferred here from Graves Registration Command? It wasn't, of course. Perhaps you've forgotten your poor colonel's experience with the press last winter. The Army was going to get rid of you if they had to carry you out in an oblong box. The Army is understandably sensitive to bad publicity, justified or not. Perhaps you've forgotten that several newspapers were calling for the withdrawal of all American service units from France. The fact that the colonel is here simply to count and bury our dead—dead who died, among other reasons, to lift the yoke off France's neck—this makes no difference in a time of fear and unreason. And we can't blame the French too much, either. Their lot was not a happy one last winter."

"I owe you a debt for arranging my transfer. I feel that I've never properly thanked you."

"It was very simple. You were a qualified civilian. There was no reason why you *had* to remain associated with the Army. My military attaché was short a man. I did the colonel a favor. Rather, he did me one. I asked for you, you see. But that information is for your personal enlightenment, yours and no one else's. As you say, you may become a pariah, and I can't afford to compromise my own position."

Stone smiled with difficulty.

"You think I'm joking? Here, look at this." The Ambassador darted a hand into a file basket and pulled out a clipping. He dangled it from two fingers. "Clipped from last week's Congressional Record. A demand for my resignation. And do you know what that demand is grounded on? Do you have any idea?"

Stone shook his head, surprised.

"Let me read you the key paragraph. It's from a speech by an old friend of yours."

"You mean Kreuger's still at it, eh?" Stone tightened his lips in exasperation.

"The same. Pay attention to this. '. . . at this very moment there are people in key posts in the Department of State who have repeatedly demonstrated their unfitness to serve on the bridge deck of our great ship of state, and I would like to take this opportunity to remind the estimable gentleman from Rhode Island that despite his blind faith in the excellence of our Foreign Service, these people I'm talking about, these people who have already proven their unfitness, are not mere flunky typists, nor are they of the vast legion of professional cookiepushers who infest the Department here in Washington. No, gentlemen, these are men we have sent abroad to represent us before the heads of state—the very heads whom the estimable gentleman from Rhode Island seems to hold in such high regard. (Laughter from the gallery.) In fact, I have personal knowledge of one recent deplorable incident where an Ambassador of the United States of America, an Ambassador, gentlemen, knowingly hired, knowingly took into the employ of this government, a man who formerly ran arms and munitions to the Communist underground in Europe. This is a man who knowingly supplied these agents of the Comintern with the weapons which they will someday use against us. These weapons came from the United States. (Disturbance in the gallery. The Speaker of the House directs the Sergeant-at-Arms to remove two spectators from the gallery and restore order. After a short delay, the Speaker returns the floor to Representative Kreuger.) It is hard to blame taxpayers for being angry when they are told that we can't afford to send arms to the brave defenders of China, and then hear that we could afford to send them to the Communists in Europe. My committee plans to investigate this matter thoroughly. We want to be fair, of course, and the guilty parties will have every chance to answer these charges. But I will demand the resignations of these people. Even if they should prove themselves innocent of designing to wreck this government, we cannot entrust our great destinies as a nation into the hands of dupes and incompetents.' " The Ambassador paused and looked at Stone.

"There's more, but it's hardly worth reading. What do you think of that?"

Stone sat stunned. "How was it that it didn't get into the papers? This is the first I knew of it."

"It didn't get into the papers because it's preposterous, I suppose. He names no names, you notice. He probably planted the two people in the gallery in the hope that that would catch the press's eye."

"But it's a complete lie."

"It's a great deal worse than that. It's a twisted half-truth. But I wouldn't worry about it. The American electorate will never fall for that sort of demagoguery. That sort of recklessness divided the country after Lincoln's death. I don't think we're foolish enough to divide the country any further now. That kind of thing is a Pandora's box. Fortunately, Kreuger is as inept as a lockpicker as he is as a legislator. The Senate, however, is another matter."

"I hope you're right. How do men like that ever get into Congress in the first place?"

"The Congress represents all the people, I suppose. Otherwise how did this young rascal McCarthy get into the Senate? And in some mysterious way that's probably a civilized good thing. If the broad avenues of law are barred to such men they will always find their way through the more devious back streets and alleyways of revolution. The American Congress has one of its most important functions in the taming of demagogues. It's a reform school for revolutionaries."

"That is certainly a charitable way to look at it."

"Not charitable, really. Public office lawfully attained, and the pressure of responsibility that goes with it, have a curious way of making the man grow up to the office. Why, for an artilleryman, I've made a pretty fair imitation of a cookiepusher, don't you think?"

"I still can't get over it. Why, he's using me to get at *you*."

"You begin to see the light. This is the Alice in Wonderland they call politics. But there's even more to it than that. Do you have any idea where his information about your wartime activities came to the congressman from? True, it is known that you worked with the underground in France, but you'll be interested to know that Dujardin's lawyers have provided Kreuger and the Senator with a summary of your activities, with particular emphasis on the fact that you were in contact with a local group of *Francs-tireurs et Partisans*. Do you see the irony of that?"

"But, my God, that doesn't make any sense. Isn't the Party . . ."

"It makes a great deal of sense, of course. Dujardin has a lot of friends who would like to vindicate themselves by vindicating him— people who during the thirties were not exactly unhappy over the rise of Adolf Hitler, let's say. Now perhaps you recall that on more than one occasion certain of our senators have expressed the opinion that it was a mistake bordering on treason to destroy Germany and leave Europe to Russia. It is an attitude that's more common than fashionable, so it tends to be played down these days. In the Army I heard a great deal of that sort of foolishness from men who should know better. A map of Europe in 1939 is usually enough to bring them back to reality. Dujardin had two sets of lawyers. One set worked quietly preparing briefs behind the scenes, mainly because many of them are still definitely not welcome in public places. The French have long memories for certain aristocratic faces that were prominent during the occupation. On the other hand, there is the other group of lawyers, the Johnny-come-latelys who were taking over his cause for their own peculiar reasons. Each group thinks they're using the other. It makes perfect sense, because in a way they are. Extremists become what they are through departure from principle. Once you have abandoned principles the only guide you have for action is expediency, and since expediency is in itself a principle—of a rather negative sort—it makes brothers of all those who serve it. For if a principle does nothing else, it unites men in action and common feeling. And here we have a perfect example of it. It's the kind of thing that makes no sense in textbooks or novels, because the historian's object is to reduce human behavior to discernible patterns. But in life there are no discernible patterns except as we discern them in and through ourselves. And there's the confusion. You can't comprehend this because it refutes your sense of the order of things, your sense of fitness. It's a discord in the harmony of your universe."

"You mean you don't find it so?"

"I'd be less than human if I didn't. But it all dovetails, don't you see? History has a curious way of doing that—after the fact. It lends credence to a belief in the Devil."

"The Devil?"

"The way evil seeks out evil. It ignores frontiers and language barriers. If one of the Devil's children is threatened the others seem to know, no matter where in the world they may be, how to come to his aid."

"No one would believe this," Stone said, shaking his head. "I still don't really believe it myself, I guess."

"One of the things Georges Merseault told me once was that a good conspiracy must fulfill two requirements. The first is that it must operate completely in the open, without cloak, without dagger. The second is that it must be so preposterous that no one would believe it if you told them what was happening. And he told me a story to illustrate that. Before the Revolution in Russia, several former revolutionaries suddenly confessed their misdeeds and made a public renunciation. They had themselves rebaptized in the Orthodox Church and became loyal subjects of the Czar again. They proved their loyalty by providing the Cheka with the names of people in the government who they said could be counted on to cooperate with a revolutionary government. The Czar eliminated these people, of course. But slowly it became apparent that his government was riddled with disloyal subjects. By the time the Revolution did come everyone in his government who might have been able to cope intelligently with the panic had been either executed or discredited. The only remedy the others knew was repression. Where bread would have done they used bullets. And of course you know the rest. The point to the story is that one of these reformed revolutionaries lost his nerve and fled to France. He lived out his days here in France in anonymity. Merseault knew him in line of business, I expect. But shortly before he died—imagine, he'd kept his secret for nearly thirty years—he confessed to Merseault that he had been ordered by the Revolutionary Council to renounce his activities and become respectable. He was specifically ordered to join the church and do homage to the Czar. But they provided him with a list of names he should inform on, university professors, government officials, even certain churchmen."

"You mean Communists they wanted to purge from their own ranks without being held responsible?"

"That's the first thing that occurred to me, too. No, that wasn't the reason. You see, for some time prior to the Revolution the Czar had been promising reforms. But he knew nothing of the science of government and he lacked the means of putting the reforms through. But among younger functionaries there was a strong reformist element who had the brains and the ability to rescue the country from chaos. The Czar was beginning to let them have his ear, and this in the opinion of the revolutionary theoreticians was a threat to them. There were so few Communists at that time that they knew they had to count on the discontent of the peasants and the workers to propel them into power. So they headed off the reform movement before it could damage their position. The missionaries they sent into the Czar's camp were dedicated revolutionists especially picked for their nerve. They took an oath that they would never again communicate with anyone in the Party or ever again try to join it. They were forced to swear—they were even coached in the ideological arguments *against* the Revolution. It's ironic, but you'll have to admit that it shows a profound grasp of the mechanism of fear psychology. Several prominent people pointed out what the informers were accomplishing, but of course the Czar paid no attention to the warnings. The tendency in times of great fear is to look *under* the bed when you should look *in* it."

The Ambassador leaned back in his chair, placed his fingertips together, and continued.

"It all seems obvious now, but that's the inscrutable way with history and destiny. It's logical after it happens, but it depends on men's lack of ability to believe the preposterous, their inability to imagine the impossible. Even when I tell you, you find yourself unable to believe. The one thing human beings can't stand is to have their worldly illusions of order upset. A world without illusions is a world without order, and a world without order is terrifying. It leaves the soul in chaos. To be so deprived is the one torture beyond human capacity to survive. But this isn't helping to solve your problem, I'm afraid."

"You've solved it for me already," Stone said.

"Oh? What will you do?" asked Sheppard.

"I'll probably resign. I never thought I would, but I won't be a pawn in a chess game between Congress and the President. As your boy Lasher predicted, they swept the Dujardin thing under the rug as soon as they could, and the whole thing is practically forgotten. But I'm pretty bitter about this. I've never asked for any medal but I didn't expect this, either."

"It's not exactly a hero's reward. However, I'm sorry to see you resign after you've stuck it out this long. If you resign, the case is closed for good."

"I thought you'd be the first one to . . ."

"Not exactly. It's true that sooner or later they'll find something against you, and under the law I would have to terminate your appointment here. But on the other hand . . . Look, let me put this as bluntly as possible. This is not advice, merely a point of information: If you resign that ends it. However, if you're fired you have a right to demand a formal hearing. After that you have recourse under the law to the appeal machinery in Washington. There's no guarantee that you'd have the finding reversed, but at least you'd have fought it as far as anyone can go."

"They already have something against me. I'm not a loyalty risk, it seems, I'm a security risk, whatever that is."

"Alcohol?"

"You know?"

"Yes, I had myself briefed. You see, *I* was just about to call *you* when you put in your request to see me. It would have been more appropriate that way, but no matter. You're here."

"You were going to call me?"

"To show you this." The Ambassador dangled the clipping. "This affects you as much as it affects me, and I wanted to talk to you about it in person. Mainly, I want you to keep clearly in mind that I have no personal animus toward you, even if I have to fire you for reasons beyond my control. However, you might outlast me here, in which case my successor will have to deal with you."

"Your successor, sir?"

"Just for your very private information, I have asked to be relieved of my public responsibilities. I trust to your discretion to keep that knowledge to yourself for a few days. Only a few of my personal staff have been told."

"It will be a great loss to the government and the country, sir."

"John Stone, that's very kind of you to say that. I actually think that perhaps you even mean it," the Ambassador said, smiling.

"I do."

"You make me feel as though I haven't wasted your time here this afternoon. I hoped that I could make you understand my position a little better if we had it out face to face. Now I'll tell you one other thing."

"Yes, sir?"

"You were with my son during the war," the Ambassador said, glancing down at his hands. "So far we have never discussed him."

"I never got a chance to know him well," Stone said quietly.

"But you *were* with him. You probably don't know his history. It's an unhappy one, I'm afraid, and some of the blame for that attaches directly to me. I never had much time for him when he was a boy. He was raised in his early years by his maternal grandmother, my mother-in-law. His own mother died in bringing him into the world, right here in Paris—he had dual citizenship. I met my wife here during the Peace Conference. I was in Panama when she died and he was born. I don't quite know how to put this to you, except that somehow I feel that it's essential that you know. When she died . . . well, I tried, but I failed. Without her to share the experience of his growing up, somehow . . ."

Stone sensed uneasily that the Ambassador was persuading himself that he, Stone, had really known his son, had known him well and was dissembling the fact—perhaps out of charity. Stone watched him search out his feelings, probing carefully for the words to express them, felt suddenly as though he were eavesdropping on a man talking indiscreetly to himself. After a reflective pause the Ambassador resumed, speaking slowly, with measured hesitation.

"I have great difficulty, even after all these years, in putting feelings into words. Perhaps that is one of the things that stood between the boy and me. I think it was a mistake to allow his grandmother to raise him. She was not entirely pleased with the marriage. The old woman wore her nobility like a hair shirt, and I think she turned the boy's mind against me. I know she held me responsible for my wife's death. Perhaps I hold myself responsible. These things are not entirely rational. The point is I feel very acutely my failure as a father. But by the time I was old enough to have the wisdom to understand what I was doing the twig was already bent. The boy's roots were always in France. Until he came to school in America he spoke English with the accent of his British governess. He always treated me like a distant uncle. I think now that he wanted my approval, but I didn't know quite how to give it. It takes a woman to teach a man how to express his love. I was lost without her. I found a remedy for my ailment in the Army. I worked day and night until suddenly I was an old man and the country was at war again. However, it hasn't been without reward."

The Ambassador waved his hand at the mute surrounding room. The walls hung silent with rich brocade that waxed even richer in the mellowing light of the afternoon sun.

"Perhaps now you can understand why I went to Montpelle. Perhaps you can understand what was in my mind as I watched you explain what happened there."

"Yes," Stone said, "I think I know."

"So now I have a question to ask you."

There was a long silence. Stone sat motionless, being careful not to let his eyes drop from the Ambassador's searching gaze. He could see that the Ambassador was phrasing the question in his mind before he asked it.

"Did he—did he acquit himself well?" the Ambassador asked without lowering his eyes.

"Yes, sir. He saved my life."

"Did he have a reason to do that?"

The question caught Stone by surprise. He couldn't allow himself to hesitate. "No more reason than I might have had to save his. He was first out of the truck."

"Did you know he was going to make the break?"

"I—I thought he might. I was ready."

"You didn't *order* him to do it?"

Stone's eyes shifted involuntarily. "No, sir. I didn't. I must admit that it crossed my mind. We were together. He would have to have been the first one out. But he didn't have to be ordered." Stone took a deep breath. He felt guilty; it was senseless. "I think he wanted to."

"Did you have any knowledge which might have caused you to think that he might have been the one . . . ?"

"I know what you're going to ask. No. I had no such knowledge, then or now."

"If you did, would you tell me?"

"No, I would not, sir," Stone blurted. "But that's beside the point."

"Yes, I suppose it is."

Stone remained silent, waiting.

"One final question. Do you know what happened to him?"

"No, sir. I don't."

"Do you know if he was the missing . . . do you know if he escaped the pyre?"

"No, sir."

"In your opinion, is he . . . ?"

"Alive? No."

"That is your considered opinion?"

"Yes."

"Do you have—"

"Sir," Stone interrupted. "He drew the fire of several automatic weapons. The very fact that two men got out alive . . ." He trailed off, suddenly aware that his irritation had taken on a note almost of pleading.

Very quietly the Ambassador said, "Three men."

"Yes, sir. I'm sorry—I keep thinking of it the old way."

"You said it was getting dark."

"Not so dark that they couldn't aim."

"I see."

"I *am* sorry, sir."

"It's I who should be sorry for not talking to you sooner. I was afraid, I suppose, of what I might hear. I'm ashamed to say that to you, but I feel that I must be completely honest. I hope this doesn't demean me in your eyes, Mr. Stone. But you see I've very dimly come to see this as a test of myself—the way he died, I mean. I can't expect you to understand the state of my feelings. I don't quite understand them myself. In a way he has redeemed my failure. It's the flaw in my own soul that makes me search out the flaw in his. I feel compelled to put him twice through the final test. I'm not proud of my little faith, but it's all I have left. It's the faith I lack in myself."

Stone was uncomfortable. Not being able to find something to say, he remained awkwardly silent. The Ambassador gazed at the window oblivious of his embarrassment. He even seemed serene, a totally different man from the terse interrogator of a few moments before. He was speaking with tired resignation, not looking directly at Stone any more. In fact, he might have been thinking out loud, addressing his thoughts to an empty room. Suddenly he stopped short and looked at his watch.

"I have to send you away. I forgot all about Merseault. He's been waiting. We'll have another talk about this when this unhappy Foreign Ministers' Conference is over and all the visiting firemen have gone home." He rose to shake Stone's hand.

In a smooth unbroken path of movement and small events, Stone found himself shown from one portal to another; and finally was standing alone in the carpeted corridor outside the closed doors of the outer office trying to remember what he had forgotten. Then he realized that he had unconsciously picked up the clipping from the Congressional Record. He held it rolled in a loose tube in his left hand. Without thinking, he reversed his steps and went through the two doors, past the secretary, and back into the Ambassador's office before he realized that he had simply burst in unannounced. Flustered, he was about to apologize when he realized that the Ambassador hadn't even looked up. He was on the telephone again.

". . . twelve million tons capacity. But coal is still the major problem," the Ambassador was saying. "No. No. No. You'll have to take that out. I don't want the Saar singled out for special mention. Lump it in with the overall . . . yes, that will do nicely. The problem is to avoid problems. We'll have enough of those when the circus tent finally goes up. Fine." Stone quietly laid the clipping back on the Ambassador's desk, where it unrolled. The Ambassador was facing the windows, his back to Stone.

As Stone withdrew he bumped into Mrs. Steele, who was coming to arrest his unannounced re-entry into the privy chamber. Mrs. Steele stepped aside to let him out, smiling and frowning all at once.

"I nearly took that clipping," he whispered. She nodded in great relieved comprehension and smiled broadly. She looked like a worried English housekeeper.

She went into the Ambassador's office and closed the door gently behind her, leaving Stone outside. Just as the door slid to, Stone heard the Ambassador say, "Not now. I have someone waiting . . ." The door closed on the last words.

He walked down the hall, quietly refusing to think about any of it until he got outside. He'd gone only a few steps, however, when he was overtaken by a vaguely disquieting feeling, a feeling of having been swindled of a moment of opportunity—the original complaint had been lost, engulfed, in the talk. He'd frittered away the fine anger he'd husbanded so long. It was his own fault for not pursuing it, yet justly or not, he felt shorn.

He'd think about it later; for whatever else was clear, the old man had troubles too.

II

Carnot telephoned before coming, as usual. He never called before midnight for fear the servants would still be up. Merseault was sitting in bed, documents spread about him, reading under the cone of light. He just finished lighting a fresh cigarette when the telephone rang by his bed. He knew it would be Carnot even before he answered it.

He let it ring twice, trying to decide whether he was up to talking to him. The last session with Carnot had been fruitless and emotionally trying. Still, there was no choice. He would have to see him. He sighed and reached outside the circle of light to pick up the receiver, shifting the bed lamp with his other hand.

"Yes?" He held the mouthpiece aslant, the cigarette bobbing in his mouth. There was a long pause as he listened. He closed one eye; cigarette smoke curled in a blue ribbon up along the puffy curve of his cheek and disappeared into the darkness over his head.

"Does it have to be tonight?" he asked.

Another long wait while Carnot's voice murmured urgently in the earpiece.

Then, "Where are you?" Merseault glanced at his wristwatch.

Carnot told him.

"In five minutes, then. The inside door will be open." Merseault's cigarette dribbled ashes down the faded black lapel of his dressing gown. He put the telephone back in its cradle, sighed again. He ground out the cigarette in the ashtray on the night table and threw back the thin blanket across his lap. Automatically his feet found their slippers and slid into them. He got up and went out of the room.

In the library there were a few embers left in the fireplace. Merseault was still stoking life into the charred logs when he heard the outside gate buzzer. He went to the wall and pushed a button. A moment later he heard the gate close in the courtyard; then the door in the lower hall. A moment later Carnot came into the room. Merseault was bent again over the blackened hearth.

"Sit down," Merseault said without turning around. "There's brandy in the small decanter, whiskey in the other." He jabbed viciously at the logs with the poker. Behind him, he heard Carnot drop heavily into a chair. Merseault said, "This is a chilly evening for spring." Carnot said nothing.

The stone fireplace was big enough for a man to stand in. The logs across the huge owl andirons were long and crooked and awkward, more tree limb than logs. Merseault scooped an armful of new kindling out of the box and threw it among the logs; then he jabbed several balls of newspaper under them with his toe. The newspaper smoked, smoked more, and then caught with a puff; the smoke vanished, changed into flame. Merseault straightened up, replaced the poker, and turned to the armchair where Carnot was sitting, tense and unrelaxed. He poured two whiskeys and handed one to Carnot. Carnot took it without saying anything. Merseault went to a couch and sat down, turned slightly so that he could see Carnot's face.

The stone hearth was raised a step from the floor; the two enormous leather couches jutted out into the room and completed three sides of a square. The armchair facing the fireplace made the fourth. A conical lamp with a shade of billiard-green glass hung from a long cord that went up and was lost in the shadows of the ancient beamed ceiling overhead. The lamp hung down to within an arm's length of Merseault's head. Merseault sat on the right-hand couch; the brilliant cone of white light spilled in a tight circle around him. The rest of the room was in shadow. He had to squint to see Carnot.

"You've lost weight," Merseault said.

"I've thought over your proposition," Carnot opened. Merseault noticed that Carnot's right sleeve wasn't pinned inside his pocket as it usually was. It simply hung loose and empty from the shoulder in a mute fold across the arm of the stuffed leather chair. Carnot leaned forward, ignoring the glass in his hand, his face intense in a half-smile. His eyes glinted black in the hard light of the fire, two dancing points of firelight that gave him the look of a captive animal. His black hair was wild and uncombed, and a stubble of beard hardened the hollow shadows under the cheekbones.

"You look terrible," Merseault said.

"I've been sick," Carnot said. "I'm all right now. I've thought over your proposition."

Merseault was beginning to sense what was wrong. Carnot seemed tense with a sort of restrained enthusiasm, utterly different from the bored resignation that had so irritated Merseault on the last occasion. Merseault had an uneasy sense of something awry. Even Carnot's voice had changed. He had been sick, that explained part of it. He still looked feverish, although his skin was sallow white around the eyes and forehead. It was the eyes, Merseault decided; they never blinked and were open too wide. Carnot showed none of his old sullen self-assurance. Perhaps it was simply that he was still sick, but the fever that showed in his eyes was not the fever of the body. Carnot was too different, too eager. It was the eagerness of a man obsessed with a single idea, a madman.

Merseault said very carefully, "I made you that proposition over three months ago. That's a long time. You turned it down."

"I didn't know he was *his* son," Carnot said. "Berger."

"What difference does that make? No one knew."

"You knew."

Merseault said nothing. There was a long silence.

Then Carnot said, "You should have told me."

"It had nothing to do with the offer."

"I don't believe you," Carnot said, a trace of his old insolence in his expression. "But I'm prepared to do what you want."

"No one wanted anything of you. You were offered asylum. Political asylum."

Carnot's eyes glinted in a smile. "Why should you offer me asylum? I'm a French citizen, and I'm in France."

Merseault nodded. "It's not usual. But perhaps you would prefer to be elsewhere when the Dujardin case is"—Merseault shrugged—"is finally adjudicated."

Carnot interrupted. "Why should I be afraid?"

"What would you say if the Party turned on you?"

"What could they do?" Carnot asked.

"They could demand your prosecution for giving false testimony."

"I'm not interested in leaving France for that reason. I'm not trying to escape anything."

"You said you've thought over my proposition. I made you no proposition. I made you a simple offer. Even a month ago you said—"

"I have never believed that America exists. Especially New York. Now I want to find out. I want to travel somewhere I've never been."

"Why not Moscow?"

"They won't let me go there. I asked."

Merseault put his glass down on the table. He had hardly touched it. Carnot hadn't tasted his. He still held it in his one hand.

Merseault looked at Carnot. "What do you want?" he asked him flatly.

"I will go to America provided Ambassador Sheppard makes me the offer in person," Carnot said. Then he added with a careful show of diffidence, "Also, I have documents."

Merseault was also careful. "Documents," he repeated flatly. "It's a little late for documents. Dujardin will probably be released. The damage has been done."

"I can change everything," Carnot said. "I didn't realize it before, but I can do whatever I please. I have . . ."

"Does Picard know you have these, ah, documents?"

"They don't concern him," Carnot said. "He thought he could use me."

"Where are these documents?" Merseault asked casually, skeptically.

"I finally have a way. I have made a plan."

"A plan," Merseault repeated, nodding.

"I have finally figured out a perfect plan. They will do what I say. Even if I leave the country, they will have to do what I say." Carnot leaned forward in his chair, confidingly. "When I tell you my plan, you'll see how it is."

Merseault remained silent, waiting.

"You said the last time that something might happen to me," Carnot said. "I don't believe you, of course. You were trying to panic me into doing what you wanted. The Party doesn't work that way."

Merseault shrugged noncommittally.

"But I have figured out how I can make them do what I want, not what they want. Do you want to hear how?"

Merseault said, "A good plan is always interesting."

"You said that dead men tell no tales, like in the American movies. But I have figured out my plan so that dead men *do* tell tales." Carnot put down his glass in a flush of excitement. The fire snapped in the fireplace and the logs shifted softly. Carnot's eyes seemed to snap points of fire as he fumbled in his trouser cuff for something. Finally he held up a dangling key. A brass key that hung on a short string. It turned in the light, glinting brightly as it wound and unwound on the end of its string. "This is the key to everything," Carnot said.

Merseault kept silent. The only sound was the murmuring of the flame draft in the chimney and the soft wet hissing of the charred green logs.

"If anything happens to me you will have this key. I will call you on the telephone every Friday afternoon at three o'clock. If anyone else ever calls you and asks you if you have this key, you will first demand to speak to me. You will tell whoever is calling that you will not say anything until you have my permission. The first thing I will say when I get on the telephone will be a number followed by the last name of a certain man. It will be the number of the safe-deposit box that this key fits. The last name of the certain man will be the last name of the manager of the bank. You will have to find out the bank from that. Then you can tell them you have the key."

Was Carnot insane? Merseault started to speak, but before he could open his mouth Carnot cut him off again.

"It will work," Carnot said. "I've thought it all out. The Party is always realistic. They will have no choice but to do as I say. If anything happens to me, you'll have the key. If you don't get a telephone call from me by at least six o'clock every Friday then you will go to the bank and take out the documents and give them to the newspapers."

"I see several things wrong," Merseault began.

"There's nothing wrong," Carnot said sharply.

"The banks are closed at night. They wouldn't be open until Monday morning."

"I'll call at noon every Thursday then," Carnot said angrily.

"Second, if you don't call, how will I know the number of the safe-deposit box and which bank to go to? That key is unmarked."

Carnot frowned. "Nothing will happen to me," he said.

"But you just said—"

"If I don't call, you will know something has happened to me and you will go to the bank and take out the . . ." Carnot stopped in mid-sentence. "Be sure you give them to the newspapers and not the police. The police will destroy them. They don't want the Dujardin case opened up again."

"These are his private files?"

"It doesn't matter what they are. As far as you know they are nothing," Carnot said. "You've never seen them. As far as you or anyone else knows, they don't exist."

"You expect to ransom yourself by—"

"I won't have to ransom myself," Carnot said. "Nothing will happen, I tell you."

"But how am I to know which bank to—"

Carnot snapped, "Go to all of them. Try all the boxes."

"But, my dear fellow—"

"There's no other way. If I tell you, you'll go tomorrow."

"But if you've trusted me this far and I haven't—"

"I don't trust anyone. You'd plot against me just like the rest of them."

"My dear Carnot—"

"Yes or no? Will you take this key or not?" Carnot asked. "I don't want to talk about it any more. Will you make an appointment for me to see him?"

"Who?"

"The Ambassador."

"He won't be the Ambassador," Merseault said. "He's resigning. You should have acted a little soon—"

"He can still arrange it," Carnot said. "The asylum."

"Yes, I think perhaps he can," Merseault said reasonably. "But why do you want to see him personally?"

"I don't trust anyone, I told you."

"You will have to trust him, I should imagine," Merseault said.

There was soft settling of logs. A curtain of sparks flew up from the low-burning wood, and the two iron owls stared impassively into the room. Despite the fire it was cold in the gloom of the stone-paneled room. Carnot said nothing. He closed the key in his fist, and stared at his feet.

Then Merseault said, "Alexi, you're in trouble."

Carnot lifted his head and stared into the fire. He was silent. The fire, in collapsing, had stoked itself to flame again. It burned brightly with false life. The hard orange light flickered and danced in reflection off the angular planes of Carnot's stubbled face. A thin grease of sweat gave his forehead the changing colors of the fire. He no longer looked like a young man, Merseault observed. In the fire's imperfect light the rough contours of his face, the heavy-boned forehead and cheeks, the dark-socketed eyes, all made the skin look stretched and tired. Carnot was cracking from something beyond simple fear.

"Don't call me by my first name," Carnot said finally.

"You realize, of course, that besides exposing your own role in the affair, these documents would completely explode the Party's position. They are all originals?"

Carnot said nothing.

"Won't they be missed?" Merseault pursued.

Carnot looked up in surprise. "You think I stole them?" he asked. "They were never in Party files. I got them myself during the war."

"With a pistol?"

"What does it matter how I got them. They were never in Party files."

Merseault shifted his position. Then he said, "It's time to be open with you. I know more than you think. I know, for example, that you are in trouble. I know also that you were unwise to threaten Picard."

Carnot's eyes narrowed. He started to say something.

"Wait. Let me finish," Merseault said, holding up his hand. "You know that I know that the Dujardin defense was a complete fabrication. We both know he was never in the Resistance. Nor did he ever cooperate with the Resistance, as his defense claimed."

"You know that from the documents I gave you," Carnot said.

There was a startled moment of silence. Then Merseault said very gently, "You haven't given me any documents yet." Carnot's mental lapse made him suddenly merely pitiable.

Carnot frowned. "I'm sick of hearing about Dujardin," he said.

Merseault could think of nothing except to continue. It seemed weird and senseless, yet he went on. "I know that Dujardin was implicated in the Resistance to make him useless to the Gestapo. And I know *how* you did it."

Carnot said nothing. He seemed to be listening to something far away.

Merseault went on. "You tried to put the kiss of death on him by planting false evidence. Dujardin's lawyers produced certain transcripts of captured German files. Those files contain a correspondence concerning certain evidence turned up in a raid sometime in 1943 implicating one Théophile Dujardin in the local movement. In other words, you tried to get rid of Dujardin by making it appear that you were smuggling arms into Mediterranean ports with his complicity and under his protection. You forged that evidence and left it where the SD would find it."

"If that's the case," Carnot asked sullenly, "why didn't it succeed?"

"You thought then that the Germans didn't fall for it, didn't you? Well, you were wrong. They did. But they decided not to arrest Dujardin in the hope of waiting and getting the whole network. *You* planted those fictitious membership lists of code names and tipped off the Gestapo. The irony is that your fiction was too successful. They didn't arrest Dujardin and never could, because the particular network they were hoping he'd expose never existed."

Carnot looked into the fire.

"Dujardin must have known he was under suspicion, because in the final days of the war he redoubled his efforts to prove his zeal to his masters. It ended with the massacre at Montpelle."

Carnot stared dully at the dying flames and said nothing.

"You did it. And you gave Picard the information that told him where he could look. The false evidence that you planted to eliminate Dujardin is what Picard turned up in Germany and used in his defense —to prove that Dujardin was working in the Resistance movement. Did you engineer the affidavit, too? Or was that Picard's work?"

Carnot said, "The affidavit was true. The Americans beat him."

"No doubt they roughed him up. At least they got their confession from the right man."

Carnot shrugged.

"And now it appears that you kept track of Dujardin after the war. Did you take his personal files before or after Montpelle?"

Carnot shrugged. "As far as anyone knows the files don't exist."

"Why did you sit on them all this time?"

Carnot shrugged again. Then he said, "Will you arrange an appointment with the Ambassador or not?"

"Can you give me a reason why I should?" Merseault asked.

"I'll tell *him* my reason. I'll give it to him when I see him."

The fire shifted again. It made a scuffing sound. For a few seconds the flame brightened and then subsided again. There was a steady subdued hissing somewhere under the intermittent tongue of tiny flame.

Merseault shrugged. "I can't do anything but relay your—"

"That's all you'll have to do," Carnot said. "I could meet him here."

"About the documents, I don't know," Merseault said.

Carnot put the key in his pocket. "I'm not leaving the key," he said. His suspicions were aroused again; Merseault knew he'd gone too far.

"I'm not sure I want to involve myself in . . ." Merseault shrugged, bluffing.

Carnot stood up abruptly. "You'd rather see my life's work wiped out?" he demanded. He was suddenly shaking with anger.

Merseault looked up at him incredulously. "Your life's work?" he said.

"They'll see that I'm right. It's only a matter of time. They've been wrong . . . they've forced me."

"If you insist on leaving the key . . ."

"I won't stand by and see my life's work . . . I've worked hard," Carnot said. "I don't have to bargain with anybody." His voice was shaking with deep anger and frustration, almost as though he was on the edge of tears. "I've worked hard. I won't be anyone's scapegoat, not yours or theirs." The empty sleeve swung in a jerky arc as he turned away from the fire. "I'll telephone you," he said.

Carnot was on his feet heading for the door, his head down and his face set in a hard cast of furious indignation. Merseault limped into step a few paces behind him and calmly followed him across the room to the door, down the wide flight of stone stairs to the lower hall. At the door leading out to the courtyard Carnot suddenly stopped and turned, about to say something, but Merseault cut him off.

Merseault said soothingly, "You'll call me."

Carnot stood for a moment in the darkened entranceway, hesitating, his face completely obscured in the shadow. He faced Merseault, watching him. Suddenly he turned without a word, opened the door, and went out. Merseault watched him cross the silent court and go out through the main gate. He waited until he heard the click-clack of the automatic lock as the gate secured itself. He shrugged in the obscuring dark.

Merseault locked the night door on the court and went back upstairs to the room he had just left with Carnot, the disjointed conversation still turning in his mind. The words seemed still to hang in the shadows of the room. He wanted to clear the whole episode out of his mind and relax before going to bed. He could think about the rest of it tomorrow. He sat down and poured Carnot's untouched whiskey back into the crystal decanter on the table.

Then, sipping his own unfinished drink, he rose and stared at the fireplace. Carrying his glass, he walked across and ran his fingers over the smoke-and-time-blackened oak caryatids that supported the wood-and-stone mantel. It was cold in the room. The fire was nearly out. The logs weren't consumed; the cold stone had merely leached the heat out of them, had slowly sapped the fire of its life. The stones were as cold as ever; the hearth threw no heat. The great vault of the fireplace was empty, black, like a deserted tomb now that the fire was dying. Earlier, when the newspaper was kindled under the charred used logs, the fire had raised a soft voice in the draft of the chimney. The huge misshapen branches, cut to span the enormous andirons, were all crooked, bent like knees and monstrous elbows; and as a result had been stacked awkwardly and burned badly. Once the kindling was consumed, the fire had quickly diminished to narrow tongues of soft flame licking at the velvet-black limbs. Now there were only small ringlets of smoky orange fire curling out from under the base.

Merseault gazed at the great unblinking pair of cast-iron owls that stared saucer-eyed from their perch on the grate posts. He thought about Carnot and pitied him, a man destroyed, a man trapped in his own misshapen longings. Longings, thought Merseault. Longings for what? Power? Love? Merseault stared into the dark maw of the fireplace, his face crossed with a frown of deep fatigue, and underlined a mental note: Carnot had finally kept the key. The charcoaled logs, already eaten thin and cracked by flame, were checked with living veins of fire, delicate and corrosive; charred black skin decked with ember lace. Tiny jets of running flame entwined the logs, forked in and out like flickering snake-tongues, diminishing; until finally there was only a single hissing flame that popped silently on and off.

For a long time Merseault stood watching the dying fire, not moving. Suddenly there was a soft rattle of logs, like a sigh, and the fire collapsed, settled to its death in a showering vapor of sparks. The orange sparks mounted the blackening shadow of the cold hearth and vanished, leaving the charred limbs a broken black bundle of faggots laced with a single ribbon of cold flame, fragile, transparent, ice-blue, gone.

III

Two days later Merseault received a telephone call from the office of Maurice Picard. A male secretary asked whether Merseault would be prepared to receive Monsieur Picard for a short visit that evening. Merseault covered his surprise with an affable invitation for the deputy to have dinner with him. The invitation seemed to take the secretary by surprise. There was a pause on the other end of the line, a hand covering the mouthpiece, and then the secretary was back on the line. The invitation was accepted.

Merseault immediately went upstairs and got out the file on Picard and began reading it. He interrupted the course of his reading every now and then to make a few telephone calls to clarify points of information with people who knew Picard, people whom Merseault trusted. To no one did he disclose the fact that Picard was dining with him. In conversation with the Ministry of Justice he asked casually if anyone was watching Carnot's movements. When told no one was, he pointedly suggested that it might be well to locate him and keep an eye on him. He gave no reason, nor was a reason asked for.

The object of Picard's call was clear. At least, by Merseault's reasoning, partly clear: Picard must have learned of Carnot's visit, but it was not clear why he had waited two days before moving. Merseault had to make a careful judgment of how much Picard knew. Picard, he calculated, was in the same position. The fact that Picard had asked for an appointment was an indication that he felt free to approach the matter directly. Therefore, either he had the advantage, or he was bluffing the advantage. It was not like Maurice Picard to take the open approach without having the clear advantage, unless—and this was what Merseault hoped—he had no other choice. For the moment Merseault knew he had no choice himself but to assume that Picard would be bluffing. He would want to know why Carnot visited him, or, if he knew why, what Carnot had given him. Merseault was curious to know whether Picard suspected the existence of the Dujardin files, or whether their existence might come as a surprise.

Hours later, Merseault interrupted his reading to have his secretary bring the usual afternoon tea. It was a custom Merseault had picked up in London during the war, and had continued on his return to France. He found it a good way to clear his mind and temper his digestion before dinner. Only in this case he wasn't trying to clear his mind, but to limber it.

Merseault's secretary was a young man. He wore glasses and had the look of a scholar, which in fact he was. His morning hours were usually spent in the library at the Faculté de Droits preparing his dissertation. Each afternoon, however, he bicycled to Merseault's house in the Rue de Varennes, where he spent the rest of the day working over the drafts that Merseault had completed that morning. Merseault was a late riser, often working in bed for several hours before emerging from his room in his old black silk dressing gown. He wrote in longhand, making marginal instructions as he went in order to guide his secretary in his researches. The secretary had his own room off the upstairs library, where the noise of the typewriter was inaudible except in the hallway above the landing of the second-floor stairway. The sound reached there only by accident of a common heating duct. It was the only way Merseault ever knew his secretary was in the house—he had his own key—until the time came for tea. Usually, over tea, Merseault would discuss the progress of the work, and give miscellaneous instructions for the following day's research. It was the young man's job to supply Merseault with a continuing stream of documents, both from Merseault's own files and from other sources as he needed them.

The secretary's name was Alain. He was about twenty-four and had worked for Colonel Owl during the war as a sort of adjutant without portfolio. Both his father and mother had died early in the war, when the family house in Garches burned down. The boy was away at school. The house burned completely because the nearest fire apparatus didn't have enough gasoline to reach it. The boy was taken in by a neighboring family after the funeral, and remained with them until 1942, when he joined a Resistance group. Merseault found him a job carrying towels in a steam bath popular with German administrative officers in the first *arrondissement*. His knowledge of German served him well.

After the war Merseault helped him enroll in law school and gave him the afternoon job. He was an intelligent young man whose extraordinary memory made him a perfect researcher. Merseault trusted him completely.

A few minutes after Merseault pushed the buzzer on his desk, Alain appeared in the doorway carrying the teatray, with a sheaf of manuscript under his arm. He put the tray down on the low table, a stuffed elephant foot someone had given Merseault, and advanced formally, as he always did in the course of the daily ritual, and solemnly shook hands with Merseault. Merseault took the typed manuscript and sat down again at his desk. The young man took a seat by the table and poured the two cups of tea, passing one across his knees into Merseault's outstretched hand. Then the younger man sat back and waited. He always waited for Merseault to speak first. Behind his glasses, his gray eyes were intelligent, alert, respectful.

"Alain, let's put this aside for tomorrow," Merseault said, pushing the day's manuscript to one side. "There's something I'd like to ask your opinion on."

"Yes, sir."

"I borrowed a few file folders before you arrived."

"Yes, sir. I know. The Picard file, the Carnot file, and the Dujardin chronological file."

"Did I leave the file cabinet unlocked again?"

"No, sir. It was locked. But I have a system of arranging the tabs so that when one looks at them over the tops of the folders they make a regular pattern. I always check them when I come in. These were missing. I came down to tell you but you were telephoning, and I saw them on your desk so I didn't bother you."

"Picard is coming here for dinner," Merseault said. The secretary's eyebrows lifted only slightly. "It surprised me too," Merseault added.

The secretary waited politely, saying nothing.

"I didn't tell you that I had a conversation two nights ago with Carnot. In fact, I've seen him several times. I suspect that Picard knows he was here and is curious to know why."

The secretary didn't ask why. He only said dryly, "I'm surprised you invited him."

"I didn't precisely. His office called to ask me whether I would receive him for a short visit. By inviting him for dinner, I was merely trying to confuse him a little. I made it sound as if he were just the man I've been wanting to see."

"Yes," the secretary said, approving.

"What I want from you is an opinion. You remember when Picard first got into the Dujardin case, I asked you to try and track down exactly what he did during the war?"

"Yes, sir. I couldn't find much."

"It leads me to think that Picard has taken some pains to keep his wartime activities quiet. He's been very valuable to the Party in the role of sympathizer. But I'm beginning to think he has a place in higher councils."

"He's fairly intelligent."

"He's also the most ambiguous figure in the whole case," Merseault said. He sipped his tea, and made a sour face. "Forgot to put sugar in," he said, and added it.

"He's been very active."

"Yes, true. But he's always able to make it appear that he's outside the Party's battles. He's maintained a posture . . . it's difficult to explain."

"You mean he's made it appear that the Party's interests only happen to coincide with his own."

"Precisely," Merseault said. "He's never made any effort to conceal his sympathies. At the same time I find his candor a little too studied."

"Is that what you want my view on?"

"What do you think?" Merseault asked. He sipped at his tea, waiting.

The secretary weighed his answer. "I'd agree with you for the most part. Except there was one thing I noticed."

"Yes?"

"The Party seemed to be following *his* lead. I mean, each time there was a new development, Picard would make the first move. He seemed to be a sort of spearhead."

"Exactly," Merseault said, tapping the desk. "Now what do you think?"

"Yes," the secretary said, nodding soberly. "It *could* be."

"It would explain why he's buried his past," Merseault said.

"But he's ridiculed the Party several times. Criticism, yes—but would they tolerate ridicule? He's been damagingly sarcastic on a few occasions."

"If he's valuable enough he could do anything."

"What about the American?" the secretary asked.

"Stone? I don't know. If that was really Picard in that farmhouse near St. Tropez, then we'd have a link. But it would be a weak one. Stone said he couldn't be sure, so I threw him off the scent. And we haven't been able to prove that Picard made the trip to Moscow after the war."

"Perhaps if you suggested . . ."

"Yes," Merseault said. "I plan to. He may be assuming that Stone made a positive identification. He may tip his own hand, although that wouldn't prove much more than the fact that he was in touch with Carnot during the war and knew him before the trial started. That in itself would not be criminal or even unusual, although it would embarrass him to explain why he never said so."

"And Carnot?"

"Nothing. He won't discuss Picard."

"You think Picard knew the whole background on Dujardin before he contacted Carnot?"

"You must admit, it gave him a perfect opportunity to embarrass the government."

"But wouldn't he be taking a rather heavy risk?"

"What did he have to lose? He could always claim he'd been duped —as half the people in the nation were duped. He wouldn't be alone. He could merely wash his hands of it. Issue an indignant statement demanding a redisposition of the case. Certainly he'd have to repudiate Carnot."

"And the Party would follow his lead," the secretary said, nodding reflectively.

"They never had anything to lose. Carnot could always be made the scapegoat."

"It's possible. What about this investigation in the American Congress?"

"I don't know. The Americans seem to have gone crazy. There's no question that it was Picard who sent them the affidavit. But why he should do that eludes me. I can't see any gain in it, except perhaps to embarrass their Embassy through Stone. But there's always the risk that the Americans will upset Picard's whole applecart. *If* they investigate seriously."

"Yes, I suppose there's *some* chance they might find something."

"Unfortunately they seem more interested in indicting their own Army officers than they do in vindicating them. Something very strange is going on when the American Senate begins wrecking the morale of their own Army in order to vindicate one French *collabo*."

"Picard has made no secret of the fact?"

"That he was the one who sent the affidavits? He had no choice after it came out in the Washington hearing. Once his name came into it, he had to deny it or else boast about it. Simple admission would have seemed suspicious. Deny sin, or boast of it; never defend it."

"He took a risk."

"But you have to admit it makes his action look more moral if not more logical. He tried to get the Quai d'Orsay to lodge a complaint against the American Army's handling of Dujardin. When that failed the logical move was to put the complaint directly in the hands of the American Congress, in the hope that some politician could use it to advance his political fortunes. It's a strange country, the United States. Even stranger after one has been there."

"I'd like to go there someday. It's difficult for me to understand Americans without seeing where they come from. I always know more about a person after I've been inside his room and looked on his dressing table."

"So you don't think it's too fantastic?" Merseault asked.

"I've always been sure that he was more than a simple commissar during the war. He's admitted as much publicly."

"Yes," Merseault said. "And he also keeps in touch with his old comrades in arms. He goes to their reunions every chance he gets. It's a perfectly sound front. Urbane lawyer. Independent. A political lone wolf."

"But I'd be surprised if he was under Party discipline today. Especially at high level."

"Of course," Merseault began, changing the tack, "there's always the possibility that he's coming here to talk about an entirely different matter. We can't rule out the possibility that he really believed Dujardin was innocent."

The secretary looked skeptically at Merseault. "Haven't you been able to get anything at all out of Carnot?"

"I'm playing for the grand prize. I haven't wanted to seem to press him. He's very frightened."

"You mean, induce him to confess to perjury?" the secretary asked, still skeptical. "Reopen the case again?"

"He won't do that. He's afraid of prosecution. But we might get him to talk out of the country. Dujardin is unimportant, but it still galls me that they've been able to paint black white and get away with it. It's a thorn in my vanity."

"There's not much you can do now."

"That's what I've been hearing." Merseault got up abruptly and paced back and forth. "The Cabinet is not anxious to have the dirt swept out from under the rug again. I've been making a pest out of myself. I've nearly worn out my welcome over at Quai d'Orsay. They think they got off cheaply, and they resent my tampering with the adjusted solution. But I'm still curious to know how Picard managed it precisely, and whether by luck or by design."

The secretary shook his head. "This is going to interfere with your writing again."

Merseault laughed. "That's not what's worrying you, Alain. You're worried that I'll have you running errands all over Paris again. I think you prefer typing to bicycling."

The secretary smiled politely and said nothing.

Dinner with Picard that evening passed without Picard once referring to the reason for his visit. The talk was of general things. Picard was greatly interested in the long history of the house. It wasn't until later, when Merseault had invited his guest into the library, that Picard's relaxed manner underwent a subtle change.

Abruptly Picard put down his brandy glass and leaned back into the pillows of the couch. Merseault watched him. Then Picard said, "I imagine you know what I wanted to discuss with you."

Merseault said, "No," simply and deliberately.

Picard raised his eyebrows ironically. "You had a young visitor the other night, two nights ago, that is. Alexi Carnot."

Merseault nodded. "Yes," he said.

"I'll come to the point. I have reason to believe he left certain papers in your keeping, papers that don't belong to him."

Merseault shook his head. "Your information is not correct," he said. "I see no reason why I shouldn't be honest with you."

542

"The papers are not in your possession, then?"

"He left no papers in my possession," Merseault said.

"They comprise the missing Dujardin file," Picard said. "You realize that."

Merseault was genuinely surprised that Picard should advance the subject so openly. The only explanation was that Picard was convinced that Merseault was already aware of what they were.

"I wasn't ever certain that such a file even existed," Merseault said. "I'm being perfectly candid with you, you realize. Carnot left no documents with me. Of course I'm not at liberty to discuss the conversation we had, not without his permission."

"Why did he come to you?"

"Purely a personal matter, I assure you. Quite personal."

"But why did he come to *you?*"

"I asked him to. Very simple," Merseault said.

"I see," Picard said. He seemed perfectly at ease.

"I am very interested in certain things he appears qualified to discuss."

"Such as the Dujardin affair?"

"That, too."

Picard sipped his brandy. "Are you still working on your memoirs, Doctor?"

"You could hardly call them *my* memoirs." Merseault smiled.

"Yes, of course," Picard said. "Do you plan to re-enter the political life? When your book is finished, that is."

"No."

"A pity. The country needs men of your experience and intelligence."

"Ah, yes," Merseault sighed. "But I have no flair for modesty. Without modesty one is doomed in politics."

"Well, if you ever change your mind . . ."

". . . you would be glad to enlist my allegiance," Merseault said flatly.

"I might be able to help you in small ways," Picard said, smiling his ironic smile again.

There was a short silence. Then Picard said, "I had hoped you'd be more open with me on this matter. However, I suppose you are somewhat in the position of a lawyer who must consider the interest of his client."

"A great deal of the material I obtain in the course of my researches must be obtained in confidence."

"Naturally," Picard said. "Perfectly understandable."

Merseault judged the moment for making his opening gambit. He shifted his position and said casually, "I was interested in Major Stone's account of your meeting each other during his work with Carnot's group."

Picard's face didn't change. He said, "Stone seemed a very capable agent."

There it was. The link. Picard—Carnot—Stone.

"You'll be interested in reading my analysis of the Dujardin case," Merseault said. "I've decided to include it."

Picard raised his hand lazily and twirled the amber brandy against the light. "Yes, the Dujardin case has its classic aspects. When do you expect your manuscript to be ready for publication?"

Merseault shrugged. "A history, like a work of art, is never finished. It is simply abandoned."

"Ah, yes," Picard said, as though only half-listening. "Perhaps someday I can give you a little more material on the backstage handling of the case. However, it's not over yet."

"I was rather surprised you took an interest in it," Merseault said.

"Politics requires risks," Picard said, shrugging.

"What will you do if it blows up under you? These files you mentioned . . ."

"I plan to blow it up myself. There's nothing further in it. The juice is all squeezed out of the lemon."

"That explains why you want the files."

"Before I break the news, I want to be sure that they at least exist." Picard smiled at his glass, turning it in the light. "I can't risk making a fool of myself by reversing my position without good reason. It will need a little drama. I'd like to produce copies of the files on the floor of the Assembly."

"Wouldn't the Party suffer rather unduly?" Merseault asked.

Picard looked at Merseault, smiled slightly. "Are you trying to trap me into revealing my connection with the Party?"

Merseault smiled in return. "I hope you don't think it's a secret," he said.

Picard smiled to himself and said, "No, I suppose a professional like yourself must be caught up on the details of Party organization."

Merseault nodded, accepted the implied compliment.

Picard continued, "I plan to make my conversion public in a few weeks."

"I should think you'd be throwing away an advantage," Merseault said.

"One must join the Party before one can break with it," Picard said, with an offhand wave of his hand. "It will be necessary to be expelled if I am to regain useful freedom of action." He smiled.

"How will you avoid blame for the Dujardin case?"

"Oh, I don't know precisely. It's not a pressing problem, really. There are several right-wing deputies on the committee."

"Committee?" Merseault said.

"The financing committee, the committee for the Liberation of Théophile Dujardin. The 'private' committee. The Party used very little of its own money. Just for propaganda expenses. The legal fees were paid mostly by public subscription."

"I see. A matter of common interest."

"Precisely," Picard said, nodding pedantically. "There are always political forces at work. It's simply a matter of harnessing them."

"So you will have been 'deceived' by the monarchists, is that how you'll explain it?"

Picard said, "Something like that. A right-wing plot—some such nonsense." He sounded bored, but he laughed. Picard was acting a role.

"Anything that will make the best newspaper headlines."

Picard looked at Merseault. "You sound sarcastic. I suppose it does appear rather cynical to a historian. I've always thought of historians as moralists."

"History is the moralist, not the historian," Merseault said.

"I wish I could agree with you," Picard said. "Unhappily I haven't found that to be true."

"Yet."

"Quite true. The last chapter of history will never be written, will it?" He smiled. "So we never will know the moral of the idiot's tale, will we?"

"I'd be curious to know how you justify your position," Merseault said.

"I have no position."

"Communism is a position, wouldn't you say?"

Picard looked at the ceiling. He appeared to be weighing the question. Then he said, "I don't know. *Is* communism a position? For the man in a factory it represents a position, I suppose. But for me? I don't think so. It's a moral expedient, that is to say, a historical necessity."

"You take a rather abstract view of it."

"Not at all. I thought this all out years ago. Long before the war. I'm not a Communist, really. I knew long ago that I could never tailor my mind to the philosophical mediocrities of pamphlet writers. I'm precisely the kind of individual Marx would enjoy and the Stalinist state would never tolerate. Lenin would merely find me useful."

"You don't think highly of Stalin?"

"You think I'm not aware of the perversion?" Picard asked. "Don't take me for a fool. Stalin is nothing more than a suspicious peasant. And yet he is historically right for Russia."

"Why do you work for them?"

"I don't. They work for me. I'm not a Communist. I'm a professional revolutionary. A mature man dedicated to pure revolution. It's my only honest passion. I have no ideology except revolution. I'm rather proud of it."

"I find that surprising."

"Yes. It surprised me when I found it out. It was the war, I think, that gave me my first taste of blood. I'm more honest than most men, in that respect, I mean. I enjoyed working to destroy authority. Does that surprise you too?"

"You mean the Germans, of course."

"No. That is precisely what I don't mean. I didn't work against the Germans simply because they were the enemy. I worked against them simply because they had power. I would work against the USSR if I were living there."

"I see why you say you're not a Communist."

"I don't think you do. I work with the Communists because they further me in my gratifications. But I am not a Communist simply because they are not revolutionaries. They aren't *pure* revolutionaries. The Kremlin is terrified of revolutionaries, real revolutionaries. A professional revolutionary is a man with no dogma, no beliefs, only an appetite for chaos. He will seek to overturn whoever is in power. If the Communists came into control of France I would be ideally placed to destroy them. That's why I look forward to the day when they'll take power. They'll make an excellent adversary."

"Aren't you being a little indiscreet in announcing your intentions?"

Picard smiled. "The Devil always gives warning. It's the secret of his success. Hitler warned you. But you thought he was a madman."

"Wasn't he?"

"He drank his own poison. Power always destroys the holder. It's like grasping the sword by the blade instead of the handle."

"You have no ambitions?"

"None. If I accepted power I would have to defend it."

"Against revolutionaries."

Picard smiled. "Yes. Against the eternal underground."

Merseault said nothing.

"Revolutionaries are the power that drives the state," Picard continued. "If you consider the meaning of the word . . ."

"Revolution?"

"Precisely. To turn over. To overturn. Think of the old metaphor of the ship of state. It's an excellent metaphor if you carry it out to the end. What is the force that drives a ship under sail?"

"Wind?" Merseault accepted the gratuitous role of pupil thrust on him by Picard.

"No. Not wind alone. Perhaps you recall the famous Newton's third law of motion."

Merseault shrugged. "I did very badly in physics."

" 'Every action has an equal and opposite reaction.' Do you recall it now? Do you notice that the Party believes in action, direct and indirect? And the dragon they think they'll slay is reaction. Reactionary. There's no worse crime in their doctrinaire lexicon, except counter-revolution—which is merely revolution in its pure form again. Politics and physics have very much of a common vocabulary. Physicists should make excellent politicians someday."

"If the physicists don't first make politics unnecessary."

Ignoring Merseault's remark, Picard continued, "A ship is driven forward by counteraction of two forces—the action of wind on the sail countered by the reaction of water on the keel. But wind is the force which gives rise to the reaction on the keel. Wind is the driving force, wind is the revolutionary force."

"I don't quite see . . ."

"Revolution is a term from physics also." Picard laughed. He was sitting forward on the couch, warming to his subject and gesturing with both hands to emphasize his words. "When a ship capsizes it commits revolution. It turns over. It's overturned."

Merseault nodded. "I see how you're going to extend the metaphor."

"Certainly. It's obvious. As long as a state is in balance between the forces of action and reaction it makes safe progress. If a ship is well designed, well ballasted, and well managed, it will be difficult to overturn. But there are always methods by which revolution can be accomplished if one works at it."

"I see."

"In America, for example. I mean North America, the United States. We must first create the proper conditions before we can achieve revolution. In the United States there is a large body of phlegmatic thought—the American middle class—who provide rather heavy ballast in the American ship of state. I feel foolish for pushing the metaphor so far, but I have an extremely literal mind. The bourgeoisie is ballast. Revolution is impossible in a state where there is a large body of moderate opinion. Lenin understood this. He understood that the European socialists were the greatest enemy of the Bolshevik Revolution. The moderates and socialists must be driven out. Lenin hated reformers. He was at first a pure revolutionary. Pure. He had no credo but revolution. In the end he accepted power, and that was his end. It was too bad."

"Power is the aim of revolution, I should imagine."

"Power is the enemy of revolution. Power is always to be rejected, overthrown."

"It seems a purposeless occupation," Merseault said. "You're committed to a completely negative view . . ."

"The alternative is belief in Utopia. That is why I use the Communists but am not one myself. Revolution, for a pure revolutionary, is endless. There can be no Utopia. Even Utopia must be overthrown. I believe in revolution as profoundly and passionately as those fools who march in the streets believe in Utopia. The only value of the Utopian ideal is as a tool in the hands of a revolutionary. Utopia is merely an instrument of discontent. It is the mirage on the horizon that keeps the dying man upright and walking. It's a lovely thing."

"I must say I find this very curious. You apparently find beauty in discontent?"

"If you were the Prince of Hell you'd find beauty in darkness," Picard said. "There is beauty in all things, including the eye of the witness."

"Have you ever wondered if you're mad?" Merseault asked, smiling.

Picard didn't show any reaction. "Of course," he said. "I've even suspected that I'm a true paranoiac—not paranoid, please, but para-noiac."

Merseault grunted. "I'm not sure I'm educated to the difference."

"But I can tell you a great many things. I could tell you for instance what you already know: that the Dujardin affair was my handiwork. That I have worked a fraud on an entire nation. And if I *told* them it was a fraud, do you think it would change anything?"

"People believe what they need to believe."

"Ah, very astute. I could announce in the public square that I knew Dujardin was guilty. It would make no difference. They would hang *me,* and set him free. By the time historians set the record straight, it will no longer matter. History will have served its purpose. Dujardin is really an upside-down scapegoat. Usually the scapegoat is a person of great virtue—a sixteen-year-old virgin, for example. The group visits all their sins on the scapegoat's head, and then kills him. In Dujardin's case they've found a person of great evil, invested him with their virtues, and granted him his life."

"Very cynical."

"Precisely. But better cynicism than bourgeois hypocrisy."

"Now you sound more like a representative of the true Party . . ."

"I find a few of their clichés useful," Picard said. He continued, "We don't preach that virtue is its own reward. The bourgeoisie is fond of preaching that work is a noble virtue. They preach it to the working classes through their hired clergymen, and yet none of them will permit his daughter to marry a man who has worked with his hands. In England a man who has ever worked with his hands is not a gentleman. That is the hypocrisy. They preach noble maxims to the men who sweat in the mills they own for profit, and then they devote their lives to demonstrating the falseness of their maxims. I prefer cynicism."

"In America—"

"Revolution will come in America," Picard said flatly. "But first we have to strengthen the forces of reaction. Why do you think we sent the Dujardin affidavit to that young Senator? Because he is a pure revolutionary. He has no credo except to disrupt and overturn the existing order. He confounds Americans because he seems to have no ambitions, which in America makes a man a saint beyond common flesh. He has no scruples, either. He knows what he is. That's why I helped him."

"Does he know you work with the Party?"

"Do you think it would make a difference?"

Merseault said nothing.

"In America we have expelled members from the Party so that they could cooperate with such men. We will eliminate the inertia of moderate opinion. We will destroy them between the hammer and the anvil. The socialists, the reformers, all the swine who swill themselves on dreams. We will finger them out one by one and let stupid reactionaries destroy them. The socialists will be ground to dust between the millstones of left and right."

Merseault laughed. Instantly Picard was on his feet, his face red and suddenly angry. "You think I'm a Quixote. You'll live to see the joke."

"But, my dear fellow," Merseault said placatingly, surprised by Picard's sudden irrational anger. "You must admit it sounds a bit fantastic. With a handful of unknown junior senators you won't change a hundred and fifty years of American history. I'm sorry I laughed. Please sit down."

Picard was not to be calmed. "First we will send out our agents. You will live to see Communists being paid by the American secret police. You will see them on the staffs of investigating committees. Don't you think we've made a study of it? We've studied for the past twenty years. We know exactly where to place them. The American Communist Party, of course, *is* a joke. But I am not."

"Really, you mustn't get so excited. Pardon me if I'm skeptical, but even assuming you can place them, what will you do with them?"

"It doesn't matter if I tell you. I could publish the whole detailed plan in a book and no one would believe it. There are always political forces, and those forces, once we harness them, will not be turned back. Then revolution will be possible. It is impossible now. But we are making progress. You notice that every American is now subject to loyalty checks."

"Not every American. Just those who work in government."

Picard actually sneered. "Wait. When we're through, every man who works in the sewers of New York will have to sign an oath. Hog butchers. Tailors. Everyone. Then it will be industries, schools. They will fire teachers for knowing the Russian language. They will thus create a new reserve of malcontents who won't be able to work at their ordinary jobs. A new crop of future recruits for us. In the next depression they will form the nucleus of an army for us. There will be no moderates. Moderates will be stamped out, ground to powder in the jaws of the vise. They will be forced to take sides or be destroyed. We will discredit high government officials. We will—"

"My dear fellow, how will you accomplish that last item?"

"You forget that the Party plans its different historical phases, not years, but decades in advance. In every country in the world we have evidence compromising key government officials. Evidence that we manufactured fifteen years ago when they were obscure clerks and bright functionaries."

"Manufactured?" Merseault inquired. *"We* manufactured?"

"Real or false—what difference will it make? Any evidence fifteen years old is old enough to be believed without question. And why will they believe it? Because they will never believe we would take such pains. Because the American Communists are fools, they think we all are. They don't think for the future. Therefore they can't believe that anyone else would."

"What kind of evidence?"

"How would I know that? These things aren't written down. Films, papers, photographers. Hidden away for the day they'll be needed."

"I think you're crazy," Merseault said soberly.

"Carnot was here two nights ago. Did he think I was crazy?"

Merseault shrugged. "Picard, you're mad. You actually are mad."

"Things will follow a logical order. First foreign policy must be paralyzed. The American Foreign Office will be discredited—"

"In America they call it the State Department."

Picard ignored the correction. "Their propaganda departments will be silenced, neutralized, exposed for what they are. The Voice of America, the information libraries, the—"

Merseault laughed.

Picard still ignored him. He was angry and very red in the face. "There will be no reforms, no reforms anywhere. They will be afraid to make them. Reformists will be hunted down and exposed. They will be discredited and ruined."

"You forget you're talking about a country that has just survived one of the worst wars in history. The Germans tried to sow disunity but failed miserably even to—"

"We are not Germans. Germans have always been fools politically. After we have paralyzed the reformist social democrats, neutralized them, the next thing will be the Army. The Army. You will see junior officers informing on the generals. Then the research programs. First the scientists will be approached, compromised. Many of them have been approached already."

"Approached?"

"Approached. Merely approached, you understand. It will be enough."

"You mean by agents? Your agents?" Merseault shook his head at Picard, as though in mock pity. "You think that in a country where scientists are revered nearly as gods, you'll be able to destroy a man's career merely by approaching him? Really, you don't know the country. I have lived there for several years. I know how—"

"You are a very stupid man," Picard said rudely.

Merseault raised his eyebrows but said nothing.

Picard continued on his own thoughts. "You have never seen Americans when they are living in fear. Already they are afraid of war. The USSR will not go to war. They have more to gain by . . . don't you see? The United States can be made to destroy itself."

"You make it sound like a new form of political jujitsu."

"Ah!" Picard said. "Excellent. Precisely. Make the aggressive weight of your opponent work against him. Ah, good. Good. I will remember that. It saves a great deal of explanation."

Merseault smiled. "I still think you're being a little indiscreet in telling me your . . . ah . . . your plans. What's to prevent my writing a report of our conversation and forwarding it to the affected parties?"

"You would be a fool if you didn't," Picard said disgustedly. "You think I'm simply a madman or a fool. You don't understand the forces at work politically. These are forces, historical forces, which are beyond anyone's power to influence. Write all the reports you wish. They will be discounted and filed, or they will be believed and accelerate the panic of the right-wing reactionaries. Either way, we win."

"Isn't it a symptom of paranoia to . . . ah . . . boast of your, your accomplishments?"

"I believe so. After the fact. I'm boasting before the fact. All it will do is help insure success. Amuse yourself. Write a report. Send it to the director of American Intelligence. Do you know what will happen to it? It will be thrown into a file by an amused staff officer and be forgotten. The secret of success in—I suppose *you* would call it conspiracy —is never to work in the dark. Work in the light. In full view of all. Nothing up your sleeve. Cellar conspiracy is for fools and children. We will openly harness political forces that the United States will create. Fear is the key. The Soviet Union merely has to exist. That fact alone will drive the capitalists into a frenzy of fear. We will give them the gun, and they will shoot themselves. The United States will never recover. They will write laws of suppression and the laws will remain. The balance between action and reaction will be upset permanently. They will be most suspicious of individuals who think. They will make all science a military secret. They will slip behind the rest of the world in science, in everything. They will sabotage their scientists, paralyze them with secrecy. They are doomed."

"What will happen if your false apostates are uncovered?"

"How can they be? They will be in league with the capitalists, leading them in a search for the secret enemies. They will walk the investigators in a circle following their own footprints. How can they be exposed? They will lead the pack. They will be eyes for the blind. The Party will cut off all contact with them for the rest of their lives. They will replace the teachers whom they drive out of their posts. They will join the church, and be happy for the haven. You know the saying, that there is more joy in heaven over one sinner saved? They will enjoy an easy life full of years and honor."

Merseault nodded. He raised his hand to mask a yawn, covertly looking at his watch.

"Once the reformist element is cleaned out, once the socialists are discredited, the capitalists will come back into unrestricted power. It will be only a matter of time before they undo the damages of Roosevelt and his middle-class reformers. The Soviet Union will suddenly relax the pressure and start another popular front. As soon as the tension vanishes, the United States will be demoralized with joy. They will have more and more big automobiles, and more unemployment. The big monopolies will compete to make more iceboxes and radios . . ."

"And television sets."

"Television will never be anything but a toy for the rich." Picard gulped the last of his brandy. "They will compete. They will make a million automobiles in two months and none for the rest of the year. It will be like the twenties. We have studied it. They will become greedy. They will try to maintain their export surplus by cutting off foreign-aid gifts, until other countries stop buying from them. They will collapse. They will destroy the farmers, then the workingmen, and finally themselves. They will do it because they can't help it. When they no longer have to compete in an arms race with the USSR they will compete among themselves in a race to extinction. They will be destroyed. The depression of the thirties will be nothing. This time it will be total collapse, and then revolution. It almost happened the last time. But there will be no Roosevelt this time. We're strong enough to see to that. And the capitalists will gnash their teeth about Communists and continue making more of them for us. Greed. Ha! Greed. What a lovely thing it is!"

"You forget about—"

"I forget about nothing."

Merseault shrugged. Not being able to resist a final goad, he smiled tolerantly.

Picard suddenly leaned back on the couch and relaxed carefully. "I'd be interested to see if you're still smiling ten years from now, Doctor. I'll be very unhappy if you are, of course, for it will mean that I am the fool after all."

"I don't approve of your ideas," Merseault said, as though coming to a conclusion. He stood up. "I'm sorry I wasn't able to help you with the documents you're looking for."

"Are you expecting someone else this evening?" Picard asked, getting to his feet.

"No," Merseault said, stretching deliberately. "No, I'm going to bed. I've had a difficult day. It's been an interesting conversation. I'm sorry if my skepticism prevents me from seeing the full feasibility of your endeavors."

"Not at all," Picard said affably. "It's your skepticism that makes them feasible in the first place."

"You mustn't think me rude if I don't wish you the best success."

"We'll manage," Picard said. He smiled and shook Merseault's hand.

Merseault showed Picard downstairs, and out to his car. The chauffeur was asleep behind the wheel, his visored cap cocked down over his eyes against the streetlight that showed over the wall of the courtyard. It was a mild, cloudless night and the air was fresh with the smell of lilacs from an adjoining courtyard. Picard got in his car and Merseault opened the courtyard gate for him, since the chauffeur made no move to do it. Picard waved a gloved hand as the car turned out into the street.

Merseault closed the gate and went back to the house. He locked up and turned off the downstairs light. Upstairs, he removed his jacket and shoes and put on slippers and his dressing gown. Then, unlocking the door, he went into the tiny office off the library, the office the secretary used. He had a worried frown on his face. He went to the corner and unlocked the bottom drawer of the second file cabinet. The drawer opened smoothly, to reveal a recording machine. The machine was still running with silent glistening efficiency. He switched it off and closed the file drawer again and locked it. Then he crossed to the desk, yawning, and dialed a number.

Merseault stood waiting while the telephone rang. He yawned again. Then he spoke into the mouthpiece: "I'd like to leave a message for Inspector de Rougement. Have you a paper and pencil?" A pause. "All right, the message is this: *You were right, but diagnosis was off. Suggest paranoia. Same old story.* Have you got that? Read it back to me." There was a pause. Then Merseault said, "No, that will be fine. He'll know who it's from. Thank you. Oh, wait a minute . . . Add this: *A.C. may need moral support. Keep an eye on him.* Got that? No, they're initials, *A.C.* That's right. Fine, see that he gets that before he goes off duty at midnight."

Merseault hung up the telephone, placing the instrument gently in its cradle. He stood a moment in the doorway, as though listening, before turning out the light and locking the door from the outside. He was tired. His expression was thoughtful as he walked through the library; in his preoccupation he nearly tripped over one of the two cats his housekeeper let roam the house at night. The cat slid gently between his legs, ghosted into the shadow of the hallway, and disappeared. He ignored it. The only thing to think about now was sleep.

IV

Most of the members present at the Thursday Club dinner were Embassy officers or men whose interests lay close to the American Government. A few businessmen came at the urging of the president, a businessman himself; three doctors, several lawyers, the editor of the *Paris Tribune,* and two clergymen rounded out the gathering. But most of the forty-odd men around the long table were State Department advisers, high-level consultants, and regular officers of the foreign service. The six young men—initiates in the foreign service—for whom the special dinner was being held were distributed along the table facing the president, who served as his own able toastmaster for the occasion. He sat not at the end but in the middle, his back to the Great Seal of the United States hung on the wall for the occasion. He was a round, jovial man, a former United States consul now director of the Paris branch of a San Francisco bank; he had the relaxed, confident manner of a man accustomed to being listened to and appreciated. The guest of honor would be arriving later. The chair reserved for him at the president's right, empty and expectant, was the only vacancy at the table.

After hors d'oeuvres and two wines—a Château de Varrains of recent vintage and a Sancerre Sauvignon 1937—in the foyer, the members and guests repaired to the adjoining room and the dinner got under way. It was prepared under the supervision of the chef of Maison Prunier, and commenced with Bar Farci a L'Angevine and Paté de Saumon Rabelaisienne served with a Grand Vouvray 1933. Out of consideration for Catholic members the dinner had been skillfully planned without a meat course. As usual since the war, the Thursday Club was dining on Friday.

The salmon with its solid core of truffles drew a sober toast from the president for the chef, who, after his masterwork was reduced to a pleasant memory, was brought from the kitchen to receive applause. He stood in the doorway nodding happily, like a diva taking an encore. When he returned to the kitchen there was an interlude of talk, mostly directed toward the new young foreign service initiates, who answered the questions politely, each in turn.

They seemed younger by contrast than they really were, more stiff-mannered. Scattered among the older hands around the table, their new black silk lapels were immaculately stiff and flat, and they sat poised and straight at their places. The older men were more relaxed, wore their dinner jackets rumpled, like fatigue uniforms, carelessly knowing and well practiced in the rituals of formal occasions.

Out of respect for the chef, the president autocratically signaled for the ashtrays to be removed before any of the younger men could commit the indiscretion of smoking while the repast was in progress. The president was a strict and accomplished gourmet, one of the few Americans in Paris who was a bona fide Chevalier de Tastevin. It was he who had arranged the menu in consultation with the chef a week before, and he took obvious pride in its enjoyment.

The salmon was followed by Asperges Nouvelles. New glasses were brought and an Anjou Rablay 1928 was served. One of the older men at the end of the table complimented the felicity of the choice and a standing toast was drunk to the president.

The asparagus was followed by assorted cheeses with still another wine, a Bourgueil 1947, and the talk flowed easily on. The cheese platter was passed and repassed, and finally remained on the table.

A young man entered the room from the door to the great hall, and went to the president's place and leaned down to whisper in his ear. Everyone turned expectantly toward the great carved doors as the young man hurried back from the table to open them. All conversation ceased. The president rose heavily from his place just as the doors opened.

The Ambassador entered the room; there was a scraping of chairs, and everyone stood up.

"Gentlemen," the president said solemnly, "His Nibs the guest of honor is here."

There was relaxed laughter. Someone said, "Hear. Hear."

The Ambassador was supporting himself slightly on a black cane. He looked extraordinarily tall in evening dress, clothed impeccably in the strong dignity of age. His hair was still cut very short, although longer than when he'd been in office, and he was markedly thinner. Against the contrast of his black dinner jacket and black tie his hair looked white rather than gray. That he walked slowly only added to the dignity of his bearing.

Everyone stood smiling; there was a pattering of informal warm applause. The president left his place and greeted Sheppard as he rounded the end of the table. The young man who had preceded him turned and departed, inconspicuously closing the doors behind him.

Sheppard was ceremoniously seated by the president, and everyone sat down. There was relaxed talk, louder and less restrained now; several men greeted Sheppard by his first name. Good-natured grumbling came from the knot of lawyers at the end of the table as one of them fished awkwardly under the table to retrieve his napkin. The dinner resumed; it was going to finish well. With the arrival of the guest of honor, there was no more furtive glancing at watches; the managers of the evening relaxed with the rest of the guests. The robust satisfaction of a dinner well enjoyed was beginning to settle on the company, along with the subtler warmth of the five delicate wines. The arrival of the distinguished guest completed the harmony.

The cheeses, twelve varieties in all, were removed and dessert was brought: Poire des Ducs d'Anjou. The dessert wine was a recent Château Moncontour. The Ambassador joined in the dessert but left his wine untouched.

Finally cigars were passed, coffee was brought, and the brandy served. The table was ringed with private talk and a pleasure of relaxed laughter. The younger men had nearly all followed the lead of the older ones in unbuttoning their dinner jackets. It was warm with the first touch of April heat in the room, and the doors onto the terrace were opened and left ajar. A light evening breeze played behind the curtains. It was a fitful breeze, sullen, as before a summer storm.

A light fragrance of mellow cigar smoke hung in a sharp blue layer over the table, when finally the president tapped on his brandy *ballon* and rose effortfully from his chair. Conversations were hastily terminated in nodding whispers, chairs were pushed back and turned slightly to face the speaker, and everyone made himself comfortable. After a short wait there was silence. The president stood looking down at his plate, silent, as though lost in private thoughts. With the timing of an accomplished raconteur he carefully let the silence around the table draw out dramatically. Finally the only sound was the rustle of work from the distant kitchen and the lifting of the breeze on the terrace. The atmosphere in the room had suddenly changed completely. As toastmaster, the president stood like an orchestra conductor, his hands at his sides, head bowed, as though to mark the pause between the allegro and the slow movement. When he finally spoke, even the key and tempo of his voice had changed.

"When the arrangements for this celebration were made several weeks ago, none of us knew then that Bruce Peel Sheppard would be finally leaving the service of our country to take the rest he's deserved for so long." He paused, looked around. "The penalty for being a great servant of people is that people come to depend on you for wisdom and guidance. We are reluctant to let our counselor go." He paused again. "Bruce Sheppard has served his country through two wars. He wanted to retire after the last one, but he couldn't. There was still much to be done, much at stake. No one was more aware than the men who fought the last war of the fact that military victory was not enough. Never in history has military victory been enough, for war always creates more problems than it solves.

"As a selfish citizen, I am reluctant to allow Bruce Sheppard to leave his post. For the world is still in narrow straits, and the waters of this unhappy decade are uncharted. The threat of war faces us in Berlin, in Trieste, in Greece, Turkey, the Far East, almost everywhere, and the problem of diplomacy is to avoid war. Never before has that problem been so acute and so baffling. Never before have we so badly needed men of wisdom and imagination to help us toward solutions. For the problems are endless, and solutions never anything but temporary.

"That is why there is such peculiar meaning in this present occasion. We are witnessing part of the continuing solution to the problem of survival, right here in this room tonight. For the six young men we are honoring are among those on whose shoulders our future destiny will weigh. As citizens we would do well to keep that fact clearly in mind. They will need our firmest support in the hard days ahead.

"It is my dedicated honor to present to you His Excellency, the Ambassador of the United States of America."

There was applause. Everyone stood up. The clapping continued unabated until the Ambassador slowly rose from his chair and nodded his appreciation of the tribute. Everyone sat down again; the room grew silent.

"Mr. President, honored friends." The Ambassador spoke without notes. "I am greatly pleased to join in welcoming the younger guests whose celebration this is. It is an admirable way to welcome them to Paris and to the foreign service. I hope this will be the first of many more dinners for other young men in years to come." The Ambassador paused, and looked at each of the six young men in turn. "Therefore, tonight I wish to address myself to you.

"We old men too often overlook the necessity of passing on the questionable experience of our years." He spoke slowly, as though gauging the fit of each word, pausing between each sentence. "Too often we merely pass on the knowledge of our successes, and keep to ourselves the experiences of our failures. A man speaks of his failures only to his trusted friends, and that is why a dinner like this is important. If friendships come out of this dinner, we will have accomplished a very real thing. For no one needs a friend today more than a young man, especially if that young man is working in the Department of State."

There was satisfied laughter around the table.

The Ambassador smiled and went on. "Times of confusion are always times of fear, and fear compounds confusion. And this is the state of the world today. It is a time of failure and misunderstanding, and nothing so bedevils the human mind and spirit as failure and misunderstanding. Yet this is the atmosphere in which you younger men will have to work—not only work, but succeed. The safety of the nation will depend on your success, and in this century the safety of one nation is the safety of all nations. A nation that ignores its own safety is not only a threat to itself but to the world, for nations are no longer isolated one from another. They are tied together like men on the side of a mountain. If one slips, they may all fall. We've seen it happen twice.

"Twice the world has fallen into the abyss of total war. If the world falls a third time, our world and all its knowledge will be forgotten. No man in Caesar's Rome foresaw the centuries of the Dark Ages. That Roman traveled roads as fine as ours, and had a vision of progress as grand. If you had told him that a few hundred years later the technology of making concrete would be lost, the ingredients a vanished secret, he would have thought you were mad. But consider: What would happen to our dream of progress if all *our* libraries were burned? Who would live long enough to remember all the intricate formulas, all the trillions of words of explanation? The ideas and techniques that made the atomic weapon possible are understood by less than a handful of the world's human beings, and no one man completely embraces them all. The man who understands Einstein's conclusions is not likely to know how to run a precision lathe.

"There are perhaps a dozen libraries in the world that contain enough books to enable a team of brilliant men to deduce roughly how our nuclear technology was evolved from start to finish. Who would rewrite these books if they were destroyed? And if they were written, who would print them? And if they were printed, who by then could read them? People have no time even to read books if their every waking minute is taken up with scraping survival out of a doomed and blasted earth.

"Books are fragile things, and subject to rot. But knowledge decays even faster. The Dark Ages would again be here, and grass would grow in the streets. In three generations, the stones and monuments of our fallen cities would be carried off, to make sheep fences. In four generations, no man would be able to state what destroyed them."

There was silence in the room. There was no more noise from the kitchen. The muted clatter of dishes had ceased. One of the glass doors swung softly shut and then open again in the breeze rising on the terrace. The draperies moved uneasily.

"A third total war would probably not destroy man. I believe man is indestructible. But it would destroy civilization. Seven cities: New York, London, Paris, Rome, Moscow, Peiping, Tokyo. Their destruction would be enough to rupture the continuity of civilization and knowledge, so that each succeeding generation would lose successively more ground in the assimilation of knowledge. For even if the libraries in other parts of the world survived, as Greek libraries survived in Asia, there would be fewer and fewer men capable of using them.

"Men of learning and understanding are drawn like bees to the hive to cities. The very word civilization derives from the Latin word for city. Destroy the cities, and you destroy the men in whom the knowledge of civilization is preserved. You destroy the writers of books, the teachers of men. The world would never again catch up with the vast amount that must be taught, the vast amount that must be learned. Each generation would leave fewer teachers behind for the next. And in the struggle to rebuild shattered livelihoods, fewer and fewer people would have time to spend nearly a third of their lives in schools, in order to know and learn to teach what they know. This is the specter that confronts us.

"That is why it is more important than ever to pass on to younger men what we can of our failures. Very little can be learned from our successes, since successes, by their very nature, are rarely exactly repeatable—in fact, most of our failures are born of attempts to repeat former successes. But in failure we have an instrument of instruction, because failures by their nature are repeatable. Men nearly all make the same mistakes; rarely do they make the same successes. A man wise in mistakes is a man schooled to success, for success most often consists exactly in making a new and original mistake. There is no final success in human affairs. Only in dying can a man be completely successful. And dying requires no instruction.

"You young men are beginning your career. Most of you, if you are any good and live long enough, will experience the illusion of simple success. But never rest on it. Seek simplicity and then distrust it. Every fruitful solution carries in it the seed of a new problem. The more striking and original the solution, the more immense will be the problem that grows out of it. The new weapon that ended this war is an example of what I'm talking about. Seek solutions for the new problems in them, and you'll have a full life. There's the key to prophecy."

The door on the terrace suddenly swung full open, then gently shut as the fit of breeze diminished. No one got up to latch it; it opened slowly again.

"A diplomat, to my way of thinking, must be something of a weather prophet." The Ambassador smiled, glanced toward the terrace, then continued. "He must be a see-er. He must always keep one eye on the horizon and the other one on the compass. But the strongest advice I can give you is this: *Never let go of the wheel.*

"We live in a time which you'll find will often reward your dedication with contempt. Your best efforts will be misrepresented, misunderstood. And, worst of all, *misquoted.*"

The emphasis brought appreciative laughs from several of the older men among the listeners.

"You will be called everything from Communists to cookiepushers. If you speak the truth, people will call you liars; if on the other hand you tell lies, people will call you liars also. So you may as well tell the truth. In this profession, as you will learn in time, the best way to conceal a fact from scrutiny is simply to tell the truth. If you are a good diplomat, no one will believe you.

"But no matter how confused things get, one thing you must never do: Never let go of the wheel. I could make a long tiresome lecture on the elements of helmsmanship, but there's no point in buttressing tired advice with tired rhetoric. If you learn how to hang on, you'll learn how to steer on your own instruction. There will be times when every one of you young men will have stood all the abuse you can take. When that time comes, take a vacation, get sick, do anything. *But don't quit.* Because if you quit, someone else will take over, and that someone else will probably be the fool who thinks he has all the answers. When an intelligent man quits in disgust, it is difficult to find an honest man to replace him. It's always easy to find a rascal or a dolt. And in the press of events, that is usually what happens.

"If you ever do quit, never make your grievances public. It will only degrade the service, and make your replacement harder to find. If, on the other hand, you are fired, consider it a duty to your country to air your legitimate complaints. If your superior is ignorant, keep it a secret from him, otherwise he's liable to rely on his own judgment instead of yours. If, rather, you tell him he's intelligent, he'll count you a young man of rare wisdom and act always on your opinions. And after a while the flattery will work its magic in reverse. Because he values your opinions you'll evaluate them more carefully and finally come to revise them, including the opinion you first held about him."

There were a few smiles around the table. The men looked more comfortable, the occasional breeze from the terrace relieved the humid warmth in the room.

"Always keep in mind that the foreign service officers you work under once passed the same kind of examination you did. None of them, despite their modesty, are ignorant. They may be stubborn, cautious, unimaginative, or conservative, but none of them are *really* ignorant. They simply slow down with age. But they are all the clay you'll have to work with, so you'd better make the best of them. They mold policy; you mold them. You'll be doing most of the work. You'll write the reports, and they'll sign them. This may annoy you, if you're looking for personal glory. But glory will come faster if you pretend she's an uncivil woman and ignore her a little."

One of the lawyers laughed loudly, comfortably.

"The older men in the diplomatic service are not necessarily wiser, but they're more tractable. They started their careers like you, full of beans and opinions. But foreign policy, for better or for worse, is made to be executed. And they soon learn that to be efficient agents of that execution they have to submerge a great many of their opinions. The Secretary of State is paid to have an opinion; you are paid to help him form and execute it. Some of you even may rise someday to the position where you are paid, as I am, to dispute it. Until then, disputation is a questionable pastime. You will have all you can do to write the reports your superiors will sign. And the way you can best shape policy, if you have a mind for that, is through those reports. Consider yourself the true musicians; your superiors are your instruments. By the time you get to my age, you'll have learned to distrust your own opinions so profoundly that you won't have any. You become a true instrument, like an oboe, which blows true only for someone skilled in the art.

"Perhaps it sounds as though I'm asking you to compromise your principles. And of course I am. If principles didn't conflict there would be no need for compromise; but in human affairs, principles always conflict. But never compromise in bad conscience. If you can't reconcile one compromise with your conscience, then find another. One principle you must never compromise until last: Never abandon your post—except, of course, in time of war, in which case make sure you take it with you. Often the most difficult compromise is with another branch of the government, particularly Congress."

There were a few ironic laughs. The Ambassador took no notice.

"Keep in mind the difference between your aims and theirs. If faced with the choice of accepting a cut in your budget or resigning, accept the cut. Accept anything, even indignity. But don't abandon your post. Don't quit. For if you do, you'll be abdicating *all* control instead of just a little. Policy is a continuous and delicate thing, like the thread in the Cretan labyrinth. It can't survive constant rupture. Your satisfaction should be in preserving that thread intact, with all the creative ingenuity at your command. If that abstract reward isn't enough, your soul will never find satisfaction in the foreign service. It's a delicate pleasure to pursue, and you'll need a thick skin and a nimble foot to do it.

"When the time comes finally to resign, you'll find, as I am finding now, that it's a bitter-sweet experience. A lifetime of activity is not easily ended. And yet we old wheelhorses should not deprive the younger men of their comeuppance, in and through the ranks."

Several of the older men smiled and nodded.

"If younger men are to come up through the ranks, someone has to move off the stools at the top. This dinner will be the last function I'll attend in my official capacity as your Ambassador, for as you know my formal resignation takes effect tomorrow. I leave the office and the service with real regret, all the stronger for being so unexpected. I have been looking forward to the pleasures of retirement for over ten years. And yet now that the time has actually come, I find myself looking backward rather than forward. My time in the service of the government is like a long corridor, a tunnel of love's labor into the past. There have been failures, grotesque mistakes, comic blunders. I feel like a small boy at a carnival, backing out of the hall of mirrors.

"The pleasant memories, the few pleasures of accomplishment, these are what make the experience sweet. The failures make it bitter. But it's more mellow regret than true bitterness, a recognition that life's impossibilities are still impossible. One sees that the deeper significance of man lies in his dreams and failures, rather than his successful monuments of achievement. Man cannot be content with the merely possible; it is the impossible that drives him. The impossibility of flying across oceans is symbolized in the fall of Icarus, an old man's myth. All that the young men learned from the myth was that you had to use something better than feathers and wax to make your wings. In the cocksure inexperience and ignorance of youth, they made them. And now even old men like me can fly.

"The impossibility facing your generation is the creation of a world without war. It has been said over and over that men will always fight wars, that it's not in the nature of man to live in peace. I can only reply that neither is it in the nature of man to fly across oceans. It's not in his nature; it's in his will. Man's blind insensible will to bend his reason in service to the impossible. An old man's thoughts dwell on the past, because the future is unthinkable. There is no reason to pretend he doesn't think of death and its mystery, because he does. And of what lies beyond death. He tends finally to see life as immutable because death is immutable, and it pervades his vision. But don't let the old men fool you. Life is not immutable. Life is the very opposite of immutability. Life is change, creation, growth, rebirth, re-creation. Death is merely another task, the final feat, the final accomplishment. It is the ultimate test of life's will and life's vigor. The final severe question a man must come to ask himself is not whether life has been worth living, but whether it's been worth dying. That is the meaning of dedication.

"All of you young men are entering on a career of service to your fellow citizens. By sheerest circumstance of time and events, the profession you have chosen is the one profession that is faced with a truly significant impossibility. When I was a young man, the significant impossibility was flight across oceans. Engineers and scientists suddenly emerged as the honor guard of civilization's march. They met the challenge and conquered the significant impossibility of their day. But as always, the solution of that problem only engendered a larger one. For they have given the world the Apple of Cataclysm. They have given mankind the means of destroying the world in precisely the miraculous fashion predicted by the Prophets of the Old Testament: by fire. That prophecy always seemed remote and ridiculous in the days of my youth, and I can still hear the militant atheist of our small New England town asking, "How can sand, stone, and water burn?" He believed in science. He died before science could give him his answer.

"The significant impossibility of an age is rarely recognized for its significance, but always for its impossibility. Fifty years ago if you talked of flying, you were a visionary lunatic. Today if you talk of a world without war, you are still—a visionary lunatic. The difficulty is that perhaps you are. But I dimly suspect not. Science, in the days of my youth, was most commonly associated with cataloguing birds and giving insects Latin names. The scientists who appeared in the novels of my youth invariably carried a butterfly net as their badge of office. And today when people talk of politics they think of a large man with a cigar. But you young men resemble him as nearly as a modern physicist resembles the man with the butterfly net and pith helmet. For diplomacy is not your profession, really. Diplomacy is your specialty, your job. Your profession is politics."

A sudden gust of wind blew the doors inward, banging. Someone got up to stop their motion by wedging table napkins under them, leaving them still ajar. The breeze freshened the smell in the room.

"It will be another twenty years before the public wakes up to the fact that you are the new honor guard. When the realization comes, it will come abruptly. The politician grasping for the idiot's illusion of power will vanish into oblivion, along with the alchemist who mixed chemicals merely to find the Elixir of Eternal Life. For they both are naïve brothers under the skin. If a man would live, let him create; for creation is life. Let him work for the love of his creation, the love of life. Ideas are creations; power is an illusion. Ideas live; men die.

"You young men, whatever they call you, economists, industrial analysts, management specialists, mathematicians, who staff our embassies nowadays, are a new breed of politician. But you're the coming breed. You'll be laughed at, scorned, investigated, humiliated, but just remember: Men die. And they die off from the top. The last man of your diverse abilities with a desk in our Paris Embassy was Benjamin Franklin. I hope each one of you does as well and lives as long as he did." The Ambassador paused, looked at each of the younger men.

"I wish you all the best of luck."

For an instant there was abrupt intense silence, a moment of suspended motion and surprise. The wind moved the draperies, a smell of rain. Everyone was simply sitting still looking at him, as the Ambassador looked from one face to another. His expression was uncertain, as though he'd just remembered where he was. The breeze romped, hissed in the shrubbery on the terrace outside the stopped doors. Then for no reason, self-consciously, he shrugged. He lifted his hands as though to show them empty. The speech was over.

The spell broke. Applause came with a single loud crack, crashed like a tree felled on the silence. A scraping of chairs. Everyone rose. Sheppard stood, his hands awkward at his sides, and smiled a full smile of shy gratitude, embarrassment. As the tension drained from his features, he looked spent and happily exhausted; his face betrayed strong sudden emotion. He seemed shaken, bewildered at the applause. He sat down, feeling behind him for the chair, and covered his eyes with his hand, as though to wipe perspiration from his forehead. The dinning applause kept on. Then he looked up, smiling broadly. He was the only man in the room sitting. He nodded over and over to the repeated shouts of the several old gentlemen who kept saying, "Brav-*o*, Shep!" They accented the "o" so that it punctured the coursing applause like pistol shots from a grandstand. The Ambassador was moved, could no longer make any effort to hide it. He sat straight in his chair, dignified in surrender, restrained, tired; his broad smile was difficult, rigid, betrayed completely by the glistening tracery of age on his wet cheeks.

The standing ovation continued for several minutes. Then someone shouted, "Toastmaster!" Instantly the room was hushed. Outside there was a surprise flicker of dry summer lightning. The president looked nearly as moved as the guest of honor. He waited a moment before picking up his glass, as though listening to the soft thrashing of the wind, gathering his thoughts. Then he reached for his wine.

"Gentlemen, a toast." Everyone picked up his glass and waited, expectant. No one moved. The toastmaster turned to the Ambassador. "To a public servant," he said, "a young man with an old dream."

The Ambassador tossed his head back, capitulating with a complete and thankful laugh. Several toasters shouted, "Hear, hear!" and lifted their glasses to him.

As the toast was drunk there was silence, abrupt, complete. Then came the far-off rumble of summer thunder.

V

The meeting of foreign ministers in Paris had been scheduled for very early spring, and had twice been postponed. The preparations were long and arduous. But now the advance guard had arrived. Hundreds of underlings, advisers, experts, consultants, staff officers, procurement specialists, had to precede the arrival of the foreign ministers themselves. Tons of files, furniture, bales of paper, everything had to be shipped in and laid out before the top echelons arrived. It took time.

The Palais Rose was being completely refurbished for the occasion, and the winter strikes and shortages had delayed even this priority work. Now it was almost finished. And in the week that remained before the conference, when all the detailed final touches were done, the toiling harbingers took a holiday. It was like an early tourist season. Minor functionaries rubbed shoulders with major functionaries in an eager competition to absorb as much as Paris had to offer, before their masters arrived to chain them to desks again. They shopped, night-clubbed, saw sights, bought everything from women to hot chestnuts. They brought a small prosperity to a city emerging from winter. Parties were struck up in their honor. They went, danced and drank, and counted not the days to their lords' arrival.

The agonies of winter, the privations of the general strike, the fuel shortages once so grindingly real, seemed dim and faraway. They were not forgotten but merely postponed, memories stored carefully away like winter clothing; memories shed, as animals shed thick winter fur. The seasons had arranged life according to their purposes; survival gave way to regeneration. The sun's slow courtship of the earth was well begun. Already the trees were prematurely heavy with leaves.

The best party of that week's furious round was given by Adelaide Bleibtreu, a Franco-American lady who for the night of her party charmed even the elements. She planned it for the eve of the conference's opening, to snare the real dignitaries.

In her walled garden, weather permitted; it was a fine evening for a party in a garden. Doors, long shut throughout the bitter winter, were left open to the languid air of early evening; across the city soft curtains blew listlessly from windows not yet screened, white silent ghosts that brushed over sills and billowed in the blue-black dusk. And with spring came music. Radios murmured, invisible melodies drifted like intimate perfume on the satisfying garlic of the after-dinner air. It had been the first really hot day, the first warm evening. Adults mingled with cats and late children, whole families sitting in doorways content with the darkness, rich and vibrant with animal promise. Spring brought new life as it brought music. Spring had arrived late, and was welcome. Old men, glad merely to greet another season, savored it in silence. Old enough to know the folly of talk, they sat in profound little groups, or alone in windows, friends thankful for every last tag-end minute of an unvouchered life. They satisfied the evening mood with their silence, sucked on slow-winking coals as they drew on pipes, laced the blue gloom of twilight with ribbons of smoke rising straight and undisturbed; except when a fitful breeze lifted and drained a few final motions from the stillness. Younger males leaned in alert exhibitions against walls, talking quietly, watching movements for signs, their cigarettes winking hot-eyed in the darkness as girls like wraiths passed before their shadows. It was the first real night of awakening, a night when all the shadows had eyes, a night to be possessed carefully, a night of adventure for the young; for the old, thanksgiving.

A night not to be adulterated with lights, or unessential purposes, a night to be mingled with music. An accidental night. A night unforeseen.

Adelaide Bleibtreu was the one American woman among all others in Paris society whose high connections were well published, and whose credentials were so genuine that she could, on the shortest kind of notice, gather the brightest galaxies under the huge crystal chandeliers that dominated her ballroom. She was the granddaughter of the old banker Amos Bleibtreu, a man of taste and breeding whose quiet philanthropies had restored and preserved many of the architectural treasures of France. The old man's passion for anonymity during his lifetime had, even after his death, only extended his power and influence. Among the powerful and the influential he was admired; among the jealous he was envied; among the public he was unknown. It was said at the time of his death that only six people in the whole world knew the total value of his aggregate holdings, and five were his partners, and they kept their knowledge to themselves. The sixth was his granddaughter. The old man was one of those whose advice was sought by heads of sober states, whose knowledge was as broad as his loyalty to friends was firm, who never put his name to any promise that he did not keep. His philanthropies, like his financial operations, were conducted through agents who kept his name private. As he lived, so he died. In private. The only newspaper in the world to carry an extended obituary was the omniscient *London Times* three thousand miles from his New York deathbed. The *Times* reported the event as though it might have been a distant earthquake detected on a local seismograph. By the time the news got back to New York the old man was already buried, as he requested, under a blank tombstone, the location of which was known only to members of his immediate family and their issue. He named his only granddaughter, whose judgment he trusted beyond all others, sole trustee of his will, a will which was quietly probated in twelve countries around the world.

Adelaide Bleibtreu had a head for long matters, but she never married. Her only constant companion was a confirmed bachelor, an old man, the last surviving member of the partnership. Like her grandfather she read widely, enjoyed music, and never kept a secretary. She had loved three men in her life; the last, her only fiancé, had been killed, as her own father and mother had been killed, in an automobile accident that she survived. Her one eccentric indulgence now was racing sports cars. She did it, it was said, in a dispassionate effort to overcome a fear, or, perhaps, to die trying.

The night was perfect for her party, and the party was perfect for her house. The house, a *hôtel particulier*, with a walled fruit orchard behind its formal garden, had once been part of the Rothschilds' landed interests. It was cut off from the city by a high wall, and its sumptuous existence would have been hard to guess from the plan of its unpretentious exterior.

A discerning eye might have read the history of France in its interior woodwork; the latest chapter was incised in the waxed parquet of the ballroom floor by broken glass and German boot heels. No amount of polishing would erase completely the deep scars of wine-drenched revelry. But tonight the floor, still empty of guests, shone under the reflected splendor of a hundred points of light. The three enormous chandeliers had been dug up prism by prism after the war from the sawdust under the floor of the potting shed, cleaned, and reassembled. They hung huge and blazing, three whimsical grape clusters of diamonds, overpowering baubles of crystal brilliance. The orchestra played punctiliously to an empty room.

Most of the early guests, eager young men and correct old countesses, mingled outside in the garden or on the ground floor, exploring the restoration. Diplomatic people were beginning to arrive; having business to conduct in the morning, they arrived ahead of film stars and would leave earlier. Most of them were merely formally attired, leaving display to their thoughtfully gowned wives, but a few bemedaled old gentlemen sailed in like ships of the line flying an alphabet of code flags. One had a huge sunburst pendant on a broad ribbon of watered blue silk that hung around his neck; it dangled like a cycloptic monocle and swung pendulously as he walked toward the garden. His severely gowned wife, following an intimidated pace behind, carried her black velvet train over her arm. Another gentleman had a real monocle. And yet another displayed a chest full of decorations on a diagonal slash of red satin; his elderly wife too had a sashed decoration amid her other jewelry; as they stood before the double doors open on the garden, young people glanced in passing as they might at a gem dealer's showcase.

The hostess extended each guest a hand in delighted greeting.

Outside in the garden, tables were gowned in white tablecloths that fell to the grass. Under the particolored paper lanterns the tables looked like wonderland toadstools. At the farther end was a wooden stage over a wooden dance floor. Lanterns hung in a horseshoe over the orchestra; it was smaller than the one in the ballroom and delicately soft in the lost acoustics of the open sky. A young couple braved the early isolation of the empty platform and enjoyed themselves in an unhampered waltz. The evening was beginning.

An old lady at one of the tables, watching the two dancers, began to tap her fan on her gloved forearm. She was with a young man who resembled her strikingly enough to be her bored son. He sat with his chair turned away from the table, eyes half closed like a somnolent lizard, knees crossed, a cigarette dribbling ashes from his hanging fingers. A white-coated servant ghosted out of the shadows with a tray of champagne and set two glasses on the table. Neither mother nor son noticed him.

The tables were beginning to fill up as guests poured into the garden from the house. Their chatter gave body to the music and made the sky seem less huge, the night less empty.

Stone would enjoy it, she said, it would take him out of himself. She was very cheerful, there was no doubt about that, but Stone's misgivings still hadn't melted. He felt a lack of credentials. And he worried fleetingly about getting drunk. He knew he had a remedy for anxiety, and that remedy was alcohol. But he also knew that he'd been leaning too hard on his crutch over the past months. It now seemed to take more than he could gracefully hold to elevate him above the restless demons he hadn't learned to live with. Fear he knew, insecurity, the feeling that he was burning his bridges; these were among the needles he slept on, but there was something deeper, something he couldn't articulate in his mind, that drove him. Despair came easy these nights. Too easy. Even amid the mindless glitter of highborn pleasures, amid this spectacle of wealth designed to assault the senses, he found himself alone and unable to purge his mind of its disease. He felt anything but easy.

Solange, looking lovely, intelligent, sensitive, seemed to feel him tense the moment she entered on his arm. She gave him a worried frown between the nods and smiles she had for everyone she saw. It surprised Stone that she knew everyone.

She made a striking entrance with this man whom no one knew. By himself Stone was not so impressive, but beside the lovely Solange, people were made to look twice to examine him carefully. The close-fitting evening clothes made a surprising man: the head, with its hard angular features, looked unfinished, the quick handiwork of a master chipping difficult stone; yet the golden proportions were there, available to the imagination's eye underneath the roughwork of the spalling hammer.

Stone didn't fit into any category among the guests. Solange was delighted—she remarked to Stone that she couldn't have got more attention if she had come with a bear in a top hat.

Solange emerged from the ladies' salon, her hair touched with light, and met him at the exit to the garden. She pulled him down and whispered spectacularly in his ear, took his arm; and together they passed through the music that cascaded from the open window of the ballroom over their heads, and descended into the walled garden.

In the garden the hostess moved about among her guests, never out of sight of the glassed-in foyer. She was a handsome woman. At thirty-eight she was younger than most of her social contemporaries, older than most of the bright crowd of younger people whose company she most enjoyed. She worked effortlessly to bridge the gap between these two groups, introducing people, reciting mutual interests, prodding conversation. She worked with the skill of an artist, mixing people as a master chef mixes ingredients for a salad. A little spice here, oil there, vinegar for tang. She sampled conversations along her circuit, as a chef lifts lids off bubbling pots and dips a finger, giving them a stir perhaps. She watched everything, saw everything. She orchestrated her feast without the slightest suggestion of careful thought, noting new arrivals out of the corner of her eye, ready to excuse herself to head off collisions between rival vanities. She directed the flow of champagne in murmured asides to the servants, as an engineer might juggle the gates of an irrigation network. It was early in the evening but she had already marked out the trouble spots. A loud drinker would merely notice that there always seemed to be a crowd of people between himself and the tray-bearing servant; and if that didn't stop him, it would at least preoccupy him. Most of the servants knew what had to be done without being told. The hostess merely accounted their oversights, and rectified them.

The old hawk-eyed countesses watched her performance, missing nothing, and nodded among themselves in grudging satisfaction with their apprentice. The men saw nothing. To them their hostess was merely a charming woman without a difficult thought in her head. The party was a success from the beginning. The older women knew why.

Solange and Stone were snapped up immediately as they descended the stairs into the garden, and were thrown into the breach between the first secretary of the Russian Embassy and an American naval attaché. The English conversation between the two men and their wives seemed to have foundered.

Stone winced inside when he heard his hostess mention the Dujardin case in the introductions. He felt Solange's hand tighten in warning. The naval attaché, it turned out, was from the Embassy in Rome, on leave in Paris with his wife. Stone didn't know him. The Russian examined Stone carefully. His wife was looking with open envy at Solange's eggshell satin gown, almost as though she might at any minute offer to buy it.

Stone shifted his weight on the soft grass and nodded acknowledgment of the introductions. The Russian's handshake was powerful, direct. Stone noticed that he'd already emptied two champagne glasses. They stood incongruously on the grass between his feet. He held a third glass in his hand. Directly over his head hung one of the Japanese lanterns that were strung between the trees in the garden. The naval attaché's wife asked Stone what he did.

"I'm with the government," Stone said. "I was with Graves Registration Command. Now I work liaison between them and the military attaché's office."

The naval officer brightened. "I know some of those people. You're with the Army at the Astoria?"

"Not exactly," Stone said. "That was my old office. Just on a different payroll."

"You're at the Embassy," the Russian said. It wasn't a question, but a statement from prior knowledge. His English was good, slightly British.

"Yes, that's right."

"You used to work under Colonel Crebbs before he went back to the United States."

Stone was impressed at the accuracy of the Russian's knowledge. "Yes."

"You have had troubles over the Dujardin case," the Russian said dryly, smiling.

"Publicity is always trouble," Stone said.

"Ha," the Russian laughed. His wife had followed the interchange like a spectator at a tennis match. From her bright puzzlement Stone concluded that she didn't speak English. The Russian turned and translated Stone's last remark to his wife. She smiled. When she smiled the corners of her mouth turned unexpectedly down. She looked slightly oriental.

"What is this Dujardin case?" the attaché's wife asked. "Was that the thing that was mixed up with that strike in the coal mines last fall?"

"Last winter," her husband corrected. "Yes, dear."

"I must have read something about it," she said defensively.

The Russian laughed. His laughter would have been rude if it hadn't been hearty.

"You should have been here, Madame."

"What did you have to do with it?" the attaché asked Stone.

"I testified at the original inquiry."

"Oh, then you're the one," the attaché said, not too tactfully.

"Your fame has spread," Solange said with thinly veiled sarcasm.

"You Americans are caught in your own net," the Russian said.

Stone ignored the remark. "It's over now," he said to the attaché.

"Perhaps," the Russian said.

There was a certain entertained smugness in the Russian's tone that irritated Stone. He took Solange's hand.

"Would you excuse us while we dance?" he asked.

As they left the group, Stone saw the hostess bringing up fresh reserves. She shot Solange a dazzling smile as they stepped away out of earshot. Solange shrugged eloquently.

"What was that for?" Stone asked.

"We helped her out," Solange said. "Were you serious about dancing?"

"No."

"That's good. I was afraid you were forgetting yourself."

Stone frowned at her. She frowned back in imitation.

"Oh, God. Leave me alone," Stone said. She stopped in her tracks.

"That conversation upset you, didn't it?"

"I didn't want to come here tonight," he said.

"John, I'm sorry. I really am. I thought . . ."

"I know. Have a drink."

"Will you join me?" she asked, serious, sobered.

"It's too early for me. You go ahead." He signaled a waiter.

"Solange"—it was their hostess overtaking them—"that was a mean thing to do to you. You've had your baptism, now come and meet some really interesting people."

She guided them skillfully across the open gravel pathway, ducking with regal grace under the low-hanging bridge of dancing paper lanterns that swung to and fro on an invisible, unfelt breeze. It was as though they moved on the music.

A group of five or six people, military men mostly, stood in a half-circle with their backs toward the gaiety. The conversation looked serious. Two older women, apparently wives used to military society, stood quietly together preserving a look of knowing professional dispassion as they listened with the rest of the men to an older man who was a head taller than the rest. The other men, whose faces were partly visible in three-quarter profile, listened carefully; each face was a study in sincere deep interest.

Stone wondered immediately who the old warrior was who formed the apex of the group. His back was squarely toward them and he stood in the shadow of a tree that fell across the group and precisely bisected it. It wasn't until they were very close that Stone caught the glint of light off the four gold stars on his right shoulder, and recognized something familiar in the tall angular stance.

They rounded the flank of the small group, the hostess in the lead, and were suddenly standing facing the semicircle. The old man had evidently just finished saying something that called for consideration, for no one except the two women seemed to take notice of the fact that their hostess had joined the group. The men were looking at the ground reflectively, two of them nodding soberly, another rubbing his chin and staring up into the open early sky. Suddenly the old general saw the new arrivals and stepped forward, offering both hands to his hostess. He was very warm and gracious. The others snapped out of their thoughts and peered in the bad light to see who had arrived out of the shadows.

"Ah, my dear," said the general. Adelaide Bleibtreu grasped his hands warmly. "We sneaked past you coming in. You seemed to have your hands full. It's a pleasure to see you again."

"I saw you out of the corner of my eye, you old rogue. You were avoiding me because you thought I'd drag you off to meet someone."

"Good evening, Adelaide," said one of the women, the general's wife.

"How are you both? I was afraid you wouldn't leave Washington in time."

"We took an early plane especially to be here, my dear. Léon sends his best. He saw us off. We have a present for you from him, but the trunks aren't unpacked yet. We just got here this afternoon."

"I'm so glad. I'd like you all to meet two people I think you'll enjoy. General and Mrs. Fletcher, Madame Récamier and Mr. John Stone. Mr. Stone is a compatriot of yours."

The general relaxed genially with unexpected laughter. "Well, now. I know you both. Young lady, I held you on my knee when you were small enough to put in my pocket. Your father and I were close friends during the First War. What do you think of that, now?"

Solange took his hand and curtsied splendidly. The general's wife beamed at her.

"And I know of Mr. Stone from—well, this is hardly the occasion—" The general laughed again. "But perhaps you remember Colonel Jay, Mr. Stone?"

"I do indeed, sir."

"He'll be General Jay in a few weeks. You should send him a note. I think he'd be glad to hear from you. He's told me something of your exploits—past *and* present, that is."

Stone smiled, shrugging. The other members of the group looked curiously at Stone, as though reassessing him. Stone recognized the air attaché from the British Embassy, and remembered that he had served on Fletcher's staff in London during the war.

"Jay thinks a great deal of you, Mr. Stone."

Stone smiled. "It gives me a great deal of pleasure to hear that, sir. I haven't seen the colonel since . . . it must have been the end of 1945."

"You should write to him. I think he feels a little responsible for some of the— Well, now, this is a *party*, isn't it. If we must talk shop, let's at least keep the discussion general. We were just talking about the Rommel book. Have you seen it? It's just out in the States."

"I haven't done much reading these last months, sir."

"Well, no, I don't imagine."

The general actually hurumphed, apologetically, and took up his stance again with his back to the tree. It was a signal for the discussion which had been interrupted to recommence.

"I agree with you," said the British air attaché. "About Rommel, that is."

"Probably for the wrong reasons," the general said with a gruff laugh.

"Probably." He nodded, smiled.

Soft laughter drifted across from another group, as though in answer. Everyone turned in surprise to look, but they were laughing at some joke of their own. A short fat girl in an expensive-looking gown was balancing a champagne glass on her head, to the delight of the others. "You see," she squealed, "I'm quite sober." Just as she said it the glass teetered and slipped, raining champagne onto the clipped turf. There was a howl of laughter and everyone in the garden paused to look and smile.

The whole evening was in a mood of indulgent high gaiety. From the open floor-length doors of the ballroom upstairs music spilled out onto the wide steps that descended into the garden. Couples stood in twos and threes in the tiny balconies that marked each window of the ballroom, like a row of opera boxes. The three huge chandeliers blazed high over the heads of the dancers invisible inside. Couples came and went on the balconies, glasses in hand, looking down on the garden, where the members of the orchestra were refreshing themselves, between waltzes, from a tray served up to them by an incredibly tall old servant. The night air was warm and perceptibly humid between the idle breaths of wind that dipped over the vine-tangled walls and stirred the leaves in the garden.

A servant bearing a tray of champagne drifted toward them from the gloom of wherever it was that the inexhaustible supply came from, somewhere behind the little construction that served as an orchestra stage. He offered it in turn to the two older women, Solange, then the general, and lastly, in order of descending rank, the others. Stone and the general were the only ones who declined. Their hostess had excused herself and vanished inconspicuously.

"It's hard to believe," the general was saying, "that Paris would ever be like this again. Bryan, did you ever think, when we were dodging buzz bombs back there in London, that we'd all meet again to stand under the stars here, with music—this calls for a toast of some sort." The general started forward, but the servant had evidently heard; he was already turning around to offer the tray again. Stone had to take the last glass—it was a toast.

"Here now, to Paris. No, better: To Peace and Paris. May there never be another war to separate them." The general held his glass high and then drank. Stone and the others drank with him. Solange drained hers also. The general's wife turned her head back, expertly not taking more than a few drops for all her gusto.

There was a long awkward silence. Suddenly the British major and the heavy-set civilian standing at the general's left both began talking at once. Both stopped instantly; the civilian determinedly deferred to the major.

"I was just going to ask—about the North African campaign—do you think Europe can be defended any better?"

"Land can always be defended. It's a question of how, and for how long. Strategically, it might not be wise to defend it with infantry. That's the point I was trying to make about Africa. The last war opened up a number of interesting questions. For example, I'd like to see a good political scientist take up the whole concept of governments-in-exile. *Can* a government be separated from the soil it governs? If so, what does it govern? The people? I'm not sure at all of that. There is some question whether De Gaulle, for one example, had the consent of the governed in setting up a government outside metropolitan France. This goes to the root of some very basic questions in political philosophy —which is not my field. But military philosophy—if you can call it that—*is* my field, and it depends in large measure on political concepts."

The general's wife smiled.

"Ladies, are we boring you?" the general asked with a slight, old-fashioned, bowing nod in their direction.

"Not at all, dear," said his wife, "I'm sure I'm the only one who's heard it all before."

"Please do go on, General," Solange said. "After all, I am French, I live in Europe."

"The ladies are forbearing," the general said.

"I don't see what difference it makes if the government survives in exile after the country is lost," the heavy-set civilian said. Stone thought he had seen his face somewhere but couldn't place it.

"Well, now, Teddy, up to the present day the object of war has always been to secure territory, the land. But there's some real question whether that will continue to be the object of war. Times have changed. In an industrial world, merely capturing territory without at the same time capturing the allegiance of the people in it, is to hang a millstone around your neck. In the old days, the land *was* the thing. But today, even farming is a highly complex undertaking. Without organization, farming reverts back to a one-mule operation. What I'm trying to say is that a country's value, since the industrial revolution, lies in something other than mere territory. It lies in its organization—or as the French say, its *organisme*. That's more accurate. A country is an organism. If you can't capture the organism alive and whole, it's not worth taking. You can't get efficient production out of people unless you have their allegiance. It's really a very simple-minded notion I have here."

"Not at all," said the civilian. Stone recognized him suddenly: Theodore Redmond, a retired director of the American Express Company in France. Stone had heard him speak at a Museum Club luncheon right after the war. "It might be simple-minded coming from a newspaper columnist. But from a military man—that's different."

"But from a military point of view, you can't just *abandon* the country," the attaché said. The others in the group seemed content to listen.

"It is no longer necessary to be *in* a country to wage a battle for the minds of the inhabitants. We have all sorts of remote means of reaching them. Radio, for example. The mere fact of instantaneous mass communication has changed the basic concepts not only of politics but of war also."

"But sooner or later you have to take the country with infantry."

"Of course. The point is how and when. There is one thing you're overlooking. Whoever starts a modern war of the territorial variety—like the last one, for instance—has the odds heavily against him."

"But the advantage of surprise . . ."

". . . may be far outweighed by the disadvantage of overextension. The hard facts of plane geometry are that a circle's perimeter increases six times as rapidly as its radius. In the case of Germany, for example, for every sixteen kilometers they pushed into surrounding territories, their battle perimeter was lengthened by a hundred kilometers. This fact was not lost on the German General Staff. They knew that their only chance to hold part of Europe was to hold all of it. They drove straight to the sea, using tanks that didn't stop to mop up infantry. Once infantry is disorganized, cut off from its command centers, it is worse than useless, because there is no greater demoralizer than disorganized infantry. The whole country knew it within a matter of hours, and the battle for France was over."

Solange said, "I can remember them coming back along the roads."

Stone looked at her profile. She looked incredibly young tonight, and very beautiful, her bare neck and shoulders strikingly white in the half-darkness. He could see the long neck tendon stretch smooth and straight as she raised her chin in a sort of defiant gesture, and turned her head away from him with a small shudder of remembrance.

"Yes," said an older man quietly.

"Infantry must be used with extreme caution in defense. The most common failure among field commanders—my opinion, of course—is not knowing when to retire their infantry. Too often they're worrying about getting their artillery moved out first. It's an old question, I suppose. There's no substitute for that uncanny knack that some commandders develop, of knowing just how to hand out hollow victories. You might say that in modern war, the strategy of defense reduces to making the adversary fight a stiff fight for a series of empty bags. Sooner or later he'll get careless. Then, when he's properly overextended from his source of supply, you let him step into what he thinks is an empty bag, and pull the drawstrings on him."

"If you haven't been pushed into the sea first," the British attaché said wryly.

"*If* you haven't been pushed into the sea first," the general agreed, nodding seriously.

At that moment a short fat man in the uniform of a British colonel came up, towed by the hostess. Behind them came another servant bearing the ever present tray of champagne. The colonel puffed into the group and literally exploded a greeting to General and Mrs. Fletcher. Everyone else drew a little aside. The colonel had a very red face, even in the poor light, and carried champagne sloshing in a glass in his right hand. He changed hands with the glass, drying his hand discreetly on his tunic, and shook hands with Mrs. Fletcher, who nevertheless seemed genuinely glad to see him. The hostess leaned near Solange and said, "Come. There's someone I want you to meet."

Stone accepted a glass of champagne without thinking, put his empty one back on the tray, and followed a dutiful few steps behind Solange and his hostess. The last thing he heard from the group was from the general, who in seeing his old friend was oblivious to the general dispersion.

"What's an old nanny like you doing still in uniform?" The general called after the departing Mr. Redmond: "Teddy, don't go away. I'd like you to meet the best M.O. ever spawned in England."

Stone walked after Solange, watching the hem of her ball gown brush across the grass with the concealed rhythm of her stride. He was sorry to leave the general. It had been like meeting someone who'd just stepped out of a newsreel; he had recognized him immediately when he saw his face clearly. He had been a little shocked when General Fletcher said that he knew about him from Jay. He wondered about Jay. He hadn't thought of him for several months, although once he *had* thought of writing him. He was astonished to feel the effects of the single glass of champagne; it came as a warning twinge. He frowned, dismissed it from his mind. He wondered what an M.O. was.

"Are you coming?" Solange stopped to wait for him. "What in the world are you thinking about?"

"Thinking about? Nothing."

"Yes, you were. Tell me," she insisted.

"I was wondering what an M.O. is," he said simply.

"It's a medical officer, silly. For a worldly one you don't know very much."

"I'm not really very worldly," he said.

"I'm beginning to believe. Do you want me to take that?" she asked, pointing to the full glass of champagne he was absent-mindedly balancing in his hand.

He looked down at it as though he hadn't realized he was carrying it.

"This? No. I've just decided that I may as well get drunk tonight too." He said it with a forced laugh.

The smile faded from her face. "You think that's clever, don't you."

"You'll take care of me."

"Yes, I will. But do you think—"

"I don't think any more," he said. "It hurts too much to think."

"I shouldn't have made you come tonight," she said, deflated.

"No, you shouldn't have." He drank off half the champagne, spilling a drop on his shirt front, and handed the glass to Solange.

"I thought it would cheer us both up to get out of the apartment for one evening."

"Well, I'm cheered up. Let's leave it at that. What happened to our guide? Weren't we supposed to meet someone else?"

"I pleaded innocence," she said. "Begged off for both of us."

"Will you really look after me?" Stone asked blandly, gazing up at a paper lantern.

"I said I would." She sipped defensively at the champagne.

Out of the corner of his eye he saw a tray of drinks passing. He left Solange and went after it, coming back a moment later with two carefully balanced glasses.

"Do you have to go at it with such a vengeance?" she said, accepting the glass, stooping to put the empty one on the grass. Her shoulders were lovely, slender in profile; sensual perceptions, forms, her gestures, were beginning to crowd his mind.

"Just get me out of here before I make a fool of myself," he said.

"You're not a fool," she said, studiedly angry, "you're tragic."

"I know it," he said. He knew she was covering real anger with false. Then he said, "On second thought, you're wrong. I'm not noble enough to be tragic."

"Does it always have to be all or nothing with you? Why can't you just relax, so I can relax?"

"It was your idea to undertake my rehabilitation, not mine," Stone said. "You said yourself that you're attracted to men with scars and broken noses. This is my broken nose." He held up the glass. "And my battle scar." She stared at it and then looked at him silently. He felt foolish holding the glass up, so he toasted her.

"If you won't take care of yourself for your own sake, why don't you do it for me?"

He looked at her, momentarily nonplused.

"For you? Why should I do it for you? The good-hearted Madame Sessions asks you to exorcise the demons from an ungifted former cellist, and you . . ."

"You're talking as if you're drunk already. The good-hearted Madame Sessions didn't ask me to live with you. That was my own idea."

"But I'm not drunk. It doesn't take much these days—God knows that's true—but I haven't even had that much. I only *wish* I were drunk."

"Even for my sake . . . ?" She laid a hand on his forearm. He looked at the white-gloved fingers for a moment and then back at her. He could feel himself perspiring under his arms.

"You wouldn't like me without my broken nose," he said finally.

"You're being impossibly childish."

"I was never childish when I was young," he said softly, gazing over her shoulder again at a swinging paper lantern, "I'm paying my debt to childhood—" And then with a self-deprecating grimace: "To my lost youth." He held up his glass. "Will you join me in a toast to my lost youth?"

Silently she raised her glass and finished it. He watched her over the brim of his without drinking. She *was* angry, that much was clear. On impulse he handed her his own glass untouched. She took it without a word and drank that one too, and then leaned over and put them both on the ground beside the other. She came up flushed and angry, and made a mock curtsy before him. He knew he should say something generous, but waited too long.

"Perhaps now we'll dance," she said. "We'll see who is going to take care of whom."

The orchestra was beginning a tango, very slow and halting. The music sounded small and delicate in the open space of the garden. In the background, even on the dancing platform, they could hear the high squeal of the larger orchestra in the ballroom—thin jazz from the far end of the walled garden—it was playing imitation American ragtime, half in the style of New Orleans; it sounded naïve, antique. People were drifting out of the garden up into the house, drawn by bursts of applause from upstairs, which gave evidence that an entertainment was on.

Stone felt the sharp point of one of her earrings digging into his chin. It was painful in a mildly pleasant way; he didn't move his head. Once he tried closing his eyes, but it gave him the feeling of falling. They danced slowly, not keeping at all to the figures of the tango, and too close together to be dancing in good form, but it hardly mattered. In a warm mood of alcohol and her sharp perfume, he wondered if he loved this woman.

After a short time they were the only couple left dancing in the garden. He could tell she hadn't forgiven him, and the knowledge pleased him in a perverse way, even though he was actively thinking how to phrase an apology for what he felt had been mere rudeness. But they didn't speak, only danced slowly, linked in the antagonistic rhythms of another tango. Several unliveried servants appeared from behind the scenes, like stagehands suddenly appearing from the wings, to take advantage of the mass exodus of guests to clean up the tables a bit, change the cloths where drinks had been spilled. One of them had a long stick with a nail on it that he used to stab cigarette butts out of the grass. They moved in a phalanx under the direction of two of their number, and having made the round of the garden, everything put to rights, vanished into the wings again along the dark paths that led to the house.

Stone closed his eyes, surrendering to the warm alarming dizziness. He could taste the aftertaste of the champagne, and his mouth felt parched and dry. It always happened. It would take a few more drinks. The palm of his left hand, against Solange's glove, felt uncomfortably hot and moist. He began to feel an urge for a drink, a real, shocking urge, the first strong one of the night. It flooded through him like a trance of slow panic, a cold dread that was almost welcome. The question was settled, at least there was that relief. He shut his mind to it, and squeezed her hand so hard that she drew back and looked at him, puzzled. Consciously he fixed his features in a melancholy smile and drew her to him gently. They danced toward the edge of the dais.

"I'm sorry for behaving like a fool," he whispered in her ear.

"It doesn't matter," she said. Her voice sounded strained.

He drew apart from her and looked at her, was shocked to find tears in her eyes. She returned his gaze fully, refusing to turn her head away. They stopped dancing and stared at each other for several seconds.

The orchestra stopped playing. One by one the men laid down their instruments and ducked off the stage under a bobbing string of paper lanterns and disappeared behind their flower-decked podium. Stone and Solange were alone.

"That's only going to make things worse," he said softly.

"It doesn't matter," she said again. "Let's go upstairs."

From the upstairs ballroom came only absolute silence. A single cricket started in the grass. Then suddenly a roar of crowded laughter and applause poured down from the ballroom.

Solange looked at him. "Please," she said. "They have comedians . . . clowns from the Cirque Medrano." She looked at him, pleading, tears sliding down her cheeks.

They left the dais and slowly crossed the soft silent grass toward the house. As they mounted the gravel path toward the broad terraced entrance the only sound was the rustle of Solange's dress and the crunch of their footsteps on the gravel. Stone waited as Solange paused to dab at her eyes. The garden was completely deserted. And then, drenched in another sudden downpour of wild hilarity from above, they left the walled garden; and mounted the red-carpeted marble stairway toward light and laughter.

Midnight supper was served, after the comedians. Stone found himself separated from Solange by a little knot of Marshall Planners, young men who looked like university instructors or advertising executives, newcomers who hadn't yet learned to blend into the social landscape. They talked earnestly, and Stone couldn't help listening idly. He was beginning to feel a warm glow from the champagne, and he listened without looking.

". . . The trouble is that no one in Congress understands the difference between an American and a European capitalist. In Europe, capitalism grew out of feudalism. It really and truly did. In America we had no feudal tradition. American capitalism grew up in the days of the frontiers. It was wide open. In Europe it was all closed up. That's why in Europe you get cartels, while in America the tendency is toward monopoly. A cartel is the more dangerous in my estimation because it's harder to prove, and therefore harder to control. A Frenchman I know told me yesterday that as soon as two businessmen enter the same room, you have a cartel. He knew what he was talking about. . . ."

The supper music in the ballroom rose to a graceful crescendo and suddenly stopped. From the tall open doors to the balcony came the drift of delicate strings on the gentle stir of night air that rose from the garden below. The few dancers not caring about food stood in their places waiting for the orchestra to begin again. A dignified couple at a nearby table watched them, morose, abstracted. The woman stole a glance at her tiny watch under her glove and leaned back in her chair. She hadn't touched her champagne.

Stone smiled to himself without turning around. He was enjoying a sudden liberating sense of solitude. From where he was standing he could hear snatches of Solange's conversation with a young Swiss she'd introduced him to earlier. He had no desire to join them. He was close enough to the windows to be able to see the late-rising moon over the wall of the garden, and he watched it for a long time, feeling light-headedly melancholy. It *was* a beautiful night. All around him people were grouped in bright clusters, eating and talking and gay. The orchestra began again, a waltz, and the brilliant din flowed around him, a broken torrent around a rock, poured out the doors and spilled over the balcony into the garden. A beautiful night. And there it was—all for him.

Stone followed Solange and his hostess into the salon off the ball-room. He had a sense of being out of things; this was a world Solange seemed to move easily in, but for Stone it was remote and vaguely unreal. The unreality was heightened by the fact that he was privately enjoying himself; he was beginning to feel the liquor take effect. It gave him a feeling of being different, irrevocably separated from the rest of the party, from the music and the dancing and the gay laughter; he took less pleasure in allowing himself to drink than he took in the heightened sense of being alone, cut off from them in a private world —a world purged and ennobled by an alcoholic sense of tragedy and futility, a world those around him could never enter because they were too content where they were. The real pleasure lay not in the drinking, but in the perversity.

They were making room for him at a circular table; several people greeted Solange as she sat down. Introductions were made; Stone nodded and smiled automatically as one by one the names flew past and escaped him. The women were middle-aged and handsome, half of them French, it seemed, half of them American. The men smoked cigars, sounded sure of themselves, smelled rich. Stone smiled and tried to look as though he was listening; actually he was listening to his own thoughts.

The talk had turned to a book Stone had never heard of, and limped along aimlessly into fishing.

Finally there were several small conversations going. The ladies were talking about another lady who wasn't present. After a further polite interval Solange turned to Stone and made a little sign of inter-rogation. He nodded, and together they got up to leave. They said good-by to everyone except a bearded man, who was looking under the table for a lady's shoe.

Stone just managed to intercept a servant and relieve him of two glasses of champagne before the man steered the huge tray out of the room.

"Dull bunch," Stone said as he raised his glass.

"I thought you'd enjoy meeting them," Solange said. She sipped her drink.

"Why should I enjoy meeting *them?*" he asked. "Who are they anyway?"

"Don't you know who the one with the beard was?"

"No," Stone said rudely.

Solange looked at him. "I think you're getting drunk," she said.

"No skin off my nose," Stone said, drinking off his champagne.

In the ballroom, dancing began again at one o'clock. In the garden, however, an American jazz band was to provide a half-hour's relaxation for those who wanted a rest; the musicians arrived carrying their own instruments, drums and a huge bass viol included, and quietly began setting up on the stage at the far end of the garden. The members of the small regular orchestra stood politely off to one side, watching with interest, smoking, talking among themselves. They seemed to defer to the American musicians; certainly the Americans were a strange and imposing group. They worked like master bricklayers squaring up their foundation; the biggest drum was set up and tested with a few smart thumps of the foot pedal, and the stool was adjusted to height with a telephone book urgently fetched from the house—a puzzled servant carried it down the graveled path as though it were a velvet cushion bearing a crown. The musicians laughed arcanely among themselves as they surveyed the crowd and began to tune their instruments. None of the glittering crowd in the garden was watching them particularly.

The players readied themselves. The leader, a huge man who used his saxophone as a baton, holding it in one hand like a club, stamped out four cannonlike beats on the booming drumlike platform; and the quiet garden disintegrated in a soaring pandemonium of sound. Every head in the crowd pivoted toward the sudden music. Transfixed by the electric excitement, talking ceased as though struck by an ax.

The six men on the bandstand played with absolute and insolent certainty that they would be listened to. The assembled society in the garden was struck dumb with hypnotic surprise. Beside the unobtrusive music they'd been not-listening to earlier, the sound that filled and overflowed the garden now was commanding, pure; it wouldn't be ignored. The leader had set a powerful tempo; and when he lifted his horn to play, he played as though wielding a hammer. The beat pounded out into the night, and the music slammed up against the walls of the house like a tidal wave, reversing the gentle stream cascading down from the open windows of the ballroom. People upstairs, curious, had stopped dancing and were squeezing out onto the narrow window balconies; younger couples fled the ballroom entirely and ran inelegantly downstairs.

After the first paralyzing impact wore off in the garden, people streamed toward the bandstand, where six powerful feet beat time on the flimsy rocking platform. Over the heads of the players the fragile string of Japanese lanterns bobbed and jumped to the stomping tempo like beads on a fiddlestring. The crowd pressed on toward the music, mere moths delighted before an open flame. In the empty ballroom upstairs the liquid decorum of tempered strings vanished, evaporated.

Stone, with Solange on his arm, was carried out into the garden on the flood of people coursing down the wide stairs toward the music. Solange looked happy and craned her neck to see over the crowd to the end of the garden.

"Come *on,*" she said to Stone, tugging with sudden excitement at his arm.

"Where did *they* come from?" Stone asked, his tongue a little thick from the champagne. "Don't pull on me. You're spilling our drink."

"Oh, you make me depressed," Solange said impatiently. She was not entirely sober herself. "I don't want to be depressed. I'll find you later and be depressed afterward."

She slipped her arm away from Stone and was suddenly gone, swallowed in the press of people. Stone started after her and then gave up, slipping out to one side of the crowd. Once out of the mainstream, he turned and walked back toward the house. Someone had jostled his arm and emptied the last of the champagne from his glass; he searched around for a white-coated servant but there were none in sight. He went inside and headed up the empty stairs to the bar.

The bar was set up in a small room off the ballroom. Besides the three bored waiters who were dispensing, the only other people there were two stout men huddled in conversation in one corner. They looked to Stone like two businessmen consummating a deal, and probably were. He hardly glanced at them, went straight to the bar.

Stone asked for champagne, but was told that the bottles had just been placed in ice and weren't chilled yet. With only a slight twinge of conscience he took whiskey and water instead, and sat down alone at one of the small tables. Through the vaulted archway to the deserted ballroom, the bored music of the ballroom orchestra commenced again, mingled fruitlessly with the distant driving rhythms of the jazzmen in the garden below.

Listening, thinking about nothing, he sipped his drink with quiet fatalistic resignation. He felt peaceful away from the crowd.

Stone finished his first whiskey slowly, refusing to think about the consequences; knew vaguely he would be hopelessly drunk in a few hours. The only excuse he could offer himself was that Solange would get him out of there before he became unmanageable or unconscious. Outside in the garden he could hear the splash of applause as the band finished the second number.

He felt relaxed and almost happy; yet he knew that the decision to get drunk had been made too easily. He drank slowly, but in his mind he was already committed, and knew he was going to regret it; he always regretted it. But as he finished his first drink the cloud vanished from his mind and he rose to get another. Outside they were clapping again.

Just as he got up from the table, one of the two men in the corner, the one with his back to him, turned around: to his confused surprise Stone saw Abe Sellers peering across the room at him. Without seeming to recognize him, Sellers went back to his conversation. Stone remembered that Sellers was near-sighted.

Stone felt intense discomfort at seeing him, and was about to turn and leave the room when Sellers ended his conversation. The man he had been talking to shook hands and turned and strode past Stone. He went out through the arch. Stone turned his back and asked for another whiskey, hoping that Sellers would pass by without noticing him. Then he heard Sellers ordering a cognac and soda; he was standing next to him.

Sellers didn't turn to look at him but said, "Is John Stone avoiding someone?"—almost as though talking to himself.

Stone felt quietly furious that Sellers had led him into thinking he hadn't recognized him, felt doubly angry at being caught in his own flimsy effort at deception.

He turned to Sellers. "Should I be overjoyed at seeing one of my examiners?" he asked with more irritation than he wanted to show. He found he had difficulty focusing his eyes.

"Come and sit down," Sellers said. "I'll ply you with drink."

"What are *you* doing here, spying for the Embassy?" Stone asked, feeling stupid for saying it. Stone was surprised at the sudden drunken bitterness he felt.

"Are you drunk?"

"I'm working on it," he said, enunciating carefully.

"I'll join you," Sellers said calmly. He preempted both drinks from the barkeeper and carried them to the table. Stone accompanied him automatically.

Sellers seated himself carefully, and then lifted his glass. "First a toast," he said. "Abe Sellers resigned from the service of his government this very morning." He looked at his watch. "No," he corrected, "time has intervened. Time—*amicus curiae*. Make that yesterday morning."

Stone looked at him. "You quit?" he said drunkenly.

"The United States Foreign Service has lost a brilliant lawyer. I am sincerely unhappy for them."

"Why did you quit?"

"I'm old—that is, I'm older. I decided that the time has come to live nobly again. I have a private income, so I can afford to."

"Did they ask you to resign?" Stone insisted. "Why did you quit?"

"No, I'm happy to say, they did not. In fact they begged me to stay. Offered bigger and better things. I *am* a brilliant lawyer, you know." Sellers paused and removed his glasses. "Or I was in my day," he added, sighing. He wiped his thick-lensed spectacles and put them back on.

"I think you're a little tight yourself," Stone said.

"The intoxication of new-found honor," Sellers said. He drank, toasting Stone. "I resent strongly that you would think I might tattle on you for getting loaded. Even though I have, apparently, stumbled on you *in flagrante delicto*."

"What will you do, go back to the States?" Sellers' face floated in and out of focus in Stone's vision. The thick lenses magnified his watery eyes, made him look wide-eyed, almost innocent, though still unblinking like an owl.

"Not for a while. Right now I'm devoting all my time to being an expatriot. I'm going to stay here for a while. I'm needed here."

"By whom?"

"By you, Stone, for one. There are others."

"Oh?" Stone focused on Sellers. The floating eyes peered back, innocent, inquiring. "You going to make a career of saving souls?"

"The Ambassador tells me that you don't want to fight your conviction."

"It's not sure that I'll be fired. And besides, it's not a conviction, as I think you yourself once reminded me," Stone said, carefully separating his words. He was trying too hard to sound diffident.

"I was wrong. Let me put you straight. First, you *will* be fired. Second—"

"Wait. Why will I be fired?"

"Because everyone is frightened. Even if you're cleared of all taint of being a security risk, no one will have the guts to keep you on their staff. Your stigmata might rub off on them, you see."

"They'll get me on *this*," Stone said, smiling foolishly into his glass. It suddenly struck him as comical, getting drunk with Sellers.

Sellers nodded. "That will be the lever they'll use to pry you loose, the club to beat you into submission, the rack on which your unhappy soul will be stretched. I wax eloquent on your demise. It's the barroom lawyer in me."

"God damn the whole business." Stone took a huge gulp of his drink.

Sellers winced visibly. "Must you drink with such deadly seriousness? Why—to defy them?"

"I don't know," Stone said, suddenly serious. "Liquor never did anything for me until recently. Now I get high just sniffing it. I don't hold it like I used to. My liver must be sick or something."

"You never drank heavily before this?" Sellers asked.

"Before what?"

"This—this whole business."

"Nothing changes. I manage. I've had bad times before. I don't know why I drink. Except that when I'm tanked I feel satisfied with myself, and warm, and the hell with it. Do you think that's funny? You know how when a drunk falls down he feels no pain? That's how I feel."

"That's fine, just fine. Security in a bottle."

"I like security. That's why I'm a security risk. If they didn't keep it locked up in a safe I'd steal it."

"And sell it to the Russians?" Sellers asked.

"Hell, no. I'd drink it. Let the Russians find their own damn security."

"Stone, if I ever buy myself an embassy, you'll be the first man I'll hire. I'll put you in charge of security."

"What's the second thing?" Stone asked, suddenly truculent again.

"What second thing?"

"You said there were two things. First I'll be fired . . ."

"You're not as drunk as I am," Sellers said, almost admiringly. "Well, the second thing is that it *is* a conviction, anyway you look at it. Ignore the doubletalk and trust your common sense. I'm a lawyer. I know a conviction when I see one."

"What am I going to be convicted of besides being an unhappy drunk?"

"That's crime enough. But that's unimportant. If you don't fight this thing . . ." Sellers paused to drink, frowning.

"Yes?"

"You're a coward. Cowardice. That's what you'll stand convicted of, my friend."

"I'm not fool enough to butt my head on a wall," Stone said thickly. "Even if I did fight it, you think for one second I'd have a chance of winning the appeal?"

"No."

"Then why fight it?" Stone shrugged and drank. "Why should I spend my last nickel betting on a fixed wheel?"

"Because unless you and all the others like you come out in the open and demand redress, there'll never be any redress. If you're so afraid or ashamed of yourself that you won't fight it, it will all be swept under the rug. And it'll be your fault. You'll deserve precisely what you'll get—nothing."

"I've got better things to do with my money than hire lawyers."

Over the rim of his glass Sellers said, "Suppose I told you that I'd take your case, at no fee." He held the glass in both hands, elbows on the table, squinting between his upright thumbs at Stone, as though measuring his features for a portrait. He had a faint smile on his face.

Stone looked at his drink and said nothing. He felt giddy.

"That makes it harder to refuse, doesn't it?" Sellers said.

"I can't think about it tonight," Stone said, looking into his glass.

"I wonder if you can think about it at all."

"They want me to resign," Stone said. He had trouble keeping Sellers' face from slipping out of his vision, tried to concentrate on the eyes.

"Don't."

"I've already caused embarrassment just by being on his staff . . ." Stone began, with thick irony. "The Ambassador . . ."

"I'll take his case too."

584

"You're a smart bastard, aren't you, Sellers?" Stone said unpleasantly.

"I know him better than you do, perhaps. He told you to fight it, didn't he? How can you fight if you resign?"

"Why did you quit?" Stone asked suddenly. "The real reason."

"Stone, I'm going to tell you something. I quit because I couldn't take it any longer. And I've got a thick skin. But . . ."

"That's no reason," Stone said. "And it's hardly a tragedy."

Sellers continued, talked without noticing that Stone didn't seem to be following. "About tragedy: Tragedy is different for each age. For the Greeks it was man against the gods. For the Elizabethans it was man against something else—I've forgotten—other men, perhaps. But for this age, it's man against himself. Tragedy for our century is the devotion of a man to a cause that he knows in his heart to be base."

"So?"

"I didn't spend all my years in the Law just so I could be privileged to read how you while away your sinful private hours. Do you know that I know more about where you spend your nights, and with whom, than I would if I was—God forbid—your wife? Do you know that?"

"Well . . ." Stone knew he wasn't following the thread of Sellers' argument, but was concentrating only on holding the watery blue eyes in focus.

"I'm a lawyer, Stone, not your conscience. Burke said something that's illuminating. He said: For me to love my country, my country must first be lovely."

"Why don't you tear up your green passport and leave the rest of us in peace?" Stone asked morosely. He finished his drink, draining the glass slowly.

"That's the easy way, my friend. But perhaps not as easy as your way, which is to stand by and let someone tear it up for you."

"I'm a drunk and a coward," Stone said. "And you have a private income. Fee-fi-fo-fum." He felt an urge to do something surprising, to stand up and sing, perhaps, make a fool of himself, embarrass Sellers. But the urge passed. He couldn't think of anything to sing.

"I don't care what you are. I don't care if you're as guilty as sin. But I can't make cases without plaintiffs. I assure you my motives are as selfish as they are selfless, if that's any consolation to you. I fancy myself as a knight without a lance. I'm sick of reading case histories, sorting other people's dirty linen. I want to get back to arguing Law. *Law*. I'm indulging myself, if you will."

"I don't know," Stone mused. "How long is the offer open?"

"As long as Abe Sellers has breath left to perform on it."

At a sudden, unpremeditated signal from Stone, the waiter brought two more drinks. Sellers sat making circles in the moisture on the table with the end of his little finger.

"When will I be fired, do you think?" Stone asked. Although he felt drunker, his speech was less fuzzy than before.

"Have you received what they call the formal interrogatory letter yet?"

"Yes." Stone laughed too loud, falsely, bitterly; he knew the alcohol was making him exaggerate.

"What do you think of it?"

"It's silly." Stone shrugged. "Did you see it before it was sent to me?"

"No. I saw the rough draft."

"One of the new charges I have to answer is . . . I'm alleged to have said that the idea of God is unspeakable."

"Did you say that?"

Stone laughed too sharply again; one of the barmen turned his head and looked at him, bored, unperturbed. "I did. I remember exactly when it was. It was at a party Solange—a party a friend took me to. Artists. Americans. I meant that if God exists, the idea is too big for human beings to comprehend. I was trying to be social, get into discussion. I meant that speech is finite, and if God is infinite, then obviously you can't speak about . . . that's what I meant. The idea of God is unspeakable." Stone put down his glass. "I'm too drunk," he said. "I get ineffable when drunk—only I don't really know what the word means. What do you care, anyway?"

Sellers put down his drink carefully and smiled. "I didn't know you were a theologian, Stone."

"I'm not. Seemed like a bunch of just nice serious kids. Left Bank. Students, artists, and a few girls . . . from Smith College. Trying to be intellectual and serious—*and* nice. They were young and pretty. Liked them. I sat on the floor with them and drank their wine. Tried to enter into . . . spirit of the thing. Felt like a damned scoutmaster."

"Unfortunately poverty has corrupted some of the more venal among them. Not the girls, of course."

A burst of applause floated in from the garden outside.

"What do you mean?" Stone asked.

"Twenty-five dollars a week doesn't mean much to us, but it can mean a lot to some kid trying to live on a G.I. check."

"You mean we pay children to inform?" asked Stone. He laughed. "God, no wonder these damned kids . . . so cynical."

"Confidential funds don't have to be accounted for, Stone," Sellers said. "You ought to know that. You spent enough of them during the war, I imagine."

"This is peacetime. These kids . . . all Americans."

Sellers sipped his drink. "Now you can see why I'm an ex-patriot. I've been a patriot too long. My head muscles were getting stiff. It's time to ask a few embarrassing questions. There's been entirely too much *unquestioning* loyalty in our fair country, Stone. Things have become unlovely."

"I'm getting drunk," Stone announced. "You're trying to subvert me. I'm drunk and the hell with you." He swallowed half his drink in one deliberate movement. Outside there was a steady roll of applause broken only by short silences, but no music.

"It's a futile remedy. You'll end by destroying yourself instead of the enemy."

"Right now, I'd like to destroy my little old self. Self is a millstone around my neck. It knows too much."

"Every man kills his own albatross sooner or later, I suppose," Sellers said resignedly. "But I'd rather not be a witness this time."

The jazz had stopped and people from the garden were filling the ballroom again. A chattering foursome of young people spilled into the bar in a rustle of silk and crinoline, flushed and excited. Sellers pushed his chair back and started to rise; Stone reached over and drunkenly restrained him with a hand on his shoulder.

"You were here first," Stone said with thick gallantry. He stood up and drained his drink. "I've got to go downstairs, anyhow. Got to look for someone. Friend." More people were coming into the bar.

"I don't really prefer this place to any other," Sellers said, tolerantly amused, pinned in his chair by Stone's hand on his shoulder. Around them, people were looking.

"No. No. You were here first. You stay here—I'll go," Stone said loudly.

Sellers laughed and turned up his hands. "If you insist . . ." he said.

Stone turned without another word and lurched determinedly toward the door; as he wove through it he brushed shoulders with a tall distinguished gentleman wearing the uniform of the Royal Air Force. Stone stopped and made an insistent overelaborate apology which only succeeded in embarrassing the man, especially as Stone made the apology in rapid blurred French which the officer obviously didn't understand.

Stone worked his way through the whirl of faces, looking for Solange. In the sudden press of bodies he was feeling sickeningly dizzy, and was doing his best to keep from lurching against people as he attempted to stem the human tide pouring from the top of the stairs. Near the staircase he was forced to stop and wait for the crowd to thin out before going down. A river of people flowed up the stairs, engulfing him. Faces swam out of focus before his eyes, and the heavy perfume of the women and the din of conversation pressed hard on his senses. He held himself as erect as possible, pinned against the stone wall by the press of the crowd, muttering thick apologies as men and women were forcibly crushed against him by the crowd behind. For support he held onto the huge bas-relief Grecian urn that was carved in the wall. The smooth stone felt waxy under his hands. The moist heat from the close bodies, the musky redolence of expensive women, aroused him to a sense of panic; suddenly it occurred to him that he might easily be sick.

The chilling panic only unsettled him more. He could feel cold sickly sweat dampening his forehead around the temples and hairline and under his shirt, and was seized with a terrible desire to take off his tail coat and simply lie down, crowd or no crowd. But he knew he had to fight it off.

He partly closed his eyes, conscious of looking as pale as death, and gritted his teeth, trying hard to overcome the spinning dizziness and maintain a composed appearance. A heavy middle-aged woman looked at him in alarm as she approached up the stairs and veered prudently off, shoving awkwardly into her companion. All around him Stone could hear, or thought he could hear, whispered remarks; the crowd pressed past in what seemed a never ending flow. He tensed every muscle in his body, again fighting the sudden wave of sickness that swept over him like a gust of fear. Chilled to his very marrow, he held onto the sculptured niche, not moving a muscle, holding his breath. Time froze.

Suddenly the stairs were empty before him; only a few last stragglers, laughing and chattering among themselves, still dallied in their ascent. At the bottom, in an instant of strange and distorted vision, he saw a bleared Negro carry a huge bass viol past. It seemed unreal. *Where is that man going, what is he doing?* He seemed to be moving furniture.

Then Stone saw Solange, saw her the same instant she saw him. She looked up; he forced a smile, made himself relax.

He felt better; the crisis of illness and claustrophobia was past. It had been the press of the crowd more than anything else, the sweet musk of perfume and sweat, and the closeness. He felt definitely better. He waved to Solange, trying hard to look careless and composed. She smiled; but as she looked at him the smile faded from her face. She started up the stairs, pausing only to gather up her gown. Male hands reached out behind her, Stone saw. Laughing young men. It was suddenly very important that he *escort her up the stairs*.

It was the last thought he had before he fell.

Solange listened to every note of the jazz entertainment. The audience had all clapped their hands red for encores, and won two. Finally the leader explained in a hilarious pleading mixture of good-natured French and happy English that they had to be back at the club where they were playing. He explained carefully that they were on tour, and gave the name, address, and hours of business of the club—a cellar place in St. Germain. Then having properly advertised themselves, and shrugging eloquently to pantomime their unhappy devotion to duty, in the face of all protests they dismantled their instruments. With that uncompromising gesture the crowd gave up, and started in full flood for the ballroom and bars in the house. Solange, having wriggled and cajoled her way to the very apron of the bandstand, found herself and her impromptu escorts bringing up the rear. The head of the crowd had abruptly become the tail.

Solange was enjoying herself with three pleasant young men, all her juniors—until she found that Stone wasn't where she had left him. Looking around for him, she covered her worry with gay and sparkling laughter. She was playing at being a belle and knew it, but in another part of her mind she was seized with anxiety, like a premonition. The music had sobered her and now she berated herself for having left him.

Stone wasn't on the terrace either. They came inside. She was laughing forcedly at some inane compliment one of the young men had made on the steps of the terrace, when finally she looked up and saw Stone standing at the head of the stairs. A surge of relief was replaced by fear as she saw his face. He was gripping the stone railing like a man drowning; the last of the crowd mounting the stairs stared openly, uncertainly, as they passed him. Behind him several men were standing in a semicircle, their faces apprehensive, each obviously wondering whether the man before them needed assistance. Stone's face was as white as the marble amphora he was holding onto. Then he looked down, saw her. He smiled grotesquely and waved. Seeing him there, swaying back and forth at the top of the stairs, she knew he was drunk beyond reason. In that instant she had to repress the urge to cry out to him to be careful; she snatched up her ball gown and started up the carpeted stone stairs, trying desperately to hold his eye.

She opened her mouth to cry out, but it was too late. With a suddenness that caught everyone by surprise he tripped and pitched forward. A woman at the top of the stairs gave a short piercing scream.

Stone struck the stairs like a dead man and tumbled on down, arms and legs flailing like a disjointed wooden toy, a thudding series of neck-wrenching somersaults—each time he struck the stairs the woman at the top uttered another shriek as though the pain were hers. Halfway down, one arm slammed against the marble at the side of the stairs and flung his smashed watch and broken band to the bottom; it landed on the heavy carpet at Solange's feet. In the galvanized instant it took for the somersaulting body to tumble the length of the stairs no one could move—and near the bottom, the roll stopped; the body straightened out with a terrible grisly thump, slid down the last few steps head first, head bumping, face up. And Solange was on her knees beside him.

There was a gash in the forehead where his head had struck on bare stone at the edge of the heavy carpet runner, and it was bleeding. He was totally unconscious. At the top of the stairs another woman was weeping hysterically; anxious men were coming down, bending to pick up scattered items—Stone's wallet, a pack of cigarettes, small change, a shirt stud. Three men gently eased the unconscious figure to the bottom. He lay on the carpet face up under the bottom step. On the top steps a gathering crowd murmured questions among themselves. A man broke through and rushed down the stairs, jamming the tails of his evening clothes inelegantly into his side pockets as he came.

"Pick that up," he said, nearly stepping on the broken watch. He spoke with professional urgency. He knelt down, and felt about the bones of Stone's neck, gently reaching underneath him to feel along the back. "Nothing obvious," he muttered, frowning.

He lifted both eyelids, looked at the sightless eyes as though comparing them.

"Bring me an overcoat," he said. The people drawn by the woman's first shriek now drifted curiously down the stairs. The doctor turned to a white-faced young man next to him. "Keep those idiots off me," he said, with a contemptuous toss of his head to indicate the crowd on the stairs. With ineffectual politeness, the young man began asking people to stand back. It did no good. Those in back pressed down on those in front, forcing them to descend another step. There was still an excited murmur of questions among the guests, one to another, women asking, men mainly answering.

The doctor stood up, frowning, and faced the crowd on the stairs. "Go back and dance," he said loudly. "All of you. It isn't a party unless someone falls down the stairs." The crowd began to retreat. "He's not hurt," the doctor said, encouraging the lapse of interest.

Then he turned to Solange, who was standing wordless, shaking, looking down at Stone. "You know the gentleman?" he asked gently.

She nodded dumbly.

"I don't know if he's hurt or not. I'd like to get him X-rayed." Then, forgetting Solange, he knelt again. He looked ridiculous, squatting with his coattails tucked in his pockets. He felt gingerly about the gash in Stone's forehead. "Bad knock," he muttered. He twisted around on his heels and looked up at Solange. "Drunk, I imagine?"

She nodded again.

The doctor examined the gash. "Nothing wrong with his clotting time," he observed, half to himself. A servant came with an overcoat.

"Roll it lengthwise and slide it under him," the doctor directed. "Four of us can take him out to my car." The doctor rose to help. "I don't want to bend him."

"Is your car in front, Doctor?" a young man asked.

The doctor glared at him distractedly. "A doctor's car is always in front," he said shortly.

A spectator in the group murmured, "It almost looked like he did it on purpose. It was like a dive."

"His face is horribly white," another voice said, "isn't it?"

Solange touched the doctor on the arm; she seemed unable to speak. The doctor looked at her a moment and then reassuringly patted her hand. "Don't worry," he said. Then he smiled gently. "He isn't dead yet."

"He's making a good start on it," a man behind them said. Both the doctor and Solange turned around. A thick-set man with thick glasses was looking down at Stone, shaking his head slowly. He looked up at Solange. "I'm a friend of the gentleman's. Abe Sellers. But I'm rather drunk, I'm afraid." He looked at Solange. "You must be Solange," he said. "I'm sorry if I'm being dire."

She nodded, still looking dazed and uncomprehending.

"I've read about you in Mr. Stone's official history," he said thickly. "I feel I've known you a long time. I admire you."

Solange didn't seem to be listening; she looked down at the inert form of Stone. He looked very still. The twisted and disheveled evening clothes made a grotesque contrast with the bleeding head and death-white face.

Their hostess appeared at Solange's side. She had found the doctor and sent him down and had sensibly stayed upstairs re-establishing order. She made no comment, as though talk was superfluous, but simply put her arm on Solange's in mute testimony of her feelings. The men and the doctor gently lifted Stone and carried him cautiously to the door.

"What hospital, Doctor?" Sellers asked. "I have my chauffeur. I'll bring the young lady."

"American," the doctor said. Then he paused. "He is one, isn't he?"

"He's one of ours, yes," Sellers said morosely. The doctor looked quizzically at Sellers a moment, and then grunted and turned and went out.

Sellers came over to Solange. Adelaide said, "Tell Mr. Stone how sorry I am for the accident. These stairs are terribly dangerous."

"Thank you," Solange said sadly. "But it wasn't your stairs."

"My dear, as far as my guests and I are concerned, it was the fault of the stairs and the carpet. I've asked one of the servants to fix it. I don't want Mr. Stone to feel bad about this. Now you go." She turned to Sellers. "Abe, you're not driving, I hope?"

"I never drive, Adelaide. Henry's outside."

"Well, I know Henry's sober," she said. "I've seen to that myself. Take care of Solange. Come calling soon."

"Yes, Addie," Sellers said. He turned to Solange. "It looks like you and I have a common cause," he said quietly.

"I'm still shaking," Solange said weakly.

"You have good reason to," Sellers said. "Because you know what the reason is."

"Abe, this is no time to be dramatic. Solange, are you certain there's no way I can help?"

Solange looked at her hostess. "He'll be all right," she said. "It was such a beautiful party." She extended her hand.

VI

Stone lay quiet, thinking, staring at the motes of sterile dust that floated in the immobile sunshine. Someone had raised the blinds and the light had awakened him; it flooded the whiteness of the room.

He had slept through most of the morning propped up on two pillows, because lying flat only made the headache worse. A nurse had awakened him at noon for lunch, a bowl of broth, with gelatin for dessert. Groggy with sedation, he found that it made him sick and irritable to look at food, but the nurse jollied him into eating whether he wanted to or not. He had fallen asleep over the gelatin. Now, as he waked again, his headache was better. He lay watching the dust motes in the empty air, trying once more to piece together the mystery of why he was in the hospital for a simple hangover. He only returned to the ominous fact that he couldn't remember leaving the party. The final thing he could remember from last night was talking to Abe Sellers. The rest was a confusion of people and faces.

A soft footstep interrupted his thoughts. An old woman in a starched smock, faded blue and very clean, came in to take away his tray. She smiled at him and carried the tray out of the room, closing the door silently behind her again. He looked at his wrist, forgetting for the third time that his watch was gone. He wished he'd been awake during the morning when the doctor came. Vaguely he recalled a man in a white jacket standing dreamlike and distant over him. That must have been quite a sedative, he thought. There was a curious taste in his mouth.

Suddenly the door opened again.

For a moment no one came in. He wondered why hospital doors always opened with the same unvarying irritating silence. It was like the nurses' rubber-soled shoes, except that the shoes at least squeaked on whatever it was they used for floors along hospital corridors. Doors never squeaked. Then a young nurse stuck her head in.

"You have a visitor," the nurse said. She spoke English with a curiously musical burr, Welsh, perhaps. She disappeared, leaving her smile in the room.

Solange came in without a word carrying a single white lily. She smiled ironically at him and placed the flower upright between the mattress and the foot of the white iron bed, where he could look at it without turning his head. She had to right it several times before it would stay vertical.

"I looked all over Paris for this," she said. "I hope you appreciate it." She drew the chair to the side of the bed. Her face was flushed and touched with light perspiration. She fluffed out her short hair with both hands and sat down. "Those stairs," she said, collapsing onto the chair. "The elevator is for patients."

"I thought they only grew those things for Easter," Stone said glumly.

"It's to celebrate your untimely resurrection. I shouldn't even speak to you after the scare you gave me last night."

"What happened last night?" Stone asked, his tone reluctant. "What am I doing in the hospital?"

"Didn't the doctor tell you?" Solange still seemed to be catching her breath.

"I was only half awake when he made his rounds. The lunch nurse said the night nurse told her I fell."

"You fell down the stairs," Solange said. "It was the fall to end all falls."

Stone winced. "Did anybody see me?"

"Only all the people at the party," Solange said. "I should think you'd hurt all over today."

Stone said nothing. Then he said, "I hurt a little."

"But your hostess covered up for you. She told everyone the carpet came loose at the top of the stairs. She even had two servants down on their hands and knees pretending to fix it."

"How kind of her," Stone said grimly. "I have an awful hangover."

"It was, really. Actually it was more intelligence than kindness. You should be grateful."

"Half the Embassy was there," Stone said. "I suppose they witnessed my descent also?"

"I telephoned the Embassy for you this morning. They were very sorry to hear you'd been hurt. They said you were to stay in the hospital and rest and not to worry about anything. The man I talked to said you had every right to take your sick leave. Someone will be around to see if you need anything. They were very kind, I thought."

"Everyone is kind today, it seems."

"Why so cynical? Don't you believe people can be concerned when someone gets hurt? You had a terrible fall. At least it looked terrible. Even the doctor thought you had broken your neck. It was the first thing he looked for."

"They called a doctor?"

"Your hostess had the foresight to invite one. A good hostess thinks of everything."

"Who brought me here?"

"The doctor—I forgot to ask his name—and a Mr. Sellers. I came in Mr. Sellers' car with him. He has a huge American car with a chauffeur. He's a rather strange person. Is he a good friend of yours?"

"You'll have to ask him. I don't know him that well."

"You're really in a sour mood. You should be glad you weren't crippled for life."

"What makes you think I wasn't?" Stone asked. "That was all the good gentlemen needed to fire me legitimately. They're probably drawing up my termination papers right this minute."

"Why be so pessimistic? Anyone can trip on a loose carpet."

"Last night wasn't the first misstep I've made. But you can rest assured, it will be my last as far as the Embassy is concerned. I've given them no choice. If I were working for me I'd fire myself." Stone shook his head disgustedly.

"You'll feel better after you've had some rest. Perhaps this vacation is just what you needed. Things at the Embassy may improve while you're away from them awhile."

"Nothing will ever improve. Least of all, human beings and government institutions."

"You make me tired," Solange said impatiently. She dropped her cheerful mask. "I came here to cheer you up, and now you're depressing me. I had a hangover myself this morning."

"Condolences."

"I have half a mind to take my flower back," Solange said. "You don't appreciate me."

"I'm glad you came," Stone said. Then he added, "Solange, I really am."

"You don't sound very convincing."

"Well, at least you cleared up the mystery of why I'm here. I'm grateful for that. It's not good when you can't remember what happened. That's the only thing that really worries me."

"What's that?"

"Not being able to remember. That's something new for me. I used to always remember everything, all the grim details. But recently . . ."

"Do you think you're becoming an alcoholic—I mean, a real one?" Solange asked seriously. "I don't really know much about it."

Stone thought for a few seconds. "I don't know why I get so drunk. I never used to. I don't remember drinking very much last night."

"You should ask the doctor about it."

"What's there to ask him? I'm simply getting old and can't hold my liquor like I used to. There's nothing to worry about, really. I just have to drink less. If you eat too much when you're old, you get fat. If you drink too much, you get drunk. I have to go on a diet."

"Still, you ought to ask the doctor about it. He took a blood test on you last night while you were passed out."

Stone sat up abruptly. He pulled back the sleeve of his hospital gown and searched his arm. In the crook of his elbow was a small spot of discolored skin, like a bruise, with a needle mark over the vein. "Damn them," he said. "Snooping around to find out how much alcohol I had in my blood. That will go into the report to the Embassy health center."

"But they always take a blood sample. It's routine."

Stone lay back on the pillows and sighed. He shrugged. "Well, at least they have proof that I was drunk. In black and white."

"The doctor wrote in red ink. I watched him when I gave him your name and everything."

"He probably filled his fountain pen from my left arm. Did you see the bruise he left?" Stone examined his punctured arm indignantly.

"That was a nurse who did that. I helped her hold your arm straight."

"So you were in league with them, were you?" Stone said. He smiled abruptly. "And I slept through all the blood-letting. Sounds like a funny scene. I can just see you two vampires jabbing at me."

"So, you can still smile." Impulsively she took his hand. "You look better when you smile."

"I don't know what I have to smile about."

"It's enough that you're alive and able to smile. If you'd been sober when you fell down those stairs, I don't think you'd be smiling."

"If I was sober I wouldn't have fallen in the first place. That's life."

"You ought to be glad you still have it."

"Have what?" Stone asked.

"Life."

"Ah, yes," Stone said. He rolled his head away from her and looked toward the barred window. "The prisoner languishes, condemned to live."

Solange released his hand. He turned his head back toward her. She looked at him, her face suddenly serious. "I wish you wouldn't talk that way," she said. "Even as a joke."

"Why not?" he said lightly. "It's true, isn't it? Look, they have bars on the windows."

"Please."

"All right," he said.

"It's not healthy to look at everything so negatively. You only drag yourself down into depression."

"Are you afraid I'm headed for suicide?" Stone asked, smiling slightly.

Solange didn't answer immediately. Then she said, "I wouldn't be so flippant about the fact that I worry about you, if I were you. I'm sorry I worry, but I'm a woman. And I can't help *that*."

"A second ago you were complaining that I'm too serious. Now I'm too flippant."

"You're trying to catch me up on words. You're flippant about the wrong things. You have everything backward."

"I'm sorry," he said. He tried to take her hand, but she pulled it away. For a moment she was silent.

Then she said, "I never told you how he died."

Suddenly he saw her agitation in a clearer light. "No, you didn't," he said. He knew she was talking about her husband.

"He killed himself."

Stone said nothing. She had the advantage after all. There was nothing to say.

"I didn't find out until after the war. From a friend of his. But I knew. I saw him a few weeks before. I could tell he wasn't coming back. He took risks. He . . ."

She hesitated, looking speculatively at Stone.

"Do you gamble?" she asked suddenly.

"No." It was clear that she was making a comparison.

She accepted the answer without comment. Then she said, "He was a lot like you in some ways. That job you had . . . in the war—why did you take it?"

"Certainly not to kill myself," he said, regretting instantly the tactless wording of the remark. He hadn't meant it that way. But she didn't take notice of it. She went on.

"Did you volunteer?"

"Yes. Well, not exactly. I sort of fell into it. I started innocently enough by just joining the Army. They put me to work teaching French in school where they trained men for jobs that required it. Are you really interested in all this?"

"Yes."

"It was in the early days of the war. They needed men to do odd jobs like working in France, but it was hard to find them at first. Recruitment was hit-or-miss at the start. I was only a schoolteacher, but I didn't want to spend the rest of the war teaching French. After you've trained a lot of men to do a job you've never done yourself, it gets to be a kind of challenge. For one thing, I had the feeling I'd be a better instructor if I had some field experience. So I put in for it. They weren't choosy in those days about making sow's ears out of silk purses, so they took me and put some meat on my bones and sent me to France. I brought back a lot of useful knowledge with me from that first trip, and I tried to pass it on to my students. All of us were part-time instructors when we weren't actually on a mission. So I didn't really volunteer. I sort of drifted in through the back door. They gave me a broom and told me to sweep."

Stone shrugged. "That's all there is to it," he said. "It seems like an odd switch from schoolteacher to special agent, but in wartime the odd switch becomes the rule rather than the exception. We had insurance agents, lawyers, we even had one who wrote poetry—published it, too. There was no logic to it in those days. Some men were good. Some were terrible. Later on, they learned to weed out the misfits. But in the beginning there were a lot of mistakes. It was mostly trial and error. Tell me why you asked about this?"

"I'm not sure. I guess I was trying to find a pattern." She paused. "I keep forgetting we hardly know each other."

"A pattern of self-destruction?" Stone asked. "I'm not being sarcastic."

"Sometimes people can be trying to destroy themselves without being aware of it. Like people who are always having accidents. I hope I'm not a Cassandra."

"Like falling downstairs?"

Solange looked at him. "I hadn't precisely thought of it that way. I guess because you were drunk."

"But, *why* was I drunk, that is the question," Stone said. He wasn't smiling.

"You said yourself you didn't remember being at the top of the stairs."

"Why should I want to remember making an ass of myself?" Stone asked. "A few times I've remembered being drunk when I've wished I hadn't."

Solange was silent. Then she asked, "Do you get very depressed about things?"

Stone sighed patiently. "The only thing that depresses me is this depressing mess at the Embassy. And that's enough to depress anybody. And that Dujardin business—but that's all over, I guess. For everybody, that is, except me."

"Maybe things will be better when you go back."

"To the Embassy?" Stone paused, smiling slightly and shaking his head slowly. "I'll never go back to the Embassy." He laughed as though at himself. "My days as a civil servant are over. I've demeaned myself long enough as it is. The only immediate ambition I ever had was to be a peaceful bachelor in Paris, and to do an honest job as a public grave-keeper. But to be without ambition is no protection from the ambitious. I'm a thorn in the bride's bouquet. I should have resigned long ago."

"Why don't you postpone thinking about that until you've had a chance to rest a few days. Your outlook might be different then."

"I don't want my outlook to be different. It took something to bring me to the light. It took a fall down a flight of stairs to open my eyes. I've been putting myself through hell trying to fight city hall."

"City hall?" Solange looked uncertain.

"It's an expression. The old Greeks fought against destiny—Americans mean the same thing when they say they're fighting city hall. I think it's a New York expression."

"It's very colorful."

"Oh, we're a very colorful people, Madame," Stone said, smiling.

"You wouldn't know it to look at you. You're still a little gray."

Stone looked at the ceiling. "Gray is the color of my true love's hair," he said meaninglessly. He paused. "What made me say that, now?"

Solange pretended a sigh. "My hair is brown," she said.

Stone took her hand and gazed out the window, smiling to himself. "Be patient," he said. "Time is on your side."

That evening Solange came again for the after-dinner visiting hour. She brought Stone magazines and newspapers and a bar of Swiss chocolate. She kept him company, sitting on the low wide window ledge by the failing evening light, knitting, making small talk. The window was open, and though it was only spring, by the light it was already summer. When it was too dark to knit without dropping stitches she put her work back into her bag and turned on the reading lamp over his bed. She sat on the foot of the bed just outside of the circle of light, and they talked until the nurse came in and announced the end of visiting hours.

After she left, Stone put the light out and tried to sleep. But there was still the last summer glow of purple sky outside his window, and somewhere he could hear the distant excitement of children playing their after-dinner games. A cooling breeze stirred through the open window, carrying the fresh smell of trees and grass into the room. It was impossible to sleep.

He lay quietly awake for more than an hour, thinking about Solange as though facing himself, trying to decide precisely what his feeling for her was. She was a comfortable person to be with, but beyond that it was hard to judge. Her presence in the room earlier was still manifest in the faint scent of perfume which lingered in the dark air.

Stone thought about the sharp disappointment he'd unexpectedly felt when the evening visiting hours came and she didn't appear immediately, and how relieved he had been to see her when, ten minutes later, just as he was resigning himself to her not coming, she suddenly burst smiling into the room with a stack of magazines in her enormous knitting bag. She kissed him and presented him with the candy bar. He told her he was glad to see her; actually, his feeling was more like joyful relief. The reaction he felt came as a surprise for its intensity. She kissed him again on both cheeks and told him he was looking better. She had looked happy and full of energy, and they had talked for an hour about nothing. More than anything, he wanted her in bed again.

Stone was sorry to see her go. The faint trace of her perfume only made the room more barren in her absence. Would she miss him, alone in the apartment at night? Stone wondered what she was doing, where she had gone when she left him. It was too warm a night to go home early.

He felt as he remembered feeling when he was a child lying awake in the resentful half-dark listening to the older children still playing outside. It was one of his earliest memories. His mother had believed in an early bedtime for her son.

He thought vaguely about his mother, trying to conjure up a vision of her face, but remembering only the sound of her voice, the inflections of her speech. It continued to puzzle him that, after her death, he could never remember exactly what she looked like. There was only the voice, disembodied, remote, but personal. Of his father, when he thought of him, he thought of his hands, the hands of a stonecutter, and the perpetual smell of red wine. He had never seen his father drunk, except once after his mother died, but there was always the smell of homemade Italian wine about him.

There was the voice of his father, but it mingled and was lost among other voices, other men, the men his father played *bocce* with in the evenings. He thought about the house on Mulberry Street, and the house in Lawrence. He thought of his mother's music pupils, of music, of the constant sound of piano exercises. Of his own cello. The cello brought him back to thinking of Solange. Unconsciously he flexed his fingers. A cello *was* like a woman, he thought.

Stone groped around the porcelain top of the night table for a cigarette. He lit it in the dark and watched the glowing tip, wondering why he should be thinking of his cello after all these years. He'd thought of it often in recent weeks. He thought of the night he sat playing by himself in his room, the night before he took the cello to New York and sold it—wasn't it to save up money to get married? He thought: To that girl. Ironic, he thought. He had to think now even to remember her name, and yet he had wanted to marry her. Even at the time, the short courtship hadn't seemed real. He tried also to remember her married name, but couldn't. Had he really sold the cello for her? The day he sold his cello marked the day he lost track of his childhood friend, himself, the boy who won a trip to Paris for being able to play so well. Even that remembered trip was dim, unreal. He could hardly remember the State Teachers College. There too time and memory tricked him. The college years had passed like anesthetic hours. Sleep had often become a substitute for food. Intent only on the daily problem of staying awake, he had sometimes lived only on coffee. He had never thought about music during those days. After the girl married someone else, the anesthesia of time had only deepened.

Stone held up his hands in the darkness. They made two clear black silhouettes against the white hospital sheets. They were no longer his mother's musician's hands, but more as he remembered his father's. In his left hand the cigarette glowed, a dull red eye in the darkness. He shook the ash off onto the floor beside the bed and blew on the tip to make it glow brighter. It made enough light to illuminate the backs of his fingers. He stubbed out the cigarette on the porcelain table top and lay back on the piled-up pillows.

Thinking of his hands made him think of his mother again, and how she had admonished him to be careful of them. *A musician has his life in his hands.* On the day before the prize recital he remembered himself digging in the front yard under the rose trellis when his mother came out on the porch and saw him. He was digging out a dead root. She threw her hands to her temples and shouted, *"Deine Klavierfingern!"* Then, flustered, she corrected herself, "You'll ruin your string fingers." She made him go inside and wash his hands and clean the dirt from under his nails. It was one of the few times he could remember her lapsing into German, as though it was a scene repeated from her own Alsatian childhood. The next day she rubbed his hands with olive oil, and made him soak them in a bowl of warm water. In honor of the occasion, he went to the concert hall in a taxicab with his father and mother. She made him flex his fingers all the way. After the concert was over and the prize announced, she broke into tears and called him *"Liebschen."* He remembered that it had never occurred to him that he wouldn't win the prize until afterward, when he saw her crying. She told him it was because she was happy, and he fell asleep that night wondering where Paris, France, was. That, at least, he remembered clearly.

Stone looked out the window to see the moon rising full and startling red behind the dark rooftops of Neuilly. Paris, he thought. *How did I know enough to wonder then?* What had made him remember that night lying awake trying to imagine Paris? He remembered the bundles of yellowed postcards from his mother's old trunk in the attic, pictures of the Arc de Triomphe and other monuments, the Opera House, Notre Dame. From these clues he had tried to form a vision of what Paris was like. But months later, when he landed in Le Havre, he was surprised to find that Paris wasn't where the boat docked.

The Gare St. Lazare had violated his basic imagining that Paris would have to be a city by the ocean like New York. In the noise and dusty confusion of arrival his disappointment was bewildering, and he remembered Madame Sessions—she seemed younger than his mother and very beautiful then—asking what was wrong. He couldn't tell her. That night in his new strange room in the Sessions' huge apartment in the Rue Babylon, he had felt homesick and lost. He wanted to get up and play his cello, but it was late at night and everyone else was asleep. Instead he turned the light on and took out the bundle of postcards from his suitcase and fell asleep trying to reconstruct the shattered dream.

Stone sat up on the edge of the high hospital bed and let his feet dangle, his toes just touching the cold floor. Outside the moon rose steadily, growing smaller and less red. From the hospital's walled garden under his window a whisper of trees rose against a background of nightsounds and insects. From the far distance came the sound of night traffic, and a pale skyglow loomed over the deeper part of the city.

He could visualize the crowds strolling on the Champs Elysées, taking their careless pleasures in the easy hospitality of a warm summer evening, the girls in light dresses, and their young men wearing collars open at the neck. It was just such a night. The outdoor cafés would be a sea of faces and wicker chairs as harried white-coated waiters hugged their trays and signaled to each other for more chairs. It was a common sight this time of year. There would always be at least one waiter hip-deep in the center of the babble, picking his way forward with two more wicker chairs held high over his head. On an evening like this the crowd seated itself wherever there was room, and grew in size like a cluster of bees until it overflowed the terrace and spilled out onto the broad sidewalks, interfering with passing pedestrians who didn't seem to care. Somewhere in just such a crowd, Stone was sure, Solange would be sitting with her young American friends. He wished he'd asked where she was going. Probably not on the Champs, he thought, more likely at the Royale St. Germain. She always said the coffee was better there, and fifty francs cheaper.

Stone hadn't told Solange about the fact that one of her American artist friends was a part-time informer for the Embassy. For one thing, it perhaps wasn't one of her friends, except that he knew it was one of the people at the party Solange had taken him to. The remark he'd made about God being an unspeakable idea was a remark he'd never made before. He couldn't help smiling to himself at the thought of some poor young fool writing it down in his little black notebook so he could report it to the Embassy security officer. It was not healthy to degrade a young man—in his mind he thought of him as a very young man—by playing on his need of money to get him to inform on his own countrymen. God is unspeakable, Stone thought. He shook his head in the darkness of the hospital room, and tried again to remember the faces of the people who had been at the party, but they remained only a blur in his memory. They all seemed happy to be the same, Stone thought, and all of them are in Paris trying to be different. Only they want to be different the same. They had called him Mr. Stone and treated him with an elder's proper due. They had seemed to form a circle around him, as though anyone Solange would bring—they called *her* by her first name—would have some pearls to cast at their feet. It had made Stone uncomfortable, sitting on the floor drinking cheap wine, and finding himself systematically quizzed about his opinions. It was as though he had been proposed for initiation into their circle and they were trying to determine his fitness. But he had liked them, made an effort to meet them halfway, and that was when the subject of the failure of religion came up. One girl, he remembered, had talked with particular intelligence on some point he had now forgotten, and it was she who challenged him for his own opinion. To avoid being dragged into a collegiate discussion of religion he had made up on the spot the answer that had later been quoted back to him in his security interrogatory. He'd said simply that he found it difficult to speak about religion because to him the very idea of God was a completely unspeakable thing. At the time he had failed to note the ambiguity, but he recalled how his remark had ended the discussion. The girl, he was certain, had understood precisely what he meant, because she nodded soberly and said she had once looked at it that way. She said that he had a point. Then someone else made a joke and said that he had a point too, but if he kept his hat on it wouldn't show. Everyone laughed and the conversation turned away. At one point Stone spoke to Solange in French without thinking, and someone complimented him and asked him where he'd learned to speak it so well. Stone was surprised to learn that almost none of the young people spoke decent French, in spite of the fact that most of them had been in France all winter. He had remarked about it in the taxi on the way home, and Solange had said it wasn't their fault, that all the Frenchmen they met used them to perfect their English.

Stone heard the hour strike in the distance. An instant later he heard it again from another church nearer by. Then it was quiet again. The moon had risen just over the iron crosspiece that held the bars in the window.

He was thirsty. The water in the carafe on the night table would be tepid by now, since it had been refilled before dinner. He felt around on the floor for his shoes, and slipped his bare feet into the cold leather.

He opened the door just in time to see another patient, an old man, vanish into the men's toilet across the hall. The old man didn't make a sound, only glanced once at Stone, then disappeared, almost as though embarrassed to be seen.

The empty corridor was lighted only by four small night lights at intervals along the ceiling. From the night nurse's office halfway down the hall, a bright slash of white light from the open door bisected the corridor. He walked toward it to ask for some fresh ice water. But the ice water was, he knew, mainly an excuse to get out of the restless confinement of his room. Even a night nurse would be someone to talk to.

The light from the open door and the music of a softly playing radio were like signs of life in a cavern. There was no one in the office. A ribbon of smoke rose from a cigarette that was nearly all ash, and a half-eaten sandwich lay on the desk on a leaf of waxed paper. An open fountain pen. A green wool sweater over the back of the chair. A glass of iced tea, the ice nearly melted. The radio was playing very low, and that was all. He looked out into the hall again but the nurse was nowhere in sight.

He stepped into the brightly lit office, squinting as the painful light struck his eyes, and sat down on a white metal stool to wait for her to come back. The hour had just struck and she was probably giving an injection or doing something in one of the rooms. He borrowed a cigarette from the pack on her desk and lit it. Under the sandwich and the fountain pen was a chart listing the occupants of all the rooms on the floor. He moved the sandwich slightly aside and looked for his own name.

The chart was printed in the form of a floor plan, like an architect's drawing, with each occupant's name and date of entry neatly printed in red ink in the rectangle that marked the position of the bed. He noticed that several of the beds were empty, as the other one in his room was. Then he read his own name: *Stone, John.* Beside the date, there were several cryptic notations similar to those after the other patient's names. It gave him an odd feeling to see his own name listed so matter-of-factly on a hospital floor plan. It was like being on the inside and the outside at the same time, for he wasn't in the room marked at the moment. He found the nurse's tiny cubicle on the chart and made an imaginary X with his fingernail. That was where he really was.

Most of the rooms were the same, doubles like his own. On the chart there were a few singles, one large ward with six beds, and a large suite at the end of the corridor. There were two large rooms in the suite and one very small one, probably a bathroom. Only one of the large rooms in the suite had a bed marked in it. The other was probably a sitting room. He looked at the single name printed in the rectangle:

> SHEPPARD

He was still staring unbelieving at the name of the occupant of the suite, when the nurse came in behind him on silent gum-soled shoes. He wasn't aware of her presence until she snatched the chart from under his eyes, almost knocking the sandwich into the wastebasket. Stone caught it in time.

"You're *not* supposed to be in here," the nurse said. She was a tall straight woman who spoke English with a strong Scandinavian accent. She looked calm and capable, very much a nurse. She had masculine features although her face was attractive, and her hair was nearly gray. She was a little older than he, perhaps forty-eight. Her hair was done in a severe bun on which a strange nurse-school cap perched, like a Spanish comb. Her tone of voice was firm, curiously liquid, but scolding. "And you're not supposed to be snooping around my desk."

"I . . ." Stone almost forgot what he'd meant to ask her for. "I came to ask you . . . if I could get some fresh water."

"What's wrong with the water in the tap?" she asked, straightening the things on her desk, blowing away the ashes where the cigarette had consumed itself into nothing, wrapping the sandwich. She worked with automatic efficiency; almost, Stone thought, like an irritated housewife cleaning up in the presence of an unexpectedly arrived visitor.

"I thought perhaps I could get some ice water," Stone said, feeling suddenly that his request was frivolous.

The nurse straightened up and looked at him. "You should comb your hair," she said decisively. "And shave. Just because you're in a hospital is no reason to let yourself go to straw."

Automatically Stone raised his hand to feel his chin. There was a heavy stubble of beard. He thought of Solange, for some reason.

"Look in the mirror," the nurse said. She pointed to a mirror on a cabinet over the sink in the corner.

Stone looked. He was surprised at his own appearance. He looked sallow.

"If I had my way," the nurse was saying, "I'd make them put a mirror in every patient's room. Then maybe they'd take care of themselves. How do you expect to take care of your soul unless you show a little concern for the body?"

Stone said, "A mirror would be a good idea."

"Now which one are you?" the nurse asked.

"I'm Stone."

She looked at the chart. "Yes, you're number nine. What's wrong with you?"

"I fell down a flight of stairs while under the influence of intoxicating spirits," Stone said. "Tripped on a loose carpet."

"Oh, you're the one. I heard about you. Last night was my night off, thank heaven."

"What did I do?" Stone asked in bewilderment. "I thought I was out cold."

"You certainly were. You vomited twice and the nurse had all she could do to lift you out of the bed so she could clean up after you."

Stone winced visibly.

"I wouldn't let it worry you. If you can take it we can. We're used to it."

"I'd like to send that poor nurse a box of candy or something."

"I wouldn't if I were you," the nurse said, sipping her iced tea. "She'd hate you for it. She's on a diet. What's the matter, can't you sleep?"

"I wanted to get a drink of cold water," Stone said.

"I'll bet you used that as an excuse when you were a little boy too," she said. "I have an order for a sedative for you if you need it. But perhaps a nice glass of iced tea and a back rub would do you more good."

"That would be very nice," Stone said. "I still ache a little from my adventure."

The nurse was studying a small file card she'd taken from a box on her desk. Suddenly she looked up at Stone, a quizzical look on her face. She pointed with the card at his right arm. "Doesn't that arm hurt you?"

"Not any more than the rest of me does," Stone said. "Why, should it?"

The nurse squinted at the card again. "You're Stone. Number nine. You have a slight fracture in your right forearm. Didn't they tell you?"

"No," Stone said, looking at his arm.

"It evidently wasn't enough to require a splint, but you're supposed to wear a sling when you're not in bed. Let's have a look at your X-rays."

She riffled through a file of large manila envelopes. "Stone, John," she said, and slid one of the envelopes out. She took out a sheaf of negatives and held them one by one to the light until she found the one she was looking for. She held it up for Stone to see. "They certainly took enough X-rays. Head. Chest. Arms. Legs. They must have thought you were in bad shape."

Stone peered at the negative of his own arm bones. "I can't see anything in the way of a crack," he said.

She pointed with the tip of a pencil. "Look there. See it? Unless you know what to look for it's hard to find."

Stone saw a tiny dark line, like a hair on the negative. "That's not much of a fracture," he said.

"It's enough to weaken the bone. Just don't use that arm until the doctor says you can. I'll order a sling for you in the morning. I can't understand why no one told you. Every time I have a day off something isn't done right. Didn't you see the doctor today?"

"I was asleep." There was a sharp burst of static from the radio, then music again.

The nurse consulted the card again. "Yes, I guess they decided to give you something to keep both you and your stomach quiet. You probably slept until noon. Now why don't you do a little of the same now? You go back to your room and I'll bring your iced tea as soon as I've finished making my entries. Here, you can take the rubbing alcohol and the talcum."

Stone took the two articles in the crook of his left arm and started toward the door. Then he turned back. "Would you mind if I asked you . . . I know I'm not supposed to have been reading what's on your desk. I wasn't doing it with any purpose in mind, but I couldn't help noticing one of the names."

Instinctively the nurse turned the floor chart face down on her desk. "You could get me fired, you know," she said.

"I'd never say anything."

"I hope you don't," she said. "I see from your admission card that you work for the Embassy."

"Yes."

"You could get yourself fired too then," she said. "He's just here for a checkup."

"Then it *is* the Ambassador?"

"If anyone finds out I told you, I'll be fired," she said. She seemed genuinely upset. "Patients aren't supposed to see hospital records. Besides, he's not an ambassador any more. I read in the papers that he's resigned."

"I really won't say anything. Please, I don't want you to worry on my account. I'm sorry."

She opened a drawer and put the chart in it. "It's my fault for leaving the door open," she said. "You get back to your bed now. I'll bring you your iced tea in a minute. I have to go to the refrigerator for it. I'll even bribe you to keep your mouth shut. I'll bring you some cookies."

Stone laughed. "Please, you don't have to bribe me."

The nurse looked slightly more relaxed. "I'll bring you the cookies," she said, uncapping her fountain pen. "He's just here for a checkup, anyway."

Feeling reluctant at the thought of going back to his room, he shuffled along the corridor in his unlaced stockingless shoes. He paused idly to inspect the patients' bulletin board, reading notices about visiting hours and the use of the hospital library. Farther on, he paused in the dim light to read the label on a fire extinguisher. Then he stopped before the open door of the darkened diet kitchen, listening for a moment to the steady vibration of the refrigerator; a water tap was dripping loudly in the dark. He wished he'd remembered to put his cigarettes in the pocket of his robe. Resignedly he started toward his own room on the other side of the corridor. He noticed that the door to the sitting room of the suite at the end of the corridor was ajar, and a night light was on. He thought: *Bruce Sheppard*. Behind him, soft music.

The door of his own room was closed. He'd remembered leaving it open. The nurse must have closed it, he thought. He shifted the bottle of rubbing alcohol and turned the knob, and the door opened before him. He stepped inside and closed it behind him. Taking his bearings on the silhouetted chair before the window, he groped his way toward his bed, intending to put the rubbing alcohol and the talcum powder on the night table.

At the foot of the bed he stopped short. A strange odor struck his senses, a strong odor like civet or musk. For a second he had a hallucination that someone was watching him from his own bed. He approached closer, instinctively reaching out his hand to dispel the trickery of the shadow-rumpled coverlet, stopped his hand in midair . . .

Someone *was* in the bed. He felt his stomach constrict sharply as he made out the apparitional outlines of a man's head propped open-eyed against the pillows.

In the split-second of imagination's panic he saw the glowing eyes as dull red orbs in the darkness, as though lit from behind like a jack-o'-lantern's. In confusion he backed away from the bed, staring at the apparition. In his mind, one clear rational thought stood out like a single marvelous headline: THIS MUST BE A HALLUCINATION. Then, suddenly, no, I'm in the wrong room. He released his breath in relief. Acute embarrassment replaced panic. He could feel the pulse beating in his temples.

From the bed, a voice that was cracked and womanish with age said, "I can still manage without you. Go back to your music."

The old man obviously thought he was the nurse. Stone felt his insides turn liquid with suppressed nervous laughter and relief. A picture of the nurse listening to her radio outside flashed across his mind. Everything suddenly became clear. This was the same furtive old man he'd seen going into the toilet earlier. It was suddenly logical: he was simply in the old man's room. The senile disembodied voice matched the aging figure. It explained the fugitive look the old man had: he was trying to outwit the nurse and the humiliation of the bedpan. Stone felt weak, felt himself shaking. The watery laughter still sloshed loose and silent inside him, threatening any second to spill over and drown the defiant old man on the bed. He knew by the reaction, he'd suffered a real fright. Stone didn't make a sound for fear of scaring the old boy out of his remaining wits. He steadied his giddy knees, groping with his free right hand for the night table, finding it. In his hand: recognition, shock. The interior laughter stopped. From the cold metal contour of the cigarette lighter on the table he recognized it instantly: his own.

He fled the room in confusion, full of unreasoning fear. Outside he looked at the number on the door. There it was: 9. It *was* his own room. He tried to visualize the floor plan—could the nurse have mistaken the number? He started toward the nurse's office just as she emerged from the doorway of the room next to his carrying an empty bedpan. He almost bumped into her. She didn't break her stride or look at him. But she was solid, real. She was no demon, no hallucination. Instantly he got control of himself.

He started uncertainly to speak, half afraid he'd find no one in the room if she went in with him. But she ignored him, brushed past him across the hall and pushed through the door marked "MEN—HOMMES." From inside he heard the metal doors of the cubicles squeak open and bang shut one after another. Then she burst out in the hall again, looking distracted and exasperated.

Stone watched her confusion for a second. Then he said, "I think he's in my bed."

She looked at him, as though venting her exasperation on him. "Oh, *God. Not* again." She turned and stalked toward Stone's room. Stone heard her mutter to herself as she opened the door and went in. The light went on in the room. Instantly Stone heard the duet of soft cajolery and cracked protest begin.

The old man was still protesting when she led him gently but firmly out into the hall a moment later. He was tiny and frail beside her, blinking in the half-light, subdued, but still babbling his toothless barefooted protest. He was bald, with a head like a clean skull. He took no notice of Stone as they passed into his own room. His old-fashioned nightshirt was almost hidden under the hospital robe she held about his thin shoulders, and his bare legs were like chair spindles. She steered him into his own room, cooing and nodding, and shot Stone a long-suffering glance of eyebrows raised heavenward. The door she shut with her heel behind her.

Stone waited in the hall. A moment later she came out again, pulling the door shut softly behind her, her fingers to her lips. She motioned Stone toward the diet kitchen. Stone followed behind her, waiting while she went in and found the light switch. The light went on, bright white and hygienic. She went to the icebox and took out a pitcher of iced tea and brought it to the steamtable. She put it down on the stainless steel top without a word, then collapsed onto one of the three folding chairs under the light, throwing her feet straight out before her. Stone put down the rubbing alcohol and talcum powder.

"I'll have to change your linen now," she said. She looked wearily at her watch. "And I haven't even started on the morning report yet."

Stone sat down, drawing his hospital robe around him, and crossed his legs.

"Don't you have any slippers?" she asked, eying the sockless untied shoes. They looked grotesque on Stone's bare bony ankles.

"I didn't have time to pack a suitcase," Stone said.

"Why didn't you ask? We have slippers." She shook her head, distracted. "That poor crazy old man. That's the second time that's happened. That used to be his room."

"I honestly thought I was having a hallucination," Stone said. "Then I thought *I* was in the wrong room."

"Oh, this time was nothing. The last time he did it, he tried to crawl in bed with a woman. He nearly scared her to death. She must have been hysterical for nearly ten minutes before she rang for me. He woke her out of a sound sleep."

"Didn't she scream?" Stone asked.

"She was in for laryngitis, poor thing. She couldn't even croak. I thought she'd sue the hospital." The nurse pointed to a wall cabinet. "Be a good sport and get two glasses down for me. My feet are killing me."

Stone got the two glasses and filled them.

"If you want ice," she said, "you'll have to break out a new tray."

"This is fine," Stone said.

"I drink this stuff all night," she said, sipping. "It's the only thing that keeps me going. The old fellow has a bottle of champagne in the icebox, but the doctor won't let him drink it. If you want sugar, there's some in the canister on the tray cart."

"This is fine," Stone said again. Then he said, "What's wrong with him? I mean, what's he here for?"

She looked at him across the rim of her glass. "He's got a disease they haven't found a cure for yet."

"What disease is that?"

The nurse didn't seem to hear his question. She took another sip of her iced tea, and looked at the huge, silently vibrating refrigerator. "Someone brought him the champagne. It's in that icebox with his name on it. I think it's stupid not to let him have it. Every time I see it in there it makes me mad. If it killed him, at least he'd die happy."

"What disease *does* he have?"

The nurse stared at the mute white refrigerator for a moment longer before she finally came to Stone's question. She turned her head and looked at him. "Age," she said.

The following morning the doctor had again come and gone before Stone was fully awake. The night before, he had lain awake until the sky began to lighten outside. He remembered hearing the first birds singing before he finally dozed off. The nurse had awakened him twice to take his temperature and once to give him breakfast, which he had eaten automatically, almost without waking up. Lunch came and he felt better afterward. After the noon rest period the nurse came in and told him the doctor had given permission for him to sit in the solarium.

The solarium was a vast tiled room walled in glass. The glass panels were open so that fresh air and sunshine filled the room. Most of the patients, Stone noticed, seemed to be invalids. Most of them were dozing in wheelchairs. In the garden below, other patients were sitting or walking on the gravel paths crisscrossing the green expanse of lawn. Two lawn sprinklers turned hypnotically in the sun, making a pale rainbow between them over the grass. It was hot, but not as hot as yesterday. There was a breeze blowing that lifted the spray of the lawn sprinklers and wafted it away in a fine mist. It was quiet.

Stone recognized immediately the old man from the room next to his. He sat in one corner of the solarium asleep in his wheelchair, his toothless mouth open, his head slightly sideways on the headrest. Stone smiled to himself, and sat down with a magazine on the other side of the room. The morning nurse had given him slippers and a white sling for his arm, which he wore out of obedience rather than necessity.

After Stone had finished four magazines and an ancient copy of the *Yale Review of Alcoholic Studies* which had found its way across the ocean, the nurse came in with the medicine cart. She doled out a few tablets to several of the patients and placed a thermometer in each of their mouths. Stone noticed that she woke all the patients up except the old man. His head had slumped a little and his mouth was closed now; she simply slipped the thermometer between his thin lips. When she came to Stone he asked her why she hadn't wakened him.

"You mean Mr. Pulver?" she asked. "It doesn't matter if he sleeps. He has no teeth."

"You mean people bite thermometers?"

"In their sleep they've been known to do it," she said, efficiently taking Stone's wrist to time his pulse. She counted to herself, not taking her eyes off her wristwatch. Then she slipped a thermometer into Stone's mouth and said, "Keep closed." She noted the pulse rate on a chart and moved on to the next patient.

When she'd finished taking pulses and distributing thermometers she started around again, retrieving them one by one and reading them. When she came to the old man she slipped out his thermometer, looked at it, and slipped it back in. When she'd taken all the other temperatures she went back to him and read the old man's thermometer again.

She stood looking at it a long time, then at the sleeping old man. Then she put it into the alcohol jar on the medicine cart with all the others, casually glanced around at the other patients, and wheeled the cart out of the room.

Stone followed her out to get his cigarettes from his room.

When Stone returned from his room he saw two nurses wheeling the old man out of the solarium. One of them pushed the chair, the other was tucking a blanket about his knees and talking in a low soothing voice. Stone passed them in the corridor. Both nurses smiled and nodded perfunctorily, the one nurse still carrying on a low reassuring conversation, speaking almost in the old man's ear, softly, as though to lull him asleep. The old man's eyes were closed and his face was perfectly relaxed. Stone smiled, remembering again the comedy of the night before of the old fellow's trying to elude the nurse. It had been a shock to find him in the wrong bed, but now by the light of day it merely seemed funny. Stone went into the solarium, still thinking of —what had the nurse just said his name was?—Pulver, that was it. Pulver, Stone thought. At least there was that advantage in being old and having no teeth: they didn't have to wake you up to take your temperature.

He sat down in a wicker armchair that earlier had been occupied. There had been a woman in it, a large middle-aged woman with faded blond hair and a blank look. She must have just left the room, Stone thought, just when I went for my cigarettes. The seat cushion was still warm.

It was only later, back in his room, that he heard the news: the old man had died in his sleep in the solarium. Even the nurses seemed surprised; at least the nurse who told him was: ". . . Why, the poor old dear was just sitting there minding his own business—just imagine, stone-dead he was—he'd be there yet. The poor old dear—off without a whistle, if you please, and not telling a soul . . ."

VII

Late that afternoon Solange brought Stone a letter in her knitting bag. It was in a long envelope and sealed with a wax seal. She said it had come that morning *exprès*. She had signed for it. He wondered who knew he was living at her apartment.

Stone broke the letter open while Solange discreetly turned her back and looked out the window into the garden below. He scanned the letter quickly to the signature: Georges Merseault. Before he even started to read it he sensed its import. It was a long letter. He started to read it, slowly and carefully.

Dear Mr. Stone:

    As I promised you I would, I have made inquiries to supplement your researches on the question of Adriane Santerre. I heard nothing until this afternoon, when a communication from Germany reached me informing me that the following information has been turned up: A woman prisoner named Santerre (no forename noted) arrived at Ravensbruck camp late in 1944. As you no doubt know, prisoners were carried on prison records mainly by their numbers, which were usually tattooed on their arms. The only reason her name was listed in this instance was in reference to a police file compiled in France. Without initials or a first name, however, it isn't yet certain that it's the same Santerre. However, this prisoner's medical record nevertheless seems to indicate that she *was* given postnatal treatment. That is, this prisoner, judging from what can be deduced from a very sketchy note, underwent either a miscarriage or a birth.

I have the details of all this here at my house. You are of course welcome to examine them, but I thought I would send you this brief letter immediately so that you would know the essentials without having to wait longer than you have.

By reckoning backward from the date of the postnatal examination, an experienced doctor, noting the remarks made on the medical record, was able to fix an approximate date of the birth. From this date it may be possible to find some record of the birth on which the number of the mother may appear. A search of all such records in the two camp areas she was known to have been in around the time of birth is now being made. For the present, all we know are these probable facts: (1) that since Adriane Santerre was known to be pregnant when she was caught in France, it is likely that the Santerre of Ravensbruck would have been she, since that prisoner was later given postnatal treatment. The date of birth coincides well with the fact that she was three months pregnant when she was captured. (2) The doctor who examined the German medical record concludes from the type of remarks that the birth was normal, although this cannot be certain. Nor is there any way of telling whether it might have been a miscarriage or a stillbirth, which, considering the conditions of these camps in late 1944, cannot be ruled out. However, the date of the postnatal examination would indicate that the child was carried at least past the eighth month and probably full term. (3) There is a chance that a record of the birth will be turned up. However, if the child was considered "Aryan" enough to be given German foster parents, it is very doubtful if we will be able to trace it further, since the practice was to eradicate all records of its origin once a child was sent to the adoption center. This was considered necessary because of the reluctance of foster parents to take children born in the camps. Once certified as sufficiently Aryan, such children were usually mixed in with the children of unwed German mothers. Thus I am pessimistic about being able to trace the child. All we will probably learn, except by the sheerest stroke of luck, will be the date of birth, the sex of the child, and whether it was deemed fit for adoption by a German family.

Please forgive me for treating these facts so impersonally. I have read over this letter and find I've sounded cold. Believe me when I tell you that in my heart I feel anything but cold. I realize what this must mean to you, but I take refuge in the official manner because there is no other way. God gave us tongues to hide our feelings.

Accept, Monsieur, my deepest sentiments of friendship and sympathy.

Georges Merseault

The letter was in English and hand-written. Stone read over the final sentence again. The stiff Anglicized version of the formal French letter ending carried an honesty that it often lacked in original language. Merseault had obviously gone to some trouble. Stone dropped the letter onto his lap and stared at the ceiling.

He'd judged Merseault lightly. When he'd met him he hadn't quite liked him. He'd seemed too calculating, even slightly inhuman, as Stone remembered him. Even during the dinner at Merseault's house the following evening. Stone had felt it. It was in Merseault's manner. He seemed to substitute wit for humor. Stone had decided then that he was someone to avoid if possible.

Merseault had seemed to want something from him besides a description of Carnot that night. He seemed to emphasize certain words when he spoke, looking for a reaction from Stone. Stone wasn't aware of it until after he got home and began to think about the strange evening. Merseault, he had decided then, had something up his sleeve. Now Stone reconsidered him in the light of his letter and the trouble he'd gone to for him. Certainly it put Merseault in a more humane light. But there was still the unanswered question: Why? After all these months, what was it Merseault still wanted?

Suddenly he heard a movement by the windows. He'd forgotten Adriane was in the room. Then, astounded at his mental slip of the tongue, he corrected himself. Not Adriane, he thought. Solange.

"Bad news?" Solange asked.

Stone looked at her. He was still thinking about having identified her with Adriane. It was the letter, of course. His mind was on Adriane. It was a natural mistake. Nevertheless, it shook him.

"What's the matter?" Solange said. "You look as if you'd seen a ghost. Did you forget I was here?"

"I was thinking about what's in this letter," he said.

"Is it something you can talk about?" she asked.

He handed her the letter. The envelope slid off the bed onto the floor. She took the letter and turned to the window to read it. Stone watched her back. She isn't at all like her, he thought.

The import of the letter from Merseault lay in his mind like a lump of lead. He couldn't even bring himself to think about it. He should have felt something, he thought, but he felt nothing. He felt numb. He had read the facts. There had been a birth. His child. He didn't know if it was living or dead. He couldn't absorb the meaning of it. It continued to weigh heavily, an undigestible gristle in his mind.

He noted aimlessly that Solange was getting tan. He gazed at her bent neck, the long line of her bent neck, at the graceful curve of muscle that rose from the hollow of her shoulder to behind her ear. She wore a blue cotton dress with an open neck and no sleeves. She held the letter in one hand, reading it slowly. When she finished it once, she raised her head slightly and started reading at the beginning again. Stone could smell her perfume on the afternoon breeze through the open windows. In the garden below, a bird was singing as usual. His eyes relaxed into a lazy out-of-focus gaze.

When she finished the letter a second time she turned and handed it back to Stone. She said nothing, but went to the window ledge and sat down. It was the way she had been sitting the night before, Stone noticed, only she was wearing different clothes and she wasn't knitting.

Finally she said: "The child was yours."

He nodded.

She pointed to the letter lying on the bed. "That explains a lot I didn't understand about you."

There was a long silence. Stone stared at the letter abstractedly.

Then she said, "I'm a little hurt that you didn't trust me enough to tell me about it. It's not right to carry something like that alone."

"I thought it was all over. I had almost convinced myself that she was delirious when she . . ."

"You saw her after the war?"

"Yes. A British medical orderly tried to do something for her. But it was too late to do anything to save her."

"What happened, do you want to tell me?" Solange asked, watching him.

"There's not much to tell," Stone said. "After the war, I checked through all the Allied lists of people found in the camps. The British found the worst ones. We had to look for missing prisoners of war of our own, but I was also looking for her. It was mostly death records I went through. Then by the simplest kind of coincidence I found a list of women who'd been treated by a British hospital unit, mostly stragglers from a forced march, women who'd been found in ditches along the roads and that sort of thing. She wasn't one of those, but her name was included on the same list because it was a list of women who had been in camps but who weren't found there. She was found by an old German farmer after they'd burned the camp down. He took care of her in his own cottage until the British came. He was crazy on a religious idea, that he had to atone for Germany's sin. He married her so that he could stay in the same house and take care of her. I also talked to the British orderly who found her."

"How did they find her?"

"The old man came to the field hospital to ask for a doctor. He knew she was French and figured the British would help her. They did what they could for her in the hospital, but the old man could take better care of her than they could at the time, so they returned her to him and detailed the orderly to visit her once a week. If the war hadn't been still on they might have been able to fly her out. But that part of Germany is remote from everything. They couldn't have moved her any distance over those roads. I saw the country myself."

"How long after was it that you found the orderly?"

"I found his commanding officer in Frankfurt. He remembered going out to see her, but he couldn't tell me much. He gave me the last name of the orderly and I traced him through the British War Ministry. I found him in Munich. He'd been discharged from the army and married a German girl. He was trying to build up an export business in German drugs after the war. I don't know what's happened to him. It was he who told me that she'd once said they'd taken her baby away from her. But he couldn't tell me whether she was lucid when she said it. When I saw her she told me the same thing herself. She could have suffered a miscarriage, or something that would make her think . . . ."

Stone stopped. He looked at Solange's face. She was pale and biting her lips unconsciously, looking at the letter lying on the bed. Stone realized that she must be thinking of the child she herself had lost during the war. She didn't seem to notice that Stone had stopped talking. She was thinking of another time and another place. Then abruptly she came back to herself.

She looked from the letter to Stone. "Go on," she said.

"That's all," Stone said, shrugging. "I arranged for—everything I could."

She rose and looked out the window, leaning on the wide ledge with one knee. Stone noticed that her legs were bare. She stood that way for a long time.

Suddenly she turned around. "Would you mind if I telephoned this Merseault person? Tonight? I mean—to see if he's heard anything new."

"Why?" Stone asked. "I mean, of course, if you want to . . . ."

"I'd like to help. I don't know. I can't explain why. I want to understand it better. You'll have to tell me about her first. I'm sorry. I didn't mean . . . ."

"I'll tell you. But not now," Stone said. "I want to think it all out first. It's been a long time—and I thought . . . I don't know how to feel about all this. It puts everything in a different light. I wouldn't let myself think about it before—I mean, the possibility that there was a . . ."

"I only hope there was a child. But there had to be a child."

"Why do you say that?"

"Otherwise . . ." Solange gestured gropingly with both hands. "Otherwise, it's just meaningless. So much—so much death—"

At that moment the door opened on its silent hinges. Solange's hands were frozen in mid-gesture. The dietitian-nurse, a large starched woman with red hands and a scrubbed face, bustled into the room. "Time for supper," she said with beefy good cheer. She was Irish. "Your tray will be here in a minute. You can stay if you want, Miss."

Solange dropped her hands and released her pent breath, forcing a smile in response to the nurse's permission. The nurse circled the room as though on wheels, cranking up the bed, arranging the tray board on Stone's lap. Without breaking her stride she circled around to the other side of the bed and scooped up the fallen envelope from the floor and stuffed the letter into it without looking at it. She opened the drawer of the night table and slid the letter in just as she closed it again, zip, bang.

"We like to keep our papers tidy," she said, as though reciting a formula she recited a hundred times a day; she squared the magazines and placed them on the bottom shelf of the bed table. Then she straightened up and surveyed the room with gimlet-eyed satisfaction. She spied the wrapper of a chocolate bar on the floor beside the chair, impaling it with her eye, like a nail on the end of a sharp stick. A barely perceptible frown of disapproval flickered in Solange's direction, as though to lay the sin to its owner. As she swooped up the paper and whisked it into her pocket, she split a quick toothsome smile, clucked her tongue twice, and turned out of the room.

The door remained open expectantly. Presently an old woman, the same one who swept under the beds and changed the water in the carafe, entered the room in her blue-faded uniform carrying a tray. She made elaborate smiles, placing the tray down before Stone, as though communicating in sign language that he should enjoy his lunch. Stone thanked her in French, and the dam of language was breached. She rattled a spate of well-wishing in her own tongue and left the room beaming. In a moment she was back with another tray which she laid on the window ledge for Solange. Solange thanked her. The old woman put a conspiratorial finger to her lips and backed out of the room, carefully closing the door.

"That was very decent of her," Stone said, continuing in French.

"She's seen me around here so much she probably knows I'm your mistress," Solange said. "Old *bonnes* love to abet young love."

"What makes you think we're so young?" Stone asked, lifting the cover off his plate.

Solange scrutinized the blade of her knife. Then without looking up she said, "What makes you think we're in love?"

Stone poked at his food with his fork. "Are we?" he asked dryly.

Solange broke a piece of bread. She shrugged almost like a man. "God knows," she said. "But I *am* your mistress. Perhaps that's real enough."

Solange stayed for a short while after supper. She couldn't stay late because she was meeting her American friends to accompany them to dinner. Afterward they were all going to an evening *vernissage* of one of their number who was exhibiting his paintings in his first one-man show.

Stone felt suddenly empty after she left. Her looking forward to an evening's amusement merely deepened the sense Stone had of being left out of her life. Again the subtle fragrance of her perfume touched the air of the room, and Stone was alone.

It was hot, but the thin perspiration felt cool on his neck and forehead. Outside the sidewalks were still hot with the passing day's heat and the children played on the same distant street again. It was another summer night in spring. The light began to soften toward night. Somewhere a window was open and soft music from a radio carried faintly on the sluggish breeze that rose and fell from the garden. Stone felt wide awake and restless again. Another night, another struggle for sleep. For the first time, his injured arm started to throb. He lit a cigarette and lay awake listening to the distant sounds from the darkness gathering over the summer city.

When the evening nurse came around at curfew time, he asked for a capsule to make him sleep. She brought it to him in a tiny medicine glass and put it on the night table beside him. It lay in the bottom of the glass, a tiny pink and white capsule, a promise of dreamless sleep. Stone turned it into his open palm and looked at it. Then he put it back. He decided he'd save it for later, and try first to sleep without it. But it was good to know it was there if he needed it, a comfort. He felt more relaxed.

The night nurse would come on at midnight. It wasn't sleep he wanted so much as someone to break the spell of loneliness Solange's departure had cast over him; suddenly he felt a twinge of unreasonable anger directed at her. He looked at the two newspapers and the candy bar she'd brought him. They were on the night table just inside the circle of light from his bed lamp.

Instantly his eye was caught by a small headline at the bottom of the folded page. He moved the medicine glass containing the sleep capsule aside so he could read the text. It was a tiny ten-line story saying that the former American Ambassador would receive the Legion of Honor for his son, who had died in France during the war. He scanned the short text to the last sentence . . . *the Ambassador soon plans to travel back to America.*

Stone read the item over slowly, then he looked at the date on the paper. It was yesterday's.

Stone lay back and looked at the ceiling, wondering whether the Ambassador had already left his suite of rooms at the end of the corridor. The imminent airplane journey probably explained the reason he was in the hospital for a checkup. He's getting to be an old man, Stone thought. He picked up the paper again and looked at the story. A few months ago, he thought, that would have been real news. Now it was simply a small one-column notice at the bottom of the first page. *The former American Ambassador . . .*

A short while later, after the evening nurse had come back a second time, he turned the light off and tried to sleep. His thoughts turned to the old man from the next room. He had simply died. He had an instant's vision of the old man lying on a bed identical to his, in an identical room, in an identical position—then he saw all the patients in the hospital lying awake on identical beds in identical rooms, alone yet strangely together in the sameness of their attitudes. It gave him a detached feeling, as though he were outside his own body, looking at the hospital with eyes that saw through mortar and brick. He saw himself as simply a name printed in red ink in a rectangle denoting a bed.

What was the old man's name again? Peavy? Parsons?

He fell asleep trying to remember it.

When he woke up it was after midnight. The luminous hands of the man's wristwatch Solange had lent him told him it was two in the morning. It seemed hotter in the room, there was no breeze at all now, and his pajamas were drenched in sweat. He kicked the sheet off his knees and lay perspiring in the dark heat, wondering if he could ask the night nurse for a change of pajamas. Under him the sheet was wet and sticky from the rubber mattress cover.

He swung his legs off the bed and sat up in the darkness, feeling around on the night table for the medicine glass with the sleeping capsule in it. But it was gone. The nurse must have taken it back. Annoyed, he searched around on the floor for his slippers and pulled his robe over his shoulders and went to the door.

The corridor seemed even more deserted that it had the night before. He started toward the nurse's office, but stopped halfway there. The door to the diet kitchen was slightly ajar and he heard her Swedish-accented voice from within. He knocked softly. There was a rustle of agitated silence from within. Then he heard the night nurse's voice.

"Who's that?" she asked. The door opened and he found himself staring into the brilliant white light. He had to shield his eyes. "Oh, it's you again, is it?"

He started to apologize when he realized that there were two other nurses sitting at the table behind her. They stared at him with blank white faces. Before he could open his mouth the night nurse turned and said over her shoulder to the other two, "It's all right. It's just number nine, the one I was telling you about." Then she turned back to Stone. "You may as well come in," she said. Stone noticed that one of the other nurses frowned as he stepped into the brightly lighted room. The door was closed behind him.

"Sit down," his own nurse said. Stone assumed the other two were night nurses from the other floors in the wing. Stone sat down. Then his nurse looked around the table and said, "What did you do with it?"

Reluctantly one of the other nurses—she looked American, thin, middle-aged—reached under the table and retrieved an open bottle of champagne. "If they ever find us in here with a patient . . ." she began.

"Oh, Thelma, relax." Stone's night nurse reached into the closet for a glass for him. "If they find us they fire us all anyway, with a patient or without." For the first time Stone noticed that she looked a little flushed. "Besides, they're all in bed. I checked."

The other two nurses relaxed slightly. But the one called Thelma glanced at her watch, still looked dubious as she poured out champagne into Stone's water tumbler. "I guess we can't drink it all, anyway," she said without conviction.

Stone's nurse giggled in a high unexpected way. "We'd better finish it tonight," she said. "It'll be flat by morning."

Suddenly the name came to him, the name he'd fallen asleep trying to remember. It was penciled on the label of the champagne bottle: PULVER. He stopped the glass halfway to his lips. The one called Thelma saw him looking at the name on the bottle and said, "You're not superstitious, are you?"

Stone looked at her in confusion. "No, it's just that I couldn't remember the name. I was trying earlier to recall—"

"At least we should drink him a toast, don't you think?" the other nurse said to Thelma, ignoring Stone.

"Someone may as well enjoy it," the other one said. She was small and mousy. "Poor man."

Stone's nurse turned to her. "You sound like we're robbing his grave, Alice. He would have wanted us to have it."

Alice said, "I hope they don't find a patient in here." Stone took her to be English.

Suddenly Thelma laughed.

"What are you laughing at?" Alice asked. "The poor man's gone."

"I know," Thelma said, regaining control, embarrassed. "I don't know why—"

"Can't we drink to the poor man's memory without you thinking it's funny?" Alice continued. She was clearly offended. She might also be a little tipsy.

Stone apologized and started backing toward the door. "I'm sorry," he said. "I didn't mean to barge in . . ."

"I should hope not," Alice said. "After all, you're a patient here just like he was, poor man."

"That's not a nice thing to say, Alice," Stone's nurse said. "I told you number nine was all right. Last night . . ." She suddenly turned to Stone. "I told them about last night. You didn't make a fuss, did you?"

"No," Stone said.

She turned to the other two. "You remember the trouble that Mrs. Marston made when it happened to her. She almost got me fired."

"It wasn't anything really," Stone said. "Just an old man who got in the wrong room."

"I hope you don't think we drink champagne every night," Alice said accusingly.

"Not at all," Stone said.

"It's just that the hospital is half empty every year about this time," Thelma put in.

"This is against all the rules," Alice said, shaking her head. "All the rules."

Stone's nurse gave an unfeminine grunt of laughter.

"You'll think we're terrible nurses, drinking on the job," Alice continued. She looked at Stone's nurse. "Herta, you shouldn't have brought him in here."

Herta shrugged and laughed. "I didn't bring him. He came."

"You didn't have to invite him in."

"I didn't have to ask you either," Herta said. "But I did. He's got as much right to it as you have. Sit down, number nine. I insist, as a friend of the deceased." She laughed.

Alice looked primly into her glass. "Well, at least I've got some respect for the dead," she said, stiffly. She raised her glass awkwardly in a silent toast.

Stone sat with the three nurses for nearly a quarter of an hour, silently sipping champagne. Alice filled her own glass twice, pointedly ignoring the others. Twice she shook her head and muttered, "Poor man," to herself.

When Stone got up to leave, Alice had tears in her eyes and was glaring at Herta. Stone left quietly.

Back in his room, Stone turned on the bed lamp and sat for a long time on the edge of the bed before the window looking out. The champagne had done nothing for him except make his stomach roll gaseously. He wondered who had written the name on the bottle. Mr. Pulver, who had been so alive and protesting not very many hours ago, would protest no longer. His battle with the nurse was over. He thought: Old Mr. Pulver is gone. The bed in the next room was empty. Absently he fished a cigarette out of the nearly empty pack in the pocket of his robe, and put it in his mouth without lighting it, content to leave it. The unlit cigarette tasted sweet as he sucked the flavored air through it. The bed lamp made the room seem emptier.

Unwillingly almost, as though finally compelled by habit, he turned away from the dark window and reached across the bed to the night table for his cigarette lighter. It had disappeared with the medicine glass and the sleeping capsule. Then he noticed that the newspaper Solange had brought had been placed on the shelf below. The nurse must have done it while I was asleep, he thought. He got off the bed and came around the foot to the night table, and opened the drawer. The lighter and the medicine glass were both there, although the nurse had indeed taken the capsule away. He knew patients weren't allowed to save sleeping pills, but it annoyed him that she had taken it. It must have been the early nurse going off duty, he thought. He flicked the sparking wheel of the lighter, and it flamed on the first try. Then he noticed the envelope. His hand stopped in midair. Merseault's letter. He stared at it.

He picked up the letter and looked at it in vague amazement. It had lain in the drawer all evening without his thinking about it once. Nor had he once thought again of the conversation he'd had with Solange about it. He'd completely forgotten about the letter from the moment the diet nurse had closed the drawer on it before supper. The unlit cigarette hung soggy, leached between his lips; automatically he turned it around and lit the wet end, the fresh end in his mouth. He closed the lighter and laid it back in the drawer unthinkingly.

He dropped the letter back into the drawer and closed it. In the back of his mind he resolved to leave the hospital in the morning. Carefully he took off his robe and folded it over the foot of the bed.

He got in bed and turned the light off and lay still. Discovering the letter had bewildered him. How could he have submerged the matter so completely? He had meant to study the letter more carefully as soon as Solange left, but had forgoten about it. It worried him. Through hours of utter boredom the thought of drafting a reply to Merseault had never once entered his head. Also, it struck him as odd that Solange hadn't mentioned the subject again after supper. I'll get out of here tomorrow, he thought. In the darkness after a while he found himself thinking again of Mr. Pulver, whose bed next door was empty. The thought made his own room seem emptier. Restless in the summer dark, he turned the light on again. And then fell asleep.

When Stone woke it was still early in the morning. The nurse had turned his lamp off. It was light outside the window and the sun was coming up in the cool blue sky. He felt rested despite the fact that he had only a few hours' sleep. His resolve of the night before was still clear in his mind; he awoke with the thought of leaving. He got out of bed and went over to the window. It was going to be another hot day.

He picked up the phone, forgetting that the switchboard for private calls would not be open till nine. The line was dead.

Outside in the corridor the lights were still on and the night nurse was still on duty. He walked quietly past her door, making no sound in his cloth slippers, and proceeded toward the telephone booth at the end of the hall. The nurse hadn't seen him. She was making entries in her log, the radio playing softly at her elbow.

Inside the cramped booth he closed the glass door and telephoned Solange. When she answered her voice was heavy with sleep. He told her he was leaving the hospital.

"Today?" she asked sleepily.

"Yes," he said. "I want to talk to you."

"Now? What do you want to talk about?" She laughed sleepily.

He heard voices approaching outside in the hallway. He heard the nurse, and a man laughing. He lowered his voice.

"Did you telephone Merseault?"

She hesitated before answering. Then she said, "Last night. After I left you. I was going to wait before telling you."

"Telling me what? You talked to him?"

There was a long pause. Then she said, "They've confirmed her identity. She gave birth to a child, and they've found the record of the birth. The birth was normal and the child healthy."

"What happened to it?" Stone asked.

"It was given out for adoption by a German family."

"Any chance of . . ."

"They don't know if they'll be able to trace it."

"What was it?"

"Male."

At that moment, he saw the night nurse glide past the glass doors. She didn't see him. She stood just outside his vision, holding open the swinging doors that led off the corridor toward the elevator. A young man pushing a wheelchair went past. The Ambassador sat in the wheelchair, fully dressed, with a blanket across his knees. He had a small valise in his lap. Stone didn't see his face in the brief instant because Sheppard was looking the other way.

"What's the matter?" Solange's voice said in the earpiece.

"The nurse just passed. I didn't want her to hear me."

"Do you want me to come for you?" she asked. "I brought clean clothes yesterday for you. I left them with the nurse."

"No. I'll be there sometime today. You go back to sleep."

After he hung up, he hurried back down the corridor to his room. He didn't want to be in the corridor when the nurse came back from taking Sheppard down in the elevator. It seemed a strange hour for a patient to be leaving.

He stopped outside his own door. The door to the suite was wide open at the end of the hall. All the lights were still on inside.

It was a strange hour, even for an ambassador.

Stone knew he wouldn't be able to leave right away. The key to the room where the clothes lockers were was in the keeping of the chief nurse, and she wouldn't be on until nine. Besides, he knew he should at least try to get the doctor's permission first.

After breakfast, when the doctor came, Stone explained that he wished to leave the hospital as soon as possible. The doctor, a young American with close-cropped hair, studied Stone's chart for a few moments and then said, "Nothing wrong with you. You can leave any time you want to." Then he smiled and said, "Just stop at the cashier's on the way out."

The nurse attending the medicine cart on the threshold of the room informed the doctor that Stone was an Embassy patient. The doctor said, "In that case forget about the cashier. You're free to go whenever you wish. You may as well stay for lunch, since Uncle Sam will be charged for it anyway."

Stone thanked him, and the doctor turned to leave. At the door he stopped and suggested that Stone wear the sling for another week, and be careful about putting undue strain on the injured arm. Then he left.

Alone in the room, Stone lay back on the bed and smoked a leisurely cigarette. Now that he was free to go when he pleased he felt no hurry to leave. He decided to make use of the time before lunch to make up for the sleep he had missed the night before. He was just falling asleep when the nurse came in and said he had a visitor. He sat up in bed.

The last person he expected to see was MacNaughton. He hadn't talked to the reporter since the day he had blundered into the meeting of officers in Stone's old office in the Graves Registration Command. Before that he'd seen him only once or twice since the one time during the war.

MacNaughton said, "So they're chucking you out today."

"How did you know I was here?" Stone asked.

"I had to come over on some other business, and saw the clerk writing your name on the discharge roster—over his shoulder, of course. I'm glad to see you."

"I'm not sure I'm glad to see you," Stone said.

"I hope you don't hold the past against me, old boy. After all, it wasn't my fault."

"I suppose it wasn't."

"You would have been smoked out sooner or later," MacNaughton said. "I only went to the Astoria to see if I could trace you. I didn't know you'd taken a civilian job there."

"It doesn't matter," Stone said. "What do you want now?"

"I wish I could say I didn't want anything."

"What is it?" Stone asked.

"I got a tip this morning that your former boss is here," MacNaughton said. "Sheppard."

"How would I know if he was here?"

622

"I thought you might know, that's all. Thought I'd stop by as long as I was here. I've heard the old boy is rather sick."

"I didn't know he was still in Paris," Stone said. "I would have thought he'd be back in the States by now."

"No," MacNaughton said. "He didn't leave town after he left the Embassy. He's been living quietly at the Residency. Shunning publicity, that sort of thing. There's no reason for him to leave until they appoint his successor."

"I see."

"You don't know if he's here?"

"Have you looked in all the rooms?" Stone asked sarcastically.

"The information came from a good source," MacNaughton said.

Stone shrugged. "Maybe you don't get up early enough in the morning."

MacNaughton rose from the chair. "I hope you'll let me buy you a drink when you get out."

"I won't be seeing you," Stone said.

MacNaughton reached into his wallet and took out a card. "I'm always here when I'm not elsewhere," he said. Stone took the card and looked at it. It was a card for a free drink at a bar in Pigalle. "Friend of mine runs it. I get my drinks free for bringing in customers. Nice place. American chap from Oregon. Married a French girl after the war. Morgan's Bar."

Stone looked at the card again.

"If you don't use it," MacNaughton said, "give it to someone who will. He's just starting and needs the business."

"All right," Stone said. He opened the drawer of the bed table, slipped the card in, and closed it.

"If you come," MacNaughton said, "look for me upstairs. Corner table in the back. It's my office."

After MacNaughton left, a young redheaded nurse Stone had never seen before brought in Stone's clean clothes and laid them out on the unused bed. She was red in the face and seething with anger.

She stood at the bottom of the bed and faced Stone. "He a friend of yours?" she asked, jerking her head in the direction of the door through which MacNaughton had just left a minute earlier. She was a short girl, well built, wearing a tight uniform, and spoke with a midwestern American twang.

Stone said, "I only know him."

"The next time you see him, tell him to keep his fresh hands to himself," she said crisply, unconsciously smoothing her starched skirt with her palms. Still ruffled, she said, "If I see him again, I'll tell him myself." She turned and stalked out of the room, muttering under her breath. She closed the door firmly behind her.

Stone smiled to himself, wondering what MacNaughton had done to earn the nurse's ire. She was the first really attractive nurse Stone had seen. He looked at his watch and decided that he ought to try to sleep before lunch. Getting up from the bed he decided against putting on his clothes until after lunch. Before trying to nap again, he decided to take a bath and shave. It would help kill time.

The telephone rang. He answered it. It was Merseault.

VIII

Merseault was out of the car almost before it stopped moving. He shouldered his way rudely through a clutch of tourists silently waiting for their luggage to be handed down from the top of the autobus they'd just descended from, and pushed through the glass doors into the air terminal building. Inside, a larger crowd milled about the departure gate, animated, smiling, strangely silent. Some few sat on their suitcases, looking like drab birds of passage sitting out an adverse wind, but most moved about excitedly, silently gesturing among themselves. Around the neck of each one of them hung a huge yellow shipping tag. Merseault glanced around the room and noticed the tags without pausing to speculate on their oddity. His mind turned about one preoccupying question.

Outside the Air France ticket office a uniformed police officer was waiting for him. Merseault didn't bother to return the salute. He was slightly breathless:

"Were you able to detain him?"

The officer nodded silently toward a closed door farther on. Merseault didn't break his stride.

He reached the door, conscious of the police officer's eyes on him, and paused before opening it. Lettered across the door before his eyes was the single word: POLICE. He listened for an instant to the muffled angry voice of Picard inside, then turned the knob.

Carnot was the first to notice his entry. He smiled a smile of almost infantile delight and sighed loudly with relief as he saw Merseault. Picard halted in angry mid-sentence and turned. He fixed a venomous eye on Merseault.

"Is this your doing, Merseault?" Picard was pale with anger.

Merseault ignored him, addressed himself to the police officer Picard had been abusing. "I would like to speak to Monsieur Carnot alone. Ask these gentlemen if they will please wait outside."

For a moment truculence hung in the air. Picard started to protest that he was Carnot's lawyer, halted, then twisted his face into a smile and abruptly left the room. Two heavy-set silent men followed him. Only the doctor hesitated.

"I am responsible for the patient . . ." he began nervously, fingering the bridge of his spectacles.

Merseault turned to Carnot and asked gently, "Do you have any objections to my talking to you alone?"

Carnot said, "It doesn't matter."

The doctor shrugged. The police captain started to follow him out.

"Please," Merseault said, "I'd like you to remain here with us."

The police officer closed the door after the doctor and returned to his desk. He remained standing. Carnot was still seated.

Merseault gazed at Carnot a moment, then offered him a cigarette. The captain struck a match and lighted it.

"Alexi, how are you?" Merseault said finally. The police captain seemed surprised by the casual tone. Merseault explained, "We're old friends."

"Yes," Carnot said instantly. "I was hoping you'd come."

"Why, Alexi?"

"They are trying to keep me here. They don't want me to get well again."

"Are you leaving France of your own free will, Alexi?" Merseault asked. "You can talk to me. No one can hear us."

"Free will?" Carnot's eyes focused on Merseault's forehead. "They are going to make me well again. I have a piece of metal"— he tapped the white scar that showed through the cropped hair over his right ear— "inside, here." He smiled, forgetful a moment as though reminded of something, his expression full of vacant affection for some distant paradise. Then he said again, mechanically, "There are great surgeons. They are going to take it out with a magnet. They learned how to do it in the war."

"You want to go, then."

"They are going to take out a piece of bone about the size of a five-franc piece. I still have a piece of the German war in my head." He tapped his head with his fingers again, disturbing the ribbon of smoke that dangled upward from the cigarette in his mouth. He closed one eye against the sting of the smoke over his sallow cheek.

A knock came at the door. The captain moved to open it. He held it ajar and listened to a few muttered words from beyond it. Then he turned to Merseault.

"Monsieur Sweet?" he inquired warily.

Merseault nodded, "It's all right. Tell your man to ask him to come in."

Byron Sweet came in looking worried. Without a word he crossed the room and stood looking out the window with his hands in his pockets.

Merseault watched Carnot's reaction; there was none. He continued: "You have not been subjected to duress?"

Carnot smiled, patient, tolerant, "You don't understand. There is something wrong with my head. But they are going to make it all right again."

"There are no surgeons in France . . ."

"Of course not."

". . . or in the United States who might be able to perform such . . . ?"

Carnot suddenly blazed. "No. Nowhere. The Russian surgeons are the finest in the world. They don't work for money." Carnot subsided just as abruptly as he'd flared up. He smiled. "And there's a university where anyone can go, after my brain is fixed again."

Merseault abruptly changed his tack. "Alexi, tell me something. Who suggested that you get in touch with Stone—the time you met him in the park near the Embassy?" Sweet's hand halted in mid-gesture, arrested in the act of lighting a cigarette; Merseault saw the hesitation.

"No one. I did."

"Why did you do it?"

Carnot looked at Merseault in amazement. "I had to explain to him, didn't I? I had to explain to him why?"

"Why did you have to explain?"

Carnot paused. Then he said, "He trusted me."

Sweet turned his head slightly from the window. Merseault caught the movement and wished he could see his face for a moment.

"You were the only one who knew about the meeting beforehand?"

Carnot nodded.

"Then do you have any idea who it was that telephoned the American Embassy and told them Stone was going to meet you?"

"Yes."

"Who."

"I did."

"Why?"

"Why?" Carnot's mind seemed to wander off for an instant.

"Yes, why? To compromise Stone?"

Carnot seemed to smile in spite of himself, a twisted, unwilling smile. "Why should I want to compromise Stone? I am not an *agent provocateur.*"

"Perhaps you were worried about justifying yourself to the Party. Am I right?"

The smile vanished. Carnot looked bewildered. "I knew they'd be there. They even open the letters I send to myself. Of course, they were right to watch me." He smiled a smile that could have meant anything from shrewdness to madness. "Even I know that I'm not responsible for what I do all the time." Then just as suddenly, as though blown by a different wind, he became angry. "They opened the letters. I sent them to myself to see. They opened them."

"Why did you telephone the security officer before your meeting with Stone?"

"Stone?" Carnot thought a moment. "He trusted me." His manner became lucid and matter-of-fact. "I knew they'd protect him. The Americans are afraid of me—everyone is afraid of me. They'd have men around us. They probably had the whole park surrounded with hundreds of men. I was safe with them watching. Nothing happened. Otherwise that madman Boris might have . . . I don't know. I took a risk, yes, but I had to explain it to him dialectically. I owed it to him. I am not a coward, you see."

"Yes," Merseault said, "I see. What about the documents?"

"You spoke to me about them several times."

"You were going to leave them with me."

Carnot smiled. "That key I gave you. It's the key to the whole thing."

Merseault was puzzled. "Key? You gave me a key?"

Carnot laughed, his eyes knowing, forgiving Merseault his little joke. "Would you like me to tell you what the key fits?"

"If you wish."

Carnot simply laughed, said nothing more.

The door sprung open and Picard stepped into the room, the police guard remonstrating, restraining him by an arm. Picard had a piece of paper in his hand.

Picard said, his tone almost taunting, "I thought you ought to see this." He handed Merseault the document and stood silent as Merseault scanned it. "So if you're thinking of using him as a witness again, forget it. You can detain him if you want to, but it will do you no good."

Carnot looked up interested. "What's that?" he asked Merseault.

"Your certification of insanity," Merseault said matter-of-factly. "It makes your attorney your legal guardian."

Carnot stood up theatrically, angry. "I'm not insane!" he shouted. "I was wounded."

Merseault turned the document back to Picard. "What makes you think we would want to detain him?"

Carnot turned triumphantly to Picard. "You see! I told you he would help me."

Merseault continued, "Actually, we have no reason to want to detain him. As long as he is not being forced to leave the country against his will, I can see no reason why . . ."

The door opened again. An angry press of silent people crowded through it pushing a small man in a black suit before them. The nonplused police guard was simply ignored, shoved aside. Merseault realized that they were all part of the group he had seen coming in; they all had yellow tags around their necks. They were angry yet absolutely silent, and suddenly Merseault realized from their jabbering fingers that they were all deaf mutes.

It was clear that they were impervious to the curses of the hapless police officer guarding the door; they couldn't hear him. They merely shouldered him aside and propelled the small black-suited man into the room. From their gestures it was clear that they had caught the pickpocket in the act.

The police captain was speechless, not from surprise, but merely because speech was obviously useless. The mutes stood in an indignant circle, a babble of silent fingers. Then suddenly the captain had an inspiration. From the center drawer of the desk he took out a pair of handcuffs and snapped them on the sullen culprit. The small man glared defiantly at the circle of satisfaction around him; the mutes, justice done, merely stared back. Then, as though on some silent signal, they turned and filed past Merseault and out again.

Picard watched them go, his mouth open, arrested. The last one out pulled the door closed behind him; his yellow tag had been reversed, hung down between his shoulder blades. Merseault noticed only the word ROME stamped on it in red ink.

"Pilgrims," the police captain said. "They've been coming in since dawn."

"Pilgrims?"

"Deaf mutes from all over the world. They will meet here all day for registration. Then they divide into smaller groups and fly to Lourdes by chartered planes. From there to Rome for a special audience." He shook his head. "Pilgrims," he said again.

The pickpocket was taken out by two gendarmes, and another went to find some one of the pilgrims to sign a formal charge against him. The police captain wiped his brow wearily and sat down.

Merseault said, "Monsieur Carnot is free to leave any time, as far as I am concerned." He turned to Picard. "However, I would like to say good-by to him privately, Monsieur."

Picard turned and opened the door. "I'll tell the pilot to ask for another flight clearance." His tone was undisguised, sarcastic.

The door closed. Silence.

"Alexi, you're not afraid to leave?"

Carnot looked at the floor, muttered, "I'm *not* insane. I'm wounded."

Merseault exchanged a glance with the police captain. Sweet hadn't moved from his position by the window. He'd turned around once when the pickpocket was brought in; now he was looking out the window again, his back to the room.

Merseault changed his tactics again. "The key you gave me," he began, phrasing the gambit carefully, "what do you want me to do with it?"

Carnot became suddenly irritated, lucid. "I'm not insane. I didn't give you any key."

"I know," Merseault said.

"I gave it to a friend of ours."

Merseault shrugged. "It doesn't matter," he said, "since no one knows what lock it fits."

"It has a number on it."

Merseault remained silent, watching Sweet's back. Sweet seemed to show no interest in the business of the key.

Carnot went on, looking at the floor, "Safe-deposit box. Boulevard St. Germain."

"Where on the Boulevard St. Germain?"

Carnot fell silent.

"It's all right," Merseault said. "I'll find it. You can trust me."

"I threw the duplicate key into the Seine. I shouldn't talk any more."

"It's all right, Alexi."

Suddenly the door opened and the doctor came in. He was wringing his hands in uncontrolled agitation. "This man is too ill. He is a sick man, I tell you. He can't possibly . . ."

"What's wrong?" Merseault asked. "Come in. Close the door."

"There are two reporters outside. They know who's in here. You can't let them in. This is my patient. I'm responsible for anything—"

On impulse Merseault turned to Carnot. "Are you afraid of newspaper reporters, Alexi?"

Carnot's eyes narrowed to weasel slits. He accused the doctor, "You said I wasn't insane."

"You're not. But you are a sick man. I don't think you ought—"

"I would like to see the reporters," Carnot said, openly defiant.

The doctor looked as though he was in agony. "I must get Monsieur Picard." he said. He turned and fled out the door.

There were two of them, Lutelacker and a younger man. Merseault knew Douglas Lutelacker; the young man looked like an American also.

"Monsieur, my assistant, Mr. Striker." Lutelacker introduced the young man first to Merseault, then to the police officer. Sweet turned around and nodded.

"Hello, Sharkie," Sweet said. He looked embarrassed.

"Byron Sweet," Sharktooth said, in a casual aside to Willie Stryker. "He shows up every now and then in these things." Sweet might have been a piece of mildly unusual furniture for all the direct attention Lutelacker paid him.

Sharktooth turned directly to Carnot. "Willie tells me they are detaining you, sir."

Merseault interposed. "No, no. Just routine checking of papers. How did you know he was here, Mr. Lutelacker?"

"Willie was out here to see the pilgrims. He keeps his ears open."

"I see."

"There'll be more along in a minute. The word got around." He turned back to Carnot. "Then you'll be summering in Moscow this year?"

"I'm going for an operation and to go to school."

"What is your opinion of Dujardin's release?"

"He is not released."

"No, but from what I hear he will be soon."

"He is not important," Carnot said.

Picard burst into the room followed by the doctor. "Merseault, what is this? This man is not in any condition to be subjected to this kind of an ordeal."

"Isn't this a little unusual?" Sharktooth asked Merseault. "After all, he could still theoretically be called upon as a witness if there *were* another trial."

"He is not competent to testify," Picard shouted, waving his document. "I am his guardian as long as he is in France and I demand that you gentlemen leave him alone."

Merseault watched Picard narrowly, calculating the proper moment to try his bluff. "We have no reason to detain him, now that we are in possession of the documents we were looking for."

For an instant there was utter silence in the room. Carnot smiled at the reporters like a guilty child. Picard cooled instantly, then laughed.

Abruptly Carnot said, "There's something else no one knows except me. Berger kept a diary in English, which proves he wasn't afraid of the Germans. He is probably still alive."

Sharktooth leaped into the opening. "Do you have reason to believe that the Ambassador's son is still alive?"

Picard: "Please, gentlemen."

The doctor: "He can't be held responsible for what he says now."

Carnot: "No. I saw him killed."

"Are you sure he was killed?"

"No."

Picard broke out laughing, a nervous laugh, full of sweat. He laughed too loud, too long. It ended the interview.

Outside in the terminal the crowd of pilgrims had swelled to twice its size. They stood around in excited groups gesticulating on their fingers, talking in grimaces, tugging and tapping at each other's sleeves to open conversations. It was a bedlam of absolute silence, with only the occasional rustle of breath and clothing and the scraping of milling shoes and suitcases on the concrete floor. Now there were green and red tags as well as yellow ones. All of them had shipping tags around their necks, and they went among themselves comparing them. There were almost as many women as men, even a few children. One child, a lovely little girl, was asleep on a woman's lap clutching a large blue balloon in an armsround embrace.

One after another, the two-engined charter planes were towed up to the gate outside; group on group of waving gesturing pilgrims departed in a silent confusion of baggage and paper bags and umbrellas and even tennis rackets. One woman waiting had what appeared to be several dozen rosaries strung around her neck with her shipping tag. One after another the small groups managed to count their number through the gate out to the waiting ramp.

Merseault waited with the police captain. The two reporters had been joined by three more, including MacNaughton; they formed another group. Two Russian Embassy chauffeurs stood off by themselves, waiting, while outside on the ramp a Russian diplomatic courier, briefcase chained to his wrist, paced irritatedly back and forth eying the pilgrims morosely as they filed past in gay silent gesticulating groups on their way to their blessing in Rome and beatitude.

The airport personnel had long ago given up trying to direct the pilgrims' movement into the planes. By some mysterious process they merely organized themselves and moved on. Words of direction were not only useless; they were smiled at and ignored. The key to the operation lay in the cryptic numbers on the shipping tags. It was like watching the orderly confusion of a beehive; the human tongue was powerless to direct its activity.

So when the special Russian-built aircraft rolled up empty to the ramp in its turn, no one paid much attention until a phalanx of pilgrims sallied out across the asphalt to board it. One of the officials from the Russian Embassy, seeing what was happening, dropped the passenger manifests he was clearing through the customs counter, and fled out onto the ramp to head them off. The bemused pilgrims tolerantly ignored him, marched in a straight unaltered line toward the plane. He circled about them in a bewildered helpless circle, like a small dog trying to herd a platoon of infantry. Finally he ran ahead and mounted the passenger stairs. Turning, he faced them from halfway up. There he stood like Horatio at the bridge, shouting at the airport personnel to do something. The determined pilgrims, not hearing a syllable of this, hardly bothered to look up as they started up the passenger stairway.

It was the uniform of the Russian pilot that halted them. He backed them down the stairs, gently gesturing, and beckoned them to follow him out under the wing. There he halted, raised his arm, and pointed to the huge red Russian star painted there.

The Russian *ensigne* was like a rock thrown into an anthill. The bewildered group that had been turned back from boarding the alien craft returned bristling with signaling fingers, and soon the word was spread in a pandemonium of gesticulating arms and fingers in a dozen languages. The exaggerated silence and excitement made the whole terminal look like a comedy disaster scene from an ancient silent movie.

When the Russians' nondiplomatic baggage was finally assembled and loaded into the aircraft, Carnot came over to Merseault to shake hands and say good-by. Picard sulked behind him with the doctor. MacNaughton stepped in front of Carnot and tried to ask a question. but the two silent Russians closed in and brushed him aside.

"I say good-by," Carnot said.

"Bon voyage."

Nothing more was said.

Except for one more small incident, the Russians' departure went smoothly. At the door, the woman with the garland of rosaries stepped forward and gave one to Carnot. As she did so, she pointed directly at Carnot's empty sleeve; the very tactlessness of the gesture made it sympathetic. Carnot hesitated, then nodded. He took the rosary, glanced at it, dropped it into his pocket. They went out.

As the passenger stairs were rolled away from the door of the plane the pilot began revving the engines. Slowly, as the plane turned its silver flank toward the building, the blood-red star on its rudder became visible. A sound like a sigh went up from the insulted pilgrims.

The engines roared one by one as the pilot checked them out. The din made the glass walls rattle and vibrate. Then the plane lumbered off down the pavement to begin its run from the far end of the runway. A moment later another plane was rolled to the waiting ramp by a small red tractor; the squad of pilgrims was already marching across the asphalt to meet it.

Merseault felt someone at his elbow and took his eyes away from the scene beyond the glass. It was MacNaughton and a young journalist he didn't know. Lutelacker was standing behind them, just within earshot.

"What is this about some documents? Do the Dujardin files really exist?"

"There are no such files." It was Picard speaking. Merseault turned to find him standing behind him.

Merseault faced MacNaughton again. He shrugged. "Carnot has a mind for fantasy, I'm afraid."

"You don't believe such files exist?"

Merseault noticed that Lutelacker was listening closely, although pretending to be absorbed in the progress of the pilgrims as they boarded the aircraft outside.

"I don't believe they exist," Merseault said. "Although I won't know until I make certain inquiries. Carnot is a very sick man. He can hardly be held entirely responsible for what he says."

"You've changed your opinion rather quickly," Picard said. "A moment earlier you said something about having found—"

"Yes, I have changed my opinion, Monsieur," Merseault said shortly.

At that moment the building roared. The silver hull of the Russian plane slipped past, its wheels just lifting off the runway. It flashed in the sun and was gone. The sound diminished to a whisper. Out of the corner of his eye Merseault noticed that Lutelacker was gone. Very casually he turned his head and saw him slipping out toward the parking lot. Byron Sweet was with him. Merseault made a note of the time on his watch. He knew where they were going. It didn't matter; there was time enough to reach Stone at the hospital by telephone.

MacNaughton hung on, searching his mind for a question. Merseault surmised from the look around his eyes that he was suffering from a hangover.

Then MacNaughton said, "And what's this about Sheppard's son keeping a diary?"

Merseault shrugged. "If such a document existed it would have been brought forward at the trial."

MacNaughton grunted and fell silent, his brows knitted. "All this nonsense at this time of day," he said. "Gives me a headache."

Merseault decided he would stand a moment longer, so as not to appear in a hurry. Then he would turn, be cordial to Picard, make a joke for the reporters. Then leave. He noticed that MacNaughton seemed to be getting interested in the pilgrims. Merseault thought: He probably doesn't want to go back empty-handed.

"Interesting pilgrimage," Merseault mused, for MacNaughton's benefit.

"Where're they going?"

"Rome, of course." Then Merseault added, "I think they're stopping at Lourdes."

"Catholics, eh?" MacNaughton said. "Too bad."

"Might make a good story," Merseault said. "They come from different countries all over the world."

"It wouldn't make much difference in Glasgow," MacNaughton said sadly.

One of the other reporters looked puzzled. "Did you say Moscow?"

"Glasgow, imbecile. Glasgow."

"Oh." The reporter still looked puzzled. He didn't say anything else.

Merseault decided he had dallied long enough and turned around to be cordial to Picard. But Picard was also gone. At that precise instant there was a sharp report like a pistol shot. Everyone turned toward the direction of the sound, everyone except the pilgrims, who heard nothing.

"What was that?" MacNaughton asked of nobody.

Merseault smiled privately, said nothing. He alone saw: For no apparent reason the blue balloon had popped in the sleeping child's arms. The woman who was holding the little girl was slumbering now also. The sound hadn't disturbed them. Both still slept, oblivious. In her arms, the child still hugged the momentary circle of empty air, the imagined blue balloon.

IX

Stone was waiting, sitting up in bed reading, when Merseault arrived. He was freshly shaved, but still not dressed. Merseault entered, put the question without preamble:

"Have you got it?"

Stone took the key out of the drawer of the night table and handed it to Merseault. "I found it in my wallet. I had forgotten all about it until you telephoned. You caught me just as I was thinking of leaving."

"The reporters haven't been here yet?" Merseault asked.

"Not about Carnot."

"What do you mean?"

"Early this morning MacNaughton was here looking for the Ambassador."

Merseault nodded. "That was before I called. MacNaughton showed up at the airport too. What did he want?"

Stone shrugged. "I told him I knew nothing. He left."

"Sheppard left here this morning before breakfast. He's resting at home."

"I know."

"You knew he was here all the time?"

Stone nodded. "When is he leaving for America?" he asked.

"Tomorrow. He wants to avoid a crowd at the airport."

"How is he?"

Merseault shrugged, avoided answering. He took out a small black notebook and looked at it. "Carnot gave you no idea of what this key . . . ?"

"No."

"I see." Merseault put the notebook back in his pocket and walked to the windows and looked down. He looked puzzled. "I can't understand where Sweet went. I was certain he'd come straight here. Do you know an American journalist named Lutelacker?"

"The one they call Sharktooth? I know who he is, that's all."

"He and Sweet left together."

"I know." Stone said. "You told me that when you telephoned. They didn't come here."

"I gave them plenty of time. You are sure you didn't tell anyone else about this key Carnot gave you?"

"No one. Frankly, I didn't think much about it afterward. Carnot was crazy. I humored him, that's all. He left the key on the bench. I picked it up. That's all. I couldn't ask him about it because he was already gone."

Merseault looked at his watch, frowning. "It's been nearly two hours since they left the airport."

Stone gazed at the ceiling. "Carnot's probably halfway to Moscow by now," he mused.

Merseault glanced at him impatiently. "Not quite," he said, and looked back at his watch as though somehow the watch held the answer. He started to pace back and forth past the foot of the bed. Then he stopped, looked straight at Stone.

In a more gentle tone, he asked, "Did you get my letter about . . . ?"

Stone nodded. "Yes. Thank you. I talked to Solange. She told me the rest."

"I should have more detailed information. I've asked the British Zone Archives Custodian to cross check the camp records with the refugee relief organizations. It's possible that they might turn up something on the adoption. Possible . . ."

". . . but not probable."

Merseault nodded wearily. "But not probable."

The telephone beside Stone's bed rang. He answered it, listened a moment, handed it to Merseault. "It's your secretary."

"Yes, Alain?"

Merseault listened long and intently, holding the receiver close to his head so that not the slightest sound escaped into the room. Stone could hear his watch ticking. Merseault's face was a mask. He listened steadily for what seemed an impossibly long time. Finally he grunted and hung up. He didn't bother to say good-by. Stone remembered Merseault's doing the same thing to him the first time he'd talked to him on the telephone. It wasn't that he meant to be rude apparently, simply that he had nothing further to add to the conversation. The secretary was probably used to it.

Merseault sat down on the bed suddenly like a man deflated, his face a mixture of worry and annoyance. He looked up at Stone.

"I'm going to have to take you into my confidence. Don't betray me."

Stone felt suddenly bewildered. He nodded passively.

"Dujardin has dictated and signed a full confession."

The news had no impact on Stone at all. It simply seemed a monumental anticlimax. "I thought they were working behind the scenes to release him."

Merseault shrugged impatiently, as though Stone's words were foolish, irrelevant. Stone felt they were the instant he'd uttered them.

Stone tried again. "Why?" he asked.

Merseault sighed. "Everything is upside down and backward. The files," he said.

Obviously "the files" meant something, explained something, but Stone missed it. "The files? What files?"

Merseault simply held up the key Stone had given him. He shook his head incredulously. "It's a miracle we haven't all gone mad," he said. "I'll tell it to you just as I heard it over the telephone. Listen carefully."

Merseault paused, as though gathering strength.

"When I called you from the airport I thought Sweet would come here to see you. I couldn't know whether he had deduced you had this key or not, but I thought you might have told him. That's why I told you to tell him you'd given it to me. If Carnot really has Dujardin's files locked up I want to see them first, before they are edited and swallowed up into the government's archives. Such files, if they exist, might contain embarrassments other than . . . so, you understand."

Merseault took a deep breath and licked his lips.

"I worked in that area during the war. I have my private reasons for wanting to check some old suspicions, as I'm certain you can understand. I lost several close friends in the south, including a man who was a close friend of yours."

Stone's eyebrows went up.

Merseault looked at him. "Lautrec," he said.

"You worked with Lautrec?" Stone's voice was incredulous.

"I trained Lautrec. He was my good friend. Why do you think I have followed your activities so closely? How do you think I knew so much about you? Do you remember the time when you first met Mac-Naughton? At the weapons drop?"

Stone nodded.

"This is something you must never repeat, because I suspect Mac-Naughton may still be active—he still goes to Berlin from time to time. MacNaughton was at one time my SOE courier, my main link with London."

Stone said nothing.

"For reasons which you can well understand, I was very anxious to keep track of those weapons you brought in. I knew what you were doing, and I knew why you were doing it. I could only assume you had good reasons. You see, I too expected the invasion to come in the south. But the British were unwilling for you to have those weapons unless I could guarantee to keep track of where they went. The British were much more alive to the possibility of civil war than the Americans."

"I see."

"Lautrec trusted you. I trusted Lautrec. Understand?"

Stone nodded.

"When Berger arrived in the south from Paris I got word from Lautrec that something was wrong. That was the last word I had from him before the mass arrests."

"New Year's Day, 1944." Stone nodded, sardonically nostalgic.

"Precisely. There was nothing I could do. I couldn't leave Paris. The best I could do was to hope you knew what you were doing."

"You knew I was coming?"

"It was I who approved your mission—that is to say, I was consulted on the hazards of arming Picard's group."

"*Picard's* group?"

"You do remember meeting him, don't you?"

"Then that *was* Picard in the farmhouse? Why did you lead me to believe that Picard was never in the south?"

"I was afraid you'd put your foot in it. You almost did. Picard couldn't be sure that you didn't remember him. Because, you see, *he'd forgotten meeting you.* At least he didn't seem to connect you with the man he'd met."

"But what's the point? I don't see why . . ."

636

"Never mind why. Leave Picard to me. Picard is a politician. We can't destroy him, but we can frustrate his ambitions by forcing him to be cautious."

Stone shrugged. "I suppose that's your battle."

"You realize that I am violating my every instinct in discussing these matters with you, especially since it involves a third party."

"MacNaughton."

"I assume you know how to keep your mouth shut or you wouldn't have survived the war. Have you told your friend Solange about that girl?—By the way, the first name tallies with the birth record."

"Yes. I told her."

"Does she know that Adriane was Carnot's mistress?"

"No."

Merseault went on. "While we are about that, what was her relationship to Berger?"

"I don't know."

"Did you trust her?"

"Yes."

"Did you trust Berger because of her?"

"I didn't trust Berger. I arrested him. I was trying to get him out, on orders."

"Do you think it was Berger who informed on you?"

"No, I don't."

"Why?"

"He didn't have the opportunity. He was under guard."

"Perhaps he got word out."

"Look here, Merseault. The war is over. I don't believe he informed because I don't *want* to believe it. It is not *necessary* to believe it."

"You know his father . . ."

". . . thinks he was a traitor. Well, he wasn't. He was sick with fear and he had a lot of sick ideas about putting the Count of Paris back on the throne of France. But he did a lot of good work in Paris . . ."

"How do you know?"

"I don't know!" Stone made no effort to hide his anger. "Do you?"

"Yes," Merseault said quietly. "He has been recommended for the Legion of Honor."

Stone looked cynically at Merseault. "Because of his father?"

"No. Because of the father's son."

Stone shrugged, frowned at his open palm.

Merseault began, "Is it because he saved your . . . ?"

"Yes! He saved my life. If he hadn't shoved into that guard I wouldn't be sitting here telling you."

"Did you push him?"

"Did I *what?*"

"Did you push him into the guard?"

Stone turned his hand over and studied his knuckles. Suddenly he was quiet, completely quiet. His mind seemed to have wandered off the subject, and for a long moment Merseault's question was left hanging in the white silence of the hospital room. Muffled in the hall outside was the slip-slop sound of someone mopping the corridor.

Finally Stone dropped his hands into his lap. They lay lifeless on the sterile white sheet. He looked directly at Merseault, and said, "I don't know."

Merseault said nothing.

Stone went on, repeated, "I just don't know."

Merseault's face registered no emotion; polite interest, nothing else.

"I thought about pushing him . . . you think of a thousand things. You can't help it. Your mind has been trained to sift all the possibilities. I thought of throwing a fit. I thought of diving under the truck to give the others a chance. I thought of running for the staff car and trying to drive off in it. I thought of trying to snatch a weapon—I thought of everything, every possible way out. And I also thought of pushing him into the guard."

"You said once you were tied together."

"They untied us as we got out of the truck."

"Yes, that would be the way," Merseault said, almost to himself.

"What made you ask if I had . . ."

". . . if you pushed him?" Merseault paused. "I don't know. I thought of myself in the same situation, perhaps."

"The Ambassador asked me if I had ordered him to."

"You've thought about it a great deal, haven't you?"

"I remember getting out of the truck. I remember calculating the distance between me and Berger. I remember running and seeing him go down. I remember the guard's face, the one Berger knocked down. He was just a youngster and he was crying."

"I don't believe you pushed him," Merseault said.

"Why?"

"As you say, it's not necessary to believe it."

Stone shrugged and looked away from Merseault. There was a pause. Then Stone asked, "Why are you bringing all this up now?"

"Dujardin confessed because he believes we have found his personal files. He confessed in order to be spared another public trial with their contents made public."

"*Do* you have the files?"

"I don't believe they exist. I won't know until I track down the safe-deposit box that this key fits. Carnot lived in a world of his own invention."

"You think it's a hoax."

"Yes, don't you?"

Stone shrugged. "I still don't see why—"

"You and I are the only ones in the world who know of the existence of this key. I want you to forget you ever had it."

"And if I'm asked under oath?"

"In that case tell the truth. I don't believe you'll ever be asked. I think I know what's in that safe-deposit box, if there's anything at all."

"Not the files?"

"No."

"Didn't Sweet hear Carnot tell you about the key?"

Merseault shrugged, irritated. "Carnot was obviously insane. Besides, he didn't mention your name. Just let me manage it, and say nothing unless you are asked. Agreed?"

"You know what you're doing," Stone said casually. "How did Dujardin get the idea that you had the files if you just came from the airport yourself?"

"That's where our missing reporters went. Lutelacker picked up a photographer from *France-Soir* and went straight to Dujardin's cell. Sweet went along for the ride. They got there just before Picard showed up. Picard tried to stop the whole thing, but Dujardin just sat there asking for a stenographer. I think he *wanted* to confess. I think he was terrified of leaving prison."

Stone shook his head. He felt depressed. He looked at Merseault, then smiled faintly and let his head fall back on the pillow and stared at the ceiling. "You get attached to prison," he said. "I remember telling the doctor in the truck that all I wanted in the world was to be back in that stinking black cell listening to the bombardment."

"Well, you don't have to go back to it now."

Stone looked at Merseault. "Go back? Hell, I never really left it."

After Merseault left, Stone got dressed, and removed his few belongings from the drawer of the bed table. Cigarettes. Lighter. The letter from Merseault he slipped into its envelope, hesitating before deciding what to do with MacNaughton's free-drink card. Finally he slipped the card into the envelope also, and closed the drawer. The magazines he would leave. When the nurses finished with them, they would find their way into the solarium, there to be thumbed slowly to destruction, by a future generation of patients. He felt a little as he had as a child on the last day of school. It seemed as though he'd been here longer than he had.

In the hall he almost ran into the redheaded nurse. Evidently she had forgotten her anger over MacNaughton, because she stepped back and smiled at Stone, looking him up and down. Stone noticed that she'd combed her hair and put lipstick on. She handed Stone an envelope.

"What's this?" he asked.

"Every departing guest has to get one," she said. "If you have any suggestions or complaints you're supposed to write them down and leave it with the cashier."

"What does the cashier do with them?" Stone asked.

"How should I know? I'm just supposed to hand them out. Someone else has the responsibility of throwing them away. I just check you out."

"Is that why they picked a pretty girl for the job?" Stone asked.

"You're a friend of his, all right," she said. "Well, I've done my part, the rest is up to you." She pointed to the envelope in Stone's hand. "Give them hell for me while you're at it. Tell them the nurses are overworked."

Stone laughed. She smiled and slipped past him and disappeared into one of the other rooms.

At the end of the corridor, near the bath, Stone met the chief nurse. He'd only seen her once before. She was a huge authoritative middle-aged woman with a dead-pan face. She stopped and looked him up and down critically.

Stone started to say something polite, but she cut him off.

"Where's the sling for that arm?" she asked, pointing sternly.

Stone looked down at his arm. He was at a loss for a moment. "I . . . I must have left it in the room," he said.

"Well, you just turn right around and go back there and get it," she commanded. "The trouble with you government people is that you don't have to pay your own bills. If you did, you'd take better care."

She strode past Stone, and rammed her bulk through the swinging glass doors to the stairway and left Stone standing alone in the hall. In one of the rooms off the corridor behind a closed door he suddenly heard a woman's voice. For a few moments, she was alternately singing and moaning. Then it was quiet again, dishes shuffling in the diet kitchen. From far away, in some distant part of the building, he heard the sullen vibration of a heavy machine. He started back along the empty corridor toward his abandoned room, just in time to see a cleaning woman emerge from it, cross the hall, and disappear into the room opposite carrying an armful of his old bed linen. Already he was one of the dispossessed. He went back.

The sling was where he'd left it, hanging on the foot of the bed-stead. Everything else had been stripped clean off the bed, everything except the brown rubber half-sheet. It was as though the cleaning woman had known he'd be back for the sling. He put it over his head and adjusted it under his forearm, and looked around the bare room. Even the magazines were gone. It gave him an odd feeling, as though the hours in this room had marked the passing of a crisis. He was leaving here into a completely uncertain future, a future he hadn't even thought about. After months of clinging to a job by his fingernails, he had finally let go, starting afresh in a direction he hadn't even considered yet. In any event, time had stopped for a few days within this room, and it was here, without knowing exactly when, that he had made the decision.

He was glad to be released into the world again, but still there was a certain regret. He was beginning to feel he had submerged the past without understanding it. Now it was becoming necessary to resurrect it again and examine it. In this room, he realized, the whole meaning of it had changed. It was as though he hadn't paid close enough attention to the experiences, had carelessly and wastefully forgotten them. He remembered how, as a young man back from Paris, he had been besieged with questions. What was it like? Only as he grew older he realized that he didn't really know. He had seen and forgotten, had seen only with a boy's eyes and a mind careless of its treasures. It was only on returning in the full awareness of an adult's miserly mind that the meaning of the earlier experience had come alive again, and he had rediscovered a part of himself that he never knew existed. But there would be time, plenty of time, to think about everything that had happened. To pursue the new meaning of his life through the labyrinth of mind and memory, to evoke the phantom of the past. At the center of the problem he felt he'd find something of his own nature, something he'd submerged and ignored since the day he'd imprisoned it.

What had happened to him in the hospital? Had he loved Solange? There seemed to be a thread running through the last few days, a powerful interconnection between events, but it eluded his grasp. And why had Sheppard been in this place at this time? It excited him a little to think that he was almost within reach of discovery. He had the confident sense, as he stood looking at the stripped bed, that something important had come to pass in this room. He could even feel the subtle change in himself. He didn't care about the job that had meant so much a few days ago. In fact, he didn't care about anything. It was a dangerous feeling, and he sensed that he hadn't yet felt its full impact. It was like the trickle that forewarns of the crashing of the dike, and the flood. The only regret he had, and it was regret only in the mildest sense of nostalgia, was in leaving this strange bare unhospitable room, a room that was no longer even his. It was a curiously unexpected feeling, and it surprised him. He surveyed the room for the last time.

And there was also the older pleasure: Solange. He looked forward to seeing her in the world outside again. Somehow his regret in leaving this room was tied in with his uncertain feeling about Solange. He felt he had come to know her here, as though for the first time, as a human being, a woman. For an instant as he thought of her, he even thought he could imagine her scent again. What his heart could not imagine, his flesh could.

He decided to leave without waiting for lunch.

Outside, closing the door behind him, he saw that the corridor was still empty. The nurses were occupied with their mysterious forenoon duties behind the closed doors of pain and suffering and healing and death. Behind the door in the diet kitchen he could hear two muffled women arguing amid a shuffle of crockery and silverware. He couldn't make out their words but the strident irritation was clear even through the closed door. He looked at his watch. They were late starting lunch today. He walked down the corridor slowly, feeling for the first time in a long while that he had no reason to hurry. There was no place he had to be. He had all the time in the world, a lifetime, to get where he was going. Behind him, in the diet kitchen, someone dropped a plate on the tiled floor. It shattered with a muted crash.

X

The table was set in Merseault's ground-floor study—the Ambassador was thus saved the difficulty of mounting stairs. It was a pleasant day and the heavy drapes that normally kept sunlight out of the room were drawn back and tied, and the doors to the small side terrace were open. The table was set in the wide doorway, in full receipt of the noon sun, and a clear fragrance of lilac reinforced the warm spring air. The Ambassador sat to the small table in his wheelchair, his jacket removed, his shirt open at the neck and tieless.

"What arrangements did you finally make with Douglas?" the Ambassador asked Merseault.

Merseault shrugged. "I did precisely as you suggested. He will stop by here for coffee—he should be here shortly."

"Quid pro quo?"

"He understands your desire for privacy—I made that clear. He gave me his word."

"This is one time I'd like to leave this city quietly. I have no conscience about avoiding the press now that I'm a private citizen again."

"Bruce, why did you want me to invite Lutelacker? Why only Lutelacker and no one else?"

"I suppose you might say I owe it to him, Georges. I've known old Sharktooth since the days of the blitz in London, and I can always trust him to quote accurately. I knew he wanted an interview. He's done me many a small favor . . ."

"You are aware, of course, that it was he who carried Carnot's tale to the prison yesterday. I suppose you might even say that he was responsible more than any other single person . . ." Merseault trailed off.

"Responsible? Responsible for what, precisely?"

Merseault looked up, as though from other thoughts. "Hm? What?" He looked blankly at the Ambassador a moment. "Why, for the confession. If he and that photographer from *France-Soir* hadn't got to Dujardin before Picard . . ."

"Douglas has an uncanny knack of going to the right place at precisely the right time—at least, so I'm told by his confreres."

"He was in the right place yesterday," Merseault mused, shaking his head slowly. "I never thought it could be so simple."

"I would like to have seen young Stone before I left. A man would like to put his life to rights."

"Why do you call him young?" Merseault asked idly. "He's in his forties."

"It must have been a great relief to him when he heard the news."

"I don't know." Merseault frowned. "I'll have to see him again—they can't locate the child in Germany."

"It *was* born alive, though?"

"Yes. It was male, and apparently born healthy because it was taken for adoption. The mother's name was listed as Santerre, and the first name was spelled in the same curious way: 'Adriane' instead of 'Adrienne.' All the other details check with the chronology of the pregnancy."

"Then what more is there to tell him?"

"Nothing, really. Except that further search seems hopeless. But I thought I'd let him read the correspondence for himself."

"He knows for certain the child is his?"

Merseault shrugged. "It's not *whose* it is, I suppose, but *what* it is that makes it important."

"I don't follow . . ."

"It's a child—what else is there beyond that? He'll never be able to find it, but at least he knows it exists."

"Yes," Sheppard said. "There is that knowledge."

"Shouldn't we change the subject?" Merseault asked flatly.

The Ambassador smiled gently, tolerantly. "If you wish," he said. "Yet you needn't be solicitous. I know what I know."

Merseault smiled in return. "You know too much . . ."

"Did the doctor tell you to tread lightly with me? Avoid upsetting me with talk?" The Ambassador snorted. "That young fool upsets me more than all the talk in the world."

"Well, enough of that," Merseault said. "What are your plans when you reach the States?"

Sheppard shrugged. "I'm getting too old to think that far ahead, Georges. First I suppose I'll have to concentrate on getting used to this—" He gripped the rubber treads of the wheelchair. "Then, if I live long enough, I'll address myself to the task of explaining my failure to myself. That should occupy me for the rest of my life."

"Your *failure?*" Mersault sounded incredulous.

The Ambassador laughed loudly. "Oh, come now, Georges. You must have guessed what monstrous ambitions I've suffered myself to keep secret from you all these years. You must have guessed that I fancied I had larger fish to fry."

"You? Political ambitions?"

Again the Ambassador laughed. "Ambition feeds on its own success, Georges. There is a point in public life past which no honest man can rise, without revising his ambitions upward. All of us entertain secret notions of high office—and those of us in high office can only think of higher office."

"And finally the highest office."

Sheppard nodded. "Ultimately, the highest office. And yet look at me—" He looked down at his legs, gripped the wheelchair again. "Look at this wreckage of cartilage and bone. Even though I have no wife, even though . . . And yet now I haven't even a body I can faithfully command." He laughed, laughed mildly, easily, as though at a joke on himself. "No, Georges. As they say elsewhere, the jig is up."

"You do seriously mean that you . . . ?"

"No, of course not." Sheppard smiled mischievously. "And yet why not? Why not, indeed? Can any of us read our futures? More worthy men than I have been quickened by impossible ambitions. Did you know that I had an opportunity to stand for elective office after the war? I had that chance and refused it. It might, by now, have led to the Senate. A dead end? I thought so. I felt that the future was to be unlocked in solving the problem of Europe. Europe had to be united. Do you suppose it was mere accident that led me into military government during the war?"

"I see," Merseault said.

"And yet it was not that I wanted office. No. I wanted peace." Sheppard smiled the same quizzical smile again. "And yet who is to say that had I solved the problem of peace in Europe—who is to say that I might not have been directed to apply my talents in broader measure? I believe passionately in what I am doing—what I *was* doing. Yet, was I not also ambitious?" Sheppard shrugged. "A short time ago I would have said no. But now? A man never knows how hard he is running till he collides with a tree. I don't know what to think."

"You are disappointed."

"I am enraged," Sheppard said grimly. "My legs . . . my . . . I am simply enraged. The Foreign Ministers Council. The General Assembly. The Council of Europe. There was work to be done, large words to be said . . ."

Merseault was growing restless, uneasy. "Bruce, you—"

". . . and where was *I*? I was flat on my back. In Walter Reed, in Boston, here in Paris. You know, Georges, there was that one idea that failed . . ."

"Yes, I know. We all know. And yet perhaps . . ."

". . . . perhaps it was doomed to failure? No. It failed because we lacked vision and common sense. Alas, the shining vision tarnished. In my own mind I saw it: the Free States of Federal Europe. Think of that . . ."

Merseault laughed. "Bruce, you never cease to amaze me. If this was a failure, then you are in good company."

Sheppard shrugged. "Well, politically we have all failed. Perhaps something can still be done economically."

Merseault made an offhand gesture. "Perhaps. Harriman couldn't have picked a better office than 2 Rue St. Florentin. Only two men in history have come close to unifying Europe previously; both sat in that same office."

"So?" Sheppard asked. "Which two?"

"Talleyrand and the Baron de Rothschild."

The Ambassador threw back his head and laughed. "Harriman will appreciate that."

"I'm sure he already has," Merseault said dryly. "But no matter. Europe will survive."

"Georges, you're exactly like all the rest. Europe will survive, indeed! Of course Europe will survive with the help of such men. But what about the rest of the world?"

"What time is your plane?" Merseault asked, abruptly changing course.

Sheppard waved off the question. "Don't worry. It won't leave until I get there. I'm the sole passenger, this time."

"And the doctor?"

Sheppard frowned. "I'm hoping he stays here. If I'm going to rest in North Africa, I'd just as soon do it without an amateur psychiatrist along. He's more interested in my head than in my knees."

"Are you being wise?"

Sheppard said, "I'm old enough now to be a little foolish, don't you think?"

The servant entered with a silver ice bucket from which protruded the graceful slender neck of a brown wine bottle. Merseault remarked that *Liebfraumilch* went particularly well with chilled rock lobster, observed also that the mayonnaise should always be freshly whipped from cold ingredients, as indeed, he said, this mayonnaise was.

"Conversation and a little cheese," Merseault said mildly, as the servant left. "That's what you said you wanted for lunch; that's what you're having."

Sheppard stared aghast, laughing; the double-tiered cheeseboard was laden with different shapes and sizes of cheese. There must have been well over a dozen varieties. Merseault turned the contrivance slowly around on its pivot, naming them.

". . . *Septmoncel*. *Pont L'Evêque*. A superb *Port-Salut* from *Mont-des-Chats*—this one looks particularly handsome." Merseault paused, picked up a knife and opened a wedge in the next one, murmured, "Ah . . . I was worried about this one—it's almost the last of this year's season. We won't see it again until the leaves are brown and blowing in the streets." Merseault gently removed the creamy yellow wedge; it sagged a little, bulged at the sides, but it didn't run. "Ah, *you* are perfect, perfect."

"What kind is that one?"

"It's a *Petit-moule*, a *Brie de Coulommiers*."

"Ah, yes. Talleyrand's 'King of Cheeses.' "

"He was more likely referring to the larger Bries—*de Meaux, de Melun*," Merseault said. "This over here is a *Cendré Champenois*—should be very fine."

"It looks as though it's been kicked through the streets," Sheppard observed.

"It is cured under hearth ashes," Merseault said, his enthusiasm undamped.

"I know that, of course. Nevertheless, it does look as though . . ."

"Trauben." He slowly turned the server. "Here are three different goat cheeses"—pointing as he named them—*"Sénecterre* from the Auvergne; *Saint-Marcellin* from the Dauphiné, and *Gavot* from the Hautes-Alpes. I tried to get you some *Saint-Affrique*—I wanted you to try it. But . . ."

"Good Lord, Georges, I had no idea you had developed into such a devoted caseophile. I'll have all I can do just to sample a few of these."

"I'm hardly a caseophile," Merseault said. "I merely like cheese in variety. And you said you wanted conversation . . ."

". . . and a little cheese." Sheppard said precisely, shaking his head, laughing.

Merseault surveyed the tiered platter, gave it another easy turn. It was an enjoyable sight, no question; he smiled and tilted his head, sighed with frank pleasure. "It's the only vice I can afford these days."

"Ah, sweet gluttony," Sheppard said, studying the platter for his first selection, knife raised hovering, probing. Merseault showed a host's true pleasure, gazed on Sheppard as a priest might on a proselyte entering the mysteries; he beamed, a man full at ease, secure in his benignity.

"After the cheese, we'll have more conversation," Merseault said. He paused a moment longer, the smile softening; then he fell to with solemn decision, smiling no more, deftly wielding the knife.

"Georges, tell me why things are as they are. What is the root of this intellectual anti-Americanism?"

"It is not intellectual. Simple," Merseault said. "It is, emotionally and spiritually, penance. It satisfies a very sensible need."

"But there must be some more precise explanation."

Merseault nodded slowly. "I have lived in nearly every major city in the Western world. I can only say that I've seen it before. It's nothing new, although it's unfamiliar to French intellectuals."

"You're not being clear."

"Guilt," Merseault said. "Existentialism is a reasoned attempt to make guilt bearable. In that, it is both a brilliant conception and courageous—and humane. But as a system it is open at both ends. Before the nausea comes the empoisonment. After the *engagement* comes the penance. French intellectuals failed rather miserably to excite the public imagination during the thirties. Their wits failed them; their rhetoric also. For one thing, they still have the death of the Spanish Republic on their consciences. Perhaps the Loyalist cause was doomed anyway, but no one will ever know. Yet the stuff of poetic rhetoric was there—one clearly written book might have changed history. But none of us wrote it. Picasso finally wrote it with a brush— Guernica—but he was a Catalan, and no one listened. We were content to sink in peace and quiet and hope. Instead of genuine eloquence, we forged indignation."

"We?"

"I was one of them in my day," Merseault said. "I even thought about volunteering to go and fight. But I didn't. It was because I didn't fight in Spain that I fought later in France—I chose military action rather than pamphleteering. I have done my penance. Others never found absolution for their failures. Even existential survival won't satisfy them. They flagellate themselves under the whip of unreason."

"You mean existentialism is a hair shirt?"

"Existentialism is a hair shirt that keeps a man warm, at least."

"And that is too much comfort? I see. How do we get to the Stalinist heresy?"

"There is no greater torture for the academic mind than to submit to an intellectual discipline of rigorous mediocrity. The professional intellectual is a deeply injured soul. I can only partly identify with him now. Since my work in the war further penance seems to me rather unimportant. I did my penance in direct military action. Nothing is more repugnant to me than killing a human being with my own hands, even if he is my enemy. I would much prefer to be killed than to kill."

"Yes," Sheppard said. "That's not an uncommon feeling among military men when depression overtakes them."

"In doing a thing repugnant to my nature I performed my absolution. The intellectuals who force themselves into service of a cause they know in their hearts to be false are committing the same kind of suicide. Theirs is a more grueling penance than mine was."

"I have not been able to fathom the appeal of existentialism," Sheppard said. "I suspect it's because I grew up in a safer age."

"No American, unless he has been in a prison camp, could possibly understand its profound emotional meaning. In the last war there were times when it was easier to die than to live. But each of us chose to live. Why?" Merseault shrugged. "Unless you can rationalize this ridiculous choice, it becomes senseless; you'll go insane. One takes final refuge in the idea that the *technique* of life is the meaning of life. The reason for living becomes a little like the reason for playing chess—not to win, but to perfect your game. It's not a senseless notion. One makes his choices, and takes his comforts. The purpose of playing chess is to play chess. The purpose of existence is to exist."

"I'm not sure I follow you."

"Mine is a highly personal view. An existentialist might understand me, but I doubt if a good old Victorian like you will."

Sheppard smiled.

"It's an attempt to force logic on the incomprehensible. For those who have been deprived of everything else, existentialism is a humane and compassionate philosophy. It's a perfect philosophy for the damned. Man values his sanity over life. I'm sure a man in Hell would teach himself to love his Tormentor. Otherwise Hell would be unbearable."

"Interesting. It's true that existence without order is terrifying."

"Man must create that rational order for himself. The universe is not naturally rational, nor for that matter is man himself. It is what makes being human more difficult than being animal. The prime requisite for human life is integrity of the mind. A man who can no longer construct meaning for himself is a man in the process of insanity. Usually he will kill himself rather than suffer the torment of a meaningless existence. However, by designing the universe as meaningless to start with, he reinvests that universe with meaning. By giving chaos a name he circumscribes chaos and can live with it. The long aim of philosophy is to conceptualize and thereby order chaos. It always amuses me to think that the physicists have come to understand this before anyone. The old concept of causality is being shored up by the new concept of total randomness."

"Georges, this is rather beyond my Edwardian formation."

"The universe is no longer seen as a piece of clockwork. The apparent order is due simply to the fact that chaos always tends to totality—the second law of thermodynamics. Entropy always increases. I usually pretend I don't understand these things—it's the only way to avoid discussing them."

"You sound very educated today, Georges," the Ambassador said pleasurably.

"I am, of course," Merseault said. "I merely pretend modesty. Fortunately there aren't many people who have the wit to dispute me."

Sheppard laughed heartily.

"How did we get onto this subject?" Merseault asked.

"You were explaining to me why French intellectuals don't like America."

Merseault frowned. "Yes," he said.

"What I can't understand is that they see all sorts of sinister things in American advertising and such silliness as Hollywood, and yet they find something enigmatically right about Soviet slave labor camps. It's very upsetting to an innocent like myself, who grew up in the train of a less subtle century. Is it that they secretly hanker after imprisonment?"

"The camps are a thorn in their consciences: Stalin—the purges—all of it. Men of inaction are always bemused by evil, mainly because ultimately evil *is* inaction. Action is life. Inaction is death. With the death of Lenin action stopped in the Soviet Union. Nothing new has come about. Stalin is the arch-conservative, the true preserver of the status quo. A rightist. Have you ever heard the story that he was a Czarist agent before Lenin came to power? It's probably not true, but it's persistent. Anyone who has ever worked in intelligence has heard it a dozen times from a dozen different sources."

"Is this another tale from your collection?" Sheppard asked, laughing.

"You never heard anything like that of Lenin," Merseault said. "It's just a curiosity, I suppose. But it makes one think."

Sheppard said, "Then you're contending that the French intellectuals have deliberately consigned themselves to a hell of their own making, is that it?"

"They didn't make it. Guilt always seeks its own torture. If they didn't have this means of seeking their own punishment, they'd find another. During the war I tried to kill myself physically. They are trying to do it spiritually. I rather admire their courage and tenacity. They live a very unrewarded existence. I hope they find their absolution."

"You seem to see it as a religious problem."

"I know nothing about religious problems. Psychologically, perhaps it is a religious problem. More accurately it is just what they say it is, a philosophical problem."

"But why should they not simply remain neutral? Why do they *actively* impugn the United States? Lord knows, we're doing the best we can with our limited vision. We have no territorial ambitions. We have never shown any predilection for aggressive military ventures."

"Those in Hell probably find the thought of Heaven bitter," Merseault said, smiling. "The United States can afford not to have ambitions."

"It's very frustrating to be misunderstood by men of obvious integrity and intelligence. I wonder if perhaps the State Department might do something by taking them on a tour of the United States?"

"Most of them couldn't qualify for visas under your laws. Picasso couldn't get into the United States, for example."

"Nonsense. The State Department isn't totally devoid of imagination."

"I hope he never puts you to the test," Merseault said.

Sheppard sighed. "Congress is very sensitive to the mood of the people. That's how such foolish laws get passed. The people are living in fear of something they don't understand. Communism has come to represent a sort of witchcraft, a baffling kind of black magic. Actually the motive behind the law is so innocent as to be naïve."

"I don't quite agree that the motive is innocent," Merseault said.

"If you look at our laws in context, it is. Americans unconsciously think of foreign political ideologies in the same terms as they think of such things as the European fruit fly and hoof-and-mouth disease—the way to keep unpleasantness out is to stop the carriers at the border. It's almost a matter of superstition."

"Fear is the handmaiden of defeat."

"Yes," Sheppard said. "That worries me."

"You see the workings of destiny?"

"Every man in public life nurses a secret dream that somehow he will see the world put to rights before he dies. Every man has a vision of a world united in peace, of one world, a world without war. It is a dangerous and foolish dream. Some have tried to unite the world by violence, some by persuasion. All of them have failed. The dream of perfect peace has spawned conquerors and madmen, as well as saints. Imperfect union might someday be possible. Perfect union, never. We all fail. We know before we start that we will fail. But the vision remains to goad a man even after he's seen its folly. I had a dream the other night."

"A dream?"

"A real dream—that is," Sheppard said slowly, "if there is any such thing as a real dream. I dreamed of another war. I woke up with the unshakable conviction that we'd lose it. I can't get it out of my mind. It's been plaguing me for the last few days, a feeling of helplessness, of defeat. I've never experiencd anything like this in my life."

"Who do you mean by 'we'd lose it'? Who's we?"

"We? I don't know precisely. I don't know."

"Perhaps you mean those of us who think that two plus two will always be four—except when counting living beings."

"I suppose in a way that's exactly what I mean. Those of us who believe in the existence and reality of truth that eludes and is unalterable by mere human will. I'm too tired to see to the bottom of it. It has something to do with simple justice, with a compassion for suffering, with a reverence for life. Things too simple for final understanding, I suppose. Every battlefield commander has dreamed of defeat, but this was different. This was more like a vision of Armageddon."

"A dream of defeat. Terrifying."

"It's the certainty that's terrifying. I can't rid my mind of it. It's outside the realm of the mind. It's irrational. It left me in a cold sweat."

"You've been driving yourself too hard. You need this rest."

"The odd thing is that I know you're right. These last few weeks in office have unhinged me a little, I think. Even after a good night's sleep . . ."

"You need more than that. There's a kind of fatigue that isn't relieved by sleep."

"Yes. Old age is one disease you don't look forward to being cured of."

"I didn't mean that."

"I've never thought of myself as an old man until recently. But weariness of the soul is only another name for old age. Even when my legs started to give out on me, I could think of myself as a cripple but never as an old man. It's bewildering."

"You have to take yourself in hand."

"That's the irony. That's the thing I didn't count on. I've always counted on being able to reason, even on my way to the grave. But this took a grip on me that was totally irrational. I never counted on that. For the first time in my life I could understand the real power of superstition."

"You mean this dream you had?"

"Yes, that too."

"It's not like you to let yourself . . ."

"I know. It's the press of events. I'm looking forward to a long rest."

Douglas Lutelacker joined them for coffee. Arriving on the dot of two, he was announced and shown in by Merseault's young law student–secretary, who, as he retired from the room, removed the ornate iron doorstop with his toe and softly closed the door behind him—the closed door would signal the servants against intrusion.

Lutelacker greeted Sheppard formally, as though to establish that he was come on business, a friend not wanting to presume on the advantage of friendship; his handshake said that he knew the rules, would ask no privileges.

Immediately Sheppard refused the consideration, said, "Sit down Douglas, and make yourself comfortable. You're among friends." Lutelacker smiled, quick to appreciate.

The Ambassador continued, "Georges and I were just talking with our shoes off. You've met each other, I'm sure."

Lutelacker smiled at Merseault, who was standing to greet him. "We've never precisely met with our shoes off before. How are you, Doctor?"

"Douglas," the Ambassador warned, "you had better call him Georges. He gets insufferably pompous in the face of flattery."

"A common failing among academicians," Merseault acknowledged. They shook hands.

"Help yourself to coffee," Sheppard said. "We'll get to business later. I want to hear what happened yesterday—Georges tells me you were the silent hero of the noisy hour.

Merseault leaned forward. "I'm curious myself to hear what happened."

Lutelacker shrugged. "All I did was carry the mail," he said. "Dujardin did the rest."

"Did you see him yourself?"

"No. Inspector de Rougement was at the prison when I got there —I simply gave him a copy of the story . . ." He shrugged again. "And that set the wheels in motion, I guess."

Merseault smiled. "De Rougement, eh? How did he happen to be there just at the time you arrived?"

Lutelacker smiled, as though found out. "Well, I didn't think it would hurt to call him. I telephoned him from the airport. He's the one who deserves the credit if anyone does."

"When did you have time to write the story?" Sheppard asked, amused, slightly incredulous. "Or did you write it in advance?"

"I typed it out on my lap in the taxi coming back from the airport."

Merseault asked, "Did you see Picard?"

"I saw him after De Rougement came out with the new confession— the ink was still wet on the signature."

"How did he look?" Merseault asked, clearly enjoying the imagined scene of Picard fuming in anger.

"Picard? He was as cool as a cucumber."

Merseault's relish vanished. "Yes. Yes, of course. An honest lawyer whose client had gravely abused his trust. A man betrayed for his charity."

"When will we see the documents?" Lutelacker asked Merseault. "Documents?"

"The Dujardin files."

Merseault laughed, shook his head, said nothing.

"You mean Dujardin confessed for nothing?"

"I don't know," Merseault said. "We're still searching."

"Then Carnot may *really* be crazy."

"It's a crazy world," Merseault said soberly. "Carnot may really be dead."

Lutelacker shook his head. "From the way he talked about going to Moscow, you'd think he was on his way to Paradise. The poor bastard. I wonder if he knew what he was doing." He paused. "I wonder if he knows what he *did*."

"The Lord works in strange ways," Sheppard said. "Strange indeed."

Merseault grunted, nodded, admitted grudgingly, "There *may* be method in His madness"— he gazed out the window —"in this, His madness."

The Ambassador put down his coffee cup and moved his wheelchair slightly to escape the patch of warm sun that had crept up onto his lap. "Well, Douglas, I have all afternoon—in fact, I have the rest of my life—to sit around talking about the old days. But I imagine you have to be more frugal of your time. I promised you an interview, and you shall have it. Shall we to business?"

"My time is your time," Lutelacker said. "But I'm ready if you are. Do you mind if I keep a few notes?"

"On the contrary. I'm flattered and reassured."

"We'll get the routine questions out of the way first," Lutelacker said, his manner hardening almost imperceptibly in the professional mold. "Have you decided when you'll be leaving for the States?"

The Ambassador smiled. "This afternoon. Later."

Lutelacker looked up from his pad, surprised, glanced involuntarily at Merseault. Merseault said, "I'm sorry if I deliberately misled you on the telephone. Security measure. His Excellency would rather avoid your esteemed fellow tribesmen at the airport."

"Fooled me completely," Lutelacker said admiringly. "Ah, well . . ."

"I wasn't being precisely untruthful . . ." Merseault looked at Sheppard before going on.

Sheppard said, "The catch is, Douglas, that I'm not quite leaving for the States. I plan to take a rest in North Africa—mainly to mollify my young bone specialist. The Embassy plane is going in for overhaul and I'm getting a free ride. Next question."

"What are your plans?"

"When I get back? I have none. I saw the Secretary when he was here for the conference, so there won't be any debriefing."

"Have you any idea who will be appointed here?"

"None whatsoever. It's very much in the air. I really don't know. Dr. Edwards will be Acting Ambassador—but you know all that. No, I have no idea who will take the post next. Partly it will depend on who can afford it."

"Have you anything to say about that?"

Sheppard laughed. "Nothing. I only regret that I have but one life to lose for my country. The question has its pros and cons, of course."

"Do you feel that the lack of adequate representational allowances limits the President in making appointments?"

"No doubt about it."

"Do you think it limits the caliber of the appointments?"

"I haven't made up my mind on that question. There may be some wisdom in requiring a man to buttress his aspirations with cash, provided of course he is otherwise equipped ably to acquit himself of his country's ambitions along with his own. Not all rich men are stupid."

Lutelacker asked, "Would you count yourself rich? I mean, of course, in application to your job here as ambassador."

"I'm not exactly a pauper, yet I cannot count myself rich. On the other hand I haven't the problem of a family to support or a business partnership to maintain. If I had I wouldn't have had adequate resources to accept my appointment in good conscience. I knew it was going to cost money."

"You feel then that the job of ambassador carries with it enough honor to compensate for any pecuniary—"

"Of course I do. Douglas, I suspect you're trying to needle me into carrying the flag for the sans-culottes in the Department. Mind you, I have the highest respect for career officers, but I also feel that a certain tension between the professional and the innocent is desirable.

It accords more closely with reality, and diplomacy if it achieves anything must achieve reality. Have I answered your inquiry?"

"Perfectly. Now, what about France's problems in North Africa?"

"Since I am about to go there, I would rather not comment, particularly since those problems bode no easy solution. However, it seems to me rather like the problem the Union faced in the 1850's—you have Parisian abolitionists in conflict with diehard *colons* over what is basically a de facto system of peonage—with essential differences, of course. I am confident that France will eventually grant that her own best interests lie in peaceful evolution."

"You think the choice is between giving North Africans either political equality or their independence, is that right? Am I quoting you right?"

"You're not quoting me at all. You're putting words in my mouth, but—yes, that's one set of choices."

"And the other?"

"Between civil war and rebellion. That's a hasty answer, and I'd rather you didn't quote me."

"China?" Lutelacker asked, moving on.

"What can anyone say about China? It's all been said."

"Do you think an industrial China under the Communists will follow Moscow?"

Sheppard thought a moment. "My military instincts lead me to think that China will follow Moscow the way the tiger follows the man riding it."

"You think China represents a threat to Russia?"

Sheppard shrugged. "China has one indisputable weapon: infantry. Infantry walks. There is only one major country that Chinese infantry can feasibly walk to: Russia. And it wouldn't be the first time either. Remember that."

"Do you have anything to say about the charges that the State Department deliberately undercut the Generalissimo?"

"I'm inclined to believe my old friend Joe Stilwell in regard to Chiang. I knew Stilwell and am still inclined to trust his intelligence—in twenty years we'll see, perhaps. In other words, any undercutting that occurred was probably self-inflicted."

"Do you feel that De Gaulle presented a parallel case in France after the war?"

"Certainly we didn't give De Gaulle a blank check to do with lend-lease as he pleased. Also, De Gaulle was able to swallow his pride when he saw that history wasn't cooperating in his plans. Certainly our policy to nurture and support the Third Force in France might have been copied in China. But I doubt if anything could change what's happening."

"What do you think of the Senate investigation of the State Department?"

"You mean this hunt for Communists? Ridiculous. I know Department security procedures, and if a bona fide Communist could hide out in the State Department, I'd double his salary and hire him for intelligence work. They don't come that clever every day of the week."

"Your name has been mentioned in connection with the Senate committee's investigation of foreign missions . . ."

"Is this what you've been leading me up to, Douglas?" Sheppard shot a sly glance at Merseault, sitting impassively listening. "No. I wouldn't think it proper to make my views public right now. If the Secretary testifies, he'll speak for all of us. I deplore the demoralizing effect the publicity has had on my Embassy personnel."

"Have the loyalty oaths affected morale, in your opinion?"

"Ah, that's a more difficult question. Loyalty oaths may be desirable, provided they can be administered without abuse. Unfortunately the legal basis for them is still very hazily defined, and practice varies from post to post. I have made it a practice to refer most such questions to Washington, where at least they receive uniform readings . . ."

As Sheppard was speaking Merseault started to smile. Silently he rose from his chair and padded across the room to the bookshelf that covered the wall behind the Ambassador. Deliberately he searched among the books along one particular section of the shelf. Sheppard followed him out of the corner of his eye as he talked; suddenly he interrupted himself. "All right, Georges, what are you up to?" He faced Lutelacker again, explained, "I can always tell when Georges is going about his·mischief—I've indulged him in this ever since I first met him at the *Science pol'*. He'll find something and read it to us now."

Merseault, conscious of his audience, carefully removed a leather-bound book from a high shelf and blew dust off the top of its spine. Briefly he consulted the index as Sheppard and Lutelacker waited, expectant, amused. He found the place he was looking for, and looked up. "Pliny the Younger's correspondence with Trajan," he announced sententiously. "This is a letter he wrote around the year 110 while he was governor of Bithynia. I'll read all of it, and then read Trajan's reply." He held the book up and began to read:

"It is my rule, sire, to refer questions upon which I am in doubt to you: who could better guide my uncertainty or inform my ignorance? I have never been present at trials of Christians, and therefore do not know the method and limits to be observed in investigating or punishing them. I have been in no little doubt whether age is to be considered or the very young treated like the adult, whether recantation secures pardon or it is of no avail to desist being a Christian if a man has ever been one, whether the name of Christian itself even when no crime is involved or the crimes associated with the name is the punishable offense.

"In the meanwhile I have observed the following procedure

in the cases of alleged Christians. I asked whether they were Christians, and if they confessed it I repeated the question a second and third time, with a threat of capital punishment. If they persisted I ordered them executed, for whatever their profession might be there could be no doubt that obdurate contumacy should be punished. Some who possessed the privileges of Roman citizenship were touched by the same madness; these I remanded to Rome for trial.

"Because the investigation was in hand it was natural that charges should proliferate, and a variety of matters came up. An anonymous placard containing many names was posted. Those who denied they were or had been Christians, who repeated after me an invocation to the gods and offered incense and wine to your image (which I had ordered brought in with the images of the deities for the purpose), and who, moreover, cursed Christ—it is said that no real Christian can be forced to do these things—I thought it right to dismiss. Others named in the placard said they were Christians but soon denied it: they had been Christians, they said, but had ceased being so, some three years before, some many years, and a few as much as twenty-five years. They all venerated your statue and the images of the gods and cursed Christ.

"They asserted that the sum of their fault or error was that they were accustomed to assemble before dawn on a fixed day, pronounce a formula to Christ as to a god, and bind themselves by oath, not for criminal purposes but never to commit theft, brigandage, adultery, prevarication, and never to refuse a deposit on demand. When they had done this it was their custom to separate and then reassemble to take food, but of an ordinary and harmless kind. Even this they ceased to do after the publication of an edict in which, according to your mandates, I forbade secret societies. For this reason I thought it essential to determine the truth of the matter, even by torture, from two female servants who were called deaconesses; but I discovered nothing more than a depraved and excessive superstition.

"I have therefore adjourned the proceedings and have resorted to consulting you. The matter seemed sufficiently important to refer to you, especially in view of the large numbers involved. People of every age and rank and of both sexes are and will continue to be gravely imperiled. The contagion of that superstition has infected not only cities but villages and hamlets; but it seems possible to check and correct it. It is clear, at least, that the temples which had been deserted are again frequented, and the sacred festivals long intermitted are revived. Sacrificial victims for which purchasers have been rare are again in demand. This makes it easy to conjecture what a host of people can be reclaimed if opportunity for recantation is offered.

"And here is Trajan's answer to young Pliny:

"You have followed a correct procedure, my dear Pliny, in sifting the cases of those who were reported to you as Christians. No universal rule of fixed form can be set up. No search is to be made for these people; if they are reported and proven guilty they must be punished, with this proviso, however: if a man denies that he is a Christian and makes it plain that he is not, that is, by worshiping our gods, then however suspect he may have been in the past his recantation shall secure him pardon. Anonymous accusations must not constitute an indictment. That is a wicked procedure, and not in keeping with the spirit of our age."

Lutelacker had been listening, looking at his notes. When Merseault stopped reading he looked up. "That is really quite extraordinary."

Merseault smiled, continuing silently to read further before closing the book. "Extraordinary time of history," he acknowledged, mumbling. He turned slowly toward the bookshelf, still absorbed.

Sheppard smiled benevolently. "You can always count on Georges." He leaned forward slightly as though surveying the notes Lutelacker was making. "How are we progressing?"

"Fine. One more standard question . . ."

"My opinion on Hollywood morality?" Sheppard asked, smiling.

"No, not that one. Will there be another war?"

Sheppard's smile vanished. "God knows," he said, shaking his head slowly. "And God help us."

Merseault suddenly looked up from his tome and clapped it shut, smiling, gazed at the ceiling in reflection. "Of course, if those chaps had really put their foot down . . ." He shrugged, and slipped the book back into its slot between books.

It cooled toward late afternoon.

After Douglas Lutelacker left, the Ambassador turned to Merseault and said, "That was a cute performance you put on."

Merseault laughed. "You mean my friend Pliny's performance?" Merseault shrugged. "A little history won't hurt that fellow."

Sheppard shook his head, smiling. "I don't know. Was that reading really for his benefit—or was it for me alone."

Merseault shrugged, smiled. "If the shoe fits . . ." He paused. "After all, Trajan wasn't a bad emperor."

"So you think I should stop trying to rationalize his policies?"

"Times *have* changed a little," Merseault said. "But men haven't. The Romans probably had a Committee on Un-Roman Activities, as you do. But have I told you of my plans to start a Committee on Un-French Activities? We're going to look into milk-drinking to start with . . ."

"Would you seriously lean on a parallel between the United States and Imperial Rome? I should think a historian would find that slightly ingenuous. Rome was frankly dedicated to a policy of territorial expansion, of exacted tribute, of imperialism."

"Ah, so? You mean: subdue your neighbor, rather than love him. That is where the Christians crossed staves with Rome. Territorial imperialism may be a thing of the past—economic imperialism, however, is still with us. Do you think the Russians want to colonize Rhode Island? No, we are living again in a period of holy wars; the object is to convert, to punish, to exact recantations. We marvel at the folly of the Romans, of the Calvinists, of the Inquisition—they all burned human beings alive for the greater glory of God, some for the love of gentle Christ. We wonder how men could become so sick in their souls as to commit murder in the name of God, and yet will it be much different looking back a millennium from now?"

"Georges, why are you lecturing me like a schoolboy?"

"One half of the world is ready to fight for freedom, privacy, and justice for all mankind; the other half is ready to fight for an end to economic enslavement of all mankind. The first half finds it increasingly necessary to repress freedom, privacy, and justice—in the name of freedom, privacy, and justice. The other half finds it necessary to employ slave labor to put an end to economic enslavement. And if nothing else will do, there is still one issue that the whole world is ready to fight for—peace. Ha! The world is sick, the souls of men are dying, and many true and honest men are dead. And I? I am not feeling well myself."

"Well, I've had enough of the world—to hell with it," Sheppard said. "Let's talk about something more promising."

"The world's in Hell already," Merseault said.

"Then let us leave it undisturbed in its damnation."

"Shall we have a brandy?" Merseault asked. "What do you say? Against your doctor's orders, naturally—I don't trust doctors who don't drink themselves."

"You don't want to continue the conversation?"

"Let's flip a coin. Heads, we continue the conversation dry"—Merseault rummaged vainly in his pockets for a coin—"tails, we imbibe a reflective brandy or two."

"Here," Sheppard said, producing a large coin from his watch pocket. It was a talisman, a gold piece. He handed it to Merseault.

Merseault looked at the coin, examined it carefully. "This is the same louis d'or you used to carry when we were fellow students, isn't it?"

"Yes," Sheppard said, surprised. "How did you know I carried a louis then?"

"Oh, I just knew," Merseault said, smiling cryptically.

Sheppard laughed. "I couldn't ask for a more generous explanation."

Merseault flipped the coin off his thumb into the air. It fell almost soundlessly onto the thick-piled carpet, bounced and rolled over. Merseault leaned forward slightly to make out the face of the coin; it was lying near Sheppard's feet. Sheppard could see it better, looked at it, made a wry face.

"Two old men," Sheppard said, almost to himself. "Two sober old men." He shook his head resignedly and slid his glass across the polished marble table top. Merseault, with unhurried deliberation, unstoppered the bottle and tilted it over his own glass first, then poured Sheppard's. Like two imperfect lenses, the decanted liquor rocked in the twin glasses, focused amber patterns of wavering sunlight on the table.

Merseault raised his glass in a wordless toast; together they drank. The unrecovered coin lay glinting on the rug, reflecting the last rays of cold afternoon sun that streamed through the window. Motes of golden dust drifted almost imperceptibly in the light; the slanting beam of sun lay across the room like a pillar of fallen brass, motionless. Later, when finally the sun fell among the tangled silhouette of leaves, it looked itself like a great gold coin tarnished and scored, before it touched among the buildings blue beyond the river and slid from sight.

XI

The morning after his return from the hospital, Stone left the apartment without telling Solange he intended to resign. She was still asleep when he left. He dressed and made coffee without waking her.

He spent the morning in an aimless round of routine conversations at the Embassy office building. The girl in personnel gave him a mimeographed sheet entitled "Procedure before Departure," and he followed its steps to the letter—turned in his building pass, had his passport amended, picked up his final pay check. After a final handshake with the personnel officer, he left. He had intended to eat lunch downstairs in the Embassy restaurant, but couldn't get in without his pass. Instead he had a sandwich in the Crillon bar and went for a walk.

There wasn't much point in going back to the Embassy this afternoon, he felt, except perhaps to clean out his desk. But he didn't feel up to it right then. Instead he walked toward Concorde bridge and into the Tuileries along the Seine, watching the barges glide up and down the sluggish water. There were still a lot of things that needed putting together, and he needed the time to think, to work them out. The afternoon was still ahead of him, and he had nothing to do; he decided to walk along the path from the Orangerie toward the Louvre.

As he walked he thought about Solange, wondering again where she was, wondering why he was so acutely disappointed when she didn't answer the telephone. He had tried to call her twice since leaving the Embassy. Why wasn't she there when he needed her? And why did he need her right now? Something MacNaughton had said in the hospital yesterday morning . . .

Stone reflected that MacNaughton seemed to intrude into his life at critical times. The first time it was on a barren plateau in south central France. But that was during the war, when anything could happen. The second time was when MacNaughton walked into the session at Graves Registration Command, walked into the hornets' nest. He was the first reporter to discover that the missing Stone was still in France; it was from that afternoon that Stone's difficulties began, and became public. MacNaughton's presence seemed to mark the dividing line between privacy and publicity. After all, he was a reporter.

Stone watched the flat brown water of the river, thinking absently of how the reporter had affected his life, wondering what significant part he played in the present confused drama. Was this another critical time? The first time, his life had hung on the success of the weapons drop. The second time . . . but what was it? Stone wondered: Am I getting superstitious? And yet was it so superstitious to be wary of a black bird circling in a dry sky?—for that was the way he thought of MacNaughton, of reporters in general. Vultures. He was inquiring after the Ambassador yesterday, Stone thought. Was the Ambassador going to die? Unlikely. Then what was MacNaughton sniffing the air for? Something else?

It was odd, Stone thought, that he had never really thought about MacNaughton before. Reporters had become something to avoid, in mind as well as in fact.

And there was another thing: the future. That was something to avoid thinking about for the time being also. The clear and present truth, as it seemed to Stone, was that there was no future. If there was to be a future, he would have to set out and build it from scratch. He was—it seemed a grim joke of war—in his forties. It wasn't easy to think about starting from scratch, although he knew that he had nothing to preserve. Since the war he had been what they called in the States a failure. He could admit it. He'd taken the easy way, had stayed on in France. Here, during the war, he hadn't failed. Here, failure didn't seem to matter. He had succeeded here when they needed him, and even now found himself able to accept and be accepted without anyone's requiring prior knowledge of his accomplishments. He was, or had been, "with the Army." That was enough. It had been a quiet life, a sort of retirement. Now, more recently, he had been "with the Embassy." And that too was enough. Now he was "with" nothing. He was with no one but himself, totally exiled for the first time, and acutely aware of the loneliness of exile. Go home? Yet where was home now?

Solange. Where did Solange fit into the puzzle? And why should he think of it as a puzzle? Enough—it was a puzzle, felt like a puzzle. And Solange seemed to fit somewhere. But where? I am afraid to marry her, he thought abruptly. Then: What else am I afraid of? What? The inane propaganda slogan went through his head: *Yankee, go home.* He left the wall along the Seine and hailed a taxi. It halted; he got in.

Once inside the cab he couldn't decide whether to go back to the apartment. For some reason he wanted to telephone her first, to hear her voice, to make certain she was there, to give her warning. Why warning? Perhaps to tell her he'd quit the Embassy. One thing was certain: He didn't want to be there alone, to go home—he was thinking of her place as "home," he realized—unannounced. The hell with it, he thought. I'll wait and telephone again.

He rapped on the glass and directed the taxi to stop in front of a *tabac-café* on the corner of the Rue de Bac.

Inside the café he purchased a *jeton* and dialed the number. He let it ring a while, listening, then hung up. Under his shirt he was perspiring, a light sweat; he noticed for the first time that his legs were still weak from the inactivity of the hospital bed. I could use a drink, he thought, and sat down at a table under a false palm near the window, intending first to order a coffee. But he knew before the proprietor had finished wiping the marble top that he would not order coffee. Instead he ordered a cognac, and made a mental note to call her later. Outside the taxi waited.

Stone noticed that the café he was in was spruced up a bit. There were fresh flowers in cheap glass vases along the zinc bar, and the tile floor had been swept and polished. At this moment the proprietor was humming to himself as he gave the glasses and bottles on the shelf behind the bar an extra burnishing. Stone thought to himself that they were probably dusted and polished once every holiday. The day already had the atmosphere of a holiday. It was the May Day weekend, and tonight there would be celebrating in the streets.

The liquor bit his tongue. It was cheap brandy but robust and with a sharp edge. He downed the small single portion in two gulps, and almost instantly felt its raw warmth in his stomach. He had had only the one sandwich to eat since he left the Embassy.

Stone thought about the Ambassador himself. It had been a surprise to find the old man in the hospital; even more surprising was the quick glimpse he had had of him. His face was thinner, almost drawn, the profile more sharply defined. But he still had the old authoritarian bearing, even sitting in a wheelchair. He'll probably bear himself upright until the day he dies, Stone thought ironically: a military man straight and true.

He wondered whether it was the liquor that was relaxing him, or whether it was merely the knowledge that eventually it would; it seemed too short a time for it to be taking hold. The power of suggestion, he thought. Somehow he didn't feel anxious about it. Tonight half the city of Paris would be celebrating; if he ended up drunk at least he'd be in company. It wasn't bad being drunk in company.

He decided to call once more before going out to the taxi. She might have only stepped out for a minute.

In the phone booth, waiting for the connection, he looked at his watch and wondered about Sheppard. What does a man like that do when he retires? he wondered. Where does *he* go? Does he have a private life to retire to, or any family living? The last thought led to Sheppard's son. Berger. Stone still thought of him by his wartime name: Antoine Berger. Somehow the name of Anthony Sheppard refused to fit the man Stone knew as Berger. And what did the Ambassador think of his son? Of his son's end?

The telephone at Solange's apartment buzzed rhythmically in Stone's ear. In his mind's eye he could visualize it sitting on the night table beside the bed ringing clamorously to a deaf room. He counted three more rings, then slowly hung up. There was a moment of silence in the booth and then the clatter of the *jeton* coming back.

He put the *jeton* in his pocket and stepped out. Disappointment must have been written on his face as he stepped out of the phone booth, because the proprietor smiled sympathetically and shrugged. He'd been watching.

Stone paid at the bar and walked out to the taxi. There was no place to go, but he got in anyhow.

"Take me for a ride," he said. "Anywhere you'd like to go."

The driver didn't even turn around, but made one huge determined nod and jammed the taxi enthusiastically into gear—obviously he had some place in mind. Stone examined the back of his head. It was lean, gray, and shaggy.

From the moment the reins were loosed the taxi driver took full advantage of Stone's indeterminate command. Given his head, he set out on some sort of involved personal errand, an odyssey which required stopping at several widely scattered small cafés around the Left Bank. Between stops the driver drove slowly, and without once turning his head, began a running commentary that had all the sauce and tired style of a sightseeing-bus driver: ". . . on your left is a warehouse belonging to the Michelin Tire Company, publishers of the famous Michelin Guidebook, whose product is at this moment between us and the paving stones. They make rubber tires so that people can drive to the places in the guidebook."

The only time he paused in his run-on delivery was when, by the most transparent coincidence, they neared one of the cafés where he had business to attend to. Then he would slow down, roll to the curb, and cut off the engine. When they were fully stopped he would turn around in his seat to face Stone and ask, "Do you mind if I stop?"

On the first two stops Stone turned down the driver's invitation to join him in a "small glass" and waited outside in the taxi, listening to the meter tick, for the old rogue left the flag up each time he stopped.

Finally, when they stopped the third time, the game became fully apparent and Stone's curiosity got the better of him. Wondering mainly what the old boy's business was, he accepted the invitation, and together they climbed out onto the sidewalk. As they did so, Stone called attention to the ticking meter. Feigning proper distress and innocence, the driver marveled a moment at his own absent-mindedness and, still standing on the sidewalk in the arrested motion of slamming his door, made amiable ceremony over having wronged his passenger—Stone heard the meter tick another five francs. Stone assured him that it was a small matter, hoping the old thief would drop his embarrassing false face of remorse. But he seemed to enjoy his act. The old man said, "Small matters make the biggest quarrels." He ducked into the door again and reached across the seat, and flipped down the meter flag. "There," he said, and backed out of the cab. *"Le bon compte fait les bons amis,"* he added, satisfied, and slammed the door with brassy indifference. Stone couldn't help being amused as the old gaffer squared his shoulders and brushed his hands together with all the aplomb of a righteous man stamping out evil. He said again, "There."

As they crossed the sidewalk toward the café Stone thought over the old man's saying: *Good accounting makes good friends.* It lost its epigrammatic neatness in English. Good fences make good neighbors. It all came to the same thing, he thought, and at bottom was probably as wrong-headed as most mercantile aphorisms. A penny saved is a penny earned; is not, thought Stone. A penny saved is a banker's penny; then he thought: A penny postponed. In 1932 it was a penny lost. What made me think of that, he wondered: 1932.

A bell jangled as they entered the café. Stone looked around: wooden floors, zinc bar. A hole in the wall. Behind a thick curtain, sounds in the back. The curtain was black—hides the dirt, he thought. Stone listened, the fading bell still jumping on its spring over the door. Good smell, he thought. Smell of stale wine. For no reason he thought briefly of Carnot, Carnot as he first knew him, in the south, in the war. Stale wine: Auguste's café smelled of stale wine. And walking past the wineshop near the church. What was his name, the one who was killed? Max—that was his name.

The proprietor came through the curtain on slippered feet. He was in his undershirt, and perspiring as though interrupted in the midst of heavy labor. He automatically shunted his bulk through the narrow slot at the end of the bar, and before acknowledging his customers, turned his back and paused to dry his hands and face on a towel that hung beside the bar's long mirror. Across the mirror, in ancient fly-blown gilded letters, arched the legend: VINS—CHARBONS—GLACE. Stone noticed it, reflecting idly on the hundreds of small bistros around France that combined a commerce in these same three items. Occasionally he had noticed shops that had expanded the traditional line to include tobacco and cordwood as well as wine, coal, and ice. Also, once or twice in places like this he had smelled kerosene.

The proprietor's back had white hair on it, Stone noticed, but his head was as bald as a melon. He was a heavy man, a man who probably enjoyed food, but he carried his flesh solidly; except around the folds of his neck and jowls where the taut skin had gone slack with late middle age, he still gave the impression of being a strong man rather than a fat man. As he drew the towel down over his face, he glanced obliquely in the mirror and stopped and turned around still holding the towel to his cheeks.

"*Tiens,* Raymond," the proprietor said. He sounded mildly surprised. "You're early today." He proffered his hand over the counter, first to Raymond, then to Stone. Stone mumbled politely as he shook it.

"*Ça va,* André?" Stone made note of the two names—somehow the name André fit the bistro owner better than Raymond fit the taxi driver.

"*Ça va.*"

André the proprietor glanced warily at Stone. Stone caught the questioning look out of the corner of his eye, but made no move. He expected the taxi driver to answer for his presence, but Raymond ignored the proprietor's mute question. Instead the taxi driver merely said, "I can give you thirty this week."

André said, "That's what you said last week."

"I might be able to give you ten more on Thursday if some more comes in," Raymond said. He shrugged sympathetically.

André shook his head and sighed resignedly, stared gravely at the counter top. For a solemn moment neither said anything. The amenities were over, a contest begun.

Stone stood to one side, ignored. André twisted a point of the towel around his finger and absently began cleaning his ears. Though they lay flat against his massive head and weren't overconspicuous, the proprietor had huge ears. When his left ear was clean, he made a new point and began rooting about the whorls and gullies of his right ear. Stone watched the operation, fascinated; meanwhile, both men were thinking.

Finally André finished cleaning his ears and thinking, and said carefully, "I suppose I really ought to buy all I need from one man. I lose money on the price when I buy in small lots from several sources." Then he added casually, "There's one who stopped in the other day who says he can give me all I need. He may have been just talking, of course."

Raymond looked uncomfortable. Stone watched Raymond's face, wondering what commodity he was dealing in.

Stone thought: They certainly make a pair. It was like watching two wily old animals sniffing in a wary circle about each other: a bear, a white-haired bear, and a rangy old gray wolf. But the proprietor André looked more like a walrus than a bear, except that he lacked the necessary mustache. And except for the shaggy head of unkempt gray hair and the lean face, Raymond didn't quite fit the role of wolf either.

His face had something in it that reminded Stone of Adolph Menjou, a streak of comedian under the long mock-solemn expression.

Still wondering what their business was about, Stone watched the two of them; one had it; the other wanted it. But what was it? One burdened with supply; the other suffering from demand. For what? In silence he continued to watch them, two small opposing cogs in the strange machinery of postwar commerce.

The silence betrayed a quiet footfall; in the mirror Stone caught an infinitesimal movement of the rear curtain. He thought: That would be his wife, listening. Checking the progress of the transaction. In his mind he imagined her: thin, sharp-tongued, impatient. He smiled to himself.

Suddenly André turned to hang up the towel. The action had an air of finality about it. Evidently Raymond sensed it, because suddenly he said, "Well, I'll make up the difference somehow. I'll give you forty. You've always been a good customer."

André shrugged, an expression of helplessness. "What can I say? I need sixty."

Raymond shrugged in return. More silence. To Stone it looked like the impasse had really been reached.

Stone looked around the room, examining it, trying to look interested in something other than the conversation, thinking: Undoubtedly it's black-market, whatever it is. And why had the taxi driver invited him, a stranger, to witness his quasi-legal doings? Except that Stone knew that the operations were more than commonplace—even the government had more or less accepted the black market as a necessary evil, a sort of economic safety valve that popped off loudly now and then and led the way to corrective readjustments in the nation's overall financial structure. It's as good a way as any, Stone thought.

Stone's eye fell on a large sepia photograph in a black frame that hung on the wall over the mirror just under the ceiling. It was a group photograph. It seemed to be a regimental portrait, probably from the First World War, although it was hard to make out the details of the uniforms through the dusty flyspecked glass. The photograph was decked across the top with a narrow ribbon of tricolor and on the sides with black crepe that had faded to purple. The crepe had gone stiff with age, to the point where it preserved its original drape despite the fact that the frame was hanging aslant. It looked glued in place, petrified.

Stone noticed that the proprietor was watching him look at the picture but said nothing.

"Well . . ." Raymond said. He hiked his shoulders and started to button his coat. "I'll stop by next week."

André rested his large arms on the bar, and leaned forward to look at the clock over the curtained door in the rear. The clock face was in the form of an advertisement for a brand of cognac Stone had never heard of. Certainly it hadn't been produced since the war.

"It's early yet," the proprietor stated flatly. "You certainly have time for a small glass before you go." Raymond appeared to hesitate. The proprietor looked at Stone, ignoring Raymond's hesitancy. "What will you have? A little *fin* to brighten the day?"

Without waiting for an answer André turned and took a bottle from the shelf. Raymond unbuttoned his coat again, sighed, and smiled a victim's wan smile.

The drinks were served on the zinc in small glasses and consumed slowly. André talked of the water heater he was attempting to repair. He had been working on it all morning, he said. For a short while the two men's talk relaxed around the intricacies of plumbing fixtures.

As Raymond finished his drink, André said, "I tell you what, make it fifty-five litres, and I'll try to economize this week. Actually I prefer doing business with people I can drink with, to tell you the truth."

Instantly, as though he'd been waiting, Raymond said, "The absolute best I can do is forty-five. And at that you'll be getting more than any of my other customers." Raymond reached into his back pocket and extracted a small change purse, to pay for the drinks.

André protested, "No, no, no. I invited you to drink with me. Put your money away."

Raymond tried to unsnap the purse, but André reached brusquely over the bar and clamped one huge hand like a vise over the purse. "Please, please," he said, "you'll insult me if you don't put it back in your pocket."

Raymond shrugged, capitulated, and the purse slid back into its hiding place unopened. Stone finished his drink and set the glass politely on the bar, nodding his thanks. He assumed they were about to leave.

Suddenly, as if by magic, all three glasses were full again. André had simply passed his hand over the bar in a casual movement, and there they were: full again. He had masked the bottle out of sight with his enormous forearm. He had been holding it all the time as he leaned on the counter, probably letting the bottle dangle from two fingers out of sight.

It was too late for Raymond to refuse, but to make certain, André quickly raised his glass in a toast: "To your wife's health," he said.

Raymond, completely outmaneuvered, simply said, "Thank you."

They drank, Raymond finishing his at a swallow, André dallying. Stone sipped his to the half mark, but kept his glass in his hand.

Raymond said, miserably Stone thought, "You'll let me pay for this round."

André appeared shocked. "Please, please," he said. No more was said. Then André asked, "How is your wife? Is she feeling better?"

"Much better, thank you." Raymond was plainly anxious to go now. "Do the doctors know what it is?"

"The liver, they think."

"She shouldn't eat eggs. Have her fry her meat on salt crystals. Take all the fat off it, of course."

"Yes." Raymond shifted his weight again.

"It's a bad time of year for the liver."

"Yes."

André straightened up, but this time Raymond covered his glass with his hand in time. Stone was holding his. André appeared not to have noticed, but merely turned and replaced the bottle on the shelf. With his back turned, he said, "And you're sure you can't do sixty litres."

The tension was telling on Raymond.

André turned around. Certain of victory, he said, "I only mentioned fifty-five to accommodate you. Sixty is what I need."

Whatever it is, Stone thought, it's measured in litres.

Suddenly the taxi driver said flatly, "All right. Fifty. Fifty litres. Not more. Don't press me further, I warn you, or I will walk out. Fifty litres, *Mon Dieu!* You are unreasonable." He looked grim.

André shrugged, a resigned shrug, but a shrug of acceptance. The deal was closed.

Raymond reached into his pocket and extracted a blue envelope. He shook it at André. "This was going to take care of three customers," he said. "You're ruining my business." He threw the envelope on the counter. "There's fifty litres in there."

Stone thought: Gasoline?

André picked it up and slipped it in a drawer, unopened. Then he opened his cash drawer and took out a similar envelope, in fact it looked to Stone identical to the one Raymond had just given André— then it came to him that it was probably the envelope from last week's transaction, that André had saved it. It looked exactly the same only fatter. Money, Stone thought.

Raymond was suddenly completely calm and casual again. He didn't take the proffered envelope, but said, "The price is up six francs this week."

André scowled, still holding out the blue envelope.

Raymond said defensively, "Look in the newspaper. I don't make my prices."

"All right," André said. But his hand had not been played out. "You can take it off the five litres you still owe me from last week."

Raymond frowned, debating with himself. Finally he took the envelope and slipped it into his breast pocket.

As good-bys were said, Stone shook hands with André and thanked him for the drinks. The proprietor didn't accompany them to the door, but smiled from behind the bar as they stepped out into the street under the jangling bell. Outside Raymond's frown vanished. His mood changed completely. By the time they reached the parked cab, he was giggling with repressed glee.

In the taxi Raymond explained that André was an old friend from the First War, and one of his best customers, but that his wife had turned him into a stingy man. Stone asked him how much André usually got, hoping to draw out the object of the transaction. The driver said airily that he always got fifty litres. It was his regular quota. The object of the bargaining, he said, was to see how many drinks he could get out of him. "When I'm by myself, I can get one free, but he lets me pay for the other. So usually it comes out a draw. But today, with you there, I stuck him for four."

He laughed and swung the taxi into a slow U-turn at the end of the block. "Without you, I would only be two ahead. He'll be hard to deal with next week."

Stone added a detail to his mental picture of André's wife: a pinched face.

The taxi completed the U-turn and started back along the street where they'd just been. Passing slowly by the tiny café both Stone and the driver looked into it. Behind the murky plate glass, for one brief instant, the huge shape of André in his undershirt was clearly visible standing up atop the bar. He had a stick in his hand and seemed to be fishing up toward the ceiling for something. Then as they passed, the sun struck the glass at an odd angle and the shop's interior vanished from view and André melted in the golden glaze of reflected sunlight, and the café was already behind them.

Raymond's voice sounded puzzled. "What do you think he was doing?" Then he laughed. "Perhaps he hides his money in the rafters."

Stone gazed at the back of the taxi driver's graying head. Inside him the brandy was already making him feel warm and relaxed, and he smiled at the mute head of the chauffeur. He said nothing. He knew exactly what the proprietor was doing. It was the regimental photograph over the mirror. The old boy hadn't missed a trick. Stone thought: He saw me looking at it—and was thinking even then how he'd wait until we left and then do it. I wonder how long he's been meaning to straighten it? Stone thought of him standing on the bar in his undershirt. What does he think about when he looks at it? Does he think, or does an old man just remember?

The taxi rattled along, purposefully threading the narrowing streets toward another of Raymond's devious endeavors. Raymond began again his singsong delivery, never pausing, never looking to left or right: ". . . and this is where they teach the blind ones to read with their fingers. This is the street they named after him. He's dead and that's where his statue . . ." He rambled on nonstop.

And I, thought Stone, do I think? And what do I remember? He listened to the ticking of the meter under the droning voice of Raymond, and thought: I won't remember getting drunk. A penny earned is a penny lost. Poor old André's wife has made him stingy. But he gave me two drinks. Why am I doing this? Where am I going? Am I really going to hell? He thought: Who cares? He cupped his chin in his hand and looked morosely out the window just as they passed a bakery; he saw a small girl come out carrying a long loaf of bread. He was still thinking of the regimental photograph, of the tricolor ribbon, and of the rigid black crepe that once again would hang the way gravity taught before it stiffened and faded with time and the passing from memory of the youthful faces it now enshrouded. *What does a man remember?*

The taxi picked up speed along the Boulevard Raspail, and Raymond's monologue slowed down. Finally they came to a stretch of residential buildings and the driver fell silent altogether, but only for a moment. He seemed to be uncomfortable driving in silence. As though for lack of anything better to say, he asked abruptly, "Monsieur is an American?" He asked the question in heavily accented English.

For a moment Stone considered saying no, just to pique him. But he merely parried the question in French. "What makes you think I'm an American?"

"Your shoes," the driver said, switching to French without hesitation. "I tell Americans by their shoes."

Stone looked up and caught the old boy grinning at him in the rearview mirror. He nodded. "You are right. I'm an American."

"My name is Raymond," the driver said, affably continuing the conversation. "You speak good French."

"I know." He hesitated. Then he said, "Call me Jack."

The driver thought about it for a moment, then said, "O.K., Jack."

For a moment there was silence. Then Stone said, "You know some English. Where did you learn it?"

"In Moscow." Raymond said. "My father was in the Ministry of Tourism under the Czar. We left before the new tenants moved in."

"What is your business?" Stone asked.

"My business?" Raymond lifted both hands from the steering wheel and made a palms-up gesture around the taxi's interior. "You are riding in it."

Stone smiled. "I mean what is it you're selling?"

"Oh, *that,*" Raymond said evasively. "I only do that one day a week. It is not my business." He shrugged his shoulders and turned his full concentration to driving again.

Stone waited, but apparently the subject was closed. There was one thing to be thankful for, though. For the moment at least, Raymond had dropped the guided-tour monologue.

The next stop was a small café in the Rue Bonaparte. This time Stone was introduced to the proprietor, but there was no bargaining, no mention of business, simply an inconspicuous exchange of envelopes. Stone accepted with Raymond the proprietor's offering of a drink, and then excused himself briefly to use the telephone in the rear of the place. He still had the *jeton* in his pocket from earlier.

There was no light in the telephone booth. Stone inserted the *jeton* and dialed the number by the light of a match, then closed the glass door and waited. Presently he heard the buzzing in the earpiece. There was no answer. Through the glass door he watched the tableau in the front of the café. The two men were silhouetted against the diffused afternoon light in the narrow street outside; they were facing each other, leaning against the bar, with the polished counter top running like an alleyway between them, talking quietly. There was no movement in the empty room. Stone counted five more futile rings, then slowly, reluctantly, hung up. The *jeton* clattered down through the metal box and came back to him. Then silence.

He didn't open the door immediately, but stood in the muffled darkness of the telephone booth listening to the indistinct murmur of Raymond's conversation with the proprietor. He wondered who else he could telephone, thinking, Why? Why telephone anybody? To say what? And why was he so anxious to reach Solange? He had nothing to tell her really. Yet a moment ago, when the telephone didn't answer, he had experienced again the same fleeting irritation that had assailed him earlier, an irritation that bordered on anguish. She knew —she had to know—he needed her. *Why isn't she home?* He knew then he wanted to meet her outside for dinner.

Then he thought of the apartment. Why don't I go back there and wait for her? He fingered the key in his left trouser pocket, separating it from the small change and pocket lint. In his mind was a gloomy picture of the empty afternoon apartment. I want to be alone, he thought, but not there. It was all right alone in the hospital. Except the afternoons, waiting for the sun to go down. It's the waiting, he thought, the waiting. Now he had a mental picture of himself sitting in the apartment waiting, waiting for the light to fail . . . *she was always out in the afternoons* . . . waiting for her. A sudden wave of unreasoning anger came over him. *Damn her.*

He looked again at the two men talking at the bar, at the slow tableau of the proprietor holding an amber bottle up to the glowing light, the other nodding his slow appreciation as it turned and glinted from pale to topaz in the light of afternoon. They were framed in the square light of the plate-glass window, a placid composition full of warmth and easy balance. Stone's moment of bitterness slowly consumed itself. He dropped the *jeton* back into his pocket and opened the door of the booth. At least, he thought, old Raymond won't fail me, not as long as I have money. He felt a sudden affection for this old White Russian, this exiled taxi driver who neither questioned nor complained but seemed to accept friendship as he found it. That he did it for payment seemed for the moment to Stone all the more to the old man's credit; it made friendship, however temporary, a real and dependable thing. He stepped out of the booth.

Stone insisted on paying for the third round himself. Raymond had paid for the second, the proprietor having stood the first. Raymond thanked him, calling him "Jack," and explained to the proprietor for the second time that Jack was an American. Whereupon the proprietor hailed a toast to America; Stone held up his glass to France; and Raymond shrugged and lifted his glass to "Mother Russia."

"Old Russia or new Russia?" the proprietor asked, joking.

Raymond blinked, his face a solemn dead-pan mask, and asked, "Is there a difference?"

The proprietor laughed humorlessly, and said, "Well . . ." and tossed off his brandy. Raymond drank his slowly and in silence, and when he finished the glass rotated it between his fingers and gazed morosely into it, a distant expression on his long face. Then he said, half aloud, half to himself: "Russia never changes." And shook his head sadly. Then he stood up straight and extended his hand to the proprietor, saying, "I'll see you next week."

Stone finished his drink and put the glass on the bar. By the time they were off again in the taxi, Stone was beginning to feel truly pleasant and relaxed. He felt almost cheerful as he rested his head against the side of the glass and watched the afternoon scene as it fled past. Bicycles. There seem to be more bicycles than usual. Holiday tomorrow, he thought. Dancing tonight.

Raymond was unusually silent in the front; suddenly Stone noticed that he had forgotten to turn on the meter again as they got into the cab.

"You've forgotten to turn on the meter."

"I left it off. The meter cheats." Raymond sounded suddenly less exuberant.

"Cheats?"

"The last time it was set I had large wheels on. I changed to smaller wheels because it is easier to get tires. Now they have to roll over faster in order to keep up with us."

"I see," Stone said. "You mean the meter is fast." He leaned forward to examine it.

Raymond came to himself, snorted. "Fast? You have no idea how fast my meter is." He was beginning to find his former mood again. "It gets home an hour before I do."

Stone relaxed back into his seat again. He was about to ask how he would know how much to pay when the ride was over. But Raymond was reading his thoughts.

"Don't worry. I'm going to charge you a *prix fixe.*" He paused. "Do you have dollars?"

"You mean greenbacks? Or traveler's checks?"

"Either. For five American dollars I'll drive you around until I have to go home for dinner, anywhere you want to go. There are still a few places I have to stop, you understand, but they are nice people and we'll have a drink there."

Stone said, "All right." He felt in his back pocket to see if he had the small wallet he carried his twenty emergency greenbacks in. It was there. He took out a single five-dollar bill and quietly slipped it into his right-hand trouser pocket.

Raymond said, "I need dollars to buy a hearing aid for my wife."

"Can't you get one in France?"

"The French ones are too big. She is very vain—was once very beautiful, my wife. And she saw this American one. Very small." He sighed. "Anyway, she wants that one. So I am collecting dollars for her birthday. She was born under Taurus. That'll give you an idea of her temperament. She was very lovely once."

"Do you have any children?"

Raymond shook his head. "No," he said. "No children. I am the last of my father's house. All my brothers were killed."

"In the war?"

"Wars, revolutions. One got drunk on his wedding night and fell in the Dnieper. That was the oldest. I was the youngest. I came here with my mother before Kerensky came to power. Then my father lost his post in Moscow. There was no money. I joined the French Army—that is where I knew André—and fought out the end of the war. But after the Treaty of Brest-Litovsk I knew we'd never go back to Russia. My father got out, but died in Nice a month later. Then my mother—" He paused and shrugged. "And that left me. I have no roots. My wife is another rootless one, otherwise she would never have married me. She was beautiful. She could have married anyone she wanted—but I spoke Russian." He shrugged again. "She still refuses to learn to speak French properly. I think she became deaf so she wouldn't have to listen to it. When I speak to her in French she can't hear me."

"You speak Russian at home?"

Raymond nodded. "She was older than me when I married her, and very beautiful. But I am her roots." He shrugged. "But life is not so bad. I drive a taxi. I'm independent. She has a few friends who come to visit her, although now she is very heavy and they are getting old." He paused. "She has liver trouble now, and the doctor keeps telling her to stop eating . . ." He trailed off, thinking his own thoughts. Then he said sadly, "She still talks about the day we'll go home—back to Russia. She is like Russia herself. She says that in Russia we could have had children, that we could have . . ." He left the sentence unfinished. Then after a moment's silence he said, "It's hard for a woman not to have children. And I'm the last of my father's children. My mother had seven, seven brothers. You'd think that with seven there would have been a chance . . ."

Ahead of them a bus slowed to turn and a young man carrying a leather briefcase jumped nimbly off the back. The taxi swerved to avoid him. Raymond pressed on the horn and muttered, "Idiot," skirting around the bus as it turned into the Boulevard St. Michel. As they continued across the intersection the ride straightened out. Raymond peered into the rear-view mirror, scowling backward at the corner. "They all try to kill themselves for nothing. They never wait until the bus stops. *Crétins.*" Stone smiled and looked out the window.

The westering sun in the Boulevard St. Germain glinted off the fretwork of high windows and iron railings and made them glow like burnished brass. As the taxi passed beneath them, the lower parts of the buildings were in shadow, a warm shadow of lowering afternoon, but the upper parts caught the full blaze and glory of the warm sun's yellow wash and shone in the clear afternoon air. Overhead the sky was subtly changing color, deepening to a greener blue with the descending sun. The people in the streets were not the aimless promenaders of midafternoon, but purposeful homegoers, bent in their strides, intent on destination rather than diversion. The buses were beginning to look less than half empty; and once a chic-looking woman raised a handbag in a white-gloved hand to hail Stone's taxi, not seeing its passenger. He wondered where she was going.

Stone made a mental note to call Solange again.

It wasn't until they had completed their stopover at the next café that Stone realized that the bibulous itinerary was having real effects. Not only on himself but on Raymond; as Stone felt better, Raymond, it appeared, was feeling worse. Raymond's intervals of reflective silence became longer and longer, and finally, after the fifth café, Stone found himself talking more to uplift his driver than to reassure himself. For if Raymond's driving was affected by alcohol at all, it was only that it made him drive more slowly.

By the time they had enjoyed the friendly good spirits of the sixth café, a café owned by another Russian where Raymond was particularly welcome, Stone realized that it was rapidly getting dark and that he was just about as drunk as it was dark. It was not quite dark yet. Twilight was just beginning.

Raymond was driving even slower. They threaded their way to the seventh café almost at a walking pace, with Raymond turning the slow corners with exaggerated precision. Raymond said the seventh café was the last. After that he would probably have to take the taxi home with him. Stone said that that was perfectly all right since it was Raymond's taxi anyway. Stone looked out the window, but the neighborhood wasn't familiar. At the snail's pace they were moving, the trip from the sixth to the last café seemed to be lasting a long time.

"Where are we going now?" he asked. He found himself speaking slowly to avoid tripping over his thickening tongue. The back of Raymond's gray head wavered slightly before his vision, although Raymond was sitting bolt upright.

"Cemetery Montparnasse," Raymond said. He wasn't thinking at all now except to answer Stone's questions, but was concentrating on his driving.

"Who is the man we're going to see here?"

"Not a man," Raymond said. "Woman. Café Monumentale. Madame Rocquier."

"Oh," Stone said, and relaxed back in his seat. Suddenly he remembered that he'd meant to try and call Solange again. He'd meant to call her two cafés ago. He sat forward on his seat.

"Raymond."

"*Oui*, Jack."

"I have to remember to make a telephone call when we get . . . wherever it is we're going."

"Café Monumentale," Raymond said.

"Yes," Stone agreed. "Café Monumentale. That's it. When we get there I have to make a very important telephone call. Don't let me forget."

"I'm not sure I'll remember to remember."

"Well, try not to let me forget. It's very important."

Raymond fell silent. Stone sat back in his seat. Looking out the window he recognized the back street they were in as being near the Pantheon. Satisfied now that he knew roughly where they were, he let his head fall back and closed his eyes. In some part of his sober consciousness he analyzed how he felt. He felt good. It was simply too bad about the alcohol, in any case. Life's too short. He weighed the effects; no whirling feeling when he closed his eyes, not yet, anyway. He felt very warm and comfortable with his eyes closed; his balance was perfect. The main thing was not to forget to call Solange. You won't forget, he told himself, and smiled. He felt the muscles in his face relax into a smile, felt each tiny contributing muscle individually; it was surprising how clearly he could separate them one from another. He wondered why he had never discovered that before. A smile was a complicated thing, at least at the moment it was—not just one action, but a complex of many separate but interrelating actions. Then he wondered: Can I pick them out and work them separately? He found he could smile on the left side of his face only, and was trying to smile with only his chin, when Raymond interrupted.

"Why don't you use a string?" he asked.

"A string?"

"Tie it around your finger and then you won't forget."

Stone realized that Raymond was still thinking about how to remember to telephone. Stone said, "I'm glad you remembered. I had forgotten already."

"My wife makes me do that sometimes," Raymond said. "Once I forgot what the string was for, though. Things like that really happen."

"Doesn't it get in your way?"

"I tie it around my wrist. It's easier that way."

"Do you have any string?" Stone asked.

"No, but Madame Rocquier will have some. We'll ask her when we get there."

Stone thought about that.

"But I won't need it then. I will be able to make my telephone call."

"That's true, of course," Raymond said. He sighed heavily. "And besides, there's no way to be sure we'll remember to ask her about the string, anyway."

Stone suddenly threw his head back and laughed. He liked Raymond, and he felt good.

Raymond simply shrugged and said, "Ah, well, that's the way it is."

They drove the rest of the way in silence.

From its name, Café Monumentale, Stone had expected something grander than it was. But if anything, it was smaller than the others, at least from the outside; when the taxi finally yielded to its creaking brakes and rolled to a halt, Stone had to look twice before he found it. *"Nous voici,"* said Raymond. They were directly in front of it.

The reason for the name of the place was immediately apparent in its surroundings; on getting out of the cab Stone recognized the neighborhood. On the opposite side of the drab boulevard ran the gaunt blank length of the Montparnasse Cemetery wall, gray and unadorned, broken only by the narrow entrances to the *allées*. In the late afternoon twilight the whole neighborhood seemed colorless and empty; the line of funereal buildings facing the boulevard opposite the wall reflected its empty solemnity. Apparently it had been a dead day for business; the funeral houses were lit only by the reflected sun, and the funeral-wreath florists were already closed. But the Café Monumentale, flanked as it was on either side by the blank samples of two gravestone dealers, seemed dimly aglow with life behind its small glass front.

Once the responsibilities of driving and parking his taxi had been properly discharged—Stone noticed that this time he locked it—Raymond again turned his talents to conversation. In the short space from the cab to the door of the café, Stone learned that Madame Rocquier had been married twice, widowed twice, that her last late husband had sold tombstones, and, indeed, had been laid to rest across the street under one of his own products. Not that he made tombstones; he merely sold them. He also sold burial insurance on the side. Madame Rocquier kept up the insurance business after his death, but sold the monument business to the café owner next door. A month later, out of mourning, she bought the café. Now, Raymond said, she stood in a fair way to have both the café *and* her husband's old business, since the man to whom she had sold the latter, from whom she purchased the former, spent most of his time in his old café courting the new owner. Raymond added significantly that the monument that graced her husband's last resting place was just tall enough to be seen over the wall from her place at the cash register. Madame was a woman of practical sentiments. She chose her husband's monument herself, he said, from stock. They'd had it for years; it was too large to sell.

Raymond paused before the door, nodding confidentially to Stone. "This one has a head for business, she does," he said seriously. Then he laughed.

For one brief suspended instant as they entered the café, at the signal of the clicking latch, everything stopped in mid-motion and all eyes flickered toward the stranger at the door, and Stone saw the still-life scene with an acute sense of detail, an impression he knew was exaggerated by alcohol. He was aware of this peculiar satisfying effect that alcohol had on him, of elongating moments of time and sharpening his sense of detail, and soberly recognized it for what it was: a pleasant signal that he had already drunk too much. He was still of two contesting minds; one sober and tensely rational, the other in gaudy revolt and not caring. The latter seemed to control his sense of time and used it as a weapon to confound his will, his remembering self. He stood inside the door, the click of the latch in his ears, as though on the threshold of a photograph: the woman, her head tilted back, arrested in mid-laugh; the ice pick raised, motionless, held poised to stab down behind the counter; even the billiard player, blind under his crystal tent of light, with his emerald face toward the camera, his arm cocked and ready. The scene wavered before his vision, there was a sharp click of billiard balls, ice chips spangled the air behind her as the woman drew another breath, and Stone stepped forward like Alice into the looking glass. Behind him there was another click as Raymond lifted his hand from the thumb latch.

The first thing Stone saw on entering the café was the café's proprietress, Madame Rocquier, sitting on a high stool in front of the bar with her head thrown back, laughing. She was a huge blond woman, generously buxom with startlingly prominent front teeth, who wore her hair tied in a large bun directly atop her head. Stone guessed her to be in her early fifties, although striving with some success at ten years less. Even sitting, she looked to be a head taller than any man in the room. She sat with her back against the bar, leaning on her elbows, carefully composing her generous charms for the appreciation of the three male customers beside her who sat before the bar in conventional fashion looking slantwise at her profile. Behind the bar, a rotund little man with a florid face was stabbing at a hidden block of ice with a large ice pick that threw sparkling chips into the air with each blow. Stone instantly decided he was the former owner.

The inside of the café was much bigger than Stone had assumed on seeing it from outside. It widened out into a room with a billiard table in the back. The billiards part was on a slightly stepped-down level, separated by a decorative iron railing entwined with false vines of red crepe-paper flowers. Two men in shirt sleeves were engaged in a slow and serious game of billiards; the younger one leaned on his cue, sipping from a glass in his hand, while the other bent over his stick under the low hanging lights about to make his shot. His face reflected a greenish cast from the billiard cloth, and he bit his lip in a study of concentration.

If anyone had noticed them enter, there was no sign of it. The proprietress was enjoying an animated conversation with the three customers at the bar, while the fourth joined from the other side of the counter, where he stood with a glass in his hand still chopping ice. In the rear the two players were circling the billiard table, glasses in hand, stalking victory with upraised spears.

The atmosphere in the place was easy and relaxed, reflecting the buxom good nature and pleasant laughter of the proprietress. The café was different from the others Stone had visited with Raymond, precisely in that it did mirror the personality of its owner. For one thing, there were small tables with blue-and-white cloths in the middle section of the long premises, where patrons could enjoy some small privacy instead of the publicity of the bar. They were empty. The colors in the place were fresh-looking and bright, and gone from the walls were the usual outdated calendars advertising vermouth and *digestifs*. In their place hung framed sketches of elaborate burial monuments, mostly crypts and mausoleums of Greek and neoclassical influence. Madame Rocquier catered to the neighborhood trade, but was, withal, a woman of obvious taste. Over the cash register, in the place of honor, hung a monument architect's rendering of a massive grave marker that might have been a deceased pawnbroker's: a stubby triangular obelisk that rested at the lower corners on three stone balls. But from the tiny crepe rosette attached to the lower corner and from Raymond's previous brief description, Stone deduced that this was the sculpture that honored her late husband's final square of earth in the park across the street.

But Madame Rocquier, in catering to the professional interests of the neighborhood trade, was herself anything but morbid. Her café was cheerful, and she was a full vision of warm-blooded womanly life. It was no wonder, Stone thought as she slid sideways off her stool and came to greet them, that she had survived two husbands; from the look of the small courtier anxiously mixing himself a drink behind the bar, she'd probably survive another.

She was near-sighted. Interrupting her entertainment at the bar, she approached her two newcoming customers with uncertain curiosity written on her face. She peered closely for an instant at Stone, and he could see her mental reaction: No, I don't know this one. Then Raymond said, *"Bonjour,"* and she turned to the familiar voice.

"My dear Raymond," she scolded, "I thought you were never coming. I was beginning to think you had forgotten us." She kissed him on both cheeks, then drew back looking at him. "This is your day, isn't it?" Stone noticed that her French had a trace of Provence in it.

Raymond passed her the blue envelope. Stone caught the movement only out of the corner of his eye, but knew before she did, what she was going to do with it. She hesitated a moment, smiled her satisfaction and silent thanks at Raymond, then, glancing over her shoulder at the bar, tucked the envelope undetected into her bosom. As Stone smiled, she turned her full attention to him, asking Raymond, without taking her smiling eyes off Stone, if she had met his friend. The elemental flattery of being looked at by a woman as she talks with someone else was not lost on Stone; he thought, a woman knows a woman's trick, and decided instantly that he liked her.

Raymond fumbled for a moment, obviously trying to remember the name Stone had told him. Madame Rocquier's gaze never wavered; Stone let him fumble, thinking to himself that near-sighted women nearly always had soft attractive eyes, never quick, never hard. Perhaps because they had to keep them open in order to see, perhaps because they had to gaze openly to follow the expressions on a face, or perhaps simply because the eyes themselves saw the world in soft outlines. Madame Rocquier's eyes were clearly brown, large with innocence.

Raymond finally said, "This is a friend of mine—from America." Then, suddenly remembering, he said, "His name is Jack."

"Ah, Jacques," Madame Rocquier said, nodding approval. Stone smiled politely. But Raymond wouldn't let it go at that.

"Not Jacques," he said, "Jack. It is an American name."

Stone interjected softly, "It's a nickname for John, Madame."

"Ah, well, Jean. This is a name I know very well. My first husband was named Jean." She extended her arm. As Stone shook her hand the silver bracelets jangled on her forearm. "Monsieur speaks beautiful French for an American." Stone nodded graciously. But Raymond, his single-mindedness reinforced by alcohol, was unwilling to let it rest there.

"My dear Françoise," he began patiently and politely, "you have it wrong. It was not Jean, but . . ."

Françoise placed both hands on her ample hips and tilted her head from one side to the other in a show of mock exasperation. "Now you're going to tell me I don't know the name of my own first husband? Ça alors."

". . . John." Raymond finished doggedly. He pointed a finger at Stone and said, "His name I'm talking about, not Jean's. You forget, Françoise, that I knew Jean as well as you did."

"That I doubt very much," she said decisively, arching a provocative eyebrow at Stone. "After all, he was my husband and we were well married." Stone smiled with her at Raymond.

Raymond shook his head and shrugged, almost resigned. But he had to make one final try. He drew a breath and pounced on the error: "John," he said. "J-O-H-N. Like King John of England."

"The King of England is Georges," she said, satisfied, and shooed Raymond toward the bar. "Go have a drink while I introduce Jean."

She turned to Stone and took his hand, saying, "I allow no strangers in here," and, preceded by Raymond, towed Stone toward the bar.

Raymond was known to everyone present. He greeted each one and continued on to the rear to greet the billiard players. Then it was Stone's turn. Madame Rocquier announced unsorted the names of the four men at the bar. The one behind the bar dried his hand and reached across to shake Stone's, something he hadn't done for Raymond. The only name Stone positively identified with its proper owner was the last one, that of one Monsieur Devrue, who was sitting on the stool next to the one temporarily vacated by the proprietress. As Stone shook his hand, he murmured helpfully, "I'm the one named Devrue." To his own satisfied amusement Stone heard himself introduced simply as "Monsieur Jean-Jacques from America." Madame Rocquier then went behind the bar to fetch a drink for him and Raymond. Stone found himself standing alone before Devrue.

The conversation started with slow decorum, Devrue asking where Stone was from in America. Stone said he was from near New York City.

"What is the name of the town?" Devrue asked, and Stone realized that they were speaking English. Devrue's English inflection was so correct that there had been nothing unnatural to signal the transition from French. Stone had simply answered him unconsciously in English.

"I'm from New Jersey," he said, "Trenton."

"Ah, yes," Devrue said. "I have been there. It's halfway between New York and Philadelphia. I went to look at a purification plant on the Delaware River. It was a very interesting place."

"I haven't been in Trenton for some years," Stone said, "but I hardly remember it as interesting. In fact I remember it was rather dull."

"Oh, I don't mean the town. I mean the purification plant was interesting. I didn't see anything of the town except the railroad station, and there you are right. That was dull, as I remember."

"I see," Stone said, not quite seeing.

"However, that is the way it is. Some of the world's dullest cities have the world's most fascinating sewage problems. You can never tell a sewage system by its cover." Devrue smiled at his small joke, and shrugged.

"You are in the—ah, sewer business?" Stone asked uncertainly.

"Well, you could hardly call it a business, since we're not in it for profit," Devrue said. "But otherwise you're quite correct. That is my line of work. I am a city engineer, assistant to the chief engineer for the Paris sewer system." Devrue clasped his hands together and rocked slowly on his stool, looking over Stone's head. "Ah, yes," he said, "I remember America. Amazing country. I have visited nearly every major city there—the underside of every major city, that is. I might not be able to cite their local monuments and tourist attractions, but I can still draw you the sewer plan of Kalamazoo, Michigan, from memory. Of course, it's changed since then. They've no doubt made changes, additions. That's an amazing name, isn't it, Kalamazoo? Like something out of Swift."

"Swift?" Stone eased his weight onto Madame Rocquier's empty stool. He was having difficulty following Devrue. Madame was still busy behind the bar.

"*The Travels of Lemuel Gulliver.* One of my favorite works of the English eighteenth century. I first read Swift while I was traveling in America. It was from him I learned a proper English style."

"You speak English extremely well," Stone said.

"I write it even better. Of course that would be an idle boast except that English is not my mother tongue, and I am proud of doing well what I do, all the more so when it is difficult."

Madame Rocquier suddenly placed a glass of cognac before Stone. "Raymond told me what you were having," she said. Stone turned and looked down the bar. Raymond was sitting at the end talking to the former owner of the place. He saw Stone and raised his glass in generous salute to their liquor-thickened friendship. Stone nodded and looked with misgivings at the ample glass before him. In the back of his mind he had been half-seriously considering ordering something slower, a glass of white Bordeaux or something.

Devrue was sharper than he looked, for after watching Stone for a moment he said, "You don't have to worry about getting drunk. Tonight's a holiday. Tomorrow's a holiday. Sunday's a holiday."

"Holiday? Yes. It is, isn't it?"

"Tomorrow is the day before May Day. No one works. It's like your Labor Day in America."

"Only different."

Devrue laughed and nodded. "Only different, that's right."

"I forgot it was a holiday," Stone said, lying.

"There'll be dancing in the streets later tonight, especially in the workers' quarters. They'll have a good time, get perhaps a little drunk, and finish the evening singing the *Internationale*. Tomorrow they will bicycle out to the country and pick flowers. And there will be a parade. Tonight I'll probably get drunk myself." Devrue nodded to himself in a satisfied way, then laughed. "Sunday we'll see the *muguet*—what do you call it? Lily of the valley?" He raised his glass; he was drinking pernod. "In fact I'm well started on my way."

Stone looked at Monsieur Devrue, re-examining him. Devrue was smiling fondly into his glass, lost in brief reflection. He was a curious sort, Stone thought, different from his looks. Dressed in brown, slightly balding, with steel-rimmed glasses, he was completely undistinguished in outward appearance, and Stone had at first taken him to be a man of rather limited humors. But when he talked his features changed, became curiously animated, and his mobile eyes shone, actually twinkled when he laughed. But as soon as he was silent he reverted to the drab functionary, looked almost morose.

Suddenly Devrue said, still looking into his glass, "When Romans have a holiday, do as the Romans do." Then he looked up. "Have you ever been in Rome?"

"Once, during the war," Stone said. "I'd like to spend some time there someday."

"Beautiful city, Rome," Devrue said. "My first wife died there. She was a passionate admirer of Shelley."

"And your second wife?" Stone asked, unintentionally tactless.

"My second wife?" Devrue looked surprised. "Oh, I haven't got a second wife yet." He gestured with his left hand around the room. "This is a sort of widowers' club we have here. Françoise is the bait in her own trap. Comfortable trap, don't you think?"

Stone looked around the café. "Very charming place," he said.

There was an awkward silence. Devrue seemed perfectly content to allow it to continue; Stone felt uncomfortable.

Stone said, "You live in the neighborhood?"

"Oh, no. My office is near here." He gestured vaguely in the direction of the street. "I have a commanding if not too cheerful view of the cemetery."

"And the others here?" Stone glanced over Devrue's shoulder and indicated the other clients talking quietly at the bar. Madame Rocquier, behind the bar with her back turned, was busy adding a column of figures on the margin of a newspaper.

"The others? They are mostly in the solemn trade."

"It seems you would have little in common professionally," Stone said.

Devrue cocked his head to one side and thought a moment. "I don't know," he said. "We both deal in the nitrogenous end products of mankind."

Stone expected to laugh, but Devrue was suddenly talking seriously.

He continued without pause, "Disposal is our main concern, speaking practically. In a sense, however, we're competitors in that respect."

Stone smiled in spite of himself, and asked, "How so?" Devrue took no notice of the smile.

"Sewers are a major weapon in the battle for lower mortality rates. In fact, the sewer system here in Paris really didn't begin to develop until 1832. A cholera epidemic was killing eight hundred people a day. That got them started, but it took until the last half of the nineteenth century to get the property laws passed that enabled work to start on the present integrated system." Devrue jerked his head in the direction of the other men talking among themselves behind him and smiled. "My business is to limit theirs."

"I see what you mean." Stone laughed. As he listened to Devrue, Stone absently watched the two billiard players circle oppositely about the table in their tensely graceful slow-motion ballet. They played fluently, advancing, retreating, halting to pose their shots with all the formal rhythm of a slow minuet.

"Do you realize," Devrue asked, abruptly serious again, "that the life expectancy of a male child born, say, in Burma, is only twenty-six years?"

"No," Stone said, feeling slightly outpaced. Obviously Devrue, when it came to his work, was dedicated and deadly earnest. "I hadn't realized that."

"If I could build them a sewage system . . ." He stopped, made a frustrated gesture with his hands, shrugged. He shook his head slowly, and picked up his drink. Then he put his glass back down on the bar decisively and said, "I know more about sewer design than almost any man in the world, but they won't erect any monuments to me. Nor will they mint me a medal, or name a street after me. People imagine sewers as something low, something not to be mentioned." He shot a withering glance at one of the sketched monuments hanging on the wall. "People despise their mortality. They put more faith in stone. It's childish, even touching, but it's true. There's no art to it, no science. My friends here are peddlers of simple immortality."

Devrue relaxed abruptly into silence, and picked up his glass. From the back of the café came the sharp solid click of a cue ball, a loud strangled groan of dismay; the wild ball thumped emptily around the cushions. Stone abstractedly saw the other player tilt his quick birdlike head in silent confidential laughter, then bend forward over the lighted table as the other retreated backward into sullen shadow.

Stately, like fencers in an oriental dance of ritual swords, the players had been moving in circles of silence to the rhythmic clicking of the three balls, two red, one white; until suddenly, just at the moment when Devrue fell silent, one of them completely missed his close-shaved shot full of power, and voiced anguish, a dancer fallen from grace on a turned ankle. Stone felt a sharp sympathy for him, admiration even; the other man played on with hawkish hunchbacked ease, a slick and evil competence that intuitively told Stone he was expert and playing for money.

Seen another way, the two players were stalkers of each other; the one still young and full of rash courage, the other older, more cautious, wily, who disciplined himself to wait, to take no chances but to play on his adversary's error. And that error had been made. He bent over the table now, carefully lining up his shot, a hawk swooping on a wounded rabbit. Back and forth he swung his wrist, drawing the suspense, flexing his certain aim to discomfit his opponent. The stick hung at the balance from his graceful springing wrist and only his wrist moved, not his arm, not his head, not his adder's unblinking eye; the stick glided in his fingers as though oiled.

The balls hardly made a sound as they kissed, barely moved. He scored once, leaving the balls in easy position; straightened and moved around the table, to score again. Then he circled again, scored again. Then again. The tempo increased as he scored twice again. Circling the table like a cat on padded feet, oblivious now of his human opponent, he closed to the kill. There was only him, the brilliant square of emerald cloth, the three balls; the stick now seemed part of him. Each shot was less cautious, more spectacular than the last; he loped about the table like an artist sure of grace, certain of his mastery, testing it now to the limit. It was no longer a game, but a performance under lights. Even the victim leaned on his cue hypnotically watching his own destruction.

Devrue had looked at Stone for a moment, then turned on his stool to follow his gaze. Now they were both watching the demonstration in the rear. One by one the others at the bar noticed that Stone and Devrue were no longer talking their English together, and they too turned to look. Finally, when all conversation had stopped and there was only

682

the clicking of the billiards, Madame Rocquier also looked up and watched.

Around and around he went, making one score after another. He seemed to have the three balls tamed, bent to his will, for each scoring situation was skillfully set up from the one before.

Abruptly he halted, looking around him as though he'd misplaced something. Then he bent over and shot a deliberate miss. He bounced the cued ball off the end cushion and watched it oscillate several times back and forth down the center line of the table. Then he straightened up. Stone suspected he had suddenly realized that everyone was watching him, and quit. There was a congratulatory murmur from the bar, then a turning around on stools, and conversation started again. Madame Rocquier sighed unhappily and adjusted her spectacles—she hadn't been wearing them before—and returned to whatever calculation she was making in the newspaper margin.

Stone watched the proprietress a moment, puzzled. Then Devrue said, "She doesn't like the boy to play for money. Mainly because he loses."

"Her son?" Stone asked. He guessed the "boy" was about thirty years old.

"By her first marriage. He inherited the streak from her, though, but he doesn't have her head to go with it. She gambles all the time—but wins." Devrue pointed surreptitiously to the proprietress. "I brought the newspaper in with me when I came."

"What's she doing?" Stone asked, still puzzled. Madame frowned over the newspaper in deep-furrowed concentration.

"The horses," Devrue said. "Tomorrow will be a big day."

Stone understood, nodded. He looked back at the billiard table. "And who's the other one?" he asked. "The one playing with him."

"Armand? He's an old friend of Madame's. She brought him in to teach the boy billiards," Devrue said. He shrugged. "Since she can't stop him from playing for money, she's decided at least to try and teach him not to lose."

"What does he do?" Stone asked.

"Her son? Nothing. She's spoiled him. He plays billiards and writes poetry. It would be all right, except that he loses at billiards and writes bad poetry. Françoise has no old friends to teach him poetry, only billiards." He shrugged. "But it's a start."

Devrue turned to the bar and sipped his drink. Stone reached for his, stopped his hand in midair, staring at his glass: it was empty.

He thought: Did I drink it? There was no question that the glass was empty. He remembered having it in his hand while he watched the billiard players, sipping it, remembered even putting it down on the bar. I must have finished it, he thought. Guiltily he closed his fingers around the empty glass, hiding the fact that it was empty, and pretended to sip it. If Devrue noticed that it was empty he'd probably order a refill. You have to slow down, Stone thought.

Suddenly Devrue said, "You've never seen our sewers, have you?"

"No," Stone said. Then he added quickly, "Of course, I'd like to. It just that I've never thought of—never had the chance."

"It's an extraordinary system. Almost entirely gravity flow, except for a few places where we have to lift it with pumps. Were you in the war?"

"The war? Yes, I was in it. Did you say the war?"

"The sewers were very handy during the war. For those who knew how to use them, of course. All the tunnels are large enough for a man to walk upright in. In the smaller tunnels, however, there's often no walkway, and there you need wading boots. But you can go almost anywhere underground, except across the Seine. There were several Resistance groups among the sewer workers. *Egoutiers* could travel almost anywhere around the city without passes. Or anybody else, for that matter."

"I should imagine it would be easy to get lost," Stone said. "Unless you knew your way around, I mean."

"Not at all. Oh, not at all. You see, the sewers follow the exact plan of the streets. We even have little signs down there in the tunnels— blue and white, just like the ones upstairs—telling you what street you're under. It's very convenient."

"You mean the sewers follow the streets exactly?"

"Even around the Arc de Triomphe," Devrue said, nodding. "The sewer under the Etoile runs in a large circle, just like the street over it. Some of the larger boulevards have two tunnels running parallel, but in general the tunnels shadow the streets exactly."

"You say the sewers bear names of the streets they follow?"

"That's right."

"That's interesting," Stone said. "A duplicate city. Upside down. Do you have streetlights down there?"

Devrue laughed. "No. We haven't gone that far yet. In time, maybe. But for the present you have to carry your own light. It's entirely dark in the tunnels. It's eternally night down there, and that's why *égoutiers* work only six hours and forty minutes a day. It's unhealthy to keep men in darkness too long. *Egoutiers* were the first workers in France to obtain the eight-hour workday, you realize. That was over fifty years ago. We are very progressive."

"You mean they took Lenin's advice literally," Stone said.

"Lenin?" Devrue looked uncertain. "I don't quite see . . ."

"Went underground."

"Oh, yes." Relieved of his uncertainty, Devrue laughed. "Went underground, of course. They certainly did do that. They do it every day, in fact."

"How many people live in this, this cave city?"

"Live?"

"Live, work. Whatever they do down there. How many do you have working for you."

"Oh, they don't work for *me*. They work for the department. We have slightly over seven hundred *égoutiers* who work in the tunnels."

"What *do* they do?"

"Most of their time is taken in keeping the tubes cleaned out. We have one thousand, four hundred and thirty-two kilometers—that's about nine hundred miles, I've worked it out—of elementary sewers and large collector tunnels. And all of the water from these tunnels goes through various purification plants before it is disposed of through the north end of the city. Some of it is used for irrigation, some of it passes back into the Seine downstream from Paris. Thence to the sea, of course."

Absently Stone raised his glass. Devrue saw immediately that it was empty, and as Stone had foreseen, signaled Madame Rocquier. "You'll accept a glass on my account?" he said to Stone. "Françoise, please, another for me, and a *fin sec* for Monsieur Jean-Jacques." He seemed to be afraid that Stone, his only audience, would escape.

"No, please, I think I'd rather . . ."

"You can buy me one later if you wish," Devrue said, with decisive finality. Obviously he thought Stone was demurring over the question of his paying for it. "But this round is mine. After all, I'm host in my own country."

Stone murmured, "Thank you." Refusal seemed hopelessly complicated. Besides, he liked Devrue, and Devrue *wanted* to buy him a drink. Why refuse him?

"Would you really like to see our sewers?" Devrue asked suddenly.

"Very much," Stone said. Actually he didn't care one way or the other about seeing sewers, but Devrue seemed hungry for human interest. Stone calculated it wouldn't hurt to humor him. Devrue appeared to be a man in love with his work and frustrated by the world's unconcern for its importance, deeply grateful for the slight interest Stone showed in it. Even in their short conversation Stone had seen him slowly change from a drab functionary to a glowing enthusiast, though liquor obviously had helped the transformation along. Stone noticed that Devrue wasn't exactly a slow drinker.

"Well, then. I'll have to arrange something sometime."

Devrue looked abruptly at his watch as though he'd just remembered something. "Excuse me. I have to make a telephone call." He slid off his stool and went toward the rear of the café.

Madame Rocquier seemed to sense that Stone was alone, for she put down her pencil and took off her glasses, and gave her hair a pat in the mirror behind the row of bottles. Then she turned and came to his end of the bar.

"Are you all taken care of?" she asked, looking at his glass. Stone defended his drink with his left hand. Out of the corner of his eye, at the other end of the bar he saw Raymond draining his.

"Everything's fine," he said.

685

"How do you like our little place? Not at all like New York, I imagine."

"Very charming," Stone said, looking around appreciatively. His eye came accidentally to rest on the framed sketch over the cash register. She noticed.

"Some people think my wall decorations are macabre. I don't think so, do you?"

"They go very well with the name of the place," Stone said. It was the best he could think to say.

"That's what I thought. A lot of expensive art talent went into those drawings, and there they were just lying around gathering dust."

"Lying around?" Stone didn't follow.

"Oh, they were in drawers and things. They were sketches my husband may he rest in peace had done for select clients. Rich people, of course, very rich. They're the architects' renderings of how the finished monuments would look. That's what he used to sell them. I think they're pretty, don't you? That one you're looking at is his God rest his soul."

"Yes, I agree with you."

"Eh?"

"That they're very pretty."

"Oh, yes. I think so, don't you?"

"Yes. Very pretty."

"I think so myself." She cast a quick, worried glance at the back of the room, at the pool table. Her son's losses were her losses. But it was only an instant's distraction. She turned again to Stone. "I suppose Devrue has been talking to you about his sewers," she stated.

"Yes."

"That's all he thinks about." She shook her head. "And with his money. Sewers." She wrinkled her nose in disgust.

"He seems to know a lot about them."

She went on as though she hadn't heard Stone. "His father left him a pile, lead mines in North Africa or some such thing. He wouldn't have to work a day in his life if he didn't want to. Went to the Sorbonne. Been all over the world. Then he decided to go to the Ecole Speciale des Travaux Publiques and learn about sewers. Can you understand that?"

"He seems to like what he's doing."

"Do you know what I'd do if I had his money? I'd start a funeral parlor. Always a steady business, a changing clientele. You don't even have to smile at them once they're in the box, and they never come back to plague you with their troubles. I tell you it's not easy being a woman in *this* business." She knocked her knuckles on the counter top to show what business she meant.

"Does your son help you with it?" Stone asked innocently.

"Him? Ha! He's got too much of his father in him. He can't even help himself yet." Then she softened. "But he's a good boy. He writes poetry but he's honest, always keeps track of his debts." She shook her head ruefully. "If he didn't *look* so much like his father, I'd have thrown him out long ago."

"I imagine it's hard to make a living writing poetry," Stone offered.

She smiled a wry smile. "That's why I'm trying to teach him to play billiards." Then she shrugged resignedly. "At least he likes girls. Thank God for that."

Stone laughed politely.

"Only you should see the girls. They all look like orphans. Thin like sticks. Straight black hair. Turtle-neck sweaters. Existentialists. I don't know where he finds them, but each one's like all the rest. If he has to go out shooting up the farmer's pigs, you'd think at least he could bring back one with some meat on it. Then we could save a hind leg for winter. But these . . ."

Stone felt a hand on his shoulder, and turned to find Raymond gently supporting himself. He was weaving hardly at all, but his eyes had a stony straight-ahead look to them. He smiled and groped for Stone's hand to shake it.

"I have to go home," he said sadly. He spoke very slowly, but sounded less than sober. "My wife . . ." He shrugged and smiled stupidly at Madame Rocquier. She grunted and turned to the cash register.

Stone asked Raymond, whispering, "Did you get your envelope?"

Raymond reacted as though stabbed. He'd meant to register a simple sudden nod of remembrance, but his reflexes momentarily escaped his tight control and his whole frame was jerked erect as though by a gigantic convulsive hiccup. "Oh, God," he said. "I nearly forgot." He turned stiffly around to the bar, like a grotesque mechanical toy.

But the proprietress had not forgotten. She had taken the ready envelope out of the cash drawer with bored efficiency, and now handed it across the counter to Raymond. He took it and bowed his exaggerated thanks.

Then he turned to Stone, grinning thickly. "I'll bet *you* forgot to ask her for the string . . ."

For a moment Stone only smiled tolerantly, wondering what Raymond was going on to say now. Then it hit him: Solange. *How* had he forgotten? Time flashed backward through his head to the moment when they'd entered. Even when Devrue had mentioned making a telephone call of his own—even then he had forgotten. What's the matter with me? He felt his smile fading.

Raymond was still talking. ". . . to tie around your wrist. You asked me to remind you to get a string."

"It was a telephone call I asked you to remind me to make," Stone said, his voice unintentionally sharp with irritation.

"I'm sorry," Raymond apologized. "I only just remembered because I forgot my . . ." He stopped in confusion. "And *you* reminded *me*. That reminded me of reminding you—to get the string. See?"

"I'm not angry with you, Raymond. I'm angry with myself. I'm sorry."

"I'm the one who should be sorry," Raymond insisted. He turned to Madame Rocquier. "Shouldn't I be the one to be sorry, Françoise? You see, in the taxi he asked me to remind him to . . ."

Françoise patted his wrist. "You let him be sorry if he wants to be. It's his turn. You've been sorry enough."

Raymond's mood suddenly changed. "I remember something else," he said, turning to Stone. He pointed a dramatic forefinger at Stone's chest. "You haven't paid me."

Stone was startled for a moment. Then he reached guiltily into his pocket and extracted the five-dollar bill and handed it to Raymond. Raymond tucked it into the palm of his driving glove. He looked prim and satisfied. The talk of money nearly forgotten had almost sobered him. He turned and waved good-by from the door.

Back on his stool at the bar, Stone found Madame Rocquier dangling before him a piece of knitting wool from a ball of white yarn. "Will this do?" she asked, breaking off a short length. She dropped the ball of wool back into an enormous knitting basket on the shelf beside the cash register.

Stone, still fishing in his pocket, finally found the *jeton*. He smiled, holding up the *jeton* for her to see. "Thank you, but I'm going to make my telephone call right now. Before I forget again."

"You can't," she said, insisting. "Brother Devrue is still using it." She held out the piece of yarn.

Stone grinned, resigned, held out his left arm. She tied it around his bared wrist alongside his watch, finishing it with a pretty bow, which she doubled so it wouldn't come loose. Stone noticed that her hands were soft, very warm.

"There," she said, tilting her head to admire her handiwork. "Give a man enough rope and he'll hang himself." She gave Stone's hand a small intimate pat as she let it go.

"It will take more rope than that," Stone said, amusedly parrying her remark.

Without hesitation she snatched the ball of white yarn out of the knitting bag again, held it up, dropped it back, and said archly, "There's plenty more where that came from, Monsieur." She dropped her eyes in modesty.

Stone had to laugh. She was quite extraordinary in her role of coquette. Notwithstanding her fifty-odd years, she was still a warm and charming woman, witty, attractive, and quite sure of herself. Her flirting was mostly conscious parody, yet beneath the humorous mask there was still the proud woman herself, fickle, half-serious, inviting. Stone laughed, laughed in pure admiration.

Knowing she'd won the advantage, she turned and strode back to her newspaper, her chin held high. Stone watched her go, feeling for the instant pleasant and relaxed, still laughing to himself. She seemed very real, very solid, an ordinary woman in full life, with warm commanding hands. Secretly Stone felt for the piece of yarn tied around his wrist, her token to him, and thought to himself: Queen bee. No wonder her customers all seem to be men; another woman wouldn't last one round.

Stone saw Devrue come out of the telephone booth in the rear, and got off his stool. As Devrue approached, Stone passed him and said, "I have to make a telephone call myself."

Devrue nodded, beaming. "Fine. Everything's arranged," he said. He gestured toward the drinks. "I'll take care of these."

"No, you don't. You promised me I could pay for this round."

But Devrue had his money on the bar and held it out of Stone's reach. "Later. Later," he said. "This is my café. We'll go to yours later."

It was useless. Stone shrugged, irritated that he hadn't thought to pay for the drinks while Devrue was away.

The light inside the telephone booth worked. Stone closed the door and the light went on. The air inside was close and the earpiece still warm from Devrue's having used it.

He dialed the number, and was halfway through when he realized he'd forgotten to drop in the *jeton*. He inserted it in the slot and started all over. Then he waited.

In the earpiece he listened to the slow intervals of buzzing, counting the rings. . . .*four*. It was impossible that she wouldn't be home by now. . . .*five*. She *had* to be home. He remembered that she'd asked him yesterday to buy wine. . . .*six*. He'd forgotten the wine. There was still time to get it, if . . . . . .*seven*. I'll wait until ten, he thought. She couldn't be asleep. . . .*eight*. But even if she was, the telephone is beside the bed. She'd . . . . . .*nine*. Viciously he slammed the receiver back into its hook. He didn't wait for the tenth ring.

This is ridiculous, he thought, staring at the mute mouthpiece. Suddenly his *jeton* clattered through the innards of the black box and fell into the cup at the bottom. Without thinking he picked it out and dropped it in again and urgently dialed the number over, knowing it was futile. I'm not that drunk, he thought. I dialed it right the first time. But he waited, listening. This time he refused to count.

There was no answer. He hung up again.

Back at the bar, he made no effort to hide his irritation. Immediately Devrue asked, "What happened?"

"No answer," Stone said shortly.

"Oh, that can be very irritating," Devrue said placatingly. "Well, have a drink. It's the only antidote for civilization."

Still standing, Stone lifted his glass and took a long grim swallow; the wavering surface of the amber liquid reflected a dozen pinpoints of light from the distorted mirror behind the bottles. He stopped and held the glass motionless for a moment, not drinking, but simply holding it against his closed lips, peering into the world of flooded light within it, fighting off a sudden petulant impulse to eradicate it, to smash the glass; he stood immobile a moment and felt the sweat start under his arms. Then he shut his eyes, relaxed, put the glass down gently on the bar, and let his weight slump back onto the edge of the stool.

"The devil," he said. "To hell with it." Out of the corner of his eye he was aware of Madame Rocquier studying him.

"You shouldn't let it upset you," Devrue said kindly. He raised his hands in a gesture of freedom. "After all, we don't have to go to work tomorrow. We have the whole night ahead of us. We can get drunk, do as we please. Monday's the day to start worrying again." Suddenly Devrue looked anxiously at Stone, and leaned toward him, inquiring, "You *don't* have any work to go to tomorrow, do you?"

Stone shook his head.

"Do you have to be anywhere tonight?"

Again he shook his head no.

Devrue relaxed, sat back again. "Well, then, as you say. To hell with it. Let the whole world go to hell."

Madame Rocquier looked up from her newspaper. "You're the one who's going to hell," she observed tartly. "What are you so happy about, my cabbage?"

"We're all going to hell," Devrue said. He was getting drunk.

"True," Madame said. "But it takes money to go in style. Would you and Monsieur Jean-Jacques care for another drink before I throw you out on your ear?"

Hypnotically Stone watched her reach for the bottle without looking. The extended arm stopped, glinting silver in the mirrored light, the bracelets slid apart and hung motionless for an instant as though spinning on her arm, the blind fingers felt the bottle's neck. Wrong bottle. Still not looking, but eying Devrue, she moved her fingers to the next bottle, felt its shape, grasped it in recognition, plucked it out of the garden of lights and glassware. All in the same instant, Stone knew he was still gazing at the empty place where the bottle had been.

Beside him he heard Devrue saying, "I make it a habit never to drink in places I'm thrown out of." And the soft suck of the cork being twisted out. The voices seemed faraway.

Madame Rocquier (wistfully): "I don't know—alcohol cushions the fall."

Devrue (laughing): "I've been thrown out of a place only once in my life, and that wasn't in France. It was a long long time ago. I'm not so young any more."

Stone's gaze relaxed out of focus.

Madame Rocquier: "You're still young enough to make mischief." The clink of the bottle on the glass's lip.

Without turning his head Stone could see her in his mind's eye: woman eternal, arch, coquettish, flattering. And Devrue, whose father left him lead mines in North Africa. Stone smiled to himself, relaxing slightly.

Devrue (protesting): "That's enough! Stop! You want to make me drunk. I can't drink all this."

"You'll manage." Outside the edge of his gaze Stone saw her turn. Then the arm, the bracelets again, and the bottle thumped back in its place. He watched the liquid rocking inside.

"I told you I'm not a young man any more," Devrue said.

"You're young enough," Madame Rocquier said. Then she placed herself directly before Stone's vision, smiling, her hands on her hips. "And now," she said, reminding herself aloud, "this one's drinking *fin sec.*" She pirouetted and picked a different bottle from the bright flower bed before the mirror. The liquid in the first one was still rocking.

"A small one for me," he said, breaking his gaze away from the mirror. She uncorked the bottle and tilted it over his glass, nodding gravely.

Before he could stop her she poured enough for three small ones. In the back of his mind he had known she would. "I like my customers to come back," she said righteously. "I give good measure, especially when they're about to leave." She looked straight at Stone.

Devrue said, "You've slowed us down, that's sure. I only hope you don't have to carry us out."

"Don't worry, my cabbage. You can sleep here." She didn't look at Devrue as she spoke, but half turned back and leaned one arm on the bar before Stone. "What does an American do here in Paris?"

Stone shrugged. "The same things a Frenchman does, I suppose."

"He doesn't pay taxes."

Stone smiled and sipped his drink to avoid her. He wished he could change the subject.

Madame Rocquier persisted. "No, truly. What do you do here? You're not a tourist, because you speak French. Do you work here?"

Stone murmured, hoping Devrue wouldn't get into it too. "I was working with the American Army, then with the Embassy. Now I am just being a tourist."

"Oh, with the Embassy. That explains how it is you speak French so well. All diplomats speak French, I suppose." Unconsciously she reached behind her head and recaptured a loose willow of hair. "Isn't it a pity about your ambassador? I wonder what could have happened?"

Devrue interrupted to correct her. "He's not their ambassador any more," he said. "He *used* to be the ambassador. Now they will have a new one."

"Yes," Stone said. "It was too bad. He was a good man. But even the good ones have to retire sooner or later." Then he added, "He's much older than he looks from his pictures."

Madame Rocquier lifted both her hands as though horrified. "Oh, no," she said. "I don't mean *that.*" Quickly she turned and went for the newspaper.

Stone's muscles involuntarily slacked. Instantly, from the look on her face, from the movement of her hands, he sensed within himself the hollow truth. He thought: The old man has finally died. He watched Madame Rocquier thrashing with the newspaper, trying to refold it in its original order. No, he thought, that's what you always think first. Saw him yesterday. Wheelchair. Probably the news is out that he can't walk. I knew before they did.

"I mean *this.*" Madame Rocquier slapped the reassembled paper onto the bar. Stone's eyes fell on a small headline . . . INFLATION . . . then something about bicycle racing.

Then he saw the photograph.

It was Sheppard all right. Standing on the stairs to an airplane, waving. Smiling. One hand on the door. Leaving? Or about to enter? Stone couldn't tell. Over the photograph was captioned the single-word question: DISPARU?

Stone's mind stumbled over the word. Disappeared. What sort of stupidity . . . ? Quickly he scanned the brief text of the accompanying story. . . . *rumored to have vanished . . . the Mediterranean* . . . That was all there was. The story was boxed as a special late-news dispatch and was only a hand's breadth long.

When? He went back to pick up the rest of the scanty details. *Last flight . . . en route to North Africa . . . short vacation before . . .* Then he stopped. Calmly he began reading again from the beginning, this time slowly, carefully. He was aware of Devrue reading along with him. *Didn't he know before?* Madame Rocquier's hips were just visible over the paper at the top edge of his vision.

The story had almost no details beyond what was "reliably rumored," and appeared to have been written at the last minute and thrown in as the newspaper went to press. Angled for sensation, full of words like "mysterious," "strange," the whole tone and tenor of the thing made Stone reluctant to credit it at its face value. It was simply too fantastic.

But then, there at the bottom—in the very last line, in fact—lay one hard irrefutable omen: *The American Embassy up to the present time has withheld comment.* Everything else was "rumored" or "reliably reported" except that last sentence. Stone looked at the smiling photograph, wondering: Is *that* the plane? He decided it was probably an old photograph they'd dug out of the files. Yesterday he had been in a wheelchair.

"What do you think happened?" Madame Rocquier asked.

Stone shrugged. Suddenly he felt completely collected. He calmly folded the paper and handed it back to her over the counter. "I doubt if he 'disappeared.' Perhaps to the press he disappeared, but people don't simply disappear."

"Perhaps he had a heart attack in the plane, and . . ." Devrue started.

". . . they took him off in a box," Madame Rocquier finished for him.

Stone turned up his hands emptily. "There's not much to go on," he said. "Mostly rumor. Nothing official yet."

Madame returned the paper to where she got it. Stone felt his mind in complete suspension; he simply watched her, thinking of nothing.

Devrue sat silent, sipping his pernod. Apparently the talk of death had touched him. He'd mentioned the possibility of a heart attack. Stone wondered if Devrue had a bad heart. He turned to him, and raised his glass.

"That's the way it goes," Stone said. "No use worrying about it."

"I'm not worrying," Devrue said. "It's just that I'm afraid of airplanes. Even talking about them makes me . . . ugh." He made a face and shuddered.

"It's safer than driving a car," Stone said. "According to statistics."

"I know. I've heard all that. It doesn't matter. It's not only airplanes, but anything high up. I have what psychologists call acrophobia. Fear of high places."

"I've heard of that." In the back of his mind Stone idly noticed that he felt more sober.

"I've tried to make myself . . ." Devrue stopped and shuddered again. "I forced myself to go up . . . on the Eiffel Tower. There's a restaurant up there." He actually seemed to shiver at the memory. "I couldn't eat. I was afraid to go down in the elevator again. I couldn't move. I just sat there with my eyes shut, actually feeling the sensation of falling. My God, it was awful."

"Have you ever fallen off anything? Say, when you were a child?"

"I've tried to think back, but there's nothing I can remember. I even had it as a child. My old governess used to say it was because my mother fell while she was carrying me. I don't know. Maybe she's right, who knows?"

"You've never flown?"

"God, no. Never. I believe flying is for birds and angels, and I have no desire to be an angel."

"It'll be hard on you if you're sent to heaven." Stone said, smiling.

Devrue shook his head. "It would be hell. I'd rather walk the earth in chains. Daedalus lived longer than Icarus, mainly because he pursued the golden mean. I'm Daedalus. I could build airplanes, but I could never fly one."

"Daedalus?"

"He's the father of us all, of engineers, that is. He built the wings that Icarus . . ."

"Oh, of course. Flew too close to the sun and melted the wax. It comes back to me now."

"He also built the Labyrinth to contain the Minotaur," Devrue said. "The Minotaur was probably the symbol of death. I have a personal theory that behind all the legendary exaggerations, Daedalus was probably the first sewer engineer."

693

Stone couldn't help turning to see if Devrue was smiling. But he wasn't joking. He was in grim earnest. He leaned closer to Stone, his face preoccupied.

"Look at it this way," Devrue went on. "Granted it's a personal theory, but all legends have to start somewhere, and archeologists have discovered that Crete had a very advanced culture. Undoubtedly they had sewers, and probably understood that sewers had something to do with containing the popular death rate. Now if the black bull stands for the mortality rate . . ."

Devrue stopped, and shrugged, as though the rest was self-evident. Stone said, "And there you are."

"Precisely." Devrue smiled and rubbed his hands. "I'm delighted that you see it. Most people need to have it explained in detail. One of these days I'm going to write it up for the *Journal of the Proceedings of the International Society of Sewage Engineers.* I think it would make interesting reading, don't you? Of course, I'd have to do a little research, perhaps try to gather a little evidence to back it up. But tell me frankly, what do you think? Do you think it sounds reasonable?"

"Oh, very reasonable," Stone said. "It amazes me that someone hasn't thought of it before this."

"Of course, that's what I'm afraid of. Ideas have a way of occurring at the same time to different people. Consider the calculus. Leibnitz and Newton both thought of it independently and both at the same time. Or the discovery of Neptune. Happens all the time. Every Gauss has his Faraday."

"You have to be careful about discussing it before you publish it."

"Oh, don't worry about that. You're one of the few people I've told about it. Just the same, I would appreciate it if you'd keep it to yourself."

Stone felt like bursting out laughing. Devrue was magnificent. Instead of laughing, Stone masked a smile behind his glass. He liked Devrue and didn't want to offend him, but the man suddenly looked for all the world like a mother hen worrying over an unhatched egg. He sat hunched on his stool, lost in his preoccupation, rolling his glass absent-mindedly between his hands.

Finally he said, "But there's no way I can keep someone else from getting the same idea. It's so obvious once you see it." He sighed deeply and shook his head. "I suppose I'll just have to stop putting it off and write it."

Stone nodded gravely. He felt a genuine sympathy with Devrue.

Devrue took a long swallow of his drink. "It's the only way." Stone watched him in profile, saw his Adam's apple bob once, twice; he put the glass down nearly empty. Then he brightened. "We've talked enough about that. Finish your drink and we'll get started. Everything's arranged."

"Get started where?"

"You said you wanted to see our sewer system. I've telephoned and made all the necessary arrangements."

"Tonight?" Stone drew back, incredulous.

"Why not? You said you didn't have to . . ."

"But the day is already over. It's nearly night." Stone turned and looked out the door. "In fact, it *is* night."

"Day or night. It makes no difference down there. It's always the same."

"Good Lord," Stone said. "I didn't realize you intended . . ."

"Well, you see, tonight's a little special. Because of the holiday—they're working an extra shift getting the boat ready."

"The *boat?*"

"Every second and fourth Thursday in May through June," Devrue recited, "and every Thursday from June to October 15, the public is permitted to take a boat ride through the large tunnel from Madeleine to the Place de la Concorde. On Monday, however, we will have an official preview for city officials, and we're working overtime to get the boat ready and the tunnel cleaned up."

Stone laughed, half at himself. "Well, I suppose . . ."

Devrue was beaming like a father with a birthday gift. "Ordinarily it would cost you twenty francs. But as my guest you'll go free. I have my car outside."

Stone squared his shoulders and raised his glass. For no reason he laughed. Simultaneously a thought flashed through another part of his mind: If Sheppard's dead—here's to him. He looked at Devrue. "To your health," he said.

"Thank you. And to yours."

Together they finished their drinks.

Devrue put his glass down hard and said, "Let's go quickly before that one hits me. I'll have to drive fast."

"We can take a taxi," Stone said.

"Bah! Why pay for a taxi when we can kill ourselves for nothing?"

"That's true."

Devrue turned and waved to Madame Rocquier. *"Bon soir,* Françoise."

The proprietress waved back with a gesture full of weary cynicism. Devrue took no notice, but was already at the door. Stone waved.

Outside, Stone was surprised to see Raymond's taxicab still parked at the curb. He pointed at it. "I thought he left."

Devrue looked briefly at the cab. "When he gets drunk he leaves it here and takes a taxi. He lives not far from here."

"I'll be damned," Stone said.

XII

It had happened like this:

The full Mediterranean moon lay long across the black water. The airplane floated easily in the unturbulent air. The navigator had gone forward to take a radio fix. Bruce Peel Sheppard, former United States Ambassador to France, sat alone in his wheelchair at his desk. He stopped in his reading, raised his head as though to listen to the unchanging drone of the engines. He put down his book, removed his wristwatch, took a letter from the pocket of the red silk dressing gown. He put his watch on top of the open book on the desk. He put the letter on the desk, removed his slippers, and placed them on top of the letter.

He turned the wheelchair about, turned out the reading light over the desk, and wheeled himself aft. In the semidarkness he positioned the wheelchair before the special loading door aft of the bath compartment. The desk had been brought aboard through this door, and the desk was wider than the wheelchair. He struck the red handle twice; nothing happened. The third time, the door vanished, ripped off by the wind. He saw the track of the moon across the water and felt the naked roar of the engines. It was like the entrance to a cave. Cold air flowed around him, engulfed him. He backed away from the exit. Light from the forward cabin fell across his knees; someone had opened the door. He pushed on the wheels, propelled the wheelchair across the short space, across the fall of light, and vanished.

That was all there was time to see. The navigator saw it, saw all there was time to see. It was the navigator also who found the letter on the desk under the slippers. The letter was sealed, addressed to Georges Merseault. The Bible was open to Jeremiah, an underlined passage:

11. Moreover the word of the Lord came unto me, saying, Jeremiah, what seest thou? And I said, I see a rod of an almond tree.
12. Then said the Lord unto me, Thou hast well seen: for I will hasten my word to perform it.
13. And the word of the Lord came unto me the second time, saying, What seest thou? And I said, I see a seething pot; and the face thereof is toward the north.
14. Then the Lord said unto me, Out of the north an evil shall break forth upon all the inhabitants of the land.

XIII

Less than an hour after leaving the Café Monumentale, Stone came up with Devrue from the tunnel under the Place de la Concorde, and was surprised to find himself emerging from a bronze door in the base of one of the statues surrounding the square. He had thought there'd be more to it. The boat trip through the sewer tunnel seemed hardly to have begun when suddenly it was over, and Stone was left with only the vaguest impression of it. It was like the trips through the tunnel of love he remembered taking as a child at amusement parks; in the darkness there had been no sensation of forward motion, only the slightest rocking of the boat. Stone was still wondering to himself when they were going to start when all of a sudden there was a slight grinding bump and the trip was over. Only then did he realize how rapidly the silent water had been flowing; he had been waiting for them to begin poling the boat along.

Devrue had given him a flashlight, but he had used it mainly to examine the boat. For the rest, he had noted only that the air was remarkably fresh, the dark echoing tunnel cavernous and chilly, and that the boat smelled strongly of fresh paint. In the chamber under the Place Madeleine where they started, Stone heard the distant clanging of iron and far down a branching tunnel briefly glimpsed several ghostly figures carrying strange white lights that cast wild galloping shadows as they walked. Devrue explained that it was an emergency work gang off to locate a leak in a fresh-water main. After they had rounded a bend in the tunnel, Stone still heard faint hollow strains of one of them singing. He was singing one of Edith Piaf's songs; Stone didn't know the name of it. Devrue had commented that the men often sang to let each other know where they were—it made them feel less lonely working alone in the dark.

As they emerged from the back of the statue's pedestal into the relative brightness of the glitter-lighted Place de la Concorde, a group of young people in a group near by, obviously on their way to a party, were standing and laughing, waiting for a bus. One of the girls saw them just as the bronze door clanged shut behind them; an *égoutier*, the one who had piloted the boat, had accompanied them to the top of the narrow winding stair in order to take the flashlights back with him. He slammed the door shut and dogged it from the inside just as the girl saw them. She pointed, and Stone heard her give a small cry of surprise. "Those two men just walked out of that statue!" The young feminine voice carried clearly on the soft night air.

Devrue said to Stone, "Sometimes people ask us where that door leads to, when they see us come out. Every *égoutier* has his own standard answer."

"What do you tell them?" Stone asked.

"I tell them I live there with my family." Then he added, "Of course I have no family."

Stone laughed. Behind them he heard another girl say, "What do you suppose they were doing in there?" He and Devrue walked away in the opposite direction, back toward the Place Madeleine, where they'd left Devrue's car. When they'd crossed the street Stone looked back over his shoulder and saw the boys in the group making a puzzled examination of the door in the back of the statue. One of them was examining the hinges by the light of a match. The girls were clustered in a knot apart, giggling privately among themselves.

Stone was feeling warmly pleasantly drunk as they turned up the Rue Royale. It was a beautiful night, neither warm nor chilly, a perfect night for festivities. It was early for tourists, but Stone had noticed several patently American couples walking the streets looking in lighted shopwindows. In seersucker jackets and pastel nylon dresses, they were like early robins hopping about looking for worms. Ahead Stone noticed one man standing before a shopwindow full of chessmen and handsome gaming boards. He still had his camera slung over his shoulder from an afternoon of sightseeing. Three shops down his wife was standing bent over before an unlighted window full of ladies' gloves, twisting her head this way and that trying to make out the prices. Stone watched them making their separate progress, calling their discoveries to each other, until finally he and Devrue came abreast and passed them.

Devrue was watching other things. "They're doing all right," he said, looking backward across the street at the expensive squad of polished limousines parked two abreast before Maxim's. Stone turned and looked. A woman in a fur stole was getting out of a taxi, helped by her escort in white tie and tails. Stone looked just in time to see her lurch slightly; three men including the doorman reached out to catch her, but she recovered her balance. With a gay peal of laughter that rose like bubbles on the champagne air, she kicked a silver slipper into the air; her escort, looking awkwardly athletic in formal clothes, made a jump backward and caught it as it came down. Just then the doorman handed him something he'd retrieved off the ground, and Stone realized that she had broken the heel off her shoe. As her escort fumbled with the broken heel she reached down and removed the other shoe and gave it to him also. He followed behind her, still worrying the broken shoe, as she entered Maxim's barefoot. The doorman and several of the liveried chauffeurs were still laughing in a circle around the entrance as Stone looked away.

"The idle rich," Stone said. Since the war he'd been to Maxim's once, and found the place to have after all a certain attractive vulgarity. Yet to his jaded eye the careful patina had finally appeared as mere corrosion; he still remembered Maxim's as the exclusive club of the German High Command. He hadn't enjoyed himself.

"Not so idle," Devrue said. "Not so rich. There's a difference between being rich and merely having money." The liquor thickened the contempt in his voice.

Stone remembered the lead mines in North Africa.

Devrue walked a few paces in silence. Then he muttered, "Money." Suddenly his hand came out of his pocket and flew into the air over his head. "What's money?" A woman and a man passing them stepped sideways, looking startled.

A moment later Stone was showered with small coins as they pelted down and bounced and rolled on the sidewalk. The woman turned and whispered to her escort, still watching. Involuntarily Stone stopped and looked at Devrue. Devrue walked straight on, his shoulders hunched forward as if he were walking into a high wind, both hands in his pockets again. Stone lagged behind, thought: He's drunker than I am.

Stone quickened his pace and walked beside Devrue again. Devrue said, "Money is garbage for pigs."

Stone said quietly, "I'm a pig."

"Why don't you go back there and get it then?"

Stone found himself giggling. "I'm only a small pig."

"Sometime I'll tell you about money," Devrue said, as though leveling a threat at Stone. Suddenly he veered right around the corner into a side street. Stone followed unthinkingly. Then he realized that the car was in the other direction.

"You wait here," Devrue said. He stepped off the curb and crossed the street.

Stone watched him and waited. Then he went back around the corner and stood. Back down the Rue Royale the woman was picking up the coins as the man stood arguing.

It wasn't a minute later that Devrue came back around the corner with a package wrapped in newspaper under each arm.

Stone greeted him. "That was quick. Where did you go?"

"Friend of mine," Devrue mumbled. "Here, take yours." He handed Stone one of the newspaper-wrapped bottles.

"What's this?"

"It's a bottle of milk. You know, very few Frenchmen ever get drunk in public. But I'm not very few Frenchmen. I was born in North Africa and I've been all around the world. And I like to drink with Americans because Americans drink to get drunk. At heart I'm a barbarian too."

"Well, thank you . . ." Stone clapped Devrue on the back, and laughed.

"It's nothing, Jean-Jacques. I would have had to buy two bottles anyhow, because he couldn't make change."

"Well, thank you again, old friend. What's your first name, any-how?"

"I don't like my first name. Besides, I want you to feel at home. Call me Devrue. Americans always call each other by their last names. I'll call you Jean-Jacques because I'm a Frenchman."

Stone wondered: How did he get so drunk all of a sudden? Then he thought of the answer: He's been saving it.

"Come on," Devrue said, "we've only started. You didn't really see anything here. Now we're going to the Place de Châtelet. That's where you can really see what a sewer looks like."

"You mean there's more?"

"Oh, we haven't really even begun yet. Certainly there's more."

Stone shrugged, grinning. "Anything you say . . . what's your first name?"

"I don't like my first name. Call me—"

"Yes, I forgot. Devrue."

"I'll tell you about money sometime," Devrue said as he fished into his pocket for the keys to the car. The car was parked directly ahead of them in the shadow of the Eglise Madeleine. Then he asked Stone abruptly, "Do you have any children?"

"No." Stone said it automatically.

Simultaneously it struck him that it wasn't true. He *did* have a child, a son, in fact. For the first time the full realization hit him; he stopped in his tracks, astounded.

Devrue said, "What's the matter? You forget something?"

"Yes," Stone said. "I have a son."

Devrue screwed up his face and looked slantwise at Stone for several seconds. Then he shook his head but said nothing. He went around the car to unlock it. Stone watched the top of Devrue's head as he fumbled with the lock. His mind suddenly felt numb. He was conscious only of the vague murmur of traffic behind him.

Suddenly he felt a powerful grip on his arm, heard a hiss loud in his ear: *"This is a dream!"* He jumped uncontrollably—startled, he whirled free, almost dropping the bottle, drew his hands up. A huge old beggar stood leering toothlessly at him—Stone almost struck him out of pure reflex. The old man hissed again: *"Where is your lost beloved?"* Stone dropped his arms in profound relief against mounting anger at having been taken unawares, thought: He's been standing in the shadows. The beggar was drunk, that was obvious. The anger sagged out of him, but his heart was still pounding with the sudden wild fright.

"What do you want?" he asked, sharply irritated.

"Buy a paper?" The man leered again, and Stone could smell the huge old man's foul breath an arm's length away. He was filthy from head to foot, red-faced, toothless, with gray hair that fell like wire across his forehead. His left cheek was bruised with dried blood.

"What?"

The drunk shoved a folded newspaper at him. "Buy a paper?" Obviously it had been read and refolded; he'd picked it up off the street, probably. Stone was just about to refuse when he saw it: there it was in bold headlines. Even in the feeble light of the streetlamp he made out the word: AMBASSADOR . . . It was no longer a small story.

He took the paper and handed the drunk twenty francs. The old man looked at the money in his hand and muttered, and something snapped inside of Stone. "Get out of here!" he roared. The impudent leer vanished from the drunk's face; stupefied, he staggered backward a pace. Stone advanced a pace, menacing. The beggar turned and retreated. Once he was out of Stone's reach, however, he turned and laughed.

Devrue abruptly started the engine, opened the door from the inside. It hit Stone in the hip. Quickly he got inside and closed the door. Almost instantly the beggar was back, huge, insolent, mocking. He squatted hugely on the sidewalk with his face before the glass, laughing. If Stone had opened the door again he would have knocked him over. As the car worked slowly out of the parking space, he made an obscene gesture. An incredible rage suddenly came over Stone, and he clawed at the door to open it. But the car pulled away from the curb and the door opened only on rushing air and empty invisible laughter behind them. Devrue didn't even turn to look. As Stone tried to close the door again he found his foot in the way; he was shaking. The newspaper had slid off his lap into the street and was gone. He slammed the door and looked back; the beggar was in the street under the streetlight reaching down to retrieve the newspaper. The imagined sound of idiot laughter still rang in Stone's ears.

He turned urgently to Devrue. "I have to stop, buy a newspaper."

Devrue nodded but said nothing, stared straight ahead over the steering wheel. His whole manner and tacit bearing suggested stern disapproval of Stone's behavior.

They rounded a corner.

Stone said, sullenly defensive, "He startled me." He was no longer shaking but his heart was still pounding. For an instant the shock of sudden rage had nearly sobered him, but now the reaction was setting in rapidly.

Devrue said nothing, merely nodded again.

"I don't like people touching me," Stone said. "I'm not trying to excuse myself."

"It's all right," Devrue said. "He was drunk. So are you. But you shouldn't have given him money. You only make the old robber lazier."

They drove several blocks in silence.

"So I am," Stone said, suddenly resigned. He really felt it now, recognized it approaching, the moment of immersion, of fear and exhilaration, moment of final submergence. Unthinking, he caressed the blind outlines of the bottle lying hard in his lap. This was the time that was worst to endure, the time when he knew it was coming; the moment out of time he both dreaded and desired, when time would escape time. "So I am." He thought: No corkscrew. Then remembered: *All we need is a stick and a rock. Adriane*—the clue. *Too young . . .*

He relaxed, let his eyes close, his head slump gently backward; submitted to the slow lethargy of pounding blood. Behind his heart he could detect it: exhilaration—the storm bending down at the sea's summer edge; the heart detached from feeling—a gull sliding sideways down a gathering wind, detached from its leewarding cry. . . . *he's got just as much right to be drunk . . .* Behind his eyes he could begin to feel it: the brain loose and sliding, a table tilting in a ship at sea. . . . *buy a newspaper . . .* Thoughts staggered, gulls in the wind, soared immobile an instant, slid sideways away, were gone. . . . *old Sheppard's dead . . .* slid across the table of his mind like careful stacks of china dinnerware sliding to crash and oblivion. . . . *my son my son my kingdom for a son. Long live the king . . .* And behind it all, the purring of a cat. . . . *you don't fool me, sonny boy. Drunk. Unto us a child is . . . Christ . . .* Later it would grow louder; later, much later, would come the whirling onslaught of the tiger he knew he would have to ride. . . . *hold that tiger, hold that . . .* thoughts changed their shape again, became detached, and were gone like words ripped on the wind, scraps of paper blown from his mouth. One wish, one desire, soared away trailing a string, like a child's slow balloon; to a pinpoint, then was gone: *Solange. O God forgive me. Our Father who art . . . watch over him.*

Stone's outburst over the beggar must have upset Devrue, for he remained silent the rest of the way. By the time the car reached the Place de Châtelet he was acting almost completely sober. He parked the car with studied efficiency, and before he got out of the car, peered at his face in the rear-view mirror and conspicuously straightened his tie; he seemed to be setting an example. Stone, chastened by Devrue's silence, did his best to follow it. Clumsily he got out of the car and stood erect, almost shutting the door on the bottle in Devrue's hand before he realized that Devrue was coming out his side. Devrue's door was blocked by the lamppost he'd parked under. Stone held the door open; Devrue followed his feet out and stood up with meticulously careful balance. Stone closed the door and shifted his bottle. Devrue nodded graciously to Stone, shifted his bottle, and locked the door.

"I have to be careful to keep my dignity before the men," Devrue said as they started down a long circular iron staircase, "otherwise discipline becomes a problem."

"Are they expecting us?" Stone asked, following behind. He clutched the railing with one hand, the bottle with the other.

"This is where we conduct special tours for engineers and administrators. The mayor is coming on Monday." Devrue produced a tiny flashlight from his vest.

"I see," Stone said. The turning stairs took full concentration.

Some thirty feet below ground they entered a huge chamber lighted by acetylene torches hung around on the walls. They threw an eerie white light. A man in hip boots rolled down to the knee came toward them. Devrue shook hands with him.

"This is Monsieur Webber, one of our most able engineers." Stone shook hands. Immediately the engineer turned and led them over to a huge wall map hanging in one corner.

Stone found himself standing before the map like a schoolboy about to be lectured. The engineer slid a pencil from his pocket to use as a pointer. "This," he began, "is the sewer plan of the city. The system is almost entirely gravity flow . . ."

Stone did his best to follow the jumping pencil point as it danced around the map. He was having trouble keeping his eyes focused.

". . . other pumps have been installed here . . ." the jumping pencil ". . . here, here, here, here, here, and here."

Some of the lecture Stone remembered hearing before: the total number of kilometers, the total number of sewer workers. The rest of the talk was all about *égouts élémentaires, branchements, reservoirs de chasse,* and *collecteurs.* Stone watched, trying to look absorbed but completely unable to grasp the total of what was being said. The engineer as he talked kept glancing furtively at Devrue like a teacher lecturing before the headmaster. Devrue kept nodding approvingly.

". . . and while drowning is one of the major occupational hazards, there have been only thirteen deaths in the system in the last thirty years. The most common danger . . ."

Devrue interrupted, saying to Stone, "That includes a woman who drowned herself on the outskirts of the city in 1939. Her body somehow ended up in the sewers so we include her in the thirteen, just to be fair."

Stone said, "Of course. Only sporting thing to do." Suddenly he remembered, "I forgot to buy a newspaper."

Devrue pointedly ignored him, turned his full attention back to the engineer, who continued.

". . . The most common danger, of course, is sudden rain from outside. The new rush of water can fill a tunnel in almost no time, and the workers have to move quickly. We instruct them to turn against their natural instinct of trying to run away from the flood. Instead they go directly upstream to the nearest branch leading to a street-gutter opening. Going downstream can easily lead to being trapped by the avalanche of water that is fed by thousands of these openings . . ."

Stone surreptitiously shifted his weight from one foot to the other. He held his left arm over the bottle cradled in his right, following Devrue's example.

". . . In the large collector tubes, where workers occasionally do become trapped, we have emergency rooms built into the ceiling for that purpose."

Stone tried to listen as the engineer gave the wage scales for the various categories of employees, but it escaped him. He was watching the wart on the lecturer's chin.

The lecture seemed to drag on endlessly as Stone shifted secretly from one foot to the other, his own thoughts weltering in endless circles. He was beginning to be acutely conscious of the need to urinate. Also he wanted to open his bottle.

". . . sewer covers are designed to require two men to lift them. They weigh approximately one hundred and fifty kilograms."

Devrue interjected, "That's over three hundred pounds."

"Lots of pounds," Stone said.

And it went on. The wall map before Stone's eyes was completely glazed over with soft indecipherable patterns. His mind returned involuntarily to Sheppard, the newspaper, the drunken beggar. The voice of the engineer droned on.

". . . retrieve objects accidentally fallen. Rings and jewelry and other heavy objects usually remain under the sewer opening where they fell. Papers, of course, float and are harder to trace. Most often, however, we are called upon to retrieve automobile keys . . ."

Stone heard him as though through a long hollow tube. He thought of Devrue standing beside the car, before the beggar came out of the shadows, fumbling for his automobile keys. He remembered watching the top of his head as he unlocked the door.

". . . dozens of carcasses of small dogs and cats . . ."

Stone saw a picture in his mind of a cat disappearing into a gutter opening. Probably following a mouse, he thought.

The voice continued, and once Stone even heard Devrue sigh. It must be worse for Devrue, he thought. Heard it before. Stone wondered where he could go to relieve himself, wondered if there were toilets under the streets. The engineer stopped a moment.

Stone thought for a moment that he was through, but he merely put the pencil back in his pocket and changed his posture. "As to the history of the system . . ." he began with renewed vigor.

Stone looked around for something, a box, anything, to sit on. But there was nothing.

". . . about as described in the famous French novel writer Victor Hugo's book entitled *Les Misérables*. Simply canals leading to the Seine. It is indicative of the medical ignorance of the time to note that in 1633 five workers were asphyxiated as they tried to clean out one of the canals. Their deaths were ascribed to bites from some kind of serpent . . ."

He might not be dead at all, Stone thought, thinking of the fragmentary headline he glimpsed when the beggar thrust the paper at him. He'd noticed only the word "ambassador." It could have been anything. A later story. Embassy denying the rumor. Maybe. Denials don't make headlines, he thought. I want to get out of here, buy a paper. Got to find out what happened to General Sheppard.

The engineer was talking about the cholera epidemic in 1832.

"Eight hundred a day," Stone heard himself say. "Killed 'em off eight hundred every single day."

The engineer faltered, hesitated, went on. ". . . at the rate of eight hundred a day, that is correct." But he was uncertain now. Abruptly he turned to Devrue and said, "Perhaps you'd like to start the tour right away, instead of . . ." He trailed off, didn't say instead of what.

Stone muttered darkly, "Have to piss."

Devrue said, "By all means, Monsieur Webber. The tour. Yes."

Stone started to speak up. "Is there any place around here where . . ."

Devrue nudged him and whispered, "Remember where you are, Jean-Jacques. At least consider my position."

"I know where I am," Stone said, irritated. "I'm in a sewer. And if I can't *faire pipi* in a sewer, then where in hell . . ."

"All right. All right. We're going into the tunnels right away."

"Fine," Stone said, nodding, "Just point me in the right direction."

The engineer looked back at Stone and asked, "Do you have rubber soles on your shoes, sir?"

Stone turned sidewise to Devrue. "Now why does a man have to have rubber shoes just to make . . . ?"

Devrue cut in, "We both have leather, Monsieur Webber." Then he turned to Stone. "It's just that rubber, particularly crepe, skids a lot down here."

Stone said, "Oh. Excuse me."

An *égoutier* in full hip boots appeared suddenly, from nowhere it seemed to Stone, and handed each of them a portable acetylene lantern. Stone took it, gazing bewilderedly at the silent white flame. Devrue explained, "We're trying out a new kind of electric lantern. It's worn on the head like a helmet."

Stone thought: I wonder what it's like to fly in an airplane in a wheelchair? You must have to go up a ramp or something. Do they chock the wheels? Strap it down? How do they keep it from rolling around inside? Maybe they were having rough weather and it tipped over. Hit his head, maybe. Could that kill him? Might hurt him, though. Old man. Bones brittle.

As they entered the tunnel Stone noticed Devrue shining his light on the street signs. They were posted at regular intervals telling what street they were under, just as Devrue had said. Neatly lettered. White on blue. Just like the ones upstairs, Stone observed to himself. Then he noticed posted every ten paces or so little numbers. He tugged at Devrue's arm and pointed at one of them as they passed it. "What are thun . . . umbers for?" He pardoned himself for belching.

"Those are the addresses of the houses directly above them," the engineer said.

"Notice how fresh the air is," Devrue said. "The rapid flow of the water and the frequent vents to the streets provide excellent ventilation. We'll turn around now and go back to the main chamber."

Stone felt a discomforting pressure on his bladder. "You said I could . . . you said, in the tunnel I could . . ."

"Yes, yes," Devrue said quickly. "We'll wait for you."

Stone stood helplessly; one hand held the bottle, the other was occupied holding the lantern. Exasperated, Devrue stepped forward and relieved him of the bottle and took the lantern and placed it down on the stone walkway.

"All right," Stone said. "I can manage everything."

A few paces away the engineer stood looking seriously concerned. In a spirit of pure respect and helpfulness he said, "Be careful not to fall in, sir." It was the first overt evidence of his having noticed Stone was drunk.

"Don't worry," Stone said, mawkishly crossing himself, "I can swim like a salmon in springtime." He wove a little and wrestled with his clothing as he stood at the edge of the walkway over the silently moving black water. He chuckled to himself, half-singing, ". . . from the elementary tunnels, to the branches, to the collector tubes, through the purification plants . . . some goes for irrigation . . . some for the Seine . . . and some for the little boy who lives down the stream . . . make my little elementary . . . contribution."

Slowly he finished his effort and stepped back, readjusting his clothing; he looked at the flowing channel a long time, ignoring Devrue and the engineer who still stood waiting. Devrue's remembered words mingled in his head with his own thoughts and the engineer's dry lecture. He suddenly felt sobered and amused.

He said aloud, "And thence to the sea, of course."

Later he was singing, to the irreverent strains of the American Marines' Hymn, "From the el-e-men-t'ry tu-uh-nels to the shores of Tripoli . . ." Devrue looked at him as though he'd gone mad. ". . . I'll fight my nation's battles, and then to hell with me . . ." The engineer looked merely uncomfortable, failing completely to understand the occasional English interchanges between his superior and the strange American who he'd been told on the telephone preferred to inspect sewer systems by night. Devrue was carrying Stone's bottle for him; the engineer his lantern. Stone walked along empty-handed, clucking to himself, occasionally bursting into lusty song, the same song. In the back of his mind he decided that the only thing to do was to cheer the other two up; the engineer looked as if all he really needed was a drink.

Coming back to the main chamber they entered a larger sewer running beneath the Boulevard de Sébastopol just as four *égoutiers* emerged dragging a long heavy chain. They carried acetylene lanterns, and shovels over their shoulders; as they passed they nodded silently each in turn to Devrue and the engineer. They passed in deferential single file, each standing aside to make room on the narrow walkway.

"They use that chain . . ." the engineer began. Then, noticing that Stone was walking behind not listening but humming to himself, the engineer finished, ". . . of course."

They walked in silence.

After a short distance they passed a large contrivance that straddled the stream of water on rails. It looked about the size of an automobile. As Stone passed it, it moved infinitesimally forward with a soft creaking noise. Startled, he jumped aside.

"*What* is that?"

"That is a *wagon-vanne,*" the engineer answered. "A scavenging device that's driven along by the flow of water. They run without attendance. Notice the large metal lip that hangs down into the water." He shone his light on it.

"You mean you have more of these things creeping around down here?" Stone asked.

"In the larger tunnels the same principle is employed with a boat, and a little machine that we call a *mitrailleuse* for the smaller tubes. They are all pushed along by water power."

Stone looked at it. Again it crept forward slightly. "Looks like a cockroach," he said.

Devrue aroused himself from his misgivings long enough to observe that the simplest cleaning device was a large wooden ball that was dropped regularly into one of the seven pipes that cross under the Seine. "The ball itself is about two meters in diameter—that's about six feet. The pipes under the Seine are always full of water and the ball is pushed through the pipe by water pressure. It pushes all the accumulated sand ahead of it."

Stone wagged his head and said, "What will they think of next?"

They resumed walking.

At the underground intersection of the Rue de Rivoli and the Boulevard de Sébastopol, the engineer stopped to explain the maze of large and small pipes and cables that surrounded them. There were fresh-water-supply pipes, compressed-air pipes, cables for telephones, cables for telegraphs, and transit tubes for *pneumatiques.* Electric-power cables and gas lines, he explained, were not allowed in the sewer because of the hazard they created.

Devrue interrupted, "Telephone and telegraph cables are safe enough because of their low voltage, you see. Between twenty-four and thirty volts."

Then Devrue turned abruptly to the engineer and said, "You can leave us here, Webber. I know you have to go on. We'll go back alone."

The engineer nodded and handed Stone his lantern again. They shook hands and Stone thanked him. He stood with Devrue watching the engineer continue on down the Rue de Rivoli, his shadow swaying grotesquely back and forth in the large tunnel as he walked swinging his acetylene torch.

"I have one more thing to show you," Devrue said, turning to go back. "The room I used during the war. I've kept it just as it was. It used to be a telephone vault, but it was abandoned when they converted the old system to dial exchanges."

"Lead on, O Kindly Light," Stone said affably. "I've come this far."

"We can sit down there," Devrue said. "And I have a corkscrew."

Retracing their steps they came finally to the large chamber where they'd started. Passing through it, Stone noticed that the *égoutiers* were sitting on the lower steps of the iron staircase eating their midnight lunches. Devrue and Stone continued in a new direction.

"I hope you don't mind the walk," Devrue said. "It's toward Bastille."

"Not if you have a corkscrew," Stone said. "I'm beginning to feel sober." Then he added, "Or a stick and a rock."

Once they passed through a smaller chamber at the intersection of two streets and Devrue stopped. "Listen!" he said, tugging at Stone's sleeve. Stone stood listening: a strange sound, a faint swishing metallic noise directly over his head. It grew louder, then suddenly died away. "That's a *pneumatique* going by," Devrue said, "maybe somebody's love letter."

"Maybe someone died," Stone said.

They turned into a smaller tunnel and continued through the confining darkness. As they walked Stone began to hear the strains of music, a weird hollow sound. It seemed to come closer as they went on: an accordion, a drum, playing a polka. Then he heard an indescribable sound, a rhythmic thumping and scraping directly overhead.

"Street dancing," Devrue said. "Someone is dancing on the manhole cover."

Stone stood amazed for a moment. "It sounds like the place is haunted. That music . . ."

They stood still a moment listening to the eerie hollow music that filtered through the dark tunnel. Devrue said, "Would you like to see them?"

"You mean come up out of the street? My God!"

"No, no. We couldn't do that. I mean through the gutter opening. There's a ladder . . ."

They turned into a smaller tube that had no walkway, but it was sharply inclined and dry. Stone had to bend over as he worked his way up. At the end there was a ladder. It was like standing in the bottom of a well; at the top feeble light filtered in along with the music.

"They must have the orchestra on the sidewalk," Devrue said. "There's a café on this corner."

Clinging to the iron ladder, Stone reached the top and leaned sideways to peer out the gutter opening. The first thing he saw was a huge hopping pair of woman's ankles like tree trunks; she had on high-heeled red leather shoes and green ankle socks, dancing in the gutter to the music. If he hadn't had to hold onto the ladder he could have reached out and touched her. The ankles vanished. Beyond where they'd been was a swirling forest of feet and legs. Suddenly the music changed without pause from a polka to a two-beat waltz. The lower edge of a pushcart wheel scraped past the gutter opening and stopped. Stone saw the shuffling worn-down shoes of the peddler, then smelled the sharp smell of roasting peanuts. Beyond, as the music's change overtook them, the multicolored whirl of hopping shoes and socks now turned in a vast dancing confusion of rhythms.

He looked down at the top of Devrue's head where he stood patiently holding the bottles and the two torches, and started down the ladder. He jumped off the ladder at the foot.

"Where in the world are we?"

Devrue looked at him, handed him back his lantern, shrugged. "What does it matter? They'll all be dancing tonight."

When they finally got to the vault, Stone noticed that it was in a side tunnel that was totally dry. It seemed completely unused. It even smelled slightly dusty. Devrue selected a key on his key ring and proceeded to unlock the huge padlock on the door as Stone held the lanterns and the bottles. The lock was difficult, and it took him several seconds to wrest it open. Inside it smelled musty but clean.

Devrue set about placing a chair to stand on and screwed a lamp bulb into a socket overhead. The room suddenly erupted in light. Devrue extinguished the acetylene torches and set them on the desk, the only piece of furniture in the room besides several chairs and three long benches. On the desk were a hotplate and a file box. The vault looked like a tiny classroom. In one corner was a litter of wires and electrical parts. In the other was a type case and an ancient printing press.

"I thought you said you had no electrical power in the sewers . . ." Stone began.

"We haven't. This is furnished through the courtesy of a shoe store up above. I occasionally buy a pair of shoes there to pay for what I use."

"How did you get the printing press in here?"

"In pieces. We floated in everything you see here. We had more during the war, but some of it we had to give back. The press I bought myself, so I kept it. I'm sentimental about this place, of course." He looked around. "I used to have a picture of De Gaulle on the wall. I got tired of looking at him."

"Do you come here often?"

"Whenever I want to be alone I come here. I used to sleep here during the war. The bed is gone because it had bedbugs."

"Where's your corkscrew?"

Devrue extracted a penknife on a long chain that hung from his vest. "Right here," he said.

"You mean you had it all the time?"

Devrue shrugged and started opening the bottles.

Devrue apologized for having only water tumblers—he took the two of them from the bottom desk drawer and blew imaginary dust off them. Stone noticed that they looked clean; they sparkled under the light. He watched without interest as Devrue poured two portions, one from each bottle; suddenly he didn't feel like drinking. He felt merely sober, the beginning edge of depression. He knew he wouldn't be able to drink fast enough now. The exhilaration he'd felt earlier in the evening was gone; he knew it wouldn't come back. He felt tired, drank anyway.

Devrue started to talk about the war, about money, about war and money. Stone let him talk, hardly listening, nodding, sipping his drink, thinking about nothing.

After a while Devrue paused, thinking to himself. Then he said, half aloud, "Money." He shook his head slowly, sadly. Abruptly he looked up at Stone. "You say you have a son," he stated matter-of-factly.

Stone said nothing.

"My father had only one son," Devrue said. "Me. Once when I was very young he told me that I was very lucky—I would never have to share his money with any sisters or brothers. He was true to his word. My mother left him when I was twenty-one. I never saw her again. She liked to paint."

Stone nodded.

"She said I was exactly like him." He paused, as though considering whether it was true or not. "I *looked* like him. But I was like her, I think."

Another pause. Devrue put his glass down.

"I have no children. My wife admired Shelley." He looked at Stone, as though asking for pardon. "I never found out if she loved me."

There was a long silence. Stone watched Devrue dabbling a finger in his glass to remove a speck of something floating. He took it out and stared at the end of his finger, frowning. "What do you suppose a mosquito is doing down here?" he asked, examining it, as though asking the insect itself. He brushed it off, as though putting it out of mind. "I suppose that sounds strange to say I loved the war. But I did and I am not afraid to admit it."

"Most of us aren't," Stone said, wondering what he meant.

"True. We still think like barbarians. Do you think there'll be another one?"

"A war? No."

Devrue ignored the answer. He looked around the room. "I'd have to get a bed in here again, I suppose. I sometimes worry if it's deep enough, though. It's so hard to know in advance how it will come." He paused, still looking around. "In any event, I'll be down here."

"If you have time."

"Ah, yes," Devrue said. "If we have time." He raised his glass in a toast. "Here's to the time we might not have."

The room was absolutely silent. Stone heard the glass click softly against Devrue's front teeth as he drank.

Devrue said, "I feel sober. How do you feel?"

Stone only nodded. They sat silent, Devrue examining the walls of the room again, Stone watching his every move.

Devrue asked, "When did you leave America to come to France?"

"A long time ago. During the war."

"You were *here* during the war?" Devrue looked narrowly at Stone. "During it?"

Stone nodded. Devrue regarded him even more closely.

"Ah, I should have known. So you were one of our wartime 'tourists,' eh? That explains a great deal. You haven't been back since?"

"No."

"What are you doing here now? Working?"

"No. Nothing."

"You said you were with the—"

"Not any more. I do nothing."

"I suppose it's a ridiculous question . . ." Devrue said, nodding slowly to himself. "Americans take it for granted. Like a birthright, I imagine."

Stone was irritated. "Take *what* for granted?"

"Power."

Stone made a small gesture of irritation, said nothing.

"It never occurs to you to be surprised that you can move mountains," Devrue continued, "It's only when you find one you can't move that you're surprised. An immovable mountain simply bewilders you. You're surprised and hurt that it won't move. Then insulted, then angry. You pour in more men, more brains, more money . . ."

Stone laughed.

". . . and if it still won't move, you throw someone in jail for treason. A mountain that refuses to move is un-American."

Stone looked at the bottle in his hand. "I'm drinking myself to death," he said. "I should stop."

"Why? Are you afraid of death?"

Stone looked up at Devrue, opened his mouth to speak, but changed his mind, merely shrugged. "I don't know," he said finally. "Who does?"

"You should find out."

"Oh?"

"Yes," Devrue said. "It is one thing to be afraid of death. It is quite another to be afraid of life."

"It was different during the war."

"Better, or worse?"

"Better," Stone said without hesitation. He paused. "I don't know why I said that."

"Perhaps because you were forced to think about it by circumstances. You were relieved of the responsibility of considering death on your own initiative."

Devrue pulled open a drawer of the battered desk before him.

Stone saw the pistol in his hand before he quite realized what it was. Devrue had taken it out of the drawer so casually that Stone had to look twice before he believed his eyes. It might have been a corkscrew or a paperweight.

"Are you all right?" Stone asked Devrue after he'd gathered his wits.

Devrue looked wistfully at the pistol a moment before answering. Without taking his eyes off it he asked Stone, "You mean, am I sane? Have I a past history of lunacy? The answer is that I believe myself to be quite normal. And you?"

"*Me?*"

"I told you before we came here that I've kept this room as my own little personal monument. It's almost exactly as it was when we used it during the war. This weapon was the cause of a bitter disagreement between my assistant and myself. I kept it here for emergency purposes." Devrue broke the pistol open and spilled the single cartridge into the palm of his hand. Then he put it back in and closed the chamber again.

"Why did you disagree?" Stone asked.

"He was a devout Catholic, preferred suicide at the hands of others. I choose to be responsible for my own life."

Stone said nothing.

Suddenly Devrue spun the cartridge chamber of the revolver.

"Give me that goddamned thing," Stone said, reaching for it. He expected Devrue to resist. Instead he gave it to him.

Stone dropped the pistol casually on the desk. He felt calm, slightly irritated at himself. Devrue was a simple morbid bore. He wanted to get out of the place.

"I thought so," Stone said, realizing suddenly that the possibility had indeed crossed his mind—he'd thought of it, neither believing it nor dismissing it but merely observing it: "What have you done, removed the firing pin?"

"Oh, no. Nothing like that," Devrue said, as though Stone had accused him of duplicity. "It happened to you as it happened to me, except that I first made sure the cartridge was under the hammer. But it was old ammunition, over twenty years old . . . a chance . . . It was my assistant, you see. He opened the cartridge and removed the powder charge so that I wouldn't notice it. He knew about me, you see, knew that I was going to try it sooner or later."

"What's happened to him," Stone asked acidly, "dead?"

712

"Oh, no. Married. Three children. Living in Bordeaux now."

"I think you're crazy."

Devrue looked up, surprised. "It's your privilege to go if you wish. I told you when we came down that you could leave whenever—"

"Are you coming with me?"

"I'll take you to the stairs. I doubt if you're in the proper mood to go dancing. I remember how I felt toward my assistant. You probably want to be alone."

XIV

Walking toward the Rue de Rivoli in search of a taxi, Stone imagined Devrue below ground shadowing his footsteps. He was glad to be rid of him, wondered how he had ever let himself be talked into going with him in the first place.

He stopped, felt his wrist. The piece of wool was still tied around it. He untied it, telling himself he didn't need it any more, refusing to need it. I'll call her once before I go home, he thought. Why? Just to be sure. Why? That fool Devrue, he thought. I don't want to be alone. He got the yarn loose from his wrist and tucked it into his top pocket, a souvenir of . . . he couldn't remember the proprietress' name. It didn't matter, he'd never be going there again, he told himself.

In his top pocket his fingers had touched a stiff card. Idly he wondered what it was. When he came to the next lamppost he took it out. It was the card MacNaughton had given him in the hospital. "Good for one drink on the house," it read in English.

MacNaughton! The Ambassador! Instantly he looked around: nothing in sight. A newspaper, he had to get a newspaper. He thought: My God, what if he is dead? Then he thought, It wouldn't make any difference. Or would it?

He caught a cruising taxi on the Rue de Rivoli. The driver stuck his arm out, stopped, and reached backward to open the door from the outside. Stone got in. MacNaughton would know the whole story, he thought. This was probably why he was . . .

"Where?" the driver asked, bored.

Stone read off the Pigalle address on the card. The question was whether he would be there; it was still early. Early? Early enough. It couldn't be much after midnight, maybe one o'clock.

The bar was in the brightly lighted heart of the Pigalle district on the Rue Blanche. Doormen stood in careless uniforms before their places like sideshow barkers spieling the inside attractions; prostitutes stood beside doorways like wooden Indians, balefully alert, watchful. Stone got out of the cab, paid, and started toward the door. The taxi driver called to him, "You forgot your bottle."

Stone hesitated a moment, then said, "Keep it. It's good stuff."

The driver tipped his hat and reached over the seat into the rear. Stone went inside the bar.

The bartender, an American, said that MacNaughton had just left for a minute but that he was expected right away. Stone ordered a drink and took a stool. He debated asking if there was a newspaper in the bar, decided against it. You can wait, he told himself.

"Aren't you Mr. Stone?"

He turned to the voice behind him, a young man he'd never seen before.

"Who's asking?"

"I'm Willie Striker, I work for Mr. Lutelacker."

"Lutelacker?" Stone tried to remember where he'd heard the name.

"Has anyone seen you yet?" Striker asked.

"Seen me? What do you mean?"

MacNaughton pushed through the door into the bar. Instantly two women waved to him. He saw Stone, stopped dead. Then he came over to him.

"Come upstairs," he said to Stone. "Bring your drink. Hello, Willie."

Willie nodded. "See you later, Mac," he said, and turned to go back to his stool.

Stone dutifully followed MacNaughton up the stairs at the back. The room upstairs was empty. "My office after hours," MacNaughton said. "Come on. Sit down. We've only got a few minutes to talk before Willie telephones Sharktooth—Lutelacker. I know he didn't bring you here, because he was here a few minutes ago when I left."

MacNaughton was half drunk but obviously trying to gather his wits. Stone sat down. MacNaughton's excitement made him suddenly wary and alert. His heart pumped hollowly in his chest. What is he going to tell me?

"All right," MacNaughton said, "we haven't got time to beat around the bush. Do you trust me to do right by you?"

Stone nodded without thinking. Then he thought: I trust him, why? Why not?

"Tell me what you know about his son," MacNaughton said.

"About whose son?" He knew whose son.

"Sheppard's, who else's?"

"What has happened to Sheppard?" Stone asked. For a second he felt as though he'd stopped breathing, wondered: Why should it bother me all of a sudden?

MacNaughton eased back, staring at Stone a long moment. "You don't know?"

Stone shook his head. His throat felt tight and dry. Why why why? Why now? The photographed image of the Ambassador floated gid-

714

dily through his mind: standing on the steps of an airplane, hatless, waving.

"Well, for Christ's sake," MacNaughton breathed. "You beat them all."

"What happened?"

"He jumped out of a goddamned airplane over the Mediterranean, for Christ's sake. Where in hell have you been? The whole story is splashed over every newspaper in town." MacNaughton sounded actually angry.

"What do you mean 'jumped'?" Stone asked levelly.

"Jumped! Jumped! Killed himself. Committed suicide. Gone. Vanished! Without a trace. Clean."

"Into the ocean?"

"I take it back. He didn't jump. He rode a wheelchair out the emergency door. Went back to go to bed, or so he told the navigator."

"Didn't any of the crew . . . ?"

"Nobody. They knew he was sick, but to go out of a plane at six thousand feet . . ."

"When?"

"When?" MacNaughton leaned back and looked narrowly at Stone. "You really didn't know about this?"

Stone shook his head.

"Then why have you been hiding out? I saw you yesterday. This morning you were at the Embassy. This afternoon you disappeared. They've searched the town for you. That girl . . . Récamier . . . seems to have disappeared too."

"Solange? What do you mean disappeared?"

"She hasn't been back to her apartment all evening. I went there to try to find you."

"How did you know about—"

"Oh, hell! Stone, look. Forget it. I've just had a bad argument with someone I owe money to. I'm sorry if—"

"Tell me what happened."

"I told you! Why don't you read the newspapers, you idiot? What do you think we write them for?"

"Please tell me what—"

"All right, all right. Visualize a beautiful Mediterranean night. The kind they tell you about in the travel folders. A full moon has just risen out of the silver water. It's shining like a bloody waterbaby across the balmy waters. The pilot notes the time in his logbook, just because it looks so beautiful. The navigator comes forward with the message that the old man is reading in his quarters, and that he's asked for coffee within the hour. They all look at the moon awhile, then the navigator goes back to check on the temperature in the cabin. The door to the old man's quarters is ajar and he sees him still sitting in his wheelchair reading—he's reading the Bible as it turns out."

Stone opened his mouth to speak, but MacNaughton held up his hand and cut him off. "Wait. I'm just coming to the good part, the part that makes it front-page for the tabloids. The navigator went forward again and started to plot a radio fix. Then they felt a thump—that was probably the door being ripped off—not much but enough to tell them. It's a miracle that door didn't hit the control surfaces aft."

MacNaughton suddenly sagged completely, and his voice changed. He spoke slowly, shaking his head sadly. "He saw him. The navigator was the only one. He said the old man must have seen him too, because he looked around toward the front of the plane. The navigator hadn't put it all together in his mind. Then he backed off his wheelchair and gave one mighty heave on the wheels—and rolled right out of the plane without a sound. He had a red silk bathrobe on."

Stone didn't move, said nothing. MacNaughton was offensively drunk; his eyes blinked heavily, like a lizard's.

"How do you suppose that kid felt looking out that door into nothing, Stone? Isn't it a funny story? With all that cold black wind rushing past. They had to come down to a thousand feet it was so cold. The door was gone with the wheelchair."

Stone said calmly, "That's enough," trying to control a mounting sense of anger.

MacNaughton smiled, said thickly, "You don't like me, do you, Stone?"

"No."

"You haven't liked me for a long time, have you, Stone?"

"That's right."

"You didn't know it until just now, did you, Stone?"

Stone said nothing.

MacNaughton took a swallow of his drink and put the glass down hard. "You know something?" he said. "I don't like you either."

"It's your privilege."

"You remind me too much of myself—maybe. Well, the hell with it. I'm not paid to like myself."

"Neither am I."

"Alexi Carnot told Sharktooth that his son had a diary. Don't you know something about that diary?"

"Carnot?" Stone pronounced the name absently. "What about Carnot?"

"It's been a busy week. Carnot left by plane yesterday for Moscow, with two big burly Russians and a Russian doctor. He's going for brain surgery. Dujardin confessed right after he left."

Stone shook his head. "Carnot's no longer sane," he said.

"I know that. That's why he went to Moscow, so he thinks. I'll give you two to one he won't even come out of the anesthesia."

"What did he say about Berger's diary?"

"He said it existed. Do you have it?"

Stone shook his head slowly. "No," he said.

"According to Sheppard's doctor, with whom I spoke today, Shep-

716

pard had not been allowed to read a magazine or a newspaper for the last week. Two weeks ago the old man evidently had a small mental crackup."

Stone muttered to himself, "He still believed he was alive . . ."

MacNaughton leaned forward quickly, but missed it. "What was that you just said?"

"Nothing."

"What was it?" MacNaughton persisted. "I heard you say something."

Stone didn't answer but got to his feet. Then he reached down for his glass, and drank it off in one swallow. MacNaughton grabbed his arm.

Stone didn't realize he'd hit MacNaughton until the reporter grunted softly and fell sideways onto the table. He'd hit him with the blade of his hand just under the right ear. MacNaughton slumped forward, knocking over his own empty glass, and lay still. For a brief second Stone felt nothing; he stared at his own left hand. Then MacNaughton moved again, trying to lift his face off the table, more drunk-stunned than hurt.

Stone turned and fled down the stairs, through the long bar, and out the door. He saw Striker bending over a telephone at the other end of the bar.

It looked like the same taxi he'd come in, waiting for another fare. The driver was casually polishing the windshield with a large chamois. Stone started to pull open the door; the driver said, "It's been taken." He pointed behind Stone. "That gentleman." Stone turned, startled. The man he hadn't noticed was standing beside the entrance to the bar. Stone couldn't quite believe his eyes: he was holding two graceful pale Afghans on twin leashes. He moved toward Stone as though in a dream. The flaxen-haired hounds followed, lifted their long pointed heads inquiringly.

"I'm terribly sorry . . ." he said in a soft, almost feminine voice. Stone saw the face suddenly by the light of the neon sign overhead. He had make-up on; an entertainer from one of the clubs. His hair was the dogs' color, combed in careful metallic waves, and his eyebrows, arched up to a point, shone like new-minted silver. But his face looked old, a mask of debauchery; the lips and cheeks were black with rouge under the sallow neon. Stone stared for a split second, and instinctively stepped back. The man came closer, brought his face close to Stone, gave a low, almost lilting laugh of apology. ". . . but I'm waiting for someone." Stone caught the acrid scent of his perfume, strong and sweet in the nostrils. One of the dogs turned under his leash and almost tripped him. He hissed at it and jerked the leather savagely. Then he looked up and smiled. "Another time, perhaps?" Stone mumbled and turned away, his heart pounding as he started up the street. The blatant shock of the cool invitation left him wordless, shamed. He had to force himself to walk. He was only a few paces away when he heard behind him the sharp slap of leather and the twisting whine of the dogs, and thought: The end of the leash.

A few steps farther he turned irresistibly to look back over his shoulder. The dogs lay cowering, but their master was still looking after Stone. Stone could still see the thin glint of his steel-bright eyebrows and knew he was smiling. "Good Lord," Stone said aloud, looking away, "I've seen the Devil himself." He picked up his pace, and as he reached the corner he looked back once again. In his convinced heart he knew that what he'd seen was true. The man still hadn't moved, still watched after him. Stone felt himself shudder with physical revulsion. Not because of what the man was, but because Stone knew what he was. Like something from a childhood dream, the conviction was terrifying, unshakably true, a thing utterly beyond reason. He'd seen the Devil. He stopped short, his heart pounding wildly, and looked up at a streetlight. Aloud he pleaded with the empty air: *"Am I going out of my mind?"*

Then he said, hearing the words first in his head in his father's cadenced Italian voice: *"Santa María,"* and stumbled forward, realizing only then that he was sobbing.

At a lighted corner, a girl in a tight black dress watched him approach. Another girl leaned against the wall. As Stone came closer, his head down, walking fast, the first one stood in his path and said, "I have a teddy bear in my room. Would you like to see my teddy bear?"

Stone brushed past without even looking up.

The other girl said, "She *does,* too," and laughed.

Then Stone overheard the first one ask the other, surprised, "Did you see his face?"

Ahead at the corner he saw a brightly lit all-night restaurant-bar. He knew the place. It had plate-glass walls, was always full of people, little people with nighttime faces putty-white.

Stone entered the brutal cage of white fluorescent lights through noisy open doors, stepped to the bar, ordered cognac. The place was filled with nervous tired-looking people; the light hurt his eyes, noise filled his ears. It was a night of revelry; this was the back door of the feast. Stone drank his drink as soon as it came. Then he turned and went out again. Anyway, he felt better.

A taxi pulled to the curb directly before him; a pouch-eyed man, American, very drunk, put his head out the window and asked Stone in execrable French if he lived in the neighborhood. Stone answered him in French, said he didn't.

"You know a girl named Chantal?" the man asked. His French was incredible. His bright hand-painted silk tie was drunkenly askew. "She lives in this street."

Stone gave up French, said in English, "I'm just a tourist here myself." He noticed the two streetwalkers eying the scene from the corner; they approached slowly, sensing game.

The man in the taxi brightened, overjoyed. "Ah ha, you speak American. Wait a minute." He opened the door and got out of the taxi. With instant misgiving, Stone was astounded to see that he was carrying a paper hat and a garbage-can lid; under his arm he had a toy cane that had been won at a carnival. "At least I *think* this is the street. It begins with an 'L.' "

Stone noticed that the total amount on the taxi meter was up to four high figures.

"My name is Snedeker." He held out his stubby hand, made an effort at sobriety. "I'm from Detroit. I'm looking for a girl named Chantal. Used to know her. Pretty. Brown hair. Been looking all over for her."

"I don't think I can help you, Mr. Snedeker," Stone said, shaking his hand.

"Oh, yes, you can. You speak this jabber-jabber they talk here. I'll pay you to be my interpreter. Just call me 'Soapy.' That's what everybody calls me." He pulled out an enormous roll of thousand-franc notes and started to peel off a handful.

"It's not a question of money, Soapy . . ."

"What business you in? I'm in scrap steel."

"I really don't think . . ."

"That's all right, boy. Everybody has their little secret. Didn't mean to be nosy. Come on, let me buy you a drink."

"Really, Soapy, I can't right now. I have to . . ."

"Go home? Home is where you go when there's no choice." He put the paper hat on his head. "First you'll have a drink with old Soapy. You've got to tell me where in hell I am."

He took Stone by the arm, propelled him toward the door he'd just come out. Stone resisted, but the small man had an amazingly large grip. "Look . . ." Stone protested, irritated.

"Now, now. You're not going to get mad at little old Soapy for wanting to buy you one little old drink, are you? Come on. You're bigger than I am."

Stone went.

Soapy entered the place as though taking it by storm. The first thing he did was beat the garbage-can lid with the cane and stop all conversation. Everyone looked, tired, bored, yet curious. Then he bulldozed through the crowd near the bar and ordered drinks for everybody to the left and right of him. Stone tried to hang back and escape his attention, but Soapy missed him instantly. "Hey!" he shouted. "Where's my interpreter?" He turned and pulled Stone through to the place of honor beside him and sat him down. "O.K., interpreter. Interpret something. How do you say bourbon in French?"

Stone looked at the bartender. Then he said, "Whiskey?" The bartender nodded.

"Hell, no, man! Bourbon ain't whiskey. It's bourbon. I've been trying all night . . ."

"I'm afraid all you'll be able to get is Scotch," Stone said.

"That's all I been getting. Some interpreter you are. O.K. Scotch. What are you having?"

Stone ordered a *fin sec.*

"Feen seck? What's that?"

"Straight brandy." Out of the corner of his eye Stone saw that the two girls had entered from the street. Surprise: one of them was pretty.

"Well, that won't hurt you, I guess. Ask if he knows a girl named Chantal who lives in this street."

No one knew a Chantal who had brown hair and was pretty.

"Maybe wrong street," Soapy mused. "Well, hell. Won't hurt to look."

An hour later, Stone was beginning to feel the effects of Soapy Snedeker's largesse. He forgot about MacNaughton, about everything, and started to enjoy himself. Everyone about him was laughing and shouting, largely because Soapy was footing a handsome bill for their entertainment. Outside the taxi still waited, meter ticking, driver asleep. Word apparently got around; new people began arriving.

It was still later when they started out to look for Chantal. Several people got in the spirit of the enterprise. A small posse fanned out up the street on both sides, calling out, "Chan—tal! Chan—tal!" A few darkened windows came to light and irate heads poked out, only to be interrogated as to the whereabouts of Chantal. Stone brought up the rear of the hunt, Soapy leading it in full cry banging his garbage-can lid with his cane. Stone was suddenly enjoying himself hugely, found himself laughing insanely until tears rolled down his cheeks. Behind Stone the empty taxi followed, creeping at a snail's pace beside the sidewalk.

The search was fruitless. The group came to the end of the street and stood around suddenly deflated. Stone recognized again the two he'd seen standing on the street. "Hell," Soapy said to Stone, "ask the driver if he knows any other streets that begin with 'L.' Short streets. It was a short street, like this one here."

The two girls managed to get into the cab ahead of Soapy while Stone conversed with the driver. Finally, the next likely street decided on, Stone got in front. As they drove off, Stone turned to Soapy. He was sitting between the two girls as though unaware of their presence. He looked suddenly sad and crestfallen. "I'll find her," he said defensively, "don't worry." He shook his head drunkenly and let it drop forward on his chest. "That girl really loved me," he mumbled. "I'll find her." The paper hat fell off into his lap.

Stone felt suddenly sorry for Soapy. "You don't know her last name?" he asked gently, realizing he himself was extremely drunk.

Soapy didn't lift his head, simply shook it in a slow negative.

"When did you last see her, Soapy?" Stone asked. He wanted Soapy to know he was concerned.

"Hell," Soapy said, "I haven't seen her for seventeen years."

The taxi went crazily through caverned streets, an antic boat through tunnels of love; the girls lost no time in making their presence felt. Hopelessly drunk, Stone knew only that he was resigned to the frolic, submerged. Later, days later, when the mists of unremembrance had effaced the valleys of this gay-grim career, only the peaks would stand above that blanketing fog; and he would remember this taxi, its musty odor of jaded elegance, would remember the girl only by taste and texture. He would remember losing track of time, would remember too the feel of the stairway carpet under his feet, the murky light of a cheap unknown hotel, a room with a taunting mirror. And finally he would remember waking and drinking on matted sheets, day into night into day behind a locked door and shuttered windows, would remember making love in the dusk—morning or night?—making love in the blind and deliberate dark. He would remember making love with all the naked fury of despair, as though trying with the point of a plow to raise a refractory root or buried rock from unyielding soil, from barren earth.

X V

Friday; Saturday; Sunday:

Awakened to the lighted room by the ringing telephone beside her bed, she reached across the vacant unslept pillow and glanced automatically at the clock—the book she'd been reading slid sideways off the coverlet in a spill of pages onto the floor. Forcing herself awake, she picked up the receiver from its cradle.

It was Georges Merseault talking to her, three hours after midnight, warning her instantly by his tone. Immediately she came awake, sat up, steeled and listening.

He began to tell her gently—and in that one sick instant she felt she already knew, felt her breath collapse with the onset of spurious certainty. Listening hardly at all to the words but to the tone, the gentle incredible tone—the telephone grew imponderably heavy in her hands—without volition she dropped her arms, let the live instrument come to rest in her lap. It looked hard and black and deadly against the delicate chiffon. She looked at it, heard the voice tiny and indistinct in her lap—it lay there passively, like a black serpent, an adder's voice.

Then she knew she must hear, knew she had to listen. The instant passed. She picked it up again and learned that the details were uncertain. It would take an hour or two to arrange. Merseault was taking care of it, would come for her.

He had been found.

How the conversation ended she didn't know—or when—yes, she would be waiting, yes, she would be all right alone, yes, she'd be dressed and waiting. The door would be open.

Carefully she fitted the receiver back into its loving cradle; then turned her head, biting her lip, and stared into the shadows.

She sat for a long time not moving.

Finally, thinking of the desperate time to kill, of the uncertain tomorrow and all small things left undone, she shook back her hair and got up; moving like a sleepwalker, she gathered up her purpose and went to water the plants.

Merseault arrived at the police station at twenty-four minutes after five in the morning. The time was noted down in the book beside the prisoner's name by the officer on duty, a ferret-faced man whose left eye twitched as he wrote. The only sound was the ticking of the wall clock and the scratching of the night officer's pen. The room was bare except for the long wooden counter and the pair of waiting benches against the opposite wall. The wood of the benches was polished smooth with wear. A definite odor of urine hung over the place, faint near the door but stronger toward the rear of the badly lit room, where a dark corridor led to the cells.

Merseault watched with dull impatience as the point of the ink-encrusted steel nib crept across the ledger line. Still only half awake, he was in no mood to engage in conversation; the police officer had read Merseault's sleepy truculence in his whitened face and kept only to the necessary questions. At the back of the room, on a signaled glance from their chief, three other ordinary gendarmes gathered up the playing cards and now stood awkwardly silent, watching the distinguished visitor. It was cold in the room. It was a dank cold, unrelieved by the single small stove in the rear. It was as though spring hadn't taken this last bastion of winter dampness. One of the policemen in the rear suddenly sneezed. He sneezed twice, and mumbled something inaudible. The clock ticked unhurriedly, and the ledger was initialed with a gritty flourish.

"You will be responsible for him?" asked the officer, carefully blotting the wet entry. He didn't look up at Merseault.

"For custody. Yes," Merseault said. He had his hands in the pockets of his black overcoat. The homburg lay on the counter between him and the officer.

"You have your identity card, Monsieur?"

"You know who I am, Captain."

"A formality."

"I know you know your routine. You don't have to prove it to me," Merseault said shortly.

"You wish to see him now, then?"

"I didn't come here to visit the zoo, Captain. I'll take him with me, if one of your men would be so kind as to bring him out."

"He is very drunk. I'm not sure he will wake up."

"Then carry him," Merseault said. "Do you have his personal effects?"

The officer made a tiny sign with his head to one of the men at the back of the room, and the gendarme went out of the room. Merseault could hear the metallic scraping of an invisible door, the turn of a key, the sharp click of a wall switch. There was a groan and a loud curse.

"They don't like the light," the captain of police said. "Interrupts their sleep. Nothing but drunks tonight." He rooted under the counter for something. Finally he came up with a large brown manila envelope. He picked up a pair of steel-rimmed glasses and squinted through them at the name scrawled across it.

"Ordinarily this is opened in the presence of the—"

"Ordinarily I am in bed at this hour," Merseault said sharply.

"As you wish," the captain said, ripping open the huge envelope with a blunt forefinger and spilling its contents on the counter. He opened the ledger again and began checking off the items one by one, pushing them across the counter to Merseault as he did so. "One wristwatch, steel, waterproof."

He drew a thin wavy line through the first item on the list and pushed the watch across the counter. Merseault pocketed it.

"Shoelaces and necktie."

The tie was rolled up and tied neatly with the laces. The pen scratched out the second item.

"Any reason for taking these from him?" asked Merseault. "Other than usual?"

"Routine. Can't ever tell."

There was a mutter of protests from deep inside the cell block as an iron door clanged shut. The sound of running water.

"Cuff links. Wallet, containing papers, no money."

The captain dipped the pen again.

"One war medal, inscribed *Dante*."

Merseault picked up the medal and scrutinized the inscription on the back. The letters were crudely incised and just barely visible in the sickly yellow light of the saucer-shaded bulb which hung on the end of a long cord from the ceiling.

"Newspaper clippings," the captain said.

Merseault picked them up and leafed through them. There were at least a dozen of them, all dating from yesterday and the day before. They were from every paper in Paris including the *Daily Mail* and the *Tribune*. They were all about Sheppard, every single one of them. Merseault stared at the clippings, fanning them out on the counter. Nearly every one of them carried a photograph of the Ambassador.

Merseault heard the police captain speaking to him and realized that he had been unconsciously shaking his head over the clippings. He gathered them up and folded them into the pocket of his overcoat with Stone's other possessions.

"Your card, Monsieur," the captain said, handing it to Merseault. "It was in the wallet, but I used it to telephone you."

Merseault recognized the card instantly as the one he had given Stone in Sheppard's office the morning several months ago when he asked him to dinner. He took the card and turned it over, wondering how Stone had managed to keep it. On the back he saw his own initials under the two words, *Laissez passer*. "This is how you got me?" Merseault asked the captain. The captain nodded. Merseault gazed at the card in his hand. "So," he said, musing.

The officer reached under the counter. "This was too large to go in the envelope," he said, bringing into the light a lumpish object. It was a stuffed animal, not the kind Stone might have won at a street arcade, but a child's plaything, well worn with loving abuse. It was a gray bear. One eye was gone and the other button hung grotesquely on the end of its loosening thread. It was patched and sewn in several places and some of its stuffing had been lost in the process, so that the bear had a limp, beaten look. The officer placed it on the counter and tried to leave it in a sitting position, but when he took his hands away the gray bear collapsed, doubled over face down in an amorphous heap as though stricken with a silent fit of laughter; the bear was too ridiculous to bear an aspect of grief. Merseault stared at the bear. The police captain was dead-pan, but the other two gendarmes weren't so successful in concealing their amusement. One of them snickered. Merseault's face hardened. He picked up the bear and examined it carefully, inspecting the patches and ruptured seams.

"The American was very reluctant to give this up," the captain said. His voice carried only the most delicate hint of irony. "He seemed very fond of it."

Merseault kneaded the bear in his fingers. "He is a great lover of animals," he said without amusement.

The police officer permitted himself a tolerant smile. Merseault didn't return it. Instead, he glanced at the two gendarmes; their smiles vanished. Then he turned slowly back to the counter.

"Tell me, Captain, you count yourself a thorough police officer, don't you?"

The captain's smile vanished also. Warily, sensing a lead to the question, he answered. "I do my best," he said.

"Then undoubtedly you looked *inside* this animal, didn't you?"

The officer stared at the bear in Merseault's hands. "Inside it? Well, no . . . that is, we are not authorized to tamper with the personal effects of—"

"Then of course you entered this bear in the ledger with everything else, is that correct?"

"Well, no. It didn't seem . . ." The officer stopped.

"Well, then, I suggest, Captain, that you make the entry."

"A bear?"

This bear. How can you be sure that this bear doesn't convey a secret message, Captain? You admit yourself that you haven't properly *looked into* this bear."

The officer picked up his pen. "What shall I put down? One bear, gray?"

"One bear, gray, *unopened.*"

The pen slowly began to scratch out the words. Out of the corner of his eye Merseault saw one of the gendarmes smile furtively and turn his back. The officer made the entry and blotted it and closed the ledger.

Merseault waited until the officer had put the pen back in the ink-well. Then he pointed to the ledger lying closed on the counter. "You forgot to cross the bear off," he said casually, and turned away from the captain of police and walked to the back of the room.

Stone was brought into the room protesting sickly, hardly able to support himself even with the gendarme's help. He stumbled to the bench and immediately tried to lie down; one of the other gendarmes gently restrained him, and succeeded in propping him upright against the wall. Stone let his head fall back against the dirty bare plaster wall and opened his eyes and saw Merseault standing over him. He stared for a moment, trying to focus his eyes. His hair was soaking wet from the dousing the gendarme had given him to wake him up.

"I had to clean him up some," the gendarme said. "You'd better have a doctor look at his hands. He cut himself up some."

"Stone," Merseault said. Stone didn't answer. Instead he closed his eyes again and let his head loll onto his shoulder. There was blood on his face and clothes, and his open-mouthed breathing rattled with phlegm. He seemed to have lost consciousness again. Merseault stepped forward and twisted his ear lobe, carefully applying pain. Stone tried drunkenly to brush the air before him with his lacerated hands. They were brown with dried blood. Finally he yielded from his stupor and painfully opened his eyes.

"Help me get him out to the taxi," Merseault said.

"Beat me," Stone said, slobbering the words. "Son-a-bitch beat me."

"Who beat you?" Merseault asked, his face close to Stone's, as though talking to a deaf man. "Who beat you?" he repeated louder, shaking Stone gently to keep his eyes from closing.

Stone stared glassily at him as though trying to place his face. "Old man beat me. Beat me to it. You . . ." Suddenly he sat up. He could hardly talk and his hands were shaking. "You. Merseault. Where is this?" He held his hands up before him and tried to open them. He could only flex them halfway. They were stiff with the dried cuts. "Something wrong. Where is this?"

"You've been in jail," Merseault said. "I'm taking you home."

Stone managed a drunken comprehending smile. "Jail," he said, and closed his eyes. ". . . ever so humble, no place like jail." He opened his eyes wide. He had to refocus them all over again. The effort took several seconds. "Oh, God," he mouthed. "Merseault. What, how're you here? Were you with me?"

"No."

Stone knitted his brows and felt his head. "Merseault," he said to himself. "What's Merseault doing here?" He started to fall sideways but the nearest gendarme caught him and propped him up again. He looked at the policeman, trying to comprehend him.

"Jail?" Stone muttered. He coughed hard and the coughing started him retching, a dry empty retching. His face was contorted with pain. Slowly the retching exhausted itself. He sat breathing hard, his face utterly white. "Need a drink," he whispered. No one said anything. Stone seemed weaker but more awake. He looked around him at the five faces gathered in a ring under the feeble light. His gaze went from one face to the next. "No one going to get me," he said. "Did I hurt anybody?"

"Not badly."

"Sorry to hurt anybody." He turned to Merseault as though seeing him for the first time. "Merseault," he said with thick surprise. "Why is he here? Where is this?"

"Can you walk?" Merseault asked him.

"Can't walk. Lost my legs. In the war. Lost both my legs. Gave me a medal to ride on."

"Stone."

"I'm Stone. Who wants Stone?"

"Can you walk for a drink?"

"Nobody wants Stone, that's who. Nobody. No-guts Stone."

"Can you walk for a drink?"

"Stone don't even want Stone. Stone, Stone, Father Time Stone. Ho. You, Merseault, you were the one and that's why you are here and now. You never had a son. I have a son, so I can't even kill Stone. Stone can't kill Stone. Not even Stone. Old right-hand man. Big friend Merseault, he beat you too. He beat us all."

"Stone, will you walk?"

"That's me. I'm sick. Sick. He had the guts to be clean about it. He beat you too, old right-hand man. He went through the narrow door. Beat us all."

"Up you come, Stone. On your feet."

"Narrow door way up high in the sky. Only one at a time through that little door. That little goddamned door. Lea' me alone. Sick."

"Take him out to the taxi," Merseault said. The two gendarmes lifted Stone to his feet and walked him slowly toward the street exit. At that moment two more gendarmes entered from outside, prodding a shrilly protesting prostitute in front of them. The trio stopped at the sight of Stone and stood aside. Stone shambled toward the door supported between the two *agents,* his laceless shoes half off. He protested unintelligibly, a muffled staccato groaning that might have passed for the laughter of the dead, as one of his shoes fell off. The prostitute leaned down and retrieved the shoe. She gave it to Merseault as he passed her. Merseault accepted the shoe and took off his hat. He had the bear under his arm.

"*Merci, Mademoiselle,*" Merseault said, distracted, polite by reflex.

The whore looked at him, poker-faced. "One shoe is no good to me," she said. "With two he can walk to his grave."

Solange was in the taxi, huddled high in the far corner of the rear seat. Stone didn't see her until he was inside. Merseault stood outside, closed the door, and spoke through the window.

"Take him to my house. I'll call a doctor from here and join you." He looked at Stone. "You smell like a dead man," he said severely.

Stone nodded weakly. "I'm sorry," he said. "I'm sick." He swung his head around clumsily and looked at Solange in mute appeal. She said nothing, kept her hands folded in a tight knot in her lap. "Why weren't you home? Telephoned . . . tried to call . . ."

"I left a message for you with the concierge. I was waiting for you at Monsieur Merseault's. He called and asked me to . . ."

"To what?"

"I'll talk to you later. I can't even think now. Just keep quiet. I don't even want to talk to you. I'm sick of you."

Merseault gave the driver instructions and paid him in advance. Then he said to Solange, "I'll bring his things. No, on second thought you take them." He dumped everything through the window into her lap. The bear landed face down. Then he peered in at Stone. "Are you going to behave? You've made enough trouble."

Stone nodded mutely, mumbled, "Sorry." Suddenly his eye fell on the bear. He tried to sit up, struggled to get upright. He pointed to the bear. "I have to return that. I stole it from . . ."

Solange turned to Merseault. "What happened to him?" she asked. "How did he cut his hands?"

Merseault looked at Stone briefly, then said, "It doesn't matter. I stopped at the hotel before I came here. I've paid for the damages. The girl left. There are no charges against him."

"What happened?"

"All I could find out was that he tried to take this"—he pointed at the bear in Solange's lap—"this object of childhood affection from . . . from someone. In the course of the resulting disagreement he attacked a large plate-glass mirror in the lobby of the hotel. I paid for the mirror and the proprietor agreed to drop the matter."

"And the girl?"

"She vanished, evidently taking her suitcase. She is in no position to prefer charges since the circumstances of her occupancy . . . ah . . ."

". . . I have to give back . . . I took it . . ." Stone tried to reach for the bear.

Solange said, "Stop it! Not another word from you."

"Please give it to me," Stone begged.

She threw it into his lap. Merseault signaled the driver and the taxi moved off. With the acceleration Stone collapsed backward into his seat again. He closed his eyes.

Stone mumbled to himself, "I'm going to give it a decent burial."

Solange sat tight-lipped and tense, looking out the window, said nothing. Outside the sky was turning from dawn black to gray. Usually at this hour there would already be people in the streets. But the streets were empty. Everything was shuttered. The gutters were full of the refuse of the holiday weekend. And the taxi spun through empty streets toward the Seine.

As the taxi swung around the long arc of the Place de la Concorde, Stone opened his eyes. When they reached the bridge he suddenly said, "Stop here!"

Without thinking, the driver jammed on the brakes and swerved to the curb. Stone had the door open and was almost out of the cab before it stopped.

"Where are you going?" Solange demanded instantly. She clawed open her own door and was out on the sidewalk in time to confront Stone as he lurched around the back. The bear dangled upside down from his hand. "Are you going to be sick again?"

Stone looked at her, weaving, then laughed, tried to laugh. "Nothing left to be sick with," he said miserably. He walked to the edge of the bridge and looked over the stone balustrade. Then he turned to Solange and said, "Is the sun going down or coming up?"

"It's morning."

He shrugged. Turning his back he dangled the bear by one arm over the edge. "Bye-bye, teddy bear," he intoned. And let it drop.

The bear didn't make much splash. Nor did it sink. Instead it floated on the surface face up, turning slowly in the eddying water below the bridge. Solange stood watching it involuntarily as it floated away downstream.

Stone watched the floating bear until it was indistinguishable on the water from the choppy shadows of the rising sun. Then he turned away from the edge and said, "I'm hungry."

Solange was looking back across the square: beyond the obelisk, beyond the classic gable of the Madeleine, on the far hill of Montmartre the morning sun just caught the bulbous domes of Sacre Coeur in a whitewash of distant light. "Do you think you ought to eat yet?" she asked without looking at him.

Stone's eye was caught by a movement of color in front of the American Embassy to the left of the square. Two Marine guards suddenly unfurled a flag. Stone watched it billow quickly up to the end of the pole, float a moment, then sink slowly back to half-mast.

XVI

The installation in this room of a concealed device to play music was an accidental extravagance of fortune. Originally it was intended for recording significant state occasions, and had in fact been used once or twice for that purpose. Until someone discovered that it could be used for playing music. Since then a collection of varied recordings had accumulated in the drawer of the writing table, a collection to which Merseault had contributed mostly Bach. It was to this room that he repaired when he wanted to escape the cubicle that had been allotted to his occasional private use in the Archives downstairs. There was no telephone here; in this room he could think, talk, or listen without interruption. Here he could receive Stone without the dreary bother of clearing his desk and removing secret documents from casual sight. But beyond that practical consideration, this room was the proper place to meet him; it accorded with Merseault's sense of the fitness of things. He'd left instructions that Stone was to be allowed to enter the outside gate without ceremony, and shown upstairs promptly, ushered in unannounced.

Now Merseault was alone, listening to music, waiting for Stone to arrive. He sat relaxed, sunk in an armchair before the tall glass doors that gave out on the narrow balcony overlooking the Quai d'Orsay and the Seine. He was listening intently, conscious now only of the music that severed his mind of all other thought; the bright thread of a single unaccompanied violin, a Bach partita, an invisible purity unspooled in his mind, pure song, abstract, difficult, intense, naked.

He had thought carefully of his meeting with Stone, had weighed out thoughts and feelings in advance, like a miser weighing precious metal dust. He sat with his back to the door, out of direct view. The scene was set. Now he waited. He knew what he was going to say and had chosen this room so that his words would be words remembered, a solemn moment, an occasion of state. From its beginnings in history this room had given place to rituals of deliberate events; intimate receptions; presentations of credentials; signings of protocols: this room lent pomp. From the dripping crystal chandelier to the chased-silver sconces on the paneled walls, every textured detail had been designed to impress the senses, the tastes, to be remembered. It had never been lived in, even by the monarch who built it; nor was it made to be lived in. Very few rooms in the Ministry were. For this was grandeur. As Merseault himself had said the first time he'd seen it, this room was France.

Even the waiting was planned. He wanted this time, to listen to music, to rest, to clear his mind of the unending problems that pressed the offices on the floors above and below. He listened to the effortless inventions of the intimate strings, a melody that dipped and soared and glided like a bird alone in a vast and empty darkening sky. He heard the loneliness in that bright performance, and behind the gay dancing song could feel the exquisite melancholy, intangible, vast, overwhelming. The single unaccompanied violin, disembodied, invisible, seemed frail, lonely in itself, like a candle shimmering in a darkened tomb; a child dancing in an empty house. The music of Bach never failed to surround him with its beauty, but these particular works evoked for him a special mystery, a tragic gaiety that baffled imagination and moved him to wonderment. Merseault abandoned his mind to the images of the music, saw the master hand writing in silence. This music seemed to illuminate the vast silence around it, as the stars punctuate the rhythms of their overwhelming void. The melody seemed transparent, a song carved in silence, crystal figures in cut glass. Each note was light, joyous, almost childlike in its simple pursuit, a chisel blow sculpturing silence. Bach was the sculptor searching out the perfect shape locked within the stone.

Sheppard was gone. Everyone else had deliberately forgotten the war. Stone was the only one left who remembered the vast intricacies of the thing that had destroyed him. Merseault knew that no one could understand his attachment to Sheppard, his devotion to the man; not Stone, not even the dead man himself. It was a secret Merseault had kept almost even from himself.

When the motion of the dance stopped, the last gay note was drawn out like a child's taffy, and broken, and in that final silence the finished work was suddenly fully present again, became whole, stood complete.

Merseault opened his eyes and stared at the blank panes of glass before him, at the afternoon sky beyond. Quietly, deliberately, he thanked God for being. A single soaring seagull stood high in the light and motionless toward the west, and he watched it, wondering, wondering why the gulls followed the river so far from the sea; until slowly the bird wheeled and slid out of its glass frame and was gone. Still gazing at the sky, he wagged his head slowly, a tiny, almost imperceptible movement, and smiled absently. His voice mixed with sorrow, admiration, disbelief, he said aloud, "Old friend, you really did it, didn't you." He sighed and dropped his unfocused gaze to his hands resting folded in his lap. "You really did it." The unseen music began again, a different recording, another partita, again the violin unaccompanied. He closed his eyes again, to listen.

The separate thread of Sheppard's destiny had been twisted with

Merseault's own to make a single yarn, a single strand that ran through the weave of three decades of depression, ambition, failure, and war. From the seminar days at the Ecole Politique, and the days of Wilson and the Fourteen Points, he and Sheppard had never been close, merely parallel. In the years between conferences he'd followed Sheppard's rise, had only once ventured upon fitful correspondence. He remembered his surprise after the war when it came out in their conversation that Sheppard had kept track also, even knew the dates of his appointments and academic promotions. He knew that Sheppard had married, and that his wife had died; he'd never known Sheppard's son.

Stone. Stone was the unwitting link—Stone who knew neither of them, whose simple survival reaffirmed the coincidence of destinies. Merseault reflected that both he and Sheppard had come to Montpelle on separate but similar errands; both of them came in search, he for an unknown murderer, Sheppard for a lost son. He remembered watching Sheppard's face, as Stone, moving in the rain like a man forsaken by God, re-enacted the grisly crime, made it happen again in the tortured imagination. Stone's face was hollow-eyed and wasted, his body thin, and his eyes were the eyes of a man who had seen Hell. Sheppard never moved, didn't speak. Not once did he take his eyes off Stone. He simply sat in the car, rigid, watching every movement; and the leaden rain came down unending.

Merseault knew that even to himself he could never explain the mystery of such private friendship as he felt for Sheppard, this student, this hurrying young captain, this tired general, bereaved father, this ambassador. This dead soldier. He knew that he had come to love in Sheppard something that was lacking in himself; yet what that thing was was as obscure to him now as it had been when Sheppard was alive. Sheppard was dead, yet his death as a man seemed abstract, unreal. A part of his mind insisted that he'd hardly known Sheppard the man; he'd known not the actor, only the roles of the actor. And it was true; he felt no familial sense of bereavement, of loss. One thing only did he feel beyond question. The grief was real. He felt the grief and it was real.

Nothing of this could he tell Stone. Nor was it necessary for Stone to know. Why then was Stone necessary to him at all? Why had he taken such pains over Stone? Why indeed had he asked him to come here? Stone, who once had played the cello?

Merseault had placed the armchair carefully. When Stone entered, the room would appear to be empty. His first impression would be of the room itself; his second impression might be the music; the final impression would be the unimpeded view of the walled river, a city two thousand years old. Merseault smiled to himself. What he was doing he knew was more than merely arranging a scene, more than just surrounding conversation with the trappings of culture and history and power. He was also indulging himself in Stone's sentimental education, indulging the human passion to change the life of another human being, the untempered passion to teach, to influence, to be remembered. Stone was hardly the quick and worthy pupil, yet there was no one else in the world for whom the lesson would have meaning.

Merseault smiled to himself, eyes shut. The questions exhausted his mind of thoughts, left it a vacuum that collapsed in the full inrush of music that filled his head. Without regret he canceled the questions and gave himself up to listening again. The image returned of Stone entering and hearing the music, seeing the room. Merseault felt pleased for Stone, felt like a citizen again, and gave himself in advance to the sensible pleasures of a subtle achievement. Music, he thought, this enduring music. It would be his gift to Stone, the memory of entering this room alone; a lasting gift, perhaps.

When Stone arrived he presented his name at the gate and was directed to the main entrance. Inside the door an old man behind a reception desk took his pass and squinted at the name. Nodding, he rose to his feet, routinely locking the desk, and beckoned Stone to follow him. The old man walked with the shuffling gait that seemed characteristic of all elderly doorkeepers, not bent, not shiftless, merely economical.

Stone followed him up the wide staircase, through a pair of matched doors into a carpeted corridor hung with tapestries of battle scenes. As he passed an open window he heard the fitful clatter of typewriters from another wing of the building. In the corridor there was no other sound except the squeaking of the old man's right shoe on the thick carpet.

The old man led him halfway. He stopped, pointed toward the paired doors at the opposite end, turned, and without another word started back the way they'd come. He seemed unconcerned, unaware of his squeaking shoe, but it sounded unusually loud in the muffled silence. He exited from the corridor without looking back, closing the door soundlessly behind him.

Stone stood before the door, debated knocking, decided against it. It was heavy figured oak, not the sort of door one knocks on with dignity; it would take a hammer to make that massive slab give sound. Instead he imitated the old man's technique, turned the handle fully down and leaned forward; the door opened easily, without a sound. He paused a moment, a polite interval, then entered. He wasn't altogether prepared for what he saw. Merseault apparently hadn't heard the door open, and for a moment he wished he could go out and make more noise coming in. But it was too late. Merseault had sensed his presence in the room and was backing out from under the table.

The sight of Merseault on his hands and knees under a table wasn't as ludicrous as it seemed to Stone it ought to be. Merseault was the kind of man who could emerge from under a table and make it seem entirely correct, a regular business, his being under a table. He backed out from beneath the table with casual dignity, turned about to face Stone, and sat cross-legged on the carpet. His mouth was set in a thin line of resigned exasperation which he was content to communicate to Stone with a slow silent shaking of the head.

"What's the matter?" Stone asked, suddenly anxious that there should be no embarrassment between them. But it was instantly obvious that his solicitude was unnecessary—Merseault, even sitting cross-legged on an oriental rug, remained in full possession of himself. With a few silken cushions around him he could have been an oriental potentate, although his blandly rounded features made him look more like a sorely tried Buddha. "Did you lose something?"

Merseault nodded, looked at him. "A violinist," he said. Then in English he said, "And all the king's horses and all the king's men can never put Heifetz together again." He shrugged, and leaned to one side so that Stone could see behind him. The wreckage of what looked like more than one phonograph record lay on the rug in pie-shaped pieces. They seemed to blend into the figure in the carpet.

"I'm surprised they broke, falling on the rug like that."

Merseault looked up at the chandelier over Stone's head, his face a mask of infinite patience and long-suffering, and recited like a litany, "Old records. Made of diatomaceous clay, I believe. Shellac for a binder, lampblack for pigment. A very brittle compound." He shrugged again. "If one is fool enough to drop them, they're fool enough to break."

"Do you want me to help you pick up the pieces?"

Merseault started heavily to rise, one hand braced on the table to take the strain off his left leg. Stone thought of helping him but refrained; Merseault might be sensitive about assistance. Merseault stood upright brushing out the creases in his trousers. He leaned down and peered sadly under the table. "We'll leave this noble debris to the brave ladies whose proper task it is. We may as well leave it there as elsewhere."

Stone looked around, but there were indeed no wastebaskets in the room.

"Besides," Merseault said, cheering himself up, "they didn't all break. I should have taken them off the machine one at a time instead of trying to turn the whole stack over." He glared malevolently at the complicated-looking device in its wall niche. "This machine has always been sullen about Bach. It will play Mozart for hours without a murmur. But Bach . . ."

"I'm sorry. My arrival brings bad luck."

Merseault looked at Stone seriously, his expression troubled. "You shouldn't say that. Really, it is quite all right." He made a slight offhand gesture. "I had planned to be under the table anyway."

For an unguarded instant Stone almost believed, Merseault's mock sincerity was so artfully compelling. Then Merseault smiled and came forward, his hand outstretched in greeting. They shook hands.

"Are you feeling rested after your enterprise of last weekend?" Merseault asked archly.

"Well rested, thank you."

"You didn't damage your arm by not wearing the sling?"

Stone looked at his arm and flexed his fingers slowly and deliberately. "No. I'm surprised I didn't break it again when I hit that mirror. I must have been out of my head."

"I'll be blunt with you," Merseault said. "You were."

Stone smiled and dropped the bruised hand out of sight.

"And Solange? Has she forgiven you?"

Stone involuntarily shifted his eyes from Merseault's inquiry. "Should she?"

Merseault laughed. "Why not? You'll both be dead soon enough without insisting on misery." Stone looked up, startled. Merseault continued, "As you probably know, I've had several long talks with her by now. She is a remarkable woman. I don't quite know what she sees in you."

"Neither do I," Stone said humorlessly. "I suppose that's the trouble."

"You don't see much in yourself, do you?"

Stone looked blankly at Merseault, as though the question had no answer.

Abruptly Merseault changed the subject. He turned his back to Stone and began adjusting the record player. "I understand from her that you used to play the cello."

"Yes."

"Were you any good?"

"I won a competition once. That's how I first came to Paris."

Merseault grunted, delicately placed some records on the machine. "Fortunately I didn't break all of them. I still have my favorite. Why did you stop?"

"Stop?" Stone felt restless, constrained by Merseault's polite effort to draw him into conversation.

"Stop playing, I mean."

Mentally Stone shrugged; the questions were harmless enough. "I'm not an artist. I was a good imitator and I had good teachers. I stopped because I sold my instrument." He knew that wasn't accurate. He hadn't sold the cello until long after his mother's death. For one sardonic instant he thought of telling Merseault that he stopped because his mother died, but it was beside the point; he didn't feel like entertaining Merseault.

"Why did you sell it?"

"Because I needed the money to get married," Stone said flatly. "It was during the Depression."

He expected Merseault to ask him about the girl, but Merseault simply said, "No woman is worth a good cello."

Surprised, Stone laughed. "I found that out," he said.

Merseault grunted. "You should have found out before you sold it. Did you ever play Bach?"

Stone nodded to himself, lied deliberately to Merseault. "No. He was over my head."

Merseault finished setting up the machine, switched it on, closed the sliding panel, and turned around to face Stone. "Let's sit down," he said. "We have business to finish."

The sound of the single violin issued invisibly from concealed speakers. The music seemed sourceless, came softly from nowhere, but was simply suddenly present. And it filled the room. It was a beautiful room, Stone thought; he looked around him quietly.

When they were seated, Merseault took a white envelope from his inside breast pocket and extracted a letter. "I can't show this to you since it contains confidential references to other pending matters, but I'll read you the pertinent paragraph." He searched through the text of the letter until his eye lighted on it, and began to read:

> "Concerning your query on our response to you dated April 13, number RB-639—et cetera, et cetera—I regret to say that we have turned up no further data. We initiated an extended inquiry as you requested and cross-checked it with adoption records compiled by UNRRA and other refugee groups, all without avail. This inquiry, as I told you, reaches only what we call 'accessible records.' There are still records which we have reason to believe existed, but which we have not been able to locate or take possession of. Undoubtedly many of these were destroyed, but since positive proof of their destruction is lacking we continue to classify them as 'inaccessible.' I have placed your inquiries in a suspension file which is automatically checked against any new records that we may from time to time discover. Since many of the adoption centers for camp-born infants were privately managed, it is possible that something may still turn up. I hesitate to remark, however, that from the information you have given us, it would appear that there would be considerable legal difficulties since there would appear to be no legal proof of parentage. There is one other thing we might be able to do, and that would be to assign an investigator. However, for this you would have to pull a wire in London since I have no authorization in my departmental budget for special assignments of this nature. If you do approach London, let me know first. Perhaps I can help grease the ways from this end.
>
> "As to your other question, I have had our records checked. Out of roughly 2700 cases of a more or less similar nature, we have been successful in only 29 instances in locating the child. Our job ends with locating them, so I have no way of knowing if the natural parent or parents gained final custody in every

case. In any case, the simple fact that the child's origin was officially concealed from foster parents has made this one of our most frustrating failures."

Merseault leafed through the two remaining pages of the letter and put it back in its envelope. "That's all," he said. "There's no point in deceiving you. The chances of locating your son are a hundred to one against you. I'll try through London if you want me to. It might take months to arrange."

Stone shook his head slowly. "For some reason I always thought of the child as a daughter." He looked at Merseault. "Perhaps because of the mother."

"Do you want me to . . . ?"

"No." Stone looked out the window at the river. "Somewhere I have a son. That will have to be enough. I have to stop somewhere."

Merseault said nothing for a moment, thinking. Then he nodded as though he was satisfied with the solution. The business was settled.

"Now I want your advice," Merseault said, changing his tone completely. He reached under the armchair he was sitting in and brought out a flat manila envelope. He looked straight at Stone. Stone stared at the envelope.

"Dujardin's papers?"

Merseault said, "I was able to find the safe-deposit box and get this out quietly. Carnot was sitting on something after all. I'm glad now that he continued to sit on it."

"So Dujardin knew what he was doing when he confessed," Stone said.

"No."

"Will they execute him now?"

"No," Merseault said, digging into the envelope. "They won't have to. He's dying of cancer. He's been dying for a long time."

"You knew?"

"Not specifically. Except that we are all dying. I can't even climb a flight of stairs any more without losing my breath." He slid a notebook out of the envelope and handed it to Stone. "The instant we're born the bones start to harden, the joints to stiffen with age. We start the long task of dying the day we come into the world." Merseault sat back watching Stone for his reaction to the notebook.

"Recognize it?" Merseault asked.

Stone turned it over in his hands before opening it. It looked like a schoolboy's copybook, cheaply made, with stiff paper covers. "No, I don't. Should I?"

"You've seen it before, I think."

Stone stared at Merseault, realization dawning on his face. He stared at the notebook in amazement. "This! This is what Carnot was . . ." He split open the pages and leafed feverishly forward to the title page. There it was, inscribed in block letters. Stone was almost stunned by the childish quality of the crudely penciled letters. He hadn't noticed that at all the first time. Were all his memories so twisted by time? He remembered the whole book as different, thicker, with white pages. Now the cheap wartime pages were yellowed, almost brown. But there was no doubt that it was Berger's diary. There it was: THE JOURNAL OF AN UNSUNG HERO. It gave him an eerie feeling. There was no question about it: this was it. Yet he remembered the handwriting as meticulously neat; this was the writing of a child or a disturbed adolescent. The slant of the letters changed from line to line, as though written now with the right hand, now with the left. Had he actually *seen* the handwriting, or had he constructed it in his imagination? He tried to remember when Carnot had showed it to him. He couldn't even place that event precisely. He was acutely aware that Merseault was watching him. He let nothing show on his face, but inside he felt shaken loose from his senses. He knew the copybook he held in his hand was genuine; what he remembered was the bogus article, the counterfeit. The war, he thought, the war. Was it *all* a dream? Suddenly he felt a full physical shock go through his whole body, like a discharge of electricity. His hands and arms quivered, out of control for the barest instant. Carefully he closed the book and looked up. Merseault hadn't noticed.

Stone said, "This is it. No question about it." It took intense control to keep his voice level.

"What are you going to do with it?" Merseault asked.

"What am *I* going to . . . ?"

"I have no use for it."

"Have you read it?"

Merseault nodded. "Evidently he thought he was writing a book."

"Did the Ambassador . . . ?"

"No. I don't think anyone suspected its existence."

"Then destroy it."

"It's not for me to destroy," Merseault said. He held up the envelope for Stone to see. "It is addressed to you."

"Does that fireplace work?" Stone asked, pointing. Merseault nodded.

Stone felt an almost frantic desire to burn the book instantly. He knew what was in it; he didn't want to examine it again in detail. It had to be destroyed before he was driven to reread it. Almost without volition he leaped up from his chair. What he felt as he stood before the cold fireplace was a paroxysm of pure fury. He felt like an avenger as he laid the book down on the iron grate full of large decorative chunks of cannel coal and touched it with the flame of a match. He poked it, fanned it, spreading the pages to let the fire in, until finally it was irreversibly burning. He stood up and watched it burn. It burned leaf on yellowing leaf. Scorched by the heat, the pages curled and turned one at a time as the fire leafed through the book. The paper was tinder-dry. Finally in their own heat the pages spread open and blazed up all at once. A few wisps of delicate black ash floated up and disappeared. After a while nothing remained but the spine and part of the stiff paper covers. Stone fanned the remains to an angry glow with the manila envelope; slowly the ashes consumed themselves and sifted down among the chunks of unburned coal. Stone became aware of the music again; the delicate melody moved unperturbed, filling the room with its mindless serenity.

Stone went back to his chair and sat down.

"And now some cheerful business. This will require a little cognac to drink a toast with. Fortunately, I have arranged for that." Merseault rose and limped over to a small commode near the fireplace. "For it is my pleasure to tell you that you are going to be received into the Legion of Honor for your services to this country."

Stone took the news in silence, waited as Merseault fetched the small silver tray with the brandy glasses and the crystal decanter. He placed the tray on the leather ottoman he had discarded as a footstool and sat down again. Stone watched him pour two careful measures, watched particularly the amber points of accidental light struck from the crystal by a single beam of the late afternoon sun.

"Do I deserve it?"

Merseault handed him his glass and raised a silent toast. Stone nodded formally, stiffly courteous, and sipped. The liquor was old and smooth, with a striking bouquet.

"When do I get my medal?" Stone asked, placing his glass back on the tray hardly touched. The words were hardly out of his mouth before he realized that they sounded coarse, not light at all, but bitter. He noted this as a revelation to himself, and it bemused him. Surprised at this, he let the whole thing out of hiding: "But first, are you sure I want it?"

"That is what I must find out," Merseault said casually.

"You mean before it's officially offered we must make certain in advance that it won't be publicly refused."

"It would be insulting to nominate you against your wish," Merseault said offhandedly.

Stone made a sudden movement, a sound of irritation, of disgust. "I don't know what's the matter with me," he said. "Of course I want it. Of course I'd be honored. I apologize for my impudence. I don't know why I said that."

"I think I know why," Merseault said. "It's because six months ago . . ."

". . . six months ago I wouldn't have had the chance to refuse. It wouldn't have been offered."

"Precisely. At least so you are inclined to think."

"Six months ago I was an untouchable because I tried to tell the truth. Now all of a sudden—"

Merseault was suddenly angry. The quiet mask of urbanity vanished from his face and for one brief instant Stone saw Merseault sitting in judgment. His voice was thick with sudden scorn. "You haven't earned the right to pity yourself yet, Monsieur. You made no conscious sacrifice. You were pushed onto the stage by events which you were unable to foresee. You didn't take the hard road to glory by your own brave choice. You took it by accident."

The sight of Merseault's unvarnished irritation surprised Stone into sober silence. In fairness, however, he conceded Merseault's right to continue by nodding reflectively at the chandelier.

"What did you do? You told the truth. You told the truth expecting to be believed. Is that such a tragedy? Some men have told the truth expecting *not* to be believed. In fact, some men have told the truth expecting to die for telling it. You didn't even expect the discomfort of not being believed. You lost a job, an unimportant job. But someone looked after you, and you got another one. You weren't important in that job—someone else can always keep track of the dead. But no other man on earth could tell the truth of what happened that night on the road to Montpelle. Is it so surprising to you that mankind is so slow to believe the truth?"

"I didn't mean to imply—"

"Or so slow to reward it? The truth hurts, Monsieur. Why do you think that the name of Dujardin is already forgotten? It is extremely disagreeable to speak to you in this manner, but I am French, French to the roots of my fingernails, and I must tell you that you are too complacent. You are smug to the point of being insufferable. And you, Monsieur, should know better. You were in this country during the war. The worst thing in war is to die. The next worst thing is to survive. Your writers are fond of referring to the Black Fall of France, to moral weakness and political decay. But I warn you. The moral weakness of France is the moral weakness of humanity. And the weakness of humanity is the simple will to survive. It has survived flood. It has survived famine. It has survived pestilence. It has survived revolutions, terror. It has survived war. And it will survive governments. It will even survive civilization."

Merseault was talking more calmly now, not looking at Stone any more, but at the nearly empty glass he was rolling slowly between his palms. Stone watched him, suddenly fascinated at the curious leap the conversation had taken. He felt uneasily that he'd missed an essential connection in Merseault's chain of statements, but that it didn't really matter. If the logic eluded him, there was something important in Merseault the man that he felt was about to be revealed to him. Very carefully he nodded, kept silent.

"The war was important," Merseault stated flatly. It was as though he was just deciding something. "The war was important not because of the battles that were fought but because of the battles that were not fought. France seemed to sense in advance what every nation knows now, that victory is merely another word for self-defeat. The stubborn fact is that war is obsolete, and every common soldier knows it. France

739

has survived the cruelest moral test a nation was ever put to, and whether by accident or by design, France is the mirror in which the world can read its own destiny. We are a nation of common psychologists, and the common psychology of France in 1939 is the psychology of the common world today. If statesmen would read their own minds, let them study the secret intentions of their people—let them study the fall of France."

"And honor?" Stone asked the question because Merseault by his pausing seemed to be waiting for it.

"There is no honor in extinction."

"And in sacrifice?"

"Understand me. A man may sacrifice his life that life may go on. But on his most sacred honor he must believe in his sacrifice. He must *believe* that life may go on. In his most sacred soul he must believe that or he becomes the most immoral of men, a criminal. Sacrifice becomes merely self-murder. It occurs to me that the very meaning of the word sacrifice is 'to make sacred.' Life is sacred. Honor is sacred only when it supports life, not just a manner of living."

"You don't believe that freedom is worth fighting for?"

"Freedom? What precisely *is* freedom? The darkest prison of all is the grave. There is no parole from a tomb. *Bon Dieu,* if a man could *believe* that he was fighting for freedom, even not for himself but for others—if he could only believe that—but man constructs his illusion of freedom in order to endure the pain of survival. He will sacrifice his own life for his children's freedom. But he will sacrifice his children's freedom for his children's life. No man who watched the destruction of Rotterdam could make himself believe that he could preserve life by sacrificing his own."

Stone tried to remember a quotation, something an admiral had said during the war. "Wars are won by remnants," he said, half certain of the wording.

Merseault nodded, looked interested, looked up at Stone as though to acknowledge his presence. "True," he said, "provided you can believe in remnants. Provided you can coax yourself to believe they'll still be men, human beings, and not irradiated brutes living in caves among the rubble. Even that would perhaps be tolerable if you could believe children could still be born whole, with all their parts, without the fetus being deformed or aborted or too sickly to survive. I for one can't believe with sufficient certainty. And I am enough of an egoist to believe that what I believe is what the rest of mankind believes, if they only had the courage to look into their hearts. But no man has the heart to look into his heart. It requires a test. He never knows what he will do until he is forced by God or by circumstances to act. France was put to that test. France was put to the agony of a moral choice with no parallel in history. Did she fail? No. She survived. And once survival was assured, she fought. Paris would never become a Rotterdam as long as German troops were quartered here. We fought.

We fought ineptly. We fought inefficiently. But we were evolving an entirely new idea of fighting, an idea in which sacrifice once again became moral. When Hitler swallowed France he swallowed a nettle."

"I take it that you have become a pacifist?"

Merseault thought a moment. Then he said, "No, I am not a pacifist. I am more than a pacifist. I am a defeatist. I believe in defeat as the surest means to victory. It is a long road, but there is no other. The only victory is survival. Man must live before he can be free. Freedom can always be fought for, even under the heel of the tyrant. That's the hard way, but there is no easy way to freedom any more."

"Do you really believe—"

"I simply believe what I have seen. I've seen with my own eyes what happened. It wasn't the politicians who betrayed France, although there were fools among them who might have made the effort if Hitler had given them time to think. It wasn't the generals. It wasn't even our home-grown fascists. If anyone betrayed France it was Hitler, who betrayed all humanity by denying it. I believe what I have seen. And I have seen what happens to human beings faced with the terror of extinction. If their fear seems groundless now, it didn't then. Nor is it groundless today, not after Hiroshima. It is not that fact but the fancy that counts. People believe and act on the fictions of their fears, not fact. It is precisely because man is endowed with the imagination to foresee death, to preview his own extinction, that he avoids it. It is this imagination that gives him dominion over animals. And it is the fact that in times of crisis he acts more on the dictates of his imagination than his five senses—this is the fact that is overlooked by military commanders and politicians. The French common soldier is as honest and as brave as any soldier in the world. He also has as much common sense. He found himself faced with a monster, a monster of steel that didn't even stop to fight him, but by-passed him, ignored him, cut him off from his supplies. This monster didn't fight, it simply destroyed. It was indifferent to fighting, oblivious to offers of battle. It merely destroyed. It wasn't even war. The tanks skirted the armed battalion in order to smash an unarmed village. It wasn't war, it was mindless insanity."

"Do you really believe what you said about being a defeatist?"

Merseault paused, brought up short. "Eh?" He thought a moment, then he said, "Perhaps I can make it clearer." His voice took on a reminiscent tone. "I remember once very early in the war, we were trying to decide on an emblem, a flag, for the Resistance. I have always been impressed by one of the early colonial flags of the United States. It shows a serpent, and the motto is *Don't tread on me*. Do you know it?"

Stone nodded.

"I proposed that we adopt that ferocious serpent for our emblem, with a slight change in the motto. I wanted to make it read *Tread on me*." Merseault shrugged. "My suggestion was turned down, largely for esthetic reasons. But no one disagreed with the chilling little message it conveyed. After all, we were already occupied by then."

"I can't quite believe you're serious, however, when you—"

"I am a realist. I know only that there are two workable solutions to an attack that threatens extinction. I know what human beings will *do,* not what they think they'll do. I know because I saw them do it. I saw the roads jammed with refugees going nowhere, just south, just escaping. The roads were so jammed that troops couldn't move forward to the front, wherever that was. And I saw whole companies of bewildered troops agree to surrender simply because there was no other conceivable choice. The war had simply passed them by, ignored them. I remember one old veteran telling me that he tried to surrender six times just to find out where his unit was and get something to eat, but each time he was told to go home. Finally he was arrested for shooting a rabbit near a gasoline dump. The Germans didn't want to slow down their advance by taking prisoners."

"You said there were two workable solutions to—"

"I just told them to you. Surrender and migration. Pétain took one course. De Gaulle took the other. And what would Churchill have done if it hadn't been for the accident of geography that put water between him and the fire? Certainly if he felt any moral responsibility to his people he would ultimately have had to choose one course or the other. There isn't much morality in going out to meet a Tiger tank with a half-empty revolver. There must be some clear affirmative purpose in martyrdom, some enterprising certainty that one is worth more to humanity dead than alive. The martyr gives men new courage in life by his one serene example of dignity in death. A single death is meaningful, a million deaths simply boggle the imagination. A single death can sustain five acts of tragedy, while a massacre of thousands is evaded with a single headline. Nor is there much martyrdom in being splashed to oblivion by a bomb. It's too impersonal, too accidental. A man will die even without dignity, even without honor, provided he finds meaning in his dying. There was a time when men at war aimed at destroying men. Now they merely wish to destroy cities—factories, railway stations, buildings—and it's only by the unhappy accident of juxtaposition that human beings vanish with the civilization. One is hurried off into an impersonal oblivion without even the polite ceremony of being aimed at. We used to say that the bullet that killed a man had his name on it. There was dignity in that, even a certain mysterious meaning, some final assertion of his individual worth as a man. In an army he was a number, at best merely a name on a list, but the bullet that killed him had only his name on it. Now the instrument of his exile from life is inscribed with the municipal census, written small, no doubt, like the Lord's Prayer on the head of a common pin. Modern War is more than Hell, it is colossal insult. Hell, at least, has its dignities. One can accept a Hell in which individuals are tortured according to the individual nature of their crimes."

Stone remained silent a long time, as though he were still listening. Merseault refilled the two brandy glasses and sat sipping his, not watching Stone. Finally Merseault said, "What are you thinking about?"

Stone looked up abruptly, nudged out of a reverie. "Thinking about? What *was* I thinking about? I was thinking about . . ." He stopped, began again. "I was wondering whether Sheppard was given his son's Legion of Honor, before he . . ."

"Yes, he got it."

Stone sat silent a minute, swirling the brandy around in his glass, gazing at it, studying it, as though distracted by the color and the fascination of the motion. Then he stopped. "Did you manage his election?"

"I don't know the intent of that question, but from what you said when you were in the hospital it's probably impertinent. Did it ever occur to you that no decisions are ever taken in these matters without the whole record being examined?"

"You mean because you know more you can forgive more?"

"I'll answer your question: No. I had nothing to do with Anthony Sheppard's name being introduced. It might help settle your mind to know that on the basis of a single piece of information he obtained, we were able to anticipate a raid that might have wiped out a whole section of the Paris organization. At that time Lautrec was part of that section. That is why he agreed to Berger's coming south even though he'd never met him face to face. Berger obtained this information by deliberately going to the SD with a harmless report of suspicious comings and goings to an apartment which we had purposely arranged to support the deception. He was shown a number of photographs in an effort to have him identify the men he had seen going in and out. He was unable to identify them because he had never seen any of them before. He got out without having his papers closely examined; although they were the finest forgeries London could provide, it was still a monumental risk. But he carried it off. And from a stack of photographs *we* showed him he was able to pick out three who had been among the group the SD was interested in. Each of those three men had nearly a dozen men under him in training. One of the three was Lautrec. We broke up the group and sent Lautrec and the other two to the Unoccupied Zone. One of them was caught passing the frontier. He died in Buchenwald."

Stone said nothing.

"It was too late to bring up the diary," Merseault said.

"Would you have?"

"I doubt it very much."

"Why not?"

Merseault fell silent, frowning slightly as though phrasing his thoughts before speaking. "Tell me something," he said abruptly. "Would you say that Sheppard—Berger, that is—was completely possessed of a sound mind and soul when you met him in the south?"

"You mean was he sane?"

"I didn't ask it that way."

"Then the answer to the question as you did ask it is no."

Merseault nodded in absent agreement. "No," he repeated. He lifted his head and gazed out the window, lacing his fingers behind his head as though watching something in the far distance. "You still live in the discomfort of a divided conscience concerning Sheppard's son, don't you?"

"Didn't his father?"

"That is a brutally callous question, if I may have your permission to say so. Are you his father?"

Stone felt suddenly irritated at Merseault's apparent complacency. "No, I am not his father, nor was I his keeper, then or now."

"You arrested him?"

"Yes. In that sense I was his keeper."

"You felt he was dangerous?"

"Yes."

"A hindrance to your mission, a burden?"

"Yes."

Merseault removed his hands from behind his head and turned his whole body from the hips to face Stone. Behind his eyes was something hidden, almost malevolent. His next words he spoke very slowly, very carefully, his voice steady with what seemed like cool contempt. "Then why didn't you kill him?"

"God knows I thought of it often enough," Stone muttered.

"And you're certain you didn't, of course."

Stone suddenly felt as though he'd stepped into quicksand, was trapped in a lie that had no bottom to it. Sheppard had asked him if he had ordered Berger . . . what was it? Why had he been unable to give a simple answer. Why had he avoided a direct answer for an ambiguous one. He couldn't remember precisely what he had answered, but it wasn't a simple no. He said something else, that it wasn't necessary to order him. And Merseault had asked him, even more directly, if he had pushed him into the guard. *I said, I don't know.* What was this perversity? He hadn't killed Berger, had never even entertained the thought. All possibilities, true. But that was never really one of them.

Merseault sat before him, not blinking, not taking his eyes off him. He was judging him for a crime he hadn't committed. Yet it was not too late to remove himself from guilt. He could tell the truth even now, that he'd colored the truth to make the truth more plausible. But even that wasn't true! Even when he was telling the lie he knew that it was implausible. Everyone knows that at a moment like that you remember every detail, every texture. The truth was he wasn't even near Berger. He'd been far enough behind him to start running without being instantly noticed in the split-second of confusion. The whole lie proliferated in his mind like a silent shower of fireworks, a shower releasing other showers. A splendid display, a splendid lie, a lie he'd come to believe. Not believe, but to forget was untrue; to ignore, to drive out of mind. He hadn't forgotten. He'd known all along: he'd run with his teeth clenched, his eyes shut, expecting any second to be ripped open up the spine, unzippered by bullets and spilled out over the ground like loose change from a money purse. He hadn't *seen* Carnot running. He hadn't *seen* Berger go down. There was only the unendurable unbelievable miraculous surprise, the unending improbable surprise, the ridiculous surprise, the surprise that mounted and grew with each lurching zigzagging step until finally he crashed into the woods believing he had to have been hit without feeling it and resolved to run until he bled to earth on his knees. He'd fled in a slow drone of bees, bullets, raindrops spattering leaves, bullets like hatchet blows thunking into trunks of trees. He'd fled, and seen nothing.

He'd lied.

Merseault was looking directly at him, into his eyes. Stone felt the instant coming quickly when he would have to decide, answer, make a gesture. If he looked away too quickly, if he held Merseault's eye too long. Why should a man in his very innocence so allow himself to be twisted into postures of guilt? *I must be careful. It's not my fault I didn't do anything. I'm not guilty for being innocent. Watch him carefully.* The lie was old and tangled. He had started it before he was out of the woods. He knew he would have to explain the impossible. The only way to explain the unexplainable was to . . . the only way to explain a miracle was to lie about it. *Ah, there. . . .*

"You have to understand me. It didn't make sense to . . ."

Merseault finished unmercifully: ". . . keep him prisoner?"

Stone looked utterly blank, taken by surprise. "No . . . that's not what I mean . . ."

Merseault suddenly relaxed, throwing Stone into complete confusion.

"I want you to know that I believe you," Merseault said, suddenly amiable. It was as though he'd snapped a briefcase shut in his mind, had decided the question, adjourned the hearing.

Stone was suddenly in complete possession of himself, calm, certain of his words, candid. "Look, I've done a very stupid thing. For reasons which I don't quite understand, I lied to you. I told you I didn't know if I pushed him. That wasn't true. I . . ."

Merseault smiled with gentle insistence, leaned forward and placed a restraining hand on Stone's forearm. "Please, I'm sorry. I shouldn't have tested you that way. I know what goes on in a man's mind when—"

". . . I didn't push him. I wasn't anywhere near him." Instantly Stone realized that he shouldn't have added the elaboration, even though it was true. "That was another part of the lie."

Merseault seemed genuinely trying to put him at his ease. "Look, I am ashamed of Dujardin so I try to explain myself instead of admitting my shame. You are ashamed of being unable to tell the truth because it hurts, even when it shouldn't. So we are both in the same dilemma. But as you said once to me, the war is over."

Stone was silent. What did Merseault believe of him?

Merseault seemed to notice Stone's uncertainty. He said firmly, too firmly perhaps, "I don't believe you laid a hand on—"

"But you wouldn't blame me if I . . ." Stone halted in sudden agony over the ambiguous intent behind his words. He had meant merely to say something quickly and lightly reasonable, to show he was objective, had nothing to conceal; instead he had overshot, almost blurted the words. It was as though instead of laughing he'd raped his own intention and bellowed, then, even worse, revealed himself by halting openmouthed in shame and silence.

Merseault actually dropped his eyes, although Stone noticed he covered the gesture instantly and fluently by reaching for his glass. Merseault sipped his drink as naturally as if that had been his simple intention. "Blame you? How could I blame you? We both know what war is."

Then it was settled. Stone felt that he had sunk to his neck in the bog of innocence and truth he'd so suddenly perceived and slipped into, and cursed himself for having been so stupid. He was in up to his neck and if he struggled once more he'd strangle. At least there might still be doubt in Merseault's mind, a straw, better than a straw, a vine he could cling to. What did it matter?

"To be perfectly honest with you, I can admit to you now that I was never even able to consider the possibility," Stone said. "I simply haven't got the kind of intellectual courage it takes to sacrifice a man. I had a radio operator on that same mission. They caught him. By all the rules in the book I should have carried on without him instead of risking the whole mission trying to rescue him. Anyway . . ." It was too slick, too pat, Merseault was too polite, too interested. Stone suddenly believed that perhaps he was interested. For one brief instant he felt like taking Merseault's balding skull in his hands and splitting it apart like an apple to see what was really inside. Instead he knew he had to go on with the story. Whatever else had happened, whether Merseault believed the earth was flat or the moon green cheese, Stone knew he had slipped in over his head. What Merseault believed Stone would never know. If Merseault believed he had murdered Sheppard's son, so much the better that it should be Merseault's secret and not his. The thought satisfied him immensely. It was an almost poetic kind of vengeance.

Stone finished his story of Mike's rescue, right up to the fact of his death the next day. Or was it the next day? It didn't matter. Merseault listened, absorbed in the tale, perhaps absorbed in his own thoughts. And when Stone finished he nodded somberly at the futility of Mike's death, and refilled the two glasses. He sipped silently for a long time without speaking. Stone was determined to wait him out.

Suddenly Merseault put down his glass. "I'm going to show you something that I swore I'd never show a living soul." He looked into his inside breast pocket again and carefully extracted an envelope, smaller than the one he'd taken out previously. "I got it this morning by hand courier from your Consul General. I've never been so shaken by anything in my life, and I swore I'd destroy it. He must have written it just before . . . They found it sealed, addressed to me." He handed the letter to Stone, folded. "If anyone in the world has a duty to read it I think you do."

Conscious of Merseault's watching him, Stone unfolded the letter and turned his chair toward the last afternoon light before the windows. He glanced down the page. It was written in a careful script that flowed in curious jerks and starts across the page, a slight trembling in the line of the pen—Stone remembered the old-fashioned fountain pen with the huge gold nib—the top half of the page clearly legible. The bottom half seemed to be in a different hand, perhaps written at a later sitting. He shifted his eyes to the top and began reading:

Dear Georges,

It was kind of you to see me off this afternoon. Lunching with you at your home set a warm and faintly tragic mood over me, for reasons which I'm at a loss to explain. At any rate the conversation is left unfinished always; like life itself there are too many turnings to take them all.

I have been thinking over some of the things we discussed. Here in the solitude of the blue and cloudless sky an old man's mind takes a sharper edge. So I am taking advantage of my lucid period—I believe that's what they call it—to answer more precisely certain of the questions you raised.

A great many events have passed since you and I were young and optimistic students of *science politique.* I wonder if you remember debating with me the question of world disarmament one night in that cramped little room you had in the Latin Quarter. We talked all night, and in the warm flush of the early twenties it seemed that peace was possible. I remember that I looked on you then as a bright youngster. I was nearly twelve years wiser, so I thought. But advancing age narrows, then reverses the advantage. Today you were talking to me with the same tolerance I visited on you then. Alas, it is true. My wits are failing me almost as fast as my body. I can't adjust to sitting in a wheelchair. I feel like a man in chains.

It's living that worries us in the end, not dying.

Here the handwriting changed markedly.

At lunch I tried to tell you what it means to fail. It was a bad choice of words. I meant fail in the sense one means when he speaks of light failing. When I accepted my last job it was because I had to have one last fling at mankind's infirmity. Peace is still a dream, as much as it was in the decade preceding the Washington Conference. As you know, I staked a great deal on the idea of a united Europe to stand strong and independent between the goliaths of East and West. But the Council of Europe is a failure. It is stillborn. It was eviscerated, and no amount of speechmaking can repair life to a dead body. I can admit now that secretly I had high hopes before. I kept them quiet for fear of putting the kiss of death on the venture through too loud an endorsement. French socialism is so uncertain of its ground that merely through agreeing with the socialists, the United States can force them to alter their adventures. It gives us a strange weapon of diplomacy, but none of us ever learned how to use it.

I hedged with Douglas, of course, on the question of war. But now I'll say it. Yes. I think, I'm compelled to believe, that we are on the brink of oblivion. What can a public man do then, when he becomes hallucinated with Armageddon? I can see no way out of it. I ask myself, am I mad? Or am I merely cursed with prophetic vision? Yet in my heart I am beyond reason; I am enslaved by the conviction. The world is nearing its end. We can sing, we can whistle, we can dance as we may, but there is no escaping it. Time? Yes, we can gain time. We can postpone it. But sooner or later there will again come to power a devil who seeks his own and the world's destruction. Sooner or later. Sooner or later. And at last, at long long last, he has the final means to do it.

Thus I am blighted, afflicted, cursed by my own whelming vision of the end. I can no longer walk, nor am I willing to run from it if I could. None of us know what to do. We are simply waiting out the centuries, waiting for the end. And the end is certain. Absolutely certain. Military men like myself know it. We all know it. We don't know what to do. So far we have simply kept the world in ignorance for fear of the panic that public knowledge would arouse. The older generations have their traditional illusions to protect them from the naked truth. Gas, they say, it will be like gas. None will use it because it is too terrible. Nonsense. The reason gas is not used is that it is an inefficient weapon, too liable to chance and error. But what desperado wouldn't use it if its destructive power were certain? The younger generations see this, and mock the duplicity of their elders, the blindness and self-deceit. We will make of them, by our example, a generation that has no respect for the truth and for the things that truth implies. We will see rising a generation of young criminals itching to "get it over with." We are teaching them to manipulate the truth because we ourselves are afraid to tell the truth. When the catastrophe finally comes no commander will be able to field an army. They'll be too busy looting, jeering, and digging holes to bury the dead. They'll be right because we've been wrong. In a world upside down, dying—dying becomes, at last resort, an act of affirmation?

And I can do nothing. If there were an act of mine that could stay disaster . . . I'm unable to walk, nibbling at the cookie's edge of senility.

What does a public man do who perceives the end of men's history on earth? To whom is he responsible then? If there were an act of mine that could stay disaster . . . but how short a man's life is!

Tomorrow lies ahead like a

XVII

It was dry, but there was the stillness and smell of incipient rain.

Stone didn't go back to the apartment when he left Merseault. Instead he walked. It was warm for May, even for late afternoon; yet it hadn't rained. The ground was dry and along the *allées* of the Tuileries the dust was almost white, fine as flour; it gave a satin patina to the shine on his shoes as he walked. He walked slowly, head down, scuffing the dry dust; just watching it made his nostrils dry.

This moment before sunset, when the parks were suddenly deserted, was a time when he liked to walk alone along the avenues between the trees along the Seine. And there was a corner in this park, near the Orangerie, where he liked to come at sunset and lean on the balustrade and watch the barges on the Seine. As he walked toward it he kept watch on the distant flagpole in front of the Embassy at the far corner of the Concorde. He caught a glimpse of the flag still being flown at half-staff, and glanced at his watch. The sun was surely down by now, he reflected. He reached the end of the park, but before turning toward the river he stopped, watching the flag, tiny across the vast square, and waited. Finally, after what seemed a long time, he saw the flag slide up the pole, touch the top, and slowly sink. It satisfied him to think that he was paying this small respect to the Old Man, of watching *his* flag. That flag that flew at half-staff was his flag. It was flown exclusively for him.

He turned away and walked slowly toward the balustrade that paralleled the river, overlooking the avenue and the quai. Crossing in front of the Orangerie, he looked up, and was instantly struck with an unshakable feeling that this had all happened before. He had done this all before, exactly as he was doing now: the dust powdering his shoes, the time of day, dressed up in his best clothes, coming from somewhere, going nowhere. He had often as a child experienced the curious phenomenon *déjà vu*, yet each time it happened he marveled at the compelling power of the conviction. It was an absolute conviction; this sequence had all happened before—it was like a motion picture being reeled past his eyes a second time; he had an exquisite *feeling* of foreknowledge, as though he knew precisely what thing would happen next, as if the instant future lay somewhere in a certain memory of the past. Yet that memory played tricks, eluded him, like a word on the tip of his tongue. He reflected idly that the Orangerie looked like a huge mausoleum. And of course!—that was what he had thought once before. With a little more effort he could have remembered.

Any second, he expected this intense fragile feeling to vanish. Never before had it lasted so long; always before it had been fleeting, abandoning him almost before he was aware of its presence in him. Yet it persisted. Everything had been exactly like this, the park deserted, his armpits cool with sweat, the light, the distant sound of traffic—everything fitted sensationally into place. He marveled, noticed far across the park an old man with a cane. No! It was a stick! And he was picking up papers. And that too he had known before.

The spell broke, rather, didn't break but subsided, like a wave sliding backward into the edge of the sea. For a minute he stood, feeling strangely rooted to the spot, absorbed in the mystery of fleeting time, and looked down at the dust on his shoes. He felt his mind drifting in lazy remembrance of remembered time, called up the experience of being a child at the beach. The same feeling. Standing in the sliding sheet of advancing surf as it rose around his bare ankles, rose and halted and then raced backward into the pull of the tide. Feeling the sand melting under his feet as the receding water sheared around them, leaving them mysteriously buried as though they were another part of him, not feet but roots buried in the earth. Dimly he remembered the pleasure of standing there immobile, imagining that he couldn't move, understanding clearly what it felt like to be a tree. Suddenly the experience was no longer dim but vivid: the remembered image of his mother's voice behind him on the sand, anxious, calling his name, and his not answering because he was a tree. There was no way of explaining why he had ignored her, and his father had risen up on one elbow and given him a sharp warning on being disrespectful to his mother. He listened and apologized, turning half around to face her as another comber rose and crashed and crumpled in a sheet of foam. But he didn't move his feet from where he was standing in the sloughing sand. The sea slithered back to the sea and left him rooted deeper than ever.

Stone looked up and started walking toward the river wall, coaxing himself to wonder at the curious experience and the state of mind induced by the *déjà vu*. The French term seemed to describe it exactly.

He reasoned that there ought to be some logical explanation for it, and tried to search his mind for a clue. But his mind seemed to balk at the effort. It seemed to prefer to enjoy the sensible pleasures of the place, the softly changing light.

Especially in this empty hour. He enjoyed coming here alone, enjoyed the sense of isolation, removal. Traffic moved in the avenues as usual, and there were noises as usual. But the park was elevated above the level of the streets, behind squat stone walls, and in spite of the movement of people and vehicles outside the park the solitude he could achieve here at this time of day was complete, delicious. It was the time of the Angelus and he felt alone in the park, the last man on earth. He looked at the lines of traffic circling the obelisk like a gigantic pinwheel in the square stone ten acres of the Place de la Concorde, and reflected that it was the hour when everyone was going home. And it was precisely because he was standing still in the midst of this hour of destination and movement that he was able to achieve the pleasure of solitude. Even the children who normally scattered the peace with their games and glad voices—even they were gone. There was only the old man with his sack and pointed stick who passed his twilight picking up the refuse of their delight.

Stone felt a leisured sense of kinship.

He thought of the Ambassador, dead, buried in the waters of the sea, and of the flag that they raised for him and lowered for him each sunrise, each sunset. Symbol of a nation. Symbol of a man. For this particular flag which hung in the listless lazy air of May, which hung to its staff half down during these lengthening days of spring and mourning—this one flag was his. When the time of grace was over they should take it down and burn it, drown it in the sea; let them have a new flag made to fly atop their pole.

It was curious that two sunsets in a row had found him here in time to watch that banner come down. Was it entirely by coincidence, or was this an unconscious duty he'd set for himself? Tonight the emotion he felt on watching it was different from last night, probably because of the letter Merseault had shown him. The brief glimpse of Sheppard's private anguish had been like looking into the roaring heart of a furnace; one recoiled before the open door, then slammed it. Yet he was glad Merseault had shown it to him. He still felt the vague sense of shock he had felt when he read the lines of Sheppard's "whelming vision." That a man as reasonable as Sheppard should be felled by such an idea as the end of the world was palpably unreal, distinctly sinister. What had happened to him in the short months since winter? *What does a public man do who perceives the end of man's history on earth? To whom is he responsible then? If there were an act of mine that could stay disaster . . .* And there was a certain mad logic in Sheppard's final act . . . yet this very madness hinted at a sanity beyond reason, a cold determined disillusion. Sheppard seemed to have penetrated all the wildly human illusions; he seemed to have

751

looked into a furnace of himself and glimpsed the whitehot holocaust, the blazing heart of truth. What if Sheppard had been in power himself? What would he have done?

Stone thought of the congressional committeeman who yesterday had hinted that Sheppard might have had something to hide, made veiled reference to the persistent rumors of his being subpoenaed in the Senate's investigation of the State Department. Thinking of the story made Stone smile with bitter contempt. Newspapers were like women gossiping; it made him bitter to think that Sheppard was ahead of them all, beyond all their finite and futile imaginations. Certainly his profound absorption with his son's ambiguous end, his son's uncertain unfinal death—certainly this had contributed cause to the final disaster. And yet even that, as Stone recalled the conversation in Sheppard's office, even that fitted into the larger obsession. For his son had been only one of millions caught in the war's bloody grinder. For Sheppard the war was more than the loss of an estranged son. Others could talk politics; Sheppard, it was clear, could not. It was all clear in retrospect, Stone thought. Death, even self-inflicted, was always clear in retrospect. The only politics that concerned Sheppard was the politics of oblivion. He had kept his counsel until hope failed him. And had ever a man been so sick with despair, despair of such colossal dimensions?

Curiously, Stone could feel no deep foreboding. Pity he could feel, perhaps, pity for the man, the suffering flesh and bone; but he found no kinship, no compassion, with the dream, the obsessive vision. Perhaps because of the pleasure he took in being alone in this place, perhaps because it was a warm spring day and the sky was cooling toward red and early evening, perhaps because his own trial was over—whatever the reason, he felt incapable of projecting himself into the vision that had driven Sheppard to his death. A few moments ago, as he walked away from the parapet after watching the flag slide down, he had felt as though something was finished. It was like walking away from a burial. He remembered himself as a young man, walking away from his mother's grave—he hadn't been there for the burial, so when he went to the grave a few days later he went by himself. It was cold and there was a dry powdery snow that dusted the frozen ground in patches, powdering his overshoes. The flowers were still on the grave, frozen beneath the monument his father had already made. He stood alone before the grave, and because he was no longer a child, he stood there a long time, determined to put an end to his sorrow. But it was in walking away that it came to him that part of his life was irrevocably behind him. It was finished, and now he was alone. Somehow, even then, he had known that his father was permanently stricken, that he would never again arise from his grief. He had understood it and accepted it. He was alone. There was a certain bitter pleasure in the memory of that moment. *And my son?*

The afternoon was failing rapidly to evening, and there was the smell of even more imminent rain. Stone looked up and saw the trees moving silently, a merest whisper of leaves. He had the distinct feeling that there was something he was leaving out, something he was failing to remember, failing to feel. In the almost perfect mood of the surrounding light, a moment of desertion overtook him, an incompleteness, a nagging sense of oversight. He looked out over the color and the movement of the square and saw himself for an instant as part of it, part of that humanity that swirled endlessly around the stone monument of a vanished civilization, heedless of its meaning, ignorant of its purpose. He saw it only for an instant, thought: *Am I worth so little after all?* He felt mindful of a failure, an omission, in what he saw and felt—it was like a string out of tune in the symphony. What was it? Was it his failure alone? Or was it something he vaguely shared with that vast leaderless army that swarmed around the square? Bees returning to hive. They are going home, he thought. Then: *Where is my son?*

Beneath the surface of his thoughts he felt an unexpected restlessness rising, a sense of black uneasiness that suddenly seemed to have been lurking there all along. A barge was passing downstream. He'd been watching it; now he gave it his full attention, studied it. What had happened to the serene mood of a moment before? The sky had changed only slightly, the traffic was a little less heavy. The gaunt bulk of the Orangerie still cast its long shadow, and the air was warm. What had changed? He took a deep breath but failed to catch it, took another, still failed to fill his lungs to satisfaction. An unreasoning irritation mounted within him. He gripped the stone parapet with both hands, forced himself to limit his appetite for air, tried to breath easily. But he felt he needed a deep breath. Again he gulped air. It was like not being able to finish a yawn. He felt himself giving way to senseless anger, caught himself. It was like a physical attack. A brief instant ago he'd been enjoying a simple few moments of peace and tranquillity, watching the scene, the barges on the Seine, and then this sudden aberration in the rhythm of his breathing. Now something was running loose inside him, driving him to fury. He blinked his eyes to make them stop watering; his eyes were tearing so badly that the outlines of the bridge were blurred. Or was something wrong with his vision?

Suddenly it was as though he were looking down a tunnel—the edges of vision were blacked out, and tiny orange lights, like sparks, danced around his darkening sight. For an instant he was certain he was going to lose consciousness, it was the only explanation. He held on, dimly seeing that his knuckles were white. The senseless fury vanished, changed, turned into pleading, into cold panic. *What is happening to me?* He thought of running, of finding the old man, another human being. But could he move? Under his very eyes his hands began to grow, his fingers, arms, become enormous, and suddenly he felt they weren't any longer a part of him. The heart beating in his chest was not his. These hands were not his, yet . . . *this is my body.* As though to escape he saw the hands clawing along the wall, *his* hands. Suddenly fear possessed him—*find the old man*—possessed him utterly. He recoiled backward, looked around him.

And fled.

As he came around the corner of the Orangerie he saw the old man; the terror vanished as instantly as it had come. The old man was standing off the path behind a bench, closer at hand than Stone had calculated, yet he kept on running. Whatever demon had tried to possess him, it couldn't follow into the presence of another human being. The old man looked up and saw him coming, but whatever the sight meant to him, it didn't alter the rhythm of his ways: he looked down and picked up another paper on the point of his stick, casually picked it off the nail and placed it in his bag. Stone slowed to an easy athletic lope, even thought of continuing past the old man—as though he were running simply because he liked to run. But as he neared the old man he slowed to a walk, came up to him and stopped.

The old man looked up without the slightest flicker of inquiry, automatically said *Bonjour*—probably because Stone was staring straight at him.

Stone said *Bonjour* and halted. The old man speared another paper behind the bench, a fluent economic motion.

Stone thought of offering him a cigarette, but somehow that seemed artificial and wrong. Nor would it explain his apparent urgency. He thought of making some remark about getting a little exercise, but dismissed that too as too transparent. The old man looked as if he didn't care, but Stone knew he had to say something. The old man was long beyond skepticism; he was content to let be. Stone knew he'd be hard to lie to.

Stone asked the question almost before he'd thought it: "Do you know any of the children who come here?" It sounded right.

The old man looked up. Stone saw his eyes: blue. Clear pale blue. The old man wasn't the challenge he'd imagined. He wasn't aloof at all, wasn't looking for advantage. It was simply that Stone hadn't noticed his eyes. The old man was an old man. Willing to help. He scratched his head and gave a small self-deprecating shrug. "I don't know their names . . ." he offered.

"Two of them." Making it up as he went, Stone said: "A boy and a girl. The boy is older."

"With a nurse? A nice young lady?"

"Yes, that's right." He searched quickly for a few descriptive words that wouldn't be too binding, took Solange's hair for a model. "Medium hair. Cut a little shorter than most . . ." He was about to add the color brown when the old man interrupted him, nodding.

"That's her. Pretty blond hair. Talks to the children in some foreign language."

"English," Stone invented instantly. "I was supposed to meet them to take them home."

"You're very late. They stayed around for quite a while. The children were probably hungry. They left about an hour ago."

"Are you sure?"

"Oh, yes. I keep track of the ones who stay late so I can find their papers when they leave. I don't like to go poking around. The mothers make a show of scolding the children for my benefit. But if they didn't throw paper on the ground I wouldn't have my job." The old man thought a moment, then turned and pointed to the opposite end of the park. "I'm pretty sure they went out the far gate."

"Yes," Stone said. "That must have been . . ."

"Nice young children, those two. That young English lady takes good care of them." The old man nodded as though to reaffirm his words. *"Bien élevé."*

Stone could think of nothing more than to thank him. The old man tipped his cap and went back to his stick and his papers.

The light in the park was changing again, sunset to twilight, not quite fully evening. There was a slight wind rising and a sudden fresh smell to the air. A single small cloud, a cloud left over from April, scudded past overhead. Stone started off toward the other end of the park, the direction the old man had given. He hadn't planned to walk this way—it was not his usual way—but it seemed crucially important not to spoil the deception he'd worked. It was the penance for success.

It was not yet nearly dark enough, but suddenly the streetlights went on, and only made the park seem darker for their feeble light. Overhead the solitary spring cloud seemed to grow more real, shedding dusk, and the fitful breeze lifted, freshened the dust in the path. Stone was alone in the park. He walked in the dust along the wide center path toward the arch near the Louvre, head bent, hands in pockets, quietly whistling to himself; mindless in his late pursuit of the imaginary children. A sudden scattering of fat raindrops fell and rolled in the dust, bejeweling the path for one instant like a handful of broadcast seeds.

And that was all the rain there was.

PHOTO: © J. N. BLEIBTREU

H. L. "Doc" Humes (1926–1992) was one of the originators of *The Paris Review* and the author of two novels, *The Underground City* and *Men Die*. His third novel, *The Memoirs of Dorsey Slade,* was never completed. He lived in Paris and Greenwich Village. Doc is also the subject of a documentary being produced by the Academy Award–nominated filmmaker Immy Humes, his daughter.

For further information, please visit www.dochumes.com.